Praise for Tad Williams'
Memory, Sorrow, and Thorn:

"This sprawling, spellbinding conclusion to the trilogy that began with *The Dragonbone Chair* weaves together a multitude of intricate strands, building to a suitably apocalyptic confrontation between good and evil."
—*Publishers Weekly*

"Tad Williams kicked-off fantasy fiction as we know it. . . . The *Memory, Sorrow, and Thorn* series redefined what traditional fantasy could be. Williams took the basics of Tolkien, deconstructed the story and put it back together in his own image; one fit for modern times."
—*National Post*

"Green Angel Tower has its mysteries, but even more fascinating is the labyrinth of tunnels, hidden passageways, and corridors hidden under the Hayholt. . . . It's one of the most striking constructions since Gormenghast, and a major part of this triumphant conclusion to a hefty trilogy."
—*Locus*

"An epic tale of the struggle of good against evil. Few fantasies have attempted the scope and depth of Williams' examination of the struggle between Being and Unbeing, and fewer still have achieved the complexity of his world-vision. In this purest of fantasies, created solely by the vigor of Williams' imagination, readers will find an exquisite rendering of the conflict between forges of light and darkness."
—*San Francisco Chronicle*

"What Williams makes of his fantasy is immeasurably better than most who assay the genre . . . a grand fantasy on a scale approaching Tolkien's *The Lord of the Rings*."
—*Cincinnati Post*

"A gripping adventure . . . refreshing and invigorating . . . *To Green Angel Tower* is a magnificent ending to a superlative high fantasy trilogy."
—*The Herald*

"Fans will not be disappointed in this well-written extravaganza."
—*Library Journal*

DAW Books Presents
The Finest in Imaginative Fiction by
TAD WILLIAMS

<u>**MEMORY, SORROW AND THORN**</u>
THE DRAGONBONE CHAIR
STONE OF FAREWELL
TO GREEN ANGEL TOWER

<u>**THE LAST KING OF OSTEN ARD**</u>
THE WITCHWOOD CROWN★

THE HEART OF WHAT WAS LOST★

★ ★ ★

<u>**THE BOBBY DOLLAR NOVELS**</u>
THE DIRTY STREETS OF HEAVEN
HAPPY HOUR IN HELL
SLEEPING LATE ON JUDGEMENT DAY

<u>**SHADOWMARCH**</u>
SHADOWMARCH
SHADOWPLAY
SHADOWRISE
SHADOWHEART

<u>**OTHERLAND**</u>
CITY OF GOLDEN SHADOW
RIVER OF BLUE FIRE
MOUNTAIN OF BLACK GLASS
SEA OF SILVER LIGHT

TAILCHASER'S SONG

THE WAR OF THE FLOWERS

★Available from DAW in 2017

TO
GREEN ANGEL TOWER

The Nornfells

RIMMERSGARD

YIQANUC

The FROSTMARCH

The Wealdhelm

HERNYSTIR

ALDHEORTE

Hayholt (Asu'a)

ERKYNLAND

HIGH THRITHING

MEADOW THRITHING

Warinsten

PERDRUIN

LAKE THRITHING

NABBAN

Osten Ard

The WRAN

TO
GREEN ANGEL TOWER

TAD WILLIAMS

BOOK THREE OF
Memory, Sorrow, and Thorn

DAW BOOKS, INC.
DONALD A. WOLLHEIM, FOUNDER
375 Hudson Street, New York, NY 10014

**ELIZABETH R. WOLLHEIM
SHEILA E. GILBERT
PUBLISHERS**
www.dawbooks.com

First Trade Printing, May 2005
New Trade Printing, September 2016

9

DAW TRADEMARK REGISTERED
U.S. PAT. AND TM. OFF. AND FOREIGN COUNTRIES
—MARCA REGISTRADA
HECHO EN U.S.A.

PRINTED IN THE U.S.A.

This series is dedicated to my mother,
Barbara Jean Evans,
who taught me to search for other worlds,
and to share the things I find in them.

This final volume, *To Green Angel Tower,*
in itself a little world of heartbreak and joy,
I dedicate to Nancy Deming-Williams,
with much, much love.

Author's Note

And death shall have no dominion.
Dead men naked they shall be one
With the man in the wind and the west moon;
When their bones are picked clean and the clean bones gone
They shall have stars at elbow and foot;
Though they go mad they shall be sane,
Though they sink through the sea they shall rise again;
Though lovers be lost love shall not;
And death shall have no dominion . . .

—DYLAN THOMAS
(from *"And Death Shall Have No Dominion"*)

Tell all the truth but tell it slant,
Success in circuit lies,
Too bright for our infirm delight
The truth's superb surprise;

As lightning to the children eased
With explanation kind,
The truth must dazzle gradually
Or every man be blind.

—EMILY DICKINSON

Many people gave me a great deal of help with these books, ranging from suggestions and moral support to crucial logistical aid. Eva Cumming, Nancy Deming-Williams, Arthur Ross Evans, Andrew Harris, Paul Hudspeth, Peter Stampfel, Doug Werner, Michael Whelan, the lovely folks at DAW Books, and all my friends on GEnie® make up only a small (but significant) sampling of those who helped me finish The Story That Ate My Life.

Particular thanks for assistance on this final volume of the Bloated Epic goes to Mary Frey, who put a bogglesome amount of energy and time into reading and—for lack of a better word—analyzing a monstrous manuscript. She gave me an incredible boost when I really needed it.

And, of course, the contributions of my editors, Sheila Gilbert and Betsy Wollheim, are incalculable. Caring a lot is their crime, and here at last is their well-deserved punishment.

To all of the above, and to all the other friends and supporters unmentioned but by no means unremembered, I give my most heartfelt thanks.

NOTE: There is a cast of characters, a glossary of terms, and a guide to pronunciation at the back of this book.

Synopsis of
The Dragonbone Chair

For eons the Hayholt belonged to the immortal Sithi, but they had fled the great castle before the onslaught of Mankind. Men have long ruled this greatest of strongholds, and the rest of Osten Ard as well. *Prester John,* High King of all the nations of men, is its most recent master; after an early life of triumph and glory, he has presided over decades of peace from his skeletal throne, the Dragonbone Chair.

Simon, an awkward fourteen year old, is one of the Hayholt's scullions. His parents are dead, his only real family the chambermaids and their stern mistress, *Rachel the Dragon.* When Simon can escape his kitchen-work he steals away to the cluttered chambers of *Doctor Morgenes,* the castle's eccentric scholar. When the old man invites Simon to be his apprentice, the youth is overjoyed—until he discovers that Morgenes prefers teaching reading and writing to magic.

Soon ancient King John will die, so *Elias,* the older of his two sons, prepares to take the throne. *Josua,* Elias' somber brother, nicknamed Lackhand because of a disfiguring wound, argues harshly with the king-to-be about *Pryrates,* the ill-reputed priest who is one of Elias' closest advisers. The brothers' feud is a cloud of foreboding over castle and country.

Elias' reign as king starts well, but a drought comes and plague strikes several of the nations of Osten Ard. Soon outlaws roam the roads and people begin to vanish from isolated villages. The order of things is breaking down, and the king's subjects are losing confidence in his rule, but nothing seems to bother the monarch or his friends. As rumblings of discontent begin to be heard throughout the kingdom, Elias' brother Josua disappears—to plot rebellion, some say.

Elias' misrule upsets many, including *Duke Isgrimnur* of Rimmersgard and *Count Eolair,* an emissary from the western country of Hernystir. Even King Elias' own daughter *Miriamele* is uneasy, especially about the scarlet-robed Pryrates, her father's trusted adviser.

Meanwhile Simon is muddling along as Morgenes' helper. The two become fast friends despite Simon's mooncalf nature and the doctor's refusal to teach him anything resembling magic. During one of his meanderings through the secret byways of the labyrinthine Hayholt, Simon discovers a secret passage and is almost captured there by Pryrates. Eluding the priest, he enters a hidden underground chamber and finds Josua, who is being held captive for use in some terrible ritual planned by Pryrates. Simon fetches Doctor Morgenes and the two of them free Josua and take him to the doctor's chambers, where Josua is sent to freedom down a tunnel that leads beneath the ancient castle. Then, as Morgenes is sending off messenger birds bearing news of what has happened to mysterious friends, Pryrates and the king's guard come to arrest the doctor and Simon. Morgenes is killed fighting Pryrates, but his sacrifice allows Simon to escape into the tunnel.

Half-maddened, Simon makes his way through the midnight corridors beneath the castle, which contain the ruins of the old Sithi palace. He surfaces in the graveyard beyond the town wall, then is lured by the light of a bonfire. He witnesses a weird scene: Pryrates and King Elias engaged in a ritual with black-robed, white-faced creatures. The pale things give Elias a strange gray sword of disturbing power, named *Sorrow*. Simon flees.

Life in the wilderness on the edge of the great forest Aldheorte is miserable, and weeks later Simon is nearly dead from hunger and exhaustion, but still far away from his destination, Josua's northern keep at Naglimund. Going to a forest cot to beg, he finds a strange being caught in a trap—one of the Sithi, a race thought to be mythical, or at least long-vanished. The cotsman returns, but before he can kill the helpless Sitha, Simon strikes him down. The Sitha, once freed, stops only long enough to fire a white arrow at Simon, then disappears. A new voice tells Simon to take the white arrow, that it is a Sithi gift.

The dwarfish newcomer is a troll named *Binabik,* who rides a great gray wolf. He tells Simon he was only passing by, but now he will accompany the boy to Naglimund. Simon and Binabik endure many adventures and strange events on the way to Naglimund: they come to realize that they have fallen afoul of a threat greater than merely a king and his counselor deprived of their prisoner. At last, when they find themselves pursued by unearthly white hounds who wear the brand of Stormspike, a mountain of evil reputation in the far north, they are forced to head for the shelter of *Geloë's* forest house, taking with them a pair of travelers they have rescued from the hounds. Geloë, a blunt-spoken forest woman with a reputation as a witch, confers with them and agrees that somehow the ancient Norns, embittered relatives of the Sithi, have become embroiled in the fate of Prester John's kingdom.

Pursuers human and otherwise threaten them on their journey to Naglimund. After Binabik is shot with an arrow, Simon and one of the rescued travelers, a servant girl, must struggle on through the forest. They are attacked by a shaggy giant and saved only by the appearance of Josua's hunting party.

The prince brings them to Naglimund, where Binabik's wounds are cared for, and where it is confirmed that Simon has stumbled into a terrifying swirl of events. Elias is coming soon to besiege Josua's castle. Simon's serving-girl companion was Princess Miriamele traveling in disguise, fleeing her father, whom she fears has gone mad under Pryrates' influence. From all over the north and elsewhere, frightened people are flocking to Naglimund and Josua, their last protection against a mad king.

Then, as the prince and others discuss the coming battle, a strange old Rim-mersman named *Jarnauga* appears in the council's meeting hall. He is a member of the *League of the Scroll,* a circle of scholars and initiates of which Morgenes and Binabik's master were both part, and he brings more grim news. Their enemy, he says, is not just Elias: the king is receiving aid from *Ineluki the Storm King,* who had once been a prince of the Sithi—but who has been dead for five centuries, and whose bodiless spirit now rules the Norns of Stormspike Moun-tain, pale relatives of the banished Sithi.

It was the terrible magic of the gray sword Sorrow that caused Ineluki's death—that, and mankind's attack on the Sithi. The League of the Scroll be-lieves that Sorrow has been given to Elias as the first step in some incompre-hensible plan of revenge, a plan that will bring the earth beneath the heel of the undead Storm King. The only hope comes from a prophetic poem that seems to suggest that "three swords" might help turn back Ineluki's powerful magic.

One of the swords is the Storm King's Sorrow, already in the hands of their enemy, King Elias. Another is the Rimmersgard blade *Minneyar,* which was also once at the Hayholt, but whose whereabouts are now unknown. The third is *Thorn,* black sword of King John's greatest knight, *Sir Camaris.* Jarnauga and others think they have traced it to a location in the frozen north. On this slim hope, Josua sends Binabik, Simon, and several soldiers off in search of Thorn, even as Naglimund prepares for siege.

Others are affected by the growing crisis. Princess Miriamele, frustrated by her uncle Josua's attempts to protect her, escapes Naglimund in disguise, ac-companied by the mysterious monk *Cadrach.* She hopes to make her way to southern Nabban and plead with her relatives there to aid Josua. Old Duke Is-grimnur, at Josua's urging, disguises his own very recognizable features and follows after to rescue her. *Tiamak,* a swamp-dwelling Wrannaman scholar, receives a strange message from his old mentor Morgenes that tells of bad times coming and hints that Tiamak has a part to play. *Maegwin,* daughter of the king of Hernystir, watches helplessly as her own family and country are drawn into a whirlpool of war by the treachery of High King Elias.

Simon and Binabik and their company are ambushed by *Ingen Jegger,* hunts-man of Stormspike, and his servants. They are saved only by the reappearance of the Sitha *Jiriki,* whom Simon had saved from the cotsman's trap. When he learns of their quest, Jiriki decides to accompany them to Urmsheim Mountain, legendary abode of one of the great dragons, in search of Thorn.

By the time Simon and the others reach the mountain, King Elias has brought his besieging army to Josua's castle at Naglimund, and though the first attacks are repulsed, the defenders suffer great losses. At last Elias' forces seem to retreat and give up the siege, but before the stronghold's inhabitants can celebrate, a weird storm appears on the northern horizon, bearing down on Naglimund. The storm is the cloak under which Ineluki's own horrifying army of Norns and giants travels, and when the *Red Hand,* the Storm King's chief servants, throw down Naglimund's gates, a terrible slaughter begins. Josua and a few others manage to flee the ruin of the castle. Before escaping into the great forest, Prince Josua curses Elias for his conscienceless bargain with the Storm King and swears that he will take their father's crown back.

Simon and his companions climb Urmsheim, coming through great dangers to discover the Uduntree, a titanic frozen waterfall. There they find Thorn in a tomblike cave. Before they can take the sword and make their escape, Ingen Jegger appears once more and attacks with his troop of soldiers. The battle awakens *Igjarjuk,* the white dragon, who has been slumbering for years beneath the ice. Many on both sides are killed. Simon alone is left standing, trapped on the edge of a cliff; as the ice-worm bears down upon him, he lifts Thorn and swings it. The dragon's scalding black blood spurts over him as he is struck senseless.

Simon awakens in a cave on the troll mountain of Yiqanuc. Jiriki and *Haestan,* an Erkynlandish soldier, nurse him to health. Thorn has been rescued from Urmsheim, but Binabik is being held prisoner by his own people, along with *Sludig* the Rimmersman, under sentence of death. Simon himself has been scarred by the dragon's blood and a wide swath of his hair has turned white. Jiriki names him "Snowlock" and tells Simon that, for good or for evil, he has been irrevocably marked.

Synopsis of
Stone of Farewell

Simon, the Sitha *Jiriki,* and soldier *Haestan* are honored guests in the mountaintop city of the diminutive Qanuc trolls. But *Sludig*—whose Rimmersgard folk are the Qanuc's ancient enemies—and Simon's troll friend *Binabik* are not so well treated; Binabik's people hold them both captive, under sentence of death. An audience with the *Herder* and *Huntress,* rulers of the Qanuc, reveals that Binabik is being blamed not only for deserting his tribe, but for failing to fulfill his vow of marriage to *Sisqi,* youngest daughter of the reigning family. Simon begs Jiriki to intercede, but the Sitha has obligations to his own family, and will not in any case interfere with trollish justice. Shortly before the executions, Jiriki departs for his home.

Although Sisqi is bitter about Binabik's seeming fickleness, she cannot stand to see him killed. With Simon and Haestan, she arranges a rescue of the two prisoners, but as they seek a scroll from Binabik's master's cave which will give them the information necessary to find a place named the Stone of Farewell—which Simon has learned of in a vision—they are recaptured by the angry Qanuc leaders. But Binabik's master's death-testament confirms the troll's story of his absence, and its warnings finally convince the Herder and Huntress that there are indeed dangers to all the land which they have not understood. After some discussion, the prisoners are pardoned and Simon and his companions are given permission to leave Yiqanuc and take the powerful sword *Thorn* to exiled *Prince Josua.* Sisqi and other trolls will accompany them as far as the base of the mountains.

Meanwhile, Josua and a small band of followers have escaped the destruction of Naglimund and are wandering through the Aldheorte Forest, chased by the *Storm King's* Norns. They must defend themselves against not only arrows and spears but dark magic, but at last they are met by *Geloë,* the forest woman, and *Leleth,* the mute child Simon had rescued from the terrible hounds of Stormspike. The strange pair lead Josua's party through the forest to a place that once belonged to the Sithi, where the Norns dare not pursue them for fear of breaking the ancient Pact between the sundered kin. Geloë then tells them they should travel on to another place even more sacred to the Sithi, the same Stone of Farewell to which she had directed Simon in the vision she sent him.

Miriamele, daughter of *High King Elias* and niece of Josua, is traveling south in hope of finding allies for Josua among her relatives in the courts of Nabban;

she is accompanied by the dissolute monk *Cadrach*. They are captured by *Count Streáwe* of Perdruin, a cunning and mercenary man, who tells Miriamele he is going to deliver her to an unnamed person to whom he owes a debt. To Miriamele's joy, this mysterious personage turns out to be a friend, the priest *Dinivan*, who is secretary to *Lector Ranessin*, leader of Mother Church. Dinivan is secretly a member of the League of the Scroll, and hopes that Miriamele can convince the lector to denounce Elias and his counselor, the renegade priest *Pryrates*. Mother Church is under siege, not only from Elias, who demands the church not interfere with him, but from the *Fire Dancers,* religious fanatics who claim the Storm King comes to them in dreams. Ranessin listens to what Miriamele has to say and is very troubled.

Simon and his companions are attacked by snow-giants on their way down from the high mountains, and the soldier Haestan and many trolls are killed. Later, as he broods on the injustice of life and death, Simon inadvertently awakens the Sitha mirror Jiriki had given him as a summoning charm, and travels on the Dream Road to encounter first the Sitha matriarch *Amerasu*, then the terrible Norn Queen *Utuk'ku*. Amerasu is trying to understand the schemes of Utuk'ku and the Storm King, and is traveling the Dream Road in search of both wisdom and allies.

Josua and the remainder of his company at last emerge from the forest onto the grasslands of the High Thrithing, where they are almost immediately captured by the nomadic clan led by March-Thane *Fikolmij,* who is the father of Josua's lover *Vorzheva*. Fikolmij begrudges the loss of his daughter, and after beating the prince severely, arranges a duel in which he intends that Josua should be killed; Fikolmij's plan fails and Josua survives. Fikolmij is then forced to pay off a bet by giving the prince's company horses. Josua, strongly affected by the shame Vorzheva feels at seeing her people again, marries her in front of Fikolmij and the assembled clan. When Vorzheva's father gleefully announces that soldiers of King Elias are coming across the grasslands to capture them, the prince and his followers ride away east toward the Stone of Farewell.

In far off Hernystir, *Maegwin* is the last of her line. Her father the king and her brother have both been killed fighting Elias' pawn *Skali,* and she and her people have taken refuge in caves in the Grianspog Mountains. Maegwin has been troubled by strange dreams, and finds herself drawn down into the old mines and caverns beneath the Grianspog. *Count Eolair,* her father's most trusted liege-man, goes in search of her, and together he and Maegwin enter the great underground city of Mezutu'a. Maegwin is convinced that the Sithi live there, and that they will come to the rescue of the Hernystiri as they did in the old days, but the only inhabitants they discover in the crumbling city are the *dwarrows,* a strange, timid group of delvers distantly related to the immortals. The dwarrows, who are metalwrights as well as stone-crafters, reveal that the sword *Minneyar* that Josua's people seek is actually the blade known as *Bright-Nail,* which was buried with *Prester John,* father of Josua and Elias. This news means little to Maegwin, who is shattered to find that her dreams have brought her people no real assistance. She is also at least as troubled by what she considers her foolish love for Eolair, so she invents an errand for him—taking news of Minneyar and maps of the dwarrows' diggings, which include tunnels below Elias' castle, the Hayholt, to Josua and his band of survivors. Eolair is puzzled and angry at being sent away, but goes.

Simon, Binabik, and Sludig leave Sisqi and the other trolls at the base of the mountain and continue across the icy vastness of the White Waste. Just at the northern edge of the great forest, they find an old abbey inhabited by children and their caretaker, an older girl named *Skodi*. They stay the night, glad to be out of the cold, but Skodi proves to be more than she seems: in the darkness, she traps the three of them by witchcraft, then begins a ceremony in which she intends to invoke the Storm King and show him that she has captured the sword Thorn. One of the undead *Red Hand* appears because of Skodi's spell, but a child disrupts the ritual and brings up a monstrous swarm of *diggers*. Skodi and the children are killed, but Simon and the others escape, thanks largely to Binabik's fierce wolf *Qantaqa*. But Simon is almost mad from the mind-touch of the Red Hand, and rides away from his companions, crashing into a tree at last and striking himself senseless. He falls down a gulley, and Binabik and Sludig are unable to find him. At last, full of remorse, they take the sword Thorn and continue on toward the Stone of Farewell without him.

Several people besides Miriamele and Cadrach have arrived at the lector's palace in Nabban. One of them is Josua's ally *Duke Isgrimnur*, who is searching for Miriamele. Another is Pryrates, who has come to bring Lector Ranessin an ultimatum from the king. The lector angrily denounces both Pryrates and Elias; the king's emissary walks out of the banquet, threatening revenge.

That night, Pryrates metamorphoses himself with a spell he has been given by the Storm King's servitors, and becomes a shadowy *thing*. He kills Dinivan and then brutally murders the lector. Afterward, he sets the halls aflame to cast suspicion on the Fire Dancers. Cadrach, who greatly fears Pryrates and has spent the night urging Miriamele to flee the lector's palace with him, finally knocks her senseless and drags her away. Isgrimnur finds the dying Dinivan, and is given a Scroll League token for the Wrannaman *Tiamak* and instructions to go to the inn named *Pelippa's Bowl* in Kwanitupul, a city on the edge of the marshes south of Nabban.

Tiamak, meanwhile, has received an earlier message from Dinivan and is on his way to Kwanitupul, although his journey almost ends when he is attacked by a crocodile. Wounded and feverish, he arrives at *Pelippa's Bowl* at last and gets an unsympathetic welcome from the new landlady.

Miriamele awakens to find that Cadrach has smuggled her into the hold of a ship. While the monk has lain in drunken sleep, the ship has set sail. They are quickly found by *Gan Itai*, a Niskie, whose job is to keep the ship safe from the menacing aquatic creatures called *kilpa*. Although Gan Itai takes a liking to the stowaways, she nevertheless turns them over to the ship's master, *Aspitis Preves*, a young Nabbanai nobleman.

Far to the north, Simon has awakened from a dream in which he again heard the Sitha-woman Amerasu, and in which he has discovered that Ineluki the Storm King is her son. Simon is now lost and alone in the trackless, snow-covered Aldheorte Forest. He tries to use Jiriki's mirror to summon help, but no one answers his plea. At last he sets out in what he hopes is the right direction, although he knows he has little chance of crossing the scores of leagues of winterbound woods alive. He ekes out a meager living on bugs and grass, but it seems only a question of whether he will first go completely mad or starve to death. He is finally saved by the appearance of Jiriki's sister *Aditu,* who has come in response to the mirror-summoning. She works a kind of traveling-magic that appears to turn winter into summer, and when it is finished, she and Simon enter the hidden Sithi stronghold of Jao é-Tinukai'i. It is a place of magical beauty and timelessness. When Jiriki welcomes him, Simon's joy is great; moments later, when he is taken to see *Likimeya* and *Shima'onari*, parents of Jiriki and Aditu, that joy turns to horror. The leaders of the Sithi say that since no mortal has ever been permitted in secret Jao é-Tinukai'i, Simon must stay there forever.

Josua and his company are pursued into the northern grasslands, but when they turn at last in desperate resistance, it is to find that these latest pursuers are not Elias' soldiers, but Thrithings-folk who have deserted Fikolmij's clan to throw in their lot with the prince. Together, and with Geloë leading the way, they at last reach Sesuad'ra, the Stone of Farewell, a great stone hill in the middle of a wide valley. Sesuad'ra was the place in which the Pact between the Sithi and Norns was made, and where the parting of the two kin took place. Josua's long-suffering company rejoices at finally possessing what will be, for a little while, a safe haven. They also hope they can now discover what property of the three Great Swords will allow them to defeat Elias and the Storm King, as promised in the ancient rhyme of *Nisses.*

Back at the Hayholt, Elias' madness seems to grow ever deeper, and *Earl Guthwulf,* once the king's favorite, begins to doubt the king's fitness to rule. When Elias forces him to touch the gray sword *Sorrow,* Guthwulf is almost consumed by the sword's strange inner power, and is never after the same. *Rachel the Dragon*, the Mistress of Chambermaids, is another Hayholt denizen dismayed by what she sees happening around her. She learns that the priest Pryrates was responsible for what she thinks was Simon's death, and decides something must be done. When Pryrates returns from Nabban, she stabs him. The priest has become so powerful that he is only slightly injured, but when he turns to blast Rachel with withering magics, Guthwulf interferes and is blinded. Rachel escapes in the confusion.

Miriamele and Cadrach, having told the ship's master Aspitis that she is the daughter of a minor nobleman, are treated with hospitality; Miriamele in particular comes in for much attention. Cadrach becomes increasingly morose, and when he tries to escape the ship, Aspitis has him put in irons. Miriamele, feeling trapped and helpless and alone, allows Aspitis to seduce her.

Meanwhile, Isgrimnur has laboriously made his way south to Kwanitupul. He finds Tiamak staying at the inn, but no sign of Miriamele. His disappointment is quickly overwhelmed by astonishment when he discovers that the old simpleton who works as the inn's doorkeeper is *Sir Camaris*, the greatest knight of Prester John's era, the man who once wielded Thorn. Camaris was thought to have died forty years earlier, but what truly happened remains a mystery, because the old knight is as witless as a very young child.

Still carrying the sword Thorn, Binabik and Sludig escape pursuing snow-giants by building a raft and floating across the great storm-filled lake that was once the valley around the Stone of Farewell.

In Jao é-Tinukai'i, Simon's imprisonment is more boring than frightening, but his fears for his embattled friends are great. The Sitha First Grandmother Amerasu calls for him, and Jiriki brings him to her strange house. She probes Simon's memories for anything that might help her to discern the Storm King's plans, then sends him away.

Several days later Simon is summoned to a gathering of all the Sithi. Amerasu announces she will tell them what she has learned of Ineluki, but first she berates her people for their unwillingness to fight and their unhealthy obsession with memory and, ultimately, with death. She brings out one of the Witnesses, an object which, like Jiriki's mirror, allows access to the Road of Dreams. Amerasu is about to show Simon and the assembled Sithi what the Storm King and Norn Queen are doing, but instead Utuk'ku herself appears in the Witness and denounces Amerasu as a lover of mortals and a meddler. One of the Red Hand is then manifested, and while Jiriki and the other Sithi battle the flaming spirit, *Ingen Jegger,* the Norn Queen's mortal huntsman, forces his way into Jao é-Tinukai'i and murders Amerasu, silencing her before she can share her discoveries.

Ingen is killed and the Red Hand is driven away, but the damage has been done. With all the Sithi plunged into mourning, Jiriki's parents rescind their sentence and send Simon, with Aditu for a guide, out of Jao é-Tinukai'i. As he departs, he notices that the perpetual summer of the Sithi haven has become a little colder.

At the forest's edge Aditu puts him in a boat and gives him a parcel from Amerasu that is to be taken to Josua. Simon then makes his way across the rainwater lake to the Stone of Farewell, where he is met by his friends. For a little while, Simon and the rest will be safe from the growing storm.

Foreword

Guthwulf, Earl of Utanyeat, ran his fingers back and forth across the scarred wood of Prester John's Great Table, disturbed by the unnatural stillness. Other than the noisy breathing of King Elias' cupbearer and the clank of spoons against bowls, the great hall was quiet—far quieter than it should be while almost a dozen people ate their evening meal. The silence seemed doubly oppressive to blind Guthwulf, although it was not exactly surprising: in these days only a few still dined at the king's table, and those who spent time in Elias' presence seemed more and more anxious to get away again without tempting fate by anything so risky as supper-table conversation.

A few weeks before, a mercenary captain named Ulgart from the Meadow Thrithing had made the mistake of joking about the easy virtue of Nabbanai women. This was a common view among Thrithings-men, who could not understand women who painted their faces and wore dresses that displayed what the wagon-dwellers thought of as a shameless amount of bare flesh. Ulgart's coarse joke would generally have gone unremarked in the company of other men, and since there were few women still living in the Hayholt, only men sat around Elias' table. But the mercenary had forgotten—if he had ever known— that the High King's wife, killed by a Thrithings arrow, had been a Nabbanai noblewoman. By the time the after-supper custard arrived, Ulgart's head was already dangling from an Erkynguardsman's saddle horn, on its way to the spikes atop the Nearulagh Gate for the delectation of the resident ravens.

It was a long time since the Hayholt's tabletalk had sparkled, Guthwulf reflected, but these days meals were eaten in almost funereal silence, interrupted only by the grunts of sweating servitors—each working hard to take up the slack of several vanished fellows—and the occasional nervous compliments offered by the few nobles and castle functionaries unable to escape the king's invitation.

Now Guthwulf heard a murmur of quiet speech and recognized Sir Fluiren's voice, whispering something to the king. The ancient knight had just returned from his native Nabban, where he had been acting as Elias' emissary to Duke Benigaris; tonight he held the place of honor at the High King's right hand. The old man had told Guthwulf that his conference with the king earlier that day had been quite ordinary, but still Elias had seemed troubled all through the meal. Guthwulf could not judge this by sight, but decades of time spent in his presence let him put images to each straining inflection, each of the High King's strange remarks. Also, Guthwulf's hearing, smell, and touch, which seemed far more acute since he had lost the use of his eyes, were sharper still in the presence of Elias' terrible sword Sorrow.

Ever since the king had forced Guthwulf to touch it, the gray blade seemed to him almost a living thing, something that knew him, that waited quietly but with terrible awareness, like a stalking animal that had caught his scent. Its mere presence lifted his hackles and made all his nerves and sinews feel tight-strung. Sometimes in the middle of the night, when the Earl of Utanyeat lay blackly awake, he thought he could feel the blade right through the hundreds of cubits of stone that separated his chambers from the king's, a gray heart whose beating he alone could hear.

Elias pushed back his chair suddenly, the squeak of wood on stone startling everyone into silence. Guthwulf pictured spoons and goblets halted in midair, dripping.

"Damn you, old man," the king snarled, "do you serve me or that pup Benigaris?"

"I only tell you what the duke says, Highness," quavered Sir Fluiren. "But I think he means no disrespect. He is having troubles along his borders from the Thrithings-clans, and the Wran-folk have been balky. . . ."

"Should I care?!" Guthwulf could almost see Elias narrowing his eyes, so many times had he watched the changes that anger worked on the king's features. His pale face would be sallow and slightly moist. Lately, Guthwulf had heard the servants whispering that the king was becoming very thin.

"I helped Benigaris to his throne, Aedon curse him! And I gave him a lector who would not interfere!"

This said, Elias paused. Guthwulf, alone of all the company, heard a sharp intake of breath from Pryrates, who was seated across from the blind earl. As though sensing he might have gone too far, the king apologized with a shaky jest and returned to quieter conversation with Fluiren.

Guthwulf sat dumbstruck for a moment, then hurriedly lifted his spoon, eating to cover his sudden fright. What must he look like? Was everyone staring at him—could they all see his treacherous flush? The king's words about the lectorship and Pryrates' gasp of alarm echoed over and over in his mind. The others would no doubt assume that Elias referred to influencing the selection of the pliable Escritor Velligis to succeed Ranessin as lector—but Guthwulf knew better. Pryrates' discomfiture when it seemed the king might say too much confirmed what Guthwulf had already half-suspected: Pryrates had arranged Ranessin's death. And now Guthwulf felt sure that Elias knew it, too—perhaps had even ordered the killing. The king and his counselor had made bargains with demons and had murdered God's highest priest.

At that moment, sitting with a great company around the table, Guthwulf felt himself as alone as a man upon a windswept peak. He could not bear up under the burdens of deception and fear any longer. It was time to flee. Better to be a blind beggar in the worst cesspits of Nabban than stay a moment longer in this cursed and haunted keep.

Guthwulf pushed open the door of his chamber and paused in the frame to let the chill hallway air wash over him. It was midnight. Even had he not heard the procession of sorrowful notes ring from Green Angel Tower, he would have recognized the deeper touch of cold against his cheeks and eyes, the sharp edge that the night had when the sun was at its farthest retreat.

It was strange to use eyes to feel with, but now that Pryrates had blasted away his sight, they had proved to be the most sensitive part of him, registering every change in wind and weather with a subtlety of perception finer even than that of his fingertips. Still, useful as his blinded orbs were, there was something horrible about using them so. Several nights he had wakened sweating and breathless from dreams of himself as a shapeless crawling *thing* with fleshy stalks that pushed out from its face, sightless bulbs that wavered like snail's horns. In his dreams he could still see; the knowledge that it was himself that he looked at dragged him gasping up from sleep, time and again, back into the real darkness that was now his permanent home.

Guthwulf moved out into the castle hallway, surprised as always to find himself still in blackness as he stepped from one room to another. As he closed the door on the chamber, and thus on his brazier of smoldering coals, the chill grew worse. He heard the muffled chinking of the armored sentries on the walls beyond the open window, then listened to the wind rise and smother the rattle of their surcoats beneath its own moaning song. A dog yipped in the town below, and somewhere, past several turns of the hallway, a door softly opened and closed.

Guthwulf rocked back and forth uncertainly for a moment, then took a few more steps away from his door. If he were to leave, he must leave now—it was useless to stand maundering in the hallway. He should hurry and take advantage of the hour: with all the world blinded by night, he was almost on equal terms again. What other choice was left? He had no stomach for what his king had become. But he must go in secret. Although Elias now had little use for Guth-wulf, a High King's Hand who could not ride to battle, still Guthwulf doubted that his once-friend would simply let him go. For a blind man to leave the castle where he was fed and housed, and also to flee his old comrade Elias, who had protected him from Pryrates' righteous anger, smacked too much of treachery—or at least it would to the man on the Dragonbone Chair.

Guthwulf had considered this for some time, had even rehearsed his route. He would make his way down into Erchester and spend the night at St. Sutrin's—the cathedral was all but deserted, and the monks there were chari-table to any mendicants brave enough to spend nights inside the city walls. When morning came, he would mix with the straggle of outgoing folk on the Old Forest Road, traveling eastward into Hasu Vale. From there, who knew? Perhaps on toward the grasslands, where rumor whispered that Josua was building a rebel force. Perhaps to an abbey in Stanshire or elsewhere, some place that would be a refuge at least until Elias' unimaginable game finally threw down everything.

Now it was time to stop thinking. Night would hide him from curious eyes; daylight would find him sheltered in St. Sutrin's. It was time to go.

But even as he started down the hallway he felt a feather-light presence at his side—a breath, a sigh, the indefinable sense of *someone there*. He turned, hand flailing out. Had someone come to stop him after all?

"Who . . . ?"

There was no one. Or, if someone was indeed near, that one now stood silent, mocking his sightlessness. Guthwulf felt a curious, abrupt unsteadiness, as though the floor tilted beneath his feet. He took another step and suddenly felt the presence of the gray sword very strongly, its peculiar force all around. For a moment he thought the walls had fallen away. A harsh wind passed over and through him, then was gone.

What madness was this?

Blinded and unmanned. He almost wept. Cursed.

Guthwulf steeled himself and walked away from the security of his chamber door, but the curious sense of dislocation accompanied him as he made his way through the Hayholt's acres of corridors. Unusual objects passed beneath his questing fingers, delicate furnishings and smooth-polished but intricately figured balusters unlike anything he remembered from these halls. The door to the quarters once occupied by the castle chambermaids swung unbolted, yet though he knew the rooms to be empty—their mistress had smuggled all of her charges out of the castle before her attack on Pryrates—he heard dim voices whispering in the depths. Guthwulf shuddered, but kept walking. The earl already knew the shifting and untrustworthy nature of the Hayholt in these days: even before he lost his sight it had become a weirdly inconstant place.

Guthwulf continued to count his paces. He had practiced the journey several times in recent weeks: it was thirty-five steps to the turning of the corridor, two dozen more to the main landing, then out into the narrow, wind-chilled Vine Garden. Half a hundred paces more and he was back beneath a roof once again, making his way down the chaplain's walking hall.

The wall became warm beneath his fingers, then abruptly turned blazingly hot. The earl snatched his hand away, gasping in shock and pain. A thin cry wafted down the corridor.

" . . . *T'si e-isi'ha as-irigú* . . . !"

He reached a trembling hand out to the wall again and felt only stone, damp and night-cold. The wind fluttered his clothing—the wind, or a murmuring, insubstantial crowd. The feeling of the gray sword was very strong.

Guthwulf hurried through the castle corridors, trailing his fingers as lightly as he could over the frighteningly changeable walls. As far as he could tell, he was the only real living thing in these halls. The strange sounds and the touches light as smoke and moths' wings were only phantasms, he assured himself—they could not hinder him. They were the shadows of Pryrates' sorcerous meddling. He would not let them obstruct his flight. He would not stay prisoned in this corrupted place.

The earl touched the rough wood of a door and found to his fierce joy that he had counted truly. He fought to restrain a cry of triumph and overwhelming relief. He had reached the small portal beside the Greater Southern Door. Beyond would be open air and the commons that served the Inner Bailey.

But when he pushed it open and stepped through, instead of the bitter night air the earl had expected, he felt a hot wind blowing and the heat of many fires upon his skin. Voices murmured, pained, fretful.

Mother of God! Has the Hayholt caught fire?

Guthwulf stepped back but could not find the doorway again. His fingers instead scrabbled at stone which grew hotter beneath his touch. The murmurs slowly rose into a drone of many agitated voices, soft and yet piercing as the hum of a beehive. Madness, he told himself, illusion. He must not give in. He staggered ahead, still counting his steps. Soon his feet were slipping in the mud of the commons, yet somehow at the same moment his heels clicked on smooth tiles. The invisible castle was in some terrible flux, burning and trembling one moment, cold and substantial the next, and all in total silence as its tenants slept on, unaware.

Dream and reality seemed almost completely interwoven, his personal blackness awash in whispering ghosts that confused his counting, but still Guthwulf struggled on with the grim resolve that had carried him through many dreadful campaigns as Elias' captain. He trudged on toward the Middle Bailey, stopping at last to rest for a moment near—according to his faltering calculations—the spot where the castle doctor's chambers had once stood. He smelled the sour tang of the charred timbers, reached out and felt them crumble into rotted powder beneath his touch, and distractedly remembered the conflagration that had killed Morgenes and several others. Suddenly, as though summoned up by his thoughts, crackling flames leaped all around him, surrounding him with fire. This could be no illusion—he could feel the deadly blaze! The heat enclosed him like a crushing fist, balking him no matter which way he turned. Guthwulf gave a choked cry of despair. He was trapped, trapped! He must burn to death!

"*Ruakha, ruakha Asu'a!*" Ghostly voices were crying from beyond the flames. The presence of the gray sword was inside him now, in everything. He thought he could hear its unearthly music, and fainter, the songs of its unnatural brothers. Three swords. Three unholy swords. They knew him now.

There was a rustle like the beating of many wings, then the Earl of Utanyeat suddenly felt an opening appear before him, an empty spot in the otherwise unbroken wall of flame—a doorway that breathed cool air. With nowhere else to turn, he threw his cloak over his head and stumbled down into a hall of quieter, colder shadows.

PART ONE

�֍

The Waiting Stone

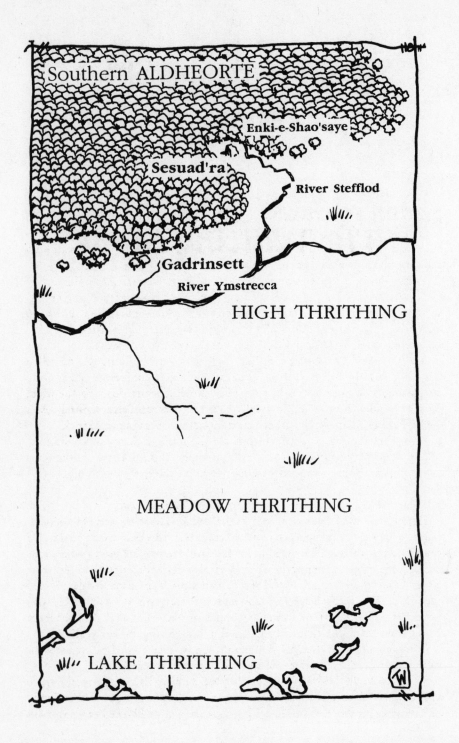

Southern ALDHEORTE

Enki-e-Shao'saye

Sesuad'ra

River Stefflod

Gadrinsett

River Ymstrecca

HIGH THRITHING

MEADOW THRITHING

LAKE THRITHING

1

Under Strange Skies

Simon squinted up at the stars swimming in the black night. He was finding it increasingly difficult to stay awake. His weary eyes turned to the brightest constellation, a rough circle of lights hovering what seemed a handsbreadth above the gaping, broken-eggshell edge of the dome.

There. That was the Spinning Wheel, wasn't it? It did seem oddly elliptical—as though the very sky in which the stars hung had been stretched into an unfamiliar shape—but if that wasn't the Spinning Wheel, what else could be so high in the sky in mid-autumn? The Hare? But the Hare had a little nubbly star close beside it—the Tail. And the Hare wasn't ever that big, was it?

A claw of wind reached down into the half-ruined building. Geloë called this hall "the Observatory"—one of her dry jokes, Simon had decided. Only the passing of long centuries had opened the white stone dome to the night skies, so Simon knew it couldn't really have been an observatory. Surely even the mysterious Sithi couldn't watch stars through a ceiling of solid rock.

The wind came again, sharper this time, bearing a flurry of snowflakes. Though it wracked him with shivers, Simon was thankful: the chill scraped some of his drowsiness away. It wouldn't do to fall asleep—not *this* night of all nights.

So, now I am a man, he thought. *Well, almost. Almost a man.*

Simon drew back the sleeve of his shirt and looked at his arm. He tried to make the muscles stand up, then frowned at the less than satisfactory results. He ran his fingers through the hair on his forearm, feeling the places where cuts had become ridged scars: here, where a Hunë's blackened nails had left their mark; there, where he had slipped and dashed himself against a stone on Sikkihoq's slope. Was that what being grown meant? Having a lot of scars? He supposed it also meant learning from the wounds, as well—but what could he learn from the sort of things that had happened to him during the last year?

Don't let your friends get killed, he thought sourly. *That's one. Don't go out in the world and get chased by monsters and madmen. Don't make enemies.*

So much for the words of wisdom that people were always so eager to share with him. No decisions were ever as easy as they had seemed in Father Dreosan's sermons, where people always got to make a clean choice between Evil's

Way and the Aedon's Way. In Simon's recent experience of the world, all the choices seemed between one unpleasant possibility and another, with only the faintest reference to good and evil.

The wind skirling through the Observatory dome grew more shrill. It put Simon's teeth on edge. Despite the beauty of the intricately sculpted pearlescent walls, this was still a place that did not seem to welcome him. The angles were strange, the proportions designed to please an alien sensibility. Like other products of its immortal architects, the Observatory belonged completely to the Sithi; it would never feel quite comfortable to mortals.

Unsettled, Simon got up and began to pace, the faint echo of his footsteps lost in the noise of the wind. One of the interesting things about this large circular hall, he decided, was that it had stone floors, something the Sithi no longer seemed to utilize. He flexed his toes inside his boots as a memory of Jao é-Tinukai'i's warm, grassy meadows tugged at him. He had walked barefoot there, and every day had been a summer day. Remembering, Simon curled his arms across his chest for warmth and comfort.

The Observatory's floor was made up of exquisitely cut and fitted tiles, but the cylindrical wall seemed to be one piece, perhaps the very stuff of the Stone of Farewell itself. Simon pondered. The other buildings here were also without visible joint or seam. If the Sithi had carved all the buildings on the surface directly from the hill's rocky bones, and had cut down into Sesuad'ra as well— the Stone seemed shot through with tunnels—how did they know when to stop? Hadn't they been afraid that if they made one hole too many the whole rock would collapse in on itself? That seemed almost as amazing as any other Sithi magic he had heard of or seen, and just as unavailable to mortals— knowing when to stop.

Simon yawned. Usires Aedon, but this night was long! He stared at the sky, at the wheeling, smoldering stars.

I want to climb up. I want to look at the moon.

Simon made his way across the smooth stone floor to one of the long staircases that spiraled gradually up around the circumference of the rooms, counting the steps as he went. He had already done this several times during the long night. When he got to the hundredth step, he sat down. The diamond gleam of a certain star, which had been midway along a shallow notch in the decayed dome when he made his last trip, now stood near the notch's edge. Soon it would disappear from sight behind the remaining shell of the dome.

Good. So at least some time had passed. The night was long and the stars were strange, but at least time's journey continued.

He clambered to his feet and continued up, walking the narrow stairway easily despite a certain light-headedness that he had no doubt would be cured by a long sleep. He climbed until he reached the highest landing, a pillar-propped collar of stone that at one time had circled the entire building. It had crumbled long ago, and most of it had fallen; now it extended only a few short ells beyond its joining with the staircase. The top of the high outer wall was just above Simon's head. A few careful paces took him along the landing to a spot where the breach in the dome dipped down to only a short distance above him. He reached up, feeling carefully for good fingerholds, then pulled himself upward. He swung one of his legs over the wall and let it dangle over nothingness.

The moon, wound in a wind-tattered veil of clouds, was nevertheless bright enough to make the pale ruins below gleam like ivory. Simon's perch was a good one. The Observatory was the only building within Sesuad'ra's outwall that stood even as high as the wall itself, which gave the settlement the appearance of one vast, low building. Unlike the other abandoned Sithi dwelling places he had seen, no towers had loomed here, no high spires. It was as though the spirit of Sesuad'ra's builders had been subdued, or as though they built for some utilitarian reason and not pure pride of craft. Not that the remains were unappealing: the white stone had a peculiar lambent glow all its own, and the buildings inside the curtain wall were laid out in a design of wild but somehow supremely logical geometry. Although it was built on a much smaller scale than what Simon had seen of Da'ai Chikiza and Enki-e-Shao'saye, the very modesty of its scope and uniformity of its design gave it a simple beauty different from those other, grander places.

All around the Observatory, as well as around the other major structures like the Leavetaking House and the House of Waters—names that Geloë had given them; Simon did not know if they were anything to do with their original purpose—snaked a system of paths and smaller buildings, or their remnants, whose interlocking loops and whorls were as cunningly designed yet naturalistic as the petals of a flower. Much of the area was overgrown by encroaching trees, but even the trees themselves revealed traces of some vestigial order, as the green space in the middle of a fairy-ring would show where the ancestral line of mushrooms had begun.

In the center of what obviously had once been a settlement of rare and subtle beauty lay a strange tiled plateau. It was now largely covered with impertinent grass, but even by moonlight it still showed some trace of its original lushly intricate design. Geloë called this central place the Fire Garden. Simon, comfortably familiar only with the workings of human habitations, would have guessed it to be a marketplace.

Beyond the Fire Garden, on the other side of the Leavetaking House, stood a motionless wavefront of pale conical shapes—the tents of Josua's company, grown now to a sizable swell by the newcomers who had been trickling in for weeks. There was precious little room left, even on the broad tabletop summit of the Stone of Farewell; many of the most recent arrivals had made themselves homes in the warren of tunnels that ran beneath the hill's stony skin.

Simon sat staring at the flicker of the distant campfires until he began to feel lonely. The moon seemed very far away, her face cold and unconcerned.

He did not know how long he had been staring into empty blackness. For a moment he thought he had fallen asleep and was now dreaming, but surely this

queer feeling of suspension was something real—real and frightening. He
struggled, but his limbs were remote and nerveless. Nothing of Simon's body
seemed to remain but his two eyes. His thoughts seemed to burn as brightly as
the stars he had seen in the sky—when there had been a sky, and stars; when
there had been something besides this unending blackness. Terror coursed
through him.

*Usires save me, has the Storm King come? Will it be black forever? God, please bring
back the light!*

And as if in answer to his prayer, lights began to kindle in the great dark.
They were not stars, as they first seemed, but torches—tiny pinpoints of light
that grew ever so slowly larger, as though approaching from a great distance
away. The cloud of firefly glimmers became a stream, the stream became a line,
looping and looping in slow spirals. It was a procession, scores of torches climbing uphill the way Simon himself had climbed up Sesuad'ra's curving path
when he had first come here from Jao é-Tinukai'i.

Simon could now see the cloaked and hooded figures who made up the
column, a silent host moving with ritual precision.

I'm on the Dream Road, he realized suddenly. *Amerasu said that I was closer to it
than other folk.*

But what was he watching?

The line of torchbearers reached a level place and spread out in a sparkling
fan, so that their lights were carried far out on either side of the hilltop. It *was*
Sesuad'ra they had climbed, but a Sesuad'ra that even by torchlight was plainly
different than the place Simon knew. The ruins that had surrounded him were
ruins no longer. Every pillar and wall stood unbroken. Was this the past, the
Stone of Farewell as it once had been, or was it some strange future version that
would someday be rebuilt—perhaps when the Storm King had subjugated all
Osten Ard?

The great company surged forward onto a flat place Simon recognized as the
Fire Garden. There the cloaked figures set their torches down into niches between the tiles, or placed them atop stone pedestals, so that a garden of fire
indeed bloomed there, a field of flickering, rippling light. Fanned by the wind,
the flames danced; sparks seemed to outnumber the very stars.

Now Simon found himself suddenly pulled forward with the surging crowd
and down toward the Leavetaking House. He plummeted through the glittering night, passing swiftly through the stone walls and into the bright-lit hall as
though he were without substance. There was no sound but a continuous rushing in his ears. Seen closely, the images before him seemed to shift and blur
along their edges, as though the world had been twisted ever so slightly out of
its natural shape. Unsettled, he tried to close his eyes, but found that his dream-
self could not shut out these visions: he could only watch, a helpless phantom.

Many figures stood at the great table. Globes of cold fire had been placed
in alcoves on every wall, their blue, fire-orange, and yellow glows casting
long shadows across the carved walls. More and deeper shadows were cast by

the thing atop the table, a construct of concentric spheres like the great astrolabe Simon had often polished for Doctor Morgenes—but instead of brass and oak, this was made entirely from lines of smoldering light, as though someone had painted the fanciful shapes upon the air in liquid fire. The moving figures that surrounded it were hazy, but still Simon knew beyond doubt that they were Sithi. No one could ever mistake those birdlike postures, that silken grace.

A Sitha-woman in a sky-blue robe leaned toward the table and deftly scribed in trails of finger-flame her own additions to the glowing thing. Her hair was blacker than shadow, blacker even than the night sky above Sesuad'ra, a great cloud of darkness about her head and shoulders. For a moment Simon thought she might be a younger Amerasu; but though there was much in this one that was like his memories of First Grandmother, there was also much that was not.

Beside her stood a white-bearded man in a billowing crimson robe. Shapes that might have been pale antlers sprouted from his brow, bringing Simon a pang of unease—he had seen something like that in other, more unpleasant dreams. The bearded man leaned forward and spoke to her; she turned and added a new swirl of fire to the design.

Although Simon could not see the dark woman's face clearly, the one who stood across from her was all too plain. That face was hidden behind a mask of silver, the rest of her form beneath ice-white robes. As if in answer to the black-haired woman, the Norn Queen raised her arm and slashed a line of dull fire all the way across the construct, then waved her hand once more to lay a net of delicately smoking scarlet light over the outermost globe. A man stood beside her, calmly watching her every move. He was tall and seemed powerfully built, dressed all in spiky armor of obsidian-black. He was not masked in silver or otherwise, but still Simon could see little of his features.

What were they doing? Was this the Pact of Parting that Simon had heard of—for certainly he was watching both Sithi and Norn gathered together upon Sesuad'ra.

The blurred figures began to talk more animatedly. Looping and crisscrossing lines of flame were thrown into the air around the spheres where they hung in nothingness, bright as the afterimage of a hurtling fire-arrow. Their speech seemed to turn to harsh words: many of the shadowy observers, gesticulating with more anger than Simon had seen in the immortals he knew, stepped forward to the table and surrounded the principal foursome, but still he could hear nothing but a dull roaring like wind or rushing water. The flame globes at the center of the dispute flared up, undulating like a wind-licked bonfire.

Simon wished he could move forward somehow to get a better view. Was this the past he was watching? Had it seeped up from the haunted stone? Or was it only a dream, an imagining brought on by his long night and the songs he had heard in Jao é-Tinukai'i? Somehow, he felt sure that it was no illusion. It seemed so real, he felt almost as though he could reach out . . . he could reach out . . . and *touch*. . . .

The sound in his ears began to fade. The lights of torches and spheres dimmed.

Simon shivered back into awareness. He was sitting atop the crumbling stone of the Observatory, dangerously close to the edge. The Sithi were gone. There were no torches in the Fire Garden, and no living things visible atop Sesuad'ra except a pair of sentries sitting near the watchfire down beside the tent city. Bemused, Simon sat for a little while staring at the distant flames and tried to understand what he had seen. Did it mean something? Or was it just a meaningless remnant, a name scratched upon a wall by a traveler which remained long after that person was gone?

Simon trudged back down the stairway from the Observatory roof and returned to his blanket. Trying to understand his vision made his head hurt. It was becoming more difficult to think with every hour that passed.

After wrapping his cloak around himself more tightly—the robe he was wearing beneath was not very warm—he took a long swallow from his drinking skin. The water, from one of Sesuad'ra's springs, was sweet and cold against his teeth. He took another swig, savoring the aftertaste of grass and shadeflowers, and tapped his fingers on the stone tiles. Dreams or no dreams, he was supposed to be thinking about the things Deornoth had told him. Earlier in the night, he had repeated them over and over in his mind so many times that they had finally begun to seem like nonsense. Now, when he again tried to concentrate, he found that the litany Deornoth had so carefully taught him would not stay in his head, the words elusive as fish in a shallow pond. His mind roved instead, and he pondered all the strange happenings he had endured since running away from the Hayholt.

What a time it had been! What things he had seen! Simon was not sure that he would call it an adventure—that seemed a little too much like something that ended happily and safely. He doubted the ending would be pleasant, and enough people had died to make the word "safely" a cruel jest . . . but still, it was definitely an experience far beyond a scullion's wildest dreams. Simon Mooncalf had met creatures out of legends, had been in battles, and had even killed people. Of course, that had proved much less easy than he had once upon a time imagined it would be, when he had seen himself as a potential captain of the king's armies; in fact, it had proved to be very, very upsetting.

Simon had also been chased by demons, was the enemy of wizards, had become an intimate of noble folk—who didn't seem much better or worse than kitchen-and-pantry folk—and had lived as a reluctant guest in the city of the undying Sithi. Besides safety and warm beds, the only thing his adventure seemed to be lacking was beautiful maidens. He *had* met a princess—one he had liked even when she had seemed just an ordinary girl—but she was long gone, the Aedon only knew where. There had been precious little else in the way of feminine company since then, other than Aditu, Jiriki's sister, but *she* had been a little too far beyond Simon's awkward understanding. Like a leopard, she was: lovely but quite frightening. He yearned for someone a little more like himself—but better looking, of course. He rubbed his fuzzy beard, felt his prominent nose. A *lot* better looking. He was tired of being alone. He wanted someone to talk to—someone who would care, who would understand, in a way that not even his troll-friend Binabik ever could. Someone who would share things with him . . .

Someone who will understand about the dragon, was his sudden thought.

Simon felt a march of prickling flesh along his back, not caused by the wind this time. It was one thing to see a vision of ancient Sithi, no matter how vivid. Lots of people had visions—madmen by the score in Erchester's Battle Square shouted about them to one another, and Simon suspected that in Sesuad'ra such things might be even more common occurrences. But Simon had met a dragon, which was more than almost anyone could say. He had stood before Igjarjuk, the ice-worm, and hadn't backed down. He had swung his sword—well, *a* sword: it was more than presumptuous to call Thorn his—and the dragon had fallen. That was truly something wonderful. It was a thing no man but Prester John had ever done, and John had been the greatest of all men, the High King.

Of course, John killed his dragon, but I don't believe Igjarjuk died. The more I think about it, the more certain I am. I don't think its blood would have made me feel the way it did if the dragon was dead. And I don't think that I'm strong enough to kill it, even with a sword like Thorn.

But the strange thing was, although Simon had told everyone exactly what happened on Urmsheim and what he thought about it all, still some of the folk who now made the Stone of Farewell their home were calling him "Dragon Killer," smiling and waving when he passed. And although he had tried to shrug off the name, people seemed to take his reticence for modesty. He had even heard one of the new settlers from Gadrinsett telling her children the tale, a version that included a vivid description of the dragon's head struck loose from its body by the force of Simon's blow. Someday soon, what really happened wouldn't matter at all. The people who liked him—or liked the story, rather—would say he had singlehandedly butchered the great snow dragon. Those who didn't care for him would say the whole thing was a lie.

The idea of those folk passing false stories of his life made Simon more than a little angry. It seemed to cheapen things, somehow. Not so much the imagined naysayers—they could never take away that moment of pure silence and stillness atop Urmsheim—but the others, the exaggerators and simplifiers. Those who told it as a story of unworrying bravery, of some imaginary Simon who sworded dragons simply because he could, or because dragons were evil, would be smearing dirty fingers across an unstained part of his soul. There was so much more to it than that, so much more that had been revealed to him in the beast's pale, emotionless eyes, in his own confused heroism and the burning instant of black blood . . . the blood that had shown him the world . . . the world. . . .

Simon straightened up. He had been nodding again. By God, sleep was a treacherous enemy. You couldn't face it and fight it; it waited until you were looking the other way, then stole up quietly. But he had given his word, and now that he would be a man, his word must be his solemn bond. So he *would* stay awake. This was a special night.

The armies of sleep had forced him to drastic measures by dawn's arrival, but they had not quite managed to defeat him. When candle-bearing Jeremias entered the Observatory, his entire frame tense with the gravity of his mission, it was to discover Simon sitting cross-legged in a puddle of fast-freezing water, wet red hair dangling in his eyes, the white streak that ran through it stark as an icicle. Simon's long face was alight with triumph.

"I poured the whole water skin over my head," he said with pride. His teeth were chattering so hard that Jeremias had to ask him to repeat himself. "Poured water over my head. To stay awake. What are you doing here?"

"It's time," the other said. "It's nearly dawn. Time for you to come away."

"Ah." Simon stood up unsteadily. "I stayed awake, Jeremias. Didn't sleep once."

Jeremias nodded. His smile was a cautious one. "That's good, Simon. Come on. There's a fire at Strangyeard's place."

Simon, who felt weaker and colder than he had thought he would, draped his arm around the other youth's lean shoulder for support. Jeremias was so thin now that it was hard for Simon to remember him as he once had been: a suety chandler's apprentice, treble-chinned, always huffing and sweating. But for the haunted look that showed from time to time in his dark-shadowed eyes, Jeremias looked just like what he now was—a handsome young squire.

"A fire?" Simon's thoughts had at last caught up with his friend's words. He was quite giddy. "A good one? And is there food, too?"

"It's a very good fire." Jeremias was solemn. "One thing I learned . . . down in the forges. How to make a proper fire." He shook his head slowly, lost in thought, then looked up and caught Simon's eye. A shadow flitted behind his gaze like a hare hunted in the grass, then his wary smile returned. "As for food—no, of course not. Not for a while yet, and you know it. But don't worry, pig, you will probably get a heel of bread or something this evening."

"Dog," Simon said, grinning, and purposefully leaned in such a way that Jeremias stumbled under the added weight. Only after much cursing and mutual insult did they avoid tumbling over onto the chilly stone flags. Together they staggered through the Observatory door and out into the pale gray-violet glow of dawn. Eastern light splashed all across the summit of the Stone of Farewell, but no birds sang.

Jeremias had been as good as his word. The blaze that burned in Father Strangyeard's tent-roofed chamber was gloriously hot—which was just as well, since Simon had stepped out of his robe and into a wooden tub. As he stared around at the white stone walls, at the carvings of tangled vines and minute flowers, the firelight rippled across the stonework so that the walls seemed to move beneath shallow pink and orange waters.

Father Strangyeard raised another pot of water and poured it over Simon's head and shoulders. Unlike his earlier self-inflicted bath, this water had at least been warmed; as it ran down his chilly flesh, Simon thought that it felt more like flowing blood than water.

". . . May this . . . may this water wash away sin and doubt." Strangyeard paused to fiddle with his eyepatch, his one squinting eye netted in wrinkles as he tried to remember the next passage of the prayer. Simon knew it was nerves, not forgetfulness: the priest had spent most of yesterday reading and rereading the short ceremony. "Let . . . let then the man so washed and made shriven fear not to stand before Me, so that I might look into the glass of his soul and see there reflected the fitness of his being, the righteousness of his oath . . . the righteousness of . . . of his oath . . ." The priest squinted again, despairingly. "Oh . . ."

Simon let the heat of the fire beat upon him. He felt quite boneless and stupid, but that was not such a bad way to feel. He had been sure he would be nervous, terrified even, but his sleepless night had burned away his fear.

Strangyeard, running his hand fitfully through his few remaining wisps of hair, at last summoned up the rest of the ceremony and hurried through to the ending, as though afraid the memory might slip away again. When he finished, the priest helped Jeremias to dry Simon off with soft cloths, then they gave him back his white robe, this time with a thick leather belt to wrap around his waist. Then, as Simon was stepping into his slippers, a small shape appeared in the doorway.

"Is he now ready?" Binabik asked. The troll spoke very quietly and gravely, as always full of respect for someone else's rituals. Simon stared at him and was filled with a sudden fierce love for the little man. Here was a friend, truly—one who had stood by him through all adversity.

"Yes, Binabik. I'm ready."

The troll led him out, Strangyeard and Jeremias following behind. The sky was more gray than blue, wild with fragmented clouds. The whole procession matched itself to Simon's bemused, wandering pace as they made their way in the morning light.

The path to Josua's tent was lined with spectators, perhaps ten score in all, mostly Hotvig's Thrithings-folk and the new settlers from Gadrinsett. Simon recognized a few faces, but knew that those most familiar to him were waiting up ahead with Josua. Some of the children waved to him. Their parents snatched at them and whispered warningly, fearful of disrupting the solemn nature of the event, but Simon grinned and waved back. The cold morning air felt good on his face. A certain giddiness had taken him over once more, so that he had to repress an urge to laugh out loud. Who would ever have thought of such a thing as this? He turned to Jeremias, but the youth's face was closed, his eyes lowered in meditation or shyness.

As they reached the open place before Josua's lodging, Jeremias and Strangyeard dropped back, moving to stand with the others in a rough semicircle. Sludig, his yellow beard new-trimmed and braided, beamed at Simon like a proud father. Dark-haired Deornoth stood beside him dressed in knightly finery, with the harper Sangfugol, the duke's son Isorn, and old Towser all close by—the jester, wrapped in a heavy cloak, seemed to be muttering quiet complaints to the young Rimmersman. Nearer the front of the tent stood Duchess Gutrun and young Leleth. Beside them stood Geloë. The forest woman's stance was that of an old soldier forced to put up with a meaningless inspection, but as Simon caught her yellow eyes she nodded once, as if acknowledging a job completed.

On the far side of the semicircle were Hotvig and his fellow randwarders, their tall spears like a thicket of slim trees. White morning light bled through the clotted clouds, shining dully on their bracelets and spearheads. Simon tried not to think about the others, like Haestan and Morgenes, who should be present but were not.

Framed in the opening between these two groups was a tent striped in gray, red, and white. Prince Josua stood before it, his sword Naidel sheathed at his side, a thin circlet of silver upon his brow. Vorzheva was beside him, her own dark cloud of hair unbound, lush upon her shoulders and moving at the wind's touch.

"Who comes before me?" Josua asked, his voice slow and measured. As if to belie his heavy tone, he showed Simon a hint of smile.

Binabik pronounced the words carefully. "One who would be made a knight, Prince—your servant and God's. He is Seoman, son of Eahlferend and Susanna."

"Who speaks for him and swears that this is true?"

"Binbiniqegabenik of Yiqanuc am I, and I am swearing that this is true." Binabik bowed. His courtly gesture sent a ripple of amusement through the crowd.

"And has he kept his vigil, and been shriven?"

"Yes!" Strangyeard piped up hurriedly. "He did—I mean, he has!"

Josua fought another smile. "Then let Seoman step forward."

At the touch of Binabik's small hand on his arm, Simon took a few steps toward the prince, then sank to one knee in the thick, rippling grass. A chill moved up his back.

Josua waited a moment before he spoke. "You have rendered brave service, Seoman. In a time of great danger, you have risked your life for my cause and returned with a mighty prize. Now, before the eyes of God and of your fellows, I stand prepared to lift you up and grant you title and honor above other men, but also to lay upon your shoulders burdens beyond those that other men must carry. Will you swear to accept them all?"

Simon took a breath so his voice would be steady, and also to make sure of the words Deornoth had so carefully taught him. "I will serve Usires Aedon and my master. I will lift up the fallen and defend God's innocents. I will not turn my eyes from duty. I will defend my prince's realm from enemies spiritual and corporeal. This I swear by my name and honor, with Elysia, Aedon's holy mother, as my witness."

Josua stepped closer, then reached down and laid his one good hand upon Simon's head. "Then I name you my man, Seoman, and lay on you the charges of knighthood." He looked up. "Squire!"

Jeremias stepped forward. "Here, Prince Josua." His voice shook a little.

"Bring his sword."

After a moment's confusion—the hilt had gotten tangled in Father Strang-yeard's sleeve—Jeremias approached bearing the sword in its tooled leather scabbard. It was a well-polished but otherwise undistinguished Erkynlandish blade. Simon felt a moment of regret that the blade was not Thorn, then chastised himself as an overweening idiot. Could he never be satisfied? Besides, think of the embarrassment if Thorn did not submit to the ritual and proved heavy as a millstone. He would look a perfect fool then, wouldn't he? Josua's hand upon his head suddenly felt as weighty as the black sword itself. Simon looked down so that no one could see his spreading flush.

When Jeremias had carefully buckled the scabbard onto Simon's belt, Simon drew the sword, kissed its hilt, then made the sign of the Tree as he set it on the ground before Josua's feet.

"In your service, Lord."

The prince withdrew his hand, then pulled slender Naidel from its scabbard and touched Simon's shoulders, right, left, then right again.

"Before the eyes of God and of your fellows—rise, Sir Seoman."

Simon rose tottering to his feet. It was done. He was a knight. His mind seemed nearly as cloudy as the lowering sky. There was a long, hushed moment, then the cheering began.

Hours after the ceremony, Simon awoke gasping from a dream of smothering darkness to find himself half-strangled in a knot of blankets. Weak, wintery sunlight was beaming down on Josua's striped tent; bars of red light lay across Simon's arm like paint. It was daytime, he reassured himself. He had been sleeping, and it had only been a terrible dream. . . .

He sat up, grunting as he unwrapped himself from the tangle of bedclothes. The tent walls throbbed beneath the wind. Had he cried out? He hoped not. It would be humiliating indeed to wake up screaming on the afternoon that he had been knighted for bravery.

"Simon?" A small shadow appeared on the wall near the door. "Are you awake?"

"Yes, Binabik." He reached over to retrieve his shirt as the little man ducked in through the tent flap.

"Were you sleeping well? It is no thing of easiness to stay awake all the night, and sometimes it is then making it hard for sleeping after."

"I slept." Simon shrugged. "I had a strange dream."

The troll cocked an eyebrow. "Do you remember it?"

Simon thought for a moment. "Not really. It sort of slipped away. Something about a king and old flowers, about the smell of earth . . ." He shook his head. It was gone.

"That, I am thinking, is just as well." Binabik bustled around the prince's tent, looking for Simon's cloak. He found it at last, then turned and tossed it to the new-made knight, who was pulling on his breeches. "Your dreams are often disturbing to you, but seldom of much help in gaining more knowledge. Probably, then, it is best you are not troubled with the memory of each one of them."

Simon felt vaguely slighted. "Knowledge? What do you mean? Amerasu said that my dreams meant something. And so did you and Geloë!"

Binabik sighed. "I was meaning only that we are not having much luck discovering their meaning. So, it seems to me better that you are not troubled by them, at least for this moment, when you should be enjoying your great day!"

The troll's earnest face was enough to make Simon thoroughly ashamed of his momentary ill humor. "You're right, Binabik." He buckled on his sword belt. Its unfamiliar weight was one more unusual thing in a day of wonders. "Today I won't think about . . . about anything bad."

Binabik gave him a hearty hand-smack. "That is my companion of many journeys that speaks! Let us go now. Besides the kindness of his tent for your sleeping comfort, Josua has made sure that a fine meal awaits us all, and other pleasures, too."

Outside, the encampment of tents that stood in the shelter of Sesuad'ra's long northeastern wall had been hung with ribbons of many colors which snapped and streamed in the powerful wind. Seeing them, Simon could not help but think of his days in Jao é-Tinukai'i, memories he usually tried to hold at bay because of the complicated and unsettling feelings that came with them. All today's fine words couldn't change the truth, couldn't make the Storm King go away. Simon was tired of being fearful. The Stone of Farewell was a refuge only for a little while—how he longed for a home, for a safe place and freedom from terror! Amerasu the Ship-Born had seen his dreams. She had said he need carry no further burdens, hadn't she? But Amerasu, who had seen so many things, had also been blind to others. Perhaps she had been wrong about Simon's destiny as well.

With the last stragglers, Simon and his companions passed through the cracked doorway and into the torchlit warmth of the Leavetaking House. The vast room was full of people seated on spread cloaks and blankets. The tiled floors had been cleared of centuries of moss and grasses; small cookfires burned everywhere. There were few enough excuses for merriment in these hard days: the exiles of many places and nations gathered here seemed determinedly joyful. Simon was called upon to stop at several fires and share a congratulatory drink, so that it took some part of an hour before he at last made his way to the high table—a massive decorated stone slab that was part of the original Sithi hall—where the prince and the rest of his company waited.

"Welcome, Sir Seoman." Josua motioned Simon to the seat at his left. "Our settlers of New Gadrinsett have spared no effort to make this feast a grand one. There is rabbit and partridge; chicken, I think; and good silver trout from the Stefflod." He leaned over to speak more quietly. Despite the weeks of peace, Simon thought the prince's face seemed gaunt. "Eat up, lad. Fiercer weather is coming soon. We may need to live on our fat, like bears."

"New Gadrinsett?" Simon asked.

"We are but visitors on Sesuad'ra," said Geloë. "The prince rightly feels that it would be presumptuous to call our settlement by the name of their sacred place."

"And since Gadrinsett is the source of many of our residents, and the name is appropriate—'Gathering Place' in the old Erkynlandish tongue—I have named our tent city after it." He lifted his cup of beaten metal. "New Gadrinsett!" The company echoed his toast.

The sparse resources of valley and forest had indeed been put to good use; Simon ate with an enthusiasm that bordered on frenzy. He had gone unfed since the midday meal of the day before, and much of his nightlong vigil had been taken up with distracted thoughts of food. Eventually, sheer exhaustion had taken his appetite away, but now it had returned at full strength.

Jeremias stood behind him, refilling Simon's cup with watered wine each time he emptied it. Simon was not yet comfortable with the idea that his Hayholt companion should wait upon him, but Jeremias would have it no other way.

When the one-time chandler's boy had reached Sesuad'ra, drawn east by the rumor of Josua's growing army of the disaffected, Simon had been surprised—not only by the change in Jeremias' appearance, but by the very unlikeliness of meeting him again, especially in such a strange place. But if Simon had been surprised, Jeremias had been astounded to discover that Simon was alive, and even more amazed by the story of what had befallen his friend. He seemed to view Simon's survival as nothing less than a miracle, and had thrown himself into Simon's service as one entering religious orders. Faced with Jeremias' unswerving determination, Simon gave way with no little embarrassment. He was made uneasy by his new squire's selfless devotion; when, as sometimes happened, a hint of their old mocking friendship surfaced, Simon was much happier.

Although Jeremias made Simon tell and retell all the things that had happened to him, the chandler's boy was unwilling to talk much about his own experiences. He would say only that he had been forced to work in the forges beneath the Hayholt, and that Inch, Morgenes' former assistant, had been a cruel master. Simon could sense much of the untold tale, and silently added to the slow-talking giant's tally of deserved retribution. After all, Simon was a knight now, and wasn't that something that knights did? Dispense justice . . . ?

"You stare at nothing, Simon," said Lady Vorzheva, waking him from his thoughts. She was beginning to show the signs of the growing child within her, but still had a slightly wild look, like a horse or bird that would suffer human touch but would never be quite tame. He remembered the first time he had seen her across the courtyard at Naglimund, how he had wondered what could make such a lovely woman look so fiercely unhappy. She seemed more contented now, but a hard edge still remained.

"I'm sorry, Lady, I was thinking about . . . about the past, I suppose." He flushed. What did one talk about at table with the prince's lady? "It is a strange world."

Vorzheva smiled, amused. "Yes, it is. Strange and terrible."

Josua rose and banged his cup on the stone tabletop until the crowded room at last fell silent. As the host of unwashed faces stared up at the prince's company, Simon had a sudden, startling revelation.

All those Gadrinsett folk, with their mouths hanging open as they watched Josua—they were him! They were like he had been! He had always been outside, looking in at the important folk. And now, wonderfully, unbelievably, *he* was one of the high company, a knight at the prince's long table, so that others stared at him enviously—but he was still the same Simon. What did it mean?

"We are gathered for many reasons," the prince said. "First, and most importantly, to give thanks to our God that we are alive and safe here upon this place of refuge, surrounded by water and protected from our enemies. Also, we are here to celebrate the eve of Saint Granis' Day, which is a holy day to be observed by fasting and quiet prayer—but to be observed the night before with good food and wine!" He lifted his cup to cheers from the throng. When the noise had died down, he grinned and continued. "We also celebrate the knighthood of young Simon, now called Sir Seoman." Another chorus of cheers. Simon blushed and nodded. "You have all seen him knighted, seen him take his sword and swear his oath. But you have not seen—his banner!"

There was much whispering as Gutrun and Vorzheva bent over and hauled up a roll of cloth from beneath the table; it had been lying right at Simon's feet. Isorn stepped forward to help them, and together they lifted and unfurled it.

"The device of Sir Seoman of New Gadrinsett," the prince declared.

On a field of diagonal gray and red stripes—Josua's colors—lay the silhouette of a black sword. Twined about it like a vine was a sinuous white dragon, whose eyes, teeth, and scales had all been meticulously stitched with scarlet thread. The crowd hooted and cheered.

"Hooray for the dragon slayer!" a man cried; several echoed him. Simon ducked his head, face reddening again, then quickly drained his wine cup. Jeremias, smiling proudly, refilled it. Simon drank down that one, too. It was glorious, all of it, but still . . . deep in his heart, he could not help feeling that some important point was being missed. Not just the dragon, although he hadn't slain it. Not Thorn, although it certainly wasn't Simon's sword, and might not even be of any use to Josua. Something was not quite right. . . .

S'Tree, he thought disgustedly, *don't you ever get tired of complaining, mooncalf?*

Josua was banging his cup again. "That is not all! Not all!" The prince seemed to be enjoying himself.

It must be nice for him to preside over cheerful events for once.

"There is more!" Josua cried. "One more present, Simon." He waved, and Deornoth stepped away from the table, heading for the back of the hall. The hum of conversation rose again. Simon drank a little more watered wine, then thanked Vorzheva and Gutrun for their work on his banner, praising the quality of the stitchery until both women were laughing. When a few people near the back of the crowd began to shout and clap their hands, Simon looked up to see Deornoth returning. The knight led a brown horse.

Simon stared. "Is it . . . ?" He leaped up, banging his knee on the table, and hurried limping across the crowded floor. "Homefinder!" he cried. He threw his arms around the mare's neck; she, less overwhelmed than he, nosed gently at his shoulder. "But I thought Binabik said she was lost!"

"She was," said Deornoth, smiling. "When Binabik and Sludig were trapped by the giants, they had to set the horses free. One of our scouting parties found her near the ruins of the Sithi city across the valley. Maybe she sensed something of the Sithi still there and felt safe, since you say she spent time among them."

Simon was chagrined to find himself weeping. He had been certain that the mare was simply one more addition to the list of friends and acquaintances lost in this terrible year. Deornoth waited until he wiped his eyes, then said: "I'll put her back with the other horses, Simon. I took her away from her feed. You can see her in the morning."

"Thank you, Deornoth. Thank you." Simon stumbled back to the high table.

As he settled in, accepting Binabik's congratulations, Sangfugol rose at the prince's request. "We celebrate Simon's knighthood, as Prince Josua has said." The harper bowed toward the high table. "But he was not alone on his journey, nor in his bravery and sacrifice. You also know that the prince has named Binabik of Yiqanuc and Sludig of Elvritshalla to be Protectors of the Realm of Erkynland. But even there, the tale is not all told. Of the six braves ones who set out, only three returned. I have made this song, hoping that in later days they will none of them be forgotten."

At a nod from Josua, he picked out a delicate succession of notes on the harp which one of the new settlers had crafted for him, then began to sing.

> *"In farthest north, where storm winds blow*
> *And winter's teeth are fierce with rime,*
> *Out of the deep eternal snows*
> *Looms the mountain, cold Urmsheim.*

At prince's call six men did ride
From out of threatened Erkynland,
Sludig, Grimmric, Binabik the troll,
Ethelbearn, Simon, and brave Haestan.

They sought Camaris' mighty sword
The black blade Thorn from old Nabban,
Splinter of fallen heaven-star
To save the prince's tortured land . . ."

As Sangfugol played and sang, the whispering stopped, and a hush fell over the gathering. Even Josua watched, as though the song could make the triumph a real one. The torches wavered. Simon drank more wine.

It was quite late. Only a few musicians were still playing—Sangfugol had exchanged his harp for his lute, and Binabik had brought out his flute late in the proceedings—and the dancing had more or less degenerated into staggering and laughing. Simon himself had drunk a great deal of wine and danced with two girls from Gadrinsett, a pretty plump one and her thin friend. The girls had whispered back and forth between themselves almost the whole time, impressed by Simon, his youthful beard and grand honors. They had also giggled uncontrollably every time he tried to talk to them. At last, bewildered and more than a little irritated, he had bid them good night and kissed their hands, as knights were supposed to do, which had occasioned more flurries of nervous laughter. They were really little more than children, Simon decided.

Josua had seen Lady Vorzheva off to bed, then returned to preside over the final hour of the feast. He sat now, talking quietly with Deornoth. Both men looked tired.

Jeremias was sleeping in a corner, determined not to go to bed while Simon was still up, despite the fact that his friend had the advantage of having slept until past noon. Still, Simon was beginning to think seriously about lurching off to bed when Binabik appeared in the doorway of Leavetaking House. Qantaqa stood beside him, sniffing the air of the great hall with a mixture of interest and distrust. Binabik left the wolf and came inside. He beckoned to Simon, then made his way over to Josua's chair.

". . . So they have made him a bed? Good." The prince turned as Simon approached. "Binabik brings news. Welcome news."

The troll nodded. "I do not know this man, but Isorn seemed to think that his coming was an important thing. Count Eolair, a Hernystirman," he explained to Simon, "has just been brought across the water by one of the fishermen, brought here to New Gadrinsett." He smiled at the name, which still seemed clumsily new-minted. "He is very tired now, but he is telling that he has important news for us, which he will give us in the morning if the prince is willing it."

"Of course." Josua stroked his chin thoughtfully. "Any news of Hernystir is valuable, although I doubt that much of Eolair's tale is happy."

"As it may be. However, Isorn was also saying," Binabik lowered his voice and leaned closer, "that Eolair claims to have learned something important about," his voice became quieter still, "the Great Swords."

"Ah!" muttered Deornoth, surprised.

Josua was silent for a moment. "So," he said at last. "Tomorrow, on Saint Granis' Day, perhaps we shall learn if our exile is one of hope or hopelessness." He rose and turned his cup over, giving it a spin with his fingers. "Bed, then. I will send for you all tomorrow, when Eolair has had a chance to rest."

The prince walked away across the stone tiles. The torches made his shadow jump along the walls.

"Bed, as the prince was saying." Binabik smiled. Qantaqa pushed forward, thrusting her head beneath his hand. "This will be a day for long remembering, Simon, will it not?"

Simon could only nod.

2

Chains of Many Kinds

Princess Miriamele considered the ocean.

When she had been young, one of her nurses had told her that the sea was the mother of mountains, that all the land came from the sea and would return to it one day, even as lost Khandia was reputed to have vanished into the smothering depths. Certainly the ocean that had beaten at the cliffs beneath her childhood home at Meremund had seemed eager to reclaim the rocky verge.

Others had named the sea as mother of monsters, of kilpa and kraken, oruks and water-wights. The black depths, Miriamele knew, did indeed teem with strange things. More than once some great, formless hulk had washed up on Meremund's rocky beaches to lie rotting in the sun beneath the fearful, fascinated eyes of the local inhabitants until the tide rolled it away again into the mysterious deeps. There was no doubt that the sea birthed monsters.

And when Miriamele's own mother went away, never to return, and her father Elias sank into brooding anger over his wife's death, the ocean even became a kind of parent to her. Despite its moods, as varied as the hours of sunlight and moonlight, as capricious as the storms that roiled its surface, the ocean had provided a constancy to her childhood. The breakers had lulled her to sleep at night, and she had awakened every morning to the sound of gulls and the sight of tall sails in the harbor below her father's castle, rippling like great-petaled flowers as she stared down from her window.

The ocean had been many things to her, and had meant much. But until this moment, as she stood at the aft rail of the *Eadne Cloud* with the whitecaps of the Great Green stretching away on all sides, she had never realized that it could also be a prison, a holdfast more inescapable than anything built of stone and iron.

As Earl Aspitis' ship coursed southeast from Vinitta, bound toward the Bay of Firannos and its scatter of islands, Miriamele for the first time felt the ocean turn against her, holding her more surely than ever her father's court had bound her with ritual or her father's soldiers had hemmed her all around in sharp steel. She had escaped those wardens, had she not? But how was she to escape a hundred miles of empty sea? No, it was better to give in. Miriamele was tired of fighting, tired of being strong. Stone cliffs might stand proudly for ages, but they fell to the ocean at last. Instead of resisting, she would do better to float where the tides took her, like driftwood, shaped by the action of the currents but moving, always moving. Earl Aspitis wasn't a bad man. True, he did not treat her with quite the same solicitude as he had a fortnight ago, but still he spoke kindly—that is, when she did as he wished. So she would do as he wished. She would float like an abandoned spar, unresisting, until time and events dropped her onto land again. . . .

A hand touched the sleeve of her dress. She jumped, surprised, and turned to find Gan Itai standing beside her. The Niskie's intricately wrinkled face was impassive, but her gold-flecked eyes, though sun-shaded, seemed to glitter.

"I did not mean to startle you, girl." She moved up to the rail beside Miriamele and together they stared out over the restless water.

"When there's no land in sight," Miriamele said at last, "you might as well be sailing off the edge of the world. I mean, it seems as if there might not be any land anywhere."

The Niskie nodded. Her fine white hair fluttered around her face. "Sometimes, at night, when I am up on the deck alone and singing, I feel as though I am crossing the Ocean Indefinite and Eternal, the one my people crossed to come to this land. They say that ocean was black as tar, but the wave crests glowed like pearl."

As she spoke, Gan Itai extended her hand and clasped Miriamele's palm. Startled and unsure of what to do, the princess did not resist, but continued to stare out to sea. A moment later the Niskie's long, leathery fingers pushed something into her hand.

"The sea can be a lonely place." Gan Itai continued as though unaware of what her own hand was doing. "Very lonely. It is hard to find friends. It is hard to know who can be trusted." The Niskie's hand dropped away, disappearing back into the wide sleeves of her robe. "I hope you will discover folk you can trust . . . Lady Marya." The pause before Miriamele's false name was unmistakable.

"So do I," said the princess, flustered.

"Ah." Gan Itai nodded. A smile tilted her thin mouth. "You look a little pale. Perhaps the wind is too much for you. Perhaps you should go to your cabin." The Niskie inclined her head briefly, then walked away, bare brown feet carrying her artfully across the rocking deck.

Miriamele watched her go, then looked up to the tiller where Earl Aspitis stood talking to the steersman. The earl lifted his arm to free himself from his golden cloak, which the wind had wrapped about him. He saw Miriamele and smiled briefly, then returned to his conversation. Nothing about his smile was unusual, except perhaps its perfunctory quality, but Miriamele suddenly felt chilled to the heart. She clutched the curl of parchment in her fist more tightly, fearful that the wind might pull it loose from her grasp and send it fluttering right up to Aspitis. She had no idea what it was, but somehow she knew beyond doubt that she did not want him to see it.

Miriamele forced herself to walk slowly across the deck, using her empty hand to clutch the rail. She was not nearly so steady as Gan Itai had been.

In the dim cabin, Miriamele carefully uncurled the parchment. She had to hold it up beside the candle flame to read the tiny, crabbed letters.

I have done many wrongs,

she read,

and I know you no longer trust me, but please believe that these words are honest. I have been many people, none of them satisfactory. Padreic was a fool, Cadrach a rogue. Perhaps I can become something better before I die.

She wondered where he had gotten the parchment and ink, and decided that the Niskie must have brought it to him. As she stared at the labored script, Miriamele thought of the monk's weak arms weighted by chains. She felt a stab of pity—what agony it must have been for him to write this! But why could he not leave her alone? Why could no one simply let her be?

If you are reading this, then Gan Itai has done as she promised. She is the only one on this ship you can trust . . . except perhaps for me. I know that I have cheated and deserted you. I am a weak man, my lady, but in my warnings at least I have served you well, and still try to do so. You are not safe on board this ship. Earl Aspitis is even worse than I guessed him to be. He is not just a gilded creature of Duke Benigaris' court. He is a servant of Pryrates.

I have told you many lies, my lady, and there are also many truths that I have kept hidden. I cannot set all to right here. My fingers are tired already, my arms are sore. But I will tell you this: there is no one alive who knows the evil of the priest Pryrates better than I. There is no one alive who bears more responsibility for that evil, since I helped him become what he is.

It is a long and complicated tale. Enough to say that I, to my eternal and horrible shame, gave Pryrates the key to a door he should never have opened. Worse, I did so even after I knew him for the ravening beast he is. I gave in to him because I was weak and frightened. It is the worst thing I have ever done in a life of grievous errors.

Believe me in this, lady. To my sorrow, I know our enemy well. I hope you will also believe me when I say that Aspitis does not only the bidding of his lord Benigaris, but the work of the red priest as well. It was common knowledge in Vinitta.

You must escape. Perhaps Gan Itai can help you. Sadly, I do not think you will ever again go under such light guard as you did on Vinitta. My cowardly attempt at flight will assure that. I know not how or why, but I beg you to leave as soon as you can. Flee to the inn called Pelippa's Bowl, *in Kwanitupul. I believe Dinivan has sent others there, and perhaps they can help you escape to your uncle Josua.*

    I must stop because I hurt. I will not ask you to forgive me. I have earned no forgiveness.

A smear of blood had stained the edge of the parchment. Miriamele stared at it, her eyes blurring with tears, until someone knocked sharply on the door and her heart erupted into frenzied pounding. She crumpled the note in her palm even as the door swung open.

"My sweet lady," said grinning Aspitis, "why do you hide yourself down here in the dark? Come, let us walk on the deck."

The parchment seemed to burn her, as though she clutched a smoldering coal.

"I . . . I do not feel well, my lord." She shook her head, trying to hide her shortness of breath. "I will walk another time."

"Marya," the earl chided, "I told you that it was your country openness that charmed me. What, are you becoming a moody court wench?" He reached her side in a long step. His hand trailed across her neck. "Come, it is no wonder you feel poorly, sitting in this dark room. You need air." He leaned forward and brushed his lips below her ear. "Or perhaps you prefer it here, in the dark. Perhaps you are merely lonely?" His fingers dragged delicately across her throat, soft as spiderwebs on her skin.

Miriamele stared at the candle. The flame danced before her, but all around it was sunken deep in shadow.

The stained glass windows of the Hayholt's throne room had been broken. Ragged curtains restrained the flurrying snow, but did not keep out the freezing air. Even Pryrates seemed to feel the cold: although he still went bareheaded, the king's counselor was wearing red robes lined with fur.

Alone of all the folk who came into the throne room, the king and his cupbearer did not seem to mind the chill air. Elias sat bare-armed and bare-footed on the Dragonbone Chair; but for the great scabbarded sword that hung from his belt, he was dressed as casually as if he lounged in his private chambers. The monk Hengfisk, the king's silent page, wore a threadbare habit and his customary lunatic grin, and appeared no less comfortable than his master in the frosty hall.

The High King slouched deep in the cage of dragon's bones, chin on chest, peering out from beneath his eyebrows at Pryrates. In contrast to the black malachite statues which stood on each side of the throne, Elias' skin seemed white as milk. Blue veins showed at his temples and along his wiry arms, bulging as though they might burst through the flesh.

Pryrates opened his mouth as if to say something, then closed it again. His sigh was that of an Aedonite martyr overwhelmed with the foolish wickedness of his persecutors.

"Damn you, priest," Elias snarled, "my mind is made up."

The king's advisor said nothing, but only nodded; the torchlight made his hairless skull gleam like a wet stone. Despite the wind that fluttered the curtains, the room seemed full of a curious stillness.

"Well?" The king's green eyes were dangerously bright.

The priest sighed again, more softly. His voice, when he spoke, was conciliatory. "I am your counselor, Elias. I only do what you would wish me to: that is, help you decide what is best."

"Then I think it best that Fengbald take soldiers and go east. I want Josua and his band of traitors driven out of their holes and crushed. I have delayed too long already with this business of Guthwulf and with Benigaris' fumblings in Nabban. If Fengbald leaves now, he and his troops will reach my brother's den in a month. You know what kind of winter it will be, alchemist—you of all people. If I wait any longer, the chance is lost." The king pulled at his face irritably.

"As to the weather, there is little doubt," Pryrates said equably. "I can only once again question the need to pursue your brother. He is no threat. Even with an army of thousands, he could not stop us before your glorious, complete, and permanent victory is assured. There is only a little while longer to wait."

The wind changed direction, making the banners that hung from the ceiling ripple like pondwater. Elias snapped his fingers and Hengfisk scuttled forward with the king's cup. Elias drank, coughed, then drank again until the goblet was empty. A bead of steaming black liquid clung to his chin.

"That is simple for you to say," the king snarled when he had finished swallowing. "Aedon's Blood, you have said it often enough. But I have waited long already. I am cursedly tired of waiting."

"But it will be worth the wait, Majesty. You know that."

The king's face grew momentarily pensive. "And my dreams have been getting more and more strange, Pryrates. More . . . real."

"That is understandable." Pryrates lifted his long fingers soothingly. "You bear a great burden—but all will soon be made right. You will author a reign of splendor unlike anything the world has seen, if you will only be patient. These matters have their own timing—like war, like love."

"Hah." Elias belched sourly, his irritation returning. "Damned little you know of love, you eunuch bastard." Pryrates flinched at this, and for a moment narrowed his coal-black eyes to slits, but the king was gazing down morosely at Sorrow and did not see. When he looked up again, the priest's face was as blandly patient as before. "So what is *your* payment for all this, alchemist? That I've never understood."

"Besides the pleasure of serving you, Majesty?"

Elias' laugh was sharp and short, like a dog's bark. "Yes, besides that."

Pryrates stared at him appraisingly for a moment. An odd smile twisted his

thin lips. "Power, of course. The power to do what I want to do . . . need to
do."

The king's eyes had swung to the window. A raven had alighted on the sill
and now stood preening its oily black feathers. "And what do you want to do,
Pryrates?"

"Learn." For a moment the priest's careful mask of statecraft seemed to slip;
the face of a child showed through—a horrible, greedy child. "I want to know
everything. For that I need power, which is a sort of permission. There are secrets
so dark, so deep, that the only way to discover them is to tear open the universe
and root about in the very guts of Death and Unbeing."

Elias lifted his hand and waved for his cup once more. He continued to
watch the raven, which hopped forward on the sill and tilted its head to return
the king's stare. "You talk strangely, priest. Death? Unbeing? Are they not the
same?"

Pryrates grinned maliciously, although at what was not clear. "Oh, no, Majesty. Not remotely."

Elias suddenly whirled in his chair, craning his head around the yellowed,
dagger-fanged skull of the dragon Shurakai. "Curse you, Hengfisk, did you not
see me call for my cup!? My throat is burning!"

The pop-eyed monk hurried to the king's side. Elias carefully took the cup
from him and set it down, then hit Hengfisk on the side of his head so swiftly
and powerfully that the cupbearer was flung to the floor as if lightning-struck.
Elias then calmly drained the steaming draught. Hengfisk lay boneless as a
jellyfish for several long moments then rose and retrieved the empty cup. His
idiot grin had not vanished; if anything, it had become wider and more deranged, as though the king had done him some great kindness. The monk
bobbed his head and backed into the shadows once more.

Elias paid him no attention. "So it is settled. Fengbald will take the Erkynguard and a company of soldiers and mercenaries and go east. He will bring me
back my brother's smirking, lecturing head on a lance." He paused, then said
thoughtfully: "Do you suppose that the Norns would go with Fengbald? They
are fierce fighters, and cold weather and darkness are nothing to them."

Pryrates raised an eyebrow. "I think it unlikely, my king. They do not seem
to like to travel by day; neither do they seem to enjoy the company of mortals."

"Not much use as allies, are they?" Elias frowned and stroked Sorrow's hilt.

"Oh, they are valuable enough, Majesty." Pryrates nodded his head, smiling.
"They will render service when we truly need them. Their master—your
greatest ally—will see to that."

The raven blinked its golden eye, then uttered a harsh noise and took wing.
The tattered curtain fluttered where it passed out through the window and into
the stinging wind.

"Please, may I hold him?" Maegwin extended her arms.

With a worried look on her dust-smeared face, the young mother handed the baby to her. Maegwin could not help wondering if the woman was frightened of her—the king's daughter, with her dark mourning clothes and strange ways.

"I'm just so afraid he'll be wicked, my lady," said the young woman. "He's been crying all day, till I nearly run mad. He's hungry, poor little thing, but I don't want him screaming 'round you, Lady. You've more important things to think about."

Maegwin felt the chill that had touched her heart thaw a little. "Never worry about that." She bounced the pink-faced baby, who did seem to be on the brink of another outburst. "Tell me his name, Caihwye."

The young woman looked up, startled. "You know me, Lady?"

Maegwin smiled sadly. "We are not so very many, any more. Far less than a thousand in these caverns all told. No, there are not so many people in Free Hernystir that I have trouble remembering them."

Caihwye nodded, wide-eyed. "It is terrible." She had probably been pretty before the war, but now she had lost teeth and was dreadfully thin. Maegwin was certain that she had been giving most of what food she had to her baby.

"The child's name?" Maegwin reminded her.

"Oh! Siadreth, my lady. It was his father's name." Caihwye shook her head sadly; Maegwin did not ask after the child's namesake. For most of the survivors, discussions about fathers, husbands, and sons were sadly predictable. Most of the stories ended with the battle at the Inniscrich.

"Princess Maegwin." Old Craobhan had been watching silently until now. "We must go. There are more people waiting for you."

She nodded. "You are right." Gently, she handed the child back to his mother. The small pink face wrinkled, preparing to shed tears. "He is very beautiful, Caihwye. May all the gods bless him, and Mircha herself give him good health. He will be a fine man."

Caihwye smiled and jiggled young Siadreth in her lap until he forgot what he had been about to do. "Thank you, Lady. I'm so glad you came back well."

Maegwin, who had been turning away, paused. "Came back?"

The young woman looked startled, frightened she'd said something wrong. "From under the ground, Lady." She pointed downward with her free hand. "From down in the deeper caverns. It is you the gods must favor, to bring you back from such a dark place."

Maegwin stared for a moment, then forced a smile. "I suppose. Yes, I am glad to be back, too." She stroked the baby's head once more before turning to follow Craobhan.

"I know that judging disputes is not so enjoyable a task for a woman as dandling babies," Old Craobhan said over his shoulder, "but this is something you must do anyway. You are Lluth's daughter."

Maegwin grimaced, but would not be distracted. "How did that woman know I had been in the caverns below?"

The old man shrugged. "You didn't work very hard to keep it secret, and you can't expect people not to be interested in the doings of the king's family. Tongues will always wag."

Maegwin frowned. Craobhan was right, of course. She had been heedless and headstrong about exploring the lower caverns. If she wanted secrecy, she should have started worrying about it sooner.

"What do they think about it?" she asked at last. "The people, I mean."

"Think about your adventuring?" He chuckled sourly. "I imagine there's as many stories as there are cookfires. Some say you went looking for the gods. Some think you were looking for a bolt hole out of this whole muddle." He peered at her over his bony shoulder. His self-satisfied, knowing look made her want to smack him. "By the middle of winter they'll be saying you found a city of gold, or fought a dragon or a two-headed giant. Forget about it. Stories are like hares—only a fool tries to run after one and catch it."

Maegwin glowered at the back of his old bald head. She didn't know which she liked less, having people tell lies about her or having people know the truth. She suddenly wished Eolair had returned.

Fickle cow, she sneered at herself.

But she did. She wished she could talk to him, tell him of all her ideas, even the mad ones. He would understand, wouldn't he? Or would it only confirm his belief in her wretchedness? It mattered little, anyway: Eolair had been gone for more than a month, and Maegwin did not even know if he still lived. She herself had sent him away. Now, she heartily wished that she had not.

Fearful but resolute, Maegwin had never softened the cold words she had spoken to Count Eolair down in the buried city of Mezutu'a. They had barely conversed during the few days that passed between their return from that place and his departure in search of Josua's rumored rebel camp.

Eolair had spent most of those days down in the ancient city, overseeing a pair of stronghearted Hernystiri clerks as they copied the dwarrows' stone maps onto more portable rolls of sheepshide. Maegwin had not accompanied him; despite the dwarrows' kindness, the thought of the empty, echoing city only filled her with sullen disappointment. She had been wrong. Not mad, as many thought her, but certainly wrong. She had thought the gods meant her to find the Sithi there, but now it seemed clear that the Sithi were lost and frightened and would be no help to her people. As for the dwarrows, the Sithi's once-servants, they were little more than shadows, incapable of helping even themselves.

At Eolair's parting, Maegwin had been so full of warring feelings that she could muster little more than a curt farewell. He had pressed into her hand a gift sent by the dwarrows—it was a glossy gray and white chunk of crystal on which Yis-fidri, the record-keeper, had carved her name in his own runic alphabet. It almost looked as though it might be part of the Shard itself, but it lacked that stone's restless inner light. Eolair had then turned and mounted his horse, struggling to hide his anger. She had felt something tearing inside her as the Count of Nad Mullach rode away down the slope and vanished into the flurrying snow. Surely, she had prayed, the gods must bear her up in this desperate time. The gods, though, seemed slow to lend their aid these days.

Maegwin had thought at first that her dreams about an underground city were signs of the gods' willingness to help their stricken followers in Hernystir. Maegwin knew now that somehow she had made a mistake. She had thought to find the Sithi, the ancient and legendary allies, to force her way in through the very gates of legend to bring help to Hernystir—but that had been prideful foolishness. The gods invited, they were not invaded.

Maegwin had been mistaken in that small thing, but still she knew that she was not altogether wrong. No matter what misdeeds her people had done, the gods would not so easily desert them. Brynioch, Rhynn, Murhagh One-Arm—they would save their children, she was sure of it. Somehow, they would bring destruction to Skali and Elias the High King, the bestial pair who had brought such humiliation on a proud and free people. If they did not, then the world was an empty jest. So Maegwin would wait for a better, clearer sign, and while she waited, she would go quietly about her duties . . . tending to her people and mourning her dead.

"What suits do I hear today?" she asked Old Craobhan.

"Some small ones, as well as a request for judgment that should prove no joy," Craobhan replied. "That one comes from House Earb and House Lacha, which were neighboring holdings on the Circoille fringe." The old man had been king's counselor since Maegwin's grandfather's day, and knew the fantastical ins and outs of Hernystiri political life the way a master smith knew the vagaries of heat and metal. "Both families shared a section of the woods as their vouchsafe," he explained, "—the only time your father had to declare separate rights to forest land and draw up a map of possession for each, like the Aedonite kings do, just to keep Earb-men and Lacha-men from slaughtering each other. They loathe each other and the two houses have fought forever. They barely took time to go to war against Skali, and they may not have noticed that we lost." He coughed and spat.

"So what is wanted of me?"

Craobhan frowned. "What would you guess, Lady? They quarrel now over cavern space—" his voice rose in mockery, " '—this place is for me, this for thee. No, no, it's mine; no, mine.' " He snorted. "They squabble like piglets over the last teat, even as we all shelter together in danger and poor conditions."

"They sound a disgusting group." Maegwin had little temper for such petty nonsense.

"I couldn't have said fairer myself," the old man said.

Neither House Lacha nor House Earb benefited much from Maegwin's presence. Their dispute proved just as petty as Craobhan had predicted. A tunnel to the surface had been dug out and widened to useful size by men from both houses with the additional help of Hernystirmen from other, less important families who shared the common cavern. Now each of the feuding houses insisted that it alone was the tunnel's owner, and that the other house and all other cavern-dwellers should pay a tithe of goatsmilk for taking their flocks up and down the tunnel each day.

Maegwin was mightily disgusted by this and said so. She also proclaimed that if such rank nonsense as people "owning" tunnels ever came up again, she would have the remainder of Hernystir's fighting men gather up the malefactors, take them to the surface, and throw them from the highest cliffs that craggy Grianspog could provide.

Houses Lacha and Earb were not pleased by this judgment. They managed to put aside their differences long enough to demand that Maegwin be replaced as judge by her stepmother Inahwen—who was after all, they said, the late King Lluth's *wife,* and not merely his daughter. Maegwin laughed and called them conniving fools. The spectators who had gathered, along with the remaining families that shared the cavern with the feuding houses, cheered Maegwin's good sense and the humbling of the haughty Earb- and Lacha-folk.

The rest of the suits went quickly. Maegwin found herself enjoying the work, although some of the disputes were sad. It was something she did well— something that had little to do with being small or delicate or pretty. Surrounded by lovelier, more graceful women, she had always felt herself an embarrassment to her father, even at a rustic court like the Taig. Here, all that mattered was her good sense. In the past weeks, she had found—to her surprise—that her father's subjects valued her, that they were grateful for her willingness to listen and be fair. As she watched her people, tattered and smoke-smudged, she felt her heart tighten within her. The Hernystiri deserved better than this low estate. They would get it, somehow, if it was within Maegwin's power.

For a while, she managed to forgot almost entirely about her cruelty to the Count of Nad Mullach.

That evening, as she lay on the edge of sleep, Maegwin found herself abruptly falling forward into a darkness vaster and deeper than the ember-lit cavern where she made her bed. For a moment she thought some cataclysm had torn open the earth beneath her; a moment later, she was certain that she dreamed. But as she felt herself slowly spinning into emptiness, the sensation seemed far too immediate for a dream, and yet too strangely dislocated to be anything so real as an earth tremor. She had felt something like this before, those nights when she had dreamed of the beautiful city beneath the earth. . . .

Even as her confused thoughts fluttered in darkness like startled bats, a cloud of dim lights began to appear. They were fireflies, or sparks, or distant torches. They spiraled upward, like the smoke of a great bonfire, mounting toward some unimaginable height.

Climb, said a voice in her head. *Go to the High Place. The time is come.*

Swimming in nothingness, Maegwin struggled toward the distant peak where the flickering lights congregated.

Go to the High Place, the voice demanded. *The time is come.*

And suddenly she was in the midst of many gleaming lights, small and intense as distant stars. A hazy throng surrounded her, beautiful yet inhuman, dressed in all the colors of the rainbow. The creatures stared at each other with gleaming eyes. Their graceful forms were vague; although they were man-shaped, she somehow felt sure they were no more human than rain clouds or spotted deer.

The time is come, said the voice, now many voices. A smear of leaping, coruscating light glowed in the midst of them, as though one of the stars had fallen down from the vaulting sky. *Go to the High Place. . . .*

And then the fantastic vision was bleeding away, draining back into darkness.

Maegwin woke to discover herself sitting upright on her pallet. The fires were only glowing coals. There was nothing to be seen in the darkened cavern, and nothing to hear but the sound of other people breathing in sleep. She was clutching Yis-fidri's dwarrow-stone so tightly that her knuckles throbbed with pain. For a moment she thought a faint light gleamed in its depths, but when she looked again she decided she had fooled herself: it was only a translucent lump of rock. She shook her head slowly. The stone was of no importance, anyway, compared to what she had experienced.

The gods. The gods had spoken to her again, even more plainly this time. The high place, they had said. The time had come. That must mean that at last the lords of her people were ready to reach out and aid Hernystir. And they wanted Maegwin to do something. They must, or they would not have touched her, would not have sent her this clear sign.

The small matters of the day just passed were now swept from her mind. *The high place*, she told herself. She sat for a long time in the darkness, thinking.

After checking carefully to make sure that Earl Aspitis was still up on deck, Miriamele hurried down the narrow passageway and rapped on the low door. A murmuring voice inside fell silent at the sound of Miriamele's knock.

The reply came some moments later. "Yes? Who is there?"

"Lady Marya. May I come in?"

"Come."

Miriamele pushed against the swollen door. It gave grudgingly, opening on a tiny, austere room. Gan Itai sat on a pallet beneath the open window, which was little more than a narrow slit near the top of the wall. Something moved there; Miriamele saw a smooth expanse of white neck and a flash of yellow eye, then the seagull dropped away and vanished.

"The gulls are like children." Gan Itai showed her guest a wrinkled smile. "Argumentative, forgetful, but sweet-hearted."

Miriamele shook her head, confused. "I'm sorry to bother you."

"Bother? Child, what a foolish idea. It is daylight, I have no singing to do for now. Why would you be a bother?"

"I don't know, I just . . ." Miriamele paused, trying to collect her thoughts. She wasn't really certain why she had come. "I . . . I need someone to talk to, Gan Itai. I'm frightened."

The Niskie reached over to a three-legged stool which appeared to serve as a table. Her nimble brown fingers swept several sea-polished stones off the seat and into the pocket of her robe, then she pushed the stool over to Miriamele.

"Sit, child. Do not hurry yourself."

Miriamele arranged her skirt, wondering how much she dared to tell the Niskie. But if Gan Itai was carrying secret messages for Cadrach, how much could there be that she still did not know? She had certainly seemed to know that Marya was a false name. There was nothing to do but roll the dice.

"Do you know who I am?"

The sea-watcher smiled again. "You are Lady Marya, a noblewoman from Erkynland."

Miriamele was startled. "I am?"

The Niskie's laugh hissed like wind through dry grass. "Are you not? You have certainly told enough people that name. But if you mean to ask Gan Itai who you *truly* are, I will tell you, or at least I will start with this: Miriamele is your name, daughter of the High King."

Miriamele was curiously relieved. "So you *do* know."

"Your companion Cadrach confirmed it for me. I had suspicions. I met your father, once. You smell like him; sound like him, too."

"I do? You did?" Miriamele felt as though she had lost her balance. "What do you mean?"

"Your father met Benigaris here on this boat two years gone, when Benigaris was only the duke's son. Aspitis, *Eadne Cloud*'s master, hosted the gathering. That strange wizard-creature was here, too—the one with no hair." Gan Itai made a smoothing gesture across her head.

"Pryrates." The name's evil taste lingered in her mouth.

"Yes, that is the one." Gan Itai sat up straighter, cocking her ear to some far-away sound. After a moment she turned her attention back to her guest. "I do not learn the names of all the folk who ride this boat. I do pay sharp attention to everyone who treads the gangplank, of course—that is part of the Navigator's Trust—but names are not usually important to sea-watchers. That time, though, Aspitis told me all their names, as my children used to sing to me their lessons about the tides and currents. He was very proud of his important guests."

Miriamele was momentarily distracted. "Your children?"

"By the Uncharted, yes, certainly!" Gan Itai nodded. "I am a great-grandmother twenty times over."

"I've never seen Niskie children."

The old woman looked at her dourly. "I know you are a southerner only by birth, child, but even in Meremund where you grew up there is a small Niskie town near the docks. Did you never go there?"

Miriamele shook her head. "I wasn't allowed."

Gan Itai pursed her lips. "That is unhappy. You should have gone to see it. We are fewer now than we once were, and who knows what will come on tomorrow's tide? My family is one of the largest, but there are fewer than ten score families all together from Abaingeat on the north coast all the way down to Naraxi and Harcha. So few for all the deep-water ships!" She shook her head sadly.

"But when my father and those others were here, what did they say? What did they do?"

"They talked, young one, but about what I cannot say. They talked the night away, but I was on deck, with the sea and my songs. Besides, it is not my place to spy on the ship's owner. Unless he wrongly endangers the ship, it is not my place to do anything at all except that which I was born for: to sing the kilpa down."

"But you brought me Cadrach's letter." Miriamele looked around to make sure the passageway door was closed. "That is not something Aspitis would want you to do."

For the first time, Gan Itai's golden eyes showed a trace of discontent. "That is true, but I was not harming the ship." A look of defiance crept onto the lined face. "We are Niskies, after all, not slaves. We are a free people."

She and Miriamele looked at each other for a moment. The princess was the first to look away. "I don't even care what they were talking about, anyway. I'm sick and tired of men and their wars and arguments. I just want to go away and be left alone—to climb into a hole somewhere and never come out."

The Niskie did not reply, only watched her.

"Still, I will never escape across fifty leagues of open water." The uselessness of it all pulled at her, making her feel heavy with despair. "Will we make land anytime soon?"

"We will stop at some of the islands in Firannos Bay. Spenit, perhaps Risa—I am not sure which ones Aspitis has chosen."

"Maybe I can escape somehow. But I'm sure I will be heavily guarded." The leaden feeling seemed to grow stronger. Then an idea flickered. "Do you ever get off the ship, Gan Itai?"

The sea-watcher looked at her appraisingly. "Seldom. But there is a family of Tinukeda'ya—of Niskies—at Risa. The *Injar* clan. Once or twice I have visited them. Why do you ask?"

"Because if you can leave the ship, you could take a message for me. Give it to someone who might get it to my Uncle Josua."

Gan Itai frowned. "Certainly I will do it, but I am not sure that it will ever get to him. It would be a piece of long luck."

"What choice do I have?" Miriamele sighed. "Of course it's foolish. But maybe it would help, and what else can I do?" Tears abruptly welled in her eyes. She wiped them away angrily. "No one will be able to do anything, even if they want to. But I have to try."

Gan Itai stared in alarm. "Do not cry, child. It makes me feel cruel for having dragged you out of your hiding place in the hold."

Miriamele waved a tear-dampened hand. "Someone would have found us."

The Niskie leaned forward. "Perhaps your companion would have some idea of who to give your note to, or some special thing that could be written in it. He seems to me a wise man."

"Cadrach?"

"Yes. After all, he knew the true name of the Navigator's Children." Her voice was grave but proud, as though knowing her people's name was evidence of godlike wisdom.

"But how . . ." Miriamele bit off the rest of her question. Of course Gan Itai knew how to get to Cadrach. She had already brought a note from him. But Miriamele was not quite sure that she wanted to see the monk. He had caused her so much pain, sparked so much anger.

"Come." Gan Itai rose from the pallet, climbing to her feet as easily as a young girl. "I will take you to him." She squinted out the narrow window. "They will not bring him food for almost another hour. That will leave plenty of time for a pleasant conversation." She grinned, then moved quickly across the small room. "Can you climb in that dress?"

The Niskie slid her fingers in behind a board on the bare wall and pulled. A panel, so closely fitted that it had been all but invisible, came free; Gan Itai set it down on the floor. A dark hole lined with pitch-smeared beams showed where the panel had been.

"Where does it lead?" Miriamele asked, surprised.

"Nowhere, particularly," Gan Itai said. She clambered through and stood up, so that only her thin brown legs and the hem of her robe showed in the opening. "It is merely a way to get quickly to the hold or the deck. A Niskie-hole, as it is called." Her muffled voice had a slight echo.

Miriamele leaned in behind her. A ladder stood against the far wall of the tiny cubicle. At the top of the confining walls, a narrow crawlspace extended in both directions. The princess shrugged and followed the Niskie up the ladder.

The passageway at the top was too low to be negotiated except on hands and knees, so Miriamele knotted the end of her skirt up out of her way, then crawled after Gan Itai. As the light of the Niskie's room disappeared behind them, the darkness pulled in closer, so that Miriamele could only follow her nose and the quiet sound of Gan Itai crawling. The beams creaked as the ship flexed. Miriamele felt as though she were creeping down the gullet of some great sea beast.

Some twenty cubits from the ladder, Gan Itai stopped. Miriamele bumped into her from behind.

"Careful, child." The Niskie's face was revealed in a growing wedge of light as she pried up another panel. When Gan Itai had peered through, she beckoned Miriamele forward. After the darkness of the crawlspace, the dim hold seemed a cheerful, sunlit place, though all that lit it was a propped hatchway at the far end.

"We must keep our voices low," the sea-watcher said.

The hold was stacked nearly to the rafters with sacks and barrels, all tied down so they would not roll free in high seas. Against one wall, as though he, too, were restrained against capricious tides, was the huddled figure of the monk. A heavy length of chain was at his ankles; another depended from his wrists.

"Learned one!" called the Niskie. Cadrach's round head came up slowly, like a beaten dog's. He stared up into the shadowed rafters.

"Gan Itai?" His voice was hoarse and weary. "Is that you?"

Miriamele felt her heart plummet in her breast. Merciful Aedon, look at him! Chained like a poor dumb brute!

"I have come to talk to you," the Niskie whispered. "Are the warders coming soon?"

Cadrach shook his head. His chains rattled quietly. "I think not. They never hurry to feed me. Did you give my note to . . . to the lady?"

"I did. She is here to talk to you."

The monk started as if frightened. "What? You brought her here?" He lifted his clanking shackles before his face. "No! No! Take her away!"

Gan Itai pulled Miriamele forward. "He is very unhappy. Speak to him."

Miriamele swallowed. "Cadrach?" she said at last. "Have they hurt you?"

The monk slid down the wall, becoming little more than a heap of shadows. "Go away, Lady. I cannot bear to see you, or to have you see me. Go away."

There was a long moment of silence. "Speak to him!" Gan Itai hissed.

"I am sorry they have done this to you." She felt tears coming. "Whatever has happened between us, I would never have wished to see you tormented this way."

"Ah, Lady, what a dreadful world this is." The monk's voice had a sobbing catch to it. "Will you not take my advice and flee? Please."

Miriamele shook her head in frustration, then realized he could not see her up in the shadow of the hatchway. "How, Cadrach? Aspitis will not let me out of his sight. Gan Itai said she would take away a letter from me and try to get it to someone who will deliver it—but deliver it to whom? Who would help me? I do not know where Josua is. My mother's family in Nabban have turned traitor. What can I do?"

The dark shape that was Cadrach slowly stood up. *"Pelippa's Bowl,* Miriamele. As I told you in my letter. There may be someone there who can help." He did not sound very convinced.

"Who? Who could I send it to?"

"Send it to the inn. Draw a quill pen on it, a quill in a circle. That will get it to someone who can help, if anyone useful is there." He lifted a weighted arm. "Please go away, Princess. After all that has happened, I want only to be left alone. I do not wish to have you see my shame any longer."

Miriamele felt her tears overspill her eyes. It took a few moments before she could talk. "Do you want anything?"

"A jug of wine. No, a wineskin: it will be easier to hide. That's all I need. Something to make a darkness within me to match the darkness around me." His laughter was painful to hear. "And you safely escaped. That, too."

Miriamele turned her face away. She could not bear to look at the monk's huddled form any longer. "I'm so sorry," she said, then hurriedly pushed past Gan Itai and retreated a few cubits up the crawlspace. The conversation had made her feel ill.

The Niskie said some last words to Cadrach, then lowered the panel and plunged the tiny passageway into darkness once more. Her thin form pushed past, then she led Miriamele back to the ladder.

The princess was no sooner back into daylight when a fresh bout of sobbing came over her. Gan Itai watched uncomfortably for a while, but when Miriamele could not stop crying, the Niskie put a spidery arm around her.

"Stop, now, stop," she crooned. "You will be happy again."

Miriamele untied her skirt, then lifted the corner and wiped her eyes and nose. "No I won't. Nor will Cadrach. Oh, God in Heaven, I am so lonely!" Another storm of weeping came over her.

Gan Itai held her until she stopped crying.

"It is cruel to bind any creature that way." The Niskie's voice was tight with something like anger. Miriamele, her head in Gan Itai's lap, was too drained to reply. "They bound Ruyan Vé, did you know? The father of our people, the great Navigator. When he would have taken the ships and set sail once more, they seized him in their anger and bound him in chains." The Niskie rocked back and forth. "And then they burned the ships."

Miriamele sniffled. She did not know who Gan Itai was talking about, nor did she care at this moment.

"They wanted us to be slaves, but we Tinukeda'ya are a free people." Gan Itai's voice became almost a chant, a sorrowful song. "They burned our ships—burned the great ships that we could never build again in this new land, and left us stranded here. They said it was to save us from Unbeing, but that was a lie. They only wanted us to share their exile—we, who did not need them! The Ocean Indefinite and Eternal could have been our home, but they took our ships away and bound mighty Ruyan. They wanted us to be their servants. It is wrong to put anyone in chains who has done you no harm. Wrong."

Gan Itai continued to hold Miriamele in her arms as she rocked back and forth and murmured of terrible injustices. The sun fell lower in the sky. The small room began to fill with shadow.

Miriamele lay in her darkened cabin and listened to the Niskie's faint song. Gan Itai had been very upset. Miriamele had not thought the sea-watcher held such strong feelings, but something about Cadrach's captivity and the princess' own tears had brought up a great outpouring of grief and anger.

Who were the Niskies, anyway? Cadrach called them Tinukeda'ya—Ocean Children, Gan Itai had said. Where did they come from? Some distant island, perhaps. Ships on a dark ocean, the Niskie had said, from somewhere far away. Was that the way of the world, that everyone longed to go back to some place or some time that was lost?

Her thoughts were interrupted by a knock at the door.

"Lady Marya? Are you awake?"

She did not answer. The door slowly swung open. Miriamele cursed herself inwardly: she should have bolted it.

"Lady Marya?" The earl's voice was soft. "Are you ill? I missed you at supper."

She stirred and rubbed her eyes, as if awakening from sleep. "Lord Aspitis? I'm sorry, I am not feeling well. We will talk tomorrow, if I feel better."

He came on cat-soft feet and sat down on the edge of her bed. His long fingers traced her cheek. "But this is terrible. What ails you? I shall have Gan Itai look to you. She is well-versed in healing; I would trust her past any leech or apothecary."

"Thank you, Aspitis. That would be kind. Now I should probably go back to sleep. I'm sorry to be such poor company."

The earl seemed in no hurry to leave. He stroked her hair. "You know, Lady, I am truly sorry for my rough words and ways of the other evening. I have come to care deeply for you, and I was upset at the idea that you might leave me so soon. After all, we share a deep lovers' bond, do we not?" His fingertips slid down to her neck, making the skin tighten and sending a chill through her.

"I fear I am not in good condition to talk about such things now, Lord. But I forgive you your words, which I know were hasty and not heartfelt." She turned her eyes to his face for a moment, trying to judge his thoughts. His eyes seemed guileless, but she remembered Cadrach's words, as well as Gan Itai's description of the gathering he had hosted, and the chill returned, bringing a tremor that she was hard-pressed to conceal.

"Good," he said. "Very good. I am glad you understand that. Hasty words. Exactly."

Miriamele decided to test that courtier's sincerity of his. "But of course, Aspitis, you must understand my own unhappiness. My father, you see, does not know where I am. Perhaps already the convent will have sent word to him that I did not arrive. He will be sick with worry. He is old, Aspitis, and I fear for his health. You can see why I feel I must forsake your hospitality, whether I wish to or not."

"Of course," said the earl. Miriamele felt a flicker of hope. Could she have misread him after all? "It is cruel to let your father worry. We will send him word as soon as we next make landfall—on Spenit Island, I think. And we will give him the good news."

She smiled. "He will be very happy to hear I am well."

"Ah." Aspitis returned her smile. His long, fine jaw and clear eyes could have served as a sculptor's model for one of the great heroes of the past. "But there will be more good news than just that. We will tell him that his daughter is to marry one into of Nabban's Fifty Families!"

Miriamele's smile faltered. "What?"

"Why, we will tell him of our coming marriage!" Aspitis laughed with delight. "Yes, Lady, I have thought and thought, and although your family is not quite so elevated as mine—and Erkynlandish, as well—I have decided for love's sake to spit in the face of tradition. We will be married when we return to Nabban." He took her cold hand in his warm grip. "But you do not look as happy as I would have hoped, beautiful Marya."

Miriamele's mind was racing, but as in a dream of fearful pursuit, she could think of nothing but escape. "I . . . I am overwhelmed, Aspitis."

"Ah, well, I suppose that is understandable." He stood, then bent over to kiss her. His breath smelled of wine, his cheek of perfume. His mouth was hard against hers for a moment before he pulled away. "After all, it is rather sudden, I know. But it would be worse than ungentlemanly of me to desert you . . . after all we have shared. And I have come to love you, Marya. The flowers of the north are different than those of my southern home, but their scent is just as sweet, the blossoms just as beautiful."

He stopped in the doorway. "Rest and sleep well, Lady. We have much to talk about. Good night." The door fell shut behind him. Miriamele immediately leaped from her bed and drove home the bolt, then crawled back under her blanket, overcome by a fit of shivering.

3

East of the World

✦

"I'm a knight now, aren't I?" Simon ran his hand through the thick fur of Qantaqa's neck. The wolf eyed him impassively.

Binabik looked up from his sheaf of parchment and nodded. "By an oath to your god and your prince." The troll turned back to Morgenes' book once more. "That is seeming to me to fit the knightly particulars."

Simon stared across the tiled expanse of the Fire Garden, trying to think of how to put his thought into words. "But . . . but I don't feel any different. I'm a knight—a man! So why do I feel like the same person?"

Caught up in something he was reading, Binabik took a moment to respond. "I am sorry, Simon," he said at last. "I am not being a good friend for listening. Please say what you were saying once more."

Simon bent and picked up a piece of loose stone, then flung it skittering across the tiles and into the surrounding undergrowth. Qantaqa bounded after it. "If I'm a knight and a grown man, why do I feel like the same stupid scullion?"

Binabik smiled. "It is not only you who has ever had such feelings, friend Simon. Because a new season has passed, or because a recognition has been given, still it is not changing a person very much on the inside. You were made Josua's knight because of bravery you showed on Urmsheim. If you were changing, it was not at the ceremony yesterday, but on the mountain that it was happening." He patted Simon's booted foot. "Did you not say that you had learned something there, and also from the spilling of the dragon's blood?"

"Yes." Simon squinted at Qantaqa's tail, which waved above the heather like a puff of smoke.

"People, both trolls and lowlanders, are growing in their own time," said the little man, "—not when someone says that it is so. Be content. You will always be extremely Simon-like, but still I have been seeing much change in the months we have been friends."

"Really?" Simon paused in mid-toss.

"Truth. You are becoming a man, Simon. Let it happen at the swiftness that it needs, and do not be worrying yourself." He rattled the papers. "Listen, I want to read something to you." He ran a stubby finger along the lines of Morgenes' spidery handwriting. "I am grateful beyond telling to Strangyeard, that he brought this book out of the ruin of Naglimund. It is our last tie to that great man, your teacher." His finger paused. "Ah. Here. Morgenes writes of King Prester John:

> ". . . *If he was touched by divinity, it was most evident in his comings and goings, in his finding the correct place to be at the most suitable time, and profiting thereby . . ."*

"I read that part," Simon said with mild interest.

"Then you will have noticed its significantness for our efforts," the troll replied.

> *"For John Presbyter knew that in both war and diplomacy—as also with love and commerce, two other not dissimilar occupations—the rewards usually do not fall to the strong or to even the just, but rather to the lucky. John also knew that he who moves swiftly and without undue caution makes his own luck."*

Simon frowned at Binabik's pleased expression. "So?"

"Ah." The troll was imperturbable. "Listen further."

> *"Thus, in the war that brought Nabban under his imperial hand, John took his far-outnumbered troop through the Onestrine Pass and directly into the spear-points of Ardrivis' legions, when all knew that only a fool would do so. It was this very foolhardiness, this seeming madness, that gave John's smaller force a great advantage of surprise—and even, to the startled Nabbanai army, an aura of God-touched irresistibility."*

Simon found the note of triumph in the little man's voice faintly disquieting. Binabik seemed to think that the point was somehow very clear. Simon frowned, thinking.

"Are you saying that we should be like King John? That we should try to catch Elias by surprise?" It was an astonishing idea. "That we should . . . attack him?"

Binabik nodded, his teeth bared in a yellow smile. "Clever Simon! Why not? We have only been reacting, not acting. Perhaps a change will be helpful."

"But what about the Storm King?" Shaken by the thought, he looked out at the beclouded horizon. Simon did not even like to say that name beneath the wide slate sky in this alien place. "And besides, Binabik, we are only a few hundred. King Elias has thousands of soldiers. Everybody knows it!"

The troll shrugged. "Who says we must be fighting army to army? In any case, our little company is growing every day, as more folk come across the meadows to . . . what was Josua's naming? Ah. New Gadrinsett."

Simon shook his head and flung another shard of wind-smoothed stone. "It seems stupid to me—no, not stupid. But too dangerous."

Binabik was not upset. He whistled for Qantaqa, who came trotting back across the stone flags. "Perhaps it is being just that, Simon. Let us walk for a little while."

Prince Josua stared down at the sword, his face troubled. The good cheer he had shown at Simon's feast seemed entirely gone.

It was not that the prince was truly any happier of late, Sir Deornoth decided, but he had learned that his self-doubts made those around him uneasy. In times like these, people preferred a fearless prince to an honest one, so Josua labored to present a mask of calm optimism to his subjects. But Deornoth, who knew him well, had little doubt that Josua's responsibilities still weighed on him as heavily as they ever had.

He is like my mother, Deornoth realized. *A strange thing to think of a prince. But like her, he feels he must take the worries and fears of all onto himself, that no one else can bear the burden.*

And, as Deornoth had seen his mother do, Josua also seemed to be aging faster than those around him. Always slender, the prince had become very thin during the company's flight from Naglimund. He had regained a little of his girth, but there was a strange aura of fragility about him now that would not go away: Deornoth thought him a little unworldly, like a man just risen from a long illness. The gray streaks in his hair had increased drastically and his eyes, although still as sharp and knowing as ever, held a slightly feverish gleam.

He needs peace. He needs rest. I wish I could stand at the foot of his bed and protect him while he slept for a year. "God give him strength," he murmured.

Josua turned to look at him. "I'm sorry, my mind was wandering. What did you say?"

Deornoth shook his head, not wishing to lie, but not caring to share his thoughts either. They both turned their attention back to the sword.

Prince and liege-man stood before the long stone table in the building Geloë had named Leavetaking House. All traces of the previous night's feast had been cleared away, and now only one gleaming black object lay upon the smooth stone.

"To think that so many have died at the end of that blade," Deornoth said at last. He touched the cord-wrapped hilt; Thorn was as cold and lifeless as the rock on which it rested.

"And more recently," the prince murmured, "think of how many have died that we might have it."

"But surely, if it cost us so dearly, we should not just leave it lying here in an open hall where anyone may come." Deornoth shook his head. "This might be our greatest hope, Highness—our only hope! Should we not hide it away safe, or put it under guard?"

Josua almost smiled. "To what purpose, Deornoth? Any treasure can be stolen, any castle thrown down, any hiding place nosed out. Better it should lie where all can see and feel what hope is in it." He narrowed his eyes as he stared down at the blade. "Not that I feel much hope looking at it. I trust you will not think me any the less princely if I say it gives me a kind of chill." He slowly ran his hand down the length of the blade. "In any case, from what Binabik and young Simon have said, no one will take this sword where it does not wish to go. Besides, if it lies here in view of all, like Tethtain's ax in the heart of the fabled beech tree, perhaps someone will come forward to tell us how it may serve."

Deornoth was puzzled. "You mean one of the common people, Highness?"

The prince grunted. "There are all kinds of wisdom, Deornoth. If we had listened sooner to the common folk living on the Frostmarch when they told us that evil was abroad in the land, who knows what anguish we might have been spared? No, Deornoth, any word of wisdom about this sword is valuable to us now, any old song, any half-remembered story." Josua could not hide his look of discontent. "After all, we have no idea of what good it can do us—in fact, no idea that it will do good at all, but for an obscure and ancient rhyme. . . ."

A harsh voice sang out, interrupting him.

> *"When frost doth grow on Claves' bell*
> *And shadows walk upon the road*
> *When water blackens in the Well*
> *Three Swords must come again."*

The two men turned in surprise. Geloë stood at the doorway. She continued the rhyme as she walked toward them.

> *"When Bukken from the Earth do creep*
> *And Hunën from the heights descend*
> *When Nightmare throttles peaceful Sleep*
> *Three Swords must come again.*

> *"To turn the stride of treading Fate*
> *To clear the fogging Mists of Time*
> *If Early shall resist Too Late*
> *Three Swords must come again.*

"I could not help hearing you, Prince Josua—I have keen ears. Your words are very wise. But as to doubting whether the sword will help . . ." She grimaced. "Forgive an old forest woman for her bluntness, but if we do not believe in the potency of Nisses' prophecy, what else do we have?"

Josua tried to smile. "I was not disputing that it means something significant to us, Valada Geloë. I only wish I knew more clearly what kind of a weapon these swords will be."

"As do we all." The witch woman nodded to Deornoth, then flicked a glance at the black sword. "Still, we have one of the three Great Swords, and that is more than we had a season ago."

"True. Very true." Josua leaned back against the stone table. "And we are in a safe place, thanks to you. I have not grown blind to good fortune, Geloë."

"But you are worried." It was not a question. "It is becoming harder to feed our growing settlement, and harder to govern those who live here."

The prince nodded. "Many of whom are not even sure why they are here, except that they followed other settlers. After such a freezing summer, I do not know how we will survive the winter."

"The people will listen to you, Highness," said Deornoth. When the witch woman was present, Josua seemed more like a careful student than a prince. He had never learned to like it, and had only partially learned to hide his annoyance. "They will do what you say. We will survive the winter together."

"Of course, Deornoth." Josua laid his hand upon his friend's shoulder. "We have come through too much to be balked by the petty problems of today."

He looked as if he would say more, but at that moment they heard the sound of footsteps on the wide stairs outside. Young Simon and the troll appeared in the doorway, followed closely by Binabik's tame wolf. The great beast sniffed the air, then snuffled at the stone on all sides of the door as well before trotting off to lie down in a far corner of the hall. Deornoth watched her go with some relief. He had seen numerous proofs of her harmlessness, but he had been raised a child of the Erkynlandish countryside, where wolves were the demons of fireplace tales.

"Ah," Josua said cheerfully, "my newest knight, and with him the honored envoy from far Yiqanuc. Come, sit down." He pointed to a row of stools left from the previous evening's festivities. "We wait on only a few more, including Count Eolair." The prince turned to Geloë. "You saw to him, did you not? Is he well?"

"A few cuts and bruises. He is thin, too—he has ridden far with little food. But his health is good."

Deornoth thought she would not say much more if the Count of Nad Mullach had been drawn and quartered—but still would have him on his feet again soon. The witch woman did not show his prince proper respect, and had few traits that Deornoth considered womanly, but he had to admit that she was very good at the things she did.

"I am happy to hear it." Josua tucked his hand under his cloak. "It is cold here. Let us make a fire so we can speak without our teeth chattering."

As Josua and the others talked, Simon fetched pieces of wood from the pile in the corner and stacked them in the firepit, happy to have something to do. He was proud to be part of this high company, but not quite able to take his membership for granted.

"Stand them touching at the top, spread at the bottom," Geloë advised.

He did as she suggested, making a conical tent of firewood in the middle of the ashes. When he had finished, he looked around. The crude firepit seemed out of place on the finely-crafted stone floor, as though animals had taken up residence in one of the great houses of Simon's own kind. There seemed no Sithi-built equivalent of the pit anywhere in the long chamber. How had they kept the room heated? Simon remembered Aditu running barefoot on the snow and decided that they might not have bothered.

"Is Leavetaking House really the name of this place?" he asked Geloë as she came forward with her flint and steel. She ignored him for a moment as she squatted beside the firepit, putting a spark to the curls of bark that lay around the logs.

"It is as close a name as any. I would have called it 'Hall of Farewell,' but the troll corrected my Sithi grammar." She showed a tight smile. A thread of smoke floated up past her hands.

Simon thought she might have made a joke, but he wasn't quite sure. "'Leavetaking' because this room was where the two families split up?"

"I believe it is the place where they parted, yes. Where the accord was struck. I imagine it has or had some other name for the Sithi, since it was in use long before the parting of those two tribes."

So he had been right: his vision had shown him the past of this place. Pondering, he stared along the pillared hall, at the columns of carved stone still clean and sharp-edged after countless years. Jiriki's people had once been mighty builders, but now their homes in the forest were as changeable and impermanent as the nests of birds. Perhaps the Sithi were wise not to put down deep roots. Still, Simon thought, a place that was always there, a home that did not change, seemed right now to be the finest treasure in the world.

"Why did the two families separate?"

Geloë shrugged. "There is never one reason for such a great change, but I have heard that mortals had something to do with it."

Simon remembered the last, terrible hour in the Yásira. "The Norn Queen—Utuk'ku. She was mad that the Sithi hadn't . . . 'scourged the mortals from the land,' she said. And she also said that Amerasu wouldn't leave the mortals be. Us mortals. Like me." It was hard to think of Amerasu the Ship-Born without shame: her assassin had claimed that he followed Simon to Jao é-Tinukai'i.

The witch woman stared at him for a moment. "I forget sometimes how much you have seen, boy. I hope you do not forget when your time comes."

"What time?"

"As to the parting of Sithi and Norn," she continued, ignoring his question, "mortals came into it, but also it is told that the two houses were uneasy allies even in the land of their origin."

"The Garden?"

"As they call it. I do not know the stories well—such tales have never been of much interest to me. I have always worked with the things that are before me, things that can be touched and seen and spoken to. There was a woman in it, a Sitha-woman, and a man of the Hikeda'ya as well. She died. He died. Both families were bitter. It is old business, boy. If you see your friend Jiriki again, ask him. It is the history of his own family, after all."

Geloë stood and walked away, leaving Simon to warm his hands before the flames.

These old stories are like blood. They run through people, even when they don't know it or think about it. He considered this idea for a moment. *But even if you don't think about them, when the bad times come, the old stories come out on every side. And that's just like blood, too.*

As Simon sat contemplating, Hotvig arrived with his right-hand man Ozhbern. They were quickly followed by Isorn and his mother, Duchess Gutrun.

"How is my wife, Duchess?" asked Josua.

"Not feeling well, your Highness," she replied, "or she would have been here. But it is only to be expected. Children aren't just difficult *after* they arrive, you know."

"I know very little, good lady," Josua laughed. "Especially about this. I have never been a father before."

Soon Father Strangyeard appeared, accompanied by Count Eolair of Nad Mullach. The count had replaced his traveling garments with Thrithings clothes, breeches and shirt of thick brown wool. He wore a golden torque at his neck, and his black hair was pulled back in a long tail. Simon remembered seeing him long ago, at the Hayholt, and once again had to marvel at the strangeness of Fate, how it moved people about the world like markers in a vast game of *shent*.

"Welcome, Eolair, welcome," Josua said. "Thanks be to Aedon, it does my heart good to see you again."

"And mine, Highness." The count tossed the saddlebags he carried against the wall by the door, then touched a knee briefly to the ground. He rose to Josua's embrace. "Greetings from the Hernystiri nation in exile."

Josua quickly introduced Eolair to those he had not met. To Simon, the count said: "I have heard something of your adventures since I arrived." The smile on his thin face was warm. "I hope you will put aside some time to speak with me."

Flattered, Simon nodded. "Certainly, Count."

Josua led Eolair to the long table where Thorn waited, solemn and terrible as a dead king upon his bier.

"The famous blade of Camaris," said the Hernystirman. "I have heard of it so many times, it is strange to see it at last and realize it is a real thing, forged of metal like any other weapon."

Josua shook his head. "Not quite like any other weapon."

"May I touch it?"

"Of course."

Eolair was barely able to lift the hilt from the stone table. The cords of his neck stood out in sharp relief as he strained at it. At last he gave up and rubbed his cramped fingers. "It is as weighty as a millstone."

"Sometimes." Josua patted his shoulder. "Other times it is as light as goose-down. We do not know why, nor do we know what good it will do us, but it is all we have."

"Father Strangyeard told me of the rhyme," the count said. "I think I have more to tell you about the Great Swords." He looked around the room. "If this is the proper time."

"This is a war council," Josua said simply. "All these folk can be told anything, and we are anxious for any news about the swords. We also wish to hear of your people, of course. I understand that Lluth is dead. You have our great sympathy. He was a splendid man and a fine king."

Eolair nodded. "And Gwythinn, too, his son."

Sir Deornoth, seated on a stool nearby, groaned. "Oh, that is foul news! He set out from Naglimund shortly before the siege. What happened?"

"He was caught by Skali's Kaldskrykemen and butchered." Eolair stared down at the ground. "They dumped his body at the foot of the mountain, like offal, and rode away."

"A curse on them!" Deornoth snarled.

"I am ashamed to call them countrymen," said young Isorn.

His mother nodded her agreement. "When my husband returns, he will deal with Sharp-nose." She sounded as certain as if she spoke of sunset coming.

"Still, we are *all* countrymen, here," Josua said. "We are all one people. From this day forward, we go together against common enemies." He gestured to the stools that stood against the wall. "Come, everybody sit down. We must fetch and carry for ourselves: I thought that the smaller this group remained, the easier it would be to speak openly."

When all were arrayed, Eolair told of Hernystir's downfall, beginning with the slaughter at the Inniscrich and Lluth's mortal wounding. He had barely started when there was a commotion outside the hall. A moment later, the old jester Towser stumbled through the door with Sangfugol tugging at his shirt, trying to restrain him.

"So!" The old man fixed Josua with a reddened stare. "You are no more loyal than your murdering brother!" He swayed as Sangfugol pulled at him desperately. Pink-cheeked and wild-haired—what little hair was left—Towser was clearly drunk.

"Come away, curse you!" the harper said. "I'm sorry, my prince, he just suddenly leaped up and . . ."

"To think that after all my years of service," Towser spluttered, "that I should be . . . should be . . . *excluded*," he pronounced the word with proud care, unaware of the strand of spittle that hung from his chin, "should be shunned, barred from your councils, when I was the one closest to your father's heart. . . ."

Josua stood up, regarding the jester sadly. "I cannot talk to you now, old man. Not when you are like this." He frowned, watching Sangfugol struggle with him.

"I will help, Prince Josua," Simon said. He could not bear to watch the old man shame himself a moment longer. Simon and the harper managed to get Towser turned around. As soon as his back was to the prince, the fight seemed to drain out of him; the jester allowed himself to be steered toward the door.

Outside, a bitter wind was blowing across the hilltop. Simon took off his cloak and draped it around Towser's shoulders. The jester sat down on the top step, a bundle of sharp bones and thin skin, and said: "I think I will be sick." Simon patted his shoulder and looked helplessly at Sangfugol, whose gaze was less than sympathetic.

"It is like taking care of a child," the harper growled. "No, children are better-behaved. Leleth, for example, who doesn't talk at all."

"*I* told them where to find that damnable black sword," Towser mumbled. "Told them where it was. Told them about the other, too, how 'Lias wouldn't hold it. 'Your father wants you to have it,' I told him, but he wouldn't listen. Dropped it like a snake. Now the black sword, too." A tear ran down his white-whiskered cheek. "He tosses me away like an orange rind."

"What is he talking about?" asked Simon.

Sangfugol curled his lip. "He told the prince some things about Thorn before you left to find it. I don't know what the rest's about." He leaned down and grasped Towser's arm. "Huh. Easy for him to complain—*he* doesn't have to play nursemaid to himself." He showed Simon a sour smile. "Ah, well, there are probably bad days in a knight's career, too, are there not? Like when people hit you with swords and so on?" He pulled the jester to his feet and waited for the old man to get his balance. "Neither Towser nor I are in a very good mood, Simon. Not your fault. Come see me later and we'll drink some wine."

Sangfugol turned and walked away across the waving grass, trying both to support Towser and simultaneously keep him as far as possible from the harper's clean clothes.

Prince Josua nodded his thanks when Simon reentered Leavetaking House; Simon felt odd being commended for such disheartening duty. Eolair was finishing his description of the fall of Hernysadharc and of his people's flight into the Grianspog Mountains. As he told of the remaining Hernystir-folk's retreat into the caves that riddled the mountain and how they had been led there by the king's daughter, Duchess Gutrun smiled.

"This Maegwin is a clever girl. You are lucky to have her, if the king's wife is as helpless as you say."

The count's smile was a pained one. "You are right, Lady. She is indeed her father's daughter. I used to think she would make a better ruler than Gwythinn, who was sometimes headstrong—but now I am not so sure."

He told of Maegwin's growing strangeness, of her visions and dreams, and of how those dreams had led Lluth's daughter and the count down into the mountain's heart to the ancient stone city of Mezutu'a.

As he told of the city and its unusual tenants, the dwarrows, the company listened in amazement. Only Geloë and Binabik did not seem astonished by Eolair's tale.

"Wonderful," Strangyeard whispered, staring up at Leavetaking House's arched ceiling as though he were even now deep in the bowels of Grianspog. "The Pattern Hall! What marvelous stories must be written there."

"You may read some of them later," Eolair said with some amusement. "I am glad that the spirit of scholarship has survived this evil winter." He turned back to the company. "But what is perhaps most important of all is what the dwarrows said about the Great Swords. They claim that they forged Minneyar."

"We are knowing some of Minneyar's story," said Binabik, "and the dwarrows—or *dvernings,* as the northmen call them—are in that story."

"But it is where Minneyar has gone that most concerns us," Josua added. "We have one sword. Elias has the other. The third . . ."

"Nearly everyone in this hall has seen the third," Eolair said, "and seen the place where it now lies as well—if the dwarrows are correct. For they say that Minneyar went into the Hayholt with Fingil, but that Prester John found it . . . and called it Bright-Nail. If they are right, Josua, it was buried with your father."

"Oh, my!" Strangyeard murmured. A moment of stunned silence followed his utterance.

"But I held it in my hand," Josua said at last, wonderingly. "I myself placed it on my father's breast. How could Bright-Nail be Minneyar? My father never said a word about it!"

"No, he did not." Gutrun was surprisingly brisk. "He would never even tell my husband. Told Isgrimnur it was an old, unimportant story." She shook her head. "Secrets."

Simon, who had been listening quietly, spoke up at last. "But didn't he bring Bright-Nail from Warinsten, where he was born?" He looked to Josua, suddenly fearful that he was being presumptuous. "Your father, I mean. That is the story I knew."

Josua frowned, considering. "That is the story that many told, but now that I think on it, my father was never one of them."

"Of course! Oh, of course!" Strangyeard sat up, slapping his long hands together. His eyepatch slid a little, so that its corner edged onto the bridge of his nose. "The passage that troubled Jarnauga so, that passage from Morgenes' book! It told how John went down to face the dragon—but he carried a spear! A spear! Oh, goodness, how blind we were!" The priest giggled like a young boy. "But when he came out, it was with Bright-Nail! Oh, Jarnauga, if only you were here!"

The prince raised his hand. "There is much to think of here, and many old tales that should be retold, but for the moment there is a more important problem. If the dwarrows are right, and somehow I feel that they are—who could doubt such a mad tale, in this mad season?—we still must get the sword, call it

Bright-Nail or Minneyar. It lies in my father's grave on Swertclif, just outside the walls of the Hayholt. My brother can stand on his battlements and see the grave mounds. The Erkynguard parade on the cliff's edge at dawn and dusk."

The giddy moment was over. In the heavy silence that followed, Simon felt the first stirrings of an idea. It was vague and unformed, so he kept it to himself. It was also rather frightening.

Eolair spoke up. "There is more, your Highness. I told you of the Pattern Hall, and of the charts the dwarrows keep there of all the delvings they have done." He rose and walked to the saddlebags he had deposited near the doorway. When he returned, he spilled them upon the floor. Several rolls of oiled sheepskin tumbled out. "These are the plans for the diggings beneath the Hayholt, a task the dwarrows say they performed when the castle was named Asu'a and belonged to the Sithi."

Strangyeard was the first down on his knees. He unfurled one of the sheepskins with the tender care of a lover. "Ah!" he breathed. "Ah!" His rhapsodic smile changed to a look of puzzlement. "I must confess," he said finally, "that I am, ah, somewhat . . . somewhat disappointed. I had not thought that the dwarrows' maps would be . . . dear me! . . . would be so crude."

"Those are not the dwarrows' maps," said Eolair, frowning. "Those are the painstaking work of two Hernystiri scribes laboring in cramped near-darkness in a frightening place, copying the stone charts of the dwarrows onto something I could carry up to the surface."

"Oh!" The priest was mortified. "Oh! Forgive me, Count! I am so sorry. . . ."

"Never mind, Strangyeard." Josua turned to the Count of Nad Mullach. "This is an unlooked-for boon, Eolair. On the day when we can finally stand before the Hayholt's walls, we will praise your name to the heavens."

"You are welcome to them, Josua. It was Maegwin's idea, if truth be told. I am not sure what good they will do, but knowledge is never bad—as I'm sure your archivist will agree." He gestured to Strangyeard, who was rooting among the sheepskins like a shoat who had uncovered a clump of truffles. "But I must confess I came to you in hope of more than thanks. When I left Hernystir, it was with the idea that I would find your rebel army and we would together drive Skali of Kaldskryke from my land. As I see, though, you are scarcely in a position to send an army anywhere."

"No." Josua's expression was grim. "We are still very few. More trickle in every day, but it would be a long wait before we could send even a small company to the aid of Hernystir." He stood and walked a little way out across the room, rubbing the stump of his right wrist as though it pained him. "This whole struggle has been like fighting a war blindfolded: we have never known or understood the strength brought against us. Now that we begin to grasp the nature of our enemies, we are too few to do anything but hide here in the remotest regions of Osten Ard."

Deornoth leaned forward. "If we could strike back *somewhere,* my prince, people would rise on your behalf. Very few beyond the Thrithings even know that you still live."

"There is truth to that, Prince Josua," Isorn said. "I know there are many in Rimmersgard who hate Skali. Some helped to hide me when I escaped from Sharp-nose's war camp."

"As far as that, Josua, your survival is only a dim rumor in Hernystir as well," said Eolair. "Just to carry that information back to my people in the Grianspog will make my journey here a great success."

Josua, who had been pacing, stopped. "You will take them more than that, Count Eolair. I swear to you, you will take them more hope than that." He passed his hand across his eyes, like one wakened too early. "By the Tree, what a day! Let us stop and take some bread. In any case, I would like to think about what I have heard." He smiled wearily. "Also, I should go and see my wife." He waved his arm. "Up, all, up. Except you, Strangyeard. I suppose you will stay behind?"

The archivist, surrounded by sheepskins, did not even hear him.

Immersed in dark and mazy thoughts, Pryrates did not for some time notice the sound.

When at last it cut through the fog of his preoccupation, he stopped abruptly, teetering on the edge of the step.

"Azha she'she t'chakó, urun she'she bhabekró . . ."

The sound that rose from the darkened stairwell was delicate but dire, a solemn melody that wove in and out of painful dissonance: it might have been the contemplative hymn of a spider winding its prey in sticky silk. Breathy and slow, it slid sourly between notes, but with a deftness that suggested the seeming tunelessness was intentional—was in fact based in an entirely different concept of melody.

"Mudhul samat'ai. Jabbak s'era memekeza sanayha-z'á
Ninyek she'she, hamut 'tke agrazh'a s'era yé . . ."

A lesser man might have turned and fled back toward the upper reaches of the daylit castle rather than meet the singer of such an unsettling tune. Pryrates did not hesitate, but set off downward once more, his boots echoing on the stone steps. A second thread of melody joined the first, just as alien, just as dreadfully patient; together they droned like wind over a chimney hole.

Pryrates reached the landing and turned into the corridor. The two Norns who stood before the heavy oaken door abruptly fell silent. As he approached, they gazed at him with the incurious and faintly insulting expression of cats disturbed while sunning.

They were big for Hikeda'ya, Pryrates realized: each was tall as a very tall man, though they were thin as starveling beggars. They held their silver-white lances loosely, and their deathly pale faces were calm within the dark hoods.

Pryrates stared at the Norns. The Norns stared at Pryrates.

"Well? Are you going to gape or are you going to open the door for me?"

One of the Norns slowly bowed his head. "Yes, Lord Pryrates." There was not the slightest hint of deference in his icy, accented speech. He turned around and pulled open the great door, exposing a corridor red with torchlight and more stairs. Pryrates stepped between the two guards and started downward; the door swung shut behind him. Before he had gone ten steps, the eerie spider-melody had begun once more.

Hammers rose and fell, clanging and clattering, pounding the cooling metal into shapes useful to the king who sat in a darkened throne room far above his foundry. The din was terrible, the stench—brimstone, white-hot iron, earth scorched to dry salt, even the savory-sweet odor of burned manflesh—even worse.

The deformity of the men who scurried back and forth across the floor of the great forge chamber was severe, as though the terrible, baking heat of this underground cavern had melted them like bad metal. Even their heavy, padded clothing could not hide it. In truth, Pryrates knew, it was only those hopelessly twisted in body or spirit or both that still remained here, working in Elias' armory. A few of the others had been lucky enough to escape early on, but most of the able-bodied had been worked to death by Inch, the hulking overseer. A few smallish groups had been selected by Pryrates himself to aid in certain of his experiments; what was left of them had eventually been returned here, to feed the same furnaces in death they had served in life.

The king's counselor squinted through the hanging smoke, watching the forge men as they struggled along beneath huge burdens or hopped back like scalded frogs when a tongue of flame came too close. One way or the other, Pryrates reflected, Inch had dealt with all those more lovely or clever than himself.

In fact, Pryrates thought, grinning at his own cruel levity, if that was the standard it was a miracle anyone at all remained to stoke the fires or tend the molten metals in the great crucibles.

There was a lull in the clangor of hammers, and in that moment of near-quiet, Pryrates heard a squeaking noise behind him. He turned, careful not to appear too hurried, in case someone was watching. Nothing could frighten the red priest: it was important that everyone know that. When he saw what made the sound, he grinned and spat onto the stone.

The vast water wheel covered most of the cavern wall behind him. The mighty wooden wheel, steel-shod and fixed on a hub cross-cut from a huge tree trunk, dipped water from a powerful stream that sluiced through the forge, then lifted it up and spilled it into an ingenious labyrinth of troughs. These directed the water to a number of different spots throughout the forge, to cool metal or to put out fires, or even—when the rare mood struck Inch—to be lapped at by the forge's parched and miserable laborers. The turning wheel also drove a series of black-scummed iron chains, the largest of which reached vertically up into the darkness to provide the motive force for certain devices dear to Pyrates' heart. But at this moment it was the digging and lifting of the wheel's paddles that engaged the alchemist's imagination. He wondered idly if such a mechanism, built mountain-large and spun by the straining sinews of several thousand whimpering slaves, could not dredge up the bottom of the sea and expose the secrets hidden for eons there in darkness.

As he contemplated what fascinating things the millennial ooze might disgorge, a wide, black-nailed hand dropped down upon his sleeve. Pyrates whirled and slapped it away.

"How dare you touch me?!" he hissed, dark eyes narrowing. He bared his teeth as though he might tear out the throat of the tall, stooping figure before him.

Inch stared back for a moment before replying. His round face was furred by a patchwork of beard and fire-scarred flesh. He seemed, as always, thick and implacable as stone. "You want to talk to me?"

"Never touch me again." Pyrates' voice was restrained now, but it still trembled with a deadly tension. "Never."

Inch frowned, his uneven brow wrinkling. The hole where one eye had been gaped unpleasantly. "What do you need from me?"

The alchemist paused and took a breath, forcing down the black rage that had climbed up into his skull. Pyrates was surprised at his own violent reaction. It was foolish to waste anger on the brutish foundrymaster. When Inch had served his purpose, he could be slaughtered like the dull beast he was. Until then, he was useful to the king's plans—and, more importantly, to Pyrates' own.

"The king wishes the curtain wall refortified. New joists, new cross-bracing—the heaviest timbers that we can bring from the Kynslagh."

Inch lowered his head, thinking. The effort was almost palpable. "How soon?" he said at last.

"By Candlemansa. A week later and you and all your groundlings will find yourselves above the Nearulagh Gate keeping company with ravens." Pyrates had to restrain a chuckle at the thought of Inch's misshapen head spiked above the gate. Even the crows would not fight over *that* morsel. "I will hear no excuses—that gives you a third of a year. And speaking of the Nearulagh Gate, there are a few other things you must do as well. A few very important things. Some improvements to the gate's defenses." He reached into his robe and produced a scroll. Inch unfurled it and held it up to better catch the fitful light of the forge fires. "That must also be finished by Candlemansa."

"Where is the king's seal?" Inch wore a surprisingly shrewd look on his puckered face.

Pryrates' hand flew up. A flicker of greasy yellow light played along his fingertips. After a moment the glow winked out; he let his hand drop back to his side, hidden in a voluminous scarlet sleeve. "If you ever question me again," the alchemist gritted, "I will blast you to flakes of ash."

The foundrymaster's face was solemn. "Then walls and gate will not be finished. No one makes them work as fast as Doctor Inch."

"Doctor Inch." Pryrates curled his thin lip. "Usires save me, I am tired of talking to you. Just do your job as King Elias wishes. You are luckier than you know, bumpkin. You will see the beginning of a great era, a golden age." *But only the beginning, and not much of that,* the priest promised himself. "I will be back in two days. You will tell me then how many men you need, and what other things."

As he strode away, he thought he heard Inch call something after him, but when Pryrates turned, the forgemaster was staring instead at the water wheel's thick spokes passing in a never-ending circle. The clatter of hammers was sharp, but still Pryrates could hear the ponderous, mournful creaking of the turning wheel.

Duke Isgrimnur leaned on the windowsill, stroking his new-sprouted beard and staring down at the greasy waterways of Kwanitupul. The storm had passed, the sprinkling of bizarrely unseasonal snow had melted, and the marshy air, though still oddly cool, had returned to its usual stickiness. Isgrimnur felt a strong urge to be moving, to do something.

Trapped, he thought. *Pinned down as surely as if by archers. It's like the damnable Battle of Clodu Lake all over again.*

But of course there were no archers, no hostile forces of any kind. Kwanitupul, at least temporarily freed from the cold's grip and restored to its usual mercenary existence, paid no more attention to Isgrimnur than it did to any of the thousands of others who occupied its ramshackle body like so many busy fleas. No, it was circumstance that had trapped the former master of Elvritshalla, and circumstance was right now a more implacable enemy than any human foes, no matter how many and how well-armed.

Isgrimnur stood up with a sigh and turned to look at Camaris, who sat propped against the far wall, tying and untying a length of rope. The old man, once the greatest knight in Osten Ard, looked up and smiled his soft, idiot-child's smile. For all his white-haired age, his teeth were still good. He was strong, too, with a grip most young tavern brawlers would envy.

But weeks of constant effort on Isgrimnur's part had not altered that maddening smile. Whether Camaris was bewitched, wounded in the head, or simply deranged with age, it all came to the same end: the duke had not been able to summon forth even a flicker of recollection. The old man did not recognize Isgrimnur, did not remember his past or even his own true name. If the duke had not once known Camaris so well he might even have begun to doubt his own senses and memory, but Isgrimnur had seen John's paramount knight at every season, in every light, in good times and evil times. The old man might no longer know himself, but Isgrimnur was not mistaken.

Still, what should be done with him? Whether he was hopelessly mad or not, he should be helped. The most obvious task was to get the old man to those who would remember and revere him. Even if the world Camaris had helped build was now crumbling, even if King Elias had laid waste to the dream of Camaris' friend and liege-lord John, still the old man deserved to spend his last years in some better place than this backwater pesthole. Also, if anyone yet survived of Prince Josua's folk, they should know that Camaris lived. The old man could be a powerful emblem of hope and of better days—and Isgrimnur, a shrewd statesman for all his bluff disavowals, knew the value of a symbol.

But even if Josua or some of his captains had somehow survived and re-grouped somewhere to the north of here, as Kwanitupul market rumor suggested, how could Isgrimnur and Camaris reach them through a Nabban full of enemies? How could he leave this inn in any case? Father Dinivan, with his dying breath, had told Isgrimnur to bring Miriamele here. The duke had not found her before being forced to flee the Sancellan Aedonitis, but Miriamele might already know of this place—perhaps Dinivan himself had mentioned it to her! She might come here, alone and friendless, and find Isgrimnur already gone. Could the duke risk that? He owed it to Josua—whether the prince was living or dead—to do his best to help her.

Isgrimnur had hoped that Tiamak—who in some unspecified way was an intimate of Dinivan's—might know something about Miriamele's whereabouts, but that hope had been immediately dashed. After much prodding, the little brown man had admitted that Dinivan had sent him here as well, but without explanation. Tiamak had been very preoccupied with the news of the deaths of Dinivan and Morgenes and afterward had offered nothing helpful to Isgrimnur at all. In fact, the duke thought him somewhat sullen. Although the marsh man's leg was obviously painful—a cockindrill had bitten him, he said—still Isgrimnur thought that Tiamak could do more to help solve the various riddles that plagued them both, Dinivan's purpose uppermost among them. But instead he seemed content just to sulk around the room—a room paid for by Isgrimnur!—or to spend long hours writing or limping along the wooden walkways of Kwanitupul, as he was doubtless doing now.

Isgrimnur was about to say something to silent Camaris when there was a knock at the door. It creaked open to reveal the landlady, Charystra.

"I've brought the food you asked for." Her tone implied that she had made some great personal sacrifice instead of merely taking Isgrimnur's money for grossly overpriced bed and board. "Some nice bread and soup. Very nice. With beans." She set the tureen on the low table and clanked down three bowls beside it. "I don't understand why you can't come down to eat with everyone else." Everyone else was two Wrannaman feather merchants and an itinerant gem cutter from Naraxi who was looking for work.

"Because I pay not to," Isgrimnur growled.

"Where's the marsh man?" She ladled out the unsteaming soup.

"I don't know, and I don't think it's business of yours, either." He glowered.
"I saw you go off with your friend this morning."

"To the market," she sniffed. "I can't take my boat, because *he*—" hands full, she waggled her head in the direction of Camaris, "—never fixed it."

"Nor will I let him, for the sake of his dignity—and I'm paying you for that, too." Isgrimnur's sour temper was rising. Charystra always tested the boundaries of the duke's chivalry. "You are very quick with your tongue, woman. I wonder what you tell your friends at the market about me and your other strange guests."

She darted an apprehensive look in his direction. "Nothing, I'm sure."

"That had better be true. I gave you money to keep silent about . . . about my friend here." He looked at Camaris, who was happily spooning oily soup into his mouth. "But in case you think to take my money and still spread tales, remember: if I find you have talked about me or my business . . . *I will make you wish you hadn't.*" He let his deep voice rumble the words like thunder.

Charystra took a step back in alarm. "I'm sure I haven't said nothing! And you've no cause to be threatening me, sir! No cause! It's not right!" She started toward the door, waving the ladle as if to fend off blows. "I said I wouldn't say anything and I won't. Anyone will tell you—Charystra keeps her word!" She quickly made the sign of the Tree, then slipped out into the hall, leaving a spatter of soup spots on the plank flooring.

"Hah," Isgrimnur snorted. He stared at the grayish fluid still rippling in the bowl. Pay for her silence, indeed. That was like paying the sun not to shine. He had been throwing money around as though it were Wran water—soon it would run out. Then what would he do? It made him angry just to think about it. "Hah!" he said again. "Damn me."

Camaris wiped his chin and smiled, staring at nothing.

Simon leaned around the standing stone and peered downward. The pale sun was nearly straight overhead; it knifed down through the undergrowth, revealing a flicker of reflection on the hillside.

"Here it is," he called back, then leaned against the wind-smoothed pillar to wait. The white stone had not yet shed its morning chill, and was even colder than the surrounding air. After a moment, Simon began to feel his bones turning to ice. He stepped away and turned to survey the line of the hill's edge. The standing stones circled Sesuad'ra's summit like the spikes of a king's crown. Several of the ancient pillars had fallen down, so the crown had a somewhat bedraggled look, but most stood tall and straight, still doing their duty after a span of unguessable centuries.

They look just like the Anger Stones on Thisterborg, he realized.

Could that be a Sithi place, too? There were certainly enough strange stories told about it.

Where were those two? "Are you coming?" he called.

When he received no answer, he clambered around the stone and made his way a short distance down the hillside, careful to keep a solid grip on the sturdy heather despite the resultant prickling: the ground was muddy and potentially treacherous. Below, the valley was full of gray water that barely rippled, so that the new lake around the hill seemed solid as a stone floor. Simon could not help thinking of the days when he had climbed to the bellchamber of Green Angel Tower and felt himself sitting cloud-high above the world. Here on Sesuad'ra, it was as though the entire hill of stone had just now been born, thrusting up from the primordial muck. It was easy to pretend there was nothing beyond this place, that this was how it must have felt when God stood atop Mount Den Haloi and made the world, as told in the Book of the Aedon.

Jiriki had told Simon about the coming of the Gardenborn to Osten Ard. In those days, the Sitha had said, most of the world had been covered in ocean, just as the west still was. Jiriki's folk had sailed out of the rising sun, across unimaginable distances, to land on the verdant coastline of a world innocent of humanity, a vast island in a great surrounding sea. Some later cataclysm, Jiriki had implied, had then changed the face of the world: the land had risen and the seas had drained away to east and south, leaving new mountains and meadows behind them. Thus, the Gardenborn could never return to their lost home.

Simon thought about this as he squinted out toward the east. There was little to see from atop Sesuad'ra but murky steppes, lifeless plains of endless gray and dull green, stretching to where vision failed. From what Simon had heard, the eastern steppes had been inhospitable territory even before this dread winter: they grew increasingly barren and shelterless the farther east of Aldheorte Forest one went. Beyond a certain point, travelers claimed, even the Hyrkas and Thrithings-folk did not journey. The sun never truly shone there and the land was sunken in perpetual twilight. The few hardy souls who had crossed that murky expanse in search of other lands had never returned.

He realized he had been staring a long time, yet he was still alone. He was just about to call again when Jeremias appeared, picking his way carefully through the brambles and waist-high grass toward the edge of the hill. Leleth, barely visible in the swaying undergrowth, held the young squire's hand. She seemed to have taken a liking to Jeremias, although it was shown only by her constant proximity. She still did not speak, and her expression remained perpetually solemn and abstracted, but when she could not be with Geloë, she was nearly always with Jeremias. Simon guessed that she might have sensed in the young squire something like her own pain, some shared affliction of the heart.

"Does it go down into the ground," Jeremias called, "or over the edge?"

"Both," said Simon, pointing.

They had been following the path of this spring from the point where it appeared in the building Geloë had named the House of Waters. Issuing mysteriously from the rocks, it did not drain away after pooling at the base of the spring—where it provided fresh drinking water for New Gadrinsett, and thus had become one of the centers of gossip and commerce for the infant settlement—but rather gurgled out of the little pond in a narrow streamlet, passing out of the House of Waters, which was at one of the highest points on Sesuad'ra, then running across the summit as a tiny rivulet, appearing and disappearing as the features of the ground changed. Simon had never seen or heard of a spring that behaved in such a way—who had ever heard of a spring on a hilltop, anyway?—and he was bound and determined to discover its path, and perhaps its origin, before the storms returned and made the hunt impossible.

Jeremias joined Simon a little way down the hillside. They both stood over the swift-flowing rivulet.

"Do you think it goes all the way down," Jeremias gestured to the vast gray moat around the base of the Stone of Farewell, "or does it go back into the hill?"

Simon shrugged. Water that sprang from the heart of a Sithi sacred mountain might indeed pass back into the rock once more, like some incomprehensible wheel of creation and destruction—like the future approaching to absorb the present, then quickly falling away again to become the past. He was about to suggest further exploration, but Leleth was making her way down the hill. Simon worried for her, although she herself seemed to pay little attention to the hazardous trail. She could easily slip, and the slope was steep and dangerous.

Jeremias took a couple of steps up and reached for her, catching her under her thin arms and lifting her down to stand beside them. As he did so, her loose dress rode up, and for a brief moment Simon saw her scars, long inflamed weals that covered her thighs. They must be far worse on her stomach, he reflected.

He had been thinking all morning about what he had heard in Leavetaking House about the Great Swords and other things. These matters had seemed abstract, as though Simon, his friends and allies, Elias, even the dreadful Storm King himself, were no more than pieces on a shent board, tiny things that could be considered in a hundred different configurations. Now, suddenly, he was reminded of the true horrors of the recent past. Leleth, an innocent child, had been terrorized and savaged by the hounds of Stormspike; thousands more just as innocent had been made homeless, been orphaned, tormented, killed. Anger suddenly made Simon sway on his feet, as if the very force of his fury might knock him stumbling. If there was any justice, someone would pay for what had happened—for Morgenes, Haestan, Leleth, for Jeremias with his now-thin face and unspoken sorrows, for Simon himself, homeless and sad.

Usires have mercy on me, I would kill them all if I could. Elias and Pryrates and their white-faced Norns—if only I could, I would kill them with my own hands.

"I saw her at the castle," said Jeremias. Simon looked up, startled. He had clenched his fists so tightly that his knuckles hurt.

"What?"

"Leleth." Jeremias nodded at the child, who was smearing her dirty face as she stared out across the flooded valley. "When she was Princess Miriamele's handmaiden. I remember thinking, 'what a pretty little girl.' She was all dressed in white, carrying flowers. I thought she looked very clean." He laughed quietly. "Look at her now."

Simon found he did not want to talk about sorrowful things. "And look at you," he said. "You're one to be talking about clean."

Jeremias would not be distracted. "Did you really know her, Simon? The princess, I mean."

"Yes." Simon didn't want to tell Jeremias that story again. He had been bitterly disappointed to find Miriamele was not with Josua, and horrified that no one knew where she was. He had dreamed of telling her his adventures, of the way her bright eyes would go wide as he told her of the dragon. "Yes," he repeated, "I knew her."

"And was she beautiful, like a princess should be?" Jeremias asked, suddenly intent.

"I suppose so." Simon was reluctant to talk about her. "Yes, she was—I mean, she is."

Jeremias was about to ask something else, but was interrupted. "Ho!" a voice cried from above. "There you are!"

A strange, two-headed silhouette was looking down at them from beside the standing stone. One of the heads had pointed ears.

"We're trying to find out where the spring comes from and where it goes, Binabik," Simon called.

The wolf tilted her head and barked.

"Qantaqa thinks you should stop your water-following for now, Simon," Binabik laughed. "Besides, Josua has asked all to be returning to the Leavetaking Hall. There is much to talk about."

"We're coming."

Simon and Jeremias each took one of Leleth's small cold hands and clambered back up toward the hillcrest. The sun stared down on them all like a milky eye.

All who had been gathered in the morning had returned to Leavetaking House. They talked quietly, perhaps overawed by the size and strange dimensions of the hall, so much more unsettling when it was not filled with a distracting crowd as it had been the night before. The sickly afternoon light leaked in through the windows, but with so little strength that it seemed to come from no direction at all, smearing all the room equally; the meticulous wall-carvings gleamed as though by their own faint inner light, reminding Simon of the shimmering moss in the tunnels beneath the Hayholt. He had been lost there in choking, strangling blackness. He had been in a place beyond despair. Surely to survive that meant something. Surely he had been spared for a reason!

Please, Lord Aedon, he prayed, *don't bring me so far just to let me die!*

But he had already cursed God for letting Haestan perish. It was doubtless too late for making amends.

Simon opened his eyes to find that Josua had arrived. The prince had been with Vorzheva, and assured them all that she was feeling better.

Accompanying Josua were two who had not been at the morning council, Sludig—who had been scouting the perimeter of the valley—and a heavyset young Falshireman named Freosel, who had been chosen by the settlers as constable of New Gadrinsett. Despite his relative youth, Freosel had the wary, heavy-lidded look of a veteran street fighter. He was liberally scarred and two of his fingers were missing.

After Strangyeard had spoken a short blessing, and the new constable had been cautioned to hold secret the things he would hear, Prince Josua stood.

"We have many things to decide," he said, "but before we begin, let me talk to you of good luck and of more hopeful days.

"When it seemed that there was nothing left but despair and defeat, God favored us. We are now in a safe place, when a season ago we were scattered over the world, the castaways of war. We undertook a quest for one of the three Great Swords, which may be our hope of victory, and that quest has succeeded. More people flock to our banner every day, so that if we only can wait long enough, we will soon have an army that will give even my brother the High King pause.

"Our needs are still great, of course. Out of those people driven from their homes throughout Erkynland, we can indeed mount an army, but to overcome the High King we will need many more. It is also certain that we are already hard-pressed to feed and shelter those who are here. And it is even possible that no army, however large and well-provided, will be great enough to defeat Elias' ally the Storm King." Josua paused. "Thus, as I see it, the important questions we must answer this day are three: What does my brother plan to do? How can we assemble a force that will prevent it? And how can we retrieve the other two swords, Bright-Nail and Sorrow, that we may have a hope of defeating the Norns and their dark master and mistress?"

Geloë lifted her hand. "Your pardon, Josua, but I think there is one more question: How much time do we have to do any of these things?"

"You are right, Valada Geloë. If we are able to protect this place for another year, we might gather a great enough force to begin disputing Elias on his own ground, or at least his outermost holdings—but like you, I doubt we will be left unmolested so long."

Others raised their voices, asking about what further strength could be expected from the east and north of Erkynland, territories that chafed beneath King Elias' heavy hand, and where other allies might be found. After a while, Josua again called the room to silence.

"Before we can solve any of these riddles," he declared, "it is my thought that we must solve the first and most important one—namely, what does my brother want?"

"Power!" said Isorn. "The power to cast men's lives around as if they were dice."

"He had that already," Josua replied. "But I have thought long, and can think of no other answer. Certainly the world has seen other kings who were not content with what they had. Perhaps the answer to this most crucial question may remain hidden from us until the very end. If we knew the shape of Elias' bargain with the Storm King, perhaps then we would understand my brother's secret intent."

"Prince Josua," Binabik spoke up, "I myself have been puzzling about a different thing. Whatever your brother is wishing to do, the Storm King's power and dark magics will be helping him. But what is the Storm King wanting in return?"

The great stone hall went silent for a moment, then the voices of those assembled rose once more, arguing, until Josua had to stamp his boot on the floor to silence them.

"You ask a dreadful question, Binabik," said the prince. "What indeed could that dark one want?"

Simon thought about the shadows beneath the Hayholt where he had stumbled in a terrible, ghost-ridden dream. "Maybe he wants his castle back," he said.

Simon had spoken softly, and others in the room who had not heard him continued to talk quietly among themselves, but Josua and Binabik both turned to stare at him.

"Merciful Aedon," said Josua. "Could it be?"

Binabik thought for a long moment, then shook his head slowly. "There is being something wrong in that thought—although it is clever thinking, Simon. Tell me, Geloë, what is it that I am half-remembering?"

The witch woman nodded. "Ineluki cannot ever come back to that castle. When Asu'a fell, its ruins were so priest-blessed and so tightly wound in spells that he could not return before the end of time. No, I do not think he *can* have it back, much as he no doubt burns to reclaim it . . . but he may wish to rule through Elias what he cannot rule himself. For all their power, the Norns are few—but as the shadow behind the Dragonbone Chair, the Storm King could reign over all the lands of Osten Ard."

Josua's face was grave. "And to think that my brother has so little care for either his people or his throne that he would sell them for some trifling prize to the enemy of mankind." He turned to the others assembled there, anger poorly hidden on his thin features. "We will take this as truth for now, that the Storm King wishes to rule mankind through my brother. Ineluki, I am told, is a creature sustained mostly by hatred, so I do not need to tell you what sort of reign his would be. Simon has told us that the Sitha-woman Amerasu foresaw

what the Storm King desired for men, and she called it 'terrible.' We must do
all that we can—even up to tithing our lives, if necessary—to halt them both.
Now the other questions must be addressed. How do we fight them?"

In the hours that followed many plans were proposed. Freosel cautiously
suggested that they merely wait in this place of refuge as disaffection with Elias
grew throughout Osten Ard. Hotvig, who for a plainsman seemed to be taking
well to stone-dweller intrigue, put forward a bold scheme to send men who,
with Eolair's maps, would sneak into the Hayholt and kill both Elias and
Pryrates. Father Strangyeard seemed distressed at the idea of sending the precious maps off with a band of brutish murderers. As the merits of these and
other proposals were introduced and debated, tempers grew hot. When at one
point Isorn and Hotvig, who normally were cheerful comrades, had nearly
come to blows, Josua at last ended the discussion.

"Remember that we are friends and allies here," he said. "We all share a
common desire to return our lands to freedom." The prince looked around the
room, calming his excited advisers with a stern gaze, as a Hyrka trainer was said
to quiet horses without touching them. "I have heard all, and I am grateful for
your help, but now I must decide." He placed his hand on the stone table, near
Thorn's silver-wrapped hilt. "I agree that we must wait yet a while before we
will be ready to strike at Elias," he nodded in Freosel's direction, "—but we
may not stand still, either. Also, our allies in Hernystir are trapped. They could
be a valuable irritant on Elias' western flank if they were free to move once
more. If the westerners were to gather together some of their scattered countrymen, they could be even more than that. Thus, I have decided to combine
two purposes and see if they cannot serve each other."

Josua beckoned forward the lord of Nad Mullach. "Count Eolair, I will send
you back to your people with more than thanks, as I promised. With you will
go Isorn, son of Duke Isgrimnur." Gutrun could not restrain a muffled cry of
sadness at this, but when her son turned to comfort her, she smiled bravely and
patted his shoulder. Josua bowed his head toward her, acknowledging her sorrow. "You will understand when you hear my plan, Duchess, that I do not do
this without reason. Isorn, take with you a half-dozen or so men. Perhaps some
of Hotvig's randwarders will consent to accompany you: they are brave fighters
and tireless horsemen. On your journey to Hernystir, you will gather as many
of your wandering countrymen as you can. I know that most of them do not
love Skali Sharp-nose, and many I hear are now unhomed on the Frostmarch.
Then, on your own judgment, you can put those you find to service—either
helping to break Skali's siege of Eolair's folk, or if that is not possible, returning
with you here to help us in our fight against my brother." Josua looked fondly
at Isorn, who was listening with eyes downcast in concentration, as though he
wished to learn each word by heart. "You are the duke's son. They respect you,
and they will believe you when you tell them that this is the first step in regaining their own lands."

The prince turned back to the assembly. "While Isorn and the others undertake this mission, we here will work to further our other causes. And there is indeed much to do. The north has been so thoroughly savaged by winter, by Skali, by Elias and his ally the Storm King, that I fear that however successful Isorn is, the lands north of Erkynland will not prove sufficient to provide all the forces we need. Nabban and the south are firmly in the grip of Elias' friends, especially Benigaris, but I must have the south myself. Only then will we truly have the number of fighting men to confront Elias. So, we will work, and talk, and think. There must be some way of cutting Benigaris off from Elias' help, but at the moment I cannot see it."

Simon had been listening impatiently, but had held his tongue. Now, when it seemed as though Josua had finished with what he had to say, Simon could not stay quiet any longer. While the others had been shouting, he had been thinking with growing excitement about the things he had discussed with Binabik that morning.

"But Prince Josua," he cried, "what about the swords?"

The prince nodded. "Those, too, we will have to think about. Do not worry, Simon: I have not forgotten them."

Simon took a breath, determined to plunge on. "The best thing to do would be to surprise Elias. Send Binabik and Sludig and me to get Bright-Nail. It's outside the walls of the Hayholt. With just the three of us, we could go to your father's grave and find it, then be away before the king even knew we'd been there. He'd never suspect that we'd do such a thing." Simon had a momentary vision of how it would be: he and his companions bearing Bright-Nail back to Sesuad'ra in glory, Simon's new dragon banner flapping above them.

Josua smiled but shook his head. "No one doubts your bravery, Sir Seoman, but we cannot risk it."

"We found Thorn when no one thought we could."

"But the Erkynguard did not march past Thorn's resting place every day."

"The dragon did!"

"Enough." Josua raised his hand. "No, Simon, it is not yet time. When we can attack Elias from west or south and thus distract his eye away from Swertclif and the grave mounds, then it will be time. You have earned great honor, and you will no doubt earn more, but you are now a knight of the realm, with all the responsibilities that go with your title. I regretted sending you away in search of Thorn and despaired of ever seeing you again. Now that you have succeeded beyond all hope, I would have you here for a while—Binabik and Sludig, too . . . whom you neglected to consult before volunteering them for this deadly mission." He smiled to soften the blow. "Peace, lad, peace."

Simon was filled with the same stifling, trapped feeling that had beset him in Jao é-Tinukai'i. Didn't they understand that to wait too long to strike could mean they would lose their chance? That evil would go unpunished? "Can I go with Isorn?" he pleaded. "I want to help, Prince Josua."

"Learn to be a knight, Simon, and enjoy these days of relative freedom.

There will be enough danger later on." The prince stood. Simon could not help seeing the weariness in his expression. "That is enough. Eolair, Isorn, and whoever Isorn chooses should make ready to leave in two days' time. Let us now go. A meal has been prepared—not as lavish as the meal celebrating Simon's knighthood, but something that will do us all good, nevertheless." With a wave of his hand, he ended the gathering.

Binabik approached Simon, wanting to talk, but Simon was angry and at first would not answer. It was back to this, was it? *Wait, Simon, wait. Let others make the decisions. You'll be told what to do soon enough.*

"It was a good idea," he muttered.

"It will still be a good idea later," said Binabik, "when we are then distracting Elias, as Josua was telling."

Simon glared at him, but something in the troll's round face made his anger seem foolish. "I just want to be useful."

"You are far more than that, friend Simon. But everything is having its season. *'Iq ta randayhet suk biqahuc,'* as we say in my homeland: 'Winter is not being the time for naked swimming.'"

Simon thought about this for a moment. "That's stupid," he said at last.

"So," Binabik responded testily. "You may be saying what you please—but do not then come weeping to *my* fire when you have chosen the wrong season for swimming."

They walked silently across the grassy hill, haunted by the cold sun.

4

The Silent Child

Although the air was warm and still, the dark clouds seemed unnaturally thick. The ship had been almost motionless all day, sails slack against the masts.

"I wonder when the storm is coming," Miriamele said aloud.

A young sailor standing nearby looked up in surprise. "Lady? You say to me?"

"I said that I wondered when the storm was coming." She gestured at the clot of overhanging clouds.

"Yes, Lady." He seemed uneasy talking with her. His command of Westerling speech was not great: she guessed that he was from one of the smaller southern islands, on some of which the residents didn't even speak Nabbanai. "Storm coming."

"I know it's coming. I was wondering *when.*"

"Ah." He nodded his head, then looked around furtively, as though the valuable knowledge he was about to impart might draw thieves. "Storm come *very soon.*" He showed her a wide, gummy smile. His gaze traveled up from her shoes to her face and his grin widened. "Very pretty."

Her momentary pleasure in having a conversation, however limited, was dashed. She recognized the look in this sailor's eyes, the insulting stare. However free he was in his inspection, he would never dare to touch her, but that was only because he considered her a toy that rightfully belonged to the ship's master, Aspitis. Her flash of indignation was mixed with a sudden uncertainty. Was he right? Despite all the doubts she now harbored about the earl—who, if Gan Itai spoke rightly, had met with Pryrates, and if Cadrach spoke rightly, was even in the red priest's employ—she at least had believed that his announced plan to marry her was genuine. But now she wondered if it might only be a ruse, something to keep her pliant and grateful until he could discard her in Nabban and go looking for new flesh. He no doubt thought she would be too ashamed to tell anyone what had happened.

Miriamele was not sure which upset her more at this point, the possibility of being forced to marry Aspitis or the conflicting possibility that he could lie to her with the same airy condescension he might show to a pretty tavern whore.

She stared coldly at the sailor until at last, puzzled, he turned and made his way back toward the bow of the ship. Miriamele watched him go, silently will-ing him to trip and bash his smug face on the deck, but her wish was not granted. She turned her eyes back to the sooty gray clouds and the dull, metal-lic ocean.

A trio of small objects were bobbing in the water off the stern, a good stone's throw from the ship. As Miriamele watched, one of the objects moved closer, then opened its red hole of a mouth and hooted. The kilpa's gurgling voice carried well across the calm waters; Miriamele jumped in surprise. At her mo-tion, all three heads swung to face her, wet black eyes staring, mouths gaping loutishly. Miriamele took a step back from the rail and made the sign of the Tree, then turned to escape the empty eyes and almost knocked over Thures, the young page who served Earl Aspitis.

"Lady Marya," he said, and tried to bow, but he was too close to her. He banged his head against her elbow and gave out a little squeak of pain. When she reached out to soothe him, he pulled away, embarrassed. "'S Lordship wants you."

"Where, Thures?"

"Cabin." He composed himself. "In his cabin, Lady."

"Thank you."

The boy stepped back as if to lead her, but Miriamele's eyes had again been caught by a movement in the water below. One of the kilpa had drifted away from the other two and now swam slowly up next to the ship. With its empty eyes fixed on hers, the sea-thing lifted a slick gray hand from the water and ran its long fingers along the hull as if casually searching for climbing holds. Miri-amele watched with fascinated horror, unable to move. After a moment, the unpleasantly manlike creature dropped away again, vanishing smoothly into the sea to reappear a few moments later a stone's throw back from the ship. It floated there, mouth glistening, the gills on its neck bulging and shrinking. Miriamele stared, frozen as if in a nightmare. Finally she tore her eyes away and forced herself back from the rail. Young Thures was looking at her curiously.

"Lady?"

"I'm coming." She followed him, turning to look back only once. The three heads bobbed in the ship's wake like fishermen's floats.

Thures left her in the narrow passageway outside Aspitis' cabin, then van-ished back up the ladder, presumably to perform other errands. Miriamele took advantage of the moment of solitude to compose herself. She could not shake off the memory of the kilpa's viscous eyes, its calm and deliberate approach toward the ship. The way it had stared—almost insolently, as though daring her to try to stop it. She shuddered.

Her thoughts were interrupted by a series of quiet clinking noises from the earl's cabin. The door was not completely closed, so she stepped forward and peered through the crack.

Aspitis sat at his tiny writing table. A book of some kind was open before him, its parchment pages reflecting creamy lamplight. The earl swept two more piles of silver coins off the table and into a sack, then dropped the clinking bag into an open chest at his feet, which seemed nearly full with other such sacks. Aspitis then made a notation of some kind in the book.

A board creaked—whether from her weight upon it or from the movement of the ship Miriamele did not know—but she moved back hurriedly before Aspitis could look up and see her in the narrow slit of open doorway. A moment later, she stepped forward and knocked firmly.

"Aspitis?" She heard him close the book with a muffled thump, then another sound she guessed was the chest being dragged across the floor.

"Yes, my lady. Come in."

She pushed on the door and walked through, then closed it gently behind her but did not let the latch fall. "You asked for me?"

"Sit down, pretty Marya." Aspitis gestured to the bed, but Miriamele pretended she had not noticed and instead perched on a stool beside the far wall. One of Aspitis' hounds rolled aside to make room for her feet, thumped its heavy tail, then fell asleep again. The earl was wearing his osprey crest robe, the one she had admired so much at their first shared supper. Now she looked at the gold-stitched talons, perfect machines for catching and clutching, and was filled with remorse for her own foolishness.

Why did I ever let myself become entrapped in these stupid lies! She would never have told him so, but Cadrach had been right. If she had said she was only a commoner, Aspitis might have left her alone; even if he had forcibly bedded her, at least he would not be planning to wed her as well.

"I saw three kilpa swimming beside the ship." She stared at him defiantly, as if he might deny that it was true. "One swam up alongside and looked like it was going to climb aboard."

The earl shook his head, but he was smiling. "They will do no such thing, Lady, do not fear. Not on *Eadne Cloud*."

"It touched the ship!" She raised her hand, shaped into a groping claw. "Like this. It was looking for handholds."

Aspitis' smile faded. He looked grim. "I will go on deck when we have finished talking. I will put a few arrows into them, the fishy devils. They do not touch my ship."

"But what do the kilpa want?" She could not get the gray things out of her mind. Also, she was in no hurry to talk with Aspitis about whatever he was thinking. She was positive now that no good could come to her out of any of the earl's plans.

"I do not know what they want, Lady." He wagged his head impatiently. "Or rather, I do know—food. But there are many easier ways for the kilpa to catch their meals than to come onto a ship full of armed men." He stared at her. "There. I should not have said it. Now you are frightened."

"They eat . . . people?"

Aspitis shook his head, this time with greater vehemence. "They eat fish,

and sometimes birds that do not take off swiftly from floating on the water."
He absorbed her skeptical look. "Yes, other things, too, when they can find
them. They have sometimes swarmed small fishing boats, but nobody knows
why for certain. Anyway, it does not matter. I told you, they will not harm
Eadne Cloud. There is no better sea-watcher than Gan Itai."

Miriamele sat silently for a moment. "I'm sure you're right," she said at last.

"Good." He stood up, ducking beneath a beam of the low cabin roof. "I am
glad Thures found you—although you could not go very far on a ship at sea,
could you?" His smile seemed a little harsh. "We have many things to discuss."

"My lord." She felt a strange sense of lassitude sweep over her. Perhaps if she
did not resist, did not protest, especially if she did not care, then things would
just go on in this unsatisfactory but impermanent way. She had promised herself
that she would drift, drift. . . .

"We are becalmed," said Aspitis, "but I think that there will be winds coming soon, far ahead of the storm. With a little luck, we could be on the island
of Spenit tomorrow night. Think of that, Marya! We will be married there, in
the church sacred to Saint Lavennin."

It would be so easy not to resist, but just to float, like *Eadne Cloud* herself,
borne slowly along on the wind's unambitious breath. Surely there would be
some chance to escape when they made landfall at Spenit? Surely?

"My lord," she heard herself saying, "I . . . there are . . . problems."

"Yes?" The earl cocked his golden head. Miriamele thought he looked like
someone's trained hound, miming civilization while he sniffed for prey. "Problems?"

She gathered the material of her dress in her damp hand, then took a deep
breath. "I cannot marry you."

Unexpectedly, Aspitis laughed. "Oh, how foolish! Of course you can! Do
you worry about my family? They will come to love you, even as I have. My
brother married a Perdruinese woman, and now she is my mother's favorite
daughter. Do not fear!"

"It's not that." She clutched her dress more tightly. "It's . . . it's just that . . .
there is someone else."

The earl frowned. "What do you mean?"

"I am already promised to someone else. Back home. And I love him."

"But I asked you! You said to me there was no one. And you gave yourself
to me."

He was angry, but so far he had kept his temper. Miriamele felt her fear ease
somewhat. "I had an argument with him and refused to marry him; that is why
my father sent me to the convent. But I have realized that I was wrong. I was
unfair to him . . . and I was unfair to you." She detested herself for saying this.
It seemed only a very slight chance that she was truly being unfair to Aspitis;
he had certainly not been over-chivalrous with her. Still, this was the time to
be generous. "But of the two of you, I loved him first."

Aspitis took a step toward her, his mouth twisting. There was a strange, trembling tension to his voice. "But you gave yourself to me."

She lowered her eyes, anxious not to cause offense. "I was wrong. I hope you will forgive me. I hope that he will forgive me, although I do not deserve it."

The earl abruptly turned his back on her. His words were still tight, barely controlled. "And that is that, you think? You will just say, 'Farewell, Earl Aspitis!' That is what you think?"

"I can only rely on your gentleman's honor, my lord." The little room seemed even smaller. She thought she could feel the very air tighten, as if the threatening storm was reaching down for her. "I can only pray for your kindness and pity."

Aspitis' shoulders began to shake. A low, moaning noise welled up from him. Miriamele shrunk back against the wall in horror, half-certain he would turn into a ravening wolf before her eyes, as in some old nurse's tale.

The earl of Eadne and Drina whirled. His teeth were indeed bared in a lupine grimace, but he was laughing.

She was stunned. *Why is he . . . ?*

"Oh, my lady!" He was barely able to control his mirth. "You are a clever one!"

"I don't understand," she said frostily. "Do you think this is funny?"

Aspitis clapped his hands together. The sudden thunder crack of noise made Miriamele jump. "You are so clever." He shook his head. "But you are not quite as clever as you think . . . Princess."

"Wh—what?"

He smiled. It was no longer even remotely charming. "You think quickly and you invent pretty little lies very well—but I was at your grandfather's funeral, and your father's coronation as well. You are Miriamele. I knew that from the first night you joined me at my table."

"You . . . you . . ." Her mind was full of words, but none of them made sense. "What . . . ?"

"I suspected something when you were brought to me." He reached out a hand and slid it along Miriamele's face into her hair, his strong fingers clasping her behind the ear. She sat unmoving, holding her breath. "See," he said, "your hair is short, but the part closest to your head is quite golden . . . like mine." He chuckled. "Now, a young noblewoman on her way to a convent *might* cut her hair before she got there—but dye it, too, when it was already such a handsome color? You can be sure I looked at your face very closely at supper that night. After that, there was not much difficulty. I had seen you before, if not closely. It was common knowledge that Elias' daughter was at Naglimund, and missing after the castle fell." He snapped his fingers, grinning. "So. Now you *are* mine, and we *will* be married on Spenit, since you might find some way to escape in Nabban, where you still have family." He chortled again, pleased. "Now they will be my family, too."

It was difficult to speak. "You really want to marry me?"

"Not because of your beauty, my lady, though you are a pretty one. And not because I shared your bed. If I had to marry all the women I have dallied with, I would need to give my army of wives their own castle, like the Nascadu desert kings." He sat down on the bedcover, leaning back until he could rest his head against the cabin wall. "No, you will be my wife. Then, when your father's conquests are over and he grows tired at last of Benigaris, as I did long ago—did you know, after he killed his father he drank wine and cried all night long! Like a child!—when your father grows tired of Benigaris, who better to rule Nabban than the one who found his daughter, fell in love with her, and brought her back home?" His smile was a knife-glint. "Me."

She stared at him, her skin turning cold; she almost felt she could spit venom like a serpent. "And if I tell him that you kidnapped and dishonored me?"

He shook his head, amused. "You are not so good a schemer as I thought, Miriamele. Many witnessed you board my boat with a false name, and saw me pay court to you, although I had been told you were a minor baron's daughter. Once it is known that you have been—dishonored, you said?—do you think your father would offend a legitimate and high-born husband? A husband who is already his ally, and who has done your father many"—he reached over and patted his hand against something Miriamele could not see—"important services?"

His bright eyes burned into hers, mocking and immensely pleased. He was right. There was nothing she could do to prevent him. He owned her. *Owned her.*

"I am going." She rose unsteadily.

"Do not cast yourself in the ocean, pretty Miriamele. My men will be watching to make sure you play no such tricks. You are far too valuable alive."

She pushed at the door, but it would not open. She was hollow, empty and hurting as if all the air had been forced out of her.

"Pull it," Aspitis suggested.

Miriamele staggered out into the corridor. The shadowed hall seemed to lurch crazily.

"I will come to your cabin later, my beloved," the earl called. "Prepare for me."

She was barely off the ladder and onto the deck before she sank to her knees. She wanted to fall into blackness and disappear.

Tiamak was angry.

He had gone through a great deal for the sake of his drylander associates—the League of the Scroll, as they called themselves, although Tiamak sometimes thought that a group of a half-dozen or so was a bit small to be called a league. Still, Doctor Morgenes had been a member and Tiamak revered the doctor, so he had always done his best when someone in the league wanted information that only the little Wrannaman could provide. The drylanders didn't often need marsh-wisdom, Tiamak had noticed, but when they did—when, for instance, one of them needed a sample of twistgrass or Yellow Tinker, herbs not to be found in any drylander marketplace—they would scratch off a note to Tiamak quickly enough. Occasionally, as when he had arduously prepared a bestiary of marsh animals for Dinivan, complete with his own painstaking illustrations, or had studied and reported to old Jarnauga which rivers reached the Wran, and what happened when their fresh water met the salt of the Bay of Firannos, he would receive a long letter of gratitude from the recipient—in fact, Jarnauga's letter had so burdened its carrier that the pigeon's journey had taken twice the usual time. In these grateful letters, League members would occasionally hint that someday soon Tiamak might be officially counted in their number.

Little appreciated by his own villagefolk, Tiamak was terribly hungry for such recognition. He remembered his time in Perdruin, the hostility and suspicion he had felt from the other young scholars, who had been astonished to find a marsh lad in their midst. If not for Morgenes' kindness, he would have fled back to the swamps. Still, beneath Tiamak's diffident exterior, there was more than a trace of pride. Had he not, after all, been the first Wrannaman ever to leave the swamplands and study with the Aedonite brothers? Even his fellow villagers knew there was no other marsh-dweller like him. Thus, when he received encouraging words from Scrollbearers, he had sensed that his time was coming. Some day he would be a member of the League of the Scroll, the very highest of scholarly circles, and travel every three years to the home of one of the other members for a gathering—a gathering of equals. He would see the world and be a famously learned man . . . or so he had often imagined.

When the hulking Rimmersman Isgrimnur came to *Pelippa's Bowl* and gave him the coveted Scrollbearer's pendant—the golden scroll and feather pen—Tiamak's heart had soared. All his sacrifices had been worth the reward! But a moment later Duke Isgrimnur had explained that the pendant came from Dinivan's dying hand, and when stunned Tiamak had asked about Morgenes, Isgrimnur gave him the shattering news that the doctor was dead, too, that he had died almost half a year ago.

A fortnight later, Isgrimnur still did not understand Tiamak's desperation. He seemed to think that although it was sad that the two men had died, Tiamak's brooding melancholy was extreme. But the Rimmersman had brought no new strategy, no useful advice; he was not, he admitted, even a member of the League! Isgrimnur did not seem to comprehend that this left Tiamak—who had waited many painful weeks for word of what Morgenes planned—terribly adrift, spinning like a flatboat in an eddy. Tiamak had sacrificed his duty to his people for a drylander errand—or so it sometimes seemed when he was angry enough to forget that it had been the crocodile attack that had forced him to give up his embassy to Nabban. In any case, he had clearly failed the people of Village Grove.

Tiamak did have to admit that at least Isgrimnur was paying for his room and board at a time when the Wrannaman's own credit had run out. That was something, anyway—but then again, it was only fair: the drylanders had made money from the sweat of the marshfolk for untold years. Tiamak himself had been threatened, chased, and abused in the markets of Ansis Pelippé.

Morgenes had rescued him then, but now Morgenes was dead. Tiamak's own people would never forgive him for failing them. And Isgrimnur was obsessed with old Ceallio the doorkeeper, who he claimed was the great knight Camaris; Isgrimnur no longer seemed to care whether the little marsh man was alive or dead. Taken all together, it was clear to Tiamak that he was now as useless as a crab with no legs.

He looked up, startled. He had wandered far away from *Pelippa's Bowl* into a section of Kwanitupul that he did not recognize. The water here was even grayer and greasier than usual, dotted with the corpses of fish and seabirds. The derelict buildings that overlooked the canals seemed almost to bend beneath the weight of centuries of grime and salt.

A dizzying sense of bleakness and loss swept over him.

He Who Always Steps on Sand, let me come safely back to my home again. Let my birds be alive. Let me . . .

"Marsh man!" The braying voice interrupted his prayer. "He's coming!"

Startled, Tiamak looked around. Three young drylanders dressed in white Fire Dancer robes stood on the far side of the narrow canal. One of them pushed back his hood to display a partially shorn head, uncut tufts of hair still sticking up like weeds. His eyes, even from a distance, seemed wrong.

"He's coming!" this one shouted again, his voice cheerful, as though Tiamak were an old friend.

Tiamak knew who and what these men were; he wanted no part of their madness. He turned and limped back along the uneven walkway. The buildings he passed were boarded up, empty of life.

"Storm King's coming! He'll fix that leg!" On the far side of the canal, the three Fire Dancers had turned as well. They paced along directly across from Tiamak, matching him step for hobbling step, shouting as they walked. "Haven't you heard yet? Sick and the lame will be scourged! Fire burn 'em, ice bury 'em!"

Tiamak saw a gap in the long wall to his right. He turned into it, hoping it was not a dead end. The jeers of the Fire Dancers followed him.

"Where do you go, little brown man? When he comes, the Storm King will find you if you hide in the deepest hole or on the highest mountain! Come back and talk with us or we will come and get you!"

The doorway led into a large open court that might once have been a shipbuilding yard, but now contained only a few castoffs of its vanished owners, a litter of weather-twisted gray spars, splintered tool handles, and pieces of shattered crockery. The planks of the courtyard floor were so warped that when he looked down he could see long stripes of the muddy canal flowing beneath him.

Tiamak made his way carefully across the dubious flooring to a door on the far side of the yard, then out onto another walkway. The cries of the Fire Dancers grew fainter, but seemed nevertheless to become more fiercely angry as he quickly strode away.

For a Wrannaman, Tiamak was quite familiar with cities, but even the residents found it easy to get lost in Kwanitupul. Few of the buildings remained in use for long, or even remained standing; the small, select group of establishments that had existed as long as a century or two had also changed location a dozen times—the sea air and the murky water chewed away at paint and pilings alike. Nothing was permanent in Kwanitupul.

After walking for a while Tiamak began to recognize a few familiar landmarks—the rickety spire of crumbling Saint Rhiappa's, the bright but decaying paint of the Market Hall dome. As his nervousness about being lost and threatened receded, he began to ponder his dilemma once more. He was trapped in an unfriendly city. If he wished to make a living, he must sell his services as a scribe and translator. This would mean living near the marketplace, since evening business, especially the small transactions on which Tiamak made his livelihood, would never wait until daylight. If he did not work, he was dependent on the continuing charity of Duke Isgrimnur. Tiamak had no urge to suffer the hospitality of the dreadful Charystra a moment longer, and in an attempt to solve this very problem he had suggested to Isgrimnur that they all move closer to the market so Tiamak could earn money while the duke nursed the idiot doorkeeper. The Rimmersman, however, had been adamant. He was certain there was a good reason Dinivan had wanted them to wait at *Pelippa's Bowl*—although what that reason might be, he could not say. So, although Isgrimnur did not like the innkeeper any more than Tiamak did, he was not ready to leave.

Tiamak was also worried about whether he was actually a member of the League of the Scroll. He had apparently been chosen to join, but the members he knew personally were dead and he had heard nothing from any of the others for months. What was he supposed to do?

Last, but certainly not the least of his problems, he was having bad dreams. Or rather, he corrected himself, not *bad* dreams so much as odd ones. For the last several weeks, his sleep had been haunted by an apparition: no matter what he dreamed, whether it was of being chased by a crocodile with an eye in every one of its thousand teeth, or of eating a splendid meal of crab and bottomfish with his resurrected family in Village Grove, a ghostly child was present—a little dark-haired drylander girl who watched everything in utter silence. The child never interfered, whether the dream was frightening or enjoyable, and in fact seemed somehow even less real than the dreams themselves. Were it not for the constancy of her presence from dream to dream, he would have forgotten her entirely. Lately she seemed to be getting fainter each time she appeared, as though her image was receding into the murk of the dreamworld, her message still unvoiced. . . .

Tiamak looked up and saw the barge-loading dock. He remembered beyond doubt that he had passed it on his way out. Good. He was back on familiar territory.

So here was another mystery—who or what was this silent child? He tried to remember what Morgenes had told him of dreams and the Dream Road and what such an apparition might signify, but he could remember nothing useful. Perhaps she was a messenger from the land of the dead, a spirit sent by his late mother, wordlessly chastising him for his failure. . . .

"The little marsh man!"

Tiamak whirled to see the three Fire Dancers standing on the walkway a few paces behind him. This time, no canal separated them from him.

The leader stepped forward. His white robe was less than pristine, smeared with dirty handprints and splotches of tar, but his eyes were even more frightening than they had been at a distance, bright and burning as if with some inner light. His stare seemed almost to jump out of his face.

"You don't walk very fast, brown man." He grinned, showing crooked teeth. "Somebody bend your leg, yes? Bend it bad?"

Tiamak backed up a few steps. The three young men waited until he stopped, then slouched forward, casually regaining their proximity. It was clear that they were not going to let him walk away. Tiamak lowered his hand onto the hilt of his knife. The bright eyes widened, as though the slender marsh man proposed a newer and more interesting game.

"I have done nothing to you," Tiamak said.

The leader laughed soundlessly, skinning his lips back and showing his red tongue like a dog. "*He* is coming, you know. You cannot run from Him."

"Does your Storm King send you to devil innocent strollers?" Tiamak tried to put strength in his voice. "I cannot believe that such a being would stoop so low." He gently eased the knife loose in its sheath.

The leader made a humorous face as he looked to his fellows. "Ah, he talks good for a little brown man, doesn't he?" He turned his gleaming eyes back on Tiamak. "The master wants to see who is fit, who is strong. It will go hard on the weak when He comes."

Tiamak began to walk backward, hoping either to reach a place where there might be others to help him—not very likely in this backwater section of Kwanitupul—or at least to find a spot where his back would be protected by a wall and where these three would not have such freedom of movement on either side of him. He prayed to They Who Watch and Shape that he would not stumble. He would have liked to be able to feel behind him with his hand, but knew he might need that arm to ward off the first blow and give himself a chance to draw his knife.

The three Fire Dancers followed him, each face as innocent of consideration as a crocodile's. In fact, Tiamak thought, trying to make himself brave, he had fought a crocodile and survived. These beasts were little different, except that the crocodile would at least have eaten him. The youths would kill him for pure pleasure, or for some warped idea of what their Storm King wanted. Even as he walked backward, locked in a strange death-dance with his persecutors, even as he desperately sought some place to make a stand, Tiamak could not help wondering how the name of a little-known demon legend from the North should these days be upon the lips of street bullies in Kwanitupul. Things had changed indeed since he had last left the swamps.

"Careful, little man." The leader looked past Tiamak. "You will fall in and drown."

Startled, Tiamak glanced backward over his shoulder, expecting to see the unfenced canal just behind him. When he realized instead that he was at the mouth of a short alleyway, and that he had been tricked, he turned back quickly to his pursuers, just in time to avoid the hurtling downstroke of an iron-tipped cudgel which crashed against the wooden wall beside him. Splinters flew.

Tiamak pulled his knife free of the sheath and slashed at the cudgel-wielding hand, missing but tearing the sleeve of a white robe. Two Fire Dancers, one of them waving a tattered sleeve in mockery, moved to either side of him as the leader took up his own position directly in front. Tiamak backed into the alley, waving his knife in an attempt to keep all three at bay. The leader laughed as he pulled his own cudgel out from beneath his robe. His eyes were full of a terrifying, guiltless glee.

The youth on the left suddenly made a quiet sound and disappeared back around the mouth of the alleyway onto the walkway they had just deserted. Tiamak guessed that he was serving as lookout while his friends finished with their victim. An instant later the vanished youth's cudgel reappeared without its owner, hurtling into the alleyway and striking the Fire Dancer on Tiamak's right hand, flinging him against the wall of the alleyway. His head left a red smear down the planking as he crumpled into a white-robed heap. As the shaven-headed leader stood, staring in astonishment, a tall shape stepped into the alley behind him, grasped him firmly around the neck and then whipped him through the air and into the walkway railing, which shattered into flinders as though struck by a catapult stone. The limp body sagged free of the remnants of the walkway and tumbled into the canal; then, within a long, silent moment, it sank out of sight in the oily water.

Tiamak discovered he was trembling uncontrollably with excitement and terror. He looked up into the kind, slightly confused face of Ceallio, the door-keeper.

Camaris. The duke said he is Camaris, was Tiamak's dazed thought. *A knight. Sworn to, sworn to . . . to save the innocent.*

The old man laid his hand on Tiamak's shoulder and led him back out of the alleyway.

That night the Wrannaman dreamed of white-shrouded figures with eyes that were flaming wheels. They came at him across the water like sails flapping. He was splashing in one of the sidestreams of the Wran, desperate to escape, but something held his leg. The more he struggled, the harder it became to keep afloat.

The little dark-haired girl watched him from the bank, solemn and silent. She seemed so faint this time that he could hardly see her, as though she were made of mist. Eventually, before the dream ended and he woke up gasping, she faded entirely.

Diawen the scryer had made her cave in the mountain's depths into something very much like the small house she had once inhabited on the outskirts of Hernysadharc, close by the Circoille fringe. The small cavern was closed off from its neighbors by woolen shawls hung across the doorway. When Maegwin gently tugged one of the curtaining shawls aside, a wave of sweetish smoke billowed out.

The dream of flickering lights had been so vivid and so obviously important that Maegwin had found it difficult to go about her business all morning. Although her people's needs were many, and she had done her best to satisfy them, she had moved all day in a kind of fog, far away in her heart and mind even as she touched the trembling hands of an old person or took one of the children in her arms.

Diawen had been a priestess of Mircha many years ago, but had broken her vows—no one knew why, or at least no one could say for certain, though speculation was constant—then left the Order to live by herself. She had a reputation as a madwoman, but was also known for true-telling, for dream-reading and healing. Many a troubled citizen of Hernysadharc, after leaving a bowl of fruit and a coin for Brynioch or Rhynn, waited until after dark and then went to Diawen for more immediate assistance. Maegwin remembered seeing her once in the market near the Taig, her long, pale brown hair fluttering like a pennant. Maegwin's nurse had quickly pulled her away, as though even looking at Diawen might be dangerous.

So, faced with a powerful but confusing dream, and having made a grave mistake in her last interpretation, Maegwin had this time decided to seek help. If anyone would understand the things that were happening to her, she felt sure, it was Diawen.

For all the smoky haze that hung thick as Inniscrich fog, the inside of the scryer's cave was surprisingly neat. She had carefully arranged the few possessions saved from her home in Hernysadharc, a collection of shiny things that might have aroused the envy of a nesting magpie. Dozens of gleaming bead necklaces hung on the cave's rough walls and caught the light of the fire like dew-spotted spiderwebs. Small mounds of shiny baubles—mostly beads of metal and polished stone—were arranged on the flat rock that was Diawen's table. In various niches around the chamber stood the equally shiny tools of the scryer's craft, mirrors ranging in size from a serving tray to a thumbnail, made of polished metal or costly glass, some round, some square, some elliptical as a cat's eye. Maegwin was fascinated to see so many in one place. A child of a rustic court, where a lady's hand mirror was, after her reputation, perhaps her most cherished possession, she had never seen anything like it.

Diawen had been beautiful once, or so everyone always said. It was hard to tell now. The scryer's upturned brown eyes and wide mouth were set in a gaunt, weathered face. Her hair, still exceptionally long and full, had turned a very ordinary iron gray. Maegwin thought she looked like nothing more than a thin woman growing old fast.

Diawen smiled mockingly. "Ah, little Maegwin. Come for a love dram, have you? If it's the count you're after, you'll have to heat his blood first or the charm won't take. He's a careful one, he is."

Maegwin's initial surprise was quickly overtaken by shock and rage. How could this woman know of her feelings for Eolair? Did everyone know? Was she the object of laughter at every cookfire? For a moment, her deep sense of responsibility for her father's subjects evaporated. Why should she fight to save such a pack of sniggering ingrates?

"Why do you say that?" she snapped. "What makes you think I love anyone?"

Diawen laughed, untouched by Maegwin's anger. "I am the one who knows. That is what I do, king's daughter."

For a long moment, her eyes smarting from the clinging smoke and her pride stinging from Diawen's bold assessment, Maegwin wanted only to turn and leave. At last, her sensible side took charge. There might be loose talk about Lluth's daughter, certainly—as Old Craobhan had pointed out, there always was. And Diawen was just the type to prowl about listening for valuable castoffs—useful little facts that, when polished up and then cunningly disclosed, would make her prophesying seem more uncanny. But if Diawen was the type to rely on such trickery, would she be any use to Maegwin's current need?

As if sensing her thoughts, Diawen gestured for her to take a seat on a smooth lump of stone covered with a shawl and said: "I have heard talk, it's true. No magical arts were needed to reveal your feelings for Count Eolair—just seeing you together once taught me all I needed to know. But there is more to Diawen than keen ears and sharp eyes." She poked at the fire and set sparks to hopping, unleashing another billow of yellowish smoke, then turned a calculating look upon Maegwin. "What do you want, then?"

When Maegwin told her that she wished the scryer's help interpreting a dream, Diawen became quite business-like. She refused Maegwin's offers of food or clothing. "No, king's daughter," she said with a hard smile, "I will help you now and you will owe me a favor. That will suit me better. Agreed?"

After being assured that the favor was not to be repaid with her firstborn son, or with her shadow, or soul, or voice, or any other such thing, she consented.

"Do not fret," Diawen chuckled. "This is no fireplace tale. No, someday I will simply want help . . . and you will give it. You are a child of Hern's House and I am only a poor scryer, yes? That is my reason."

Maegwin told Diawen the substance of the dream, and of the other strange things she had dreamed in the months before, as well as what had happened when she let the visions lead her down into the earth with Eolair.

The smoke in the little chamber was so thick that when she finished telling of Mezutu'a and its denizens, she had to step out past the hanging for a while to breathe. Her head had begun to feel very strange, as if it were floating free of her body, but a few moments out in the main cavern restored her to clear-mindedness.

"That story is almost payment enough, king's daughter," the scryer said when Maegwin returned. "I had heard the rumors, but did not know whether to believe them. The dwarrow-folk alive in the earth below us!" She made a strange hooking gesture with her fingers. "Of course, I have always thought there was something more to the Grianspog tunnels than just the dead past."

Maegwin frowned. "But what about my dream? About the 'high place'— about how the time has come."

Diawen nodded. The scryer crawled to the wall on her hands and knees. She ran her fingers over several of the mirrors, then at last selected one and brought it back to the fireside. It was small, set in a wooden frame gone nearly black from untold years of handling.

"My grandmother used to call this a 'wormglass,'" Diawen said, holding it out for Maegwin's inspection. It looked like a very ordinary mirror, the carving worn down until it was almost completely smooth.

"A wormglass? Why?"

The scryer shrugged her bony shoulders. "Perhaps in the days of Drochna-thair and the other great worms, it was used to watch for their approach. Or perhaps it was made from the claws or the teeth of a worm." She grinned, as though to show that she herself, despite her livelihood, did not hold with such superstition. "Most likely the frame was once carved to look like a dragon. Still, it is a good tool."

She held the mirror above the flames, moving it in slow circles for a long while. When at last she turned it upright once more, a thin film of soot covered its surface. Diawen held it up before Maegwin's face; the reflection was ob-scured, as though by fog. "Think of your dream, then blow."

Maegwin tried to fix in her mind the strange procession, the beautiful but alien figures. A tiny cloud of soot puffed from the mirror's face.

Diawen turned the glass around and studied it, biting her lower lip as she concentrated. With the firelight directly below her, her face seemed even thin-ner, almost skeletal. "It is strange," the scryer said finally. "I can see patterns, but they are all unfamiliar to me. It is as though someone is speaking loudly in a house nearby, but in a tongue I have never heard before." Her eyes narrowed. "Something is wrong, here, king's daughter. Are you sure this was your own

dream and not one that someone told to you?" When Maegwin angrily reaf-
firmed her ownership, Diawen frowned. "I can tell you little, and nothing from
the mirror."

"What does that mean?"

"The mirror is as good as silent. It is speaking, but I do not understand. So,
then, I will release you from your promise to me, but I will also tell you
something—give you my own advice." Her voice implied that this would be
just as good as whatever the mirror might have told them. "If the gods truly
mean for this to be made clear to you, do what they say." She briskly wiped the
mirror clean with a white cloth and set it back into its niche in the cavern wall.

"What is that?"

Diawen pointed up, as though at the ceiling of the cave. "Go to the high
place."

Maegwin felt her boots sliding on snow-slicked rock and flung out a gloved
hand to catch a prong of stone beside the steep path. She bent her knees and
edged her feet under her body until she had regained her balance, then stood
straight once more, looking back down the white hillside at the dangerous
distance she had already climbed. A slip here could easily topple her off the
narrow path; after that, nothing would stop her tumble down the slope but the
tree trunks that would dash out her brains long before she reached the bottom.

She stood panting, and found to her mild surprise that she was not very
frightened. Such a fall would certainly end in death one way or another—either
immediately, or by leaving her crippled on a snowy mountain in the
Grianspog—but Maegwin was giving her life back into the hands of the gods:
what difference could it make if they decided to take her now rather than later?
Besides, it was glorious to be out beneath the sky again, no matter how cold
and grim it might be.

She shuffled a little farther toward the outside edge of the trail and turned
her gaze upward. Almost half the height of the hill still loomed between Maegwin and her destination—Bradach Tor, which jutted from the pinnacle like
the prow of a stone ship, its underside blackly naked of the snow that blanketed
the slopes. If she went hard at it, she should reach the summit before the weak
morning sun, which now shone full in her face, had climbed far past noon.

Maegwin shouldered her pack and turned her attention back to the path,
noting with satisfaction that the fluttering snow had already erased most of the
marks of her recent passage. At the base of the hill where she had begun, the
tracks had no doubt been completely obliterated. If any of Skali's Rimmersmen
came sniffing around this part of the Grianspog, there would be no sign she had
been here. The gods were doing their share. That was a good sign.

The steep path forced her to make most of the ascent leaning forward, grasping at the handholds that presented themselves. She felt a small, sour pride at
the strength of her body, at the way her muscles stretched and knotted, pulling
her up the slope just as swiftly as most men could climb. Maegwin's height and

strength had always been more of a curse to her than a blessing. She knew how unwomanly most thought her, and had spent most of her life pretending not to care. But still, it was somehow very satisfying to feel her capable limbs work for her. Sadly, it was her body itself that was the greatest impediment to her given task. Maegwin felt sure she would be able to let it go if she had to, although it would not be easy, but it had been even harder to turn against Eolair, to pretend a contempt for him that was the opposite of her feelings. Still, she had done it, however sick it made her feel. Sometimes doing the gods' bidding required a hardened heart.

The climb did not get easier. The snowy path that she followed was really little more than an animal track. In many places it vanished altogether, forcing her to make her way awkwardly over outcroppings of stone, trusting tangles of leafless heather or the branches of wind-twisted trees to hold her weight until she could haul herself up to another area of relative safety.

She made several stops to catch her breath, or to squeeze her sodden gloves dry and rub the feeling back into her fingers. The clouded sun was well into the western sky by the time she clambered up the last rise and found herself atop Bradach Tor. She scraped away snow, then slumped down in a heap on the black, wind-polished rock.

The forested skirts of the Grianspog spread below her. Beyond the mountain's base, hidden from her eyes by swirling snow, stood Hernysadharc, the ancestral home of Maegwin's family. There, Skali the usurper strode the oaken halls of the Taig and his reavers swaggered through Hernysadharc's white-clad streets. Something had to be done; apparently it was something only the daughter of the king could do.

She did not rest long. The heat generated by her exertion was being rapidly sucked away by the wind, and she was growing chilled. She emptied her pack, pouring all the possessions she thought she would need in this world onto the black stone. She wrapped herself in the heavy blanket, trying not to dwell childishly on how the onset of night might deepen the already unpleasant cold. Her leather sack of flints and her striking stone she put to one side: she would have to clamber back off the tor to find some firewood.

Maegwin had brought no food, not only to show trust in the gods, but also because she was tired of acceding to her body's demands. The flesh she inhabited could not live without meals, without love—in truth, it was the low clay of which she was made that had confused her with its constant need for food and warmth and the good will of others. Now it was time to let such earthly things fall away so that the gods could see her essence.

There were two articles nestled in the bottommost folds of her sack. The first was a gift from her father, a carved wooden nightingale, emblem of the goddess Mircha. One day, when a younger Maegwin had cried inconsolably over some childhood disappointment, King Lluth had stood and plucked the graceful bird from the rafters of the Taig where it hung among the myriad of other god-carvings, then put it into her small hands. It was all that she had left to remind her of how things had been, of what had been lost. After pressing it for a moment against her cold cheeks, she set it on a rounded outcropping of stone where it rocked in the brisk wind.

The last treasure in the bag was the stone that Eolair had given her, the dwarrow's gift. Maegwin frowned, rolling the strange object between her palms. She had pretended that the reason she packed it was because she had been holding it when she had the god-sent dream, but really she knew better. The count had given it to her, then he had ridden away.

Tired and stupefied from her climb, Maegwin stared at the stone and her name-rune until her head hurt. It was a perfectly useless thing—her name given a sort of false immortality, as much of a cheat as the great stone city beneath the ground. All things of the heavy earth were suspect, she now understood.

At the gods' own clear urging, she had come to this high place. This time, Maegwin had decided, she would let the gods do what they wished, not struggle to anticipate them. If they wanted to bring her to stand before them, then she would plead for salvation of her folk and the destruction of Skali and the High King, the bestial pair who had brought such humiliation on a blameless people; if the gods did not wish to help her, she would die. But no matter the ultimate result, she would sit here atop the tor until the gods made their wishes known.

"Brynioch Sky-lord!" she shouted into the wind. "Mircha cloaked in rain! Murhagh Armless, and bold Rhynn! I have heard your call! I await your judgment!"

Her words were swallowed up in gray and swirling white.

Waiting, Miriamele fought against sleep, but Aspitis hovered on the edge of wakefulness for a long time, mumbling and shifting on the bed beside her. She found it very hard to keep her own thoughts fixed. When the knock came on her cabin door, she was floating in a sort of a half-slumber, and did not at first realize what the noise was.

The knock came again, a little louder. Startled, Miriamele rolled over. *"Who is it?"* she hissed. It must be Gan Itai, she decided—but what would the earl think about the Niskie visiting Miriamele in her room? A second thought followed swiftly: she did not want Gan Itai to see Aspitis here in her bed. Miriamele had no illusions about what the Niskie knew, but even in her wretchedness she wished to preserve some tiny fragments of self-respect.

"Is the master there?" The voice, to both her shame and relief, was male—one of the sailors.

Aspitis sat up in bed beside her. His lean body was unpleasantly warm against her skin. "What is it?" he asked, yawning.

"Pardon, my lord. You're needed by the helmsman. That is, he begs your pardon, and asks for you. He thinks he sees storm signs. Odd ones."

The earl sagged onto his back once more. "By the Blessed Mother! What is the hour, man?"

"The Lobster's just gone over the horizon, Lord Aspitis. Mid-watch, four hours till dawn. Very sorry, my lord."

Aspitis swore again, then reached down to the cabin floor for his boots. Although he must have known that Miriamele was awake, he did not say a word to her. Miriamele saw the sailor's bearded face etched in lamplight when the door opened, then listened as the two sets of footsteps passed down the corridor to the deck ladder.

She lay in the darkness for dragging minutes, listening to her own heartbeat, which was louder than the still-becalmed ocean. It was plain that all the sailors knew where Aspitis was—they *expected* to find the earl in his doxy's bed! Shame choked her. For a moment she thought of poor Cadrach down in the shadowed hold. He was bound by iron chains, but were her own fetters any more comfortable for being invisible?

Miriamele could not imagine how she could ever again walk across the deck under the eyes of those grinning sailors—could not imagine it any more than she could imagine standing naked before them. It was one thing to be suspected, another to be part of the casual knowledge shared by the entire ship: when he was needed in the night watches, Aspitis could be found in her bed. This latest degradation seemed to creep over her like a heavy, numbing chill. How could she ever leave the cabin again? And even if she did, what did she have to look forward to in any case but a forced marriage to the golden-haired monstrosity? She would rather be dead.

In the dark, Miriamele made a small noise. Slowly, as if approaching a dangerous animal, she considered this last idea for a moment—it was stunning in its power, even as an unvoiced thought. She had promised herself that she could outlast anything, that she could float with any tide and lie happily beneath the sun on whatever beach received her—but was it true? Could she even marry Aspitis, who had made her his whore, who had aided in murdering her uncle and was a willing catspaw of Pryrates? How could a girl—no, a woman now, she reflected ruefully—how could a woman with the blood of Prester John in her veins allow such a thing to happen to her?

But if the life that stretched before her was so unbearable that death seemed preferable, then she need be afraid no longer. She could do anything.

Miriamele slipped from the bed. After dressing quickly, she edged out into the narrow passageway.

Miriamele climbed the ladder as quietly as she could, lifting her head above the hatchway just far enough to make sure that Aspitis was still talking to the helmsman. They seemed to be having a very animated discussion, waving their lamps so that the flaming wicks left streaks across the black sky. Miriamele dropped down to the passageway as quickly as she could. A kind of cold cleverness had come over her along with her new resolution, and she moved quietly and surely along the corridor to Aspitis' doorway. When she had slipped through the door and closed it behind her, she took the hood off her lamp.

A quick examination of Aspitis' room turned up nothing useful. The earl's sword lay across his bed like some heathen wedding token, a slim, beautifully wrought blade with a hilt in the shape of a spread-winged seahawk. It was the earl's favorite possession—except perhaps for her, Miriamele thought grimly—but it was not what she sought. She began to investigate a little more thoroughly, checking the folds of all his clothing, rummaging through the caskets in which he kept his jewelry and gaming-dice. Although she knew that time was growing ever shorter, she forced herself to refold each garment and lay it back where it had been. It would do her cause no good to alert Aspitis.

When she had finished, Miriamele stared around the cabin in frustration, unwilling to believe that she could simply fail. Abruptly, she remembered the chest into which she had seen Aspitis pushing bags of money. Where had that gone? She dropped down onto her knees and pushed aside the bed's hanging coverlet. The chest was there, draped by Aspitis' second-best cloak. Certain that any moment the Earl of Eadne and Drina would walk through the door, Miriamele forced herself under the bed and dragged it out into the light, wincing at the loud scraping as its metal corners cut into the plank floor.

The chest was, as she had seen, full of bags of money. The coins were mostly silver, but each sack contained more than a few gold Imperators as well. It was a small fortune, but Miriamele knew that Aspitis and his family were the possessors of a very large fortune beside which this was a mere handful. She carefully lifted out a few of the sacks, trying to keep them from jingling, noting with some interest that her hands, which should have been shaking, were as steady as stone. Hidden beneath the top row of sacks was a leather-bound ledger. It contained lists in Aspitis' surprisingly fastidious handwriting of places the *Eadne Cloud* had stopped—Vinitta and Grenamman, as well as other names that Miriamele decided must have been ports visited on other voyages; beside each entry was a line of cryptic markings. Miriamele could make no sense of it, and after a moment's impatient study she put it aside. Beneath the ledger, rolled into a bundle, was a hooded robe of coarse white cloth—but this was not what she was looking for either. The trunk contained no further secrets, so she repacked it as well as she could, then pushed it back beneath the bed.

Time was running short. Miriamele sat on the floor, full of a dreadful, cold hatred. Perhaps it would be easiest just to slip up on deck and throw herself into the ocean. It was hours until dawn; no one would know where she had gone until it was too late to stop her. But she thought of the kilpa, patiently waiting, and could not imagine joining them in the black seas.

As she stood, she saw it at last. It had been hanging on a hook behind the door all along. She took it down and slipped it into her belt beneath her cloak, then stepped into the doorway. When she was certain that no one was coming, she hooded her lamp and made her way back to her own cabin.

Miriamele was crawling under her blanket when she suddenly understood the significance of the white robe. In her oddly detached state, this realization was only one more tally added to the earl's overloaded account, but it helped to stiffen her resolve. She lay unmoving, breathing quietly, waiting for Aspitis' return, her mind set on her course so firmly that she would not allow any thoughts to distract her—not memories of her childhood and her friends, not regrets about the places she would never see. Her ears brought her every creak of the ship's timbers and every slap of the waves on the hull, but as the trudging hours passed, his booted footsteps never sounded in the passageway. Her door did not creak open. Aspitis did not come.

At last, as dawn was glimmering in the sky above-decks, she fell into a heavy, muddy sleep with the earl's dagger still clutched in her fist.

She felt the hands that shook her, and heard the quiet voice, but her mind did not want to return to the waking world.

"Girl, wake up!"

At last, groaning, Miriamele rolled over and opened her eyes. Gan Itai peered down at her, a look of concern furrowing her already wrinkled brow. Morning light from the hatch in the passageway outside spilled in through the open door. The achingly painful memories of the day before, absent for the first few moments, rolled back over her.

"Go away," she told the Niskie. She tried to push her head back under the blanket, but Gan Itai's strong hands clutched her and pulled her upright.

"What is this I hear on deck? The sailors are saying that Earl Aspitis is to be married on Spenit—married to you! Is that true?"

Miriamele covered her eyes with her hands, trying to keep out the light. "Has the wind come up?"

Gan Itai's voice was puzzled. "No, we are still becalmed. Why do you ask such a strange question?"

"Because if we can't get there, he can't marry me," Miriamele whispered.

The Niskie shook her head. "By the Uncharted, then it is true! Oh, girl, this is not what you want, is it?"

Miriamele opened her eyes. "I would rather be dead."

Gan Itai made a little humming noise of dismay. She helped Miriamele to get her feet out of bed and onto the floor, then brought over the small mirror that Aspitis had given to Miriamele when he had still been pretending kindness.

"Do you not wish to brush your hair straight?" the Niskie asked. "It looks rumpled and windblown, and that is not how you like it, I think."

"I don't care," she said, but the look on Gan Itai's face touched her: the sea-watcher could think of no other way to help. She reached out her hand for the mirror. The hilt of Aspitis' dagger, which had been covered in the folds of blanket, caught in her sleeve and clattered onto the floor. Both Miriamele and the old Niskie stared at it for a moment. Suddenly, chillingly, Miriamele saw her one door of escape closing. She leaped from the bed to grab it, but Gan Itai had bent first. The Niskie held it up to the light, a look of surprise in her gold-flecked eyes.

"Give it to me," said Miriamele.

Gan Itai gazed at the silver osprey carved so that it seemed to be alighting on the dagger's pommel. "This is the earl's knife."

"He left it here," she lied. "Give it to me."

The Niskie turned to her, solemn-faced. "He did not leave it here. He only wears this with his best clothes, and I saw how he was dressed when he came on deck in the night. In any case, he was wearing his other dagger on his belt."

"He gave it to me as a present, a gift. . . ." Abruptly, she burst into tears, great convulsive sobs that shook her whole body. Gan Itai jumped up in alarm and pushed the cabin door shut.

"I hate him!" Miriamele moaned, rocking from side to side. Gan Itai curled a thin dry arm around her shoulders. "I hate him!"

"What are you doing with his knife?" When she received no answer, she asked again. "Tell me, girl."

"I'm going to kill him." Miriamele found strength in saying it; for a moment, her tears subsided. "I'm going to stab that whoremongering beast, and then I won't care what happens."

"No, no, this is madness," the Niskie said, frowning.

"He knows who I am, Gan Itai." Miriamele gulped air. It was hard to speak. "He knows I am the princess, and he says he will marry me . . . so he can be master of Nabban when my father has conquered all the world." The idea seemed unreal, yet what could prevent it from happening? "Aspitis helped kill my uncle Leobardis, too. And he is giving money to the Fire Dancers."

"What do you mean?" Gan Itai's eyes were intent. "The Fire Dancers, they are madmen."

"Maybe, but he has a chest filled with sacks of silver and gold, and there is a book that lists payments made. He also has a Fire Dancer's robe rolled up and hidden away. Aspitis would never wear such a coarse weave." It had been so clear, suddenly, so laughably obvious: Aspitis would die before wearing something so common . . . unless there was a reason. And to think she had once been impressed by his beautiful clothes! "I am certain he goes among them. Cadrach said that he does Pryrates' bidding."

Gan Itai lifted her arm from Miriamele's shoulder and sat back against the wall. In the silence, the sound of men moving about on deck drifted down through the cabin ceiling. "The Fire Dancers burned down part of Niskietown in Nabban," the old woman said slowly. "They wedged doors shut, with children and old ones inside. They have burned and slaughtered in other places where my people live, too. And the Duke of Nabban and other men do nothing. Nothing." She ran her hand through her hair. "The Fire Dancers always claim some reason, but in truth there never is a reason, just love of other folks' suffering. Now you say that my ship's master is bringing them gold."

"It doesn't matter. He'll be dead before landfall."

Gan Itai shook her head in what looked like astonishment. "Our old masters put Ruyan the Navigator into chains. Our new masters burn our children, and ravage and kill their own young as well." She put a cool hand on Miriamele's arm and left it there for a long time. Her upturned eyes narrowed in thought. "Hide the knife," she said at last. "Do not use it until I speak to you again."

"But . . ." Miriamele began. Gan Itai squeezed hard.

"No," the Niskie said harshly. "Wait! You must wait!" She stood and walked out of the room. When the door shut behind her, Miriamele was left alone, tears drying on her cheeks.

5

Wasteland of Dreams

※

The sky was filled with swirling streamers of gray. A thicker knot of clouds loomed like an upraised fist on the distant northern horizon, angry purple and black.

The weather had gone bitterly cold again. Simon was very grateful for his thick new wool shirt. It had been a present from a thin New Gadrinsett girl, one of the two young women who had attached themselves to him at his knighthood feast. When the girl and her mother had come to bestow the gift, Simon had been properly polite and thankful as he imagined a knight should be. He just hoped they didn't think he was going to marry the girl or something. He had met her half a dozen times now, but she had still said scarcely anything to him, although she giggled a lot. It was nice to be admired, Simon had decided, but he couldn't help wishing that someone was doing the admiring besides this silly girl and her equally silly friend. Still, the shirt was well-made and warm.

"Come, Sir Knight," Sludig said, "are you going to use that stick, or are we going to give up for the day? I'm as tired and frozen as you are."

Simon looked up. "Sorry. Just thinking. It *is* cold, isn't it?"

"It is seeming our short taste of summer has come to its ending," Binabik called from his seat on a fallen pillar. They were in the middle of the Fire Garden, with no shelter from the brisk, icy wind.

"Summer!?" Sludig snorted. "Because it stopped snowing for a fortnight? There is still ice in my beard every morning."

"It has been, in any case, an improvement of weather over what we were suffering before," said Binabik serenely. He tossed another pebble at Qantaqa, who was curled in a furry loop on the ground a few steps away. She peered at him sideways, but then, apparently deciding that an occasional pebble was not worth the trouble of getting up and biting her master, closed her yellow eyes once more. Jeremias, who sat beside the troll, watched the wolf apprehensively.

Simon picked up his wooden practice sword once more and moved forward across the tiles. Although Sludig was still unwilling to use real blades, he had helped Simon lash bits of stone to the wooden ones so that they were more truly weighted. Simon hefted his carefully, trying to find the balance. "Come on, then," he said.

The Rimmersman waded forward against the surging wind, heavy tunic flapping, and brought his sword around in a surprisingly quick two-handed swipe. Simon stepped to one side, deflecting Sludig's blow upward, then returned his own counterstroke. Sludig blocked him; the echo of wood smacking wood floated across the tiles.

They practiced on for most of an hour as the shrouded sun passed overhead. Simon was finally beginning to feel comfortable with a sword in his hand: his weapon often felt as though it were part of his arm, as Sludig was always saying it should. It was mostly a question of balance, he now realized—not just swinging a heavy object, but moving with it, letting his legs and back supply the force and letting his own momentum carry him through into the next defensive position, rather than flailing at his opponent and then leaping away again.

As they sparred, he thought of shent, the intricate game of the Sithi, with its feints and puzzling strikes, and wondered if the same things might work in swordplay. He allowed his next few strokes to carry him farther and farther off-balance, until Sludig could not help but notice; then, when the Rimmersman swept in on the heels of one of Simon's flailing misses with the aim of catching him leaning too far and smacking him along the ribs, Simon let his swing carry him all the way forward into a tumbling roll. The Rimmersman's wooden sword hissed over him. Simon then righted himself and whacked Sludig neatly on the side of his knee. The northerner dropped his blade and hopped up and down, cursing.

"*Ummu Bok!* Very good, Simon!" Binabik shouted. "A surprising movement." Beside him, Jeremias was grinning.

"That hurt." Sludig rubbed his leg. "But it was a clever thought. Let us stop before our fingers are too numb to hold the hilts."

Simon was very pleased with himself. "Would that work in a real battle, Sludig?"

"Perhaps. Perhaps not if you are wearing armor. Then you might go down like a turtle and not be able to get up in time. Be very sure before you ever leave your feet, or you will be more dead than you are clever. Still, it was well done." He straightened up. "The blood is freezing in my veins. Let us go down to the forges and warm up."

Freosel, New Gadrinsett's young constable, had put several of the settlers to work building a smithy in one of the airier caves. They had taken to the task briskly and efficiently, and were now melting down what little scrap metal could be found on Sesuad'ra, hoping to forge new weapons and repair the old ones.

"The forges, for warming," Binabik agreed. He clicked his tongue at Qantaqa, who rose and stretched.

As they walked, shy Jeremias dropped behind until he trailed them by several paces. The wind blew cuttingly across the Fire Gardens, and the sweat on the back of Simon's neck was icy. He found his buoyant mood settling somewhat. "Binabik," he asked suddenly, "why couldn't we go to Hernystir with

Count Eolair and Isorn?" That pair had departed the previous day in the gray of early morning, accompanied by a small honor guard made up mostly of Thrithings horsemen.

"I am thinking that the reasons Josua gave you were true ones," Binabik replied. "It is not good for the same people always to be having the risks—or gaining the glories." He made a wry face. "There will be enough for all to do in coming days."

"But we brought him Thorn. Why shouldn't we try to at least get Minneyar as well—or Bright-Nail, rather?"

"Just because you are a knight, boy, does not mean you will have your way all the time," Sludig snarled. "Count your good fortunes and be content. Content and quiet."

Taken by surprise, Simon turned to the Rimmersman. "You sound angry."

Sludig looked away. "Not me. I am only a soldier."

"And not a knight." Simon thought he understood. "But you know why that is, Sludig. Josua is not king. He can only knight his own Erkynlanders. You are Duke Isgrimnur's man. I'm sure he will honor you when he returns."

"*If* he returns." There was bitterness in Sludig's voice. "I am tired of talking about this."

Simon thought carefully before speaking. "We all know what part you played, Sludig. Josua told everyone—but Binabik and I were there and we will *never* forget." He touched the Rimmersman's arm. "Please don't be angry with me. Even if I am a knight, I am still the same mooncalf you've been teaching how to swing a sword. I am still your friend."

Sludig peered at him for a moment from beneath bushy yellow brows. "Enough," he said. "You are a mooncalf indeed, and I need something to drink."

"And a warm fire." Simon tried not to smile.

Binabik, who had listened to the exchange in silence, nodded solemnly.

Geloë was waiting for them at the edge of the Fire Garden. She was bundled up against the cold, a scarf wrapped about her face so that only her round yellow eyes showed. She raised a chill-reddened hand as they approached.

"Binabik. I wish you and Simon to join me just before sundown, at the Observatory." She gestured to the ruined shell several hundred paces to the west. "I need your assistance."

"Help from a magical troll and a dragon-slaying knight." Sludig's smile was not entirely convincing.

Geloë turned her raptor's stare on him. "It is no honor. Besides, Rimmersman, even if you could, I don't think you would wish to walk the Road of Dreams. Not now."

"The Dream Road?" Simon was startled. "Why?"

The witch woman waved toward the ugly boil of clouds in the northern sky. "Another storm is coming. Besides wind and snow, it will also bring closer the

mind and hand of our enemy. The dream-path grows ever riskier and soon may
be impossible." She tucked her hands back beneath her cloak. "We must use the
time we have." Geloë turned and walked away toward the ocean of rippling
tents. "Sundown!" she called.

"Ah," said Binabik after a moment's silence. "Still, there is time for the wine
and the hand-warming we were discussing. Let us go to the forges with haste."
He started away. Qantaqa bounded after him.

Jeremias said something that could not be heard over the rising voice of the
wind. Simon stopped to let him catch up.

"What?"

The squire bobbed his head. "I said that Leleth wasn't with her. When Geloë
goes out to walk, Leleth always walks with her. I hope she's well."

Simon shrugged. "Let's go and get warm."

They hurried after the retreating forms of Binabik and Sludig. Far ahead,
Qantaqa was a gray shadow in the waving grass.

Simon and Binabik stepped through the doorway into the lamplit Observatory. Beyond the sundered roof, twilight made the sky seem a bowl of blue
glass. Geloë was absent, but the Observatory was not empty: Leleth sat on a
length of crumbled pillar, her thin legs drawn up beneath her. She did not even
turn her head at their entrance. The child was usually withdrawn, but there was
something about the quality of her stillness that alarmed Simon. He approached
and spoke her name softly, but although her eyes were open, fixed on the sky
overhead, she had the slack muscles and slow breath of one who slept.

"Do you think she's sick?" Simon asked. "Maybe that's why Geloë asked us
to come." Despite worry over Leleth, he felt a glimmering of relief: thoughts
of traveling the Dream Road made him anxious. Even though he had reached
the safety of Sesuad'ra, his dreams had continued to be vivid and unsettling.

The troll felt the child's warm hand, then let it drop back into her lap. "Little there is that we could do for her that Geloë could not be doing better. We
will wait with patientness." He turned and looked around the wide, circular
hall. "I am thinking this was a very beautiful place once. My people have long
been carving into the living mountain, but we are having not a tenth of the
skill the Sithi had."

The reference to Jiriki's people as though they were a vanished race bothered
Simon, but he was not yet ready to give up the subject of Leleth's well-being.
"Are you sure we shouldn't get something for her? Perhaps a cloak? It's so cold."

"Leleth will be well," said Geloë from the doorway. Simon jumped guiltily,
as if he had been plotting treason. "She is only traveling a little way on the
Dream Road without us. She is happiest there, I think."

She strode forward into the room. Father Strangyeard appeared behind her.
"Hello, Simon, Binabik," the priest said. His face was as happy and excited as
a child's at Aedontide. "I'm going to go with you. Dreaming, I mean. On the
Dream Road. I have read of it, of course—it has long fascinated me—but I

never imagined . . ." He waggled his fingers as if to demonstrate the delightful unlikeliness of it all.

"It is not a day of berry-picking, Strangyeard," Geloë said crossly. "But since you are a Scrollbearer now, it is good that you learn some of the few Arts left to us."

"Of course it is not—I mean, of course it is good to learn. But berry-picking, no—I mean . . . oh." Defeated, Strangyeard fell silent.

"Now I am knowing why Strangyeard joins us," Binabik said. "And I may be good for helping, too. But why Simon, Valada Geloë? And why here?"

The witch woman passed her hand briefly through Leleth's hair, eliciting no response from the child, then sat down on the pillar beside her. "As to the first, it is because I have a special need, and Simon perhaps can help. But let me explain all, so no mistakes will be made." She waited until the others had seated themselves around her. "I told you that another great storm is coming. The Road of Dreams will be difficult to walk, if not impossible. There are other things coming, too." She held up her hand to forestall Simon's question. "I cannot say more. Not until I speak to Josua. My birds have brought news to me—but even they will go to their hiding places when the storm comes. Then we atop this rock will be blind."

As she spoke, she deftly built a small pile of sticks on the stone floor, then lit it with a twig she had set aflame from one of the lamps. She reached into her cloak pocket and produced a small sack. "So," she continued, "while we can, we will make a last try to gather those who may be useful to us, or who need the shelter we can give. I have brought you here because it is the best spot. The Sithi themselves chose it when they spoke with each other over great distance, using, as the old lore says, 'Stones and Scales, Pools and Pryes'—what they called their Witnesses." She poured a handful of herbs from the sack, weighing them on her palm. "That is why I named this place the 'Observatory.' As clerics in the observatories of the old Imperium once watched the stars from theirs, so the Sithi once came to this place to look over their empire of Osten Ard. This is a powerful spot for seeing."

Simon knew more than a little about the Witnesses—he had summoned Aditu with Jiriki's mirror, and had seen Amerasu's disastrous use of the Mist Lamp. He suddenly remembered his dream from the night of his vigil—the torchlit procession, the Sithi and their strange ceremony. Could the nature of this place have something to do with his clear, strong vision of the past?

"Binabik," Geloë said, "you may have heard of Tiamak, a Wrannaman befriended by Morgenes. He sent messages sometimes to your master Ookequk, I think." The troll nodded. "Dinivan of Nabban also knew Tiamak. He told me that he had instigated some well-meaning plan, and had drawn the Wrannaman into it." Geloë frowned. "I never found out what it was. Now that Dinivan is dead, I fear the marsh man is lost and without friends. Leleth and I have tried to reach him, but have not quite managed. The Dream Road is very treacherous these days."

She reached across the pillar and lifted a small jar of water from the rubble-strewn floor. "So I hope your added strength will help us find Tiamak. We will tell him to come to us if he needs protection. Also, I have promised Josua that I will try to reach Miriamele once more. That has been even stranger—there is some veil over her, some shadow that prevents me from finding her. You were close to her, Simon. Perhaps that bond will help us finally to break through."

Miriamele. Her name sent a rush of powerful feelings through Simon—hope, affection, bitterness. He had been angry and disappointed to discover that she was not at Sesuad'ra. In the back of his mind he had been somehow certain that if he won through to the Stone of Farewell she would be there to welcome him; her absence seemed like desertion. He had been frightened, too, when he discovered that she had vanished with only the thief Cadrach for company.

"I will help any way I can," he said.

"Good." Geloë stood, rubbing her hands on her breeches. "Here, Strangyeard, I will show you how to mix the mockfoil and nightshade. Does your religion forbid this?"

The priest shrugged helplessly. "I don't know. It might . . . that is, these are strange days."

"Indeed." The witch woman grinned. "Come, then, I will show you. Consider it a history lesson, if you wish."

Simon and Binabik sat quietly while Geloë demonstrated the proportions for the fascinated archivist.

"This is the last of these plants until we leave this rock," she said when they had finished. "Another encouragement to succeed this time. Here." She dabbed a little on Simon's palms, forehead, and lips, then did the same for Strangyeard and Binabik before setting down the pot. Simon felt the paste grow chill against his skin.

"But what about you and Leleth?" Simon asked.

"I can get by without it. Leleth has never needed it. Now, sit and clasp hands. Remember, the Road of Dreams is strange these days. Do not be frightened, but keep your wits about you."

They put one of the lamps on the floor and sat in a circle beside the crumbling pillar. Simon clutched Binabik's small hand on one side and Leleth's equally small hand on the other. A smile spread slowly across the little girl's face, the blind smile of someone who dreams of happy surprises.

The icy sensation spread up Simon's arms and all through him, filling his head with a kind of fog. Although twilight should still have been clinging overhead, the room swiftly grew dark. Soon Simon could see nothing but the wavering orange tongues of the fire, then even that light passed into blackness . . . and Simon fell through.

Beyond the black all was a universal, misty gray—a sea of nothingness with no top or bottom. Out of that formless void a shape slowly began to coalesce, a small, swift-moving figure that darted like a sparrow. It took only a moment before he recognized Leleth—but this was a dream-Leleth, a Leleth who whirled and spun, her dark hair flying in an unfelt wind. Although he could hear nothing, he saw her mouth curl in delighted laughter as she beckoned him forward; even her eyes seemed alive in a way he had never seen. This was the little girl he had never met—the child who, in some inexplicable way, had not survived the mauling jaws of the Stormspike Pack. Here she was alive again, freed from the terrors of the waking world and from her own scarred body. His heart soared to watch her unfettered dance.

Leleth swept along before him, beckoning, silently pleading with him to hurry, to follow her, to follow! Simon tried, but in this gray dream place it was he who was lamed and lagging. Leleth's small form quickly became indistinct, then vanished into the unending grayness. His dream-self felt a kind of warmth disappear with her. Suddenly, he was alone again and drifting.

What might have been a long time passed. Simon floated without purchase until something tugged at him with gentle, invisible fingers. He felt himself pulled forward, gradually at first, then with growing speed; he was still un-bodied, but nevertheless caught up by some incomprehensible current. A new shape began to form out of the emptiness before him—a dark tower of un-stable shadow, a black vortex shot through with red sparks, like a whirlpool of smoke and fire. Simon felt himself drawn toward it even more swiftly and was suddenly fearful. Death lay in that whirling dark—death or something worse. Panic welled up in him, stronger than he had imagined it could be. He forced himself to remember that this was a dream, not a place. He did not have to dream this dream if he did not want it. A part of him remembered that at this very moment, in some other place, he was holding the hands of friends. . . .

As he thought of them, they were there with him, invisible but present. He gained a little strength and was able to halt his slide inward toward the boiling, sparking blackness. Then, bit by bit, he pulled himself away, his dream-self somehow swimming against the current. As he put distance between himself and the black roil, the whirlpool abruptly fell in upon itself and he was free and sailing into some new place. The grayness was placid here, and there was a different quality to the light, as though the sun burned behind thick clouds.

Leleth was there before him. She smiled at his arrival, at the pleasure of having him with her in this place—although Simon knew now beyond a doubt that he could never share all she experienced.

The formlessness of the dream began to change; Simon felt as though he hovered above something much like the waking world. A shadowed city lay below him, a vast tract of structures formed from a haphazard collection of unlikely things—wagon wheels, children's toys, statues of unfamiliar animals, even toppled siege-towers from some long-ago war. The haphazard streets be-tween the madly unlikely buildings were full of scurrying lights. As he stared down, Simon felt himself drawn toward one particular building, a towering structure made entirely of books and yellowing scrolls, which seemed ready at any moment to collapse into a rubbish heap of old parchment. Leleth, who had been moving around him in circles, swift as a bumblebee, now whirled down toward a gleaming window in the book-tower.

Upon a bed lay a figure. Its shape was unclear, as something seen through deep water. Leleth spread her thin arms above the bed and the dark shape tossed in uneasy sleep.

"*Tiamak*," said Leleth—but it was Geloë's voice, and it contained traces of his other companions' voices as well. "*Tiamak! Wake to us!*"

The shape on the bed moved more fitfully, then slowly sat up. The figure seemed to ripple, and the sense of being underwater was strengthened. Simon thought he heard it speak, but the voice at first was wordless.

". . . . ? ?"

"*It is Geloë, Tiamak—Geloë of the Aldheorte Forest. I want you to come and join me and others at Sesuad'ra. You will be safe there.*"

The figure rippled again. ". . . *dreaming? . . .*"

"*Yes—but it is a true dream. Come to the Stone of Farewell. It is hard to speak to you. Here is how you can find it.*" Leleth stretched her arms over the shadowy figure once more, and this time a blurry image of the Stone began to form.

". . . *Dinivan . . . wanted . . .*"

"*I know. All is changed now. If you need refuge, come to Sesuad'ra.*" Leleth lowered her hands and the wavering picture was gone. The form on the bed also began to fade.

". . . ! . . ." It was trying to tell some urgent thing, but it was rapidly vanishing into mist, even as the tower in which it lay and the surrounding city were vanishing, too. ". . . *from the North . . . grim . . . found the old night . . .*" There was a lag, then a last heroic effort. ". . . *Nisses' book . . .*"

The dream-shadow vanished and all was murky gray once more.

As the intangible mist surrounded him once more, Simon's thoughts turned to Miriamele. Surely, since they had somehow reached Tiamak, Geloë would now turn her attention to the missing princess. And indeed, even as Miriamele's image came to his mind—he saw her as she had been in Geloë's house, dressed in boy's clothing, hair blackened and close-shorn—that very picture began to form in the nothingness before him. Miriamele shimmered for a moment—he thought her hair might have turned gold, its natural hue—then it dissolved into something else. A tree? A tower? Simon felt a sense of cold foreboding. He had seen a tower in many dreams, and it never seemed to signify anything good. But no, this was more than one tall shape. Trees? A forest?

Even as he strained to make the image clearer, the shadowy vision began to coalesce, until he at last could see that it was a ship, as blurry and imprecise as had been the dream-Tiamak in his parchment tower. The tall masts were hung with lank sails and fluttering ropes, all made from cobwebs, gray and dusty and tattered. The ship rocked as though in a great wind. The black waters beneath were studded with glowing whitecaps, and the sky overhead was just as black. Some force pushed at Simon, holding him away from the vessel despite his desperation to approach. He fought hard against it. Miriamele might be there!

Exerting his will to the utmost, Simon tried to force himself nearer to the ghostly ship, but a great dark curtain swept before him, a storm of rain and mist so thick as to be almost solid. He stopped, lost and helpless. Leleth was suddenly beside him, her smile gone, her small face set in a grimace of effort.

Miriamele! Simon cried. His voice pealed out—not from his own, but from Leleth's mouth. *Miriamele!* he shouted again. Leleth forced herself a little nearer to the phantom, as though carrying his words as close as she could before they spilled from her mouth. *Miriamele, come to the Stone of Farewell!*

The boat had now vanished entirely and the storm was spreading to cover all the black sea. At its heart, Simon thought he saw jumping arcs of red light like those that had pierced the great whirlpool. What did this mean? Was Miriamele somehow endangered? Were her dreams invaded? He forced himself to a final effort, pushing hard against the swirling dream-storm, but to no avail. The ship was gone. The storm itself had completely surrounded him. It growled and hummed through his very being like the tolling of huge brazen bells, shaking him so powerfully that he thought he could feel himself breaking apart. Now Leleth was gone, too. The spark-shot blackness held him like an inky fist, and he suddenly thought that he would die here, in this place that was no place.

A patch of light appeared in the distance, small and gray as a tarnished silver coin. He moved toward it as the blackness battered him and the red sparks sizzled through him like tiny lances of fire. He tried to feel his friends' hands but could not. The gray seemed to be no closer. He was tiring, as would a swimmer far out at sea.

Binabik, help me! he thought, but his friends were lost beyond the unending blackness. *Help me!* Even the tiny spot of gray was fading. *Miriamele*, he thought, *I wanted to see you again. . . .*

He reached for the spot of light one last time and felt a touch, as of a fingertip pressing his, although he had no hands to touch or be touched. A little strength came, and he slipped closer to the gray . . . closer, with black all around . . . closer. . . .

Deornoth thought that in different circumstances, he would have laughed. To see Josua sitting, listening with such rapt and respectful attention to this unusual pair of counselors—a hawk-faced woman with mannish hair and man's clothing, and a waist-high troll—was to see the upside-down world personified.

"So what do you hope that this Tiamak will bring, Valada Geloë?" the prince asked. He moved the lamp closer. "If he is another wise one like Morgenes and yourself, I am sure we will welcome him."

The witch woman shook her head. "He is not a wielder of the Art, Josua, and he is certainly not a planner of wars. In truth, he is a shy little man from the swamp who knows much about herbs that grow in the Wran. No, I have tried to call him here only because he was close to the League, and because I fear for him. Dinivan had some plan to use him, but Dinivan is dead. Tiamak should not be abandoned. Before the storm arrives, we must save all we can."

Josua nodded his head, but without much enthusiasm. Beside him, Vorzheva looked no happier. Deornoth thought that the prince's wife might resent any more responsibilities being piled on her husband's shoulders, even one very small responsibility from the marsh country.

"Thank you for that, Geloë," he said. "And thank you for trying again to reach my niece Miriamele. I grow increasingly worried for her."

"It is strange," the witch woman replied. "There is something odd there, something I cannot make sense of. It is almost as though Miriamele has erected some barrier to us, but she has no such talents. I am puzzled." She straightened, as if dismissing a useless thought. "But there is more to tell you."

Binabik had been shifting from foot to foot. Before Geloë could continue, he touched her arm. "Forgive me, but I should be looking to Simon, to make sure the unpleasantness of the Dream Road has left him and that he is resting well."

Geloë almost smiled. "You and I can speak later."

"Go, Binabik," urged Josua. "I will go to him later myself. He is a brave boy, although perhaps a bit overeager."

The troll bowed low and trotted out through the tent's door flap.

"I wish my other news was good, Prince Josua," Geloë said, "but the birds have brought me worrisome tidings. There is a large force of armored men coming toward us from the west."

"What?" Josua sat up, startled. Beside him, Vorzheva draped her hands protectively across her belly. "I don't understand. Who has sent you this message?"

The witch woman shook her head. "I do not mean birds like Jarnauga's, who carry little scraps of parchment. I mean the birds of the sky. I can speak with them . . . somewhat. Enough to understand the sense of things. There is a small army on the march from the Hayholt. They have ridden through the valley towns of Hasu Vale and are now following the southern border of the great forest toward the grasslands."

Deornoth stared at her. When he spoke, his voice sounded weak and querulous, even to his own ears. "You talk with *birds*?"

Geloë turned a sharp glance on him. "Your life may have been saved by it. How do you think I knew to come to you on the banks of the Stefflod, when you would have fought Hotvig's men in the dark? And how do you think I found you in the first place in all the vastness of Aldheorte?"

Josua had laid his hand on Vorzheva's shoulder as if to soothe her, although she looked quite calm. When he spoke, his voice was unusually harsh. "Why have you not told us of this before, Geloë? What other information could we have had?"

The forest woman seemed to suppress a sharp reply. "I have shared everything vital. There has been precious little to share during this yearlong winter. Most of the birds are dead, or hiding from the cold—certainly not flying. Also, do not misunderstand: I cannot talk to them as you and I are speaking now. Their thoughts are not people's thoughts, and words do not always fit them, nor can I always understand. Weather they understand, and fear, but those signs have been clear enough for us to read ourselves. Beyond that, it is only something as plain as a large body of men on foot and horseback that can even catch their attention. Unless some man is hunting them, they think very little about us."

Deornoth realized he was staring and looked away. He thought she did more than just talk with birds—he remembered the winged thing that had struck at him in the copse above the Stefflod—but he knew it was foolish to bring it up. It was more than foolish, he decided suddenly, it was rude. Geloë had been a loyal ally and helpful friend. Why did he begrudge her the secrets on which her life was plainly founded?

"I think Valada Geloë is correct, sire," he said quietly. "She has proven time and again that she is a valuable ally. What is important now is the news she brings."

Josua stared at him for a moment, then nodded once in assent. "Very well, Geloë, have your winged friends any idea how many men are coming, and how fast?"

She thought for a moment. "I would say the number is somewhere in the hundreds, Josua, although that is a guess. Birds do not count as we do, either. As for when they will be here, they seem to be traveling without hurry, but still, I should not be surprised to see them inside a month."

"Aedon's Blood," Josua swore. "It is Guthwulf and the Erkynguard, that would be my wager. So little time. I had hoped we might have until the coming spring to prepare." He looked up. "Are you sure they come here?"

"No," said Geloë simply. "But where else?"

For Deornoth, the fear this announcement brought was almost overwhelmed by a surprising sense of relief. It was not what they had wanted, not so soon, but the situation was by no means hopeless. Despite their own scant numbers, as long as they held this eminently defensible rock entirely surrounded by water, there was at least a small chance they could fight off a besieging force. And it would be the first chance to strike back at Elias since the destruction of Naglimund. Deornoth felt the knife-edge of violence pressing against him. It would not be entirely bad to simplify the world, since there seemed to be no other choice. What was it that Einskaldir used to say? *Fight and live, fight and die, God waits for all.* Yes, that was it. Simple.

"So," Josua said finally. "Caught between a bitter new storm and my brother's army." He shook his head. "We must defend ourselves, that is all. So soon after we have found this place of refuge, we must fight and die again." He stood up, then turned and bent to kiss his wife.

"Where are you going?" Vorzheva raised a hand to touch his cheek, but did not meet his eyes. "Why do you leave?"

Josua sighed. "I should go and speak to the lad Simon. Then I will walk for a while and think."

He strode out into the night and the swift wind.

In the dream, Simon was seated upon a massive throne made of smooth white stone. His throne room was not a room at all, but a great sward of stiff green grass. The sky overhead was as unnaturally blue and depthless as a painted bowl. A vast circle of courtiers stood before him; like the sky, their smiles seemed fixed and false.

"The king brings rebirth!" someone cried. The nearest of the courtiers stepped up to the throne. It was a dark-eyed woman dressed in gray with long straight hair; there was something terribly familiar about her face. She set before him a doll woven of leaves and reeds, then stepped away again and, despite the absence of hiding places on all sides, disappeared. The next person moved into place. *"Rebirth!"* someone shouted; *"Save us!"* cried another. Simon tried to tell them that he had no such power, but the desperate faces continued to circle past, continuous and indistinguishable as the spokes of a turning wheel. The pile of offerings grew larger. There were other dolls, and sheaves of summer-yellow wheat, as well as bunches of flowers whose brightly colored petals seemed as artificial as the paint-blue sky. Baskets of fruit and cheeses were placed before him, even farm animals, goats and calves whose bleating rose above the importuning voices.

"I can't help you!" Simon cried. *"There's nothing to be done!"*

The endless parade of faces continued. The cries and moans began to swell, an ocean of pleading that made his ears ache. At last he looked back down and saw that a child had been placed on the spreading mass of offerings, as though atop a funeral bier. The infant's face was somber, the eyes wide.

Even as Simon reached out to the child, his eye was caught by the doll that had been the first gift. It was rotting before his eyes, blackening and sagging until it became little more than a smear upon the obscenely bright grass. The other offerings were changing, too, decaying at a horrible rate—the fruits first bruising and dimpling, then seeming almost to froth as a blanket of mold swept over them. The flowers dried to ashy flakes, the wheat diminished to gray dust. As Simon watched in horror, even the tethered animals sagged, bloated, then were skeletonized in heartbeats by a pulsing mass of squirming white grubs.

Simon tried to clamber down off his throne, but the unlikely seat had begun buckling and sliding beneath him, pitching as though in an earth tremor. He tumbled to his knees in the muck. Where was the baby? Where? It would be consumed like the rest, crumbled into putrefaction unless he rescued it! He dove forward, shoveling through the rotting, stinking humus that had been the pile of offerings, but there was no sign of the child—unless that was a wink of gold, down there in the heap. . . . Simon scraped down into the dark mass until it was all around him, clogging his nose and filling his eyes like graveyard earth. Was that gold, there, beaming through the shadows? He must go deeper. Hadn't the child worn a golden bracelet? Or had it been a ring, a golden band . . . ? Deeper. It was so hard to breathe. . . .

He awoke in the dark. After a moment of panic, he fought free of his cloak and rolled toward the doorway, then fumbled open the flap so he could see the few stars not smothered by clouds. His heart slowed its pounding. He was in the tent he and Binabik shared. Geloë and Strangyeard and the troll had helped him stumble here from the Observatory. Once they had laid him down on his pallet, he had fallen into sleep and dreamed a strange dream. But there had been another dream as well, hadn't there—the journey on the Dream Road, a shadow house and then a haunted ship? It was hard now to remember which had been which, and where the separation was. His head felt heavy and cobwebbed.

Simon pushed his head out and breathed the cold air, drinking it in as though it were wine. Gradually his thoughts became clearer. They had all gone to the Observatory to walk the Dream Road, but they had not found Miriamele. That was the important thing, far more important than some nightmare about dolls and babies and golden rings. They had tried to reach Miriamele, but something had prevented it, as Geloë had warned might happen. Simon had refused to give up. Pushing on when the others did not, he had almost lost himself in something bad—something very bad indeed.

I almost reached her! Almost! I know I could do it if I tried again!

But they had used the last of Geloë's herbs, and in any case, the time when the Dream Road could be walked had almost ended. He would never have another chance . . . *unless* . . .

The idea—a frightening, clever idea—had just begun to make its presence felt when he was startled from his thoughts.

"I am surprised to find you awake." The lamp Josua held limned his thin face in yellow light. "Binabik said he had left you sleeping."

"I just woke up, your Highness." Simon tried to stand, but tangled himself in the tent flap and nearly fell down again.

"You should not be up. The troll said you had a difficult time. I do not quite understand all that you four were doing, but I know enough to think you should be abed."

"I'm well." If the prince thought him sickly, he would never let him go anywhere. Simon did not want to be left out of any further expeditions. "Truly. It was only a sort of bad dream. I'm well."

"Hmm." Josua stared at him skeptically. "If you say it is so. Come, then— walk with me for a little while. Perhaps afterward you will be able to go back to sleep."

"Walk . . . ?" Inwardly, Simon cursed himself. Just at a time when he truly wanted to be alone, his stupid pride had tricked him again. Still, it was a chance to talk to Josua.

"Yes, just a short way across the hilltop. Get something to wrap yourself in. Binabik will never forgive me if you catch some ague under my care."

Simon ducked back into the tent and found his cloak.

They walked for a while in silence. The light of Josua's lamp reflected eerily from the broken stones of Sesuad'ra.

"I want to be a help to you, Prince Josua," he said at last. "I want to get your father's sword back."

Josua did not reply.

"If you let Binabik go with me, we will never be noticed. We are too small to attract the king's attention. We brought you Thorn, we can bring you Bright-Nail as well."

"There is an army coming," said the prince. "It seems my brother has learned of our escape and seeks to remedy his earlier laxness."

As Josua related Geloë's news, Simon felt a surprising sense of satisfaction growing within him. So he would not be denied his chance to do something after all! A moment later he remembered the women and children and old folk who now made New Gadrinsett their home and was ashamed at his pleasure. "What can we do?" he asked.

"We wait." Josua stopped before the shadowy bulk of the House of Waters. A dark rivulet ran down the crumbling stone sluice at their feet. "All other roads are closed to us, now. We wait, and we prepare. When Guthwulf or whoever leads this troop arrives—it could even be my brother himself—we will fight to defend our new home. If we lose . . . well, then all is finished." The hilltop wind lifted their cloaks and tugged at their clothing. "If somehow God grants that we win, we will try to move forward and make some use of our victory."

The prince sat down on a fallen block of masonry, then gestured for Simon to sit beside him. He set the lamp down; their shadows were cast giant-sized on the walls of the House of Waters. "We must live our lives day to day, now. We must not think too far ahead or we will lose what little we have."

Simon stared at the dancing flame. "What about the Storm King?"

Josua drew his cloak tighter. "I do not know—it is too vast a matter. We must stick to the things we can understand." He lifted his hand toward the slumbering tent city. "There are innocents to be protected. You are a knight now, Simon. That is your sworn task."

"I know, Prince Josua."

The older man was silent for a while. "And I have my own child to think of, as well." His grim smile was a small movement in the lampglow. "I hope it is a girl."

"You do?"

"Once, when I was a younger man, I hoped my firstborn would be a son."

Josua lifted his face to the stars. "I dreamed of a son who would love learning and justice, but have none of my failings." He shook his head. "But now, I hope our child is a girl. If we lost and he survived, a son of mine would be hunted forever. Elias could not let him live. And if we were to win somehow . . ." He trailed off.

"Yes?"

"If we were to win, and I took my father's throne, one day I would have to send my son off to do something I could not do—something dangerous and glorious. That is the way of kings and their sons. And I would never sleep again, waiting to hear that he had been killed." He sighed. "That is what I hate about ruling and royalty, Simon. It is living, breathing people with whom a prince plays the games of statecraft. I sent you and Binabik and the others into danger—you, who were little more than a child. No, I know you are now a young man—who knighted you, after all?—but that does not ease my remorse. With Aedon's mercy, you survived my attention—but other companions of yours did not."

Simon hesitated a moment before speaking. "But being a woman does not save anyone from being caught by war, Prince Josua. Think of Miriamele. Think of your wife, Lady Vorzheva."

Josua nodded slowly. "I fear you are right. And now there will be more fighting, more war—and more helpless ones will die." After a moment's thought he looked up, startled. "Elysia, Mother of God, this is wonderful medicine for someone suffering from nightmares!" He grinned shamefacedly. "Binabik will kick me for this—taking his ward out and talking to him of death and misery." He put his arm around Simon's shoulder for a brief instant, then rose to his feet. "I will take you back to your tent. The wind is getting fierce."

As the prince bent to retrieve the lamp, Simon watched his spare features and felt a painful kind of love for Josua, a love mixed with pity, and wondered if all knights felt this way about their lords. Would Simon's own father Eahlferend have been stern but kind like Josua if he had lived? Would he and Simon have talked together about such things?

Most important of all, Simon thought as they pushed through the waving grass, would Eahlferend have been proud of his son?

They saw Qantaqa's gleaming eyes before they could make out Binabik, a small dark figure standing beside the tent door.

"Ah, good," the troll said. "I was, I must confess, full of worrying when I found you gone, Simon."

"It is my fault, Binabik. We were talking." Josua turned to Simon. "I leave you in able hands. Sleep well, young knight." He smiled and took his leave.

"Now," said Binabik sternly, "it is back to your bed that you should go." He directed Simon through the door, then followed him inside. Simon suppressed a groan as he lay down. Was this to be a night when everyone in New Gadrinsett would wish to talk with him?

His groan became actual as Qantaqa, following them into the tent, stepped on his stomach.

"Qantaqa! *Hinik aia!*" Binabik swatted at the wolf. She growled and backed out of the door flap. "Now, time for sleeping."

"You're not my mother," Simon muttered. How could he ever do anything about his idea with Binabik hanging about? "Are you going to sleep now, too?"

"I cannot." Binabik took an extra cloak and threw that over Simon as well. "I am on watch with Sludig this night. I will return to the tent with quietness when it is finished." He crouched at Simon's side. "Are you wishing to talk for a while? Was Josua telling you about the armed men who are coming here?"

"He told me." Simon feigned a yawn. "I'll talk to you about it tomorrow. I *am* sleepy, now that you mention it."

"You have had a day of great difficulty. The Dream Road was treacherous, as Geloë was warning."

Simon's desire to get on with his plans was blunted for a moment by curiosity. "What *was* that, Binabik—that thing on the Dream Road? Like a storm, with sparks in it? Did you see it, too?"

"Geloë is not knowing, and neither am I. Some disturbance, she called it. A storm is a good word, because I am thinking it was something like bad weather on the Road of Dreams. But what was causing it is something for guessing about, only. And even the guessing is not good for nighttime and the dark." He stood up. "Sleep well, friend Simon."

"Good night, Binabik." He listened as the troll made his way outside and whistled for Qantaqa, then he lay quietly for a long time after, counting ten score heartbeats before he slid out from beneath the sheltering cloaks and went searching for Jiriki's mirror.

He found it in the saddlebags Binabik had saved from Homefinder. The White Arrow was there, too, as was a heavy drawstring sack that momentarily puzzled him. He hefted it, then struggled with the knotted cord that held it shut. Memory came back to him suddenly: Aditu had given it to him at their parting, saying it was something sent from Amerasu to Josua. Curious, Simon wondered for a moment if he should take it with him and open it in a more private place, but he felt time pressing. Binabik might come back sooner than expected; it would be better to be berated for being absent than to be stopped before he had a chance to try out his idea. He reluctantly pushed the sack back into the saddlebag. Later, he promised himself. Then he would give it to the prince, as he had promised.

Stopping only to root out the small pouch containing his flints, he slipped out of the tent and into the cold night.

Scant moonlight leaked through the clouds, but it was enough for him to find his way across the hilltop. A few shadowy figures were moving through the tent city on one sort of errand or another, but none challenged him, and soon he had passed out of New Gadrinsett and into the central ruins of Sesuad'ra.

The Observatory was deserted. Simon crept through the deep-shadowed interior until he found the remains of the fire Geloë had made. The ashes were still warm. He added a few pieces of kindling that lay beside the embers, then sprinkled it with a handful of sawdust from his pouch. He struck at the blunt edge of his iron with his flint until he finally managed to catch a spark. It died before he could breathe it into full life, so he laboriously repeated the procedure, cursing quietly. At last he managed to start a small fire burning.

The carved rim of Jiriki's mirror seemed warm to his touch, but the reflecting surface, when he held it near his cheek, was as cold as a sheet of ice. He breathed on it as he had breathed on the hard-won spark, then held it up before his face.

His scar had lost some of its angry flame; it was now a red and white line curving down his cheek from his eye to his jaw. It gave him, he thought, a certain soldierly look—the appearance of one who had fought for what was right and honorable. The snow-white streak running through his hair also seemed to add a touch of maturity. His beard, which he could not resist fluffing with his fingers while he stared, made him look, if not like a knight, at least like a young man rather than a boy. He wondered what Miriamele would think if she could see him now.

Maybe I'll find out soon.

He tilted the mirror a little, so that the firelight illumined only half his face, leaving the remainder in red-tinged shadow. He thought carefully about what Geloë had said about the Observatory, how it had once been a place where the Sithi saw and spoke to each other over great distances. He tried to pull its antiquity and silence around him like a cape. He had found Miriamele once before in the mirror, without trying: why not now, in this potent place?

As he stared at his own halved reflection, the quality of the firelight seemed to change. The flicker became a gentle wavering, then slowed to a methodical pulse of scarlet light. The face in the mirror dissolved into smoky gray, and as he felt himself falling forward into it, he had time for a brief, triumphant thought.

And nobody wanted to teach me magic!

The frame of the mirror had vanished and the grayness was all around him. After his journeyings earlier in the day, he was undaunted: this was old and familiar territory. But even as he told himself this, another thought suddenly came to him. He had always had a guide before, and other travelers with him. This time there would be no Leleth to share his troubles, and no Geloë or Binabik to help him if he should go too far. A thin frost of fear descended, but Simon fought it back. He had used the mirror to call Jiriki once, had he not? There had been no one to help him then. Still, a small part of him guessed that calling for help might be a little less difficult than exploring the Road of Dreams by himself.

But Geloë had said that time was running short, that soon the Dream Road would be impassable. This might be his last chance to reach Miriamele, his last chance to save her and guide her back. If Binabik and the others found out, it would certainly be his last chance. He must go forward. Besides, Miriamele would be so astonished, so pleased and surprised. . . .

The gray void seemed thicker this time. If he swam, it was in gelid, muddy waters. How did one find his way here, without landmarks or signs? Simon formed the image of Miriamele in his mind, the same that he had held at sunset, dream-traveling with the others. This time, though, the picture would not hold together. Surely that was not what Miriamele's eyes looked like? And her hair, even when she had dyed it for disguise, was never that shade of sorrel brown? He fought with the recalcitrant vision, but the features of the lost princess would not come right. He was even having trouble remembering what they *should* look like. Simon felt as though he tried to build a stained glass window with colored water: the shapes ran and merged together, heedless of his efforts.

Even as he struggled, the grayness around him began to change. The difference was not immediately obvious, but if Simon had been in his body—which he suddenly wished he were—the hair on the back of his neck would have risen and goosebumps would have carbuncled his skin. Something shared the void with him, something much vaster than he was. He felt the outward wash of its power, but unlike the dream-storm that had caught at him before, this thing was no mindless force: it exuded intelligence and evil patience. He felt its remorseless scrutiny as a swimmer in the open sea might sense a great-finned thing pass beneath him in the black depths.

Simon's solitude suddenly seemed a kind of dreadful nakedness. He struggled, desperate to make contact with something that might pull him away from this shelterless void. He felt himself dwindling with fear, guttering like a candleflame—he did not know how to get away! How could he leave this place? He tried to startle himself out of the dream, to come awake, but as in childhood nightmares, there was no breaking the spell. He had entered this dream without sleeping, so how could he wake from it?

The blurry image that was not Miriamele remained. He tried to force himself toward it, to pull away from whatever great, slow thing was stalking him.

Help me! he screamed silently, and felt a glimmer of recognition somewhere on the horizon of his thoughts. He reached for it, grasping at it like a castaway at a spar. This new presence became a little stronger, but even as it grew in strength, the thing that shared the void with him extended a fraction more of its own power, just enough to keep him from escaping. He sensed a malicious alien humor that delighted in his hopeless struggle, but he also sensed that the thing was tiring of the diversion and would soon end the game. A kind of deadening force reached out and surrounded him, a coldness of the soul that froze his efforts even as he reached out one more time toward the faint presence. He touched her then, across a dreadful span of dream, and clung.

Miriamele? he thought, praying that it was so, terrified to let loose of the tenuous contact. Whoever she was, she seemed finally to realize that he was there, but the thing that had him did not falter now. A black shadow moved over and through him, smothering light and thought. . . .

Seoman!? Another presence was with him suddenly—not the hesitant feminine one, not the dark, deadly other. *Come to me, Seoman!* it called. *Come!*

A warmth touched him. The chill grasp of the other squeezed more tightly for a moment, then let go—not overpowered, he sensed from its retreating thought, but bored and unwilling to trouble with such small matters, as a cat might lose interest in a mouse that had run under a stone. The gray came back, still featureless and direction-less, then began to swirl like breeze-twisted clouds. A face formed before him—thin-boned, with eyes like liquid gold.

"*Jiriki!*"

"*Seoman,*" the other said. His face was worried. *"Are you in danger? Do you need help?"*

"I am safe now, I think." Indeed, the lurking presence seemed gone completely. *"What was that horrible thing?"*

"I do not know for sure what had you, but if it was not of Nakkiga, there is more evil in the world than even we suspected." Despite the strange disconnectedness of dream-vision, Simon could see the Sitha studying him carefully. *"Do you mean to say you did not call me for a reason?"*

"I didn't mean to call you at all," Simon replied, a little shamed now that the worst was over. *"I was trying to find Miriamele—the king's daughter. I told you about her."*

"By yourself, on the Road of Dreams?" With the anger, there was a kind of chilly amusement. *"Idiot manchild! If I had not been resting, and thus near to the place you are— near in thought, I mean—then only the Grove knows what would have become of you."* After a moment, the feeling of his presence warmed. *"Still, I am glad you are well."*

"I'm happy to see you, too." And he was. Simon had not realized how much he missed Jiriki's calm voice. *"We are at the Stone of Farewell—Sesuad'ra. Elias is sending troops. Can you help us?"*

The Sitha's angular face turned grim. *"I cannot come to you any time soon, Seoman. You must keep yourself safe. My father Shima'onari is dying."*

"I'm . . . I'm sorry."

"He slew the hound Niku'a, greatest beast ever whelped in the kennels of Nakkiga, but he took his death-wound in the doing of it. It is another knot in the overlong skein— another blood-debt to Utuk'ku and . . ." he hesitated, *"the other. Still, the Houses are gathering. When my father at last is taken to the Grove, the Zida'ya will ride to war again."* After his earlier flash of anger the Sitha had returned to his customary implacability, but Simon thought he could detect an underlying feeling of tension, of excitement.

Simon's hopes rose. *"Will you join with Josua? Will you fight with us?"*

Jiriki frowned. *"I cannot say, Seoman—and I would not make false promises. If I have my way, we will, and one last time the Zida'ya and Sudhoda'ya will fight together. But there are many who will speak when I speak, and many will have their own ideas. We have danced the year's end many hundreds of times since all the Houses were together for a war-council. Look!"*

Jiriki's face shimmered and faded, and for a moment Simon could see a cloudy scene, a vast circle of silver-leaved trees that stretched tall as towers. Gathered at their feet was a great host of Sithi, hundreds of immortals clad in armor of wildly different forms and colors, armor that glinted and shimmered in the columns of sunlight that spilled down through the treetops.

"Look. The members of all the Houses are joined at Jao é-Tinukai'i. Chekai'so Amber-Locks is here, as is Zinjadu, Lore-Mistress of lost Kementari, and Yizashi Gray-spear. Even Kuroyi the tall horseman has come, who has not joined with the House of Year-Dancing since Shi'iki and Senditu's day. The exiles have returned, and we will fight as one people, as we have not done since Asu'a fell. In this, anyway, Amerasu's death and my father's sacrifice will not be in vain."

The vision of the armored host faded, then Jiriki faced Simon once more. *"But I have only a little power to guide this gathering of forces,"* he said, *"and we Zida'ya have many obligations. I cannot promise we will come, Seoman, but I will do my best to uphold my own duties to you. If your need is great, call me. You know I will do what I can."*

"I know, Jiriki." There seemed many other things that he should tell him, but Simon's mind was in a whirl. *"I hope we see each other soon."*

At last, Jiriki smiled. *"As I said once before, manchild, a very unmagical wisdom tells me we shall meet again. Be brave."*

"I will."

The Sitha's face grew serious. *"Now go, please. As you have found, the Witnesses and the Dream Road are no longer reliable—in fact, they are dangerous. I also doubt that words spoken here are safe from listening ears. That the Houses are gathering is no secret, but what the Zida'ya will do is. Avoid these realms, Seoman."*

"But I need to find Miriamele," Simon said stubbornly.

"You will only find trouble, I fear. Leave it alone. Besides, perhaps she is hiding from things that might not find her unless, without meaning to, you lead them to her."

Simon thought guiltily of Amerasu, but realized Jiriki had not intended to remind him of that, but only to caution him. *"If you say so,"* he acceded. So it had all been for nothing.

"Good." The Sitha narrowed his eyes, and Simon felt his presence begin to fade. A sudden thought came.

"But I don't know how to get back!"

"I will help you. Farewell for now, my Hikka Staja."

Jiriki's features blurred and evaporated, leaving only shimmering gray. As even that emptiness began to fade, Simon felt again a faint touch, the feminine presence to which he had reached out in his moment of fear. Had she been with them all along? Was she a spy, as Jiriki had warned about? Or was it indeed Miriamele, separated from him somehow, but nonetheless feeling that he was near? Who was it?

As he came back to himself, shivering in the cold beneath the Observatory's broken dome, he wondered if he would ever know.

6

The Sea-Grave

Miriamele had paced back and forth across the small cabin so many times that she could almost feel the plank flooring wearing away beneath her slippered feet.

She had nerved herself to an exquisite pitch, ready to slit the earl's throat as he lay sleeping. But now, at Gan Itai's direction, she had hidden the pilfered dagger and was waiting—but she did not know for what. She was trembling, and no longer just with anger and frustration: the gnawing fear, which she had been able to suppress with the thought that all would be over quickly, had returned. How long could it be until Aspitis noticed the theft of his knife? And would he have even a moment's doubt before he fixed the blame in the obvious place? This time, he would come to her wary and prepared; then, instead of the bindings of shame and society, she would go to her impending wedding in chains as real as Cadrach's.

As she paced, she prayed to blessed Elysia and Usires for help, but in the offhand way that one spoke to an ancient relative who had long ago gone deaf and numb-witted. She had little doubt that whatever happened to her on this drifting ship was of scant interest to a God who could allow her to reach this sorry state in the first place.

She had been proved wrong twice. After a childhood surrounded by flatterers and lackeys, she had been certain the only way to make a life worth living was to listen only to her own counsel and then push forward against any impediment, letting no one stay her from whatever seemed important—but it was just that course which had brought her to this horrible position. She had fled her uncle's castle, certain that she alone could help change the course of events, but the faithless tides of time and history had not waited for her, and the very things she hoped to prevent had occurred anyway—Naglimund fallen, Josua defeated—leaving her without purpose. So it had seemed wisest to cease fighting, to put an end to a lifetime's worth of stubborn resistance and simply let events push her along. But that plan had proven as foolish as the first, for her listlessness had brought her to Aspitis' bed, and soon would make her his queen. For a while this realization had toppled Miriamele back into heedlessness—she would kill him, and then likely be killed by Aspitis' men; there would be no mucking about in the middle ground, no complicated responsibilities. But Gan Itai had stopped her, and now she drifted and circled just as the *Eadne Cloud* idled on the windless waters.

This was an hour of decision, the sort Miriamele had learned about from her tutors—as when Pelippa, the pampered wife of a nobleman, had to decide whether to declare her belief in the condemned Usires. The pictures in her childhood prayer book were still fresh in her memory. As a young princess, she had been chiefly fascinated by the silver paint on Pelippa's dress. Miriamele had given little thought to Pelippa herself, to the actual people caught up in the legends, written of in stories, painted on walls. Only recently had it occurred to her to wonder how it felt to be one of those folk. Had the warring kings immortalized in the Sancellan's tapestries walked back and forth in their ancient halls as they agonized over decisions, thinking little of what people would say in centuries unborn, but rather sorting the small facts of the moment, trying to see a pattern that might guide them to a wise choosing?

As the ship gently rocked and the sun rose into the sky, Miriamele paced and thought. Surely there must be some way to be bold without being stupid, to be resilient without becoming malleable and yielding as candle wax. Along some course midway between these two extremes, might there be a way she could survive? And if there was, could she then fashion from it a life worth living?

In the lamplit cabin, hidden from the sun, Miriamele pondered. She had not slept much the night before and she doubted she would sleep in the night that was coming . . . if she lived to see it.

When the knock came upon her door, it was a quiet one. She thought herself ready to face even Aspitis, but her fingers trembled as they reached for the door handle.

It was Gan Itai, but for a moment Miriamele thought that some other Niskie had come aboard, so changed did the sea-watcher look. Her golden-brown skin seemed almost gray. Her face was loose and haggard and her sunken, red-rimmed eyes seemed to gaze out at Miriamele across a vast distance. The Niskie had wrapped her cloak closely about her, as though even in the swollen, humid air that presaged a storm, she feared catching a chill.

"Mercy of Aedon!" Miriamele hustled her inside and pushed the door closed. "Are you ill, Gan Itai? What has happened?" Aspitis had discovered the theft and was on his way, of course—that could be the only reason for the Niskie to look so dreadful. Miriamele faced this resolution with a kind of cold relief. "Do you need something? Water to drink?"

Gan Itai raised her weathered hand. "I need nothing. I have been . . . thinking."

"Thinking? What do you mean?"

The Niskie shook her head. "Do not interrupt, girl. I have things to say to you. I made my own decision." She sat down on Miriamele's bed, moving as though two score years had been added to her age. "First, do you know where the landing boat is?"

Miriamele nodded. "Near midship on the starboard side, hanging from the windlass ropes." There was at least some advantage to having lived among waterfaring folk most of her young life.

"Good. Go to it this afternoon, when you are sure you are unobserved. Hide these there." The Niskie lifted her cloak and dumped several bundles out onto the bed. Four were water skins, tight-filled; two more were packages wrapped in sacking. "Bread, cheese, and water," Gan Itai explained. "And some bone fishhooks, so you may perhaps have some flesh to eke out your provisions. There are a few other small things that may also prove useful."

"What does this mean?" Miriamele stared at the old woman. Gan Itai still looked as though she carried some dreadful burden, but her eyes had lost some of the clouded look. They glinted now.

"It means you are escaping. I cannot sit and watch such wickedness forced on you. I would not be one of the Navigator's true children if I did."

"But it cannot happen!" Miriamele fought against the rush of witless hope. "Even if I could get off the ship, Aspitis would hunt me down within a few hours. The wind will come up long before I reach land. Do you think I can vanish in a dozen leagues of empty sea, or outrow the *Eadne Cloud?*"

"Outrow her? No." There was a strange pride in Gan Itai's expression. "Of course not. She is fleet as a dolphin. But as to how . . . leave that to me, child. That is the rest of *my* duty. You, however, must do one other thing."

Miriamele swallowed her arguments. Heedless, stubborn pushing had done her little good in the past. "What?"

"In the hold, in one of the barrels near the starboard wall, tools and other metal goods are packed in oil. There is writing on the cask, so do not fear you will not find it. Go to the hold after sunset, take a chisel and a mallet from the barrel, and strike off Cadrach's chains. Then he must hide the fact that the chains are broken, in case someone comes."

"Break his chains? But everyone on the ship will hear me." Weariness descended on her. Already it seemed clear that the Niskie's plan could never succeed.

"Unless my nose betrays me, the storm will be here soon. A ship at sea in heavy wind makes many noises." Gan Itai lifted her hand to still further questions. "Just do those tasks, then leave the hold and go to your cabin or anywhere, but *do not let anybody bolt you in.*" She waggled her long fingers for emphasis. "Even if you must feign sickness or madness, do not let anyone put a bolt between you and freedom." The golden eyes stared into her own until Miriamele felt her doubts wither away.

"Yes," she said. "I will."

"Then, at midnight, when the moon is just *there,*" the Niskie pointed at a spot on the ceiling, as if the sky were spread directly over them, "get your learned friend and help him to the landing boat. I will make sure you get a chance to put it overboard." She looked up, caught by a sudden thought. "By the Uncharted, girl, make sure that the oars are in the boat! Look for them when you hide the food and water."

Miriamele nodded. So the matter was resolved. She would do her best to live, but if she failed, she would not struggle against the inevitable. Even as her husband, Aspitis Preves could not keep her alive against her will. "And what will you do, Gan Itai?" she asked.

"What I have to."

"But it was not a dream!" Tiamak was growing angry. What did it take to convince this great brute of a Rimmersman? "It was Geloë, the wise woman of Aldheorte Forest. She talked to me through a child who has been in all my dreams of late. I have read of this. It is a trick of the Art, something adepts can do."

"Calm yourself, man. I didn't say you imagined it." Isgrimnur turned from the old man, who was waiting patiently for the next question the duke might ask him. Although unable to answer, he-who-had-been-Camaris seemed to get a quiet, childlike satisfaction from the attention, and would sit smiling back at Isgrimnur for hours. "I have heard of this Geloë. I *believe* you, man. And when we can leave, your Stone of Farewell is as good a destination as any—I have heard that Josua's camp is somewhere near where you say the place is. But I cannot let a dream of any kind, no matter how urgent it seems, take me away just yet."

"But why?" Tiamak was not even sure himself why it seemed so important that they leave. All he knew was that he was tired of feeling worthless. "What can we do here?"

"I am waiting for Miriamele, Prince Josua's niece," said the Rimmersman. "Dinivan sent me to this godforsaken inn. Perhaps he sent her as well. Since it is my sworn duty to find her, and I have lost the trail, I must stay for a time here where the track ends."

"If he sent her, then why is she not here now?" Tiamak knew he was making trouble, but could not help himself.

"Perhaps she's been delayed. It is a long journey on foot." Isgrimnur's mask of calm slipped a little. "Now be quiet, damn you! I have told you all I can. If you wish to go, then go! I won't stop you."

Tiamak closed his mouth with a snap, then turned and limped unhappily to his bundle of belongings. He began to sort through them in halfhearted preparation for departure.

Should he leave? It was a long journey, and would certainly be better made with companions, however shortsighted and uncaring of his feelings they might be. Or maybe it would be better just to slink back to his house in the banyan tree, deep in the marsh outside Village Grove. But his people would demand to know what had become of his forsaken errand to Nabban on their behalf, and what would he tell them?

He Who Always Steps on Sand, Tiamak prayed, *save me from this terrible indecision!*

His restless fingers touched heavy parchment. He drew out the page of Nisses' lost book and cradled it briefly in his hands. This small triumph, anyway, no one could take from him. It was he and no one else who had found it. But, sadness of sadnesses, Morgenes and Dinivan were no longer alive to marvel at it!

"... *Bringe from Nuanni's Rocke Garden,*"

he read silently,

> "... *The Man who tho' Blinded canne See*
> *Discover the Blayde that delivers The Rose*
> *At the foote of the Rimmer's greate Tree*
> *Find the Call whose lowde Claime*
> *Speakes the Call-bearer's name*
> *In a Shippe on the Shallowest Sea—*
> *—When Blayde, Call, and Man*
> *Come to Prince's right Hande*
> *Then the Prisoned shall once more go Free ...*"

He remembered the dilapidated shrine to Nuanni he had found in his wanderings a few days earlier. The wheezing, half-blind old priest had been able to tell him little of import, although he was quite happy to talk after Tiamak dropped a pair of cintis-pieces into the offering bowl. Nuanni was, apparently, a sea god of ancient Nabban whose glory days had passed even before the upstart Usires appeared. Old Nuanni's followers were few indeed these days, the priest had assured him: were it not for the tiny pockets of worship still clinging to life in the superstitious islands, no one living would remember Nuanni's name, although the god had once bestrode the Great Green, first in the hearts of all seafarers. As it was, the old priest guessed that his was the last shrine still on the mainland.

Tiamak had been pleased to hear the now-familiar name from his parchment at last given substance, but had thought little more of it than that. Now he let his mind run on the first line of the puzzling rhyme and wondered if "Nuanni's rock garden" might not refer to the scattered islands of Firannos Bay themselves ...?

"What do you have there, little man? A map, hey?" From the sound of his voice, Isgrimnur was trying to be friendly, perhaps in an effort to offset his earlier gruffness—but Tiamak was having none of it.

"Nothing. It is not your business." He quickly rolled the parchment and pushed it back into his clump of belongings.

"No need to bite my head off," the duke growled. "Come, man, talk to me. Are you truly leaving?"

"I do not know." Tiamak did not want to turn and look at him. The Rimmersman was so large and imposing that he made the Wrannaman feel terribly small. "I might. But it would be a long way for one to go alone."

"How would you go, anyway?" Isgrimnur's interest sounded genuine.

Tiamak considered. "If I did not go with you two, there would be no need to be inconspicuous. So I would go the straightest way possible, overland across Nabban and the Thrithings. It would be a long walk, but I am not afraid of exertion." He frowned, thinking of his injured leg. It might never heal, and certainly was not now capable of carrying him a long distance. "Or perhaps I would buy a donkey," he added.

"You certainly speak fine Westerling for a Wran-man," Isgrimnur smiled. "You use words I don't know myself."

"I told you," Tiamak replied stiffly. "I studied with the Aedonite brothers in Perdruin. And Morgenes himself taught me much."

"Of course." Isgrimnur nodded. "But, hmm, if you did have to travel—inconspicuously, I think you said? If you did have to travel without being noticed, what then? Some secret marsh-man tunnels, or something like?"

Tiamak looked up. Isgrimnur was watching him carefully. Tiamak quickly lowered his gaze, trying to hide a smile of his own. The Rimmersman was trying to trick him, as though Tiamak were a child! It was funny, actually. "I imagine I would fly."

"Fly!?" Tiamak could almost hear the look of incredulity twist the duke's features. "Are you mad?"

"Oh, no," said Tiamak earnestly, "it is a trick known to all Wran-dwellers. Why do you think that we are only observed in places like Kwanitupul, where we choose to be seen? Surely you know that great blundering drylanders come into the Wran and never see a living soul. It is because when we have to, we can fly. Just like birds." He darted a sideways glance. Isgrimnur's baffled face was everything he could hope. "Besides, if we could not fly . . . how would we reach the treetop nests where we lay our eggs?"

"S'Red Blood! Aedon on the Tree!" Isgrimnur swore explosively. "Damn you, marsh man! Mock me, will you?!"

Tiamak cringed in expectation of having some heavy object thrown at him, but a moment later looked up to see the duke grinning and shaking his head. "I suppose I asked for that. You Wrannamen have a sense of humor, it seems."

"Perhaps some drylanders do also."

"Still, the problem remains." Isgrimnur glowered. "Life seems nothing but difficult choices these days. By the Ransomer's Name, I have made mine and must live with it: if Miriamele does not appear by the twenty-first day of Octander—Soul's Day, that is—then I, too, will say 'enough' and head north. There is my choice. Now you must make yours: stay or go." He turned back to the old man, who had observed their entire conversation with benign incomprehension. "I hope you stay, little man," the duke added quietly.

Tiamak stared for a moment, then stood and walked to the window. Below, the murky canal gleamed like green metal in the afternoon sun. He pulled himself up onto the sill and dangled his wounded leg out the window.

"Inihe Red-Flower had dark hair,"

he crooned, watching a flatboat bob past,

> *"Dark hair, dark eyes. Slender as a vine she was,*
> *And she sang to the gray doves.*
> *Ah-ye, ah-ye, she sang to them all the night long.*
>
> *"Shoaneg Swift-Rowing heard her,*
> *Heard her, loved her. Strong as a banyan he was,*
> *But he had no children.*
> *Ah-ye, ah-ye, he had no one to carry his name.*
>
> *"Shoaneg called out to Red-Flower,*
> *Wooed her, won her. Swift as dragonflies their love was*
> *And she came back to his home.*
> *Ah-ye, ah-ye, her feather hung over his door.*
>
> *"Inihe, she bore a boy-child,*
> *Nursed him, loved him. Sweet as cool wind he was,*
> *And he bore Swift-Rowing's name.*
> *Ah-ye, ah-ye, water was safe to him as sand.*
>
> *"The child grew up to wander,*
> *Rowing, running. Footloose as a rabbit he was,*
> *Traveled far from his home.*
> *Ah-ye, ah-ye, he was stranger to the hearth.*
>
> *"One day his boat came empty,*
> *Spinning, drifting. Empty as a nutshell it was,*
> *Red-Flower's child was gone.*
> *Ah-ye, ah-ye, he had blown away like thistledown.*
>
> *"Shoaneg said forget him,*
> *Heartless, thoughtless. Like a foolish nestling he was,*
> *Who flies from his home.*
> *Ah-ye, ah-ye, his father cursed his name.*
>
> *"Inihe could not believe it,*
> *Missed him, mourned him. Sad as drifting leaves she was*
> *Her tears soaked the floor-reeds.*
> *Ah-ye, ah-ye, she cried for her missing son.*

"Red-Flower burned to find him,
Hoping, praying. Like a hunting owl she was,
Who would search for her son.
Ah-ye, ah-ye, she would find her lost child.

"Shoaneg said he forbade her,
Shouted, ordered. Angry as a beehive he was,
If she went, he had no wife.
Ah-ye, ah-ye, he would blow her feather from his door . . ."

Tiamak broke off. A barge, crewed by shouting Wrannaman, was being poled awkwardly into a narrow side-canal. It scraped hard against the wharf pilings which jutted at the front of the inn like rotten teeth. The surface of the water boiled with waves. Tiamak turned to look at Isgrimnur, but the duke had left the room. Only the old man remained, his eyes fixed on nothing, his face vacant but for a small, secretive smile.

It was long since Tiamak's mother had sung that song to him. The tale of Inihe Red-Flower's terrible choice had been her favorite. Thinking of her brought a tightness to Tiamak's throat. He had betrayed the trust she would have wanted him to keep—the debt he owed to his own people. Now what should he do? Wait here with these drylanders? Go to Geloë and the other Scrollbearers who had asked him to come? Or return in shame to his own Village Grove? Wherever he went, he knew that his mother's spirit would watch him, mourning because her son had turned his back on his people.

He frowned as if tasting something bitter. Isgrimnur was right about one thing, anyway. These days, these bleak days, life seemed nothing but difficult choices.

☗

"Pull her back!" the voice said. "Quickly!"

Maegwin woke to find herself staring straight down into white nothingness. The transition was so strange that for a moment she thought she still dreamed. She leaned forward, trying to move through this emptiness as she had moved through the gray dream-void, but something restrained her. She gasped as she felt the fierce, biting cold. She was leaning out over an abyss of swirling snow. Rough hands were clutching at her shoulders.

"Hold her!"

She flung herself backward, scrabbling for safety, struggling against those who held her. When she could feel stone solidly beneath her on all sides, she let out a deep rush of close-held breath and went limp. The flurrying snowflakes were quickly filling the indentations left by her knees along the outer edge of the precipice. Nearby, the ashes of her small campfire had all but disappeared under a mantle of white.

"Lady Maegwin—we are here to help you!"

She looked around, dazed. Two men still held her tightly; a third stood a few paces behind her. All were heavily cloaked, and wore scarves wrapped around their faces. One wore the tattered crest of the Croich clan.

"Why have you brought me back?" Her voice seemed slow and clumsy. "I was with the gods."

"You were about to fall, Lady," the man at her right shoulder said. She could feel from the hand that gripped her that he was shivering. "We have been searching for you three days."

Three days! Maegwin shook her head and looked at the sky. From the indistinct gleam of the sun, it was only a little after dawn. Had she really been with the gods all that time? It had seemed scarcely an instant. If only these men had not come. . . .

No, she told herself. *That is selfish. I had to come back—and I would have been of no use if I had tumbled down the mountain and died.*

After all, she now had a duty to survive. She had more than duty.

Maegwin unwrapped her chilled fingers from the dwarrow-stone, letting it tumble to the ground. She felt her heart swell inside her. She had been right! She had climbed Bradach Tor as the dream had bidden her. Now, here in the high place she had dreamed again, dreams just as compelling as the ones that had brought her here.

Maegwin had felt the messenger of the gods reaching out for her, a messenger in the form of a tall, red-haired youth. Although his features had been misted by the dream, she guessed that he was very beautiful. Perhaps he was a fallen hero of old Hernystir, Airgad Oakheart or Prince Sinnach, taken to live in the sky with Brynioch and the rest!

During the first vision back in the cavern she had merely sensed him looking for her, but when she tried to reach out to him the dream had dissolved, leaving her chill and lonely atop her rock. Then, when she had fallen back into sleep, she had felt the messenger searching for her once more. She had felt that his need was urgent, so she had strained herself to the utmost, trying to burn as bright as a lamp so that he could find her, stretching herself out through the substance of the dream so she could reach him. Then, when she had touched him at last, he had instantly carried her to the threshold of the land where the gods lived.

And surely that had been one of the gods she had seen there! Again, the dream-vision had been fogged—perhaps living mortals could not witness the gods in their true forms—but the face that had appeared before her was nothing born of man or woman. If nothing else, the burning, inhumanly golden eyes would have proved that. Perhaps she had seen cloud-bearing Brynioch himself! The messenger, whose spirit had remained with her, seemed to tell the god something about a high place—which could only be the spot where Maegwin's sleeping body lay while her soul flitted in dream—then the messenger and the god spoke of a king's daughter and a dead father. It had all been very confusing,

the voices seeming to come to her garbled and echoing, as if through a very
long tunnel or across a mighty chasm—but who else could they have been
speaking of but Maegwin herself and her own father Lluth, who had died protecting his people?

Not all the words spoken reached her, but the sense of them was clear: the
gods were readying themselves for battle. Surely that could only mean they
were going to intervene at last. For a moment she had even been vouchsafed a
glimpse into the very halls of Heaven. A mighty host of them had waited there,
fiery-eyed and streaming-haired, clad in armor as colorful as the wings of butterflies, their spears and swords shimmering like lightning in a summer's sky.
Maegwin had seen the gods themselves in their power and glory. It was true, it
must be! How could there be any doubt now? The gods meant to take the field
and to wreak revenge on Hernystir's enemies.

She swayed back and forth and the two men steadied her. She felt that if she
leaped from Bradach Tor at this moment she would not fall, but would fly like
a starling, arrow-swift down the mountain to tell her people the wonderful
news. She laughed at herself and her foolish ideas, then laughed again with joy
that she should be chosen by the gods of field, water, and sky to bear their message of coming redemption.

"My lady?" The man's worry was clear in his tone. "Are you ill?"

She ignored him, afire with ideas. Even if she could not truly fly, she must
hurry down the mountain to the cave where the Hernystiri nation labored in
its exile. It was time to go!

"I have never been better," she said. "Lead me to my people."

As her escorts helped her back along the tor, Maegwin's stomach rumbled.
Her hunger, she realized, was returning swiftly. Three days she had slept and
dreamed and stared into the snowy distance from this high place, and in that
time she had eaten almost nothing. Full of the words of heaven, she was now
also hollow as an empty barrel. How would she ever fill herself up? She laughed
uproariously and paused, smacking the snow from her clothing in powdery
bursts of white. It was bitterly cold, but she was warmed. She was far from her
home, but she had her leaping thoughts for company. She wished she could
share this sense of triumph with Eolair, but even the thought of him did not
sadden her, as it always had before. He was doing what he should do, and if the
gods had planted the seed of his going in her mind, there must be some reason
for it. How could she doubt, when all else that had seemed promised had been
given—all but the last and greatest gift, which she knew was coming soon?

"I have spoken with the gods," she told the three worried men. "They are
with us at this terrible time—they will come to us."

The man nearest her looked quickly at his companions, then did his best to
smile as he said: "Praise to all their names."

Maegwin gathered her sparse possessions into her sack so hastily that she
chipped the wooden wing of Mircha's bird. She sent one of the men back to get
the dwarrow-stone, which she had dropped in the snow at the cliff's edge.

Before the sun had moved a handsbreadth above the horizon, she was making her way down the Grianspog's snowy slope.

She was hungry and very tired, and she had also finally begun to feel the cold. Even with the help of her rescuers, the journey down was even more difficult than the climb up. Still, Maegwin felt joy pulsing quietly within her like a child waiting to be born—a joy that, like a child, would grow and become ever more splendid. Now she could tell her people that help was coming! What could be more welcome after this bleak twelvemonth?

But what else should be done, she suddenly wondered. What should the Hernystiri people do to prepare for the return of the gods?

Maegwin turned her thoughts to this as the party made its careful way down and the morning slipped away across the face of the Grianspog. She decided at last that before anything else, she must speak to Diawen again. The scryer had been right about Bradach Tor and had understood instantly the importance of the other dreams. Diawen would help Maegwin decide what to do next.

Old Craobhan met the search party, full of angry words and poorly-hidden worry, but his fury at her heedlessness rolled off Maegwin like rain from oiled leather. She smiled and thanked him for sending men to bring her safely down, but would not be hindered; she ignored him as he first demanded, then asked, then at last begged her to rest and be tended. Finally, unable to convince her to accompany them, unwilling to use force in a cavern full of curious onlookers, Craobhan and his men gave up.

Diawen was standing before her cave as though she had expected Maegwin to come at just that time. The scryer took her arm and guided her into the smoky chamber.

"I can see by your face." Diawen peered solemnly into Maegwin's eyes. "Praise Mircha, you have had another dream."

"I climbed up to Bradach Tor, just as you suggested." She wanted to shout her excitement. "And the gods spoke to me!"

She related all that she had experienced, trying not to exaggerate or glorify— surely the bare reality was marvelous enough! When she had finished, Diawen gazed back at her in silence, eyes bright with what looked like tears.

"Ah, praise be," said the scryer. "You have been given a Witnessing, as in the old tales."

Maegwin grinned happily. Diawen understood, just as Maegwin had known she would. "It's wonderful," she agreed. "We will be saved." She paused as the thought she had been holding made itself felt. "But what should we do?"

"The gods' will," Diawen replied without hesitation.

"But what is that?"

Diawen searched among her collection of mirrors, at last selecting one made of polished bronze with a handle in the shape of a coiling serpent. "Quiet now. I did not walk in dreams with you, but I have my own ways." She held the mirror above the smoldering fire, then blew away the accumulated soot. For a long time she stared into it, her dark brown eyes seemingly fixed on something beyond the mirror. Her lips moved soundlessly. At last, she put the mirror down.

When Diawen spoke, her voice was remote. "The gods help those who are bold. Bagba gave cattle to Hern's folk because they had lost their horses fighting on behalf of the gods. Mathan taught the art of weaving to the women who hid her from her husband Murhagh's rage. The gods help those who are bold." She blinked and pushed a lock of gray hair from her eyes. Her voice resumed its ordinary tone. "We must go to meet the gods. We must show them that Hern's children are worthy of their help."

"What does that mean?"

Diawen shook her head. "I am not sure."

"Should we take up arms ourselves? Go forth and challenge Skali?" Maegwin frowned. "How can I ask the people to do that, few and weak as we are?"

"Doing the will of the gods is never easy," Diawen sighed. "I know. When I was young, Mircha came to me in a dream, but I could not do what she asked. I was afraid." The scryer's face, lost in memory, was full of fierce regret. "Thus I failed in my moment and left her priesthood. I have never felt her touch since, not in all the lonely years. . . ." She broke off. When she turned her gaze to Maegwin once more, she was brisk as a wool merchant. "The will of the gods can be frightening, king's daughter, but to refuse it is to refuse their help as well. I can tell you no more."

"To take arms against Skali and his reavers . . ." Maegwin let the thought flow through her like water. There was a certain mad beauty in the idea, a beauty that might indeed please the heavens. To lift the sword of Hernystir once more against the invaders, even for one brief moment. Surely the gods themselves would shout to see such a proud hour! And surely at that moment the sky could not help but open up, and all of Rhynn's lightnings leap forth to burn Skali Sharp-nose and his army into dust. . . .

"I must think, Diawen. But when I speak to my father's people, will you stand with me?"

The scryer nodded, smiling like a prideful parent. "I will stand with you, king's daughter. We will tell the people how the gods spoke."

A shower of warm rain was falling, the first outrider of the approaching storm. The thick bank of clouds along the horizon was mottled gray and black, touched at the edges by the orange glare of the late afternoon sun it had almost swallowed. Miriamele narrowed her eyes against the spattering drops and looked carefully all around. Most of the sailors were busy preparing for the storm, and none seemed to be paying any attention to her at all. Aspitis was in his cabin, where she prayed he would be too engrossed in his charts to notice the theft of his fanciest dagger.

She slid the first of the water skins out from beneath her belted cape, then loosened a knot that held the heavy cloth cover in place over the open landing boat. After one more quick survey of the surroundings, she let the water skin slide down into the boat to nestle beside the oars, then quickly sent down the other. As she stood on tiptoe to push the parcels of bread and cheese in, somebody shouted in Nabbanai.

"Hoy! Stop that!"

Miriamele froze like a cornered rabbit, heart pounding. She let the food bundles slide out of her fingers and down into the boat, then slowly turned.

"Fool! You've put it wrongside-round!" the sailor screamed from his perch in the rigging. Twenty cubits up, he was staring indignantly at another sailor working above him on the mast. The object of his criticism gave him the goat-sign and cheerfully continued doing whatever it was that had proved so offensive. The first sailor shouted for a while longer, then laughed and spat through the wind before resuming his own labors.

Miriamele closed her eyes as she waited for her knees to stop shaking. She took a deep breath, filling her nose with the scents of tar, wet planks, and the sodden wool of her own cloak, as well as the bristly, secretive odor of the approaching storm, then opened her eyes again. The rain had grown stronger and was now running off her hood, a tiny cascade falling just beyond the tip of her nose. Time to get below-decks. It would be sunset soon and she did not want to defeat Gan Itai's plan through simple carelessness, however faint the hope of success. Also, while it was not inexplicable that Miriamele should be on deck in this rapidly worsening rain, if she encountered Aspitis it might stick in his mind as a curious thing. Miriamele did not know exactly what the Niskie was arranging, but she knew it would not be helped by putting the earl on guard.

She made her way down the hatchway stairs without attracting attention, then padded silently along the corridor until she reached the Niskie's sparsely furnished room. The door had been left unbolted and Miriamele quickly slipped inside. Gan Itai was gone—out preparing the master-stroke of her plan, Miriamele felt sure, however hopeless even the Niskie thought it to be. Gan Itai had certainly seemed weary and heartsick when she had seen her this morning.

After Miriamele had tied up her skirt, she pulled free the loose section of wall paneling, then agonized for a long moment over whether to bolt the outer door of the room. Unless she could replace the panel perfectly from the inside of the hidden passageway, anyone entering the room would instantly know someone had gone through, and might be interested enough to investigate. But if she threw the bolt, Gan Itai might return and be unable to get in.

After a little consideration, she decided to leave the door alone and take her chances with accidental discovery. She took a stub of candle from her cloak and held it to the flame of Gan Itai's lamp, then climbed through and pulled the panel closed behind her. She held the candle-end in her teeth as she climbed the ladder, saying a silent prayer of thanks that her hair was wet and still cropped short. She hastily dismissed an image of what might happen if someone's hair caught fire in a narrow place like this.

When she reached the hatchway, she dripped some wax on the passageway floor to hold the candle, then lifted the trapdoor and peered through the crack. The hold was dark—a good sign. She doubted that any of the sailors would be walking around among the precariously stacked barrels without light.

"Cadrach!" she called softly. "It's me! Miriamele!"

There was no reply, and for an instant she was sure that she had come too late, that the monk had died here in the darkness. She swallowed down the clutch in her throat, retrieved her candle, then climbed carefully down the ladder fixed to the sill of the hatchway. It ended short of the ground, and when she dropped the remaining distance she struck sooner than she expected to. The candle popped from her hand and rolled across the wooden flooring. She scrambled after it, burning herself with a panicky grab, but it did not go out.

Miriamele took a deep breath. "Cadrach?"

Still unanswered, she snaked her way through the leaning piles of ship's stores. The monk was slumped on the floor beside the wall, head sunken on his breast. She grabbed his shoulder and shook, making his head wobble.

"Wake up, Cadrach." He moaned but did not awaken. She shook harder.

"Ah, gods," he slurred, "that *smearech fleann . . .* that cursed book . . ." He flailed as if caught in a terrible nightmare. "Close it! Close it! I wish I had never opened it. . . ." His words fell away into unintelligible mumbling.

"Curse you, wake up!" she hissed.

His eyes opened at last. "My . . . my lady?" His confusion was pitiable. Some of his substance had withered away during his captivity: his skin hung loosely on the bones of his face and his eyes peered blearily out of deep sockets. He looked like an old man. Miriamele took his hand, wondering a little that she should do so without hesitation. Wasn't this the same tosspot traitor she had pushed into the Bay of Emettin and hoped to watch drown? But she knew he was not. The man before her was a miserable creature who had been chained and beaten—and not for any real crime, but only for running away, for trying to save his own life. Now she wished she had run with him. Miriamele pitied the monk, and remembered that he had not been entirely bad. In some ways, he had even been a friend.

Miriamele suddenly felt ashamed of her callousness. She had been so certain about things, so sure about what was right and what was wrong that she had been ready to let him drown. It was hard to look at Cadrach now, his eyes wounded and frightened, his head bobbing above the stained robe. She squeezed his cold hand and said: "Don't fear—I will return in a moment." She took her candle and went off to search the ranked barrels for Gan Itai's promised tools.

She squinted at faded markings as footsteps echoed back and forth overhead. The ship rolled abruptly, creaking in the grasp of the storm's first winds. At last she found a barrel helpfully marked *"Otillenaes."* When she had also located a pry-bar that hung near the ladder, she unlidded the cask. A treasure trove of tools were packed inside, all neatly wrapped in leather and floating in oil like

exotic supper birds. She bit her lip and forced herself to work calmly and carefully, unwrapping the oozing parcels one at a time until she found a chisel and
a heavy mallet. After wiping them off on the inside of her cloak, she took them
back to Cadrach.

"What are you doing, Lady? Do you plan to favor me with a blow from that
pig-slaughterer? It would be a true favor."

She frowned, fixing the candle to the floor with hot wax. "Don't be a fool.
I'm going to cut your chains. Gan Itai is helping us to escape."

The monk stared at her for a moment, his pouchy gray eyes surprisingly
intent. "You must know that I cannot walk, Miriamele."

"If I have to, I will carry you. But we will not go until tonight. That will
give you a chance to rub some life back into your legs. Perhaps you can even
stand up and try pacing a bit, if you are quiet about it." She pulled at the chain
that hung from his ankles. "I suppose I must cut this on each side or you will
rattle when you walk, like a tinker." Cadrach's smile, she guessed, was mostly
for her sake.

The long chain between his leg irons ran through one of the tying-bolts in
the floor of the hold. Miriamele pulled one side taut, then set the chisel's sharp
blade against the nearest link to the shackle. "Can you hold it for me?" she
asked. "Then I can use both hands on the hammer."

The monk nodded and clutched the spike of iron. Miriamele hefted the
mallet a few times to get the feel of it, then raised it above her head.

"You look like Deanagha of the Brown Eyes," he whispered.

Miriamele was trying to listen to the creaking rhythm of the boat's movement, hoping to find a noisy moment in which to strike. "Like who?"

"Deanagha of the Brown Eyes." He smiled. "Rhynn's youngest daughter.
When his enemies surrounded him and he lay sick, she pounded on his bronze
cauldron with her spoon until the other gods came to rescue him." He stared
at her. "Brave she was."

The boat rolled and the timbers gave out a long, shuddering groan.

"My eyes are green," Miriamele said, then brought the mallet down as hard
as she could. The clank seemed loud as thunder. Certain that Aspitis and his
men must now be racing toward the hold, she looked down. The chisel had
bitten deep, but the chain was still uncut.

"Curse it," she breathed and paused to listen for a long, anxious moment.
There seemed no unusual sounds from the deck above, so she lifted the mallet,
then had a thought. She took off her cloak and folded it over, then folded it once
more. She slid this cushion beneath the chain. "Hold this," she ordered, and
struck again.

It took several cuts, but the cloak helped soften the noise, though it also
made striking a hard blow more difficult. At last the iron link parted. Miriamele
then pounded laboriously through the other side as well, and even managed to
sever one side of Cadrach's wrist chains before she had to stop. Her arms felt as
though they were afire; she could no longer lift the heavy mallet above her

shoulder. Cadrach tried, but was too weak. After he had struck at it several times without making an appreciable dent, he handed her back the hammer.

"This will be sufficient," he said. "One side is enough to free me, and I can wrap the chain about my arm so it will make no noise. The legs were what mattered, and they are free." He wiggled his feet carefully to demonstrate. "Do you think you could find some dark cloth in this hold?"

Miriamele looked at him curiously, but got up and began a weary search. At last she returned. Aspitis' knife, which had been tied to her leg with a scarf, was in her hand. "There's nothing around. If you really need it, we'll take it off the hem of my cloak." She kneeled and held the blade over the dark fabric. "Shall I?"

Cadrach nodded. "I will use it to tie the chains together. That way they will hold unless someone pulls them hard." He exerted the effort to grin. "In this light, my guards will never notice that one of the links is made of soft Erkyn-landish wool."

When they had done this, and when all the tools had been wrapped and replaced, Miriamele picked up her candle and stood. "I will be back for you at midnight, or just before."

"How is Gan Itai planning to work this little trick?" There was a flavor of his old ironic tone.

"She has not told me. Probably she thinks it's best I know little, so I will worry less." Miriamele shook her head. "There she has failed."

"It is not likely that we will get off the boat, nor that we will get far even if we do." The painful effort of the last hour showed in Cadrach's every halting movement.

"Not likely at all," she agreed. "But Aspitis knows that I am the High King's daughter and he is forcing me to marry him, so I do not care what is likely or unlikely." She turned to go.

"No, Lady, I imagine you do not. Until tonight, then."

Miriamele paused. Somewhere in the hour just passed, as the chains were falling away, an unspoken understanding had arisen between the two of them . . . a sort of forgiveness.

"Tonight," she said. She took the candle and made her way back up the ladder, leaving the monk sitting in darkness once more.

The hours of evening seemed to inch past. Miriamele lay in her cabin listening to the mounting storm, wondering where she would be this time tomorrow.

The winds grew stronger. The *Eadne Cloud* heaved and rolled. When the earl's page came and rapped at the door to say that his master bid her come to a late supper, she claimed illness from the restless seas and declined the invitation. A while later, Aspitis himself arrived.

"I am sorry to hear you are sick, Miriamele." He lounged in the doorway, loose-jointed as any predator. "Perhaps you would like to sleep in my cabin tonight, so you will not be alone with your misery?"

She wanted to laugh at such hideous irony, but resisted. "I am sick, Lord. When you marry me, I will do what you say. Leave me this last night to myself."

He seemed inclined to argue, but shrugged instead. "As you wish. I have had a long evening, preparing for the storm. And, as you say, we still have our entire lives before us." He smiled, a line thin as a knife-slash. "So, good night." He stepped forward and kissed her cold cheek, then stepped to the small table and pinched the wick of her lamp, snuffing the flame. "This will be a rough night. You do not want to start a fire."

He walked out, pulling the door closed behind him. As soon as his steps had receded down the passageway, she leaped from her bed to make sure he had not somehow locked her in. The door swung open freely, revealing the dark corridor. Even with the upper hatchway closed, the wail of the wind was loud, full of wild power. She closed the door and went back to her bed.

Propped upright, swaying to the ship's powerful movements, Miriamele drifted in and out of a light, restless sleep, surfacing with a start from time to time, the rags of dream still clinging, then hastening to the passageway and up the ladder to sneak a look at the sky. Once she had to wait so long for the moon to reappear in the stormclouded heavens that, still not completely awake, she feared that it had vanished altogether, chased away somehow by her father and Pryrates. When it appeared at last, a winking eye behind the murk, and she saw that it was still far from the place of which the Niskie had spoken, Miriamele glided back to her bed.

It even seemed that once, as she lay half-awake, Gan Itai opened the door and peered in at her. But if it was truly her, the Niskie said nothing; a moment later, the doorway was empty. Soon after, in a lull between gusts of wind, Miriamele heard the sea-watcher's song keening across the night.

When she could wait no longer, Miriamele rose. She pulled out the bag she had hidden underneath the bed and removed her monk's clothing, which she had put away in favor of the lovely dresses Aspitis had provided. After donning the breeches and shirt and belting the loose robe close about her waist, she donned her old boots, then threw a few select articles into the bag. Aspitis' knife, which she had worn that afternoon, she now thrust under her belt. Better to have it available than to worry about discovery. If she met someone between here and Gan Itai's cabin, she would have to try to hide the blade under the robe's wide sleeve.

A quick inspection proved the corridor empty. Miriamele tucked her sack under her arm and moved as silently as she could down the passageway, aided in her stealth by the rain that was beating down on the deck above her head like a drum struck by a thousand hands. The Niskie's song, rising above the storm noises, had a weird, unsettled quality, far less pleasant to the ear than usual. Perhaps it was the Niskie's obvious unhappiness coming out in her song, Miriamele thought. She shook her head, disturbed.

Even a brief glance out through the hatchway left her drenched. The torrential rains were being swept almost sideways by the wind, and the few lamps still burning in their hoods of translucent horn banged and capered against the masts. The *Eadne Cloud*'s crewmen, wound in flapping cloaks, hurried about the decks like panicked apes. It was a scene of wild confusion, but even so, Miriamele felt her heart grow heavy. Every seaman aboard seemed to be on deck and hard at work, eyes alert for a tearing sail or a flapping rope. It would be impossible for her and Cadrach to sneak from one side of the boat to the other unobserved, let alone lower the heavy landing boat and escape over the side. Whatever Gan Itai had planned, the storm would surely bring the scheme to ruin.

The moon, though almost completely obscured, looked to be near the place that the Niskie had indicated. As Miriamele squinted into the rain, a pair of cursing sailors approached the hatchway dragging a heavy coil of rope. She quickly lowered the door and scrambled back down the ladder, then hurried along the passage to Gan Itai's room and the Niskie-hole that led to Cadrach.

The monk was awake and waiting. He seemed a little improved, but his movements were still weak and slow. As Miriamele wrapped the length of chain around his arm and secured it with the strips from her cloak, she worried about how she would manage to get him across the deck to the landing boat unobserved.

When she had finished, Cadrach lifted his arm and wagged it bravely. "It is almost no weight at all, Lady."

She stared at the heavy links, frowning. He was lying, of course. She could see the strain in his face and his posture. For a moment she considered reopening the barrel and having another try with hammer and chisel, but she feared to take the time. Also, with the ship pitching so strongly, there was a great chance she might somehow wound herself or Cadrach by accident. She doubted their escape would succeed, but it was her only hope. Now that the time had come, she was determined to do her best.

"We must go soon. Here." She pulled a slim flask out of her sack and handed it to Cadrach. "Just a few swallows."

He took it with a wondering look. After the first gulp, a smile spread over his face. He took several more long drinks.

"Wine." He licked his lips. "Good red Perdruin! By Usires and Bagba and . . . and everyone else! Bless you, Lady!" He took a breath and sighed. "Now I can die happy."

"Don't die. Not yet. Let me have that."

Cadrach looked at her, then reluctantly handed over the flask. Miriamele upended it and drank the last few swallows, feeling the warmth trickle down her throat and nestle into her stomach. She hid the empty vessel behind one of the barrels.

"Now we will go." She picked up her candle and led him to the ladder.

When Cadrach at last made his way up the ladder and into the passageway of the Niskie-hole, he stopped to catch his breath. As he wheezed, Miriamele considered the next step. Overhead, the ship hummed and vibrated beneath the downpour.

"There are three ways we can get out," she said aloud. Cadrach, steadying himself against the rocking of the ship, did not seem to be listening. "The hatchway out of the hold—but that opens directly in front of the aft deck, where there is always a steersman. In this weather someone will certainly be there and be wide awake. So that's out." She turned to look at the monk. In the small circle of candlelight, he was staring down at the passageway boards beneath him. "We have two choices. Up through the hatchway in the main passage, right past Aspitis and all his sailors, or down this passage to the far end, which probably opens onto the foredeck."

Cadrach looked up. "Probably?"

"Gan Itai never told me and I forgot to ask. But this is a Niskie-hole; she said she uses it to get across the ship quickly. Since she always sings from the foredeck, that must be the place it leads to."

The monk nodded wearily. "Ah."

"So I think we should go there. Perhaps Gan Itai is waiting for us. She didn't say how we should get to the landing boat or when she would meet us."

"I will follow you, Lady."

As they crawled along the narrow passageway, a huge concussive thump made the very air in their ears seem to burst. Cadrach let out a muffled cry of terror.

"Gods, what is it?" he gasped.

"Thunder," said Miriamele. "The storm is here."

"Usires Aedon in His mercy, save me from boats and the sea," Cadrach groaned. "They are all cursed. Cursed."

"From one boat to another, and even closer to the sea." Miriamele began inching along again. "That's where we're going—if we're lucky." She heard Cadrach come scrambling after her.

Thunder tolled two more times before they reached the end of the passage, each peal louder than the last. When at last they crouched beneath the hatchway, Miriamele turned and laid her hand on the monk's arm.

"I'm going to snuff the candle. Now be quiet."

She inched the heavy door up until the opening was as wide as her hand. Rain flew and splashed. They were just below the forecastle—the steps mounted up only a few paces from the hatch—and some twenty cubits from the portside railing. A glare of lightning momentarily illuminated the whole deck. Miriamele saw the silhouetted shapes of crewmen all around, caught in mid-gesticulation as though painted on a mural. The sky was pressing down on the ship, a roil of angry black clouds that smothered the stars. She dropped down and let the hatchway close as another smack of thunder rattled the night.

"There are people all around," she said when the echoes had faded. "But none of them are too close. If we get to the rail and wear our hoods up, they may not notice we are not of the crew. Then we can make our way aft to the boat."

Without the candle she could not see the monk, but she could hear him breathing in the narrow space beside her. She had a sudden thought.

"I did not hear Gan Itai. She was not singing."

There was a moment's silence before Cadrach spoke. "I am afraid, Miriamele," he said hoarsely. "If we are to go, let us go soon, before I lose what little nerve I have left."

"I'm afraid, too," she said, "but I need to think for a bit." She reached out and found his chilly hand, then held it while she pondered. They sat that way for some while before she spoke again. "If Gan Itai is not on the foredeck, then I don't know where she is. Maybe waiting for us at the landing boat, maybe not. When we get there, we'll have to undo the tie-ropes that hold it to the ship— all but one. I'll go look for her, and when I come back we'll drop the boat down and jump into the water. If I don't come back, you must do it yourself. It will only be one knot, though. It won't take much strength."

"Jump . . . into the water?" he stammered. "In this terrible storm? And with those demon-creatures, those *kilpa,* swimming there?"

"Of course, jump," she whispered, trying to hold down her annoyance. "If we let the boat go while we're in it, we'll probably break our backs. Don't worry, I'll go first and give you an oar to hang onto."

"You shame me, Lady," the monk said, but did not let go of her hand. "It should be me protecting you. But you know I hate the sea."

She squeezed his fingers. "I know. Come on, then. Remember, if someone calls to you, pretend you can't hear them properly and keep walking. And keep your hand on the railing, for the deck is sure to be slippery. You don't want to go overboard before we get the landing boat into the water."

Cadrach's laugh was giddy with fright. "You are right about that, Lady. God save us all."

Another sound abruptly rose over the roar of the storm, a little quieter than the thunder but somehow just as powerful. Miriamele felt it surge through her and had to brace herself against the wall for a moment as her knees became weak. She could not think what it might be. There was something terrible about it, something that went to her heart like a spike of ice, but there was no time left to hesitate. A moment later, when she had mastered herself once more, she pushed up the hatchway door and they clambered out into the driving rain.

The strange sound was all around, piercingly sweet yet as frightfully compelling as the pull of a riptide. For a moment it seemed to soar up beyond the range of mortal ears, so that only a ghost of its fullness remained and her skull was full of echoes that piped like bats; then, a moment later, it descended just as swiftly, swooping down so rumblingly deep that it might be singing the slow and stony language of the ocean's floor. Miriamele felt as though she stood inside a humming wasp's nest big as a cathedral: the sound quivered right down to her innards. A part of her burned with the need to fling her body into sympathetic motion, to dance and scream and run in circles; another part of her wanted only to lie down and beat her head against the deck until the sound stopped.

"God save us, what is that horrible noise?" Cadrach wailed. He lost his balance and tumbled to his knees.

Clenching her teeth, Miriamele put her head down and forced herself to inch away from the forecastle steps toward the rail. Her very bones seemed to rattle. She grabbed at the monk's sleeve and pulled him with her, dragging him like a sledge across the slippery planks. "It's Gan Itai," she gasped, fighting against the stunning power of the Niskie's song. "We're too close."

The velvety darkness, lit only by the yellow-streaming lanterns, suddenly went stark blue and white. The rail before her, Cadrach's hand in hers, the empty blackness of the sea beyond both—all were seared on her eyes in an explosive instant. A heartbeat later the lightning flared again, and Miriamele saw, imprisoned in the flash, a smooth round head poking up above the portside rail. As the lightning faded and thunder double-cracked, another half-dozen loose-jointed shapes came swarming onto the ship, slick and gleaming in the dim lantern light. Realization struck, hard as a physical blow; Miriamele turned, stumbling and sliding, then plunged toward the starboard side of the ship, dragging Cadrach after her.

"What is happening?" he shouted.

"It's Gan Itai!" Ahead of her sailors ran back and forth like ants from a scattered nest, but it was no longer the *Eadne Cloud*'s crew she feared. "It is the Niskie!" Her mouth filled with rainwater and she spat. "She is singing the kilpa *up*!"

"Aedon save us!" Cadrach shrieked. "Aedon save us!"

Lightning glared again, revealing a host of gray, froglike bodies slithering over the starboard rail. As the kilpa flopped down onto the deck, they swung their gape-mouthed faces from side to side, staring like pilgrims who had finally reached a great shrine. One of them threw out a thin arm and caught a reeling crewman, then seemed to fold around him, dragging the screaming man down into darkness as the thunder bayed. Sickened, Miriamele turned and hurried along the length of the ship toward the spot where the landing boat hung. Water tugged at her feet and ankles. As in a nightmare, she felt that she could not run, that she was going slower and slower. The gray things continued to spill over the side, like ghouls from a childhood tale swarming out of an unhallowed grave. Behind her Cadrach was shouting incoherently. The Niskie's maddening song hung over all, making the very night pulse like a mighty heart.

The kilpa seemed to be everywhere, moving with a terrible, lurching suddenness. Even through the noise of the storm and Gan Itai's singing, the deck echoed with despairing cries from the beleaguered crewmen. Aspitis and two of his officers were backed against one of the masts, holding off a half-dozen of the sea beasts; their swords were little more than thin glints of light, darting, flashing. One of the kilpa tottered backward, clutching at an arm that was no longer attached to its body. The creature let the limb fall to the deck, then hunched over it, gills puffing. Black blood fountained from the stump.

"Oh, merciful Aedon!" Ahead, Miriamele could finally see the dark shadow that was the boat. Even as she dragged Cadrach toward it, one of the lamps burst against the crosstree overhead, raining burning oil down onto the watery deck. Gouts of steam leaped up all around and a smoldering spark caught on Miriamele's sleeve. As she hastily beat out the flame, the night erupted into orange light. She looked up into a blinding torrent of raindrops. A sail had caught fire, despite the storm, and the mast was rapidly becoming a torch.

"The knots, Cadrach!" she shouted. Nearby, someone's choking scream was buried in the rumble of thunder. She grabbed at the rain-slicked rope and struggled, feeling one of her fingernails tear as she tried to loose the swollen rope. At last it slipped free and she turned to the one beside it. The landing boat swung with the roll of the ship, bumping her away from her task, but she hung on. Nearby, Cadrach, pale as a corpse, struggled with another of the four ropes that held the windlass over the deck of the *Eadne Cloud.*

She felt a wave of cold even before the thing touched her. She whirled, slipping and falling back against the hull of the landing boat, but the kilpa took a step closer and caught her trailing sleeve in its web-fingered hand. Its eyes were black pools that glowed with the flames of the burning sail. The mouth opened and then shut, opened and shut. Miriamele screamed as it dragged her nearer.

There was a sudden rush of movement from out of the shadows behind her. The kilpa fell back but retained its grip on her arm, dragging her down after it so that her outflung hand smacked the slippery resilience of its belly. She gasped and tried to rip herself loose, but the webbed hand gripped her too tightly. Its stench enwrapped her, brine and mud and rotting fish.

"*Run,* Lady!" Cadrach's face appeared behind the creature's shoulder. He had pulled his chain taut around its throat, but even as he tightened the strangling hold, Miriamele saw the gills on the kilpa's neck pulsing in the half-light, translucent wings of delicate gray flesh, pink at the edges. She realized with a numbing sense of defeat that the beast did not need its throat to breathe: Cadrach had the chain too high. Even as he strained, the kilpa was drawing her in toward the other reaching arm, toward its slack mouth and gelid eyes.

Gan Itai's song ended abruptly, although its echo seemed to linger for long moments. The only sounds that rose above the wind now were screams of fear and the dull hoots of the swarming sea-demons.

Miriamele had been fumbling at her belt, but at last her hand closed around Aspitis' hawk-knife. Her heart skipped as the hilt caught in a fold of her sodden robe, but with a tug it came free. She shook it hard to knock loose the sheath, then slashed at the gray arm that held her. The knife bit, freeing a line of inky blood, but failed to loosen the creature's grip.

"*Ah, God help us!*" Cadrach screeched.

The kilpa rounded its mouth but made no sound, only pulled her closer until she could see the rain beading on its shiny skin and the soft, pale wetness behind its lips. With a cry of disgusted rage, Miriamele threw herself forward, plunging the knife into the thing's gummy midsection. Now it did make a sound, a soft, surprised whistle. Blood bubbled out over Miriamele's hand and she felt the creature's grasp weaken. She stabbed again, then again. The kilpa spasmed and kicked for what seemed an eternity, but at last fell limp. She rolled away. Then, shuddering, she plunged her hands down into cleansing water. Cadrach's chain was still wrapped about the thing's neck, making a grisly tableau for the next flash of lightning. The monk's eyes were wide, his face stark white.

"Let it go," Miriamele gasped. "It's dead." Thunder echoed her.

Cadrach kicked the thing, then crawled on his hands and knees toward the landing boat, struggling for breath. Within moments he had recovered enough to fumble open his two knots, then he helped Miriamele, whose hands were shaking uncontrollably, to finish hers. With one of the oars they swung the scaffolding out from the side of the ship, guiding it until it was perpendicular to the deck and only one tie held the boat suspended from the windlass over the dark, surging water.

Miriamele turned to look back across the ship. The mast was burning like an Yrmansol tree, a pillar of flame whipped by the winds. There were pockets of struggling men and kilpa scattered across the deck, but there also seemed to be a relatively clear line between the landing boat and the forecastle.

"Stay here," she said, pulling her hood down to obscure her face. "I must find Gan Itai."

Cadrach's look of astonishment quickly turned to rage. "Are you mad? *Goirach cilagh!* You will find your death!"

Miriamele did not bother to argue. "Stay here. Use the oar to protect yourself. If I don't come back soon, drop the boat and follow it. I will swim to you if I can." She turned and trotted back across the deck with the knife clutched in her fist.

Pretty *Eadne Cloud* had become a hell-ship—something that might have been crafted by the devil's boatwrights to torment sinners on the deepest seas of damnation. Water covered much of the deck, and the fire from the central mast had spread to some of the other sails. Burning rags rode the winds like demons. The few bloodied sailors who still remained topside had the crushed, brutalized look of prisoners punished far past what any crime could warrant. Many kilpa had been slaughtered, too—a pile of their corpses lay near the mast where Aspitis and his officers had fought, although at least one human leg protruded from the heap—and quite a few more of the sea creatures seemed to have seized a meal and leaped back overboard, but others still hopped and slid after survivors.

Miriamele waded to the foredeck without being set upon, although she had to pass much closer than she wished to several groups of feeding kilpa. A part of her was amazed to find that she could look on such things without being overcome by terror. Her heart, it seemed, had hardened: a year before, any one of these atrocities would have had her weeping and searching for a place to hide. Now she felt that if she had to, she could walk through fire.

She reached the stairs and made her way swiftly up to the forecastle. The Niskie had not stopped singing altogether: a thin drone of melody still hung over the foredeck, a thin shadow of the power that had outstormed even the wind. The sea watcher sat cross-legged on the deck, bent forward so that her face nearly touched the planks.

"Gan Itai," Miriamele said. "The boat is ready! Come!"

At first the Niskie did not respond. Then, when she sat up, Miriamele gasped. She had never seen such wretchedness on the face of a living creature.

"Ah, no!" the Niskie croaked. "By the Uncharted, go away! *Go!*" She waved her hand feebly. "I have done this for your freedom. Do not make the crime pointless by failing your escape!"

"But aren't you going to come?!"

The Niskie moaned. Her face seemed to have aged a hundred years. Her eyes were sunken deep into her head, their luster burned away. "I cannot leave. I am the ship's only hope to survive. It will not change my guilt, but it will ease my ruined heart. May Ruyan forgive me—it is an evil world that has brought me to this!" She threw back her head and gave out a groan of misery that brought Miriamele to tears. "Go!" the Niskie wailed. "Go! I beg you!"

Miriamele tried again to plead with her, but Gan Itai lowered her face to the deck once more. After a long silence, she at last resumed her weak, mournful song. The rain eased for a moment as the wind changed direction. Miriamele saw that only a few figures still moved on the firelit deck below. She stared at the huddled Niskie, then made the sign of the Tree and went down the stairs. She would think later. Later she would wonder why. Later.

It was a wounded sailor, not a kilpa, who grabbed at Miriamele on her return. When she slashed at his hand the crewman let go and collapsed back onto the sloshing deck. A few steps farther along she waded past the body of Thures, the earl's young page. There were no signs of violence upon him. The boy's dead face was peaceful beneath the shallow water, his hair undulating like seaweed.

Cadrach was so happy to see her he did not utter a single word of reproach or ask any questions about her solitary return. Miriamele stared at where the last windlass-rope was tied, then reached out with the dagger and sawed through it, leaning back as the cut end whipped free. The winding-drum spun and the landing boat plummeted down. A fountain of white spray sprang up as it hit the waves.

Cadrach handed her the oar he had been clutching. "Here, Miriamele. You're tired. It will help you float."

"Me?" she said, surprised almost into a smile.

A third voice interrupted them. *"There* you are, my darling."

She whirled to see a ghastly figure limping toward them. Aspitis had been slashed bloody in a dozen places, and a long cut that snaked down his cheek had closed one eye and flecked his golden locks with gore, but he still held his long sword. He was still as beautiful and terrifying as a stalking leopard.

"You were going to leave me?" he asked mockingly. "Not stay and help clean up after our . . ." he grinned, a dreadful sight, and gestured toward him,

". . . our *wedding guests?*" He took another step forward, waving the sword slowly from side to side. It glinted in the light of burning sails like a whisker of red-hot iron. It was strangely fascinating to watch it pass back and forth . . . back and forth. . . .

Miriamele shook her head and stood up straighter. "Go to hell."

Aspitis' smile dropped away. He leveled the tip of the sword toward her eye. Cadrach, who stood behind her, cursed helplessly. "Should I kill you," the earl mused, "or will you still be useful?" His eyes were as inhuman as a kilpa's.

"Go ahead and kill me. I would die before I let you have me again." She stared at him. "You are paying the Fire Dancers, aren't you? For Pryrates?"

Aspitis shook his head. "Some only. Those who are not . . . firm believers. But they are *all* useful." He frowned. "I do not wish to talk of such unimport- ant things. You are mine. I must decide . . ."

"I have something that *is* yours," she said, and raised the dagger before her. Aspitis smiled oddly, but lifted his sword-blade to fend off a sudden throw. Instead, Miriamele tossed the knife into the water at his feet. His dreaming eye caught its glitter and followed it down. As his head dipped, ever so slightly, Miriamele thrust the oar handle into his gut. He gasped for breath and took a staggering step backward, his sword jabbing blindly like the sting of an injured bee. Miriamele brought the oar up again with both hands, then swung it with all the might of her arms and back, sweeping it around in a great arc that ended with a crunch of bone. Aspitis shrieked and fell to the deck holding his face. Blood spurted from between his fingers.

"Hah!" Cadrach shouted with exultant relief. "Look at you, you devil! Now, you will have to find something else to bait your woman-trap with!"

Miriamele fell to her knees, then pushed the oar across the slippery deck to Cadrach. "Go," she panted. "Take this and jump."

The monk stood in confusion for a moment, as if he could not remember where he was, then staggered to the side of the ship. He closed his eyes and muttered some words, then plunged overboard. Miriamele rose and took a last look at the earl, who was bubbling red froth out onto the deck, then scrambled over the railing and pushed herself out into emptiness. For a moment she was falling, flying through the dark. When the water closed on her like a cold fist, she wondered if she would ever come back up, or if instead she would just con- tinue downward into the ultimate depths, into blackness and quiet. . . .

She did come up. When she had reached the boat and helped Cadrach to clamber aboard, they fitted the oars and began to row away from the wounded ship. The storm still hovered overhead, but it was diminishing. *Eadne Cloud* grew smaller behind them until it was only a point of burning light on the black horizon, a tiny flame like a dying star.

7

Storm King's Anvil

♦

At the northernmost edge of the world the mountain stood, an upthrusting fang of icy stone that shadowed the entire landscape, towering high above even the other peaks. For long weeks the smokes and steams and vapors had crept from vents in the mountain's side. Now they wreathed Stormspike's crown, spinning in the awesome winds that circled the mountain, gathering and darkening as though they sucked the very substance of ultimate night from between the stars.

The storm grew and spread. The few scattered folk who still lived within sight of the terrible mountain huddled in their longhouses as the beams creaked and the wind howled. What seemed an unceasing blizzard of snow piled above their walls and onto their roofs, until all that remained were white mounds like so many grave barrows, marked as dwellings of the living only by the thin pennants of smoke that fluttered above the chimney-holes.

The vast expanse of open land known as the Frostmarch was also engulfed by driving snows. Only a few years before, the vast plain had been dotted with small hamlets, thriving towns and settlements fed by the traffic of the Wealdhelm and Frostmarch roads. After half a dozen seasons of continuous snow, with crops long dead and virtually all the animals fled or eaten, the land had become a desolate waste. Those who huddled in the foothills along its border or in the sheltering forests knew it as the home only of wolves and wandering ghosts, and had come to call the Frostmarch by a new name—the Storm King's Anvil. Now an even greater storm, a dreadful hammer of frost and cold, was pounding on that anvil once more.

The storm's long hand reached out even beyond Erkynland to the south, sending gusts of freezing wind across the open grasslands, turning the Thrithings bone-white for the first time in memory. And snow returned to Perdruin and Nabban—the second time in a season, but only the third time in five centuries, so that those who had once scoffed at the Fire Dancers and their dire warnings now felt a squeeze of fear on their hearts, a fear much more chilling than the powdery snow sifting down onto the domes of the two Sancellans.

Like a tide moving toward some unimaginable high water mark, the storm spread farther than ever before, bringing frost to southern lands that had never felt its touch and draping a great cold shroud over all of Osten Ard. It was a storm that numbed hearts and crushed spirits.

"That way!" the leading rider shouted, pointing to the left. *"Á prenteiz, men*—up and after!" He spurred forward so swiftly that his clouded breath was left hanging in the air behind him. Snow spouted from beneath his horse's hooves.

He bore down on the empty space between two tumbledown, snow-covered dwellings, his mount slashing through the drifts as effortlessly as through fog. A dark shape bolted out into the open from behind one of the buildings and dashed away, bounding erratically across the flat. The leading pursuer vaulted a low, snow-buried fence, landed, and followed close after. The horse's pounding strides obliterated the smaller prints of its fleeing quarry, but there was no need now for tracking: the end was in sight. Half a dozen other riders came hurtling from between the houses and spread out like an opening fan, surrounding the quarry like a riverman's fishing net. A moment to draw the net closed—the riders reining in as a narrowing circle—then the hunt was over. One of the men who had ridden the wing leaned down until his lance touched the captive's heaving side. The leader dismounted and took a step forward.

"Well run," said Duke Fengbald, grinning. "That was excellent sport."

The boy stared up at him, eyes wide with terror.

"Shall I finish him, Lord?" asked the rider with the lance. He gave the boy a hard poke. The child squealed and flinched away from the sharp lance-head.

Fengbald peeled off his gauntlet, then turned and flung it into the rider's face. Its metal beadwork left a cross-hatching on the man's cheek that welled with blood. "Dog!" Fengbald scowled. "What am I—a demon? You will be whipped for that." The rider shied away, pulling his horse a few steps back from the circle. Fengbald glared after him. "I do not murder innocent children." He turned his eyes down to the cowering boy. "We had a game, that is all. Children love games. This one has played with us as well as he could." The duke retrieved his gauntlet and put it back on, then smiled. "And a merry chase you led us, boy. What is your name?"

The child grimaced, baring his teeth like a treed cat, but made no sound.

"Ah, too bad," Fengbald said with a philosophical air. "If he will not talk, he will not talk. Put him with the rest—one of these shack-women will feed him. They say a bitch will always nurse a stranger's pups."

One of Fengbald's men-at-arms dismounted and grabbed the boy, who put up no resistance as he was draped across the front of the soldier's saddle.

"I think he is the last," said Fengbald. "The last of our sport, too. A shame—but still, better than if we let them run ahead of us and spoil our surprise." He grinned broadly, pleased with his own wit. "Come. I want a warm cup of wine to take off the chill. This was a hard, cold ride."

He vaulted up into the saddle, then swung his mount around and led his company back into the snow-smothered remnants of Gadrinsett.

Duke Fengbald's red tent sat in the middle of the snowy meadow like a ruby in a puddle of milk. The silver falcon, the duke's family emblem, stretched its wings from corner to corner above the door-flap; in the stiff winds that blew down the river valley, the great bird trembled as though longing to take flight. The tents of the duke's army were clustered all around, but set at a respectful distance.

Inside, Fengbald reclined on a pile of figured cushions, his cup of mulled wine—several times refilled since he had returned—held loosely, his dark hair unbound and trailing down across his shoulders. At Elias' coronation Fengbald had been lean as a young hound. Now the master of Falshire, Utanyeat, and the Westfold had grown a little soft in the waist and jowls. A fair-haired woman kneeled on the floor near his feet. A thin page, pale and anxious-looking, waited at his lord's right hand.

On the far side of the brazier that warmed the tent was a tall man, squint-eyed and bearded, dressed in the leather and rough wool of the Thrithings-dweller. Refusing to sit as city-folk did, he stood spread-legged, arms crossed. When he shifted, his necklace of finger-bones made a clinking music.

"What else is there to know?" he demanded. "Why more talking?"

Fengbald stared at him, eyes slowly blinking. He was a little befuddled by drink, which for once seemed to curb his belligerence. "I must like you, Lezh-draka," he said at last, "because otherwise I would have become sick of your questions long ago."

The mercenary chieftain stared back, unimpressed. "We know where they are. What more do we ask?"

The duke took another drink, then wiped his mouth with the sleeve of his silken shirt and gestured to his page. "More, Isaak." He returned his attention to Lezhdraka. "I learned some things from old Guthwulf, for all his failings. I have been given the keys to a great kingdom. They are in my hand, and I will not throw them away by acting too fast."

"Keys to a kingdom?" said the Thrithings-man scornfully. "What stone-dweller nonsense is that?"

Fengbald seemed pleased by the mercenary's incomprehension. "How do you plains-folk ever hope to drive me and the other city-dwellers into the sea, as you are always babbling about? You have no craft, Lezhdraka, no craft at all. Just go and fetch the old man. You like the night air—do your people not sleep, eat, piss, and sport beneath the stars?" The duke chuckled.

The High King's Hand, having turned to watch his page fill his cup, did not witness the Thrithings-man's venomous look as he left the tent. But for the wind strumming the fabric, the tent fell quiet.

"So, my sweet," Fengbald said at last, prodding the silent woman with his slippered foot, "how does it feel to know that you belong to the man who will one day hold all the land in his grasp?" When she did not reply, he pushed her again, more roughly. "Speak, woman."

She looked up slowly. Her pretty face was empty, drained of life as a corpse's. "It is good, my lord," she murmured at last, the Westerling words thickly accented by a Hernystiri burr. She let her head sink back down, her hair falling like a curtain before her features. The duke looked around impatiently.

"And you, Isaak? What do you think?"

"It is well, master," the page said hurriedly. "If you say it will happen, it will happen."

Fengbald smiled. "Of course it will. How can I fail?" He paused for a moment, frowning at the boy's expression, then shrugged. There were worse things than being feared.

"Only a fool," he resumed, quickly warming to the topic once more, "only a fool, I say, could not see that King Elias is a dying man." He waved his hand expansively, slopping a little wine over the rim of his cup. "Whether he has caught some wasting illness, or whether the priest Pryrates is slowly poisoning him, I do not care. The red priest is an idiot if he thinks he can rule the kingdom—he is the most hated man in Osten Ard. No, when Elias dies, only someone of noble blood will be able to rule. And who will that be? Guthwulf has gone blind and run away." He laughed shortly. "Benigaris of Nabban? He cannot even rule his own mother. And Skali the Rimmersman is no more noble or civilized than that animal Lezhdraka. So when I have killed Josua—if he even truly lives—and put down this petty rebellion, who else will be fit to rule?" Excited by his own words, he drained the remainder of his cup in a single draught. "Who else? And who would oppose me? The king's daughter, that fickle slut?" He paused and eyed the page intently, so that the young boy lowered his gaze. "No, perhaps if Miriamele came begging to me on her knees, I *might* make her my queen—but I would keep her closely watched. And she would be punished for spurning me." He smirked and leaned forward, placing his hand on the pale neck of the woman who knelt before him. "But never fear, little Feurgha, I would not cast you aside for her. I will keep you, too." As she shrunk away he tightened his hand, holding her, enjoying the tension of her resistance.

The tent flap bulged and flapped inward. Lezhdraka entered, snowflakes shimmering in his hair and beard. He held the arm of an old man whose bald head was red with too much sun and whose white ruff of beard was stained and discolored by the juices of citril root. Lezhdraka roughly shoved the man forward. The captive took a few stumbling steps, then fell stiffly to his knees at Fengbald's feet and did not look up. His neck and shoulders, exposed by the open collar of his thin shirt, were covered with yellowing bruises.

When the nervous page had filled the duke's cup once more, Fengbald cleared his throat. "You look somewhat familiar. Do I know you?" The old man wagged his head from side to side. "So. You may look up. You claim to be the Lord Mayor of Gadrinsett?"

The old man nodded slowly. "I am," he croaked.

"You *were*. Not that there would be much glory in being mayor of this pest-hole in any case. Tell me what you know about Josua."

"I . . . I don't understand, Lord."

Fengbald leaned forward and gave him a brief but solid push. The Lord Mayor toppled over to lie on his side; he did not seem to have the strength to sit up again. "Don't play the fool with me, old man. What have you heard?"

Still curled on his side, the Lord Mayor coughed. "Nothing that you have not learned, Duke Fengbald," he quavered, "nothing. Riders came from the evil-omened valley up the Stefflod. They said that Josua Lackhand had escaped from his brother, that he and a band of warriors and magicians had driven out the demons and made a stronghold on the witch-mountain in the middle of the valley. That all who came to join him there would be fed, and have places to live, and that they would be protected from bandits and from . . . and from . . ." his voice dropped, ". . . from the High King's soldiers."

"And you think it is a pity you did not listen to these treasonous rumors, eh?" Fengbald asked. "You think that perhaps Prince Josua might have saved you from the king's vengeance?"

"But we did no wrong, my lord!" the old man moaned. "We did no wrong!"

Fengbald looked at him with perfect coldness. "You harbored traitors, since everyone who joins Josua is a traitor. Now, how many are with him on this witch-mountain?"

The mayor shook his head vehemently. "I do not know, lord. In time, some few hundred of our folk went. The first riders who came said there were five or six score there already, I think."

"Counting women and children?"

"Yes, lord."

Fengbald snapped his fingers. "Isaak, go find a guardsman and bid him come to me."

"Yes, sire." The youth hurried out, happy with any errand that took him out of his master's reach for a few moments.

"A few more questions." The duke settled back against the cushions. "Why did your people believe it was Josua? Why should they leave a safe haven to go to a place of bad reputation?"

The old man shrugged helplessly. "One of the women who lived here claimed she had met Josua—that she had sent him to the rock herself. A gossipy creature, but well-known. She swore that she had fed him at her fire and had marked him instantly as the prince. Many were convinced by her. Others went because . . . because they heard you were coming, Duke Fengbald. People from Erkynland and the western Thrithings came here, fleeing . . . moving east ahead of your lordship's progress." He cringed as if expecting a blow. "Forgive me, lord." A tear ran down his wrinkled cheek.

The tent flap rustled. Isaak the page entered, followed by a helmeted Erkyn-guardsman. "You wanted me, lord?" the soldier said.

"Yes." Fengbald gestured toward the old man. "Take this one back to the pens. Treat him roughly, but do not hurt him. I will wish to speak to him again later." The duke turned. "You and I have things to talk about, Lezhdraka." The guardsman dragged the mayor to his feet. Fengbald watched the process with contempt. "Lord Mayor, is it?" he snorted. "There is not a drop of lordly blood in you, peasant."

The old man's rheumy eyes opened wide, staring at Fengbald. For a moment, it seemed he might do something entirely mad; instead, he shook his head like someone waking from a dream. "My brother was a nobleman," he said hoarsely, then a fresh outpouring of tears spilled down his cheeks. The soldier grabbed his elbow and hastened him out of the tent.

Lezhdraka stared insolently at Fengbald. " '*Do not hurt him*'? I thought you were harder than that, city-man."

A slow, drunken smile spread across Fengbald's face. "What I said was, 'treat him roughly but do not hurt him.' I don't want the rest of his folk to know he will spill his guts any time I ask. And he may prove useful to me somehow, either as a spy in the pens or as a spy among Josua's folk. Those traitors take in all who flee my terrible wrath, do they not?"

The Thrithings-man squinted. "Do you think my horsemen and your armored city-dwellers cannot smash your king's enemies?"

Fengbald waved an admonitory finger. "Never throw a weapon away. You never know when you may need it. That's another lesson that sightless fool Guthwulf taught me." He laughed, then waved his cup. His page scurried after the wine ewer.

Outside, darkness had fallen. The duke's tent glowed crimson, smoldering like an ember half-buried in fireplace ashes.

A rat, Rachel thought bitterly. *Now I'm no better than a rat in the walls.*

She peered out at the darkened kitchen and suppressed a bitter curse. It was just as well that Judith had long since quit the Hayholt. If the huge, galleon-stately Mistress of the Kitchens were to see the condition of her beloved domain, it would probably kill her dead. Rachel the Dragon's own work-callused hands itched as she felt herself torn between a desire to repair the damage and an equally strong urge to throttle whoever had let the castle fall into this dreadful state.

The Hayholt's great kitchen might have become a den of wild dogs. The pantry doors were off their hinges and the few remaining sacks of foodstuffs lay ripped and scattered about the chamber. It was the waste as much as the filth that set a fire of anger burning in Rachel's heart. Flour lay all across the floors, ground into the cracks between flagstones, crisscrossed with the prints of heedless, booted feet. The great ovens were black with grease, the baking paddles charred from inexpert use. Staring out at the wreckage from her hiding hole behind a hanging curtain, Rachel felt tears coursing down her face.

*God should strike those who did this dead. This is wickedness with no purpose—
devil's work.*

And the kitchen, for all the damage done, was one of the places least affected
by the evil changes that had overtaken the Hayholt. Rachel had seen much in
her forays out of hiding, all of it disheartening. The fires were no longer set in
most of the great chambers and the dark hallways were almost misty with cold.
The shadows seemed to have lengthened, as though a strange twilight had
settled over the castle: even on the days when the sun broke through the clouds,
the Hayholt's passages and gardens were steeped in shade. But the night itself
had become almost too frightening to bear. When the dim sun set, Rachel
found herself hiding-places in the abandoned places of the castle and did not
stir until dawn. The unearthly sounds that floated through the darkness were
enough to make her pull her shawl over her head, and sometimes as evening
came along there were shifting, unsolid shapes that hovered just at the edge of
vision. Then, when the bells rang midnight, dark-robed demons silently walked
the halls.

Clearly some dreadful magic was at work all around. The ancient castle
seemed almost to breathe, imbued with a chilling vitality that it had never had
before, for all its illustrious history. Rachel could feel a crouching presence,
patient but alert as a predatory beast, that seemed to inhabit the very stones. No,
this ruined kitchen was only the smallest, mildest sample of the evil Elias had
brought down on her beloved home.

She waited, listening, until she was certain no one was about, then pushed
her way out past the curtain. The closet behind this hanging had a false back
hung with shelves of vinegar and mustard jars; the shelves hid a passageway into
one of the network of corridors that ran behind, above, and beneath the Hayholt's walls. Rachel, who for many weeks now had made her home in these
between-places, still marveled at the web of secret ways that had surrounded
her all her life, unseen and unrecognized as a riot of mole tunnels beneath a
formal garden.

*Now I know where that rascal Simon used to disappear to. By the Blessed Mother,
no wonder I sometimes thought the boy'd been swallowed up by the earth when there was
work to be done.*

She made her way out to the center of the kitchen, moving as quietly as her
stiff old bones would allow so she would not obscure the sounds of anyone
approaching. There were few people left in the great keep these days—Rachel
did not think of the king's white-faced demons as *people*—but there were still
some mercenaries from the Thrithings and elsewhere billeted in the castle's
scores of empty rooms. It was such barbarians as those, Rachel felt sure, who
had reduced Judith's kitchen to its hideous condition. Surely abominations like
those devil-Norns did not even eat earthly food. Drank blood most likely, if
the Book of the Aedon was any guide—and it had been Rachel's only guide
since she was old enough to understand what the priests said.

There was nothing remotely fresh to be found anywhere. More than once

Rachel opened a jar to discover the contents rotted, covered with blue or white mold, but after much patient searching she was able to find two small containers of salted beef and a jug of vegetables pickled in brine that had rolled beneath a table and somehow been missed. She also discovered three loaves of bread, hard and stale, wrapped in a napkin in one of the pantries. Although the sample piece she pulled from a loaf was painfully hard to chew—Rachel had few teeth left, and felt sure that such fare as this would finish off the survivors—it was edible, and when dipped in the beef brine would make a nice change indeed. Still, this raid had turned up scant results. How much longer would she be able to keep herself alive on what she could thieve from the Hayholt's untended larders? Thinking of the days ahead, she shivered. It was horribly cold, even in the rock fastness of the castle's internal passageways. How long could she go on?

She wrapped the fruits of her scavenging in her shawl and dragged the heavy bundle across the floor toward the closet and its hidden door, doing her best to obscure the tracks she made in the flour. When she reached the closet, where the flour—so eerily like the snow outside—had not yet drifted, she unwrapped her take for a moment and used the shawl to brush away all the nearest marks, so that no one might wonder at tracks that disappeared into an abandoned closet and failed to come out again.

As she was rebundling her salvage, she heard voices in the hallway outside. A moment later, the great kitchen doors began to swing inward. Her heart suddenly beating as swiftly as a bird's, Rachel leaned forward and caught at the curtain with fumbling fingers, then pulled the hanging across the closet entrance just as the outer door thumped back against the wall and booted footsteps sounded on the flagstones.

"Damn him and his grinning face, where is he?!"

Rachel's eyes widened as she recognized the king's voice.

"I know I heard someone in here!" Elias shouted. There was a crash as something was swept off one of the knife-scarred tables, then the rhythmic clatter of someone pacing back and forth across the great length of the kitchen floor. "I hear everything in this castle, every foot-step, every murmur, until my head pounds with it! He must have been here! Who else could it be?"

"I told you, Majesty, I do not know."

The Mistress of Chambermaids' heart skipped and seemed to stumble between beats. That was Pryrates. She thought of him as he had stood before her—her knife standing from his back, no more effective than a twig—and felt herself sagging toward the floor. She reached out a hand to steady herself and brushed against a copper trivet hanging on the wall, setting it swinging. Rachel grasped it, holding its heavy weight out from the wall so that it would make no noise.

Like a rat! Her thoughts were wild and fragmented. *Like a rat. Trapped in the walls. Cats outside.*

"Aedon burn and blast him, he is not to leave my side!" Elias' hoarse voice, teetering on the edge of some strange despair, seemed almost to reflect Rachel's own panic. "Hengfisk!" he shouted. "Damn your soul, where are you!?" The sound of the king's furious pacing resumed. "When I find him, I will slit his throat."

"*I* will prepare your cup for you, Majesty. I will do it for you now. Come."

"It's not just that. What is he doing? Where could he be? He has no right to go off wandering!"

"He will be back soon, I'm sure," the priest said. He sounded impatient. "His needs are few, and easily satisfied. Come now, Elias, we should go back to your chamber."

"He's hiding!" Rachel could hear the king's steps suddenly grow louder. He stopped, and she heard a squeak of hinges as he yanked at one of the broken doors. "He is hiding in the shadows somewhere!"

The footsteps approached. Rachel held her breath, trying to be as still as stone. She heard the king come nearer, muttering angrily as he yanked at doors and kicked piles of fallen hangings out of his way. Her head whirled. Darkness seemed to descend before her eyes, a darkness threaded with fluttering sparks of light.

"Majesty!" Pryrates voice was sharp. The king stopped thrashing and quiet descended on the kitchen. "This is accomplishing nothing. Come. Let me prepare your cup. You are overtired."

Elias groaned softly, a terrible sound like a beast in final pain. At last, he said: "When will it all end, Pryrates?"

"Soon, Majesty." The priest's voice resumed its soothing tone. "There are certain rituals to be performed on Harrow's Eve. Then, after the year turns, the star will come and that will show that the final days are at hand. Soon after, your waiting will be over."

"Sometimes I cannot bear the pain, Pryrates. Sometimes I wonder if anything is worth this pain."

"Surely the greatest gift of all is worth any price, Elias." Pryrates' footfalls moved closer. "Just as the pain is beyond what others must bear, so are you brave beyond other men. Your reward will be equally splendid."

The two men moved away from her hiding spot. Rachel let out her breath in a near-silent hiss.

"I am burning up."

"I know, my king." The doors thumped shut behind them.

Rachel the Dragon sank to a crouch on the closet floor. Her hand shook as she traced the sign of the Tree.

Guthwulf could feel stone at his back and stone beneath his feet, and yet at the same moment he felt that he stood before a great abyss. He folded to his knees and reached cautiously before him, patting at the ground, certain that any moment he would feel his hand waving in empty space. But nothing was before him but more of the endless stone of the passageway floor.

"God help me, I am cursed!" he shouted. His voice rattled and echoed from a distant ceiling, obliterating for a moment the whispering chorus that had surrounded him for a length of time he could not guess. "Cursed!" He fell forward, cradling his face on his outstretched arms in an unconscious attitude of prayer, and wept.

He knew only that he must be somewhere beneath the castle. Since the moment he had stepped through the unseen doorway, fleeing from flames that burned so hot that he was certain they would char him to cinders, he had been as lost as a damned soul. He had wandered through these mazy depths so long that he could no longer remember the feeling of wind and sunshine on his face, no longer recall the taste of food other than cold worms and beetles. And always the . . . *others* . . . had accompanied him, the quiet murmurs just below the level of intelligibility, the ghostly things that seemed to move beside him but mocked his blindness by slipping away before he could touch them. Countless days he had stumbled unseeing through this netherworld of mournful whispers and shifting forms, until life was only that which made him sensible to torment. He had become little more than a cord tight-stretched between terror and hunger. He was cursed. There could be no other explanation.

Guthwulf rolled over onto his side and slowly sat up. If Heaven was punishing him for the wickedness of his life, how long would it go on? He had always scoffed at the priests and their talk of eternity, but now he knew that even an hour could stretch to a terrible, infinite length. What could he do to end this dreadful sentence?

"I have sinned!" he screamed, his voice a hoarse croak. "I have lied and killed, even when I knew it was wrong! *Sinned!"* The echoes flew and dissipated. "Sinned," he whispered.

Guthwulf crawled forward another cubit, praying that the pit he had sensed was truly there before him, a hole into which he would tumble and perhaps find the release of death—if he were not already dead. Anything was preferable to this unending emptiness. Were it not as grave a sin as the murder of another, he would have long since smashed his head against the stone that surrounded him until life fled, but he feared that he would only find himself awakened to an even more dreadful sentence after the added crime of self-slaughter. He groped ahead in desperation, but his crawling fingers found nothing but more stone, the unending, winding passageway floor.

Surely this was but another element of his punishment, the shifting reality of his prison. Just as a moment earlier he had known beyond doubt that a great chasm lay before him—a chasm that his fingers now proved did not exist—he had at other times encountered great columns that rose to the ceiling, and had run his hands over their intricate carvings, trying to read in their crafted textures some message of hope, only to find a moment later that he stood in the midst of a great and empty chamber as vacant of columns as it was of other human company.

What of the others, he suddenly wondered? What of Elias and the devil Pryrates? Surely if divine justice had been meted out, they had not escaped—not with crimes on their souls vaster and more evil by far than Guthwulf's poor tally. What had happened to them, and to all the other uncountable sinners who had lived and died on the spinning earth? Was each condemned to his or her own solitary damnation? Did others as afflicted as Guthwulf wander just on the other side of the stone walls, wondering if they, too, were the last creatures in the universe?

He clambered to his feet and stumbled toward the wall, pounding on it with the flat of his hand. "Here I am!" he cried. "I am!" He let his fingers drag down the cool, faintly damp surface as he slumped to the floor again.

In all the years when he had been alive—for he could not help but feel that his life was now over, even if he still seemed to inhabit a body that hurt and hungered—Guthwulf had never realized the simple wonder of companionship. He had enjoyed his associations with others—the rough company of men, the satisfying compliance of women—but he had always been able to do without them. Friends had died or left. Some Guthwulf had been forced to turn his back on when they opposed him, some one or two he had been forced to remove, despite previous comradeship. Even the king had turned on him at last, but Guthwulf had been strong. To need was to be weak. To be weak was not to be a man.

Now Guthwulf thought of the most precious thing he had. It was not his honor, for he knew he had given that up when he did not raise a hand to help Elias combat his growing madness; it was not his pride, for he had lost that with his sight, when he became a staggering invalid who had to wait for a servant to bring him a chamber pot. Even his courage was no longer his to give or receive, for it had fled when Elias made him touch the gray sword and he had felt the blade's horrible, cold song run through him like poison. No, the only thing left to him was the most ephemeral of all, the tiny spark that still lived and still hoped, buried though it was beneath such a weight of despair. Perhaps that was a soul, that thing the priests prattled about, and perhaps it wasn't—he no longer cared. But he did know that he would give even that last, crucial spark away if he could only have companionship once more, if there could be some end to this hideous loneliness.

The empty darkness suddenly filled with a great wind, a wind that blew through him but did not rustle a hair on his head. Guthwulf groaned weakly: he had felt this before. The void that surrounded him filled with chittering voices that brushed by him moaning and sighing words that he could not understand, but that he felt were full of loss and dread. He stretched out a hand, knowing as he did so that there was nothing to grasp . . . but his hand touched something.

With a gasp of shock, Guthwulf snatched the hand back. A moment later, as the rush of wailing shades dwindled down the endless corridor, something touched him again, this time bumping against his outstretched leg. He squeezed his eyelids shut, as though whatever was there might horrify even the eyes of a blind man. There was another insistent push at his leg. He slowly reached out once more and felt . . . fur.

The cat—for surely that was what it was: he could feel its back arching beneath his hand, the sinuous tail sliding between his fingers—thumped his knee with its small, hard head. He let his fingers rest on it, not daring to move for fear of frightening it away. Guthwulf held his breath, half-certain that this would prove to be like other things of this inconstant netherworld, that a moment's time would find it vanished into air. But the cat seemed pleased with its own substantiality; it put two paws up on his thin leg, delicately sinking its claws into his skin as it moved beneath his careful touch.

For a moment, as he scratched and patted, and as the unseen animal wriggled with pleasure, he remembered that he had eaten nothing but crawling things since he had come to this place of damnation. The warm flesh moved beneath his hand, a starving man's banquet of meat and hot, salty blood separated from him only by a thin layer of fur.

It would be so easy, he thought, his fingers gently circling the cat's neck. *Easy. Easy.* Then, as his fingers tightened just a little bit, the cat began to purr. The vibrations moved up through its throat and into his fingers, a throb of contentment and trust as piercingly beautiful as any music of angelic choirs. For the second time in an hour, Guthwulf burst into tears.

When the one-time Earl of Utanyeat awoke, he had no idea how long he had been asleep, but for the first time in many days he felt as though he had truly rested. His moment of peace ended quickly when he realized that the warm body that had nestled in his lap was gone. He was alone once more.

Just as the emptiness swept back down upon him, there was a soft pressure against his leg, then a small cold nose pressed against his hand.

"Back," he whispered. "You came back." He reached down to touch the cat's head, but instead found he was pressing something smaller, something warm and slickly wet. The cat purred as he felt the thing that it had pushed against his hip: it was a rat, recently killed.

Guthwulf sat up, saying a silent prayer of thanks, and pulled the offering apart with trembling fingers. He returned an equal portion to the founder of the feast.

♔

Deep beneath the dark bulk of Stormspike Mountain, the eyes of Utuk'ku Seyt-Hamakha suddenly opened. She lay motionless in the onyx crypt that was her bed, staring up into the perfect blackness of her stone chamber. She had wandered far along her web, into places in the dreamworld that only the eldest of the immortals could go—and in the shadows of the most distant improbabilities, she had seen something she had not expected. A sharp sliver of unease pierced her ancient heart. Somewhere at the outermost edges of her designs, a strand had snapped. What that meant, she could not know, but an uncertainty had been added, a flaw in the pattern she had woven so long and so faultlessly.

The Norn Queen sat up, her long-fingered hand clawing for her silver mask. She placed it on her face, so that once more she appeared as serenely emotionless as the moon, then she sent out a cold and fleeting thought. A door opened in the blackness and dark shapes entered, bringing with them a little light, for they, too, wore masks, theirs of faintly glowing pale stone. They helped their mistress to rise from her vault and brought her royal robes of ice-white and silver, which they wrapped about her with the ritual care of burial priests swaddling the dead. When she was dressed, they scuttled away, leaving Utuk'ku alone once more. She sat for a while in her lightless chamber; if she breathed, she made no sound doing so. Only the almost imperceptible creaking of the mountain's roots sullied the pure silence.

After some time, the Norn Queen rose and made her way out through the twisting corridors that her servants had carved from the mountain's flesh in the deeps of the past. She came at last to the Chamber of the Breathing Harp and took her seat upon the great throne of black rock. The Harp hovered in the mists that rose from the vast well, its shifting dimensions glinting in the lights that shone from the deeps below. The Lightless Ones were chanting somewhere in the depths of Stormspike, their hollow voices tracing the shapes of songs that had been old and already forbidden back in the Lost Garden, Venyha Do'sae. Utuk'ku sat and stared at the Harp, letting her mind trace its complexities as the steams of the pit met the chamber's icy air and turned to frost upon her eyelashes.

Ineluki was not there. He had gone, as he sometimes did, into that place that was no place, where he alone could go—a place as far beyond the dreamworld as dreams were beyond waking, as far beyond death as death was beyond living. For this time, the Norn Queen would have to keep her own counsel.

Although her shining silver face was as impassive as ever, Utuk'ku nevertheless felt a shadow of impatience as she stared into the untenanted Well. Time was growing short now. A lifetime for one of the scurrying mortals was a scant season for the eldest, so the short span that stretched between now and the hour of her triumph could seem scarcely more than a few heartbeats if she chose to perceive it so. But she did not choose that. Every moment was precious. Every instant brought victory closer—but for that victory to come to pass, there could be no mistakes.

The Queen of the Norns was troubled.

8

Nights of Fire

✦

Simon's blood seemed almost to boil in his veins. He looked around him, at the white-blanketed hills, at the dark trees bending in the fierce, chilling winds, and wondered how he could feel so full of fire. It was excitement—the thrill of responsibility . . . and of danger. Simon felt very much alive.

He leaned his cheek against Homefinder's neck and patted her firm shoulder. Her wind-cooled skin was damp with sweat.

"She is tired," Hotvig said, cinching the strap on his own mount's saddle. "She is not meant for such fast traveling."

"She's fine," Simon shot back. "She's stronger than you think."

"The Thrithings-folk know horses if they know anything," Sludig said over his shoulder. He turned away from the tree trunk, lacing his breeches. "Do not be so proud, Simon."

Simon stared at the Rimmersman for a moment before speaking. "It is not pride. I rode this horse a long way. I will keep her."

Hotvig raised his hand placatingly. "I did not mean to make you angry. It is just that you are thought of well by Prince Josua. You are his knight. You could have one of our fleet clan-horses for the asking."

Simon turned his stare on the braid-bearded grasslander, then tried to smile. "I know you meant it well, Hotvig, and one of your horses would be a gift indeed. But this is different. I called this horse Homefinder, and that is where she will go with me. Home."

"And where is that home, young thane?" asked one of the other Thrithings-men.

"The Hayholt," Simon said firmly.

Hotvig laughed. "The place where Josua's brother rules? You and your horse must be mighty travelers indeed, to ride into such fierce weather."

"That's as may be." Simon turned to look at the others, squinting against the oblique afternoon light streaming past the trees. "If you're all ready, it's time to go. If we wait longer, the storm may die. We'll be under the light of an almost full moon tonight. I'd rather have the snow and the sentries all hunkered down over a fire."

Sludig started to say something, then thought better of it. The Thrithings-men nodded in agreement and swung easily into their saddles.

"Lead on, thane." Hotvig's laugh was short but not unfriendly. The little company eased down out of the copse and back into the bitter clutches of the wind.

Simon was almost as grateful for the simple chance to *do* something as he was of this evidence of Josua's trust. The days of increasingly bad weather, coupled with the important duties granted to his companions but not to him, had left Simon restless and ill-tempered. Binabik, Geloë, and Strangyeard were in deep discussion over the swords and the Storm King; Deornoth oversaw the arming and preparing of New Gadrinsett's ragtag army; even Sangfugol, thankless as he found the task, had Towser to watch. Before Prince Josua had called him to his tent, Simon had begun to feel as he had in days he had hoped long past—like a drummer boy hurrying along after the Imperator's soldiers.

"Just a little spying work," Josua had called this task, but to Simon it was almost as splendid as the moment he had been knighted. He was to take some of Hotvig's grasslanders and ride out for a look at the approaching force.

"Don't do *anything*," the prince had said emphatically. "Just look. Count tents—and horses if you see them. Look for banners and crests if there's enough light. But don't be seen, and if you are, ride away. Quickly."

Simon had promised. A knight leading men to war: that was what he had become. Impatient to be off on this glorious quest, he had squirmed—unobtrusively, he hoped—as he waited for Josua to finish with his instructions.

Sludig, surprisingly, had asked to come along. The Rimmersman was still smarting over Simon's high honors, but Simon suspected that, like Simon himself, Sludig was feeling a little left out, and would even prefer being Simon's subordinate for a short time to the frustration of waiting atop Sesuad'ra. Sludig was a warrior, not a general: the Rimmersman was interested only when the fighting became real, blade on blade.

Hotvig had also offered his services. Simon guessed that Prince Josua, who had come to both like and trust the Thrithings-man, might have asked Hotvig to go along and keep an eye on his youngest knight. Surprisingly, this possibility did not bother Simon. He had begun to understand a little of the burden of power, and knew that Josua was trying to do his best for all concerned. So, Simon had decided, let Hotvig be Josua's eye: he would give the grasslander something good to report.

The storm was worsening. All the Stefflod river valley was covered with snow, the river itself only a dark streak running through a field of white. Simon pulled his cloak tight and wrapped his woolen scarf more tightly around his face.

The Thrithings-men, for all their confident bantering, were more than a little frightened by the changes the storm winds had brought to their familiar grasslands. Simon saw their eyes widen as they looked around, the uneasy way they spurred their horses through the deeper drifts, the small reflexive signs to ward evil that they made with crossed fingers. Only Sludig, child of the frozen north, seemed unaffected by the bleak weather.

"This is truly a black winter," said Hotvig. "If I had not already believed Josua when he said there was an evil spirit at work, I would believe him now."

"A black winter, yes—and summer only just ended." Sludig flicked snow from his eyes. "The lands north of the Frostmarch have not seen a spring for more than a year. We fight against more than men."

Simon frowned. He did not know how superstitious the clan men were, but he did not want to stir up any fears that might interfere with their task. "It *is* a magical storm," he said loudly enough to be heard over the cloak-snapping wind, "but it's still only a storm. The snows can't hurt you—but they might freeze off your tail."

One of the Thrithings-men turned to him with a grin. "If tails freeze, then you will suffer most, young thane, riding that bony horse." The other men chortled. Simon, pleased at the way he had changed the conversation, laughed with them.

Afternoon swiftly melted into evening as they rode, a journey almost silent but for the soft chuffing of the horses' hooves and the eternal moaning of the wind. The sun, which had been overmatched by clouds all day, at last gave up and dropped down below the low hills. A violet, shadowless light enveloped the valley. Soon it was almost too dark for the little company to see where they rode; the moon, enmeshed in clouds, was all but invisible. There was no sign of stars.

"Should we stop and make camp?" Hotvig shouted above the wind.

Simon considered for a moment. "I don't think so," he said at last. "We are not too far away—maybe another hour's riding at most. I think we could risk a torch."

"Should we also blow some trumpets?" Sludig asked loudly. "Or perhaps we could find some criers to run ahead and announce that we are coming to spy out Fengbald's position."

Simon scowled but did not rise to the bait. "We still have the hills between us and Fengbald's camp at Gadrinsett. If the people who fled his army are right about where he is, we can easily put our light out before we are within sight of his sentries." He raised his voice for emphasis. "Do you think it would be better to wait until morning light, when Fengbald's men are rested and there is sun to make us even easier to spot?"

Sludig waved his hand, conceding.

Hotvig produced a torch—a good, thick branch, wrapped in strips of cloth and soaked in pitch—and struck a spark with his flints. He shielded the flame from the winds until it was burning well, then raised the brand and rode a few paces ahead of the others, mounting the slope of the riverbank as he headed for the greater shelter of the hillside. "Follow, then," he called.

The procession resumed, moving a little more slowly now. They passed across the uneven terrain of the hills, letting the horses feel their way. Hotvig's torch became a jogging ball of flame, the only thing throughout the storm-darkened valley that could hold a wandering eye: Simon almost felt he tracked a will-of-the-wisp across the misty barrens. The world had become a long black tunnel, an endless corridor spiraling down into the earth's lightless heart.

"Anybody know a song?" Simon asked at last. His voice sounded frail lifted against the mournful wind.

"A song?" Sludig wrinkled his brow in surprise.

"Why not? We are still far off from anyone. In any case, you are an arm's length away and I can scarcely hear you over this damnable wind. So, a song, yes!"

Hotvig and his Thrithings-men did not volunteer to sing, but they seemed to have no objection. Sludig made a face, as if the very idea was foolish beyond belief.

"Up to me, then?" Simon smiled. "Up to me. Too bad that Shem Horseg-room isn't here. He knows more songs and stories than anyone." He wondered briefly what had happened to Shem. Was he still living happily in the Hayholt's great stables? "I'll sing you one of his. A song about Jack Mundwode."

"Who?" asked one of the Thrithings-men.

"Jack Mundwode. A famous bandit. He lived in Aldheorte Forest."

"If he lived at all," scoffed Sludig.

"If he lived at all," Simon agreed. "So I'll sing one of the songs about Mund-wode." He wrapped his reins around his hand once more, then leaned back in the saddle, trying to remember the first verse.

"Bold Jack Mundwode,"

he began at last, timing the song to the thudding rhythm of Homefinder's pace;

"Said: 'I'll go to Erchester,
I've heard that there's a maiden sweet
Who is a-living there.'

" 'Hruse her name is:
Hair of softly flowing gold,
Shoulders pale as winter snows,
Hruse young and fair.'

"Jack's bandits warned him,
Said: 'The town's no place for you.
Their lord has sworn to take your head,
He's a-waiting there.'

"Jack only laughed then.
Lord Constable he knew of old

Many times had Jack escaped him
By a slender hair.

"Jack put on rich dress,
Shining silks and promise-chain
Told Osgal: 'You're the servant
Who'll stand behind my chair.

" 'Duke of Flowers I'll be,'
Said Jack, '—a wealthy nobleman.
A man of grace and gifts and gold
Come to the county's fair.' "

Simon sang just loudly enough to let his voice carry above the wind. It was a long tune, with many verses.

They followed Hotvig's torch through the hills as Simon continued the story of how Jack Mundwode entered into Erchester in disguise and charmed Hruse's father, a baron who thought he had found a wealthy suitor for his daughter. Although Simon had to pause from time to time to catch his breath, or to remember words—Shem had taught him the song a very long time ago—his voice grew more sure as the ride progressed. He sang about how Jack the trickster paid court to the beautiful Hruse—sincerely, since he had fallen in love at his first sight of her—and sat beside the unknowing Lord Constable at the baron's supper. Jack even convinced the greedy baron to take a magical rose bush as Hruse's dowry, a bush whose delicate blossoms each contained a shining gold Imperator, and which, the supposed Duke of Flowers assured Hruse's father and the constable, would bear fresh coins every season as long as its roots were in the ground.

It was only as Simon neared the end of the song—he had begun the verse that told how a drunken remark by the bandit Osgal spoiled Jack's disguise and led to his capture by the constable's men—that Hotvig reined up his horse and waved his arm for silence.

"I think that we are very close." The Thrithings-man pointed. The hillside sloped downward ahead, and even through the swirling snows it was clear that open land lay before them.

Sludig rode up beside Simon. The Rimmersman's frosty breath hung in the air around his head. "Finish the song on the way back, lad. It is a good tale."

Simon nodded.

Hotvig rolled over his saddle and down onto the ground, then snuffed his torch in a drift of snow. He patted it dry on his saddle blanket before slipping it under his belt and turning to Simon with an expectant look.

"Let's go, then," Simon said. "But carefully, since we have no light."

They spurred their horses forward. Before they had gone halfway down the long hill, Simon saw distant lights, a sparse collection of gleaming dots.

"There!" he pointed, and immediately worried he had spoken too loudly. His heart was hammering. "Is that Fengbald's camp?"

"It is what is left of Gadrinsett," said Sludig. "Fengbald's camp will be near it."

In the valley before them, where the invisible Stefflod met the equally unseeable Ymstrecca, only a scatter of fires burned. But on the far side, camped near what Simon felt sure was the Ymstrecca's northern bank, a greater concentration of lights lay spread across the darkened meadows, a myriad of fiery points arranged in rough circles.

"You're right." Simon stared. "That will be the Erkynguard there. Fengbald is probably in the middle of those rings of tents. Wouldn't it be nice to put an arrow through *his* blanket."

Hotvig rode a little nearer. "He is there, yes. And I would like to kill him myself, just to pay him for the things he said about the Stallion Clan when we last met. But we have other things to do tonight."

Stung, Simon took a breath. "Of course," he said at last. "Josua needs to know the strength of armies." He paused to think. "Would it be useful to count the fires? Then we should know how many troops he has brought."

Sludig frowned. "Unless we know how many men share each fire, it will mean little."

Simon nodded, musing. "Yes. So we count the fires now, then ride closer and find out if each tent has one, or every dozen."

"Not too close," Sludig warned. "I like a fight as much as any God-fearing man, but I like odds that are a little better."

"You are very wise." Simon smiled. "You should take Binabik on as your apprentice."

Sludig snorted.

After counting the tiny points of flame, they rode down the hill.

"We are lucky," Hotvig said quietly. "I think the stone-dweller sentries will be standing close to their campfires tonight, staying out of the wind."

Simon shivered, bending a little closer to Homefinder's neck. "Not all stone-dwellers are that smart."

As they came down onto the snowy meadows, Simon again felt his heart racing. Despite his fear, there was something heady and exciting about being so close to the enemy, about moving silently through the darkness scarcely more than an arrow flight from armed men. He felt very alive, as though the wind blew right through his cloak and shirt, making his skin tingle. At the same time, he was half-convinced that Fengbald's troops had already spotted his little company—that even at this moment the entire Erkynguard was crouching with bows drawn, eyes glittering in the deep darkness between the shadowy tents.

They made a slow circuit around the outside of Fengbald's camp, trying to move from the shelter of one clump of trees to another, but trees were in unpleasantly short supply on the edge of the grasslands. It was only when they came close to the riverside and the westernmost end of the encampment that they felt themselves safe for a while from staring eyes.

"If there are less than a thousand men at arms here," Sludig declared, "then I'm a Hyrka."

"There are Thrithings-men in that camp," Hotvig said. "Men-of-no-clan from the Lake Thrithing, if I know anything."

"How can you tell?" Simon asked. At this distance the tents showed no markings or distinctive features—many of them were little more than cloth shelters staked to the ground and then roped to bushes or standing stones—and none of the inhabitants of the camp's perimeter were out in such fierce weather.

"Listen." Hotvig cupped his hand behind his ear. His scarred face was solemn.

Simon held his breath and listened. The windsong covered everything, drowning even the sound of the men riding beside him. "Listen to what?"

"Listen with more care," said Hotvig. "It is the harnesses." Beside him, one of his clansmen nodded his head solemnly.

Simon strained to hear what the grasslander did. He thought he could make out a faint clinking. "That?" he asked.

Hotvig smiled, showing the gap in his teeth. He knew it was an impressive feat. "Those horses are wearing Lakeland harnesses—I am sure of it."

"You can tell what kind of harnesses they wear by the sound?" Simon was astonished. Did these meadow-men have ears like rabbits?

"Our bridles are different as the feathers of birds," one of the other Thrithings-men said. "Lakeland and Meadow and High Thrithings harness are all different to our ears as your voice is from the northerner's, young thane."

"How else could we know our own horses at night, from a distance?" Hotvig frowned. "By the Four-Footed, how do you stone-dwellers stop your neighbors stealing from you?"

Simon shook his head. "So we know where Fengbald's mercenaries are from. But can you tell how many of the men down there are Thrithings-folk?"

"By their shelters, I guess that more than half these troops are from the un-clanned," Hotvig replied.

Simon's expression turned grim. "And good fighters, I'd wager."

Hotvig nodded. There was more than a trace of pride in the set of his jaw. "All the grasslanders can fight. But the ones without clans are the most . . ." he searched for a word, ". . . the most fierce."

"And the Erkynguard are no sweeter." Sludig's voice was sour, but his eyes held a faintly predatory spark. "It will be a strong and bloody battle when iron and iron meet."

"Time to go back." Simon looked out to the stripe of dark emptiness that was the Ymstrecca. "We've been lucky so far."

The little company crossed back over the exposed spaces. Simon again felt their vulnerability, the closeness of a thousand enemies, and thanked the heavens that the stormy weather had enabled them to come close to the camp without having to leave their horses behind. The idea of having to flee on foot if they were discovered by mounted sentries—and flee through wind and snow at that—was a disheartening one.

They reached the shelter of a copse of wind-stripped elders that stood forlornly on the slope of the lowest-lying foothills. As Simon turned to stare back at the sprinkling of lights that marked the edge of Fengbald's placid camp, the anger that had been hidden by his excitement suddenly began to well inside him—a cold fury at the thought of all those soldiers lying securely in their tents, like caterpillars that had gorged on the leaves of a beautiful garden and now lay safely wrapped in their cocoons. These were the despoilers, the Erkynguardsmen who had come to arrest Morgenes, who had tried to throw down Josua's castle at Naglimund. Under Fengbald, they had crushed the whole town of Falshire as thoughtlessly as a child might kick over an anthill. Most importantly to Simon, they had driven him from his home, and now they would try to drive him from Sesuad'ra as well.

"Which of you has a bow?" he said abruptly.

One of the Thrithings-men looked up in surprise. "I do."

"Give it to me. Yes, and an arrow, too." Simon took the bow and hooked it over his saddle horn, still staring out at the dark shapes of the clustered tents. "Now give me that torch, Hotvig."

The Thrithings-man stared at him for a moment, then pulled the unlit brand from his belt and handed it to him. "What will you do?" he asked quietly. His expression betrayed nothing but calm interest.

Simon did not reply. Instead, with his concentration on other matters freeing him for a moment from self-consciousness, he swung down from the saddle with surprising ease. He unpeeled the pitchy rag from the end of the torch and wrapped it instead around the head of the arrow, tying it tightly with the length of leather thong that had bound his Qanuc sheath against his thigh. Kneeling, sheltered from the wind by Homefinder's bulk, he produced his flints and iron bar.

"Come, Simon." Sludig sounded midway between worry and anger. "We have done what we came for. What are you up to?"

Simon ignored him, striking at the iron until a spark nestled in the sticky folds of the rag wound around the arrow's tip. He blew on it until the flame caught, then pocketed his flints and swung back up into the saddle. "Wait for me," he said, and spurred Homefinder out of the stand of trees and down the slope. Sludig started after him, but Hotvig reached out a hand and caught the harness of the Rimmersman's mount, pulling him up short. They fell into an animated, but whispered, argument.

Simon had found little chance to practice with a bow, and none at all to shoot one from horseback since the terrible, swift battle outside of Haethstad when Ethelbearn had been killed. Still, it was not accuracy or skill that was important now so much as his desire to do *something,* to send a small message to Fengbald and his confident troops. He nocked the arrow while still holding the reins, clinging with his knees to the saddle as Homefinder jounced across the uneven snow. The flame blew back along the arrow's shaft until he could feel it hot on his knuckles. At last, as he swept down onto the valley floor, he pulled up. He used his legs to turn Homefinder slowly in a wide circle, then pulled the bowstring back to his ear. His lips moved, but Simon himself did not know what he was saying, so all-absorbing was the ball of flame quivering at the end of the shaft. He took a breath, then let the arrow go.

It flew out, bright and swift as a shooting star, and arched across the night sky like a finger dipped in blood being drawn across black cloth. Simon felt his heart leap as he watched its erratic flight, watched the wind that nearly extinguished the flame carry it first to this side, then that, then drop it at last in among the crowded shadows of the camp. A few moments later a bright blossom of light arose as one of the tents caught fire. Simon watched for a moment, his heart beating as swiftly as a bird's, then turned and spurred Homefinder back up the hill.

He did not say anything about the arrow when he caught up with the rest of his companions. Even Sludig did not question him. Instead, the little company fell in around Simon and together they rode swiftly through the darkened hills with the wind blowing chill against their faces.

"I wish you would go and lie down," Josua said.

Vorzheva looked up. She was sitting on a mat beside the brazier with the cloak she was repairing spread out on her lap. The young New Gadrinsett girl who was helping her also looked up, then quickly lowered her eyes to the mending once more.

"Lie down?" Vorzheva said, cocking her head quizzically. "Why?"

Josua resumed his pacing. "It . . . it would be better."

Vorzheva ran a hand through her black hair as she watched him cross from one wall of the tent to the other then start back again, a journey of little more than ten cubits. The prince was tall enough that he could only stand upright at the very center of the tent, which gave his pacing progress an odd, hunchbacked look.

"I do not want to lie down, Josua," she said at last, still watching him. "What is wrong with you?"

He stopped and flexed his fingers. "It would be better for the baby . . . and for you . . . if you did lie down."

Vorzheva stared at him for a moment, then laughed. "Josua, you are being foolish—the child will not come until the end of winter."

"I worry for you, Lady," he said plaintively. "The bitter weather, the hard life we live here."

His wife laughed again, but this time there was a slight edge in her voice. "The women of the Stallion Clan, we give birth standing up on the grasslands, then we go back to work. We are not city women. What is wrong with you, Josua?"

The prince's thin face flushed violently. "Why must you always disagree with me?" he demanded. "Am I not your husband? I fear for your health and I do not like to see you working so strenuously, late into the night."

"I am no child," Vorzheva snapped, "I only am carrying one. Why do you walk here and back, here and back? Stand and talk to me!"

"I try to talk with you, but you quarrel with me!"

"Because you tell me what things I should do, like you tell a child. I am not a fool, even though I do not speak like your castle ladies!"

"Aedon curse it, I never said you were a fool!" he shouted. The moment the words were out of his mouth, he stopped his agitated walking. After staring at the ground for a moment, he raised his eyes to Vorzheva's young helper. The girl was huddled in mortification, doing her best to vanish into the shadows. "You," he said. "Would you leave us for a while? My wife and I would like to be alone."

"She is helping me!" Vorzheva said angrily.

Josua fixed the girl with his hard gray eyes. *"Go."*

The young woman leaped to her feet and fled out through the tent flap, leaving her mending in a heap on the floormats. The prince stared after her for a moment, then turned his attention back to Vorzheva. He seemed about to say something, then stopped and swiveled around to the tent flap.

"Blessed Elysia," he murmured. It was hard to tell whether it was a prayer or a curse. He walked toward the doorway and out of the tent.

"Where do you go?" Vorzheva called after him.

Josua squinted into the darkness. At last he saw a lighter shape against one of the tents not far away. He walked toward it, clenching and unclenching his fist.

"Wait." He reached out to touch the young woman's shoulder. Her eyes widened. She had backed herself against the tent; now she raised her hands before her as if to ward off a blow. "Forgive me," he said. "That was an ungentle thing for me to do. You have been kind to my lady and she likes you. Please forgive me."

"For-forgive *you,* Lord?" she sniffled. "Me? I am no one."

Josua winced. "God values each soul at the same measure. Now please, go to Father Strangyeard's tent over there. There, you can see the light of his fire. It will be warm, and I'm sure he will give you something to eat and drink. I will come to fetch you when I have finished talking to my wife." A sad, tired smile crept onto his lean face. "Sometimes a man and woman must have some time alone, even when they are the prince and his lady."

She sniffled again, then tried to curtsy, but was pressed back so firmly against the fabric of the tent that she could not bend. "Yes, Prince Josua."

"Go on, then." Josua watched her hurry across the snowy ground toward the circle of Strangyeard's fire. He saw the archivist and someone else stand to greet her, then he turned and walked back to the tent.

Vorzheva stared at him as he entered, curiosity clearly mixed with anger on her face. He told her what he had done.

"You are the strangest man I have ever known." She took a deep, shaky breath, then looked down, squinting at her needlework.

"If the strong can bully the weak without shame, then how are we different from the beasts of forest and field?"

"Different?" She still avoided his eyes. "How is it different? Your brother chases us with soldiers. People die, women die, children die, all for grazing land and names and flags. We *are* beasts, Josua. Have you not seen that?" She looked up at him again, more kindly this time, as a mother at a child who has not learned life's harsh lessons. She shook her head and returned to her task.

The prince moved to the pallet, then sat down among the piles of cushions and blankets. "Come sit with me." He patted the bed beside him.

"It is warmer here, close to the fire." Vorzheva seemed engrossed in her stitchery.

"It would be just as warm if we sat together here."

Vorzheva sighed, then put down her sewing, stood, and walked to the bed. She fell down beside him and leaned back upon the cushions. Together they stared up at the roof of the tent, which sagged beneath its burden of snow.

"I am sorry," Josua said. "I did not mean to be harsh. But I worry. I fear for your health, and for the child's health."

"Why is it that men think they are brave and women are weak? Women see more blood and pain than men ever do, unless men are fighting—and that is foolish blood." Vorzheva grimaced. "Women tend the hurts that cannot be helped."

Josua did not reply. Instead, he slid his arm around her shoulder and let his fingers move in the dark curls of her hair.

"You have no need to fear for me," she said. "Clan women are not weak. I will not cry. I will make our child and it will be strong and fit."

Josua maintained his silence for a while, then took a deep breath. "I blame myself. I did not give you a chance to understand what you were doing."

She turned suddenly to look at him, her face twisting in fear. She reached up and plucked his hand from her hair, then held it tightly. "What are you saying?" she demanded. "Tell me."

He hesitated, looking for words. "It is a different thing being a prince's wife than it is being a prince's woman."

She swiftly moved a little way across the bed so she could turn and face him. "What are you saying? That you would bring some other woman to take my place? I will kill you and her, Josua! I swear on my clan!"

He laughed softly, although at that moment she looked quite capable of carrying out her threat. "No, that is not what I mean. Not at all." He looked at her and his smile faded. "Please, my lady, never think anything like that." He reached out and clasped her hand again. "I meant only that as prince's wife, you are not like other women—and our child is not like other children."

"So?" The fear still lingered. She was not yet appeased.

"I cannot let anything happen to you, or to our child. If I am lost, the life you bear within you might be the only remaining link to the world as it was."

"What does that mean?"

"It means that our child must live. If we fail—if Fengbald defeats us, or even if we survive this battle, but I die—then one day our child must avenge us." He rubbed his face. "No, that is not what I mean. This is more important than vengeance. Our child could be the last light against an age of darkness. We do not know if Miriamele will come back to us, or if she even lives. If she is lost, then a prince's son—or a prince's daughter, for that matter—a grandchild of Prester John, would raise the only banner that could bring together a resistance to Elias and his ungodly ally."

Vorzheva was relieved. "I told you, we Thrithings-women bear strong children. You need have no worry—our child will live to make you proud. And we will win here, Josua. You are stronger than you know." She moved closer to him. "There is too much worry in you."

He sighed. "I pray that you are right. Usires and His mercy, is there anything worse than being a ruler? How I wish I could simply walk away."

"You would not do that. My husband is no coward." She lifted herself to look at him closely, as if he might be an impostor, then settled back once more.

"No, you are right. It is my lot—my test, perhaps . . . my own Tree. And each nail is sharp and cold indeed. But even the condemned man is allowed to dream of freedom."

"Do not talk of this any more," she said into his shoulder. "You will bring bad luck."

"I can stop speaking, my love, but I cannot so easily silence my thoughts."

She pushed her head against him like a young bird trying to force its way out of an egg. "Be quiet now."

The worst of the storm had passed, moving southeast. The moon, although curtained and invisible, still shed enough light to give a faint shine to the snow, as though all the river valley between Gadrinsett and Sesuad'ra were sprinkled with powdered diamonds.

Simon watched the snow fountain up from the hooves of Sludig's horse and wondered if he would live to look back on this year. What might he be, if by some odd chance he managed to survive? A knight, of course, which was already something so grand he had only imagined it in his most childish daydreams—but what did a knight do? Fought for his liege in war, of course, but Simon did not want to think about wars. If there were peace someday, and if he lived to see it—two possibilities that seemed sadly remote—what sort of life would he have?

What did knights do? Ruled over their fiefdoms, if they had land. That was more or less like being a farmer, wasn't it? It certainly didn't seem grand, but suddenly the idea of coming home from a wet day spent walking through the fields seemed very appealing. He would pull off his cloak and boots and wiggle into his slippers, then warm himself in front of a great roaring fire. Someone would bring him wine, and mull it with a hot poker . . . but who? A woman? A wife? He tried to conjure a suitable face out of the darkness, but could not. Even Miriamele, if she lost her legacy and consented to marry a commoner, and if she would choose Simon in any case—if the rivers ran uphill and fish flew, in other words—Miriamele would not be, he sensed, the kind of woman who would wait quietly at home for her husband to return from the fields. To imagine her thus was almost to think of a beautiful bird with its wings tied.

But if he did not marry and have a household, what then? The thought of tournaments, that staple of the knight's spring and summer entertainment which had occupied his excited thoughts for several years, nearly sickened him now. That healthy men would hurt each other for no reason, lose eyes and limbs and even their lives for a game when the world was already such a dreadful and dangerous place, made Simon furious. "Mock-war" some called it, as though any mere sport, no matter how hazardous, could approach the horror of the things Simon had seen. War was like a great wind or an earth tremor, something dreadful that should not be trifled with. To imitate it seemed almost blasphemous. Practicing at tilting and swordwork was something you did to stay alive if war caught you. When this all ended—*if* it ended—Simon wanted to get as far away from war, mock or otherwise, as he could.

But one did not always go looking for war, for pain and terror; certainly death did not need to be sought out. So shouldn't a knight always be ready to do his duty defending himself and others? That was what Sir Deornoth said, and Deornoth did not strike Simon as the kind who fought needlessly or happily. And what was it that Doctor Morgenes had said once about the great Camaris? That he blew his famous battle horn Cellian not to summon help or make himself glorious, but to let his enemies know he was coming so they could safely escape. Morgenes had written time after time in his book that Camaris took no pleasure in battle, that his mighty skills were only a burden, since they drew attackers to him and forced him to kill when he did not want to. *There* was a paradox. No matter how adept you were, someone would always wish to test you. So was it better to prepare for war or to avoid it?

A clump of snow fell from a branch overhead and, as if it had life, avoided his heavy scarf and slid easily down the back of his neck. Simon gave a muffled squeak of dismay, then quickly looked around, hoping none of the others had heard him make such an unmanly noise. No one was looking at him; the attention of all his companions seemed fixed on the silver-gray hills and spiky, shadowy trees.

So which was better? To flee war, or to try to make yourself so strong that no one could hurt you? Morgenes had told him that such problems were the stuff of kingship, the sort of questions that kept goodhearted monarchs awake at night when all their subjects were sleeping. When Simon had complained about such a vague response, the doctor had smiled sadly.

"That answer is certainly unsatisfactory, Simon," the old man had said. *"So are*

all possible answers to such questions. If there were correct answers, the world would be as orderly as a cathedral—flat stone on flat stone, pure angle mating with pure angle—and everything as solid and unmoving as the walls of Saint Sutrin's." He had cocked his beer jug in a sort of salute. *"But would there be love in such a world, Simon? Beauty or charm, with no ill-favor to compare them to? What kind of place would a world without surprises be?"* The old man had taken a long drink, wiped his mouth, then changed the subject. Simon had not thought any more of what the doctor had said again—until this moment.

"Sludig." Simon's voice was startlingly loud as it broke the long silence.

"What?" Sludig turned in his saddle to look back. "Would you rather live in a world without surprises? I mean without good ones and bad ones both?"

The Rimmersman glared at him for a moment. "Don't talk foolishness," he grunted, then turned back, using his knees to urge his horse around a boulder standing stark against the white drifts.

Simon shrugged. Hotvig, who had also looked back, stared intently for a moment, then swiveled around once more.

The thought would not quite go away, however. As Homefinder plodded along beneath him, Simon remembered a bit of a recent dream—a field of grass whose color was so even that it might have been painted, a sky as cold and unchanging as a piece of pottery, the whole landscape eternal and dead as stone.

I'll take surprises, I think, Simon decided. *Even with the bad ones included.*

They heard the music first, a thin, piping melody that wove in and out through the noise of the wind. As they came down the hillside into the bowl-shaped valley around Sesuad'ra, they saw a small fire burning at the edge of the great black tarn that surrounded the hill. A little round shape rose from beside the fire, draped in shadow, silhouetted by flame as it lowered a bone flute.

"We heard you playing," Simon said. "Aren't you worried that someone else might hear you, too? Someone unfriendly?"

"I have protection of sufficiency." Binabik smiled just a little. "So, you are returned." He sounded studiedly calm, as if worrying was absolutely the last thing he might have been doing. "Are you all well?"

"Yes, Binabik, we're well. All Fengbald's sentries were staying close to their fires."

"As I have myself been doing," the troll said. "The flatboats are over there, where I am pointing. Would you like to rest and warm yourselves, or should we be going up the hill now?"

"We should probably get the news to Josua as soon as possible," Simon decided. "Fengbald has something near a thousand men, and Hotvig says that almost half of them are Thrithings mercenaries." He was distracted by a shape moving along the shadowy shore. When it passed before a high snow drift, he saw that it was Qantaqa slipping along the water's edge like a driblet of quicksilver. The wolf turned to look toward him, her eyes reflecting the firelight, and Simon nodded. Yes, Binabik was indeed protected: no one would sneak up on Qantaqa's master without first dealing with her.

"That is not truly good news, but I am thinking it could be less good," Binabik said as he gathered together the pieces of his walking-stick. "The High King could have thrown all his forces upon us, as he was doing at Naglimund." He sighed. "Still, a thousand soldiers is not a comforting thought." The troll pushed the assembled stick through his belt and took Homefinder's reins. "Josua is gone to sleep for the night, but I think you are sensible when you say you will go straight up. Better we all go to the safeness of the Stone. Even if the king's armies are still distant, this is a wild place, and I am thinking that the storm may bring strange things out into the night."

Simon shivered. "Then let's get ourselves out of the night and into a warm tent."

They followed Binabik's short steps down to the edge of the lake. It seemed to have an odd sheen.

"Why does the water look so strange?" Simon asked.

Binabik grimaced. "That is my news, it gives me sorrow to say. I fear that this last storm has brought us more evil luck than we had guessed. Our moat, as you castle-dwellers would call it, is becoming frozen."

Sludig, who was standing close by, cursed richly. "But the lake is our best guard against the king's troops!"

The little man shrugged. "It is not all frozen yet—otherwise there would be terrible difficulties to get our boats back across. Perhaps we will be having a thaw, and then it will be a shield to us again." The look on his face, shared by Sludig, suggested that it was not very likely.

Two large flatboats waited at the lake's edge. "Men and wolves are to go in this one," Binabik said, gesturing. "The other will take the horses and one man for watching them. Although, Simon, I am thinking your horse has been with Qantaqa enough to bear the trip in our boat."

"It's me you should worry about, troll," growled Sludig. "I like boats less than I like wolves—and I don't like wolves much more than the horses do."

Binabik waved a small, dismissive hand. "You are making jokes, Sludig. Qantaqa has risked her life at your side many times, and that you are knowing."

"So now I have to risk my own again on another of your damned boats," the Rimmersman complained. He seemed to be suppressing a smile. Simon was surprised again by the strange fellowship that seemed to have grown between Binabik and the northerner. "Very well, then," Sludig said, "I will go. But if you trip over that great beast and fall in, I am the last person who will jump in after you."

"Trolls," Binabik said with great dignity, "do not 'fall in.'"

The little man plucked a burning brand from the flames, extinguished the campfire with a few handfuls of snow, then clambered onto the nearest flatboat. "Your torches have too much brightness," he said. "Put them out. Let us be enjoying this night, when some stars can at last be seen." He lit the horn-shielded lamp hanging at the front of the barge, then stepped gingerly from one rocking deck to the other and fired the wick on the other boat as well. The lamplight, lunar and serene, spread out across the water as Binabik dropped his torch overboard. It disappeared with a hiss and a belch of steam. Simon and the others doused their own brands and followed the troll aboard.

One of Hotvig's clansmen was deputed to ferry the horses in the second barge, but the mare Homefinder, as Binabik had predicted, seemed unruffled by Qantaqa's presence and so was deemed fit to ride with the rest of the company. She stood in the stern of the leading boat and gazed back at the other horses like a duchess eyeing a gang of drunkards carousing beneath her balcony. Qantaqa curled up at Binabik's feet, tongue lolling, and watched Sludig and Hotvig as they poled the first barge out onto the lake. Mist rose up all around; in a moment the land behind them had vanished and the two boats were floating through a netherworld of fog and black water.

In most places the ice was little more than a thin skin across the water, brittle as sugar candy. As the front of the boat pushed through, the ice crackled and rang, a delicate but unnerving sound that made the back of Simon's neck prickle. Overhead, the passage of this wave of the storm had left the sky almost clear; as Binabik had said, a few stars could indeed be seen blinking in the murk.

"Look," the troll said softly. "While men prepare for fighting, Sedda still goes about her business. She has not caught her husband Kikkasut yet, but she does not stop her trying."

Simon stood beside him and stared up into the deep well of the sky. But for the soft tinkling of the water's frozen crust parting before them, and an occasional muffled thump when they struck a larger piece of floating ice, the valley was supernaturally silent.

"What's that?" Sludig said abruptly. "There."

Simon leaned to follow his gaze. The Rimmersman's fur-cloaked arm pointed out across the water to the dark edge of the Aldheorte, which stood like a castle outwall above the north shore of the lake.

"I can't see anything," Simon whispered.

"It's gone now," Sludig said fiercely, as though Simon had spoken from disbelief instead of inability. "There were lights in the forest. I saw them."

Binabik stepped closer to the edge of the boat, peering out into the darkness. "That is near where the city Enki-e-Shao'saye stands, or what is remaining of it."

Hotvig now moved forward as well. The barge rocked gently. Simon thought it good that Homefinder still stood placidly in the stern, otherwise the shallow flatboat might have overbalanced. "In the ghost city?" The Thrithings-man's scarred features were suddenly childlike in their apprehension. "You see lights there?"

"I did," Sludig said. "I swear by the Blood of Aedon I did. But they are gone now."

"Hmm." Binabik looked troubled. "It could be that somehow our own lamps were shining back from some mirroring surface there in the old city."

"No." Sludig was firm. "One was bigger than any lamp of ours. But they went dark so quickly!"

"Witch lights," said Hotvig grimly.

"It is also possible," Binabik offered, "that you only saw them for a moment through trees or broken buildings, then after that we passed from where we could be seeing them." He thought for a moment, then turned to Simon. "Josua has set tonight's task for you, Simon. Should we back water for a way to see if we can be finding these forest lights again?"

Simon tried to think calmly of what was best, but he truly did not want to know what was on the far side of the black water. Not tonight.

"No." He tried to make his voice measured and steady. "No, we will not go and look. Not when we have news that Josua needs. What if it is a scouting party for Fengbald? The less they see of us, the better." Stated that way, it sounded rather reasonable. He felt a moment of relief, but that was quickly followed by shame that he should try to falsely impress these men, who had risked their lives under his command. "And also," he said, "I am tired and worried—no, frightened is what I am. This has been a hard night. Let's go and tell Josua what we've seen, including the lights in the forest. The prince should decide." As he finished, he was suddenly aware of a vast presence at his shoulder. He turned quickly, unnerved, to be confronted with the great bulk of Sesuad'ra looming up from the water beside him; it had appeared so unexpectedly through the fog that it might have just that moment pushed up from beneath the lake's obsidian surface like a breaching whalefish. He stood and stared up at it, openmouthed.

Binabik stroked Qantaqa's broad head. "I am thinking Simon speaks with good sense. Prince Josua should be deciding what to do about this mystery."

"They were there," Sludig said angrily, but shook his head as though not as sure now as he had been.

The flatboats sailed on. The forested shore vanished once more into the cloaking mist, like a dream receding before the light and noises of morning.

Deornoth watched Simon as the youth made his report, and found that he liked what he was seeing. The young man was flushed with the excitement of his new responsibilities, and the gray morning light was reflected in eyes that were perhaps a little too bright for the gravity of the things discussed—namely, Fengbald's army and its overwhelming superiority in numbers, equipment, and experience—but Deornoth noted with pleasure that the youth did not rush through his explanations, did not jump toward unwarranted conclusions, and thought carefully before answering each of Prince Josua's questions. This new-minted knight had seen and heard much in his short life, it seemed, and had paid attention. As Simon related their adventure and Sludig and Hotvig nodded agreement with the young man's conclusions, Deornoth found himself nodding, too. Though Simon's beard still had the chick-feathered look of youth, Deornoth's experienced eye saw beneath it the makings of a fine man. He guessed that the lad might someday be one such as other men might follow to their benefit.

Josua was holding his council before his tent, where a blazing fire kept the morning chill at bay and served as a centerpiece to their deliberations. As the prince questioned and probed, Freosel, New Gadrinsett's stocky constable, cleared his throat to gain Josua's attention.

"Yes, Freosel?"

"Strikes me, sire, that all things your knight here says he saw, well, they be like what the Lord Mayor told us."

Simon turned to the Falshireman. "Lord Mayor? Who's that?"

"Helfgrim, who was once mayor of Gadrinsett," Josua explained. "He came to us just after you and the others rode out. He escaped from Fengbald's camp and made his way here. He is sickly and I have ordered him to bed, otherwise he would be with us this moment. He had a long, cold journey on foot, and Fengbald's men had treated him badly."

"As I said, your Highness," Freosel resumed, polite but determined, "what Sir Seoman here says bears out all Helfgrim's talk. So when Helfgrim says he knows how Fengbald will attack, and where, and when . . ." the young man shrugged, "well, seems we should pay heed. Would be a boon to us, and we have small enough to work with."

"Your point is well taken, Freosel. You said the mayor is a trustworthy man, and you, as another Falshireman, know him best." Josua looked around the circle. "What think you all? Geloë?"

The witch woman looked up quickly, surprised. She had been staring into the shifting orange depths of the fire. "I do not pretend to be a war strategist, Josua."

"That I know, but you are a keen judge of people. How much weight can we place on the old Lord Mayor's words? We have few enough forces—we cannot spare anything on a bad gamble."

Geloë thought for a moment. "I have only spoken with him briefly, Josua, but I will say this: there is a darkness in his eyes I do not like—a shadow. I suggest you take great care."

"A shadow?" Josua looked at her intently. "Could it be a mark of his suffering, or are you saying you read treachery in him?"

The forest woman shook her head. "No, I would not go so far as to say anything about treachery. It could be pain, certainly. Or he could be addled by harsh treatment, and the thing I see is a mind hiding from itself, hiding behind imaginings of knowing what the great ones are thinking and doing. But go carefully, Josua."

Deornoth sat up straighter. "Geloë is wise, sire," he said quickly, "—but we shouldn't make the error of a caution so great we fail to use what could save us."

Even as he spoke, Deornoth wondered whether he was so concerned that the witch woman might talk his master into passivity that he was ignoring the possible truth of what she said. Still, it was important in these final days to keep Josua resolved. If the prince was bold and decisive, it would overcome many small mistakes—that, in Deornoth's experience, was the way of war. If Josua wavered and hesitated too long, over this matter or any others, it might steal away what little fighting spirit remained to New Gadrinsett's army of survivors.

"I say we pay close attention to what Helfgrim the mayor has to offer," he asserted.

Hotvig spoke up in Deornoth's support, and Freosel was clearly already in agreement. The others held their peace, although Deornoth could not help noticing that Binabik the troll had an uneasy look on his round face as he poked at the fire with a length of stick. The little man put too much stock in Geloë and her magical trappings, Deornoth thought. This was different, though. This was war.

"I think I will have a talk with the Lord Mayor tonight," Josua said at last. "Providing he is strong enough, that is. As you say, Deornoth, we cannot afford to be too proud to accept help. We are needy, and God, it is said, provides what His children need if they trust Him. But I will not forget your words, Geloë. That would also be throwing away valuable gifts."

"Your pardon, Prince Josua," Freosel said. "If you be done with this, there are other things I need speak on."

"Of course."

"We have more problems than just readying to fight," the Falshireman said. "You know food is dreadful scarce. We fished the rivers until they be nearly empty—but now ice has come, we cannot even do that. Every day hunters go farther and come back with less. This woman," he nodded toward Geloë, "helped us find plants and fruits we did not know were good to eat, but that only helps stretch stores gone mighty thin." He stopped and swallowed, anxious about speaking so forwardly, but determined to say what was needed. "Even do we win here and beat off siege . . ." at the word, Deornoth felt an almost imperceptible shudder travel around the circle, ". . . we'll not be able to stay. Not enough food to last us through winter, that is the length of it."

The baldness of his statement dropped the makeshift council into silence.

"What you say is not truly a surprise," Josua said at last. "Believe me, I know the hunger our people are feeling. I hope the settlers of New Gadrinsett are aware that you and I and these others are not eating any better than they are."

Freosel nodded. "They know, your Highness, and that's stopped any worse trouble than grumbling and complaining. But if people starve, they won't care that you be starving, too. They'll go. Some be gone already."

"Goodness!" said Strangyeard. "But where can they go? Oh, the poor creatures!"

"Don't matter." Freosel shook his head. "Back to tag along the edges of Fengbald's army begging for scraps, or back across plains toward Erkynland. Only a few be gone. So far."

"If we win," Josua said, "we will move on. That was my plan, and this only proves to me that I was right. If the wind swings in our favor, we would be fools not to move while it blows at our backs." He shook his head. "Always more troubles. Fear and pain, death and hunger—how much my brother has to answer for!"

"It's not just him, Prince Josua," Simon said, his face tight with anger. "The king didn't make this storm."

"No, Simon, you are correct. We cannot afford to forget my brother's allies." Josua seemed to think of something, for he turned toward the young knight. "And now I am reminded. You spoke of seeing lights on the northeast shore last night."

Simon nodded. "Sludig saw them—but we are certain they were there," he hastened to add, then darted a look over at the Rimmersman, who was listening attentively. "I thought it best we tell you before doing anything."

"This is another puzzle. It could be some feint of Fengbald's, I suppose—some attempt to outflank us. But it makes little sense."

"Especially with his main army still so far away," Deornoth said. It did not seem like Fengbald's method, anyway, he thought. The duke of Falshire had never been the subtle sort.

"It seems to me, Simon, that it could be your friends the Sithi coming to join us. That would be a happy chance." Josua cocked an eyebrow. "I believe you had some conversation recently with your Prince Jiriki?"

Deornoth was amused to see the young man's cheeks turn bright scarlet. "I . . . I did, your Highness," Simon mumbled. "I shouldn't have done it."

"That is not to the point," Josua said dryly. "Your crimes, such as they were, are not for this gathering. Rather, I wish to know if you think it might be them."

"The fairy-folk?" blurted out Freosel. "This lad talks to the fairy-folk?"

Simon ducked his head in embarrassment. "Jiriki seemed to say that it would be a long time before he could join us, if he even could. Also—and I cannot prove this, Highness, it is just a feeling—I think he would let me know somehow if he were coming to bring us help. Jiriki knows how impatient we mortals are." He smiled sadly. "He knows how much it would lift our spirits if we knew they were coming."

"Merciful Aedon and His mother." Freosel was still stunned. "Fairies!"

Josua nodded thoughtfully. "So. Well, if the folks who make those lights are not friends, they are most likely enemies—although, now that I think on it, perhaps you saw the campfires of some of the folk Freosel spoke of, those who have fled Sesuad'ra." He frowned. "I will think on this, too. Perhaps we will send a scouting party tomorrow. I do not wish to remain ignorant of whoever might be sharing our little corner of Osten Ard." He stood, brushing ashes from his breeches, and tucked the stump of his right wrist into his cloak. "That will be all. I release you to find what slim provender you can to break your fast."

The prince turned and walked into his tent. Deornoth watched him go, then turned to look out at the edge of the great hill, where the standing stones loomed against a gray mist, as though Sesuad'ra floated in a sea of nothingness. He frowned at the thought and moved closer to the fire.

In the dream, Doctor Morgenes stood before Simon, dressed as though for a long journey, wearing a traveling cloak with a tasseled hood and scorchmarks blackening its hem, as though its owner had ridden through flames. Little of the old man's face could be seen in the darkened depths of the hood—a glint from his spectacles, the white flash of his beard; other than that, the doctor's face was only hint and shadow. Behind Morgenes lay no familiar vista, but only a swirling patch of pearlescent nothingness like the eye of a blizzard.

"It is not enough merely to fight back, Simon," the doctor's voice said, ". . . even if you are only fighting to stay alive. There must be more."

"More?" As delighted as he was to see this dream-Morgenes, Simon somehow knew he had only moments to grasp what the old man said to him. Precious time was slipping away. "What does that mean, 'more'?"

"It means you must fight for something. Otherwise you are no more than a straw man in a wheatfield—you can scare the crows away, you can even kill them, but you will never win them over. You cannot stone all the crows in the world . . ."

"Kill crows? What do you mean?"

"Hate is not enough, Simon . . . it is never enough." The old man seemed about to say more, but the white emptiness behind him was abruptly slashed by a great stripe of vertical shadow which seemed to grow out of the very nothingness. Although without substance, still the shadow seemed oppressively heavy—a thick column of darkness that could have been a tower, or a tree, or the upright rim of an oncoming wheel; it bisected the void behind the doctor's hooded figure as neatly as a heraldic blazon.

"Morgenes!" Simon cried, but in this dream his voice was suddenly weak, almost stifled by the weight of the long shadow. "Doctor! Don't leave!"

"I had to leave a long time ago," the old man cried, his voice faint, too. "You've done the work without me. And remember—the false messenger!" The doctor's voice suddenly slid upward in pitch until it became a piping shriek. "False!" he cried. "Faaaallllsssse!"

His hooded shape began to crumple and shrink, the cloak flapping madly. At last, the old man was gone; where he had stood, a tiny silver bird beat its wings. It suddenly darted up into the emptiness, circling first sun-wise, then widdershins, until it was only a speck. An instant later it was gone.

"Doctor!" Simon squinted after it. He reached up, but something was restraining his arms, a heavy weight that clung to him and pushed him down, as though the milky void had become thick as a sodden blanket. He struggled against it. *"No! Come back! I need to know more. . . ."*

"It is me, Simon!" Binabik hissed. "More quiet, please!" The troll shifted his weight once more until he was almost sitting on the young man's chest. "Stop now! If you keep up these struggling-about movements, you will hit my nose again."

"What . . . ?" Simon gradually stopped thrashing. "Binabik?"

"From bruised nose to wounded toes," the troll sniffed. "Have you finished with your flinging of arms and legs?"

"Did I wake you up?" Simon asked.

Binabik slid down and crouched beside the pallet. "No. *I* was coming to wake *you*—that is the truth of it. But what was this dream that caused you so much worry and fearfulness?"

Simon shook his head. "It's not important. I don't remember it very well, anyway."

He actually remembered every word, but he wished to think about it a while longer before he discussed the subject with Binabik. Morgenes had seemed more vivid in this dream than he had in others—more *real*. In a way, it had almost been like having a last meeting with his beloved doctor. Simon had grown covetous of the few things he could call his own: he did not yet wish to share this small thing with anybody. "Why did you wake me?" He yawned to cover the change of subject. "I don't have to stand guard tonight."

"That is true." Binabik's surprising smile was a brief pale blur in the light of the dying embers. "But I am wishing you to get up, put on your boots and other clothes for traveling out of doors, and then be coming with me."

"What?" Simon sat up, listening for the sound of alarum or attack, but heard nothing louder than the ever-present wind. He slumped back down into his bed and rolled over, turning his back to the troll. "I don't want to go anywhere. I'm tired. Let me go back to sleep."

"This is a thing that you will be finding is worth your trouble."

"What is it?" he grumbled into his upper arm.

"A secret, but a secret of great excitingness."

"Bring it to me in the morning. I'll be very excited then."

"Simon!" Binabik was a little less jovial. "Do not be so lazy. This is being very important! Do you have no trust in me?"

Groaning as though the entire weight of the earth had been tipped onto his shoulders, Simon rolled over again and levered himself into a sitting position. "Is it really important?"

Binabik nodded.

"And you won't tell me what it is?"

Binabik shook his head. "But you will soon be discovering. That is my promise."

Simon stared at the troll, who seemed inhumanly cheerful for this dark hour of the night. "Whatever it is, it's certainly put you in a good mood," he growled.

"Come." Binabik stood up, excited as a child at the Aedontide feasting. "I have Homefinder with her saddle upon her back already. Qantaqa is also waiting with immense wolfly patience. Come!"

Simon allowed himself to be coerced into boots and a thick wool shirt. Dragging his bed-warm cloak about him, he stumbled out of the tent after Binabik, then nearly turned and stumbled right back in again. "S'Bloody Tree!" he swore. "It's cold!"

Binabik pursed his lips at the oath, but said nothing. Now that Simon had been made a knight, the troll seemed to have decided that he was a grown man and could curse if he wished to. Instead, the little man lifted a hand to gesture toward Homefinder, who stood pawing at the snowy ground a few paces away, bathed in the light of a torch thrust handle-first into the snow. Simon approached her, stopping to stroke her nose and whisper a few muzzy words in her warm ear, then dragged himself clumsily into the saddle. The troll gave a low whistle and Qantaqa appeared silently out of the darkness. Binabik sank his fingers in her thick gray fur and clambered onto her broad back, then leaned over to pick up the torch before urging the wolf forward.

They made their way out of the close-quartered tent city and across the broad summit of Sesuad'ra, across the Fire Garden where the wind whirled little eddies of snow across the half-buried tiles, then past Leavetaking House, where a pair of sentries stood. Not far beyond the armed men was a standing stone which marked the edge of the wide road that wound down from the summit. The sentries, bundled up against the cold so that only the gleam of their eyes could be seen below their helms, raised their spears in salute. Simon waved, puzzled.

"They don't seem very curious about where we're going."

"We have permission." Binabik smiled mysteriously.

The skies overhead were almost clear. As they made their way down the hill along the crumbling stones of the old Sithi road, Simon looked up to see that the stars had returned. It was a cheering sight, although he was bemused to find that none of them seemed quite familiar. The moon, appearing for a moment from behind a spit of clouds, showed him that it was earlier than he had at first thought—perhaps only a few hours after sunset. Still, it was late enough that almost the whole of New Gadrinsett was abed. Where on earth could Binabik be leading him?

Several times as they made their spiraling circuit of the Stone, Simon thought he saw lights sparkling in the distant forest, tiny points dimmer even than the stars high overhead. But when he pointed them out, the troll merely nodded as though such a sight was no more than he had expected.

By the time they reached the place where the old road widened out once more, pale Sedda had vanished behind a curtain of mist on the horizon. They came down onto the sloping shoulder of land at the hill's base. The waters of the great lake lapped against the stone. A few drowned treetops still protruded above the surface like the heads of giants sleeping beneath the black waters.

Without a word, Binabik dismounted and led Qantaqa to one of the flatboats moored near the end of the road. Simon, lulled into an unquestioning dreaminess, slid down from the saddle arid led his horse aboard. Once Binabik had lit the lamp in the bow, they lifted their poles and pushed out onto the freezing water.

"Not many more trips can we make this way," Binabik said quietly. "Luckily, that will not matter soon."

"Why won't it matter?" Simon asked, but the troll only waved his small hand.

Soon the slope of the submerged valley began to fall away beneath the boat, until at last their poles reached down and touched nothing. They took up the paddles that were lying in the barge's shallow bottom. It was hard work—the ice seemed to grab and cling to hull and paddle-blade alike, as though urging the boat to stop and become part of the greater solidification. Simon did not notice for a while that Binabik had steered them toward the northeast shore, where Enki-e-Shao'saye had once stood and where the strange glimmerings had appeared.

"We're going to the lights!" he said. His voice seemed to sigh and quickly fade, vanishing into the enormity of the darkened valley.

"Yes."

"Why? Are the Sithi there?"

"Not the Sithi, no." Binabik was staring out across the wind-rippled water, his posture that of one who could barely contain himself. "I am thinking that you spoke truly: Jiriki would not keep his coming a secret."

"Then who is there?"

"You will see."

The troll's whole attention was now fixed on the far shore, which grew ever closer. Simon saw the great breakfront of trees looming up, shadowy and impenetrable, and suddenly remembered how the writing-priests back at the Hayholt would lift their heads almost as one movement when some errand brought him into their sanctuary—a vast crowd of ancient men tugged up from their parchmenty dreams by his blundering entrance.

Soon the bottom of the boat scraped, then ran aground. Simon and Binabik stepped out and pulled it up onto a more secure spot while Qantaqa loped in wide, splashing circles around them. When Homefinder had been coaxed out onto the shore, Binabik relit his torch and they rode into the forest.

The trees of the Aldheorte grew close together here, as though huddling for warmth. The torch revealed an incredible profusion of leaves in an uncountable variety of shapes and sizes, as well as what seemed to be every variety of creeper, lichen, and moss, all grown together into a disordered riot of vegetation. Binabik led them onto a narrow deer track. Simon's boots were wet and his feet were cold and getting colder. He wondered again what they were doing in this place at such an hour.

He heard the noise long before he could see anything but the choke of trees, a whining, discordant skirling of flutes that wound in and out around a deep, almost inaudible drumbeat. Simon turned to Binabik, but the troll was listening and nodding and did not see Simon's inquiring glance. Soon they could see light, something warmer and less steady than moonlight, flickering through the thick trees. The odd music grew louder, and Simon felt his heart began to beat more swiftly. Surely Binabik knew what he was doing, he chided himself. After all the dreadful times they had survived together, Simon could trust his friend. But Binabik seemed so strangely distracted! The little man's head was cocked to one side in an attitude that mirrored Qantaqa's, as though he heard things in the weird melody and incessant drums that Simon could not even guess at.

Simon was full of nervous anticipation. He realized that he had been smelling something vaguely familiar for a long while. Even after he could no longer ignore it, he was at first certain that it was nothing more than the scent of his own clothing, but soon the pungency, the *aliveness* of it could no longer be denied.

Wet wool.

"Binabik!" he cried—then, recognizing the truth, he began to laugh.

They came down into a wide clearing. The crumbled ruins of the old Sithi city lay all around, but now the dead stone was painted with leaping flames: life had returned, if not the life its builders had intended. All along the upper part of the dell, crowding and quietly clamoring, bumped a great herd of snow-white rams. The bottom of the dell, where the fires burned merrily, was equally filled with trolls. Some were dancing or singing. Others were playing on trollish instruments, producing the skittering, piping music. Most simply watched and laughed.

"*Sisqinanamook!*" Binabik shouted. His face was stretched in an impossibly delighted smile. "*Henimaatuq! Ea kup!*"

A score of faces, two score, three score or more, all turned to stare up at the spot where he and Simon stood. In an instant a great crowd was pushing up past the disgruntled, sour-bleating rams. One small figure outstripped the rest and within moments had reached Binabik's widespread arms.

Simon was surrounded by chattering trolls. They shouted and chuckled as they tugged at his garments and patted him; the good will on their faces was unmistakable. He felt himself suddenly in the midst of old friends and found that he was beaming back at them, his eyes overbrimming. The strong scent of oil and fat that he remembered so well from Yiqanuc rose to his nostrils, but at this moment it was a very pleasant scent indeed. He turned, dazed, and looked for Binabik.

"How did you know?" he cried.

His friend stood a little way distant, an arm wrapped around Sisqi. She was smiling almost as widely as he, and the color had come out in her cheeks. "My clever Sisqinanamook was sending me one of Ookequk's birds!" Binabik said. "My people have been at camp here for two days, building boats!"

"Building boats?" Simon felt himself gently jostled from side to side by the ocean of little people that hemmed him close.

"To come across our lake for joining Josua," Binabik laughed. "One hundred brave trolls is Sisqi bringing to help us! Now you will truly see why the Rimmersmen still frighten their children with whispered stories of Huhinka Valley!" He turned and embraced her again.

Sisqi ducked her head into the side of his neck for a moment, then turned and faced Simon. "I read Ookequk book," she said, her Westerling awkward but understandable. "I speak more now, your talk." Her nod was almost a bow. "Greetings, Simon."

"Greetings, Sisqi," he said. "It is good to see you again."

"This is why I was wanting you to come, Simon." Binabik waved his hand around the clearing. "Tomorrow will be enough time for talking of war. Tonight, friends are being together again. We will sing and dance!"

Simon grinned at the joy evident in Binabik's face, a happiness that was mirrored in the dark eyes of his betrothed. Simon's own weariness had melted away. "I'd like that," he said, and meant it.

9

Pages in an Old Book

✦

Clawlike hands grasped at her. Empty eyes stared. They were all around her, gray and shiny as frogs, and she could not even scream.

Miriamele awakened with her throat so tightly constricted that it ached. There were no clutching hands, no eyes, only a sheet of cloth above her and the sound of slapping waves. She lay on her back for long moments, fighting for breath, then sat up.

No hands, no eyes, she promised herself. The kilpa, apparently sated by their feast on the *Eadne Cloud,* had scarcely troubled the landing boat.

Miriamele slid out from beneath the makeshift awning she and the monk had constructed from the boat's oiled broadcloth cover, then squinted, trying to find some trace of the sun so she could gauge the time of day. The ocean that surrounded her had a dull, leaden look, as though the vast sheet of water surrounding the boat had been hammered out by a legion of blacksmiths. The gray-green expanse stretched in every direction, featureless but for the wave-crests glimmering in the diffuse light.

Cadrach was sitting before her on one of the front benches, the oar handles held beneath his arms while he stared down at his hands. The bits of cloak he had wrapped around his palms for protection were in tatters, shredded by the repetitive slide of the oar handles.

"Your poor hands." Miriamele was surprised by her own rasping voice. Cadrach, more startled than she, flinched.

"My lady." He peered at her. "Is all well?"

"No," she said, but tried to smile. "I hurt. I hurt all over. But look at your hands, they are terrible."

He stared ruefully at his ragged skin. "I have rowed a little too much, I fear. I am still not strong."

Miriamele frowned. "You are mad, Cadrach! You have been in chains for days—what are you doing pulling at oars? You will kill yourself!"

The monk shook his head. "I did not work at it long, my lady. These wounds on my hands are a tribute to the weakness of my flesh, not the diligence of my labors."

"And I have nothing to put on them," Miriamele fretted, then looked up suddenly. "What time of the day is it?"

It took the monk a moment to answer the unexpected question. "Why, early evening, Princess. Just after sunset."

"And you let me sleep all day! How could you?"

"You needed to sleep, Lady. You had bad dreams, but I'm sure that you are still much better for . . ." Cadrach trailed off, then lifted his curled fingers in a gesture of insufficiency. "In any case, it was best."

Miriamele hissed her exasperation. "I will find something for those hands. Perhaps in one of Gan Itai's packages." She kept her mouth firm, despite the quiver she felt at the corners when she spoke the Niskie's name. "Stay there, and do not move those oars an inch if you value your life."

"Yes, my lady."

Moving gingerly for the comfort of her painful muscles, Miriamele at last turned up the small oilcloth packet of useful articles that Gan Itai had bundled with the water skins and food. It contained the promised fishhooks, as well as a length of strong and curiously dull-colored cord of a type Miriamele had not seen before; there was also a small knife and a sack that contained a collection of tiny jars, none of them bigger than a man's thumb. Miriamele unstoppered them one by one, sniffing each cautiously.

"This one's salt, I think," she said, "—but what would someone at sea need with salt, when they could get their own by drying water?" She looked to Cadrach, but he only shook his round head. "This one has some yellowish powder in it." She closed her eyes to take another sniff. "It smells fragrant, but not like something to eat. Hmm." She opened three more, discovering crushed petals in one, sweet oil in the second, and a pale unguent in the third which made her eyes water when she leaned close.

"I know that scent," said Cadrach. "Mockfoil. Good for poultices and such—the staple of a rustic healer's apothecary."

"Then that's what I was looking for." Miriamele cut some strips from the nightshirt she still wore underneath her masculine clothing, then rubbed the unguent into some of the strips and bound them firmly around Cadrach's blistered hands. After she had finished, she wrapped a few bits of dry cloth around the outside to keep the others clean.

"There. That will help some, anyway."

"You are too kind, Lady." Although his tone was light, Miriamele saw an unexpected glimmer in his eye, as though a tear had blossomed. Embarrassed and a little unsure, she did not look too closely.

The sky, which had long since bled out its brighter colors, was now rapidly going purple-blue. The wind quickened, and Miriamele and Cadrach both drew their cloaks closer about their necks. Miriamele leaned back against the railing of the boat for a long, silent moment, feeling the long craft roll from side to side on the cradling waters.

"So what do we do now? Where are we? Where are we going?"

Cadrach was still prodding at the dressings on his hands. "Well, as to where we are at this moment, Lady, I would say we were somewhere between Spenit and Risa Islands, in the middle of the Bay of Firannos. We're most likely about three leagues off shore—a few days' rowing, even if we pull oars the day long. . . ."

"There's a good thought." Miriamele crawled forward to the bench Cadrach had occupied and lowered the oars into the water. "Might as well keep moving while we're talking. Are we facing the right direction?" She laughed sourly. "But how could you say when we probably don't know where we're going?"

"In truth, we should do well as we are headed, Princess. I'll look again when the stars come out, but the sun was all I needed to know that we are pointing northeast, and that is as fine as we need to be for now. But are you sure you should tire yourself? Perhaps I can manage a little more. . . ."

"Oh, Cadrach, you with your bleeding hands!? Nonsense." She dipped the oarblades into the water and pulled, slipping backward on the seat when one of them popped free of the water. "No, don't show me," she said quickly. "I learned how when I was little—it's only that I haven't done it for a long time." She scowled in concentration, searching for the half-remembered stroke. "We used to practice on some of the Gleniwent's small backwaters. My father used to take me."

The memory of Elias on a rowing bench before her, laughing as one of the oars floated away across green-scummed water, blew through her. In that snatch of recollection, her father seemed scarcely older than she now was herself—perhaps, she suddenly realized with a kind of startled wonder, he had been in some ways still a boy, for all his manly age. There was no question that the imposing weight of his mighty, fabled, and beloved father had pressed down upon him hard, forcing him to wilder and wilder feats of valor. She remembered her mother fighting back fearful tears at some report of Elias' battlefield madness, tears that the tale-bringers never understood. It was strange to think about her father this way. Perhaps for all his bravery he had been unsure and afraid—terrified that he would stay a child forever, a son with an undying sire.

Unsettled, Miriamele tried to sweep the curiously clinging memory from her mind and concentrate instead on finding the ancient rhythm of oars in water.

"Good, my lady, you do very well." Cadrach settled back, his bandaged hands and round face pale as mushroom flesh in the swiftly darkening evening. "So, we know where we are—add or subtract a few million buckets of seawater. As to where we are going . . . well, what say you, Princess? *You* are the one who rescued *me,* after all."

She suddenly felt the oars heavy as stone in her hands. A fog of purposelessness rolled over her. "I don't know," she whispered. "I have nowhere to go."

Cadrach nodded his head as though he had expected her answer. "Then let me cut you a bit of bread and a cintis-worth of cheese, Lady, and I will tell you what I am thinking."

Miriamele did not want to stop rowing, so the monk kindly consented to feed her bites between strokes. His comical look while dodging the backswing of the oars made her laugh; a dry crust stuck in her throat. Cadrach thumped her back, then gave her a swig of water.

"That is enough, Lady. You must stop for a moment and finish your meal. Then, if you wish, you may start again. It would fly in the face of God's mercy to escape the kil . . . the many dangers we have, then to die of a foolish strangulation." He watched her critically as she ate. "You are thin, too. A girl your age should be putting meat on her bones. What did you eat on that cursed ship?"

"What Gan Itai brought me. The last week, I could not bear to sit at the same table with . . . that man." She fought back another wave of despair and instead waved her heel of bread indignantly. "But look at you! You are a skeleton—a fine one to talk!" She forced the lump of cheese he had given her back into his hand. "Eat that."

"I wish I had a jug." Cadrach washed the morsel down with a small swallow of water. "By Aedon's Golden Hair, a few dribbles of red Perdruin would do wonders."

"But you don't have any," Miriamele replied, irritated. "There is no wine for . . . for a very long way. So do something else instead. Tell me where you think we should go, if you really do have an idea." She licked her fingers, stretched until her bruised muscles twinged, then reached for the oars. "And tell me anything else you want as well. Distract me." She slowly resumed her rhythmic pulling.

For a while, the chop-swish of the blades diving and surfacing was the only sound except for the endless murmuration of the sea.

"There is a place," said Cadrach. "It is an inn—a hostel, I suppose—in Kwanitupul."

"The marsh-city?" Miriamele asked, suspicious. "Why would we want to go there—and if we did, what difference would it make which inn we chose? Is the wine so good?"

The monk put on a look of injured dignity. "My lady, you wrong me." His expression became more serious. "No, I suggest it because it may be a place of refuge in these dangerous times—and because it is where Dinivan was going to send you."

"Dinivan!" The name was a shock. Miriamele realized that she had not thought about the priest in many days, despite his kindness, despite his terrible death at Pryrates' hands. "Why on earth would you know what Dinivan wanted to do? And why should it matter now anyway?"

"How I know what Dinivan wanted is easy enough to explain. I listened at keyholes—and other places. I heard him discuss you with the lector and tell of his plans for you . . . although he did not inform the lector of all the reasons why."

"You did such a thing!?" Miriamele's outrage was quickly dampened by the memories of doing just such a thing herself. "Oh, never mind. I am beyond surprise. But you must change your ways, Cadrach. Such skulking—it goes with the drinking and lying."

"I do not think you know much about wine, my lady," he said with a wry smile, "so I may not consider you much of a teacher in that study. As for my other flaws—well, 'necessity beckons, self-interest comes following,' as they say in Abaingeat. And those flaws may prove the saving of us both, at least from our current situation."

"So why did Dinivan plan to send me to this inn?" she asked. "Why not let me stay at the Sancellan Aedonitis, where I would be safe?"

"As safe as Dinivan and the lector were, my lady?" Despite the harshness, there was real pain in his voice. "You know what happened there—although, the gods be thanked, you were spared seeing it with your poor young eyes. In any case, Dinivan and I had a falling out, but he was a good man and no fool. Too many people in and out of that place, too many folk with too many different needs and wants and problems to solve . . . and most of all, too many wagging tongues. I swear, they call Aedon's monument Mother Church, but at the Sancellan she is the most babble-breathed old gossip in the history of the world."

"So he planned to send me to some inn in the marshes?"

"I think so, yes—he spoke in a general way even to the lector, with no naming of names. But I am convinced I have it right because it is a place we all knew. Doctor Morgenes helped its owner to buy it. It is a place closely entangled with the secrets Dinivan and Morgenes and I shared."

Miriamele brought the oars to an awkward stop, leaning on the poles as she stared at Cadrach. He gazed back calmly, as though he had said nothing unusual. "My lady?" he asked at last.

"Doctor Morgenes . . . of the Hayholt?"

"Of course." He lowered his chin until it seemed to rest on his collarbone. "A great man. A kind, kind man. I loved him, Princess Miriamele. He was like a father to so many of us."

Mist was beginning to hover above the surface of the water, pale as cotton wool. Miriamele took a deep breath and shivered. "I don't understand. How did you know him? Who is 'us'?"

The monk let his gaze pass from her face out onto the shrouded sea. "It is a long story, Princess—a very long one. Have you ever heard of something called the League of the Scroll?"

"Yes! At Naglimund. The old man Jarnauga was part of it."

"Jarnauga." Cadrach sighed. "Another good man, although the gods know, we have had our differences. I hid from him while I was at Josua's stronghold. How was he?"

"I liked him," Miriamele said slowly. "He was one of those people who really listen—but I only talked with him a few times. I wonder what happened to him when Naglimund fell." She looked sharply at Cadrach. "What does all that have to do with you?"

"As I said, it is a long tale."

Miriamele laughed; it quickly turned into another shiver. "We don't have much else to do. Tell me."

"Let me first find something else to keep you warm." Cadrach crawled back into the shelter and brought out her monk's cloak. He draped it around Miriamele's shoulders and pulled the hood over her short hair. "Now you look like the convent-bound noblewoman you once claimed to be."

"Just talk to me—then I won't notice the cold."

"You are still weak, though. I wish you would put the oars down and let me take a turn, or at least lie down under the awning, out of the wind."

"Don't treat me like a little girl, Cadrach." Although she frowned, she was strangely touched. Was this the same man she had tried to drown—the same man who had tried to sell her into slavery? "You're not going to touch the oars tonight. When I get too tired, we'll drop the anchor. Until then, I'll row slowly. Now talk."

The monk waved his hands in a gesture of surrender. "Very well." He fluffed his own cloak around him, then settled down with his back against a bench and his knees drawn up before him so that he looked up at her from the darkness of the boat's bottom. The sky had gone almost completely black, and there was just enough moonlight to show his face. "I am afraid that I don't know where exactly to begin."

"At the beginning, of course." Miriamele raised the oars from the water and slid them back in again. A few drops of spray spattered her face.

"Ah. Yes." He thought for a moment. "Well, if I go back to the true beginnings of my story, then perhaps the later parts will be easier to understand—and that way I can also postpone the most shameful tales for a little while longer. It is not a happy story, Miriamele, and it winds through a great deal of shadow . . . shadow that has now fallen over many people besides a drunken Hernystiri monk.

"I was born in Crannhyr, you know—when I say I am Cadrach ec-Crannhyr, only the last part is true. I was born Padreic. I have had other names, too, few of them pleasant, but Padreic I was born, and Cadrach I now am, I suppose.

"I stretch no truth when I say that Crannhyr is one of the strangest cities in all of Osten Ard. It is walled like a great fortress, but it has never been attacked, nor is there anything particularly worth stealing in it. The people of Crannhyr are secretive in a way that even other Hernystiri do not understand. A Crannhyr-man, it is said, would sooner buy everyone at the inn a drink than let even his closest friend into his home—and no one yet has seen a Crannhyr-man buy anyone's drink but his own. Crannhyr folk are close; that is the best word, I think. They talk in few words—how unlike the rest of the Hernystiri, in whose blood runs poetry!—and they make no show of wealth or luck at all, for fear that the gods will become jealous and take it back. Even the streets are close as conspirators, the buildings leaning so near together in some spots that you have to blow out all your breath before you go in and cannot suck in more air until you come out at the far end.

"Crannhyr was one of the first cities built by men in Osten Ard, and that age breathes in everything, so that people talk quietly from birth, as though they are afraid that if they speak too loud the old walls will tumble down and expose all their secrets to the light of day. Some people say that the Sithi had a hand in the making of the place, but although we Hernystirmen are never foolish enough to disbelieve in the Sithi—unlike some of our neighbors—I for one do not think the Peaceful Ones had anything to do with Crannhyr. I have seen Sithi ruins, and they are nothing like the cramped and self-protective walls of the city in which I spent my childhood. No, men built it—frightened men, if my eye tells me anything."

"But it sounds a terrible place," Miriamele said. "All that whispering!"

"Yes, I did not like it much myself." Cadrach smiled, a tiny gleam in the shadow. "I spent most of my childhood wanting to get away. My mother died when I was young, you see, and my father was a hard, cold man, fitly made for that hard, cold city. He never spoke a word more to me or my brothers and sisters than was necessary, and did not embellish even those words with kindness. He was a coppersmith, and I suppose that hammering at a hot forge all day to put food into our mouths showed that he recognized his obligations, so he felt bound to do no more. Most Crannhyri are like that—dour, and scornful of those who are not. I could not wait to make my own way in the world.

"Strangely, though—and it is often the way—for one so bedeviled by secrets and quietude, I developed a surprising love for old books and ancient learning. Seen through the eyes of the ancients—scholars like Plesinnen Myrmenis and Cuihmne's Frethis—even Crannhyr was wonderful and mystical, its secretive ways hiding not just old unpleasantness, but strange wisdoms that freer, less arcane places could not boast. In the Tethtain Library—founded in our city centuries ago by the great Holly King himself—I found the only kindred souls in that entire walled prison, people who, like myself, lived for the lights of earlier days, and who enjoyed running down a bit of lost lore the way some men revel in chasing down a buck deer and putting an arrow in its heart.

"And that is where I met Morgenes. In those days—and this is almost two score years ago, my young princess—he was still inclined to travel. If there is a man who has seen more than Morgenes, who has been to more places, I have never heard of him. The doctor spent many hours among the scrolls of the Tethtain Library and knew the archives better than even the old priests who watched over them. He saw my interest in matters of history and forgotten lore and took me in hand, guiding me toward useful paths that I would otherwise never have found. When some years had passed, and he saw that my devotion to learning was not a thing to be sloughed off with childhood, he told me of the League of the Scroll, which was formed long ago by Saint Eahlstan Fiskerne, the Hayholt's Fisher King. Eahlstan inherited Fingil's castle and his sword Minneyar, but he wanted nothing to do with the Rimmersman's heritage of destruction—especially the destruction of learning. Eahlstan wanted instead to conserve knowledge that might otherwise vanish into shadow—and to use that knowledge when it seemed necessary."

"Use it for what?"

"We often argued about that, Princess. It was never 'for Good' or 'for Righteousness'—the Scrollbearers realized that once such a broad ideal is in place, one must meddle in *everything*. I suppose the clearest explanation is that the League acts to protect its own learning, to prevent a dark age that would bury again the secrets it has so laboriously unearthed. But at other times the League has acted only to protect itself rather than its products.

"However, I knew little of such difficult questions then. For me, the League sounded like a dream of heaven—a happy brotherhood of extraordinary scholars searching out the secrets of Creation together. I was deliriously eager to join. Thus, when our shared love of scholarship had ripened into a friendship—although on my part it was more like a love for a kind father—Morgenes took me to meet Trestolt, who was Jarnauga's father, and old Ookequk, a wise man of the troll people who live in the far north. Morgenes put me forward as fit for the League, and those two took me in without hesitation, as wholeheartedly and trustfully as if they had known me all their lives—but that was because of Morgenes, you see. With the exception of Trestolt, whose wife had died a few years before, none of the other Scrollbearers was married. This has often been the case throughout the League's centuries of existence. Its members are generally the kind of folk—and it is true of the women who have carried the Scroll as well—who are more in love with knowledge than with mankind. Not that they do not care for other people, you must understand, but they love them better when they can keep them at a distance; in practice, people are a distraction. So for the Scrollbearers, the League itself became a kind of family. Thus, it was no surprise that any candidate put forward by the doctor should be warmly greeted. Morgenes—although he resisted any move to grant him power—was in a way a father to all the League's members, despite the fact that some of them seemed older than he did. But who will ever know when or where Morgenes was born?"

Down in the darkness of the hull, Cadrach laughed. Miriamele slowly dipped the oars into the water, listening dreamily to his words as the boat rose and fell.

"Later," he continued, "I met the other Scrollbearer, Xorastra of Perdruin. She had been a nun, although by the time I met her she had left her order. The inn at Kwanitupul that I spoke of earlier belongs to her, by the way. She was a fiercely clever woman, denied by her sex the life she would otherwise have led: she should have been a king's minister, that one. Xorastra also accepted me, then introduced me to a pair of her own candidates, for she and Morgenes had long had it in their minds to bring the numbers of the League back up to seven, which had traditionally been its full measure.

"Both of them were younger than I was. Dinivan was a mere youth at the time, studying with the Usirean brothers. Sharp-eyed Xorastra had seen the spark in him, and thought that if he were brought into contact with Morgenes and the others, that spark might become a great and warming fire by which the church she still loved could greatly benefit. The other that she put forward was a clever young priest, just ordained, who came from a poor island family, but who had made his way into a small sort of prominence by the swiftness of his mind. Morgenes, after much talk with Xorastra and their two northern colleagues, accepted these two new additions. When we all met the next year in Tungoldyr at the longhouse of Trestolt, the numbers of the League of the Scroll were seven once more."

Cadrach's words had become heavy and slow, and when at last he paused, Miriamele thought he might be falling asleep. But instead, when he spoke again there was a terrible hollowness to his voice. "Better they had kept us all out. Better that the League itself had fallen back into the dust of history."

When he did not speak more, Miriamele straightened up. "What do you mean, Cadrach? What could you have done that was so bad?"

He groaned. "Not me, Princess—my sins came later. No, it was in the moment we brought that young priest into our midst . . . for that was Pryrates."

Miriamele sucked in a deep breath, and for a moment, despite her warming feelings for Cadrach, felt the web of some terrible conspiracy gathering around her. Were all her enemies in alliance? Was the monk playing some deeper game, so that now she was in his hands utterly, adrift on an empty sea? Then she remembered the letter that Gan Itai had brought her.

"But you told me that," she said, relieved. "You wrote to me and said something about Pryrates—that you had made him what he was."

"If I said that," Cadrach replied sadly, "then I was exaggerating in my grief. The seeds of great evil must have been in him already, otherwise it could never have flowered so swiftly and so forcefully . . . or such is my guess. My own part came much later, and my shame is that although I already knew him for a black-souled and heartless creature, I helped him anyway."

"But why? And helped him how?"

"Ah, Princess, I feel the drunken honesty of the Hernystiri on me tonight without even tasting a swallow of wine—but still there are things I would rather not tell. The story of my downfall is mine alone. Most of my friends who were near me in those years are dead now. Let me say only this: for many reasons, both because of the things that I studied, many of which I wish I had left alone, and because of my own pain and the many drunken nights I spent trying to kill it, the joy that for a time I found in life soon faded away. When I was a child, I believed in the gods of my people. When I was older, I came to doubt them, and believed instead in the single god of the Aedonites—single, though

He is dreadfully mixed up with Usires His son and Elysia the blessed mother. Later, in the first blossoming of my scholarship, I came to disbelieve in all gods, old and new. But a certain dread gripped my heart when I became a man, and now I believe in the gods once more . . . Ah, how I believe! . . . for I know myself to be cursed." The monk quietly wiped his eyes and nose on his sleeve. He was sunken now in a shadow even the moonlight could not pierce.

"Cursed? What do you mean? Cursed how?"

"I do not know, or I would have found some hedge-wizard to grind me up a powder-charm a long time ago. No, I am joking, my lady, and a bleak joke it is. There are curses in the world no spell can dismiss—just as, I presume, there is good luck that no evil eye or envious rival can overthrow, but which can only be lost by its possessor. I only know that long ago the world became a heavy burden on me, one that my shoulders have proved too weak to bear. I became a drunkard in earnest—no local clown who drinks too many pots and sings the neighbors awake on his way home, but a chill-spirited, heart-lonely seeker of oblivion. My books were my only solace, but even they seemed to me full of the breath of tombs: they spoke only of dead lives, dead thoughts, and worst of all, dead and juiceless hopes, a million of them stillborn for every one that had a brief butterfly moment under the sun.

"So I drank, and I railed at the stars, and I drank. My drunkenness sent me down into the pit of despond, and my books, especially the volume with which I was then most deeply involved, only made my dread worse. So oblivion seemed even more desirable. Soon I was not wanted in the places where once I had been everyone's friend, which made me even more bitter. When the keepers of the Tethtain Library told me I would no longer be welcomed there, I fell down as into a deep hole, a season-long riot of black drunkenness from which I awoke to find myself by the side of a road outside Abaingeat, naked and without a cintis-piece. Clothed only in brambles and leaves like the lowest beast, I made my way by night to the house of a nobleman I knew, a good man and a lover of learning who had been, from time to time, my willing patron. He let me in, fed me, then gave me a bed for the night. When the sun rose, he gave me a monk's gown that had belonged to his brother and wished me good luck and Godspeed away from his house.

"There was disgust in his eyes that morning, Lady, a kind of loathing that I pray you never see in the eyes of another person. He knew of my habits, you see, and my tale of abduction and robbery did not fool him. I knew, as I stood in his doorway, that I had passed beyond the walls that surrounded my fellow men, that I was now as one unclean from plague. You see, all my drinking and wretched acts had only done this: it had made my curse as plain for others to see as it had been to me long before."

Cadrach's voice, which had grown more deathly during this recitation, now trailed off in a hoarse whisper. Miriamele listened to him breathing for a long while. She could think of nothing to say.

"But what had you actually done?" she tried at last. "You speak of being cursed, but you hadn't done anything wrong—besides drinking too much wine, that is."

Cadrach's laugh was unpleasantly cracked. "Oh, the wine was only to dull the pain. That is the thing with these stains, my lady. Though others, especially innocents like yourself, cannot always see them, the stain is there nevertheless, and others sense it, as the beasts of the field sense one of their number who is sick or mad. You tried to drown me yourself, didn't you?"

"But that was different!" Miriamele said indignantly. "That was for something you did!"

"Never fear," the monk murmured. "I have done enough wrong since that night by the road in Abaingeat to justify any punishment."

Miriamele pulled the oars in. "Is it shallow enough to drop the anchor?" she asked, trying to keep her voice calm. "My arms are tired."

"I will find out."

While the monk rooted the anchor out of the hold and made sure that its cord was tied firmly to the boat, Miriamele tried to think of something she could do to help him. The more she made him talk, the deeper the wounds seemed to be. His earlier good cheer, she sensed, was nothing but a thin skin that had grown over these raw places. Was it better to make him speak, when it was obviously painful, or simply to let it go? She wished that Geloë were here, or little Binabik with his shrewd and careful touch.

When the anchor had splashed over the side and the rope had fizzed down into the depths behind it, the two of them sat quietly for a while. At last, Cadrach spoke, his voice a little lighter than it had been.

"The cord only played out twenty ells or so before it struck bottom, so we may be closer to shore than I had thought. Still, you should try to sleep again, Miriamele. The day will be long tomorrow. If we are to reach shore, we will have to take turns at those oars so we can keep moving all day."

"Might there not be a ship around somewhere that might see us and pick us up?"

"I don't know if that would be the luckiest thing for us. Do not forget that Nabban now belongs utterly to your father and Pryrates. I think we will be happiest if we can make our way quietly to shore and disappear into the poorer parts of Nabban, then find our way to Xorastra's inn."

"You never explained about Pryrates," she said boldly, inwardly praying that it was not a mistake. "What happened between the two of you?"

Cadrach sighed. "Would you really force me to tell you such black things, Lady? It was only weakness and fear that led me to mention them in my letter, when I was frightened you would mistake the Earl of Eadne for something better than he was."

"I would not force you to do anything that would hurt you more, Cadrach. But I would like to know. These are the secrets that are behind our troubles, remember? It is not the time to hold them back, however bad they are."

The monk nodded slowly. "Spoken like a king's daughter—but spoken well.

Ah, gods of earth and sky, if I had known that one day I would have to tell such stories and say 'that is my life,' I think I would have pushed my head into my father's kiln."

Miriamele made no reply but pulled her cloak tight. Some of the mist had blown away, and the sea stretched away beneath them like a great black table-top. The stars overhead seemed too small and chill to give off light; they hung unsparkling, like flecks of milky stone.

"I did not leave the fellowship of ordinary men completely empty-handed," Cadrach began. "There were certain things I had obtained—many of them legitimately, in my early days of scholarship. One was a great treasure which no one knew that I had. My possessions—those I had not sold to buy wine— remained in the care of an old friend. When it was decided I was no longer fit for the company of those I had known, I took them back from him . . . against his protestations, for he knew I was not a reliable keeper. Thus, when times became particularly bad, I could usually find a dealer in rare manuscripts or church-forbidden books and—usually at prices so low as to approach robbery— get some money in exchange for one of my prized books. But, as I said, one thing that I had found was worth a thousandfold more than all the rest. The story of its getting is a night's tale in itself, but it was for long the one thing with which I would not part, however desperate my circumstances. For you see, I had found a copy of *Du Svardenvyrd,* the fabled book of mad Nisses, the only copy that I have ever heard to exist in modern days. Whether it was the origi-nal I do not know, for the binding had long since disappeared, but the . . . person from whom I obtained it swore that it was genuine; indeed, if it was a forgery, it was a work of brilliance in itself. But copy or no, it contained the actual words of Nisses—of that there was no doubt. No one could read the dreadful things that I did, then look at the world around him, and disbelieve."

"I have heard of it," said Miriamele. "Who *was* Nisses?"

Cadrach laughed shortly. "A question for the ages. He was a man who came out of the north beyond Elvritshalla, from the land of the Black Rimmersmen who live below Stormspike, and presented himself to Fingil, King of Rimmers-gard. He was no court conjuror, but it is said that he gave Fingil the power that enabled him to conquer half of Osten Ard. That power may have been wisdom, for Nisses knew the facts of things that no one else had even dreamed existed. After Asu'a was conquered and Fingil died at last, Nisses served Fingil's son Hjeldin. It was during those years that he wrote his book—a book that con-tained part of the dreadful knowledge he had brought with him when he ap-peared in a murderous snowstorm outside Fingil's gates. He and Hjeldin both died in Asu'a—the young king by throwing himself out the window of the tower that bears his name. Nisses was found dead in the room from which Hjeldin had leapt, with no mark upon him. There was a smile on his face; the book was clutched in his hands."

Miriamele shuddered. "That book. They spoke of it at Naglimund. Jarnauga said that it supposedly tells of the Storm King's coming and other things."

"Ah, Jarnauga," Cadrach said sadly. "How he would have loved to see it! But I never showed it to him, nor to any of the Scrollbearers."

"But why? If you had it, even a copy, why didn't you show it to Morgenes and the others? I thought that was just the sort of thing that your League was for."

"Perhaps. But by the time I had finished reading it, I was no longer a Scroll-bearer. I knew it in my heart. From the moment I turned the last page I gave up the love of learning for the love of oblivion—the two cannot live together. Even before I found Nisses' book, I had gone far down the wrong paths, learning things that no man should learn who wishes to sleep well at night. And I was jealous of my fellow Scrollbearers, Miriamele, jealous of their simple happiness with their studies, angry with their calm assurance that all that could be examined could be understood. They were so certain that if they could look closely enough at the nature of the world they could divine all its purposes . . . but *I* had something they did not, a book the mere reading of which would not only prove to them things I had already suggested, but would crumble the pillars of their understanding. I was full of rage, Miriamele, but I was also full of despair." He paused, the pain clear in his voice. "The world is different once Nisses has explained it. It is as though the pages of his book were dipped in some slow poison that kills the spirit. I touched them all."

"It sounds horrible." Miriamele remembered the image she had seen in one of Dinivan's books, a homed giant with red eyes. She had seen that image since, in many troubling dreams. Could it be better not to know some things, to be blind to certain pictures and ideas?

"Horrible indeed, but only because it reflected the true terror that lurked beneath the waking world, the shadows which are the obverse image of sunlight. Still, even such a powerful thing as Nisses' book eventually became nothing more to me than another instrument of forgetting: when I had read it so many times that it made me sick even to stare at it, I began to sell its pages off, one by one."

"Elysia, Mother of Mercy! Who would buy such a thing?"

Cadrach chortled harshly. "Even those who were sure it was a deft forgery stumbled over themselves in their haste to take a single page from my hands. A banned book has a powerful fascination, young one, but a truly evil book—and there are not many—draws the curious as honey lures flies." His laughter grew for a moment, then was choked off in what sounded like a sob. "Sweet Usires, I wish that I had burned it!"

"But what about Pryrates?" she prodded. "Did you sell pages to him?"

"Never!" Cadrach almost shouted. "Even then, I knew he was a demon. He was forced out of the League long before my own downfall, and every one of us knew what a danger he was!" He recovered his composure. "No, I suspect that he merely frequented the same peddlers of antiquities that I did—it is a rather small community, you know—and that some scraps made their way into his hands. He is tremendously learned in dark matters, Princess, particularly the most dangerous areas of the Art. It was not difficult, I'm sure, for him to discover who had possessed the powerful thing from which those pages came. Neither was it hard for him to find me, despite the fact that I had sunk myself as deeply into shadows as I could, bending all my own learning into making myself unimportant to the point of invisibility. But, as I said, he found me. He sent some of your father's own guardsmen after me. You see, he had already become a counselor to princes—or in your sire's case, kings-to-be."

Miriamele thought of the day she had first met Pryrates. The red priest had come to her father's apartments in Meremund, bringing Elias information about events in Nabban. Young Miriamele had been having a difficult time speaking to her father, struggling to think of something she could tell him that might make him smile even for a moment, as he often had in the days when she was the light of his eye. Matters of state providing a useful excuse for avoiding another uncomfortable conversation with his daughter, Elias had sent her away. Curious, she had caught Pryrates' gaze on her way out the door.

Even as a young girl, Miriamele had become used to the variety of different looks she inspired among her father's courtiers—irritation from those who considered her an impediment to their affairs, pity from those who recognized her loneliness and confusion, honest calculation from those who wondered who she might marry someday, or whether she would grow into an attractive woman, or whether she would be a pliable queen after her father's death. But never until that moment had she been examined with anything like Pryrates' inhuman regard, a stare cold as a plunge in ice water. There seemed not the slightest bit of human feeling in his black eyes: she had known somehow that had she been flayed meat on a butcher's table his expression would have been no different. At the same time, he had seemed to see right into her and through her, as though her every thought were being made to walk naked before him, squirming beneath his inspection. Aghast, she had turned from his terrible gaze and fled down the corridor, inexplicably weeping. Behind, she heard the dry buzz of the alchemist's voice as he began to speak. She realized she meant no more to this new intimate of her father's than would a fly—that he would ignore her with never another thought, or crush her without a qualm if it suited his purposes. To a girl raised in the nurturing certainty of her own importance, an importance that had even outlasted her father's love, it was a horrifying realization.

Her father, for all his faults, had never been a monster of that sort. Why, then, had he brought Pryrates into his inner circle, so that eventually the devil-priest became his closest and most trusted advisor? It was a deeply troubling question, and one for which she had never discovered an answer.

Now, in the gently pitching boat, she struggled to keep her voice steady. "Tell me what happened, Cadrach."

The monk plainly did not want to start. Miriamele could hear his fingers scratching quietly against the wooden seat, as though he searched for something in the darkness. "They found me in the stable of an inn in south Erchester," he said slowly, "sleeping in the muck. The guardsmen dragged me out, then threw me in the back of a wagon and we rode toward the Hayholt. It was during the worst year of that terrible drought, and in the late afternoon light everything was gold and brown, even the trees stiff and dull as dried mud. I remember staring, my head ringing like a church bell—I had been sleeping off a long bout of drinking, of course—and wondering if the same dryness that made my eyes and nose and mouth feel as though they were packed with dust had somehow leached away all the colors of the world as well.

"The soldiers, I'm sure, thought I was nothing but another criminal, and one not fated for a long life beyond that afternoon. They talked as though I were already dead, complaining about the onerous duty of having to carry out and bury a corpse as fetid and unwashed as mine. A guardsman even said he would demand an extra hour's pay for the unpleasant labor. One of his companions smirked and said: 'From Pryrates?'. The braggart fell silent. Some of the other soldiers laughed at his discomfort, but their voices were forced, as though the mere thought of demanding anything from the red priest was enough to spoil the day. This was the first time I had any inkling of where I was going, and I knew it to be a great deal worse than simply being hung as a thief or a traitor—both of which I was. I tried to throw myself out of the cart, but was quickly pulled back in again. 'Ho,' one of them said, 'he knows the name!'

" 'Please,' I begged, 'do not take me to that man. If there is Aedonite mercy in you, do anything else with me you like, but do not give me to the priest.' The soldier who had last spoken stared at me, and I think there might have been some pity in his hard eyes, but he said: 'And bring his anger down on us? Leave our children fatherless? No. Bear up, and face it like a man.'

"I wept all the way to the Nearulagh Gate.

"The cart stopped at the iron-banded front door of Hjeldin's Tower and I was dragged inside, too weak with despair to resist—not that my wasted body would have served me for much against four armed Erkynguards. I was half-carried through the anteroom, then up what seemed like a million steps. At the top, two great oaken doors swung open. I was shoved through like a sack of meal and fell to my knees on the hard flags of a cluttered chamber.

"The first thing I thought, Princess, was that I had tumbled somehow into a lake of blood. The entire room was scarlet, every niche and cranny; my very hands held before my face had changed their color as well. I looked up in horror to the tall windows. Every one was fitted from top to bottom with panes of bright red glass; the setting sun streamed through them, dazzling the eye, as though each window were a great ruby. The red light stripped everything inside the room of color, just as evening does. There seemed no shades but black and red. There were tables and tall, leaning shelves, none of which touched the chamber's single curving outer wall, but instead were clustered toward the middle of the room. Every surface was draped in books and scrolls and . . . and other things, many of which I could not bear to look at for long. The priest has a terrible curiosity. There is nothing he will not do to discover the truth about something—or such truths as are important to him. Many of the subjects of his inquiries, mostly animals, were locked in cages stacked haphazardly among the books; most of them were still alive, although it would have been better for them if they had not been. Considering the chaos in the center of the room, the wall was curiously uncluttered, naked except for certain painted symbols.

"'Ah,' a voice said. 'Greetings, fellow Scrollbearer.' It was Pryrates, of course, seated on a narrow, high-backed chair at the center of this strange nest. 'I trust your journey was a comfortable one?'

"'Let us not bandy words,' I said. With despair had come a certain resignation. 'You are a Scrollbearer no longer, Pryrates, nor am I. What do you want?'

"He grinned. He was in no mood to speed what was, for him, an enjoyable diversion. 'Once a member of the League, always a member, I should think,' he chuckled. 'For are we not both still intimately concerned with old things, old writings . . . old books?'

"When he said this last, my heart stumbled in my chest. At first I had thought he wanted only to torment me, to take revenge for his ousting from the League—although others were more responsible for that than I was; I had already begun my slide into darkness when he was forced out. Now I realized he wanted something quite different. He plainly desired some book he thought I had—and I had little doubt as to which book that might be.

"I dueled with him for part of an hour, using words as a swordsman does his blade, and for a while held my own—the last thing a drunkard loses, you see, is his cunning: it outlasts his soul by a long season—but we both knew that I would give in at the end. I was tired, you see, very tired and sick. As we spoke, two men came into the room. These were not more Erkynguardsmen, but rather somber-robed, shaven-headed men who had the dark-haired, dark-skinned look of southern islanders. They neither of them spoke—perhaps they were mutes—but nevertheless, their purpose was clear: they would hold me so that Pryrates might have his hands and attention unimpeded as he moved on to more strenuous means of negotiation. When the two grabbed my arms and dragged me close to the priest's chair, I gave up. It was not the pain I feared, Miriamele, or even the other soul-horrors that he could have inflicted. I swear that to you, although why it should matter I don't know. Rather, I simply no longer cared. Let him have what he would of me, I thought. Let him do what he pleased with it. It was not, I told myself, as though this sin-blackened world might receive undeserved punishment . . . for I had dwelt in the depths so long that I saw nothing left that was good but nothingness itself.

"'You have been making free with pages from a certain old volume, Padreic,' he said. 'Or do I remember that you call yourself something different now? No matter. I need that book. If you tell me where you keep it hidden, you will walk free into the evening air.' He gestured to the world beyond the scarlet windows. 'If not . . .' He pointed at certain objects that were lying on the table close by his hand, objects already filthy with hair and blood.

"'I do not have it anymore,' I told him. That was the truth. I had sold the remaining few pages a fortnight earlier: I had been sleeping off the last of the proceeds in that noisome stable.

"He said: 'I do not believe you, little man,' then his servants did something to me until I screamed. When I still could not tell him where it was, he began to take a more active hand himself, stopping only when I could shriek no longer and my voice was a cracked whisper. 'Hmm,' he said, scratching his chin as though aping Doctor Morgenes, who would often muse that way over a delicate translation. 'Perhaps I must believe you after all. I find it hard to think that offal such as you would stay silent on purely moral grounds. Tell me who you sold it to—all the pieces.'

"Damning myself silently for the murder of these various merchants—for Pryrates, I knew, would have them killed and their wares confiscated without a moment's hesitation—I told him all the names I could remember. When I hesitated, I was helped along by . . . by . . . his servants. . . .'"

Cadrach suddenly broke into deep, chesty sobs. Miriamele heard him trying to repress them, then he broke off in a fit of coughing. She leaned forward and caught his cold hand, squeezing hard to let him know that she was there. After a while, his breathing became more regular.

"I am sorry, Princess," he rasped. "I do not like to think of it."

There were tears in Miriamele's eyes as well. "It's my fault. I should never have made you talk about it. Let's stop, and you can sleep."

"No." She could feel him shaking. "No, I have begun it. I will not sleep well in any case. Perhaps it will help me if I finish the tale." He reached out and patted her head. "I thought he had gotten everything from me he could wish, but I was wrong. 'What if these gentlemen no longer have the pieces I need, Padreic?' he asked. Ah, gods, there is nothing fouler than that priest's smile! 'I think you should tell me what you remember—there is still some wit left in that wine-soaked head, is there not? Come, recite for me, little acolyte.'

"And tell him I did, every bit and every line that I could recall, the order as tumbled as you would expect from a creature as wretched as I was. He seemed most interested in Nisses' cryptic words on death, especially something termed 'speaking through the veil,' which I gathered to be the rituals that allow one to reach what Nisses had called 'songs of the upper air'—that is, the thoughts of those who are somehow beyond mortality, both the dead and the never-living. I disgorged it all, aching to please, with Pryrates sitting there nodding, nodding, his shiny head gleaming in the strange light.

"Somehow, in the middle of this terrible experience, I noticed something strange. It took a while, as you can imagine, but since I had begun to talk freely about my memories of Nisses' book I had been left unharmed—one of the unspeaking servitors even gave me a cup of water so that I could speak more clearly. While I rattled on, answering Pryrates' every question as eagerly as a child at its first holy mansa, I noticed something disturbing about the way the light was moving across the room. At first, in my weary, pained state, I was convinced that somehow Pryrates had managed to make the sun roll backward in its tracks, for the light that should have been passing from east to west across the bloody windows was slipping the other way instead. I mused on this—at such times, it is good to have something to think about other than what is happening to you—and realized at last that the laws of heaven had not been countermanded after all. Rather, it was the tower itself, or at least the topmost section where we were, that was spinning slowly sunward, a little faster than the passage of the sun itself—so slowly that, when combined with the sameness of the tower's uppermost story, I would guess that none have ever marked it from the outside.

"So that was why nothing was allowed to lean against the stones of these chamber walls, I thought! Even in the extremity of my pain and terror, I marveled at the huge gears and wheels that must be moving silently behind the mortar or below my feet. Such things were once a joy of mine—I spent many hours of my youth studying the mechanical laws of the spinning globe and the heavens. And, the gods help me, it gave me something to think about beside what had been done to me, and what I, in turn, was doing to my fellow men.

"Looking around the circular room as I continued my prattling, I saw for the first time the subtle marks incised in the red window glass, and how those marks, thrown forward as faint lines of darker red, crossed over the strange symbols marked all around on the tower's interior wall. I could think of no other explanation but that Pryrates had turned the top of Hjeldin's Tower into some kind of vast water clock, a time-keeping device of fantastic size and intricacy. I have pondered and pondered, but to this day I still can think of nothing else that fits the facts as well. The black arts in which Pryrates has become involved, I suppose, have made hourglass and sundial unhelpfully imprecise."

Miriamele let him pause for a long time. "So what happened, Cadrach?"

Cadrach still hesitated. When he resumed, he spoke a little more swiftly, as though this part was even more troubling than what had preceded it. "After I had finished telling Pryrates all I knew, he sat thinking for the time it took the last sliver of the sun to drop out one of the windows and appear at the edge of the next. Then he stood, waved a hand, and one of his servants stepped up behind me. Something struck me on the head and I knew no more. I woke up lying in a thicket in the Kynslagh, my torn clothes stained with the fluids of my own body. I believe they thought me dead. Certainly Pryrates did not believe me worth any more effort, not even the effort to kill me properly." Cadrach stopped to take a deep breath.

"You would think that I would have been deliriously happy to be alive, to have survived when I did not expect to, but all I could do was crawl deeper into the underbrush and wait for death. But those were warm, dry days; I did not die. When I was enough recovered, I made my way down into Erchester. There I stole some clothing and some food. I even bathed in the Kynslagh, so that I could go to into the places where wine was sold." The monk groaned. "But I could not leave the town, although I burned to. The sight of Hjeldin's Tower looming up above the Hayholt's outwall terrified me, but still I could not flee:

I felt as though Pryrates had pulled out a part of my soul to keep me tethered, as though he could call me back any time he wished and I would go. This despite the fact that he clearly did not care if I was alive or dead. I remained in the town, thieving, drinking, trying without success to forget the terrible, treacherous thing I had done. I have not forgotten it, of course—I will *never* forget it—although I eventually grew strong enough to wrench myself free of the tower's shadow and flee Erchester." He looked for a moment as though he might say something more, but shuddered and fell silent.

Miriamele again clutched the monk's hand, which had been scraping fretfully at the wooden bench. Somewhere to the south a seagull raised its lonely cry. "But you can't blame yourself, Cadrach. That is foolish. Anyone would have done what you did."

"No, Princess," he murmured sadly. "Some would not have. Some would have died before telling such dreadful secrets. And more importantly, others would not have given up a treasure in the first place—especially a dangerous treasure like Nisses' book—for the price of a few jugs of wine. I had a sacred trust. That is what the League of the Scroll is meant for, Miriamele—to preserve knowledge, and also to preserve Osten Ard from those like Pryrates who would use the old knowledge for power over others. I failed on both those counts. And the League was also meant to watch for the return of Ineluki, the Storm King. There I failed most miserably of all, for it seems clear to me that I gave Pryrates the means of finding that terrible spirit and interesting it in humankind once more—and all this evil I accomplished simply so I could guzzle wine, so I could make my already dim brain a little darker."

"But why did Pryrates want to know all that? Why was he so interested in death?"

"I don't know." Cadrach was weary. "His is a mind that has gone rotten like a piece of old fruit—who knows what strange prodigies will hatch from such a thing?"

Angry, Miriamele squeezed his hand. "That is no answer."

Cadrach sat up a little straighter. "I'm sorry, my lady, but I have no answers. The only thing I can say is that from the questions Pryrates asked me, I do not think that he was seeking to contact the Storm King—not at first. No, he had some other interest in, as he called it, 'speaking through the veil.' And I think that when he began to explore in those lightless regions, he was noticed. Most living mortals who are discovered there are destroyed or made mad, but my guess is that Pryrates was recognized as a possible tool for a vengeful Ineluki. From what you and others have told me, he has been a very useful tool indeed."

Miriamele, chilled by the night breeze, crouched lower. Something in what Cadrach had just said tugged at her mind, asking to be examined. "I want to think," she said.

"If I have disgusted you, my lady, it is only reasonable." He seemed very distant. "I have grown unutterably disgusted with myself."

"Don't be an idiot." Impulsively, she lifted his cold hand and pressed it against her cheek. Startled, he left it there for a moment before pulling it back again. "You have made mistakes, Cadrach. So have I, so have many others." She yawned. "Now we need to sleep, so we can get up in the morning and start rowing again." She crawled past him toward the boat's makeshift cabin.

"My lady?" the monk said, surprise evident in his voice, but she did not say anything more.

Some time later, as Miriamele was drifting toward sleep, she heard him crawl in beneath the oilcloth shelter. He curled up near her feet, but his breathing stayed quiet, as though he, too, were thinking. Soon, the gentle smack of the waves and the rocking of the anchored boat pulled her down into dreams.

10

Riders of the Dawn

✹

Despite the chill morning mists that covered Sesuad'ra like a gray cloak, New Gadrinsett was in almost a festival mood. The troop of trolls, led back across the slowly freezing lake by Binabik and Simon, were a new and pleasant wonder in a year whose other oddities had been almost entirely bad. As Simon and his small friends made their way up the last winding stretch of the old Sithi road, a rush of chattering children who had legged out ahead of their parents and older siblings began to gather around them. The mountain rams, hardened by the din of Qanuc villages, did not break stride. Some of the smaller children were lifted up by rough brown hands and dropped into the saddle to ride with troll herders and huntresses. One little boy, not expecting such a sudden and intimate introduction to the newcomers, broke into loud crying. Grinning worriedly through his sparse beard, the troll-man who had picked him up held the struggling lad gently but firmly in place lest he fall and be hurt among the horn-bumping rams. The boy's wailing outstripped even the shouting of the other children and the unrestrained banging and tootling of Qanuc marching music.

Binabik had told Josua of his folk's arrival before taking Simon down to the forest; in turn, the prince had done his best to see that a suitable welcome was prepared. The rams were taken to warm cavern stables where they cropped hay contentedly beside New Gadrinsett's horses, then Sisqi and the rest of her troll contingent marched to the wind-burnished hulk of Leavetaking House, still surrounded by a flock of gaping settlers. Sesuad'ra's meager stores were combined with the traveling food of the trolls and a modest meal was shared. There were now enough citizens in New Gadrinsett that the addition of five score of even such diminutive men and women filled the cavernous Sithi hall to its limits, but the closeness made it a warmer place. There was little food, but the company was exotically exciting.

Sangfugol stood, dressed in his best—if perhaps a little threadbare—doublet and hose, and presented a few favorite old songs. The trolls applauded by smacking their boots with the palms of their hands, a custom that much amused the citizens of New Gadrinsett. A man and woman of the Qanuc, urged on by their fellows, next presented an acrobatic dance that employed two of their hooked sheep-herder's spears and involved much leaping and tumbling. Most of the people of New Gadrinsett, even those who had entered the hall suspicious of these small strangers, found themselves warming to the newcomers. Only among those few settlers originally from Rimmersgard did there seem to be any lingering ill-feeling: the longtime enmity of trolls and Rimmersmen would not be banished by a single banquet and a little dancing and singing.

Simon sat and watched proudly. He did not drink, since the blood was still thudding uncomfortably in his head from the previous night's *kangkang,* but he felt as pleasurably giddy as if he had just downed a skinful. All Sesuad'ra's defenders were grateful for the arrival of new allies—any allies. The trolls were small, but Simon remembered from Sikkihoq what brave fighters they were. There was still little chance that Josua's folk would be able to hold off Fengbald, but at least the odds were better than they had been the day before. Best of all, however, Sisqi had solemnly asked Simon to fight alongside the trolls. From what he could gather, they had never asked another *Utku,* which made it an honor indeed. The Qanuc thought very highly of his bravery, she told him, and the loyalty he had shown to Binabik.

Simon could not help gloating a little, although he had decided to keep it to himself for the time being. Still, he could not keep from grinning cheerfully down the long table at anyone whose eye he caught.

When Jeremias appeared, Simon forced him to sit down beside him. In the company of the prince and the other "high folk," as Jeremias called them, the onetime chandler's boy was still generally more comfortable waiting on Simon as his body-servant—something that Simon did not find comfortable at all.

"It's not right," Jeremias grunted, staring down at the cup that Simon had placed in front of him. "I'm your squire, Simon. I shouldn't be sitting at the prince's table. I should be filling *your* cup."

"Nonsense." Simon waved his hand airily. "That's not the way things work here. Besides, if you had gotten out of the castle when I did, it would have been you that had the adventures, and me who wound up in the cellar with Inch. . . ."

"Don't say that!" Jeremias gasped, eyes full of sudden fright. "You don't know . . . !" He struggled to control himself. "No, Simon, don't even say it—you'll bring bad luck, make it come true!" His expression changed, the fear gradually giving way to a look of wistfulness. "Besides, you're wrong. Such things wouldn't have happened to me, Simon—the dragon, the fairy-folk, any of that. If you can't see that you're special, then . . ." He took a deep breath, ". . . then you're just being stupid."

This kind of talk made Simon even more uncomfortable. "Special or stupid, make up your mind," he growled.

Jeremias stared at him as if sensing his thought. He seemed to consider pursuing the subject, but after some moments his face twisted into a mocking smile instead. "Hmm. 'Specially stupid' would be about right, now that you mention it."

Relieved to find himself back on safer footing, Simon dipped his fingers in his wine cup and flicked droplets onto Jeremias' pale face, making his friend splutter. "And you, sirrah, are no better. I have anointed thee, and now I dub thee 'Sir Stupidly Special.'" He gravely flicked a few more drops. Jeremias snarled and swiped at the cup, spilling the dregs onto Simon's shirt, then they began to arm-wrestle, laughing and swatting back and forth with their free hands like sportive bear cubs.

"Specially Stupid!"

"Stupidly Special!"

The contest, although still good-natured, soon became a little more heated; those guests seated closest to the combatants moved back to give them room. Prince Josua, despite certain reservations, found it hard to maintain his look of detached propriety. Lady Vorzheva laughed outright.

The trolls, whose state occasions took place in the awesome vastness of Chidsik ub Lingit and never included anything as trivial as two friends wrestling and rubbing wine in each other's hair, watched the proceedings with grave interest. Several wondered aloud if any particular augury or prophesy was determined by the result of this contest, others whether it would be insulting to their hosts' religious beliefs if they made a few quiet wagers on who might be the winner. Regarding this last, a quiet consensus developed that what was not noticed could not offend; the odds changed several times as one or the other of the combatants seemed on the brink of crushing defeat.

As long moments passed and neither warrior showed any sign of surrender, the interest of the trolls grew. For such a thing to go on so long at a celebratory banquet in the cavern of these lowlanders' Herder and Huntress—well, clearly, the more cosmopolitan of the Qanuc folk explained, it must be more than a mere contest. Rather, they told their fellows, it was obviously a very complicated sort of dance that solicited luck and strength from the gods for the upcoming battle. No, others said, it was likely nothing more intricate than a combat for the right to mate. Rams did it, so why not lowlanders?

When Simon and Jeremias realized that almost everyone in the room was watching them, the arm-wrestling match suddenly came to a halt. The two embarrassed contestants, red-faced and sweating, straightened their chairs and addressed themselves to their food, not daring to look up at any of the other guests. The trolls whispered sadly. What a shame it was that neither Sisqi nor Binabik had been present to translate their many questions about the odd ritual. A chance for a greater appreciation of *Utku* customs had been lost, at least for the time being.

Outside Leavetaking Hall, Binabik and his betrothed stood ankle-deep in the snow that blanketed the crumbling tiles of the Fire Garden. The cold bothered them not at all—late spring in Yiqanuc could be far worse, and they had not been alone together in a long time.

The hooded pair stood close, face to face, warming each other's cheeks with their breath. Binabik reached up a gentle hand and brushed a melting particle of sleet from Sisqi's cheek.

"You are even more beautiful," he said. *"I had thought that my loneliness was play-ing tricks on me, but you are more lovely even than I remembered."*

Sisqi laughed and pulled him close. *"Flattery, Singing Man, flattery. Have you been practicing on these huge lowland women? Be careful, one of them might take offense and smash you flat."*

Binabik made a mock-frown. *"I see no one else but you, Sisqinanamook, nor have I since the first time your eyes opened before mine."*

She wrapped her arms about his chest and squeezed as tightly as she could. When she let him go, she turned and began walking once more. Binabik fell into step beside her.

"Your news was welcome," he said. *"I have worried for our people since the day I left Blue Mud Lake."*

Sisqi shrugged. *"We will get on. Sedda's children always do. Still, it was like taking a stone from the foot of an angry ram to convince my parents to let me bring even this small mustering of our folk."*

"The Herder and Huntress may be reconciled to the truth of what Ookequk wrote," said Binabik, *"but just because an unpleasant thing is known to be true does not make it more palatable. Still, Josua and the others are truly grateful—every arm, every eye, will help. The Herder and Huntress have done a good thing, however unwillingly."* He paused. *"And you have done a good thing also. I thank you for your kindness to Simon."*

Sisqi looked at him, puzzled. *"What do you mean?"*

"Asking him to join the Qanuc troop. That meant much to him."

She smiled. *"It was no favor, beloved. It is a deserved honor, and our choice—and not just mine, Binabik, but that of the folk who came with me."*

Binabik stared at her, surprised. *"But they do not know him!"*

"Some do. A few of those who survived our march down Sikkihoq are among this hundred. You saw Snenneq, surely? And those who were at Sikkihoq brought back stories to the rest. Your young friend has made a strong impression on our folk, beloved."

"Young Simon." Binabik thought about this for a moment. *"It is strange to think it, but I know you speak the truth."*

"He has grown much, your friend, even since we parted at the lake. Surely you have seen that?"

"I know you do not mean in size—he has always been large, even for one of his folk."

Sisqi laughed and squeezed him again. *"No, of course not. I mean that since he came down from our mountains, he looks like one who has taken the Walk of Manhood."*

"The lowlanders do not do as we do, my love—but I think that the whole of the last year has been, in a way, his manhood-walk. And I do not think it is over yet." Binabik shook his head, then folded her hand in his. *"But still, I have done Simon a disser-vice by guessing you had given this as a kindness. He is young and he is changing quickly. I am so close to him, perhaps I do not see the changes as clearly as you do."*

"You see more clearly than any of us, Binbiniqegabenik. That is why I love you—and that is also why no harm must come to you. I gave my parents no rest until I could be at your side with a troop of your own folk."

"Ah, Sisqi," he said wistfully, *"a thousand thousand of the stoutest trolls could not*

keep us safe in these terrible times—but better than a million spears is having you close
to me again."

"Flattery again," she laughed. *"But so wonderfully spoken."*

Arm in arm, they walked through the snow.

Provisions were scarce, but wood was not: inside Leavetaking House, the fire had been banked high with logs so that the smoke blackened the ceiling. Normally, Simon would have been upset by such a smirching of the Sithi's sacred place, but tonight he saw it as no more than what was needed—a brave and happy gesture in a time scant of hope. He looked toward the circle of people that had formed around the blaze once supper was finished.

Most of the settlers had wandered back to their tents and sleeping caves, tired after a long day and an unexpected celebration. Some of the trolls had also gone off, a few to look in on the rams—for what, they had asked themselves, did lowlanders *truly* know about sheep?—and others to bed down in the caverns the prince's folk had prepared for them. Binabik and Sisqi were now sitting at the high table with the prince, talking quietly, their faces far more serious than those of the rest of the revelers, who were passing a few precious wineskins around the fire-circle. Simon debated for a moment, then headed toward the group gathered near the fire.

Lady Vorzheva had left the prince's table and was moving toward the door—Duchess Gutrun was walking beside her, delicately holding the Thrithings-woman's elbow like a mother ready to restrain an impulsive child—but when Vorzheva saw Simon, she paused. "There you are," she said, and beckoned. The child growing in her was beginning to show, a bulge at her middle.

"My lady. Duchess." He wondered if he should bow to them, then remembered that they had both seen him thumping Jeremias earlier. He blushed and bent hastily to hide his face.

Vorzheva sounded as though she was smiling. "Prince Josua says that these trolls are your sworn allies, Simon—or should I call you Sir Seoman?"

It was getting worse and worse. His cheeks felt woefully hot. "Please, my lady, just Simon." He sneaked a look, then slowly straightened.

Duchess Gutrun chuckled. "Heaven help you, lad, don't get so worried. Let him go and join the others, Vorzheva—he's a young man and wants to stay up late, drinking and bragging."

Vorzheva looked at her sharply for a moment, then her expression softened. "I wanted only to tell him . . ." She turned to Simon. "I wanted only to tell you that I wish I knew more about you. I had thought *our* lives since going from Naglimund were strange, but when Josua tells me things you have seen . . ." She laughed again, a little sadly, and spread her long fingers on her stomach. "But it is good of you to bring help to us. I have never seen anything like these trolls!"

"You have known . . . *mmmmhh* . . . Binabik for a long time," Gutrun said, yawning behind her hand.

"Yes, but seeing one small person is different than seeing many, so many." Vorzheva turned to Simon as if for help. "Do you understand?"

"I do, Lady Vorzheva." He grinned, remembering. "The first time I saw the city where Binabik's people live—hundreds of caves in the mountainside, and swinging rope bridges, and more trolls than you can imagine, young and old—yes, it was far different than knowing only Binabik."

"Just so." Vorzheva nodded. "Well, again I thank you. Perhaps one day you will come to tell me more of your travels. I am sick now some days, and Josua worries so much for me when I go out and walk around—" she smiled again, but there was a touch of bitterness in it, "—so it is good to have company."

"Of course, Lady. I would be honored."

Gutrun tugged at Vorzheva's sleeve. "Come along now, Vorzheva. Let the young man go and talk to his friends."

"Yes. Well, good night to you, Simon."

"Ladies." He bowed again as they left, a little more gracefully this time. Apparently it was something that improved with practice.

Sangfugol glanced up as Simon reached the fire. The harper looked tired. Old Towser was seated beside him, carrying on one half of a rambling argument—an argument that Sangfugol seemed to have abandoned a while earlier.

"There you are," said the harper. "Sit down. Have some wine." He offered a skin.

Simon took a swallow just to be friendly. "I liked that song you did to-night—the one about the bear."

"The Osgal tune? It is a good one. I remembered you saying that they have bears up in the trollish country, so I thought they would like it."

Simon did not have the heart to reveal that only one of their hundred new guests spoke even a single word of Westerling—that the harper could have sung about swamp fowl for all they would have noticed. However, although the subject matter had been a complete mystery, the Qanuc *had* enjoyed the song's energetic choruses and Sangfugol's goggling facial expressions. "They certainly clapped for it," Simon said. "I thought the roof would come down."

"Smacked on their boots—did you see?" Thinking back on such a triumph, Sangfugol visibly lifted himself straighter. He might be the only harper ever to be applauded by troll feet—such a thing was not said even of the legendary Eoin-ec-Cluias.

"Boots?" Towser leaned forward and clutched at Sangfugol's knee. "And who taught 'em to wear boots at all, that's what I'd like to know. Mountain savages don't wear boots."

Simon started to reply, but Sangfugol shook his head, irritated. "You're talking nonsense again, Towser. You don't know the first thing about trolls."

Abashed, the jester looked around, the lump in his throat bobbing. "I just thought it strange that . . ." He looked at Simon. "And you know them, son? These little people?"

"I do. Binabik is my friend—you've seen him here often, haven't you?"

"So I have, so I have." Towser nodded, but his watery eyes were vague; Simon was not sure that he truly did remember.

"Well, after we left Naglimund and went to the dragon-mountain," Simon said carefully, "—the mountain that *you* helped us find, Towser, with your memories about the sword Thorn—after we were on the mountain, we went to the place where Binabik's people live and met their king and queen. And now they have sent these folks to be our allies."

"Ah, very kind. That's very kind." Towser squinted suspiciously across the fire at the nearest group of trolls, half a dozen men who were laughing and throwing dice in the damp sawdust. The aged jester looked up, brightening. "And they're here because of what I said!"

Simon hesitated, then said: "In a way, yes. That's true."

"Hah!" Towser grinned, exposing the stumps of his few remaining teeth. He looked truly happy. "I told Josua and all those others about the sword, didn't I? About both swords." He looked at the trolls again. "What are they doing?"

"Throwing dice."

"Since I brought 'em here, I should show 'em how a real game is played. I should teach 'em Bull's Horn." Towser rose and stumbled a few paces to where the trolls were gambling, then flopped himself down cross-legged in their midst and began to try to explain the playing of Bull's Horn. The trolls chortled at his obvious drunkenness, but also seemed to be enjoying his visit. Soon the jester and the newcomers were engaged in a hilarious dumb show as Towser, already befuddled by drink and the excitement of the evening, tried to explain the more delicate nuances of the dice game to a group of tiny mountain men who could not understand his words.

Laughing, Simon turned back to Sangfugol. "That will probably keep him occupied for a few hours, at least."

Sangfugol made a sour face. "I wish I'd thought of that myself. I would have sent him over to pester them a long time ago."

"You don't have to be Towser's keeper. I'm sure that if you told Josua how much you dislike the task, he'd ask someone else to do it."

The harper shook his head. "It's not that simple."

"Tell me." From close up, Simon could see dark grit in the shallow creases around Sangfugol's eyes, a smudge on his forehead beneath his curly brown hair. The harper seemed to have lost more than a little of his fastidiousness, but Simon was not sure that this was a good thing: an unkempt Sangfugol seemed a blow against nature, like a slovenly Rachel or a clumsy Jiriki.

"Towser was a good man, Simon." The harper's words came out slowly, grudgingly. "No, that is not fair. He *is* a good man still, I suppose, but these days he is mostly old and foolish—and drunk whenever he can be. He is not wicked, he is just tiresome. But when I first began my craft, he took the time to help me although he owed me nothing. It was all from kindness. He taught me songs and tunings I did not know, helped me learn to use my voice properly so that it would not fail me in time of need." Sangfugol shrugged. "How can I turn away from him just because he wearies me?"

The voices of the trolls nearby had risen, but what seemed for a moment the beginning of an argument was instead the swelling of a song, a guttural arid jerky chant; the melody was strange as could be, but the humor so evident even in an unfamiliar tongue that Towser, in the midst of the singers, giggled and clapped his hands.

"Look at him," Sangfugol said with a touch of bemusement. "He is like a child—and so may we all be, someday. How can I hate him, any more than I would hate an infant that did not know what it did?"

"But he seems to drive you mad!"

The harper snorted. "And do children not sometimes drive parents mad? But someday, the parents become as children themselves and are revenged on their sons and daughters, for then it is the old parents who cry and spit and burn themselves at the cookfire, and it is their children who must suffer." There was little mirth in his laugh. "I thought myself well away from my own mother when I went off to make my fortune. Now, see what I have inherited for my unfaithfulness." He gestured at Towser, who, with head thrown back, was singing along with the trolls, baying wordlessly and tunelessly as a dog beneath a harvest moon.

The smile that this sight engendered faded quickly from Simon's face. At least Sangfugol and others had a choice about staying or not staying with parents. It was different for orphans.

"Then there is the other side." Sangfugol turned to look at Josua, who was still in deep conversation with the Qanuc. "There are those who, even when their parents die, still cannot get free of them." The gaze he leveled at his prince was full of love and, surprisingly, anger. "Sometimes he seems to be almost afraid to move, for fear he might have to step across the shadow of old King John's memory."

Simon stared at Josua's long, troubled face. "He worries so much."

"Yes, even when there is no use in it." As Sangfugol spoke, Towser came swaggering back. The *kangkang* of his Qanuc dicing partners seemed to have lifted the old man to a newer and more alert stage of drunkenness.

"We are about to be attacked by Fengbald and a thousand troops, Sangfugol," Simon growled. "That is certainly some reason for Josua to worry. Sometimes worry is called 'planning,' you know."

The harper waved his hand in apology. "I know, and I do not criticize him as a war-leader. If anyone can think of a way of winning this fight, it will be our prince. But I swear, Simon, I sometimes think that if he ever looked down at his feet and noticed the ants and fleas he must kill with every pace, he would never walk again. You cannot be a leader—let alone a king—when every hurt done to one of your people galls as though it happened to you. Josua suffers too much, I think, ever to be happy on a throne."

Towser had been listening, his eyes bright and intent. "He is his father's child, that's certain."

Sangfugol looked up, annoyed. "You are talking nonsense again, old fellow. Prester John was the very opposite, as everybody knows—as *you* should know better than anybody!"

"Ah," Towser said solemnly, his face unexpectedly serious. "Ah. Yes." After a moment's silence, when it seemed he might say more, the jester turned abruptly and walked away again.

Simon shrugged off the old man's strange remark. "How can a good king not hurt when his people are in pain, Sangfugol?" he asked. "Shouldn't he care?"

"Certainly he should. Aedon's Blood, yes!—otherwise he'd be no better than Josua's mad brother. But when you cut your finger, do you lay down and not move until it is healed again? Or do you staunch the blood and get on with what you have to do?"

Simon considered this. "You mean that Josua is like the farmer in that old story—the one who bought the finest, fattest pig at the fair, then couldn't bear to slaughter it, so he and his family starved but the pig lived."

The harper laughed. "I suppose, yes. Although I am not saying that Josua should let his people be butchered like swine—just that sometimes bad things happen, no matter how hard a kind prince tries to prevent it."

They sat staring into the fire as Simon thought about what his friend had said. When Sangfugol at last decided that Towser would be safe in the company of the Qanuc—the old jester was laboriously teaching them ballads of dubious propriety—the harper wandered off to sleep. Simon sat and listened to the concert for a while until his head began to hurt, then went to have a few words with Binabik.

His troll friend was still talking with Josua, although Sisqi was now practically asleep, her head propped on Binabik's shoulder, her long-lashed eyes half-closed. She smiled muzzily as Simon approached, but said nothing. The two lovers and Josua had been joined by the burly constable Freosel and a thin old man Simon did not recognize. After a moment he realized that this must be Helfgrim, the onetime Lord Mayor of Gadrinsett who had fled from Fengbald's camp.

As he watched Helfgrim, Simon remembered Geloë's doubts about him. He certainly looked anxious and unsettled as he spoke to the prince, as though at any moment he might say the wrong thing and bring some terrible punishment down on himself. Simon could not help wondering how far they should trust this twitchy old man, but a moment later he chided himself for such callousness. Who knew what torments poor old Helfgrim had suffered that made him look the way he did? Hadn't Simon himself wandered like a wild animal in the woods after his escape from the Hayholt? Who could have seen him then and still thought him reliable?

"Ah, friend Simon." Binabik looked up. "I am glad to see you. I am doing a thing for which your help will be needed tomorrow."

Simon nodded to show his availability.

"In truth," Binabik said, "it is being two things. One is that I must teach you some Qanuc, so that you can be talking to my folk in battle."

"Of course." Simon was pleased that Binabik remembered. It made it more real, to hear it spoken in the serious presence of Josua. "If I have the prince's leave to fight with the Qanuc, of course." He looked at Josua.

The prince said: "Binabik's folk will help us most if they can understand what we need from them. Their own safety will also be best served that way. You have my leave, Simon."

"Thank you, Highness. What else, Binabik?"

"We must also be collecting all the boats that belong to the folk of New Gadrinsett." Binabik grinned. "There must be two score of them all counted together."

"Boats? But the lake around Sesuad'ra is frozen. What good will they do us?"

"Not the boats themselves will be doing good," said the troll. "But parts of them will."

"Binabik has a plan for the defense of this place," Josua elaborated. He looked doubtful.

"It is not just being a plan." Binabik was smiling again. "Not just an idea that has landed on me like a stone. It is a certain Qanuc way that I will show to you *Utku*—and that is a great luckiness for you." He chuckled with self-satisfaction.

"What is it?"

"I will tell you tomorrow as we are at our boat-hunting task."

"One other thing, Simon," Josua said. "I know I have spoken of it before, but I feel it is worth asking again. Do you think there is any chance that your friends the Sithi will come? This is their sacred place, is it not? Will they not defend it?"

"I do not know, Josua. As I said, Jiriki seemed to think that his people would need a great deal of convincing."

"A pity." Josua drew his fingers through his short-cropped hair. "In truth, I fear we are just too few, even with the arrival of these brave trolls. The aid of the Fair Ones would be a great boon. Ha! Life is strange, is it not? My father prided himself that he had driven the last of the Sithi into hiding; now his son prays for them to come and help defend the remnants of his father's kingdom."

Simon shook his head sadly. There was nothing to say. The old Lord Mayor, who had listened silently to this exchange, now looked up at Simon, examining him closely. Simon tried to see some hint of the old man's thoughts in his watery eyes, but could make out nothing.

"Wake me up when it's time to go, Binabik," Simon said at last. "Good night, all. Good night, Prince Josua." He turned and walked toward the doorway. The singing of the trolls and lowlanders around the fire had quieted, the tunes grown slow and melancholy. The fire, dwindling, set red light shimmering along the shadowy walls.

The late morning sky was almost empty of clouds. The air was bitterly cold; Simon's breath clouded before his face. He and Binabik had been practicing a few important words in the Qanuc speech since first light, and Simon, showing greater than usual patience, was making good progress.

"Say 'now.'" Binabik cocked an eyebrow.

"Ummu."

Qantaqa, trotting beside them, lifted her head and huffed, then found her voice for a short bark. Binabik laughed.

"She is not understanding why you are now speaking to her," he explained. "These are words she hears only from me."

"But I thought you said that your people had a whole different language that you spoke to your animals." Simon banged his gloved hand together to keep his fingers from turning into icicles.

Binabik gave him a look of reproach. "I am not talking to Qantaqa as we trolls are speaking to our rams, or to birds or fish. She is my friend. I speak to her as I would to any friend."

"Oh." Simon eyed the wolf. "How do you say 'I'm sorry,' Binabik?"

"Chem ea dok."

He turned and patted the wolf's wide back. *"Chem ea dok,* Qantaqa." She grinned hugely up at him, panting steam.

After they had walked a little farther, Simon said: "Where are we going?"

"As I was telling the night before: we are going to go and collect the boats. Or rather, we are to be sending the boat-owners to the forge, where Sludig and others will be breaking the boats up. But we will give each person one of these—" he displayed a wad of parchment scraps with Josua's rune printed large on each, "—so that they know they are having the prince's word that they will be repaid."

Simon was puzzled. "I still don't understand what you're going to do. Those people need their boats to catch fish, to feed themselves and their families."

Binabik shook his head. "Not when even the rivers are now so thick with ice. And if we do not win here, it will matter little what plans the folk of New Gadrinsett are having."

"So are you going to tell me what *your* plan is?"

"Soon, Simon, soon. When we are finished with this morning's work, I will take you to the forge and you will then be seeing."

They strode along toward the settlement.

"Fengbald will probably attack soon."

"I am certain," said Binabik. "This cold must wear down the spirits of his men, even if they are having payment from the king's gold."

"But they'll be too few to lay siege, don't you think? Sesuad'ra is quite large, even for a thousand men."

"I am agreeing with your thought, Simon." Binabik considered. "Josua and Freosel and others were speaking of this last night. They are thinking that Fengbald will not try to besiege the hill. In any case, I am doubting that he knows how sad is our preparedness or scant our supplies."

"So what will he do, then?" Simon tried to think like Fengbald. "I guess that he'll simply try to overwhelm us. From what I've heard about him, he's not the patient type."

The troll looked up at him appraisingly, a twinkle in his dark eyes. "I think that you have thought well, Simon. That is seeming most likely to me, also. If you could lead a force of spying men to Fengbald's camp, it is only sense that he has sent spies here as well—Sludig and Hotvig think they have seen evidence of this, tracks of horses and such. So, he will know that there is a broad road that leads up the hill, and while it is something we can be defending, it is not like a castle wall where stones can be thrown down from above. I am guessing that he will try to overwhelm the resistance with his more strong and fearsome soldiers and drive all the way to the hilltop."

Simon pondered this. "We have more men than he may know, now that your folk are here. Maybe we can hold him longer than he thinks."

"Without doubt," Binabik said briskly. "But ultimately we will fail. They will be finding other ways up the slope—also unlike a castle, the hill can be climbed by men of determination, even in this cold and slippery weather."

"Then what can we do—nothing?"

"We can be using our brains as well as our hearts, friend Simon." Binabik smiled—a gentle, yellow smile. "That is why we are now hunting for boats—or rather, for the nails that are holding boats together."

"Nails?" Simon was even more puzzled.

"You will see. Now quick, give me the word that is meaning 'attack'!"

Simon thought. *"Nihuk."*

Binabik reached over and gave him a little shove on the hip. *"Nihut.* With the sound of 't,' not 'k.'"

"Nihut!" Simon said loudly.

Qantaqa growled and looked around, searching for an enemy.

☸

Simon dreamed that he stood in the great throne room of the Hayholt, watching Josua and Binabik and a host of others search for the three swords. Although they were hunting in every corner, lifting each tapestry in turn and even looking beneath the malachite skirts of the statues of the Hayholt's former kings, only Simon seemed able to see that black Thorn, gray Sorrow, and a third silvery blade that must be King John's Bright-Nail were propped in plain sight on the great throne of yellowing ivory, the Dragonbone Chair.

Although Simon had never seen this third sword from any nearer than a hundred feet when he had lived at the Hayholt, it was remarkably clear to his dream-vision, the golden hilt worked in the curve of a holy Tree, the edge so polished that it sparkled even in the dim chamber. The blades leaned against each other, hilts in the air, like some unusual three-legged stool; the great, grinning skull of the dragon Shurakai stretched over them, as though at any moment it would gobble them down, sucking them out of sight forever. How could Josua and the others not see them? It was so obvious! Simon tried to tell his friends what they were missing, but could find no voice. He tried to point, to make some sound that would draw their attention, but he had somehow lost his body. He was a ghost, and his beloved friends and allies were making a terrible, terrible mistake. . . .

"Damn you, Simon, get up!" Sludig was shaking him roughly. "Hotvig and his men say Fengbald is marching. He will be here before the sun is above the tree line."

Simon struggled to a sitting position. "What?" he gurgled. "What?"

"Fengbald is coming." The Rimmersman had retreated to the doorway. "Get up!"

"Where is Binabik?" His heart was beating swiftly even as he fought toward full wakefulness. What was he supposed to do?

"He is already with Prince Josua and the others. Come now." Sludig shook his head, then grinned with fierce exhilaration. "Finally—someone to fight!" He ducked through the tent flap and was gone.

Simon scrambled out from beneath his cloak and fumbled on his boots, snagging a thumbnail in his chill-fingered hurry. He swore quietly as he threw on his outer shirt, then found his Qanuc knife and strapped on the sheath. The sword Josua had given him was wrapped in its polishing cloth beneath his pallet; when he unwrapped it, the steel was icy against his hand. He shuddered. Fengbald was coming. It was the day they had talked of for so many weeks. People would die, perhaps some of them before the gray sun even reached noon. Perhaps Simon himself would be one of them.

"Bad thoughts," he mumbled as he buckled his sword belt. "Bad luck." He made the sign of the Tree to ward off his own ill-speaking. He had to hurry. He was needed.

As he foraged in the corner of the tent for his gloves he came upon the strangely-shaped bundle that Aditu had given him. He had forgotten it since the night he had stolen out to the Observatory. What was it? He had a sudden and sickening recollection that Amerasu had wanted it given to Josua.

Merciful Aedon, what have I done?

Was it something that might have saved them? Had he, in his foolishness, in his mooncalf forgetfulness, neglected a weapon that might help keep his friends alive? Or was it something with which to summon the aid of the Sithi? Would it now be too late?

Heart thudding at the magnitude of his mistake, he snatched up the bag—noticing even in his fearful haste the odd, slithering softness of its weave—then dashed out into the icy dawn light.

*   *   *

A huge crowd was gathering in the Leavetaking House, caught up in a frenzy of activity that seemed ready at any moment to spill over into panicked flailing. At the center of it all Simon found Josua and a small group that included Deornoth, Geloë, Binabik, and Freosel. The prince, any trace of indecision vanished, was calling out orders; reviewing plans and arrangements, and exhorting some of the more anxious of New Gadrinsett's defenders. The brightness of Josua's eye made Simon feel like a traitor.

"Your Highness." He took a step forward, then dropped to a knee before the prince, who looked down in mild surprise.

"Up, Simon," Deornoth said impatiently. "There is work to do."

"I'm afraid I've made a terrible mistake, Prince Josua."

The prince paused, visibly willing himself to calm attention. "What do you mean, son?"

Son. The word struck Simon very hard. He wished that Josua could truly have been his father—there was certainly something in the man that he loved. "I think I have done a foolish thing," he said. "Very foolish."

"Speak with care," said Binabik. "Tell just the facts that have importance."

Prince Josua's alarmed expression eased as he listened to Simon's worried explanation. "Give it to me, then," he said when Simon had finished. "There is no point in tormenting yourself until we know what it is. I feared from the look on your face that you had done something to leave us open to attack. As it is, your bundle is most likely only some token."

"A fairy gift?" Freosel asked doubtfully. "Be those not perilous?"

Josua squatted and took the bag from Simon. It was difficult for him to untie the knotted drawstring with only one hand, but no one dared offer him aid. When the prince had at last worked it open, he upended the bag. Something wrapped in an embroidered black cloth rolled out into his lap.

"It is a horn," he said as he pulled away the covering and held it up. It was made of a single piece of ivory or unyellowed bone, chased all over with fine carvings. The lip and mouthpiece were sheathed in a silvery metal, and the horn itself hung on a black baldric as sumptuously worked as the wrapping. There was something unusual in the shape of it, some compelling but not quite recognizable essence. Although age and much use were suggested by its every line, still at the same time it shone as though newly made. It was potent, Simon saw: though it was not like Thorn, which sometimes almost seemed to breathe, the horn had something in it which drew the eye.

"It is a beautiful thing," Josua murmured. He tilted it from side to side, squinting at the carvings. "I can read none of these, although some look like writing-runes."

"Prince Josua?" Binabik held out his hands. Josua passed the horn to him. "They are all Sithi runes—not a surprising thing on a present from Amerasu."

"But the winding-cloth and the baldric are of mortal weave," Geloë said abruptly. "That is a strange thing."

"Can you read any of the writing?" Joshua asked.

Binabik shook his head. "Not now. It might be so with some studying."

"Perhaps you can read this." Deornoth leaned forward and plucked a scrap of shimmery parchment out of the bell of the horn. He opened it, whistled in surprise, then handed it to Joshua.

"It is written in our Westerling letters!" said the prince. " '*May this be given to its rightful owner when all seems lost.*' Then there is a strange sign—like an 'A.' "

"Amerasu's mark." Geloë's deep voice was sorrowful. "Her mark."

"But what can it mean?" Joshua asked. "What is it, and who could be its rightful owner? It is clearly something of worth."

"Beggin' pardon, Prince Joshua," Freosel said nervously, "but p'raps would be best not to meddle with such things—p'raps there be curse on it or somewhat like that. The gifts of the Peaceful Ones, they say, can cut both ways."

"But if it is meant to summon aid," said Joshua, "then it seems a shame not to use it. If we are vanquished today, all will not just *seem* lost, it will *be* lost."

He hesitated for a moment, then lifted the horn to his lips and blew. Astonishingly, there was no sound at all. Joshua stared into the bell of the horn in search of some obstruction, then puffed his cheeks again and blew until he was bent almost double, but still the horn was silent. He straightened with a shaky laugh. "Well, I do not seem to be the thing's rightful owner. Someone else try—anyone, it matters not."

Deornoth at last accepted it from him and lifted it, but had no more luck than Joshua. Freosel waved it away. Simon took it, and although he puffed until black flecks whirled before his eyes, the horn remained mute.

"What is it for?" Simon panted.

Joshua shrugged. "Who can say? But I do not think you have done any harm, Simon. If it is meant to serve some purpose, that purpose has not yet been revealed to us." He wrapped the horn again, then placed it back into the sack and put it down beside his feet. "We have other things to occupy us now. If we survive this day, then we will look at it again—perhaps Binabik or Geloë will be able to puzzle out its carvings. Now, bring me the tally of men, Deornoth, and let us make final dispositions."

Binabik pulled away from the group and came and took Simon's arm. "There are still a few things you should have," he said, "then you should go to be with your Qanuc troop."

Simon followed his small friend across the milling confusion of the Leave-taking House. "I hope your schemes work, Binabik."

The troll made a hand sign. "As I am hoping, too. But we will do what is our best to do. That is all the gods, or your God, or our ancestors can be expecting."

Against the far corner of the western wall a line of men stood before a dwindling pile of wooden shields, some of which still bore river-moss stains from their previous existence as boat timbers. Sangfugol, wearing a sort of battle-dress of ragged gray, was overseeing the distribution.

The harper looked up. "There you are. It's in the corner. Ho, stop that, you!" he snarled at a bearded older man who was pawing through the pile. "Take the one that's on top."

Binabik went to the place Sangfugol had indicated and drew something out from beneath a pile of sacking. It was another wooden shield, but this one had been painted with the arms Vorzheva and Gutrun had created for Simon's banner, the black sword and white dragon intertwined over Josua's gray and red.

"It is not done with the hand of art," the troll said. "But it was done with the hand of friendship."

Simon bent and embraced him, then took the shield and thumped it with the heel of his hand. "It's perfect."

Binabik frowned. "I am only wishing that you were having more time for practicing with its use, Simon. It is not easy to be riding and using a shield and fighting, too." His look grew more worried as he gripped Simon's fingers in his own small fist. "Do not be foolish, Simon. You are yourself of great importance, and my people are being very important as well . . . but the finest of *all* things that I am knowing will be with you, also." He turned his round face away. "She is a huntress of our folk and brave as a thunderstorm, but— *Qinkipa!*—how I wish Sisqi were not in this fighting today."

"Aren't you going to be with us?" Simon asked, surprised.

"I will be with the prince, acting as messenger since Qantaqa and I can be moving with swiftness and quiet where a bigger man on a horse might be observed." The troll laughed softly. "Still, I will be carrying a spear for the first time since my manhood-walk. It will be a strangeness to have that in my hand." His smile vanished. " 'No' is the answer to your questioning, Simon—I will not be with you, at least not closely by. So please, my good friend, keep an eye out for Sisqinanamook. If you are keeping her from harm, you keep away a blow to my own heart that might be the killing of me." He squeezed Simon's hand again. "Come. There are things we must still be doing. It is not enough to have clever schemes," he tapped his forehead and smiled mockingly, "if they are not completed with properness."

They met at last in the Fire Garden, all of Sesuad'ra's defenders, those who would fight and those who would stay behind, gathered together on the great commons-yard of tiles. Although the sun was well into the sky, the day was dark and very cold; many had brought torches. Simon felt a pang at seeing the flames fluttering in this open place, as they had in his vision of the past. A thousand Sithi had once waited here, just as his friends and allies now waited, for something that would change their lives forever.

Josua stood on a section of broken wall so that he could look out over the hushed crowd. Simon, standing close beside him, saw the prince's look of disappointment. The defenders were so few, his face said clearly, and so poorly prepared.

"People of New Gadrinsett and our kind allies of Yiqanuc," Josua called, "there is little need to speak about what we are doing. Duke Fengbald, who slaughtered the women and children of his own fiefdom in Falshire, is coming. We must fight him. There is little more to it than that. He is the tool of a great evil, and that evil must be stopped here or there will be none left to resist it. A victory here will not by any means overthrow our enemies, but if we lose it will mean that those enemies have won a great and total victory. Go and do your best, both those who will fight and those who will remain behind with their own tasks to do. Surely God is watching and will see your bravery."

The murmurs that had risen when Josua spoke of evil turned into cheers as he finished. The prince then reached down to help Father Strangyeard climb into place to say the benediction.

The archivist fretfully smoothed his few strands of hair. "I am certain I will muddle it," he whispered.

"You know it perfectly," said Deornoth. Simon thought he meant it kindly, but the knight could not keep impatience from his voice.

"I fear I am not meant to be a war-priest."

"Nor should you be," Josua said harshly. "Nor should any priest, if God were doing all that he ought to."

"Prince Josua!" Startled, Father Strangyeard sucked in air and coughed. "Beware of blasphemy!"

The prince was grim. "After these last two years of torment across the land, God must have learned to be a little . . . flexible. I am sure He will understand my words."

Strangyeard could only shake his head.

When the priest had finished his blessing, much of which was inaudible to the large crowd, Freosel mounted the wall with the ease of one used to climbing. The heavyset man had taken on an increasing burden of the defense, and seemed to be thriving under the responsibility.

"Come on, then," he said loudly, his rough voice reaching out to every one of the several hundred gathered in that cold, windy place. "You heard what Prince Josua said. What more need you know? Defending our home's what we be doing. Even a badger'll do that without thinking a moment. Will you let Fengbald and them come and take your home, kill your families? Will you?"

The assembled folk called back a ragged but heartfelt denial.

"Right. So, let's go to it."

Simon was caught up for a moment by Freosel's words. Sesuad'ra was his home, at least for now. If he had any hope of finding something more permanent, he would have to survive this day—and they would also have to beat back Fengbald's army. He turned to Snenneq and the other trolls who were waiting quietly a little apart from the rest of the defenders.

"Nenit, henimaatuya," Simon said, waving them toward the stables where the rams—and Simon's horse—were waiting patiently. "Come on, friends."

Despite the chill of the day, Simon found himself sweating heavily beneath his helmet and chain mail. As he and the trolls turned off from the main road and started downslope through the clinging brush, he realized that he was, in a way, all alone—that no one would be near who could truly understand him. What if he showed himself a coward in front of the trolls, or something happened to Sisqi? What if he let Binabik down?

He pushed the thoughts away. There were things to do that would require his concentration. There could be no mooncalf foolishness, as with the forgotten gift from Amerasu.

As they neared the base of the hill and the hidden places near the foot of the road, Simon's company dismounted and led their beasts into place. The hill slope was covered here with ice-blasted bracken that snatched at feet and tore cloaks, so it took them a good part of an hour before they had finally selected their spots and the crackling and rustling had ceased. When all the troop was settled in, Simon climbed up out of the shallow gulley so that he could see the barricade of felled trees that Sludig and others had built at the skirt of the hill, blocking entrance to the wide, stone-paved road. It was to be his responsibility to relay the prince's commands.

Out beyond the expanse of ice that had once been Sesuad'ra's floodwater moat, the near shore was covered with a dark, seething mass. It took Simon a few startled moments to realize that this was Fengbald's army, settled in along the edge of the frozen water. It was more than an army, for the duke appeared to have brought a large section of the squatter town of Gadrinsett with him: tents and cookfires and makeshift forges spread lumpily into the distance, filling the small valley with smokes and steams. Simon knew it was an army of only a thousand or so, but to one who had not seen the army ten times larger that had besieged Naglimund, it seemed as vast as the legendary Muster of Anitulles that had covered the hills of Nabban like a blanket of spears. Chill sweat began to bead on his forehead once more. They were so near! Two hundred ells or more separated Fengbald's forces from Simon's hidden perch, yet he could clearly see individual faces among the armored men. They were people, living people, and they were coming to kill him. Simon's companions would in turn try to kill as many of these soldiers as possible. There would be many new widows and orphans at the end of this day.

An unexpected trill of melody behind him made Simon jump. He whirled to see one of the trolls rocking slowly from side to side, his head lifted in quiet song. The troll, alerted by Simon's sudden movement, looked up at him questioningly. Simon tried to smile and waved for the little man to continue. After a moment the troll's plaintive voice rose once more into the freezing air, lonely as a bird in a leafless tree.

I don't want to die, thought Simon. *And God, please, I want to see Miriamele again—I truly, truly do.*

A vision of her came to him suddenly, a memory of their last desperate moment near the Stile, when the giant had come crashing down on them just as Simon had finally sparked his torch alight. Her eyes, Miriamele's eyes . . . they had been frightened but resolute. She was brave, he remembered helplessly, brave and lovely. Why had he never told her how much he admired her—even if she *was* a princess?

There was a movement downslope near the barricade of tumbled trunks. Josua, his crippled right arm marking him even at a distance, was climbing onto the makeshift wall. A cloaked and hooded trio mounted to stand beside him.

Josua cupped his hand before his mouth. *"Where is Fengbald?"* he shouted. His voice echoed out across the frozen lake and reverberated in the hollows of the close-looming hills. *"Fengbald!"*

After some moments a small group of figures detached themselves from the horde along the shore and came a short way out onto the ice. In their midst, mounted on a tall charger, rode one who was armored in silver and cloaked in bright scarlet. A silver bird flared its wings upon his helmet, which he removed and tucked beneath his arm. His long hair was black, and fluttered in the stiff wind.

"So you are there after all, Josua," the rider shouted. "I was wondering."

"You are trespassing on free lands, Fengbald. We do not acknowledge my brother Elias here, for his crimes have stolen away his right to rule my father's kingdom. If you leave now, you may go away freely and tell him so."

Laughing, Fengbald threw back his head in what seemed quite genuine amusement. "Very good, Josua, very good!" he bellowed. "No, it is you who must consider *my* offer. If you will surrender yourself to the king's justice, I promise that all but the guiltiest few of your traitorous mob will be allowed back to take their place as honorable subjects. Surrender, Josua, and they will be spared."

Simon wondered what effect this promise would have on the frightened and unhopeful army of New Gadrinsett. Fengbald was doubtless wondering the same.

"You lie, murderer!" someone shouted from near Josua, but the prince lifted his hand in a calming gesture.

"Did you not make that same promise to the wool merchants of Falshire," Josua called, "before you burned their wives and children in their beds?"

Fengbald was too distant for his expression to be discernible, but from the way he straightened in the saddle, pushing against his stirrups until he was al- most standing, Simon could guess at the anger surging through him. "You are in no position to speak so insolently, Josua," the duke shouted. "You are a prince of nothing but trees and a few tattered, hungry sheepherders. Will you surrender and save much bloodshed?"

Now one of the other figures standing beside Josua stepped forward. "Hear me!" It was Geloë; she pulled back her hood as she spoke. "Know that I am Valada Geloë, protectress of the forest." She waved her cloaked arm toward the shadowy face of the Aldheorte, which loomed on the hillcrest like a vast and silent witness. "You may not know me, lord from the cities, but your Thrith- ings allies have heard of me. Ask your mercenary friend Lezhdraka if he recog- nizes my name."

Fengbald did not reply, but appeared to be in conversation with someone standing near him.

"If you would attack us, think of this," Geloë called. "This place, Sesuad'ra, is one of the Sithi's most sacred spots. I do not think they would like it spoiled by your coming. If you try to force your way in, you may find that they make a more terrible enemy than you can guess."

Simon was sure, or at least thought he was sure, that the witch woman's speech was an idle threat, but he found himself wishing again that Jiriki had come. Was this what a condemned man felt as he sat looking through the window slit at his gallows a-building? Simon felt a dull certainty that he and Josua and the rest could not win. Fengbald's army seemed a great infection upon the snowy plain beyond the lake, a plague that would destroy them all.

"I see," Fengbald shouted suddenly, "that you have not only gone mad yourself, Josua, but that you have surrounded yourself with other mad folk as well. So be it! Tell the old woman to hurry and call out to her forest spirits—perhaps the trees will come and rescue you. I have lost patience!" Fengbald waved his hand and a flurry of arrows spat out from the men along the shoreline. They all fell short of the barricade and skittered along the ice. Josua and the others clambered down into the undergrowth surrounding the pile of logs, disappearing once more from Simon's view.

At another cry from Fengbald, something that looked like a huge barge moved slowly out onto the ice. This war-engine was pulled by stout dray horses who were themselves covered in padded armor, and as it scraped along the ice it made a continual shrieking noise. From the dreadful sound, it might have been a market cart full of damned souls. The bed of the sledge was piled high with bulging sacks.

Simon could not help shaking his head, impressed despite his sudden fear. Someone in Fengbald's camp had been planning well.

As the great sledge moved out across the ice, the meager swarm of arrows coming back from the defenders—they had few to begin with, and Josua had warned them repeatedly against waste—bounced ineffectually from its steel-shod sides, or stuck harmlessly in the armor of the horses that drew it until they began to resemble some fabulous species of long-legged porcupines. Where the sledge passed, its crosswise runners scraped the ice raw. From holes in the mountain of sacks, a wide shower of sand dribbled down the sledge's sloping bed and spattered across the frozen surface of the lake. Fengbald's soldiers, following the sledge in a wide column, found much firmer footing than Josua and the defenders had ever suspected they might.

"Aedon curse them!" Simon felt his heart sink within his breast. Fengbald's army, a pulsing column like a stream of ants, moved forward across the moat.

One of the trolls, eyes wide, said something Simon could only partially understand.

"*Shummuk.*" For the first time Simon felt real fear coiling inside him like a serpent, crushing hope. He must keep to the plan, although all now seemed doubtful. "Wait. We will wait."

Far from Sesuad'ra, and yet somehow strangely near, there was a movement in the heart of the ancient forest Aldheorte. In a deep grove that was touched only lightly by the snows that had blanketed the woods for many months, a horseman rode out from between two standing stones and turned his impatient mount around and around at the center of the clearing.

"Come out!" he cried. The tongue he spoke was the oldest in Osten Ard. His armor was blue and yellow and silver-gray, polished until it gleamed. "Come through the Gate of Winds!"

Other riders and their mounts began to make their way out between the tall stones until the dell was foggy with the clouds of their breath.

The first rider reined up his horse before the assembled throng. He lifted a sword before him, lifted it as though it might pierce the clouds. His hair, bound only by a band of blue cloth, had once been lavender. Now it was as white as the snow clinging to the tree branches.

"Follow me, and follow Indreju, sword of my grandfather," Jiriki cried. "We go to the aid of friends. For the first time in five centuries, the Zida'ya will ride."

The others lifted their weapons, shaking them at the sky. A strange song began to build, deep as the booming of marsh bitterns, wild as a wolf cry, until all were singing and the glade shook with the force of it.

"Away, Houses of the Dawn!" Jiriki's thin face was fierce, his eyes alight, burning like coals. "Away, come away! And let our enemies tremble! The Zida'ya ride again!"

Jiriki and the rest—his mother Likimeya on her tall black horse, Yizashi of the gray spear, bold Chekai'so Amber-Locks, even Jiriki's green-clad uncle Khendraja'aro with his longbow—all spurred their horses out of the clearing with a great shout and a singing. So great was the tumult of their going that the trees seemed to bend away before them and the wind, as if abashed, was momentarily silent in their wake.

11

The Road Back

✦

Miriamele slouched lower inside her cloak, trying to vanish. It seemed that every person who passed by slowed to look at her, the slender Wrannamen with their calm brown eyes and rigorously expressionless faces as well as the Perdruinese traders in their slightly shabby finery. All seemed to be pondering the appearance of this crop-haired girl in a stained monk's habit, and it was making her very anxious. Why was Cadrach taking so long? Surely she should have known better by now than to let him go into an inn by himself.

When the monk appeared at last he wore an air of self-satisfaction, as though he had completed some immensely difficult task.

"It is down by Peat Barge Quay, as I should have remembered. A none-too-savory district."

"You have been drinking wine." Her tone was harsher than she wanted it to be, but she was cold and fretful.

"And how could I expect a publican to give me good directions if I bought nothing?" Cadrach was not to be so easily thrown off stride. He seemed to have rebounded from the despair that had filled him on the boat, although Miriamele could see where it was imperfectly hidden, where the deadly bleakness peered past the ragged edges of the jollity he had drawn over himself like a cloak.

"But we have no money!" she complained. "That's why we have to walk all over this cursed town, trying to find a place you said you knew!"

"Hush, my lady. I made a small wager on a coin-flip and won—and just as well, too, since I'd no coin to match the bet. But all's well now. In any case, it is traveling on foot through this city of canals that has confused me, but with the innkeeper's instructions, we will have no more problems."

No more problems. Miriamele had to laugh at that, if bitterly. They had been living like beggars for three weeks—parched on the boat for several days, then slogging through the coast towns of southeastern Nabban begging meals where they could and taking rides on farm wagons when they were lucky enough to get them. The largest portion of the time had been spent walking, walking, walking, until Miriamele felt that if she were to somehow remove her legs from her body they would continue pacing along without her. This kind of life was not unfamiliar to Cadrach, and he seemed to have returned to it complacently, but Miriamele was growing more than tired of it. She could never live in her father's court again, but suddenly the stifling surroundings of Uncle Josua's castle at Naglimund seemed a great deal more appealing than they had a few months before.

She turned to say something else sharp to Cadrach—she could smell the wine on his breath at an arm's distance—and caught him by surprise, un-guarded. He had let his buoyant expression slip; the hollowness in his once round cheeks and the shadows beneath his haunted eyes chastened Miriamele into a kind of irritated love.

"Well . . . come on, then." She took his arm. "But if you don't find this place soon, I'm going to push you into the canal."

Since they did not have the price of a boatman's fare, it took the better part of the morning for Cadrach and Miriamele to make their way through the daunting maze of Kwanitupul's wooden walkways to Peat Bog Quay. Every turn seemed to bring them to another dead end, another passage that ended in an abandoned boatyard or a locked door with rusty hinges or a rickety fence beyond which was only yet another of the ubiquitous waterways. Thwarted, they would retrace their steps, try another turning, and the maddening process would begin again. At last, with the noon sun whitening the cloudy sky, they stumbled around the corner of a long and very deteriorated warehouse and found themselves staring at a salt-rotted wooden sign that proclaimed the inn before which it hung as *Pelippa's Bowl*. It was indeed, as Cadrach had warned, in a rather unsavory district.

While Cadrach searched for the door—the front of the building was an almost uniform wall of gray, weathered wood—Miriamele wandered out onto the inn's front deck and stared down at a wreath of yellow and white flowers floating on the choppy canal near the wharf ladder.

"That's a Soul's Day wreath," she said.

Cadrach, who had found the door, nodded.

"Which means it was more than four months ago that I left Naglimund," she said slowly. The monk nodded again, then pulled the door open and beckoned. Miriamele felt a wild sorrow course through her. "And it was all for nothing! Because I was a headstrong fool!"

"Things would have gone no better, and perhaps worse, if you had stayed with your uncle," Cadrach pointed out. "At least you are alive, my lady. Now, let us go and see if *Soria* Xorastra will remember an old, if fallen, friend."

They entered the inn through the dooryard, past the corroding hulks of a pair of fishing boats, and quickly received two unpleasant surprises. The first was that the inn itself was ill-kept and smelled distinctly of fish. The second was that Xorastra had been dead for three years, and her jut-jawed niece Charystra quickly proved to be quite a different sort of innkeeper than her predecessor.

She stared at their threadbare and travel-stained clothing. "I don't like the look of you. Let me see your money."

"Come, now," Cadrach said as soothingly as he could. "Your aunt was a good friend of mine. If you let us have a bed for the night, we will have money to pay you by the morning—I am well known in this town."

"My aunt was mad and worthless," Charystra said, not without some satisfaction, "—and her stinking charities left me with nothing but this tumbledown barn." She waved her hand at the low-ceilinged common room, which seemed more like a burrow belonging to some disheartened animal. "The day I let a monk and his doxy stay without paying is the day they take me back to Perdruin in a wooden box."

Miriamele could not help looking forward to such a day, but she knew better than to let the innkeeper know it. "Things are not as they appear," she said. "This man is my tutor. I am a nobleman's child—Baron Seoman of Erkynland is my father. I was kidnapped, and my tutor here found me and saved me. My father will be very kind to anyone who helps with my return." Beside her, Cadrach straightened up, pleased to be the hero of even a mythical rescue.

Charystra squinted. "I've heard more than a few wild stories lately." She chewed at her lip. "One of them turned out to be true, but that doesn't mean yours will." Her expression turned sour. "I've got to make a living, whether your father is a baron or the High King at the Hayholt. Go out and get the money, if you say it's so easy. Let your friends help you."

Cadrach began once more to wheedle and flatter, now taking up the strands of story Miriamele had begun and weaving them into a richer tapestry, one in which Charystra would retire with bags of gold, a gift from the grateful father. Hearing the wild way in which the story grew beneath Cadrach's manipulation, Miriamele almost began to feel sorry for the woman, whose practicality was obviously being strained by her greed, but just before Miriamele was about to ask him to give it up, she saw a large man coming slowly down the stairway into the commons room. Despite his clothes—he wore a cowled cloak much like Cadrach's, belted with a rope—and a beard that was scarcely a finger's breadth thick, he was so instantly familiar that for a moment Miriamele could not believe what she was seeing. As he came down into the light of the tallow lamps, the man also stopped, wide-eyed.

"Miriamele?" he said at last. His voice was thick and hesitant. "Princess?"

"Isgrimnur!" she shrieked. "Duke Isgrimnur!" Her heart seemed to expand within her breast until she thought she might choke. She ran across the cluttered room, dodging past the crooked-legged benches, then flung herself against his broad belly, weeping.

"Oh, you poor thing," he said, squeezing her, crying himself. "Oh, my poor Miriamele." He lifted her away for a moment, staring with reddened eyes. "Are you hurt? Are you well?" He caught sight of Cadrach and his eyes narrowed. "And there's the rogue who stole you!"

Cadrach, who like Charystra had been staring openmouthed, flinched. Isgrimnur cast a large shadow.

"No, no," Miriamele laughed through her tears. "Cadrach is my friend. He helped me. I ran away—don't blame him." She hugged him again, burying her face in his reassuring bulk. "Oh, Isgrimnur, I have been so unhappy. How is Uncle Josua? And Vorzheva, and Simon, and Binabik the troll?"

The duke shook his head. "I know little more than you do, I would guess." He sighed, his breath trembling out. "This is a miracle. God has heard my prayers at last. Blessed, blessed. Come, sit down." Isgrimnur turned to Charystra and waved his hand impatiently. "Well? Don't just stand there, woman! Bring us some ale, and some food, too!"

Charystra, more than a little stunned, went lurching away.

"Wait!" Isgrimnur shouted. She turned to face him. "If you tell anyone about this," he roared, "I'll pull your roof down with my own hands."

The innkeeper, beyond surprise or fear, nodded slackly and headed for the sanctuary of her kitchen.

Tiamak hurried along, although his lame leg allowed him scarcely more speed than what would have been a normal walking pace. His heart was thumping against his ribs, but he forced himself to keep the worry from his face.

He Who Always Steps on Sand, he murmured to himself, *let no one notice me! I am almost there!*

Those who shared the narrow walkways with him seemed determined to hinder his progress. One burly drylander carrying a basket full of sandfish thumped into him and almost knocked him down, then turned to shout insulting names as Tiamak limped on. The little man ached to say something— Kwanitupul was a Wrannaman town, after all, no matter how many drylander traders built expensive stilt houses on the edge of Chamul Lagoon, or had their massive trading barges poled through the canals by sweating crews of Tiamak's folk—but he dared not. There was no time to waste in quarrels, however justified.

He hurried through *Pelippa's Bowl's* common room, sparing barely a glance for the proprietress, despite Charystra's strange expression. The innkeeper, clutching a board laid with bread and cheese and olives, was swaying at the foot of the stairs as though deciding whether to go up or not was an overwhelming strain.

Tiamak angled past her and hobbled up the narrow staircase, then onto the landing and the first warped, ill-hung door in the passageway. He pushed it open, his chest already filling with air to spill out his news, then stopped, surprised by the odd tableau before him.

Isgrimnur was sitting on the floor. In the corner stood a short, husky man, dressed as was the duke in the costume of a pilgrim Aedonite monk, his squarish face curiously closed. Old Camaris sat on the bed, his long legs crossed sailor-style. Beside him sat a young woman with yellow hair close-cropped. She, too, wore a monk's robe, and her pretty, sharp-featured face was set in an expression of bemusement almost as complete as Charystra's.

Tiamak closed his jaw with a snap, then opened it once more. "What?" he said.

"Ah!" Isgrimnur seemed immensely cheerful, almost giddy. "And this is Tiamak, a noble Wrannaman, a friend of Dinivan and Morgenes. The princess is here, Tiamak. Miriamele has come."

Miriamele did not even look up, but continued to stare at the old man. "This is . . . Camaris?"

"I know, I know," Isgrimnur laughed. "I couldn't credit it myself, God strike me—but it is him! Alive, after all this time!" The duke's face suddenly became serious. "But his wits are gone, Miriamele. He is like a child."

Tiamak shook his head. "I . . . I am glad, Isgrimnur. Glad that your friends are here." He shook his head again. "I have news, too."

"Not now." Isgrimnur was beaming. "Later, little man. Tonight we celebrate." He lifted his voice. "Charystra! Where are you, woman!?"

The inn's proprietress had just begun to push the door open when Tiamak turned and shut it in her face. He heard a surprised grunt and the thud of a heavy bread loaf bounding down the stairway. "No," Tiamak said. "This cannot wait, Isgrimnur."

The duke frowned at him, thick brows beetling. "Well?"

"There are men searching for this inn. Nabbanai soldiers."

Isgrimnur's impatience suddenly dropped away. He turned his full attention to the little Wrannaman. "How do you know?"

"I saw them down by Market Hall. They were asking questions of the boatmen there, treating them very roughly. The leader of the soldiers seemed desperate to find this inn."

"And did they find out?" Isgrimnur rose to his feet and walked across the room, taking up his sword Kvalnir from where it stood bundled in the corner.

Tiamak shrugged. "I knew I would not be able to go much faster than the soldiers, even though I am sure I know the city better than they do. Still, I wanted to delay them, so I stepped forward and told the soldiers that *I* would talk to the boatmen since they were all Wrannamen like me." For the first time since beginning his recitation, Tiamak turned to look at the young woman. Her face had gone quite pale, but the dazed expression had vanished. She was listening carefully. "In our swamp-language I told the boatmen that these were bad men, that they should talk only to me, and only in our tongue. I told them that when the soldiers left, they should leave, too, and not come back to the Market Hall until later. After I had talked with them for a few moments longer, pretending to receive directions from them—in truth they were merely telling me that these drylanders acted like madmen!—I told the leader of the soldiers where he and his men could find *Pelippa's Bowl*. Don't scowl so, Duke Isgrimnur! I told them that it was on the other side of town from here, of course! But it was so strange: when I told that man, he shivered all over, as though knowing where this place was made him itch."

"What . . . what did the leader look like?" There was strain in Miriamele's voice.

"He was very odd." Tiamak hesitated. He did not know how to address a drylander princess, even one dressed like a man. "He was the only one not dressed as a soldier. Tall and strong-looking, wearing rich drylander's clothes, but his face was purple with bruises, his eyes red as a boar's, full of blood. He looked as though his head had been crushed in a crocodile's jaws. He was missing teeth, as well."

Miriamele groaned and slid down from the pallet onto the floor. "Oh, Elysia, save me! It is Aspitis!" Her ragged voice was now entirely given over to desperation. "Cadrach, how could he know where we were going?! Have you betrayed me again?"

The monk winced, but his words held no anger. "No, my lady. Obviously he got back to shore, and I would guess that he then somehow exchanged messages with his true master." Cadrach turned toward Isgrimnur. "Pryrates knows this place well, my lord Duke, and Aspitis is his creature."

"Aspitis?" Isgrimnur, strapping his sword belt around his broad middle, shook his head in bafflement. "I do not know him, but I gather that he is no friend."

"No." Cadrach looked to Miriamele where she sat on the floor, head in hands. "He is no friend."

Isgrimnur made a noise deep in his throat. Tiamak turned to him with a startled look, for the duke sounded like nothing less than an angry bear, but Isgrimnur was only thinking, twisting his fingers in his short beard. "Enemies are at our heels," he said at last. "Even were we sitting with the Camaris of forty years ago—ah, Lord love him, Miriamele, he was the mightiest man of all— still I would not like the odds. So, then, we must leave . . . and leave quickly."

"Where can we go?" asked Cadrach.

"North to Josua." Isgrimnur turned to Tiamak. "What did you say that time, little man? That if you were traveling with Camaris and me as fugitives, you would find another way?"

Tiamak felt his throat tighten. "Yes. But it will not be easy." He felt a chill, as though the cold breath of She Who Waits to Take All Back whispered against his neck. He suddenly did not like the idea of taking these drylander friends into the mazy Wran.

Miriamele arose. "Josua is alive?"

"So rumor says, Princess." Isgrimnur shook his head. "Northeast of the Thrithings, it is claimed. But it may be false hope."

"No!" Miriamele's face, still tearstained, wore a strange look of surety. "I believe it."

Cadrach, still leaning in the corner like a neglected house-god, shrugged. "There is nothing wrong with belief, if it is all we can cling to. But what is this other way?" He turned his brooding eyes on the marsh man.

"Through the Wran." Tiamak cleared his throat. "It will be nearly impossible for them to follow us, I think. We can make our way north to the outermost part of the Lake Thrithing."

"Where we will be trapped on foot in the middle of a hundred leagues of open ground," said Cadrach grimly.

"Damn it, man," Isgrimnur snarled, "what else can we do? Try to make our way through Kwanitupul, past this Aspitis fellow, then across all of hostile Nabban? Look at us! Can you imagine a more unlikely and memorable company? A girl, two monks—one bearded—a childish old giant and a Wrannaman? What choice do we have?"

The Hernystirman seemed prepared to argue, but after a moment's hesitation he shrugged once more, drawing back into himself like a tortoise retreating inside its shell. "I suppose there is no choice," he said quietly.

"What should we do?" Miriamele's fear had receded a little. Though still shaken, she seemed bright-eyed and determined. Tiamak could not help admiring her spirit.

Isgrimnur rubbed his large paws together. "Yes. We must leave, certainly by the time an hour has passed, sooner if we can, so there is no more time to waste. Tiamak, go and watch from the front of the inn. Someone else may give these soldiers better directions than you did, and if they catch us unaware, we are lost. You will be the least likely to be noticed." He looked around, thinking. "I will put Camaris to work patching the less mangled of those boats in the dooryard. Cadrach, you will help him. Remember, he is simple-witted, but he has been working here for years—he knows what to do and he understands many words, though he does not speak. I will finish gathering up the rest of our things, then I will come help you finish the boat and carry it down to the water."

"What about me, Isgrimnur?" Miriamele was actually bouncing from one foot to the other in her need for something to do.

"Take that shrew of an innkeeper and go down to the kitchens and provision us. Get things that will keep, since we don't know how long we must go without . . ." He paused, snagged by a sudden thought. "Water! Fresh water! Sweet Usires, we are going to the swamps. Get all you can, and I will come help you carry the jugs or whatever you find to put it in. There is a rain barrel in the yard behind the inn—full, I think. Hah! I knew this foul weather would be good for something!" He tugged at his fingers, thinking frantically. "No, Princess, don't go yet. Tell Charystra she will be paid for everything we take, but don't dare say a word of where we are going! She would peddle our immortal souls for a bent cintis-piece each. I wish I were the same, but I will pay her for what we take, though it will empty my purse." The duke took a deep breath. "There! Now go to. And wherever you are, all of you, listen for Tiamak's call and run to the dooryard if you hear it."

He turned and pulled open the door. Charystra was sitting on the top step in a scattering of foodstuffs, her face a mask of confusion. Isgrimnur looked at her for a moment, then stepped over to Miriamele and bent to her ear; Tiamak was close enough to hear his whisper.

"Don't let her stray from you," the duke murmured. "We may have to take her with us, at least far enough away to protect the secret of which way we've gone. If she kicks up rough, just shout and I'll be there in a moment." He took Miriamele's elbow and guided her toward Charystra's seat on the steps.

"Greetings again, goodwife," the princess said to her. "My name is Marya. We met downstairs. Come now, let us go to the kitchen and get some food for my friends and me—we have been traveling and we are very hungry." She leaned down and helped Charystra to her feet, then bent again to retrieve the bread and cheese that had fallen. "See?" she said cheerfully, taking the dumb-founded woman by the arm. "We will be sure to waste nothing, and we will pay for all."

They disappeared down the stairs.

Miriamele found herself working in a sort of haze. She was concentrating so intently on the task at hand that she lost all track of the reasons for what she was doing until she heard Tiamak's excited cry and his rabbitlike thumping on the roof overhead. Her heart speeding, she snatched up a last handful of wizened onions—Charystra went to few pains to keep her larder well-stocked—and bolted for the dooryard, hurrying the protesting innkeeper along before her.

"Here, what do you think you're at?" Charystra complained. "There's no cause to be treating me this way, whoever you are!"

"Hush! All will be well." She wished she believed it.

As she reached the common room door, she heard Isgrimnur's heavy foot-steps on the stairs. He quickly moved up behind, allowing the balking Charys-tra no room for escape, and together they pushed through into the dooryard. Camaris and Cadrach were working so intently that they did not look up at the entrance of their comrades. The old knight held a pitch-smeared brush, the monk a strip of heavy sailcloth which he was hacking at with a knife.

A moment later Tiamak came slithering down from the rafters. "I saw sol-diers, not far distant," he said breathlessly. "They are a thousand paces away, maybe fewer, and they are coming here!"

"Are they the same ones?" Isgrimnur asked. "Damn me, of course they are! We must go. Is the boat patched?"

"I would guess that it will keep the water out for a while," Cadrach said calmly. "If we bring these things with us," he indicated the pitch and sailcloth, "we can do a better and more thorough job when we stop."

"If we get a chance to stop at all," the duke growled. "Very well. Miriamele?"

"I have stripped the larders. Not that it took much work."

Charystra, who had regained a little of her haughtiness, drew herself up. "And what are my guests and I going to eat?" she demanded. "The finest table in Kwanitupul, I'm known for."

Isgrimnur's snort fluttered his whiskers. "It's not your table that's the prob-lem, it's the muck you put on top of it. You'll be paid, woman—but first you're going to take a little voyage."

"What?" Charystra shrieked. "I'm a God-loving Aedonite woman! What are you going to do with me?"

The duke grimaced and looked at the others. "I do not like this, but we cannot leave her here. We will put her off somewhere safe—with her money." He turned to Cadrach. "Take some of that rope and tie her up, will you? And try not to hurt her."

The last few preparations were finished to the accompaniment of Charystra's outraged protests. Tiamak, who seemed quite worried that Isgrimnur might have forgotten some precious items of their baggage, ran upstairs to make certain nothing had been left behind. When he returned, he joined the others in their efforts to move the large boat out through the broad side door of the yard.

"Any decent boatyard would have a windlass," Isgrimnur complained. Sweat was pouring down his face. Miriamele worried that one of the two older men might hurt themselves, but Camaris, for all his years, seemed utterly untroubled by carrying his share of the weight, and Isgrimnur was still a powerful man. Rather, it was Cadrach, wrung out by their misadventures, and slender Tiamak who had the most trouble. Miriamele wanted to help, but did not dare leave bound Charystra alone for a moment for fear she would raise an alarm or fall into the water and drown.

As they staggered down the ramp to the rear dock, Miriamele was certain she could hear the tramping bootsteps of Aspitis and his minions. The progress of the boat seemed horrifically slow, a blind eight-legged beetle that snagged itself on every narrow turning.

"Hurry!" she said. Her charge Charystra, understanding nothing but her own plight, moaned.

At last they reached the water. As they eased the boat over the edge of the floating dock, Cadrach reached down between the benches and lifted out the heavy maul from the pile of tools they had brought for patching the hull, then went back up the ramp toward the inn.

"What are you doing?" Miriamele shouted. "They'll be here at any moment!"

"I know." Cadrach broke into an uneven trot, the huge hammer cradled against his chest.

Isgrimnur glowered. "Is the man mad?"

"I don't know." Miriamele urged Charystra toward the boat, which was scraping gently against the side of the dock. When the innkeeper resisted, old Camaris stood up and lifted her down as easily a father might his small daughter, then placed her on the bench beside him. The woman huddled there, a tear snaking down her cheek; Miriamele could not help but feel sorry for her.

A moment later Cadrach reappeared, pelting down the gangway. He clambered into the boat with the help of the others, then pushed it away from the dock. The nose swung out toward the middle of the canal.

Miriamele helped the monk squeeze onto the bench. "What were you doing?"

Cadrach took a moment to catch his breath, then carefully laid the maul back down atop the bundle of sailcloth. "There was another boat. I wanted to make sure that it would take them a lot longer to patch it than we took on this. You can't chase anyone through Kwanitupul without a boat."

"Good man," said Isgrimnur. "Although I'm sure they will get a boat soon enough."

Tiamak pointed. "Look!" A dozen blue-cloaked, helmeted men were passing along the wooden walkway toward *Pelippa's Bowl.*

"First they will knock," Cadrach said quietly. "Then they will push down the door. Then they will see what we've done and start searching for a boat."

"So we'd better take advantage of our head start. Row!" Suiting action to word, Isgrimnur bent to his sweep. Camaris also bent, and as their two oar-blades bit at the green water the little boat leaped forward.

In the stern, Miriamele peered back at the diminishing inn. In the antlike movement of people near the entranceway, she thought she could discern a momentary flash of golden hair. Stricken, she dropped her eyes to the choppy canal and prayed to God's mother and several saints that she would never have to see Aspitis again.

"It is only a little farther." The wall-eyed Rimmersman looked at the palisade of gnarled pine trees as fondly as at a familiar street. "There you can rest and eat."

"Thank you, Dypnir," Isorn said. "That will be good." He might have said more, but Eolair had caught at his bridle and slowed his horse. Dypnir, who had not seemed to notice, let his own mount carry him a little ahead until he was only a shadow in the forest dusk.

"Are you sure you can trust this man, Isorn?" the Count of Nad Mullach asked. "If you are not, let us demand some further proof of him now, before we ride into an ambush."

Isorn's wide brow furrowed. "He is of Skoggey. Those folk are loyal to my father."

"He *says* that he is from Skoggey. And they *were* loyal to your father." Eolair shook his head, amazed that the son of a duke could have so little craft. Still, he could not help admiring Isorn's kind and open heart.

Anyone that can keep himself so, in the midst of all this horror, is someone to be treasured, the count thought, but he felt a responsibility for, among other things, his own skin that would not let him be silent, even if it risked offending Duke Isgrimnur's son.

Isorn smiled at Eolair's worry. "He knows the folk he should know. In any case, this is a rather tricksy way to go about ambushing a half-dozen men. Don't you think that if this fellow was Skali's we would simply have been fallen upon by a hundred Kaldskrykemen?"

Eolair frowned. "Not if this fellow is only a scout, and looking to earn his spurs with a clever capture. Enough, then. But I will keep my sword loose in the sheath."

The young Rimmersman laughed. "As will I, Count Eolair. You forget, I spent much of my childhood with Einskaldir, Aedon rest him—the most mistrusting man who ever drew breath."

The Hernystirman found himself laughing a little, too. Einskaldir's impatience and quick temper had always seemed more in keeping with the old pagan Rimmersgard whose gods were as volatile as the weather, hard as the Vestivegg Mountains.

Eolair and Isorn and the four Thrithings-men sent by Hotvig had been traveling together for several weeks now. Hotvig's men were friendly enough, but the journey through the civilized lands of eastern Erkynland—civilized with houses and fields that bore the marks of cultivation, though at the moment it seemed largely unpopulated—had filled them with a certain unease. More and more, as the trek wore on and the grasslanders found themselves farther each day from the plains of their birth, they became moody and sullen, speaking almost entirely to each other in the guttural Thrithings tongue, sitting up at night around the fire singing the songs of their homeland. As a result, Isorn and Eolair had been thrown back almost entirely on each other's company.

To the count's relief, he had found there was a great deal more to the duke's yellow-haired bear of a son than was at first apparent. He was brave, there was little doubt of that, but it seemed unlike the courageousness of many brave men Eolair had known, who felt that to be otherwise was to fail somehow in the sight of others. Young Isorn simply seemed to know little fear, and to do the things he did only because they were right and necessary. Not that he was completely nerveless. His shuddersome story about his captivity among the Black Rimmersmen, of the torture he and his fellows had suffered and of the haunting presence of pale-skinned immortal visitors, still affected him so strongly that he found it difficult to tell. Yet Eolair, with his sharp intriguer's eye, thought that anyone else who had suffered such an experience would have taken it even more to heart. To Isorn it was a terrible time that was now over, and that was that.

So, as the little company had passed along the hillsides above eerily empty Hasu Vale and through the fringes of the Aldheorte, wide-skirting the menace of snowbound Erchester and the Hayholt—and also, Eolair could not help recalling, of tall Thisterborg—the Count of Nad Mullach had found himself growing more and more fond of this young Rimmersman, whose love for his father and mother was so firm and uncomplicated, whose love of his people was almost as strong and was virtually inseparable from his feelings for his family. Still, Eolair, tired and bruised by events, sick already of the horrors of war before this most recent one had begun, could not help wondering if he himself had *ever* been as young as Isorn.

"Almost there." Dypnir's voice brought Eolair's mind back to the dim forest track.

"I only hope they have something to drink," Isorn said, grinning, "and enough of it to share."

As Eolair opened his mouth to reply, a new voice cracked through the evening.

"Hold! Stand where you are!" It was Westerling, spoken with the thickness of Rimmersgard. Isorn and Eolair reined up. Behind them, the four Thrithings-men brought their horses to an effortless halt. Eolair could hear them whispering among themselves.

"It's me," their guide called, leaning his bearded head to the side so the hidden watcher could mark him. "Dypnir. I bring allies."

"Dypnir?" There was a note of doubt in the question. It was followed by a flurry of Rimmerspakk. Isorn seemed to be listening carefully.

"What do they say?" Eolair whispered. "I cannot follow when they speak so fast."

"About what you would expect. Dypnir has been gone several days, and they ask him why. He explains about his horse."

Eolair and his companions had found Dypnir beside a forest trail in the western Aldheorte, hiding near the corpse of his mount, whose leg had been broken in a hole and whose throat Dypnir himself had slit a few moments before. After sharing out the burdens of one of the pack horses, they had given that mount to the Rimmersman in exchange for his aid in finding men who could help them—they had not been too specific about the type of help they needed, except that it seemed understood by all parties that it would not be to the benefit of Skali Sharp-nose.

"Very well." The hidden sentry returned to Westerling speech. "You will follow Dypnir. But you will go slow, and with your hands where we can see them. We have bows, so if you think to play foolish games with us in a dark forest, you will be sorry."

Isorn sat straighter. "We understand. But play no games with us, either." He added something in Rimmerspakk. After a moment of silence, some sign was given and Dypnir started forward, Eolair's party behind him.

They plodded on for a little while into the deepening evening.

At first all that the Count of Nad Mullach could see were tiny sparks like red stars. As they rode forward and the lights wavered and danced, he realized that he was seeing the flames of a fire through close-knit, needled branches. The company turned abruptly and rode through a hedge of trees, ducking at Dypnir's whispered insistence, and the warm light of the blaze rose up all around them.

The camp was what was called a woodsman's hall, a clearing in a copse of trees that had been walled against the wind by bundles of pine and fir branches tied between the trunks. In the center of the open space, ranged about the firepit, sat perhaps three or four dozen men, their eyes glinting with reflected light as they silently observed the strangers. Many of them wore the dirty and tattered remnants of battle costumes; all bore the look of men who had long slept out-of-doors.

Rhynn's Cauldron, it is a camp of outlaws. We will be robbed and killed. Eolair felt a brief clutch of dismay at the thought that his quest should end so pointlessly, and of disgust that they should have ridden so trustingly to their deaths.

Some of the men nearest the entrance to the copse drew their weapons. The Thrithings-men shifted on their horses, hands snaking down to their own hilts. Before anyone's untoward movement could touch off a fatal confrontation, Dypnir flapped his hands in the air and slid down from his borrowed steed. The husky Rimmersman, far less graceful on land than on horseback, stumped to the center of the clearing.

"Here," he said. "These men are friends."

"No one is a friend who comes to eat out of our pot," one of the grimmest-looking growled. "And who is to say they are not Skali's spies?"

Isorn, who had been watching as quietly as Eolair, suddenly leaned forward in the saddle. "Ule?" he said wonderingly. "Are you not Ule, the son of Frekke Grayhair?"

The man stared at him, eyes narrowed. He was perhaps Eolair's age. So much dirt was on his lined, weathered face that he seemed to be wearing a mask. A hand ax with a pitted blade was thrust through his belt. "I am Ule Frekkeson. How do you know my name?" He was stiff, tensed as if to spring.

Isorn dismounted and took a step toward him. "I am Isorn, son of Duke Isgrimnur of Elvritshalla. Your father was one of my own father's most loyal companions. Do you not remember me, Ule?"

A dry rustle of movement around the clearing and a few whispered comments were all this revelation engendered. If Isorn expected the man before him to leap up and joyfully embrace him, he was disappointed. "You have grown since I last saw you, manling," said Frekke's son, "but I see your father's face in yours." Ule stared at him. Something was moving behind the man's quiet anger. "Your father is duke no longer, and all of his men are outlaws. Why do you come to plague us?"

"We come to ask your help. There are many beside yourself unhomed, and they have begun to gather together to take back what was stolen from them. I bring you tidings from my father, the rightful duke—and from Josua of Erkynland, who is his ally against Skali Sharp-nose."

The murmur of surprise grew louder. Ule paid no attention. "This is a sad trick, boy. Your father is dead at Naglimund, your Prince Josua with him. Do not come to us with goblin-stories because you think it would be nice to rule over a pack of house-carls again. We are free men now." Some of his companions growled their agreement.

"Free men?" Isorn's voice suddenly grew tight with fury. "Look at you! Look at this!" He gestured around the clearing. Watching, Eolair marveled to see this sudden passion in the young man. "Free to skulk in the woods like dogs who have been whipped from the hall, do you mean? Where are your homes, your wives, your children? My father is alive . . . !" He paused, steadying his voice. Eolair wondered if the thought had entered Isorn's head that Isgrimnur's safety was not quite so sure as he made it sound. "My father will have his lands back," he said. "Those who help him will have their own steadings back as well—and more beside, because when we are finished Skali and his

Kaldskrykemen will leave behind many unhusbanded women, many an untended field. Any true men that we find to follow us will be well rewarded."

A harsh laugh rose up from the watching men, but it was one of enjoyment at the boast, not mockery. Eolair, sensibilities honed by years of courtly sparring, could feel the spirit of the moment beginning to turn their way.

Ule suddenly rose, his bearlike body wide in his ragged furs. The noise of the onlookers dwindled away. "Tell me then, Isorn Isgrimnurson," he demanded. "Tell me what happened to my father, who served your father all his life. Does he wait for me at the end of your road, like the man-hungry widows and the wide, masterless fields you speak of? Will he be waiting to embrace his son?" He was shaking with rage.

Clear-eyed Isorn did not flinch. He took a slow breath. "He was at Naglimund, Ule. The castle fell before the siege of King Elias. Only a few escaped, and your father was not one of them. If he died, though, he died bravely." He paused, lost for a moment in memory. "He was always very kind to me."

"The damned old man loved you like his own grandchild," Ule said bitterly, then took a lurching step forward. In the moment of stunned silence Eolair fumbled for his sword, cursing his own slowness. Ule grabbed Isorn in a rib-cracking embrace, dragging the duke's son forward and lifting the taller man off the ground.

"God curse Skali!" Tears made pale tracks on Ule's dirty face. "The murderer, the devil-cursed murderer! It is blood feud forever." He let Isorn go and wiped his face with his sleeve. "Sharp-nose must die. Then my father will laugh in heaven."

Isorn stared at him for a moment, then tears came to his eyes. "My father loved Frekke, Ule. I loved him, too."

"Blood on the Tree, is there nothing to drink in this wretched place!?" Dypnir shouted. All around, the tattered men came pressing forward to welcome Isorn home.

"What I am going to say to you will sound most strangely," Maegwin began. More nervous than she had thought she would be, she took a moment to smooth the folds of her old black dress. "But I am the daughter of King Lluth, and I love Hernystir more than I love my own life. I would sooner tear out my own heart than lie to you."

Her people, gathered together in the largest of the caverns beneath the Grianspog, the great high-ceilinged catacomb where justice was dispensed and food was shared out, listened attentively. What Maegwin said might indeed prove strange, but they were going to hear her out. What could be so odd as to be unbelievable in a world as mad as the one in which they found themselves?

Maegwin looked back to Diawen, who stood just behind her. The scryer, eyes radiant with some personal happiness, smiled her approval. "Tell them!" Diawen whispered.

"You know that the gods have spoken to me in dreams," Maegwin said loudly.

"They put a song of the elder days into my head and taught me to bring you here into the rocky caverns where we would be safe. Then Cuamh Earthdog, the god of the depths, led me to a secret place that had not been seen since before Tethtain's time—a place where the gods had a gift in store for us. You!" She pointed at one of the scribes who had descended to Mezutu'a with Eolair to copy the dwarrow's maps. "Stand and tell the people what you saw."

The old man rose unsteadily, leaning for support on one of his young pupils. "It was indeed a city of the gods," he quavered, "deep in the earth—bigger than all Hernysadharc, set in a cavern wide as the bay at Crannhyr." He threw his thin arms apart in a helpless attempt to indicate the stone city's vastness. "There were creatures in that place like none I have seen, whispering in the shadows." He raised his hand as several of the onlookers made signs against evil. "But they did us no harm, and even led us to their secret places, where we did what the princess asked us to do."

Maegwin gestured for the scribe to sit down. "The gods showed me the city, and there we found things that will help turn the tide of battle against Skali and his master, Elias of Erkynland. Eolair has taken those gifts to our allies—you all saw him go."

Heads nodded throughout the crowd. Among people as isolated as these earth-dwellers had become, the departure of the Count of Nad Mullach on a mysterious errand had been the subject of several weeks' worth of gossip.

"So twice the gods have spoken to me. Twice they have been correct."

But even as she spoke, Maegwin felt a twinge of worry. Was that really true? Hadn't she cursed herself for misinterpreting—even at times blamed the gods themselves for sending her cruel, false signs? She paused, suddenly beset by doubt, but Diawen reached forward and touched her shoulder, as if the scryer had heard her troubled thoughts. Maegwin found the courage to go on.

"Now the gods have spoken to me—a third time, and with the mightiest words of all. I saw Brynioch himself!" For surely, she thought, it must have been him. The strange face and golden stare burned in her memory like the afterimage of sun against the blackness of closed eyelids. "And Brynioch told me that the gods would send help to Hernystir!"

A few of the audience, caught up in Maegwin's own fervor, raised their voices in a cheer. Others, unsure but hopeful, exchanged glances with their neighbors.

"Craobhan," Maegwin called. "Stand and tell our people how I was found."

The old counselor got up with obvious reluctance. The look on his face told all: he was a statesman, a practical man who did not hold with such high-flown things as prophecies and the gods speaking to princesses. The folk gathered in the cavern knew that. For this reason, he was Maegwin's master stroke.

Craobhan looked around the chamber. "We found Princess Maegwin on Bradach Tor," he intoned. His voice could still carry powerfully despite his years; he had used it to great effect in the service of Maegwin's father and grandfather. "I did not see, but the men who brought her down are known to me, and . . . and trustworthy. She had been three days on the mountain, but had taken no hurt from the cold. When they found her she was . . ." he looked helplessly at Maegwin, but saw nothing in her stern face that would allow him to escape this moment, ". . . she was in the grip of some deep, deep dream."

The gathering buzzed. Bradach Tor was a place of strange repute, and it was stranger still that it should be climbed by a woman during frozen winter.

"Was it just a dream?" Diawen said sharply from behind Maegwin. Craobhan looked at her angrily, then shrugged.

"The men said it was like no dream they had ever seen," he said. "Her eyes were open, and she spoke as though to someone who stood before her . . . but nothing was there but empty air."

"Who was she speaking to?" Diawen asked.

Old Craobhan shrugged again. "She . . . was speaking as though she addressed the gods—and she listened betimes, as though they were speaking to her in turn."

"Thank you, Craobhan," Maegwin said gently. "You are a loyal and honest man. It is no wonder my father valued you so highly." The old counselor sat down. He did not look happy. "I know that the gods have spoken to me," she continued. "I was given a sight of the place where the gods dwell, of the gods themselves in their invincible beauty, caparisoned for war."

"For war?" someone shouted. "Against who, my lady? Who do the gods fight?"

"Not who," Maegwin said, raising an admonitory finger. "But *for whom*. The gods will fight for *us*." She leaned forward, quelling the rising murmur of the crowd. "They will destroy our enemies—but only if we give our hearts to them wholly."

"They have our hearts, lady, they do!" a woman cried.

Someone else shouted: "Why have they not helped us before now? We have always honored them."

Maegwin waited until the clamor died down. "We have always honored them, it is true, but in the manner that one honors an old relative, out of grudging habit. We have never shown them honor worthy of their power, their beauty, worthy of the gifts they have given our people!" Her voice rose. She could feel again the nearness of the gods; the sensation rose inside her like a spring of clear water. It was such an odd, heady feeling that she burst out laughing, which brought amazement to the faces of the people around her. "No!" she shouted. "We have performed the rites, polished the carvings, lit the sacred fires, but very few of us have ever asked what more the gods might wish as proof that we are worth their aid."

Craobhan cleared his throat. "And what do they want, Maegwin, do you think?" He addressed her in a way that seemed untowardly familiar, but she only laughed again.

"They want us to show our trust! To show our devotion, our willingness to put our lives in their hands—as our lives have been all along. The gods will help us, this I have seen for myself—but only if we show that we are worthy! Why did Bagba give cattle to men? Because men had lost their horses fighting in the wars of the gods, in the time of the gods' truest need."

Even as she spoke, it all suddenly became clear to Maegwin. How right Diawen had been! The dwarrows, the frightened Sitha-woman who had spoken through the Shard, the frighteningly endless winter—it was all so clear now!

"For you see," she cried, "the gods themselves are at war! Why do you think that snow has fallen, that winter has come and never left although more than a dozen moons have changed? Why do ancient terrors walk the Frostmarch— things not seen since Hern's day? Because the gods are at war even as we are at war. As the soldiering games of children ape the combats of warriors, so is our small conflict beside the great war that rages in the heavens." She took a breath and felt the god-feeling bubbling inside her, filling her with joyful strength. She was sure now that she had seen the truth. It was bright as sunlight to a new-wakened sleeper. "But just as the learning of childhood is what shapes the wars of grown folk, so does our strife here on the green earth affect the wars of heaven. So if we wish the help of the gods, we must help them in turn. We must be bold, and we must trust in their beneficence. We must work the greatest magic against darkness that we have."

"Magic?" a voice cried, an old man's distrustful rasp. "Is that what the scryer woman's taught you?"

Maegwin heard Diawen's hiss of indrawn breath, but she was feeling too bold for anger. "Nonsense!" she shouted. "I do not mean the fumblings of conjurors. I mean the sort of magic that speaks as loudly in heaven as it does upon the earth. The magic of our love for Hernystir and the gods. Do you wish to see our enemies vanquished? Do you wish to walk your green land again?"

"Tell us what we must do!" a woman near the front shouted.

"I will." Maegwin felt a great sense of peace and strength. The cavern had grown silent, and several hundred faces peered intently up at her. Just before her, old Craobhan's deep-lined, skeptical brow was creased with anger and worry. Maegwin loved him at that moment, for she saw in his defeated look the vindication of her suffering and the proof of the power of her dreams. "I will tell you all," she said again, louder, and her voice echoed and echoed again through the great cavern, so strong, so full of triumphant certainty that few could doubt that they were indeed hearing the chosen messenger of the gods.

❧

Miriamele and her companions lingered only a few moments to put Charystra ashore on an isolated dock in the furthest outskirts of Kwanitupul. The innkeeper's violated feelings were only partially soothed by the bag of coins Isgrimnur tossed onto the weathered boards at her feet.

"God will punish you for treating an Aedonite woman this way!" she cried as they rowed away. She was still standing on the edge of the rickety dock, waving a fist and shouting incomprehensibly, as their slow-sliding boat nosed down a canal lined by twisted trees and she was lost from view.

Cadrach winced. "If what we have experienced lately has been God's way of showing His favor, I think I would be willing to try a little of His punishment, just for a change."

"No blasphemy," Isgrimnur growled, leaning hard on his oar. "We are still alive, against all reason, and still free. That is indeed a gift."

The monk shrugged, unimpressed, but said no more.

They floated out into an open lagoon, so shallow that stalks of marsh-grass poked from the surface and wavered in the wind. Miriamele watched Kwani-tupul slipping away behind them. In the late afternoon light, the low gray city seemed a collection of drifting flotsam that had snagged on a sandbar, vast but purposeless. She felt a terrible longing for some place to call home, for even the most mindless and stifling routines of everyday life. At the moment, there was not a single scrap of charm left in the idea of adventuring.

"There is still no one behind us," Isgrimnur said with some satisfaction. "Once we reach the swamps, we will be safe."

Tiamak, sitting in the bow of the boat, gave a curious, strangled laugh. "Do not say such a thing." He pointed to the right. "There, head for that small canal, just between those two large baobab trees. No, do not talk like that. You might attract attention."

"What attention?" asked the duke, irritated.

"They Who Breathe Darkness. They like to take men's brave words and bring them back to them in fear."

"Heathen spirits," Isgrimnur muttered.

The little man laughed again, a sad and helpless giggle. He slapped his hand against his bony thigh so that the smack rang echoing across the sluggish water, then he sobered abruptly. "I am so ashamed. You people must think me a fool. I studied with the finest scholars in Perdruin—I am as civilized as any dry-lander! But now we are going back to my home . . . and I am frightened. Suddenly the old gods of my childhood seem more real than ever."

Next to Miriamele, Cadrach was nodding in a coldly satisfied way.

The trees and their raiment of clinging vines grew thicker as the afternoon wore on, and the canals down which Tiamak directed them grew progressively smaller and less well-defined, full of thick weeds. By the time the sun was scudding toward the leafy horizon, Camaris and Cadrach—Isgrimnur was taking a well-deserved rest—could hardly drag their oars through the mossy water.

"Soon we will have to use the oars as poles only." Tiamak squinted at the murky waterway. "I hope that this boat is small enough to go where we must take it. There is no doubt we will soon have to find something with a more shallow draft, but it would be good to be farther in, so that there will be less chance our pursuers will discover what we have done."

"I don't have a cintis-piece left." Isgrimnur fanned away the cloud of tiny insects that hovered around his head. "What will we use to trade for another boat?"

"This one," Tiamak said. "We will not get anything so sturdy in return, but whoever trades with us will know that they can sell this in Kwanitupul for enough to buy two or three flatboats, and also a barrel of palm wine."

"Speaking of boats," Cadrach said, resting against his sweep for a moment, "I can feel more water around my toes than I like. Should we not stop soon and patch this one, especially if we are condemned to keep it for a few more days? I would not care to look for a camping place on this mucky ground in the dark."

"The monk is right," Tiamak told Isgrimnur. "It is time to stop."

As they glided slowly along, with the Wrannaman standing in the bow inspecting the tangled coastline for a suitable mooring place, Miriamele occasionally caught a glimpse through the close-leaning trees of small, ramshackle huts. "Are those your people's houses?" she asked Tiamak.

He shook his head, a slight smile curving his lips. "No, lady, they are not. Those of my folk who must live in Kwanitupul for their livelihood live *in* Kwanitupul. This is not the true Wran, and to live in this place would be worse for them than simply enduring the two seasons a year they spend in the city, then returning to their villages after their money is earned. No, those who live here are drylanders mostly, Perdruinese and Nabbanai who have left the cities. They are strange folk who are not much like their brethren, for many of them have lived long on the edge of the marshes. In Kwanitupul they are called 'shoalers' or 'edge-hoppers,' and are thought to be odd and unreliable." He smiled again, bashfully, as if embarrassed by his long explanation, then returned to his search for a campsite.

Miriamele saw a wisp of smoke trailing upward from one of the hidden houses, and wondered what it would be like to live in such an isolated place, to hear no human voice from the start of the day until the end. She looked up at the overarching trees and their strange shapes, the roots twisted like serpents where they ran down to the water, the branches gnarled and grasping. The narrow watercourse, now shadowed from the dying sun, seemed lined by lonely shapes that reached out as if to clutch at the small boat and hold it fast, to pinion it until the waters would rise and the mud and roots and vines would swallow it. She shivered. Somewhere in the shaded hollows, a bird screeched like a frightened child.

12

Raven's Dance

At first the battle did not seem real to Simon. From his position on the lower slopes of Sesuad'ra, the great expanse of frozen lake lay before him like a marble floor, and beyond it the snow-stippled downs stretched to the snow-blanketed, wooded hills across the valley. Everything was so small—so far away! Simon could almost trick himself into believing that he had returned to the Hayholt and was peering down from Green Angel Tower on the busily harmless movements of castle folk.

From Simon's vantage point, the initial sally of Sesuad'ra's defenders—meant to keep Duke Fengbald's troops out on the ice and away from the log barricade that protected the entrance to the Sithi road—seemed a capering display of intricate puppetry. Men waved swords and axes, then fell to the ice pierced by invisible arrows, dropping as suddenly as if some titanic master had loosed their strings. It all seemed so distant! But even as he marveled at the miniature combat, Simon knew that what he was watching was in deadly earnest, and that he would be seeing it closer soon enough.

The rams and their riders were both growing restive. Those of Simon's Qanuc troop whose hiding places did not allow them a view of the frozen lake were calling whispered questions to those who could see. The steamy breath of the entire company hung close overhead. All around, the branches of the trees shimmered with droplets of melting snow.

Simon, as impatient as his trollish companions, leaned into Homefinder's neck. He inhaled her reassuring smell and felt the warmth of her skin. He wanted so to do the right thing, to help Josua and his other friends; at the same time, he was mortally afraid of what might happen down there on the glassy surface of the frozen lake. But for now, he could only wait. Both death and glory would have to be put off, at least for Simon and these small warriors.

He watched carefully, trying to make sense of the chaos before him. The line of Fengbald's soldiers, which was holding tightly to the sandy path laid for them by their battle-sledges, rippled as the wave of defenders struck them. But although they wavered, Fengbald's force held, then struck back at their attackers, hitting and then dispersing the initial clump into several smaller groupings. The leading company of Fengbald's soldiers then swarmed around their attackers, so that the firm line of the Duke's forces quickly became a number of actively moving points, each small skirmish largely self-contained. Simon could not help thinking of wasps clustering around a scatter of scraps.

The muffled sounds of combat were rising. The faint clanking as swords and axes struck armor, the dim bellows of rage and terror, all added to the sense of remoteness, as though the battle were being fought beneath the frozen lake instead of atop it.

Even to Simon's untrained eye, it quickly became obvious that the defenders' opening sally had failed. The survivors were breaking away from Fengbald's line, which was still swelling as more and more of his army made its way out onto the lake. Those of Josua's soldiers who could pull free were skidding and crawling back over the naked ice to the dubious safety of the barricade and the wooded hillside.

Homefinder snorted beneath Simon's stroking hand and wagged her head restively. Simon gritted his teeth. They had no choice, he knew. The prince wished them to wait until they were called, even if it looked as if all might be lost before their time came.

Waiting. Simon let out an angry sigh. Waiting was so hard. . . .

Father Strangyeard was hopping about in an agony of worry.

"Oh!" he said, almost slipping on the muddy earth. "Poor Deornoth!"

Sangfugol reached out a hand and snagged the archivist's sleeve, saving the priest from a long tumble down the hillside.

Josua was standing upslope, peering down at the battle site. His red Thrithings-horse, Vinyafod, stood nearby, reins tied loosely around a low branch. "There!" Josua could not keep the exultation from his voice. "I see his crest—he is still on his feet!" The prince leaned forward, teetering precariously. Below, Sangfugol made a reflexive gesture to go toward him, as though the harper might have to catch his master as he had rescued the priest. "Now he has broken free!" Josua cried, relief in his voice. "Brave Deornoth! He is rallying the men and they are falling back, but slowly. Ah, God's Peace, I love him dearly!"

"Praise Aedon's name." Strangyeard made the sign of the Tree. "May they all come back safely." He was flushed with exertion and excitement, his eyepatch a black spot atop the mottled pink.

Sangfugol made a bitter noise. "Half of them are lying bloody on the ice, already. What is important is that some of Fengbald's men are doing the same." He clambered atop a stone and squinted down at the milling shapes. "I think I see Fengbald, Josua!" he called.

"Aye," the prince said. "But has he taken the feint?"

"Fengbald is an idiot," Sangfugol replied. "He will take it like a trout takes a shadfly."

Josua looked away from the battle for a moment, turning to the harper with a look of cool, if somewhat distracted, amusement. "Oh, he will, will he? I wish I had your confidence, Sangfugol."

The harper flushed. "I beg your pardon, Highness. I only meant that Fengbald is not the tactician that you are."

The prince returned his attention to the lake below. "Don't waste time with flattery, harper—at this moment, I fear I'm too busy to appreciate it. And don't make the mistake of underestimating an enemy, either." He stared, shading his eyes against the glare of the shrouded sun, which was climbing behind the clouds. "Damnation! He *hasn't* taken it, not entirely! There, see, he has only brought part of his troop forward. The rest are still huddled at the edge of the lake."

Embarrassed, Sangfugol said nothing. Strangyeard was hopping up and down again. "Where is Deornoth? Oh, curse this old eye!"

"Still falling back." Josua leaped down from his perch, then made his way down the hill to where they stood. "Binabik has not yet returned from Hotvig and I cannot wait any longer. Where is Simon's boy?"

Jeremias, who had been crouching beside a toppled log, trying to stay out of the way, now leaped to his feet. "Here, Your Highness."

"Good. Go now, first to Freosel, then down the hill to Hotvig and his riders. Tell them to make ready—that we will strike now after all. They will hear my signal shortly."

Jeremias bowed quickly, his face pale but composed, then turned and dashed up the trail.

Josua was frowning. Down on the ice, Fengbald's army of Erkynguardsmen and mercenaries indeed seemed to be moving forward only hesitantly, despite their success in the first engagement. "Welladay," said the prince, "Fengbald has grown more cautious with his advancing years and greater burdens. Damn his eyes! Still, we have no choice but to pull the trapdoor shut on whatever of his force we can catch." His laugh was sour. "We will leave tomorrow for the Devil."

"Prince Josua!" gasped Strangyeard, so shocked that he ceased hopping. He sketched another hasty Tree in the air before him.

The hot breath of men and horses hung over the lake as a mist. It was hard to see clearly for more than a few ells in any direction, and even those men Deornoth could see were dim and insubstantial, so that the clamor of combat seemed to come from some ghost battle.

Deornoth caught the guardsman's downward stroke on his hilt. The impact nearly shivered his blade loose from his grip, but he managed to retain it in his tingling fingers long enough to bring it up for a counterswipe. His stroke missed, but slashed the guardsman's mount on an unprotected leg. The dappled horse shrieked and bounced back a few steps, then lost its footing and tumbled to the ragged ice with a crash and a spurt of powdery snow. Deornoth reined in Vildalix; they danced away from the fallen charger, who was thrashing wildly. Its rider was trapped beneath, but unlike the horse, he was making no noise.

Breath whistling in the confines of his helmet, Deornoth raised his sword and hammered it against his shield as loud as he could. His hornsman, one of the young and untrained soldiers from New Gadrinsett, had gone down in the first crush, and now there was no one to blow the retreat.

"Hark to me!" Deornoth shouted, redoubling the clatter. "Fall back, all men, fall back!"

As he looked around, his mouth filled with something salty and he spat. A gobbet of red flew out through the helmet's vertical slot and onto the ice. The wetness on his face was blood, probably the wound he had gotten when another of the guardsmen had dented his headgear. He could not feel it—he never did feel such small hurts while the fight was raging—but he offered a quick prayer to Mother Elysia that the blood would not run into his eyes and blind him at an important moment.

Some of his men had heard and were collapsing back around his position. They were not true fighting men yet, God knew, but so far they had shown themselves bravely against a formidable line of Erkynguards. They were not meant to break Fengbald's leading force, but only to slow them, and perhaps to lure them incautiously toward the barricade and the first of Josua's surprises: New Gadrinsett's few dependable archers and their small hoard of arrows. Bowmen alone would not change the course of this battle—the mounted knights on both sides were too well-armored—but they would wreak some havoc, and force Fengbald's men to think twice before launching an unbridled assault against the base of Sesuad'ra. So far, very few arrows had flown from either side, although a few of Deornoth's makeshift troops had gone down in the first moments of their assault with shafts quivering in their throats or even punched through chain mail into a chest or stomach. Now the fog caused by the rising sun would make it even more difficult for Fengbald's men to make use of their bows.

Thank God it is Fengbald we are fighting, Deornoth thought. He was almost immediately forced to duck, surprised by the flailing blade of a mounted guardsman who appeared without warning out of the murk. The horse clattered by, receding into insubstantiality once more. Deornoth took a few quick, deep breaths.

Mounted knights and kerns we can deal with, at least for a while. Only Fengbald would be so foolhardy as to besiege a fortified hill without a company or two of longbowmen! They could have cut us all down in the first moments.

Of course, for all his arrogance, Fengbald had not proved quite as foolish as Josua and the others had hoped. They had prayed that he would send at least a major force of the Thrithings-men in first, trusting to their superior horsemanship on the treacherous ice. The grasslanders were fearsome fighters, but they loved the heroism of individual combat. The prince had felt sure that a few nettling attacks from Deornoth's troop would lure the mercenaries out of formation, where they would be more easily dealt with, and which would also throw Fengbald's advance into confusion. But they had all reckoned without the sledges—and whose clever plan was *that,* Deornoth could not help wondering—and the improved footing brought by the blanket of sand had allowed the duke to send in his disciplined Erkynguard.

There was a sound as of a swelling drum roll. Deornoth looked up to see that the guardsman who had missed on his first pass had finally turned his horse around—the footing was so dreadful and necessitated such careful movement by both sides that the entire battle had the look of some strange underwater dance—and was now bearing down on him out of the fog again, slowly this time, urging his horse forward at no more than a cautious walk. Deornoth gave Vildalix a polite heel, bringing the bay around to face the attacker, then lifted his sword. The Erkynguardsman raised his in turn, but still continued his approach at little more than a man's hiking pace.

It was strange to see the green livery of the Erkynguard draping an enemy. It was stranger still to have so much time to deliberate on the oddness of it while waiting for that enemy to make his measured way across the ice. The guardsman ducked a wild sword-swing from one of Deornoth's comrades, a blow that flashed out of the mist like a serpent's darting tongue—Josua's men were all around, fighting desperately now to pull close enough together for an orderly retreat—and came on, undaunted. Deornoth could not help wondering for a brief moment if the face beneath this bold soldier's helm was one he would recognize, someone he had drunk with, diced with. . . .

Vildalix, who despite his bravery seemed sometimes as sensitive as flayed skin, took Deornoth's minute pull on the reins and lurched heavily to one side just as the attacker reached them, so that the guardsman's first stroke scraped harmlessly across Deornoth's shield. Vildalix then danced in place for a moment, trying to avoid stepping on the crumpled form of the rider who had earlier gone down beneath his own mount, and thus Deornoth's own return blow missed widely. The attacking guardsman pulled up, his horse's legs spreading slightly as it skidded in an attempt to make a sudden stop. Seeing his opening, Deornoth dragged Vildalix around and went after him. The Thrithings-horse, who had been trained on ice as Josua's men prepared, was able to turn fairly easily, so that Deornoth caught up with the Erkynguard before he had completed his own awkward revolution.

Deornoth's first blow caromed off the guardsman's lifted shield, raising a brief plume of sparks, but he let the sword's own momentum carry it around for a second blow, rotating his wrists and leaning almost sideways in the saddle so he would not be forced to break his grip. He caught the green-liveried guardsman a powerful backhand blow to the head just as the man lowered his shield once more; the side of the Erkynguardsman's helmet crumpled inward at a hideous angle. Blood already sluicing down his neck and onto his byrnie, the guardsman toppled out of his saddle, tangling for a moment in his stirrups, then clanged to the ice where he lay twitching feebly. Deornoth turned away, pushing any regrets from his mind with the ease of long experience. This bleeding hulk might once have been someone he knew, but now any Erkynguardsman was only an enemy, no more.

"Hark, men, hark!" Deornoth shouted, standing upright in his stirrups so that he could better view their position through the mist. "Follow me on the retreat! Careful as you go!" It was hard to tell, but he thought he saw something more than half the force he had taken out now ringing him round. He raised his sword high, then spurred Vildalix in the direction of the great log barricades. An arrow whipped past his head, then another, but the aim was poor, or else the archers were confused by the mist. Deornoth's men lifted a thin cheer as they rode.

"Where is Binabik?" Josua fumed. "He was to be my messenger, but he has not come back from Hotvig." The prince made a face. "God grant me patience, listen to me! Perhaps something has happened to him." He turned to young Jeremias, who stood by, panting. "And Hotvig said Binabik left his side some time ago?"

"Yes, Highness. He said the sun has lifted a hand since the troll left, whatever that means."

"Damnable luck." Josua began pacing, but his eyes never left the battle below. "Well, there is nothing for it. I do not trust the call to carry so far, lad, so go to Simon and tell him that if hears nothing by the time he has counted five hundreds or so after Hotvig's men have ridden out, then he and the trolls are to rush in. Do you have that?"

"If he doesn't hear the horn, wait to a count of five hundreds after Hotvig appears, then rush in, yes." Jeremias considered before adding: "Your Highness."

"Fine. Go, then—run. We are at the time when moments matter." Josua waved him off, then turned to Sangfugol. "And you are ready, too?"

"Yes, sire," the harper said. "I have been trained by the best. I should have little difficulty wringing a few honking sounds out of something so simple as a horn."

Josua chuckled grimly. "There is something reassuring about your insolence, Sangfugol. But remember, master musician, you must do more than honk: you must play a victory call."

Simon was looking over the small company, mostly to keep himself busy, when he suddenly realized that Sisqi was not among the gathered trolls. He quickly went among the Qanuc, checking every face but finding no sign of

Binabik's betrothed. She was their leader—where could she have gone? After a moment's thought, Simon realized that he had not seen her since the muster before Leavetaking House.

Oh, Aedon's mercy, no, he thought desperately. *What will Binabik say? I've lost his beloved before the battle even begins!*

He turned to the nearest of the trolls. "Sisqi?" he asked, trying to show by shrugs and gestures that he wished to know her whereabouts. Two troll women looked at him uncomprehendingly. Damn, that was what Binabik called her. What was her full name? "Sis—Sisqimook?" he tried. "Sisqinamok?"

One of the women nodded urgently, pleased to have understood. *"Sisqinanamook."*

"Where is she?" Simon could not think of the troll words. "Sisqinanamook? Where?" He pointed around to all sides and then shrugged again, trying to convey his question. His small companions seemed to grasp his meaning: after a long round of murmuring Qanuc-speech, those nearest indicated to him with perfectly understandable gestures that they did not know where Sisqinanamook had gone.

Simon was cursing roundly when Jeremias arrived.

"Hullo, Simon, isn't this glorious?" his squire asked. Jeremias seemed quite excited. "It's just like what we used to dream of back in the Hayholt."

Simon made a pained face. "Except we were hitting each other with barrel staves, and those men down there will use sharp steel instead. Do you know where Sisqi is—you know, the one Binabik is going to marry? She was supposed to be here with the other trolls."

"No, I don't, but Binabik's missing, too. Stop, though, Simon—I have to give you Josua's message first." Jeremias proceeded to relay the prince's instructions, then dutifully ran through them a second time, just in case.

"Tell him that I'm ready . . . that *we're* ready. We'll do what we're supposed to. But Jeremias, I have to find Sisqi. She's their leader!"

"No, you don't." His squire was complacent. "You've become a trollish war chieftain now, Simon, that's all. I have to run back to Josua. With Binabik gone, I'm his chief messenger. It happens that way in battles." He said it lightly, but with more than a touch of pride.

"But what if they won't follow me?" Simon stared at Jeremias for a moment. "You seem very cheerful," he growled. "Jeremias, people are being killed here. We may be next."

"I know." He became serious. "But at least it's our choice, Simon. At least it's an honorable death." A strange look flitted over his face, twisting his features as though he might suddenly burst into tears. "For a long time, when I was . . . under the castle . . . a quick, clean death seemed like it would be a wonderful thing." Jeremias turned away, hunching his shoulders. "But I suppose I must stay alive now. Leleth needs me as a friend—and you need someone to tell you what to do." He sighed and then straightened up, gave Simon an oddly flat smile and a half-wave, then trotted back into the shrouding greenery, disappearing in the direction from which he had come. "Good luck, Simon—Sir Seoman, I mean."

Simon started to call after him, but Jeremias was already gone.

Binabik's return was abrupt and somewhat startling. Josua heard a soft rustling noise and looked up to find himself staring into the yellow eyes and sharp-toothed maw of Qantaqa, panting on a rise just above him. The troll, seated atop her back, pushed some branches away from his round face and leaned forward. "Prince Josua," he said calmly, as though they were meeting at some court function.

"Binabik!" Josua took a backward step. "Where have you been?"

"I ask your pardoning, Josua." The troll slid off Qantaqa and made his way down to the level place where the prince stood. "I saw some of Fengbald's men who were exploring where they should not be going. I followed them." He gave Josua a significant look. "They were looking for a place with better climbing. Fengbald is not being so foolish as we were thinking—it is clear he is knowing he may not dislodge us with this first attack."

"How many were there?"

"Not a great number. Six . . . five."

"You couldn't tell? How closely did you watch them?"

Binabik's gentle smile did not reach his eyes. "There were six at first." He patted his walking-stick, and the hollow tube and darts contained therein. "Then one was falling down the hill again."

Josua nodded. "And the rest?"

"After they had been led away from the places they should not be, I left Sisqi behind for distracting them while I went quickly up the hill. Some of the women of New Gadrinsett came down to help us."

"The women? Binabik, you are not to place women and children in danger."

The little man shook his head. "You know that they will be fighting just as bravely for saving their home as any men—we have never known any other thing among the Qanuc. But be of quieter heart. All they did was come for helping Sisqi and myself in the rolling of some large stones." He flattened his hand in a gesture of completion. "Those men will be no danger to us anymore, and their searching will bring no reward for Fengbald."

Josua sighed in frustration. "I trust that at least you did not drag my wife along to help roll your stones?"

Binabik laughed. "She was eager to go, Prince Josua, that I will say. You have a wife of some fierceness—she would make a good Qanuc bride! But Gutrun was not allowing her a step out of camp." The troll looked around. "What is happening below? I could not easily be watching as I made my way back."

"Fengbald, as you said, was better prepared than we expected. They have built some kind of sleds or carts that roughen the ice so that the soldiers can move more easily. Deornoth's attack was pushed back, but Fengbald's Erkynguard did not chase him; they are still massing on the lake. I am about to—but enough. You will see what I am about to do."

"And do you need me to go to Hotvig?" Binabik asked.

"No. Jeremias has taken on your tasks while you were introducing Fengbald's spies to the ladies of New Gadrinsett." Josua smiled briefly. "Thank you, Binabik. I knew that if you were not hurt or trapped, you would be doing something important—but try to let me know next time."

"Apologies, Josua. I was fearing to wait too long."

The prince turned and beckoned to Sangfugol, who came quickly to his side. Father Strangyeard and Towser were both standing solemnly, watching the battle, although Towser seemed to be listing slightly, as if even the deadly combat below was not enough excitement to keep him from his midday nap much longer.

"Blow for Freosel," Josua said. "Three short bursts, three long."

Sangfugol lifted the horn to his lips, puffed out his thin chest, and blew. The call echoed down the wooded hillside, and for a moment the flurry of battle on the ice seemed to slow. The harper gasped in another great draught of air, then blew again. When the echoes died, he gave the call a third time.

"Now," Josua said firmly, "we shall see how ready Fengbald is for a real fight. Do you mark him down there, Binabik?"

"I think I am seeing him, yes. In the red flapping cape?"

"Yes. Watch and see what he does."

Even as Josua spoke, there was a sudden convulsion in the front line of Fengbald's army. The clot of soldiers nearest the wooden barricades abruptly stopped and swirled back in disorder.

"Hurrah!" Strangyeard shouted and leaped; then, seeming to remember his priestly gravity, he donned his look of worried concern once more.

"Aedon's Blood, see how they jump!" Josua said with fierce glee. "But even this will not stop them for long. How I wish we had more arrows!"

"Freosel will be making good use of those we are having," Binabik said. "'A well-aimed spear is worth three,' as we say in Yiqanuc."

"But we must use the confusion Freosel's bowmen have given us." Josua paced distractedly as he watched. When a little time had passed, and he evidently could bear the waiting no longer, he cried: "Sangfugol—Hotvig's call, now!"

The trumpet blared again, two long, two short, two long.

The flight of arrows from Sesuad'ra's defenders caught Fengbald's men by surprise: they spilled back in confusion, leaving several score of their fellows lying skewered on the ice, some trying to crawl back across the slippery surface, trailing smears of blood like the tracks of snails. In the chaos, Deornoth and his remaining force were able to make their escape.

Deornoth himself went back three times to help carry the last of the wounded past the great wall of logs. When he was sure there was no more he could do, he slumped to the trampled mud in the shadow of the high barricade and pulled off his helmet. The sounds of struggle still raged close by.

"Sir Deornoth," someone said, "you are bleeding."

He waved the man away, disliking to be fussed over, but took the piece of cloth that was offered to him. Deornoth used the rag and a handful of snow to wipe the blood from his face and hair, then probed at his head wound with chilled fingers. It was only a shallow cut. He was glad he had sent the man off to aid those in greater need. A strip of the now bloodied cloth made an adequate bandage, and the pressure as he knotted it helped to soothe the ache in his head.

When he had finished looking over his other injuries—all quite minor, none as bloody as the nick in his scalp—he pulled his sword out of its scabbard. It was a plain blade, the hilt leather-wrapped, the pommel a crude hawk's head worn almost featureless by long handling. He wiped it down with an unbloodied corner of the cloth, frowning in displeasure at the new notches it had gained, however honorably. When he had finished, he held it up to catch the faint sunlight and squinted to make sure he had not left any blood to gnaw at the honed edge.

This is no famous blade, he thought. *It has no name, but it has still served well for many years. Like me, I suppose.* He laughed quietly to himself; a few of the other soldiers resting nearby looked at him. *No one will remember me, I think, no matter how long the names of Josua and Elias are spoken. But I am content with that. I do what the Lord Usires would have me do—was He any less humble?*

Still, there were times when Deornoth wished that the people of Hewenshire could see him now, see the way he fought loyally for a great prince, and how that prince depended on him. Was that too prideful for a good Aedonite? Perhaps. . . .

Another horn call shrilled from the hillside above, disrupting his thoughts. Deornoth scrambled to his feet, anxious to see what was afoot, and began to climb the barricade. A moment later, he dropped down and went back for his helmet.

Pointless to take an arrow between the eyes if I can avoid it, he decided.

He and several other men carefully lifted themselves so they could nose over the topmost logs and peer out through the crude observation slots that Sludig and his helpers had cut with their hand-axes. As they squeezed into place, they heard a great shout: a company of riders was breaking from the trees a short distance to the east, heading out onto the ice and directly toward Fengbald's rallying forces. There was something different about this company, but in the confusion of mists and flailing men and horses it took a moment to see what it was.

"Ride, Hotvig!" Deornoth shouted. The men beside him picked up the cry, cheering hoarsely. As the Thrithings-men pounded across the frozen lake, it quickly became apparent that they were moving far more easily and skillfully than Fengbald's men. They might almost have been riding on firm ground, so sure was their horsemanship.

"Clever Binabik," Deornoth breathed to himself. "You may save us yet!"

"Look at them ride!" one of the other men called, a bearded old fellow who had last joined a battle when Deornoth was a swaddled baby. "Those troll-tricks work, sure enough."

"But we are still far outnumbered," cautioned Deornoth. "Ride, Hotvig! Ride!"

In a matter of moments, the Thrithings-men were sweeping down on Fengbald's guardsmen, the horses' hooves making an oddly clangorous thunder on the ice. They struck the first lines of men like a club, smashing a path through them without difficulty. The noise, the clashing of weapon and shield, the shrieking of men and horses, seemed to double in a moment. Hotvig himself, his beard festooned with scarlet war-ribbons, was plying his long spear as swiftly as an expert river-fisher; every time he darted it forward it seemed to find a target, bringing forth flaring sprays of blood as red as the silken knots in his whiskers. He and his grasslanders sang as they fought, a shouting chant with little tune but a horrible sort of rhythm which they used to punctuate each thrust and slash. They wheeled around Fengbald's men with amazing ease, as though the battle-hardened Erkynguardsmen were swimming in mud. The leading edges of the duke's forces wavered and fell back. The Thrithings-men's fierce song grew louder.

"God's Eyes!" Fengbald screamed, waving his long sword in purposeless fury, "hold your lines, damn you!" He turned to Lezhdraka. The mercenary captain was staring with slitted, feral eyes at Hotvig and his riders. "They have some damnable Sithi magic," the duke raged. "Look, they move across the ice as though they were on a tourney field."

"No magic," Lezhdraka growled. "Look at their horses' hooves. They wear some special shoe—see, the spikes are flashing! Somehow your Josua has shod his horses with metal nails, I think."

"Damn him!" Fengbald stood high in his stirrups and looked around. His pale, handsome face was beaded with sweat. "Well, it is a brave trick, but it is not enough. We are still far too many for him, unless he has an army three times that size hidden up there—which he has not. Bring up your men, Lezhdraka. We will shame my Erkynguard into giving a better account of themselves." He rode a little way toward his leading forces and raised his voice in a shriek. "Traitors! Hold your lines or you will go to the king's gibbet!"

Lezhdraka grunted in disgust at Fengbald's frenzy, then turned to his first company of Thrithings mercenaries, who had been sitting stolidly in their saddles, caring little for what happened until their own turn should come to ply their trade. They all wore boiled leather cuirasses and metal-rimmed leather helmets, the armor of the grasslands. At Lezhdraka's gesture, the large company of scarred and silent men straightened. A light seemed to kindle in their eyes.

"You carrion dogs," Lezhdraka shouted in his own tongue, *"listen! These stone-dwellers and their High Thrithing pets think that because they have ice-shoes on their horses, they will scare us off. Let us go and bare their bones!"* He spurred his horse forward, taking care to stay on the path provided by one of the battle sledges. With a single grim shout, his mercenaries fell in behind him.

"Kill them all," Fengbald shouted, riding in circles beside their column and waving his sword. "Kill them all, but especially, *do not let Josua leave the field alive.* Your master, King Elias, demands his death!"

The mercenary captain stared at the duke with poorly hidden contempt, but Fengbald was already spurring his horse forward, screeching at his faltering Erkynguard. *"I care little for these stone-dweller quarrels,"* Lezhdraka shouted to his men in the Thrithings-tongue, *"but I know something that idiot does not: a live prince will get us better pay than Fengbald would ever give us—so I want the one-handed prince alive. But if Hotvig or any other whelp of the High Thrithing walks living from this field, I will make you scum eat your own guts."*

He waved again and the column surged forward. The mercenaries grinned in their beards and patted their weapons. The smell of blood was in the air—a very familiar smell.

Deornoth and his men were struggling back into their battle array when Josua appeared, leading Vinyafod. Father Strangyeard and the harper Sangfugol straggled after him, muddy and disarrayed.

"Binabik's ice-shoes have worked—or at least they have helped us catch Fengbald off-guard," Josua called.

"We have been watching, Highness." Deornoth gave the inside of his helmet another thump with his sword-hilt, but the dent was too deep for such simple repairs. He cursed and pulled it on anyway. There was nowhere near enough armor to go around; New Gadrinsett had strained to supply even what small weaponry and gear they had, and if Hotvig's Thrithings-men had not brought their own leather chestplates and headware, less than a quarter of the defenders would have been armored. There were certainly no replacements available, Deornoth knew, except those which could be gleaned from the newly dead. He decided he would stick with his original helm, dented or not.

"I am glad to see you ready," said Josua. "We must press whatever advantage we have, before Fengbald's numbers overwhelm us."

"I only wish we had more of the troll's boot-irons to pass around." As he spoke, Deornoth strapped on his own set, numbed hands fumbling awkwardly. He fingered the metal spikes that now jutted from his soles. "But we have used every piece of metal we could spare."

"Small price if it saves us, meaningless if it does not," Josua said. "I hope you gave preference to the men who must fight on foot."

"I did," Deornoth replied, "although we had enough for nearly all the horses, anyway, even after outfitting Hotvig's grasslanders."

"Good," Josua said. "If you have a moment, help me fit these on Vinyafod." The prince smiled an uncharacteristically straightforward smile. "I had the good sense to put them aside yesterday."

"But my lord!" Deornoth looked up, startled. "What do you want them for?"

"You do not think that I will watch the whole battle from this hillside, do you?" Josua's smile vanished. He seemed honestly surprised. "It is for my sake that these brave men are fighting and dying down on the lake. How could I not stand with them?"

"But that is precisely the reason." Deornoth turned to Sangfugol and Strangyeard, but those two merely looked away shamefacedly. Deornoth guessed that they had already argued this point with the prince and lost. "If something happens to you, Josua, any victory will be a hollow one."

Josua fixed Deornoth with his clear gray eyes. "Ah, but that is not true, old friend. You forget: Vorzheva now bears our child. You will protect her and our baby, just as you promised you would. If we win today and I am not here to enjoy it, I know that you will carefully and skillfully lead the people on from here. People will flock to our banner—people who will not even know or care if I am alive, but will come to us because we are fighting my brother, the king. And Isorn will soon return, I am sure, with men of Hernystir and Rimmersgard. And if his father Isgrimnur finds Miriamele—well, what more legitimate name could you have to fight behind than King John's granddaughter?" He watched Deornoth's face for a moment. "But, here, Deornoth, do not put on such a serious face. If God means me to overthrow my brother, not all the knights and bowmen of Aedon's earth can slay me. If He does not—well, there is no place to hide from one's fate." He bent and lifted one of Vinyafod's feet. The horse shifted anxiously but held its position. "Besides, man, this is a moment when the world is delicately balanced. Men who see their prince beside them know that they are not being asked to sacrifice themselves for someone who does not value that sacrifice." He fitted the leather sack with the stiffened bottom and protruding spikes over Vinyafod's hoof, then wrapped the long ties back and forth around the horse's ankle. "It is no use arguing," he said without looking up.

Deornoth sighed. He was desperately unhappy, but a part of him had known his prince might do this—indeed, would have been surprised if he had not. "As you wish, Highness."

"No, Deornoth." Josua tested the knot. "As I must."

❧

Simon cheered as Hotvig's riders smashed into Fengbald's line. Binabik's clever stratagem appeared to be working: the Thrithings-men, although still riding more slowly than normal, were far swifter than their opponents, and the difference in maneuverability was startling. Fengbald's leading troops were falling back, forced to regroup several hundred cubits back from the barricade.

"Hit them!" Simon shouted. "Brave Hotvig!" The trolls cheered, too, strange bellowing whoops. Their time was fast approaching. Simon was counting silently, although he had already lost track once or twice and had to guess. So far, the battle was unfolding just the way Josua and the others had said.

He looked at his strange companions, at their round faces and small bodies, and felt an overwhelming affection and loyalty sweep through him. They were his responsibility, in a way. They had come far to fight in someone else's cause—even if it might ultimately prove to be everyone's cause—and he wanted them all to reach their homes safely once more. They would be fighting bigger, stronger men, but trolls were accustomed to fighting in these wintry conditions. They, too, wore boot-irons, but of a far more elaborate type than those Binabik had taught the forge men to make. Binabik had told Simon that among his people these boot-spikes were precious now, since the trolls had lost the trade routes and the trading partners which had once made it possible to bring iron into Yiqanuc; in this present era, each pair of boot-spikes was handed down from parent to child, and they were carefully oiled and regularly repaired. To lose a pair was a terrible thing, for there was now almost no way to replace them.

Their saddled rams, of course, had no need for such trifles as iron shoes: their soft, leathery hooves would cling to the ice like the feet of wall-walking flies. A flat lake was little challenge when compared to the treacherous frozen trackways of high Mintahoq.

"I come," someone said behind him. Simon turned to find Sisqi looking up at him expectantly. The troll woman's face was flushed and pearled with sweat, and the fur jacket she wore beneath her leather jerkin was tattered and muddy, as if she had crawled through the undergrowth.

"Where were you?" he said. He could see no trace of a wound on her, and was grateful for that.

"With Binabik. Help Binabik fight." She lifted her hands to mime some complicated activity, then shrugged and gave up.

"Is Binabik well?" Simon asked.

She thought for a moment, then nodded. "Not hurt."

Simon took a deep breath, relieved. "Good." Before he could say more, there was a flurry of movement down below. Another group of shapes suddenly scrambled forth from near the log barricade, hurrying to join the battle. A moment later Simon heard the faint, mournful cry of a horn. It blew a long note, then four short, then two long blasts that echoed thinly along the hillside. His heart leaped and he felt suddenly cold and yet tingling, as though he had fallen into icy water. He had forgotten his count, but it did not matter. That was the call—it was time!

Despite his nervous excitement, he was careful not to scrape Homefinder's side with his irons as he scrambled into the saddle. Most of the Qanuc words Binabik had so carefully taught him were blasted from his head.

"*Now!*" he shouted. "Now, Sisqi! Josua wants us!" He drew his sword and waved it in the air, catching it for a moment in a low-hanging tree branch. What was the word for "attack"? *Ni*-something. He turned and caught Sisqi's eye. She stared back, her small face solemn. She knew. The troll woman waved her arm and called out to her troops.

Everybody knows what happens now, he realized. *They don't need me to tell them anything.*

Sisqi nodded, giving him permission.

"*Nihut!*" Simon shouted, then spurred down the muddy trail.

Homefinder's hooves skidded as they struck the frozen lake, but Simon—who had ridden her unshod on the same surface a few days before—was relieved when she quickly caught her balance. The noise of conflict was loud before them, and now his trollish comrades were shouting too, bellowing strange war-cries in which he could discern the names of one or two of the mountains of Yiqanuc. The din of battle swiftly rose until it crowded all other thoughts from his mind. Then, before it seemed that he even had time to think, they were in the thick of it.

Hotvig's initial attack had split Fengbald's line and scattered it away from the safety of the sledge-scraped track. Deornoth's soldiers—all but a few on foot—had then surged out from behind the barricade and flung themselves on those Erkynguard who had been cut off from their own rearguard by Hotvig's action. The fighting near the barricade was particularly fierce, and Simon was startled to see Prince Josua in the thick of it, standing tall in red Vinyafod's saddle, his gray cloak billowing, his shouted words drowned in the confusion. Meanwhile, though, Fengbald had brought up his Thrithings mercenaries, who, instead of helping to stiffen the line behind the retreating Erkynguardsmen, were swarming around the broken column in their haste to engage Hotvig's horsemen.

Simon's troop struck the mercenaries from the blind side; those closest to the oncoming Qanuc had only a moment to look around in amazement before being skewered by the short spears of the trolls. A few of the Thrithings-men seemed to regard the onrushing Qanuc with a shock that seemed closer to superstitious terror than mere surprise. The trolls howled their Qanuc war-cries as they charged, and whirled stones on oiled cords over their head, which made a dreadful buzzing sound like a swarm of maddened bees. The rams moved swiftly between the slower horses, so that several of the mercenaries' mounts reared and threw their masters; the trolls also used their darting spears to poke at the horses' undefended bellies. More than one Thrithings-man was killed beneath his own toppled steed.

The din of battle, which at first had seemed to Simon a great roaring, quickly changed as the conflict drew him in, and became instead a kind of silence, a terrible humming quiet in which snarling faces and the steaming, white-toothed and red-throated mouths of horses loomed up from the mist. Everything seemed to move with a horrible sluggishness, but Simon felt that he was moving even more slowly. He swung his sword around, but although it was mere steel, it seemed at that moment as heavy as black Thorn.

A hand-ax struck one of the troll-men beside Simon. The small body was flung from the saddled ram and seemed to tumble slowly as a falling leaf until it disappeared beneath Homefinder's hooves. Through the droning emptiness, Simon thought he heard a faint, high-pitched shriek, like the cry of a distant bird.

Killed, he thought distractedly as Homefinder stumbled and again found her footing. He *was killed.* A moment later he had to fling his own blade up before him to ward off a swordstroke from one of the mounted mercenaries. It seemed to take forever for the two swords to meet; when they did, with a thin *clink,* he felt the shock down his arm and into his chest. Something brushed by him from the other side. When he looked down, he saw that his makeshift corselet had been torn and blood was rilling up in a wound along his arm; he could feel only a line of icy numbness from wrist to elbow. Gaping, he lifted his sword to strike back, but there was no one within reach. He pulled Homefinder around and squinted through the mist rising off the ice, then spurred her toward a knot of tangled shapes where he could see some of the trolls at bay.

After that the battle rose around him like a smothering hand and nothing made very much sense. In the midst of the nightmare, he was struck in the chest by someone's shield and tumbled from his saddle. As he scrambled to find purchase, he quickly realized that even shod with Binabik's magic spikes, he was still a man struggling for footing on a glassy sheet of ice. By luck, the reins had stayed tangled around his hand so that Homefinder did not bolt, but this same luck almost killed him.

One of the mounted Thrithings-men came out of the murk and pressed Simon backward, trapping him against Homefinder's flank. The gaunt swordsman had a face so covered with ritual scars that the skin showing beneath his helm looked like tree bark. Simon was in a terrible position, his shield arm still snagged in the reins so that he could barely get half of his shield between himself and his attacker. The grinning mercenary wounded him twice, a shallow gouge along his sword arm parallel to his first blooding of the day and a stab in the fat part of his thigh below his mail shirt. He would almost certainly have killed Simon in a few more moments, but someone else came up suddenly out of the fog—another Thrithings-man, Simon noted with dazed surprise—and accidentally collided with Simon's adversary, knocking the man's horse toward Simon and pushing the mercenary part of the way out of his saddle. Simon's half-desperate thrust, more in self-defense than anything else, slid up the man's leg and into his groin; he fell to the ground, blood fountaining from his wound, then screamed and writhed until his convulsions shook his helmet from his head. The man's thin, staring-eyed face, contorted with pain, brought back to Simon a Hayholt memory of a rat that had fallen into a rain barrel. It had been horrible to see it paddling desperately, teeth bared, eyes bulging. Simon had tried to save it, but in its terror the rodent had snapped at his hand, so he had run away, unable to bear watching it drown. Now an older Simon stared at the shrieking mercenary for a moment, then stepped on his chest to stop him rolling and pushed his sword blade into the man's throat, holding it there until all movement had stopped.

He felt curiously light-headed. Several long moments passed during which he tore loose the corpse's baggy sleeve and cinched it tightly around the wound in his own leg. It was only when he had finished and put his foot into Homefinder's stirrup that he realized what he had just done. His stomach heaved, but he had not made the mistake of eating that morning. After a brief pause he was able to drag himself up into the saddle.

Simon had thought he would be a sort of second-in-command of the trolls, Josua's hand among the prince's Qanuc allies, but he quickly discovered that it was hard enough work just to stay alive.

Sisqi and her diminutive troops were scattered all over the misty battlefield. At one point he had managed to find the area where they were most concentrated, and for a while he and the trolls had stood together—he saw Sisqi then, still alive, her slim spear as swift as a wasp sting, her round face set in a mask so fierce she looked like a tiny snow-demon—but at last the ebb and flow of combat had broken them apart again. The trolls did not do their best fighting in an orderly line, and Simon quickly saw that they were more useful when they moved quickly and unobtrusively among Fengbald's bigger horsemen. The rams seemed sure-footed as cats, and although Simon could see many small shapes of Qanuc dead and wounded scattered here and there among the other bodies, they seemed to be giving as good as they were getting, and perhaps better.

Simon himself had survived several more combats, and had killed another Thrithings-man, this time in a more or less fair fight.

It was only as he and this other were hacking at each other that Simon abruptly realized that to these enemies he was no child. He was taller than this particular mercenary, and in his helmet and mail-shirt, he doubtless seemed a large and fearsome fighter. Abruptly heartened, he had renewed his attack, driving the Thrithings-man backward. Then, as the man stopped and his horse came breast to breast with Homefinder, Simon remembered his lessons from Sludig. He feinted a clumsy swing and the mercenary seized the bait, leaning too far forward with his return stroke. Simon let the man's sword carry him well off-balance, then slammed his shield against the man's leather helm and followed with a sword thrust that slid between the two halves of the man's chest armor and into his unprotected side. The mercenary stayed in his saddle as Simon pulled Homefinder back, tugging loose his sword, but before Simon turned away his opponent had already fallen awkwardly to the bloody ice.

Panting, Simon had looked around him and wondered who was winning.

★   ★   ★

Whatever beliefs about the nobility of war that Simon still retained died during that long day on the frozen lake. In the midst of such terrible carnage, with fallen friends and enemies alike scattered about, maimed and bloodied, some even made faceless by terrible wounds; with the crying and pleading of dying men ringing in his ears, their dignity ripped away from them; with the air rank with the stenches of fear-sweat, blood, and excrement, it was impossible to see warfare as anything other than what Morgenes had once termed it: a kind of hell on earth that impatient mankind had arranged so it would not have to wait for the afterlife. To Simon, the grotesque unfairness of it was almost the worst of all. For every armored knight dragged down, half a dozen foot-soldiers were slaughtered. Even animals suffered torments that should not have been visited on murderers and traitors. Simon saw screaming horses, hamstrung by a chance blow, left to roll on the ice in agony. Although many of the horses belonged to Fengbald's troops, no one had asked them if they wanted to go to war; they had been forced to it, just as had Simon and the rest of the folk of New Gadrinsett. Even the king's Erkynguard might have wished to be elsewhere, rather than here on this killing ground where duty brought them and loyalty prisoned them. Only the mercenaries were here by choice. To Simon, the minds of men who would come to this of their own will were suddenly as incomprehensible as the thoughts of spiders or lizards—less so, even, for the small creatures of the earth almost always fled from danger. These were madmen, Simon realized, and that was the direst problem of the world: that madmen should be strong and unafraid, so that they could force their will on the weak and peace-loving. If God allowed such madness to be, Simon could not help thinking, then He was an old god who had lost His grip.

The sun was vanished high above, hiding behind clouds: it was impossible to tell how long the battle had raged when Josua's horn blew again. This time it was a summons note that sliced through the misty air. Simon, who did not think he had ever been wearier in his life, turned to the few trolls nearby and shouted: *"Sosa!* Come!"

A few moments later he nearly ran down Sisqi, who stood over her slaughtered ram, her face still strangely emotionless. Simon leaned toward her and extended his hand. She grasped it in her cold dry fingers and pulled herself up to his stirrup. He helped her into the saddle.

"Where is Binabik?" she asked him, shouting above the din.

"I don't know. Josua is calling us. We go to Josua now."

The horn blew again. The men of New Gadrinsett were falling back rapidly, as though they could not have fought a moment longer—which might not have been far from the truth—but they were retreating so swiftly that they seemed almost to evaporate around Simon, like the deposited foam of a sea-wave vanishing into the beach. Their departure left a knot of half a dozen trolls and a couple of Deornoth's foot-soldiers encircled by a ring of mounted Erkynguardsmen some fifty ells out on the ice. Without help, Simon knew, the defenders would be smothered. He looked around at the small company and grimaced. Too few to do any good, certainly. And those trolls had heard the retreat just as Simon and the others had—was it his duty to rescue everyone? He was tired and bleeding and frightened, and sanctuary was only a few moments away—he had survived, and that was almost a miracle!—but he knew he could not leave those brave folk behind.

"We go there?" he said to Sisqi, pointing to the clump of beleaguered defenders.

She looked and nodded wearily, then screamed something to the few surrounding Qanuc as Simon pulled Homefinder around and moved toward the Erkynguards at a slithering trot. The trolls fell in behind. There were no howls this time, no singing: the little company rode in the silence of utter exhaustion.

And then there was another nightmare of hacking and slashing. The top of Simon's shield was smashed by a sword blow, splinters of painted wood flying through the air. Several of his own blows struck against solid objects, but the chaos prevented him knowing what he had hit. The encircled trolls and men, seeing that help had come, redoubled their effort and managed to cut their way out, although at least one more of the Qanuc fell. His blood-spattered ram, when it had shaken its dead master's boot loose from the stirrup, leaped away from the corpse and ran off across the lake as though pursued by demons, zigzagging wildly until it vanished into the darkening mist. The weary Erkynguards, who after the initial moments seemed no more willing to prolong the struggle than Simon and his company, fought fiercely but gave ground, trying to herd Simon and the rest back toward the strength of Fengbald's forces. Simon finally saw an opening and shouted to Sisqi. With a last convulsion of soldiers and horses and trolls and rams, Simon's company broke away from the Erkynguards and fled toward Sesuad'ra and the waiting barricades.

Josua's horn was blowing again as Simon and the trolls—less than two score gathered together, he noted with dismay—reached the great wall of logs at the base of the hill-trail. Many of Sesuad'ra's other defenders were around them, and even those who were unwounded looked as beaten down and gray as dying men. A few of Hotvig's Thrithings-folk, however, were singing hoarsely, and Simon saw one of them had what looked like a pair of bloody heads dangling from his saddle-horn, bouncing to the horse's strides.

An immense feeling of relief struck Simon as he saw Prince Josua himself standing before the barricade, waving Naidel in the air like a banner and shouting to the returning combatants. The prince was grim, but his words were meant to be heartening.

"Come on," he cried. "We have given them a taste of their own blood! We have showed them some teeth! Back now, back—they will come no more this day!"

Again, even through the chill that had settled on his heart like a frost, Simon felt a deep and loving loyalty toward Josua—but he also knew that the prince had little left to offer except brave words. Sesuad'ra's defenders had nearly held their own against better trained and better equipped forces, but they could hardly match Fengbald body for body—the duke had almost three times as many men—and now any element of surprise, such as Binabik's boot-irons, had been played to its utmost. From here on, the war would be one of attrition, and Simon knew that he would be on the losing side.

On the ice behind them, the ravens were already feeding on the fallen. The birds hopped and pecked and argued raucously among themselves. Half-hidden by the mist, they might have been tiny black demons come to gloat at the destruction.

Sesuad'ra's defenders limped up the hillside, leading their panting mounts. Although he felt curiously numb, Simon was still pleased to see that more of the Qanuc had survived than just those he and Sisqi had led off the ice. These other survivors rushed forward to greet their kin with cries of happiness, although there were sounds of keening sorrow, too, as the trolls counted their losses.

For Simon, an even greater joy came when he saw Binabik standing with Josua. Sisqi saw him, too. She leaped down from Simon's saddle and rushed to her betrothed. The two of them embraced at Josua's side, heedless of the prince or anyone else.

Simon watched them for a moment before staggering on. He knew he should look for his other friends, but at the moment he felt so battered and wrung out that it was as much as he could do just to put one foot before the other. Someone walking beside him passed him a cup of wine. When he had drunk it off and handed the cup back, he took a few limping steps up the hill to where the campfires had been lit. Now that the day's fighting had ended, some of the women of New Gadrinsett had come down to bring food and to help care for the wounded. One of them, a young girl with stringy hair, handed Simon a bowl of something that faintly steamed. He tried to thank her, but could not summon the strength to speak.

Although the sun was just now touching the western horizon and the day was still quite light, Simon had no sooner finished his thin soup than he found himself lying on the muddy ground, still wearing all of his armor but for his helm, his head cushioned on his cloak. Homefinder stood nearby, cropping at the few thin stalks of grass that had survived the general trampling. A moment later Simon felt himself sliding down toward sleep. The world seemed to tilt back and forth around him, as though he lay on the deck of some huge, slow-rolling ship. Blackness was coming on fast—not the black of night, but a deep and smothering dark that welled up from inside him. If he dreamed, he knew, for once it would not be of towers or giant wheels. He would see screaming horses, and a rat drowning in a rain barrel.

Isaak, the young page, leaned close to the brazier, trying to absorb some warmth. He was chilled right through. Outside, the wind strummed on the ropes and poked at the rippling walls of Duke Fengbald's vast tent as though seeking to uproot it and carry it away into the night. Isaak wished he had never been forced to leave the Hayholt.

"Boy!" Fengbald cried. There was an edge of violence in his voice, barely contained. "Where is my wine?"

"Just mulling, Lord," Isaak said. He took the iron out of the pitcher and hurried to replenish the duke's goblet.

Fengbald ignored him as he poured, turning his attention to Lezhdraka, who stood by scowling, still dressed in his bloodied leather armor. By contrast, the duke was bathed—Isaak had been forced to heat innumerable pots of water on the one small bed of coals—and wore a robe of scarlet silk. He had put on a pair of doeskin slippers, and his long, black hair hung on his shoulders in wet ringlets. "I will listen to no more of this nonsense," he told the mercenary captain.

"Nonsense?" Lezhdraka snarled. "You say that to me! I saw the magic folk with my own eyes, stone-dweller!"

Fengbald's eyes narrowed. "You had better learn to speak more respectfully, plainsman."

Lezhdraka clenched his fists, but kept his arms at his side. "Still, I saw them—you did, too."

The duke made a noise of disgust. "I saw a troop of dwarfs—freaks, such as can be seen tumbling and capering before most of the thrones of Osten Ard. Those were not the Sithi, whatever Josua and this scrub-woman Geloë might claim."

"Dwarfs or fairy-folk I cannot prove, but that other is no ordinary woman," Lezhdraka said darkly. "Her name is well-known in the grasslands—well-known and well-feared. Men who go into her forest do not return."

"Ridiculous." Fengbald drained his cup. "I do not quickly mock the dark powers . . ." he trailed off, as though some uncomfortable memory was clamoring for attention, ". . . I do not mock, but neither will I *be* mocked. And I will not be frightened by conjuring tricks, however they may affect superstitious savages."

The Thrithings-man stared at him for a moment, his face suddenly gone serenely cold. "Your master, from what you have said before, has dabbled much in what you call 'superstition.'"

Fengbald's return glance was equally chilly. "I call no man master. Elias is the king, that is all." The moment of imperiousness quickly dissolved. "Isaak!" he called petulantly. "More wine, damn you." As the page scurried to serve him, Fengbald shook his head. "Enough quibbling. We have a problem, Lezhdraka. I want to solve it."

The mercenary chief folded his arms. "My men do not like the idea of Josua having magical allies," he growled, "—but do not fear. They are not womanish.

They will fight anyway. Our legends have long told us that fairy-blood spills just as man-blood does. We proved that today."

Fengbald made an impatient gesture. "But we cannot afford to beat them this way. They are stronger than I thought. How can I return to Elias with most of his Erkynguard dead at the hands of a few cornered peasants?" He tapped his finger on the rim of his goblet. "No, there are other ways, ways that will assure, that I return to Erkynland in triumph."

Lezhdraka snorted. "There are no other ways. What, some secret track, some hidden road as you talked of before? Your spies did not come back, I notice. No, the only way now is the way we have started. We will beat them down until none are left."

Fengbald was no longer paying attention. His gaze had shifted to the door flap of the tent and a soldier who stood there, unsure of whether to come in. "Ah," the duke said. "Yes?"

The soldier dropped to one knee. "The captain of the guard has sent me, Lord . . ."

"Good." Fengbald settled back in his chair. "And you have brought with you a certain person, yes?"

"Yes, Lord."

"Bring him in, then wait outside until I summon you again."

The soldier went, trying to hide a look of dismay at having to stand outside the tent in the jagged wind. Fengbald threw a mocking glance toward Lezhdraka. "One of my spies *has* come back, it appears."

A moment later the tent flap opened again. An old man stumbled in, his ragged clothes speckled with snowflakes.

Fengbald grinned hugely. "Ah, you have returned to us! Helfgrim, is it not?" The duke turned to Lezhdraka, his good humor returning as he played out his little show. "You remember the Lord Mayor of Gadrinsett, don't you, Lezhdraka? He left us for a while to go a-visiting, but now he has returned." The duke's voice became harsh. "Did you get away unseen?"

Helfgrim nodded miserably. "Things are confused. No one has seen me since the battle started. There are others missing, too, and bodies still lost on the ice and in the forest along the hill's base."

"Good." Fengbald snapped his fingers, pleased. "And of course you have done what I asked?"

The old man lowered his head. "There is nothing, Lord."

Fengbald stared at him for a moment. Color rose in the duke's face and he began to stand, then sat down again, clenching his fists. "So. You seem to have forgotten what I told you."

"What is all this?" Lezhdraka asked, irritated.

The duke ignored him. "Isaak," he called, "fetch the guard."

When the shivering soldier had come in, Fengbald summoned him to his side, then whispered a few words in his ear. The soldier went out through the flap once more.

"We will try again," Fengbald said, turning his attention back to the Lord Mayor. "What did you find out?"

Helfgrim could not seem to meet his eyes. The old man's weak-chinned, reddish face worked as though with some barely hidden grief. "Nothing of use, my lord," he said at last.

Fengbald had evidently gained control of his anger, for he only smiled tightly. A few moments later, the tent flap bulged once more. The guard came in, accompanied this time by two more guardsmen. They were escorting a pair of women, both of middle years, with threads of gray in their dark hair, both of them grimy and dressed in threadbare cloaks. The ashen, fearful expressions of the women changed to startlement as they saw the old man who cringed before Fengbald.

"Father!" one of them cried.

"Oh, merciful Usires," the other said, and made the sign of the Tree.

Fengbald surveyed the scene coolly. "You seemed to have forgotten who holds the whip hand, Helfgrim. Now, let me try again. If you lie to me, I will have to cause your daughters pain, much as it troubles my Aedonite conscience. Still, it will be your conscience that will suffer most, for it will be your fault." He smirked. "Speak."

The old man looked at his daughters, at the terror on their faces. "God forgive me," he said. "God forgive me for a traitor!"

"Don't you do it, Father," one of the women cried. The other daughter was sobbing helplessly, her face buried in the sleeve of her cape.

"I cannot do other." Helfgrim turned to the duke. "Yes," he said quaveringly. "There is another way onto the hill, one that only a few of the folk there know. It is another old Sithi track. Josua has put a guard onto it, but only a token force, since the bottom of it is hidden by overgrowth. He showed it to me when we were planning his defense."

"A token force, eh?" Fengbald grinned and looked triumphantly at Lezhdraka. "And this track, it is wide enough for how many?"

Helfgrim's voice was so low as to be almost inaudible. "A dozen could march abreast, once the first few cubits of brambles are cleared away."

The mercenary captain, who had listened quietly for a long time, now stepped forward. He was angry, and his scars showed white against his dark face. "You are too trusting," he snarled at Fengbald. "How do you know this is no trap? How do you know that Josua will not be waiting for us with his whole army?"

Fengbald was unmoved. "You grasslanders are too simple-minded, Lezhdraka—did I not tell you that before? Josua's army will be busy trying to fight off our frontal assault tomorrow—far too busy to spare any more soldiers than his token force—when we go to make our surprise visit on Helfgrim's other road. *We* will take a sizable company. And just to make sure that there is no treachery, we will take the Lord Mayor with us."

At this, the two women burst into tears. "Please, do not take him into battle," one said desperately. "He is but an old man!"

"That is true." Fengbald appeared to consider the point. "And hence he might not be afraid to die, if there *is* some kind of trap—if Josua's force is more than token. So we will take you, too."

Helfgrim leaped up. "No! You cannot risk their lives! They are innocent!"

"And they will be safe as doves in a dovecote," Fengbald grinned, "as long as your story has been true. But if you have tried to betray me, they will die. Quickly, but painfully."

The old man begged him again, but the duke slouched back in his chair, unmoved. At last the Lord Mayor went to his daughters. "It will be well." He patted them awkwardly, inhibited by the presence of cruel strangers. "We will be together. No harm will come." He turned to Fengbald, anger showing beneath his trembling features; for a moment his voice almost lost its quaver. "There is no trap, damn you—you will see—but there are a few dozen men, as I said. I have betrayed the prince for you. You must show honor toward my children, and keep them out of danger if there is fighting. Please."

Fengbald waved his hand expansively. "Never fear. I promise on my honor as a nobleman that when we hold this dreadful hill and Josua is dead, you and your daughters will go free. And you will tell those you meet that Duke Fengbald keeps his bargains." He rose and gestured to the guards. "Now take them all three away—and keep them separate from the rest of their folk."

After the prisoners had been removed, Fengbald turned to Lezhdraka. "Why so silent, man? Can you not admit you were wrong—that I have solved our problem?"

The Thrithings-man seemed to want to argue, but instead reluctantly nodded his head. "These stone-dwellers are soft. No Thrithings-man would betray his people for the sake of two daughters."

Fengbald laughed. "We stone-dwellers, as you call us, treat our women differently than you louts do." He walked to the brazier and warmed his long hands over the coals. "And tomorrow, Lezhdraka, I shall show you how *this* stone-dweller treats his enemies—especially those who have defied him as Prince Josua has." He narrowed his lips. "That cursed fairy-hill will run red with blood."

He stared into the gleaming embers, a smile curling the corners of his mouth. The wind wailed outside and rubbed against the tent cloth like an animal.

13

The Nest Builders

✹

Tiamak stared at the still water. His mind was only half on his task, so when the fish appeared, a dark shadow flitting between the water lilies, the Wrannaman's strike was far too late. Tiamak stared down at the handful of dripping vegetation in disgust and dropped the clump of weeds back into the muddied water. Any fish in the vicinity would be long gone now.

They Who Watch and Shape, he thought miserably, *why have you done this to me?*

He moved closer to the edge of the waterway and sloshed as delicately as he could down to the next backwater, then set himself in place to begin his wait once more.

Ever since he had been a small boy, it seemed, he had gotten less than he wanted. As the youngest of six children, he had always felt that his brothers and sisters ate better than he did, that when the bowl came at last to Tiamak, there was little left. He had not grown up as large as any of his three brothers or his father Tugumak, nor had he ever been able to catch fish as well as his swift sister Twiyah, or find as many useful roots and berries as his clever sister Rimihe. When at last he had found something he could do better than anyone else—namely, master the drylander skills of reading and writing, and even learn to speak the drylander tongues—this also proved too small a gift. This scurrying after the knowledge of drylanders made scant sense to his family, or to the other residents of Village Grove. When he went away to Perdruin to study in a drylander school, were they proud? Of course not. Despite the fact that no other Wrannaman in memory had done it—or perhaps because of that—his family could not understand his ambitions. And the drylanders themselves, all but a very few, were openly scornful of his gifts. The indifferent teachers and mocking students had let young Tiamak know in no uncertain terms that no matter how many scrolls and books and learned discussions he devoured, he would never be anything better than a savage, a performing animal who had mastered a clever trick.

So it had been for all of his life until this fatal year, his only meager comforts found in his studies and the occasional correspondence of the Scrollbearers. Now, as if They Who Watch and Shape sought to pay all back in a single season, everything that came to him was *too much*—far, far too much.

This is how the gods mock us, he thought bitterly. *They take our fondest wish, then grant it in such a way that we beg to be released from it. And to think that I had stopped believing in them!*

They Who Watch and Shape had set the trap neatly enough, of that there was no doubt. First they had forced him to choose between his kin and his friends, then they had sent the crocodile that forced him to fail his kin. Now his friends needed to be conducted through the vast marshlands, in fact depended on him for their very lives, but the only safe route would take him back through Village Grove, back to the people he had forsaken. Tiamak only wished that he himself could have learned to build such a faultless snare—he would have eaten crabs for supper every night!

He stood hip-deep in the greenish water and pondered. What could he do? If he returned to his village, his shame would be known to all. It might even be possible that they would not let him go again, holding him as a traitor against the clan. But if he tried to avoid the wrath of the villagers, he would have to go leagues out of the way to find a suitable boat. The only other villages close to this end of the Wran, High Branch Houses, Yellow Trees, or Flower-in-the-Rock, were all farther to the south. To go to one would mean leaving the main arterial waterways and crossing some of the most dangerous stretches of the entire marsh. Still, there was no choice: they had to stop in Village Grove or one of the farther settlements, for without a flatboat Tiamak and his companions would never reach the Lake Thrithing. As it was, their present craft was leaking badly. They had already been forced to make several dangerous trips across the unpredictable mud, carrying the boat around places in the waterway that were too shallow. ˙

Tiamak sighed. What was it that Isgrimnur himself had said? Life seemed nothing but difficult choices these days—and he was right.

There was a flirt of shadow between his knees. Tiamak swiftly darted a hand down and felt his fingers close around something small and slippery. He lifted it high, holding tightly. It was a fish, a pinch-eye, although not a very large one. Still, it was better than no fish at all. He turned and pulled up the cloth sack that floated beside him, anchored to a thick root. He dropped the wriggling thing in, tightened the drawstring, then lowered the sack back into the water. A good omen, perhaps. Tiamak closed his eyes to make a short prayer of thanks, hoping that the gods, like children, could be confirmed in good behavior by praise. When he had finished, he gave his attention back to the green water once more.

Miriamele was doing her best to keep the fire going, but it was difficult. Since entering the marshes they had found nothing that resembled dry wood, and the small blazes they had been able to light burned fitfully at best.

She looked up as Tiamak returned. His thin brown face was closed, and he only nodded as he put down a leaf-wrapped bundle, then continued to where Isgrimnur and the others were working on the boat. The Wrannaman seemed very shy: he had said only a few words to Miriamele in the two days since they had left Kwanitupul. She wondered briefly if he might be embarrassed by his lilting Wrannaman accent. Miriamele dismissed the thought: Tiamak spoke the Westerling tongue better than most people who had grown up with it, and Isgrimnur's thick consonants and Cadrach's musical Hernystiri vowels were far more noticeable than the slight up and down quality of the marsh man's speech.

Miriamele unbundled the fish Tiamak had brought and gutted them, wiping her knife clean on the leaves before sheathing it again. She had never cooked in her life before fleeing the Hayholt, but traveling with Cadrach she had been forced to learn, if only to avoid starving on those frequent nights when he was too drunk to be of any help. She wondered if there was some marsh plant that might add flavor—perhaps she could wrap the fish in the leaves and steam them. She wandered over to ask the Wrannaman for advice.

Tiamak stood watching as Isgrimnur, Cadrach, and Camaris tried for the fourth or fifth time to seal the leaks that kept the bottom of their small boat almost constantly full of water. The marsh man held himself a little apart, as though to stand shoulder to shoulder with these drylanders might be presumptuous, but Miriamele suddenly found herself wondering if she might have it backward: maybe Wrannamen did not feel that those who lived outside the marsh were worth very much. Could Tiamak's stolidity be pride rather than shyness? She had heard that some savages, like the Thrithings-men, actually looked down on those who lived in cities. Could that be true with Tiamak, too? She realized now that she knew little about people outside the courts of Nabban and Erkynland, although she had always thought herself a shrewd judge of humanity. However, it was a much larger and more complicated world on the other side of the castle walls than she had ever suspected.

She reached out a hand toward the Wrannaman's shoulder, then pulled it back again. "Tiamak?" she said.

He jumped, startled. "Yes, Lady Miriamele?"

"I would like to ask you some questions about plants—for the cook-pot, that is."

He lowered his eyes and nodded. Miriamele could not believe that this was a man too proud to speak. The two of them walked back to the fire. After she had asked him a few questions and had shown that she was genuinely interested, he began to talk more freely. Miriamele was astonished. Although his reserve did not completely vanish, the Wrannaman turned out to be so full of plant lore, and so pleased to share some of it, that she quickly found herself overwhelmed with information. He found for her half a dozen flowers and roots and leaves that could be safely used to add savor to food, plucking them as he walked her around the campsite and down to the water's edge, and he listed a dozen more that they would encounter as they traveled through the Wran. Caught up, he began to point out other bits of greenery that were useful as medicine or ink or countless other things.

"How do you know so much?"

Tiamak stopped as if he had been struck. "I am sorry, Lady Miriamele," he said quietly. "You did not wish to hear all this."

Miriamele laughed. "I think it's wonderful. But where did you learn it all?"

"I have studied these things for many years."

"You must know more than anyone in the world!"

Tiamak averted his face. Miriamele was fascinated. Was he blushing? "No," he said, "no, I am just a student." He looked up shyly, but with a hint of pride. "But someday I do hope that my studies will be known—that my name will be remembered."

"I'm sure that it will." She was still somewhat awed. This slender little man with his unruly mop of thinning black hair, dressed now like any other Wran-naman in nothing but a belt and a loincloth, seemed as learned as any of the writing-priests of the Hayholt! "No wonder Morgenes and Dinivan were your friends."

His pleased look abruptly evaporated, leaving behind a kind of sadness. "Thank you, Lady Miriamele. Now I will leave you to do what you will with those small fish. I have bored you long enough."

He turned and walked back across the marshy clearing, stepping without visible attention from one tussock of solid earth to another, so that when he reached the far side and sat down on a log his feet were still dry. Miriamele, who had mud up to her shins, was forced to admire his sure-footedness.

But what did I say to upset him? She shrugged and took her handful of marsh-blossoms back to the waiting fish.

After supper—Tiamak's savory touches had proven most welcome—the company stayed seated around the fire. The air remained warm, but the sun had gone down behind the trees and the marsh was filling with shadows. An army of frogs that had begun booming and croaking at the first onset of evening was contesting with a vast array of whistling, chirping, and screeching birds, so that the twilight was as noisy as a holiday fair.

"How big is the Wran?" Miriamele asked.

"It is almost as large as the peninsula of Nabban," said Tiamak. "But we will only have to cross a small part of it, since we are already in the northernmost region."

"And how long will it take, O guide?" Cadrach was leaning back against a log, trying to make a flute out of a marsh reed. Several crumpled stalks, the victims of previous attempts, lay beside him.

The sad look that Miriamele had seen earlier returned to the Wrannaman's face. "That depends."

Isgrimnur cocked a bushy eyebrow. "Depends on what, little man?"

"On which way we go." Tiamak sighed. "Perhaps it is best I share my worries with you. I suppose it is not a decision I should make alone."

"Speak, man," the duke said.

Tiamak told them of his dilemma. He made it plain that it was not only the shame of returning to his village-folk after having failed their errand that he feared, but that even if the rest of the company were allowed to leave again, Tiamak himself might not be, stranding them deep in the Wran without a guide.

"Could we not hire another of the villagers?" Isgrimnur asked. "Not that we want to see anything happen to you, of course," he added hastily.

"Of course." Tiamak's glance was cool. "As to your question, I do not know. Our clan has never been one to cause trouble for others, unless actual harm is done to someone of Village Grove, but that does not mean that the elders might not prevent anyone in the settlement from helping you. It is hard to say."

The company debated as night came on. Tiamak did his best to explain the distance and the dangers involved in a trip to any alternate settlement south of Village Grove. At last, as a troop of chittering apes scrambled past overhead, making the tree branches dip and waver, they arrived at a decision.

"It's hard, Tiamak," Isgrimnur said, "and we will not force you against your will, but it seems best we go to your village."

The Wrannaman nodded solemnly. "I agree. Even though I have done no wrong to the clanfolk of High Branch Houses or Yellow Trees, there is no certainty that they would take kindly to strangers. At least my people have been tolerant of the few drylanders that have come." He sighed. "I think I will walk for a short while. Please, stay near the fire." He rose and ambled down toward the waterway, quickly vanishing in the shadows.

Camaris, bored by the others' talk, had long since curled up with his head on a cloak and gone to sleep, his long legs drawn up like a small child's. Miriamele, Isgrimnur, and Cadrach faced each other over the flickering blaze. The hidden birds, who had quieted as Tiamak walked out of the campsite, swelled into raucous voice again.

"He seems very sad," Miriamele said.

Isgrimnur yawned. "He's been steady enough, in his way."

"Poor man." Miriamele lowered her voice, worried that the Wrannaman might return and hear them. No one liked to be pitied. "He knows a lot about plants and flowers. It's too bad that he has to live so far away from people who could understand him."

"He is not the only one with such a problem," said Cadrach, mostly to himself.

Miriamele was watching a small deer, white-spotted and round-eyed, that had come down to the watercourse to drink. She held her breath as it stilted along the sandy bank, a bare three cubits from the boat; her companions had all fallen silent in the afternoon heat, so there was nothing to frighten the deer away. Miriamele rested her chin on the railing of the boat, marveling at the creature's graceful movements.

As it dipped its nose to the muddy river, a toothy snout suddenly erupted from the water. Before it could leap back, the little deer was seized by the crocodile and dragged down thrashing into the brown darkness. Nothing remained but ripples. Miriamele turned away, revolted and more than a little frightened. How swiftly death had come!

The more she watched, the more fickle the Wran seemed, a place of waving fronds, shifting shadows, and constant movement. For every beauty—great bell-like scarlet flowers as heavily scented as any Nabbanai dowager, or hummingbirds like streaks of jeweled light—Miriamele saw what seemed to be a corresponding ugliness, like the great gray spiders, large as supper bowls, that clung to the overhanging branches.

In the trees she saw birds of a thousand colors, and mocking apes, and even dappled snakes that hung from the branches like swollen vines. At sunset, clouds of bats leaped out from the upper branches and turned the sky into a whirling storm of wings. Insects, too, were everywhere, buzzing, stinging, wings shimmering in the uneven sunlight. Even vegetation moved and shifted, the reeds and trees bending in the wind, the water plants bobbing with every ripple. The Wran was a tapestry in which every thread seemed to be in motion. Everything was alive.

Miriamele remembered the Aldheorte, which had also been a place of life, of deep roots and quiet power, but that forest had been old and settled. Like an ancient people, it seemed to have found its own stately music, its own measured and unchanging pace. She remembered thinking that the Aldheorte could easily remain just as it was until the end of time. The Wran seemed to be inventing itself every moment, as though it were a curl of foam on the boiling edge of creation. Miriamele could just as easily imagine returning in twenty years to find it a howling desert, or a jungle so thick that there would be no passage through it, a clot of green and black where the twining leaves would shut out the very light of the sun.

As the days passed and the boat and its small crew moved deeper into the marshlands, Miriamele felt a weight lift from her being. She felt anger still, at her father and his terrible choices, at Aspitis who had tricked her and violated her, at the supposedly kindly God that had so twisted her own life from her grasp . . . but it was an anger that did not bite so fiercely now. When all around her was so full of weirdly vibrant and changing life, it was hard to hold on to the bitter feelings that had ruled her in the weeks before. When the world was ceaselessly recreating itself on every side, it was almost impossible for her not to feel as though she, too, were being made anew.

"What are all these bones?" Miriamele asked. On either side of the waterway, the shoreline was littered with skeletons, a jumble of spines and rib cages like the bleached staves of ruined ships, strangely white against the mud. "I hope they belong to animals."

"We are all animals," said Cadrach. "We all have bones."

"What are you trying to do, monk, frighten the girl?" Isgrimnur said angrily. "Look at those skulls. Those were cockindrills, not men."

"Ssshh." Tiamak turned from the prow of the boat. "Duke Isgrimnur is right. They are the bones of crocodiles. But you must be quiet for a while now. We are coming to the Pool of Sekob."

"What is that?"

"It is the reason for all these remains." The Wrannaman's eyes lit on Camaris, who was trailing his veined hand in the water, watching the ripples with the absorbed stare of childhood. "Isgrimnur! Do not let him do that!"

The duke turned and lifted Camaris' hand out of the water. The old man looked at him with mild reproach, but kept his dripping hand in his lap.

"Now, please be quiet for a little while," said Tiamak. "And row slowly. Do not splash."

"What is this all about?" Isgrimnur demanded, but at a look from the Wrannaman he fell silent. He and Miriamele did their best to make their touch on the oars gentle and steady.

The boat floated down a waterway so draped with the fronds of leaning willows that it seemed hung with a solid green curtain. When they had passed the willows, they discovered that the passage had suddenly opened before them into a wide, still lake. Banyan trees grew down to the water's edge, serpentine roots forming a wall of curling wood around most of the lake. On the far side the banyans fell away and the lake floor sloped up into a broad beach of pale sand. A few small islands, mere bumps on the surface of the water near the beach, were the only thing that marred the lake's glassy smoothness. A pair of bitterns stalked along the water's edge at the near end, bending to probe in the mud. Miriamele thought that the wide strand looked like a wonderful place to camp—the lake itself seemed an airy paradise after some of the wet and tangled places they had stopped—and she was about to say so when Tiamak's fierce look stilled her. She supposed that this was some kind of sacred spot for the Wrannaman and his folk. Still, there was no cause for him to treat her like a misbehaving child.

Miriamele turned away from Tiamak and looked out across the lake, memorizing it so that someday she would be able to summon up the feeling of pure peace it represented. As she did, she had a sudden disquieting sensation that the lake was moving, that the water was flowing away to one side. A moment later she realized that it was the small islands that were moving instead. Crocodiles! She had been fooled before, seen other logs and sandbars that abruptly lurched into life; she smiled at her own city-bred innocence. Perhaps it would not be such a wonderful choice for camp after all—still, a few crocodiles did not spoil the looks of the place. . . .

The moving bumps rose farther out of the water as they neared the beach.

It was only when the immense, impossible thing finally crawled up onto the sand, dragging its bloated form into the clear light of the sun, that Miriamele finally realized that there was only one crocodile.

"God's mercy on us!" Cadrach said in a strangled whisper. Isgrimnur echoed him.

The great beast, long as ten men, wide as a mason's barge, turned its head to regard the little boat slipping across the lake. Both Miriamele and Isgrimnur ceased rowing, hands clammy and nerveless on the sweeps.

"Don't stop!" Tiamak hissed. "Slowly, slowly, but keep going!"

Even across the expanse of water, Miriamele thought she could see the creature's eye glitter as it watched them, feel its cold and ancient stare. When the immense legs shifted and the clawed feet dug briefly at the ground as though the giant would turn and re-enter the water, Miriamele feared her heart would stop. But the great crocodile did no more than send a few gouts of sand into the air, then the huge, knobby head dropped down to the beach and the yellow eye closed.

When they had made their way across to the waterway's outlet, Miriamele and Isgrimnur began rowing hard, as if by silent agreement. After a few moments they were breathing heavily. Tiamak told them to stop.

"We are safe," he said. "The time has long gone when he could follow us up this way. He has gotten far too big."

"What was it?" Miriamele gasped. "It was horrible."

"Old Sekob. My folk call him the grandfather of all crocodiles. I do not know if that is true, but he is certainly the master of all his kind. Year after year other crocodiles come to fight him. Year after year he feeds on these challengers, swallows them whole, so he never has to hunt any more. The strongest of all sometimes escape the lake and crawl as far away as the riverbank before they die. Those were the bones you saw."

"I've never seen anything like it." Cadrach had gone quite pale, but there was a quality of exhilaration in his tone. "Like one of the great dragons!"

"He is the dragon of the Wran," Tiamak agreed. "There is no doubt of that. But unlike drylanders, we marsh-folk leave our dragons alone. He is no threat to us, and he kills many of the largest man-eaters that would otherwise prey on the Wran people. So we show him respect. Old Sekob is far too well-fed to need to chase such a puny morsel as we would make."

"So why did you want us to be quiet?" asked Miriamele.

Tiamak gave her a dry look. "He might not need to eat us, but you do not go into the king's throne room and play children's games, either. Especially when the king is old and quick to temper."

"Elysia, Mother of God." Isgrimnur shook his head. Sweat beaded his forehead, although the day was not particularly warm. "No, we certainly would not want to get that old fellow upset."

"Now come," said Tiamak. "If we keep on until first dark, we should be able to reach Village Grove by tomorrow midday."

*   *   *

As they traveled, the Wrannaman became more talkative. When they had reached waters so shallow that rowing was no use, there was little else to do but listen to each other's stories as Tiamak stood and poled the boat along. Under Miriamele's questioning he told them much about the life of the Wran, as well as about his own unusual choices which had marked him out from his fellow villagers.

"But your people have no king?" she asked.

"No." The small man thought for a moment. "We have elders, or we call them that, but some of them are no older than I am. Any man can become one."

"How? By asking to?"

"No. By giving feasts." He smiled shyly. "When a man has a wife and children—and whatever other family lives with him—and can feed them all with some left over, he begins to give what is left to others. In return, he might ask for something like a boat or new fishing floats, or if he chooses he can say: 'I will ask payment when I give my feast.' Then, when he is owed enough, he 'calls for the crabs,' as we say, which means he asks all those who owe him things to pay him back; then he invites everyone in the village for a feast. If everyone is satisfied, that man becomes an elder. He must then give such a feast once every year, or he will not be an elder in that year."

"Sounds daft," Isgrimnur grumbled, scratching. He had been by far the greatest target for the local insect life; his broad face was covered in bumps. Miriamele understood, and forgave him his short temper.

"No more daft than passing land down from father to son." Cadrach's response was mild, but held an edge of sarcasm. "Or getting it in the first place by braining your neighbor with an ax—as your folk did until fairly recently, Duke."

"No man should have what he is not strong enough to protect," Isgrimnur responded, but he seemed more preoccupied with digging at a difficult spot between his shoulder blades than with continuing the debate.

"I think," Tiamak said quietly, "that it is a good way. It makes certain that no one starves and that no one hoards his wealth. Until I studied in Perdruin, I could not imagine that there was another way of doing things."

"But if a man doesn't wish to be an elder," Miriamele pointed out, "then there's nothing to make him give up the things he is gathering."

"Ah, but then no one in the village thinks very highly of him." Tiamak grinned. "Also, since the elders decide what is best for the village, they might just decide that the excellent fish pond beside which a rich and selfish man has built his house now belongs to all the village. There is little sense in being rich and not being an elder—it causes jealousy, you see."

Duke Isgrimnur continued to scratch. Tiamak and Cadrach fell into a quiet conversation about some of the more intricate points of Wran theology. Miriamele, who had grown tired of talk, took the opportunity to watch old Camaris.

Miriamele could stare without embarrassment: the tall man seemed quite uncaring, no more interested in the business of his fellows than a horse in a paddock might be with the traders talking by the fence. Observing his bland but certainly not stupid face, it was almost impossible to believe that she was in the presence of a legend. The name of Camaris-sá-Vinitta was nearly as famous as that of her grandfather Prester John, and both of them, she felt sure, would be remembered by generations yet unborn. Yet here he was, old and witless, when all the world had thought him dead. How could such a thing have come to pass? What secrets hid behind his guileless exterior?

Her attention was drawn down to the old knight's hands. Gnarled and callused by decades of toil at *Pelippa's Bowl* and on countless battlefields, they were still somehow quite noble, huge and long-fingered but gentle. She watched him twisting aimlessly at the material of his ragged breeches and wondered how such deft, careful hands could have dealt death as swiftly and terribly as his legend said. Still, she had seen his strength, which would have been impressive even in a man half his age, and in the few moments of danger the little company had experienced in the Wran, when the boat had threatened to overturn or someone had fallen into a pit of sucking mud, he had responded with amazing quickness.

Miriamele's eyes strayed back to Camaris' face once more. Before encountering him at the inn, she had never met him, of course—he had disappeared a quarter of a century before her birth—but there was something troublingly familiar about his face. It was something that she only saw at certain angles, a phantom glint that left her feeling as though she were on the verge of some revelation, of some profound recognition . . . but the moment would always pass and the familiarity would disappear. Just now, for instance, the nagging sensation was not present: at this moment, Camaris looked like nothing but a handsome old man with a particularly serene and other-worldly expression.

Perhaps it was only the paintings and tapestries, Miriamele reasoned—after all, she had seen so many pictures of this famous man! There were likenesses of him in the Hayholt, in the ducal palace at Nabban, even in Meremund . . . although Elias had only hung them when his father John was coming, to honor the old man's friendship with Osten Ard's greatest knight. Her father Elias, who had considered himself the paramount knight of his father's kingdom in latter days, had shown little patience with stories of the old times of the Great Table, and particularly with tales about the splendor of Camaris. . . .

Miriamele's thoughts were interrupted by Tiamak's announcement that they were nearing Village Grove.

"I hope you will forgive me if we stop and spend the night at my little house," he said. "I have not seen it for several months and I would like to make sure that my birds have survived. It would take us another hour or so to reach the village anyway, and it is later in the day than I thought it would be." He waved a hand toward the reddening western sky. "We may as well wait until morning to go see the elders."

"I hope your house has curtains to keep the bugs out," Isgrimnur said somewhat plaintively.

"Your birds?" Cadrach was interested. "From Morgenes?"

Tiamak nodded. "To begin with, although I have long since been raising my own. But Morgenes taught me the art, it is true."

"Could we use them to send a message to Josua?" Miriamele asked.

"Not to Josua," Tiamak said, frowning in thought. "But if you know of any Scrollbearers who might be with him we could try. These birds cannot find just anybody. Except for certain people whom they have been trained to seek out, they only know places, like any ordinary messenger birds. In any case, we will talk about this when we are under my roof."

Tiamak guided the boat through a succession of tiny streamlets, some so shallow that the whole company was forced to stand waist-deep in the water to lift the rowboat over the sandbars. At last they entered a slow-moving waterway that took them down a long alley of banyan trees. They drew up at last before a hut so cunningly hidden that they would surely have drifted past if its owner were not guiding the boat. Tiamak hooked down the ladder of twisted vines and one by one they climbed up into the Wrannaman's house.

Miriamele was disappointed to find the interior of the hut so spare. It was obvious that the little scholar was a man of humble means, but she had at least hoped in this, her first experience of a Wran dwelling, to find a little more in the way of exotic furnishings. There were neither beds, tables, nor chairs. Other than the firepit set into the floor of the house beneath a cleverly vented smoke hole, the only household belongings were a small chest of wickerwork, another much larger and sturdier wooden chest, a stretched-bark writing board, and a few other odds and ends. Still, it was dry, and that alone was such a change from the last few days that Miriamele was grateful.

Tiamak showed Cadrach the wood piled beneath the eaves outside one of the high windows, then left the monk to start a fire while he himself clambered up onto the roof to see to his birds. Camaris, whose height made him seem a giant in the small house—although Isgrimnur was not much shorter and was certainly a great deal heavier—squatted uncomfortably in the corner.

Tiamak appeared at the window, upside down. He was leaning over the edge of the roof, and he was clearly delighted. "Look!" He held up a handful of powdery gray. "It is Honey-Lover! She has come back! Many of the others, too!" He disappeared from sight as though jerked up by a string. After a moment, Camaris went to the window and climbed out after him with his usual surprising dexterity.

"Now if we could only find something to eat," Isgrimnur said. "I don't really trust Tiamak's marsh-muck—not that I'm not grateful." He wet his lips. "It's just that I wouldn't turn down a joint of beef or something like. Keep our strength up."

Miriamele could not help laughing. "I don't think there are many cows in the Wran."

"Can't be sure," Isgrimnur muttered distractedly. "It's a strange place. Could be anything here."

"We met the grandfather of all crocodiles," Cadrach said as he fumbled with the flints. "Could it be, Duke Isgrimnur, that somewhere in the dank shrubbery lurks the gigantic grandmother of all cows? With a brisket big as a wagon?"

The Rimmersman would not be baited. "If you mind your manners, sirrah, I might even leave you a bite or two."

There was no beef. Isgrimnur, along with the rest of the company, was forced to make do with a thin soup made from various kinds of marsh-grass and a few slivers from the one fish Tiamak was able to catch before dark. Isgrimnur made an offhand remark about the charm of an ember-roasted pigeon, but the Wrannaman was so horrified that the duke quickly apologized.

"It's just my way, man," he grumbled. "I'm damned sorry. Wouldn't touch your birds."

Even had he been serious, he might have found it more difficult than expected. Camaris had taken to Tiamak's pigeons as though to a long-lost family. The old knight spent most of the evening up on the roof of the house with his head stuck in the dovecote. He came down for only a few moments to drink his share of the soup, then climbed back to the roof again, where he sat in silent communion with Tiamak's birds until everyone else had curled up in their cloaks on the board floor. The old man returned at last and lay down, but even then he stared fixedly at the shadow-darkened ceiling as though he could see through the thatch to where his new friends roosted; his eyes were still open long after the sound of Isgrimnur and Cadrach snoring had filled the small room. Miriamele watched him until drowsiness began to send her own thoughts spinning slowly around like a whirlpool.

So Miriamele fell asleep in a house in a tree with the quiet slapping of water beneath her, the questioning cries of night birds above.

Different birds were shrilling when the tree-filtered sunlight awoke her. Their voices were coarse and repetitive, but Miriamele did not find it too distracting. She had slept astonishingly well—she felt as though she had gotten the first solid night's sleep since leaving Nabban.

"Good morning!" she said cheerily to Tiamak, who was huddled over the firepit. "Something smells nice."

The Wrannaman bobbed his head. "I found a pot of flour I had buried in the back. How it stayed dry I will never know. Usually my seals don't hold." He pointed his long fingers at the flat cakes bubbling on a hot stone. "It is not much, but I always feel better when I get hot food."

"Me, too." Miriamele took a deep, savoring sniff. How astonishing yet reassuring it was that someone raised around the groaning banquet tables of Erkynlandish royalty could still find herself so pleased by unleavened biscuits cooked on a rock—if only the circumstances were right. There was something profound in that, she knew, but it seemed a shame to brood so early in the morning. "Where are the others?" she asked.

"Trying to clear some rocks out of the narrow part of the waterway. If we can get the boat past this spot, we will have an easy time in to Village Grove. We will be there long before noon."

"Good." Miriamele considered for a moment. "I want to wash. Where should I go?"

"There is a rainwater pool not too far away," Tiamak said. "But I should take you there."

"I can go by myself," she said, a little briskly.

"Of course, but it is very easy to make a bad step here, Lady Miriamele." The slender man was embarrassed to have to correct her, and Miriamele immediately felt ashamed.

"I'm sorry," she said. "It's very kind of you to take me, Tiamak. Whenever you're ready, we'll go."

He smiled. "Now. Just let me pull these cakes off, so they do not burn. The first crabs should go to the one who made the trap, don't you think?"

It was not easy to climb down from the house while juggling hot cakes. Miriamele almost fell off the ladder.

Their three companions were a little way up the estuary, waist-deep in green, scummy water. Isgrimnur straightened up and waved. He had doffed his shirt, and his great chest and stomach, covered with reddish-brown fur, were revealed in all their glory beneath the murky sun. Miriamele giggled. He looked just like a bear.

"There is food inside," Tiamak called to them. "And batter in the bowl to make more."

Isgrimnur waved again.

After wading through the thick, clinging underbrush for a few moments, skirting patches of sucking mud, Miriamele and Tiamak began to climb a short, low rise. "This is one of the little hills," Tiamak said. "There are a few in this part of the Wran—the rest is very flat." He pointed into the distance, which was just as tree-choked where he pointed as in any other direction. "You cannot see from here, but the highest point in the Wran is there, half a league away. It is called *Ya Mologi*—Cradle Hill."

"Why?"

"I don't know. I think that She Who Birthed Mankind is supposed to have lived there." He looked up, shy again. "One of our gods."

When Miriamele did not comment, the little man turned around and pointed along the rise a short distance to a place where the land folded in upon itself. A row of tall trees grew there—willows again, Miriamele noticed. They seemed far more robust than the surrounding vegetation. "There." Tiamak headed toward the spot where the land dipped down.

It was a tiny canyon, a mere wrinkle in the hillside, less than a stone's throw from end to end. The bottom was almost entirely filled with a standing pond choked with hyacinths and water lilies and long trailing grasses. "It is a rainwater pond," Tiamak said proudly. "It is the reason my father Tugumak built his house here, although we were far from Village Grove. There are a few other such ponds in this part of the Wran, but this is much the nicest."

Miriamele looked it over a little doubtfully. "I can bathe in it?" she asked. "No crocodiles or snakes or anything else?"

"A few water beetles, nothing more," the Wrannaman assured her. "I will go and leave you to your washing. Can you find your way back?"

Miriamele thought for a moment. "Yes. I'm close enough to shout if I get lost, in any case."

"True." Tiamak turned and made his way back up the shallow defile, then disappeared through the hedge of willows. When she heard his voice again, it was quite faint. "We will save some food for you, Lady!"

He did that to let me know he was far away, Miriamele thought, smiling. *So I wouldn't worry that he was staying to watch. Even in the swamp, there are gentlemen.*

She undressed, enjoying the morning warmth that was one of the few nice things about the swamp, then waded into the pond. She sighed with pleasure as the water reached her knees: it was quite comfortable, only a little cooler than a tub bath. Tiamak had given her a small gift, she realized; it was one of the nicest she had been given in a long while.

The bottom of the pond was covered with soft, firm mud that felt good beneath her toes. The willows that loomed so closely and drooped so low, as if greedy for the pondwater, made her feel almost as protected and private as if she had been in her chamber at Meremund. After wading partway around the rim of the pool, she found a spot where the grass grew thick beneath the surface. She sat on it as though it were a carpet, sinking down until the water almost reached her chin. She splashed water on her face, then wetted her hair and tried to loosen the tangles. Now that it was beginning to grow out again, she could not treat it as carelessly as she had of late.

After she had finished, she simply sat for a while, listening to the racket of birds and the warm wind moving the trees.

As Miriamele was belting her dirty and somewhat odoriferous monk's robe around her waist once more—and grumbling to herself as she did because she had not been foresighted enough to bring a change of clothing with her out of *Pelippa's Bowl*—the rustle of leaves overhead suddenly became louder. Miriamele looked up, expecting a large bird or perhaps even one of the marsh apes, but what she saw instead caused her to suck in her breath in shocked surprise.

The thing hanging from the branch was only as big as a young child, but that was still unpleasantly large. It looked something like a crab and something like a spider, but despite its crustacean exterior it had, as far as Miriamele could tell, only four limbs; each was jointed, ending in a recurved claw. The creature's body was covered in a horny, leathery shell, gray and brown splashed with inky black, crisscrossed with uneven trails of lichen. Its eyes were the worst part, though: their beady black glimmer—somehow so oddly intelligent, despite the malformed head and chitinous body—sent her stumbling backward until she was sure it could not reach her, no matter how prodigious a leaper it might be. The thing did not move. It seemed to watch her in a disturbingly human way, but the creature was otherwise not human in the least; it did not even have a mouth that she could see, unless the little clicking things in the cleft at the bottom of its blunt head served that purpose.

Miriamele shivered in disgust. "Go away!" she cried, waving her hands as she might try to shoo a dog. The glittering eyes stared at her with what almost seemed an attitude of amused malice.

But it has no face, she told herself. *How can it have feelings?!* It was an animal, and it was either dangerous or not. How could she think she saw feelings in something that was no more than a huge bug? Still, she found the creature terrifying. Although it made no hostile movement, she circled the tree widely as she made her way up out of the little canyon. The thing made no move to follow her, but it turned to watch her go.

"A ghant," Tiamak explained as they were all climbing back into the boat. "I am sorry it frightened you, Lady Miriamele. They are ugly things, but they seldom attack people, and almost never anyone larger than a child."

"But it looked at me like a person would!" Miriamele shuddered. "I don't know why, but it was dreadful."

Tiamak nodded his head. "They are not just low animals, Lady—or at least I do not think so, although others of my folk insist they are no cleverer than crayfish. I wonder, though: I have seen the huge nests they build, and the clever way they hunt for fish and trap birds."

"So you would suggest they are thinking creatures?" Cadrach asked dryly. "That would come as a disturbing thought to the hierarchy of Mother Church, I should think. Must they not then have souls? Perhaps Nabban will have to send missionary priests out to the Wran to bring them to the bosom of the True Faith."

"Enough of your mockery, Hernystirman," Isgrimnur grunted. "Help me get this damnable boat off the sandbar."

It was a short journey to Village Grove, or so Tiamak had said. The morning was bright and only comfortably warm, but even so, the ghant had darkened Miriamele's mood. It had reminded her of the terrible, alien nature of the marsh country. This was not her home. Tiamak might be able to live happily here—although she doubted that such was the case even with him—but she herself certainly never could.

The Wrannaman, poling now with the oar handle, directed them down an ever-turning succession of interwoven canals and streamlets, each one hidden from the next by the thick shield of vegetation that grew along its sandy, un-stable banks—dense walls of pale reeds and dark, tangled growth festooned with bright but somehow feverish-looking flowers—so that every time that a side course took them from one waterway to the next, the previous one had vanished behind them almost as soon as the stern of the boat had crossed over to the new one.

Soon the first houses of Village Grove began to appear on either side of the waterway. Some were built in trees, like Tiamak's; others loomed on tree-trunk stilts. After they had floated past a few, Tiamak pulled the boat up beneath the landing of a large stilt-house and loudly hailed the occupants.

"Roahog!" he called. When there was no reply, he banged the oar handle against one of the pilings; the rattling drove a bevy of green and scarlet birds shrieking from the trees overhead, but brought no other response. Tiamak shouted again, then shrugged.

"The potter is not home," he said. "I saw no one in the other houses, either. Perhaps there is a gathering at the landing-place."

They poled on. The houses that now began to appear were closer together. Some of the dwellings seemed to be composed of many small houses of different shapes and sizes that had been grafted onto an original hut—clumps of muddled shapes pocked with irregular black windows, like the nests of cliff-dwelling owls. Tiamak stopped and called at several of them, but no one ever answered his hail.

"The landing-place," he said firmly, but Miriamele thought he looked worried. "They must be at the landing-place."

This proved to be a great, flat dock that protruded halfway out into the middle of the widest part of the watercourse. Houses gathered thickly around it on all sides, and parts of the landing-place itself were equipped with thatched roofs and walls. Miriamele guessed these areas might be used for market stalls. There were other signs of recent life—large decorated baskets set back in the leafy shade, boats bobbing at the end of their painters—but no people.

Tiamak was clearly shaken. "They Who Watch and Shape," he breathed, "what has happened here?"

"They're gone?" Miriamele looked around. "How could a whole village be gone?"

"You've not seen the north, my lady," Isgrimnur said dourly. "There are many towns on the Frostmarch that are empty as old pots."

"But those people have been chased out by war. Surely there's no war here. Not yet."

"Some in the north have been chased out by war," Cadrach murmured. "Some by fear of things more difficult to name. And fear is everywhere in these days."

"I do not understand." Tiamak wagged his head as though he still could not believe what he saw. "My people would not just run away, even if they were afraid of the war—which I doubt they have even heard about. Our life is here. Where would they go?"

Camaris stood up suddenly, setting the boat rocking and filling the other passengers with alarm; but when the old man had balanced himself, he merely reached up and plucked a long yellowish seedpod from one of the tree branches hanging overhead, then sat back down again to examine his prize.

"Well, there are boats here, anyway," Isgrimnur said. "They're what we need. I don't mean to be cruel, Tiamak, but we should pick one and be on our way. We'll leave our boat for trade, as you said." He made a face, trying to think of the knightly thing to do. "Maybe you can scratch a letter on one of your parchments or somesuch—let 'em know what we've done."

Tiamak stared for a moment as though he had suddenly forgotten the Westerling language. "Oh," he said at last. "A new boat. Of course." He shook his head. "I know we have need for haste, Duke Isgrimnur, but would you mind if we stopped here a little time? I must look around—see if my sisters or anyone else left word of where they have gone."

"Well . . ." Isgrimnur peered at the deserted dock. Miriamele thought the duke seemed a little reluctant. There was indeed something eerie about the empty village. The inhabitants seemed to have vanished quite suddenly, as though they had been swept away by a strong wind. "I suppose that's all right, certainly. We thought it might take us the whole day, after all. Certainly."

"Thank you." Tiamak nodded. "I would have felt . . ." He started again. "So far I have not done all that I could do for my people. It would not be right just to take a flatboat and float away without even looking about."

He caught hold of one of the tie posts and made their boat fast to the landing-place.

The people of Village Grove did seem to have left in a hurry. A cursory inspection showed that many useful things had been left behind, not least of which were several baskets of fruits and vegetables. While Tiamak went off to search for some indication of why and where his people had fled, Cadrach and Isgrimnur began to harvest this unexpected bounty, loading their new vessel— a large and well-constructed flatboat—until it floated rather lower in the water than Tiamak might think was best. On her own, Miriamele found some flower-colored dresses in one of the huts near the landing-place. They were baggy and shapeless, quite unlike anything she would ever have worn at home, but in these conditions they would serve nicely for a change of clothing. She also discovered a pair of leather slippers, thong-stitched, that seemed as though they might make a nice change from the boots she had been wearing almost continuously since leaving Naglimund. After a moment's hesitation over the propriety of taking someone's belongings without leaving anything in return, Miriamele steeled herself and appropriated the clothes. After all, what did she have to exchange?

As morning slid into afternoon, Tiamak returned occasionally to pass on his news, which was generally no news. He had discovered the same curious evidence of hasty retreat, but could find nothing to indicate why the flight had occurred. The only possible clue was that several spears and other weapons were missing from the hut where the village's elders met—weapons that

Tiamak said were not the property of individuals but of the village as a whole, important weapons which were only taken down in time of battle or other conflict.

"I think I will go to Older Mogahib's house," said the Wrannaman. "He is our chief elder, so anything important would be there. It is a good distance up the watercourse, so I will take a boat. I should be back before the sun hits the treeline." He pointed to indicate the sun's westward path.

"Do you want to eat before you go?" Isgrimnur asked. "I'll have the fire going in a moment."

Tiamak shook his head. "I can wait until I return. As I said, there will still be much of the day left when I get back."

But the afternoon waned and Tiamak did not return. Miriamele and the others ate turnips—or at least something that looked like turnips, bulbous, starchy things which Tiamak had assured them were safely edible—and a squishy yellow fruit that they wrapped in green leaves and baked in the coals of the fire. A brown, dovelike bird that Cadrach captured with a snare, when boiled for soup, helped to fill out the meal. As the shadows lengthened across the green water and the hum of insects began to rise, Miriamele became worried.

"He should have been back by now. The sun went below the trees a long time ago."

"The little fellow's fine," Isgrimnur assured her. "He's probably found something interesting—some damned marsh-man scroll or something. He'll be back soon."

But he did not come back, not even when the sun had gone and the stars came out. Miriamele and the others made their beds out on the landing dock—more than a little reluctantly, since they still had no idea what had happened to Village Grove's vanished citizens—and were glad for the embers of the fire. Miriamele did not fall asleep for a long time.

The morning sun was high when Miriamele awoke. One look at Isgrimnur's worried face was enough to confirm what she had feared.

"Oh, poor Tiamak! Where is he? What could have happened!? I hope he isn't hurt!"

"Not just poor Tiamak, Lady." Cadrach's studiedly sour tone did not entirely cover his deep unease. "Poor us as well. How will we ever find our way out of this godless swamp by ourselves?"

She opened her mouth, then shut it again. There was nothing to say.

"There's nothing else to do," Isgrimnur said on the second Tiamak-less morning. "We have to try and find our way out by ourselves."

Cadrach made a bitter face. "We might as well give ourselves to the grandfather crocodile, Rimmersman. At least it would save time."

"Damn you," Isgrimnur snarled, "don't expect *me* to crawl off and die! I've never given up in my life, and I've been in some tight spots."

"You've never been lost in the Wran before," Cadrach pointed out.

"Stop it! Stop it now!" Miriamele's head hurt. The wrangling had been going on since the middle of the day before. "Isgrimnur's right. We have no other choice."

Cadrach seemed about to say something unpleasant, but shut his mouth instead and stared off at the empty houses of Village Grove.

"We will go the same direction Tiamak went," declared Isgrimnur. "That way, if something has happened to him—I mean if he is hurt or holed his boat or something like—at least we may chance upon him."

"But he said he was not going far—just to the other end of his people's village," she said. "When we leave the last houses, we will not know where he meant us to go next, will we?"

"No, curse it, and I was too foolish to think to ask him when I could have." Isgrimnur scowled. "Not that anything he said would have made much sense—this damnable place just turns my head around."

"But the sun is still the same, even over the Wran," Miriamele said, a touch of desperation now making itself felt. "The stars, too. We should be able to decide which direction is north toward Uncle Josua, at least."

Isgrimnur smiled sadly. "Aye. That's true, Princess. We will do our best."

Cadrach stood suddenly, then walked to the flatboat they had selected, stepping around the old man Camaris, who was dangling his feet off the dock into the green water. Earlier Miriamele had dangled her own feet similarly and been bitten by a turtle, but the old man seemed to have established more amicable relations with the river's inhabitants.

Cadrach bent and hefted one of the sacks piled on the dock. He heaved it to Camaris, who caught it with ease and dropped it into the boat. "I will not argue any further," the monk said as he stooped for a second sack. "Let us load what food and water we can. At least we will not die from hunger or thirst—although we soon may wish we had."

Miriamele had to laugh. "Elysia, Mother of God, Cadrach, could you be more gloomy if you tried?! Maybe we should just kill you now and put you out of your misery."

"I've heard worse ideas," grunted Isgrimnur.

Miriamele watched with apprehension as the center of Village Grove disappeared behind them. Although it had been empty, nevertheless it had clearly been a place where people had lived: the marks of their recent habitation were everywhere. Now she and her remaining friends were leaving this bastion of comparative familiarity and heading back into the unknowable swamps. She suddenly wished they had decided to wait a few more days for Tiamak.

They continued to float past deserted houses well into the morning, although the dwellings were becoming ever more widely separated from each

other. The greenery was as dense as ever. Watching the endless mural of vegetation unroll on either side, Miriamele for the first time found herself wishing
they had not followed Tiamak into this place. The Wran seemed so heedless in
its vegetative enterprise, so busily unconcerned with anything as meaningless
as people. She felt very small.

It was Camaris who saw it first, although he did not speak or make any noise;
it was only by his stance, the sudden alertness like a hound on the point, that
the others were drawn to squint down the waterway at the drifting speck.

"It's a flatboat!" Miriamele cried. "Someone's in it—lying down! Oh, it must
be Tiamak!"

"It's his boat, all right," Isgrimnur said, "—the one with the yellow and
black eyes painted on the front."

"Oh, hurry, Cadrach!" Miriamele almost toppled the monk into the waterway as she pushed at his arm. "Pole faster!"

"If we tip over and drown," Cadrach said through clenched teeth, "then we
will do the marsh man little good."

They approached the flatboat. The dark-haired, brown-skinned figure lay
curled in the bottom with one arm hanging over the side, as though he had
fallen asleep trying to reach his hand down to the water. The boat was drifting
in a slow circle as Miriamele and her companions pulled alongside. The princess was the first to cross over, setting both boats rocking as she hurried to the
Wrannaman's aid.

"Careful, my lady," Cadrach said, but Miriamele had already lifted the small
man's head onto her lap. She gasped at the blood that had dried on the dark face,
then a moment later, gasped again.

"It's not Tiamak!"

The Wrannaman, who had obviously suffered much in recent days, was
stouter and a little lighter-skinned than their companion. His skin was covered
with some sticky substance whose odor made Miriamele wrinkle her nose in
discomfort. Nothing else could be discovered, though, for he was completely
insensible. When she lifted the water skin to his cracked lips, Miriamele had to
be very careful not to choke him. The stranger managed to down a few swallows without ever appearing to wake.

"So how did this blasted other marsh man wind up with Tiamak's boat?"
Isgrimnur grumbled, digging the mud from his bootheels with a stick. They
had come ashore to make a temporary camp while they decided what to do; the
ground in this spot was somewhat soggy. "And what's happened to Tiamak? Do
you think this fellow waylaid him for his flatboat?"

"Look at him," Cadrach said. "This man could not strangle a cat, I am sure.
No, the question is not how he got the boat, but why Tiamak isn't in it with
him, and what happened to this unlucky fellow in the first place. Remember,

this is the first of Tiamak's folk we've seen since we left Kwanitupul for the marshes."

"That's true." Miriamele stared at the stranger. "Maybe whatever happened to Tiamak's villagers happened to this man, too! Or maybe he was running away from it . . . or . . . or something." She frowned. Instead of finding their guide, they instead had discovered a new mystery to make things even more complicated and unpleasant. "What do we do?"

"Take him with us, I suppose," Isgrimnur said. "We will want to ask him questions when he wakes up—but the Aedon only knows how long that will be. We can't afford to wait."

"Ask him questions?" Cadrach murmured. "And how, Duke Isgrimnur, will we do that? Tiamak is a rarity among his people, as he told us himself."

"What do you mean?"

"I doubt this fellow can speak anything other than the Wran-tongue."

"Damn! Damn and damn and thrice damned!" The duke colored. "Begging your pardon, Princess Miriamele. He's right, though." He pondered a moment, then shrugged. "Still, what else can we do? We'll bring him."

"Maybe he can draw pictures, or maps," Miriamele offered.

"There!" Isgrimnur was relieved. "Maps! Clever, my lady, very clever. Maybe he can do that, indeed."

The unknown Wrannaman slept through the rest of the afternoon, not stirring even when the boat was scraped down the muddy bank and relaunched into the watercourse. Before departure, Miriamele had cleaned his skin, discovering to her relief that most of his wounds were not serious—at least the ones she could see. She could think of nothing else to do.

Isgrimnur's thankless task of trying to find a safe passage through this treacherous and unfamiliar land was made easier by the relatively straightforward nature of this section of the waterway. Because there were few side streams and few forks, it had seemed easiest to simply remain in the center of the watercourse, and so far it was working. Although there had been a few junctures at which Isgrimnur could have gone a different way, they were still seeing occasional houses, so there seemed no cause yet for worry.

Somewhat after the sun had passed the midpoint of the sky, the strange Wrannaman suddenly woke up, startling Miriamele, who was shading his eyes with a broad leaf as she mopped his brow. The man's brown eyes widened in fear as he saw her, then darted from side to side as though he were surrounded by enemies. After a few moments his hunted look softened and he became calmer, although he still did not speak. Instead, he lay for a long while staring up at the canopy of branches sliding past overhead. He breathed shallowly, as though just to keep his eyes open and watching represented the farthest limit of his strength. Miriamele talked softly to him and continued moistening his brow. She was certain that Cadrach was right when he guessed that this man could not speak her tongue, but she was not trying to tell him anything important: a quiet and friendly voice, she hoped, might make him feel better even if he did not understand any of her words.

A little over an hour later the man was at last recovered enough to sit partway up and take a little water. He still seemed quite confused and ill, so it was no surprise when the first noises he made were moans of discomfort, but the unhappy sounds continued even as Miriamele offered him another drink. The Wrannaman pushed away the skin bag, gesturing up the watercourse and showing every sign of extreme disquiet.

"Is he mad?" Isgrimnur peered at the man suspiciously. "Just what we need, some mad swamp fellow."

"I think he's trying to tell us to turn back," Miriamele said, then realized with a sudden vertiginous drop in her innards what she was saying. "He's telling us it's . . . *bad* to go the way we're going."

The Wrannaman at last found his words. *"Mualum nohoa!"* he gabbled, obviously terrified. *"Sanbidub nohoa yia ghanta!"* When he had said this again several times, he tried to drag himself over the side and into the water. He was weak and distracted; Miriamele was able to restrain him with little difficulty. She was shocked when he burst into tears, his round brown face as defenseless and unashamed as a child's.

"What can it be?" she asked, alarmed. "He thinks it's dangerous, whatever it is."

Isgrimnur shook his head. He was helping Cadrach keep the boat off the tangled bank as they negotiated a bend in the waterway. "Who knows? Could be some animal, or some other group of marsh men who are at war with these fellows. Or it could be some heathen superstition—a haunted pond or something like."

"Or it could be what emptied Tiamak's village," Cadrach said. "Look."

The Wrannaman sat up again, straining to escape Miriamele's grip. *"Yia ghanta!"* he burbled.

"Ghanta," Miriamele breathed, staring across the waterway. "Ghants? But Tiamak said . . ."

"Tiamak may have found out that he was wrong." Cadrach's voice had dropped to a whisper.

On the far side of the watercourse, now revealed as the flatboat made its way past the bend, sprawled a huge and bizarre structure. It might almost have been built in parody of Village Grove, for like that place it was obviously the dwelling place of many. But where the village had clearly been the work of human hands, this lopsided agglomeration of mud and leaves and sticks, although it stretched up from the water's edge into the trees to many times a man's height, and along the bank for what looked like well over a furlong, was just as clearly not built by human beings at all. A buzzing, clicking sound issued from it and out across the Wran, a great cloud of noise like an army of crickets in an echoing, high-arched room. Some of the builders of the huge nest could be seen clearly, even from the far side of the wide canal. They moved in their distinctive manner, dropping deftly from one stump of branch to a lower, scuttling swiftly in and out of the black doors of the nest.

Miriamele felt both terror and a certain disgusted fascination. A single ghant had been disturbing. From the size of the dwelling, she did not doubt that hundreds of the unpleasant creatures were sheltering in this pile of dirt and sticks.

"Mother of Usires," Isgrimnur hissed. He turned the boat and poled rapidly back up the waterway until the bend in the river shielded them once more from the alarming sight. "What kind of hell-thing is that?"

Miriamele squirmed as she remembered the mocking eyes that had watched her bathe, dots of jet pivoting in an inhuman face. "Those are the ghants Tiamak told us about."

The sick Wrannaman, who had fallen into deathly silence when the nest came into view, began to waggle his hands. *"Tiamak!"* he said hoarsely. *"Tiamak nib dunou yia ghanta!"* He pointed back to where the nest lay hidden from their view by a wall of greenery. Miriamele did not need to speak the Wrantongue to know what the strange man was saying.

"Tiamak's in there. Oh, God help him, he's in that nest. The ghants have him."

14

Dark Corridors

✦

The stairs were steep and the sack was heavy, but Rachel felt a
certain joy, nevertheless. One more trip—just one more time that she would be
forced to brave the haunted upper rooms of the castle—and then she would be
finished.

Just off the shadowy landing, halfway down the stairs, she stopped and set
down her burden, careful not to let the jars clank. The doorway was hidden by
what Rachel the Dragon felt sure was the oldest, dustiest arras in the entire
castle. It was a measure of the importance of her hiding hole remaining inconspicuous that she could pass it every day and leave it uncleaned. Her very soul
rebelled each time she had to lay her hands on the moldering fabric, but there
were circumstances when even cleaning had to take second place. Rachel grimaced. *Hard times make odd changes,* her mother had always said. Well, if that
wasn't Aedon's holy truth, what was?

Rachel had taken great care to oil the ancient hinges, so when she lifted the
tapestry and pushed at the handle, the door swung in almost silently. She lifted
her bag over the low threshold, then let the heavy tapestry slip back into place
behind her so it would again hide the door. She unshielded her lamp, set it in a
high niche, and went to work unpacking.

When the last jar had been removed and Rachel had drawn a picture of the
contents on its outside with a straw dipped in lamp-black, she stepped back to
survey her larder. She had labored hard over the last month, surprising even
herself with her daring pilferage. Now she wanted only the sack of dried fruit
she had spotted on today's raid, then she would be able to last out the entire
winter without risking capture. She needed that sack: a lack of fruit to eat
would mean the clenches, if not something worse, and she could not afford to
become ill with no one to tend her. She had planned everything with great care
so that she could be alone: there was certainly no one left in the castle she could
trust.

Rachel had searched patiently for just the right place to make her sanctuary.
This monk's hole, far down in one of the long-unused sections of the Hayholt's
underground rooms, had worked out perfectly. Now, thanks to her ceaseless
hunting, it was stocked with a larder that many a lord of troubled Erkynland

might envy. Also, just up a few flights she had found another unused room—not as well hidden, but with a small slit window that protruded just above ground level. Outside that window hung the drain spout from one of the Hayholt's stone gutters. Rachel already had a full barrel of water in her cell; as long as the snows and rains lasted, she would be able to fill a bucket every day from the spout outside the room above, and not have to touch her precious store of drinkable water at all.

She had also scavenged spare clothing and several warm blankets, as well as a straw mattress, and even a chair to sit in—a fancy chair, as she marveled, with a back on it! She had wood for the tiny fireplace, and so many rows of jars of pickled vegetables and meats and wrapped piles of hard-baked bread were stacked along the walls that there was scarcely room to walk from the door to the bed. But it was worth it. Here, in her hidden room filled with provender, she knew she could last the better part of a year. What might happen by the time the provisions ran out, what event might take place that would allow her to leave her den and reemerge into daylight, Rachel wasn't sure . . . but that was something she could not worry about. She would spend her time staying safe, keeping her nest clean, and waiting. That lesson had been pounded into her since childhood: Do what you can. Trust God for the rest.

She thought about her youth a great deal these days. The constant solitude and the secretive nature of her daily life conspired, limiting her activities and throwing her back on her memories for entertainment and solace. She had remembered things—an Aedonmansa when her father had been feared lost in the snow, a straw doll that her sister had once made for her—that she had not thought of for years. The memories, like the foodstuffs floating in the briny darkness of the jars she was rearranging, were only waiting to be taken out once more.

Rachel pushed the last jar back a little farther, so that they made an even row. The castle might be falling apart, but here in her haven she would have order! *Only one more trip,* she thought. *Then I won't have to be afraid any more. Then I can finally have a little rest.*

The Mistress of Chambermaids had reached the top of the stairway and was reaching for the door when a feeling of immense cold suddenly swept over her. Footsteps were approaching on the other side of the door, a dull ticking sound like water dripping on stone. Someone was coming! She would be caught!

Her heart seemed to be beating so swiftly she feared it would climb right up out of her chest. She was gripped by a nightmarish immobility.

Move, idiot woman, move!

The footsteps were growing louder. She finally pulled back her hand, then, seeing that movement was possible after all, forced herself to back down onto a lower step, looking around wildly. Where to go, where to go? Trapped!

She backed farther down the slippery steps. Where the stairway bent around the corner there was a landing, much like the one where she had discovered her new home. This landing, too, was graced with a musty, ragged arras. She grabbed at it, struggling as the heavy, dusty cloth resisted her. It seemed too much to hope that a room was hidden behind this one, too, but at least she could press herself flat against the wall and hope that the person who was even now pulling at the door above her was shortsighted, or in a hurry.

There *was* a door! Rachel wondered momentarily if there hung a single tapestry in the sprawling castle that didn't shield some hidden portal. She tugged at the ancient handle.

Oh, Aedon on the Tree, she mouthed silently—surely the hinges would creak! But the hinges did not make a sound, and the door swung open quietly, even as the door at the top of the stairs above her scraped across the stone flags. The noise of bootheels grew louder as they descended the steps. Rachel pushed herself through and pulled the door after her. It swung most of the way closed, then stopped with a little less than a hand's width remaining. It would not shut.

Rachel looked up, wishing she dared to unshutter her lantern, but grateful that at least there was a torch burning fitfully in the stairwell outside. She forced herself to search carefully, even though black spots were swirling before her eyes and her heart was rabbiting in her breast. There! The top of the arras was caught in the door . . . but it was far above where she could reach. She grasped the thick, dust-caked velvet to shake it free, but the footsteps were almost on the landing. Rachel shrank back from the open crack of the doorway and held her breath.

As the noise came closer, so, too, did the sensation of cold—a bone-deep chill like walking out of a hot room into mid-winter winds. Rachel began shivering uncontrollably. Through the crack of the doorway she saw a pair of black-clad figures. The quiet noise of their conversation, which had just become audible, abruptly ceased. One of them turned so that its pale face was momentarily visible from Rachel's hiding place. Her heart lurched, seeming to lose its beat. It was one of those witch-things—the White Foxes! It turned away again, speaking to its companion in a low but oddly musical voice, then looked back up the steps they had just descended. Another clatter of footsteps came echoing down the stairwell.

More of them!

Rachel, despite a horror of moving or doing anything at all that might make a noise, began to back away. As she stared at the partially opened doorway, praying that the things would not notice how it was ajar, Rachel kept feeling behind her for the rear wall. She took several steps backward, until the doorway was only a thin vertical line of yellowish torch-glow, but still her hand encountered no resistance. She stopped at last and turned to look, terrified by the sudden idea that she might stumble over something stored in this room and send it clattering to the ground.

It was not a room. Rachel stood in the mouth of a corridor that led away into darkness.

She paused for a moment, forcing herself to think. There was no sense in remaining here, especially with a flock of those creatures just beyond the door.

The stark stone wall was devoid of hiding places, and she knew that any moment now she might make an involuntary noise, or worse, grow faint and fall noisily to the floor. And who knew how long those things might stand there, murmuring to themselves like carrion birds on a branch? When their fellows all arrived, they might next enter this very passageway! At least if she went now, she might find some better place to hide or another way out.

Rachel tottered down the corridor, trailing one hand along the wall—the horrible, grimy things that she felt beneath her fingers!—and holding the darkened lantern in front of her with the other, trying to make sure that it did not bump against the stone. The thin sliver of light from the doorway disappeared behind a bend in the hallway, leaving her in utter darkness. Rachel carefully pulled back the lantern's hood a little way, allowing a single beam to leap out and shine on the flagstones before her, then began to walk swiftly down the passageway.

Rachel held the lamp high, squinting down the featureless corridor into the unexplored darkness beyond the pool of light. Was there no end to the castle's maze of passageways? She had thought she knew the Hayholt as well as anyone, yet the last few weeks had been a revelation. There seemed to be another entire castle beneath the basement storehouses that had once been the downward limit of her experience. Had Simon known about these places?

Thinking of the boy was painful, as always. She shook her head and trudged forward. There had been no sound of pursuit yet—she had finally caught her fear-shortened breath—but there was no sense standing around waiting.

But there *was* a problem to be solved, of course: if she dared not go back, what could she do? She had long ceased trusting her ability to find her way in this warren. What if she took a wrong turn and went wandering into darkness forever, lost and starving . . . ?

Fool woman. Just don't turn off from this hall—or at least mark the turn if you do. Then you can always find the landing and the stairs again.

She snorted, the same chuff of sound that had reduced many a novice chambermaid to whimpers. Rachel knew discipline, even if it was she herself that needed it this time.

No time for nonsense.

Still, it was strange to be wandering here in these lonely, between-ish spaces. It was a little like what Father Dreosan had said about the Waiting Place—that spot between Hell and Heaven where dead souls waited for judgment, where they remained for a timeless time if they were not bad enough for the former but not ready for the latter. Rachel had found this a rather uncomfortable idea: she liked her distinctions clean and forthright. Do wrong, be damned and burnt. Lead a life of cleanliness and Aedonite rigor and you could fly up to heaven and sing and rest beneath eternal blue skies. This middle place that the priest had spoken of just seemed unpleasantly mysterious. The God that Rachel worshiped should not work in such a way.

The lamp's light fell upon a wall before her: the corridor had ended in a perpendicular hallway, which meant that if she wished to continue, she had to go right or left. Rachel frowned. Here she was already, having to leave the straight path. She didn't like it. The question was, did she dare go back, or even remain in the hallway? She didn't think she'd traveled very far since leaving the staircase.

The memory of the whispering, white-faced things gathering on the steps decided her.

She dipped a finger in lampblack, then stood on tiptoe to mark the left wall of the corridor in which she stood. That would be what she would see on returning. She then turned reluctantly down the right-hand side of the intersecting corridor.

The passageway wound on and on, crisscrossed by halls, opening out from time to time into small, unwindowed galleries, each as empty as a plundered tomb. Rachel dutifully marked each turn. She was beginning to worry about the lamp—surely she would run out of oil if she went much farther before turning back—when the passageway ended abruptly at an ancient door.

The door had no markings, nor any bolt or lock. The wood was old and warped and so waterstained that it was splotched like the shell of a tortoise. The hinges were great clumsy chunks of iron, fastened by nails that seemed little more than shards of rough metal. Rachel squinted at the floor to make sure that no recent footprints other than her own were there, then made the Tree before her breast and pulled at the stubby handle. The door gritted open partway before grinding to a halt, wedged by what must have been a century's worth of dust and rubble on the floor. Beyond lay another darkened space, but this darkness was glazed with reddish light.

It's Hell! was Rachel's first thought. *Out of the Waiting Place and through the door to Hell!* Then: *Elysia the Mother! Old woman, you aren't even dead! Be sensible!* She stepped through.

The passageway on the far side was different than those through which she had come. Instead of being lined with cut and fitted stone, it was walled with naked rock. The glimmers of red light which writhed across the rough walls seemed to be coming from farther up the corridor to the left, as though somewhere just around a corner a fire was burning.

Despite her uncertainty over this new development, Rachel was just about to take a few steps up the passage toward the source of the red glow when she heard a sudden noise from the opposite direction, down the new corridor to her right. She hurriedly stepped back into the doorway, but it was still stuck fast and would not close. She pushed herself back into the shadows and tried to hold her breath.

Whatever made the new noise did not move very quickly. Rachel cringed as the faint scraping slowly grew louder, but mixed with the fear was a deep anger. To think that she, the Mistress of Chambermaids, should be made to cower in her own home by . . . by things! Trying to slow her racing heart, she relived the moment when she had struck out at Pryrates—the hellish excitement of it, the odd satisfaction of being able to actually do something after all those bleak months of suffering. But now? Her strongest blow had not seemed to affect the red priest at all, so what could she hope to do against a whole gang of demons? No, it was better to stay hidden and save the anger for when it might do her some good.

When the figure passed the stuck doorway, Rachel was at first tremendously relieved to see that it was only a mortal after all, a dark-haired man whose form was barely distinguishable against the red-lit rocks. A moment later her curiosity came rushing back, buoyed by the same fury she had felt earlier. Who felt so free to walk these dark places?

She poked her head out through the doorway to watch the retreating figure. He was walking very slowly, trailing his hand along the wall, but his head was back and waving from side to side, as though he tried to read something written on the corridor's shadowed ceiling.

Mercy, he's blind! she suddenly realized. The hesitation, the questing hands—it was obvious. A moment later, she realized that she knew the man. She flung herself back into the darkness of the doorway.

Guthwulf! That monster! What is he doing here? For a moment she had the dreadful certainty that Elias' henchmen were still looking for her, combing the castle hall by hall in meticulous search. But why send a blind man? And when had Guthwulf gone blind?

A memory came back, fragmented but still unsettling. That *had* been Guthwulf on the balcony with the king and Pryrates, hadn't it? The Earl of Utanyeat had grappled with the alchemist even as he, with Rachel's dagger standing in his back, rounded upon the Mistress of Chambermaids who lay stunned on the floor. But why would Guthwulf have done that? Everyone knew that Utanyeat was the High King's Hand, most hardhearted of Elias' minions.

Had he actually saved her life?

Rachel's head was whirling. She peered out through the open doorway again, but Earl Guthwulf had disappeared around a bend in the corridor, heading toward the red glow. A tiny shadow detached itself from the greater darkness and skittered past her feet, following him into the shadows. A cat? A gray cat?

The world beneath the castle had become altogether too confusingly dreamlike for Rachel. She unshuttered her lantern again and turned back in the direction she had come, leaving the door to the rough passageway ajar. For now, she wanted no dealings with Guthwulf, blind or not. She would follow her own careful marks back toward the staircase landing and pray that the White Foxes had gone on about their unholy business. There was much to think about—too much. Rachel wanted only to shut herself safely away in her sanctuary and go to sleep.

As Guthwulf trudged along, his head was full of seductive, poisonous music—a music that spoke to him, that summoned him, but that also frightened him as nothing else ever had.

For a long time in the endless darkness of his days and nights he had heard that song only in dreams, but today the music had come to him at last in his waking hours, summoning him up from the depths, driving even the whispering voices that were his regular companions out of his mind. It was the voice of the gray sword, and it was somewhere nearby.

A part of the Earl of Utanyeat knew perfectly well that the sword was only an object, a mute stem of metal that hung on the king's belt, and that the last thing in the world he should want to do was seek it out, since where it was, King Elias would also be. Guthwulf certainly did not want to be caught—he cared little for his safety, but he would rather die alone in the pits below the castle than be seen by the people who had known him before he had become such a pitiable wreck—but the presence of the sword was hugely compelling. His life was now little more than echoes and shadows, cold stone, ghostly voices, and the tapping and scraping of his own footsteps. But the sword was alive, and somehow its life was more powerful than his own. He wanted to be near it.

I will not be caught, Guthwulf told himself. *I will be clever, careful.* He would merely venture close enough to feel its singing strength. . . .

His thoughts were disrupted by something twining through his ankles—the cat, his shadow-friend. He bent to touch the animal, running his fingers along its bony back, feeling its lean muscles. It had come with him, perhaps to keep him out of trouble. He almost smiled.

Sweat dripped down his cheek as he straightened. The air was getting warmer. He could half-believe that after all the stairs he had climbed, all the long upward ramps he had trudged, he might be approaching the surface—but could things have changed so much in his time below-ground? Could the winter be fled, replaced by hot summer? It did not seem that so much time could have passed, but perpetual darkness was deceptive. Blind Guthwulf had already learned that while still in the castle. As for the weather . . . well, in such ill-omened and confusing times as these, anything was possible.

Now the stone walls were beginning to feel warm beneath his questing fingers. What was he walking into? He pushed the thought down. Whatever it was, the sword was there. The sword that was calling to him. Surely he should go just a little farther. . . .

That moment when Sorrow had sung inside him, filling him . . .

In the moment Elias had forced him to touch it, it had seemed that Guthwulf had become a part of the sword. He had been subsumed in an alien melody. For that moment at least, he and the blade were one.

Sorrow needed its brothers. Together they would make a music greater still.

In the king's throne room, despite his horror, Guthwulf had also yearned for that communion. Now, remembering, he ached for it again. Whatever the risks, he needed to feel the song that had haunted him. It was a kind of madness, he knew, but he did not have the strength to resist it. Instead, it would take all his reserves of cunning and self-restraint just to get closer without being revealed. It was so near now. . . .

The air in the narrow corridor was stifling. Guthwulf stopped and felt around. The little cat was gone, probably retreated to some place less injurious to its pads. When he put his hand back onto the corridor wall, he could only drag it for a short distance before he had to snatch it away once more. From somewhere ahead he could now hear a faint but continuous rush of sound, a near-silent roar. What could lie before him?

Once a dragon had made its lair beneath the castle—the red worm Shurakai, whose death had made Prester John's reputation and provided the bones for the Hayholt's throne, a beast whose fiery breath had killed two kings and countless castle-dwellers in an earlier century. Might there still be a dragon, some whelp of Shurakai, grown to adulthood in darkness? If so, let it kill him if it would— let it roast him to ashes. Guthwulf was beyond caring much about such things. All he wished was to bask first in the song of the gray sword.

The pathway took a sharp upward angle, and he had to lean forward to make any headway. The heat was fierce; he could imagine his skin blackening and shriveling like the cooked flesh of a holiday pig. As he struggled against the slope, the roaring noise became louder, a deep unsteady growl like thunder, or an angry sea, or the troubled breath of a sleeping dragon. Then the sound began to change. After a moment, Guthwulf realized that the passageway was widening. As he turned the corner, his blind man's senses told him that the hall had not only widened but grown higher as well. Hot winds billowed toward him. The grumbling noise echoed strangely.

Another few steps and he knew the reason. There was some much larger chamber beyond this one, something vast as the great dome of Saint Sutrin's in Erchester. A fiery pit? Guthwulf felt his hair wafting in the hot breeze. Had he somehow arrived at the fabled Lake of Judgment where sinners were cast into a pool of flame forever? Was God Himself waiting down here in the rocky fastnesses? In these confused, distracted days Guthwulf did not remember much of his life before the blinding, but what he did remember now seemed full of foolish, meaningless actions. If there was such a place, such a punishment, he doubtless deserved it, but it would be a pity never to feel the strong magic of the gray sword again.

Guthwulf began taking smaller steps, dragging each foot in a careful side-to-side arc before setting it down. His progress slowed as he devoted all his attention to feeling his way forward. At last his foot touched air. He stopped and squatted, tapping his fingers along the hot passage floor. A lip of stone lay before him, stretching on either side farther than he could reach. Beyond that was nothing but emptiness and scorching winds.

He stood, shifting from foot to foot as the heat worked its way through his boot soles, and listened to the great roaring. There were other sounds, too. One

was a deep, irregular clanging, as of two massive pieces of metal crashing together; the other was that of human voices.

The sound of metal on metal came again, and the noise finally pushed up a
memory from his life in the castle of old. The thunderous clanging was the
great forge doors being opened and closed. Men were throwing fuel into the
blaze—he had seen it many times when he had inspected the foundries in his
role as King's Hand. He must be standing at one of the tunnel mouths almost
directly above the huge furnace. No wonder his hair was about to catch fire!

But the gray sword was here. He knew that as certainly as a foraging mouse
knows when an owl is on the wing overhead. Elias must be down among the
forges, the sword at his side.

Guthwulf backed away from the edge, thinking frantically of ways he could
descend to the foundry floor without being observed.

When he had stood in one place long enough to burn his feet, he had to move
farther away. He cursed as he went. There was no way to approach the thing.
He might wander through these tunnels for days without finding another route
down, and surely Elias would be gone by then. But neither could he simply give
up. The sword called to him, and it did not care what stood in his way.

Guthwulf stumbled farther down the passageway, away from the heat, although the sword called to him to come back, to leap down into fiery oblivion.

"Why have you done this to me, sweet God?!" he shouted, his voice swiftly
disappearing in the roar of the furnace. "Why have you hung me with this
curse?!"

The tears evaporated from his eyelids as swiftly as they emerged.

Inch bowed before King Elias. In the flickering forge light, the huge man
looked like an ape from the southern jungles—an ape dressed in clothes, but
still a poor mockery of a man. The rest of the foundrymen had cast themselves
to the floor upon the king's entrance; the scatter of bodies all round the great
chamber made it seem as though his very presence had struck a hundred men
dead.

"We are working, Highness, working," Inch grunted. "Slow work, it is."

"Working?" Elias said harshly. Though the foundrymaster dripped with
sweat, the king's pale skin was dry. "Of course you are working. But you are
not finished with the task I have set, and if I do not hear a reason quickly, your
filthy skin will be flayed and hung to dry over your own furnace."

The large man dropped to his knees. "We work as fast as we can."

"But it is not fast enough." The king's gaze wandered across the cavern's
shadowy roof.

"It is hard, master, hard—we only have parts of the plans. Sometimes we
must make everything over when we see the next drawing." Inch looked up,
his single eye keen in his dull face as he watched for the king's reaction.

"What do you mean, 'parts of the plans'?" Something was moving in a tunnel mouth, high on the wall above the great furnace. The king squinted, but the flirt of pale color—a face?—was obscured by risking smoke and heat-jumbled air.

"Your majesty!" someone called. "Here you are!"

Elias turned slowly toward the scarlet-robed figure. He lifted an eyebrow in mild surprise, but said nothing.

Pryrates hurried up. "I was surprised to find you gone." His raspy voice was sweeter, more reasonable than usual. "Can I assist you?"

"I do not need you every moment, priest," Elias said curtly. "There are things I can do by myself."

"But you have not been well, Majesty." Pryrates lifted his hand, the red sleeve billowing. For a moment it seemed he might actually take Elias' arm and try to lead him away, but he lifted his fingers to his own head instead, brushing at his hairless scalp. "Because of your weakness, Majesty, I only feared you might stumble on these steep stairs."

Elias looked at him, narrowing his eyes until they were scarcely more than black slits. "I am not an old man, priest. I am not my father in his last years." He flicked a glance at the kneeling Inch, then turned back to Pryrates again. "This clod says that the plans for the castle's defense are difficult."

The alchemist darted a murderous look at Inch. "He lies, Majesty. You approved them yourself. You know that is not so."

"You give us only part at a time, priest." Inch's voice was deep and slow, but the anger prisoned behind it was more apparent than ever.

"Do not bandy words before the king!" Pryrates snarled.

"I tell truth, priest!"

"*Silence!*" Elias drew himself up. His knob-knuckled hand fell onto the hilt of the gray sword. "I will have silence!" he shouted. "Now, what does he mean? Why does he get the plans only in pieces?"

Pryrates took a deep breath. "For secrecy, King Elias. You know that several of these foundrymen have run away already. We dare not let anyone see all the plans for defense of the castle. What would prevent them running straight to Josua with what they knew?"

There was a long moment of silence as Pryrates stared at the king. The air in the forge seemed to change slightly, thickening, and the roar of the fires grew strangely muffled. The flickering lights threw long shadows.

Elias suddenly seemed to lose interest. "I suppose." The king's gaze went drifting back to the spot along the cavern wall where he thought he had seen movement. "I will send a dozen more men here to the forges—there are at least that many mercenaries whose looks I do not care for." He turned to the overseer. "Then you will have no excuse."

A tremor ran through Inch's wide frame. "Yes, Highness."

"Good. I have told you when I wish the work on walls and gate to be done. You *will* have it finished."

"Yes, Highness."

The king turned toward Pryrates. "So. I see it takes the king to make certain things go as they should."

The priest bowed his shiny head. "You are irreplaceable, sire."

"But I am also a little tired, Pryrates. Perhaps it is as you said—I have not been well, after all."

"Yes, Highness. Perhaps your healing drink, then a little sleep?" And now Pryrates did insinuate his hand beneath Elias' elbow, turning him gently toward the staircase leading back up to the castle proper. The king went, docile as a child.

"I might lie down for a while, Pryrates, yes . . . but I do not think I will sleep just now." He stole a look back at the wall above the furnace, then shook his head dreamily.

"Yes, sire, an excellent idea. Come, we will let the forgemaster get on with his work." Pryrates stared pointedly at Inch, whose one eye looked fixedly back, then the red priest turned away, his face expressionless, and led the king out of the cavern.

Behind them, the prostrated workers slowly began clambering to their feet, too beaten and exhausted even to whisper about such an unusual happening. As they trudged back to their tasks, Inch remained kneeling for some time, his features as frozen as the priest's had been.

Rachel carefully retraced her steps and found the original landing once more. To her even greater relief, when she stared out through the crack, the stairwell was empty. The White Foxes had gone.

Off to work some kind of deviltry, no doubt. She made the sign of the Tree.

Rachel pushed a strand of graying hair out of her eyes. She was exhausted, not only by the dreadful corridor-tramping—she had walked for what seemed like hours—but by the shock of near-discovery. She was not a girl anymore, and she did not like to feel her heart beating as it had beat today: that was not the racing blood of good honest work.

Old—you're getting old, woman.

Rachel was not so foolish as to lose all caution, so she kept her footsteps light and quiet as she made her way down the stairs, peering cautiously around each corner, holding her shuttered lantern behind her so it would not give her away. Thus she saw the king's cupbearer Brother Hengfisk standing on the stairway below her a moment before she would have otherwise run into him in the shadows between wall-torches. As it was, her surprise was still so great that she gave a startled shriek and dropped her lantern. It rolled thumping down to the landing—her landing, the location of her sanctuary!—to lie at the monk's sandal-shod feet as it dripped blazing oil onto the stone. The pop-eyed man looked down at the flames burning around his feet with calm interest, then lifted his gaze to Rachel once more, mouth stretched in a wide grin.

"Merciful Rhiap," Rachel gasped. "Oh, God's mercy!" She tried to retreat back up the stairwell, but the monk moved as swiftly as a cat; he was past her in a moment, then turned to block her passage, still smiling his horrid smile. His eyes were empty pools.

Rachel took a few tottering steps back down toward the landing. The monk moved with her, one step at a time, absolutely silent as he matched his movements to hers. When Rachel stopped, he stopped. When she tried to move more swiftly, he headed her off, forcing her to shrink back against the stone walls of the stairwell to avoid contact with him. He gave off a feverish warmth, and there was a strange, alien stink about him, like hot metal and decaying plants.

She began to cry. Shoulders quivering, unable to hold up a moment longer, Rachel the Dragon slid down the wall into a crouch.

"Blessed Elysia, Mother of God," she prayed aloud, "pure vessel that brings forth the Ransomer, take mercy on this sinner." She squeezed her eyes shut and made the Tree sign. "Elysia, raised above all other mortals, Queen of the Sky and Sea, intercede for your supplicant, so that mercy may smile upon this sinner."

To her horror, she could not remember the rest of the words. She huddled, trying to think—oh, her heart, her heart, it was beating so swiftly!—and waited for the thing to take her, to touch her with its foul hands. But when long moments had passed and nothing had happened, her curiosity overcame even her fear. She opened her eyes.

Hengfisk still stood before her, but the grin was gone. The monk was leaning against the wall, tugging at his garments as though surprised to find himself wearing them. He looked up at her. Something had changed. There was a new sort of life in the man—cloudy, muddled, but somehow more human than what had stood before her moments earlier.

Hengfisk looked down at the pool of burning oil, at the blue flames licking at his feet, then leaped back, startled. The flames flickered. The monk's lips moved, but at first nothing came out.

". . . *Vad es*. . .?" he said at last. ". . . *Uf nammen Hott, vad es . . . ?*"

He continued to stare at Rachel as if bewildered, but now something else was working behind his eyes. A tightness came to his features, like an invisible hand clutching the back of his tonsured head. The lips pulled taut, the eyes emptied. Rachel gave a little squeak of alarm. There was something going on that she could not understand, some struggle inside the pop-eyed man. She could only stare, terrified.

Hengfisk shook his head like a dog emerging from the water, looked at Rachel once more, then all around the stairwell on either side. The expression on his face had changed again: he looked like a man trapped beneath a crushing weight. A moment later, without warning, Hengfisk turned and stumbled up the stairs. She heard his uneven footfalls winding away into darkness.

Rachel lurched to the tapestry and pulled it aside with clumsy, shaking fingers. When she had fumbled open the door, she fell through and pushed it closed behind her. She shot the bolt before throwing herself onto her mattress and pulling her blanket all the way over her head, then lay trembling as though she had a fever.

The song that had tempted him up from the safer depths was growing more faint. Guthwulf cursed weakly. He was too late. Elias was going, taking the gray sword back up to his throne room, back to that dusty, bloodless tomb of malachite statues and dragon's bones. Where the sword's music had been there was now only emptiness, a gnawing hollow in his being.

Hopelessly, he chose the next corridor that seemed to slope downward, retreating from the surface like a worm unearthed by a shovel. There was a hole in him, a hole through which the wind would blow and the dust sift. He was empty.

As the air became more breathable and the stones grew cool beneath his touch, the little cat found him again. He could feel its buzzing purr as it wound itself around his feet, but he did not stop to give it comfort: at that moment, there was nothing in him to give. The sword had sung to him, then it had gone away once more. Soon the idiot voices would return, the ghost-voices, meaningless, meaningless. . . .

Feeling his way, slow as Time's great wheel, Guthwulf trudged back down into the depths.

15

Lake of Glass

✦

The noise of their coming was like a great wind, a roaring of bulls,
a wildfire sweeping through dry lands. Although they ran on roads unused for
centuries, the horses did not hesitate, but sped along the secret paths that twined
through forest and dale and fen. The old ways, untraveled for scores of mortal
generations, were on this day opened again, as though Time's wheel had been
stopped in its rut and turned back on itself.

The Sithi had ridden out of summer into a country shackled by winter, but
as they passed through the great forest and across the places of their ancient
sovereignty—hilly Maa'sha, cedar-mantled Peja'ura, Shisae'ron with her
streams, and the black earth of Hekhasór—the land seemed to move restlessly
beneath the tread of their hooves, as though struggling to awaken from a cold
dream. Birds flew startled from their winter nests and hung in the air like bum-
blebees as the Sithi thundered past; squirrels clung, transfixed, on frozen
boughs. Deep in their dens in the earth, the sleeping bears groaned with hungry anticipation. Even the light seemed to change in the wake of the bright
company, as beams of sunlight came needling down through the shrouded sky
to sparkle on the snows.

But winter's grip was strong: when the Sithi had passed by, its fist soon closed
on the forest once more, dragging everything back down into chill silence.

The company did not stop to rest even as the red glow of sunset drained
from the sky and stars glistened between the tree branches overhead. Nor did
the horses need more than starlight to find their way along the old roads,
though all those tracks were covered with the growth of years. Mortal and
earthly the horses were, made only of flesh and blood, but their sires had been
of the stock of Venyha Do'sae, brought out of the Garden in the great flight.
When the native horses of Osten Ard still ran untamed and frightened on the
grasslands, ignorant of hand or bridle, the forebears of these Sithi steeds had
ridden to war against the giants, or carried messengers along the roads that
spanned from one end to the other of the bright empire. They had borne their
riders as swiftly as a sea breeze, and so smoothly that Benayha of Kementari was
said to have painted meticulous poems while in the saddle, with never a smeared

character. The mastery of these roads was bred into them, a knowledge carried in their wild blood—but their endurance seemed almost a kind of magic. On this endless day, when the Sithi rode once more, their steeds seemed to grow stronger as the hours wore by. As the company sped onward and the sun began to warm beyond the eastern horizon, the tireless horses still ran like a surging wave rushing toward the forest's edge.

If the horses carried ancient blood, their riders were the history of Osten Ard in living flesh. Even the youngest, born since the exile from Asu'a, had seen centuries pass. The eldest could remember many-towered Tumet'ai in its springtime, and the glades of fire-bright poppies, miles of blazing color, that had surrounded Jhiná-T'seneí before the sea swallowed her.

Long the Peaceful Ones had hidden from the eyes of the world, nursing their sadnesses, living only in the memories of other days. Today they rode in armor as brilliant as the plumage of birds, their spears shining like frozen lightning. They sang, for the Sithi had always sung. They rode, and the old ways unfolded before them, forest glades echoing to their horses' hoofbeats for the first time since the tallest trees had been seedlings. After a sleep of centuries, a giant had awakened.

The Sithi were riding.

Although he had been battered and bruised to exhaustion during the day's fighting, and had then spent over an hour after sunset helping Freosel and others to hunt loose arrows in the icy mud—a chore that would have been hard in daytime and was cruelly difficult by torchlight—Simon still did not sleep well. He awoke after midnight with his muscles aching and his mind running in circles. The camp was quiet. Wind had swept the skies clean, and the stars glittered like knife-points.

When it became obvious that sleep was indeed lost, at least for a while, he got up and made his way to the watchfires that burned on the hillside above the great barricades. The largest blazed beside one of the weathered Sithi monument stones, and there he found Binabik and a few others—Geloë, Father Strangyeard, Sludig, and Deornoth—sitting with the prince, talking quietly. Josua was drinking soup from a steaming bowl. Simon guessed that it was the first nourishment the prince had taken that day.

The prince looked up as Simon stepped into the circle of light. "Welcome, young knight," he said. "We are all proud of you. You fulfilled my trust today, as I knew you would."

Simon inclined his head, unsure of what to say. He was glad of the praise, but troubled by the things he had seen and done on the ice. He did not feel very noble. "Thank you, Prince Josua."

He sat huddled in his cloak and listened as the others discussed the day's battle. He sensed that they were talking around the central point, but he also guessed that everyone at the fire knew it as well as he did: they could not win a battle of attrition with Fengbald. They were too badly outnumbered. Sesuad'ra was not a castle to be defended against a long siege—there were too many places where an invading army could gain a foothold. If they could not stop the earl's forces upon the frozen lake, there was little else to do but sell their lives as dearly as they could.

As Deornoth, his head bandaged with a strip of cloth, told of the fighting tendencies he had seen in the Thrithings mercenaries, Freosel strode up to the fire. The constable was still wearing his battle-stained gear, his hands and wide face dirt-smeared; despite the freezing temperatures, his forehead was dotted with sweat, as though he had run all the way down the hill-trail from New Gadrinsett.

"I come from the settlement, Prince Josua," Freosel panted. "Helfgrim, Gadrinsett's mayor, is gone."

Josua looked at Deornoth for a moment, then at Geloë. "Did anyone see him go?"

"He was with others, watching the fighting. No one saw what happened to him."

The prince frowned. "I do not like that. I hope no harm has befallen him." He sighed and put down his bowl, then stood up slowly. "I suppose we must see what we can find out. There will be scant chance in the morning."

Sludig, who had come up behind Freosel, said: "Your pardon, Prince Josua, but there is no need to bother yourself with it. Let others do this so you can rest."

Josua smiled thinly. "Thank you, Sludig, but I have other tasks up at the settlement as well, so it is no great effort. Deornoth, Geloë, perhaps you would accompany me. You, too, Freosel. There are things I would finish discussing with you." He pushed absently at one of the fire logs with the toe of his boot, then drew his cloak about him and moved to the path. Those he had summoned followed, but Freosel turned back for a moment and came and put his hand on Simon's shoulder.

"Sir Seoman, I spoke quick the other day, without thinking."

Simon was confused, and more than a little embarrassed to hear his title in the mouth of this powerful and competent young man. "I don't know what you mean."

"About the fairy-folk." The Falshireman fixed him with a serious look. "You may think I made fun, or showed disrespect. See now, I fear the Peaceful Ones like any God-fearing Aedonite man, but I know they can be powerful friends, for all that. If summon 'em you can, go to it. We need any help we can get."

Simon shook his head. "I have no power over them, Freosel—none at all. You don't know what they're like."

"Nor do I, that's true. But if they be your friends, tell 'em we be in hard straits. That's all I have to say." He turned and went up the path, hurrying to catch the prince and the others.

Sludig, who had remained, made a face. "Summon the Sithi. Hah! It would be easier to summon the wind."

Simon nodded in sad agreement. "But we do need help, Sludig."

"You are too trusting, lad. We mean little to the Sithi-folk. I doubt we will see Jiriki again." The Rimmersman frowned at Simon's expression. "Besides, we have our swords and our brains and our hearts." He hunkered down before the flames and warmed his hands. "God gives a man what he deserves, no more, no less." A moment later he straightened up, restless. "If the prince has no need of me, I will go and find a place to sleep. Tomorrow will be bloodier work than today." He nodded at Simon and Binabik and Strangyeard, then walked down toward the barricade, the chain on his sword belt clinking faintly.

Simon sat watching him go, wondering if Sludig was right about the Sithi, dismayed because of the feeling of loss that idea brought.

"The Rimmersman is angry." The archivist sounded surprised by his own words. "I mean, that is, I scarcely know him . . ."

"It is my thinking you speak the truth, Strangyeard." Binabik looked down at the piece of wood he had been carving. "Some folk there are who are not liking much to be beneath others, especially when it was once being otherwise. Sludig has become again a foot-soldier, after being chosen for questing and bringing back a great prize." The troll's words were thoughtful, but his face was unhappy, as though he shared the Rimmersman's pain. "I am afraid for him to be fighting in battle with that feeling in his heart—we have shared a friendship since our travels in the north, but he has seemed dark and sad-hearted to me since coming here."

A silence fell on the little gathering, broken only by the crackle of the flames.

"What about what he said?" Simon asked abruptly. "Is he right?"

Binabik looked at him inquiringly. "What are you meaning, Simon? About the Sithi?"

"No. 'God gives a man what he deserves, no more, no less,' that's what Sludig said." Simon turned to Strangyeard. "Is that true?"

The archivist, flustered, looked away; after a moment, though, he turned back and met Simon's gaze. "No, Simon. I don't think that is true. But I cannot know the mind of God, either."

"Because my friends Morgenes and Haestan certainly didn't get what they deserved—one burned and one crushed by a giant's club." Simon could not keep the bitterness from his voice.

Binabik opened his mouth as though he would say something, but seeing Strangyeard had done the same, the troll stayed silent.

"I believe that God has plans, Simon." The archivist spoke carefully. "And it may be that we simply do not understand them . . . or it may be that God Himself does not quite know how His plans will work out."

"But you priests are always saying that God knows everything!"

"He may have chosen to forget some of the more painful things," Strang- yeard said gently. "If you lived forever, and experienced every pain in the world as though it were your own—died with every soldier, cried with every widow and orphan, shared every mother's grief at the passing of a beloved child— would you not perhaps yearn to forget, too?"

Simon looked into the shifting flames of the fire. *Like the Sithi*, he thought, *trapped with their pain forever.* Craving an ending, as Amerasu had said.

Binabik carved a few more chips from the piece of wood. It was beginning to take a shape that might be a wolf's head, prick-eared and long of muzzle. "If I am allowed the asking, friend Simon, is there a reason that Sludig's saying struck you with such strongness?"

Simon shook his head. "I just don't know how to . . . to be. These men have come to kill us—I want them all to die, painfully, horribly. . . . But Binabik, these are the Erkynguard! I knew them at the castle. Some of them used to give me sweets, or lift me up on their horses and tell me I reminded them of their own sons." He fidgeted with a stick, scuffing at the muddy soil. "Which is right? How could they do these things to us, who never did them any harm? But the king is making them, so why should they be killed, any more than us?"

Binabik's lips curled in a tiny smile. "I notice you are not having worries about the mercenaries—no, say nothing, there is no need! It is hard to feel sorry for those who are searching out war for gold." He slipped the half-finished carving into his jacket and began to reassemble his walking-stick, socketing the knife back into the long handle. "The questions you are asking are important ones, but they are also questions without answers. This is what being a man or woman means, I am thinking, instead of a boy or girl child: you must be finding your own solution to questions that are having no true answers." He turned to Strangyeard. "Do you have Morgenes' book somewhere that is near, or is it now up in the settlement?"

The archivist had been staring into the flames, lost in thought. "What?" he said, suddenly rousing. "The book, you say? Oh, heavenly pastures, I carry it with me everywhere! How could I trust it left in some place unwatched?" He turned abruptly and looked shyly at Simon. "Of course, it is not mine—please do not think I have forgotten your kindness, Simon, in letting me read it. You cannot imagine how wonderful it has been, having Morgenes' words to savor!"

Simon felt an almost pleasurable twinge of regret at the memory of Morgenes. How he missed that good old man! "It is not mine, either, Father Strangyeard. He merely gave it to me for safekeeping so that eventually people like you and Binabik would be able to read it." He smiled gloomily. "I think that is what I am learning these days—that nothing is really mine. I thought for a time that Thorn was meant for me, but I doubt it now. I have been given other things, but none of them quite do what they are supposed to. I'm glad someone is getting good use of Morgenes' words."

"We all are getting such use." Binabik smiled back, but his tone was serious. "Morgenes planned for us all in this dark time."

"Just a moment." Strangyeard scrambled to his feet. He returned a moment later with his sack, inadvertently spilling its contents—a Book of the Aedon, a scarf, a water skin, a few small coins and gewgaws—in his effort to get to the manuscript lodged firmly at the bottom. "Here it is," he said in triumph, then paused. "Why was I looking for it?"

"Because I was asking if you had it," Binabik explained. "There is a passage I think Simon would find of great interestingness."

The troll took the proffered manuscript and leafed through it with delicate care, frowning as he tried to read by the uncertain light of the campfire. It did not seem that it would be a very swift process, so Simon got up to empty his bladder. The wind was chilly along the hillside, and the white lake below, which he glimpsed through a break in the trees, looked like a place for phantoms. When he got back to the fire he was shivering.

"Here, I have found it." Binabik waved the page. "Would you prefer reading for yourself, or should I go to reading it for you?"

Simon smirked at the troll's solicitousness. "You love to read things at me. Go ahead."

"It is in the interest of your continuing education, only," Binabik said mock-severely. "Listen: *'In fact,'* Morgenes writes,

'the debate as to who was the greatest knight in Aedondom was for many years a source of argument everywhere, in both the corridors of the Sancellan Aedonitis in Nabban and the taverns of Erkynland and Hernystir. It would be difficult to claim that Camaris was the inferior of any man, but he seemed to take so little joy in combat that for him warfare might have been a penance, his own great skills a form of punishment. Often, when honor compelled him to fight in tournaments, he would hide the kingfisher-crest of his house beneath a disguise, thus to prevent his foes from being overmatched simply by awe. He was also known to give himself incredible handicaps, such as fighting with his left hand only, not out of bravado, but out of what I myself guess was a dreadful desire to have someone, somewhere, finally best him, thus removing from his shoulders the burden of being Osten Ard's preeminent knight—and hence a target for every drunken brawler as well as the inspiration of every balladeer. When fighting in war, even the priests of Mother Church agreed, his admirable humility and mercy to a beaten foe seemed almost to stretch too far, as though he longed for honorable defeat, for death. His feats of arms, which were talked about across the length and breadth of Osten Ard, were to Camaris acts almost shameful.

'Once Tallistro of Perdruin had been killed by ambush in the first Thrithings War— a treachery made famous in almost as many songs as tell of Camaris' exploits—it was only John himself who could ever be considered a rival to Camaris for the title of Aedondom's greatest warrior. Indeed, none would have suggested that even Prester John, as mighty as he was, could have defeated Sir Camaris in an open fight: after Nearulagh, the battle in which they met, Camaris was careful never even to spar with John again, for fear of upsetting the delicate balance of their friendship. But where Camaris' skills were to him an onerous burden, and the prosecution of war—even those wars that Mother Church sanctioned and, some might say, occasionally encouraged—was for Nabban's greatest knight a trial and a source of grief, Prester John was a man who never seemed happier than on the battlefield. He was not cruel—no defeated foe was ever shown less than fairness by him, except for the Sithi, against whom John held some private but powerful ill-feelings, and whom he persecuted until they have all but vanished from the sight of mortal men. But since some would argue that the Sithi are not men, and therefore

do not have souls—although I myself would not so argue—it could then be said that all John's enemies were treated in a way that even the most scrupulous churchman would have to call just and merciful. And to his subjects, even the pagan Hernystiri, John was a generous king. It was only in those times when the carpet of war was spread before him that he became a dangerous weapon. Thus it was that Mother Church, in whose name he conquered, named him—in gratitude and perhaps a bit of quiet fear—the Sword of the Lord.

'So the argument raged, and does to this day: who was the greater? Camaris, the most skillful man to lift a sword in human memory? Or John, only slightly less proficient, but a leader of men, and himself a man who welcomed a just and godly war . . . ?'"

Binabik cleared his throat. "And, as he is telling that the argument went on, so Morgenes himself is going on for several pages more, talking in greater depth of this question, which was of great importantness in its day—or was anyway *thought* to be of such importantness."

"So Camaris killed better but liked it less than King John did?" Simon asked. "Why did he do it, then? Why not become a monk, or a hermit?"

"Ah, that is being the nub of what you were earlier wondering, Simon," Binabik said, his dark eyes intent. "That is why the writing of great thinkers is being such a help to the rest of us in our own thinking. Here Morgenes has put the words and names in a different way, but it is the same questioning as yours: is it right to be killing, even if it is what your master or country or church wishes? Is it better to kill but not to enjoy it, or to not kill at all, and then perhaps be seeing bad things happen to those who you are loving?"

"Does Morgenes give an answer?"

"No." Binabik shook his head. "As I said, the wise know that these questions have no true answers. Life is made from these wonderings, and from the answers that we each and every one are finding for ourselves."

"Just for once, Binabik, I want you to tell me there *is* an answer for something. I'm tired of thinking so much."

The troll laughed. "The punishment for being born . . . no, perhaps that is too much to be calling that. The punishment for being truly alive—that is fair to say. Welcome, Simon, to the world of those who are every day condemned to thinking and wondering and never ever knowing with certainness."

Simon snorted. "Thank you."

"Yes, Simon." There was strange, somber earnestness in Strangyeard's voice. "Welcome. I pray that someday you will be glad that your decisions were not simple ones."

"How could that be?"

Strangyeard shook his head. "Forgive me for saying the kind of things that old men say, Simon, but . . . you will see."

Simon stood up. "Very well. Now that you have made my head spin, I will do as Sludig did: go away in disgust and try to sleep." He put his hand on Binabik's shoulder, then turned to the archivist, who was reverently placing

Morgenes' book back in his bag. "Good night, Father Strangyeard. Be well. Good night, Binabik."

"Good night, friend Simon."

He heard the troll and the priest talking quietly as he walked back to his sleeping spot. It made him feel a little safer, for some reason, to know that such folk were awake.

In the last moments before dawn, Deornoth had run out of tasks. His sword had been sharpened, then sharpened again. He had reattached several buckles that had been torn from his byrnie, which had required hard, finger-cramping work with a tack-needle, and then laboriously cleaned the mud from his boots. Now he would either have to remain barefoot but for the rags that wrapped his feet—a cold, cold condition—until it was time to move out onto the ice, or put his boots back on and stay where he was. A single step across the muddy ruin that was the encampment would certainly undo his careful work. The footing was going to be bad enough without slick mud on his boot soles to make it worse.

As the sky began to pale, Deornoth listened to some of his men singing quietly. He had never fought beside any of them before yesterday. They were a tattish army, no doubt: many of them had never wielded a sword before, and of those who had, more than a few were so old that back in their shareholdings they had not come to the seasonal muster for years. But fighting in defense of home could turn even the mildest farmer into an enemy to be reckoned with, and this bare stone was home now to many. Deornoth's men, under the leadership of those few of their number who had actually served under arms, had acquitted themselves bravely—very bravely indeed. He only wished he had something better to offer them in the way of reward than this coming day's slaughter.

He heard the sucking noise of horses' hooves in mud; the quiet murmur of the men around him died away. He turned to see a small group of riders winding their way down the trail that ran through the camp. Foremost among them was a tall, slender figure mounted on a chestnut stallion, his cloak rippling in the strong wind. Josua was ready at last. Deornoth sighed and stood up, waving for the rest of his troops as he grabbed his boots. The time for woolgathering was past. Still unshod, still postponing that inevitable moment, he went to join his prince.

At first there were few surprises in the second day's fighting. It was bloody work, as Sludig had prophesied, breast to breast, blade against blade; by mid-morning the ice was washed in red and ravens were feasting on the outskirts of combat.

Those who survived this battle would call it by many names: to Josua and his closest company, it was the Siege of Sesuad'ra. For the captains of Fengbald's Erkynlandish troops, it was Stefflod Valley; to the mercenary Thrithings-men, the Battle of the Stone. But for most who remembered it, and few did without a shudder, the name that was most evocative was the Lake of Glass.

War surged back and forth across Sesuad'ra's icy moat all morning long as first one side and then the other gained a momentary advantage. At first the Erkynguard, embarrassed by their showing the day before, pressed the attack so strongly that the Stone's defenders were driven back against their own barricades. They might have been cut down then, overwhelmed by superior numbers, but Josua rode forth on fiery Vinyafod, leading a small mounted group of Hotvig's Thrithings-men, and caused enough dismay in the flanks of the king's soldiers that they could not push their advantage to its fullest extent. The arrows that Freosel and the other defenders had scavenged flew down from the hillside, and the green-liveried Erkynguard were forced to draw back out of range, waiting until the missiles were spent. Red-cloaked Duke Fengbald rode back and forth in a clear section of ice at mid-lake, waving his sword and gesticulating.

His troops attacked again, but this time the defenders were ready and the wave of mounted Erkynguard broke against the great log walls. A sallying force from the hillside then pierced the green line and stabbed deep into the middle of Fengbald's forces. They were not strong enough to split the duke's army, or the battle might have gone very differently, but even when they were thrown back with heavy losses, it was clear that Deornoth's farmer-soldiers had found a renewed determination. They knew they could fight on this field as near-equals; it was clear that they would not give up their home to the king's swords without exacting a bloody price.

The sun reached the tips of the treeline, morning light just spilling onto the far side of the valley. The ice was again thick with mist. Down in the murk, the fighting grew desperate as men struggled not just with each other but with the treacherous battlefield as well. Both sides seemed determined that things would be finished by nightfall, the issue settled forever. From the number of unmoving shapes that already lay sprawled across the frozen lake, there seemed little doubt that by afternoon, there would be few of Sesuad'ra's defenders left to contest the matter.

Within the first hour after dawn, Simon had forgotten about Camaris, about Prester John, even about God. He felt like a boat caught in a terrible storm, but the waves that threatened to drown him had faces and carried sharp blades. There was no attempt today to hold the trolls in reserve. Josua had felt sure that Fengbald would simply throw his men against Sesuad'ra's defenders until they were beaten down, so there was little point in trying to surprise anyone. There was no order of battle, only a skeleton of battlefield command, tattered banners and distant horns. The opposing armies rushed together, hit, and clung to each other like drowning men, then withdrew again to rest before the next surge, leaving the bodies of the fallen splayed across the misty lake.

As the Erkynguard's assault pressed the defenders back against the barricades, Simon saw the troll-herder Snenneq skewered by an Erkynguardsman's lance, lifted completely out of his ram-saddle and pinned against one of the barricade tree trunks. Although the troll was undoubtedly dead or dying, the armored guardsman jerked his weapon free and pierced the small body again as it slid down the wall, twisting the lance as though killing an insect. Simon, maddened, spurred Homefinder through a gap in the crush of men and brought his sword around with all the strength he could muster, nearly beheading the guardsman, who crashed off his horse and fell to the frozen lake, fountaining blood. Simon bent and caught at Snenneq's hide jacket, pulling him up from the ground with one hand without even feeling the weight. The troll's head bobbed; his brown eyes stared sightlessly. Simon cradled the small, stocky form against his own body, heedless of the blood that soaked his breeches and saddle.

Sometime later he found himself on the edge of the battle. Snenneq's body was gone. Simon did not know if he had put it down or dropped it; he did not remember anything but the dead troll's astonished, frightened face. There had been blood on the little man's lips and between his teeth.

It was easy to hate if he did not think, Simon discovered. If he saw the faces of enemies only as pale smears within their helmets, if he saw their open mouths as horrid black holes, it was easy to ride at them and smash them with all his strength, to try to separate the knobby heads and flailing limbs from the bodies until the hated things were dead. He also found that if he was not afraid of dying—and at this moment he was not: he felt as though all his fear had been charred away—it was easy to survive. The men against whom he rode, even though they were trained fighting men, many of them veterans of several battles, seemed frightened by Simon's single-minded assaults. He swung and swung, each blow as hard or harder than the last. When they lifted their own weapons, he swung at their arms and hands. If they fell back to try to lure him off-balance, he rode Homefinder full into their sides and battered away as Ruben the Bear had once pounded red-hot metal in the Hayholt's stables. Sooner or later, Simon discovered, the look of fear would creep into their eyes, the whites flashing in the depths of their helmets. Sooner or later they would shy back, but Simon would hammer on, slashing and hewing, until they fled or fell. Then he would suck air deep into his lungs, hearing little but the impossibly fast drumbeat of his own heart, until anger rebirthed his strength and he went riding on in search of something else to hack.

Blood spurted, hovering for long moments like a red mist. Horses fell, legs kicking convulsively. The noise of battle was so loud as to be virtually unbearable. As he pushed through the carnage, Simon felt his arms turn to iron—rigid, hard as the blade he held in his hand; he had no horse, but rather four strong legs that took him where he wished to go. He was spattered in red, some of it his own, but he felt nothing but fire inside his chest and a spastic need to beat down the things that had come to steal his new home and slaughter his friends.

Simon did not know it, but beneath his helm, his face was wet with tears.

★   ★   ★

A curtain seemed to draw away at last, letting light into the dark room of Simon's bestial thoughts. He was somewhere near the middle of the lake and someone was calling his name.

"Simon!" It was a high voice, yet strange. For a moment he was not quite sure where he was. "Simon!" the voice called again.

He looked down, searching for the one who had spoken, but the foot-soldier who lay crumpled there would never call to anyone again. Simon's horrifying numbness melted a little further. The corpse belonged to one of Fengbald's soldiers. Simon turned away, unwilling to look at the man's slack face.

"Simon, come!" It was Sisqi, followed by two of her troll-kin, riding toward him. Even as he brought Homefinder around to face the new arrivals, he could not help looking at the yellow slot-eyes of their saddle-rams. What were they thinking? What could animals think of such a thing as this?

"Sisqi." He blinked. "What . . . ?"

"Come, come fast!" She gestured with her spear toward a place closer to the barricades. The battle was still swirling, and although Simon stared hard, he knew it would take someone like old Jarnauga to make any sense out of such chaos.

"What is it?"

"Help your friend! Your *Croohok!* Come!"

Simon kicked his heels against Homefinder's ribs and followed the trolls as they neatly wheeled their rams about. Homefinder lurched as she struggled across the slippery lake surface after them. Simon could tell that the horse was tired, dreadfully tired. Poor Homefinder! He should stop and give her water . . . let her sleep . . . sleep . . . Simon's own head was pounding, and his right arm felt as though it had been beaten with clubs.

Aedon's mercy, what have I done? What have I done today?

The trolls led him back into the knot of battle. The men he saw around him were exhausted almost to heedlessness, like South Islander slaves sent to fight in the old Nabbanai arenas. Foes seemed to hold each other up as they struck, and the clang of weaponry had a dolorous, off-key sound, like a hundred cracked bells pealing.

Sludig and a knot of defenders were surrounded by Thrithings mercenaries. The Rimmersman had an ax in each hand. He had been unhorsed, but even as he struggled to keep his footing on the ice he held two scarfaced Thrithings-men at bay. Simon and the trolls came on as swiftly as the footing would allow, falling on Sludig's attackers from behind. Although Simon's cramping arm failed to strike a clean blow, his blade struck near the unprotected tail of one of the Thrithings-men's horses, making the creature rear suddenly. Its rider crashed to the ice, where he was quickly savaged by Sludig's companions. The Rimmersman used the skidding, riderless horse as a shield against his other enemy, then was able to get a foot into the stirrup and clamber into the saddle, bringing one of his axes up just in time to ward a blow from the Thrithings-man's curved sword. Their weapons clanked together twice more, then Sludig, roaring wordlessly, hooked the man's blade from his grip with one ax and buried the other in the mercenary's head, smashing down through the stiff leather helmet as though it were an eggshell. He put his boot in the man's chest and wrenched the ax free; the mercenary flopped over his horse's neck, then slid heavily to the ground.

Simon shouted to Sludig, then turned quickly as another surge of the struggle pushed a riderless horse heavily against Homefinder's shoulder, almost jarring him out of his seat. He clutched at the reins, then righted himself and kicked at the panicking creature, which whinnied and scrambled for purchase on the ice before scrambling away.

The Rimmersman stared at Simon for a moment as though he did not recognize him. His yellow beard was spattered with drops of blood, and his chain mail was broken and torn in several places. "Where is Deornoth?"

"I don't know! I just got here!" Simon lifted himself higher in the saddle to look around, clutching Homefinder with his knees.

"He was cut off." Sludig stood in his own stirrups. "There! I see his cloak!" He pointed into a clot of Thrithings-men nearby, in whose midst there was a flash of blue. "Come!" Sludig spurred the mercenary's horse ahead. The beast, fitted with no special iron spikes, slipped and skidded.

Simon called for Sisqi and her friends, who were calmly spearing wounded Thrithings-men. The daughter of the Herder and Huntress barked something to her companions in the Qanuc tongue and they all cantered after Simon and Sludig.

The sky had grown darker overhead as clouds had covered the sun. Now a flurry of tiny snowflakes began to fill the air. The mist seemed to be growing thicker, too. Simon thought he saw a flash of crimson moving in the dark sea of struggling men not far beyond Sludig. Could it be Fengbald? Here, in the middle of things? It seemed impossible the duke would take such a risk when numbers and experience were on his side.

Simon had less than a moment to ponder this unlikely possibility before Sludig had crashed into the clump of Thrithings-men, laying about indiscriminately with his axes. Although two men fell wounded before the Rimmersman, opening his way, Simon saw that others were moving into the gap, several of them still on horseback: Sludig would be surrounded. Simon's sense of unreality became even stronger. What was he doing here? He was no soldier! This was madness. Yet what else could he do? His friends were being hurt and killed. He spurred forward, slashing at the bearded mercenaries. Each blow now leaped up his arm, a pain like a tongue of fire that he felt through his shoulders into the base of his skull. He heard the strange yipping cries of Sisqi and her Qanuc behind him, then suddenly he was through.

Sludig had climbed down off his horse. He was kneeling beside a figure in a cloak the color of an early evening sky. It was Deornoth, and his face was very pale. Beneath Josua's knight, half-covered by his blue cloak, a hugely-muscled Thrithings-man lay on his back, staring sightlessly at the cloudy sky, a crust of blood on his lips. With the sharpened clarity of near-madness, Simon saw a snowflake flutter down to land on the mercenary's opened eye.

"It is the leader of the mercenaries," Sludig shouted over the clamor. "Deornoth has killed him."

"But Deornoth, is he alive?"

Sludig was already struggling to lift the knight from the ice. Simon looked around to see if they were in immediate danger, but the mercenaries had been lured away to some other pocket of the shifting chaos. Simon quickly dismounted and helped Sludig lift Deornoth onto the saddle. The Rimmersman climbed up and clutched at the knight, who sagged like an understuffed doll.

"Bad," Sludig said. "He is bad. We must get him back to the barricades."

He set out at a trot. Sisqi and the other two trolls fell in behind him. The Rimmersman steered his horse in a wide arc, heading for the outer fringe of the killing ground and comparative safety.

Simon could only lean against Homefinder's side, panting, staring at Sludig's back and Deornoth's slack face bouncing beside the Rimmersman's shoulder. Things were as bad as could be imagined. Jiriki and his Sithi were not coming. God had not seen fit to rescue the virtuous. If only this whole nightmarish day could be wished away. Simon shivered. It seemed almost that if he closed his eyes this would all be gone, that he would wake in his bed in the Hayholt's serving quarters, the spring sunlight crawling across the flagstones outside. . . .

He shook his head and struggled into the saddle, legs trembling. He spurred Homefinder forward. No time to let the mind wander. No time.

There was the flash of red again, just to his right. He turned and saw a figure in crimson, sitting on a white horse. The mounted man's helm was furnished with silver wings.

Fengbald!

Slowly, as though the ice had turned to sticky honey beneath his horses' hooves, Simon reined up and turned toward the armored man. Surely this was a dream! The duke was behind a small knot of Erkynguardsmen, but his attention seemed fixed on the fighting just before him. Simon, at the outer edge of the battle, had a clear path. He spurred Homefinder forward.

As he moved closer, picking up speed, the silver helmet seemed to grow before him, dazzling even in the murky light. The crimson cloak and bright chain mail were like a wound on the dim darkness of the far-away trees.

Simon shouted, but the figure did not turn. He kicked his boot-irons against Homefinder's side. She made a huffing noise and increased her pace; foam flew from her lips. "Fengbald!" Simon screamed again, and this time the duke seemed to hear. The closed helm swiveled toward Simon, the eye-slit blankly inscrutable. The duke lifted his sword with one hand and tugged at his reins to bring his horse around to face this attacker. Fengbald seemed slow, as if underwater, as though he, too, found himself in some terrible dream.

Beneath his own helm, Simon's lips skinned back from his teeth. A nightmare, then. He would be Fengbald's nightmare, this time. He swung his own sword back, feeling the muscles in his shoulders jump and strain. As Homefinder swept down on the duke, Simon brought his sword around with both hands. It met the duke's blade with a shivering impact that nearly pushed Simon backward out of the saddle, but something yielded at the blow. When he was past, and had straightened himself in the saddle, he turned Homefinder around in a careful half-circle. Fengbald had fallen from his horse and his sword had been knocked from his hand. The duke lay on his back, struggling to rise.

Simon vaulted from the saddle and promptly slipped, falling forward to land painfully on elbows and knees. He crawled to where the duke still fought for balance, then rose on his knees and brought the flat of his sword against the shining helm as hard as he could. The duke fell back, arms spread wide like the wings of the silver eagle on his surcoat. Simon clambered on top of him and squatted on his chest. He, Simon, had beaten Duke Fengbald! Had they won, then? Panting, he darted a quick look around him, but no one seemed to have seen. Neither was there any sign that the fighting had been resolved—clots of figures still thrashed in the mist all across the lake. Could he have won the battle without anyone noticing?

Simon pulled his Qanuc knife from the sheath and pressed it against Fengbald's throat, then fumbled at the duke's helm. He worked it free at last, tugging it loose with little regard for its owner's comfort. He tossed it aside. It spun on the ice as Simon leaned forward.

His prisoner was a middle-aged man, bald where he was not gray. His bloodied mouth was missing most of its teeth. He was not Fengbald.

"'S Bloody Tree!" Simon swore. The world was collapsing. Nothing was real. He stared at the surcoat, at the falcon-winged helmet lying just inches away. They were Fengbald's, there was no question. But this was not the duke.

"Tricked!" Simon groaned. "Oh, God, we have been tricked like children." There was a cold knot in his stomach. "Mother of Aedon—*where is Fengbald!?*"

♔

Far across Osten Ard to the west, far from the concerns of Sesuad'ra's defenders, a small procession emerged from a hole in the Grianspog mountainside like a troop of white mice released from a cage. As they left the shadowy tunnels they stopped, blinking and squinting in the snow-glare.

The Hernystiri, only a few hundred all told, most of them women, children, and old men, milled in confusion on the rocky shelf outside the cavern. Maegwin sensed that with any prompting at all they would quickly dash back into the safety of the caves once more. The balance was very delicate. It had taken a great effort on Maegwin's part, all her powers of persuasion, to convince her people even to set out on this seemingly doomed journey.

Gods of our forefathers, she thought, *Brynioch and Rhynn, where is our backbone!?* Only Diawen, breathing deeply of the cold air with her arms lifted as if in ritual celebration, seemed to understand the glory of this march. The expression on the lined face of Old Craobhan left no doubt as to what he thought of this foolishness. But the rest of her subjects seemed mostly fearful, looking for some portent, some excuse to turn back again.

They needed prodding, that was all. It was frightening for mortals to live as their deities wished them to—it was a greater responsibility than most wished to bear. Maegwin took a deep breath.

"Great days are before us, people of Hernystir," she cried. "The gods wish us to go down the mountain to face our enemies—the enemies who have stolen our houses, our farms, our cattle and pigs and sheep. Remember who you are! Come with me!"

She strode forward onto the path. Slowly, reluctantly, her followers fell into step behind her, shivering despite being wrapped in the warmest clothing they had been able to find. Many of the children were crying.

"Arnoran," she called. The harper, who had been walking a little distance behind—perhaps hoping that he could fall far enough back that his presence would not be missed—came forward, leaning against the force of the wind.

"Yes, my lady?"

"Walk beside me," she directed. Arnoran took a look down at the mountain's sheer, snowy face just beyond the narrow path, then quickly looked away again. "I want you to play a song," Maegwin said.

"What song, Princess?"

"Something that everyone knows the words to. Something that lifts the heart." She pondered as she walked. Arnoran looked nervously down at his feet. "Play 'The Lily of the Cuihmne.'"

"Yes, my lady." Arnoran lifted his harp and began to pick out the opening strains, working it through a few times to let his chilled fingers warm. Then he began in earnest, playing loudly so that those behind could easily hear.

"The Hernysadharc rose is fair."

he sang, lifting his voice above the wind that prowled the mountainside and stirred the trees,

"As red as blood, as white as snow,
But still unplucked I'll leave it there
For I have somewhere else to go."

One by one at first, then in bunches, others of Maegwin's band began to pick up the verses of the familiar song.

"At Inniscrich the violets grow
As dark as skies of early night,
But I'll not have them, even so
For I prefer my beauties bright.

"Near Abaingeat the daisies bloom
Like stars a-twinkle in the sky,
But I will leave them in the coomb
I cannot stop; I must pass by.

"The sweetest flower of all, she grows
Where river past sweet meadow flows,
And where she blossoms I will go:
The Lily of the Cuihmne.

"When someday winter's winds shall blow
When leaves are withered, sap is slow,
I will recall this love, I know:
The Lily of the Cuihmne . . ."

By the refrain, scores of people had joined in. The pace of the marching feet seemed to increase, to match itself to the rhythm of the old song. The voices of Maegwin's people rose until they outshouted the wind—and strangely, the wind grew weaker, as if acknowledging defeat.

The remnants of Hernysadharc marched down from their mountain retreat, singing.

They stopped on a shelf of snow-swept rock, and ate their midday meal beneath the dim and straining sun. Maegwin walked among her people, paying special attention to the children. She felt happy and fulfilled for the first time in long memory: Lluth's daughter was finally doing what she was meant to do. Satisfied at last, she felt her love for the people of Hernystir come bubbling up—and her people felt it, too. Some of the older folk might still have misgivings about this mad undertaking, but to the children it was a wonderful lark; they followed Maegwin through the camp, laughing and shouting, until even the worried parents were able to forget for a while the danger into which they were traveling, to put aside their doubts. After all, how could the princess be so full of light and truth if the gods were not with her?

As for Maegwin, virtually all her own doubts had been left on Bradach Tor. She had the entire company singing again and on their way before the noon hour had passed.

When they reached the bottom of the mountain at last, her people seemed to gain hope. For all but a few of them, this was the first time they had touched the meadows of Hernystir since the Rimmersgard troops had driven them into the high places half a year before. They were returning home.

The first of Skali's pickets came forward in a rush as they saw a small army descending from the Grianspog, but reined up in surprise, the hooves of their horses digging up great gouts of powdery snow, when they saw that the army bore no weapons—in fact, carried nothing at all in their arms but swaddled infants. The Rimmersmen, hardened warriors every one, undaunted by the confusion and horror of battle, stared in consternation at Maegwin and her troop.

"Stop!" the leader cried. He was all but hidden in his helmet and fur-lined cloak, and for a moment seemed a startled badger blinking in the door of its sett. "Going where are you?"

Maegwin made a haughty face at his poor command of the Westerling tongue. "We are going to your master, Skali of Kaldskryke."

The soldiers looked, if possible, even more bewildered. "So many to surrender are not needed," the leader said. "Tell the women and children for waiting here. Men with us will come."

Maegwin scowled. "Fool. We do not come to surrender. We come to take our land back." She waved. Her followers, who had stopped while she spoke to the soldiers, surged forward once more.

The Rimmersmen fell in beside them like dogs trying to herd a flock of unimpressed and hostile sheep.

As they made their way across the snowy meadowlands between the foothills and Hernysadharc, Maegwin felt anger growing within her once more, anger that for a while had been overwhelmed by the glory of positive action. Here stand after stand of ancient trees, oak and beech and alder, had been leveled by Rimmersgard axes, their carcasses stripped of bark and dragged away across the rutted ground. Skali's soldiers and their horses had churned the earth around their camps to frozen mud, and the ashes of their countless fires blew across the gray snow. The very face of the land was wounded and suffering—no wonder the gods were unhappy! Maegwin looked around and saw her own fury mirrored in the faces of her followers, their few lingering doubts now vanishing like water drops on a hot stone. The gods would make this place clean again, with their help. How could anyone doubt that it would be so?

At last, as the afternoon sun hung swollen in the gray sky, they reached the outskirts of Hernysadharc itself. They were now part of a much larger crowd: during the slow approach of Maegwin's folk, many of the Rimmersmen had drifted in from the encampments to watch this odd spectacle, until it seemed that the whole occupying army trailed along after them. The combined company, nearing perhaps a thousand souls, made its way through the narrow, spiraling streets of Hernysadharc toward the king's house, the Taig.

When they reached the great cleared place atop the hillock, Skali of Kaldskryke was waiting for them, standing before the Taig's vast oaken doors. The Rimmersman was dressed in his dark armor as though waiting for a fight, and he carried his raven-helm under his arm. He was surrounded by his household guard, a legion of grim, bearded men.

Many of Maegwin's people now, at this late moment, felt their courage suddenly falter. As Skali's own Rimmersmen kept to a respectful distance, so, too, did many of Maegwin's company slow and begin to hang back. But Maegwin and a few others—Old Craobhan, always the loyal servant, was one of them—strode forward. Maegwin moved without fear or hesitation toward the man who had conquered and brutally subjugated her country.

"Who are you, woman?" Skali demanded. His voice was surprisingly soft, with a suggestion of a stutter. Maegwin had only heard him once before—Skali had shouted up at the Hernystiri's hiding place on the mountain side, trumpeting the gift of her brother Gwythinn's mutilated body—but that one horrid time was enough: shouting or whispering, Maegwin knew that voice and loathed it. The nose that had given Skali his nickname stood out starkly from a broad, wind-burned face. His eyes were intent and clever. She did not see a hint of any sort of kindness in their depths, but she had not expected to.

Face-to-face at last with the destroyer of her family, she was pleased by her own icy calm. "I am Maegwin," she proclaimed. "Daughter of Lluth-ubh-Llythinn, the king of Hernystir."

"Who is dead," Skali said shortly.

"Whom you killed. I have come to tell you that your time is over. You are to leave this land now, before the gods of Hernystir punish you."

Skali stared at her carefully. His guardsmen were smirking at the ridiculousness of the situation, but Sharp-nose was not. "And if I do not, king's daughter?"

"The gods will decide your fate." She spoke serenely despite the hatred boiling within her. "It will not be a kind one."

Skali looked at her a moment longer, then gestured to some of his guardsmen. "Pen them. If they resist, kill the men first." The guards, laughing openly now, moved to surround Maegwin's people. One of the children began to cry, then more joined in.

As the guards began to lay rough hands on her folk, Maegwin felt her confidence waver. What was happening? When would the gods make things right? She looked around, expecting deadly lightnings to leap from the skies, or the ground to heave and swallow the defilers, but nothing happened. She sought frantically for Diawen. The scryer's eyes were closed in rapt concentration, her lips soundlessly moving.

"No! Do not touch them!" Maegwin cried as the guardsmen prodded with their spears at some of the crying children, trying to round them back into line with the others. "You must quit this land!" she shouted with all the authority she could summon. "It is the will of the gods!"

But the Rimmersmen paid no attention. Maegwin's heart was racing as though it would burst. What was happening? Why had the gods betrayed her? Could this have all been some incomprehensible trick?

"Brynioch!" she cried. "Murhagh One-Arm! Where are you!?"

The skies did not answer.

The light of early dawn was filtering through the treetops, shimmering faintly on the crumbling stones. The company of fifty mounted knights and twice that many foot-soldiers passed yet another ruined wall, a precarious stack of eroded, snow-dusted blocks glazed with brilliant rose and shining lavender which seemed more alive than any mere stones should. They rode by in silence, then began to wind down the hillside toward the icy lake, an expanse of white streaked with blue and gray hanging behind the outermost trees like a painter's catch-cloth.

Helfgrim, the Lord Mayor, craned his head to look back at the ruins, although it was no little strain to do so with his hands tied to the pommel of a saddle.

"So that is it," he said softly. "The fairy city."

"I may need you to lead me to the path," Fengbald snapped, "but that doesn't mean I can't break your arm. I will hear no more about any 'fairy cities.'"

Helfgrim turned, a hint of a smile curling his puckered mouth. "It is a shame to pass so near such a thing and not look, Duke Fengbald."

"Look all you want. Just keep your mouth shut." And he glared at the mounted soldiers, as if daring any of them to share Helfgrim's interest.

When they reached the shore of the frozen lake, Fengbald looked up, smoothing his unbound black hair away from his face. "Ah. The clouds are gathering. Good." He turned to Helfgrim. "It would be best of all to have done this in darkness, but I am not such a fool as to trust an old dotard to find his way by night. Besides, Lezhdraka and the rest should be making enough of a ruckus on the far side of the hill by now to keep Josua nicely occupied."

"I'm sure." Helfgrim gave the duke a wary glance. "My lord, could we at least have my daughters to ride here beside me?"

Fengbald stared at him suspiciously. "Why?"

The old man paused a moment. "It is hard for me to say it, my lord. I trust your word, please don't believe I don't. But I fear that your men—well, if they're out of your sight, Duke Fengbald, they might perform some mischief."

The duke laughed. "Surely you do not fear for the virtue of your daughters, old fellow? Unless I miss my guess, their maiden days are far behind them."

Helfgrim could not conceal a flinch. "Even so, my lord, it would be a kindness to put a father's heart at ease."

Fengbald considered for a moment, then whistled for his page. "Isaak, tell the guardsmen who carry the women to come ride nearer to me. Not that any should complain at being asked to ride beside their liege-lord," he added for the old man's benefit.

Young Isaak, who seemed to wish that he himself had the option of riding anything at all, bowed and went sloshing back up the muddy trail.

A few moments later the guardsmen appeared. Helfgrim's two daughters were not bound, but each one sat in the saddle before an armored man, so that they looked not unlike Hyrka brides—who, it was reputed in the cities, were frequently stolen in midnight raids and unceremoniously carried away, draped across their captor's saddles like sacks of meal.

"Are you well, daughters?" Helfgrim asked. The younger of the two, who had been crying, wiped her eyes with the hem of her cloak and tried to smile bravely.

"We are quite well, Father."

"That is good. No tears, then, my little coney. Be like your sister. There is nothing to fear—you know that Duke Fengbald is a man of his word."

"Yes, Father."

The duke smiled beneficently. *He* knew what sort of man he was, but it was good to see that the common folk knew it, too.

The wind blew harder as the first horses stepped out onto the ice. Fengbald cursed as his mount misstepped and had to splay its legs to stay afoot. "Even had I no other reasons," he hissed, "I would kill Josua just for bringing me to this godforsaken spot."

"Men must run far to elude your long arm, Duke Fengbald," said Helfgrim. "There is no place that far."

Snow came flurrying around the great hill's northern flank, moving almost horizontally in the strong wind. Fengbald squinted and pulled up his hood. "Are we almost there?"

Helfgrim squinted, too, then nodded and pointed to a blot of deeper shadow ahead. "There is the foot of the hill, Lord." He continued to stare into the darting snow.

Fengbald smiled. "You look very glum," he called over the noise of the wind. "Can it be that you still do not trust my word?"

Helfgrim looked down at his bound wrists and pursed his lips before speaking. "No, Duke Fengbald, but surely I must feel some grief that I am betraying folk who were kind to me."

The duke waved his hand at the nearest riders. "To save your daughters—a noble enough reason. Besides, Josua was doomed to lose in any case. You are no more to blame for his fall than the worm that devours the corpse is to blame for Death's reaping." He grinned, pleased with his turn of phrase. "No more to blame than a worm, do you see?"

Helfgrim looked up. His wrinkled skin, speckled by snow, seemed gray. "Perhaps you are right, Duke Fengbald."

The hill now loomed overhead like a finger raised in warning. The company was only a few hundred ells from the edge of the ice when Helfgrim pointed again.

"There is the path, Duke Fengbald."

It was a tiny break in the vegetation, barely visible even from their near vantage point. Still, Fengbald could see enough to be satisfied that Helfgrim told the truth.

"Now, then . . ." the duke said, when suddenly a voice came rolling down from the mountainside.

"Stop, Fengbald! You may not pass!"

The duke pulled up, startled. A small group of shadowy figures had appeared at the lip of the path. One of them raised his hands to cup his mouth. *"Go back,*

Fengbald—go away and leave this place. Ride away back to Erkynland and we will let you live."

The duke turned suddenly and slapped Helfgrim on the side of the head. The old man swayed and almost fell, but his bound wrists held him in the saddle. "Traitor! You said there would be only a few guards!"

Helfgrim's face sagged in fear. Fengbald's mark showed red on his pale cheek. "I did not lie, my lord! Look, they are a few only."

Fengbald waved for his troops to hold their position, then rode a little distance forward, staring. "I see only a handful of you," he shouted up at the men on the path. "How will you stop me?"

The man nearest the edge stepped forward. "We will, Fengbald. We will give our lives and more to stop you."

"Very well." The duke had evidently decided it was a bluff after all. "Then I will let you hurry and give them." He raised his arm to order his troops forward.

"Stop!" the figure called. "I will give you one last chance, damn you! You don't recognize my face I know, but how about my name? I am Freosel, Freobeorn's son."

"What do I care, you madman?" Fengbald shouted. "You are nothing to me!"

"Nor were my wife and children, my father and mother, nor any of the others you murdered!" The stocky figure had stepped out onto the ice with the rest of his companions. They were less than a dozen all told. "You burned half of Falshire, you great whoreson bastard! Now the time has come for you to pay!"

"Enough!" Fengbald turned to wave his men forward. "Up now and clean the madmen out. It is a rat's nest!"

Freosel and his companions bent and lifted what at first seemed like axes, or swords, or some other weapons with which to defend themselves. A moment later, as his men began to guide their slipping mounts past him, Fengbald saw to his astonishment that the hill's defenders were swinging heavy mallets. Freosel brought his own down first, smashing it onto the ice as though in idiot frustration. His companions on either side strode forward and joined him.

"What are they doing!?" Fengbald bellowed. The furthermost of his soldiers were still a hundred ells from the shore. "Have all of Josua's people gone starvation-mad?"

"They are killing you," a calm voice said beside him.

The duke whirled to see Helfgrim, still lashed to the saddle of his horse. His daughters and their guards were close by, the soldiers looking both excited and confused.

"What are you babbling about?" Fengbald snarled, lifting his sword as if to swipe off the old man's head. Before he could move a pace closer, there was a horrible, deafening crack, like the splitting of a giant's bones. A moment later it sounded again. Somewhere at the foremost edge of Fengbald's company there was a sudden roar of men's voices and, even more chillingly, the almost human screaming of terrified horses.

"What is happening?" the duke demanded, straining to see past the crush of mounted men.

"They prepared the ice for you, Fengbald. I helped them plan it. You see, *we* are of Falshire, too." Helfgrim spoke just loudly enough to be heard above the wind. "My brother was its Lord Mayor, as you would have known instantly if you had ever bothered to come there except to steal our bread, our gold, even our young women for your bed. Surely you did not think we would stand by and let you also destroy the few of our people who had escaped your brutality?"

There was another jarring crack, and suddenly, just yards away from the Lord Mayor and the duke, a crevice foamed with black water where there had been ice a moment before. More ice crumbled along the opening and sheared loose; a pair of horsemen toppled in, flailing for an instant until they were sucked down into darkness.

"But you will die, too, damn you!" Fengbald shouted, urging his horse toward the old man.

"Of course I will. It is enough that my daughters and I avenge the others—their souls will welcome us." And then Helfgrim smiled, a cold smile without a scintilla of mirth.

Fengbald suddenly found himself flung sideways as the white surface erupted beneath him, snapping upward like dragon's jaws. A moment later the duke's horse was gone and he was clutching a jagged-edged sheet of ice which rocked precariously. His boots and breeches were already submerged in freezing water. "Help me!" he shrieked.

Eerily, Helfgrim and his daughters were still upright, seated on their frantic horses just cubits away. Their guards were scrambling away across the remaining sheet of unbroken ice, struggling toward the shelter of the standing stone. "Too late," the old man cried. The two women stared down at the duke, eyes wide as they struggled to contain their terror. "Too late for you, Fengbald," Helfgrim repeated. A moment later, with a sudden grinding crunch, the entire section on which the trio and their mounts stood broke and collapsed into the choppy black waters. The Lord Mayor and his daughters vanished like ghosts chased by the dawn-knell.

"Help!" Fengbald screamed. His fingers were slipping. As he slid, the piece of ice to which he clung began to tilt, the far end reaching for the gray sky even as his own end plunged inexorably downward. Fengbald's eyes bulged. "No! I can't die! I *can't!*"

The ragged pane of ice, almost vertical now, overbalanced and abruptly flipped over. The duke's gloved hand snatched briefly at the air, then was gone.

The sun was in Maegwin's eyes. Doubt dug into her heart, sending black rays of pain through all her limbs. Around her, Skali's Rimmersmen were rounding up her people, prodding them at spear-point, herding them as though they were beasts.

"*Gods of our people!*" Her voice tore in her throat. "Save us! *You promised!*"

Skali Sharp-nose approached, laughing, his hands tucked into his belt. "Your gods are dead, girl. Like your father. Like your kingdom. But I may find a use for you yet." Maegwin could smell the stink of him, like the tangy, rotten scent of over-aged venison. "You are plain, *haja,* but your legs are long . . . and I like long legs. Better than being a whore to my men, eh?"

Maegwin stepped back, raising her arms as though to ward a blow. Before she could say anything, the air was ripped by the sound of a distant horn. Skali and some of his men turned, surprised. The horn sounded again, louder now, clear and shrill and powerful. It played a cascade of notes that echoed around the Taig and out over the fields of Hernysadharc. Maegwin stared.

It was only a gleam at first, a rippling shimmer out of the east. The hooves made a rushing sound, like a river after strong rains. Skali's men began to scramble for the helmets they had tossed aside when they had discovered the nature of Maegwin's company of partisans; Skali himself began screaming for his horse.

It was an army, Maegwin realized—no, it was a dream, a dream made flesh and unleashed upon the snowy meadows. They were coming at last!

The horn echoed again. The riders were thundering toward Hernysadharc, impossibly swift. Their armor shone in every color the rainbow had—sky-blue, ruby-crimson, leaf-green, the orange and vermilion of sunset fog. She could hear them singing now as they rode, a high, brilliant keening like a flock of impossibly musical birds. They could have been a hundred riders or ten thousand: Maegwin could not even try to guess, for in the beautiful terror of their coming it was almost impossible to stare at them too long. They streamed with color and noise and light, as though the world had been torn open and the raw stuff of dream allowed to spill through.

Again the horn sounded. Maegwin, suddenly all alone, stumbled toward the Taig, not even conscious at that moment that this was the first time she had touched its wooden walls since Skali had put her people to flight. The Rimmersmen, dismayed, were gathering on the hillside below her father's great hall, milling and shouting as they struggled to make their horses face this incomprehensible enemy. The horns of the oncoming army sounded again.

The gods have come! Maegwin turned in the doorway to watch. The culmination of all her agonies and hope was here at last, burning across the snowy fields to rescue her people. The gods! The gods! She had brought the gods!

There was a clatter from within the Taig. More of Skali's men came streaming forth, pulling on helmets, fumbling with sword belts. One of them pushed into Maegwin and sent her spinning into the path of another, who raised his mailed fist and brought it crashing against her head.

Maegwin's world abruptly vanished.

It was Binabik who found Simon at last, with Sisqi helping him search—or rather it was Qantaqa, whose nose could discern the proper scent even in the madness that surrounded Sesuad'ra. They found him sitting cross-legged on the ice beside a motionless figure wearing Fengbald's armor. Homefinder stood over him, shivering in the terrible wind, her muzzle near Simon's ear. Qantaqa pawed at the young man's leg and made a soft sound as she waited for her master.

"Simon!" Binabik scrambled toward him across the rough surface of the lake. There were bodies scattered all about, but the troll did not stop to look at any of them. "Are you injured?"

Simon lifted his head slowly. His throat was so rough that his voice was barely a whisper. "Binabik? What happened?"

"Are you safe, Simon?" The little man bent to examine his friend, then straightened. "You have many wounds. We must get you back."

"What happened?" Simon asked again. Binabik was pulling at his shoulders, trying to help him stand, but Simon could not seem to gather the strength. Sisqi approached and stood nearby, waiting to see if Binabik would need her help.

"We have won," said Binabik. "The price we have been paying is great, but Fengbald is dead."

"No." A look of concern flitted across Simon's haggard face. "It wasn't him. It was someone else."

Binabik darted a look at the figure lying nearby. "I know, Simon. It is elsewhere that Fengbald is being dead—a horrible death, and for many others than him only. But come. You are needing a fire, and food, and some attending to your wounds."

Simon let out a deep groan as he let the little man urge him to his feet, a hollow noise that drew another worried look from Binabik. Simon limped a few steps, then stopped and caught at Homefinder's reins. "I can't get into the saddle," he murmured sadly.

"Walk, then, if you can," Binabik said. "With slowness. Sisqi and I will be walking with you."

With Qantaqa in the lead once more, they turned and trudged toward the Stone, whose summit was painted with rosy light from the dying sun. Thickening mist hung over the icy lake, and all around the ravens hopped and scuttled from body to body like tiny black demons.

"Oh, God," Simon said. "I want to go home."

Binabik only shook his head.

16

Torches in the Mud

🔥

"Stop." Cadrach's voice was nearly a whisper, but the straining tone was evident. "Stop now."

Isgrimnur pushed the pole down until it touched the muddy bottom of the watercourse, arresting their progress. The boat floated gently back into the reeds once more. "What is it, man?" he said irritably. "We have gone over everything a dozen times. Now it's time to move."

In the bow of the boat, ancient Camaris fingered a long spear Isgrimnur had made from a stiff swamp reed. It was thin and light, and the point had been scraped against a stone until it was sharp as an assassin's dirk. The old knight, as usual, seemed oblivious to the conversation of his fellows. He hefted the spear and made a slow, mock stab, slipping the point into the still water.

Cadrach took a deep, shaky breath. Miriamele thought he looked as though he were on the brink of tears. "I cannot go."

"Cannot?" Isgrimnur almost shouted. "What do you mean, cannot? It was your idea we wait for morning before going into the nest! What are you talking about now!?"

The monk shook his head, unable to meet the duke's eyes. "I tried to nerve myself all night. I have been saying prayers all the morning—me!" He turned to Miriamele with a look of bleak irony. "Me! But I still cannot do it. I am a coward, and I cannot go into . . . that place."

Miriamele reached out a hand and touched his shoulder. "Even to save Tiamak?" She let the hand rest gently, as though the monk had turned to fragile glass. "And as you said, even to save ourselves? For without Tiamak, we may never get out of this place at all."

Cadrach buried his face in his hands. Miriamele felt a hint of her old distrust come sneaking back. Could the monk be play-acting? What else could he have in mind?

"God forgive me, Lady," he moaned, "but I simply cannot go down into that hole with those creatures. I *cannot.*" He shuddered, a convulsive movement so uncontrolled that Miriamele doubted it could be trickery. "I have given over my right to be called a man long ago," Cadrach said through his splayed fingers. "I do not even care for my life, believe me. But—I—cannot—go."

Isgrimnur grumbled his frustration. "Well, damn you, that is the end. I should have broken your skull when we met, as I wanted to." The duke turned to Miriamele. "I should never have let you talk me out of it." He shifted his scornful gaze back to Cadrach. "A kidnapper, a drunkard, and a coward."

"Yes, you probably should have killed me when you first had the chance," Cadrach agreed tonelessly. "But I promise you would still be better off doing it now than dragging me down into that mud nest. I will not go in there."

"But why, Cadrach?" Miriamele asked. "Why won't you?"

He looked at her. His sunken eyes and sun-reddened face seemed to plead for understanding, but his grim smile suggested he expected none. "I simply cannot, Lady. It . . . it reminds me of a place I was in before." Again he shuddered.

"What place?" she prodded, but Cadrach would not answer.

"Aedon on the Holy Tree," Isgrimnur swore. "So what do we do now?"

Miriamele stared at the waving reeds, which at this moment hid them from the sight of the ghant nest a few hundred ells up the waterway. The muddy bank nearby had a low-tide smell. She wrinkled her nose and sighed. What could they do, indeed?

They had not even been able to make a plan until late the afternoon before. There was a strong chance that Tiamak was already dead, which made any decision more difficult. Although no one had wanted to say it directly, there was some sentiment that the best thing to do would be to go on, hoping that the Wrannaman they had found floating in Tiamak's boat might recover enough to guide them. Failing that, they might discover another swamp native who would help them find their way out of the Wran. No one had been comfortable with the idea of abandoning Tiamak, although it seemed by far the least risky course, but it was dreadful to think about what it would take to find out if he still lived, and to save him if he did.

Still, when Isgrimnur at last said that leaving Tiamak would not be the Aedonite thing to do, Miriamele had been relieved. She had not wanted to run away without at least trying to save the Wrannaman, however terrifying the idea of entering that nest. And, she reminded herself, she had faced at least as bad in the past months. In any case, how could she live with herself if she made it to safety and had to remember the shy little scholar left to those clicking monstrosities?

Cadrach—even then he had seemed more frightened of the nest than the rest of them—had argued strenuously for waiting until morning. His reasons had seemed good: there was little sense in trying such a foolhardy thing without a battle plan, and even less sense starting when it would soon be dark. As it was, Cadrach had said, they would need not just weapons but torches, because even though the nest seemed to have holes that let in the light, who knew what dark passages might run through the heart of the thing? So it had been agreed.

They found a rattling grove of heavy green reeds along the edge of the watercourse and made camp near it. The site was muddy and wet, but it was also a good distance from the nest, which was recommendation enough. Isgrimnur took his sword Kvalnir and cut a great bundle of the reeds, then he and Cadrach hardened them over the embers of the campfire. Some of the stalks they had cut and sharpened to make short stabbing spears; they split the ends of others and forced stones between the halves, then tied the stones in place with thin vines to make clubs. Isgrimnur lamented the lack of good wood and rope, but Miriamele admired the job. It was much more reassuring to go into the nest with even such primitive arms than to walk in empty-handed. Lastly, they sacrificed some of the clothes Miriamele had brought out of Village Grove, shredding them for rags which they wound tightly around the remaining reeds. Miriamele crushed one of the leaves of a tree which Tiamak had named as an oil palm during his botanical tour a few days before, then dabbed a rag in it and held the cloth to the campfire. It held a flame, she discovered, although nothing like true lamp oil; the scent of its burning was acrid and foul. Still, it would keep the torches blazing a little while longer, and she had a feeling that they would need all the time they could buy. She plucked an armful of fronds and rubbed crushed pulp on the torch rags until her hands were so coated with sap that her fingers stuck together.

When the night sky had at last begun to lighten, just before dawn, Isgrimnur had awakened the company. They had decided to leave the wounded Wrannaman in camp: there was little sense in bringing him into further danger, since he seemed already to be exhausted and starved nearly to death. If they survived their attempt to rescue Tiamak, they could always come back for him; if they did not, at least he would have a small chance to survive and make his own escape.

Isgrimnur lifted his pole to the surface of the water and swished off the mud that clung to the end. "So, then? What do we do? The monk is worthless."

"There may still be a way he can help." Miriamele looked meaningfully at Cadrach. He kept his face averted. "In any case, we can certainly go on with the first part of what we planned, can't we?"

"I suppose." Isgrimnur stared at the Hernystirman as though he would have liked to test one of the reed clubs on him. He thrust the pole into the monk's hands. "Let's get to it. You can damn well make yourself useful."

Cadrach poled the boat out of the waving forest of reeds and onto the wide part of the watercourse. The morning sun was not very bright today, hidden behind a smudgy sheet of clouds, but the air was even hotter than it had been the day before. Miriamele felt a sheen of sweat on her forehead and wished that she dared to flout the crocodiles by taking off her boots and dangling her feet in the murky water.

They slipped along the waterway until they finally came into view of their objective, then moved close to the bank and slowly and cautiously up the canal, trying to use the cover of reeds and trees to stay out of direct sight. The nest looked just as sinister as it had the day before, although there seemed to be fewer ghants scuttling about outside. When they had gotten as close as they dared, Isgrimnur let the boat drift toward the outer edge of the waterway until a tree-lined bend in its course blocked them completely from view of the nest.

"Now we wait," he said quietly.

They sat in silence for no little time. The insects were a misery. Miriamele, afraid to slap at them because of the noise, tried to pick them off with her fingers as they landed, but they were too numerous and too persistent: she was bitten many times. Her skin itched and throbbed so completely that she felt she would go mad, and the idea of leaping into the river and drowning all the bugs at once grew stronger and stronger, until it seemed that any moment she would be able to hold it off no longer. Her fingers clutched the wales of the boat. It would be cool. It would stop the stinging. Let the crocodiles come, damn them. . . .

"There," Isgrimnur whispered. Miriamele looked up.

Not twenty cubits from where they sat, a lone ghant was coming down a long tree branch that snaked out over the water. Because of its jointed legs, its movements seemed strangely awkward, but it traveled swiftly and confidently on the thin, swaying branch. From time to time it would stop suddenly, becoming so utterly motionless that, gray and lichen-streaked as it was, it seemed part of the bark, just a particularly large tree gall.

"*Push*," Isgrimnur mouthed, gesturing at Cadrach. The monk prodded the boat away from the bank and sent it idling down the watercourse toward the branch. Miriamele and all the company remained as still as they could.

The ghant did not seem to notice them at first. As they drew closer, it continued to creep out along the bough, moving patiently toward a trio of small birds that had lit at the end. Like the thing that hunted them, the birds seemed oblivious to the presence of danger.

Isgrimnur replaced Camaris in the prow of the boat, then leaned forward, steadying himself as well as he could. The ghant finally seemed to see the boat floating toward it; black eyes glittered as it swayed in place, trying to decide whether the approaching object was a menace or a potential meal. As Isgrimnur raised the reed spear, the ghant seemed to come to a conclusion: it turned and began to shinny back toward the tree trunk.

"Now, Isgrimnur!" cried Miriamele. The Rimmersman flung the spear as hard as he could; the boat rocked treacherously with the force of his throw. The birds lifted from the branch, squawking and flapping. The spear hissed through the air, a length of Tiamak's precious rope falling away behind it, and struck the ghant but did not pierce its shell; the spear bounced away and fell to the water, but the force of the blow was enough to knock the animal from the bough. It splashed into the green water and surfaced a moment later with legs flexing wildly, then righted itself and began a strange, jerky swim toward the bank.

Cadrach swiftly poled the boat forward until they were beside the creature.

Isgrimnur leaned low and struck it hard twice with the flat of his sword. When it floated back up, clearly beyond struggling, he looped a bit of Tiamak's rope around one clawed leg so they could tow it back to shore.

"Don't want to put the thing in the boat," he said. Miriamele could not have agreed more.

The ghant seemed dead—the carapace of its lumpish head was cracked, oozing gray and blue fluids—but no one stood too near as they used the steering pole to turn it onto its back on the sandy bank. Camaris remained in the boat, although he seemed to be watching as curiously as the rest of the company.

Isgrimnur scowled. "God help us. They are ugly bastards, aren't they?"

"Your spear couldn't kill it." Miriamele's feelings about their chances had sunk even lower.

Isgrimnur waved his hand reassuringly. "Got thick armor, these things. Have to make the spears a little heavier. A stone spliced in the end should do it. Don't worry yourself more than you need, Princess. We'll be able to do what we need to."

Strangely, she believed him and felt better. Isgrimnur had always treated her like a favorite niece, even when his relations with her father had become strained, and she in turn treated him with the loving, mocking familiarity she had never been able to use on Elias. She knew he would do his best to keep them all safe—and the Duke of Elvritshalla's best was usually very good. Although he allowed his comrades and even his house-carls to make fun of his fierce but short-lived temper and his underlying softheartedness, the duke was a tremendously capable man. Miriamele was again grateful that Isgrimnur was with her.

"I hope you're right." She reached out and squeezed his broad paw.

They all stared at the dead ghant. Miriamele could now see that it did have six legs, just like a beetle, not four as she had thought. The two she had missed on her first ghant were tiny, withered things tucked just below the place where the neckless head met the rounded body. The thing's mouth was half-hidden behind an odd featherlike fringe and its shell was dull and leathery as a sea-turtle's egg.

"Turn away, Princess," Isgrimnur said as he lifted Kvalnir. "You won't want to see this."

Miriamele suppressed a smile. What did he think she had been doing the last half year? "Go ahead. I'm not squeamish."

The duke lowered his sword and placed it against the creature's abdomen, then pushed. The ghant slid across the mud a little way. Isgrimnur grunted, then held the carcass steady with his foot before pushing again. This time, after a moment of effort, he was able to push the blade through the shell, which gave with a faint popping noise. A salty, sour smell wafted up and Miriamele took a step back.

"The shells are tough," Isgrimnur said thoughtfully, "but they can be pierced." He tried to smile. "I was worried that we might have to besiege a castle of armored soldiers."

Cadrach had gone quite pale, but continued to stare at the ghant, fascinated. "It is disturbingly manlike, as Tiamak said," he murmured. "But I will not be too sorry about this one or any others we kill."

"*We* kill?" Isgrimnur began angrily, but Miriamele gave him another hand-squeeze.

"What else can this tell us?" she asked.

"I don't see any poison stingers or teeth, so I suppose they don't bite like spiders do—that's a relief." The duke shrugged. "They can be killed. Their shells are not as hard as tortoise shells. That is enough, I think."

"Then I suppose it's time to go," Miriamele said.

Cadrach poled the flatboat in to the bank. They were only a few hundred steps from the edge of the nest now. So far, they seemed to be unnoticed.

"But what about the boat?" Isgrimnur whispered. "Can we leave it so we can get back to it in a hurry?" His expression soured. "And what about this damnable monk?"

"That's my idea," Miriamele whispered back. "Cadrach, if you keep the boat in the middle of the waterway until we come out, you can land right at the front of the nest and get us. We'll probably be in a hurry," she added wryly.

"What!?" Isgrimnur struggled to keep his voice soft, with only partial success. "You're going to leave this coward in our boat, free to paddle away if he wants to? Free to strand us here? No, by the Aedon, we will take him with us—bound and gagged if need be."

Cadrach clutched the steering pole, his knuckles white. "You might as well kill me first," he said hoarsely. "Because I will die if you drag me in there."

"Stop it, Isgrimnur. He may not be able to go into the nest, but he would never leave us here. Not after all he and I have been through." She turned and gave the monk a purposeful glance. "Would you, Cadrach?"

He looked at her carefully, as though he suspected a trick. A moment passed before he spoke. "No, my lady, I would not—whatever Duke Isgrimnur thinks."

"And why should I let you make such a decision, Princess?" Isgrimnur was angry. "Whatever you think you know of this man, you also said yourself that he stole from you and sold you out to your enemies."

Miriamele frowned. It was true, of course—and she had not told Isgrimnur everything. She had never mentioned Cadrach's attempt to escape and leave her behind on Aspitis' ship, which would certainly not argue in his favor. She found herself wondering why she *was* so certain that Cadrach could be trusted to wait for them, but it was no use: there was no answer. She just believed that he would be there when they got out . . . *if* they got out.

"We really have very little choice," she told the duke. "Unless we force him to go along—and it will be hard enough to find our way and do what we must without also dragging a prisoner with us—we would have to tie him up some-where to prevent him taking the boat if he wanted to. Don't you see, Isgrimnur, it's just the best way! If we leave the boat untended, even if we try to hide it from the ghants . . . well, who knows what could happen?"

Isgrimnur pondered for a long moment, his bearded jaws working as though he chewed on the various possibilities. "So," he said at last. "I suppose that is true. Very well—but if you are *not* there when we need you," he whirled on Cadrach menacingly, "I will find you some day and crush your bones. I will eat you like a game hen."

Cadrach smiled sadly. "I'm sure you would, Duke Isgrimnur." The monk turned to Miriamele. "Thank you for trusting me, my lady. It is not easy to be a man like myself."

"I should hope not," Isgrimnur growled. "Otherwise there'd be more of you."

"I think it will all be well, Cadrach," said Miriamele. "But pray for us."

"Every god I know."

The duke, still muttering angrily, struck a spark with his flint and lit one of the torches. The rest he and Miriamele stuck in their belts until they were both spined like hedgehogs. Miriamele carried a club and one of the weighted spears, as did Camaris, who handled his weapons distractedly while the other two prepared. Isgrimnur had Kvalnir sheathed on his belt, and a pair of short spears clutched in his free hand.

"Going into battle armed with sticks," he growled. "Going to fight bugs."

"It will make a wretched song," Miriamele whispered. "Or a glorious one, perhaps. We'll see." She turned to the old man. "Sir Camaris, we're going to help Tiamak. Your friend—do you remember? He's in there." She pointed with her spear at the dark bulk of the nest looming behind the trees. "We have to find him and bring him out." She stared at his unexcited expression. "Do you think he understands, Isgrimnur?"

"He has become simple . . . but not as simple as he seems, I think." The duke grabbed at a low branch and helped himself over the side of the boat and into the shin-deep water. "Here, Princess, let me help you." He lifted her and set her on the bank. "Josua will never forgive me if anything happens to you. I still think it is foolish to bring you along—especially when *that* one is staying be-hind, cozy and safe."

"You need me," she said. "It will be difficult enough with three."

Isgrimnur shook his head, unconvinced. "Just stay near me."

"I will, old uncle."

As Camaris sloshed to shore, Cadrach began to push the boat out into deeper water.

"Hold," said Isgrimnur. "Wait until we are inside at least. We don't need to attract their attention until we're ready."

Cadrach nodded and used the pole to stop the boat.

"Bless you all," he said softly. "Good luck to you."

The duke snorted and moved away into undergrowth, boots squelching in the mud. Miriamele nodded to Cadrach, then took Camaris' hand and led him after the duke.

"Good luck," Cadrach said again. He spoke in a whisper, and none of the others seemed to hear him.

"See!" Miriamele hissed. "There's one that's big enough!"

A soft humming filled the air. They were very close to the nest, so close that had Miriamele dared to stretch her hand out from where they hid in a tangle of flowering brush, she could almost have touched it. Upon approaching the huge mud structure, they had quickly realized that many of the doors—mere holes in the walls, actually—were far too small for even the princess to enter, let alone broad Isgrimnur.

"Right," said the duke. "Let's get to it, then." He started to reach for his torch, then stopped and waved for his companions to do the same. A few cubits away, a pair of ghants came creeping along the perimeter of the nest. Although they walked in file, one behind the other, they were clicking and hissing back and forth as though they conversed. Again Miriamele wondered how smart the things were. The ghants walked past on all fours, jointed legs ticking as they went. The trio watched them until they were gone around the curve of the huge nest.

"Now." Isgrimnur plucked his torch out of the mud; he had set it behind him so that his broad frame masked its light. Even in the morning sun, its flame made Miriamele feel a little safer.

After looking cautiously in all directions, the duke crossed the short distance to the nest and leaned into the ragged opening. He stepped through, then reached back to beckon to Miriamele and Camaris.

Increasingly reluctant as the actual moment approached, Miriamele hesitated before following the duke inside, taking a deep breath as if to dive into water. She understood Cadrach's decision better than she did her own. The place would be full of those crawling, clicking, many-legged things. . . . Her knees grew weak. How could she walk into that black hole? But Tiamak was already there, alone with the ghants. He might be screaming for help down in the darkness.

Miriamele swallowed, then stepped into the nest.

She found herself in a circular passageway as wide as her outstretched arms and only a little taller than her own height. Isgrimnur had to hunch down, and Camaris, who followed Miriamele, had to bend even lower. The mud walls were spiky with loose stones and bits of splintered sticks, all covered with pale froth that looked like spittle. The tunnel was dark and steamily humid and smelled of rotting vegetation.

"Ugh." Miriamele wrinkled her nose. Her heart was pounding. "I don't like this at all."

"I know," Isgrimnur whispered. "It's foul. Come on, let's see what we can see."

They followed the winding passageway, struggling for footing on the slippery mud. Isgrimnur and Camaris had to lean forward, which made balancing even more difficult. Miriamele felt her courage beginning to fail. Why had she been so anxious to prove herself? This was no place for a girl. This was no place for anyone.

"I think Cadrach was right." She tried to keep the quaver out of her voice.

"No sensible person would want to come in here," the duke said quietly, "but that's not the question. Besides, if this is as bad as it gets, I'll be happy. I'm afraid we might find ourselves in a smaller tunnel and have to go on our knees."

Miriamele thought of being chased by the scuttling ghants but not being able to run. She stared at the slickly glistening tunnel floor and shuddered.

The light from the entrance began to dim as they put several bends of the tunnel behind them. The rotten smell grew stronger, accompanied now by a strange spicy odor, musty and cloyingly sweet. Miriamele slipped her club into her belt and lit one of her brands from Isgrimnur's, then lit another and gave it to Camaris, who took it as placidly as an infant handed a crust of bread. Miriamele envied his idiot calm. "Where are the ghants?" she whispered.

"Don't look for trouble." Isgrimnur made the Tree sign in the air with his torch before moving on.

The uneven passage turned and turned again, as though they clambered through the guts of some vast animal. After a few more squishing steps, they reached a point where a new tunnel crossed theirs. Isgrimnur stood and listened for a moment.

"I think I hear more noise from this one." The duke pointed down one of the side branches. Indeed, the dull humming did seem stronger there.

"But should we go toward it or away from it?" Miriamele tried to wave the choking torch smoke away from her face.

Isgrimnur's expression was fatalistic. "I think that Tiamak or any other prisoners would be at the heart of the thing. I say, follow the noise. Not that I like it," he added. He reached up and scraped a circle in the froth with one of his reed spears, exposing the muddy wall beneath. "We have to remember to mark our way."

The froth on the walls was thicker in the new passage; in places it hung from the tunnel roof in viscous, ropy strands. Miriamele did her best to avoid touching the stuff, but there was no way to avoid breathing. She could almost feel the damp, unpleasant air of the tunnels congealing inside her chest. Still, Miriamele told herself, she had no real cause for complaint: they had been in the nest for no little time, and still had not met any of the inhabitants. That alone was an incredible piece of luck.

"This place doesn't look nearly so big from outside," she said to Isgrimnur.

"We never saw the back of it, for one thing." He stepped carefully over a glob of pale muck in the passageway. "And I think that these tunnels may be looping back on themselves. I'd wager that if you broke through this . . ." he prodded at the wall with his torch; the froth hissed and bubbled, ". . . you'd find another tunnel just on the other side of it."

"Round and round. Farther and farther in. Like a chamber-shell," Miriamele whispered. It was more than a little dizzying to think of such an endless spiral of mud and shadows. Again she fought down rising panic. "Still . . ." she began.

There was a scuttling movement in the tunnel before them.

The ghant had apparently stepped out of another side tunnel; it crouched motionless in the middle of the passage as though stunned. Isgrimnur also froze for a moment, then slowly walked forward. The ghant, devoid of anything that could truly be called a face, stared at their approach, the tiny legs below its head straightening and contracting. Suddenly it turned and scuttled away up the tunnel. Isgrimnur hesitated for a moment, then ran heavily after it, struggling to keep his balance. He stopped and hurled his spear, then pulled up suddenly with a hiss of pain that made Miriamele's heart race.

"*Damn!* I've hit my head. Careful, the cursed roof is low here." He rubbed at his forehead.

"Did you get it?"

"I think so. I can't quite see it yet." He went forward a little way. "Yes. It's dead—or it looks it, anyway."

Miriamele came up beside him, peering around the duke's wide shoulders at the thing in the pool of torchlight. The ghant lay in the mud of the passageway with Isgrimnur's spear protruding from the armor of its back; the wound oozed a thin fluid a shade paler than blood. The jointed legs twitched a few times, then slowly came to rest as Camaris stepped forward and reached out his long arm to turn the creature over. The ghant's face was as blank in death as in life. The old man, with a contemplative look, scooped a handful of mucky earth from the tunnel floor and dropped it onto the dead thing's chest. It was a strange gesture, Miriamele thought.

"Come," Isgrimnur muttered.

The new tunnel did not twist as much as the first had. It ran steeply downward, bumpy and sodden, the walls as uneven as if they had been chewed out of the mud by monstrous jaws: looking at the gleaming strands of foam, Miriamele decided that was not a pleasant thought to pursue.

"Curse it," Isgrimnur said suddenly. "I'm stuck."

His boot had sunk deep into the squelching mud of the tunnel floor. Miriamele held out her arm to him so he could balance as he pulled. A terrible odor rose from the disturbed mud, and tiny wet things brought to light by Isgrimnur's struggles quickly buried themselves again. The Rimmersman, for all his efforts, only seemed to sink deeper.

"It's like that sucking sand Tiamak said they have in the swamp. Can't get free." There was an edge of panic in Isgrimnur's voice.

"It's just mud." Miriamele tried to sound calm, but she could not help wondering what would happen if the ghants came upon them suddenly. "Leave the boot if you have to."

"It's my whole leg, not just the boot." Indeed, one leg had now sunk to the knee, and the foot of the other boot was also lodged in the slime. The carrion smell grew worse.

Camaris stepped forward, then braced his own legs to either side of Isgrimnur's foot before taking the Rimmersman's leg in his hands; Miriamele prayed there was only one patch of treacherous mud. If not, they might both become trapped. What would she do then?

The old knight heaved. Isgrimnur grunted in pain, but his foot did not come loose. Camaris pulled again, so strenuously that the cords on his neck grew taut as ropes. With a sucking gasp, Isgrimnur's leg came free; Camaris tugged him away to a firmer patch of ground.

The duke stood bent over for a moment, examining the glob of mud below his knee. "Just stuck," he said. He was breathing heavily. "Just stuck. Let's keep moving." The fear was not entirely gone from his voice.

They sloshed on, trying to find the driest spots to walk. The smoke of the torches and the stench of the mud was making Miriamele feel ill, so she was almost heartened when the narrow passage opened at last into a wider room, a sort of grotto in which the white froth hung like stalactites. They entered it cautiously, but it seemed as deserted as the tunnel had been. As they made their way across the chamber, stepping around the larger puddles, Miriamele looked up.

"What are those?" she asked, frowning. Large, faintly luminous sacs sagged from the ceiling, hanging unpleasantly close overhead. Each was as long as a crofter's hammock, with thin, cobwebby white tendrils depending from its center, a wispy fringe that drifted lazily in the warm air rising from the torches.

"I don't know, but I don't like them," Isgrimnur said with a grimace of distaste.

"I think they're egg pouches. You know, like the spider eggs you see on the bottoms of leaves."

"Haven't looked much at the bottoms of leaves," the duke muttered. "And I don't want to look at these any longer than I have to."

"Shouldn't we do something? Kill them or something? Burn them?"

"We're not here to kill all these bugs," said Isgrimnur. "We're here to get in and find that poor little marsh fellow, then get out. God only knows what would happen if we started mucking around with these things."

With mud sucking at their bootheels, they made their way quickly to the other side of the chamber, where the tunnel resumed its former size. Miriamele, drawn by a horrid sort of interest, turned back for a last glance. In the fading light of the torch, she thought she saw a shadowy movement in one of the sacs, as though something was pawing at the maggot-white membrane, seeking a way out. She wished she hadn't looked.

Within a few steps the passageway turned and they found themselves facing a half-dozen ghants. Several had been climbing up the tunnel wall and now hung in place, clicking in apparent surprise. The others squatted on the floor, mud-smeared shells glimmering dully in the torchglow. Miriamele felt her heart turn over.

Isgrimnur stepped forward and wagged Kvalnir from side to side. Swallowing hard, Miriamele moved up behind him and lifted her torch. After a few more seconds of chittering indecision, the ghants turned and scrambled away down the tunnel.

"They're afraid of us!" Miriamele was exhilarated.

"Perhaps," said Isgrimnur. "Or perhaps they're going for their friends. Let's get on." He began walking swiftly, head hunched beneath the low ceiling.

"But that's the direction *they* went," Miriamele pointed out.

"I said, it's the heart of this wretched place we want."

They passed numerous side tunnels as they traveled downward, but Isgrimnur seemed certain of where he was going. The humming continued to grow louder; the stench of putrefaction grew stronger, too, until Miriamele's head ached. They passed through two more of the egg chambers—if that was indeed what they were—hurrying through both. Miriamele no longer felt any urge to linger and stare.

They came upon the central chamber so suddenly that they almost fell through the tunnel mouth and tumbled down the sloping mud into the vast swarm of ghants.

The room was huge and dark; the torches of Miriamele and her companions cast the only light, but it was enough to reveal the great crawling horde, the faint wink of their shells as they clambered over each other in the darkness at the bottom of the chamber, the muted glimmering of their countless eyes. The chamber was a long stone's throw in width, with walls of piled and smoothed mud. The entire floor was covered with many-legged things, hundreds and hundreds of ghants.

The humming sound that arose from the squirming mass was stronger here, a pulsing throb of sound so powerful that Miriamele could feel it in her teeth and the bones of her head.

"Mother of Usires," Isgrimnur swore brokenly.

Miriamele felt chilly and light-headed. "W-what . . ." She swallowed bile and tried again. "What . . . do we do?"

Isgrimnur leaned forward, squinting. The swarm of ghants did not appear to have noticed them, though the nearest was only a dozen cubits away: they seemed enmeshed in some dreadful and all-consuming activity. Miriamele fought to catch her breath. Maybe they were laying their eggs here and, caught up in the grip of Nature, would not notice the interlopers.

"What's that at the middle?" Isgrimnur whispered. The duke was having trouble keeping his voice from breaking. "That thing they're all gathered around?"

Miriamele strained to see, although at that moment there was nothing she would less rather look at. It was like the worst vision of hell, a writhing pile of muddy things without hope or joy, legs kicking pointlessly, shells scraping as they rubbed against each other—and always the terrible droning, the ceaseless grinding sound of the assembled ghants. Miriamele blinked and forced herself to concentrate. At the center, where the activity seemed the most fervid, stood a row of pale, shining lumps. The nearest had a dark spot at the top which seemed to be moving. It took her a moment to realize that the spot atop the gleaming mass was a head—a human head.

"It's Tiamak," she gasped, horrified. Her stomach heaved. "He's stuck in something terrible—it's like a pudding. Oh, Elysia Mother of God, we have to help him!"

"Ssshhh." Isgrimnur, who looked as sickened as Miriamele felt, gestured her to silence. "Think," he murmured. "Got to think."

The tiny ball that was Tiamak's head began to wiggle back and forth atop the gelatinous mound. As Miriamele and Isgrimnur stared in amazement, the mouth opened and Tiamak began to shout in a loud voice. But instead of words, what roared out was the tormented sound of buzzing, clicking ghant-speech— something that sounded so cruelly wrong coming from the little Wrannaman's mouth that Miriamele burst into tears.

"What have they done to him!?" she cried. Suddenly there was movement beside her, a rush of hot air as a torch swished past, then the flame was bobbing down the slope toward the floor and the squirming congregation of ghants.

"Camaris!" Isgrimnur shouted, but the old man was already forcing his way through the outermost ghants, swinging his torch like a scythe. The great humming sound faltered, leaving echoes in Miriamele's ears. The ghants around Camaris started to buzz shrilly, and others in the vast gathering took up the cries of alarm. The tall old man waded through them like a master of hounds come to take the fox away. Agitated creatures swirled around his legs, some clutching at his cloak and breeches even as he knocked others away with his club.

"Oh, God help me, he can't do it himself," Isgrimnur groaned. He began making his way down the slippery mud, spreading his arms for balance. "Stay there," he called to Miriamele.

"I'm coming with you," she shouted back.

"*No,* damn it," the duke cried. "Stay there with the torch so we can find our way back to this tunnel! If we lose the light, we're done for!"

He turned, lifting Kvalnir over his head, and swung it at the nearest ghants. There was an awful hollow smack as he struck the first one. He took a few steps forward into the swarm and the noise of his struggle was lost in the greater uproar.

The humming had completely died out. The great chamber was now filled instead with the staccato cries of angry ghants, a dreadful chorus of wet clicking. Miriamele tried to make out what was happening, but Isgrimnur had already lost his torch and was now little more than a dark shape in the middle of a seething mass of shells and twitching legs. Somewhere closer to the center, Camaris' torch still cut the air like a banner of fire, swinging back and forth, back and forth, as he waded toward the spot where Tiamak was prisoned.

Miriamele was terrified but furious. Why should she wait while Isgrimnur and Camaris risked their lives? They were her friends! And what if they died or were captured? Then she would be alone, forced to try and find her way out, pursued by those horrible things. It was stupid. She wouldn't do it. But what else could she do?

Think, girl, think, she told herself, even as she hopped up and down anxiously, trying to see if Isgrimnur was still on his feet. *Do what? What?*

She couldn't stand waiting. It was too horrible. She took the two remaining torches from her belt and lit them. When they were burning, she thrust them down into the mud on either side of the tunnel mouth, then took a deep breath and followed Isgrimnur's track down the slope, her legs so wobbly she feared she might fall down. Unreality gripped her: she couldn't be doing this. Her skin was pricklingly cold. No one with their wits left would go down into that pit. But somehow her booted feet kept moving.

"Isgrimnur!" she shrieked. "Where are you?"

Cold muddy legs clutched at her, chitinous things like animate tree branches. The hissing creatures were all around; knobby heads butted at her legs and she felt her stomach thrash again. She kicked out like a horse, trying to drive them back. A claw caught at her leg and hooked itself into her boot top; the torch momentarily illuminated her target, which gleamed like a wet stone. She lifted her short spear, almost dropping the torch, which was clutched awkwardly in the same hand, and stabbed down as hard as she could. The spear thumped into something which gave satisfyingly. When she jerked it back, the claw let go.

It was easier to swing the club, but it did not seem to kill the things. At every blow they fell and tumbled, but a moment later they were back again, scratching, clasping, worse than any nightmare. After a few moments she pushed the cudgel into her belt and took up the torch in her free hand, which seemed at least to keep them at bay. She hit one of the ghants full in its empty face, and some of the burning palm oil spattered and stuck. The thing shrieked like a fool's whistle and dove forward, digging itself into the mud, but another clambered over its quivering shell to take its place. She shouted in fear and disgust as she kicked it aside. The army of ghants was never-ending.

"Miriamele!" It was Isgrimnur, somewhere ahead of her. "Is that you!?"

"Here!" she cried, her voice tearing along the edge, threatening to become a shriek that would never stop. "Oh, hurry, hurry, hurry!"

"I told you to stay!" he shouted. "Camaris is coming back! See the torch!"

She stabbed at one of the things before her, but her spear only scraped along the shell. Out in the churning mass there was suddenly a glint of flame. "I see it!"

"We're coming!" The duke was barely audible above the rattling voices of the ghants. "Stay where you are and wave your torch!"

"I'm here," she howled, "I'm here!"

The sea of writhing creatures seemed to pulse as though a wave rolled through it. The light of the torch jiggled above them, moving closer. Miriamele fought desperately—there was still a chance! She swung her torch in as wide an arc as she could, trying to keep her attackers at a distance. A clawing leg caught at the brand and suddenly it was gone, sizzling into the mud and leaving her in darkness. She thrust out wildly with the spear.

"Here!" she screamed. "My torch is gone!"

There was no reply from Isgrimnur. All was lost. Miriamele wondered briefly if she would be able to use the spear on herself—certainly she could never let them have her alive. . . .

Something grasped her arm. Shrieking, she struggled but could not break free.

"It's me!" cried Isgrimnur. "Don't stick me!" He pulled her against his broad side and shouted to Camaris, who was still some distance away. The torch came closer, the ghants dancing around it like water drops on a hot stone. "How will we find our way out?" Isgrimnur bellowed.

"I left torches by the door." Miriamele turned to look, even as something snatched at her cloak. "There!" She realized Isgrimnur could not see her pointing. She kicked and the snagging claw fell away. "Behind you."

Isgrimnur lifted her bodily and carried her for a few steps, clearing the way with Kvalnir until they had pushed through a clump of buzzing creatures and found their feet on the upward slope.

"We have to wait for Camaris."

"He's coming," Isgrimnur bellowed. "Move!"

"Did he get Tiamak?"

"Move!"

Slipping back half as far as each step took her forward, Miriamele struggled up the muddy incline toward the light of the twin torches. She could hear Isgrimnur's grunting breath behind her, and at intervals the muffled crack of Kvalnir's steel against the shells of their pursuers. When she reached the top, she grasped the two torches and pulled them from the mud, then turned, ready to fight again. Isgrimnur was right behind her, and the flickering brand that she knew must belong to Camaris was at the bottom of the slope.

"Hurry!" she called down. The torch paused, then waved from side to side, as though Camaris used it to keep the swarm away as he climbed. Now she could see his hair gleaming silver-yellow in the torchlight. "Help him," she pleaded with Isgrimnur. The duke took a few steps down, Kvalnir moving in a blurry arc, and in a moment Camaris had broken free and the two of them came tripping and sliding up the slope to the tunnel mouth. Camaris had lost his club. Tiamak, covered with white jelly and apparently senseless, hung over his shoulder. Miriamele stared at the Wrannaman's slack features in dismay.

"Go, damn it!" Isgrimnur pushed Miriamele toward the tunnel. She tore her eyes from Tiamak's sticky form and began to run, waving her burning brand as she went, making shadows leap and streak madly across the dun walls.

The floor of the chamber behind them seemed to erupt as the ghants came scurrying in pursuit. Isgrimnur pushed through into the tunnel; a mass of angrily clicking shapes followed him, a wave of armored flesh. The pursuing ghants might have caught the duke and his companions within moments, but their numbers were so great that they filled the passage almost completely, tangling themselves. Those following tried to force their way past; within instants the tunnel mouth was clogged with writhing, leg-waving bodies.

"Lead the way!" the duke cried.

It was difficult to move quickly with her head hunched down and her back bent, and the muddy floor had been difficult to traverse even at walking speed. Miriamele fell down several times, once giving her ankle a nasty twist. She scarcely felt the pain, but a dim part of her thoughts knew that if she survived, she would certainly feel it later. She did her best to look for the marks Isgrimnur had so conscientiously scraped in the foamy walls, but by the time they had gone a few hundred paces from the great chamber, Miriamele realized in horror that she had missed a turning. She knew that they should have passed through at least one of the egg-chambers by now, but instead they were still in one of the featureless tunnels—and this one was sloping downward, when the return trip should have led up.

"Isgrimnur, I think we're lost!" She slowed to a trot, holding her torch close to the dripping walls as she looked desperately for something that she recognized. She could hear Camaris' heavy tread just behind.

The Rimmersman swore floridly. "Just keep running, then—can't be helped!"

Miriamele sped her pace again. Her legs were aching, and each breath pushed at her lungs with sharp needles. Positive now that they had lost their course, she chose the next of the cross tunnels that seemed to lead upward. The slope was not steep, but the slippery mud made climbing difficult. Above the sound of her own ragged breath she could hear the clatter of the ghants rising again behind them.

The top of the rise came into view, another tunnel running perpendicularly to theirs, about a hundred ells above; but even as Miriamele's heart lightened a little, a swarm of ghants came scuttling into the tunnel below them. Moving low to the ground and traveling on four legs instead of two, the creatures were making much swifter time up the sloping pathway. Miriamele dug harder, forcing herself up the final slope. She only hesitated an instant before choosing the right-hand side of the cross-tunnel. Even Camaris' breathing was loud and harsh now. A few of the fastest ghants reached Isgrimnur, who was bringing up the rear. Bellowing with anger and disgust, the duke made a broad sweep with Kvalnir; hissing, the ghants tumbled back down into the boiling mass of their fellows.

Before Miriamele and her companions had gone fifty paces down the new passage, the ghants reached the top of the rise behind them and spilled out into the tunnel. On flat ground they traveled even more swiftly, hopping forward at a terrifying pace. Some ran directly up the walls before swiveling to pursue the fleeing company.

"We must turn and fight," Isgrimnur gasped. "Camaris! Put the marsh man down!"

"Oh, God love us, no!" cried Miriamele, "I hear more of them ahead!" It was a nightmare, a dreadful, endless nightmare. "Isgrimnur, we're trapped!"

"Stop, damn it, stop! We'll fight here!"

"No!" Miriamele was horrified. "If we stop here, we'll have to fight both swarms, front and back. Keep running!"

She took a few steps farther down, but she could tell no one was following her. She turned to see Isgrimnur staring grimly at the ghants behind them, who had slowed when their prey did and now came forward with deliberate caution, their numbers swelling as dozens more scrambled up from the tunnel below. Miriamele turned and saw jiggling spots down the corridor before her as the glossy, dead eyes of the ghants there began to catch the torchlight.

"Oh, Merciful Elysia," Miriamele breathed, utterly defeated. Camaris, who stood beside her, was staring at the floor as though musing on some odd but not terribly important thought. Tiamak lay against his shoulder, eyes closed and mouth open like a sleeping child. Miriamele felt a moment of sadness. She had wanted to save the marsh man . . . it would have been so lovely to save him. . . .

With a bellow, Isgrimnur abruptly turned. To Miriamele's complete astonishment, he kicked the wall behind him as hard as he could. Caught up in what must be some fit of insane frustration, he slammed his boot sole against it again and again.

"Isgrimnur . . . !" Miriamele began, but at that moment the duke's boot smashed through the wall, making a hole the size of his head in the crumbling mud. He lashed out again and another section fell through.

"Help me!" he grunted. Miriamele stepped forward, but before she could lend any aid, Isgrimnur's next blow knocked out a large section. There was now a hole in the wall almost two cubits high, with nothing beyond but blackness.

"Go on!" the duke urged her. A dozen paces away the ghants were clicking madly. Miriamele pushed the torch through the gap, then forced her head and shoulders after it, half-certain she would feel jointed claws reach down and clutch her. Slipping and struggling, she scrambled through, praying that there was some solid ground there, that she would not fall into nothingness. Her hands touched the muck of another tunnel floor; she caught a momentary glimpse of the empty passage that surrounded her before she turned back to help the others. Camaris pushed Tiamak's limp form through to her. She nearly dropped him—the slender Wrannaman did not weigh much, but he was sagging dead weight covered with slippery ooze. The old knight followed, then Isgrimnur squeezed his own broad body through a moment later. Almost on his heels, the hole filled with the reaching arms of ghants, hard and shiny as polished wood.

Kvalnir slashed out, bringing fizzing squeals of pain from the far side of the hole. The arms were quickly withdrawn, but the chittering of the ghants continued to grow.

"They'll decide to come through in a moment, sword or no sword," the duke panted.

Miriamele stared at the gap for a moment. The stench of the ghants was strong, as was the coarse noise they made as they rubbed against each other. They were gathering for another attack, and they were only a few scant inches away.

"Give me your shirt," she told Isgrimnur suddenly. "And his, too." She pointed at Camaris.

The duke looked at her for a moment in alarm, as though she might have suddenly lost her wits, then quickly stripped off his tattered shirt and handed it to her. Miriamele held it to the flame of her torch until it caught—it was a maddeningly slow process, since that shirt was damp and mud-streaked—then used her spear-point to push the burning cloth into the gap in the wall. Surprised hisses and quiet snicking noises came from the ghants on the other side. Miriamele pushed Camaris' shirt in beside it; when it had caught fire and both garments were burning steadily, she took Isgrimnur's heavy cloak as well and crammed it into the remaining space.

"Now we run again," she said. "I don't think they like fire." She was surprised at how calm she suddenly felt, despite a certain light-headedness. "But it won't hold them long."

Camaris scooped up Tiamak and they all hastened on. At each turning they chose the tunnel that seemed to lead upward. Two more times they broke through sections of the passageway walls and sniffed at the holes like dogs, hunting for outside air. At last they found a tunnel that, although lower and narrower than many through which they had passed, seemed somehow fresher.

The clamor of pursuit had begun again, although as yet none of the creatures had come into view. Miriamele ignored the gelatinous froth beneath her hands as she half-walked, half-crawled through the low tunnel. Strands of pale foam fell wetly across her face and fouled her hair. A curl of it touched her open lips, and before she could spit it out, she tasted bitter musk. At the next bend in the passage the tunnel suddenly became larger. After a few more lurching steps, they turned another corner and found light splashed across the mud.

"Daylight!" Miriamele shouted. She had never been happier to see it.

They stumbled along until the tunnel turned again, then found themselves facing a round but ragged hole in the tunnel wall, beyond which hung the sky—gray and dim, but the sky nonetheless, the glorious sky. She threw herself forward, clambering through the hole and out onto a rounded floor of lumpy mud.

Treetops waved below them, so green and intricate that Miriamele's muck-deadened mind almost could not take them in. They were standing atop one of the upper parts of the nest; a scant two hundred cubits away lay the watercourse, tranquil as a great snake. There was no flatboat waiting.

Camaris and Isgrimnur followed her out onto the roof of the nest.

"Where is the monk?" Isgrimnur howled. "Damnation! Damnation! I knew he couldn't be trusted!"

"Never mind that now," said Miriamele. "We have to get off this thing."

After a quick search they found a way down onto a lower roof. They teetered across a slender ridge of mud for some dozen paces before reaching the safety of the next level, then continued from flat spot to flat spot, moving always toward the front of the nest and the waiting watercourse. As they reached the outermost point, from which it was only a leap of three or four ells down to the ground, a company of ghants surged out of the hole near the top of the nest.

"Here they come," Isgrimnur wheezed. "Jump down!"

Before Miriamele could do so, another, larger swarm of the creatures came spilling out of one of the nest's large front entrances, gathering quickly into an agitated mass directly below them. Miriamele felt a deathly, terrible weariness settle over her. To be so close—it wasn't fair!

"Holy Aedon, save us now." There was little strength left in the duke's voice. "Move back, Miriamele. I'll jump first."

"You can't!" she cried. "There are too many of them."

"We can't stay here." Indeed, the other ghants were moving rapidly down across the uneven upper levels of the nest, leggy as spiders, nimble as apes. They were clicking in anticipation and their black eyes glittered.

A bright streak abruptly flashed across the beach. Startled, Miriamele looked down at the ghants below, who were milling wildly. Their percussive cries were even wilder and more shrill than they had been, and several of them seemed to have caught fire. Miriamele looked out to the watercourse, trying to make sense of what was happening. The flatboat had floated into view. Cadrach, who stood spread-legged in the square bow, held something in his hand that looked like a large torch, its upper end burning brightly.

As Miriamele stared in numb astonishment, the monk swung the thing forward and a ball of fire seemed to leap from the end, arcing across the water to land amid the ghants clustered on the sand below her. The fiery blob burst, scattering great splashes of flame which stuck to the creatures like burning glue. Some of those who were struck fell to the ground with their shells bubbling from the heat and began to pipe like boiling lobsters, while others ran back and forth, tearing ineffectually at their own armor, clacking and clattering like broken wagon wheels. Out on the flatboat, Cadrach bent; when he straightened, another flame had blossomed at the end of his strange stick. He threw once more and another gout of liquid fire spattered across the shrieking ghants. The monk raised his hands to his mouth.

"Jump now!" he cried, his voice echoing faintly. "Hurry!"

Miriamele turned and looked briefly at Isgrimnur. The duke's face was slack with wonder, but he drew himself together long enough to give Miriamele a gentle but purposeful shove.

"You heard him," he growled. *"Jump!"*

She did, then landed hard in the sand and rolled. A fiery bit of something caught in her cloak, but she thumped it out with her hands. A moment later, with a *whoof* of outrushing breath, Isgrimnur crashed down beside her. The ghants, who were squealing and dashing madly back and forth across the grass-strewn beach, paid little attention to their former quarry. The duke turned and climbed to his feet, then reached up his hands. Camaris, leaning far over the uneven edge of the nest, dropped Tiamak down to him. The duke was knocked back to the sand, but cradled the unmoving Wrannaman; a moment later Camaris had vaulted down as well. The company dashed across the strand. A few ghants who had not been struck by Cadrach's fiery attack scuttled toward them, but Miriamele and Camaris kicked them out of the way. The fleeing company stumbled down the bank and waded out into the sluggish green water.

Miriamele sprawled in the bottom of the flatboat, gasping for air. With a few shoves of the pole, the monk sent the boat bobbing out toward the middle of the waterway, well out of reach of the capering ghants.

"Are you hurt?" Cadrach's face was pale, his eyes almost feverishly bright.

"What . . . what did you . . . ?" She could not find the breath to finish her sentence.

Cadrach dipped his head, shrugging. "The oil-palm leaves. I had an idea after you went into . . . that place. I cooked them. There are things I know how to do." He held up the tube he had made from a large reed. "I used this to throw the fire." The hand that clutched the tube was covered with angry blisters.

"Oh, Cadrach, look what you've done."

Cadrach turned to look at Camaris and Isgrimnur, who were huddled over Tiamak. Behind them on the shoreline, the ghants were leaping and hissing like damned souls made to dance. Smears of flame still burned along the nest's front walls, sending knots of inky smoke into the late afternoon sky.

"No, look what *you've* done," the monk said, and smiled a grim but not entirely unhappy smile.

PART TWO

※

The Winding Road

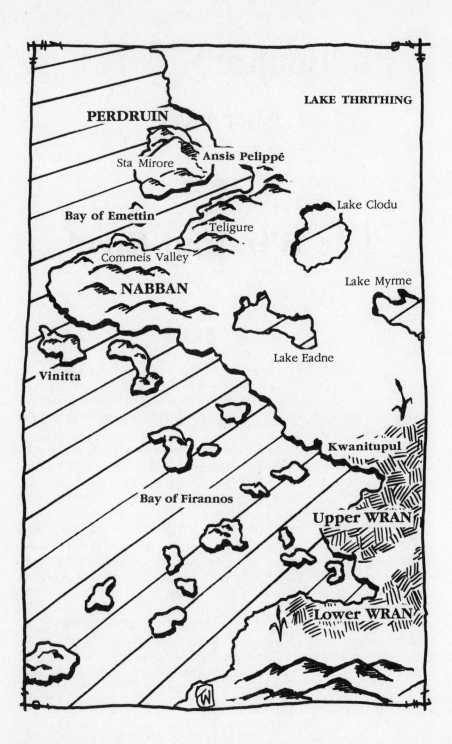

LAKE THRITHING

PERDRUIN

Sta Mirore   Ansis Pelippé

Bay of Emettin   Teligure

Lake Clodu

Commeis Valley

NABBAN

Lake Myrme

Vinitta

Lake Eadne

Kwanitupul

Bay of Firannos

Upper WRAN

Lower WRAN

17

Bonfire Night

❦

"I don't think I want to go, Simon." Jeremias was doing his best, with a rag and a smoothing stone, to clean Simon's sword.

"You don't have to." Simon grunted in pain as he pulled on his boot. Three days had passed since the battle on the frozen lake, but every muscle still felt as though it had been pounded on a blacksmith's anvil. "This is just something he wants me to do."

Jeremias seemed relieved, but was unwilling to accept his freedom so easily. "But shouldn't your squire go along when the prince calls for you? What if you need something that you've forgotten—who would go back for it?"

Simon laughed, but broke off as he felt a band of pain tighten around his ribs. The day after the battle he had barely been able to stand. His body had felt like a bag of broken crockery. Even now, he still moved like an old, old man. "I'll just have to go and get it myself—or I'll call for you. Don't worry. It's not like that here, which you should know as well as anybody. It's not a royal court, like at the Hayholt."

Jeremias peered closely at the blade's edge, then shook his head. "You say that, Simon, but you never can tell when princes will get squinty on you. You can never tell when they might suddenly feel their blood and go all royal."

"It's a risk I'll have to take. Now give me that damned sword before you polish it away to a sliver."

Jeremias looked up anxiously. He had regained a little weight since coming to New Gadrinsett, but provisions were scarce and he was still far from being the chubby boy Simon had grown up with; he had a drawn look that Simon doubted would ever completely go away. "I would never harm your sword," he said seriously.

"Oh, God's Teeth," Simon growled, swearing with the practiced indifference of a blooded soldier. "I was joking. Now give it here. I've got to go."

Jeremias gave him a haughty look. "One thing about jokes, Simon—they're supposed to be funny." Despite the grin that was beginning to crinkle his lips, he handed the blade over carefully. "And I'll let you know if you're ever actually funny, I promise."

Simon's witty reply—which in truth he had not yet formulated—was forestalled by the opening of the tent flap. A small figure appeared in the door-way, silent and solemn.

"Leleth!" Jeremias said. "Come in. Would you like to go for a walk with me? Or I could finish telling you that story about Jack Mundwode and the bear."

The little girl moved a few steps into the tent, which was her way of show-ing assent. Her eyes, as they turned momentarily to Simon's, were disturbingly adult. He remembered how she had looked on the Dream Road—a free crea-ture in its element, flying, exulting—and felt an obscure sense of shame, as if he were somehow helping to keep a beautiful thing prisoned.

"I'll be on my way," he said. "Take care of Jeremias, Leleth. Don't let him handle anything sharp."

Jeremias flung the polishing cloth at him as he stepped through the tent flap.

Outside, Simon took a deep breath. The air was chill, but he thought it felt subtly warmer than it had a few days before, as though somewhere nearby Spring was looking for a way in.

We only beat Fengbald, he cautioned himself. *We didn't hurt the Storm King at all. So there's not much chance we've driven the winter away.*

But the thought raised another question. Why hadn't the Storm King sent help to Fengbald as he had to Elias at the siege of Naglimund? Survivors' stories of the horror of the Norns' attack were almost as vivid in Simon's mind as the memories of his own strange adventures. If the swords were so important, and if Josua was known by the Hikeda'ya to have one of them—which, according to the prince and Deornoth, was almost certainly the case—why hadn't Ses-uad'ra's defenders found themselves staring down at an army of ice-giants and armored Norns? Was it something about the Stone itself?

Perhaps because it is a Sithi place. But they weren't afraid to attack Jao é-Tinukai'i, finally.

He shook his head. It was something to share with Binabik and Geloë, al-though he was sure it had already occurred to them. Or had it? It might be almost too overwhelming to add another unsolvable puzzle to the pile they already faced. Simon was so tired of questions without answers.

His boots crunched in the thin snow as he made his way across the Fire Garden toward Leavetaking House. He had gladly played the fool with Jer-emias, since it seemed to bring his friend out of his worries and evil memo-ries, but Simon was not in a particularly cheerful frame of mind. His last nights had been filled with dreams of the battle's carnage, of madness and blood and screaming horses. Now he was going to see Josua, and the prince was in an even blacker mood than he was. Simon was not looking forward to this at all.

He stopped, his frosty breath rising around his head in a cloud, and stared at the broken dome of the Observatory. If only he dared take the mirror and try to speak with Jiriki again! But the fact that the Sithi had not come, despite the defenders' great need, made it clear that Jiriki had more important things on his mind than the doings of mortals. Also, the Sitha had expressly warned

Simon that this was a perilous time to walk the Road of Dreams. Perhaps if he tried, he would somehow bring the Storm King's attention to Sesuad'ra— Simon might shatter the very indifference that seemed to have been the single greatest reason for their unbelievable victory.

He was a man now, or might as well be. There could be no more mooncalf tricks, he decided. The stakes were far too high.

Leavetaking House was poorly lit: only a few torches burned in the sconces, so that the great room seemed half-dissolved in shadow. Josua was standing by the bier.

"Thank you for coming, Simon." The prince barely raised his eyes before returning his gaze to Deornoth's body, which was laid out on the slab of stone with the Tree and Drake banner draped across it, as though the knight were only sleeping beneath a thin blanket. "Binabik and Geloë are there," the prince said, gesturing to a pair of figures sitting beside the firepit near the far wall. "I will join you in a moment."

Simon walked to the fire with a careful tread, trying to avoid disrespectful noise. The troll and the witch woman were talking quietly.

"Greetings, friend Simon," said Binabik. "Come, sit and be warm."

Simon sat cross-legged on the stone floor, then moved forward to a warmer spot. "He seems even sadder than yesterday," he whispered.

The troll looked at Josua. "It has struck him with a great weightiness. It is as though all the people he was loving, and for whose safety he was fearing, were all killed with Deornoth."

Geloë made a noise of mild exasperation. "You cannot fight battles without losses. Deornoth was a good man, but others died, too."

"Josua is now mourning for all of them, I am thinking—in his way." The troll shrugged. "But I have certainty he will recover."

The witch woman nodded. "Yes, but we have little time. We must strike while the advantage is ours."

Simon looked at her curiously. Geloë seemed as ageless as ever, but she seemed to have lost a little of her vast assurance. Not that it would be surprising if she had: the past year had been a dreadful one. "I wanted to ask you something, Geloë," he said. "Did you know about Fengbald?"

She turned her yellow eyes on him. "Did I know he would send someone onto the field wearing his armor, to fool us? No. But I did know that Josua had conspired with Helfgrim, the Lord Mayor. I did *not* know whether Fengbald would take the bait."

"I am afraid that I was also knowing, Simon," said Binabik. "My help was needed for planning how to split the ice. It was done with the helping of some of my Qanuc fellows."

Simon felt a little warmth rise to his cheeks. "So everybody knew but me?"

Geloë shook her head. "No, Simon. Besides Helfgrim, Josua and myself, there were only Binabik, Deornoth, Freosel, and the trolls that helped prepare the trap—that was all who knew. It was our last hope, and we dared not take a chance of it being even rumored to Fengbald."

"Didn't you trust me?"

Binabik laid a calming hand on his shoulder. "Trust was not the thing that was mattering, Simon. You and any others who were fighting on the ice could have been captured. Even the bravest will tell all they know if they are under torturing—and Fengbald was not being the sort for scruples in such things. The fewer who knew, the better were being chances that the secret would hold. If there had been need to tell you, as there was with those others, we would have told you with no hesitating."

"Binabik is right, Simon." Josua had come up silently as they spoke and now stood over them. The firelight threw his shadow across the ceiling, a long empty stripe of darkness. "I trust you as fully as I trust anyone—anyone living, that is." A hint of something darted across his face. "I ordered that only those necessary to the plan should know. I am sure you can understand."

Simon swallowed. "Of course, Prince Josua."

Josua lowered himself down onto a stone and gazed absently at the wavering flames. "We have won a great victory—it is a miracle, truly. But the price was so very high. . . ."

"No price that kept innocent people alive could be too high," Geloë replied.

"Perhaps. But there is a possibility that Fengbald would have let the women and children go. . . ."

"But now they are alive and *free,*" said Geloë shortly. "And a good number of the men are, too. And we have had an unexpected victory."

The ghost of a smile flickered on Josua's lips. "Are you to take Deornoth's place, then, Valada Geloë? For that is what he always did for me—reminded me when I began to brood."

"I cannot take his place, Josua, but I do not think we need to apologize for winning. Mourning is honorable, of course. I do not seek to take that away from you."

"No, of course not." The prince looked at her for a moment, then pivoted slowly and surveyed the long hall. "We must honor the dead."

There was a scrape of leather in the doorway. Sludig stood there, a pair of saddlebags draped over his brawny arm. Looking at the strain on the Rimmersman's face, Simon wondered if they were packed full of stones. "Prince Josua?"

The prince turned. "Yes, Sludig?"

"These are all that were found. They have Fengbald's crest on them. They are soaking wet, though. I have not opened them."

"Put them down here by the fireside. Then please sit and speak with us. You have been a great help, Sludig."

The Rimmersman bobbed his head. "Thank you, Prince Josua. But I also have another message for you. The prisoners are ready to talk now—or so Freosel says."

"Ah." Josua nodded. "And Freosel is no doubt right. He is rough, but very clever. Not unlike our old friend Einskaldir, eh, Sludig?"

"Just as you say, Highness." Sludig seemed uncomfortable talking to the prince. He was finally getting the attention and credit he seemed to have wanted, Simon noted, but did not seem completely happy with it.

Josua laid his hand on Simon's shoulder. "I suppose I must go and do my duty, then," he said. "Would you come with me, Simon?"

"Of course, Prince Josua."

"Good." Josua made a gesture toward the others. "If you would be so good, attend me after supper. There is much to speak about."

As they approached the door, Josua put the stump of his right wrist beneath Simon's elbow and led him toward the bier where Deornoth lay. Simon could not help noticing that he was a little taller than the prince. It had been a long time since he had stood so close to Josua, but he was still surprised. He, Simon, was tall—and not just for a youth, but for a man. It was a strange thought.

They stopped before the bier. Simon stood on the balls of his feet, respect-fully silent but anxious to move on. Being so close to the knight's body made him uncomfortable. The pale, angular face that lay upon the stone slab looked less like the Deornoth he remembered than like something carved in soap. The skin on his face, especially on his eyelids and nostrils, was bloodlessly translu-cent.

"You did not know him well, Simon. He was the best of men."

Simon swallowed. His mouth felt dry. The dead were . . . so *dead*. And someday Josua, Binabik, Sludig, everyone in New Gadrinsett would be that way. Even he would be that way, Simon realized with a feeling of distaste. What was it like? "He was always very kind to me, Highness."

"He knew no other way. He was the truest knight I have ever known."

The more Josua had spoken of Deornoth in the last few days, the more Simon had come to realize that he had apparently not known the man at all. He had seemed a simple man, kind and quiet, but hardly an exemplar of knight-liness as Josua seemed to think him, a modern Camaris.

"He died bravely." It seemed a lame sort of condolence to offer, but Josua smiled.

"He did. I wish you and Sludig could have reached his side sooner, but you did your best." Josua's face changed abruptly, like clouds blowing across a spring sky. "I do not mean to suggest that you two failed in some way, Simon. Please forgive me—I have grown thoughtless in my grief. Deornoth could always chivvy me out of my self-indulgence. Ah, God, I will miss him. I think he was my best friend, although I never knew it until he was dead."

Simon was further discomfited to see tears forming in Josua's eyes. He wanted to look away, but was suddenly reminded of the Sithi, and of what Strangyeard had said. Perhaps it was the highest and the greatest who always bore the largest griefs. How could there be shame in such sadness?

Simon reached up and took the prince's elbow. "Come, Josua. Let's walk. Tell me about Deornoth, since I never had the chance to know him properly."

The prince tore his gaze away from Deornoth's alabaster features. "Yes, of course. We will walk."

He let Simon lead him out the door and into the hilltop wind.

". . . And he actually came to me and apologized!" Josua was laughing now, although there seemed little joy in it. "As though he himself had transgressed. Poor, loyal Deornoth." He shook his head and wiped at his eye. "Aedon! Why is it that this cloud of regret seems to surround me, Simon? Either I am pleading forgiveness, or those around me are—it is no wonder that Elias thought I was soft-headed. Sometimes I think he was right."

Simon suppressed a grin. "Perhaps the problem is only because you are too quick to share your thoughts with people you do not know well—like escaped scullions."

Josua looked at him narrowly for a moment, then laughed, but this time his mirth seemed less constrained. "Perhaps you are right, Simon. People like their princes strong and unswerving, don't they?" He chuckled. "Ah, Usires the Merciful, could they ever have a prince less like that than me?" He looked up, squinting across the field of tents. "God help me, I have wandered. Where is the cave where the prisoners are kept?"

"There." Simon pointed to a rocky outcropping just inside Sesuad'ra's outer barrier, barely visible behind the wind-shimmied walls of the tent city. Josua altered his course and Simon followed, moving slowly to ease the ache of his several wounds.

"I have let myself run far afield," Josua said, "and not only in my search for the prisoners. I asked you to come to me so I could ask you a question."

"Yes?" Simon could not help but be interested. What could the prince possibly want of him?

"I wish to bury our dead on this hill." Josua waved his arm, spanning the breadth of Sesuad'ra's grassy summit. "You of all the people here know the Sithi best, I think—or at least the most intimately, for certainly Binabik and Geloë have studied them. Do you think that it would be allowed? This is their place, after all."

Simon thought about this for a moment. "Allowed? I can't imagine the Sithi preventing it, if that's what you mean." He smiled wryly. "They didn't even show up to defend it, so I don't think that they would suddenly arrive with an army to keep us from burying our dead."

They walked on a short way in silence. Simon pondered before speaking again. "No, I don't think they would object—not that I could ever claim to speak for them," he added hurriedly. "After all, Jiriki buried his kinsman An'nai with Grimmric, back on Urmsheim." The days on the dragon-mountain seemed so far away now, as though they had been spent there by another Simon, a distant relative. He kneaded the muscles of his painfully stiff arm and sighed. "But, as I said, I cannot speak for the Sithi. I was there for—what, months? And I still could never hope to understand them."

Josua looked at him keenly. "What was it like to live with them, Simon? And what was their city like—Jao . . . Jao . . . ?"

"*Jao é-Tinukai'i.*" Simon was more than a little proud at how easily the difficult syllables fell from his lips. "I wish I could explain, Josua. It's sort of like trying to describe a dream—you can tell what happened, but you can't quite make someone understand how it felt. They are old, Highness, very, very old. But to look at them, they are young and healthy and . . . and beautiful." He remembered Jiriki's sister Aditu, her lovely, bright, predatory eyes, her smile full of secret amusement. "They have every right to hate us, Josua—at least I think they do—but instead they seem . . . puzzled by us. As we would feel if sheep became mighty and drove us out of our cities."

Josua laughed. "Sheep, Simon? Are you saying that the Imperators of Nabban and King Fingil of Rimmersgard . . . and my father, for that matter . . . were woolly, harmless creatures?"

Simon shook his head. "No, I only mean that we are that *different* from the Sithi. They don't understand us any more than we understand them. Jiriki and his grandmother Amerasu might not be as different as some—they certainly treated me with kindness and understanding—but the other Sithi . . ." He stopped, at a loss. "I don't know how to explain it."

Josua looked at him kindly. "What was the city like?"

"I tried to describe it before, when I came here. I said then that it was like a huge boat, but that it was also like a rainbow in front of a waterfall. That's terrible, but I still can't describe it any better than that. It's all made of cloth strung between the trees, but it seems as solid as any city I've ever seen. But it looks as though they could pack it up any moment and take it somewhere else." He laughed despairingly. "You see, I keep running out of words!"

"I think you explain it very well, Simon." The prince's thin features were pensive. "Ah, how I would like to truly know the Sithi someday. I cannot understand what made my father fear and hate them so. What a storehouse of history and lore they must possess!"

They had reached the cave entrance, which was barred with a makeshift portcullis of heavy, rough-cut timbers. A guard posted there—one of Hotvig's Thrithings-men—left the jug of coals over which he had been warming his hands to raise the gateway and let them in.

Several more guards, an even mix of Thrithings-men and Freosel's Erkynlanders, stood in the antechamber. They saluted both the prince and Simon respectfully, much to the bemused chagrin of the latter. Freosel, rubbing his hands together, appeared from the depths of the cavern.

"Your Highness . . . and Sir Seoman," he said, inclining his head. "I think time has come. They be starting to get frisky-like. If we wait longer, we may have trouble—if you pardon my saying so."

"I trust your judgment, Freosel," said Josua. "Take me to them."

The inner part of the wide cavern, which was separated from the front by a bend in the stone walls and thus hidden from the sun, had been divided by the use of more stout timbers into two stockades with a sizable open space between them.

"They do shout at each other 'cross the cave." Freosel's grin revealed the gap in his teeth. "Blaming each other, like. Take turns keeping each other awake nights. Do our job for us, they do."

Josua nodded as he approached the left-hand stockade, then turned to Simon. "Say nothing," he said firmly. "Just listen."

In the dim, torchlit cavern, Simon at first had trouble making out its occupants. The smell of urine and unwashed bodies—something Simon had thought he could no longer notice—was strong.

"I wish to speak with your captain," Josua called. There was slow movement in the shadows, then a figure in the tattered green surcoat of an Erkynguardsman stepped up to the rough bars.

"That is me, your Highness," the soldier said.

Josua looked him over. "Sceldwine? Is that you?"

The man's embarrassment was plain in his voice. "It is, Prince Josua."

"Well." Josua seemed to be taken aback. "I never dreamed to see you in a place like this."

"Nor did I, Highness. Nor expected to be sent to fight against you either, sire. It's a shame . . ."

Freosel abruptly stepped forward. "Don't you listen to him, Josua," he sneered. "He and his murdering cronies will say anything to save their lives." He thumped his powerful hand against the stockade wall hard enough to make the wood quiver. "The rest of us haven't forgot what your kind did to Falshire."

Sceldwine, after drawing back in alarm, leaned forward to see better. His pale face, exposed now by the torchlight, was drawn and worried. "None of us were happy about that." He turned to the prince. "And we did not want to come against you, Prince Josua. You must believe us."

Josua started to say something, but Freosel, astonishingly, interrupted him. "Your people won't have it, Josua. This ben't the Hayholt or Naglimund. We don't trust these armored louts. If you let them live, there'll be trouble."

A mumbling growl ran through the prisoners, but there was more than a little fear in it.

"I don't want to execute them, Freosel," Josua said unhappily. "They were sworn to my brother. What choice did they have?"

"What choice have any of us got?" the Falshireman shot back. "They made the wrong one. Our blood be on their hands. Kill them and have done. Let God worry about choices."

Josua sighed. "What do you say, Sceldwine? Why should I let you live?"

The Erkynguardsman seemed momentarily at a loss. "Because we are just fighting men, serving our king, Highness. There is no other reason." He stared out between the bars.

Josua beckoned for Freosel and Simon and walked away from the stockade to the center of the cavern, out of earshot.

"Well?" he said.

Simon shook his head. "Kill them, Prince Josua? I don't . . ."

Josua raised his hand. "No, no. Of course I won't kill them." He turned to the Falshireman, who was grinning. "Freosel has been working on them for two days. They are convinced he wants their hides, and that the citizens of New Gadrinsett are demanding they be hung before Leavetaking House. We just want them in the proper mood."

Simon was again embarrassed: he had misjudged. "What are you going to do, then?"

"Watch me." After stalling for a few moments more, Josua assumed an air of solemnity and walked slowly back to the stockade and the nervous prisoners. "Sceldwine," he said, "I may regret this, but I am going to let you and your men live."

Freosel, scowling, snorted a great angry snort and marched away. An audible sigh of relief rose from the prisoners.

"But," Josua raised his finger, "we will not keep you and feed you. You will work to earn your lives. My people would hang *me* if I did any less—they will already be very displeased to be cheated of your executions. If you prove yourselves trustworthy, we may let you fight at our side when we push my mad brother from the Dragonbone Chair."

Sceldwine gripped the wooden bars with both his hands. "We will fight for you, Josua. No one else would show us such mercy in these mad times." His comrades gave ragged shouts of agreement.

"Very well. I will think further on how this is to be accomplished." Josua nodded stiffly, then turned his back on the prisoners. Simon followed him out into the middle of the room once more.

"By the Ransomer," said Josua, "if they *will* fight for us, what a boon! A hundred more disciplined soldiers. They may be the first of many more defections, when word begins to spread."

Simon smiled. "You were very convincing. Freosel, too."

Josua looked pleased. "I think that there may be a few strolling players in the constable's family history. As for me—well, all princes are born liars, you know." His expression turned serious. "And now I must deal with the mercenaries."

"You will not make them the same offer, will you?" Simon asked, suddenly worried.

"Why not?"

"Because . . . because someone who fights for gold is different."

"All soldiers fight for gold," Josua said gently.

"That's not what I mean. You heard what Sceldwine said. They fought because they thought they must—that's at least partly true. Those Thrithings-men fought because Fengbald paid them. *You* can't pay them with anything but their lives."

"That's not an inconsiderable sum," Josua pointed out.

"But after they're armed again, how much weight will that have? They're different than the Erkynguard, Josua, and if you want to make a kingdom that's different than your brother's, you can't build it on men like the mercenaries." He stopped abruptly, horrified to discover he was lecturing the prince. "I'm sorry," he blurted. "I have no right to speak this way."

Josua was watching him, eyebrow raised. "They are right about you, young Simon," he said slowly. "There is a good head under that red hair of yours." He laid his hand on Simon's shoulder. "I had not planned to deal with them until Hotvig could join me, in any case. I will think carefully on what you have said."

"I hope you can forgive me my forwardness," Simon said, abashed. "You have been very kind with me."

"I trust your thoughts, Simon, as I do Freosel's. A man who will not listen carefully to advice honestly given is a fool. Of course, a man who blindly takes any advice he receives is a bigger fool." He gave Simon's shoulder a squeeze. "Come, let us walk back. I would like to hear more about the Sithi."

It was strange to use Jiriki's mirror for such a mundane purpose as trimming his beard, but Simon had been told by Sludig—and none too subtly—that he was looking rather straggly. Propped on a rock, the Sithi glass winked in the failing afternoon light. There was a faint mist in the air which continually forced Simon to clean the mirror with his sleeve. Unfamiliar with the art of grooming with a bone knife—he could have borrowed a sharper steel blade from Sludig, but then the Rimmersman probably would have stood by and made comments—Simon had accomplished little more than causing himself a few twinges of pain when the three young women approached.

Simon had seen all three of them around New Gadrinsett—he had even danced with two of them the evening he had become a knight, and the thinnest one had made him a shirt. They seemed terribly young, even though he was probably no more than a year older than any of them. One of them, though, a dark-eyed girl whose round figure and curly brown hair was a little reminiscent of the chambermaid Hepzibah, he thought was rather fetching.

"What are you doing, Sir Seoman?" the thin one asked. She had large, serious eyes which she hooded with her lashes whenever Simon looked at her too long.

"Cutting my beard," he said gruffly. Sir Seoman, indeed! Were they making fun of him?

"Oh, don't cut it off!" the curly-haired girl said. "It makes you look so grand!"

"No, don't," her thin friend echoed.

The third, a short girl with straight yellow hair and a few spots on her face, shook her head. "Don't."

"I'm just trimming it." He marveled at the silliness of women. Just days before, people had been killed defending this place! People that these girls knew, most likely. Yet here they were, bothering him about his beard. How could they be so flittery? "Do you really think it looks . . . grand?" he said.

"Oh, yes," Curly-Hair blurted, then reddened. "That is, it makes you . . . it makes a man look older."

"So you think I need to look older?" he asked in his sternest voice.

"No!" she said hurriedly. "But it looks nice."

"They say you were very brave in the battle, Sir Seoman," said the thin girl.

He shrugged. "We were fighting for our home . . . for our lives. I was just trying not to be killed."

"Just like Camaris would have said," the thin girl sighed.

Simon laughed aloud. "Nothing like Camaris. Nothing at all."

The small girl had sidled around and was now looking intently at Simon's mirror. "Is that the Fairy Glass?" she asked.

"Fairy Glass?"

"People say . . ." She faltered and looked to her friends for help.

Thin One jumped in. "People say that you are a fairy-friend. That the fairies come when you call them with your magic looking-glass."

Simon smiled again, but hesitantly. Bits of truth mixed up with silliness. How did that happen? And who was talking about him? It was odd to think about. "No, that's not quite right. This was given to me by one of the Sithi, yes, but they do not simply come when I call. Otherwise, we would not have fought by ourselves against Duke Fengbald, now would we?"

"Can your looking-glass grant wishes?" Curly-Hair asked.

"No," Simon said firmly. "It's never granted any of mine." He paused, remembering his rescue by Aditu in Aldheorte's wintery depths. "I mean, that's not really what it does," he finished. So he, too, was mixing truth with lies. But how could he possibly explain the madness of this last year so that they could understand it?

"We were praying that you would bring us allies, Sir Seoman," the thin girl said seriously. "We were so frightened."

As he looked at her pale face, he saw that she was telling the truth. Of course they had been upset—did that mean that they could not be glad that they were alive? That wasn't the same as being flittery, really. Should they brood and mourn like Josua?

"I was frightened, too," he said. "We were very lucky."

There was a pause. The curly-haired girl arranged her cloak, which had fallen open to reveal the soft skin of her throat. The weather *was* getting warmer, Simon realized. He had been standing motionless here for some time, but had not shivered once. He looked up at the sky, as if hoping to find some confirmation of winter's dwindling.

"Do you have a lady?" the curly-haired girl said suddenly.

"Do I have a what?" he asked, although he had heard her perfectly well.

"A lady," she said, blushing furiously. "A sweetheart."

Simon waited for a moment before replying. "Not really." The three girls were staring at him raptly, expectant as puppies, and he felt his own cheeks grow hot. "No, not really." He had been clutching his Qanuc knife so long that his fingers had begun to ache.

"Ah," said Curly-Hair. "Well, we should leave you to your work, Sir Seoman." Her slender friend pulled at her elbow, but she ignored her. "Will you be coming to the bonfire?"

"Bonfire?" Simon furrowed his brow.

"The celebration. Well, and the mourning, too. In the middle of the settlement." She pointed toward the massed tents of New Gadrinsett. "Tomorrow night."

"I didn't know. Yes, I suppose I might." He smiled again. These were really quite sensible young women when you talked with them a while. "And thank you again for the shirt," he told Thin One.

She blinked rapidly. "Maybe you will wear it tomorrow night."

After saying good-bye, the three girls turned and walked off across the hillside, leaning their heads very close together, wriggling and laughing. Simon felt a moment's indignation at the thought that they might be laughing at him, but then he let it pass. They seemed to like him, didn't they? That was just the way that girls were, as far as he could tell.

He turned to his mirror once more, determined to finish with his beard before the sun began to set. A bonfire, was it . . . ? He wondered if he should wear his sword.

Simon pondered his own words. It was true, of course, that he had no lady love, as he supposed knights should—even the ragtag sort of knight he had become. Still, it was hard not to think about Miriamele. How long had it been since he had seen her? He counted the months on his hand: Yuven, Anitul, Tiyagaris, Septander, Octander . . . almost half a year! It was easy to believe she had forgotten him entirely by now.

But he had not forgotten her. There had been moments, strange and almost frightening moments, when he had been certain that she felt as drawn to him as he was to her. Her eyes had seemed so large when she looked at him, so careful to take him in, as though she memorized his every line. Could it be only his imagination? Certainly they had shared a wild and almost unbelievable adventure together, and almost equally certainly, she considered him a friend . . . but did she think anything more of him than that?

The memory of how she had looked at Naglimund swept over him. She had been dressed in her sky-blue gown and had been suddenly almost terrible in her completeness—so different from the ragged serving girl who had slept on his shoulder. And yet, the very same girl had been inside that blue dress. She had been almost hesitant when they had met in the castle courtyard—but was it out of shame at the trick she had played him, or worry that her resumption of station might have separated them?

He had seen her on a Hayholt tower top: her hair had been like golden floss. Simon, a poor scullion, had watched and felt like a mud-beetle catching a glimpse of the sun. And her face, so alive, so quick to change, full of anger and laughter, more mercurial and unpredictable than that of any woman he had ever met . . .

But it was fruitless to go on mooning this way, he told himself. It was unlikely in the extreme that she even thought of him as anything more than a friendly scullion, like the servants' children with whom the nobility were raised, but who they quickly forgot upon reaching adulthood. And of course, even if she did care for him at all, there was no chance that anything could ever come of it. That was just the way of things, or at least so he had been taught.

Still, he had been out in the world long enough now and had seen enough oddities that the immutable facts of life Rachel had taught him seemed much less believable. How were common folk and those of royal blood different, anyway? Josua was a kind man, a clever and earnest man—Simon had little doubt that he would make a fine king—but his brother Elias had proved to be a monster. Could any peasant dragged from the barley fields do any worse? What was so sacred about royal blood? And, now that he thought about it, hadn't King John himself come from a family of peasants—or as good as peasants?

A mad thought suddenly occurred to him: what if Elias should be defeated, but Josua died? What if Miriamele never returned? Then someone else must be king or queen. Simon knew little of the affairs of the world—at least those outside his own tangled journey of the past half year. Were there others of royal blood who would step forward and claim the Dragonbone Chair? That fellow in Nabban, Bigaris or whatever his name was? Whoever was the heir of Lluth, dead king of Hernystir? Or old Isgrimnur, perhaps, if he should ever come back. He, at least, Simon could respect.

But now the fleeting thought was glowing like a hot coal. Why shouldn't he, Simon, be as likely as anyone else? If the world were turned upside down, and if all those with claims were gone when the dust settled, why not a knight of Erkynland—one who had fought a dragon just as John had, and who had been marked by the dragon's black blood? One who had been to the forbidden world of the Sithi, and who was a friend of the trolls of Yiqanuc? Then he would be fit for a princess or anyone else!

Simon stared at his reflection, at the curl of white hair like a dab of paint, at his long scar and his disconcertingly fuzzy beard.

Look at me, he thought, and suddenly laughed aloud. *King Simon the Great! Might as well make Rachel the Duchess of Nabban, or that monk Cadrach the Lector of Mother Church. Might as well wait for the stars to shine in the middle of the day!*

And who would want to be the king, anyway?

For that was it, after all: Simon saw little but pain in store for whoever re-placed Elias on the chair of bones. Even if the Storm King could be defeated, which seemed a possibility small to the point of nonexistence, the whole of the land was in ruins, the people starved and frozen. There would be no tourna-ments, no processions, no sunlight gleaming on armor, not for many years.

No, he thought bitterly, *the next king should be someone like Barnabas, the sexton of the Hayholt's chapel—someone good at burying the dead.*

He pushed the mirror back into the pocket of his cloak and sat down on a rock to watch the sun slipping behind the trees.

Vorzheva found her husband in Leavetaking House. The long hall was empty but for Josua and the pale form of Deornoth. The prince himself scarcely seemed like one of the living, standing motionless as a statue beside the altar that bore his friend's body.

"Josua?"

The prince turned slowly, as though waking from a dream. "Yes, lady?"

"You are here too much. The day is ending."

He smiled. "I have only just returned. I was walking with Simon, and I had some other duties."

Vorzheva shook her head. "You returned long ago, even if you do not re-member. You have been in this place most of the afternoon."

Josua's smile faltered. "Have I?" He turned to look at Deornoth. "I feel, I don't know, that it is wrong to leave him alone. He was always looking after me."

She stepped forward and took his arm. "I know. Come, walk with me."

"Very well." Josua reached out and touched the shroud draped across Deor-noth's chest.

Leavetaking House had been little more than a shell when Josua and his company had first come to Sesuad'ra. The settlers had built shutters for the gaping windows and stout wooden doors to make it a place where the business of New Gadrinsett could take place in warmth and privacy. There was still something of the makeshift about it, though—the crude contrivances of the latest residents made an odd contrast when set against the graceful handiwork of the Sithi. Josua let his fingers trail across a bloom of carvings as Vorzheva led him toward one of the doors in the back wall and out into the failing sunlight.

The garden's walls were crumbled, the stone walkways broken and upended. A few hardy old rosebushes had survived winter's onslaught, and although it might be months or years before they would bloom again, their dark leaves and gray, thorny boughs looked strong and vigorous. It was hard not to wonder how long they had grown there, or who had planted them.

Vorzheva and Josua walked past the knotted trunk of a huge pine tree which grew in the breach of one of the walls. The dying sun, a blur of burning red, seemed hung in its branches.

"Do you still think of her?" Vorzheva asked suddenly.

"What?" Josua's mind seemed to have been wandering. "Who?"

"That other one. The one you loved, your brother's wife."

The prince inclined his head. "Hylissa. No, not often. There are far more important things to think on these days." He put his arm about his wife's shoulders. "I have a family now which needs my care."

Vorzheva looked at him suspiciously for a moment, then nodded her head with quiet satisfaction. "Yes," she said. "You do."

"And not just a family, but a whole people, it seems."

She made a quiet noise of despair. "You cannot be everyone's husband, everyone's father."

"Of course not. But I must be the prince, whether I wish to or not."

They walked on for a while without talking, listening to the irregular music of a lone bird perched high in the swaying branches. The wind was chilly, but the edge seemed a little less than it had been in the days before, which might have been why the bird sang.

Vorzheva pressed her head against Josua's shoulder so that her black hair fluttered around his chin. "What will we do now?" she asked. "Now the battle is ended?"

Josua led her toward a stone bench, fallen to shards at one end, but still with much of its surface unbroken. They brushed off a few melting spatters of snow and sat down. "I do not know," he said. "I think it is time for another Raed—a council. We have much to decide. I have many doubts about what is the wisest course. We should not wait long after . . . after we have buried our fallen."

Vorzheva looked at him, surprised. "What do you mean, Josua? Why such hurry to have this thing?"

The prince raised his hand and examined the lines on his palm. "Because there is a possibility that if we do not strike now, an important chance will be lost."

"Strike?" She seemed astounded. "Strike what? What madness is this? We have lost one of every three! You would take these few hundred against your brother!?"

"But we have won an important victory. The first anyone has had against him since he began his mad campaign. If we strike out now, while memory is fresh and Elias is unaware of what has happened, our people here will take heart; when others see we are moving, they will join us, too."

Vorzheva stood, her eyes wide. She held an arm around her middle as if to protect their unborn child. "No! Oh, Josua, that is too stupid! I thought you were to wait at least until the winter had passed! How can you go off to fight now?"

"I never said I was going to do anything," he said. "I have not decided yet—nor will I, until I have called a Raed."

"Yes, you men will sit around and talk of the great battle you fought. Will the women be there?"

"Women?" He looked at her quizzically. "Geloë will be a part of it."

"Oh, yes, Geloë," she said with scorn. "Because she is called a 'wise woman.' That is the only sort of woman you will listen to—one who has a name for it, like a fast horse or a strong ox."

"What should we do—invite everyone from all of New Gadrinsett?" He was growing annoyed. "That would be foolish."

"No more foolish than listening to only men." She stared at him for a moment, then visibly forced herself to become calm. She took several breaths before speaking again. "There is a story the women of the Stallion Clan tell. It is about the bull who would not listen to his cows."

Josua waited. "Well," he said at last. "What happened to him?"

Vorzheva scowled and moved away down the broken path. "Go on as you are doing. You will find out."

Josua's expression seemed half-amusement, half-displeasure. "Wait, Vorzheva." He rose and followed her. "You are right to chide me. I should listen to what you have to say. What happened to the bull?"

She looked him over carefully. "I will tell you some other time. I am too angry now."

Josua took her hand and fell into step beside her. The path curled through the disarranged stones, bringing them close to the tumbled blocks of the outer garden wall. There was a noise of voices from beyond.

"Very well," she said abruptly. "The bull was too proud to listen to his cows. When they told to him that a wolf was stealing the calves, he did not believe, because he did not see it himself. When all the calves were stolen, the cows drove the bull away and found a new bull." Her stare was defiant. "Then the wolves ate the old bull, since he had no one to protect him while he slept."

Josua's laugh was harsh. "And is that a warning?"

She squeezed his arm. "Please, Josua. The people are tired of the fighting. We make a home here." She pulled him closer to the breach in the stone. From the far side rose the noise of the ragtag marketplace that had sprung up in the shelter of Leavetaking House's outer walls. Several dozen men, women, and children were bartering with old possessions carried out of their former homes and new things gathered on and about Sesuad'ra. "See," Vorzheva said, "they make a new life. You told them they fought for their home. How can you make them move again?"

Josua stared at a group of bundled children playing tug-o-war with a colorful rag. They were shrieking with laughter and kicking up puffs of snow; nearby, someone's mother was calling angrily for her child to come in out of the wind. "But this is not their true home," he said quietly. "We cannot stay here forever."

"Who is staying forever?" Vorzheva demanded. "Until spring! Until our child is born!"

Josua shook his head. "But we may never have a chance like this again." He turned away from the wall, his face grave. "Besides, I owe it to Deornoth. He gave his life, not for us to quietly disappear, but so that we could pay back the wrongs my brother has done."

"Owe it to Deornoth!" Vorzheva sounded angry, but her eyes were sad. "What a thing to say! Only a man would say such a thing."

Josua turned and caught her up, pulling her toward him. "I do love you, Lady. I only try to do what is right."

She averted her eyes. "I know. But . . ."

"But you do not think I am making the best decision." He nodded, stroking her hair. "I am listening to everyone, Vorzheva, but the final word must be mine." He sighed and held her for a while without speaking. "Merciful Aedon, I would not wish this on anyone," he said at last. "Vorzheva, promise me something."

"What?" Her voice was muffled in his cloak.

"I have changed my mind. If something happens to me . . ." He thought. "If something happens to me, take our child away from this. Do not let anyone put him on a throne, or use him as the rallying symbol for some army."

"Him?"

"Or her. Do not let our child be forced into this game as I was."

Vorzheva shook her head fiercely. "No one will take my baby away from me, not even your friends."

"Good." He looked out through the blowing tendrils of her hair. The sun had fallen behind Leavetaking House, reddening the entire western sky. "That makes whatever will come easier to bear."

Five days after the battle, the last of Sesuad'ra's dead were buried—men and women of Erkynland, Rimmersgard, Hernystir and the Thrithings, of Yiqanuc and Nabban, refugees from half a hundred places, all laid to rest in the shallow earth on the summit of the Stone of Farewell. Prince Josua spoke carefully and seriously about their suffering and sacrifice as his cloak billowed in the winds that swirled around the hilltop. Father Strangyeard, Freosel, and Binabik all rose in turn to say words of one sort or another. The citizens of New Gadrinsett stood, hard-faced, and listened.

Some of the graves had no markers, but most had some small monument, a carved board or rough-chiseled piece of stone that bore the name of the fallen one. After great labors to hack into the icy ground, the Erkynguard had buried their own dead in a mass grave beside the lake, crowning it with a single slab of rock that bore the legend: "Soldiers of Erkynland, killed in the Battle of Stefflod Valley. *Em Wulstes Duos."* By God's will.

Only the fallen Thrithings mercenaries were unmourned and unmarked. Their living comrades dug a vast barrow for them on the grasslands below Sesuad'ra—half believing it would be their own, that Josua planned to execute them. Instead, when the labor was finished they found themselves escorted by armed men far out onto the open lands and then set free. It was a terrible thing for a Thrithings-man to lose his horse, but the surviving mercenaries decided quickly that walking was better than dying.

So, at last, all the dead were buried and the ravens were cheated of their holiday.

As solemn music played, vying with the harsh wind to be heard, the thought came to many of those who watched that although Sesuad'ra's defenders had won an improbable and heroic victory, they had paid dearly for it. The fact that they had defeated only the tiniest portion of the forces arrayed against them, and had lost nearly half their number in doing so, made the winter-shrouded hillcrest seem an even colder and lonelier place.

Someone caught Simon's arm from behind. He turned swiftly, tugging his arm loose, and raised it to strike.

"Here, lad, here, don't be so hasty-quick!" The old jester cowered, hands held over his head.

"I'm sorry, Towser." Simon rearranged his cloak. The bonfire was glowing in the near distance and he was impatient to be going. "I didn't know who it was."

"No offense taken, laddie." Towser swayed slightly. "The thing is . . . well, I was just wondering if I could walk with you a way. Over to the celebration. I'm not as steady on my feet as I was."

Not surprising, Simon thought: Towser's breath was heavily scented with wine. Then he remembered what Sangfugol had said and fought down his urge to hurry on. "Of course." He extended a discreet arm for the old man to lean on.

"Kind, lad, very kind. Simon, isn't it?" The old man looked up at him, his shadowed face a puzzle of wrinkles.

"That's right." Simon smiled in the darkness. He had reminded Towser of his name a dozen different times.

"You'll do well, you will," the old man said. They moved toward the flickering light, walking slowly. "And I've met them all."

Towser did not stay with him long once they reached the celebration. The old jester quickly found a group of drunken trolls and went off to reintroduce them to the glories of Bull's Horn—and himself to the glories of *kangkang,* Simon suspected. Simon wandered for a while on the periphery of the gathering.

It was a true feast night, perhaps the first that Sesuad'ra had seen. Fengbald's camp had proven to be groaningly full of stocks and stores, as though the late duke had plundered all Erkynland to insure he would be as comfortable in the Thrithings as if he had remained at the Hayholt. Josua had wisely made sure that most of the food and other useful things were hidden away for later—even if the company was to leave the Stone, it would not be tomorrow—but a generous portion had been made available for the celebration, so that tonight the hilltop had a genuinely festive air. Freosel, in particular, had derived no little pleasure from breaching Fengbald's casks, draining off the first mug of Stanshire Dark himself with as much pleasure as if it had been the duke's blood instead of only his beer.

Wood, one of the other things not in short supply, had been piled high in the center of the vast flat surface of the Fire Garden. The bonfire was burning brightly, and most of the people were gathered on the wide field of tiles. Sangfugol and some of the other musical citizens of New Gadrinsett were strolling here and there, playing for knots of appreciative listeners. Some of the listeners were more enthusiastic than others. Simon had to laugh as a particularly sodden trio of celebrants insisted on joining the harper in his rendition of "By Greenwade's Shore." Sangfugol winced but gamely played on; Simon silently congratulated the harper on his fortitude before wandering away.

The night was chilly but clear, and the wind that had bedeviled the hilltop during the burial rites was all but gone. Simon, after pondering for a moment, decided that considering the time of the year, the weather was actually rather nice. Again he wondered if the Storm King's power might somehow be slipping, but this time the thought was followed by an even more worrisome question.

What if he's only gathering his strength? What if he's going to reach out now and do what Fengbald couldn't?

That was not a line of thought Simon wished to pursue. He shrugged and readjusted his sword belt.

The first cup of wine offered to him went down very nicely, warming his stomach and loosening his muscles. He had been part of the small army put to work burying the dead—a ghastly task made worse by the occasional familiar face glimpsed beneath a mask of hoarfrost. Simon and the others had worked like demons to breach the stony ground, digging with whatever they could find—swords, axes, limbs of fallen trees, but as difficult as it had been to scrape in the frozen earth, the cold had slowed putrefaction, making a horrible job just a little more bearable. Still, Simon's sleep had been raddled by nightmares the past two nights—endless visions of stiffened bodies tumbling into ditches, bodies rigid as statues, contorted figures that might have been carved by some mad sculptor obsessed by pain and suffering.

War's rewards, Simon thought as he walked through the noisy throng. And if Josua were to be successful, the battles to come would make this look like an Yrmansol dance. The corpses would be piled higher than Green Angel Tower.

The thought made him feel cold and sick. He went in search of more wine.

The festival had a certain air of heedlessness, Simon noted. Voices were too loud, laughter too swift, as though those who talked and made merry were doing so for the benefit of others more than themselves. With the wine came fighting, too, which seemed to Simon as though it should be the last thing anyone would desire. Still, he passed more than a few clumps of people gathered around a pair or more of swearing, shouting men, calling encouragement and mockery as the combatants rolled in the mud. Those in the crowd who were not laughing looked disturbed or unhappy.

They know we are not saved, Simon thought, regretting his own mood on what should be a wonderful night. *They are happy to be alive, but they know the future may be worse.*

He wandered on, taking a drink when it was offered. He stopped for a while near Leavetaking House to watch Sludig and Hotvig wrestle—a friendlier kind of combat than he had seen elsewhere. The northerner and the Thrithings-man were stripped to the waist and grappling fiercely, each trying to throw the other out of a circle of rope, but both men were laughing; when they stopped to rest, they shared a wineskin. Simon called out a greeting to them.

Feeling like a lonely seagull circling the mast of a pleasure boat, he walked on.

Simon was not sure what time it was, whether it was just an hour or so after dark or approaching midnight. Things had begun to grow a little blurry somewhere after his half-dozenth drink of wine.

However, at this exact moment, time did not seem very important. What *did* seem that way was the girl who walked beside him, the light of the fading bonfire glinting in her dark, wavy hair. She wasn't named Curly-Hair, but Ulca, as he had recently learned. She stumbled and he put his arm around her, amazed at how warm a body could feel, even through thick clothing.

"Where are we going?" she asked, then laughed. She did not seem terribly worried about possible destinations.

"Walking," Simon replied. After a moment's thought he decided he should make his plan more clear. "Walking around."

The noise of the celebration was a dull roar behind them, and for a moment Simon could almost imagine that he was in the middle of the battle once more, on the frozen lake, slick with blood. . . .

His hackles rose. Why would he want to think about something like that!? He made a noise of disgust.

"What?" Ulca swayed, but her eyes were bright. She had shared the wineskin Sangfugol had given to him. She seemed to have a natural talent for holding her wine.

"Nothing," he replied gruffly. "Just thinking. About the fighting. The battle. Fighting."

"It must have been . . . horrible!" Her voice was full of wonder. "We watched. Welma 'n' me. We were crying."

"Welming you?" Simon glared at her. Was she trying to confuse him? "What does that mean?"

"Welma. I said 'Welma an' me.' My friend, the slender one. You met her!" Ulca squeezed his arm, amused by his clever jest.

"Oh." He reflected on the recent conversation. What had they been talking about? Ah. The battle. "It was horrible. Blood. People killed." He tried to find some way to sum up the totality of the experience, to let this young woman know what he, Simon, had experienced. "Worse than anything," he said heavily.

"Oh, Sir Seoman," she cried, and stopped, losing her balance for a moment on the slippery ground. "You must have been frightened!"

"Simon. Not Seoman—Simon." He considered what she had said. "Little. A little." It was hard not to notice her proximity. She had a very nice face, really, full-cheeked and long-lashed. And her mouth. Why was it so close, though?

He refocused his eyes and discovered that he was leaning forward, toppling toward Ulca like a felled tree. He put his hands on her shoulders for balance, and was interested by how small she felt beneath his touch. "I'm going to kiss you," he said suddenly.

"You shouldn't," Ulca said, but closed her eyes and did not move away.

He kept his own eyes open for fear of missing his mark and tumbling to the snow-flecked ground. Her mouth was strangely firm beneath his, but warm and soft as a blanketed bed on a winter's night. He let his lips stay there for a moment, trying to remember if he had ever done this before and if so, what to do next. Ulca did not move, and they stood in place, breathing air gently scented with wine into each other's mouths.

Simon discovered soon enough that kissing was more than just standing lip to lip, and after a short while the cold air, the horrors of battle, even the ruckus of the bonfire a short distance away had disappeared from his mind. He stretched his arms around this wonderful creature and pulled her close, enjoying the feeling of sweetly yielding girl pressed against him, never wanting to do anything else in his whole life, however long it might be.

"Ooh, Seoman," Ulca said at last, pulling back to catch her breath, "you could make a girl faint."

"Mmmm." Simon drew her back again, bending his neck so that he could nibble at her ear. If only she were a little taller! "Sit down," he said. "I want to sit down."

They struggled along for a few joined steps, clumsy as a crab, until Simon found a chunk of fallen masonry of appropriate height. He wrapped his cloak around both of them as they sat down, then pulled Ulca close once more, squeezing and kneading even as he continued to kiss her. Her breath was warm against his face. She was soft in some places, firm in others. What a wonderful world this was!

"Ooh, Seoman." Her voice was muffled as she spoke into his cheek. "Your beard, it scratches so!"

"Yes, it does, doesn't it?"

It took Simon a moment to realize that someone other than himself had answered Ulca. He looked up.

The figure standing before them was dressed all in white—jacket, boots, and breeches. It had long hair that streamed in the light breeze, a mocking smile, and upturned eyes no more human than those of a cat or a fox.

Ulca stared for a moment, her mouth open. She let out a tiny squeak of amazement and fear.

"Who . . . ?" She rose unsteadily from their seat. "Seoman, who . . . ?"

"*I* am a fairy woman," said Jiriki's sister, her voice suddenly stony. "And *you* are a little mortal girl . . . who is *kissing my husband-to-be!* I think I shall have to do something dreadful to you."

Ulca gasped for breath and screamed in earnest this time, pushing herself away from Simon so strongly that he was almost toppled from the rock. Curly hair unbound and flying behind her, she ran back toward the bonfire.

Simon stared after her stupidly for a moment, then turned back to the Sitha-woman. "Aditu?"

She was watching the disappearing form of Ulca. "Greetings, Seoman." She spoke calmly, but with a hint of amusement. "My brother sends his regards."

"What are you doing here?" Simon could not understand what had just happened. He felt as though he had fallen out of bed during a wonderful dream and landed on his head in a bear pit. "Merciful Aedon! And what do you mean, 'husband-to-be'?!"

Aditu laughed, her teeth flashing. "I thought it would be a good story to add to the other Tales of Seoman the Bold. I have been haunting the shadows all evening and have heard many people mention your name. You slay dragons and wield fairy-weapons, so why not have a fairy-wife?" She reached out a hand, enclosing his wrist with cool, supple fingers. "Now come, we have much to talk about. You can rub faces with that little mortal girl some other time."

Simon followed, stunned, as Aditu led him back toward the light of the bonfire. "Not after this I can't," he mumbled.

18

The Fox's Bargain

Eolair's sleep had been shallow and troubled, so he woke instantly when Isorn touched his shoulder.

"What is it?" He fumbled for his sword, fingers scrabbling through the damp leaves.

"Someone coming." The Rimmersman was tense, but there was an odd look on his face. "I don't know," he muttered. "You had better come."

Eolair rolled over and clambered to his feet, then paused to buckle on his sword belt. The moon hung solemnly above the Stagwood; from its position, Eolair guessed that dawn could not be far away. There *was* something odd in the air: the count could feel it already. This forest the Hernystiri called *Fiadhcoille,* which spread in a contented clump a few leagues southeast of Nad Mullach beside the river Baraillean, was a place he had hunted every spring and fall as a young man, a spot he knew like his own hall. When he had rolled himself in his cloak and blanket to sleep, it had been familiar as an old friend. Now, suddenly, it seemed different in a way he could not understand.

The camp was stirring into wakefulness. Already most of Ule's men were pulling on their boots. Their numbers had almost tripled since he and Isorn had found them—there were quite a few masterless men wandering the edges of the Frostmarch who were happy to join an organized band, regardless of its purpose—and Eolair doubted that anything but a major force of arms could threaten them.

But what if Skali had received word of their presence? They were a sizable company, but against an army like Kaldskryke's they could not hope to be more than a brief annoyance.

Isorn stood just ahead at the forest fringe, beckoning. Eolair moved toward him, trying to move as quietly as he could, but even as he listened to the soft crunching of his own footfalls, he became aware of . . . something else.

At first he thought it was the wind, wailing like a chorus of spirits, but the trees around him were still, clumps of soft snow balanced delicately at the ends of the branches. No, it was not the wind. The sound had a regular quality, rhythmic, even musical. It sounded, Eolair thought, like . . . singing.

"Brynioch!" he swore as he moved up beside Isorn. "What is it?"

"The sentries heard that an hour gone," the duke's son muttered. "How loud must it be, that we have not seen them yet?"

Eolair shook his head. The snow-dappled plain of the lower Inniscrich lay before them, pale and uneven as rumpled silk. Men were moving up on either side, crawling to the edge of the trees to look out, until Eolair felt as though he were surrounded by a crowd awaiting a royal procession. But the anticipatory looks of the hard-faced men around him were more than a little fearful. Many sword-hilts were already clutched in damp palms.

The singing rose in pitch, then abruptly stopped. In its wake, the sound of many hoofbeats echoed along the Stagwood's fringe. Eolair, still wiping sleep from his eyes, drew breath to say something to Isorn. As it turned out, he held that breath for a long time, and when he let it go, it was only to suck in another.

They appeared from the east, as though they had come out of northern Erkynland—or, Eolair thought distractedly, out of the depths of Aldheorte Forest. They were little more than a shimmer of moonlight on metal at first, a distant cloud of silvershine in the darkness. Hoofbeats rumbled like heavy rain on a wooden roof, then a horn winded, an oddly haunting note that pierced the night, and suddenly they seemed almost to burst into full view. One of Ule's men went mad when he saw them. He ran shouting into the forest, slapping at his head as though it burned, and was not seen again by any of his fellows.

Although none of the others were so badly afflicted, no one who passed that night in the Stagwood was ever after the same, nor could any of them quite say why. Even Eolair was stunned, Eolair who had traveled most of the length and breadth of Osten Ard, who had seen sights that reduced most men to tongue-tied awe. But even the worldly count would never be able to explain just how it had felt to watch the Sithi ride.

As the wild company thundered past, the very quality of the moonlight seemed to change. The air became pale and crystalline; objects seemed to glitter at the edges, as though every tree and man and blade of grass was limned in diamond. The Sithi rolled past like a great ocean wave capped with gleaming spear-points. Their faces were hard and fierce and beautiful as the faces of hunting hawks, and their hair streamed in the wind of their passage. The immortals' steeds seemed to race more swiftly than any horses could run, but they moved in a way that seemed fit only for dreams, pace smooth as melting honey, hooves carving the darkness into pale streaks of fire.

Within moments the bright company had dwindled to a dark mass vanishing in the west, their hoofbeats a fading murmur. They left behind them silence and, in some of the watchers, tears.

"The Fair Ones . . ." Eolair breathed at last. His own voice seemed as thick and hoarse as the croaking of a frog.

"The . . . Sithi?" Isorn shook his head as though he had been struck a blow. "But . . . but why? Where are they going?"

And suddenly Eolair knew. "The Fox's Bargain," he said, and laughed. His heart felt buoyant in his chest.

"What do you mean?" Isorn watched in bewilderment as the Count of Nad Mullach turned and headed back into the forest.

"An old song," he called back. "The Fox's Bargain!" He laughed again and sang, feeling the words leap out as though they sought the night air of their own accord.

> " 'We never forget,' the Fair Ones said,
> 'Though Time may ancient run.
> You will hear our horns beneath the moon,
> You will see our spears shine in the sun . . .' "

"I do not understand!" Isorn cried.

"Never mind!" Eolair was almost out of sight, moving rapidly toward the camp. "Get the men! We must ride to Hernysadharc!"

As if to echo him, a silvery horn sounded in the distance.

"It is an old song of our people," Eolair called across to Isorn. Although they had been riding at speed since before the sun had risen, there was no sign of the Sithi but for a trample of hoofprints on the snowy grass, hoofprints already fading as the grass sprang back and the snow liquefied in the morning's warmth. "It tells of the promise the Fair Ones made to the Red Fox—Prince Sinnach—before the battle of Ach Samrath: they swore they would never forget the faithfulness of Hernystir."

"So you think they are riding against Skali?"

"Who can say? But look where they are bound!" The count stood in the saddle and pointed out across the broad grasslands at the tracks disappearing into the west. "True as an arrow's flight to the Taig!"

"Even if that is where they are going, we cannot ride all the way there at this pace," said Isorn. "The horses are flagging already, and we have only traveled a few leagues."

Eolair looked around. The company was beginning to slide apart, some of the riders falling well back. "Perhaps. But, Bagba bite me, if they are going to Hernysadharc, I want to be there!"

Isorn grinned, his wide face crinkling. "Not unless your fairy-folk left us some of their fairy-horses, with wings on their feet. But we will get there eventually."

The count shook his head, but pulled gently back on the reins, slowing his gray horse to a canter. "True. We'll do no one any good if we kill our mounts."

"Or ourselves." Isorn waved his hand to slow the rest of the company.

They stopped for a midday meal. Eolair balanced his impatience against what he knew to be the wisdom of having his troop at least somewhat rested: if there was to be fighting, men who were ready to drop in their tracks and horses who could not walk another step would make a very indifferent contribution.

After an hour's rest they were back in the saddle again, but Eolair now kept the pace more reasonable. By the time darkness arrived, they had crossed the Inniscrich to the outskirts of the territory of Hernysadharc, although they were still several hours' ride from the Taig. They had passed some encampments that Eolair guessed had belonged to Skali's men. All were deserted, but signs indicated that the tenancy had been recent: in one of them, the cookfires still smoldered. The count wondered if the Rimmersmen had fled before the onrushing Sithi, or had suffered some other, stranger fate.

At Isorn's insistence, Eolair finally brought the company to a halt near Ballacym, a walled town on a low hillside that looked back over the western edge of the Inniscrich. Much of the town had been destroyed during Lluth's losing battle with Skali nearly a year before, but enough of the walls remained to offer some shelter.

"We do not want to arrive in the midst of any struggle at night," Isorn said as they rode through the shattered gates. "Even if you are correct and your fairy-folk have come to fight for Hernystir, how will they know the difference between the right and wrong sort of mortal in the dark?"

Eolair was not pleased, but he could not dispute the wisdom of Isorn's words. As he had already known, there was little his small band could do against a large army like Skali's, but the thought of having to wait was still infuriating. His heart had sung to match the Sithi themselves as he had watched them ride. To do something—to finally strike a blow at those who had devastated his land! The idea had pushed at him like a strong wind. And now he must wait until morning.

Eolair drank more than his usual modest portion of wine that night, though it was in short supply, then lay down early, uninterested in talking about what they all had seen and what they might be riding toward. He knew that even with the wine-fumes in his head, sleep would be a long time coming. It was.

"I do not like this," Ule Frekkeson growled, drawing back on his reins. "Where have they gone? And, by the Holy Aedon, what has happened here?"

The streets of Hernysadharc were strangely deserted. Eolair knew that few of his people had remained after Skali's conquest, but even if all the Rimmersmen had been driven out by the Sithi—which seemed impossible, since scarcely more than a day had passed since the Fair Ones rode past, half a hundred leagues west—there should still be at least a few of the native Hernystir-folk.

"I do not like it any more than you do," the count replied, "but I cannot imagine Skali's entire army would be hiding in ambush for our seven or eight score."

"Eolair is right." Isorn shaded his eyes. The weather was still cold, but the sun was surprisingly bright. "Let's ride in and take our chances."

Ule bit back a rejoinder, then shrugged. The trio rode in through the crude gates the Rimmersmen had built; the men followed, talking among themselves.

It was disturbing enough to see a wall around Hernysadharc. Never in Eolair's memory had there been one, and even the ancient wall that circled the Taig remained only out of the Hernystiri reverence for past days. Most of the older wall had collapsed long ago, so that the remaining sections stood vastly separated, like the few remaining teeth in an old man's jaw. But this rough yet sturdy barrier around the innermost section of the city had been built very recently.

What was Skali afraid of? Eolair wondered. *The remaining Hernystiri, a beaten people? Or perhaps it was his own ally, the High King Elias, that he did not trust.*

Disturbing as it was to see the new wall, it was even more so to see what had happened to it. The timbers were scorched and blackened as though they had been lightning-struck, and a section wide enough for a score of riders to pass through abreast had been blasted away entirely. A few wisps of smoke still curled above the wreckage.

The mystery of what had happened to Hernysadharc's inhabitants was partially solved as Eolair's company swung out onto the wide road that had once been named Tethtain's Way. That name had passed not long after the great Hernystiri King, and people usually called it the Taig Road, for it led directly up the hill to the great hall. Now, as the company entered the muddy thoroughfare, they saw a great crowd of people standing at the summit of the hill, clustered around the Taig like sheep at a salt lick. Curious but still careful, Eolair and the others rode forward.

When Eolair saw that most of the crowd swarming on the lower slopes of Hern's Hill seemed to be Hernystiri, his heart rose. When a few of the outermost people turned, alarmed at the sight of a troop of mounted and armored men, he hastened to reassure them.

"People of Hernysadharc!" he cried, standing in his stirrups. Several more members of the crowd turned at the sound of his voice. "I am Eolair, Count of Nad Mullach. These men are my friends and will do you no harm."

The reaction was surprising. While several of those nearest cheered and waved to him, they seemed little moved. After staring for a moment, they turned their attention back to the hilltop again, despite the fact that none of them had a better vantage point than mounted Eolair, and he himself could see nothing before him but the stretching crowd.

Isorn was puzzled, too. "What are you doing here?" he shouted to the people standing nearby. "Where is Skali?"

Several shook their heads as though they did not understand, and several others made joking remarks about Skali being headed back to Rimmersgard, but no one seemed inclined to waste too much time or energy enlightening the duke's son and his companions.

Eolair cursed quietly and spurred his horse forward, letting the beast make room for him. Although no one actively contested his passage, it was slow going to push through the crush of people, and no short while before they passed between two of the standing remnants of ruined fortress wall and onto the ancient grounds of the Taig. Eolair squinted, then whistled with astonishment.

"Bagba bite me," he said, and laughed, although he could not have said why.

The Taig and its outbuildings still stood on the hilltop, solid and impressive, but now all the fields across the summit of Hern's Hill were covered with wildly colorful tents. They were every shade imaginable and a hundred different sizes and shapes; someone might have emptied a giant basket of quilt-squares across the snowy grass. What had been the capital of the Hernystiri nation, the royal seat, had suddenly become a village constructed by wild, magical children.

Eolair could see movement among the tents—slender shapes in garb as colorful as the newly-erected dwellings. He spurred forward, passing the last of the Hernystiri onlookers as he climbed the hill. These stared hungrily at the bright cloth and the strange visitors, but seemed reluctant to cross the last open space and draw too close. Many watched the count and his company with something like envy.

As they rode into the wind-billowed city of tents, a lone figure came toward them. Eolair reined up, prepared for anything, but was astonished to find that the one who came forward to greet them was Craobhan, the royal family's most elderly but also most loyal advisor. The old man seemed almost thunderstruck to see them; he stared at Eolair for a long time without speaking, but at last tears came to his eyes and he opened his arms wide.

"Count Eolair! Mircha's wet blessing upon us, it's good to see you."

The count scrambled down from his horse and embraced the counselor. "And you, Craobhan, and you. What has happened here?"

"Ha! More than I can tell you standing in the wind." The old man chuckled strangely. He seemed genuinely befuddled, a state in which Eolair had never thought to find him. "By all the gods, more than I can tell you. Come to the Taig. Come in and have something—food, drink."

"Where is Maegwin? Is she well?"

Craobhan looked up, his watery gaze suddenly intent. "She is alive and happy," he said. "But come. Come see . . . well, as I said, more than I can tell you now." The old man took his elbow and tugged.

Eolair turned and waved to the others. "Isorn, Ule, come!" He patted Craobhan's shoulder. "Can our men have something to eat?"

Beyond worrying, Craobhan waved his bony hand. "Somewhere. Some of the people from the town have probably hoarded a few things. There's much to do, though, Eolair, much to do. Hardly know where to start."

"But what's happened? Did the Sithi drive off Skali?"

Craobhan pulled at his arm, leading him toward the great hall.

The Count of Nad Mullach got scarcely more than a glance at the score or so of Sithi who were on the hilltop. Those he saw seemed absorbed in the task of building their camp, and did not even look up as Eolair and the others walked by, but even from a distance he could see the strangeness of them, their odd but graceful motions, their quiet serenity. Although in some places more than a few Sithi were working together, men and women both, they uttered no words that he could hear, going about their tasks with a smooth uniformity of purpose that was somehow as unsettling as their alien faces and movements.

As they drew closer to the Taig, it was easy to see the marks of Skali's occupation. The carefully cultivated gardens had been dug up, the stone pathways torn apart. Eolair cursed Sharp-nose and his barbarians, then wondered again what had happened to the occupiers.

Inside the Taig's great doors things were no different. The walls had been denuded of tapestries, relics had been stolen from their niches, and the floors were scarred with the ruts of countless booted feet. The Hall of Carvings, where King Lluth had held court, was in better condition—Eolair guessed it had been Thane Skali's seat—but still there were signs that the northern reavers had not been overly reverent. Many scores of arrows bristled in the high-arched ceilings, where the hanging wooden carvings had proven tempting targets for Kaldskryke's winter-bound soldiers.

Craobhan, who seemed to wish to avoid talking, seated them in the hall and went to find something to drink.

"What do you suppose has happened, Eolair?" Isorn shook his head. "It makes me feel ashamed to be a Rimmersman when I see what Skali and his cutthroats have done to the Taig." Beside him, Ule was peering suspiciously into the corners of the hall, as though Kaldskrykemen might be hiding there.

"You have nothing to be ashamed of," said Eolair. "They did not do this because they were Rimmersmen, but because they were in someone else's country in a bad time. Hernystiri or Nabbanai or Erkynlanders might do the same."

Isorn was not mollified. "It is wrong. When my father has his dukedom back, we will see that the damage is repaired."

The count smiled. "If we all survive and this is the worst we have to deal with, then I will gladly sell my own home at Nad Mullach stone by stone to make it right again. No, this will be mild, I'm afraid."

"I fear you are right, Eolair." Isorn frowned. "God knows what has happened in Elvritshalla since we were driven out. And after the terrible winter, too."

They were interrupted by Craobhan, who tottered back in with a young Hernystiri woman who carried four large hammered silver tankards decorated with the leaping stag of the royal house.

"Might as well use the best," Craobhan said with a crooked smile. "Who's to say no in these strange days?"

"Where is Maegwin?" Eolair's apprehension had grown when she had not appeared to greet them.

"Sleeping." Again Craobhan made a dismissive gesture. "I'll take you when you've finished. Drink up."

Eolair stood. "Forgive me, old friend, but I'd like to see her now. I'll be better able to enjoy my beer."

The old man shrugged. "In her old room. There's a woman seeing to her." He seemed more interested in his tankard than in the fate of the king's only living child.

The count looked at him for a moment. What had happened to the Craobhan he knew? The old man seemed muddle-headed, as though he'd been struck with a club.

There were far too many other things that needed worrying over. Eolair walked out of the hall, leaving the others to drink and stare up at the shattered carvings.

Maegwin was indeed sleeping. The wild-haired woman who sat beside the bed looked slightly familiar, but Eolair gave her scarcely more than a glance before he kneeled down and took Maegwin's hand. A wet cloth lay across her forehead.

"Has she been wounded?" There seemed to be something Craobhan was keeping from him—perhaps she was badly hurt.

"Yes," the woman said. "But it was a glancing blow only, and she has already recovered." The woman lifted the cloth to show Eolair the bruise on Maegwin's pale brow. "She is merely resting now. It has been a great day."

Eolair turned sharply at the sound of her voice. She looked as distracted as Craobhan, her eyes wide and fey, her mouth twitching.

Has everyone here gone mad? he wondered.

Maegwin stirred at the sound of his voice. As he turned back, her eyes fluttered open, closed again, then opened once more and stayed that way.

"'Eolair. . . ?" Her voice was groggy with sleep. She smiled like a young child, with no trace of the fretfulness he had seen the last time they had spoken. "Is that you, truly? Or just another dream. . . ."

"It is me, Lady." He squeezed her hand again. She looked little different at that moment than when she had been a girl and he had first felt his heart stirring with interest. How could he have ever been angry with her, no matter what she had said or done?

Maegwin tried to sit up. Her sorrel hair was disarranged, her eyes still heavy-lidded. She seemed to have been put to bed fully dressed; only her feet, which protruded from beneath the blanket, were bare. "Did . . . did you see them?"

"Did I see who . . . ?" he asked gently, although he felt sure he knew. Her answer, though, surprised him.

"The gods, silly man. Did you see the gods? They were so beautiful. . . ."

"The . . . gods?"

"I made them come," she said, and smiled sleepily. "They came for me. . . ." She let her head fall back into the pillow and closed her eyes. "For me," she murmured.

"She needs sleep, Count Eolair," the woman said from behind him. There was something peremptory in her voice that lifted Eolair's hackles.

"What is she talking about, the gods?" he demanded. "Does she mean the Sithi?"

The woman smiled, a smugly knowing smile. "She means what she says."

Eolair stood, holding back his anger. There was much to discover here. He would bide his time. "Take good care of Princess Maegwin," he said as he moved toward the door. It was more of an order than a request. The woman nodded.

Musing, Eolair had just re-entered the Hall of Carvings when there was a clatter of boots at the front doors behind him. He stopped and turned, his hand reflexively dropping to his sword-hilt. A few paces away, Isorn and husky Ule also rose, alarm plain on their faces.

The figure that appeared in the door of the hall was tall but not overly so, dressed in blue armor that, strangely, had the look of painted wood—but the armor, an intricate collection of plates held together by shiny red cords, was not the strangest thing about him. His hair was white as a snow-drift; bound in a blue scarf, it fell past his shoulders. He was slender as a young birch tree, and despite the color of his hair, looked to be scarcely into his manhood, insofar as Eolair could read a face so angular, so different from a human face. The stranger's upturned eyes were golden, bright as noon sun reflected in a forest pond.

Surprised into immobility, Eolair stared. It was as though some creature out of elder days stood before him, one of his grandmother's stories appearing in flesh and bone. He had expected to meet the Sithi, but he was no more prepared than someone told about a deep canyon could be when they suddenly discovered they were standing on its rim.

When the count had stood frozen for some seconds, the newcomer took a step backward. "Forgive me." The stranger made an oddly articulated bow, sweeping his long-fingered hand past his knees, but although there was something light in his movements, there was no mockery. "I forget my manners in the heat of this memorable day. May I enter here?"

"Who . . . who are you?" Eolair asked, startled out of his normal courtesy. "Yes, come in."

The stranger did not seem offended. "I am Jiriki i-Sa'onserei. At this moment I speak for the Zida'ya. We have come to repay our debt to Prince Sinnach of Hernystir." After this formal speech, he suddenly flashed a cheerfully feral grin. "And who are you?"

Eolair hastily introduced himself and his companions. Isorn was staring, fascinated, and Ule was pale and unsettled. Old Craobhan wore an odd, mocking smile.

"Good," Jiriki said when he had finished. "This is very good. I have heard your name mentioned today, Count Eolair. We have much to talk about. But first, who is the master here? I understand that the king is dead."

Eolair looked dazedly to Craobhan. "Inahwen?"

"The king's wife is still up in the caves in the Grianspog." Craobhan wheezed with what might have been laughter. "Wouldn't come down with the rest of us. I thought she was being sensible at the time. Then again, perhaps she was."

"And Maegwin, the king's daughter, is asleep." Eolair shrugged. "I suppose then I am the one with whom you must speak, at least for the present."

"Would you be kind enough to come with me to our camp? Or would you rather we came here to talk?"

Eolair was not sure exactly who "we" might be, but he knew he would never forgive himself if he did not experience this moment to its fullest. Maegwin, in any case, obviously needed her rest, which would not be best accomplished with the Taig full of men and Sithi.

"We will be pleased to accompany you, Jiriki i-Sa'onserei," the count said.

"Jiriki, if it is acceptable." The Sitha stood waiting.

Eolair and his companions walked with him out the Taig's front doors. The tents billowed before them like a field of oversized wildflowers. "Do you mind my asking," Eolair ventured, "what happened to the wall Skali built around the city?"

Jiriki seemed to ponder for a moment. "Ah. That," he said at last, and smiled. "I think you probably are speaking of the handiwork of my mother, Likimeya. We were in a hurry. The wall was in our way."

"Then I hope *I* am never in her way," Isorn said earnestly.

"As long as you do not come between my mother and the honor of Year-Dancing House," said Jiriki, "you need not worry."

They continued across the wet grass. "You mentioned the bargain with Sinnach," the count said. "If you can defeat Skali in a day . . . well, forgive me, Jiriki, but how was the battle at Ach Samrath ever lost?"

"First, we have not quite defeated this Skali. He and many of his men have fled into the hills and out onto the Frostmarch, so there is work still to be done. But your question is a good one." The Sitha's eyes narrowed as he considered. "I think we are, in some ways, a different people from what we were five centuries gone. Many of us were not born then, and we children of the Exile are not as cautious as our elders. Also, we feared iron in those days, before we learned how to protect ourselves from it." He smiled, that same fierce cat-grin, but then his face grew somber. He brushed a strand of his pale hair from his eyes. "And these men, Count Eolair, these Rimmersmen here, they were not prepared for us. Surprise was on our side. But in the battles ahead—and there will be many, I think—no one will be so unprepared. Then it will be like Ereb Irigú all over again—what you men call 'the Knock.' There will be much killing, I fear . . . and my people can afford it even less than yours."

As he spoke, the wind that rippled the tents changed direction, swinging around until it blew from the North. It was suddenly much colder on Hern's Hill.

Elias, High King of all Osten Ard, staggered like a drunkard. As he made his way across the Inner Bailey courtyard he lurched from one shadowy spot to another as though the direct light of the sun made him ill, even though it was a gray, cold day and the sun itself, even at noon, was invisible behind a choke of clouds. The Hayholt's chapel dome loomed behind him, strangely asymmetrical; a mass of dirty snow, long uncleared, had dimpled several of the leaded panes inward so that the great dome looked like an old, rumpled felt hat.

Those few shivering peasants who were compelled to live within the Hayholt's walls and tend the castle's crumbling facilities seldom left their quarters unless forced by duty, which usually appeared in the form of a Thrithings-man overseer, whose commands were upheld by the possibility of sudden and violent retribution. Even the remainder of the king's army now barracked itself in the fields outside Erchester. The story given out was that the king was unwell and wished his peace, but it was commonly whispered that the king was mad, that his castle was haunted. As a result, only a handful of people were creeping about the Inner Bailey this gray, murky afternoon, and of those few—a soldier bearing a message for the Lord Constable, a pair of fearful rustics carting a wagon full of barrels away from Pryrates' chambers—not a one watched Elias' uneven passage for more than a moment before looking away. Not only would it be dangerous, possibly even fatal, to be caught staring at the king in his infirmity, but there was something so dreadfully *wrong* in his stiff-legged gait, some quality so terrifyingly unnatural, that those who saw him felt compelled to turn aside and furtively make the sign of the Tree before their breasts.

Hjeldin's Tower was gray and squat. With the red windows in its upper story gleaming dully, it might have been some ruby-eyed pagan god of the Nascadu wastes. Elias came to a stop before the heavy oak doors, which were three ells high and painted an unglossy black, studded with bronze hinges going splotchily green. On either side of the entrance stood a figure hooded and robed in a black even darker and flatter than the door. Each bore a lance of strange, filigreed design, a fantastic weave of curlicues and whorls, sharp as a barber's razor.

The king swayed in place, staring at the twin apparitions. It was clear that the Norns filled him with unease. He moved another step closer to the door. Although neither of the sentries moved, and their faces were invisible in the depths of their hoods, they seemed to become suddenly more intent, like spiders feeling the first trembling steps of a fly on the outskirts of a web.

"Well?" Elias said at last, his voice surprisingly loud. "Are you going to open the damned door for me?"

The Norns did not reply. They did not move.

"Blast you to hell, what ails you?!" he growled. "Don't you know me, you miserable creatures? I'm the king! Now open the door!" He took a sudden step forward. One of the Norns allowed his lance to sag a handspan into the doorway. Elias stopped and leaned back as though the point had been waved in his face.

"So this is the game, is it?" His pale face had begun to take on a gleam of madness. "This is the game? In my own house, eh?" He began to rock back and forth on his heels as though preparing to fling himself toward the door. One of his hands slithered down to clutch at the double-guarded sword which hung at his belt.

The sentry turned slowly and thumped twice on the heavy doors with the butt of his lance. After a moment's pause, he banged three more times before resuming his settled stance.

As Elias stood staring, a raven screeched on one of the tower's parapets. After what seemed like only a few heartbeats, the door grated open and Pryrates stood in the gap, blinking.

"Elias!" he said. "Your Majesty! You honor me!"

The king's lip curled. His hand was still tightening and loosening on Sorrow's hilt. "I don't honor you at all, priest. I came to talk to you—and *I* am dishonored."

"Dishonored? How?" Pryrates' face was full of shocked concern, but there was an unmistakable trace of mirth as well, as though he played mocking games with a child. "Tell me what has happened and what I can do to make it up to you, my king."

"These . . . things wouldn't open the door." Elias jerked his hand toward the silent warders. "When I tried to do it myself, one of them blocked my path."

Pryrates shook his head, then turned and conversed with the Norns in their own musical speech, which he seemed to speak well if somewhat haltingly. He faced the king again. "Please do not blame them, Highness, or even me. You see, some of the things I do here in the pursuit of knowledge can be hazardous. As I told you before, I fear that someone coming in suddenly might find himself endangered. You, my king, are the most important man in the world. Therefore I have asked that *no one* be allowed to walk in until I am here to escort them." Pryrates smiled, an unmodified baring of teeth that would have seemed appropriate on the face of an eel. "Please understand that it was for your safety, King Elias."

The king looked at him for a moment, then peered at the two sentries; they had returned to their positions and were stiff as statues once more. "I thought you were using mercenaries to stand guard. I thought these things didn't like the daylight."

"It does not harm them," said Pryrates. "It is just that after several score centuries living in the great mountain Stormspike, they prefer shade to sun." He winked, as though over the foibles of some eccentric relative. "But I am at an important point in my studies, now—*our* studies, Majesty—and thought they would be better warders."

"Enough of this," Elias said impatiently. "Are you going to let me in? I came here to talk to you. It can't wait."

"Of course, of course," Pryrates assured him, but the priest seemed suddenly distracted. "I always look forward to speaking with you, my king. Perhaps you would prefer it if I came to your apartments . . . ?"

"Damn it, priest, let me in. You don't make a king stand on the doorstep, curse you!"

Pryrates shrugged and bowed. "Of course not, sire." He stepped aside, extending his arm toward the staircase. "Come up to my chambers, please."

Inside the great doors, in the high-ceilinged anteroom, a single torch burned fitfully. The corners were full of shadows that leaned and stretched as though struggling to free themselves. Pryrates did not pause, but went immediately up the narrow staircase. "Let me go ahead and make sure things are ready for you, Majesty," he called back, his voice echoing in the stairwell.

Elias stopped on the second landing to catch his breath. "Stairs," he said direly. "Too many stairs."

The door to the chamber was open, and the light of several torches spilled out into the passageway. As he entered, the king looked up briefly at the windows, which were masked by long draperies. The priest, who was closing the lid of a large chest on what seemed to be a pile of books, turned and smiled. "Welcome, my king. You have not favored me with a visit here in some time."

"You have not invited me. Where can I sit down—I am dying."

"No, my lord, not dying," Pryrates said cheerfully. "The opposite, if anything—you are being reborn. But you have been very sick of late, it's true. Forgive me. Here, take my chair." He ushered Elias to the high-backed chair; it was innocent of any decorations or carvings, yet somehow carried an air of great antiquity. "Would you like some of your soothing drink? I see Hengfisk has not accompanied you, but I could arrange to have some made." He turned and clapped his hands. *"Munshazou!"* he called.

"The monk is not here because I have knocked in his head, or near to," Elias growled, shifting uncomfortably on the hard seat. "If I never see his pop-eyed face again, I will be a happy man." He coughed, his fever-bright eyes blinking closed. At this moment, he did not look in the least like a happy man.

"He caused you some trouble? I am so unhappy to hear that, my king. Perhaps you should tell me what happened, and I will see that he is . . . dealt with. I am your servant, after all."

"Yes," Elias said dryly. "You are." He made a noise in his throat and shifted again, trying to find a better position.

There was a discreet cough from the doorway. A small dark-haired woman stood there. She did not look particularly aged, but her sallow face was lined with deep wrinkles. A mark of some kind—it might have been a letter from some foreign script—was scribed on her forehead above her nose. She moved ever so slightly as she stood, weaving in a slow, circular motion so that the hem of her shapeless dress brushed against the floor and the tiny bone-colored charms she wore at waist and neck tinkled gently.

"Munshazou," Pryrates said to Elias, "my servant from Naraxi, from my house there." He told the dark woman: "Bring something the king can drink. And for me—no, I need nothing. Go now."

She turned with a rattle of ivory and was gone. "I apologize for the interruption," said the alchemist. "You were telling me of your problem with Hengfisk."

"Don't worry about the monk. He is nothing. I just woke suddenly and found him standing over me, staring. Standing over my bed!" Remembering, the king shook himself like a wet dog. "God, but he has a face only a mother could bear. And that cursed smile always . . ." Elias shook his head. "I struck him—gave him my fist. Knocked him right across the bedchamber." He laughed and then coughed. "Teach him to come spying on me while I sleep. I *need* my sleep. I've been getting precious little. . . ."

"Is that why you came to me, Lord?" Pryrates asked. "For your sleep? I could perhaps make something for you—there is a sort of wax I have that you could burn in a dish by your bedside. . . ."

"No!" Elias said angrily. "And it's not the monk, either. I came to you because I had a dream!"

Pryrates looked at him carefully. The patch of skin above his eye—a spot where others had eyebrows—rose in a questioning look. "A dream, lord? Of course, if that is what you wish to speak with me about . . ."

"Not that sort of dream, damn you! You know what kind I mean. I had a *dream!*"

"Ah." The priest nodded. "And it disturbed you."

"Yes it bloody well did, by the Sacred Tree!" The king winced and laid his hand on his chest, then burst into another round of wracking coughs. "I saw the Sithi riding! The Dawn Children! They were riding to Hernystir!"

There was a faint clicking noise from the door. Munshazou had reappeared, bearing a tray on which stood a tall goblet glazed in a deep rust-red. It steamed.

"Very good." Pryrates strode forward to take it from the woman's hand. Her small, pale eyes watched him, but her face remained expressionless. "You may go now," he told her. "Here, Majesty, drink this. It will help your clouded chest."

Elias took the goblet suspiciously and sipped. "It tastes like the same swill you always give me."

"There are . . . similarities." Pryrates moved back to his position near the trunk full of books. "Remember, my king, you have special needs."

Elias took another swallow. "I saw the immortals—the Sithi. They were riding against Skali." He looked up from his cup to fix his green gaze on Pryrates. "Is it true?"

"Things seen in dreams are not always wholly true or wholly false . . ." Pryrates began.

"God damn you to the blackest circles of hell!" Elias shouted, half-rising from the chair. "*Is it true?!*"

Pryrates bowed his hairless head. "The Sithi have left their home in the fastness of the forest."

Elias' green eyes glittered dangerously. "And Skali?"

Pryrates moved slowly toward the door, as though preparing to flee. "The thane of Kaldskryke and his Ravens have . . . decamped."

The king hissed out a long breath and his hand tugged at Sorrow's hilt, sinews jumping in his pale arm. A length of the gray sword appeared, mottled and shiny as a pikefish's back. The torches in the room seemed to bend inward, as though drawn toward it. "Priest," Elias growled, "you are listening to your last few heartbeats if you don't speak quickly and plainly."

Instead of cringing, Pryrates drew himself upright. The torches fluttered again, and the alchemist's black eyes lost their luster; for a moment, the whites seemed to vanish, almost as though they had drawn back into his head, leaving only holes in a darkened skull. An oppressive tension filled the tower room. Pryrates raised his hand and the king's knuckles tightened on the sword's long hilt. After a moment's stillness, the priest lifted his fingers to his neck, carefully smoothed the collar of his red robe as though adjusting the fit, then let the hand drop again.

"I am sorry, Highness," he said, and allowed himself a small, self-mocking smile. "It is often a counselor's wish to shield his liege from news that might be upsetting. You have seen rightly. The Sithi have come to Hernystir and Skali has been driven out."

Elias stared at him for a long moment. "What does this mean to all your plans, priest? You said nothing about the Dawn Children."

Pryrates shrugged. "Because it *means* nothing. It was inevitable once things reached a certain point. The increasing activity of . . . of our benefactor was bound to draw them in. It should not disrupt any of our plans."

"*Should* not? Are you saying that what the Sithi do doesn't matter to the Storm King?"

"That one has planned long. There is nothing that will surprise him in any of this. In truth, the Norn Queen told me to expect it."

"She did, did she? You seem very well informed, Pryrates," Elias' voice had not lost its edge of fury. "Then tell me: if you knew this, why can you not tell me what is happening with Fengbald? Why have we no knowledge of whether he has driven my brother from his lair?"

"Because our allies deem it of little account." Pryrates lifted his hand again, this time to forestall the king's angry reply. "Please, majesty, you asked for candor and so I give it to you. They feel that Josua is beaten and that you waste your time with him. The Sithi, on the other hand, have been the enemies of the Norns since time out of mind."

"But still of no account, apparently, if what you said before is correct." The king glowered. "I do not understand how they can be more important than my treacherous brother and yet not important enough for us to worry about—even when they have destroyed one of my chief allies. I think you are playing a double game, Pryrates. God help you if I find that to be true!"

"I serve only my master, Highness, not the Storm King, not the Norn Queen. It is all a matter of timing. Josua was a threat to you once, but you defeated him. Skali was needed to protect your flank, but he is no longer necessary. Even the Sithi are no threat, because they will not come against us until they have saved Hernystir. They are cursed by ancient loyalties, you see. That will be far too late for them to be any hindrance to your ultimate victory."

Elias stared into his steaming cup. "Then why did I see them riding in my dreams?"

"You have grown close to the Storm King, sire, since you accepted his gift." Pryrates gestured to the gray sword, now sheathed once more. "He is of the Sithi blood—or was when he still lived, to speak rightly. It is only natural that the mustering of the Zida'ya should draw his attention and thus make its way to you." He moved a few steps closer to the king. "You have had other . . . dreams . . . before this, have you not?"

"You know I have, alchemist." Elias drained the cup, then made a face as he swallowed. "My nights, those few when sleep actually comes, are full of him. Full of him! Of that frozen thing with the burning heart." His eyes wandered across the shadowed walls, suddenly full of fear. "Of the dark spaces between . . ."

"Peace, your Majesty," Pryrates said. "You have suffered much, but the reward will be splendid. You know that."

Elias shook his head heavily. His voice, when he spoke, was a straining rasp. "I wish I had known the way this would feel, the things . . . the things it would do to me. I wish I had known before I made that devil's bargain. God help me, I wish I had known."

"Let me get my sleeping-wax for you, Highness. You need rest."

"No." The king lifted himself awkwardly from the chair. "I do not want any more dreams. It would be better never to sleep again."

Elias moved slowly toward the door, waving away Pryrates' offer of assistance. He was a long time going down the stairs.

The red-robed priest stood and listened to his entire descent. When the great outer doors creaked open and then crashed closed, Pryrates shook his head once, as if dismissing an irritating thought, then went to retrieve the books he had hidden.

♔

Jiriki had gone ahead, his smooth strides carrying him deceptively quickly. Eolair, Isorn, and Ule followed at a slower pace, trying to take in the strange sights.

It was particularly unsettling for Eolair, to whom Hernysadharc and the Taig had been a second residence. Now, following the Sitha across Hern's Hill, he felt like a father come home to find that all his children were changelings.

The Sithi had built their tent city so swiftly, the billowing cloths stretched artfully between the trees that ringed the Taig, that it almost seemed it had always been there—that it belonged. Even the colors, which had been so jarringly bright when seen from a distance, now seemed to him more muted—tones of summer sunset and dawn more in keeping with a king's house and gardens.

If their lodgings already seemed like a natural part of the hilltop, the Zida'ya themselves seemed scarcely less at home. Eolair saw no sign of diffidence or meekness in those Sithi who surrounded him; they paid scant attention to the count and his companions. The immortals walked proudly, and as they worked they sang lilting songs in a language that, although strange to him, seemed oddly familiar in its swooping vowels and birdlike trills. Although they had been in the place scarcely a day, they seemed as comfortable on the snowy grass and beneath the trees as swans scudding across a mirror-still pond. Everything they did seemed to speak of immense calm and self-knowledge; even the act of looping and knotting the many ropes that gave their tent city its shape became a kind of conjuror's trick. Watching them, Eolair—who had always been judged a nimble, graceful man—felt bestial and clumsy.

The new-made house into which Jiriki had vanished was little more than a ring of blue and lavender cloth which hemmed one of the hilltop's magisterial oak trees like a paddock around a prize bull. As Eolair and the others stood, uncertain, Jiriki reemerged and beckoned them forward.

"Please understand that my mother may stray a little beyond the bounds of courtesy," Jiriki murmured as they stood at the opening. "We are mourning for my father and First Grandmother." He ushered them forward into the enclosure. The grass was dry, swept clean of snow. "I bring Count Eolair of Nad Mullach," he said, "Isorn Isgrimnurson of Elvritshalla, and Ule Frekkeson of Skoggey."

The Sitha-woman looked up. She was seated on a cloth of pale, shining blue, surrounded by the birds which she had been feeding. Despite the soft feathered bodies perched on her knees and arms, Eolair had the immediate impression that she was hard as sword-steel. Her hair was flaming red, bound by a gray scarf across her forehead; several long, soot-colored feathers hung in her braids. Like Jiriki, she was armored in what looked to be wood, but hers was shiny and black as a beetle's shell. Beneath the armor she wore a kirtle of dove-gray. Soft boots of the same color rose above her knees. Her eyes, like her son's, were molten gold.

"Likimeya y'Briseyu no'e-Sa'onserei," Jiriki intoned. "Queen of the Dawn Children and Lady of the House of Year-Dancing."

Eolair and the rest dropped to a knee.

"Get up, please." She spoke in a throaty murmur, and seemed less comfortable with the mortal tongue than Jiriki. "This is your land, Count Eolair, and it is the Zida'ya who are guests here. We have come to pay our debt to your Sinnach."

"We are honored, Queen Likimeya."

She waved a long-nailed hand. "Do not say 'queen.' It is a title, only—it is the nearest mortal word. But we do not call ourselves such things except at certain times." She cocked an eyebrow at Eolair as he and his companions rose. "You know, Count Eolair, there is an old story that Zida'ya blood is in the House of Nad Mullach."

For a moment the count was confused, thinking she meant some kind of injustice had been done against the Sithi in his ancestral home. When he realized what she had truly said, he felt his own blood turn cold and the hairs lift on the back of his arms. "An old story?" Eolair felt as though his head was about to float away. "I'm sorry, my lady, I am not sure I understand. Do you mean to say that there was Sithi blood among my ancestors?"

Likimeya smiled, a sudden, fierce gleam of teeth. "It is an old story, as I said."

"And do the Sithi know whether it is true?" Was she playing some sort of game with him?

She fluttered her fingers. A cloud of birds leaped up and into the tree branches overhead, momentarily hiding her from view with the blur of their wings. "Long ago, when mortals and Zida'ya were closer . . ." She made a strange gesture. "It could be. We know it *can* happen."

Eolair definitely felt himself on shaky ground, and was surprised at how swiftly his training in diplomacy and politicking had deserted him. "It has happened, then? The Fair Folk have . . . mingled with mortals?"

Likimeya seemed to lose interest in the subject. "Yes. Long ago, for the most part." She motioned to Jiriki, who came forward with more of the shimmery, silken cloths, which he spread for the count and his companions before gesturing for them to sit. "It is good to be on *M'yin Azoshai* again."

"That is what we call this hill," Jiriki explained. "It was given to Hern by Shi'iki and Senditu. It was, I suppose you would say, a sacred place for our folk. That it was granted to a mortal for his steading is a mark of the friendship between Hern's people and the Dawn Children."

"We have a legend that says something much like that," Eolair said slowly. "I had wondered if there was truth to it."

"Most legends have a kernel of truth at their center." Jiriki smiled.

Likimeya had turned her cat-bright eyes from Eolair to his two comrades, who almost seemed to flinch beneath the weight of her gaze. "And you are Rimmersmen," she said, looking at them intently. "We have little cause to love your folk."

Isorn hung his head. "Yes, Lady, you do." He took a deep breath, steadying his voice. "But please, do not forget that we live short lives. That was many years ago—a score of generations. We are not much like Fingil."

Likimeya's smile was brief. "You may not be, but what about this kinsman of yours we have put to flight? I have seen his handiwork here on M'yin Azoshai, and it looks little different than what your Fingil Bloodfist did to the Zida'ya lands five centuries ago."

Isorn shook his head slowly, but did not reply. Beside him, Ule had turned quite pale and looked as though he might bolt at any moment.

"Isorn and Ule fought *against* Skali," Eolair said hurriedly, "and we were bringing more men here to take up the battle when you and your folk passed us by. You have done these two as great a favor by putting the murderer to flight as you have done for my own people. Now there is hope that someday Isorn's father can retain his rightful dukedom."

"Ah." Likimeya nodded. "Now we come to it. Jiriki, have these men eaten?"

Her son looked at the count inquiringly. "No, my lady," Eolair replied.

"Then you will eat with us, and we will talk."

Jiriki got up and vanished through a gap in the rippling walls. There followed a long and, for Eolair, uncomfortable silence which Likimeya seemed uninclined to break. They sat and listened to the wind in the oak tree's upper branches until Jiriki returned bearing a wooden tray piled with fruit, bread, and cheese.

The count was astonished. Didn't these creatures have servants to perform such humble tasks? He watched while Jiriki, as commanding a presence as he had ever encountered, poured something from a blue crystal flask into drinking cups carved from the same wood as the tray, then handed the cups to Eolair and his companions with a simple but elegant bow. The queen and prince of the eldest folk, yet they waited on themselves? The gap between Eolair and these immortals seemed broader than ever.

Whatever was in the crystal flask burned like fire but tasted like clover-honey and smelled like violets. Ule sipped his cautiously, then drained it at a swallow and gladly let Jiriki refill his cup. As he drank his own cup dry, Eolair felt the pain of two days' hard riding dissolve in the warm glow. The food was excellent as well, each piece of fruit at the peak of ripeness. The count wondered briefly where the Sithi could have found such delicacies in the middle of a year-long winter, but dismissed it as only another small miracle in what was rapidly becoming a vast catalog of wonders.

"We have come to war," Likimeya said suddenly. Of all, only she had not eaten, and she had taken no more than a sip of the honey cordial. "Skali eludes us for a moment, but the heart of your kingdom is free. We have made a start. With your help, Eolair, and those of your people whose wills are still strong, we will soon lift the yoke from the neck of our old allies."

"There are no words for our gratitude, Lady," Eolair replied. "The Zida'ya have shown us today that they honor their promises. Few mortal tribes can say the same."

"And what then, Queen Likimeya?" Isorn asked. He had drunk three glasses of the pale elixir, and his face had gone a bit red. "Will you ride with Josua? Will you help him take the Hayholt?"

The look she turned on him was cool and austere. "We do not fight for mortal princes, Isorn Isgrimnurson. We fight to honor our debts, and to protect ourselves."

Eolair felt his heart sink. "So you will stop here?"

Likimeya shook her head, then lifted her hands and wove her fingers together. "It is nothing like that simple. I spoke too quickly. No, there are things that threaten both your Josua Lackhand and the Dawn Children as well. Lackhand's enemy has made a bargain with our enemy, it seems. Still, we will do what we alone are fit for: once Hernystir is free, we will leave the wars of mortals to mortals—at least for now. No, Count Eolair, we owe other debts, but these are strange times." She smiled, and this time the smile was a little less predatory, a little more like something that might stretch across a mortal face. Eolair was struck by her angular beauty. At the same moment, in lightning juxtaposition, he realized that he sat before a being who had seen the fall of Asu'a. She was as old as the greatest cities of men—older, perhaps. He shivered.

"Yet," Likimeya continued, "although we will not ride to the aid of your embattled prince, we *will* ride to the aid of his fortress."

There was a moment of confused silence before Isorn spoke. "Your pardon, Lady. We do not understand what you mean."

It was Jiriki who answered. "When Hernystir is free, we will ride to Naglimund. It is the Storm King's now, and it stands too close to the house of our exile. We will take this place back from him." The Sitha's face was grim. "Also, when the final battle comes—and it is coming, mortal men, do not doubt it— we wish to be sure that the Norns have no bolt hole left in which to hide themselves."

Eolair watched Jiriki's eyes as the Sitha spoke, and fancied that he saw a hatred there that had smoldered for centuries.

"A war unlike any the world has seen," Likimeya said. "A war in which many matters will be settled for once and all." If Jiriki's eyes smoldered, hers blazed.

19

A Broken Smile

⚜

"I have done all I can do for either of them—unless . . ." Cadrach rubbed fretfully at his damp forehead, as though to bring out some idea hiding there. He was obviously exhausted, but just as obviously—with the duke's slurs still fresh in his mind—he was not going to let that stop him.

"There is nothing else to be done," Miriamele said firmly. "Lie down. You need some sleep."

Cadrach looked up at Isgrimnur, who stood at the bow of the flatboat with the pole clasped firmly in his broad hands. The duke only tightened his lips and returned to his inspection of the watercourse. "Yes, then, I suppose I should." The monk curled up beside the still forms of Tiamak and the other Wrannaman.

Miriamele, recently awakened from her own evening-long nap, leaned forward and draped her cloak across the three of them. There was little use for the garment anyway, except to keep off bugs. Even near midnight, the marsh was warm as a midsummer day.

"If we snuff the lamp," Isgrimnur rumbled, "maybe these creepy-crawlies will go make a meal on something else for a change." He slapped at his upper arm and held the resultant smear up for inspection. "The damnable light draws them. You'd think a lamp that comes from that marsh-man town would keep 'em away." He snorted. "How people can live here year-round is a puzzle to me."

"If we're going to do that, we should drop the anchor." Miriamele did not much like the idea of floating along in the dark. So far, they seemed to have left the ghants behind, but she still looked carefully at every low-hanging branch or dangling vine. But Isgrimnur had gone long without sleep; it only seemed fair to try to bring him some relief from the flying insects.

"That's good. I think this bit is wide enough to make us as safe as we'd be anywhere else," Isgrimnur said. "Don't see any branches. The little bugs are bad enough, but if I never see one of those Aedon-cursed big ones again . . ." He did not need to finish. Miriamele's shallow sleep had been full of dreams of clacking, scuttling ghants and sticky tendrils that held her in place when she wanted only to run.

"Help me with the anchor." Together they heaved the stone up and dumped it over the side. When it had struck bottom, Miriamele tested the rope to make sure there was not too much slack. "Why don't you sleep first," she told the duke. "I'll watch for a little while."

"Very well."

She glanced quickly at Camaris, sleeping soundlessly in the stern with his white head propped on his cloak, then she reached out and shuttered the lamp.

At first, the darkness was frighteningly complete. Miriamele could almost feel jointed legs reaching silently toward her, and fought the impulse to turn around and wave her hands in the blackness to keep the phantoms at bay. "Isgrimnur?"

"What?"

"Nothing. I just wanted to hear your voice."

Her sight began to come back. There was little enough light—the moon was gone, either blocked by clouds or by the close-tangled trees that roofed the watercourse, and the stars were only faint specks—but she could make out forms around her, the dark bulk of the duke, the patchy shadows of the river banks on either side.

She heard Isgrimnur rattling the pole around until he got it well-situated, then his shadowy form sank down. "Are you sure you don't need to sleep more yourself?" he asked. Weariness was making his voice muddy.

"I'm rested. I'll sleep a little later. Go on now, put your head down."

Isgrimnur did not protest further—a sure sign of his exhaustion. Within moments he was snoring noisily. Miriamele smiled.

The boat moved so smoothly that it was not hard to imagine they were floating like a cloud through the night sky. There was no tide, and no discernible current, only the minute push of the swamp breezes that sent them slowly circling around the anchor, moving smoothly as quicksilver on a tilted pane of glass. Miriamele sat back and stared up at the murky sky, trying to make out a familiar star. For the first time in some days, she could afford the luxury of homesickness.

I wonder what my father is doing now? Does he think about me? Does he hate me?

Thoughts of Elias set other things to stirring inside her head. Something Cadrach had mentioned their first night after escaping the *Eadne Cloud* had been nagging at her. During his long and difficult confession, the monk had said that Pryrates had seemed particularly interested in communicating with the dead—"speaking through the veil," Cadrach had said it was called—and that those were the parts of Nisses' book on which he had been most fixated. For some reason, that phrase had made her think of her father. But why? Was it something Elias had said?

Try as she might to summon the idea that had snagged at the back of her mind, it remained elusive. The boat spun slowly, silent beneath dim stars.

She had drowsed a little. The first light of morning was creeping into the skies above the marsh, turning them pearly gray. Miriamele straightened, groaning quietly. Her bruises and aches from the ghant nest had begun to stiffen: she felt as though she had been rolled down a hill in a bag of rocks.

"L-L-Lady?" It was a breathy sound, little more than a sigh.

"Tiamak?!" She turned abruptly, causing the boat to pitch. The Wrannaman's eyes were open. His face, though pale and slack-featured, held the spark of intelligence once more.

"Y-yes. Yes, Lady." He took a deep breath, as though even those few words had tired him out. "Where . . . are we?"

"We are on the waterway, but I have no idea where. We poled for most of a day after leaving the ghant nest." She looked at him carefully. "Are you in pain?"

He tried to shake his head, but could only move it slightly. "No. But water. Would be kind."

She leaned across the boat to take the water skin lying near Isgrimnur's leg. She unstoppered it and gave the Wrannaman a few careful swallows.

Tiamak turned a little to eye the still form next to him. "Younger Mogahib," he whispered. "Is he alive?"

"Barely. At least he seems very close to . . . he seems very sick, although Cadrach and I couldn't find any wounds on him."

"No. You would not. Nor on me." Tiamak let his head fall back and closed his eyes. "And the others?"

"Which others?" she asked cautiously. "Cadrach, Isgrimnur, Camaris, and I are all here, and all more or less well."

"Ah. Good." Tiamak's eyes remained closed. In the prow, Isgrimnur sat up groggily. "What's this, then?" he mumbled. "Miriamele . . . what?"

"Nothing, Isgrimnur. Tiamak's woken up."

"Has, has he?" The duke settled back, already sliding down into slumber once more. "Brains not scrambled? Talks like himself? Damnedest thing I ever saw . . ."

"You were speaking another language in the nest," Miriamele told Tiamak. "It was frightening."

"I know." His face rippled, as though he fought down revulsion. "I will talk about it later. Not now." His eyes opened partway. "Did you bring anything out with me?"

Miriamele shook her head, thinking. "Just you. And the muck you were covered with."

"Ah." Tiamak looked disappointed for a moment, but then relaxed. "Just as well." A moment later, his eyes opened wide. "And my belongings?" he demanded.

"Everything you had in the boat is still here." She patted the bundle.

"Good . . . good." He sighed his relief and slid down into the cloak.

The sky was growing paler, and the foliage on either side of the river was beginning to emerge from shadow into color and life.

"Lady?"

"What?"

"Thank you. Thank you all for coming after me."

Miriamele listened as his breathing grew slower. Soon the little man was asleep again.

"As I told Miriamele last night," Tiamak said, "I wish to thank you all. You have been better friends to me than I could have hoped—certainly better than I have earned."

Isgrimnur coughed. "Nonsense. Couldn't have done anything else." Miriamele thought the duke looked a little shamefaced. Perhaps he was remembering the debate on whether to try to save the Wrannaman or to leave him behind.

The company had set up a makeshift camp near the watercourse. The small fire, its flames almost invisible in the bright late-morning light, was burning merrily, heating water for soup and yellowroot tea.

"No, you do not understand. It was not merely my life you saved. If I have a ka—a soul, you would call it—it would not have survived another day in that place. Perhaps not another hour."

"But what were they doing to you?" Miriamele asked. "You were babbling away—you sounded almost like a ghant yourself!"

Tiamak shuddered. He was sitting up, wrapped in her cloak, but he had so far moved very little. "I will tell you as best I can, although I do not understand much myself. But you are certain that you brought nothing out of that place with me?"

The rest of the company shook their heads.

"There was . . ." he began, then stopped, thinking. "It was a piece of what looked like a mirror—a looking glass. It was broken, but there was still a bit of the frame in place, carved with great art. They . . . the ghants . . . they put it in my hands." He lifted his palms to show them the healing cuts. "As soon as I held it, I felt cold running through me, from my fingers right into my head. Then some of the creatures vomited forth that sticky substance, covering me with it." He took a deep breath but could not immediately continue. For a moment he just sat, tears shining in his eyes.

"You don't have to talk about it, Tiamak," Miriamele said. "Not now."

"Or at least just tell us how they got hold of you," Isgrimnur said. "If that's not so bad, I mean."

The Wrannaman looked down at the ground. "They caught me as easily as if I were a just-hatched crablet. Three of them dropped on me out of the trees," he looked up quickly, as though it might happen again, "and while I struggled with them, a dozen more came swarming down and overwhelmed me. Oh, they are clever! They wrapped me in vines, just as you or I would bind a prisoner, although they did not seem able to tie knots. Still, they held the vines tight enough that I could not escape. Then they tried to lift me into the trees, but I suppose I was too heavy. Instead, they were forced to grab at vines and sunken branches and pull the flatboat against the sandbank. Then they took me to the nest. I cannot tell you how many times I wished that they would kill me, or at least knock me senseless. To be carried alive and awake through that horrible pitch-black place by those chattering *things* . . . !" He had to pause for a moment to regain his composure.

"What they did with me, they had already done with Younger Mogahib." He nodded toward the other Wrannaman, who lay on the ground nearby, still locked in feverish slumber. "I think he lived because he had not been there long: perhaps he had not proved as useful a tool as they thought I would. In any case, they must have had to free him to get the mirror-shard for me. When they dragged him past, I cried out. He was half-mad, but he heard my voice and called back. I recognized him then, and shouted that my boat was still on the bank outside, that he should escape if he could and take it."

"Did you tell him to find us?" Cadrach asked. "It was an unbelievable stroke of luck if he was trying to."

"No, no," Tiamak said. "There were only moments. Later, though, I hoped that if he did get free and made his way back to Village Grove, he might find you there. But even then, I only hoped that you would find out I had not deserted you by choice." He frowned. "It was too much to hope that someone would come into that place after me. . . ."

"Enough of that, man," Isgrimnur said quickly. "What were they doing to you?"

Miriamele was certain now that the duke wished to avoid the subject of their decision. She almost smiled. As if anyone would ever doubt his good will and bravery! Still, after what he had said about Cadrach, perhaps Isgrimnur was a little sensitive.

"I am still not sure." Tiamak squinted, as if trying to summon an image to his mind's eye. "As I said, they . . . put the mirror in my hand and covered me with that ooze. The feeling of cold grew stronger and stronger. I thought I was dying—smothering and freezing at the same moment! Then, just when I was certain I had breathed my last, something even stranger happened." He looked up, meeting Miriamele's eyes as though to make sure that she would believe him. "Words began to come into my head—no, not words. There were no words to it at all, merely . . . visions." He paused. "It was as though a door had been opened—as though someone pushed an entrance through into my head and other thoughts came flooding in. But, worst of all, they . . . they were not *human* thoughts."

"Not human? But how could you know such a thing?" Cadrach was interested now, leaning forward, his gray eyes intent on the Wrannaman.

"I cannot explain, but just as you could hear a red knifebill squawk in the trees and know it was not a human voice, so I could tell that these were thoughts that had never known a mortal mind. They were . . . cold thoughts. Slow and patient and so hateful to me that I would have torn my head from my shoulders if I had not been imprisoned in that muck. If I did not quite believe in They

Who Breathe Darkness before, I do now. It was h-horrible to have them inside of my sk—skull."

Tiamak was shaking. Miriamele reached forward to pull the cloak up around his shoulders. Isgrimnur, nervous and fidgeting, threw more sticks onto the flames. "Perhaps you have told enough," she said.

"I am almost f-f-finished. F-forgive me, my t-t-teeth are banging together."

"Here," Isgrimnur said, relieved to have something to do. "We'll move you closer to the fire."

When Tiamak was relocated, he began again.

"I half-knew that I was speaking like a ghant, although it did not feel like that. I felt as though I was taking the terrible, crushing thoughts inside my head and speaking them aloud, but somehow it came out as clicks and buzzing and all the noises those creatures make. Yet it made sense, somehow—it was what I wanted to do, to talk and talk, to let all the thoughts of the cold thing inside me just bleed out for the ghants to understand."

"What were the thoughts about?" Cadrach asked. "Can you remember?"

Tiamak scowled. "Some. But as I said, they were not words, and they were so unlike the things I think or you think that I find it difficult even to explain what I *do* remember." He snaked a hand out from the folds of the cloak to take a bowl of yellowroot tea. "They were visions, really, just pictures as I told you. I saw ghants swarming out of the swamps into the cities—thousands upon thousands, like flies on a sugar-bulb tree. They were just . . . just swarming. And they were all singing in their buzzing voices, all singing the same song of power and food and never dying."

"And this was what the . . . the cold thing was telling them?" Miriamele asked.

"I suppose. I was speaking as a ghant, I was seeing things as they did—and that was terrible, too. He Who Always Steps on Sand, preserve me from ever seeing such a thing again! The world through their eyes is cracked and skewed, the only colors are blood-red and tar-black. Shimmery, too, as though every-thing were covered in grease, or as if one's eyes were full of water. And—this is the hardest to explain—nothing had a face, not the other ghants, not the people running screaming from the invaded cities. Every living th-thing was just a muddy l-l-lump with l-legs."

Tiamak fell silent, sipping his tea, the bowl trembling in his hands.

"That is all." He took a deep, shaky breath. "It seemed as though it lasted for years, but it cannot have been more than a few days."

"Poor Tiamak!" Miriamele said with feeling. "How did you keep your wits!?"

"I would not have if you had been any longer in coming," he said firmly. "I am sure of that. I could feel my own mind straining and slipping, as though I hung by my fingertips over a long drop. A drop into darkness without end." He looked down into his tea-bowl. "I wonder how many of my fellow villagers besides Younger Mogahib served them as I did, but were *not* rescued?"

"There were lumps." Isgrimnur spoke slowly. "Other lumps in a row beside you—but bigger, with no heads sticking out. I came close to them." He hesitated. "There were . . . there were shapes under that white ooze."

"Others of my tribe, I am sure," Tiamak murmured. "Ah, it is horrible. They must have been used up like candles, one at a time." His face sagged. "Horrible."

No one said anything for a while.

Miriamele finally spoke. "You said that the ghants had never been dangerous before."

"No. Although I am sure now that they became dangerous enough after I left that the villagers made a raid on the nest. That is why the weapons were missing from Older Mogahib's house, almost certainly. And the things Isgrimnur saw tells what happened to the raiders." He looked over to the other Wrannaman. "This one was probably the last of the prisoners."

"But I still don't understand all this about a mirror," the duke said. "Ghants don't use mirrors, do they?"

"No. Nor do they make anything so fine." Tiamak offered the duke a weak smile. "I wonder too, Isgrimnur."

Cadrach, who had been pouring out a bowlful of tea for silent Camaris, turned to look over his shoulder. "I have some ideas, but I must think on them. However, one thing is sure. If some sort of intelligence does guide those creatures, or is capable of guiding them sometimes, then we cannot afford to tarry. We must escape the Wran as swiftly as we possibly can." His tone was cold, as though he spoke of events that barely concerned him. Miriamele did not like the distant look in his eyes.

Isgrimnur nodded. "The monk's right, for once. I don't see that we have any time to waste."

"But Tiamak is sick!" Miriamele said angrily.

"There is nothing to be done, Lady. They are right. If I can be propped up with something to lean against, I can give directions. I can at least take us far enough from the nest by nightfall that we might risk sleeping on land."

"Let's to it, then." Isgrimnur rose. "Time is short."

"It is indeed," said Cadrach. "And growing shorter every day."

His tone was so flat and somber that the others turned to look at him, but the monk only sloshed to the water's edge and began loading their belongings back into the flatboat.

By the next day, Tiamak was much recovered, but Younger Mogahib was not. The Wrannaman slid in and out of fever-madness. He thrashed and raved, shouting things that, when Tiamak translated them, sounded much like the nightmarish visions he himself had experienced; when he was quiet, Younger Mogahib lay like one dead. Tiamak fed him concoctions made from healing herbs gathered along the banks of the watercourse, but they seemed little use.

"His body is strong. But I think his thoughts are wounded, somehow." Tiamak sadly shook his head. "Perhaps they had him longer than I suspected."

They sailed on through the Wran, bearing north in the large part, but going there by a circuitous route that only Tiamak could follow. It was clear that without him, they would indeed have been doomed to wander the swamp's backwaters for a long time. Miriamele did not like to think about what their end might have been.

She was growing tired of the swamp. The descent into the nest had filled her with a disgust for mud and stench and odd creatures that now spread to include all the wild Wran. It was stunningly alive, but so was a tub full of worms. She would not want to spend a moment longer than necessary in either of them.

On the third night after their escape from the nest, Younger Mogahib died. He had been shouting, according to Tiamak, about "the sun running backward" and about blood pouring through the drylander cities like rainwater, when suddenly his face darkened and his eyes bulged. Tiamak tried to give him water to drink, but his jaws were clamped shut and could not be opened. A moment later, the Wrannaman's entire body went rigid. Long after the gleam of life had faded from his wide eyes he remained as stiff as a wooden post.

Tiamak was upset, although he tried to maintain his composure. "Younger Mogahib was not a friend," he said as they drew a cloak over the staring face, "but he was the last link to my village. Now I will not know if they were all captured—taken to the nest . . ." his lip quivered, ". . . or fled to another, safer village when the raiding party failed."

"If there *are* safer villages," said Cadrach. "You say there are many ghant nests in the Wran. Could this be the only one that has become so dangerous?"

"I do not know." The small man sighed. "I will have to come back and search for an answer to that."

"Not by yourself," Miriamele said firmly. "Stay with us. When we find Josua, he will help you find your people."

"Now, Princess," Isgrimnur cautioned, "you can't know that for certain. . . ."

"Why not? Am I not of the royal blood as well? Doesn't that count for anything? Besides, Josua will need all the allies he can find, and the Wrannamen are nothing to scoff at—as Tiamak has proven to us time and again."

The marsh man was dreadfully embarrassed. "You are kind, Lady, but I could not hold you to such a promise." He looked down at Younger Mogahib's shrouded form and sighed. "We must do something with his body."

"Bury him?" Isgrimnur asked. "How do you, when the ground's so wet?"

Tiamak shook his head. "We do not bury our dead. I will show you in the morning. Now, if you will forgive me, I need to walk for a while." He limped slowly out of the campground.

Isgrimnur looked uncomfortably at the body. "I wish he hadn't left us with this."

"Do you fear ghosts, Rimmersman?" Cadrach asked with an unpleasant smile.

Miriamele frowned. She had hoped that when the monk's oil-fire missiles had helped them escape, the hostility between Cadrach and Isgrimnur would diminish. Indeed, the duke seemed ready to call a truce, but Cadrach's anger had hardened into something cold and more than a little unpleasant.

"There's nothing wrong with caution . . ." Isgrimnur began.

"Oh, be quiet, both of you," Miriamele said irritably. "Tiamak has just lost his friend."

"Not a friend," Cadrach pointed out.

"His clansman, then. You heard him: this man was the only one of his village he's found since he returned. This is the only other Wrannaman he's seen! And now he's dead. You'd want a little time alone, too." She turned on her heel and walked over to sit next to Camaris, who was twining grasses to make a sort of necklace.

"Well . . ." Isgrimnur said, but then fell silent, chewing his beard. Cadrach, too, said no more.

When Miriamele awoke the next morning, Tiamak was gone. Her fears were allayed a short while later when he returned to the camp bearing a huge sheaf of oil-palm fronds. As she and the others watched, he wrapped Younger Mogahib with them, layer after layer, as if in parody of the priest of Erchester's House of Preparing; soon there was nothing to be seen but an oblong bundle of oozing green leaves.

"I will take him now," Tiamak said quietly. "You need not come with me if you do not wish it."

"Would you like us to?" Miriamele asked.

Tiamak looked at her for a moment, then nodded. "I would like that, yes."

Miriamele made sure that the others came along—even Camaris, who seemed far more interested in the fringe-tailed birds in the branches overhead than in corpses and funeral parties.

With Isgrimnur's help, Tiamak carefully laid Younger Mogahib's leaf-wrapped body in the flatboat. A short way up the watercourse, he poled against a sand bank and led them ashore. He had built a sort of frame of thin branches in a flat clearing. Beneath the frame, wood and more oil-palm leaves had been stacked. Again with Isgrimnur's assistance, Tiamak lifted the bundle up onto the slender frame, which swayed gently beneath the weight of the corpse.

When everything had been arranged to his satisfaction, Tiamak stepped back and stood beside his companions, facing the frame and the unlit pyre.

"She Who Waits to Take All Back," he intoned, "who stands beside the last river, Younger Mogahib is leaving us now. When he drifts past, remember that he was brave: he went into the ghant nest to save his family, his clansmen and clanswomen. Remember also that he was good."

Here Tiamak had to pause and think for a moment. Miriamele remembered that he had said he and the other Wrannaman had not been friends. "He always respected his father and the other elders," Tiamak declared at last. "He gave his feasts when they were allotted, and did not stint." He took a deep breath. "Remember your agreement with She Who Birthed Mankind. Younger Mogahib had his life and lived it; then, when They Who Watch and Shape touched his shoulder, he gave it up. She Who Waits to Take All Back, do not let him drift by!" Tiamak turned to his companions. "Say it with me, please."

"Do not let him drift by!" they all cried together. In the tree overhead, a bird made a sound like a squeaky door.

Tiamak went and kneeled beside the pyre. With a few strokes of flint and steel, he set a spark among the scraps of oil palm. Within moments, the fire was burning strongly, and soon the leaves wrapped around Younger Mogahib's body began to blacken and curl.

"You do not need to watch," said Tiamak. "If you wait for me a little downstream, I will join you soon."

This time, Miriamele sensed, the Wrannaman did not want company. She and the others boarded the boat and poled a little way along the watercourse, until a bend in the stream hid from their view all but the growing plume of dark gray smoke.

Later, when Tiamak came wading through the water, Isgrimnur helped him aboard. They poled the short distance back to camp. Tiamak said little that night, but sat and stared at the campfire long after the others had bedded down.

"I think I understand something of Tiamak's story, now," Cadrach said.

It was late morning, six days since they had left the ghant nest behind. The weather was warm, but a breeze made the watercourse more pleasant than it had been in days. Miriamele was beginning to believe they might actually see the last of it soon.

"What do you mean, understand?" Isgrimnur tried to keep the surliness out of his voice, but without complete success. Relations between the Rimmersman and the monk had continued to worsen.

Cadrach favored him with a magisterial stare, but directed his reply to Miriamele and Tiamak, who sat in the middle of the boat. Camaris, watching the banks intently, was poling in the stern. "The shard of mirror. The ghant speech. I think I may know what they mean."

"Tell us, Cadrach," Miriamele urged.

"As you know, Lady, I have studied many ancient matters." The monk cleared his throat, not entirely averse to having an audience. "I have read of things called Witnesses. . . ."

"Was that in Nisses' book?" Miriamele asked, then was startled to feel Tiamak cringe beside her as if dodging a blow. She turned to look at him, but the slender man was staring at Cadrach with what looked oddly like suspicion—a fierce, intent suspicion, as if it had just been revealed that the Hernystirman was half-ghant.

Puzzled, she looked at the monk to find that *he was* looking at *her* with fury.

I suppose he doesn't much want to think about that, Miriamele realized, and felt bad that she had not kept quiet. Still, Tiamak's reaction was what truly puzzled her. What had she said? Or what had Cadrach said?

"In any case," Cadrach said heavily, as if unwillingly forced to continue, "there were once things called Witnesses, which were made by the Sithi in the depths of time. These things allowed them to speak to each other over great distances, and perhaps even let them show dreams and visions to each other. They came in many forms—'Stones and Scales, Pools and Pyres,' as the old books say. 'Scales' are what the Sithi called mirrors. I do not know why."

"Are you saying that Tiamak's mirror was . . . one of those things?" Miriamele asked.

"That is my guess."

"But what would the Sithi have to do with the ghants? Even if they hate men, which I have heard, I can't believe they would like those horrid bugs any better."

Cadrach nodded. "Ah, but if these Witnesses still exist, it could be that others beside the Sithi can use them. Remember, Princess, all the things you heard at Naglimund. Remember who plans and waits in the frozen north."

Miriamele, thinking of Jarnauga's strange speech, suddenly felt a chill quite unrelated to the mild breeze.

Isgrimnur leaned forward from his seat before Camaris' knees. "Hold, man. Are you saying that this Storm King fellow is doing some magic with the ghants? Then what did they need Tiamak for? Doesn't make sense."

Cadrach bit back a sharp reply. "I don't claim to know anything with certainty, Rimmersman. But it could be that the ghants are too different, too . . . simple, perhaps . . . for those who now use these Witnesses to be able to speak with them directly." He shrugged. "It is my guess that they needed a human as a sort of go-between. A messenger."

"But what could the Stor . . ." Miriamele caught herself. Even though Isgrimnur had uttered the name, she had no desire to do the same. "What could someone like that want with the ghants down in the Wran?"

Cadrach shook his head. "It is far beyond me, Lady. Who could hope to know the plans of . . . someone like that?"

Miriamele turned to Tiamak. "Do you remember anything else of what you were being made to say? Could Cadrach be right?"

Tiamak appeared reluctant to talk about it. He stared cautiously at the monk. "I do not know. I know little about . . . about magic or ancient books. Very little." The Wrannaman fell into silence.

"I thought I disliked the ghants before," Miriamele said finally. "But if that's true—if they're somehow part of . . . of what Josua and the others are fighting against . . ." She wrapped her arms around herself. "The sooner we leave here, the better."

"That's something we all agree on," Isgrimnur rumbled.

In Miriamele's dreams that night, as the boat gently rocked on the slow-moving waters, voices spoke to her from behind a veil of shadow—thin, insistent voices that whispered of decay and loss as though they were things to be desired.

She woke up beneath the faint stars and realized that even surrounded by friends, she was terribly lonely.

👑

Tiamak's recovery proved to be incomplete. Within a day after Younger Mogahib's ceremonial burning, he had fallen back into a kind of fever that left him weak and listless. When darkness fell, the Wrannaman had terrible dreams, visions that he could not remember in the morning but which made him writhe in his sleep and cry out. With Tiamak suffering his nightly tortures, the remainder of the company was nearly as ill-rested as he was.

More days passed, but the Wran lingered like a guest that had outstayed his welcome: for every league of marshy tangle they crossed—floating beneath the steamy sky or wading through clinging, foul-scented mud as they struggled with the heavy flatboat—another league of swamp appeared before them. Miriamele began to feel that some sorcerer was playing a cruel trick on them, spiriting them back to their starting place each night while they lay in shallow sleep.

The hovering insects who seemed to delight in finding each person's tenderest spot, the shrouded but potent sun, the air as hot and damp as the steam over a soupbowl, all helped bring the travelers' tempers close to the snapping point—and many times to push them past it. Even the arrival of rain, which at first seemed like such a blessing, turned out to be another curse. The monotonous, blood-warm downpour persisted for three whole days, until Miriamele and her companions began to feel that demons were pounding on their heads with tiny hammers. The unpleasant conditions were even beginning to affect old Camaris, who had previously been unmoved and untouched by almost everything, so calm that he allowed the biting bugs to crawl across his skin without reprisal—something that made Miriamele itch uncontrollably just watching. But the three days and nights of unbroken rain reached even the old knight at last. As they poled along through the third day's storm, he pulled a hat he had made from fronds lower over his white brows and stared miserably out at the rain-pocked watercourse, his long face so sorrowful that Miriamele finally went and put her arm around him. He gave no clear sign of it, but something in his posture suggested he was grateful for the contact; whether that was true or not, he stayed in place for some time, seemingly a little more content. Miriamele marveled at his broad back and shoulders, which seemed almost indecently solid on an old man.

Tiamak found it a labor just to sit upright in the stern of the boat, wrapped in a blanket, and call directions through his chattering teeth. He told them they had nearly reached the Wran's northern fringe, but he had already told them that many days earlier, and the Wrannaman's eyes now had an odd, glazed look. Miriamele and Isgrimnur were being careful not to let each other see they were worrying. Cadrach, who more than once seemed on the verge of coming to blows with the duke, was openly scornful about their chances of finding the way out. Isgrimnur at last told him that if he made any more pessimistic predictions he would be thrown over the side, so that if he wished to make the rest of the journey it would have to be by swimming. The monk ceased his carping, but the looks he directed at the duke when Isgrimnur's back was turned made Miriamele uneasy.

It was clear to her that the Wran was finally wearing them all down. It was not a place for people, ultimately—especially drylanders.

"Over here should do well," she said. She took a few more awkward steps, struggling to stay upright as the mud squelched beneath her bootsoles.

"If you say so, Lady," Cadrach murmured.

They had moved a little way from their camp to bury the remains of their meal, mostly fish bones and scaly skin and fruit pits. During the long course of their journey, the inquisitive Wran apes had proved all too willing to come into camp in search of leavings, even if one of the human company stayed up and sat sentry. The last time the offal had not been removed to at least a few score yards from the campsite, the travelers had spent all night in the middle of what seemed a festival of brawling, screeching apes, all in mad competition for the rights to the finest scraps.

"Go to, Cadrach," she said crossly. "Dig the hole."

He gave her a quick sidelong look, then bent and began scraping at the moist soil. Pale wriggling things came up with each stroke of the hollowed reed spade, gleaming in the torchlight. When he had finished, Miriamele dropped in the leaf-wrapped bundle and Cadrach pushed the mud over it, then turned and began to make his way back toward the glow of the campfire.

"Cadrach."

He turned slowly. "Yes, Princess?"

She took a few steps toward him. "I . . . I am sorry that Isgrimnur said what he did to you. At the nest." She lifted her hands helplessly. "He was worried, and he sometimes speaks without thinking. But he is a good man."

Cadrach's face was expressionless. It was as though he had drawn some curtain across his thoughts, leaving his eyes curiously flat in the torchlight. "Ah, yes. A good man. There are so few of those."

Miriamele shook her head. "That is not an excuse, I know. But please, Cadrach, surely you can understand why he was upset!"

"Of course. I can well understand it. I have lived with myself for many years, Lady—how can I fault someone else for feeling the same way, someone who doesn't even know all that I know?"

"Damn you," Miriamele snapped. "Why must you be this way? I don't hate you, Cadrach! I don't loathe you, even though we have caused trouble for each other!"

He stared at her for a moment, seeming to struggle with conflicting emotions. "No, my lady. You have treated me better than I deserve."

She knew better than to argue. "And I don't blame you at all for not wanting to go into that nest!"

He shook his head slowly. "No, Lady. Nor would any man, even your duke, if they knew . . ."

"Knew what?" she said sharply. "What happened to you, Cadrach? Something more than what you told me about Pryrates—and about the book?"

The monk's mouth hardened. "I do not wish to speak of it."

"Oh, by Elysia's mercy," she said, frustrated. She took a few steps forward and reached out and grasped his hand. Cadrach flinched and tried to pull back, but she held him tightly. "Listen to me. If you hate yourself, others will hate you. Even a child knows that, and you are a learned man."

"And if a child is hated," he spat, "that child will grow to hate itself."

She did not understand what he meant. "But, please, Cadrach. You must forgive, starting with yourself. I cannot bear to see a friend so mistreated, even by himself."

The steady pressure with which the monk had tried to pull away suddenly slackened. "A friend?" he said roughly.

"A friend." Miriamele squeezed his hand and then released it. Cadrach pulled back a step, but went no further. "Now please, we must try to be kind to each other until we reach Josua, or we shall all go mad."

"Reach Josua . . ." The monk repeated her words without inflection. He was suddenly very distant.

"Of course." Miriamele started to walk toward the camp, then stopped again. "Cadrach?"

He did not reply for a moment. "What?"

"You know magic, don't you?" When he remained silent, she plunged on. "I mean, you know a great deal about it, at least—you've made that clear. But I think that you actually know how to do it."

"What are you talking about?" He sounded irritated, but there was a trace of fear in his words. "If you are talking about the fire-missiles, that was no magic at all. The Perdruinese invented that long ago, although they made it with a different sort of oil. They used it for sea-battles. . . ."

"Yes, it was a clever thing to do. But there is more than that to you, and you know it. Why else would you study things like . . . like that book. And I know all about Doctor Morgenes, so if you were part of his—what did you call it? The Scroll League . . . ?"

Cadrach made a gesture of annoyance. "The Art, my lady, is not some bag of wizard's tricks. It is a way of understanding things, of seeing how the world works just as surely as a builder understands a lever or a ramp."

"You see! You *do* know about it!"

"I do not 'do magic,'" he said firmly. "I have, once or twice, used the knowledge I have from my studies." Despite his straightforward tone, he could not meet her eyes. "But it is not what you think of as magic."

"But even so," Miriamele said, still eager, "think of the help you could be to Josua. Think of the aid we could give him. Morgenes is dead. Who else can advise the prince about Pryrates?"

Now Cadrach did look up. He looked hunted, like a cur backed into a corner. "Pryrates?" He laughed hollowly. "Do you think that I can be any help against Pryrates? And he is the smallest part of what is arrayed against you."

"All the more reason!" Miriamele reached out for his hand again, but the monk pulled it away. "Josua needs help, Cadrach. If you fear Pryrates, how much more do you fear the kind of world he will make if he and this Storm King are not defeated?"

At the sound of that terrible name, a muffled purr of thunder could be heard in the distance. Startled, Miriamele looked around, as though some vast, shadowy thing might be watching them. When she turned back, Cadrach was stumbling across the mud, headed back toward camp.

"Cadrach!"

"No more," he shouted. He kept his head lowered as he vanished into the shadowy undergrowth. She could hear him cursing as he made his way back across the treacherous mud.

Miriamele followed him to camp, but Cadrach refused all her attempts at conversation. She berated herself for having said the wrong thing, just when she had thought she was reaching him. What a mad, sad man he was! And, equally infuriating, in the confusion of their talk she had forgotten to ask him about her Pryrates-thought, the one that had been tugging at her mind the other night—something about her father, about death, about Pryrates and Nisses' book. It still seemed important, but it might be a long time until she could bring up the subject with Cadrach again.

Despite the warm night, Miriamele rolled herself tightly in her cloak when she lay down, but sleep would not come. She lay half the night listening to the swamp's strange, incessant music. She also had to put up with the continual misery of crawling and fluttering things, but the bugs, annoying as they might be, were as nothing compared to the irritation of her restless thoughts.

To Miriamele's surprise and pleasure, the next day brought a marked change in their surroundings. The trees were less thickly twined, and in places the flatboat slid out from the humid tangle onto wide shallow lagoons, mirrors compromised only by the faint rippling of the wind and the forests of swaying grasses which grew up through the water.

Tiamak seemed pleased with their progress, and announced that they were very close to the Wran's outermost edge. However, their approaching escape did not cure his weakness and fever, and the thin brown man spent much of the morning slipping in and out of uncomfortable sleep, waking occasionally with a startled movement and a mouthful of wild jabber before slowly coming back to his ordinary self.

In late afternoon, Tiamak's fever became stronger, and his discomfort increased to the point where he sweated and babbled continuously, experiencing

Tad Williams

only short spans of lucidity. During one of these, the Wrannaman regained his wits enough to play apothecary for himself. He asked Miriamele to prepare for him a concoction of herbs, some of which he pointed out where they grew along the watercourse, a flowering grass called quickweed and a ground-hugging, oval-leafed creeper which, in his weakened state, he could not name.

"And yellowroot, too," Tiamak said, panting shallowly. He looked dreadful, his eyes red, his skin shiny with perspiration. Miriamele tried to keep her hands steady as she ground the ingredients already gathered on a flat stone she held in her lap. "Yellowroot, to speed the binding," he mumbled.

"Which is that?" she asked. "Does it grow here?"

"No. But it does not matter." Tiamak tried to smile, but the effort was too much, and instead he gritted his teeth and groaned quietly. "Some in my bag." He rolled his head ever so slightly in the direction of the sack he had appropriated in Village Grove, which now held all the belongings he had guarded so zealously.

"Cadrach, would you find it?" Miriamele called. "I'm afraid I'll spill what I have here."

The monk, who had been sitting at Camaris' feet while the old man poled, stepped gingerly across the rocking flatboat, avoiding Isgrimnur without a glance. He kneeled and began to lift out and examine the contents of the bag.

"Yellowroot," Miriamele said.

"Yes, I heard, Lady," Cadrach replied with a little of his old mocking tone. "A root. And I know that it is yellow, too . . . thanks to my many years of study." Something that he felt beneath his fingers made him pause. His eyes narrowed, and he pulled from Tiamak's bag a package wrapped in leaves and tied with thin vines. Some of the covering had dried and peeled away. Miriamele could see a flash of something pale inside. "What is this?" Cadrach eased the wrappings back a little further. "A very old parchment . . ." he began.

"No, you demon! You witch!"

The loud voice startled Miriamele so much that she dropped the blunt rock she had been using as a pestle; it bounced painfully on her boot and thumped down into the bottom of the boat. Tiamak, his eyes bulging, was struggling to lift himself.

"You won't have it!" he shouted. Flecks of spittle gathered at the corners of his mouth. "I knew you would come after it!"

"He's fever-mad!" Isgrimnur was more than a little alarmed. "Don't let him tip the boat over."

"It's just Cadrach, Tiamak," Miriamele said soothingly, but she, too, was startled by the look of hatred on the Wrannaman's face. "He's just trying to find the yellowroot."

"I know who it is," Tiamak snarled. "And I know just what he is, too, and what he wants. Curse you, demon-monk! You wait until I am ill to steal my parchment! Well, you may not have it! It is mine! I bought it with my own coin!"

"Just put it back, Cadrach," Miriamele urged. "It will make him stop raving."

The monk, whose initial look of startlement had changed to something even more unsettled—and, to Miriamele, unsettling as well—slowly eased the leaf-wrapped bundle back into the sack, then handed the whole thing to Miriamele.

"Here." His voice was once again strangely flat. "You take out what he wants. I cannot be trusted."

"Oh, Cadrach," she said, "don't be foolish. Tiamak is ill. He doesn't know what he's saying."

"I know." The Wrannaman's wide eyes were still fixed on the monk. "He gave himself away. I knew then that he was after it."

"For the love of Aedon," Isgrimnur growled, disgusted. "Just give him something to make him sleep. Even *I* know the monk wasn't trying to steal anything."

"Even you, Rimmersman?" Cadrach murmured, but with none of his usual sharpness. Rather, there was an echo of some great hopelessness in the monk's voice, and something else, too—some peculiar edge that Miriamele could not identify.

Worried and confused, she turned her concentration onto the search for Tiamak's yellowroot. The Wrannaman, his hair damp and tousled by sweat, continued to glare at Cadrach like a maddened blue jay who had found a squirrel sniffing about his nest.

Miriamele had thought the entire incident merely the product of Tiamak's illness, but that night she woke up suddenly in the camp they had made on a rare dry sandbank, and saw Cadrach—who had been delegated the first watch—rummaging through Tiamak's bag.

"What are you doing?!" She crossed the camp in a few swift paces. Despite her anger, she kept her voice low so as not to wake any of the rest of her companions from their sleep. She could not escape the feeling that somehow Cadrach was her responsibility alone, and that the others should not be brought in if she could avoid it.

"Nothing," the monk grumbled, but his guilty face belied him. Miriamele reached forward and plunged her hand into the sack, closing her fingers on his own and the leaf-wrapped parchment.

"I should have known better," she said, full of fury. "Is there truth to what Tiamak said? Have you been trying to steal his belongings, now that he is too sick to protect them?"

Cadrach snapped back like a wounded animal. "You are no better than all the rest, with your talk of friendship! At the first moment, you turn on me, just like Isgrimnur."

His words stung, but Miriamele was still angry to find him doing this low thing after she had given him her trust. "You haven't answered my question."

"You are a fool," he snarled. "If I wanted to steal something from him, why would I wait until he had been saved from the ghant's nest?!" He pulled his hand from the sack, bringing hers with it, then took the package and thrust it into her hands. "Here! I was merely interested in what it could be, and why he turned *goirach* . . . why he became so angry. I had never seen it before—didn't even know that it was there! You keep it, then, Princess. Safe from grubby little thieves like me!"

"But you could have asked him," she said, more than a little ashamed now that the heat had passed, and angry to feel that way. "Not come creeping after it when everyone was asleep."

"Oh, yes, asked him! You saw the kindly way he looked at me when I merely touched it! Do you have any idea what it is, my headstrong lady? Do you?"

"No. Nor will I until Tiamak tells me." Hesitantly, she stared at the cylindrical object. In other circumstances, she knew, she would have been the first to try to find out what the Wrannaman was protecting. Now, she was caught by her own high-handedness, and she had offended the monk as well. "I will keep it safe, and I will not look at it," she said slowly. "When Tiamak is well, I will ask him to show it to us."

Cadrach stared at her for a long moment. His moonlit features, touched with crimson by the last few embers of the fire, were almost frightening. "Very well, my lady," he whispered. She thought she could hear his voice hardening like ice. "Very well. By all means keep it out of the hands of thieves." He turned and walked to his cloak, then dragged it to the edge of the sand, far from the others. "Keep watch, then, Princess Miriamele. Make sure no evil men come near. I am going to sleep." He lay down, becoming only another lump of shadow.

Miriamele sat listening to the night noises of the swamp. Although the monk did not speak again, she could almost feel his unsleeping presence in the darkness a few short steps away. Something raw and painful in him had been exposed again, something that, for the last few weeks, had been almost completely hidden. Whatever it was, she had thought it might have been exorcised after Cadrach's long revelatory night on Firannos Bay. Now Miriamele found herself wishing desperately that she had slept through the night tonight and not awakened until morning, when the light of day would have made everything safe and ordinary.

The Wran fell away at last, not in a single broad stroke, but with the gradual dwindling of trees and narrowing of waterways, until finally Miriamele and her companions found themselves floating across an open scrubland crisscrossed with small channels. The world was wide again, something that spread from horizon to horizon. She had grown so used to the hemming-in of her vision that she found it almost uncomfortable to be confronted with so much space.

In some ways, the last stage of the Wran was the most treacherous, since they had to carry the boat over land more frequently than before. Once, Isgrimnur became stuck in a waist-deep sandhole, and was only rescued by the combined efforts of Miriamele and Camaris.

The Lake Thrithing lay before them, a vast expanse of low hills and, except for the ever-present grass, sparse vegetation. Trees clung near to the hillsides; but for a few copses of tall pines, they were dwarfish, barely distinguishable from bushes. In the late afternoon light it seemed a lonely, windswept land, a place where few creatures and no people would live by choice.

Tiamak had at last brought them beyond the bounds of his territorial knowledge, and they found increasing difficulty in choosing streams wide enough to carry the boat. When the latest channel narrowed beyond the point of navigability, they clambered from the boat and stood silent for a while, collars lifted against the cold breeze.

"It looks as though it's time to walk." Isgrimnur gazed out across the wilderness to the north. "This is the Lake Thrithing, after all, so at least there'll be drinking water, especially after this year's weather."

"But what about Tiamak?" Miriamele asked. The potion she had brewed for the Wrannaman had certainly helped, but it had not provided a miraculous cure: although he was standing, he was weak and his color was not good.

Isgrimnur shrugged. "Don't know. I suppose we could wait a few days until he gets better, but I hate to spend any more time than we need to out here. P'raps we could make some kind of sling."

Camaris abruptly stooped and put his long hands under Tiamak's armpits, startling the Wrannaman into a whoop of surprise. With an astounding absence of effort, the old man lifted Tiamak high and lowered him onto his shoulders; the Wrannaman, who began to understand in midair, spread his knees to either side of Camaris' neck, settling like a pickaback child.

The duke grinned. "There's your answer, looks like. I don't know how long he can go, but maybe at least until we can find better shelter. That would be more than fine."

They took their belongings from the boat, packing them in the few cloth sacks they had brought out of Village Grove. Tiamak took his own bag and clutched it in the arm he was not using to hold on to Camaris. He had not spoken of the bag and its contents again since the incident in the boat, and Miriamele had not yet felt inclined to press him to reveal what he carried.

With more regret than she had expected, Miriamele and the others bade a silent farewell to the flatboat and marched out onto the fringes of the Lake Thrithing.

Camaris proved more than equal to the task of carrying Tiamak. Although he stopped to rest when the others did, and moved very slowly through the few patches of swampy ground that still remained, he kept the same pace as the less burdened members of the company and did not seem inordinately tired. Miriamele could not help staring at him from time to time, full of awe. If he was like this as an old man, what prodigious feats must he have performed when he was in the bloom of youth? It was enough to make one believe that all the old legends, even the wildest ones, might be true after all.

Despite the old man's uncomplaining strength, Isgrimnur insisted on taking

the Wrannaman onto his own shoulders for the last hour until sunset. When
they stopped at last to make their camp, the duke was puffing and blowing, and
looked as though he regretted his decision.

They made camp while the light was still in the sky, finding a spot in a grove
of low trees and building a fire from deadwood. The snow that had covered
much of the north had apparently not lingered on the Lake Thrithing, but as
the sun finally dipped below the horizon, the evening grew cold enough to
keep them all huddled by the fire. Miriamele was suddenly grateful she had not
discarded her tattered, travel-stained acolyte's habit.

Chill wind sawed in the branches close over their heads. The surrounded
feeling of the Wran had been replaced by a sensation of being dangerously exposed, but at least the ground beneath them was dry: that, Miriamele decided,
was something to be thankful for, anyway.

Tiamak was a little better the next day, and was able to walk most of the morning before having to be hoisted onto Camaris' broad shoulders again. Isgrimnur,
out of the confining and confusing swamps, was almost his old self, full of songs
of questionable taste—Miriamele enjoyed counting how many verses he finished
of each before stopping, flustered, to beg her pardon—and stories of battles and
wonders he had seen. Cadrach, on the other hand, was as silent as he had been
since they had escaped the *Eadne Cloud*. When spoken to, he responded, and he
was strangely courteous to Isgrimnur, acting almost as if they had never had harsh
words, but the rest of the day's trip he might have been as mute as Camaris for all
he contributed. Miriamele did not like the hollow look of him, but nothing she
said or did changed his calm, withdrawn manner, and at last she gave up.

The low-lying ravel of the Wran had long since disappeared behind them:
even from the highest of the hills, there was little to see back on the southern
horizon but a dark smear. As they set up camp in another copse of trees, Miriamele wondered how far they had come—and, more important, how long a
journey still awaited them.

"How far are we going to have to walk?" she asked Isgrimnur as they shared
a bowl of stew made with dried Village Grove fish. "Do you know?"

He shook his head. "Not sure, my lady. More than fifty leagues, perhaps
sixty or seventy. A long, long hike, I'm afraid."

She made a worried face. "That could take weeks."

"What else can we do?" he said, then smiled. "In any case, Princess, we are
far better off than we were—and closer to Josua."

Miriamele felt a momentary pang. "If he is really there."

"He is, young one, he is." Isgrimnur squeezed her hand in his broad paw.
"We've come through the worst."

Something awakened Miriamele abruptly in the bruised light just before
dawn. She had scarcely an instant to gather her wits before she was grabbed by
the arm and jerked upright. A triumphant voice spoke in rapid Nabbanai.

"Here she is. Dressed like a monk, Lord, as you said."

A dozen men on horseback, several of them carrying torches, had surrounded them. Isgrimnur, who was sitting on the ground with one of the horsemen's lances at his throat, groaned.

"It was my watch!" the duke said bitterly. "My watch . . ."

The man who held Miriamele's arm pulled her a few steps across the copse toward one of the riders, a tall figure in a capacious hood, his face invisible in the gray of night's end. She felt a claw of ice clutch at her.

"So," the rider said in accented Westerling. "So." Despite the strange mushiness of his speech, his voice was unmistakably smug.

Miriamele's horror was warmed a little by anger. "Take off your hood, my lord. You have no need to play such a game with me."

"Truly?" The rider's hand rose. "Do you wish to see what you have done, then?" He pushed the hood back with a sweeping gesture like a traveling player's. "Am I as beautiful as you remember me?" asked Aspitis.

Miriamele, despite the soldier's restraining hand, stepped back. It was hard not to. The earl's face, once so handsome that, after their first meeting, it had haunted her dreams for days, was now a distorted ruin. His fine nose was a blob of flesh skewed to one side like a lump of ill-handled clay. His left cheekbone had been cracked like an egg and dented inward, so that the torchlight made a shadow in the deep hollow. All around his eyes black blood had gathered beneath the skin and the rumple of scars, as though he wore a mask. His hair was still beautiful, still golden.

Miriamele swallowed. "I have seen worse," she said quietly.

Half of Aspitis Preves' mouth curled in an eerie grin, displaying the stumps of teeth. "I am glad to hear it, my sweet lady Miriamele, since you will be waking up to it the rest of your life. Bind her!"

"No!" It was Cadrach who shouted, lurching up from where he lay in the darkness. A moment later, an arrow shivered in the gnarled trunk of a tree, a handspan from his face.

"If he moves again, kill him," said Aspitis calmly. "Perhaps I should let you kill him anyway—he was as responsible as she for what happened to me, to my ship." He shook his head slowly, savoring the moment. "Ah, you are such fools, Princess, you and your monk. Once you had slipped away into the Wran, what did you think? That I would let you go? That I would forget what you had done to me?" He leaned forward, fixing her with bloodshot eyes. "Where else would you go but north, back to the rest of your friends? But you forget, my lady, that this is *my* fiefdom." He chuckled. "My castle on Lake Eadne is only a few leagues away. I have been combing these hills, hunting you for days. I knew you would come."

She felt miserably numb. "How did you get off the ship?"

Aspitis' crooked smirk was horrible. "I was slow to realize what had happened, it is true, but after you had gone and my men found me, I had them kill the treacherous Niskie—Aedon burn her! She had finished her devil's work.

She did not even try to escape. After that, the rest of the kilpa went back over the side—I do not think they would have had the courage to attack without the sea witch's spell. We had enough men to row my poor damaged *Eadne Cloud* to Spenit." He slapped his hands on his thighs. "Enough. You are mine again. Save your prattling questions until I ask for them."

Full of anger and sorrow over Gan Itai's fate, Miriamele struggled toward him, dragging the soldier who gripped her arm a full pace forward. "God's curse on you! What kind of man are you? What kind of knight? You, with all your talk about the fifty noble families of Nabban."

"And you, a king's daughter, who willingly gave herself to me—who brought me to her bed? Are you so high and pure?"

She was ashamed that Isgrimnur and the others should hear, but a sort of high, clear anger followed, sharpening her thoughts. She spat on the ground. "Will you fight for me?" she demanded. "Here, before your people and mine? Or will you take me as a sneak thief, as you tried to take me before—with lies, and with force used against those who were your guests?"

The earl's eyes narrowed to slits. "Fight for you? What nonsense is this? Why should I? You are mine, by capture and maidenhead."

"I will never be yours," she said in her haughtiest tones. "You are lower than the Thrithings-men, who at least fight to claim their brides."

"Fight, fight, what trick is this?" Aspitis glared. "Who would fight for you? One of these old men? The monk? The little swamp boy?"

Miriamele let her eyes fall closed for a moment, struggling to contain her fury. He was vile, but this was not the moment to let emotions rule her. "Anyone in this camp can beat you, Aspitis. You are not a man at all." She looked around, making sure that she had the attention of the earl's soldiers. "You are a stealer of women, but you are no man."

Aspitis' osprey-hilted blade slid from its sheath with a metallic hiss. He paused. "No, I see your game, Princess. You are a clever one. You think to make me so maddened that I kill you here." He laughed. "Ah, to think that a woman exists who would rather die than wed the Earl of Eadne." He lifted his hand and touched his shattered face. "Or rather, to think that you felt that way even *before* you did this to me." He held his sword out; the point wavered in the air not a cubit from her neck. "No, I know what punishment will best pay you back, and that is marriage. My castle has a tower that will keep you well. Within the first hour, you will know its every stone. Think how it will feel when years have passed."

Miriamele lifted her chin. "So you will not fight for me."

Aspitis slapped his fist on his thigh. "Enough of this! I grow weary of the joke."

"Do you hear?" Miriamele turned toward the rest of Aspitis' company, who sat, waiting. "Your master is a coward."

"Silence!" Aspitis shouted. "I will whip you myself."

"That old man can thrash you," she said, pointing to Camaris. The old knight sat wrapped in his blanket, watching wide-eyed. He had made no move since Aspitis and his soldiers had arrived. "Isgrimnur," she called, "give the old man your sword."

"Princess . . ." Isgrimnur's voice was rough with worry. "Let me . . ."

"Do it! Let the earl's men see him cut to ribbons by an old, old man. Then they will know why their master has to steal women."

Isgrimnur, keeping a careful eye on the watching soldiers, pulled Kvalnir out from beneath his sack of belongings. The buckles of the sword belt clinked as he slid it across the ground toward Camaris. For a moment, that was the only sound.

"My lord?" the soldier who held Miriamele said hesitantly. "What . . . ?"

"Shut your mouth," Aspitis snapped as he dismounted. He walked to Miriamele and grabbed her face with his hand, staring at her intently for a moment. Then, before she had a chance to react, he leaned forward suddenly and kissed her with his broken mouth. "We will have many interesting nights." The earl then turned to Camaris. "Go on, put it on so I can kill you. Then I will finish the rest of you, too. But I will allow you to defend yourselves or run as you choose." He turned and looked at Miriamele. "I am, after all, a gentleman."

Camaris stared at the sword by his feet as though it were a serpent.

"Put it on!" Miriamele urged.

Elysia's mercy, she thought frantically, *what if he won't do it! What if, after all this, he won't do it?*

"For the love of God, man, put it on," Isgrimnur shouted. The old man looked at him, then bent and picked up the sword belt. He withdrew Kvalnir and let the belt and sheath slide back to the ground. He held it loosely, unwillingly.

"Matra sá Duos," Aspitis said disgustedly, "he does not even know how to swing a sword." He unbelted his robe and let it fall, revealing a surcoat of yellow-gray trimmed in black, then took a few steps toward Camaris, who looked up bemusedly. "I will kill him quickly, Miriamele," the earl declared. *"You* are the cruel one, to make an old man fight." He raised his weapon, which gleamed beneath the white dawn sky, then aimed a cut at Camaris' unprotected neck.

Kvalnir rose awkwardly and Aspitis' blade rebounded. The earl, with a noise of irritation, swung again. Once more his steel clanked against the duke's sword and flew back. Miriamele heard her warder grunt in soft surprise at his master's frustration.

"You see!" she said, and forced herself to laugh, though there was no mirth in her. "The coward earl cannot even best a man in his dotage."

Aspitis attacked more strongly. Camaris, moving almost like a man sleep-walking, kept Kvalnir weaving before him in deceptively slow arcs. Several more wicked blows were deflected.

"I see your old man *has* wielded a sword." The earl was beginning to breathe a little more heavily. "That is good. I will not feel that I have been forced to kill one who cannot defend himself."

"Fight back!" Miriamele shouted, but Camaris would not. Instead, as his movements became more fluid, ancient reflexes gradually awakening after a long sleep, he merely defended himself more diligently, blocking every thrust, guiding every slash away, spinning a web of steel that Aspitis could not breach.

The fighting was in deadly earnest now. It was plain that the Earl of Eadne and Drina was a very good swordsman, and he in turn had quickly grasped the fact that his opponent was something unusual. Aspitis eased his attack, pursuing a more cautious, probing strategy, but he did not back down from the challenge. Something, whether pride or some deeper, more animalistic urge, had caught him up. Camaris, meanwhile, seemed to fight only because he was forced to. Miriamele thought she saw several times when he could have pressed his own attack but chose not to, waiting until his enemy came at him once more.

Aspitis feinted, then slid in a thrust beneath Camaris' guard, but somehow Kvalnir was there to push the earl's blade aside. Aspitis cut at the old man's feet, but Camaris shuffled back without visible haste, keeping his balance firm and his shoulders level even as he avoided the earl's blow. He was like water, flowing always to where there was an opening, giving way but never breaking, absorbing every blow from Aspitis and directing its force up or down, to one side or the other. A thin film of sweat broke on the old man's forehead, but his face remained calmly regretful, as though he were being forced to sit and watch two of his friends trade unpleasant words.

The duel went on for what seemed to Miriamele a dreadfully long time. Although she knew that her heart was racing, each beat seemed to come long moments apart. The two men, the crack-faced earl and the tall, long-legged Camaris, worked their way out from the stand of pine trees and down onto the hillside, circling their way along the weedy slope like two moths revolving around a candle, their blades whirling and flickering beneath the gray sky. As the earl pressed forward once again, Camaris stepped in a hole and lost his balance; Aspitis took advantage of the opportunity and landed a swipe across the old man's arm, drawing a streak of blood. Behind her, Miriamele heard Isgrimnur curse in heartbreaking impotence.

The cut seemed to awaken something in Camaris. Although he still would not attack aggressively, he began to beat back the earl's attacks with greater strength, striking hard enough to make the rattle of steel echo across the plains of the Lake Thrithing. Miriamele worried that it would not be enough, since despite his almost unbelievable fortitude, he seemed to be tiring at last. He stumbled again, this time with no hole to blame, and Aspitis brought home a thrust that skimmed off Kvalnir and found Camaris' shoulder, freeing more blood. But the earl was flagging, too: after a swift flurry in which several of his strokes were blocked, he took a few steps back, panting, and bent low to the ground as if he might collapse. Miriamele saw him pick something from the ground.

"Camaris! Watch out!" she screamed.

Aspitis flung the handful of dirt in the old man's face and followed it with a swift and aggressive attack, seeking to end the combat with a single stroke. Camaris staggered backward, clawing at his eyes as Aspitis closed with him. A moment later, the earl fell to his knees, yowling.

Camaris, his greater reach enabling him to extend past the earl's outstretched blade, had struck his opponent a flat blow across the upper arm, but the blade had bounced and continued upward, slashing diagonally across the earl's forehead. Aspitis, his face quickly vanishing behind a sheet of blood, scrabbled across the ground toward Camaris, still waving his blade before him. The old man, who was rubbing the dirt from his watering eyes, stepped aside and brought the hilt of his sword down atop the earl's head. Aspitis dropped like a maul-slaughtered ox.

Miriamele pulled free from the grip of her thunderstruck guard and dashed down the hillside. Camaris sank to the ground, gasping for breath. He looked tired and vaguely unhappy, like a child asked to do too much. Miriamele glanced at him quickly to make sure his wounds were not dangerous, then took Kvalnir from his unresisting grasp and kneeled down beside Aspitis. The earl was breathing, too, although shallowly. She turned him over, staring for a moment at his bloody, shattered-doll face . . . and something changed inside of her. A bubble of hatred and fear that had been in her since the *Eadne Cloud,* a bubble that had grown chokingly large at finding Aspitis still pursuing her, abruptly burst. Suddenly, he seemed so small. He was nothing important at all, just a tattered, damaged thing—no different than the cloak draped over a chair-back that had given her the screaming night-terrors when she was a small child. Morning's light had come, and the demon had become a rumpled cloak again.

A sort of smile crossed Miriamele's face. She pressed the sword blade against the earl's throat.

"You men!" she shouted at Aspitis' soldiers. "Do you want to explain to Benigaris how his best friend was killed?"

Isgrimnur stood, pushing away the lance-point of the soldier who had held him.

"Do you?" Miriamele demanded.

None of the earl's men spoke.

"Then give us your bows—all of them. And four horses."

"We will not give you any horses, witch!" one of the soldiers shouted angrily.

"So be it. Then you can take Aspitis back with his gullet slit and tell Duke Benigaris it was done by an old man and a girl, while you stood watching—that is, if you get away unharmed, and you will have to kill us all to do that."

"Do not bargain with them," Cadrach shouted suddenly. There was desperation in his tone. "Kill the monster. Kill him!"

"Be quiet." Miriamele wondered if the monk was trying to convince the soldiers that the danger to their master was real. If so, he was a fine actor: he sounded remarkably sincere.

The soldiers looked at each other worriedly. Isgrimnur took advantage of the moment's confusion to begin relieving them of their bows and arrows. After the Rimmersman growled at him, Cadrach scrambled forward to help. Several of the men cursed them and looked as though they wished to resist, but no one made the move that would have sparked open conflict. When Isgrimnur and the monk each had an arrow nocked on a bow, the soldiers began to talk angrily among themselves, but Miriamele could see that the fight had gone out of them.

"Four horses," she said calmly. "I will do you a favor and ride with the man that *this* scum," she prodded Aspitis' still form, "called a 'swamp boy.' Otherwise you would be leaving us five."

After more arguing, Aspitis' troop turned over four horses, first removing the saddlebags. When riders and baggage were redistributed upon the remaining horses, two of the earl's household guard came forward and lifted their liege-lord from the ground, then draped him unceremoniously across the saddle of one of the remaining horses. His soldiers had to ride two-to-a-mount, and looked positively embarrassed as the little caravan rode off.

"And if he lives," Miriamele shouted after them, "remind him of what happened!"

The mounted company vanished quickly, riding east into the hills.

Wounds were tended, the newly acquired horses were loaded with the travelers' scant baggage, and by the middle of the day they were on their way once more. Miriamele felt curiously light-headed, as though she had just woken up from a terrible dream to find a sunny spring morning outside her window. Camaris had returned to his normal placidity; the old man seemed scarcely the worse for his experience. Cadrach did not speak much, but that was no different than any day of the last few.

Aspitis had been a shadow at the back of Miriamele's mind since the night of the storm and her escape from the earl's ship. Now that shadow was gone. As she rode across the hilly Thrithings-country with Tiamak nodding in the saddle before her, she almost felt like singing.

They covered several leagues that afternoon. When they stopped for the night, Isgrimnur, too, was in an excellent mood.

"We shall make far better time now, Princess." He was grinning in his beard. If he thought less of her now that Aspitis had revealed her shame, he was too much a gentleman to show it. "By Dror's Mallet, did you see Camaris? Did you see him? Like a man half his age."

"Yes." She smiled. The duke was a good man. "I saw him, Isgrimnur. It was like an old song. No, it was better."

He woke her in the morning. She could tell by his face that something was wrong.

"Is it Tiamak?" She had a sickened feeling. They had come through so much! Surely the little man had been getting better?

The duke shook his head. "It's the monk. He's gone."

"Cadrach?" Miriamele was not prepared for that. She rubbed her head, fighting to wake up. "What do you mean, gone?"

"Gone away. Took one of the horses. He left a note." Isgrimnur pointed to a piece of the Village Grove cloth which lay on the ground near where she had been sleeping; the furl of cloth had been anchored by a rock against the stiff hillside breeze.

Where Miriamele's feelings about Cadrach's flight should have been, there was nothing. She lifted the stone and spread the sheet of pale fabric. Yes, he had written this: she had seen Cadrach's hand before. It looked as though he had done his writing with the burned tip of a twig.

What could have been so important to say, she wondered, *that he spent so much time writing a note before he left?*

> *Princess,*

it said,

> *I cannot go with you to Josua. I do not belong with those people. Do not blame yourself. No one has been kinder to me than you, even after you knew me for what I am.*
>
> *I fear that things are worse than you know, much worse. I wish there was something more that I could do, but I am unable to help anyone.*

He had not signed it.

"What 'things'?" Isgrimnur asked, irritated. He was reading over her shoulder. "What does he mean, 'things are worse than you know'?"

Miriamele shrugged helplessly. "Who can say?" *Deserted again,* was all she could think.

"Maybe I was too hard on him," the duke said gruffly. "But that's no cause to steal a horse and ride off."

"He was always afraid. Ever since I have known him. It's hard to live with fear all the time."

"Well, we can't waste tears on him," Isgrimnur grumbled. "We have troubles of our own."

"No," Miriamele said, folding the note, "we shouldn't waste tears."

20

Travelers and Messengers

✦

"I have not been here for many seasons," Aditu said. "Many, many seasons."

She stopped and raised her hands, circling the fingers in a complicated gesture; her slim body swayed like a dowser's rod. Simon watched in wonder and more than a little apprehension. He was quickly becoming sober.

"Shouldn't you come down?" he asked.

Aditu only glanced down at him, a moonlit smile playing around the corners of her mouth, then turned her eyes upward to the sky once more. She took a few more steps along the Observatory's slender, crumbling parapet. "Shame to the House of Year-Dancing," she said. "We should have done more to preserve this place. It grieves me to see it fallen to pieces."

Simon did not think she sounded very grieved. "Geloë calls this place the Observatory," Simon said. "Why is that?"

"I do not know. What is 'observatory'? It is not a word that I know in your tongue."

"Father Strangyeard said it's a place like they used to have in Nabban in the days of the Imperators—a tall building where they look at the stars and try to figure out what will happen."

Aditu laughed and raised one foot in the air to take off her boot, then lowered it and did the same with the other, as calmly as though she stood on the ground beside Simon instead of twenty cubits in the air on a thin cornice of stone. She tossed the boots down. They thumped softly on the damp grass. "Then she is making fun, I think, although there is some meaning behind her jest. No one looked at the stars here, except as one would look at them anywhere. This was the place of the *Rhao iye-Sama'an*—the Master Witness."

"Master Witness?" Simon wished she wouldn't move along the slippery parapet so quickly. For one thing, it forced him to walk briskly just to stay within hearing. For another . . . well, it *was* dangerous, even if she didn't think so. "What's that?"

"You know what a Witness is, Simon. Jiriki gave you his mirror. That is a minor Witness, and there are many of those still in existence. There were only a few Master Witnesses, each more or less bound to a place—the Pool of Three

Depths in Asu'a, the Speakfire in Hikehikayo, the Green Column in Jhiná-T'seneí—and most of those are broken or ruined or lost. Here at Sesuad'ra it was a great stone beneath the ground, a stone called the Earth-Drake's Eye. Earth-Drake is another name—it is difficult to explain the differences between the two in your tongue—for the Greater Worm who bites at his own tail," she explained. "We built this entire place on top of that stone. It was not quite a Master Witness—in fact, it was not even a Witness by itself, but such was its potency that a minor Witness like my brother's mirror would be a Master Witness if used here."

Simon's head was whirling with names and ideas. "What does that *mean,* Aditu?" he asked, trying to keep from sounding cross. He had been doing his best to remain calm and well-spoken once the wine had begun to wear off. It seemed important that she see how much he had grown in the months since they had last met.

"A minor Witness will lead you onto the Road of Dreams, but will usually show you only those you know, or those who are looking for you." She raised her left leg and leaned backward, her back arched like a drawn longbow as she bent gracefully into balance, looking for all the world like a little girl playing on a waist-high fence. "A Master Witness, if used by someone who knew the ways of it, could look on anyone or anything, and sometimes into other times and . . . *other* places."

Simon could not help remembering the night-visions of his vigil, as well as what he had seen when he had brought Jiriki's mirror to this place on a later night. He pondered this as he watched Aditu tilt backward until her palms touched the crumbling stone. A moment later, both her feet were in the air as she swayed upside down, standing on her hands.

"Aditu!" Simon said sharply, then tried to make his voice calm. "Shouldn't we go see Josua now?"

She laughed again, a swift sound of pure animal pleasure. "My frightened Seoman. No, there is no need to hurry to Josua, as I told you on the way here. The tidings from my folk can wait until morning. Give your prince a night of rest from worries. From what I saw of him, he needs some relief from woe and care." She inched along on her hands. Her hair, unbound, hung down over her face in a white cloud.

Simon felt sure she could no longer see what she was doing. It frustrated him and made him more than a little angry. "Then why did you come all the way from Jao é-Tinukai'i, if it wasn't important?" He stopped following. "Aditu! What are you doing this for?! If you've come to talk to Josua, then let's go and talk to Josua!"

"I did not say it was not important, Seoman," she replied. There was something of her old mocking tone, but there was a hint of something sharper, almost angry. "I merely said that it would best wait until tomorrow. And that is what will happen." She brought her knees down between her elbows and delicately placed her feet between her hands. Then she lifted her arms and stood up all in one motion, as though preparing to dive out into empty space. "So until then I will spend my time as *I* please, no matter what a young mortal might think."

Simon was stung. "You've been sent to bring news to the prince, but you'd rather do tumbling tricks."

Aditu was wintery cool. "In fact, if I had been given my choice, I would not be here at all. I would have ridden with my brother to Hernystir."

"Well, why didn't you?"

"Likimeya willed otherwise."

So quickly that Simon barely had time to draw in a surprised breath, she bent, catching the parapet in one long-fingered hand, then dropped over the edge. She found a grip on the pale stone wall with her free hand and lodged the toe of one bare foot while probing with the other. She descended the rest of the way as quickly and effortlessly as a squirrel skittering down a tree trunk.

"Let us go inside," she said.

Simon laughed and felt his anger ease.

Standing beside the Sitha made the Observatory seem even eerier. The shadowed staircases which wound up the walls of the cylindrical room made him think of the insides of some huge animal. The tiles, even in the near-darkness, glimmered faintly, and seemed to be assembled in patterns that would not quite lie still.

It was odd to realize that Aditu was almost as much a youngling as he, since the Sithi had built this place long before her birth. Jiriki had once said that he and his sister were "children of the Exile," which Simon understood to mean that they had been born after the fall of Asu'a five centuries ago—a short time indeed in Sithi terms. But Simon had also met Amerasu, and *she* had come to Osten Ard before a single stone had been set on another stone anywhere in the land. And if his own vigil-night dream had been correct, Amerasu's elder Utuk'ku had stood in this very building when the two tribes had separated. It was disturbing to think of anything living as long as First Grandmother or the Norn Queen.

But the most disturbing thing of all was that the Norn Queen, unlike Amerasu, was *still* alive, still powerful . . . and she seemed to have nothing but hatred for Simon and his mortal kind.

He did not like thinking about that—did not, in fact, like thinking about the Norn Queen at all. It was almost easier to understand crazed Ineluki and his violent anger than the spiderlike patience of Utuk'ku, someone who would wait a thousand years or more, full of brooding malice, for some obscure revenge. . . .

"And what did you think of war, Seoman Snowlock?" Aditu asked suddenly. He had sketched for her the bare outlines of the recent struggle as they exchanged news during their walk to the Observatory.

He considered. "We fought hard. It was a wonderful victory. We didn't expect it."

"No, what did *you* think?"

Simon took a moment before replying. "It was horrible."

"Yes, it is." Aditu took a few steps away from him, sliding into a spot beneath the wall where the moonlight did not penetrate, vanishing into shadow. "It is horrible."

"But you just said you wanted to go to war in Hernystir with Jiriki!"

"No. I said I wanted to be with them. That is not the same thing at all, Seoman. I could have been one more rider, one more bow, one more set of eyes. We are very few, we Zida'ya—even mustered together riding out of Jao é-Tinukai'i, with the Houses of Exile reunited. Very few. And none of us wished to go into battle."

"But you Sithi have been in wars," Simon protested. "I know that's true."

"Only to protect ourselves. And once or twice in our history, as my mother and brother are doing in the west now, we have fought to protect those who stood by us in our own need." She sounded very serious now. "But even now, Seoman, we have only taken up our arms because the Hikeda'ya brought the war to *us*. They entered our home and killed my father and First Grandmother, and many more of our folk as well. Do not think that we rush out to fight for mortals at the waving of a sword. These are strange days, Seoman—and you know that as well as I."

Simon took a few steps forward and tripped on a piece of broken stone. He bent to rub his toe, which throbbed painfully. "S'Bloody Tree!" he cursed under his breath.

"It is hard for you to see here at night, Seoman," she said. "I am sorry. We will go now."

Simon did not want to be babied. "In a moment. I'm well." He gave the toe a final squeeze. "Why is Utuk'ku helping Ineluki?"

Aditu appeared from out of the moon-shadow and took his hand in her cool fingers. She seemed troubled. "Let us talk outside." She led him out the door. Her long hair lifted and fluttered in the wind, caressing his face as he walked beside her. It had a strong but pleasing scent, savory-sweet as pine bark.

When they were out on open ground once more, she took his other hand in hers and fixed him with her bright eyes, which seemed to gleam amber in the moonlight. "That is most certainly not the place to name their names, nor to think of them too much," she said firmly, then smiled a wicked smile. "Besides, I do not think I should let as dangerous a mortal boy as you be alone with me in a dark place. Oh, the tales they tell of you around your camp, Seoman Snow-lock."

He was irritated but not altogether displeased. "Whoever 'they' are, they don't know what they're talking about."

"Ah, but you are a strange beast, Seoman." Without another word, she leaned forward and kissed him—not a short, chaste touch as she had given him at their parting many weeks ago, but a warm lover's kiss that sent a shiver of amazement running up his back. Her lips were cool and sweet as morning rose petals.

Far before he would have wished to stop, Aditu gently pulled away. "That little mortal girl liked kissing you, Seoman." Her smile returned, mocking, insolent. "It is an odd thing to do, is it not?"

Simon shook his head, at a loss.

Aditu took his arm and tugged him into motion, falling into step beside him. She bent to pick up the boots she had discarded, then they walked a little farther through the wet grass beside the Observatory wall. She hummed a brief snatch of melody before speaking. "What does Utuk'ku want, you asked?"

Simon, confused by what had happened, did not respond.

"That I could not tell you—not with certainty. She is the oldest thinking creature in all of Osten Ard, Seoman, and she is far more than twice as old as the next most ancient. Be assured, her ways are strange and subtle beyond even the understanding of anyone except perhaps First Grandmother. But if I had to guess, I would say this: she longs for Unbeing."

"What does that mean?" Simon was beginning to wonder if he was truly sober after all, for the world was slowly spinning and he wanted to lie down and sleep.

"If she wished death," Aditu said, "then that would be oblivion just for herself. She is tired of living, Seoman, but she is *eldest*. Never forget that. As long as songs have been sung in Osten Ard, and longer, Utuk'ku has lived. She alone of any living thing saw the lost home that birthed our kind. I do not think she can bear to think of others living when she is gone. She cannot destroy everything, much as she might desire to, but perhaps she hopes to help create the greatest cataclysm possible—that is, to assure that as many living folk accompany her into oblivion as she can drag with her."

Simon stopped, horrified. "That's terrible!" he said with feeling.

Aditu shrugged, a sinuous gesture. She had a lovely neck. "Utuk'ku *is* terrible. She is mad, Seoman, although it is a madness as tightly woven and intricate as the finest *juya'ha* ever spun. She was perhaps the cleverest of all the Gardenborn."

The moon had freed itself from a bank of clouds; it hung overhead like a harvester's scythe. Simon wanted to go to sleep—his head felt very heavy—but at the same time he was loath to give up this chance. It was so rare to find one of the Sithi in a mood to answer questions, and even better, to answer them directly, without the usual Sithi vagueness.

"Why did the Norns go into the north?"

Aditu bent and picked a sprig of some curling vine, white-flowered and dark-leaved. She knotted it in her hair so that it hung against her cheek. "The two families, Zida'ya and Hikeda'ya, had a disagreement. It concerned mortals. Utuk'ku's folk felt your kind to be animals—worse than animals, actually, since we of the Garden do not kill any creature if we can avoid doing so. The Dawn Children did not agree with the Cloud Children. There were other things, too." She lifted her head to the moon. "Then Nenais'u and Drukhi died. That was the day the shadow fell, and it has never been lifted."

No sooner had he congratulated himself on catching Aditu in a forthright mood than she had begun to grow obscure. . . . Still, Simon did not linger over her unsatisfying explanation. He did not really want any more names to learn— he was already overwhelmed with all the things she had told him tonight; in any case, he had another purpose in asking. "And when the two families parted," he said eagerly, "it was here, wasn't it? All the Sithi came to the Fire Garden with torches. And then in Leavetaking House they stood around some thing built of glowing fire and made their bargain."

Aditu lowered her eyes from the sliver of moon, fixing him with her cat-bright stare. "Who told you this tale?"

"I saw it!" He was almost sure by the look on her face that he had been right. "I saw it when I had my vigil. The night I became a knight." He laughed at his own words. Fatigue was making him feel silly. "My knight-night."

"Saw it?" Aditu folded her hand around his wrist. "Tell me, Seoman. We will walk a little while longer."

He described his dream-vision for her—then, for good measure, he told her of what had happened later when he used Jiriki's mirror.

"What happened when you brought the Scale here shows that there is still potency in *Rhao iye-Sama'an*," she said slowly. "But my brother was right to warn you off the Dream Road. It is very dangerous now—otherwise I would take the glass and try to find Jiriki myself, tonight, and tell him of what you told me."

"Why?"

She shook her head. Her hair drifted like smoke. "Because of the thing you saw during your vigil. That is fearful. For you to see something from the Elder Days, *without* a Witness . . ." She made another of her strange finger gestures, this one tangled and complex as a basket of wriggling fish. "Either you have things in you that Amerasu did not see—but I cannot believe that First Grandmother, even in her preoccupation, would fail so abjectly—or there is something happening beyond anything we suspected. That worries me greatly. For the Earth-Drake's Eye to show a vision of the past that way, unbidden . . ." She sighed. Simon stared. She *looked* worried—something he would not have believed possible.

"Maybe it was the dragon's blood," Simon offered. He raised his hand to indicate his scar and shock of white hair. "Jiriki said I was marked somehow."

"Perhaps." Aditu did not seem convinced. Simon felt slightly insulted. So she didn't think he was special enough, did she?

They walked on until they had crossed back over the ruptured tiles of the Fire Garden and were approaching the tent city. Most of the merrymakers had gone to their beds; only a few fires still burned. Beside them, a few shadowy shapes still talked and laughed and sang.

"Go and rest, Seoman," Aditu said. "You are staggering."

He wanted to argue, but knew that what she said was true. "Where will you sleep?"

Her serious expression changed to one of genuine amusement. "Sleep? No, Snowlock, I will walk tonight. I have much to think about. In any case, I have not seen the moon on Sesuad'ra's broken stones for almost a century." She reached out and squeezed his hand. "Sleep well. In the morning we will go to Josua." She turned and walked away, silent as dew. Within moments she was only a slender shadow disappearing across the grassy hilltop.

Simon rubbed at his face with both hands. There was so much to think about. What a night this had been! He yawned and headed toward the tents of New Gadrinsett.

"A strange thing has happened, Josua."

Geloë stood in the door of his tent, unusually hesitant.

"Come in, please." The prince turned to Vorzheva, who was sitting up in bed beneath a mound of blankets. "Or perhaps you would prefer we go elsewhere?" he asked his wife.

Vorzheva shook her head. "I do not feel well today, but if I must lie here this morning, at least there will be some people to keep me company."

"But perhaps Valada Geloë's news will distress you," the prince said worriedly. He looked to the wise woman. "Can she hear it?"

Geloë's smile was sardonic. "A woman with a baby inside her is not like someone who is dying of old age, Prince Josua. Women are strong—bearing a child is hard work. Besides, this news should not frighten anyone . . . even you." She softened her expression to let him know she was joking.

Josua nodded. "I deserved that, I suppose." His own answering smile was wan. "What strange thing has happened? Please, come in."

Geloë shrugged off her dripping cloak and dropped it just inside the doorway. A light rain had begun to fall soon after dawn, and had been pattering on the tent roof for the better part of an hour. Geloë ran her hand through her wet, cropped hair, then seated herself on one of the stools Freosel had built for the prince's residence. "I have just received a message."

"From whom?"

"I do not know. It came to me with one of Dinivan's birds, but the writing is not his hand." She reached into her jacket and pulled forth a bundle of damp feathers, which softly cheeped; its black eye gleamed through the gap between her fingers. "Here is what it bore." She held up a small curl of oilcloth. With some difficulty, she managed to pull a twist of parchment from the cloth and open it without unduly discommoding the bird.

"Prince Josua."

she read,

"Certain signs tell me that it may be propitious for you to begin thinking about Nabban. Certain mouths have whispered in my ear that you might find more

support there than you suspect. The kingfishers have been taking too much of the boatmen's catch. A messenger will arrive within a fortnight, bearing words that will speak more clearly than this brief message can. Do nothing until that one has arrived, for your own fortune's sake."

Geloë looked up as she finished reading, her yellow eyes wary. "It is signed only with the ancient Nabbanai rune for 'Friend.' Someone who is either a Scrollbearer or of equivalent learning wrote this. Perhaps someone who would wish us to *believe* that a Scrollbearer wrote it."

Josua gave Vorzheva's hand a gentle squeeze before he stood up. "May I see it?" Geloë gave him the note, which he scrutinized for a moment before handing it back. "I do not recognize the hand, either." He took a few steps toward the tent's far wall, then turned and paced back toward the door. "The writer is obviously suggesting that there is unrest in Nabban, that the Benidrivine House is not as loved as it once was—not surprising with Benigaris in the saddle and Nessalanta pulling the reins. But what could this person want of me? You say it came to you with Dinivan's bird?"

"Yes. And that is what most worries me." Geloë was about to say more when there was an apologetic cough from the doorway. Father Strangyeard stood there, the wisp of red hair atop his head plastered to his skull by rainwater.

"Your pardon, Prince Josua." He saw Vorzheva and colored. "Lady Vorzheva. Goodness. I hope you can forgive my . . . my intrusion."

"Come in, Strangyeard." The prince beckoned as though to summon a skittish cat. Behind him, Vorzheva smiled to show she did not mind.

"I asked him to come, Josua," said Geloë. "Since it was Dinivan's bird—well, you can understand, I think."

"Of course." He waved the archivist to one of the vacant stools. "Now, tell me about the birds. I remember what you told me about Dinivan himself—although I can still scarcely credit that the lector's secretary would be part of such a company."

Geloë looked a little impatient. "The League of the Scroll is a thing that many would be proud to be part of, and Dinivan's master would never have been troubled by anything that he did on its behalf." Her eyelids lowered as some new thought came to her. "But the lector is dead, if the rumors that have come to us here are true. Some say that worshipers of the Storm King murdered him."

"I have heard of these Fire Dancers, yes," Josua said. "Those of New Gadrinsett who fled here from the south can talk of little else."

"But the troubling thing is that since this rumored event, I have heard nothing from Dinivan," Geloë continued. "So who would have his birds, if not him? And if he survived the attack on the lector—I am told there was a great fire in the Sancellan Aedonitis—then why would he not write himself?"

"Perhaps he was burned or injured," Strangyeard said diffidently. "He might have had someone else write on his behalf."

"True," Geloë mused, "but then I think he would have used his name, unless he is somehow so frightened of discovery that he cannot even send a message by bird that bears his rune."

"So if it is not Dinivan," said Josua, "then we must accept that this could be a trick. The very ones who were responsible for the lector's death may have sent this."

Vorzheva raised herself a little higher in the bed. "It could be *not* either of those things. Someone who found Dinivan's birds could send it for their own reasons."

Geloë nodded slowly. "True. But it would have to be someone who knew who Dinivan's friends were, and where they might be: this message has your husband's name at the top of it, as though whoever sent it knew it would come straight to him."

Josua was pacing again. "I have thought about Nabban," he muttered. "So many times. The north is a wasteland—I doubt Isorn and the others will find more than a token force at best. The people have been scattered by war and weather. But if we could somehow drive Benigaris out of Nabban . . ." He stopped and stared up at the tent ceiling, frowning. "We could raise an army, then, and ships. . . . We would have a real chance to thwart my brother." His frown deepened. "But who can know whether this is real or not? I do not like to have someone pull at my strings like this." He slapped his hand against his leg. "Aedon! Why can nothing be simple?"

Geloë shifted on her stool. The wise woman's voice was surprisingly sympathetic. "Because nothing *is* simple, Prince Josua."

"Whatever it is," Vorzheva pointed out, "whether it is a true thing or a lie, it says that a messenger will be sent. Then we will learn more."

"Perhaps," Josua said. "If it is not just a ploy to keep us hesitant, to make us delay."

"But that does not seem likely, if you will pardon my saying so," Strangyeard piped up. "Which of our enemies is so powerless that they would stoop that low . . . ?" He trailed off, looking at Josua's hard, distracted face. "I mean . . ."

"I think that makes sense, Strangyeard," Geloë agreed. "It is a weak play, and I think Elias and his . . . ally . . . are beyond such things."

"Then you should not hurry to have your Raed, Josua." There was something like triumph in Vorzheva's voice. "It would not make sense to have plans until you know if this is true or not. You must wait for this messenger. At least a little while."

The prince turned to her; a look passed between them, and although the others did not know what the silence between husband and wife meant, they waited. At last Josua nodded stiffly.

"I suppose that is true," he said. "The note says a fortnight. I will wait that long before calling the Raed."

Vorzheva smiled in satisfaction.

"I agree, Prince Josua," said Geloë. "But there is still much that we do not . . ."

She stopped as Simon appeared in the doorway. When he did not immediately enter, Josua beckoned to him impatiently. "Come in, Simon, come in. We are discussing a strange message, and what may be an even stranger messenger."

Simon started. "Messenger?"

"A letter was sent to us, perhaps from Nabban. Come in. Do you need something?"

The tall youth swallowed. "Perhaps now is not the best time."

"I can assure you," Josua said dryly, "there is nothing that you could ask me that would not seem simple when set beside the quandaries I have already discovered today."

Simon still seemed hesitant. "Well . . ." he said, then stepped inside. Someone followed him in.

"Blessed Elysia, Mother of our Ransomer," Strangyeard said in a curiously choked voice.

"No. My mother named me Aditu," replied Simon's companion. For all her fluency, her Westerling was strangely accented; it was hard to tell whether she meant mockery or not.

She was slender as a lance, with hungry golden eyes and a great spilling froth of snowy white hair tied with a gray band. Her clothes were white, too, so that she seemed almost to glow in the shadowed tent, as though a little piece of the winter sun had rolled through the doorway.

"Aditu is my friend Jiriki's sister. She's a Sitha," Simon added unnecessarily.

"By the Tree," Josua said. "By the Holy Tree."

Aditu laughed, a fluid, musical noise. "Are these things you all say magical charms to chase me away? If so, they do not seem to be working."

The witch woman stood. Her weathered face worked through an unreadable mixture of emotions. "Welcome, Dawn Child," she said slowly. "I am Geloë."

Aditu smiled, but gently. "I know who you are. First Grandmother spoke of you."

Geloë lifted her hand as if to touch this apparition. "Amerasu was dear to me, although I never met her face-to-face. When Simon told me what had happened . . ." Astonishingly, tears formed and trembled on her lashes. "She will be missed, your First Grandmother."

Aditu inclined her head for a moment. "She *is* missed. All the world mourns her."

Josua stepped forward. "Forgive me my discourtesy, Aditu," he said, pronouncing the name carefully. "I am Josua. Besides Valada Geloë, these others are my wife, the lady Vorzheva, and Father Strangyeard." He ran his hand across his eyes. "Can we offer you something to eat or drink?"

Aditu bowed. "Thank you, but I drank from your spring just before dawn, and I am not hungry. I have a message from my mother, Likimeya, Lady of the House of Year-Dancing, which you may be interested to hear."

"Of course." Josua could not seem to help staring at her. Behind him, Vorzheva was also staring at the newcomer, although her expression was different than the prince's. "Of course," he repeated. "Sit down, please."

The Sitha sank to the floor in a single movement, light as thistledown. "Are you certain this is a good time, Prince Josua?" Her tuneful voice contained a hint of amusement. "You do not look well."

"It has been a strange morning," the prince replied.

"So they have already ridden to Hernystir?" Josua spoke carefully. "This is unexpected news indeed."

"You do not seem pleased," Aditu commented.

"We had hoped for Sithi aid—although we certainly did not expect it, or even think that it was deserved." He grimaced. "I know you have no cause to love my father, and so no reason to love me or my people. But I am glad to hear that the Hernystiri will hear the Sithi's horns. I have wished I could do more for Lluth's folk."

Aditu stretched her arms high over her head, a gesture that seemed oddly childlike, out of place with the gravity of the discussion. "As have we. But we have long exiled ourselves from the doings of all mortals, even the Hernystiri. We might have remained that way, even at the expense of honor," she said with casual frankness, "but events forced us to admit that Hernystir's war was ours, too." She turned her luminous eyes on the prince. "As is yours, of course. And that is why, when Hernystir is free, the Zida'ya will ride to Naglimund."

"As you said." Josua looked around the circle, as though to confirm that the others had heard the same thing as he. "But you did not say why."

"Many reasons. Because it is too close to our forest, and our lands. Because the Hikeda'ya must not have any foothold south of Nakkiga. And other worries I am not at leave to explain."

"But if the rumors are true," Josua said, "the Norns are already at the Hayholt."

Aditu cocked her head on one side. "A few are there, no doubt to reinforce your brother's bargain with Ineluki. But, Prince Josua, you should understand that there is a difference between the Norns and their undead master, just as there is a difference between your castle and your brother's. Ineluki and his Red Hand *cannot* come to Asu'a—what you call the Hayholt. So it falls to the Zida'ya to make sure that they cannot make a home for themselves in Naglimund either, or anywhere else south of the Frostmarch."

"Why can't the . . . why can't he come to the Hayholt?" Simon asked.

"It is an irony, but you can thank the usurper Fingil and the other mortal kings who have held Asu'a for that," Aditu said. "When they saw what Ineluki had done in his final moments of life, they were terrified. They had not dreamed that anyone, even the Sithi, could wield such power. So prayers and spells—if there is a difference between the two—were said over each handspan of what remained of our home before the mortals made it their own. As it was rebuilt, the same was done over and over again, until Asu'a was so wrapped in protections that Ineluki can never come there until Time itself ends, when it will not matter." Her face tightened. "But he is still unimaginably strong. He can send his living minions, and they will help him rule over your brother and, through him, mankind."

"So you think that is what Ineluki plans?" Geloë asked. "Is that what Amerasu thought?"

"We will never know for certain. As Simon has no doubt told you, she died before she could share with us the fruits of her pondering. One of the Red Hand was sent into Jao é-Tinukai'i to help silence her—a feat that must have exhausted even Utuk'ku and the Unliving One below Nakkiga, so it says much of how greatly they feared First Grandmother's wisdom." She briefly crossed her hands over her breast, then touched a finger to each eye. "So the Houses of Exile came together in Jao é-Tinukai'i to consider what had happened and to make plans for war. That Ineluki plans to use your brother to rule mankind seemed to all the gathered Zida'ya the most likely possibility." Aditu leaned down to the brazier and picked up a piece of wood that smoldered at one end. She held it before her, so that its glow crimsoned her face. "Ineluki is, in a way, alive, but he can never truly exist in this world again—and in the place he covets most, he has no direct power." She looked around the gathering, sharing her golden stare with each in turn. "But he will do what he can to bring the upstart mortals under his fist. And if he can also humble his family and tribe while he does so, then I do not doubt he will." Aditu made a noise that sounded a little like a sigh and dropped the wood back into the embers. "Perhaps it is fortunate that most heroes who die for their people cannot come back to see what the people *do* with that hard-bought life and freedom."

There was a pause. Josua at last broke the silence.

"Has Simon told you that we buried our fallen here on Sesuad'ra?"

Aditu nodded. "We are not strangers to death, Prince Josua. We are immortal, but only in the sense that we do not die except by our own choice—or the choice of others. Perhaps we are all the more enmeshed with dying because of it. Just because our lives are long when held against yours does not mean we are any more eager to give them up." She allowed a slow, coolly measured smile to narrow her lips. "So we know death well. Your people fought bravely to defend themselves. There is no shame to us in sharing this place with those who died."

"Then I would like to show you something else." Josua stood and extended his hand toward the Sitha. Vorzheva, watching closely, did not look pleased. Aditu rose and followed the prince toward the door.

"We have buried my friend—my dearest friend—in the garden behind Leavetaking House," he said. "Simon, perhaps you will accompany us? And Geloë and Strangyeard, too, if you would like," he added hurriedly.

"I will stay and talk with Vorzheva for a while," the wise woman said. "Aditu, I look forward to a chance to speak with you later."

"Certainly."

"I think I will come, too," Strangyeard said, almost apologetically. "It's very pretty there."

"*Sesu-d'asú* is a sad place now," said Aditu. "It was beautiful once."

They stood before the broad expanse of Leavetaking House; its weatherworn stones glinted dully in the sunlight.

"I think it is still beautiful," Strangyeard said shyly.

"So do I," Simon echoed. "Like an old woman who used to be a lovely young girl, but you can still see it in her face."

Aditu grinned. "My Seoman," she said, "the time you spent with us has made you part Zida'ya. Soon you will be composing poems and whispering them to the passing wind."

They walked through the hall and into the ruined garden, where a cairn of stones had been built over Deornoth's grave. Aditu stood silently for a moment, then laid her hand atop the uppermost stone. "It is a good, quiet place." For a moment, her gaze grew distant, as though she beheld some other place or time. "Of all the songs we Zida'ya sing," she murmured, "the closest to our hearts are those which tell of things lost."

"Perhaps that is because none of us can know something's true value until it is gone," said Josua. He bowed his head. The grass between the broken paving stones rippled in the breeze.

Strangely, of all the mortals living on Sesuad'ra, it was Vorzheva who most quickly befriended Aditu—if a mortal could truly become a friend to one of the immortals. Even Simon, who had lived among them and had rescued one of them, was not at all certain that he could count any of them as friends.

But despite her initial coolness toward the Sitha-woman, Vorzheva seemed to be drawn by something in Aditu's alien nature, perhaps the mere fact that Aditu *was* alien, the only one of her kind in that place, as Vorzheva herself had been for all the years in Naglimund. Whatever Aditu's attraction, Josua's wife made her welcome and even sought her out. The Sitha also seemed to enjoy Vorzheva's company: when she was not with Simon or Geloë, she could often be found walking with the Thrithings-woman among the tents, or sitting by her bedside on days when Vorzheva felt ill or tired. Duchess Gutrun, Vorzheva's usual companion, did her best to show good manners to the strange visitor, but something in her Aedonite heart would not let her be fully comfortable. While Vorzheva and Aditu talked and laughed, Gutrun watched Aditu as though the Sitha were a sort of dangerous animal that she had been assured was now tame.

For her part, Aditu seemed oddly fascinated by the child Vorzheva carried. Few children were born to the Zida'ya, especially in these days, she explained.

The last had come over a century before, and he was now as much of an adult as the eldest of the Dawn Children. Aditu also seemed interested in Leleth, although the little girl was no more expressive with her than with anyone else. Still, she would allow Aditu to take her for walks, and even to carry her occasionally, something that almost no one else was permitted to do.

If Aditu was interested in some of the mortals, the ordinary citizens of New Gadrinsett were in turn both fascinated and terrified by her. Ulca's tale—the truth of which was strange enough—had grown in the telling and retelling until Aditu's arrival had come in a flash of light and puff of smoke; the Sitha, the story continued, enraged by the mortal girl's flirtation with her intended, had threatened to turn Ulca into stone. Ulca quickly became the heroine of every young woman on Sesuad'ra, and Aditu, despite the fact that she was seldom seen by most of the hill-dwellers, became the subject of endless gossip and superstitious mumbling.

To his chagrin, Simon also continued to be a subject of rumor and speculation in the small community. Jeremias, who frequently loitered in the marketplace beside Leavetaking House, would gleefully report the latest strange tale—the dragon from whom Simon had stolen the sword would come back someday and Simon would have to fight it; Simon was part Sitha and Aditu had been sent to bring him back to the halls of the Fair Folk; and so on. Simon, hearing the fantasies that seemed to be woven from empty air, could only cringe. There was nothing he could do—every attempt he made to quell the stories merely convinced the folk of New Gadrinsett that he was either manfully modest or slyly deceptive. Sometimes he found the fabrications amusing, but he still could not help feeling more closely observed than was comfortable, leading him to spend his time only with people he knew and trusted. His evasiveness, of course, only fueled more speculation.

If this was fame, Simon decided, he would have preferred to stay a lowly and unknown scullion. Sometimes when he walked through New Gadrinsett these days, when people waved to him or whispered to each other as he passed, he felt quite naked, but there was nothing to do but walk by with a smile on his face and his shoulders back. Scullions could hide or run away; knights could not.

"He is outside, Josua. He swears you are expecting him."

"Ah." The prince turned to Simon. "This must be the mysterious messenger I spoke of—the one with news of Nabban. And it *has* been a fortnight—almost to the day. Stay and see." To Sludig he said: "Bring him in, please."

The Rimmersman stepped out, then returned a moment later leading a tall, lantern-jawed fellow, pale-complected and—Simon thought—a little sullen-looking. The Rimmersman stepped back beside the wall of the tent and remained there with one hand on the handle of his ax, the other toying with the hairs of his yellow beard.

The messenger dropped slowly to one knee. "Prince Josua, my master sends his greetings and bids me give you this." As he put his hand in his cloak Sludig took a step forward, even though the messenger was several paces away from the prince, but the man withdrew only a roll of parchment, beribboned and sealed in blue wax. Josua stared at it for a moment, then nodded to Simon to fetch it to him.

"The winged dolphin," Josua said as he gazed at the emblem stamped into the melted wax. "So your master is Count Streáwe of Perdruin?"

It was hard not to call the look on the messenger's face a smirk. "He is, Prince Josua."

The prince broke the seal and unrolled the parchment. He scanned it for a few long moments, then curled it up and set it on the arm of his chair. "I will not hurry through this. What is your name, man?"

The messenger nodded his head with immense satisfaction, as though he had been long expecting this crucial question. "It is . . . Lenti."

"Very well, Lenti, Sludig will take you and see that you get food and drink. He will also find you a bed because I will want some time before I send my answer—maybe several days."

The messenger looked around the prince's tent, assessing the possible quality of New Gadrinsett's accommodations. "Yes, Prince Josua."

Sludig came forward and, with a jerk of his head, summoned Lenti to follow him out.

"I didn't think much of the messenger," Simon said when they had gone.

Josua was inspecting the parchment once more. "A fool," he agreed "jumped up beyond his capabilities, even for something as simple as this. But don't confuse Streáwe with his minions—Perdruin's master is clever as a marketplace cutpurse. Still, it doesn't speak well of his ability to deliver on this promise if he can find no more impressive servitor to bear it to me."

"What promise?" Simon asked.

Josua rolled the message and slid it into his sleeve. "Count Streáwe claims he can deliver me Nabban." He stood. "The old man is lying, of course, but it leads to some interesting speculation."

"I don't understand, Josua."

The prince smiled. "Be glad. Your days of innocence about people like Streáwe are fast disappearing." He patted Simon's shoulder. "For now, young knight, I would as soon not talk about it. There will be a time and place for this at the Raed."

"You're ready to have your council?"

Josua nodded. "The time has come. For once, *we* will call the tune—then we will see if we can make my brother and his allies dance to it."

"That is a most interesting deception, clever Seoman." Aditu stared down at the game of shent she had constructed from wood and root-dyes and polished stones. "A false thrust played falsely: a seeming that is revealed as a sham, but underneath is a true thing after all. Very pretty—but what will you do if I place my Bright Stones here . . . here . . . and here?" She suited action to words.

Simon frowned. In the dim light of his tent, her hand moved almost too swiftly to be seen. For an unpleasant moment he wondered if she might be cheating him, but another instant's reflection convinced him that Aditu had no need to cheat someone to whom the subtleties of shent were still largely a mystery, any more than Simon would trip a small child with whom he was running a race. Still, it raised an interesting question.

"Can you cheat at this game?"

Aditu looked up from arranging her pieces. She was wearing one of Vorzheva's loose dresses; the combination of her unusually modest attire and her unbound hair made her look a little less dangerously wild—in fact, it made her seem disconcertingly human. Her eyes gleamed in the light of the brazier. "Cheat? Do you mean lie? A game can be as deceptive as the players wish it to be."

"That's not what I mean. Can you do something on purpose that is against the rules?" She was eerily beautiful. He stared at her, remembering the night she had kissed him. What had that meant? Anything? Or was it just another way for Aditu to toy with her one-time lap-dog?

She considered his question. "I am not sure how to answer. Could you cheat against the way you are made and fly by flapping your arms?"

Simon shook his head. "A game that has so many rules must have some way to break them. . . ."

Before Aditu could try again to answer, Jeremias burst into the tent, out of breath and agitated. "Simon!" he shouted, then drew up short, seeing that Aditu was there. "I'm sorry." Despite his embarrassment, he was having trouble containing his excitement.

"What is it?"

"People have come!"

"Who? What people?" Simon looked briefly to Aditu, but she had returned to her study of the arrangement before her.

"Duke Isgrimnur and the princess!" Jeremias waved his arms up and down. "And there are others with them, too! A strange little man, sort of like Binabik and his trolls, but almost our size. And an old man—he's taller than you, even. Simon, the whole town has gone down to see them!"

He sat for a moment in silence, his mind whirling. "The princess?" he said at last. "Princess . . . Miriamele?"

"Yes, yes," Jeremias panted. "Dressed as a monk, but she took off her hood and waved to people. Come on, Simon, everyone is going down to meet them." He turned and took a few steps toward the doorway, then pivoted to look at his friend in astonishment. "Simon? What's wrong? Don't you want to go see the princess and Duke Isgrimnur and the brown man?"

"The princess." He turned helplessly to Aditu, who gazed back at him with feline disinterest.

"It sounds like something you will enjoy, Seoman. We will play our game later."

Simon stood and followed Jeremias out of the tent and into the hilltop wind, moving as slowly and unsteadily as a sleepwalker. As if he passed through a dream, he heard people shouting all around, a rising murmur of sound that filled his ears like the roar of the ocean.

Miriamele had come back.

21

Answered Prayers

✧

It had grown steadily colder as Miriamele and her companions made their way across the wide grasslands. By the time they reached the seemingly endless plain of the Meadow Thrithing, there was snow on the ground, and even in full afternoon the sky remained a dull pewter stained with streaks of black cloud. Huddled in her traveling cloak against the predatory wind, Miriamele found herself almost grateful that Aspitis Preves had found them; it would have been a long and miserable journey indeed if they had been forced to make it on foot. Cold and uncomfortable as she was, however, Miriamele was also experiencing a curious sense of freedom. The earl had haunted her, but now, although he lived, and might still conceivably seek some kind of vengeance, she no longer feared him or anything he might do. But Cadrach's flight was another thing altogether.

Since their escape together from the *Eadne Cloud,* she had begun to see the Hernystirman in a different way. He had betrayed her several times, certainly, but in his odd way he had seemed to care for her as well. The monk's own self-hatred had continued to loom between them—and had apparently driven him away at last—but her own feelings had changed.

She deeply regretted the argument over Tiamak's parchment. Miriamele had thought she might slowly continue to draw him out, might somehow reach through to the man beneath—a man she liked. But, as though she had tried to tame a wild dog and had moved too quickly to pet it, Cadrach had startled and bolted. Miriamele could not rid herself of the obscure feeling that she had missed an opportunity that was more important than she could understand.

Even on horseback, it was a long journey. Her thoughts were not always good company.

✧

They rode a full week to reach the Meadow Thrithing, traveling from first light until after the sun had vanished . . . on those days that they saw the sun at all. The weather grew steadily colder, but remained something just short of unlivable: by mid-afternoon of most days the sun struggled through like a tired but determined messenger and chased away the chill.

The meadowlands were wide and, for the most part, flat and featureless as a carpet. What slope there was to the land was almost more depressing: after a long day's ride up a gradual incline, Miriamele found it hard to rid herself of the idea that they would eventually reach a summit and that it would be *somewhere.* Instead, at some point they would cross a flat table of meadow no more interesting than the upward slope, then gradually find themselves moving down an equally uninspiring decline. Even the *idea* of having to make such a monotonous journey on foot was disheartening. Acre after empty acre, mile after trying mile, Miriamele whispered quiet prayers of gratitude for Aspitis' unwitting gift of horses.

Riding on the saddle before her, Tiamak quickly recovered his strength. After some encouragement, the Wrannaman told her—and Isgrimnur, who was happy to have someone else share the burden of storytelling—more about his childhood in the marshes and his difficult year as an aspiring scholar in Perdruin. Although his natural reticence prevented him from dwelling on his ill-treatment, Miriamele thought she could feel every slight, every little cruelty that wound through his tale.

I'm not the first person to feel lonely, to feel misunderstood and unwanted. This seemingly obvious fact now struck her with the force of revelation. *And I'm a princess, a privileged person—I've never been hungry, never been afraid that I would die unremembered, never been told that I wasn't good enough to do something that I wished to do.*

Listening to Tiamak, watching his wiry but somehow fragile form, his precise, scholarly gestures, Miriamele was dismayed by her own willful ignorance. How could she, with all her native good fortune, be so consumed with the few inconveniences that God or fate had put in her way? It was shameful.

She tried to tell Duke Isgrimnur something of her thoughts, but he would not let her slide too far into self-loathing.

"Each one of has our own sorrows, Princess," he said. "It's no shame to take them to heart. The only sin is to forget that other folk have theirs, too—or to let pity for yourself slow your hand when someone needs help."

Isgrimnur, Miriamele was reminded, was more than just a gruff old soldier.

On their third night in the Meadow Thrithing, as the four sat close to their campfire—very close, since wood was scarce on the grasslands and the fire was a small one—Miriamele finally worked up the courage to ask Tiamak about his sack and its contents.

The Wrannaman was so embarrassed he could scarcely meet her eye. "It is terrible, Lady. I remember only a little, but in my fever I was certain that Cadrach meant to steal it from me."

"Why would you think that? And what *is* it, anyway?"

After a moment's consideration, Tiamak reached into his bag, drew out the leafy bundle, and peeled away the wrappings. "It was when you spoke of the monk and Nisses' book," he explained shyly. "I can believe now that it was innocent, since Morgenes also said something about Nisses in his message to me—but in the depth of my illness, I could only think that it meant my treasure was in danger."

He handed her the parchment. As she unrolled it, Isgrimnur moved around the fire to look over her shoulder. Camaris, seemingly oblivious as always, stared out into the empty night.

"It's some kind of song," Isgrimnur said crossly, as though he had been expecting more.

". . . *'The manne who though blinded canne see'* . . ." Miriamele read. "What is it?"

"I am not sure myself," Tiamak replied. "But look, it is signed 'Nisses.' I think it is part of his lost book, *Du Svardenvyrd.*"

Miriamele took a sudden breath. "Oh. But that's the book Cadrach had—the one he sold off page by page." She felt something squeeze in the pit of her stomach. "The book that Pryrates wanted. Where did you get this?"

"I bought it in Kwanitupul almost a year ago. It was part of a pile of scraps. The merchant could not have known it was worth anything, or else he never inspected what he had probably bought as scrap himself."

"I don't think Cadrach actually knew what you had," said Miriamele. "But, Elysia, Mother of Mercy, how strange! Perhaps this is one of the pages that he sold!"

"He sold pages of Nisses' book?" Tiamak asked. Outrage mingled with wonder. "How could that be?"

"Cadrach told me he was poor and desperate." She weighed the idea of telling them the rest of the monk's story, then decided she should consider the matter more carefully. They might not understand his actions. Even though he had fled, she felt the urge to protect Cadrach from those who did not know him as she did. "He had a different name then," she offered, as though somehow it might absolve him. "He was called Padreic."

"Padreic!" Now Tiamak was nothing short of astounded. "But I know that name! Can he be the same man? Doctor Morgenes knew him well!"

"Yes, he knew Morgenes. He has a strange history."

Isgrimnur snorted, but now he, too, sounded a little defensive. "A strange history indeed, it seems."

Miriamele hurried to change the subject. "Perhaps Josua will understand this."

The duke shook his head. "I think Prince Josua, if we find him, will have other things to do than look at old parchments."

"But it may be important." Tiamak looked sideways at Isgrimnur. "As I said, Doctor Morgenes wrote in a letter to me that he thought these were the times that Nisses warned about. Morgenes was a man who knew many things hidden from the rest of us."

Isgrimnur grunted and moved back to his own place in the fire-circle. "It's beyond me. Well beyond me."

Miriamele was watching Camaris, who was surveying the darkness as calmly and possessively as an owl poised to glide from a tree branch. "There are so many mysteries these days," she said. "Won't it be nice when things are simple again?"

There was a pause, then Isgrimnur laughed self-consciously. "I'd forgotten the monk was gone. I was waiting for him to say, 'Things will never be simple again,' or something like it."

Miriamele smiled despite herself. "Yes, that's just what he would have said." She held her hands closer to the fire's reassuring warmth and let out a sigh. "Just what he would have said."

Days passed as they rode north. Snow thickened on the ground; the wind became an enemy. As the last leagues of the Meadow Thrithing disappeared behind them, Miriamele and the rest grew more and more downhearted.

"It's hard to imagine Josua and the rest are having any luck in this weather." Isgrimnur was almost shouting to be heard above the wind. "Things are worse now than when I came south."

"If they are alive, that will be enough," Miriamele said. "That will be a start."

"But, Princess, we don't really know where to look for them." The duke was almost apologetic. "None of the rumors I heard said much more than that Josua was somewhere in the High Thrithing. There's more than a hundred leagues of grassland up ahead, no more settled or civilized than this." He waved his broad arm at the bleak, snowy expanses on either side. "We could hunt for months."

"We will find him," Miriamele said, and in her own heart she felt almost as certain as she sounded. Surely the things she had been through, the things she had learned, must be for *something*. "There are people who live on the Thrithings," she added. "If Josua and the others have made themselves a settlement, the Thrithings-folk will know."

Isgrimnur snorted. "The Thrithings-folk! Miriamele, I know them better than you may think. These are not town-dwellers. For one thing, they do not stay in one place, so we may not even find them. And we might be just as glad if we don't. They are barbarians, just as likely to knock our heads off as offer us news of Josua."

"I know you fought against the Thrithings-men," Miriamele replied. "But that was long ago." She shook her head. "And we have no choice that I can see, in any case. We will solve that when we come to it."

The duke stared at her with a mixture of frustration and amusement on his face, then shrugged. "You are your father's daughter."

Strangely, Miriamele was not displeased by this remark, but she frowned anyway—as much to keep the duke in his place as anything. A moment later she laughed.

"What's funny?" Isgrimnur asked suspiciously.

"Nothing, in truth. I was just thinking of all the times when I was with

Binabik and Simon. Several times I had decided that within a few moments I would be dead—once when some terrible dogs almost got us, another time a giant, and men shooting arrows at us . . ." She shook her hair from her eyes, but the maddening wind immediately flung it back. She tucked the offending strands back into her hood. "But now I don't think that any more, no matter how dreadful things are. When Aspitis captured us, I never believed that he would truly manage to take me away. And if he had, I would have escaped."

She slowed her horse for a moment, trying to put her thought into words. "You see, in truth it's not funny at all. But it seems to me now that there are things happening that are beyond our strength. Like waves on the ocean, huge waves. I can fight them—and drown—or I can let them carry me, and swim just enough to keep my head above the water. I *know* I'm going to see Uncle Josua again. I just know. And Simon and Binabik and Vorzheva—there's more to be done, that's all."

Isgrimnur looked at her warily, as though the little girl he had once knee-dandled had become a Nabbanai star-reader. "And then? When we're all together again?"

Miriamele smiled at him, but it was only the bittersweet tip of a great sorrow that washed through her. "The wave will crash, dear old Uncle Isgrimnur . . . and some of us will go down and never come up. I don't know how it will be, of course not. But I'm not as frightened as I used to be."

They were silent then, three horses and four riders fighting their way into the wind.

Only the amount of time they had been riding told them when they had crossed over into the High Thrithing: the snow-mantled meadows and hills were no more memorable than anything they had crossed in the first week of their journey. Strangely, though, the weather did not worsen as they continued to move northward. Miriamele even began to believe that it was growing a bit warmer, the wind a little less biting.

"A hopeful sign," she said one afternoon when the sun actually appeared. "I told you, Isgrimnur. We'll get there."

"Wherever 'there' is, exactly," the duke grumbled.

Tiamak stirred in the saddle. "Perhaps we should make our way to the river. If there are people still living in this place, they are most likely to be near moving water, where there might still be fish to catch." He shook his head sadly. "I wish that what I remembered from my dream was more precise."

Isgrimnur pondered. "The Ymstrecca is just south of the great forest. But it runs most of the length of the Thrithings—a long way to go a-searching."

"Is there not another river that crosses it?" Tiamak asked. "It has been long since I looked at a map."

"There is. The Stefflod, if I remember rightly." The duke frowned. "But it is little more than a large stream."

"Still, in the places where rivers meet you often find villages," Tiamak said with surprising assuredness. "So it is in the Wran, and in all the other places that I have heard of."

Miriamele started to say something, but stopped, watching Camaris. The old man had ridden a little way off to the side and was watching the sky. She followed his stare but saw only dingy clouds.

Isgrimnur was considering the Wrannaman's idea. "P'raps you're right, Tiamak. If we continue north, we can't help but strike the Ymstrecca. But I think the Stefflod must be a little to the east." He looked around as though seeking some landmark; his eyes stopped on Camaris. "What's he looking at?"

"I don't know," Miriamele replied. "Oh. It must be those birds!"

A pair of dark shapes were swooping toward them out of the east, whirling like cinders caught in the draught of a fire.

"Ravens!" said Isgrimnur. "Gore crows!"

The birds wheeled in a circle above the travelers as if they had found what they had been seeking. Miriamele thought she could see their yellow eyes glint. The sensation of being watched, marked, was very strong. After a few more turns, the ravens dove, their feathers shining oily-black as they approached. Miriamele ducked her head and covered her eyes. The ravens flew past, shrieking; a moment later they banked upward and hurtled away. In moments, the birds were two dwindling specks vanishing into the northern sky.

Only Camaris had not lowered his head. He watched their retreating forms with an absorbed, contemplative look.

"What are they?" Tiamak asked. "Are they dangerous?"

"Birds of ill omen," the duke growled. "In my country, we chase them with arrows. Carrion eaters." He made a face.

"I think they were looking at us," Miriamele said. "I think they wanted to know who we were."

"That's no way to talk." Isgrimnur reached over and squeezed her arm. "And what would birds care who we were, anyway?"

Miriamele shook her head. "I don't know. But that's the feeling I have: someone wanted to know who we were—and now they do."

"They were just ravens." The duke's smile was grim. "We have other things to worry about."

"That's true," she said.

A few more days' riding brought them at last to the Ymstrecca. The swiftly flowing river was almost black beneath the faint sun. Patchy snow cloaked its banks.

"The weather *is* getting warmer," Isgrimnur said, pleased. "This is scarcely colder than it should be at this time of the year. It is Novander, after all."

"Is it?" Miriamele was unsettled. "And we left Josua's keep in Yuven. Half a year. Elysia's mercy, we have been traveling a long time."

They turned and followed the river eastward, stopping at dark to make camp with the sound of the water loud in their ears. They started early the next morning beneath a gray sky.

In late afternoon they reached the edge of a shallow valley of wet grass. Before them, like the leavings from some ruinous flood, lay the weather-battered remains of a vast settlement. Hundreds of makeshift houses had stood here, and most of them seemed to have been recently inhabited, but something had drawn or driven out the residents; but for a few lonely birds poking among the abandoned dwellings, the ramshackle city seemed deserted.

Miriamele's heart sank. "Was this Josua's camp? Where have they gone?"

"It is on a great hill, Lady," Tiamak said. "At least, that was what I saw in my dream."

Isgrimnur spurred his horse down toward the empty settlement.

On inspection, much of the impression of disaster was revealed to be the nature of the settlement itself, since most of the building materials were scraps and deadwood. There did not seem to be a nail in the whole of the city; the crudely woven ropes that had held together most of the better-constructed buildings appeared to have frayed and given way in the clutch of storms that had lately battered the Thrithings—but even at the best of times, Miriamele decided, none of the dwellings could have been much more than hovels.

There was also some sign of orderly retreat. Most of the people who had lived here seemed to have had time to take their possessions with them—although, judging by the quality of the shelters, they could not have had much to start. Still, there was little left of the everyday necessities: Miriamele found a few broken pots and some rags of clothing so miserably tattered and mud-soaked that even in a cold winter they had probably not been missed.

"They left," she told Isgrimnur, "but it looks as though they chose to."

"Or were forced to," the duke pointed out. "They could have been marched out in a careful manner, if you see what I mean."

Camaris had climbed down from his horse and was rooting in a pile of sod and broken branches that had once been someone's home. He stood up with something shiny in his hand.

"What is that?" Miriamele rode over. She held out her hand, but Camaris was staring at the piece of metal. At last she reached out and gently pried it from the old knight's long, callused fingers.

Tiamak slid forward onto the horse's shoulders and turned to examine the object. "It looks like a clasp to hold a cloak," he offered.

"It is, I think." The silvery object, bent and muddy, had a rim of molded holly leaves. At the center was a pair of crossed spears and an angry reptilian face. Miriamele felt a wisp of fear rise inside her once more. "Isgrimnur, look at this."

The duke brought his mount alongside hers and took the brooch. "It's the badge of the king's Erkynguard."

"My father's soldiers," Miriamele murmured. She could not restrain the urge to look around, as though a company of knights could have been lying in wait unobserved somewhere nearby on the empty grass slope. "They have been here."

"They could have been here after the people left," Isgrimnur said. "Or there could be some other reason we can't guess." He did not sound very convinced himself. "After all, Princess, we don't even know who was living here."

"*I* know." She was angry just imagining it. "They were people who had fled my father's reign. Josua and the others were probably with them. Now they have been driven away or captured."

"Pardon, Lady Miriamele," Tiamak said cautiously, "but I think it would not be good to make our minds up so quickly. Duke Isgrimnur is right: there is much we do not know. This is not the place I saw in the dream Geloë sent me."

"So, then, what should we do?"

"Continue," said the Wrannaman. "Follow the tracks. Perhaps those who lived here have gone to join Josua."

"That looks promising over there." The duke was shading his eyes against the gray sun. He pointed toward the edge of the settlement, where a series of wide ruts wound out from the trampled acres of mud toward the north.

"Then let us follow." Miriamele handed the brooch back to Camaris. The old knight looked at it for a moment, then let it drop to the ground.

The ruts ran close enough together to make a large muddy scar through the grasslands. On either side of this makeshift road lay the marks of the people who had used it—broken wagon spokes, sodden fire ashes, numerous holes dug and filled in. Despite the look of it, the ugly scatter across an otherwise pristine land, Miriamele was heartened by how new the signs seemed: it could not have been more than a month or two at most since the road had been traveled.

Over a supper culled from their dwindling Village Grove stores, Miriamele asked Isgrimnur what he would do when they reached Josua at last. It was nice to talk about that day as something that *would* happen, not just as something that *might*: it made it seem certain, real and tangible, even though she still felt a wisp of superstitious fear at talking of good things not yet come to pass.

"I'll show him that I kept my word," the duke laughed. "Show you to him. Then I think I will catch up my wife and hug her until she squeaks."

Miriamele smiled, thinking of plump, always-capable Gutrun. "I want to see that." She looked over at Tiamak, who slept, and Camaris, who was polishing Isgrimnur's sword with the fascinated absorption he usually gave only to the movements of birds in the sky. Before the duel with Aspitis, the old knight had not wanted even to touch the blade. She felt a little sad now as she watched him. He handled the duke's sword as though it were an old but not quite trusted friend.

"You really miss her, don't you?" she said, turning back to Isgrimnur. "Your wife."

"Ah, sweet Usires, I do." He stared at the fire as though unwilling to meet her eyes. "I do."

"You love her." Miriamele was pleased and a little surprised: Isgrimnur had spoken with a heat she had not expected. It was strange to think that love could burn so strongly in the breast of someone who seemed as old and familiar as the duke—and that grandmotherly Duchess Gutrun could be the object of such powerful feelings!

"Of course I love her, I suppose," he said, frowning. "But it's more than that, my lady. She's a part of me, my Gutrun—we've grown together through the years, twined 'round each other like two old trees." He laughed and shook his head. "I always knew. From the moment I saw her first, carrying mistletoe from the ship-grave of Sotfengsel . . . Ah, she was so beautiful. She had the brightest eyes I've ever seen! Like something in a story."

Miriamele sighed. "I hope someone feels that way about me someday."

"They will, my girl, they will." Isgrimnur smiled. "And when you are married, if you are lucky enough to marry the right one, you will know just what I mean. He will be a part of you, just like my Gutrun is for me. Forever until we die." He made the Tree on his breast. "None of this southlander nonsense for me—widows and widowers taking another spouse! How could anyone ever match her?" He fell silent as he considered the monumental impertinence of second marriages.

Miriamele, too, reflected in silence. Would it be her lot someday to find such a husband? She thought of Fengbald, to whom her father had once offered her, and shuddered. Horrid, swaggering oaf! That Elias, of all people, should attempt to marry her to someone she did not love, when he himself had been so crippled by the death of Miriamele's mother Hylissa that he had been like a man lost in the dark since the hour of her death. . . .

Unless he was trying to spare me from such awful loneliness, she thought. *Maybe he thought it would be a blessing not to love so, and never to feel such a loss. That was the heartbreaking thing, to see him so lonely for her. . . .*

With the suddenness and enormity of a lightning flash, Miriamele saw the thing that had been teasing her mind since Cadrach had first told her his story. It was all there before her, and it was so clear—so clear! It was as though she had groped in a blackened chamber, but now a door had abruptly opened, spilling light, and she could finally see all the strange shapes she had touched in darkness.

"Oh!" she said, gasping. "Oh! Oh, Father!"

She astonished Isgrimnur by bursting into tears. The duke tried his best to soothe her, but she could not stop crying. Neither would she tell him what had caused it, except to say that Isgrimnur's words had reminded her of her mother's death. It was a cruel half-truth, although she did not intend cruelty: when Miriamele crawled away from the fire, the duke was left perturbed but helpless, blaming himself for her misery.

Still sniffling quietly, Miriamele rolled herself in her blanket to stare at the stars and think. There was suddenly so much to think about. Nothing important had changed, but at the same time, everything was vastly different.

Tears came to her again before she finally fell asleep.

W

A brief flurry of snow came up in the morning, not enough to slow the horses much, but sufficient to make Miriamele shiver most of the day. The Stefflod was sluggish and gray, like a twining stream of fluid lead, and the snow seemed thickest just above it, so that the fields on the river's far side were much murkier than the nearer bank. Miriamele had the illusion that the Stefflod drew snow like the lodestone in Ruben the Bear's smithy drew scraps of iron.

The land sloped upward, so that by late afternoon, when the light had already fled and they rode in cold twilight, they found themselves climbing into a rank of low hills. Trees were nearly as scarce as they had been in the Lake Thrithing, and the wind was sharp and raw on Miriamele's cheeks, but there was a sort of relief in the changing scenery.

They climbed high into the hills that night before making camp. When they arose in the morning, feet and fingers and noses bright pink and smarting, the company lingered over the fire longer than usual. Even Camaris got on his horse with a look of obvious reluctance.

The snow grew less, then vanished by late morning. Toward noon the sun emerged brilliantly from the clouds, sending down great arrow-flights of beams. By the time they had reached what seemed to be the summit of the hills in mid-afternoon, the clouds had returned, this time bearing a chill but delicate rain.

"Princess!" Isgrimnur shouted. "Look here!" He had ridden a short way ahead, looking for any possible hazards in their journey downslope: an easy ascent did not guarantee an equally simple descent, and the duke was taking no chances in unknown country. Half in fear, half in exhilaration, Miriamele rode forward. Tiamak leaned forward in the saddle before her, straining to see. The duke stood in a break in the sparse treeline, waving his hand toward the gap between the trunks. "Look!"

Spread below them was a wide valley, a bowl of green patched with white. Despite the soft rain, a sense of stillness hung over it, the air somehow taut as an indrawn breath. At the center, rising up from what looked like a partially frozen lake, was a great stony hill mantled in snow-flecked greenery. The slanting light played across it so that its western face seemed almost to glow, warmly inviting. From the top, pale smoke rose from a hundred different sources.

"God be praised, what is it?" Isgrimnur said in astonishment.

"I think it is the place from my dream," Tiamak murmured.

Miriamele hugged herself, awash in feeling. The great hill seemed almost too real. "I hope it is a good place. I hope Josua and the others are there."

"*Somebody* is living there," Isgrimnur said. "Look at all the fires!"

"Come!" Miriamele spurred her horse down the trail. "We can be there before nightfall."

"Don't be in such a hurry." Isgrimnur urged his own mount forward. "We don't know for certain that it's anything to do with Josua."

"I would willingly be captured by almost anyone if they'd take me to a fire and a warm bed," Miriamele called back over her shoulder.

Camaris, who had brought up the rear, paused at the gap in the trees to stare down into the valley. His long face did not change expression, but he remained where he was for a long time before following the others.

Although it was still light when they reached the lake shore, the men who came to meet them carried torches—flowers of fire that reflected yellow and scarlet in the black lake water as the boats made their way slowly through floating ice. Isgrimnur held back at first, cautious and protective, but before the first boat touched shore he recognized the yellow-bearded figure in the bow and swung down from his saddle with a shout of delight.

"Sludig! In God's name, in Aedon's name, bless you!"

His liege-man sloshed the last few steps to shore. Before he could bend his knee before the duke, Isgrimnur snatched him up and crushed him to his broad chest. "How fares the prince?" Isgrimnur cried, "and my lady wife? And my son?"

Although Sludig was himself a large man, he had to free himself from the duke's clutches and catch his breath before he could assure Isgrimnur that all were fine, although Isorn had left on a mission for the prince. Duke Isgrimnur did a clumsy, enthusiastic, bearlike dance of glee. "And I've brought the princess back!" the duke said. "And more, and more! But lead on! Ah, this is as fine as Aedonmansa!"

Sludig laughed. "We have been watching you since midday. Josua said: 'Go down and find out who they are.' He will be quite surprised, I think!" He quickly arranged for the horses to be loaded on one of the barges, then helped Miriamele onto the boat.

"Princess." His touch was firm as he helped her to one of the benches. "You are welcome to New Gadrinsett. Your uncle will be happy to see you."

The guardsmen who had accompanied Sludig examined Tiamak and Camaris with great interest as well, but the Rimmersman did not allow them to waste time. Within moments they were heading back across the ice-studded lake.

Waiting on the far side was a cart drawn by two thin and disgruntled oxen. When the passengers were loaded on board, Sludig smacked one of the beasts on the flank and the cart began to roll creakily up the stone-shod road.

"What is this?" Isgrimnur peered over the side of the cart to look at the pale stones.

"It is a Sithi road," Sludig said with more than a touch of pride. "This is a Sithi place, very ancient. They call it 'Sesuad'ra.'"

"I have heard of it," Tiamak whispered to Miriamele. "It is famous in lore—but I had no idea it still existed, or that it was the Stone Geloë showed me!"

Miriamele shook her head. She cared little where they were being taken. With Sludig's appearance, she felt as though a vast load had been taken from her back; only now did she realize how tired she truly was.

She felt herself nodding a little with the movement of the ox cart, and tried to fight back a wave of exhaustion. Children were running down the mountainside to join them. They fell in behind the travelers, shouting and singing.

By the time they reached the top of the hill, a great crowd had gathered. Miriamele found the immense sea of people almost sickening; it had been a long time since the swarming wooden streets of Kwanitupul, and she found herself unable to look at so many hungry, expectant faces. She leaned against Isgrimnur and closed her eyes.

At the top, the faces suddenly became familiar. Sludig helped her down from the cart and into the arms of her uncle Josua, who pulled her to him and hugged her almost as firmly as Isgrimnur had embraced Sludig. After a moment he held her out at arm's length to stare at her. He was thinner than she remembered, and his garments, although colored his habitual gray, were odd and rustic. Her heart opened a little wider, letting in both pain and joy.

"The Ransomer has answered my prayers," he said. There could be no doubt, despite his lined and troubled face, that he was very happy to see her. "Welcome back, Miriamele."

Then there were more faces—Vorzheva, wearing an odd, tentlike robe, and the harper Sangfugol, and even little Binabik who bowed with mocking courtliness before taking her hand in his small, warm fingers. Another who stood silently by seemed oddly familiar. He was bearded, and a streak of white marred his red hair and capped the pale scar on his cheek. He looked at her as though he would memorize her, as though someday he might carve her in stone.

It took a long moment.

"Simon?" she said.

Astonishment turned rapidly to a kind of strange bitterness—she had been cheated of so much! While she had been busy elsewhere, the world had changed. Simon was no longer a mere boy. Her friend had disappeared, and this tall young man had taken his place. Had she been away that long?

The stranger's mouth worked, but it was a moment before she heard him speak. Simon's voice seemed deeper, too, but his words were halting. "I am glad you're safe, Princess. Very glad."

She stared at him, her eyes burning as tears began to come. The world seemed topside-round.

"Please," she said abruptly, turning to Josua. "I think . . . I need to lie down. I need to sleep." She did not see the one-time kitchen boy lower his head as though he had been spurned.

"Of course," said her uncle, full of concern. "Of course. As long as you like. Then, when you arise, we will have a feast of thanksgiving!"

Miriamele nodded, dazed, then let Vorzheva lead her away toward the rippling sea of tents. Behind her, Isgrimnur's arms were still locked about his giggling, weeping wife.

22

Whispers in Stone

The water poured out of the great crevice and splashed across the shelf of flat black basalt before surging over the edge and down into the pit. For all its fury, the waterfall was nearly invisible in the dark cavern, which was lit only by a few small, glowing stones embedded in the walls. The impossibly high-ceilinged chamber was called *Yakh Huyeru,* which meant Hall of Trembling; and although the cavern had been given that name for another reason, the walls did seem to shiver ever so slightly as *Kiga'rasku,* the Tearfall, rolled ceaselessly down into the depths. It made very little noise in its passage, whether because of some trick of the vast chamber's echo or because of the void into which it fell. Some of the mountain's residents whispered that Kiga'rasku had no bottom, that the water fell through the bottom of the earth, pouring endlessly into the black Between.

As she stood at the chasm's edge, Utuk'ku was a minute stitch of silvery white against the tapestry of dark water. Her pale robes fluttered slowly in the wind of the falls. Her masked face was lowered as though she sought Kiga'rasku's depths, but at the moment she was not seeing the mighty rush of water any more than she saw the dim sun that rolled past the mountaintop overhead, on the far side of many hundred furlongs of Stormspike stone.

Utuk'ku considered.

Odd and unsettling shifts had begun to take place in the intricate pattern of events that she had undertaken so long ago, events she had studied and delicately modified over the course of more than a thousand thousand sunless days. One of the first of those shifts had caused a small tear in her design. It was not irreparable, of course—Utuk'ku's weavings were strong, and more than a few strands would have to snap completely before her long-planned triumph would be threatened—but patching it would require care, and work, and the diamond-sharp concentration that only the Eldest could bring to bear.

The silver mask turned slowly, catching the faint light like the moon emerging from behind clouds. A trio of figures had appeared in the doorway of Yakh Huyeru. The nearest kneeled, then placed the heels of her hands over her eyes; her two companions did the same.

As Utuk'ku considered them and the task she would set for them, she felt a moment of regret for the loss of Ingen Jegger—but it was a moment only. Utuk'ku Seyt-Hamakha was the last of the Gardenborn: she had not survived all of her peers by many centuries through wasting time on useless emotions. Jegger had been eager and blindly loyal as a coursing hound, and he had possessed the particular virtues, for Utuk'ku's purposes, of his own mortal nature, but he had still been only a tool—something to be used and then discarded. He had served what had been at the time her greatest need. For other tasks, there would be other servitors.

The Norns bowing before her, two women and a man, looked up as though awakening from a dream. The desires of their mistress had been poured into them like sour milk from a pitcher, and now Utuk'ku raised her gloved hand in a brittle gesture of dismissal. They turned and were gone, smooth, swift, and silent as shadows fleeing the dawn.

After they had vanished, Utuk'ku stood for another long silent time before the falling water, listening to the ghostly echoes. Then, at last, the Norn Queen turned and made her unhurried way toward the Chamber of the Breathing Harp.

As she took her seat beside the Well, the chanting from the depths of Stormspike below her rose in pitch: the Lightless Ones, in their unfathomable, inhuman way, were welcoming her back to her frost-mantled throne. Except for Utuk'ku herself, the Chamber of the Harp was empty, although a single thought or flick of her hand would have raised a thicket of bristling spears clutched in pale hands.

She lifted her long fingers to the temples of her mask and stared into the shifting column of steam that hung above the Well. The Harp, its outlines shiftingly imprecise, glinted crimson, yellow and violet. Ineluki's presence was muted. He had begun to withdraw into himself, drawing strength from whatever ultimate source nurtured him as air fed the flame of a candle. He was preparing for the great test that would be coming soon.

Although it was in some ways a relief to be free of his burning, angry thoughts—thoughts that often were not intelligible even to Utuk'ku except as a sort of cloud of hatred and longing—the Norn Queen's thin lips nevertheless compressed into a thin line of discontent behind her gleaming mask. The things she had seen in the dreamworld had troubled her; despite the machinations she had set underway, Utuk'ku was not altogether content. It would have been a relief of sorts to share them with the thing that was focused in the heart of the Well—but it was not to be. The greatest part of Ineluki would be absent from now until the final days when the Conqueror Star stood high.

Utuk'ku's colorless eyes suddenly narrowed. Somewhere on the fringes of the great tapestry of force and dream that wove through the Well, something else had begun to move in an unexpected way. The Norn Queen turned her gaze inward, letting her mind reach out and probe along the strands of her delicately balanced web, along the uncountable lines of intention and calculation and fate. There it was: another parting of her careful work.

A sigh, faint as the velvet wind across a bat's wing, fluted through Utuk'ku's lips. The singing of the Lightless Ones faltered for a moment at the wave of irritation that washed out from Stormspike's mistress, but a moment later their voices rose again, hollow and triumphant. It was only someone dabbling with one of the Master Witnesses—a youngling, even if of the line of Amerasu Ship-Born. She would treat the whelp harshly. This damage, too, could be repaired. It would merely require a bit more of her concentration, a bit more of her straining thought—but it would be done. She was weary, but not so weary as that.

It had been perhaps a thousand years since the Norn Queen had smiled, but if she had remembered how, she might have smiled at that moment. Even the oldest of the Hikeda'ya had known no other mistress but Utuk'ku. Some of them could be pardoned, perhaps, for thinking that she was no longer a living thing, but like the Storm King a creature made entirely of ice and sorcery and endless, vigilant malignity. Utuk'ku knew better. Although even the millennial lives of some of her descendants spanned but a small portion of her own, beneath the corpse-pale robes and shimmering mask was still a living woman. Inside her ancient flesh a heart still beat—slow and strong, like a blind thing crawling at the bottom of a deep, silent sea.

She was weary, but she was still fierce, still powerful. She had planned so long for these coming days that the very face of the land above had shifted and altered beneath Time's hand as she waited. She would live to see her revenge.

The lights of the Well flickered on the empty metal face she showed the world. Perhaps in that triumphant hour, Utuk'ku thought, she would once more remember what it was to smile.

⚔

"Ah, by the Grove," Jiriki said, "it is indeed Mezutu'a—the Silverhome." He held his torch higher. "I have not seen it before, but so many songs are sung of it that I feel I know its towers and bridges and streets as though I had grown here."

"You haven't been here? But I thought your people built it." Eolair moved back from the stair's precipitous edge. The great city lay spread below them, a fantastic jumble of shadowed stone.

"We did—in part—but the last of the Zida'ya had left this place long before *my* birth." Jiriki's golden eyes were wide, as though he could not tear his gaze from the roofs of the cavern city. "When the Tinukeda'ya severed their fates from ours, Jenjiyana of the Nightingales declared, in her wisdom, that we should give this place to the Navigator's Children, in partial payment of the debt we owed them." He frowned and shook his head, hair moving loosely about his shoulders. "Year-Dancing House, at least, remembered something of honor. She also gave to them Hikehikayo in the north, and sea-collared Jhiná-T'seneí, which has long since disappeared beneath the waves."

Eolair struggled to make sense of the barrage of unfamiliar names. "Your people gave this to the Tinukeda'ya?" he asked. "The creatures that we called *domhaini?* The dwarrows?"

"Some were called that," Jiriki nodded. He turned his bright stare on the count. "But they are not 'creatures,' Count Eolair. They came from The Garden that is Lost, just as my people did. We made the mistake of thinking them less than us then. I wish to avoid it now."

"I meant no insult," said Eolair. "But I met them, as I told you. They were . . . strange. But they were kind to us, too."

"The Ocean Children were ever gentle." Jiriki began to descend the staircase. "That is why my people brought them, I fear—because they felt they would be tractable servants."

Eolair hastened to catch up to him. The Sitha moved with assured swiftness, walking far nearer to the edge than the count would have dared, and never looking down. "What did you mean, 'some of them were called that'?" Eolair asked. "Were there Tinukeda'ya who were *not* dwarrows?"

"Yes. Those who lived here—the dwarrows as you call them—were a small-ish group who had split off from the main tribe. The rest of Ruyan's folk stayed close to water, since the oceans were always dear to their hearts. Many of them became what the mortals called 'sea-watchers.'"

"Niskies?" In his long career, during which he had traveled often in southern waters, Eolair had met many sea-watchers. "They still exist. But they look nothing like the dwarrows!"

Jiriki paused to let the count catch up, and thereafter, perhaps out of courtesy, kept his pace slower. "That was the Tinukeda'ya's blessing as well as their curse. They could change themselves, over time, to better fit the place that they lived: there is a certain mutability in their blood and bones. I think that if the world were to be destroyed by fire, the Ocean Children would be the only ones to survive. Before long, they would be able to eat smoke and swim in hot ashes."

"But that is astounding," said Eolair. "The dwarrows I met, Yis-fidri and his companions, seemed so timid. Who would ever dream they were capable of such things?"

"There are lizards in the southern marshes," Jiriki said with a smile, "that can change their color to match the leaf or trunk or stone on which they crouch. They are timid, too. It does not seem odd to me that the most frightened creatures are often the best at hiding themselves."

"But if your people gave the dwarrows—the Tinukeda'ya—this place, why are they so afraid of you? When the lady Maegwin and myself first came here and met them, they were terrified that we might be servants of yours come to drag them back."

Jiriki stopped. He seemed to be transfixed by something down below. When he turned to Eolair once more, it was with an expression so pained that even his alien features did not disguise it. "They are right to be frightened, Count

Eolair. Amerasu, our wise one who has just been taken from us, called our dealings with the Tinukeda'ya our great shame. We did *not* treat them well, and we kept from them things that they deserved to know . . . because we thought they would make better servants if they labored in ignorance." He made a gesture of frustration. "When Jenjiyana, Year-Dancing House's mistress, gave them this place in the distant past, she was opposed by many of the Houses of Dawn. There are those among the Zida'ya, even to this day, who feel we should have kept Ruyan Ve's children as servants. They are right to fear, your friends."

"None of these things were in our old legends of your folk," Eolair marveled. "You paint a grim, sad picture, Prince Jiriki. Why do you tell me all this?"

The Sitha started down the pitted steps once more. "Because, Count Eolair, that era will soon be gone. That does not mean I think that happier things are coming—although there is always a chance, I must suppose. But for better or worse, this age of the world is ending."

They continued downward, unspeaking.

Eolair relied on his dim memories of his previous visit to lead Jiriki through the crumbling city—although, judging by the Sitha's impatience, which seemed bridled only by his natural courtesy, Jiriki might have been just as capable of leading him. As they walked through the echoing, deserted streets, Eolair again had the impression of Mezutu'a as not so much a city as a warren for shy yet friendly beasts. This time, though, with Jiriki's words about the ocean still fresh in his mind, Eolair saw it as a sort of coral garden, its countless buildings growing one from another, shot through with empty doorways and shadowed tunnels, its towers joined together by stone walkways thin as spun glass. He wondered absently if the dwarrows had harbored some longing for the sea deep inside themselves, so that this place and its additions—even now, Jiriki was once again pointing out some feature that had been added to Mezutu'a's original buildings—had gradually become a sort of undersea grotto, shielded from the sun by mountain stone instead of blue water.

As they emerged from the long tunnel and its carvings of living stone into the vastness of the great stone arena, Jiriki, who had now taken the lead, was surrounded by a nimbus of pale, chalky light. As he stared down into the arena, the Sitha raised his slim hands to shoulder height, then made a careful gesture before striding forward, only his deerlike grace hiding the fact that he was moving very quickly.

The great crystalline Shard still stood at the center of the bowl, throbbing weakly, its surfaces full of slow-moving colors. Around it, the stone benches were empty. The arena was deserted.

"*Yis-fidri!*" Eolair shouted. "*Yis-hadra! It is Eolair, Count of Nad Mullach!*"

His voice rolled across the arena and reverberated along the cavern's distant walls. There was no reply. "*It is Eolair, Yis-fidri! I have come back!*"

When no one answered him—there was no sign of life at all, no footfalls, no gleam of the dwarrows' rose-crystal batons—Eolair walked down to join Jiriki.

"This is what I feared," said the count. "That if I brought you, they would vanish. I only hope they have not fled the city completely." He frowned. "I imagine they think me a traitor, bringing one of their former masters here."

"Perhaps." Jiriki seemed distracted, almost tense. "By my ancestors," he breathed, "to stand before the Shard of Mezutu'a! I can feel it singing!"

Eolair put his hand near the milky stone, but could feel nothing but a slight warming of the air.

Jiriki raised his palms to the Shard but paused short of touching it, bringing his hands to a stop as though he embraced an invisible something that followed the stone's outline but was nearly twice as large. The light patterns began to glow a little more colorfully, as though whatever moved in the stone had swum closer to the surface. Jiriki watched the play of colors carefully as he moved his fingers in slow orbits, never touching the Shard directly, positioning his hands around the stone as though partnering the unmoving object in some ritual dance.

A long time passed, a time in which Eolair felt his legs beginning to ache. He sat down on one of the stone benches. A cold draft was wafting down the arena and scraping at the back of his neck. He huddled a little deeper into his cloak and watched Jiriki, who still stood before the gleaming stone, locked in some silent communion.

More than a little bored, Eolair began to fidget with his long horsetail of black hair. Although it was hard to tell exactly how much time had passed since Jiriki had approached the stone, the count knew it had not been a brief interval: Eolair was famous for his patience, and even in these maddening days, it took a great deal to make him restless.

Abruptly, the Sitha flinched and took a step back from the stone. He swayed in place for a moment, then turned to Eolair. There was a light in Jiriki's eyes that seemed more than just a reflection of the Shard's inconstant glow.

"The Speakfire," Jiriki said.

Eolair was confused. "What do you mean?"

"The Speakfire in Hikehikayo. It is another witness—a Master Witness, like the Shard. It is very close, somehow—close in a way that has nothing to do with distance. I cannot shake it free and turn the Shard to other things."

"What other things do you want to turn it to?"

Jiriki shook his head. He glanced quickly at the Shard before beginning. "It is hard to explain, Count Eolair. Let me put it this way—if you were lost and surrounded by fog, but there was a tree you could climb that would allow you to move *above* the mist, would you not do it?"

Eolair nodded. "Certainly, but I still do not quite see what you mean."

"Simply this. We who are used to the Road of Dreams have been denied it of late—as surely as thick fog can make a person afraid to wander any distance from his home, even when his need is great. The Witnesses I can use are minor; without the strength and knowledge of someone like our First Grandmother Amerasu, they are of use only for small purposes. The Shard of Mezutu'a is a Master Witness—I had thought of searching for it even before we rode out of Jao e-Tinukai'i—but I have just found that its use is denied me, somehow. It is as though I had ascended that tree I spoke of, clambering up to the upper limits of the fog, only to find that someone else was above me, and that they would not let me climb high enough to see. I am balked."

"I'm afraid it is all still largely a mystery to a mortal like me, Jiriki, although I think I see a little of what you are trying to explain." Eolair considered for a moment. "Saying it another way: you wish to look out a window, but someone on the other side has covered it. Is that right?"

"Yes. Well put." Jiriki smiled, but Eolair saw weariness beneath the Sitha's alien features. "But I dare not go away without trying to look through the window again, as many times as I have the strength."

"I will wait for you, then. But we have brought little food or water—and besides, although I cannot speak for yours, I fear *my* people will have need of me before too long."

"As to food and drink," Jiriki said distractedly, "you may have mine." He turned back to the Shard once more. "When you feel it is time for you to return, tell me—but do not touch me until I say it is permitted, Count Eolair, if you will promise. I do not know exactly what I must do, and it would be safer for both of us if you leave me alone, no matter what it may seem is happening."

"I will not do anything unless you ask me to," Eolair promised.

"Good." Jiriki raised his hands and began making the slow circles once more.

The Count of Nad Mullach sighed and leaned back against the stone bench, trying to find a comfortable position.

Eolair awakened from a strange dream—he had been fleeing before a vast wheel, treetop-tall, rough and splintered as the beams of an ancient ceiling—into the abrupt realization that something was wrong. The light was brighter, pulsing now like a heartbeat, but it had turned a sickly blue-green. The air in the huge cavern was as tense and still as before a storm, a smell like the aftereffects of lightning burned Eolair's nostrils.

Jiriki still stood before the gleaming Shard, a mote in the sea of blinding light—but where before he had been as poised as a Mircha-dancer readying a rain prayer, now his limbs were contorted, his head thrown back as though some invisible hand was squeezing the life out of him. Eolair rushed forward, desperately worried but unsure of what to do. The Sitha had told the count not to touch him, no matter what seemed to be happening, but when Eolair drew close enough to see Jiriki's face, nearly invisible in the great outwash of nauseating brilliance, he felt his heart plummet. Surely this could not be what Jiriki had planned!

The Sitha's gold-flecked eyes had rolled up, so that only a crescent of white showed beneath the lids. His lips were skinned back from his teeth in the snarl of a cornered beast, and the writhing veins in his neck and forehead seemed about to burst from his skin.

"Prince Jiriki!" Eolair shouted. "Jiriki, can you hear me!?"

The Sitha's mouth opened a little wider. His jaws worked. A loud rumble of sound spilled out and echoed across the great bowl, deep and unintelligible, but so obviously full of pain and fear that even as Eolair clapped his hands over his ears in desperation he felt his heart lurch with sympathetic horror. He reached out a tentative hand toward the Sitha and watched in amazement as the hairs on his arm lifted straight up. His skin was tingling.

Count Eolair only thought for a moment longer. Cursing himself for the fool he was, then flicking off a quick, silent prayer to Cuamh Earthdog, he took a step forward and grasped Jiriki's shoulders.

At the instant his fingers touched, Eolair felt himself suddenly overrun by a titanic force from nowhere, a rushing black river of terror and blood and empty voices that poured through him, sweeping his thoughts away like a handful of leaves in a cataract. But even in the brief moment before his real self spun out into nothingness, he could see his hands still touching Jiriki, and saw the Sitha, overbalanced by Eolair's weight, toppling forward into the Shard. Jiriki touched the stone. A great bonfire of sparks leaped up, brighter even than the blue-green radiance, a million gleaming lights like the souls of all the fireflies in the world set free at once, dancing and swooping. Then everything faded into darkness. Eolair felt himself falling, falling, cast down like a stone into an endless void. . . .

"You live."

The relief in Jiriki's voice was clear. Eolair opened his eyes to a pale blur that gradually became the Sitha's face bent close to his. Jiriki's cool hands were on his temples.

Eolair feebly waved him off. The Sitha stepped back and allowed him to sit up; Eolair was obscurely grateful to be allowed to do it himself, even though it took him no little time to steady his shaking body. His head was hammering, ringing like Rhynn's cauldron in full battle cry. He had to close his eyes for a moment to keep himself from vomiting.

"I warned you not to touch me," Jiriki said, but there was no displeasure in his voice. "I am sorry that you should have suffered so for me."

"What . . . what happened?"

Jiriki shook his head. There was a certain new stiffness in his movements, but when Eolair thought of how much longer the Sitha had endured what he himself had survived for only a moment, the count was awed. "I am not sure," Jiriki answered. "Something did not want me to reach the Dream Road, or did not want the Shard tampered with—something with far more power or knowledge than I have." He grimaced, showing his white teeth. "I was right to warn Seoman away from the Road of Dreams. I should have heeded my own advice, it seems. Likimeya my mother will be furious."

"I thought you were dying." Eolair groaned. It felt as though someone was shoeing a large plow-horse behind his forehead.

"If you had not pushed me out of the alignment in which I was trapped, worse than death would have awaited me, I think." He laughed suddenly, sharply. "I owe you the Staja Ame, Count Eolair—the White Arrow. Sadly, someone else already has mine."

Eolair rolled toward his side and struggled to stand. It took several tries, but at last, with Jiriki's help, which Eolair accepted gladly this time, he managed to drag himself upright. The Shard again seemed quiescent, flickering mutedly in the center of the empty arena, casting hesitant shadows behind the stone benches. "White Arrow?" he murmured. His head hurt, and his muscles felt as though he had been dragged behind a cart from Hernysadharc to Crannhyr.

"I will tell you some day soon," said Jiriki. "I must learn to live with these indignities."

Together they began to walk toward the tunnel that led out of the arena, Eolair limping, Jiriki steadier, but still slow. "Indignities?" Eolair asked weakly. "What do you mean?"

"Being saved by mortals. It has become a sort of habit for me, it seems."

The sound of their halting footsteps sent echoes fluttering across the vast cavern and up among the dark places.

👑

"Here, puss, puss. Come now, Grimalkin."

Rachel was a little embarrassed. She wasn't quite sure what one said to cats— in the old days, she had expected them to do their job keeping the rat population down, but she had left the petting and pampering of them to her chambermaids. As far as she had been concerned, handing out endearments and sweetmeats was no part of her obligation to *any* of her charges, two-footed or four. But now she had a need—if admittedly a daft and soft-headed one—and so she was humbling herself.

Thank merciful Usires no human creature is around to see me.

"Puss, puss, puss." Rachel waved the bit of salt-beef. She slid forward half a cubit, trying to ignore the ache in her back and the rough stone beneath her knees. "I'm trying to *feed* you, you Rhiap-preserve-us filthy thing." She scowled and waggled the bit of meat. "Serve you right if I *did* cook you."

Even the cat, standing just a short distance out of Rachel's reach in the middle of the corridor, seemed to know that this was an idle threat. Not because of Rachel's soft heart—she needed this beast to take food from her, but otherwise would just as happily have smacked it with her broom—but because eating cat flesh was as inconceivable to Rachel as spitting upon a church altar. She could not have said why exactly cat meat was different than the flesh of rabbit or roe deer, but she did not need to. It was not done by decent folk, and that was enough to know.

Still, in the last quarter of an hour, she had more than once or twice toyed with the idea of kicking this recalcitrant creature down the steep staircase and then turning to some idea that did not require the assistance of animals. But the most irritating thing was that even the idea itself was of no practical use.

Rachel looked at her quivering arm and greasy fingers. All of this to help a monster?

You're slipping, woman. Mad as a mooncalf.

"Puss . . ."

The gray cat took a few steps closer and paused, surveying Rachel with eyes widened by suspicion as much as the bright lamplight. Rachel silently said the Elysia prayer and tried to move the beef enticingly. The cat approached warily, wrinkled its nostrils, then took a cautious lick. After a moment's mock-casual washing of whiskers, it seemed to gain courage. It reached out and pulled loose some of the meat, stepping back to swallow it, then came forward once more. Rachel brought up her other hand and let it brush the cat's back. It started, but when Rachel made no sudden move, the cat took the last piece of beef and gulped it down. She let her fingers trail lightly against its fur as the cat nosed her now-empty hand questioningly. Rachel stroked it behind the ears, gamely resisting the impulse to throttle the particular little beast. At last, when she had worked loose a purr, she clambered heavily to her feet.

"Tomorrow," she said. "More meat." She turned and stumped wearily up the corridor toward her hidden room. The cat watched her go, sniffed around on the stone floor for any scraps it might have missed, then lay down and began to groom itself.

Jiriki and Eolair emerged into the light blinking like moles. The count was already regretting his decision to choose this entrance into the underground mines, one that was so far from Hernysadharc. If they had come in through the caverns where the Hernystiri had sheltered, as he and Maegwin had the first time, they could have spent the night in one of the recently-inhabited dens of the cave-city, saving themselves a long ride back.

"You do not look well," the Sitha commented, which was probably no more than the truth. Eolair's head had at last stopped ringing, but his muscles still ached mightily.

"I do not feel well." The count looked around. There was still a little snow on the ground, but the weather had improved greatly in the last few days. It was tempting to consider staying right here and traveling back to the Taig in the morning. He squinted up at the sun. Only mid-afternoon: their time underground had seemed much longer . . . if this was still the same day. He grinned sourly at the thought. Better a painful ride back to the Taig, he decided, than a night in the still-cold wildlands.

The horses, Eolair's bay gelding and Jiriki's white charger, which had feathers and bells braided into its mane, stood cropping the meager grass, stretched to the ends of their long tethers. It was the work of only a few moments to make them ready, then human and Sitha spurred away toward the southeast and Hernysadharc.

"The air seems different," Eolair called. "Can you feel it?"

"Yes." Jiriki lifted his head like a hunting beast scenting the breeze. "But I do not know what it might mean."

"It's warmer. That's enough for me."

By the time they reached the outskirts of Hernysadharc, the sun had finally slipped down behind the Grianspog and the base of the sky was losing its ruddiness. They rode side by side up the Taig Road, threading through the not inconsiderable foot- and cart-traffic. Seeing his people once more out and about their business eased the pain of Eolair's aches. Things were far from ordinary, and most of the people on the road had the gaunt, staring look of the hungry, but they were traveling freely in their own country again. Many seemed to have come from the market; they clutched their acquisitions jealously, even if they held no more than a handful of onions.

"So what did you learn?" Eolair asked at last.

"From the Shard? Much and little." Jiriki saw the count's expression and laughed. "Ah, you look like my mortal friend Seoman Snowlock! It is true, we Dawn Children do not give satisfactory answers."

"Seoman . . . ?"

"Your kind call him 'Simon,' I think." Jiriki nodded his head, milk-white hair dancing in the wind. "He is a strange cub, but brave and good-natured. He is clever, too, although he hides it well."

"I met him, I think. He is with Josua Lackhand at the Stone—at Ses . . . Sesu . . ." He gestured, trying to summon the name.

"Sesuad'ra. Yes, that is him. Young, but he has been caught up by too many currents for chance alone to be the explanation. He will have a part to play in things." Jiriki stared into the east, as if looking for the mortal boy there. "Amerasu—our First Grandmother—invited him into her house. That was a great honor indeed."

Eolair shook his head. "He seemed little more than a tall and somewhat awkward young man when I met him—but I stopped putting trust in appearances long ago."

Jiriki smiled. "You are one in whom the old Hernystiri blood runs strong, then. Let me consider what I found in the Shard a while longer. Then, if you come with me to see Likimeya, I will share my thoughts with both of you."

As they made their way up Hern's Hill, Eolair saw someone walking slowly across the damp grass. He raised his hand.

"A moment, please." Eolair passed the Sitha his reins, then swung down from his saddle and walked after the figure, which bent every few moments as though plucking flowers from among the grass-stems. A loose scatter of birds hovered behind, swooping down and then starting up again with a flurry of wings.

"Maegwin?" Eolair called. She did not stop, so he hurried his steps to catch up to her. "Maegwin," he said as he came abreast of her. "Are you well?"

Lluth's daughter turned to look at him. She was wearing a dark cloak, but beneath it was a dress of bright yellow. Her belt buckle was a sunflower of hammered gold. She looked pretty and at peace. "Count Eolair," she said calmly, and smiled, then bent at the waist and let another handful of seed corn dribble from her fist.

"What are you doing?"

"Planting flowers. The long battle with winter has withered even Heaven's blooms." She stooped and sprinkled more corn. Behind her, the birds fought noisily over the kernels.

"What do you mean, 'Heaven's blooms'?"

She looked up at him curiously. "What a strange question. But think, Eolair, of what beautiful flowers will spring from these seeds. Think of how it will look when the gardens of the gods are a-blossom once more."

Eolair stared at her helplessly for a moment. Maegwin continued to walk forward, sprinkling the corn in little piles as she went. The birds, stuffed but not yet sated, followed her. "But you are on Hern's Hill," he said. "You are in Hernysadharc, the place where you grew up!"

Maegwin paused and pulled her cloak a little tighter. "You do not look well, Eolair. That is not right. Nobody should be ill in a place like this."

Jiriki was making his way lightly across the grass leading the two horses. He stopped a short distance away, unwilling to intrude.

To Eolair's surprise, Maegwin turned to the Sitha and dropped into a curtsy. "Welcome, Lord Brynioch," she called, then rose and lifted her hand to the reddening western horizon. "What a beautiful sky you have made for us today. Thank you, O Bright One."

Jiriki said nothing, but looked to Eolair with a catlike expression of calm curiosity.

"Do you not know who this is?" the count asked Maegwin. "This is Jiriki of the Sithi. He is no god, but one of those who saved us from Skali." When she did not reply, but only smiled indulgently, his voice rose. "Maegwin, this is not Brynioch. You are not among the gods. This is Jiriki—immortal, but of flesh and blood just like you and I."

Maegwin turned her sly smile onto the Sitha. "Good my Lord, Eolair seems fevered. Did you perhaps take him too close to the sun on your journeying today?"

The Count of Nad Mullach stared. Was she truly mad or playing some unfathomable game? He had never seen anything like this. "Maegwin!" he snapped.

Jiriki touched his arm. "Come with me, Count Eolair. We will talk."

Maegwin curtsied again. "You are kind, Lord Brynioch. I will continue with my task now, if I have your leave. It is little enough to repay your kindness and hospitality."

Jiriki nodded. Maegwin turned and continued her slow walk across the hillside.

"Gods help me," Eolair said. "She is mad! It is worse than I had feared."

"Even one who is not of your kind could see that she is gravely troubled."

"What can I do?" the count mourned. "What if she does not recover her wits?"

"I have a friend—a cousin, by your terms—who is a healer," Jiriki offered. "I do not know that this young woman's problem can be helped by her, but there could be no harm in trying, I think."

He watched Eolair clamber back into his saddle, then mounted his own horse in a single, fluid movement and led the silent count up the hillside toward the Taig.

When she heard the approaching footfalls, Rachel almost pushed herself farther back into the shadows before she remembered that it would make no difference. Inwardly, she cursed herself for a fool.

The steps were slow, as if the one making them was very weak or was carrying a huge burden.

"Now where are we going?" It was a harsh whisper, deep and rough, a voice that was not used very often. "Going. Where are we going? Very well, then, I'm coming." There was a thin wheeze of sound that might have been laughing or crying.

Rachel held her breath. The cat appeared first, head up, certain now after nearly a week that what was waiting was dinner rather than danger. The man followed a moment later, trudging forward out of the shadows into the lamplight. His pale, scarred face was covered in a long, gray-shot beard and the parts of him that were not covered by his ragged, filthy clothes were starvation-thin. His eyes were closed.

"Slow down," he said raspingly. "I'm weak. Can't go fast." He stopped, as though he sensed the lamplight on his face, on the lids of his ruined eyes. "Where are you, cat?" he quavered.

Rachel leaned down to pet the cat, which was butting at her ankle, then slipped it a bit of its expected salt-beef. She straightened up.

"Earl Guthwulf." Her voice seemed so loud after Guthwulf's whisper that it even shocked her. The man flinched and fell back, almost toppling over, but instead of turning to run he raised his trembling hands before him.

"Leave me alone, you damnable things!" he cried. "Haunt someone else! Leave me with my misery! Let the sword have me if it wants."

"Don't run, Guthwulf!" Rachel said hastily, but at the renewed sound of her voice, the earl turned and begin to stagger back down the corridor.

"There will be food for you here," she called after him. The tattered apparition did not answer, but vanished into the shadows beyond the lampglow. "I will leave it and then go away. I will do that every day! You do not need to speak to me!"

When the echoes had died, she put down a small helping of jerked meat for the cat, which began to chew hungrily. The bowl full of meat and dried fruit she placed in a dusty alcove on the wall, above the cat's reach, but where the living scarecrow could not fail to find it when he worked up the nerve to return.

Still not quite sure what her own purpose was, Rachel picked up her lamp and started back toward the stairwell that would lead to the higher, more familiar parts of the castle's labyrinth. Now she had done it and it was too late to turn back. But *why* had she done it? She would have to risk the upper castle again, since the stores she had laid in were planned to feed one frugal person only, not two adults and a cat with a bottomless stomach.

"Rhiap, save me from myself," she grumbled.

Perhaps it was the fact that it was the only charity she could perform in these terrible days—although Rachel had never been obsessed with charity, since so many mendicants were, as far as she could tell, perfectly able-bodied and most likely merely frightened of work. But perhaps it *was* charity after all. Times had changed, and Rachel had changed, too.

Or perhaps she was just lonely, she reflected. She snorted at herself and hurried up the corridor.

23

The Sounding
of the Horn

❧

Several odd things happened in the days after Princess Miriamele and her companions arrived at Sesuad'ra.

The first and least important was the change that came over Lenti, Count Streáwe's messenger. The beetle-browed Perdruinese man had spent his first days in New Gadrinsett strutting around the small marketplace, annoying the local women and picking fights with the merchants. He had shown several people his knives, with the thinly veiled implication that he was prone to use them when the mood was upon him.

However, when Duke Isgrimnur arrived with the princess, Lenti immediately retired to the tent he had been given as his billet and did not come out for some time. It took a great deal of coaxing to get him to emerge even to receive Josua's reply to his master Streáwe, and when Lenti saw that the duke was to be present, the knife-flourishing messenger became weak in the knees and had to be allowed to sit down for Josua's instructions. Apparently—or so the story was later told in the market—he and Isgrimnur had met before, and Lenti had not found the acquaintanceship a pleasant one. Once given a reply for his master, Lenti left Sesuad'ra hurriedly. Neither he nor anyone else much regretted his departure.

The second and far more astounding event was Duke Isgrimnur's announcement that the old man he had brought to Sesuad'ra out of the south was in fact Camaris-sá-Vinitta, the greatest hero of the Johannine Age. It was whispered throughout the settlement that when Josua was told this on the evening of the return, he fell to his knees before the old man and kissed his hand—which seemed proof enough that Isgrimnur spoke truly. Oddly, however, the nominal Sir Camaris seemed almost entirely unmoved by Josua's gesture. Conflicting rumors quickly swept through the community of New Gadrinsett—the old man had been wounded in the head, he had gone mad from drink or sorcery or any number of other possible reasons, even that he had taken a vow of silence.

The third and saddest occurrence was the death of old Towser. On the same night that Miriamele and the others returned, the ancient jester died in his sleep. Most agreed that the excitement had been too much for his heart. Those who knew the terrors through which Towser had already passed with the rest of Josua's company of survivors were not so sure, but he was after all a very old man, and his passing appeared to be natural. Josua spoke kindly of him at the burial two days later, reminding the small party gathered there of Towser's long service to King John. It was noted by some, though, that despite the prince's generous eulogy, the jester was interred near the other casualties of the recent battle rather than beside Deornoth in the garden of Leavetaking House.

The harper Sangfugol made sure that the old man was buried with a lute as well as his tattered motley, in memory of how Towser had taught him his musical art. Together, Sangfugol and Simon also gathered snowflowers, which they scattered atop the dark earth after the grave was filled.

"It's sad that he should die just when Camaris had returned." Miriamele was stringing the remaining snowflowers, which Simon had given to her, into a delicate necklace. "One of the few people he knew in the old days, and they never had a chance to talk. Not that Camaris would have said anything, I suppose."

Simon shook his head. "Towser *did* speak to Camaris, Princess." He paused. Her title still felt strange, especially when she sat before him in the flesh, living, breathing. "When Towser saw him—even before Isgrimnur said who it was—Towser went pale. He stood in front of Camaris for a moment, rubbing his hands like this, then whispered, 'I did not tell anyone, Lord, I swear!' Then he went off to his tent. Nobody heard him say it but me, I think. I had no idea what it meant—I still don't."

Miriamele nodded. "I suppose we never will, now." She glanced at him, then immediately dropped her gaze back to her flowers.

Simon thought she was prettier than ever. Her golden hair, the dye now worn away, was boyishly short, but he rather liked how it emphasized the firm, sharp line of her chin and her green eyes. Even the slightly more serious expression she now wore just made her all the more appealing. He admired her, that was the word, but there was nothing he could do with his feelings. He longed to protect her from anything and everything, but at the same time he knew very well that she would never allow anyone to treat her as though she were a helpless child.

Simon sensed something else changed in Miriamele as well. She was still kind and courteous, but there was a remoteness to her that he did not remember, an air of restraint. The old balance forged between the two of them seemed to have been altered, but he did not quite understand what had replaced it. Miriamele seemed a little more distant, yet at the same time more aware of him than she had ever been before, almost as though he frightened her in some way.

He could not help staring at her, so he was grateful that for the moment her attention was fixed on the flowers in her lap. It was so strange to face the real Miriamele after all the months of remembering and imagining that he found it hard to think clearly in her presence. Now that the first week since her return had passed, a little of the awkwardness seemed to be gone, but there was still a gap between them. Even back in Naglimund, when he had first seen her as the king's daughter she was, there had not been this quality of separation.

Simon had told her—not without some pride—of his many adventures in the last half-year; to his surprise, he had then discovered that Miriamele's experiences had been almost as wildly improbable as his own.

At first he had decided that the horrors of her journey—the kilpa and ghants, the deaths of Dinivan and Lector Ranessin, her not-quite-explained confinement on the ship of some Nabbanai nobleman—were quite enough to explain the wall that he felt between them. Now he was not so sure. They had been friends, and even if they could never be more than that, the friendship had been real, hadn't it? Something had happened to make her treat him differently.

Could it be me, Simon wondered. *Could I have changed so much that she doesn't like me anymore?*

He unthinkingly stroked his beard. Miriamele looked up, caught his eye, and smiled mockingly. He felt a pleasant warmth: it was almost like seeing her in her old guise as Marya, the servant girl.

"You're certainly proud of that, aren't you?"

"What? My beard?" Simon was suddenly glad he had kept it, for he was blushing. "It just . . . sort of grew."

"Mmmm. By surprise? Overnight?"

"What's wrong with it?" he asked, stung. "I'm a knight, by the Bloody Tree! Why shouldn't I have a beard!"

"Don't swear. Not in front of ladies, and especially not in front of princesses." She gave him a look that was meant to be stern, but was spoiled in its effect somehow by her suppressed smile. "Besides, even if you are a knight, Simon—and I suppose I'll have to take your word for that until I remember to ask Uncle Josua—that doesn't mean you're old enough to grow a beard without looking silly."

"Ask Josua? You can ask anyone!" Simon was torn between pleasure at seeing her act a little more like her old self and irritation at what she had said. "Not old enough! I'm almost sixteen years! Will be in another fortnight, on Saint Yistrin's day!" He had only just realized himself that it was near when Father Strangyeard had made a remark about the saint's upcoming holy day.

"Truly?" Miriamele's look became serious. "I had my sixteenth birthday while we were traveling to Kwanitupul. Cadrach was very nice—he stole a jam-tart and some Lakeland pinks for me—but it wasn't much of a celebration."

"That thieving villain," Simon growled. He still had not forgotten his purse and the shame he had endured over its loss, no matter how much had happened since then.

"Don't say that." Miriamele was suddenly sharp. "You don't know anything about him, Simon. He has suffered much. His life has been hard."

Simon made a noise of disgust. "*He's* suffered!? What about the people he steals from?"

Miriamele's eyes narrowed. "I don't want you to say another word about Cadrach. Not a word."

Simon opened his mouth, then shut it again. *Damn me,* he thought, *you can get in trouble with girls so quickly! It's like they're all practicing to grow up to be Rachel the Dragon!*

He took a breath. "I'm sorry your birthday wasn't very nice."

She eyed him for a moment, then relented. "Perhaps when yours comes, Simon, we can both celebrate. We can give each other gifts, like they do in Nabban."

"You already gave me one." He reached into the pocket of his cloak and removed a wisp of blue cloth. "Do you remember? When I was leaving to go north with Binabik and the others."

Miriamele stared at it for a moment. "You kept it?" she asked quietly.

"Of course. I wore it the whole time, practically. Of course I kept it."

Her eyes widened, then she turned away and rose abruptly from the stone bench. "I have to go, Simon," she said in an odd tone of voice. She would not meet his eye. "Your pardon, please." She swept up her skirts and moved swiftly off across the black and white tiles of the Fire Garden.

"Damn me," said Simon. Things had seemed to be going well at last. What had he done? When would he ever learn to understand women?

Binabik, as the nearest thing to a full-fledged Scrollbearer, took the oaths of Tiamak and Father Strangyeard. When they had sworn, he in turn spoke his oath to them. Geloë looked on sardonically as the litanies were spoken. She had never held much with the formalities of the League, which was one reason she had never been a Scrollbearer, despite the immense respect in which she was held by its members. There were other reasons as well, but Geloë never spoke of those, and all of her old comrades who might have been able to explain were now gone.

Tiamak was torn between pleasure and disappointment. He had long dreamed that this might happen someday, but in his imagination he had received his scroll-and-pen from Morgenes, with Jarnauga and Ookequk beaming their approval. Instead he had brought Dinivan's pendant up from Kwanitupul himself after Isgrimnur delivered it, and now he sat with the largely unproved successors of those other great souls.

Still, there was something unutterably exciting even in such a humble realization of his dream. Perhaps this would be a day long remembered—the coming of a new generation to the League, a new membership which would make the Scrollbearers as important and respected as they had been in the days of Eahlstan Fiskerne himself . . . !

Tiamak's stomach growled. Geloë turned her yellow eyes on him and he smiled shamefacedly. In the excitement of the morning's preparations he had forgotten to eat. Embarrassment spread through him. There! That was They Who Watch and Shape reminding him of how important he was. A new age, indeed—those gathered here would have to labor mightily to be half the Scroll-bearers that their predecessors had been. That would teach Tiamak, the savage from Village Grove, to allow himself to become so heady!

His stomach growled again. Tiamak avoided Geloë's eye this time and pulled his knees closer in to his body, huddling on the mat floor of Strangyeard's tent like a pottery merchant on a cold day.

"Binabik has asked me to speak," Geloë said when the oaths were done. She was brisk, like an Elder's wife explaining chores and babies to a new bride. "Since I am the only one who knew all the other Scrollbearers, I have agreed." The fierceness in her stare did not make Tiamak particularly comfortable. He had only corresponded with the forest woman before his arrival in Sesuad'ra, and had possessed no idea of the force of her presence. Now, he was frantically trying to remember the letters he had sent her and hoping that they had all been suitably courteous. She was clearly not the sort of person one wanted to upset.

"You have become Scrollbearers in what may be the most difficult age the world has yet seen, worse even than Fingil's era of conquest and pillage and destruction of knowledge. You have all heard enough now to understand that what is happening seems clearly far more than a war between princes. Elias of Erkynland has somehow enlisted the aid of Ineluki Storm King, whose undead hand has reached down out of the Nornfells at last, as Eahlstan Fiskerne feared centuries ago. That is the task set before us—to somehow prevent that evil from turning a fight between brothers into a losing struggle against utter darkness. And the first part of that task, it seems, is to solve the riddle of the blades."

The discussion of Nisses' sword-rhyme went far into the afternoon. By the time Binabik thought to find something for them all to eat, Morgenes' precious manuscript was scattered about Strangyeard's tent, virtually every page having been held up for scrutiny and argued over until the incense-scented air seemed to ring.

Tiamak saw now that Morgenes' message to him must have referred to the rhyme of the Three Swords. The Wrannaman had thought it impossible that anyone could have knowledge of his own secret treasure: it was clear that no one had. Still, if he hadn't already developed a scholar's healthy respect for co-incidence, this day's revelations would have convinced him. When bread and wine had been passed around, and the sharper disagreements had been softened by full mouths and the necessity of sharing a jug, Tiamak at last spoke up.

"I have found something myself that I hope you will look at." He placed his cup down carefully and then withdrew the leaf-wrapped parchment from his sack. "I found this in the marketplace at Kwanitupul. I had hoped to take it to Dinivan in Nabban to see what he would say." He unrolled it with great caution as the other three moved forward to look. Tiamak felt the sort of worried pride a father might feel on first bringing his child before the Elders to have the Naming confirmed.

Strangyeard sighed. "Blessed Elysia, is it real?"

Tiamak shook his head. "If it is not, it is a very careful forgery. In my years in Perdruin, I saw many writings from Nisses' time. These are Rimmersgard runes as someone in that age would have written them. See the backward spirals." He pointed with a trembling finger.

Binabik squinted. "*. . . From Nuanni's Rocke Garden . . .*" he read.

"I think that it means the Southern Islands," Tiamak said. "Nuanni . . ."

"—Was the old Nabbanai god of the sea." Strangyeard was so excited that he interrupted—an amazing thing from the diffident priest. "Of course— Nuanni's rock garden—the islands! But what does the rest mean?"

As the others bent close, already arguing, Tiamak felt a glow of pride. His child had met with the Elders' approval.

⚜

"It's not enough to stand our ground." Duke Isgrimnur sat on a stool facing Josua in the prince's darkened tent. "You have won an important victory, but it means little to Elias. Another few months and no one will remember it ever happened."

Josua frowned. "I understand. That is why I will call the Raed."

Isgrimnur shook his head, beard wagging. "That's not enough, if you'll pardon my saying so. I'm being blunt."

The prince smiled faintly. "That is your task, Isgrimnur."

"So then let me say what I need to say. We need more victories, and soon. If we do not push Elias back, it won't matter whether this 'three swords' nonsense will work or not."

"Do you really think it is nonsense?"

"After all I've seen in the last year? No, I wouldn't quickly call *anything* nonsense in these times—but that misses the point. As long as we sit here like a treed cat, we have no way to get to Bright-Nail." The duke snorted. "Dror's Mallet! I am still not used to thinking that John's blade is really Minneyar. You could have knocked my head off with a goose feather when you told me that."

"We all must become used to surprises, it seems," Josua said dryly. "But what do you suggest?"

"Nabban." Isgrimnur spoke without hesitation. "I know, I should urge you to hasten to Elvritshalla to free my people there. But you're right in your fears. If what I have heard is true, half the able-bodied men in Rimmersgard were forced into Skali's army: it would mean a drawn-out struggle to beat him.

Kaldskryke's a hard man, a canny fighter. I hate his treacherous innards, but I'd be the last to call him an easy match."

"But the Sithi have ridden to Hernystir," Josua pointed out. "You heard that."

"And what does that mean? I can make neither hide nor hair of the lad Simon's stories, and that white-haired Sitha witch-girl doesn't strike me as the kind of scout whose information should be used to plan an entire campaign." The duke grimaced. "In any case, if the Sithi and the Hernystiri drive Skali out, wonderful. I will cheer louder and longer than any. But those of Skali's men we would even *want* to recruit will still be scattered far and wide across the Frostmarch: even with the weather getting a little better, I would not want to have to try to round them up and convince them to attack Erkynland. And they're *my* people. It's my country, Josua . . . so you'd better listen to what I say." He worked his bushy eyebrows furiously, as if the mere thought of the prince's possible disagreement called his own good sense into question.

The prince sighed. "I always listen to you, Isgrimnur. You taught me tactics as you held me on your knee, remember."

"I'm not *that* much older than you, pup," the duke grumbled. "If you don't mind your manners, I'll take you out in the snow and give you an embarrassing lesson."

Josua grinned. "I think we will have to put that off for some other day. Ah, but it is good to have you back with me, Isgrimnur." His expression grew more sober. "So, then, you say Nabban. How?"

Isgrimnur slid his stool closer and dropped his voice. "Streáwe's message said the time is right—that Benigaris is very unpopular. Rumors of the part he played in his father's death are everywhere."

"The armies of the Kingfisher Crest will not desert because of rumors," said Josua. "There have been more than a few other patricides who ruled in Nabban, remember. It is hard to shock those people. In any case, the elite officers of the army are loyal to the Benidrivine House above all. They will fight any foreign usurper—even Elias, were he to assert his power directly. They certainly would not throw Benigaris over on my behalf. Surely you remember the old Nabbanai saying, 'Better our whoreson than your saint.'"

Isgrimnur grinned wickedly in his whiskers. "Ah, but who is talking about convincing them to throw Benigaris over for *your* sake, my prince? Merciful Aedon, they'd let Nessalanta lead the armies before they'd let *you* do it."

Josua shook his head in irritation. "Well, who, then?"

"Camaris, damn you!" Isgrimnur thumped his wide hand down on his thigh for emphasis. "He's the legitimate heir to the ducal throne—Leobardis only became duke because Camaris disappeared and was thought dead!"

The prince stared at his old friend. "But he's mad, Isgrimnur—or at least simple-minded."

The duke sat up. "They've accepted a cowardly patricide. Why wouldn't they prefer a heroic simpleton?"

Josua shook his head again, this time in wonder. "You are astounding, Isgrimnur. Where did you get such an idea?"

Isgrimnur grinned fiercely. "I've had a lot of time to think since I found Camaris in that inn at Kwanitupul." He ran his fingers through his beard. "It's a pity that Eolair isn't here to see what a skulker and intriguer I've become in my old age."

The prince laughed. "Well, I'm not certain that it would work, but it bears thinking about at least." He rose and walked to the table. "Would you like some more wine?"

Isgrimnur raised his goblet. "Thinking is thirsty work. Fill it, would you?"

"It is *prise'a*—Ever-fresh." Aditu lifted the slender vine to show Simon the pale blue flower. "Even after it has been picked, it does not wilt, not until the season has passed. It is said that it came from the Garden on our people's boats."

"Some of the women here wear it in their hair."

"As do our folk—men and women both," the Sitha replied with an amused glance.

"Please, hello!" someone called. Simon turned to see Tiamak, Miriamele's Wrannaman friend. The small man seemed tremendously excited. "Prince Josua wishes you to come, Sir Simon, Lady Aditu." He started to sketch a bow, but was too full of nervous exhilaration to complete it. "Oh, please hurry!"

"What is it?" asked Simon. "Is something wrong!"

"We have found something important, we think." He bounced on his tiptoes, anxious to be going. "In my parchment—mine!"

Simon shook his head. "What parchment?"

"You will learn all. Come to Josua's tent! Please!" Tiamak turned and began trotting back toward the settlement.

Simon laughed. "What a strange man! You'd think he had a bee in his breeches."

Aditu set the vine carefully back into place. She lifted her fingers to her nose. "This reminds me of my house in Jao é-Tinukai'i," she said. "Every room is filled with flowers."

"I remember."

They made their way back across the hilltop. The sun seemed quite strong today, and though the northern horizon was aswim with gray clouds, the sky overhead was blue. Almost no snow remained except in the hollows of the hillside below them, the deep places where shadows lingered late into the day. Simon wondered where Miriamele was: he had gone looking for her in the morning, hoping to convince her to take a walk with him, but she had been absent, her tent empty. Duchess Gutrun had told him that the princess had gone out early.

Josua's tent was crowded. Beside Tiamak stood Geloë, Father Strangyeard, and Binabik. The prince sat on his stool, looking closely at a parchment which was spread across his lap. Vorzheva sat near the far wall, stitching at a piece of cloth. Aditu, after nodding her greetings to the others, left Simon and went to join her.

Josua glanced up briefly from the parchment. "I am glad you are here, Simon. I hope you can help us."

"How, Prince Josua?"

The prince raised his hand without looking up again. "First you must hear what we have found."

Tiamak inched forward shyly. "Please, Prince Josua, may I tell what has happened?"

Josua smiled at the Wrannaman. "When Miriamele and Isgrimnur arrive, you may."

Simon eased over next to Binabik, who was talking with Geloë. Simon waited as patiently as he could and listened to them discuss runes and errors of translation until he was nearly bursting. At last the Duke of Elvritshalla arrived with the princess. Her short hair was wind-tousled and her cheeks had a delicate flush. Simon could not help staring at her, full of mute longing.

"I had to climb halfway down this damnable hill to find her," Isgrimnur muttered. "I hope this is worth it."

"You could have just called to me and I would have come up," Miriamele replied sweetly. "You didn't have to nearly kill yourself."

"I didn't like where you were climbing. I was afraid I'd startle you."

"And having a huge, sweating Rimmersman come crashing down the hillside *wouldn't* startle me?"

"Please." Josua's voice was a little strained. "This is not the time for teasing. It is worth it, Isgrimnur—or I hope it will be." He turned to the Wrannaman and handed him the parchment. "Explain to the newcomers, Tiamak, if you will."

The slender man, his eyes bright, quickly described how he had acquired the parchment, then showed them the ancient runes before reading it aloud.

> ". . . *Bringe from Nuanni's Rocke Garden,*
> *The Man who tho' Blinded canne See*
> *Discover the Blayde that delivers The Rose*
> *At the foote of the Rimmer's greate Tree*
> *Find the Call whose lowde Claime*
> *Speakes the Call-bearer's name*
> *In a Shippe on the Shallowest Sea—*
> *—When Blayde, Call, and Man*
> *Come to Prince's right Hande*
> *Then the Prisoned shall once more go Free . . .*"

Finished, he looked around the room. "We . . ." He hesitated. "We . . . Scrollbearers . . . have discussed this and what it might mean. If Nisses' other words are important for our purposes, it seemed likely that these might be, too."

"So what does it mean?" Isgrimnur demanded. "I looked at it before and couldn't make horns nor hind-quarter out of it."

"You were not having the advantage that some others were having," said Binabik. "Simon and myself and some others were already facing one part of this riddle for ourselves." The troll turned to Simon. "Have you seen it yet?"

Simon thought hard. "The Rimmer's Tree—the Uduntree!" He looked over to Miriamele with more than a little pride. "That's where we found Thorn!"

Binabik nodded. The tent had grown quiet. "Yes—the 'blade that delivers the Rose' was being found there," the troll said. "The sword of Camaris called Thorn."

"Ebekah, John's wife." Isgrimnur breathed. "The Rose of Hernysadharc." He pulled vigorously at his beard. "Of course!" he said to Josua. "Camaris was your mother's special protector."

"So we were seeing that the rhyme spoke in part of Thorn," Binabik agreed.

"But the rest," said Tiamak, "we think we know, but we are not sure."

Geloë leaned forward. "It seems possible that if the rhyme speaks of Thorn, it may also speak of Camaris himself. A 'man who though blinded can see' could certainly describe a man who is blind to his past, even his own name, although he sees as well as anyone here."

"Better," said Miriamele quietly.

"That seems right." Isgrimnur scowled, considering. "I don't know how such a thing could be in some old book from hundreds of years ago, but it seems right."

"So what does that leave us?" Josua asked. "This part about 'the Call' and the last lines about the prisoned going free."

A moment of silence followed his remark.

Simon cleared his throat. "Well, perhaps this is stupid," he began.

"Speak, Simon," Binabik urged him.

"If one part is about Camaris, and another is about his sword—maybe the other parts are about other things of his and other places he's been."

Josua smiled. "That is not at all stupid, Simon. That is what we think, too. And we even think we know what the Call might be."

From her seat by the far wall, Aditu suddenly laughed, a clear, musical trill like falling water. "So you did remember to give it to them, Seoman. I was afraid you might forget. You were very tired and sad when we parted."

"Give it to them?" said Simon, confused. "What . . . ?" He stopped short. "The horn!"

"The horn," Josua said. "Amerasu's gift to us, a gift we could see no use for."

"But how does that fit with the call-bearer's name . . . ?" Simon asked.

"It was under our noses, so to speak," Tiamak said. "When Isgrimnur found Camaris at the inn in Kwanitupul, he was called 'Ceallio'—that means 'shout' or 'call' in the Perdruinese tongue. The famous horn of Camaris was named 'Cellian,' which is the same thing in the Nabbanai tongue."

Aditu rose, smoothly as a hawk taking wing. "It was called Cellian by mortals only. It has a far older name than that—its true name, its name of Making. The horn that Amerasu sent you belonged to the Sithi long before your Camaris sounded it in battle. It is called *Ti-tuno.*"

"But how did it come to be in Camaris' hands?" Miriamele asked. "And if he had it, how did the Sithi get it back again?"

"I can answer the first part of your question easily," Aditu told her. "Ti-tuno was made of the dragon Hidohebhi's tooth, the black worm that Hakatri and Ineluki slew. When Prince Sinnach of the mortal Hernystiri came to our aid before the battle of Ach Samrath, Iyu'unigato of Year-Dancing House gave it to him as a token of gratitude, a gift from friend to friend."

When Aditu paused, Binabik looked for her permission to continue. When she nodded, he spoke. "Many centuries after Asu'a was falling, when John came to his power in Erkynland, he was having the chance to make the Hernystiri his vassals. He did not choose to do that thing, and in gratitude King Llythinn sent the horn Ti-tuno as part of Ebekah's bridal dower when she was sent for being Prester John's wife." He raised his small hand in a gesture of gift giving. "Camaris was guarding her on that journey, and brought her with safety to Erkynland. John was finding his Hernystiri bride so beautiful that he gave the horn to Camaris to commemorate the day of her coming to the Hayholt." He waved his hand again, a broader flourish, as though he had painted a picture he now wished the others to admire. "As for how it was returned to Amerasu and the Sithi—well, perhaps that is a story Camaris himself can be telling to us. But that is where it was brought from: the 'ship on the shallowest sea.'"

"I do not understand that part," Isgrimnur said.

Aditu smiled. "Jao é-Tinukai'i means 'Boat on the Ocean of Trees.' It is hard to imagine an ocean shallower than one with no water."

Simon was growing confused by the flood of words and the changing litany of speakers. "What do you mean when you say Camaris can tell the story, Binabik? I thought Camaris couldn't talk—that he was mute, or mad, or under a spell."

"Perhaps he is being all those things," the troll replied. "But it is also perhaps true that the last line of the poem is speaking to us about Camaris himself—that when these things are brought together, he will be then released from the prison of sorts that he is in. We hope it will be bringing back his wits."

Again the room fell silent for several heartbeats.

"Of course," Josua added at last, "there is still the problem of how that will come to be, if the second-to-last line is to be believed." He held up his arms— his left hand with Elias' manacle still clasped about the wrist, his right arm that ended in a leather-clad stump. "As you can see," he said, "the one thing this prince does *not* have is a right hand." He allowed himself a mocking grin. "But we hope that it is not meant to be taken word for word. Perhaps just bringing them into my presence will do the trick."

"I tried to show Camaris the blade Thorn once already," Isgrimnur remembered. "Thought it might jog his mind, if you see my meaning. But he wouldn't go near it. Acted like it was a poisonous snake. Pulled free and walked right out of the room." He paused. "But maybe when everything is together, the horn and all, maybe then . . ."

"Well?" said Miriamele. "Why don't we try it, then?"

"Because we can't," Josua said grimly. "We have lost the horn."

"What?" Simon looked up to see if, improbably, the prince might be joking. "How can that be?"

"It vanished sometime during the battle with Fengbald," Josua said. "It is one of the reasons I wanted you here, Simon. I thought you might have taken it back for safekeeping."

Simon shook his head. "I was glad to be rid of it, Prince Josua. I was so afraid that I had doomed us all by forgetting to give it to you. No, I haven't seen it."

No one else in the tent had either. "So," Josua said at last. "We must search for it, then—but quietly. If there is a traitor in our midst, or even just a thief, we must not let him know that it is an important thing or we may never recover it."

Aditu laughed again. This time it seemed shockingly out of place. "I am sorry," she said, "but this is something that the rest of the Zida'ya would never believe. To have lost Ti-tuno!"

"It's not funny," Simon growled. "Besides, can't you use some magic or something to locate it?"

Aditu shook her head. "Things do not work that way, Seoman. I tried to explain that to you once before. And I am sorry to laugh. I will help look for it."

She didn't look very sorry, Simon thought. But if he couldn't understand mortal women, how could he ever in a thousand years hope to understand Sithi women?

The company slowly filed out of Josua's tent, talking quietly among themselves. Simon waited for Miriamele outside. When she emerged, he fell in beside her.

"So they are going to give Camaris back his memories." Miriamele looked distracted and tired, as though she had not slept much the night before.

"If we can find the horn, I suppose we'll try." Simon was secretly quite pleased that Miriamele had been present to see how involved he was in Prince Josua's counsels.

Miriamele turned to look at him, her expression accusatory. "And what if he doesn't want those memories back?" she demanded. "What if he is happy now, for the first time in his life?"

Simon was startled, but could think of no reply. They walked back across the settlement in silence until Miriamele said good-bye and went off to walk by herself. Simon was left wondering at what she had said. Did Miriamele, too, have memories that she would be just as happy to lose?

Josua was standing in the garden behind Leavetaking House when Miriamele found him. He was staring into the sky, across which the clouds were drawn in long ribbons like torn linen.

"Uncle Josua?"

He turned. "Miriamele. It is a pleasure to see you."

"You like to come here, don't you?"

"I suppose I do." He nodded slowly. "It is a place to think. I worry too much about Vorzheva—about our child and what kind of a world it will live in—to feel very comfortable most places."

"And you miss Deornoth."

Josua turned his gaze back to the cloud-strewn sky again. "I miss him, yes. But more importantly, I want to make his sacrifice worthwhile. If our defeat of Fengbald *means* something, then it will be easier for me to live with his death." The prince sighed. "He was still young, compared to me—he had not seen thirty summers."

Miriamele watched her uncle in silence for a long while before speaking. "I need to ask you a favor, Josua."

He extended his hand, indicating one of the time-worn benches. "Please. Ask me whatever you wish."

She took a deep breath. "When you . . . when we come to the Hayholt, I want to speak to my father."

Josua tilted his head, raising his eyebrows so that his high, smooth forehead creased. "What do you mean, Miriamele?"

"There will be a time before any final siege when you and he will talk," she said hurriedly, as though speaking words that had been practiced. "There has to be, no matter how bloody the fighting. He is your brother, and you will speak to him. I wish to be there."

Josua hesitated. "I am not certain that would be wise. . . ."

"And," Miriamele continued, determined to have her say, "I wish to speak to him alone."

"Alone?" The prince shook his head, taken aback. "Miriamele, such a thing cannot be! If we are able to lay siege to the Hayholt, your father will be a desperate man. How could I leave you alone with him—I would be giving you over as a hostage!"

"That's not important," she said stubbornly. "I must speak with him, Uncle Josua. I *must!*"

He bit back a sharp reply; when he spoke, it was gently. "And why must you, Miriamele?"

"I cannot tell you. But I must. It could make a difference—a very great difference!"

"Then you must tell me, my niece. For if you do not, I can only say no; I cannot allow you alone with your father."

Tears glistened in Miriamele's eyes. She angrily wiped them away. "You don't understand. It's something I can only talk to him about. And I must! Please, Josua, please!"

A weary anguish seemed to settle on his features like the work of long years. "I know you are not frivolous, Miriamele. But neither do you have the lives of hundreds, maybe thousands, weighing down your decisions. If you cannot tell me what you feel is so important—and I believe that you think it is true—then I certainly cannot let you risk your life for it, and perhaps the lives of many others as well."

She stared at him intently. The tears were gone, replaced by a cold, dispassionate mask. "Please reconsider, Josua." She gestured toward Deornoth's cairn. A few blades of grass were already growing up between the stones. "Remember your friend, Uncle Josua, and all the things you wish you had said to *him.*"

He shook his head in frustration. The sunlight showed that his brown hair was thinning near the top. "By Aedon's blood, I cannot allow it, Miriamele. Be angry at me if you must, but surely you can see that I have no other choice." His own voice grew a little more chill. "When your father surrenders at last, I will do everything I can to see that he is not harmed. If it is within my power, you will have a chance to speak with him. That is the most I can promise."

"It will be too late then." She rose from the bench and walked rapidly back across the garden.

Josua watched her go; then, as motionless as if he were rooted to the ground, he watched a sparrow flutter down to alight briefly atop the cairn of stones. After a few bouncing steps and a chain of piping notes, it rose again and flew away. He let its departure lift his gaze back to the streaming clouds.

"Simon!"

He turned. Sangfugol was hurrying across the damp grass.

"Simon, may I talk to you?" The harper pulled up, breathing heavily. His hair was mussed and his clothing seemed to have been thrown on without a thought for color or style, which was very unusual; even in the days of exile, Simon had never seen the musician looking quite this unkempt.

"Certainly."

"Not here." Sangfugol looked around furtively, although there was no one in sight. "Somewhere where we won't be overheard. Your tent?"

Simon nodded, puzzled. "If you wish."

They walked through the tent city. Several of the residents waved or called greetings to them as they passed. The harper seemed almost to flinch each time, as though every person was a potential source of danger. At last they reached Simon's tent and found Binabik just preparing to go out. As the troll pulled on his fur-lined boots, he chatted amiably about the missing horn—the hunt had been afoot for three days, and was still unsuccessful—and other topics. Sangfugol was quite visibly anxious for him to leave, a fact which Binabik could not help noticing; he cut short the conversation, made his farewells, then went off to join Geloë and the rest.

When the troll was gone, Sangfugol let out a sigh of released tension and sank to the floor of the tent, unmindful of the dirt. Simon was beginning to be alarmed. Something was very wrong indeed.

"What is it?" he asked. "You seem frightened."

The harper leaned close, his voice a conspiratorial near-whisper. "Binabik says they are still searching for that horn. Josua seems to want it very much."

Simon shrugged. "No one knows if it will do any good. It's for Camaris. They hope it will bring him back to his senses somehow."

"That doesn't make sense." The harper shook his head. "How could a horn do something like that?"

"*I* don't know," Simon said impatiently. "What is so important that you needed to talk about?"

"I imagine that when they find the thief, the prince will be very angry."

"I'm sure they'll hang him on the wall of Leavetaking House," Simon said in irritation, then stopped as he saw the expression of horror on Sangfugol's face. "What's wrong? Merciful Aedon, Sangfugol, did *you* steal it?"

"No, no!" the harper said shrilly. "I didn't, I swear!"

Simon stared at him.

"But," Sangfugol said at last, his voice trembling with shame, "but I know where it is."

"What?! Where?"

"I have it in my tent." The harper said this in the doomful voice of a condemned martyr forgiving his executioners.

"How could that be? Why is it in your tent? And you didn't take it?"

"Aedon's mercy, Simon, I swear I didn't. I found it in with Towser's things after he died. I . . . I loved that old man, Simon. In my way. I know he was a drunkard, and that sometimes I talked as though I wanted to knock his head in. But he was good to me when I was young . . . and, curse it, I *miss* him."

Despite the sadness of the harper's words, Simon was losing patience again. "But why did you keep it? Why didn't you tell anybody?"

"I just wanted something of his, Simon." He was as ashamed and sorrowful as a wet cat. "I buried my second lute with him. I thought he wouldn't have minded . . . I thought the horn was his!" He reached out to grab Simon's wrist, thought better, and pulled his hand back. "Then, by the time I realized what all the fuss and searching was for, I was afraid to admit that I had it. It will seem like I stole from Towser when he was dead. I would never do that, Simon!"

Simon's moment of anger faded. The harper seemed close to tears. "You should have told," he said gently. "No one would have thought ill of you. Now we had better go speak to Josua."

"Oh, no! He'll be furious! No, Simon, why don't I just give it to you—then you can say that *you* found it. You'll be the hero."

Simon considered for a moment. "No," he said at last. "I don't think that would be a good idea. For one thing, I'd have to lie to Prince Josua about where I found it. What if I told him I found it somewhere, then it turned out they'd already looked there. It would seem like *I* stole it." He shook his head emphatically. For once, it hadn't been Simon who had made the mooncalf mistake. He was in no hurry to take this particular blame. "In any case, Sangfugol, it won't be as bad as you think. I'll come with you. Josua's not like that—you know him."

"He told me once that if I sang 'Woman from Nabban' again he'd have my head off." Sangfugol, the worst of his fear past, was dangerously close to sulking.

"And well he should have," Simon replied. "We're all tired of that song." He stood and extended a hand to the harper. "Now get up and let's go see the prince. If only you hadn't waited so long to tell, this would be easier."

Sangfugol shook his head miserably. "It just seemed easier not to say anything. I kept thinking I could take it out and leave it somewhere that it would be found, but then I got frightened that someone would catch me at it, even if I did it in the middle of the night." He took a deep breath. "I haven't slept the last two nights for worrying."

"Well, you'll feel better once you've talked to Josua. Come on, up now."

When they emerged from the tent, the harper stood for a moment in the sun, then wrinkled his thin nose. He offered a weak smile, as though he scented possible redemption in the damp morning air. "Thank you, Simon," he said. "You are a good friend."

Simon made a noise of mocking derision, then clapped the harper on the shoulder. "Let's talk to him now, when he's just eaten breakfast. *I'm* always in a better mood when I've just eaten—maybe it works for princes, too."

They all gathered at Leavetaking House after the midday meal. Josua stood solemnly before the altar of stone on which Thorn still lay. Simon could feel the prince's tension.

The others gathered in the hall talked quietly among themselves. The conversations seemed strained, but silence in the great room might have been even more daunting. The sunlight streamed through the doorway, but did not reach the room's farthest reaches. The place seemed a kind of chapel, and Simon could not help wondering if they would see a miracle. If they could bring back Camaris' wits, the senses and memories of a man forty years gone from the world, would it not be a sort of raising of the dead?

He remembered what Miriamele said and had to repress a shiver. Perhaps it was wrong, somehow. Perhaps Camaris was indeed meant to be left alone.

Josua was turning the dragon's-tooth horn over and over in his hands, looking distractedly at the inscriptions. When it had been brought to him, he had not been as angry as Sangfugol had feared, but instead openly puzzled as to why Towser might have taken the horn and hidden it away. Josua had even been so generous, once his initial flash of annoyance had passed, as to invite Sangfugol to stay and witness whatever might happen. But the harper, reprieved, wanted nothing more to do with the horn or the doings of princes; he had returned to his bed to get some much-needed rest.

Now there was a stir among the dozen or so gathered in the hall as Isgrimnur entered leading Camaris. The old man, dressed in formal shirt and hose like a child who had been readied for church, stepped inside and looked around squinting, as if trying to see the nature of the trap into which he was being led. It did seem almost as though he had been brought to answer for some criminal act: those who waited in the hall stared at his face as though memorizing it. Camaris looked more than a little frightened.

Miriamele had said that the old man had been door warden and man-of-all-work at a hostel in Kwanitupul, and not particularly well treated there, Simon remembered; perhaps he thought he was to be punished for something. Certainly, from his nervous, sidelong glances, Camaris looked as though he would rather be anywhere than this place.

"Here, Sir Camaris." Josua lifted Thorn from the altar—by the ease with which he hefted it, it must have seemed light as a twig; remembering the sword's changing character, Simon wondered what this meant. He had thought once that the sword had wishes of its own, that it cooperated only when going where and doing what it desired. Was this its goal, now almost in reach? To return to its former master?

Prince Josua presented the blade to Camaris hilt first, but the old man would not take it. "Please, Sir Camaris—it is Thorn. It was yours, and still is."

The old man's expression became even more desperate. He stepped back, half-raising his hands as though to fend off an attack. Isgrimnur took his elbow and steadied him.

"All is well," the duke rumbled. "It's yours, Camaris."

"Sludig," Josua called. "Do you have the sword belt?"

The Rimmersman stepped forward, carrying a belt from which depended a heavy sheath of black leather studded with silver. With his master Isgrimnur's help, he strapped it around Camaris' waist. The old man did not resist. In fact, Simon thought, he might as well have been turned to stone. When they were finished, Josua carefully slid Thorn into the scabbard, so that its hilt came to rest in the space between Camaris' elbow and his loose white shirt.

"Now the horn, please," said Josua. Freosel, who had been holding it while the prince carried the blade, handed him the ancient horn. Josua slipped the baldric over Camaris' head so that the horn hung beside his right hand, then stepped back. The long-bladed sword seemed made to fit its tall owner. A shaft of sunlight from the doorway glinted in the knight's white hair. There was an unquestionable *rightness* to it; everyone in the room could see it. Everyone except the old man himself.

"He's not doing anything," Sludig said quietly to Isgrimnur. Simon again had the impression of attending a religious service—but now it felt as though the sexton had neglected to put out the reliquary, or the priest had forgotten part of the mansa. Everyone was caught up in the embarrassing pause.

"Perhaps if we are reading the poem?" Binabik suggested.

"Yes." Josua nodded. "Please read it."

Binabik instead pushed Tiamak forward. The Wrannaman held up the parchment in a trembling hand and, in an equally unsteady voice, read Nisses' poem.

> "*. . . When Blayde, Call, and Man,*"

he finished in firmer tones—he had gained courage with each line,

> "*Come to Prince's right Hande*
> *Then the Prisoned shall once more go Free . . .*"

Tiamak stopped and looked up. Camaris stared back at him, offering a faintly wounded look to the companion of many weeks who was now doing this inexplicable thing to him. The old knight might have been a dog expected to perform some degrading trick for a previously kind master.

Nothing had changed. A shock of disappointment went through the room.

"We have perhaps been making some mistake," Binabik said slowly. "We shall have to be at studying it further."

"No." Josua's voice was harsh. "I don't believe that." He stepped up to Camaris and lifted the horn to the level of the old man's eyes. "Don't you recognize this? This is Cellian! Its call used to strike fear into the hearts of my father's enemies! Sound it, Camaris!" He moved it toward the old man's lips. "We need you to come back!"

With a hunted look, a look almost of terror, Camaris pushed Josua away. So unexpected was the old man's strength that the prince stumbled and nearly fell before Isgrimnur caught him. Sludig snarled and took a step toward Camaris as though he might strike the old knight.

"Leave him be, Sludig!" Josua snapped. "If anyone is at fault here, it is me. What right do I have to trouble a simple-minded old man?" Josua bunched his fist and stared at the stone tiles for a moment. "Perhaps we *should* leave him be. He fought his battles—we should fight ours and leave him to rest."

"He never turned his back on any fight, Josua," said Isgrimnur. "I knew him, remember. He always did what was right, what was . . . needful. Don't give up so easily."

Josua lifted his gaze to the old man's face. "Very well. Camaris, come with me." He gently took his elbow. "Come with me," he said again, then turned and led the unresisting knight toward the door that led to the garden behind the hall.

Outside the afternoon was growing chill. A light mist of rain had darkened the ancient walls and stone benches. The rest of the company gathered in the doorway, uncertain of what the prince meant to do.

Josua led Camaris to the pile of stones that marked Deornoth's grave. He lifted the old man's hand and placed it on the cairn, then pressed his own down atop the knight's.

"Sir Camaris," he said slowly. "Please listen to me. The land that my father tamed, the order that you and King John built, is being torn to pieces by war and sorcery. Everything you worked for in your life is threatened, and if we fail this time, I fear there will be no rebuilding.

"Beneath these stones my friend is buried. He was a knight, as you. Sir Deornoth never met you, but the songs of your life he heard as a child led him to me. 'Make me a knight, Josua,' he told me on the day I first saw him. 'I wish to serve as Camaris served. I wish to be your tool and God's, for the betterment of our people and our land.'

"That is what he said, Camaris." Josua laughed abruptly. "He was a fool—a holy fool. And he found out, of course, that sometimes the land and people do not seem worth saving. But he took a vow before God that he would do what was right and he lived all his days in an effort to measure up to that pledge."

Josua's voice rose. He had found some wellspring of feeling within himself; the words came tumbling out, strong and effortless. "He died defending this place—a single battle, a single skirmish took his life, yet without him, the chance of a greater victory would have been lost long ago. He died as he lived, trying to do what was not humanly possible, blaming himself when he failed, then getting up and trying again. He died for this land, Camaris, the same land that you fought for, the order that you struggled to create, where the weak could live their lives in peace, protected from those who would use strength to force their wishes on others." The prince leaned close to Camaris' face, catching and holding the old man's reluctant gaze. "Will his death mean nothing? For if we do not win this fight, there will be too many graves for one more to make a difference, and there will be no one left to mourn for people like Deornoth."

Josua's fingers tightened on the knight's hand. "Come back to us, Camaris. Please. Don't let his death be meaningless. Think of the battles of your time, battles I know you would prefer not to have fought, but did because the cause was just and fair. Must all that suffering become meaningless, too? *This is our last chance.* After us comes darkness."

The prince abruptly let go of the old man's hand and turned away, eyes glistening. Simon, watching from the doorway, felt his own heart catch.

Camaris still stood as if frozen, his fingers splayed atop Deornoth's cairn. At last he turned and looked down at himself, then slowly raised the horn and stared at it for a long time, as though it were something never before seen on the green earth. He closed his eyes, lifted it carefully to his lips with shaking hand, and blew.

The horn sounded. Its first thin note grew and strengthened, becoming louder and louder until it seemed to shake the very air, a shout that seemed to have the clash of steel and the thunder of hooves in it. Camaris, his eyes squeezed shut, sucked in a deep breath and blew again, louder this time. The piercing call winded out across the hillside and reverberated in the valley; the echoes chased themselves through the air. Then the noise died away.

Simon discovered he had his hands over his ears. Many others in the company had done the same.

Camaris was staring at the horn again. He lifted up his face to those who watched him. Something had changed. His eyes had become deeper somehow, sadder: there was a glint of awareness that had not been there before. His mouth worked, striving for speech, but no sound came out except a rasping hiss. Camaris looked down at the hilt of Thorn. With slow and deliberate movements, he drew it from the scabbard and held it up before him, a line of glinting black that seemed to slice right through the light of the failing afternoon. Tiny drops of misty rain gathered on the blade.

"*I . . . should have known . . . that my . . . torment was not yet finished, my guilt not forgiven.*" His voice was painfully dry and rough, his speech strangely formal. "Oh, my God, my loving and terrible God, I am humble before You. I shall serve out my punishment."

The old man fell to his knees before the astonished company. For a long time, he said nothing, but seemed to be praying. Tears ran down his cheeks, merging with the raindrops to make his face shine in the slanting sunlight. Finally, Camaris clambered to his feet and allowed Isgrimnur and Josua to lead him away.

Simon felt something tugging at his arm. He looked down. Binabik's small fingers had caught his sleeve. The troll's eyes were bright. "Do you know, Simon, it is what we had all forgotten. Sir Deornoth's men, the soldiers of Naglimund, do you know what they were calling him? 'The prince's right hand.' And even Josua did not remember, I am thinking. Luck . . . or something else, friend Simon." The little man squeezed Simon's arm again, then hurried after the prince.

Overwhelmed, Simon turned, trying to catch a last glimpse of Camaris. Miriamele was standing near the doorway. She caught Simon's eyes and gave him an angry look that seemed to say: *you are to blame for this, too.*

She turned and followed Camaris and the others back into Leavetaking House, leaving Simon alone in the rainy garden.

24

A Sky Full of Beasts

Four strong men, sweating despite the cold night breeze and panting from the exertion of heaving the covered litter up the narrow stairway, carefully lifted out the chair containing the litter's passenger and carried it to the middle of the rooftop garden. The man in the chair was so swaddled in furs and robes as to be practically unrecognizable, but the tall, elegantly dressed woman immediately rose from her own seat and came forward with a glad cry.

"Count Streáwe!" said the dowager duchess. "I'm so glad you could come. And on such a chill evening."

"Nessalanta, my dear. Only an invitation from you would bring me out in such ghastly weather." The count took her gloved hand in his own and drew it to his lips. "Forgive me for being so discourteous as to remain seated."

"Nonsense." Nessalanta snapped her fingers at the count's bearers and indicated they should bring his chair closer to hers. She seated herself again. "Although I think it is growing a little warmer. Nevertheless, you are a jewel, a splendid jewel for coming tonight."

"The pleasure of your company, dear lady." Streáwe coughed into his kerchief.

"It will be worth your while, I promise." She gestured floridly at the star-sprinkled sky as though she herself had commanded it spread before them. "Look at this! You will be so glad you came. Xannasavin is a brilliant man."

"My lady is too kind," said a voice from the stairwell. Count Streáwe, somewhat limited in his mobility, craned his neck awkwardly to see the speaker.

The man who emerged from the entranceway onto the rooftop garden was tall and thin, with long fingers clasped as though in prayer. He wore a great curling beard of gray-shot black. His robes, too, were dark, and bespotted with Nabbanai star symbols. He moved between the rows of potted trees and shrubs with a certain storklike grace, then bent his long legs to kneel before the dowager duchess. "My lady, I received your summons with great pleasure. It is always a joy to serve you." He turned to Streáwe. "The Duchess Nessalanta would have been a splendid astrologer, had she not her greater duties to Nabban. She is a woman of great insight."

Beneath his hood, Perdruin's count smiled. "This is known to all."

Something in Streáwe's voice made the duchess hesitate for a moment before she spoke. "Xannasavin is too kind. I have studied a few rudiments only." She crossed her hands demurely before her breast.

"Ah, but could I have had you for an apprentice," Xannasavin said, "the mysteries that we might have plumbed, Duchess Nessalanta. . . ." His voice was deep and impressive. "Does my lady wish me to start?"

Nessalanta, who had been watching his lips move, shook herself as though suddenly coming awake. "Ah. No, Xannasavin, not yet. We must wait for my eldest son."

Streáwe looked at her with real interest. "I did not know that Benigaris was a follower of the mysteries of the stars."

"He is interested," Nessalanta said carefully. "He is . . ." She looked up. "Ah, he is here!"

Benigaris strode onto the rooftop. Two guards, their surcoats kingfisher-blazed, followed a few paces behind him. The reigning duke of Nabban was going a little to fat around the middle, but was still a tall, broad-shouldered man. His mustache was so luxuriant as to hide his mouth almost entirely.

"Mother," he said curtly as he reached the small gathering. He took her gloved hand and nodded, then turned to the count. "Streáwe. I missed you at dinner last night."

The count lifted his kerchief to his lips and coughed. "My apologies, good Benigaris. My health, you know. Sometimes it is just too difficult for me to leave my room, even for hospitality as famed as that of the Sancellan Mahist-revis."

Benigaris grunted. "Well, then you probably shouldn't be out here on this freezing roof." He turned to Nessalanta. "What *are* we doing here, Mother?"

The dowager duchess put on a look of girlish hurt. "Why, you know perfectly well what we are doing here. This is a very favorable night to read the stars, and Xannasavin is going to tell us what the next year will bring."

"If you so desire, Highness." Xannasavin bowed to the duke.

"I can *tell* you what the next year will bring," Benigaris growled. "Trouble and more trouble. Everywhere I turn there are problems." He looked to Streáwe. "You know how it is. They want bread, the peasants do, but if I give it to them they just want more. I tried to bring in some of those swamp men to help work the grain fields—I have had to expend a lot of soldiers in those border skirmishes with the Thrithings savages and now all the barons are screaming about having their peasants levied and their fields fallow—but the damnable little brown men won't come! What am I to do, send troops into that cursed swamp? I'm better off without them."

"How well do I know the burdens of leadership," Streáwe said sympathetically. "You have been doing a heroic job in difficult times, I am told."

Benigaris jerked his head in acknowledgment. "And then those damned, damned, thrice-damned Fire Dancers, setting themselves on fire and frightening the common folk." His expression turned dark. "I should never have trusted Pryrates. . . ."

"I'm sorry, Benigaris," said Streáwe. "I didn't hear you—my old ears, you know. Pryrates . . . ?"

The Duke of Nabban looked at the count. His eyes narrowed. "Never mind. Anyway, it's been a filthy year, and I doubt the next will be any better." A sour smile moved his mustache. "Unless I convince some of the troublemakers here in Nabban to become Fire Dancers. There are more than a few that I think would look very good in flames."

Streáwe laughed, then broke into a fit of dry coughing. "Very good, Benigaris, very good."

"Enough of this," Nessalanta said pettishly. "I think you are wrong, Benigaris—it should be a splendid year. Besides, there is no need to speculate. Xannasavin will tell you everything you need to know."

"I am but a humble observer of the celestial patterns, Duchess," the astrologer said. "But I will do my best. . . ."

"And if you can't come up with something better than the year I've just gone through," Benigaris muttered, "I may just toss you off the roof."

"Benigaris!" Nessalanta's voice, which had so far been wheedling and childlike, turned suddenly sharp as the crack of a drover's whip. "You will not speak that way before me! You will *not* threaten Xannasavin! Do you understand!?"

Benigaris almost imperceptibly flinched. "It was only a jest. Aedon's Holy Blood, Mother, don't take on so." He walked to the half-canopied chair with the ducal crest and sat down heavily. "Go on, man," he grunted, waving at Xannasavin. "Tell us what wonders the stars hold."

The astrologer pulled a sheaf of scrolls from his voluminous robe, brandishing them with a certain drama. "As the duchess mentioned," he began, his voice smooth and practiced, "tonight is an excellent night for divination. Not only are the stars in a particularly favorable configuration, but the sky itself is clear of storms and other hindrances." He smiled at Duke Benigaris. "An auspicious sign in and of itself."

"Continue," said the duke.

Xannasavin lifted a furled scroll and pointed up at the wheel of stars. "As you can see, Yuvenis' Throne is directly overhead. The Throne is, of course, much tied to the ruling of Nabban, and has been since the old heathen days. When the lesser lights are moving through its aspect, the heirs of the Imperium do well to take notice." He paused for a moment to let the import of this sink in. "Tonight you can see that the Throne is upright, and that on its topmost edge, the Serpent and Mixis the Wolf are particularly bright." He swung around and pointed to another part of the sky. "The Falcon, there, and the Winged Beetle are now visible in the southern sky. The Beetle always brings change."

"It is like one of the old Imperators' private menageries," Benigaris said impatiently. "Beasts, beasts, beasts. What does it all mean?"

"It means, my lord, that there are great times ahead for the Benidrivine House."

"I knew it," Nessalanta purred. "I knew it."

"What tells you that?" Benigaris asked, squinting at the sky.

"I could not do justice to your majesties by trying to make an explanation that was too brief," the astrologer said smoothly. "Suffice it to say that the stars, which have long spoken of hesitation, of unsureness and doubt, now proclaim that a time of change is coming. Great change."

"But that could be anything," Benigaris grumbled. "That could mean the whole city burned down."

"Ah, but that is only because you have not heard all that I have to say. There are two other factors, factors most important. One is the Kingfisher itself—there, do you see it?" Xannasavin gestured toward a point in the eastern sky. "It is far brighter than I have ever seen it—and at this time of year it is generally quite hard to see. Your family's fortunes have long risen and fallen with the waxing and waning of the Kingfisher's light, and it has not been so gloriously illuminated before in my lifetime. Something of great moment is about to happen to the Benidrivine House, my lord. Your house."

"And the other?" Benigaris appeared to be growing interested. "The other thing you mentioned?"

"Ah." The astrologer unrolled one of his scrolls and examined it. "That is something that you cannot see at this moment. There will be a reappearance soon of the Conqueror Star."

"The bearded star that we saw last year and the year before?" It was Streáwe who spoke, his voice eager. "The great red thing?"

"That is the one."

"But when it came, it frightened the common folk out of their shallow wits!" Benigaris said. "I think that is what started all this doom-saying nonsense in the first place!"

Xannasavin nodded. "The celestial signs are often misread, Duke Benigaris. The Conqueror Star will return, but it is not a precursor of disaster, merely of change. Throughout history it has come to herald a new order appearing out of conflict and chaos. It trumpeted the end of the Imperium, and shone over the final days of Khand."

"And this is good!?" Benigaris shouted. "You are saying that something which speaks of the downfall of an empire should make me happy!?" He seemed ready to leap from his chair and manhandle the astrologer.

"But my lord, remember the Kingfisher!" Xannasavin said hurriedly. "How could these changes be to your dismay when the Kingfisher is burning so brightly? No, my lord, pardon your humble servant for seeming to instruct you in any way, but can you think of no situation in which a great empire might fall, yet the fortunes of the Benidrivine House might improve?"

Benigaris sat back swiftly, as though repelled by a blow. He stared at his hands. "I will talk to you of this later," he said at last. "Leave us now for a while."

Xannasavin bowed. "As you wish, my lord." He bowed again, this time in the direction of Streáwe. "A pleasure to meet you at last, Count. I have been honored."

The count absently bobbed his head, as lost in thought as Benigaris.

Xannasavin kissed Nessalanta's hand, swept the rooftop with a low bow, then stowed his scrolls once more and walked to the stairwell. His footsteps gradually dwindled down into echoing darkness.

"Do you see?" Nessalanta asked. "Do you see why I value him so? He is a brilliant man."

Streáwe nodded. "He is most imposing. And you have found him reliable?"

"Absolutely. He predicted my poor husband's death." Her face assumed a look of profound sorrow. "But Leobardis would not listen, despite all my warnings. I told him if he set foot on Erkynlandish soil, I would never see him again. He told me it was nonsense."

Benigaris looked at his mother sharply. "Xannasavin told you Father would die?"

"He did. If only your father had listened."

Count Streáwe cleared his throat. "Well, I had hoped to save these matters for a different time, Benigaris, but hearing what your astrologer had to say—hearing of the splendid future he sees for you—I think perhaps I should share my thoughts with you now."

Benigaris turned from his dissatisfied contemplation of his mother to the count. "What are you talking about?"

"Certain things I have learned." The old man looked around. "Ah, forgive me, Benigaris, but would it be an imposition to ask your guards to step back out of hearing?" He made a crabbed gesture toward the two armored men, who had stood motionless and silent as stone throughout the proceedings. Benigaris grunted and gestured them back.

"So?"

"I have, as you know, many sources of information," the count began. "I hear many things that even others more powerful than myself are not able to discover. Recently I have heard some things that you might wish to know. About Elias and his war with Josua. About . . . other things." He paused and looked to the duke expectantly.

Nessalanta, too, was sitting forward. "Go on, Streáwe. You know how much we value your counsel."

"Yes," Benigaris said, "go on. I will be very interested to discover what you have heard."

The count smiled, a vulpine grin that showed his still-bright teeth. "Ah, yes," he said. "You *will* be interested. . . ."

Eolair did not recognize the Sitha who stood in the doorway of the Hall of Carvings. He was dressed conservatively, at least in Sithi terms, in shirt and breeches of a pale creamy cloth that shimmered like silk. His hair was nut-brown—the closest to a human shade the count had yet seen—and had been pulled into a knot on top of his head.

"Likimeya and Jiriki say that you must come to them." The stranger's Hernystiri was as awkward and as archaic as that of the dwarrows. "Must you wait for a moment, or is it that you can come now? It is good that you come now."

Eolair heard Craobhan take a breath as if to protest the summons, but the count laid a hand on his arm. It was only this immortal's imperfect speech that made it sound peremptory—Eolair guessed that the Sithi would wait for him for days without impatience.

"One of your people, a healer, is with the king's daughter—with Maegwin," he told the messenger. "I must talk to her. Then I will come."

The Sitha, face impassive, bobbed his head swiftly in the manner of a cormorant seizing a fish from a river. "I will tell to them." He turned and left the room, his booted feet soundless on the wooden floors.

"Are they the masters here now?" Craobhan asked irritatedly. "Should we step to their measures?"

Eolair shook his head. "That is not their way, old friend. Jiriki and his mother simply wish to speak to me, I am sure. Not all of them speak our tongue as well as those two."

"I still do not like it. We had to live with Skali's boot on our necks long enough—when are the Hernystiri going to take their rightful place in their own land again?"

"Things are changing," Eolair said mildly. "But we have always survived. Five centuries ago, Fingil's Rimmersmen drove us into the hills and the seacliffs. We came back. Skali's men are on the run now, so we have outlasted them, too. The weight of the Sithi is a far easier burden, don't you think?"

The old man stared at him, eyes wrinkling in a suspicious squint. At last, he smiled. "Ah, my good count, you should have been a priest or a general. You take the long view."

"As you do, Craobhan. Else you would not be here today to complain."

Before the old man could respond, another Sitha appeared in the doorway, this one a gray-haired woman dressed in green with a cloak of cloudy silver. Despite the color of her hair, she looked no older than the just-departed messenger.

"Kira'athu," the count said, rising. His voice lost its lightness. "Can you help her?"

The Sitha stared at him for a moment, then shook her head; the gesture seemed curiously unnatural, as though she had learned it from a book. "There is nothing wrong with her body. But her spirit is somehow hidden from me, gone deep inside, like a mouse when the owl's shadow is upon the night-fields."

"What does that mean?" Eolair struggled to keep impatience out of his words.

"Frightened. She is frightened. She is like a child who has seen its parents killed."

"She has seen much death. She has buried her father and her brother."

The Sitha-woman waved her fingers slowly, a gesture that Eolair could not translate. "It is not that. *Anyone,* Zida'ya or Sudhoda'ya—Dawn Child or mortal—who has lived enough years understands death. It is horrible, but it is understandable. But a child does not understand it. And something has come to the woman Maegwin in this way—something that is beyond her understanding. It has frightened her spirit."

"Will she get better? Is there anything you can do for her?"

"I can do nothing more. Her body is sound. Where the spirit goes, though, is another matter. I must think on this. Perhaps there is an answer I cannot see at this time."

It was difficult to read Kira'athu's high-boned, feline face, but Eolair did not think she sounded very hopeful. The count balled his fists and held them hard against his thighs. "And is there anything *I* can do?"

Something very much like pity showed in the Sitha's eyes. "If she has hidden her spirit deep enough, only the woman Maegwin can lead herself back. You cannot do it for her." She paused as though searching for words of solace. "Be kind. That is something." She turned and glided from the hall.

After a long silence, Old Craobhan spoke. "Maegwin's mad, Eolair."

The count held up his hand. "Don't."

"You can't change it by not listening. She grew worse while you were gone. I told you where we found her—up on Bradach Tor, raving and singing. She'd been sitting unprotected in the wind and snow for Mircha only knows how long. Said she'd seen the gods."

"Perhaps she did see them," Eolair said bitterly. "After all *I* have seen in this cursed twelve-month, who am I to doubt her? Perhaps it was too much for her. . . ." He stood, rubbing his wet palms on his breeches. "I will go now and meet Jiriki."

Craobhan nodded. His eyes were moist, but his mouth was set in a hard line. "Don't ruin yourself, Eolair. Don't give in. We need you even more than she does."

"When Isorn and the others come back," the count said, "tell them where I've gone. Ask them to wait up for me, if they would be so good—I don't think I will be too long with the Sithi." He looked out at the sky deepening toward twilight. "I want to talk to Isorn and Ule tonight." He patted the old man's shoulder before walking out of the Hall of Carvings.

"*Eolair.*"

He turned in the outer doorway to find Maegwin standing in the entrance hallway behind him. "My lady. How are you feeling?"

"Well," she said lightly, but her eyes belied her. "Where are you going?"

"I am going to see . . ." He caught himself. He had almost said "the gods." Was madness contagious? "I am going to speak with Jiriki and his mother."

"I do not know them," she said. "But I would like to go with you in any case."

"Go with me?" Somehow it seemed strange.

"Yes, Count Eolair. I would like to go with you. Is that so dreadful? We are not such dire enemies, surely?" There was a hollowness to her words, like a jest made on a gibbet's top step.

"Of course you may, my lady," he said hurriedly. "Maegwin. Of course."

Although Eolair could not discern any new additions to the Sithi camp that stretched across the broad expanse of Hern's Hill, still it seemed more intricate than it had just a few days before, more connected to the land. It looked as though, instead of the product of a few days' work, it had stood here since the hill was young. There was a quality of peace and soft, natural movement: the multicolored tent houses shifted and swayed like plants in an eddying stream. The count felt a moment of irritation, an echo of Craobhan's dissatisfaction. What right did the Sithi have to make themselves so comfortable here? Whose land was this, after all?

A moment later, he caught himself. It was just the nature of the Fair Ones. Despite their great cities, mere bat-haunted ruins now if Mezutu'a was any indication, they were people who were not rooted to a place. From the way Jiriki had talked about the Garden, their primordial home, it seemed clear that despite their eon-long tenancy in Osten Ard they still felt themselves to be little more than travelers in this land. They lived in their own heads, in their songs and memories. Hern's Hill was only another place.

Maegwin walked silently beside him, her features set as though she hid troubled thoughts. He remembered a time many years before when she had brought him to watch one of her beloved pigs give birth. Something had gone wrong, and near the end of the birthing the sow had begun to squeal in pain. By the time the two dead piglets had been removed, one still wrapped in the bloody umbilicus that had strangled it, the sow in her panic had rolled on one of her other newborns.

All through that blood-spattered nightmare, Maegwin had worn a look much like the one she bore now. Only when the sow had been saved and the rest of the litter were nursing had she allowed herself to break down and cry. Remembering, Eolair realized suddenly that it had been the last time she had let him hold her. Even as he had sorrowed for her, trying to understand her grief over the deaths of what to him were only animals, he had felt her in his arms, her breasts against him, and had realized that she was a woman now, for all her youth. It had been a strange feeling.

"Eolair?" There was just a hint of a tremor in Maegwin's voice. "May I ask you a question?"

"Certainly, Lady." He could not lose the memory of himself as he had held her, blood on their hands and clothes as they kneeled in the straw. He had not felt half so helpless then as he did now.

"How . . . how did you die?"

At first he thought he had misheard her. "I am sorry, Maegwin. How did I what?"

"How did you die? I am ashamed I have not asked you before. Was it the sort of death you deserved, a noble one? Oh, I hope it was not painful. I don't think I could bear that." She looked at him quickly, then broke into a shaky smile. "But of course that doesn't matter, for here you are! It is all behind us."

"How did I die?" The unreality of it struck him like a blow. He pulled at her arm and stopped. They were standing in an open stretch of grass with Likimeya's enclosure only a stone's throw away before them. "Maegwin, I am not dead. Feel me!" He extended his hand and took her cool fingers. "I am alive! So are you!"

"I was struck down just as the gods came," she said dreamily. "I think it was Skali—at least his ax being raised is the last thing I remember before I woke up here." She laughed shakily. "That's funny. Can you wake up in Heaven? Sometimes, since I have been here, it feels as though I sleep for a little while."

"Maegwin." He squeezed her hand. "Listen to me. We are not dead." Eolair felt himself about to weep and shook his head angrily. "You are still in Hernystir, the place where you were born."

Maegwin looked at him with a curious gleam in her eyes. For a moment the count thought he might have finally reached her. "Do you know, Eolair," she said slowly, "when I was alive, I was always frightened. Frightened that I would lose the things I cared about. I was even frightened to talk to you, the closest friend I ever had." She shook her head. Her hair streamed in the breeze moving across the hill, exposing her long pale neck. "I could not even tell you that I loved you, Eolair—loved you until it burned inside me. I was frightened that if I told you, you would push me away and I would not even have your friendship."

Eolair's heart felt as though it would crack right through, like a flawed stone struck by a hammer. "Maegwin, I . . . I didn't know." Did he love her, too? Would it help her to tell her he did, whether it was true or not? "I was . . . I was blind," he stammered. "I didn't know."

She smiled sadly. "It is no matter now," she said with terrible certainty. "It's too late to worry about such things." She clutched his hand and led him forward once more.

He took the last few steps toward the blue and purple of Likimeya's compound like a man arrow-shot in the dark, so surprised that he walks on without realizing he has been murdered.

Jiriki and his mother were in quiet but intense conversation when Eolair and Maegwin stepped through the ring of cloth. Likimeya still wore her armor; her son was attired in softer clothing.

Jiriki looked up. "Count Eolair. We are happy you could come. We have things to show you and tell you." His eyes lit on Eolair's companion. "Lady Maegwin. Welcome."

Eolair felt Maegwin tense, but she made a curtsy. "My Lord," she said. The count could not help wondering what she saw. If Jiriki was the sky-god

Brynioch, what did she make of his mother? What did she see when she looked at the rippling cloth all around them, the fruit trees and the dying afternoon light, at the alien faces of the other Sithi?

"Please sit." It was strange how musical Likimeya's voice was, for all its roughness. "Will you have refreshment?"

"Not for me, thank you." Eolair turned to Maegwin. She shook her head, but her eyes were distant, as though she were somehow pulling away from what lay before her.

"Then let us not wait," Likimeya said. "We have something to show you." She looked over to the brown-haired messenger who had earlier visited the Taig. This one stepped forward, lowering the sack that he held in his hands. With a deft movement, he unlaced the drawstring and turned it upside-down. Something dark rolled out onto the grass.

"Tears of Rhynn!" Eolair choked.

Skali's head lay before him, mouth open, eyes wide. The full yellow beard was now almost entirely crimson, stained by the gore that had wicked up from his severed neck.

"There is your enemy, Count Eolair," said Likimeya. A cat who had killed a bird might drop it at her master's feet with just such calm satisfaction. "He and a few dozen of his men turned at last, in the hills east of Grianspog."

"Take it away, please." Eolair felt his gorge rising. "I did not need to see him like this." For a moment he looked worriedly to Maegwin, but she was not even watching: her pale face was turned toward the darkening sky beyond the walls of the compound.

Unlike her flame-red hair, Likimeya's eyebrows were white, two streaks like narrow scars above her eyes. She raised one of them in a curiously human expression of mocking disbelief. "Your Prince Sinnach displayed his defeated enemies this way."

"That was five hundred years past!" Eolair recovered a little of his usual calm. "I am sorry, Mistress, but we mortals change in such a length of time. Our ancestors were perhaps fiercer than we are." He swallowed. "I have seen much death, but this was a surprise."

"We meant no offense." Likimeya gave Jiriki what appeared to be a significant glance. "We thought it would gladden your heart to see what came to the one who conquered and enslaved your people."

Eolair took a breath. "I understand. And I mean no offense either. We are grateful for your help. Grateful past telling." He could not help looking again at the blood-matted thing on the grass.

The messenger stooped and plucked Skali's head up by the hair and dropped it back into the sack. Eolair had to restrain an urge to ask what had happened to the rest of Sharp-nose. Probably left for the vultures somewhere in those cold eastern hills.

"That is good," replied Likimeya. "Because we wish your aid."

Eolair steadied himself. "What can we do?"

Jiriki turned to him. His face was blandly indifferent, even more so than usual. Had he disapproved somehow of his mother's gesture? Eolair pushed the thought aside. To try to understand the Sithi was to invite perplexity bordering on madness.

"Now that Skali is dead and the last of his troops scattered across the land, our purpose here is fulfilled," Jiriki said. "But we have only set our feet to the path. Now the journey begins in earnest."

As he spoke his mother reached behind her and drew out a jar, a squat but oddly graceful object glazed in dark blue. She reached two fingers into it and then withdrew them. The tips were stained gray-black.

"We told you that we cannot stop here," Jiriki continued. "We must go on to *Ujin e-d'a Sikhunae*—the place you call Naglimund."

Slowly, as if performing a ritual, Likimeya began to daub her face. She began by drawing dark lines down her cheeks and around her eyes.

"And . . . and what can the Hernystiri do?" Eolair asked. He was having trouble tearing his gaze away from Jiriki's mother.

The Sitha lowered his head for a moment, then raised it and held the count's eye, compelling him to pay attention. "By the blood that our two peoples have spilled for each other, I ask you to send a troop of your countrymen to join us."

"To join you?" Eolair thought of the shining, trumpeting charge of the Sithi. "What help could we possibly be?"

Jiriki smiled. "You underestimate yourselves—and you overestimate us. It is very important that we take the castle that once belonged to Josua, but it will be a fight like no other. Who knows what surprising part mortals may play when the Gardenborn fight? And there are things you can do that we cannot. We are few now. We need your folk, Eolair. We need you."

Likimeya had drawn a mask around her eyes, on her forehead and cheeks, so that her amber gaze seemed to flame in the darkness like jewels in a rock crevice. She drew three lines down from her bottom lip to her chin.

"I cannot compel my people, Jiriki," Eolair told him. "Especially after all that has happened to them. But if I go, I think that others would join me." He considered the needs of honor and duty. Revenge against Skali had been taken from him, but it seemed the Rimmersman had only been a catspaw for Elias—and for an even more frightening enemy. Hernystir was free, but the war was by no means ended. The count also found a certain seductiveness in the idea of something as straightforward as battle. The tangle of reoccupying Hernysadharc and coping with Maegwin's madness had already begun to overwhelm him.

The sky overhead was dark blue, the color of Likimeya's pot. Some of the Sithi produced globes of light which they set on wooden stands around the enclosure; the branches of the fruit trees, lit from below, burned golden.

"I will come with you to Naglimund, Jiriki," he said at last. Craobhan could watch over the folk of Hernysadharc, he decided, and watch over Maegwin and Lluth's wife Inahwen as well. Craobhan would continue the work of rebuilding the land—it was a task that would suit the old man perfectly. "I will bring as many of my fighting men as will come."

"Thank you, Count Eolair. The world is changing, but some things are always true. The hearts of the Hernystiri are constant."

Likimeya put down her pot, wiped her fingers on her boots—they left a broad smear—and stood up. By her face-painting, she had changed herself into something even more alien, more unsettling.

"Then it is agreed," she said. "When the third morning from tonight comes, we will ride to Ujin e-d'a Sikhunae." Her eyes seemed to spark in the light of the crystal globes.

Eolair could not brave her gaze for long, but neither could he still his curiosity. "Your pardon, Mistress," he said. "I hope I am not being impolite. May I ask what you have put on your face?"

"Ashes. Mourning ashes." She made a sound in the back of her throat, a thin exhalation that could have been a sigh or a huff of exasperation. "You cannot understand, mortal men, but I will tell you anyway. We go to war on the Hike-da'ya."

After a moment's pause, while Eolair tried to puzzle out what she meant, Jiriki spoke up. His voice was gentle, mournful. "Sithi and Norns are of a single blood, Count Eolair. Now we must fight them." He lifted a hand and made a gesture like a candle flame being extinguished—a flutter, then stillness. "We must kill members of our own family."

Maegwin was silent most of the way back. It was only when the Taig's sloping roofs loomed before them that she spoke.

"I am going with you. I will go to see the gods make war."

He shook his head violently. "You are going to stay here with Craobhan and the rest."

"No. If you leave me behind, I will follow you." Her voice was calm and certain. "And in any case, Eolair, what makes you sound so fearful? I cannot die twice, can I?" She laughed a little too loudly.

Eolair argued with her in vain. At last, just as he was on the verge of losing his temper, a thought came to him.

The healer said she must find her own way back. Perhaps this is part of it?

But the danger. Surely he could not think of letting her take such a risk. Not that he *could* stop her from following if he left her behind—mad or no, there was no one in all of Hernysadharc half as stubborn as Lluth's daughter. Gods, was he cursed? No wonder he almost longed for the brutal simplicity of battle.

"We will speak of this later," he said. "I am tired, Maegwin."

"No one should be tired in this place." There was a subtle note of triumph in her voice. "I worry about you, Eolair."

Simon had picked an open, unshaded spot near Sesuad'ra's outer wall. The sun was actually shining today, although it was windy enough that both he and Miriamele wore their cloaks. Still, it was pleasant to have his hood down and to feel the sun on his neck. "I brought some wine." Simon produced a skin bag and two cups from his sack. "Sangfugol said it's good—I think it's from Per-druin." He laughed nervously. "Why would it be better from one place than another? Grapes are grapes."

Miriamele smiled. She seemed tired: shadows lay beneath her green eyes. "I don't know. Maybe they grow them differently."

"It doesn't really matter." Simon carefully aimed a stream from the winesack into first one cup, then the other. "I'm still not sure I even like wine—Rachel would never let me drink it. 'The Devil's blood,' she called it."

"The Mistress of Chambermaids?" Miriamele made a face. "She was a nasty woman."

Simon handed her a cup. "I used to think so. She certainly had a temper. But she tried to do her best for me, I suppose. I made it hard on her." He lifted the wine to his lips, letting the sourness run over his tongue. "I wonder where she is now? Still at the Hayholt? I hope she's well. I hope she hasn't been hurt." He grinned—to think of having such feelings for the Dragon!—then looked up suddenly. "Oh, no. I've already drunk some. Shouldn't we say something—have a toast?"

Miriamele lifted her cup solemnly. "To your birth-day, Simon."

"And to yours, Princess Miriamele."

They sat and drank for a while in silence. The wind pressed the grass side-ways, flattening it in changing patterns as though some great invisible beast rolled in restless sleep. "The Raed is beginning tomorrow," he said. "But I think that Josua has already decided what he wants to do."

"He will go to Nabban." There was quiet bitterness in her voice.

"What's wrong with that?" Simon motioned for her cup, which was empty. "It's a start."

"It's the wrong start." She stared at his hand as she took the cup. The scru-tiny made him uneasy. "I'm sorry, Simon. I am just unhappy with things. With lots of things."

"I will listen if you want to talk. I've gotten to be a good listener, Princess."

"Don't call me 'Princess'!" When she spoke again, her tone was softer. "Please, Simon, not you, too. We were friends once, when you didn't know who I was. I need that now."

"Certainly . . . Miriamele." He took a breath. "Aren't we friends now?"

"That's not what I meant." She sighed. "It's the same problem as I have with Josua's decision. I don't agree with him. I think we should move directly to Erkynland. This is not a war like my grandfather fought—it's much worse, much darker. I am afraid we will be too late if we try to conquer Nabban first."

"Too late for what?"

"I don't know. I have these feelings, these ideas, but I have nothing that I can use to prove they are real. That's bad enough, but because I am a princess—because I am the High King's daughter—they listen to me anyway. Then they all try to find a polite way to ignore me. It would almost be better if they just told me to be quiet!"

"What does that have to do with me?" Simon asked quietly. Miriamele had closed her eyes, as though she looked at something inside herself. The red-gold of her eyelashes, the minute fineness of them, made him feel as though he were coming apart.

"Even you, Simon, who met me as a serving-girl—no, a serving-boy!" She laughed, but her eyes remained shut. "Even you, Simon, when you look at me, you are not just looking at me. You are seeing my father's name, the castle I grew up in, the costly dresses. You are looking at a . . . a *princess.*" She said the word as though it meant something terrible and false.

Simon stared at her for a long time, watching her wind-shifted hair, the downy line of her cheek. He burned to tell her what he really saw, but knew he could never find the proper words; it would all come out as a mooncalf babble. "You are what you are," he said at last. "Isn't it just as false to try to be something else as it is for others to pretend they're talking to *you* when they're only talking to some . . . princess?"

Her eyes opened suddenly. They were so clear, so searching! He suddenly had an idea of what it must have been like to stand before her grandfather, Prester John. It reminded him, too, of what he himself was: a servant's awkward child, a knight only by virtue of circumstance. At this moment she seemed closer than she had ever been, but at the same time the gulf between them also seemed as wide as the ocean.

Miriamele was staring at him intently. After a few moments, he looked away, abashed. "I'm sorry."

"Don't be." Her voice was brisk, but it somehow did not match the fretful expression on her face. "Don't be, Simon. And let's talk of something else." She turned to look across the swaying grass of the hilltop. The strange, fierce moment passed.

They finished the wine and shared bread and cheese. For a treat, Simon produced a leaf-wrapped package of sweetmeats that he had bought from one of the peddlers at New Gadrinsett's small market, little balls made of honey and roasted grain. The talk turned to other things, of the places and strange things they had both seen. Miriamele tried to tell Simon of the Niskie Gan Itai and her singing, of the way she had used her music to stitch sky and sea together. In his turn, Simon tried to explain something of what it had been like to be in Jiriki's house by the river, and to see the Yásira, the living tent of butterflies. He tried to describe gentle, frightening Amerasu, but faltered. There was still a great deal of pain in that memory.

"And what about that other Sitha-woman?" Miriamele asked. "The one who is here. Aditu."

"What do you mean?"

"What do you think of her?" She frowned. "I think she has no manners."

Simon snorted softly. "She has her own manners, is more like it. They're not like us, Miriamele."

"Well, then I think little of the Sithi. She dresses and acts like a tavern harlot."

He had to suppress another smile. Aditu's current style of dress was almost bogglingly reserved in comparison to the garb she had worn in Jao é-Tinukai'i. It was true that she still often exhibited more of her tawny flesh than the citizens of New Gadrinsett found comfortable, but Aditu was obviously doing her best not to outrage her mortal companions. As for her behavior . . . "I don't think she's so bad," he said.

"Well, you wouldn't." Miriamele was definitely cross. "You moon after her like a puppy."

"I do not!" he said, stung. "She is my friend."

"That's a nice word. I have heard my father's knights use that word also, to describe women who would not be allowed across the threshold of a church." Miriamele sat up straight. She was not just teasing. The anger he had sensed earlier was there, too. "I do not blame you—it is the nature of men. She is very fetching, in her strange way."

Simon's laugh was sharp. "I will never understand," he said.

"What? Understand what?"

"No matter." He shook his head. It would be good to move the conversation back to safer ground, he decided. "Ah, I almost forgot." He turned and reached for the drawstring bag which he had leaned against the weather-polished wall. "This is a celebration of our birth-days. It is time for the giving of gifts."

Miriamele looked up, stricken. "Oh, Simon! But I don't have anything to give you!"

"Just your being here is enough. To see you safe after all this time . . ." His voice broke, making an embarrassing squeak. To cover his chagrin, he cleared his throat. "But in any case, you have already given me a fine present—your scarf." He pulled his collar wide so she could see it where it nestled about his long neck. "The finest gift that anyone ever gave me, I think." He smiled and hid it again. "Now I have something to give to you." He reached into his bag and pulled out a long slender something wrapped in a cloth.

"What is it?" The care seemed to slide from her face, leaving her childlike in her attention to the mysterious bundle.

"Open it."

She did, unwinding the cloth to disclose the white Sithi arrow, a streak of ivory fire.

"I want you to have it."

Miriamele looked from the arrow to Simon. Her face went pale. "Oh, no," she breathed. "No, Simon, I can't."

"What do you mean? Of course you can. It's my gift to you. Binabik said that it was made by the Sithi fletcher Vindaomeyo, longer ago than either of us can imagine. It's the only thing I have to give that's worthy of a princess, Miriamele—and like it or not, that's what you are."

"No, Simon, no." She pushed the arrow and its cloth into his hands. "No, Simon. That's the kindest thing anyone has ever done for me, but I can't take it. It's not just a thing, it's a promise from Jiriki to you—a pledge. You told me so. It means too much. The Sithi do not give these things away for no reason."

"Neither do I," said Simon angrily. So even this was not good enough, he thought. Under a thin layer of fury he felt a great reserve of hurt. "I want *you* to have it."

"Please, Simon. I thank you—you do not understand how kind I think you are—but it would hurt me too much to take it from you. I cannot."

Baffled, pained, Simon closed his fingers on the arrow. His offering had been rejected. He felt wild and full of folly. "Then wait here," he said, and rose. He was on the verge of shouting. "Promise me you won't leave this spot until I come back."

She looked up at him uncertainly, shielding her eyes from the sun. "If you want me to stay, Simon, I will stay. Will you be gone long?"

"No." He turned toward the crumbling gateway of the great wall. Before he had gone ten steps, he quickened his pace to a run.

When he returned, Miriamele was still seated in the same place. She had found the pomegranate he had hidden as a last surprise.

"I'm sorry," she said, "but I was restless. I got this open, but I haven't eaten any yet." She showed him the seeds lined up on the split fruit like rows of gems. "What have you got in your hand?"

Simon drew his sword out of the tangle of his cloak. As Miriamele watched, her apprehension far from gone, he kneeled before her.

"Miriamele . . . Princess . . . I will give you the only gift I have left to give." He extended the hilt of his sword toward her, lowering his head and staring fixedly at the jungle of grass around his boots. "My service. I am a knight now. I swear that you are my mistress, and that I will serve you as your protector . . . if you will have me."

Simon looked up out of the corner of his eye. Miriamele's face was awash in emotions, none of which he could identify. "Oh, Simon," she said.

"If you will not have me, or cannot for some reason I'm still too stupid to know, then just tell me. We can still be friends."

There was a long pause. Simon looked down at the ground again and felt his head spinning.

"Of course," she said at last. "Of course I will have you, dear Simon." There was an odd catch in her voice. She laughed raggedly. "But I will never forgive you for this."

He looked up, alarmed, to see if she was joking. Her mouth was curved in a trembling half-smile, but her eyes were closed again. There was a gleam like tears on her lashes. He could not tell if she was happy or sad.

"What do I do?" she asked.

"I'm not sure. Take the hilt and then touch my shoulders with the blade, I suppose, like Josua did to me. Say: 'You will be my champion.'"

She took the hilt and held it for a moment against her cheek, then lifted the sword and touched his shoulders in turn, left and right.

"You will be my champion, Simon," she whispered.

"I will."

The torches in Leavetaking House had burned low. It was long past time for the evening meal, but no one had said a word about eating.

"This is the third day of the Raed," Prince Josua said. "We are all tired. I beg your attention for just a few moments more." He drew his hand across his eyes.

Isgrimnur thought that of all those assembled in the room, it was the prince himself who most showed the strain of the long days and the acrimonious arguments. In attempting to let everyone have his or her fair say, Josua had been dragged along through many a side issue—and the onetime master of Elvritshalla did not approve at all. Prince Josua would never survive the rigors of a campaign against his brother if he did not harden himself. He had improved some since Isgrimnur had seen him last—the journey to this strange place seemed to have changed everyone who made it—but the duke still did not think Josua had grasped the trick of listening without being led. Without that, he thought sourly, no ruler could long survive.

The disagreements were many. The Thrithings-men did not trust the hardiness of the New Gadrinsett folk and feared that they would become a burden on the wagon-clans when Josua moved his camp down onto the grasslands. In turn, the settlers were not certain that they wanted to leave their new lives to go somewhere else since they would not even have new lands to settle until Josua took some territory from his brother or Benigaris.

Freosel and Sludig, who had become Josua's war commanders after the death of Deornoth, also disagreed bitterly over where the prince should go. Sludig sided with his liege-lord Isgrimnur in urging an attack on Nabban. Freosel, like many others, felt an excursion into the south missed the true point. He was an Erkynlander, and Erkynland was not only Josua's own country, but also the place that had been most blighted by Elias' misrule. Freosel had made it clear that he felt they should move westward to the outer fiefdoms of Erkynland, gathering strength from the High King's disaffected subjects before marching on the Hayholt itself.

Isgrimnur sighed and scratched his chin, indulging for a moment in the pleasure of his regrown beard. He longed to stand up and simply tell everyone what they should do and how to do it. He even sensed that Josua would secretly welcome having the burden of leadership lifted from his shoulders—but such a thing could not be allowed. The duke knew that as soon as the prince lost his preeminence, the factions would dissolve and any chance of an organized resistance to Elias would collapse.

"Sir Camaris," Josua said abruptly, turning to the old knight. "You have been mostly silent. Yet if we are to ride on Nabban, as Isgrimnur and others urge us, you will be our banner. I need to hear your thoughts."

The old man had indeed remained aloof, although Isgrimnur doubted it was from disapproval or disagreement. Rather, Camaris had listened to the arguments like a holy man on a bench in the midst of a tavern brawl, present and yet separate, his attention fixed on something that others could not see.

"I cannot tell you what is the right thing to do, Prince Josua." The old knight spoke, as he had since regaining his wits, with a sort of effortless dignity. His old-fashioned, courtly speech was so careful as to seem almost a parody; he might have been the Good Peasant from the proverbs of the Book of the Aedon. "That is beyond me, nor would I presume to interpose myself between you and God, who is the final answerer of all questions. I can only tell you what I think." He leaned forward, staring down at his long-fingered hands, which were twined on the table before him as if he prayed. "Much of what has been said is still incomprehensible to me—your brother's bargain with this Storm King, who was only a dim legend in my day; the part you say the swords are to play, my black blade Thorn among them—it is all most strange, most strange.

"But I do know that I loved well my brother, Leobardis, and from what you said, he served Nabban honorably in the years I was insensible—better than I ever could have, I think. He was a man who was made to govern other men; I am not.

"His son Benigaris I knew only as a bawling infant. It gnaws at my soul to think that someone of my father's house could be a patricide, but I cannot doubt the evidence I have heard." He shook his head slowly, a tired war-horse. "I cannot tell you to go to Nabban, or to Erkynland, or anywhere else upon the Lord's green earth. But if you decide to march on Nabban, Josua . . . then, yes, I will ride before the armies. If the people will use my name, I will not stop them, although I do not find it knightly: only our Ransomer should be exalted by the voices of men. But I cannot let such shame to the Benidrivine House go unheeded.

"So if that is the answer you seek from me, Josua, then you have it now." He raised his hand in a gesture of fealty. "Yes, I will ride to Nabban. But I wish I had not been brought back to see my friend John's kingdom in ruins and my own beloved Nabban ground beneath the heel of my murderous nephew. It is cruel." He dropped his gaze to the table once more. "This is one of the sternest tests God has given me, and I have failed Him already more times than I can count."

When he had finished speaking, the old man's words seemed to linger in the air like incense, a fog of complicated regret that filled the room. No one dared to break the stillness until Josua spoke.

"Thank you, Sir Camaris. I think I know what it will cost you to ride against your own countrymen. I am heartsick that we may have to force it upon you." He looked around the torchlit hall. "Is there anyone else who would speak before we are finished?"

Beside him, Vorzheva moved on the bench as though she might say something, but instead she stared angrily at Josua, who slipped her gaze as though he found it uncomfortable. Isgrimnur guessed what had passed between them—Josua had told him of her desire to stay until the child was born—and frowned; the prince did not need any further doubts clouding his decision.

Many cubits down the long table, Geloë stood. "I think there is one last thing, Josua. It is something that Father Strangyeard and I discovered only last night." She turned to the priest, who was sitting beside her. "Strangyeard?"

The archivist stood up, fingering a stack of parchments. He lifted a hand to straighten his eyepatch, then looked worriedly at some of the nearby faces, as though he had suddenly found himself called before a tribunal and charged with heresy.

"Yes," he said. "Oh, yes. Yes, there is something important—your pardon, something that *may* be important . . ." He riffled through the pages before him.

"Come, Strangyeard," the prince said kindly. "We are anxious to have you share your discovery with us."

"Ah, yes. We found something in Morgenes' manuscript. In his life of King John Presbyter." He held up some of the parchment sheets for the benefit of those who had not already seen Doctor Morgenes' book. "Also, from speaking to Tiamak of the Wran," he gestured with the sheaf toward the marsh man, "we found that it was something that much concerned Morgenes even after he began to see the outlines of Elias' bargain with the Storm King. It worried him, you see. Morgenes, that is."

"See what?" Isgrimnur's rear end was beginning to hurt from the hard chair, and his back had been griping him for hours. "*What* worried him?"

"Oh!" Strangyeard was startled. "Apologies, many apologies. The bearded star, of course. The comet."

"There was such a star in the skies during my brother's regnal year," Josua mused. "As a matter of fact, it was the night of his coronation we first saw it. The night my father was buried."

"That's the one!" Strangyeard said excitedly. "The *Asdridan Condiquilles*—the Conqueror Star. Here, I'll read what Morgenes wrote about it." He pawed at the parchment.

". . . *Strangely enough,*"

he began,

"*the Conqueror Star, instead of shining above the birth or triumph of conquerors as its name might suggest, seems instead to appear as a herald of the death of empires. It trumpeted the downfall of Khand, of the old Sea Kingdoms, and even the ending of what may have been the greatest empire of all—the Sithi mastery of Osten Ard, which came to an end when their great stronghold Asu'a fell. The first records collected by scholars of the League of the Scroll tell that the Conqueror Star was bright in the night sky above Asu'a when Ineluki, Iyu'unigato's son, pondered the spell that would soon destroy the Sithi castle and a large part of Fingil's Rimmersgard army.*

"It is said that the only event of pure conquest that ever saw the Conqueror Star's light was the triumph of the Ransomer, Usires Aedon, since it shone in the skies above Nabban when Usires hung on the Execution Tree. However, the argument could be made that there, too, it heralded decline and collapse, since Aedon's death was the beginning of the ultimate collapse of the mighty Nabbanai Imperium. . . ."

Strangyeard took a breath. His eyes were shining now: Morgenes' words had driven out his discomfort at speaking to a crowd. "So you see, there is some significance to this, we think."

"But why, exactly?" Josua asked. "It already appeared at the beginning of my brother's regnal year. If the destruction of an empire has been forecast, what of it? No doubt it is my brother's empire that will fall." He showed a weak smile. There was a small rustle of laughter from the assembly.

"But that is not the whole story, Prince Josua," Geloë said. "Dinivan and others—Doctor Morgenes, too, before his death—studied this matter. The Conqueror Star, you see, is not yet gone. It will be coming back."

"What do you mean?"

Binabik rose. "Every five hundreds of years, Dinivan was discovering," he explained, "the star is in the sky not once, but three times. It is appearing for three years, bright the first, then almost too dim for seeing the second, then most bright of all for the last."

"So it is coming back this year, at the end of the winter," Geloë said. "For the third time. The last time it did that was the year Asu'a fell."

"I still don't understand," Josua said. "I believe that what you say may be important, but we already have many mysteries to think about. What does the star mean to us?"

Geloë shook her head. "Perhaps nothing. Perhaps, as in the past, it heralds the passing of a great kingdom—but whether that would be the High King's, the Storm King's, or your father's if we are defeated, none of us can say. It seems unlikely that an occurrence with such a fateful history would mean *nothing*, however."

"I am in agreement," Binabik said. "This is not the season for the dismissing of such things as coincidence."

Josua looked around in frustration, as though hoping someone else at the long table could provide an answer. "But what does it *mean*? And what are we supposed to do about it?"

"First, it could be that only when the star is in the sky will the swords be of use to us," Geloë offered. "Their value seems to be in their otherworldliness. Perhaps the heavens are showing us when they will be most useful." She shrugged her shoulders. "Or perhaps that will be a time when Ineluki will be strongest, and most able to help Elias against us, since it was five centuries ago he spoke the spell that made him what he is now. In that case, we will need to reach the Hayholt before that time comes 'round again."

Silence descended on the vast chamber, broken only by the quiet murmuring of the fireplace flames. Josua shuffled absently through a few pages of Morgenes' manuscript.

"And you have learned nothing further about the swords on which we have staked so much—nothing which would be of use to us?" he demanded.

Binabik shook his head. "We have been speaking now many times with Sir Camaris." The little man gave the old knight a respectful nod. "He has been telling us what he knows of the sword Thorn and its properties, but we have not yet learned of anything that tells us what we may do with it and the others."

"Then we can't afford to bet our lives on them," Sludig said. "Magic and fairy-tricks will turn traitor every time."

"You speak about things you do not know . . ." Geloë began grimly.

Josua sat up. "Stop. It is too late in the day to abandon the three swords. If it was my brother alone we fought, then perhaps we might chance it. But the Storm King's hand has apparently been behind him at every step of his progress, and the swords are our only thin hope against that dark, dark scourge."

Miriamele now stood. "Then let me ask again, Uncle Josua . . . *Prince* Josua, that we go directly to Erkynland. If the swords are valuable, then we need to take Sorrow back from my father and recover Bright-Nail from my grandfather's grave. From what Geloë and Binabik are saying, we seem to have little time."

Her face was solemn, but Duke Isgrimnur thought he sensed desperation behind her words. That surprised him. Important, all-important as these decisions were, why should little Miriamele sound like her own life was so absolutely dependent on going straight to Erkynland and confronting her father?

Josua's look was cool. "Thank you, Miriamele. I have listened to what you say. I value your counsel." He turned to face the rest of the assembly. "Now I must tell you my decision." The desire to be finished with all this was audible in his every word.

"Here are my choices. To remain here—to build up this place, New Gadrinsett, and hold out against my brother until his misrule turns the tide in our favor. That is one possibility." Josua ran his hand through his short hair, then held up two fingers. "The second is to go to Nabban, where with Camaris to march at the head of our army, we may quickly gain adherents, and thus eventually field an army capable of bringing down the High King." The prince raised a third finger. "The third, as Miriamele and Freosel and others have suggested, is to move directly into Erkynland, gambling that we can find enough supporters to overcome Elias' defenses. There is also a possibility that Isorn and Count Eolair of Nad Mullach may be able to join us with men recruited in the Frostmarch and Hernystir."

Young Simon rose. "I beg your pardon, Prince Josua. Don't forget the Sithi."

"Nothing is promised, Seoman," said the Sitha woman Aditu. "Nothing can be."

Isgrimnur was a little taken aback. She had sat so quietly during the debate that he had forgotten she was here. He wondered if it had been wise to talk so openly before her. What did Josua and the rest truly know about the immortals, anyway?

"And perhaps the Sithi will join with us," Josua amended, "although as Aditu has told us, she does not know what is happening in Hernystir, or what exactly her folk plan to do next." The prince closed his eyes for a long moment.

"Added to these possibilities," he said at last, "is the need to recover the other two Great Swords, and also what we have learned here today about the Conqueror Star—which is little, I must say frankly, except that it may have some bearing on things." He turned to Geloë. "Obviously, if you learn more I ask to hear it at once."

The witch woman nodded.

"I wish that we *could* stay here." Josua looked quickly at Vorzheva, but she would not meet his eyes. "I would like nothing better than to see my child born here in something like safety. I would love to see all our settlers make of this ancient place a new and living city, a refuge for all who sought one. But we cannot stay. We are nearly out of food as it is, and more outcasts and war victims are arriving every day. And if we stay longer, we invite my brother sending a more formidable army than Fengbald's. It is also my sense that the time for a defensive game is past. So, we will move on.

"Of our two alternatives, I must, after much thought, choose Nabban. We are not strong enough to confront Elias directly now, and I fear that Erkynland is so much reduced that we might find it hard to raise an army there. Also, if we failed, we would have nowhere to run but back across the empty lands to this place. I cannot guess how many would die just trying to flee a failed battle, let alone in the battle itself between Elias' troops and our ragtag army.

"So it will be Nabban. We will go far before Benigaris can bring an army to bear, and in that time Camaris may lure many to our banner. If we are lucky enough to force Benigaris and his mother out, Camaris will also have the ships of Nabban to put at our service, making it easier for us to move against my brother."

He raised his arms, silencing the gathering as whispers began to fill the room. "But this much of the Scroll League's warnings about the Conqueror Star will I take to heart. I would rather not ride out in winter, especially since it has long seemed the tool of the Storm King, but I think that the sooner we can make our way from Nabban to Erkynland, the better. If the star is a herald of empire's fall, still it need not be *our* herald as well: we will try to reach the

Hayholt before it appears. We will hope that this mildness in the weather will hold, and we will leave this place in a fortnight. That is my decision." He lowered his hand to the tabletop. "Now go, all of you, and get some sleep. There is no point in further arguing. We leave this place for Nabban."

Voices were raised as some of those gathered began to call out questions. "Enough!" Josua cried. "Go and leave me in peace!"

As he helped herd the others out, Isgrimnur looked back. Josua was slumped in his chair, rubbing his temples with his fingers. Beside him Vorzheva sat and stared straight ahead, as though her husband were a thousand miles away.

Pryrates emerged from the stairwell into the bellchamber. The high-arching windows were open to the elements, and the winds that swirled around Green Angel Tower fluttered his red robe. He stopped, his boot heels clicking once more on the stone tiles before silence fell.

"You sent for me, Your Highness?" he asked at last.

Elias was staring out across the jumble of the Hayholt's roofs, looking toward the east. The sun had dropped below the western rim of the world and the sky was full of heavy black clouds. The entire land had fallen into shadow.

"Fengbald is dead," the king said. "He has failed. Josua has beaten him."

Pryrates was startled. "How could you know!?"

The High King whirled. "What do you mean, priest? A half-dozen Erkynguardsmen arrived this morning, the remnants of Fengbald's army. They told me many surprising tales. But you sound as though *you* knew already."

"No, Highness," the alchemist said hastily. "I was just surprised that I was not informed immediately when the guardsmen arrived. It is usually the king's counselor's task . . ."

". . . To sift through the news and decide what his master is allowed to hear," Elias finished for him. The king's eyes glittered. His smile was not pleasant. "I have many sources of information, Pryrates. Never forget that."

The priest bowed stiffly. "If I have offended you, my king, I beg your forgiveness."

Elias contemplated him for a moment, then turned back to the window. "I should have known better than to send that braggart Fengbald. I should have known he would muck it up. Blood and damnation!" He slapped his palms on the stone sill. "If only I could have sent Guthwulf."

"The Earl of Utanyeat proved himself a traitor, Highness," Pryrates observed mildly.

"Traitor or not, he was the finest soldier I have ever seen. He would have ground up my brother and his peasant army like pig meat." The king bent and picked up a loose stone, holding it before his eyes for a moment before flinging it out the window. He watched its fall in silence before speaking again. "Now Josua will move against me. I know him. He has always wanted to take the throne from me. He never forgave my being firstborn, but he was too clever to say so aloud. He is subtle, my brother. Quiet but poisonous, like an adder." The king's pale face was drawn and haggard, but he seemed nevertheless full of an awful vitality. His fingers curled and uncurled spasmodically. "He will not find me unready, will he, Pryrates?"

The alchemist allowed a smile to curl his own thin lips. "No, my lord, he will not."

"I have friends, now—powerful friends." The king's hand dropped to the double hilt of Sorrow, sheathed at his waist. "And there are things afoot that Josua could never dream of if he lived for centuries. Things he will never guess until it is too late." He drew the sword from its scabbard. The mottled gray blade seemed a living thing, something pulled against its will from beneath a rock. As Elias held it before him, the wind lifted his cloak, spreading it above him like wings; for a moment, the blotchy twilight made him a pinioned *thing*, a demon out of dark ages past. "He and all he leads will die, Pryrates," the king hissed. "They do not know who they meddle with."

Pryrates regarded him with genuine uneasiness. "Your brother does not know, my king. But you will show him."

Elias turned and brandished the sword at the eastern horizon. In the distance, a flicker of lightning played across the turbulent darkness.

"Come, then!" he shouted. "Come, all of you! There is death enough to be shared! No one will take the Dragonbone Chair from me. No one can!"

As if in answer, there came a dim rumble of thunder.

25

The Semblance of Heaven

⚜

They rode down out of the north on black horses—steeds raised in cold darkness, surefooted in deep night, unafraid of icy wind or high mountain passes. The riders were three, two women and one man, all Cloud Children, and their deaths were already being sung by the Lightless Ones, since there was little chance they would ever return to Nakkiga. They were the Talons of Utuk'ku.

As they departed Stormspike, they rode through the ruins of the old city, Nakkiga-that-was, sparing hardly a glance to the tumbled relics of an age when their people had still lived beneath the sun. By night they passed through the villages of the Black Rimmersmen. There they met no one, since the inhabitants of those settlements, like all the mortals in that ill-fated land, knew better than to stir out of doors once twilight had fallen.

Despite the speed and vigor of their mounts, the three riders were many nights crossing the Frostmarch. Except for those sleepers in remote settlements who suffered unexpectedly bad dreams, or the rare travelers who noticed an added chill to the already freezing wind, the riders went unperceived. They continued on in silence and shadow until they reached Naglimund.

They stopped there to rest their horses—even the cruel discipline of the Stormspike stables could not prevent a living animal from tiring eventually—and to confer with those of their kind who now made Josua of Erkynland's desolated castle their home. The leader of Utuk'ku's Talons—although she was only first-among-equals—paid uncomfortable homage to the castle's shrouded master, one of the Red Hand. He sat in his gray winding sheets peeping ember-red at every crease, on the smoldering wreckage of what had once been Josua's princely throne of state. She was respectful, although she did nothing more than that which was necessary. Even to the Norns, hardened through the long centuries, blasted by their cold exile, the Storm King's minions were unsettling. Like their master, they had gone *beyond*—they had tasted Unbeing and then returned; they were as different from their still-living brethren as a star was from a starfish. The Norns did not like the Red Hand, did not like the singed emptiness of them—each one of the five was little more than a hole in the stuff of reality, a hole filled by hatred—but as long as their mistress made Ineluki's war her own, they had little choice but to bow before the Storm King's chief servants.

They also found themselves distanced from their own brethren. Since the Talons were death-sung, the Hikeda'ya of Naglimund treated them with reverent silence and boarded them in a cold chamber far from the rest of the tribe. The three Talons did not stay long in the wind-haunted castle.

From there they rode over the Stile, through the ruins of Da'ai Chikiza, and then westward through the Aldheorte, where the travelers made a wide circle around the borders of Jao é-Tinukai'i. Utuk'ku and her ally had already had their confrontation with the Dawn Children and received its full benefit: this task was one that required secrecy. Although at times the forest seemed actively to resist them with paths that abruptly vanished and tree limbs so close-knit they made the filtered light of the stars seem different and confusing, still the trio rode on, heading inexorably southeast. They were the Norn Queen's chosen: they were not so easily put off their quarry.

At last they reached the forest's edge. They were close now to that which they sought. Like Ingen Jegger before them, they had come down from the north bearing death for Utuk'ku's enemies, but unlike the Queen's Huntsman, who had met defeat the first time he had turned his hand against the Zida'ya, these three were immortals. There would be no hurry. There would be no mistakes.

They turned their horses toward Sesuad'ra.

👑

"Ah, by the good God, I feel a weight lifted from my shoulders." Josua took a deep breath. "It is something fine to be moving at last."

Isgrimnur smiled. "Even if all do not agree," he said. "Yes. It's good."

Josua and the Duke of Elvritshalla were sitting their horses by the gate stones that marked the hilltop's edge, watching the citizens of New Gadrinsett decamp in a most disorderly fashion. The parade wound past them down the old Sithi road, spiraling around the bulk of the Stone of Farewell until it vanished from sight. As many sheep and cows seemed to be setting out as people, an army of unhelpful animals bleating, lowing, bumping along, causing chaos among the overloaded citizenry. Some of the settlers had built crude wagons and had piled their possessions high on them, which added to the strange air of festival.

Josua frowned. "As an army, we look more like a town fair being moved."

Hotvig, who had just ridden up with Freosel the Falshireman, laughed. "This is how our clans always look when they travel. The only difference is that most of these are your stone-dwellers. You will become accustomed."

Freosel was watching the process critically. "We need all cattle and sheep we can get, Highness. Many mouths that need feeding." He awkwardly urged his horse forward a few paces—he was still not used to riding. "Ha, there!" he shouted. "Give that wagon some room!"

Isgrimnur thought that Josua was right: it *did* look like a traveling fair, although this company showed something less than the cheerfulness that usually attended such things. There were children crying—although not all the children were displeased to be traveling, by any means—as well as a steady undercurrent of bickering and complaint from the citizens of New Gadrinsett. Few among them had wanted to leave this place of relative safety: the idea of somehow forcing Elias from his throne was remote to them, and almost all the settlers would have preferred to stay on Sesuad'ra while others dealt with the grim realities of war—but it was also clear that staying in this remote place after Josua had taken all the men-at-arms away was no real alternative. So, angry but unwilling to risk more suffering without the protection of the prince's makeshift army, the inhabitants of New Gadrinsett were following Josua toward Nabban.

"We would not fright a nest of scholars with this lot," the prince said, "let alone my brother. Yet, I do not think the less of them—of any of us—for our rags and poor weaponry." He smiled. "In truth, I think I know for the first time what my father felt. I have always treated my liege-men as well as I could, since that is what God would have me do, but I never felt the strong love that Prester John did for all his subjects." Josua stroked Vinyafod's neck meditatively. "Would that the old man could have saved some of that love for both his sons as well. Still, I think I finally know what he felt when he rode out through the Nearulagh Gate and down into Erchester. He would have given his life for those people, as I would give mine for these." The prince smiled again, shyly, as if embarrassed by what he had revealed. "I will bring this beloved rabble of mine safe through Nabban, Isgrimnur, whatever it takes. But when we get to Erkynland, we are putting the dice into the hands of God—and who knows what He will do with them?"

"Not a one of us," Isgrimnur said. "And good deeds do not buy His favor, either. At least your Father Strangyeard said that to me the other night, that he thought it might be as much a sin to try to buy God's love by good deeds as it is to do bad ones."

A mule—one of the few such on all of Sesuad'ra—was balking at the rim of the road. His owner was pushing at the cart to which the mule was tethered, trying to urge him along from behind. The beast had gone stiff and spread-legged, silent but implacable. The owner moved forward and laid a switch across the mule's back, but the creature only dropped back its ears and lifted its head, accepting the blows with mutely stubborn hostility. The owner's curses filled the morning air, echoed by the people trapped behind his stalled cart.

Josua laughed and leaned closer to Isgrimnur. "If you would see what I look like to myself, gaze on that poor beast. If it were uphill, he would pull all day and never show a moment's weariness. But now he has a long and dangerous downward track before him and a heavy cart behind him—no wonder he digs in his heels. He would wait until the Day of Weighing-Out if he could." His grin faded and he turned to fix the duke with his gray eyes. "But I have interrupted you. Say again what Strangyeard told you."

Isgrimnur stared at the mule and its drover. There was something both comic and pathetic about it, something that seemed to hint at more than it revealed. "The priest said that trying to buy God's favor with good deeds was a sin. Well, first he apologized for having any thoughts at all—you know how he is, skittery mouse of a man—but said it anyway. That God owes us nothing, and we owe Him all, that we should do right things because they are right and that is closest to God, not because we will be rewarded like children given sweetmeats for sitting quietly."

"Father Strangyeard is a mouse, yes," said Josua. "But a mouse can be brave. Small as they are, though, they learn it is wiser not to challenge the cat. So it is with Strangyeard, I think. He knows who he is and where he belongs." Josua's eyes strayed upward from the futile flogging of the mule to the western hills that walled the valley. "I will think on what he said, though. Sometimes we *do* act as God bids us out of fear or hope of reward. Yes, I will think on what he said."

Isgrimnur suddenly wished he had kept his mouth closed.

That's all Josua needs—another reason to fault himself. Keep him moving, old man, not thinking. He is magical when he throws away his cares. He is a true prince, then. That is what will give us a chance of living to talk about such things over the fire someday.

"What do you say we move this idiot and his mule out of the road?" Isgrimnur suggested. "Otherwise, this place is going to be less like a town fair and more like the Battle of Nearulagh soon."

"Yes, I think so." Josua smiled again, sunny as the cold, bright morning. "But I don't think it's the idiot drover who will need convincing—and mules are no respecters of princes."

"Yah, Nimsuk!" Binabik called. "Where is Sisqinanamook?"

The herder turned and raised his crook-spear in greeting. "She is by the boats, Singing Man. Checking for leaks so the rams' feet don't get wet!" He laughed, displaying an uneven mouthful of yellow teeth.

"And so you don't have to swim, since you'd sink to the bottom like a rock," Binabik grinned back. "They'd find you in the summer when the water went away, a little man of mud. Show some respect."

"It's too sunny," Nimsuk replied. "Look at them frisk!" He pointed to the rams, who were indeed very lively, several of them playing at mock combat, something they almost never did.

"Just don't let them kill each other," Binabik said. "Enjoy your rest." He bent and whispered into Qantaqa's ear. The wolf leaped forward over the snow with the troll clinging to her hackles.

Sisqi was indeed inspecting the flatboats. Binabik released Qantaqa, who shook herself vigorously and trotted off to the nearby skirts of the forest. Binabik watched his betrothed with a smile. She was examining the boats as distrustfully as a lowlander might count the lashings on a Qanuc chasm-bridge.

"So careful," Binabik chided her, laughing. "Most of our people are crossed already." He waved his arm at the stippling of white rams dotted across the valley floor, the knots of troll herdsmen and huntresses enjoying the short hour of peace before the journeying began once more.

"And I will see every single one across safely." Sisqi turned and opened her arms to him. They stood face-to-face for a while, unspeaking. "This traveling-on-water is one thing when a few are fishing on Blue Mud Lake," she said eventually, "another when I must trust the lives of all my people and rams."

"They are fortunate in your care," Binabik said, serious now. "But for a moment, forget the boats."

She squeezed him hard. "I have."

Binabik lifted his head and looked out across the valley. The snow was melted in many places, with tufts of yellow-green grass showing through. "The herds will eat until they are sick," he said. "They are not used to such abundance."

"Is the snow going away?" she asked. "You said before that these lands were normally not snowbound at this time of year."

"Not always, but the winter has spread far south. Still, it does seem to be falling back again." He looked up into the sky. The few clouds did not in the least diminish the strength of the sun. "I do not know what to think. I cannot believe that he who made the winter reach down so far has given up. I do not know." He freed a hand from Sisqi's side and bumped it once against his breastbone. "I came to say that I am sorry I have seen you so little of late. There has been much to decide. Geloë and the others have been working long hours with Morgenes' book, trying to find the answers we yet seek. We have been studying Ookequk's scrolls as well, and that cannot be done without me."

Sisqi raised the hand of his she retained up to her cheek, pressing it there before letting it go. "You have no need for sorrow. I know what you do . . ." she inclined her head toward the boats bobbing at the water's edge, ". . . just as you know what I must do." She lowered her eyes. "I saw you stand at the lowlander's council and speak. I could not understand most of the words, but I saw them watching you with respect, Binbiniqegabenik." She gave his full name a ritual sound. "I was proud of you, my man. I only wish my mother and father could see you as I did. As I do."

Binabik snorted, but he was obviously pleased. "I do not think that the respect of lowlanders would count for much on your parents' tally stick. But I thank you. The lowlanders think highly of you, too—of all our people, after having seen us in battle." His round face grew serious. "And that is the other thing I wished to speak of. You told me once that you thought to go back to Yiqanuc. Will you do that soon?"

"I am still considering," she said. "I know we are needed by my mother and father, but I also think there are things we can do here. Lowlanders and trolls fighting together—perhaps that is something that will make our people safer in days ahead."

"Clever Sisqi," Binabik smiled. "But the fighting may grow too fierce for our folk. You have never seen a war for a castle—what the lowlanders call a 'siege.' There might be scant place for our people in such a battle, yet much danger. And at least one or two battles of that kind lie before Josua and his people."

She nodded her head solemnly. "I know. But there is a more important reason, Binabik. I would find it very hard to leave you again."

He looked away. "As I found it hard to leave you when Ookequk took me south—but both of us know that there are duties that make us do what we wish we did not have to." Binabik slid his arm through hers. "Come, let us walk for a while, since we will not have much time to be together in days ahead."

They turned and made their way back toward the base of the hill, avoiding the press of people waiting for boats. "I regret most that these troubles prevent us from our marriage," he said.

"The words, only. The night I came for you, to set you free, we were married. Even had we never seen each other again."

Binabik hunched his shoulders. "I know. But you should have the words. You are the daughter of the Huntress."

"We have separate tents," Sisqi smiled. "All that is honorable is observed."

"And I do not mind sharing mine with young Simon," he shot back. "But I would prefer sharing with you."

"We have our times." She squeezed his hand. "And what will you do when this is all over, my dear one?" She kept her voice steady, as if there were little question whether there would be an afterward. Qantaqa appeared from the curve of the forest and loped toward them.

"What do you mean? You and I will go back to Mintahoq—or, if you have already gone, I will come to you."

"But what about Simon?"

Binabik had slowed his pace. Now he stopped and pushed snow from a hanging branch with his stick. Here in the hill's long shadow, the raucous noise of the departing throngs was less. "I do not know. I am bound to him by promises, but the day will come when those can be discharged. After that . . ." He shrugged, a trollish gesture made with his palms held out. "I do not know what I am to him, Sisqi. Not a brother, not a father, certainly. . . ."

"A friend?" she suggested gently. Qantaqa was beside her, nosing at her hand. She scratched the wolf's muzzle, running her fingers along jaws that could swallow her arm to the elbow. The wolf growled contentedly.

"Certainly that. He is a good boy. No, he is a good man, I suppose. I have watched him growing."

"May Qinkipa of the Snows bring us all through this safely," she said gravely.

"Simon to grow happily old, you and I to love each other and raise children, our kind to keep our mountains as our home. I am not frightened of lowlanders any more, Binabik, but I am happier among people I understand."

He turned and pulled her close. "May Qinkipa grant what you ask. And don't forget," he said, reaching out to lay his fingers next to hers where they touched the wolf's neck, "we must wish for the Snow Maiden to protect Qantaqa, too." He grinned. "Come, go with me a little farther. I know a quiet spot on the hillside, sheltered from the wind—the last private place we may see for day upon day upon day."

"But the boats, Singing Man," she teased. "I must look at them again."

"You have looked at each one a dozen times," he said. "Trolls could swim laughing through that water if they had to. Come."

She put her arm around him and they went, heads leaning close together. The wolf padded after them, silent as a gray shadow.

♛

"Blast you, Simon, that hurt!" Jeremias fell back, sucking on his wounded fingers. "Just because you're a knight doesn't mean you have to break my hand."

Simon straightened up. "I'm just trying to show you something Sludig taught me. And I need the practice. Don't be a baby."

Jeremias gave him a disgusted look. "I'm not a baby, Simon. And you're not Sludig. I don't even think you're doing it right."

Simon took a few deep breaths, fighting down a cross remark. It wasn't Jeremias' fault that he was restless. He hadn't been able to speak to Miriamele for days, and despite the huge and complicated process of breaking camp on Sesuad'ra, there still seemed little of importance for Simon to do. "I'm sorry. I was stupid to say that." He lifted the practice sword, made of timbers rescued from the war barricade. "Just let me show this to you, this thing where you turn the blade . . ." He reached out and engaged Jeremias' wooden weapon. "Like . . . *so* . . ."

Jeremias sighed. "I wish you would just go and talk to the princess instead of beating on me, Simon." He raised the sword. "Oh, come on, then."

They feinted and engaged, the blades clacking loudly. Some of the sheep pasturing nearby looked up long enough to see if the rams were fighting again; when it proved instead to be a contest of two-legged younglings, they turned back to their grass.

"Why did you say that about the princess?" Simon asked, panting.

"What?" Jeremias was trying to stay out of reach of his opponent's longer arms. "Why do you think? You've been moping around after her since she got here."

"I have not."

Jeremias stepped back and let the point of his stave-sword sag to the ground. "Oh, you haven't? It must have been some other hulking, red-haired idiot."

Simon smiled, embarrassed. "That easy to tell, is it?"

"Usires Ransomer, yes! And who wouldn't? She's certainly pretty, and she seems kind."

"She's . . . more than that. But why aren't *you* moping after her, then?"

Jeremias darted him a quick, hurt look. "As if she would notice me if I fell dead at her feet." His face grew mocking. "Not that she seems to be flinging herself at *you,* either."

"That's not funny," said Simon darkly.

Jeremias took pity. "I'm sorry, Simon. I'm sure being in love is horrible. Look, go ahead and break the rest of my fingers if it will make you feel better."

"It might." Simon grinned and raised his blade once more. "Now, damn you, Jeremias, do this *right.*"

"Make someone a knight," Jeremias huffed, dodging a downward blow, "and you ruin his friends' lives forever."

The noise of their conflict rose again, the irregular smack of blade on blade fierce as the hammering of a huge and drunken woodpecker.

They sat gasping on the wet grass, sharing a water skin. Simon had untied the neck of his shirt to let the wind at his heated skin. Soon he would be uncomfortably chilly, but at the moment the air felt wonderful. A shadow fell between the two of them and they looked up, startled.

"Sir Camaris!" Simon struggled to rise. Jeremias just stared, wide-eyed.

"Hea, sit, young man." The old man spread his fingers, gesturing Simon back down. "I was only watching the two of you at your bladework."

"We don't know much," Simon said modestly.

"That you do not."

Simon had been half-hoping that Camaris would contradict him. "Sludig tried to teach me what he could," he said, trying to keep his voice respectful. "We haven't had much time."

"Sludig. That is Isgrimnur's liege-man." He looked at Simon intently. "And you are the castle-lad, are you not? The one that Josua knighted?" For the first time, it was apparent that he had a faint accent. The slightly over-rounded roll of Nabbanai speech still clung to his stately phrases.

"Yes, Sir Camaris. Simon is my name. And this is my friend—and my squire—Jeremias."

The old man flicked his gaze to Jeremias and dipped his chin briefly before returning his pale blue eyes to Simon. "Things have changed," he said slowly. "And not for the better, I think."

Simon waited a moment for Camaris to explain. "What do you mean, sire?" he asked.

The old man sighed. "It is not your fault, young fellow. I know that a monarch must sometimes make knights upon the field, and do not doubt that you have done noble deeds—I heard you helped find my blade Thorn—but there is more to knighthood than a touch of a sword. It is a high calling, Simon . . . a high calling."

"Sir Deornoth tried to teach me what I needed to know," Simon said. "Before I had my vigil, he taught me about the Canon of Knighthood."

Camaris sat down, astonishingly nimble for a man of his age. "But even so, lad, even so. Do you know how long I was in service to Gavenaxes of Honsa Claves, as page and squire?"

"No, sire."

"Twelve years. And every day, young Simon, every single day was a lesson. It took me two long years simply to learn how to care for Gavenaxes' horses. You have a horse, do you not?"

"Yes, sire." Simon was uncomfortable yet fascinated. The greatest knight in the history of the world was talking to him about the rules of knighthood. Any young nobleman from Rimmersgard to Nabban would have given his left arm to be in Simon's place. "She's called Homefinder."

Camaris gave him a sharp look, as though he disapproved of the name, but went on as though he did not. "Then you must learn to care for her properly. She is more than a friend, Simon, she is as much a part of you as your two legs and two arms. A knight who cannot trust his horse, who does not know his horse as well as he knows himself, who has not cleaned and repaired every piece of harness a thousand times—well, he will be of little use to himself *or* to God."

"I am trying, Sir Camaris. But there is so much to learn."

"Admittedly it is a time of war," Camaris continued. "So it is quite permissible to slight some of the less crucial arts—hunting and hawking and suchlike." But he did not look as though he was entirely comfortable with this thought. "It is even conceivable that the rules of precedence are not so important as at other times, except insofar as they impinge on military discipline; still, it is easier to fight when you know your place in God's wise plan. Little wonder the battle here with the king's men was a brawl." His look of severe concentration abruptly softened; his eyes turned mild. "But I am boring you, am I not?" His lips quirked. "I have been as one asleep for two score years, but still I am an old man, for all that. It is not my world."

"Oh, no," Simon said earnestly. "You are not boring me, Sir Camaris. Not at all." He looked at Jeremias for support, but his friend was goggle-eyed and silent. "Please, tell me anything that will help me be a better knight."

"Are you being kind?" asked the greatest knight in Aedondom. His tone was cool.

"No, sire." Simon laughed in spite of himself, and had a momentary fear that he would dissolve into terrified giggling. "No, sire. Forgive me, but to have you ask if you're boring me . . ." He could not summon words to describe the magnificent folly of such an idea. "You are a hero, Sir Camaris," he said at last, simply. "A hero."

The old man rose with the same surprising alacrity with which he had seated himself. Simon was afraid he had somehow offended him.

"Stand, lad."

Simon did as he was told. "You, too . . . Jeremias." Simon's friend rose to the knight's beckoning finger. Camaris looked at them both critically. "Lend me your sword, please." He pointed to the wooden blade still clutched in Simon's hand. "I have left Thorn scabbarded in my tent. I am still not quite comfortable having her near me, I confess. There is a restless quality to her that I do not like. Perhaps it is only me."

"Her?" Simon asked, surprised.

The old man made a dismissive gesture. "It is the way we talk on Vinitta. Boats and swords are 'she,' storms and mountains are 'he.' Now, attend me well." He took the practice-sword and drew a circle in the wet grass. "The Canon of Knighthood tells that, as we are made in the image of our Lord, so is the world . . ." He made a smaller circle inside the first. ". . . made in the semblance of Heaven. But, woefully, without its grace." He examined the circle critically, as if he could already see it populated with sinners.

"As the angels are the minions and messengers of God the Highest," he went on, "so does the fraternity of knighthood serve its various earthly rulers. The angels bring forth God's good works, which are absolute, but the earth is flawed, and so are our rulers, even the best. Thus, there will be disagreement as to what is God's will. There will be war." He divided the inner circle with a single line. "By this test will the righteousness of our rulers be made known. It is war that most closely reflects the knife edge of God's will, since war is the hinge on which earthly empires rise or fall. If strength alone were to determine victory, strength unmitigated by honor or mercy, then there would *be* no victory, because God's will can never be revealed by the mere exercise of greater strength. Is the cat more beloved of God than the mouse?" Camaris shook his head gravely, then turned his sharp eyes on his audience. "Are you listening?"

"Yes," Simon said quickly. Jeremias only nodded, still silent as if struck dumb.

"So. All angels—excepting The One Who Fled—are obedient to God above all, because He is perfect, all-knowing and all-capable." Camaris drew a series of ticks on the outer circle—representing the angels, Simon supposed. In truth, he was a little bit confused, but he also felt that he could grasp much of what the knight was saying, so he clung to what he could and waited. "But," the old man continued, "the rulers of men are, as aforesaid, flawed. They are sinners, as are we all. Thus, although each knight is loyal to his liege, he must also be loyal to the Canon of Knighthood—all the rules of battle and comportment, the rules of honor and mercy and responsibility—which is the same for *all* knights." Camaris bisected the line through the inner circle, drawing a perpendicular. "So no matter which earthly ruler wins a struggle, if his knights are true to their canon, the battle will have been won according to God's law. It will be a just reflection of His will." He fixed Simon with his keen gaze. "Do you hear me?"

"Yes, sire." In truth, it did make a kind of sense, although Simon wanted to think about it on his own for a while.

"Good." Camaris bent and wiped the mud-daubed wooden blade as carefully as if it had been Thorn, then handed it back to Simon. "Now, just as God's priest must render His will understandable to the people, in a form that is pleasing and reverent, so, too, must His knights prosecute His wishes in a similar fashion. That is why war, however horrible, should not be a fight between animals. That is why a knight is more than simply a strong man on a horse. He is God's vicar on the battlefield. Swordplay is prayer, lads—serious and sad, yet joyful."

He doesn't look very joyful, Simon thought. *But there is something priestlike about him.*

"And that is why one does not become a knight just by the passing of a vigil and the tapping of a sword, any more than one might become a priest by carrying the Book of the Aedon from one side of a village to another. There is study, study in every part." He turned to Simon. "Stand and hold up your sword, young man."

Simon did. Camaris was a good handspan taller than he, which was interesting. Simon had become accustomed to being taller than nearly everyone.

"You are holding it like a club. Spread your hands, thus." The knight's long hands enfolded Simon's own. His fingers were dry and hard, as rough as if Camaris had spent his life working the soil or building stone walls. Abruptly, by his touch, Simon realized the enormity of the old knight's experience, understood him as far more than just a legend made flesh or an aged man full of useful lore. He could feel the countless years of hard, painstaking work, the unnumbered and largely unwanted contests of arms that this man had suffered to become the mightiest knight of his age—and all the time, Simon sensed, enjoying none of it any more than a kind-hearted priest forced to denounce an ignorant sinner.

"Now feel it as you lift," said Camaris. "Feel how the strength comes from your legs. No, you are off your balance." He pushed Simon's feet closer together. "Why does a tower not fall? Because it is centered over its foundation."

Soon he had Jeremias working, too, and working hard.

The afternoon sun seemed to move swiftly through the sky; the breeze turned icy as evening approached. As the old man put them through their rigorous paces, a certain gleam—chill, but nevertheless bright—came to his eye.

Evening had descended by the time that Camaris finally turned them loose; the bowl of the valley was filled with campfires. This day's work to bring everyone across the river would enable the prince's company to leave with the first light in the morning. Now the people of New Gadrinsett were laying out their temporary camps, eating belated suppers, or wandering aimlessly in the deepening dark. A mood of stillness and anticipation hung over the valley, as real as the twilight. It was a little like the Between World, Simon thought—the place before Heaven.

But it's also the place before Hell, Simon thought. *We're not just traveling—we're going to war . . . and maybe worse.*

He and Jeremias walked silently, flushed with exertion, the sweat on their faces rapidly growing cold. Simon had a soreness in his muscles that was pleasant now, but experience told him that it would be less pleasant tomorrow, especially after a day on horseback. He was suddenly reminded of something.

"Jeremias, did you see to Homefinder?"

The young man looked at him in irritation. "Certainly. I said I would, didn't I?"

"Well, I think I'm going to go have a look at her anyway."

"Don't you trust me?" Jeremias asked.

"Of course I do," Simon said hastily. "It's nothing to do with you, truly. What Sir Camaris said about a knight and his horse just . . . just made me think about Homefinder." He was also feeling an urge to be on his own for a little while: other things Camaris had said needed to be thought about as well. "You understand, don't you?"

"I suppose so." Jeremias scowled, but didn't seem too upset. "I'm going to go and find something to eat, myself."

"Meet me at Isgrimnur's fire later. I think Sangfugol is going to sing some songs."

Jeremias continued on toward the busiest part of the camp and the tent that he, Simon, and Binabik had erected that morning. Simon peeled off, heading for the hill-slope where the horses were tethered.

The evening sky was a misty violet and the stars had not yet appeared. As Simon picked his way across the slushy meadowland in growing darkness, he found himself wishing for a little moonlight. Once he slipped and fell, cursing loudly as he wiped the mud off his hands onto his breeches, which were muddy and damp enough after the long hours of swording. His boots had already become thoroughly soaked.

A figure coming toward him through murk turned out to be Freosel, returning from seeing to his own horse as well as to Josua's Vinyafod. In this way, if no other, Freosel had taken Deornoth's place in the prince's life, and he seemed to fulfill the role admirably. The Falshireman had told Simon once that he came from a smithying family—something that Simon, looking at the broad-shouldered Freosel, could readily believe.

"Greetings, Sir Seoman," he said. "See you didn't bring torch either. If you don't be too long, y'may not need it." He squinted upward, gauging the fast-diminishing light. "But have a care—there be a great mud pit half a hundred steps behind me."

"I already found one of those," Simon laughed, gesturing to his mud-clotted boots.

Freosel looked at Simon's feet appraisingly. "Come by my tent and I'll give you grease for 'em. Won't do to have that leather crack. Or be you comin' to hear the harper sing?"

"I think so."

"Then I'll bring it with." Freosel gave him a courtly nod before walking on. "Mind that mud pit!" he called back over his shoulder.

Simon kept his eyes open and managed to make his way without incident around a patch of sucking slime that was indeed a larger brother of the one with which he had already made acquaintance. He could hear the gentle whickering of the horses as he approached. They were tethered on the hillside, a dark line against the dim sky.

Homefinder was where Jeremias had said he had left her, staked to a longish rope not far from the twisted black form of a spreading oak. Simon cupped the horse's nose in his hand and felt her warm breath, then laid his head on her neck and rubbed her shoulder. The horse scent was thick and somehow reassuring.

"You're my horse," he said quietly. Homefinder flicked an ear. "My horse."

Jeremias had draped her with a heavy blanket—a gift to Simon from Gutrun and Vorzheva, one which had been his own cover until the horses were moved from their warm stables in Sesuad'ra's caves. Simon made sure that it had been tied in place well but not too tightly. As he turned from his inspection, he saw a pale shape flitting through the darkness before him, passing through the scatter of horses. Simon felt his heart jump within his chest.

Norns?

"Wh-who's that?" he called. He forced his voice lower and shouted again. "Who's there? Come out!" He let his hand fall to his side, realizing after a moment that he carried no weapon but his Qanuc knife, not even the wooden practice sword.

"Simon?"

"Miriamele? Princess?" He took a few steps forward. She was peering around at him from behind one of the horses, as if she had been hiding. As he moved closer, she moved out. There was nothing unusual in her dress, a pale gown and a dark cloak, but she had an oddly defiant look on her face.

"Are you well?" he asked, then cursed himself for the stupid question. He was surprised to see her out here by herself and couldn't think of anything to say. Another time, he supposed, when it would have been better to say nothing than to speak and prove himself a mooncalf.

But why did she look so guilty?

"I am, thank you." She looked past his shoulders on either side as if trying to decide whether Simon was alone. "I was out seeing to my horse." She indicated an undifferentiated mass of shadowy shapes farther down the hill. "He's one of those we took from . . . from the Nabbanai nobleman I told you about."

"You startled me," Simon said, and laughed. "I thought you were a ghost or . . . or one of our enemies."

"I am *not* an enemy," Miriamele said with a little of her usual lightness. "I'm not a ghost either, so far as I can tell."

"That's good to know. Are you finished?"

"Finished . . . with what?" Miriamele looked at him with a strange intensity.

"Seeing to your horse. I thought you might . . ." He paused and started again. She seemed very uncomfortable. He wondered if he had done something to offend her. Offering her the White Arrow as a gift, perhaps. The whole thing seemed dreamlike now. That had been a very odd afternoon.

Simon started again. "Sangfugol and a few others are going to play and sing tonight. At Duke Isgrimnur's tent." He pointed down the hillside to the rings of glowing fires. "Are you going to come and listen?"

Miriamele appeared to hesitate. "I'll come," she said at last. "Yes, that would be nice." She smiled briefly. "As long as Isgrimnur doesn't sing."

There was something not quite right in her tone, but Simon laughed at the joke anyway, as much from nervousness as anything else. "That will depend on whether any of Fengbald's wine is left over, I'd guess."

"Fengbald." Miriamele made a noise of disgust. "And to think that my father would have married me to that . . . that *pig.* . . ."

To distract her, Simon said: "He's going to sing a Jack Mundwode tune—Sangfugol is, I mean. He promised me he would. I think he's going to sing the one about the Bishop's Wagons." He took her arm almost without thinking, then had a moment of apprehension. What was he doing, grabbing her like that? Would she be insulted?

Instead, Miriamele seemed almost not to notice. "Yes, that would be very nice," she said. "It would be good to spend a night singing by the fire."

Simon was puzzled again, since something like that had been going on most nights somewhere in New Gadrinsett, and even more frequently of late, when people had been gathered for the Raed. But he said nothing, deciding just to enjoy the feeling of her slender, strong arm beneath his.

"It will be a very good time," he said, and led her down the hillside toward the beckoning campfires.

After midnight, when the mists had finally fallen away and the moon was high in the sky, bright as a silver coin, there was a stir of movement on the hilltop that the prince and his company had so recently abandoned.

A trio of shapes, dark forms almost completely invisible despite the moonlight, stood near one of the standing stones at the outermost edge of the hilltop and looked down at the valley below. Most of the fires had burned low, but still a perimeter of flickering flames lay around the encampment; a few dim figures could be seen moving in the reddish light.

The Talons of Utuk'ku watched the camp for a long, long time, still as owls. At last, and without a word spoken between them, they turned away and walked silently through the high grasses, back toward the center of the hill. The pale bulk of Sesuad'ra's ruined stone buildings lay before them like the teeth in a crone's mouth.

The Norn Queen's servants had traveled far in a short time. They could afford to wait for another night, a night that would doubtless come soon, when the great, shambling company beneath them was not quite so vigilant.

The three shadows slipped noiselessly into the building the mortals called the Observatory, and stood for a long time looking up through the cracked dome at the newly emergent stars. Then they sat together on the stones. One of them began very quietly to sing; what floated within the crumbling chamber was a tune bloodless and sharp as splintered bone.

Although the sound did not even make an echo in the Observatory, and certainly could not have been heard across the windy hilltop, some sleepers in the valley below still moaned in their sleep. Those sensitive enough to feel the song's touch—and Simon was one of them—dreamed of ice, and of things broken and lost, and of nests of twining serpents hidden in old wells.

26

A Gift for the Queen

The prince's company, a slow-moving procession of carts and animals and straggling walkers, left the valley and edged out onto the plains, following the snaking course of the Stefflod south. The fray-edged army took close to a week to reach the place where the river joined with its larger cousin, the Ymstrecca.

It was a homecoming of sorts, for they made camp in the hill-sheltered valley that had once been the site of the first squatter town, Gadrinsett. Many of those who laid down their bed rolls and scavenged for firewood in the desolation of their former home wondered if they had gained anything by leaving this place to throw in their lot with Josua and his rebels. There was a little mutinous whispering—but only a little. Too many remembered the courage with which Josua and others had stood against the High King's men.

It could have been a more bitter homecoming: the weather was mild, and much of the snow that had once blanketed this part of the grasslands had again melted away. Still, the wind raced through the shallow gulleys and bent the few small trees as it flattened the long grass, and the campfires jigged and capered: the magical winter had abated somewhat, but it was still nearly Decander on the open plains of the Thrithings.

The prince announced that the great company would rest there three nights while he and his advisers decided what route would best serve them. His subjects, if they could be called by such a name, seized eagerly at the days of rest. Even the short journey from Sesuad'ra had been difficult for the wounded and infirm, who were many, and for those with young children. Some passed rumors that Josua had reconsidered, that he would rebuild New Gadrinsett here on the site of its predecessor. Although the more serious-minded tried to point out the foolishness of leaving a protected high place for an unprotected low one, and the fact that whatever else he might be, Prince Josua was no fool, enough of the homeless army found the idea a hopeful one that the rumors proved impossible to quell.

"We can't stay here long, Josua," Isgrimnur said. "Every day we remain will add another score of folk that won't follow us when we go."

Josua was scrutinizing a tattered, sun-faded map. The ragged prize had once belonged to the late Helfgrim, New Gadrinsett's onetime Lord Mayor, who had become, along with his martyred daughters, a sort of patron saint of the squatters. "We will not stay long," the prince said. "But if we bring these folk to the grasslands, away from the river, we must be sure of finding water. The weather is changing in ways none of us can foretell. It is quite possible we will suddenly be without rain."

Isgrimnur made a noise of frustration and looked to Freosel for support, but the young Falshireman, still unreconciled to Nabban as a destination, only stared back defiantly. They could have followed the Ymstrecca all the way west to Erkynland, his expression said clearly. "Josua," the duke began, "finding water will not trouble us. The animals can get theirs from dew if need be, and we can fill a mountain of water bags from the rivers before we leave them— there are dozens of new streams just sprung up from snowmelt, for that matter. Food is more likely to be a problem."

"And that is not solved either," Josua pointed out. "But I don't see that our choice of routes will help us much with that. We *can* pick our track to bring us near the lakes—I just don't know how much I trust Helfgrim's map. . . ."

"I had never . . . never realized how hard it is to feed this many people." Strangyeard had been reading quietly from one of the translations Binabik had made of Ookequk's scrolls. "How do armies manage?"

"They either drain their king's purse dry, like sand from a sackhole," Geloë said grimly, "or they simply eat everything around them as they pass through, like marching ants." She stood up from where she had squatted by the archivist. "There are many things growing here that we can use to feed people, Josua— many herbs and flowers and even grasses that will make sustaining meals, although some who have only lived in cities might find them strange."

"'Strange becomes homely when people are hungry,'" Isgrimnur quoted. "Don't remember who said it, but it's true, sure enough. Listen to Geloë: we'll make do. What we need is haste. The longer we stay in any place, the sooner we do what she said, eat the place up like ants. We'll do better if we keep moving."

"We have not halted just so I can think about things, Isgrimnur," the prince said a little coldly. "It is too much to expect an entire city, which is what we are, to get up and walk to Nabban in one march. The first week was a hard one. Let us give them a little time to grow used to it."

The Duke of Elvritshalla tugged at his beard. "I didn't mean . . . I know, Josua. But from now on, we need to move quickly, as I said. Let those who are slow catch up when we do finally stop. They won't be the fighters, anyway."

Josua pursed his lips. "Are they any the less God's children because they cannot wield a sword for us?"

Isgrimnur shook his head. The prince was in one of *those* moods. "That's not what I mean, Josua, and you know it. I'm just saying that this is an army, not a religious procession with the lector walking at the back. We can start whatever we have to do without waiting for every last soul who pulls up lame, or every horse that throws a shoe."

Josua turned to Camaris, who sat quietly by the small fire, staring intently at the smoke rising up to the hole in the tent roof. "What do you think, Sir Camaris? You have been on more marches than any of us, except perhaps for Isgrimnur. Is he right?"

The old man slowly turned his gaze away from the flickering fire. "I think that what Duke Isgrimnur says is just, yes. We owe it to the people as a whole to do what we have set out to do, and even more than that, we owe it to our good Lord, who has heard our promises. And we would be presumptuous to try to do God's work by holding the hand of every foot-weary traveler." He paused for a moment. "However, we also wish—nay, need—the people to join us. People do not join a hurrying, furtive band, they join a triumphant army." He looked around the tent, his eyes calm and clear. "We should go as swiftly as we can while still maintaining our company in good order. We should send riders out, not just to search what lies before us, but to be our heralds as well, to call to the people: 'The prince is coming!'" For a moment it seemed he might say more, but his expression grew distant and he fell silent.

Josua smiled. "You should have been an escritor, Sir Camaris. You are as subtle as my old teachers, the Usirean brothers. I have only one disagreement with you." He pivoted slightly to include the others in the tent. "We are going to Nabban. Our criers will shout: 'Camaris has come back! Sir Camaris has returned to lead his people!'" He laughed. "'And Josua is with him.'"

Camaris frowned slightly, as if what the prince said made him uneasy.

Isgrimnur nodded. "Camaris is right. Haste with dignity."

"But dignity does not allow us to plunder inhabited lands," Josua said. "That is not the way to gain the people's hearts."

Isgrimnur shrugged; again, he thought the prince was cutting the point too fine. "Our people are hungry, Josua. They have been cast out, some of them living in the wildlands for almost two years. When we reach Nabban, how will you tell them not to take the food they see growing from the ground, the sheep they see grazing the hills?"

The prince squinted wearily at the map. "I have no more answers. We will all do our best, and may God bless us."

"May God have mercy on us," Camaris corrected him in a hollow voice. The old man was again staring at the rising smoke.

Night had fallen. Three shapes sat in a copse of trees overlooking the valley. The music of the river rose up to them, muted and fragile. They had no fire, but a blue-white stone that lay between them glowed faintly, only a little brighter than the moon. Its azure light painted their pale, long-boned faces as they spoke quietly in the hissing tongue of Stormspike.

"Tonight?" asked the one named Born-Beneath-Tzaaihta's-Stone.

Vein-of-Silverfire made a finger-gesture of negation. She laid her hand on the blue stone for a long moment and sat in unmoving silence. At last, she let out a long-held breath. "Tomorrow, when Mezhumeyru hides in the clouds. Tonight, in this new place, the mortals will be watchful. Tomorrow night." She looked meaningfully at Born-Beneath-Tzaaihta's-Stone. He was the youngest, and had never before left the deep caverns below Nakkiga. She could tell by the tautness in his long, slender fingers, the gleam in his purple eyes, that he would bear watching. But he was brave, of that there was no doubt. Anyone who had survived the endless apprenticeship in the Cavern of Rending would fear nothing except the displeasure of their silver-masked mistress. Overeagerness, though, could be as harmful as cowardice.

"Look at them," said Called-by-the-Voices. She was staring raptly at the few human figures visible in the encampment below. "They are like rockworms, always wriggling, always squirming."

"If your life were but a few seasons," Vein-of-Silverfire replied, "perhaps you, too, would feel that you could never pause." She stared down at the twinkling constellation of fires. "You are right, though—they are like rockworms." The line of her mouth hardened minutely. "They have dug and eaten and laid waste. Now we will help put an end to them."

"By this one thing?" Called-by-the-Voices asked.

Vein-of-Silverfire looked at her, face cold and hard as ivory. "Do you question?"

There was a moment of tight-stretched silence before Called-by-the-Voices bared her teeth. "I seek only to do as She wishes. I want only to do what will serve Her best."

Born-Beneath-Tzaaihta's-Stone made a musical sound of pleasure. The moon reflected tombstone-white in his eyes. "She wishes a death . . . a *special* death," he said. "That is our gift to Her."

"Yes." Vein-of-Silverfire picked up the stone and placed it inside her raven-black shirt, next to her cool skin. "That is the gift of the Talons. And tomorrow night, we will give it to Her."

They fell silent, and did not speak again through the long night.

"You are still thinking too much of yourself, Seoman." Aditu leaned forward and pushed the polished stones into a crescent that spanned the shore of the Gray Coast. The shent-stones winked dully in the light of one of Aditu's crystalline globes, which sat on a tripod of carved wood. A little more light, this from the afternoon sun, leaked in through the flap of Simon's tent.

"What does that mean? I don't understand."

Aditu looked from the board to Simon, her eyes suggesting a deep-hidden amusement. "You are too much in yourself, that is what I mean. You are not thinking about what your partner is thinking. Shent is a game played by two."

"It's hard enough to try to remember the rules without having to think as well," Simon complained. "Besides, how am I supposed to know what you're thinking about while we're playing? I *never* know what you're thinking about!"

Aditu seemed poised to make one of her sly remarks, but instead she paused and laid her hand flat over her stones. "You are upset, Seoman. I have seen it in your play—you play well enough now that your moods carry over to the House of Shent."

She had not asked what was bothering him. Simon guessed that even if a companion showed up with a leg missing, Aditu or any other Sitha might wait while several seasons passed without asking what had happened. This evidence of what he thought of as her Sithi-ness irritated him, but he was also flattered that she thought he was becoming good at shent—although she probably only meant "good for a mortal," and since he was the only mortal he'd ever heard of who played, that was a rather lackluster compliment.

"I'm not upset." He glared down at the shent board. "Maybe I am," he said at last. "But it's nothing you could tell me anything about."

Aditu said nothing, but leaned back on her elbows and stretched her long neck in her oddly-jointed way, then shook her head. Pale hair fell loose from the pin that held it and gathered around her shoulders like fog, one thin braid coiling in front of her ear.

"I don't understand women," he said suddenly, then set his mouth in a scowl as though Aditu might contradict him. Evidently she agreed that he didn't, for she still said nothing. "I just don't understand them."

"What do you mean, Seoman? Surely you understand some things. I often say I do not understand mortals, but I know what they look like and how long they live, and I can speak a few of their languages."

Simon looked at her in irritation. Was she playing with him again? "I suppose it's not all women," he said grudgingly. "I don't understand Miriamele. The princess."

"The thin one with the yellow hair?"

She *was* playing with him. "If you like. But I can see it's stupid to talk to you about it."

Aditu leaned forward and touched his arm. "I am sorry, Seoman. I have made you angry. Tell me what is bothering you, if you would like. Perhaps even if I know little about mortals, speaking will make you feel happier."

He shrugged, embarrassed that he had brought it up. "I don't know. She's kind to me sometimes. Then, other times, she acts as if she hardly knows me. Sometimes she looks at me like I frighten her. *Me!*" He laughed bitterly. "I saved her life! Why should she be frightened of me?"

"If you saved her life, that is one possible reason." Aditu was serious. "Ask my brother. Having your life saved by someone is a very great responsibility."

"But Jiriki doesn't act like he hates me!"

"My brother is of an old and reserved race—although among the Zida'ya, he and I are thought to be quite youthfully impulsive and dangerously unpredictable." She gifted him with a catlike smile; there might as well have been a mouse tail-tip protruding from the corner of her pretty mouth. "And no, he does not hate you—Jiriki thinks very highly of you, Seoman Snowlock. He would never have brought you to Jao é-Tinukai'i otherwise, which confirmed in the minds of many of our folk that he is not entirely trustworthy. But your Miriamele is a mortal girl, and very young. There are fish in the river outside that have lived longer than she has. Do not be surprised that she finds owing someone her life to be a difficult burden."

Simon stared at her. He had expected more teasing, but Aditu was talking sensibly about Miriamele—and she was telling him things about the Sithi he had never heard her say. He was torn between two fascinating subjects.

"That's not all. At least, I don't think it is. I . . . I don't know how to be with her," he said finally. "With Princess Miriamele. I mean, I think about her all the time. But who am I to think about a princess?"

Aditu laughed, a sparkling sound like falling water. "You are Seoman the Bold. You saw the Yásira. You met First Grandmother. What other young mortal can say that?"

He felt himself blushing. "But that's not the point. She's a princess, Aditu—the High King's daughter!"

"The daughter of your enemy? Is that why you are troubled?" She seemed honestly puzzled.

"No." He shook his head. "No, no, no." He looked around wildly, trying to think of a way to make her see. "You are the daughter of the king and queen of the Zida'ya, aren't you?"

"That is more or less how it would be said in your speech. I am of the Year-Dancing House, yes."

"Well, what if someone who was from, I don't know, an unimportant family—a bad house or something like that—wanted to marry you?"

"A . . . bad house?" Aditu looked at him carefully. "Do you ask whether I would consider another of my folk to be beneath me? We have long been too few for that, Seoman. And why must you marry her? Do your people never make love without being married?"

Simon was speechless for a moment. Make love to the king's daughter without a thought of marrying her? "I am a knight," he said stiffly. "I have to be honorable."

"Loving someone is not honorable?" She shook her head, mocking smile now returned. "And you say you do not understand *me*, Seoman!"

Simon rested his elbows on his knees and covered his face with his hands. "You mean that your people don't care who marries who? I don't believe it."

"That is what tore asunder the Zida'ya and Hikeda'ya," she said. When he looked up, her gold-flecked gaze had become hard. "We have learned from that terrible lesson."

"What do you mean?"

"It was the death of Drukhi, the son of Utuk'ku and her husband Ekimeniso Blackstaff, that drove the families apart. Drukhi loved and married Nenais'u, the Nightingale's daughter." She raised her hand and made a gesture like a book being closed. "She was killed by mortals in the years before Tumet'ai was swallowed by the ice. It was an accident. She was dancing in the forest when a mortal huntsman was drawn to the glimmer of her bright dress. Thinking he saw a bird's plumage, he loosed an arrow. When her husband Drukhi found her, he went mad." Aditu bent her head, as though it had happened only a short while before.

After she had gone some moments without speaking, Simon asked: "But how did that drive the families apart? And what does that have to do with marrying whoever you want?"

"It is a very long story, Seoman—perhaps the longest that our people tell, excepting only the flight from the Garden and our coming across the black seas to this land." She pushed at one of the shent-stones with her finger. "At that time, Utuk'ku and her husband ruled all the Gardenborn—they were the keepers of the Year-Dancing groves. When their son fell in love with Nenais'u, daughter of Jenjiyana and her mate Initri, Utuk'ku furiously opposed it. Nenais'u's parents were of our Zida'ya clan—although it had a different name in those long-ago days. They were also of the belief that the mortals, who had come to this land after the Gardenborn had arrived, should be permitted to live as they would, as long as they did not make war on our people."

She made another, more intricate arrangement of the stones on the board before her. "Utuk'ku and her clan felt that the mortals should be pushed back across the ocean, and that those who would not leave should be killed, as some mortal farmers crush the insects they find on their crops. But since the two great clans and the other smaller clans allied with one or the other were so evenly divided, even Utuk'ku's position as Mistress of Year-Dancing House did not permit her to force her will on the rest. You see, Seoman, we have never had 'kings' and 'queens' as you mortals have.

"In any case, Utuk'ku and her husband were fiercely angry that their son had married a woman of what they considered to be the traitorous, mortal-loving clan that opposed them. When Nenais'u was slain, Drukhi went mad and swore that he would kill every mortal he could find. The men of Nenais'u's clan restrained him, although they were, in their own way, as bitterly angry and horrified as he. When the Yásira was called, the Gardenborn could come to no decision, but enough feared what might happen if Drukhi was free that they decided he must be confined—something that had never happened this side of the Ocean." She sighed. "It was too much for him, too much for his madness, to be held prisoner by his own people while those he deemed his wife's murderers went free. Drukhi made himself die."

Simon was fascinated, although he could tell from Aditu's expression how sad the story was to her. "Do you mean he killed himself?"

"Not as you think of it, Seoman. No, rather Drukhi just . . . stopped living. When he was found lying dead in the Si'injan'dre Cave, Utuk'ku and Ekimeniso took their clan and went north, swearing that they would never again live with Jenjiyana's people."

"But first everyone went to Sesuad'ra," he said. "They went to Leavetaking House and they made their pact. What I saw during my vigil in the Observatory."

She nodded. "From what you have said, I believe you had a true vision of the past, yes."

"And that is why Utuk'ku and the Norns hate mortals?" he asked.

"Yes. But they also went to war with some of the first mortals in Hernystir, back long before Hern gave it the name. In that fighting, Ekimeniso and many of the other Hikeda'ya lost their lives. So they have other grudges to nurse, as well."

Simon sat back, wrapping his arms about his knees. "I didn't know. Morgenes or Binabik or someone told me that the battle of the Knock was the first time that mortals had killed Sithi."

"Sithi, yes—the Zida'ya. But Utuk'ku's people clashed with mortals several times before the shipmen came from over the western sea and changed everything." She lowered her head. "So you can see," Aditu finished, "why we of the Dawn Children are careful not to say that someone is above someone else. Those are words that mean tragedy to us."

He nodded. "I think I understand. But things are different with us, Aditu. There are rules about who can marry who . . . and a princess can't marry a landless knight, especially one who used to be a kitchen boy."

"You have seen these rules? Are they kept in one of your holy places?"

He made a face. "You know what I mean. You should hear Camaris if you want to find out how things work. He knows everything—who bows to who, who gets to wear which colors on what day . . ." Simon laughed ruefully. "If I ever asked him about someone like me marrying the princess, I think he'd cut my head off. But nicely. And he wouldn't enjoy doing it."

"Ah, yes, Camaris." Aditu seemed to be about to say something significant. "He is a . . . strange man. He has seen many things, I think."

Simon looked at her carefully but could not discern any particular meaning behind her words. "He has. And I think he means to teach them all to me before we reach Nabban. Still, that's nothing to complain about." He stood up. "As a matter of fact, it's going to be dark before too long, so I should go and see him. There was something he wanted to show me about using a shield . . ." Simon paused. "Thank you for talking to me, Aditu."

She nodded. "I do not think I have said anything to help you, but I hope you will not be so sad, Seoman."

He shrugged as he swept his cloak up from the floor.

"Hold," she said, rising. "I will come with you."

"To see Camaris?"

"No. I have another errand. But I will walk with you down to where our paths part."

She followed him out through the tent flap. Untouched, the crystal globe flickered and dimmed, then went dark.

"So?" asked Duchess Gutrun. Miriamele could clearly hear the fear beneath her impatient tone.

Geloë stood. She squeezed Vorzheva's hand for a moment, then set it down atop the blanket. "It is nothing too bad," the witch woman said. "A little blood, that is all, and stopped now. You have had your own children, Gutrun, and grandmothered many more. You should know better than to fret her this way."

The duchess set her chin defiantly. "I have had and raised my own children, yes, which is more than some can say." When Geloë did not even raise an eyebrow at this sally, Gutrun continued with only a little less heat. "But I never bore any of my children on horseback, and I swear that is what her husband means for her to do!" She looked to Miriamele as though for support, but her would-be ally only shrugged. There was little point in arguing now—the deed was done. The prince had chosen to go to Nabban.

"I can ride in the wagon," Vorzheva said. "By the Grass-Thunderer, Gutrun, the women of my clan ride on horses sometimes until their last moon!"

"Then the other women of your clan are fools," Geloë said dryly, "even if you are not. Yes, you can ride in a wagon. That should not be too bad on open grassland." She turned to Gutrun. "As for Josua, you know he is doing what seems best. I agree with him. It is harsh, but he cannot halt everybody for a hundred days so his wife can bear their child in peace and quiet."

"Then there should be some other way to do things. I told Isgrimnur that it was cruelty, and I meant it. I told him to tell Prince Josua as well. I don't care what the prince thinks of me, I can't bear to see Vorzheva suffer this way."

Geloë's smile was grim. "I am sure your husband listened to you carefully, Gutrun, but I doubt that Josua will ever hear it."

"What do you mean?" the duchess demanded.

Before the forest woman could reply—although Miriamele thought she looked in no hurry to do so—there was a soft noise at the door of the tent. The flap slid back, revealing for the merest instant a spatter of stars, then Aditu's lithe form slipped through and the cloth fell back into place.

"Do I intrude?" the Sitha asked. Oddly, Miriamele thought that she sounded as though she meant it. To a young woman raised on the false politeness of her father's court, it was strange to hear someone asking that as though they wanted an answer. "I heard you were ill, Vorzheva."

"I am better," said Josua's wife, smiling. "Come in, Aditu, you are very welcome here."

The Sitha sat on the floor near Vorzheva's bed, her golden eyes intent on the sick woman, her long, graceful hands folded in her lap. Miriamele could not help staring. Unlike Simon, who seemed quite accustomed to the Sithi, she had not yet grown used to having such a foreign creature among them. Aditu seemed as strange as something from an old story, but stranger still because she was sitting right here in the dim rushlight, as real as a stone or a tree. It was as though the past year had turned the entire world upside down, and all the hidden things remembered only in legends had come tumbling out.

Aditu pulled a pouch from her gray tunic and held it up. "I have brought something to help you sleep." She spilled a small cluster of green leaves into her palm, then showed them to Geloë, who nodded. "I will brew them for you while we talk."

The Sitha appeared not to notice Gutrun's disgruntled stare. Using a pair of sticks, Aditu levered a hot stone from the fire, knocked off the ashes, then dropped it into a bowl of water. When a cloud of steam hung over it, she crumbled in the leaves. "I am told we will remain here one more day. That will give you a chance to rest, Vorzheva."

"I do not know why everyone is so frightened for me. It is only a child. Women bear children every day."

"Not the prince's only child," Miriamele said quietly. "Not in the middle of a war."

Aditu was using the hot stone to further crush the leaves, pushing it about with a stick. "You and your mate will have a healthy child, I am sure," she said. To Miriamele, it sounded incongruously like the kind of thing a mortal might have said—polite, cheerful. Maybe Simon was right after all.

When the stone was removed, Vorzheva sat up to take the bowl, which still steamed. She took a small sip. Miriamele watched the muscles in the Thrithingswoman's pale neck move as she swallowed.

She's so lovely, Miriamele thought.

Vorzheva's eyes were huge and dark, though heavy-lidded with fatigue; her hair was a thick black cloud about her head. Miriamele's fingers crept up to her own shorn locks and felt the ragged ends where the dyed hair had been cut off. She could not help feeling like an ugly little sister.

Be still, she told herself angrily. *You're as pretty as you need to be. What more do you want—do you need?*

But it was hard to be in the same room with boldly beautiful Vorzheva and the feline, graceful Sitha and not feel a little frowsy.

But Simon likes me. She almost smiled. *He does, I can tell.* Her mood soured. *But what does it matter? He can't do what I have to do. And he doesn't know anything about me, anyway.*

It was strange, though, to think that the Simon who had pledged her his service—it had been a strange and painful moment, but sweet, too—was the same person as the gangling boy who had accompanied her to Naglimund. Not that he had changed so much, but what *had* changed . . . He was older. Not just his height, not just the fuzzy beard, but in his eyes and in the way he stood. He would be a handsome man, she now saw—something she would never have said when they stopped in Geloë's forest house. His prominent nose, his long-boned face, had gained something in the intervening months, a rightness that they hadn't had before.

What was it that one of her nurses had said once of another Hayholt child? "He has to grow into that face." Well, that was definitely true of Simon. And he was doing just that.

Little surprise, though, she supposed. He had done so many things since leaving the Hayholt—why, he was almost a hero! He had faced a dragon! What had Sir Camaris or Tallistro ever done that was braver? And although Simon played down his meeting with the ice-worm—while at the same time, Miri-amele had seen, he was dying to boast a little—he had also stood at her side when a giant had charged. She had seen his bravery then. *Neither* of them had run, so she was brave, too. Simon was indeed a good companion . . . and now he was her protector.

Miriamele felt warm and strangely fluttery, as though something swift-winged moved inside of her. She tried to harden herself against it, against any such feelings. This was not the time. This was definitely not the time—and soon there might not be time for anything. . . .

Aditu's quietly musical voice pulled her back to the tent and the people who surrounded her. "If you have done all that you wished to do for Vorzheva," the Sitha was saying to Geloë, "I would like to have your company for a little while. I wish to speak to you of something."

Gutrun made a rumbling noise, which Miriamele guessed was meant to convey the duchess' impression of people who would go off and tell secrets. Geloë either ignored or did not hear her wordless comment, and said: "I think what she needs now is sleep, or at least some quiet." Now she turned at last to Gutrun. "I will look in on her later."

"As you wish," said the duchess.

The witch woman nodded to Vorzheva, then to Miriamele, before following Aditu out of the tent. The Thrithings-woman, who was lying back now, raised her hand in farewell. Her eyes were almost closed. She appeared to be falling asleep.

The tent was silent for some moments except for the tuneless humming of Gutrun as she sewed, which continued even as she held the cloth close to the fire to examine her stitchery. At last, Miriamele stood up.

"Vorzheva is tired. I will leave, too." She leaned forward and took the Thrithings-woman's hand. Her eyes opened; it took them a moment to fix on Miriamele. "Good night. I'm sure it will be a fine baby, one that will make you and Uncle Josua very proud."

"Thank you." Vorzheva smiled and closed her long-lashed eyes again.

"Good night, Auntie Gutrun," Miriamele said. "I'm glad you were here when I came back from the south. I missed you." She kissed the duchess' warm cheek, then delicately untangled herself from Gutrun's motherly embrace and slipped out through the door.

"I haven't heard her call me that for years!" Miriamele heard Gutrun say in surprise. Vorzheva mumbled something sleepily. "The poor child seems so quiet and sad these days," Gutrun went on. "But then again, why shouldn't she . . . ?"

Miriamele, walking away through the wet grass, did not hear the rest of what the duchess had to say.

Aditu and Geloë walked beside the whispering Stefflod. The moon was covered in a net of clouds, but stars glinted higher up in the blackness. A soft breeze was blowing from the east, carrying the scent of grass and wet stones.

"It is strange, what you say, Aditu." The witch woman and the Sitha made a peculiar pair, the immortal's loose-limbed stride reined in to match Geloë's more stalwart tread. "But I do not think there is harm in it."

"I do not say that there is, only that it bears thinking about." The Sitha laughed hissingly. "To think that I have grown so embroiled in the doings of mortals! Mother's brother Khendraja'aro would grind his teeth."

"These mortal concerns *are* your family's concerns, at least in part," Geloë said matter-of-factly. "Otherwise, you would not be here."

"I know that," agreed Aditu. "But many of my people will walk a long way around to find some other reason for what we do than anything that smacks of mortals and their affairs." She leaned down and plucked a few blades of grass, then held them to her nose and sniffed. "The grass here is different than that which grows in the forest, or even on Sesuad'ra. It is . . . younger. I cannot feel as much life in it, but it is sweet for all that." She let the loose blades flutter to the ground. "But I have let my words wander. Geloë, I do not see any harm in Camaris at all, except that in him which would harm himself. But it is odd that he keeps his past a secret, and odder still when there are so many things he might know that could aid his people in this struggle."

"He will not be pushed," said Geloë. "If he tells his secrets, it will be in his own time, that is clear. We have all tried." She shoved her hands into the pocket of her heavy tunic. "Still, though, I cannot help being curious. Are you sure?"

"No," Aditu said thoughtfully. "Not sure. But an odd thing Jiriki told me has been at the back of my thoughts for some time. We both, he and I, thought that Seoman was the first mortal to set foot in Jao é-Tinukai'i. Certainly that is what my father and mother thought. But Jiriki told me that when Amerasu met Seoman she said that he was *not* the first. I have long wondered about that, but First Grandmother knew the history of the Gardenborn better than anyone—perhaps even better than silver-faced Utuk'ku, who has long brooded on the past, but never made its study an art, as Amerasu did."

"But I still don't know why you think the first might have been Camaris."

"In the beginning it was only a sense I had." Aditu turned and wandered down the bank toward the soft-singing river. "Something in the way he looked at me, even before he recovered his wits. I caught him staring at me several times when he did not think I was looking. Later, when his sense had returned, he continued to watch me—not slyly, but like someone who remembers something painful."

"That could have been anything—a resemblance to someone." Geloë frowned. "Or perhaps he was feeling shame over the way his friend John, the High King, hunted your people."

"John's persecution of the Zida'ya occurred almost entirely before Camaris came to the court, from what the archivist Strangyeard has told me," Aditu replied. "Don't stare!" she laughed. "I am curious about many things, and we Dawn Children have never been afraid of inquiry or scholarship, although we would not use either of those words."

"Still, there could be many reasons Camaris stared. You are not a common sight, Aditu no-Sa'onserei—at least not for mortals."

"True. But there is more. One night, before his memory was returned, I was walking by the Observatory, as you named it—and I saw him walking slowly toward me. I nodded, but he seemed absorbed in his shadow-world. I was singing a song—a very old song from Jhiná-T'seneí, a favorite of Amerasu's—and as I passed him, Geloë, I saw that his lips were moving." She stopped and squatted by the riverside, but looked up at the forest woman with eyes that even in the darkness seemed to glimmer like amber coals. "He was mouthing the words to the same song."

"Are you sure?"

"As certain as I am that the trees in the Grove are alive and will blossom again, and I feel that in my blood and heart. Amerasu's song was known to him, and although he still wore his faraway look, he was singing silently along with me. A playful song that First Grandmother used to sing. It is not the sort of tune that is sung in the cities of mortal men, or even in the oldest sacred grove in Hernystir."

"But what could it mean?" Geloë stood over Aditu, looking out across the river. The wind slowly shifted direction, blowing now from behind the encampment that lay just uphill. The normally imperturbable forest woman seemed faintly agitated. "Even if Camaris somehow knew Amerasu, what could it mean?"

"I do not know. But considering that Camaris' horn was once our enemy's, and that our enemy was also Amerasu's son—and once the greatest of my people—I feel a need to know. It is also true that the sword of this knight is very important to us." She made what was, for a Sitha, an unhappy face, a faint thinning of the lips. "If only Amerasu had lived to tell us her suspicions."

Geloë shook her head. "We have been laboring in shadows too long. Well, what can we do?"

"I have approached him. He does not wish to talk to me, although he is polite. When I try to guide him toward the subject, he pretends to misunderstand, or simply pleads some other necessity, then leaves." Aditu rose from the grass beside the river. "Perhaps Prince Josua can compel him to talk. Or Isgrimnur, who seems the nearest thing to a friend Camaris has. You know them both, Geloë. They are suspicious of me, for which I do not blame them—many mortal generations have passed since we could consider the Sudhoda'ya to be our allies. Perhaps at your urging, one of them may convince Camaris to tell us whether it is true that he was in Jao é-Tinukai'i, and what it might mean."

"I will try," promised Geloë. "I am to see the two of them later tonight. But even if they can convince Camaris, I am not sure there will be any value in what he has to say."

She ran her thick fingers through her hair. "Still, we have learned precious little else that is of use lately." She looked up. "Aditu? What is it?"

The Sitha had gone rigid, and stood with her head cocked in a most unhuman way.

"Aditu?" Geloë said again. "Are we attacked?"

"*Kei-vishaa,*" Aditu hissed. "I smell it!"

"What?"

"Kei-vishaa. It is . . . there is no time to explain. It is a smell that should not be in the air here. Something bad is happening. Follow me, Geloë—I am suddenly fearful!"

Aditu sprang away up the river bank, swift as a flushed deer. Within a moment she had vanished into the darkness, heading back toward the encampment. Following her, the witch woman ran a few more paces, muttering words of worry and anger. As she passed into the shadow of a congregation of willows that grew on a hill overlooking the streambank, there was a convulsive movement; the faint starlight seemed to bend, the darkness to coalesce and then burst outward. Geloë, or at least Geloë's shape, did not reemerge from the treeshadows, but a winged form did.

Yellow eyes wide in the moonlight, the owl flew in pursuit of swift Aditu, following the whisper-faint mark of her passage across the wet grass.

Simon had been restless all evening. Talking with Aditu had helped, but only a little. In a way, it had made him even more unsettled.

He desperately wanted to speak with Miriamele. He thought about her all the time—at night when he wanted just to fall asleep, during the day whenever he saw a girl's face or heard a woman's voice, at odd moments when he should be thinking of other things. It was strange how she had come to mean so much to him in the short time since she had returned: the smallest change in the way she treated him stayed in his mind for days.

She had seemed so strange when he had met her by the horses the night before. And yet, when she had accompanied him to Isgrimnur's fire to hear the singing, she had been kind and friendly, if a little distracted. But now she had avoided him all day today—or at least so it seemed, for everywhere he looked for her he was told that she was somewhere else, until it began to feel as though she was staying a step ahead of him on purpose.

The twilight had gone and darkness had settled in like a great black bird folding its wings. His visit with Camaris had been brief—the old man had seemed fully as preoccupied as he was, barely able to fix his attention on explaining the rank of battle and the rules of engagement. To Simon, consumed with worries more heated and more current, the knight's litany of rules had seemed dry and pointless. He had made excuses and departed early, leaving the old man sitting by the fire in his sparsely-furnished campsite. Camaris seemed just as happy to be left alone.

After a fruitless exploration of the camp, Simon had looked in on Vorzheva and Gutrun. Miriamele had been there, the duchess said—whispering so as not to wake the prince's sleeping wife—but had left some time before. Unrewarded, Simon had returned to his search.

Now, as he stood at the outer edge of the field of tents, at the beginnings of the wide halo of fires that marked the camps of those members of Josua's company to whom a tent was, at this moment, an unimaginable luxury, Simon puzzled over where Miriamele might be. He had walked along the riverbank earlier, thinking that she might be there keeping company with her thoughts by the water, but there had been no sign of her, only a few New Gadrinsett folk with torches, night-fishing with what appeared to be little success.

Maybe she's seeing to her horse, he thought suddenly.

That was, after all, where he had found her the night before, not too much earlier in the evening than it was now. Perhaps she found it a quiet place after everyone else had gone down to supper. He turned and headed for the dark hillside.

He stopped first to say hello to Homefinder, who received his greeting with a certain aloofness before condescending to snuffle at his ear, then he headed uphill toward the spot where the princess had said her horse was picketed. There was indeed a shadowy figure moving there. Pleased with his own cleverness, he stepped forward.

"Miriamele?"

The hooded figure started, then whirled. For a moment he could see nothing but a smear of pallid face in the depths of the hood.

"S-Simon?" It was a shocked, fearful voice—but it was her voice. "What are you doing here?"

"I was looking for you." The way she spoke alarmed him. "Are you well?" This time the question seemed tremendously appropriate.

"I am . . ." She moaned. "Oh, why did you come?"

"What's wrong?" He took a few paces toward her. "Have you . . . ?" He stopped.

Even in the moonlight, he could see that the silhouette of her horse seemed somehow wrong. Simon put out his hand and touched the bulging saddlebags.

"You're going somewhere . . ." he said wonderingly. "You're running away."

"I am *not* running away." The earlier tone of fear gave way to pain and fury. "I am not. Now leave me alone, Simon."

"Where are you going?" He was caught up in the strange dreaminess of it—the dark hillside with its few lonely trees, Miriamele's hooded face. "Is it me? Did I make you angry?"

Her laugh was bitter. "No, Simon, it's not you." Her voice softened. "You have done nothing wrong. You have been a friend when I didn't deserve one. I can't tell you where I'm going—and please wait until tomorrow to tell Josua you've seen me. Please. I beg this of you."

"But . . . but I can't!" How could he tell Josua that he had stood by and watched as the prince's niece had ridden away by herself? He tried to slow his excited heart and think. "I will go with you," he said finally.

"What!?" Miriamele was astonished. "You can't!"

"I can't let you go off by yourself, either. I am your sworn protector, Miriamele."

She seemed on the verge of crying. "But I don't want you to go, Simon. You are my friend—I don't want you hurt!"

"And I don't want you hurt, either." He felt calmer now. He had a strange but powerful feeling that this was the right decision . . . although another part of him was simultaneously crying *mooncalf, mooncalf!* "That's why I'm going with you."

"But Josua needs you!"

"Josua has lots of knights, and I'm the least of them. *You* only have one."

"I can't let you, Simon." She shook her head violently. "You don't understand what I'm doing, where I'm going. . . ."

"Then tell me."

She shook her head again.

"Then I'll just have to find out by going with you. Either you take me, or you stay. I'm sorry, Miriamele, but that is all."

She looked at him for a moment, staring hard, as though she would see into his very heart. She seemed to be in a kind of ecstasy of indecision, pulling distractedly at her horse's bridle until Simon feared the animal might startle and bolt. "Very well," she said at last. "Oh, Elysia save us all, very well! But we must go now, and you must ask me no more questions about where or why tonight."

"Fine," he said. The doubting part of him was still screaming for attention, but he had decided not to listen. He could not bear the idea of her riding away into the dark alone. "But I must go and get my sword and a few other things. Do you have food?"

"Enough for me . . . but you dare not try to steal more, Simon. There's too much chance someone would see you."

"Well, we'll worry about it later, then. But I must have a sword, and I must leave something to explain. Did you?"

She stared at him. "Are you mad?"

"Not to say where you're going, but just to tell them that you're gone of your own will. We have to, Miriamele," he explained firmly. "It's cruel, otherwise. They'll think we were kidnapped by the Norns, or that we've, we've . . ." he smiled as the thought came, ". . . we've run away to be married, like in the Mundwode song."

Her look turned calculating. "Very well, get your sword and leave a note."

Simon frowned. "I'm off. But remember, Miriamele, if you aren't here when I get back, I'll have Josua and every man of New Gadrinsett after you tonight."

She jutted her chin defiantly. "Go on, then. I want to ride until dawn and be well away, so hurry."

He threw her a mock-bow, then turned and ran down the hillside.

It was strange, but when Simon thought of that night later, during moments of terrible pain, he could no longer remember how he had felt as he hastened toward the camp—as he had prepared to steal off with the king's daughter, Miriamele. The memory of all that came afterward crowded out what had throbbed in him as he pelted down the hill.

On that night he felt all the world singing about him, all the stars hanging close and attentive above. As Simon ran, the world seemed poised on some vast fulcrum, teetering, and every possibility was both beautiful and terrible. It seemed for all the world as though the dragon Igjarjuk's molten blood had come alive in him again, opening him up to the vast sky, filling him with the pulse of the earth.

He dashed through the encampment with hardly a glance for any of the night life that surrounded him, hearing none of the voices that were raised in song or laughter or argument, seeing nothing but the twisting track through the tents and small camps toward his own sleeping place.

Happily for Simon, as it seemed, Binabik was away from the tent. He had not given a moment's thought to what he would have done if the little man had been waiting for him—he might have been able to come up with some practical reason for needing his sword, but could certainly not have left a note. Fumble-fingered with hurry, he ransacked the tent for something to write on, and at last found one of the scrolls Binabik had brought from Ookequk's cave in the Trollfells. With a bit of charcoal plucked from the cold firepit, he laboriously scrawled his message on the back of the sheep-leather.

"Mirimel has gon away and I hav gon after Her."

he wrote, tongue gripped between his teeth.

"We will be well. Tell Prince Josua I am sory but I hav to go. I will bring Her bak soon as I can. Tell Josua I am a bad knigt but I am tring to do wat is the best thing. Your frend Simon."

He thought for a moment, then added:

"You can hav my things if I dont cum bak. I am sory."

He left the note on Binabik's bedroll, grabbed his sword and scabbard and a few other necessities, then left the tent. At the doorway he hesitated for a moment, recalling his sack of beloved treasures, the White Arrow, Jiriki's mirror. He turned and went to retrieve it, although every moment he kept her waiting—she would wait; she *must* wait—felt like an hour. He had told Binabik he could have them, but Miriamele's earlier words returned to him. They were entrusted; they were promises. He could not give them away any more than he could give away his name, and there was not time now to sort out the things that could safely be left behind. He dared not even take the time to think or he knew that he would lose courage.

We will be alone together, just us two, he kept thinking in wonderment. *I will be her protector!*

It took him what seemed an agonizingly long time to find the sack where he had hidden it in a hole under a flap of sod. With sack and scabbard clutched under his arm, his worn saddle over his shoulder—he winced at the noise the harness buckles made—he ran as quickly as he could back through the camp to where the horses were tied, to where Miriamele—he prayed—was waiting.

She *was* there. Seeing her impatiently pacing, he felt a moment of giddiness. She had waited for him!

"Hurry up, Simon! The night is slipping away!" She seemed to feel none of his pleasure, but only a sense of frustration, a terrible need to be moving.

With Homefinder saddled and Simon's few belongings hastily pushed into the saddlebags, they were soon leading the horses up toward the hilltop, moving silently as spirits through the damp grass. They turned for a last look down at the glowing quilt of campfires spread in the river valley.

"Look!" Simon said, startled. "That's no cookfire!" He pointed to a large, moving billow of orange-red flame near the middle of the encampment. "Someone's tent is on fire!"

"I hope no harm comes to them, but at least it will keep people busy until we are away," said Miriamele grimly. "We must ride, Simon."

Suiting action to words, she clambered deftly into the saddle—she was once more wearing the breeches and shirt of a man beneath her heavy cloak—and led him down the hill's far side.

He took one last look back at the lights, then urged Homefinder after her, into shadows that even the emergent moon could not pierce.

PART THREE

The Turning Wheel

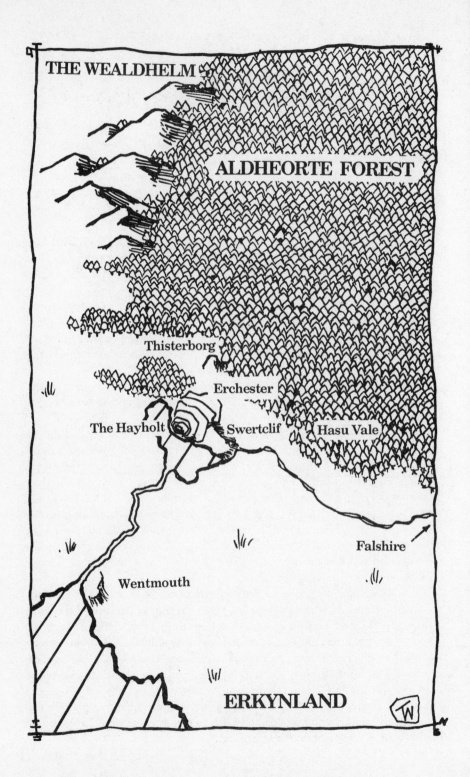

27

Tears and Smoke

✦

Tiamak found the empty treelessness of the High Thrithing oppressive. Kwanitupul was strange, too, but he had been visiting that place since childhood, and its tumbledown buildings and ubiquitous waterways at least reminded him a little of his marshy home. Even Perdruin, where he had spent time in lonely exile, was so filled with close-leaning walls and narrow pathways, so riddled with shadowy hiding places and blanketed in the salt smell of the sea, that Tiamak had been able to live with his homesickness. But here on the grasslands he felt tremendously exposed and utterly out of place. It was not a comforting feeling.

They Who Watch and Shape have indeed made a strange life for me, he often reflected. *The strangest, perhaps, of any they have made for my people since Nuobdig married the Fire Sister.*

Sometimes there was solace in this thought. To have been marked out for such unusual events was, after all, a sort of repayment for the years of misunderstanding that his own people and the drylanders on Perdruin had shown him. Of course he was not understood—he was special: what other Wrannaman could speak and read the drylander tongues as he could? But lately, surrounded again by strangers, and with no knowledge of what had happened to his own folk, it filled him with loneliness. At such times, disturbed by the emptiness of these queer northern surroundings, he would walk down to the river that ran through the middle of the camp to sit and listen to the calming, familiar sounds of the waterworld.

He had been doing just that, dangling his brown feet in the Stefflod despite the chill of water and wind, and was returning to camp a little heartened, when a shape flashed past him. It was someone running, pale hair streaming, but whoever it was seemed to move as swiftly as a dragonfly, far faster than anyone human should travel. Tiamak had only a moment to stare after the fleeing form before another dark shape swept past. It was a bird, a large one, flying low to the ground as though the first figure was its prey.

As both shapes vanished up the slope toward the heart of the prince's encampment, Tiamak stood in stunned amazement. It took some moments for him to realize who the first shape had been.

The Sitha-woman! he thought. *Chased by a hawk or an owl?*

It made no sense, but then she—Aditu was her name—made little sense to Tiamak either. She was like nothing he had ever seen and, in fact, frightened him a little. But what could be chasing her? From the look on her face she had been running from something dreadful.

Or *to* something dreadful, he realized, and felt his stomach clench. She had been heading toward the camp.

He Who Always Steps on Sand, Tiamak prayed as he set out, *protect me—protect us all from evil.* His heart was beating swiftly now, faster than the pace of his running feet. *This is an ill-omened year!*

For a moment, as he reached the nearest edge of the vast field of tents, he was reassured. It was quiet, and few campfires burned. But there was *too much* quiet, he decided a moment later. It was not early, but still well before midnight. People should be about, or at least there should be some noise from those not yet asleep. What could be wrong?

It had been long moments since he had caught his most recent glimpse of the swooping bird—he was certain now it was an owl—and he hobbled on in the direction he had last seen it, his breath now coming in harsh gasps. His injured leg was not used to running, and it burned him, throbbed. He did his best to ignore it.

Quiet, quiet—it was still as a stagnant pond here. The tents stood, dark and lifeless as the stones drylanders set in fields where they buried their dead.

But there! Tiamak felt his stomach turn again. There was movement! One of the tents not far away shook as though in a wind, and some light inside it threw strange moving shadows onto the walls.

Even as he saw it, he felt a tickling in his nostrils, a sort of burning, and with it came a sweet, musky scent. He sneezed convulsively and almost tripped, but caught himself before falling to the ground. He limped toward the tent, which pulsed with light and shadow as though some monstrous thing was being born inside. He tried to raise his voice to cry out that he was coming and to raise an alarm, for his fear was rising higher and higher—but he could not make a sound. Even the painful rasp of his breathing had become faint and whispery.

The tent, too, was strangely silent. Pushing down his fright, he caught at the flap and threw it back.

At first he could see nothing more than dark shapes and bright light, almost an exact reflection of the shadow puppets on the outside walls of the tent. Within a few instants, the moving images began to come clear.

At the tent's far wall stood Camaris. He seemed to have been struck, for blood rilled from some cut on his head, staining his cheek and hair black, and he reeled as though his wits had been addled. Still, bowed and leaning against the fabric for support, he was yet fierce, like a bear beset by hounds. He had no blade, but held a piece of firewood clenched in one fist and waved it back and forth, holding off a menacing shape that was almost all black, but for a flash of white hands and something that glinted in one of those hands.

Kicking near Camaris' feet was an even less decipherable muddle, although Tiamak thought he saw more black-clothed limbs, as well as the pale nimbus of Aditu's hair. A third dark-clad attacker huddled in the corner, warding off a swooping, fluttering shadow.

Terrified, Tiamak tried to raise his voice to call for help, but could make no sound. Indeed, despite what seemed to be life-or-death struggles, the entire tent was silent but for the muffled sounds of the two combatants on the floor and the hectic flapping of wings.

Why can't I hear? Tiamak thought desperately. *Why can't I make a sound?*

Frantic, he searched the floor for something to use as a weapon, cursing himself that he had carelessly left his knife behind in the sleeping-place he shared with Strangyeard. No knife, no sling-stones, no blow-darts—nothing! She Who Waits to Take All Back had surely sung his song tonight.

Something vast and soft seemed to strike him in the head, sending Tiamak to his knees, but when he looked up, the several battles still raged, none of them near him. His skull was throbbing even more painfully than his leg and the sweet smell was chokingly strong. Dizzy, Tiamak crawled forward and his hand encountered something hard. It was the knight's sword, black Thorn, still sheathed. Tiamak knew it was far too heavy for him to use, but he dragged it out from beneath the tangle of bedding and stood, as unsteady now on his feet as Camaris. What was in the air?

The sword, unexpectedly, seemed light in his hands, despite the heavy scabbard and dangling belt. He raised it high and took a few steps forward, then swung it as hard as he could at what he thought was the head of Camaris' attacker. The impact shivered up his arm, but the thing did not fall. Instead, the head turned slowly. Two eyes, shining black, stared out of the corpse-white face. Tiamak's throat moved convulsively. Even had his voice remained, he could not have made a sound. He lifted his shaking arms, holding the sword up to strike again, but the thing's white hand flashed out and Tiamak was knocked backward. The room whirled away from him; the sword flew from his nerveless fingers and tumbled to the grass that was the tent's only floor.

Tiamak's head was as heavy as stone, but he could not otherwise feel the pain of the blow. What he could feel were his wits slipping away. He tried to lift himself to his feet once more but only got as far as his knees. He crouched, shaking like a sick dog.

He could not speak but, cursedly, could still see. Camaris was stumbling, wagging his head—as damaged, seemingly, as Tiamak. The old man was trying to hold off his attacker long enough to reach something on the ground—the sword, the Wrannaman realized groggily, the black sword. Camaris was prevented from reaching it as much by the dark, contorted forms of Aditu and her enemy rolling on the ground beneath him as by the foe he was trying to keep at bay with his firelog club.

In the other corner, something glittered in the hand of one of the pale-faced things, a shining something red as a crescent of firelight. The scarlet gleam moved, swift as a striking snake, and a tiny cloud of dark shapes exploded outward, then drifted to the ground, slower than snowflakes. Tiamak squinted helplessly as one settled on his hand. It was a feather. An owl's feather.

Help. Tiamak's skull felt as though it had been staved in. *We need help. We will die if no one helps us.*

Camaris at last bent and caught up the sword, almost over-balancing, then managed to lift Thorn in time to hold off a strike by his enemy. The two of them circled each other, Camaris stumbling, the black-clad attacker moving with cautious grace. They fell together once more, and one of the old knight's hands shot out and pushed away a dagger blow, but the blade left a trail of blood down his arm. Camaris fell back clumsily, trying to find room to swing his sword. His eyes were half-closed with pain or fatigue.

He is hurt, Tiamak thought desperately. The throbbing in his head grew stronger. *Maybe dying. Why does no one come?*

The Wrannaman dragged himself toward the wide brazier of coals that provided the only light. His dimming senses were beginning to wink out like the lamps of Kwanitupul at dawn. Only a dim fragment of an idea was in his mind, but it was enough to lift his hand toward the iron brazier. When he felt—as dimly as a distant echo—the heat of the thing against his fingers, he pushed. The brazier tumbled over, scattering coals like a waterfall of rubies.

As Tiamak collapsed, choking, the last things he saw were his own soot-blackened hand curled like a spider and, beyond it, an army of tiny flames licking at the bottom of the tent wall.

"We don't *need* any more damnable questions," Isgrimnur grumbled. "We have enough to last three lifetimes. What we need are answers."

Binabik made an uncomfortable gesture. "I am agreeing with you, Duke Isgrimnur. But answers are not like a sheep that is coming when a person calls."

Josua sighed and leaned back against the wall of Isgrimnur's tent. Outside, the wind rose for a moment, moaning faintly as it vibrated the tent ropes. "I know how difficult it is, Binabik. But Isgrimnur is right—we need answers. The things you told us about this Conqueror Star have only added to the confusion. What we need to know is how to use the three Great Swords. All that the star tells us—if you are right—is that our time to wield them is running out."

"That is what we are giving the largest attention to, Prince Josua," said the troll. "And we think we may perhaps be learning something soon, for Strangyeard has found something that is of importantness."

"What is that?" Josua asked, leaning forward. "Anything, man, anything would be heartening."

Father Strangyeard, who had been sitting quietly, squirmed a little. "I am not as sure as Binabik, Highness, that it is of any use. I found the first of it some time ago, while we were still traveling to Sesuad'ra."

"Strangyeard was finding a passage that is written in Morgenes' book," Binabik amplified, "something about the three swords that are so much concerning us."

"And?" Isgrimnur tapped his fingers on his muddy knee. He had spent a long time trying to secure his tentstakes in the loose, damp ground.

"What Morgenes seems to suggest," the archivist said, "is that what makes the three swords special—no, more than special, *powerful*—is that they are not of Osten Ard. Each of them, in some way, goes against the laws of God and Nature."

"How so?" The prince was listening intently. Isgrimnur saw a little ruefully that these sorts of inquiries would always interest Josua more than the less exotic business of being a ruler, such as grain prices and taxes and the laws of freeholding.

Strangyeard was hesitant. "Geloë could explain better than I. She knows more of these things."

"She should have been coming here by now," Binabik said. "I wonder if we should be waiting for her."

"Tell me what you can," said Josua. "It has been a very long day and I am growing weary. Also, my wife is ill and I do not like being away from her."

"Of course, Prince Josua. I'm sorry. Of course." Strangyeard gathered himself. "Morgenes tells that there is something in each sword that is not of Osten Ard—not of our earth. Thorn is made from a stone that fell from the sky. Bright-Nail, which was once Minneyar, was forged from the iron keel of Elvrit's ship that came over the sea from the West. Those are lands that our ships can no longer find." He cleared his throat. "And Sorrow is of both iron and the Sithi witchwood, two things that are inimical. The witchwood itself, Aditu tells me, came over as seedlings from the place that her people call the Garden. None of these things should be here, and also, none of them should be workable . . . except perhaps the pure iron of Elvrit's keel."

"So how were these swords made, then?" asked Josua. "Or is that the answer you still seek?"

"There is something that Morgenes is mentioning," Binabik offered. "It is also written in one of Ookequk's scrolls. It is called a Word of Making—a magic spell is what we might be naming it, although those who are knowing the Art do not use those words."

"A Word of Making?" Isgrimnur frowned. "Just a word?"

"Yes . . . and no," Strangyeard said unhappily. "In truth, we are not sure. But Minneyar we know was made by the dwarrows—the dvernings as you would call them in your own tongue, Duke Isgrimnur—and Sorrow was made by Ineluki in the dwarrow forges beneath Asu'a. The dwarrows alone had the lore to make such mighty things, although Ineluki learned it. Perhaps they had a hand in Thorn's forging as well, or their lore was used somehow. In any case, it is possible that if we knew the way in which the swords were created, how the binding of forces was accomplished, it might teach us something about how we can use them against the Storm King."

"I wish I had thought to question Count Eolair more carefully when he was here," said Josua, frowning. "He had met the dwarrows."

"Yes, and they told him of their part in the history of Bright-Nail," Father Strangyeard added. "It is also possible, however, that it is *not* the making of them that is important for our purpose, but just the fact that they exist. Still, if we have some chance in the future to send word to the dwarrows, and if they will speak with us, I for one would have many questions."

Josua looked at the archivist speculatively. "This chore suits you, Strangyeard. I always thought you were wasted dusting books and searching out the most obscure points of canon law."

The priest reddened. "Thank you, Prince Josua. Whatever I can do is because of your kindness."

The prince waved his hand, dismissing the compliment. "Still, as much as you and Binabik and the rest have accomplished, there is still far more to do. We remain afloat in deep waters, praying for a sight of land . . ." He paused. "What is that noise?"

Isgrimnur had noticed it, too, a rising murmur that had slowly grown louder than the wind. "It sounds like an argument," he said, then waited for a moment, listening. "No, it is more than that—there are too many voices." He stood. "Dror's Hammer, I hope that someone has not started a rebellion." He reached for Kvalnir and was calmed by its reassuring heft. "I had hoped for a quiet day tomorrow before we are to ride again."

Josua clambered to his feet. "Let us not sit here and wonder."

As Isgrimnur stepped out of the door flap, his eyes were abruptly drawn across the vast camp. It was plain in an instant what was happening.

"Fire!" he called to the others as they spilled out after him. "At least one tent burning badly, but it looks like a few more have caught, too." People were now rushing about between the tents, shadowy figures that shouted and gesticulated. Men dragged on their sword belts, cursing in confusion. Mothers dragged screaming children out of their blankets and carried them into the open air. All the pathways were full of terrified, milling campfolk. Isgrimnur saw one old woman fall to her knees, crying, although she was only a few paces from where he stood, a long distance from the nearest flames.

"Aedon save us!" said Josua. "Binabik, Strangyeard, call for buckets and waterskins, then take some of these mad-wandering folk and head for the river—we need water! Better yet, pull down some of the oiled tents and see how much water you can carry in them!" He sprang away toward the conflagration; Isgrimnur hastened after him.

The flames were leaping high now, filling the night sky with a hellish orange light. As he and Josua approached the fire, a flurry of dancing sparks sailed out, hissing as they caught in Isgrimnur's beard. He beat them out, cursing.

Tiamak awakened and promptly threw up, then struggled to catch his breath. His head was hammering like a Perdruinese church bell.

There were flames all around him, beating hot against his skin, sucking away the air. In a blind panic, he dragged himself across the crisping grass of the tent floor toward what looked like a patch of cool darkness, only to find his face pushed up against some black, slippery fabric. He struggled with it for a moment, dimly noting its strange resistance; then it flopped aside, exposing a white face buried in the black hood. The eyes were turned up, and blood slicked the lips. Tiamak tried to scream, but his mouth was full of burning smoke and his own bile. He rolled away, choking.

Suddenly, something grabbed at his arm and he was yanked forward violently, dragged across the pale-skinned corpse and through a wall of flame. For a moment he thought he was dead. Something was thrown over him, and he was rolled and pummeled with the same swift violence that had carried him away, then whatever covered him was lifted and he found himself lying on wet grass. Flames licked at the sky close beside him, but he was safe. Safe!

"The Wrannaman is alive," someone said near him. He thought he recognized the Sitha-woman's lilting tones, although her voice was now almost sharp with fear and worry. "Camaris dragged him out. How the knight managed to stay awake after he had been poisoned I will never know, but he killed two of the Hikeda'ya." There was an unintelligible response.

After he had lain in place for a few long moments, just breathing the clean air into his painful lungs, Tiamak rolled over. Aditu stood a few paces away, her white hair blackened and her golden face streaked with grime. Beneath her on the ground lay the forest woman Geloë, partially wrapped in a cloak, but obviously naked beneath it, her muscular legs shiny with dew or sweat. As Tiamak watched, she struggled to sit up.

"No, you must not," Aditu said to her, then took a step backward. "By the Grove, Geloë, you are wounded."

With a trembling effort, Geloë lifted her head. "No," she said. Tiamak could barely hear her voice, a throaty whisper. "I am dying."

Aditu leaned forward, reaching out to her. "Let me help you. . . ."

"No!" Geloë's voice grew stronger. "No, Aditu, it is . . . too late. I have been stabbed . . . a dozen times." She coughed and a thin trickle of something dark ran down her chin, glinting in the light of the burning tents. Tiamak stared. He saw what he took to be Camaris' feet and legs behind her, the rest of the knight's long form stretched out in the grass hidden by her shadow. "I must go." Geloë tried to clamber to her feet but could not do so.

"There might be something . . ." Aditu began.

Geloë laughed weakly, then coughed again and spat out a gobbet of blood. "Do you think I . . . do not . . . know?" she said. "I have been a healer for . . . a long time." She held out a shaking hand. "Help me. Help me up."

Aditu's face, which for a moment had seemed as stricken as any mortal's, grew solemn. She took Geloë's hand, then leaned forward and clasped her other arm as well. The wise woman slowly rose to her feet; she swayed, but Aditu supported her.

"I must . . . go. I do not wish to die here." Geloë pushed away from Aditu and took a few staggering steps. The cloak fell away, exposing her nakedness to the leaping firelight. Her skin was slick with sweat and great smears of blood. "I will go back to my forest. Let me go while I still can."

Aditu hesitated a moment longer, then stepped back and lowered her head. "As you wish, Valada Geloë. Farewell, Ruyan's Own. Farewell . . . my friend. *Sinya'a du-n'sha é-d'treyesa inro.*"

Trembling, Geloë raised her arms, then took another step. The heat from the flames seemed to grow more intense, for Tiamak, where he lay, saw Geloë begin to shimmer. Her outline grew insubstantial, then a cloud of shadow or smoke seemed to appear where she stood. For a moment, the very night seemed to surge inward toward the spot, as though a stitch had been taken in the fabric of the Wrannaman's vision. Then the night was whole again.

The owl circled slowly for a moment where Geloë had been, then flew off, close above the wind-tossed grasses. Its movements were stiff and awkward, and several times it seemed that it must lose the wind and fall tumbling to the earth, but its lurching flight continued until the night sky had swallowed it.

His head still full of murk and painful clangor, Tiamak slumped back. He was not sure what he had seen, but he knew that something terrible had happened. A great sadness lurked just out of his reach. He was in no hurry to bring it closer.

What had been the thin sound of voices in the distance became a raucous shouting. Legs moved past him; the night seemed suddenly full of movement. There was a rush and sizzle of steam as someone threw a pail of water into the flames of what had been Camaris' tent.

A few moments later he felt Aditu's strong hands under his arms. "You will be trampled, brave marsh man," she said into his ear, then pulled him farther away from the conflagration, into the cool darkness beside some tents untouched by the blaze. She left him there, then returned shortly with a water skin. The Sitha pressed it against his cracked lips until he understood what it was, then left him to drink—which he did, greedily.

A dark shadow loomed, then abruptly sank down beside him. It was Camaris. His silvery hair, like Aditu's, was scorched and blackened. Haunted eyes stared from his ash-smeared face. Tiamak handed him the water skin, then prodded him until he lifted it to his lips.

"God have mercy on us . . ." Camaris croaked. He stared dazedly at the spreading fires and the shouting mob that was trying to douse them.

Aditu returned and sat down beside them. When Camaris offered her the water skin, she took it from him and downed a single swallow before handing it back.

"Geloë . . . ?" Tiamak asked.

Aditu shook her head. "Dying. She has gone away."

"Who . . ." It was still hard to speak. Tiamak almost did not want to, but he suddenly felt a desire to *know,* to have some reasons with which to balance off the terrible events. He also needed something—words if nothing else—to fill the emptiness inside of him. He took the skin bag from Camaris and moistened his throat. "Who was it . . . ?"

"The Hikeda'ya," she said, watching the efforts to quell the flames. "The Norns. That was Utuk'ku's long arm that reached out tonight."

"I . . . I tried to . . . to call for help. But I couldn't."

Aditu nodded. "Kei-vishaa. It is a sort of poison that floats on the wind. It kills the voice for a time, and also brings sleep." She looked at Camaris, who had leaned back against the tent wall that sheltered them. His head was thrown back, his eyes closed. "I do not know how he stood against it for the time he did. If he had not, we would have been too late. Geloë's sacrifice would have been for nothing." She turned to the Wrannaman. "You, too, Tiamak. Things would have been different without your aid: you found Camaris' sword. Also, the fire frightened them. They knew they did not have much time, and that made them careless. Otherwise, I think we would all be there still." She indicated the burning tent.

Geloë's sacrifice. Tiamak found his eyes filling with tears. They stung.

She Who Waits to Take All Back, he prayed desperately, *do not let her drift by!* He covered his face with his hands. He did not want to think any more.

Josua ran faster. When Isgrimnur caught him at last, the prince had already stopped to make sure that the fires were being mastered. The original blaze had spread only a little way, catching perhaps a half-dozen other tents at most, and all but some in the first tent had escaped. Sangfugol was one of them. He stood, clothed only in a long shirt, and blearily watched the proceedings.

After assuring himself that everything possible was being done, Isgrimnur followed Josua to Camaris and the other two survivors, the Sitha-woman and little Tiamak, who were resting nearby. They were all bloodied and singed, but Isgrimnur felt sure after looking them over quickly that they would all live.

"Ah, praise merciful Aedon that you escaped, Sir Camaris," said Josua, kneeling at the side of the old knight. "I feared rightly that it might be your tent when we first saw the blaze." He turned to Aditu, who seemed to have her wits about her, which could not quite be said of Camaris and the marsh man. "Who have we lost? I am told there are bodies inside the tent still."

Aditu looked up. "Geloë, I fear. She was badly wounded. Dying."

"God curse it!" Josua's voice cracked. "Cursed day!" He pulled a handful of grass and flung it down angrily. With an effort, he calmed himself. "Is she still in there? And who are the others?"

"They are none of them Geloë," she said. "The three inside the tent are those you call Norns. Geloë has gone to the forest."

"What!" Josua sat back, stunned. "What do you mean, gone to the forest? You said she was dead."

"Dying." Aditu spread her fingers. "She did not want us to see her last moments, I think. She was strange, Josua—stranger than you know. She went away."

"Gone?"

The Sitha nodded slowly. "Gone."

The prince made the sign of the Tree and bowed his head. When he looked up, there were tears running on his cheek; Isgrimnur did not think they were caused by the smoke. He, too, felt a shadow move over him as he thought of the loss of Geloë. With so many pressing tasks he could not dwell on it now, but the duke knew from long experience in battle that it would strike him hard later.

"We have been attacked in our very heart," the prince said bitterly. "How did they get past the sentries?"

"The one I fought was dripping wet," said Aditu. "They may have come down the river."

Josua swore. "We have been dangerously lax, and I am the worst miscreant. I had thought it strange we had escaped the Norns' attentions so long, but my precautions were inadequate. Were there more than those three?"

"I think there were no more," Aditu replied. "And they would have been more than enough, but that we were lucky. If Geloë and I had not guessed something was amiss, and if Tiamak had not somehow known and arrived when he did, this tale would have had a different ending. I think they meant to kill Camaris, or at least to take him."

"But why?" Josua looked at the old knight, then back to Aditu.

"I do not know. But let us carry him, and Tiamak, too, to some warm place, Prince Josua. Camaris has at least one wound, perhaps more, and Tiamak is burned, I think."

"Aedon's mercy, you are right," said Josua. " 'Thoughtless, thoughtless. One moment." He turned and called some of his soldiers together, then sent them off with orders for the sentries to search the camp. "We cannot be sure there were not more Norns or other attackers," Josua said. "At the very least, we may find something to tell us how these came into our camp without being seen."

"None of the Gardenborn are easily seen by mortals—if they do not wish to be seen," said Aditu. "May we take Camaris and Tiamak away now?"

"Of course." Josua called two of the bucket carriers. "You men! Come and help us!" He turned to Isgrimnur. "Four should be enough to carry them, even though Camaris is large." He shook his head. "Aditu is right—we have made these brave ones wait too long."

The duke had been in such situations before, and knew that too much haste was as bad as too little. "I think we would be better to find something to carry them on," he said. "If one of those outer tents has been saved from the fire, we might use it to make a litter or two."

"Good." Josua stood. "Aditu, I did not ask if *you* had wounds that needed tending."

"Nothing I cannot care for myself, Prince Josua. When these two have been seen to, we should gather those that you trust and talk."

"I agree. There is much to talk about. We will meet at Isgrimnur's tent within the hour. Does that suit you, Isgrimnur?" The prince turned aside for a moment, then turned back. His face was haggard with grief. "I was thinking that we should find Geloë to come nurse them . . . then I remembered."

Aditu made a gesture, fingers touching fingers before her. "This is not the last time we shall miss her, I think."

♚

"It is Josua," the prince called from outside the tent. When he stepped inside, Gutrun still had the knife held before her. The duchess looked fierce as an undenned badger, ready to protect herself and Vorzheva from whatever danger might show itself. She lowered the dagger as Josua entered, relieved but still full of worry.

"What is it? We heard the shouting. Is my husband with you?"

"He is safe, Gutrun." Josua walked to the bed, then leaned forward and pulled Vorzheva to him in a swift embrace. He kissed her brow as he released her. "But we have been attacked by the Storm King's minions. We have lost only one, but that is a great loss."

"Who?" Vorzheva caught his arm as he tried to straighten.

"Geloë."

She cried out in grief.

"Three Norns attacked Camaris," Josua explained. "Aditu, Geloë, and the Wrannaman Tiamak came to his aid. The Norns were killed, but Aditu says that Geloë took a fatal wound." He shook his head. "I think she was the wisest of us all. Now she is gone and we cannot replace her."

Vorzheva fell back. "But she was just here, Josua. She came with Aditu to see me. Now she is dead?" Tears filled her eyes.

Josua nodded sadly. "I came to see that you were safe. Now I must go meet with Isgrimnur and the others to decide what this means, what we will do." He stood, then bent and kissed his wife again. "Do not sleep—and keep your knife, Gutrun—until I can send someone here to guard you."

"No one else was hurt? Gutrun said that she saw fires."

"Camaris' tent. He seems to have been the only one attacked." He began to move toward the door.

"But Josua," Vorzheva said, "are you sure? Our camp is so big."

The prince shook his head. "I am sure of nothing, but we have not heard of any other attacks. I will have someone here to guard you soon. Now I must hurry, Vorzheva."

"Let him go, Lady," Gutrun told her. "Lie back and try to sleep. Think of your child."

Vorzheva sighed. Josua squeezed her hand, then turned and hastened from the tent.

♔

Isgrimnur looked up as the prince strode into the light of the campfire. The cluster of men waiting for the prince stepped back respectfully, letting him pass. "Josua . . ." the duke began, but the prince did not let him finish.

"I have been foolish, Isgrimnur. It is not enough to have sentries running through the camp looking for signs of invading Norns. Aedon's Blood, it took me long enough to realize it—Sludig!" he shouted. "Is Sludig somewhere nearby?"

The Rimmersman stepped forward. "Here, Prince Josua."

"Send soldiers through the camp to see if everyone is accounted for, especially those of our party who might be at risk. Binabik and Strangyeard were with me until the fire started, but that does not mean they are safe still. It is late in the day for me to realize this might have been a diversion. And my niece, Miriamele—send someone to her tent immediately. And Simon, too, although he may be with Binabik." Josua frowned. "If they wanted Camaris, it seems likely it was about the sword. Simon carried it for a while, so perhaps there is some danger to him as well. Damn me for my slow wits."

Isgrimnur made a throat-clearing noise. "I already sent Freosel to look after Miriamele, Josua. I knew you would want to see Lady Vorzheva as soon as you could and I thought it should not wait."

"Thank you, Isgrimnur. I did go to her. She and Gutrun are fine." Josua scowled. "But I am shamed you have had to do my thinking."

Isgrimnur shook his head. "Let's just hope the princess is safe."

"Freosel has been sent after Miriamele," Josua told Sludig. "That is one less to hunt for. Go and see to the rest now. And post two guards at my tent, if you would. I will think better knowing that someone is watching over Vorzheva."

The Rimmersman nodded. He commandeered a large portion of the soldiers who were milling aimlessly around Isgrimnur's camp and went off to do as he had been bid.

"And now," Josua said to Isgrimnur, "we wait. And think."

★ ★ ★

Before the hour was too much older, Aditu reappeared; Father Strangyeard and Binabik were with her. They had gone with the Sitha to make sure Camaris and Tiamak were resting comfortably in the care of one of New Gadrinsett's healing-women—and also, apparently, to talk, for they were all three deep in conversation when they reached Isgrimnur's tent.

Aditu told Josua and the rest all the details of the night's events. She spoke calmly, but Isgrimnur could not help noticing that, although she chose her words with as much care as ever, the Sitha seemed profoundly troubled. She and Geloë had been friends, he knew: apparently the Sithi felt grief just as mortals did. He liked her better for it, then dismissed the thought as unworthy. Why should immortals *not* take hurt like humans? From what Isgrimnur knew, they had certainly suffered at least as much.

"So." Josua sat back and looked around the circle. "We have found no trace of anyone else being attacked. The question is, why did they single out Camaris?"

"There *must* be something to this Three Swords rhyme after all," said Isgrimnur. He didn't like such things: they made him feel as though the ground beneath his feet was unsolid, but that seemed to be the kind of world he found himself in. It was hard not to yearn for the clean edge that things had when he was younger. Even the worst of matters, like war, terrible as it was, had not been so shot through with strange sorceries and mysterious enemies. "They must have been after Camaris because of Thorn."

"Or perhaps it was Thorn alone they were seeking for," Binabik said soberly. "And Camaris was not of the most importance."

"I still do not understand how they were able almost to overcome him," Strangyeard said. "What is that poison you spoke of, Aditu?"

"Kei-vishaa. In truth, it is not just a poison: we Gardenborn use it in the Grove when it is time to dance the year's end. But it can also be wielded to bring a long, heavy sleep. It was brought from Venyha Do'sae; my people used it when they first came here, to remove dangerous animals—some of them huge creatures whose like have long passed from Osten Ard—from the places where we wished to build our cities. When I smelled it, I knew that something was wrong. We Zida'ya have never used it for anything except the year-dancing ceremonies."

"How is it used there?" the archivist asked, fascinated.

Aditu only lowered her eyes. "I am sorry, good Strangyeard, but that is not for me to say. I perhaps should not have mentioned it at all. I am tired."

"We have no need to pry into your people's rituals," said Josua. "And we have more important things to speak of, in any case." He turned an irritated look on Strangyeard, who hung his head. "It is enough that we know how they were able to attack Camaris without his raising an alarm. We are lucky that Tiamak had the presence of mind to set the tent ablaze. From now on, we will be absolutely rigid in the arrangement of our camp. All who are in any way at risk will set their tents close together in the very center, so we all sleep within sight of each other. I blame myself for indulging Camaris' wish for solitude. I have taken my responsibilities too lightly."

Isgrimnur frowned. "We must all be more careful."

As the council turned to talk of what other precautions should be taken, Freosel appeared at the fireside. "Sorry, Highness, but the princess be not anywhere 'round her tent, nor did anyone see her since early."

Josua was clearly upset. "Not there? Aedon preserve us, was Vorzheva right? Did they come for the princess after all?" He stood up. "I cannot sit here while she may be in danger. We must search the entire camp."

"Sludig is doing that already," said Isgrimnur gently. "We will only confuse things."

The prince slumped down again. "You are right. But it will be hard to wait."

They had barely resumed the discussion when Sludig returned, his face grim. He handed Josua a piece of parchment. "This was in young Simon's tent."

The prince read it quickly, then flung it down on the ground in disgust. A moment later he stooped for it, then handed it to the troll, his face stiff and angry. "I am sorry, Binabik, I should not have done that. It seems to be for you." He stood. "Hotvig?"

"Yes, Prince Josua." The Thrithings-man also stood.

"Miriamele has gone. Take as many of your riders as you can quickly find. The chances are good that she has headed toward Erkynland, so do most of your searching west of the camp. But do not ignore the possibility that she might go some other way to throw us off before she turns back to the west."

"What?" Isgrimnur looked up in surprise. "What do you mean, gone?"

Binabik looked up from the parchment. "This was written by Simon. It is seeming that he has gone with her, but he also says he will try to bring her back." The troll's smile was thin and obviously forced. "There is some question in my head about who is leading who. I am doubting Simon will convince her for coming back very soon."

Josua gestured impatiently. "Go, Hotvig. God only knows how long they have been gone. As a matter of fact, since you and your riders are the fastest horsemen we have here, go west; leave the other part of the search to the rest of us." He turned to Sludig. "We will ride around the camp, making our circle wider each time. I will saddle Vinyafod. Meet me there." He turned to the duke. "Are you coming?"

"Of course." Silently, Isgrimnur cursed himself. *I should have known something was coming,* he thought. *She has been so quiet, so sad, so distant since we came here. Josua hasn't seen the change as I have. But even if she thinks we should have marched on Erkynland, why would she go on her own? Fool of a headstrong child. And Simon. I thought better of that boy.*

Already unhappy at the thought of a night in the saddle and what it would do to his sore back, Isgrimnur grunted and rose to his feet.

"Why won't she wake up!?" Jeremias demanded. "Can't you do something?"

"Hush, boy, I'm doing what I can." Duchess Gutrun bent and felt Leleth's face again. "She is cool, not feverish."

"Then what's wrong with her?" Jeremias seemed almost frantic. "I tried to wake her for a long time, but she just lay there."

"Let me give another cover for her," Vorzheva said. She had made room in the bed for the girl to lie beside her, but Gutrun had disallowed it, frightened that Leleth had some sickness which Vorzheva might catch. Instead, Jeremias had carefully set the girl's limp form on a blanket upon the ground.

"You just lie still and I'll worry about the child," the duchess told her. "This is altogether too much noise and fretting."

Prince Josua stepped through the door, unhappiness etched on his face. "Is there not enough gone wrong? The guard said someone was sick. Vorzheva? Are you well?"

"It is not me, Josua. The little girl Leleth, she cannot be wakened."

Duke Isgrimnur stumped in. "A damned long ride and no sign of Miriamele," he growled. "We can only hope that Hotvig and his Thrithings-men have better luck than we did."

"Miriamele?" Vorzheva asked. "Has something happened to her, also?"

"She has ridden off with young Simon," Josua said grimly.

"This is a cursed night," Vorzheva groaned. "Why does this all happen?"

"To be fair, I don't think it was the lad's idea." Isgrimnur bent and put his arm about his wife's shoulders, then kissed her neck. "He left a letter which said he would try to bring her back." The duke's eyes narrowed. "Why is the girl here? Was she hurt in the fire?"

"I brought her," Jeremias said miserably. "Duchess Gutrun asked me to look after her tonight."

"I didn't want her underfoot with Vorzheva so sick." Gutrun could not entirely hide her own discomfort. "And it was just for a while, when Geloë was going to meet with you men."

"I was with her all evening," Jeremias explained. "After she was asleep, I fell asleep, too. I didn't mean to. I was just tired."

Josua turned and looked at the young man kindly. "You did nothing wrong to fall asleep. Go on."

"I woke up when everyone was shouting about the fire. I thought Leleth would be frightened, so I went over to let her know I was still there. She was sitting up with her eyes open, but I don't think she heard a word I said. Then she fell back and her eyes closed, like she was sleeping. But I couldn't wake her up! I tried for a long time. Then I brought her here to see if Duchess Gutrun could help." As Jeremias finished, he was on the verge of tears.

"You did nothing wrong, Jeremias," the prince repeated. "Now, I need you to do something for me."

The young man caught his breath on the verge of a sob. "W-What, your Highness?"

"Go to Isgrimnur's tent and see if Binabik has returned. The troll knows something of healing. We will have him look at young Leleth."

Jeremias, only too glad to have something useful to do, hurried out.

"In truth," Josua said, "I no longer know what to think of all that has happened tonight—but I must admit that I am very fearful for Miriamele. Damn her forwardness." He clutched Vorzheva's blanket in his fingers and twisted it in frustration.

There had been no change in Leleth's condition when Jeremias returned with Binabik and Aditu. The little man inspected the girl closely.

"I have seen her being like this before," he said. "She is gone away somewhere, to the Road of Dreams or some other place."

"But surely she has never been like this for so long," Josua said. "I cannot help but think it has something to do with the night's happenings. Could the Norn poison have made her this way, Aditu?"

The Sitha kneeled beside Binabik and lifted the little girl's eyelids, then laid her slim fingers below Leleth's ear to feel how swiftly her heart beat. "I do not think so. Surely this one," she indicated Jeremias, "would also have been struck if the Kei-vishaa had spread so far."

"Her lips are moving!" Jeremias said excitedly. "Look!"

Although she still lay as if deeply asleep, Leleth's mouth was indeed opening and closing as though she would speak.

"Silence." Josua leaned closer, as did most of the others in the room.

Leleth's lips worked. A whisper of sound crept out. "*. . . hear me . . .*"

"She said something!" Jeremias exulted, but was stilled by a look from the prince.

"*. . . I will speak anyway. I am fading. I have only a short time left.*" The voice that issued from the little girl's mouth, though thin and breathy, had a familiar cadence.

"*. . . There is more to the Norns than we suspect, I think. They play some double game . . . Tonight was not a feint, but something even more subtle . . .*"

"What's wrong with the child?" Gutrun said nervously. "She's never spoken before—and she sounds wrong."

"That is Geloë speaking." Aditu spoke calmly, as though she identified a familiar figure coming up the road.

"What?" The duchess made the Tree sign, her eyes wide with fear. "What witchcraft is this?"

The Sitha leaned close to Leleth's ear. "Geloë?" she said. "Can you hear me?"

If it was the wise woman, she did not seem to hear her friend's voice. "*. . . Remember what Simon dreamed . . . the false messenger.*" There was a pause. When the voice resumed it was quieter, so that all in the room held their breath in an effort not to obscure a word. "*. . . I am dying. Leleth is here with me somehow, in this . . . dark place. I have never understood her completely, and this is strangest of all. I think I can speak through her mouth, but I do not know if anyone is listening. My time is short. Remember: beware a false messenger. . . .*"

There was another long, silent interval. When everyone was certain that they had heard the last, Leleth's lips moved again. *"I am going now. Do not mourn me. I have had a long life and did what I wished to do. If you would remember me, remember that the forest was my home. See that it is respected. I will try to send Leleth back, although she does not want to leave me. Farewell. Remember . . ."*

The voice faded. The little girl again lay like one dead.

Josua looked up. His eyes were bright with tears. "To the last," he said, almost in anger, "she tried to help us. Oh, God the Merciful, she was a brave soul."

"An old soul," Aditu said quietly, but did not elaborate. She seemed shaken.

Though they sat around the bedside in heavy, mournful silence for some time, Leleth did not stir any more. Geloë's absence seemed even more powerful, more devastating than it had earlier in the evening. Other eyes besides Josua's filled with tears of sorrow and fear as the realization of the company's loss settled in. The prince began to speak quietly of the forest woman, praising her bravery, wit, and kindness, but no one else seemed to have the heart to join in. At last he sent them all off to rest. Aditu, saying that she felt no need to sleep, stayed to watch over the child in case she awakened in the night. Josua lay down fully dressed beside his wife, ready for whatever calamity might befall next. Within moments, he had fallen into a deep, exhausted slumber.

In the morning, the prince awakened to discover Aditu still watching over Leleth. Wherever the child's spirit had journeyed with Geloë, it had not yet returned.

Not long afterward, Hotvig and his men rode into camp, weary and empty-handed.

28

Ghost Moon

✦

Simon and Miriamele rode in near-silence, the princess leading as they made their way down into the valley on the far side of the hills. After they had gone a league or more, Miriamele turned them north so that they were riding back along the same track the company had taken on its way to Gadrinsett.

Simon asked her why.

"Because there are already a thousand fresh hoofprints here," Miriamele explained. "And because Josua knows where I'm going, so it would be stupid to head straight that way in case they find out we've left tonight."

"Josua knows where we're going?" Simon was disgruntled. "That's more than I do."

"I'll tell you about it when we're far enough that you can't ride back in one night," she said coolly. "When I'm too far away for them to catch me and bring me back."

She would not answer any more questions.

Simon squinted at the bits of refuse that lined the wide, muddy track. A great army of people had crossed this way twice now, along with several other smaller parties that had made their way to Sesuad'ra and New Gadrinsett; Simon thought it would be a long time before the grass grew on this desolated swath again.

I suppose that's where roads come from, he thought, and grinned despite his weariness. *I never thought about it before. Maybe someday it will be a real king's road, with set stones and inns and way stations . . . and I saw it when it was nothing but a hoof-gouged track.*

Of course, that was presuming that whatever happened in the days to come, there would *be* a king who cared about roads. From what Jeremias and others had told him about the state of affairs at the Hayholt, it didn't seem very likely that Elias was worrying about such things.

They rode on beside the Stefflod, which glowed silver in the moon's ghostly light. Miriamele remained uncommunicative, and it seemed to Simon that they rode for days on end, although the moon had not yet moved much past the midpoint of the sky. Bored, he watched Miriamele, admiring how her fair skin took the moonlight, until she, irritated, told him to stop staring at her. Desperate for diversion, he then considered the Canon of Knighthood and Camaris' teachings; when that failed to hold his interest for more than half a league, he quietly sang all the Jack Mundwode songs he knew. Later, after Miriamele had rebuffed several more attempts at conversation, Simon began counting the stars that dotted the sky, numerous as grains of salt spilled on an ebony tabletop.

At last, when Simon was certain that he would soon go mad—and equally certain that a full week must have passed during this one long night—Miriamele reined up and pointed to a copse of trees standing on a low hill some three or four furlongs from the wide rut of the infant road.

"There," she said. "We'll stop there and sleep."

"I don't need to sleep yet," Simon lied. "We can ride longer if you want to."

"There's no point. I don't want to be out in the open in daylight tomorrow. Later, when we're farther away, we can ride when it's light."

Simon shrugged. "If you say so." He had wanted this adventure, if that was what it was, so he might as well endure it as cheerfully as possible. In the first moments of their escape he had imagined—during those few brief instants in which he had allowed himself to think at all—that Miriamele would be more pleasant once the immediate worry of discovery had lessened. Instead, she had seemed to grow even more morose as the night wore on.

The trees at the top of the hill grew close together, making an almost seamless wall between their makeshift camp and the road. They did not light a fire—Simon had to admit he could see the wisdom of that—but instead shared some water and a little wine by moonlight, and gnawed on a bit of Miriamele's bread.

When they had wrapped themselves in their cloaks and were lying side by side on their bedrolls, Simon suddenly found that his weariness had fled—in fact, he did not feel the least bit sleepy. He listened, but although Miriamele's breathing was quiet and regular, she did not sound like she was sleeping either. Somewhere in the trees, a lone cricket was gently sawing away.

"Miriamele?"

"What?"

"You really should tell me where we're going. I would do better as your protector. I could think about it and make plans."

She laughed quietly. "I'm certain that's true. I will tell you, Simon. But not tonight."

He frowned as he stared up at the stars peeping through the branches. "Very well."

"You should go to sleep now. It will be harder to do once the sun is up."

Did all women have a little Rachel the Dragon in them? They certainly seemed to enjoy telling him what he should do. He opened his mouth to tell her he didn't need any rest just yet, but yawned instead.

He was trying to remember what he had meant to say even as he passed over into sleep.

★   ★   ★

In the dream Simon stood on the edge of a great sea. Extending from the beach before him was a thin causeway of land that extended out right through the teeth of the waves, leading to an island some long distance offshore. The island was bare except for three tall white towers which shimmered in the late afternoon sun, but the towers were not what interested Simon. Walking on the island before them, passing in and out of their threefold shadow, was a tiny figure with white hair and a blue robe. Simon was certain it was Doctor Morgenes.

He was considering the causeway—it would be easy enough to walk across, but the tide was growing higher, and soon might cover the thin spit of land entirely—when he heard a distant voice. Out on the ocean, midway between the island and the rocky shoal where Simon stood, a small boat was rocking and bobbing in the grip of strong waves. Two figures stood in the boat, one tall and solid, the other small and slender. It took a few moments to recognize Geloë and Leleth. The woman was calling something to him, but her voice was lost in the roar of the sea.

What are they doing out in a boat? Simon thought. *It will be night soon.*

He moved a few steps out onto the slender causeway. Geloë's voice wafted to him across the waves, barely audible.

". . . *False!*" she cried. "*It's false . . . !*"

What is false? he wondered. The spit of land? It seemed solid enough. The island itself? He squinted, but although the sun had now dropped low on the horizon, turning the towers into black fingers and the shape of Morgenes into something small and dark as an ant, the island seemed indisputably substantial. He took another few steps forward.

"*False!*" Geloë cried again.

The sky abruptly turned dark, and the roar of the waves was overwhelmed by the cry of rising wind. In an instant the ocean turned blue and then blue-white; suddenly, all the waves stiffened, freezing into hard, sharp points of ice. Geloë waved her arms desperately, but the sea around her boat surged and cracked. Then with a roar and an out-wash of black water as alive as blood, Geloë, Leleth, and the boat disappeared beneath the frozen waves, sucked down into darkness.

Ice was creeping up over the causeway. Simon turned, but it was now as far back to the beach as it was toward the island, and both points seemed to be receding from him, leaving him stranded in the middle of an ever-lengthening spit of rock. The ice mounted higher, crawling up to his boots. . . .

Simon jerked awake, shivering. Thin dawn light filled the copse and the trees swayed to a chill breeze. His cloak was curled in a hopeless tangle around his knees, leaving the rest of him uncovered.

He straightened the cloak and lay back. Miriamele was still asleep beside him, her mouth partially open, her golden hair pushed out of shape. He felt a wave of longing pass over and through him, and at the same time a sense of shame. She was so defenseless, lying here in the wilderness, and he was her protector—what sort of knight was he, to have such feelings? But he longed to pull her close to him, to warm her, to kiss her on that open mouth and feel her breath on his cheek. Uncomfortable, he rolled over and faced the other direction.

The horses stood quietly where they had been tied, their harnesses wrapped around a low-hanging tree branch. The sight of the saddlebags in the flat morning light suddenly filled him with a hollow kind of sadness. Last night this had seemed a wild adventure. Now, it seemed foolish. Whatever Miriamele's reasons might be, they were not his own. He owed many, many debts—to Prince Josua, who had lifted him up and knighted him; to Aditu, who had saved him; to Binabik, who had been a better friend than he deserved. And there were also those who looked up to Simon as well, like Jeremias. But he had deserted them all on a moment's whim. And for what? To force himself on Miriamele, who had some sad purpose of her own in leaving her uncle's camp. He had left the few people who wanted him to tag along after someone who did not.

He squinted at his horse and felt his sadness deepen. Homefinder. That was a pretty name, wasn't it? Simon had just run away from another home, and this time there was no good reason for it.

He sighed and sat up. He was here and there was little to be done about it, at least right now. He would try again to talk Miriamele into going back when she woke up.

Simon pulled his cloak about him and got to his feet. He untied the horses, then stood at the edge of the copse and peered cautiously around before leading them down the hill to the river to drink. When he brought them back, he tied them to a different tree where they could easily reach the long shoots of new-grown grass. As he watched Homefinder and Miriamele's unnamed steed contentedly break their fast, he felt his mood lighten for the first time since awakening from his frightening dream.

He gathered up deadwood from around the copse, taking only what seemed dry enough to burn with little smoke, and set about making a small fire. He was pleased to see that he had brought his flint and striking-steel, but wondered how long it would be until he discovered something he needed just as much but had forgotten in the hurry to leave camp. He sat before the fire for a while, warming his hands and watching Miriamele sleep.

A bit later, as he was looking through the saddlebags to see what there might be to eat, Miriamele began to toss in her sleep and cry out.

"No!" she mumbled. "No, I won't . . . ." She half-raised her arms, as though to fight something off. After watching in consternation for a moment, Simon went and kneeled beside her, taking her hand.

"Miriamele. Princess. Wake up. You're having a bad dream."

She tugged against his grip, but strengthlessly. At last her eyes opened. She stared at him, and briefly seemed to see someone else, for she brought her free hand up as though to protect herself. Then she recognized him and let the hand fall. Her other hand remained clutched in his.

"It was just a bad dream." He squeezed her fingers gently, surprised and gratified by how much larger his hand was than hers.

"I'm well," she muttered at last, and drew herself up into a sitting position, pulling the cloak tightly about her shoulders. She glared around at the clearing as though the presence of daylight was some silly prank of Simon's. "What time of day is it?"

"The sun's not over the treetops yet. Down there, I mean. I walked down to the river."

She didn't reply, but clambered to her feet and walked unsteadily out of the copse. Simon shrugged and went back to his search for something on which they could break their fast.

When Miriamele returned a short time later, he had turned up a lump of soft cheese and round loaf of bread; he had split the latter open and was toasting it on a stick over the small fire. "Good morning," she said. She looked tousled, but she had washed the dirt from her face, and her expression was almost cheerful. "I'm sorry I was so cross. I had a . . . a terrible dream."

He looked at her with interest, but she did not elaborate. "There's food here," he said.

"A fire, too." She came and sat near, holding out her hands. "I hope the smoke doesn't show."

"It doesn't. I went out a little way and looked."

Simon gave Miriamele half the bread and a hunk of the cheese. She ate greedily, then smiled with her mouth full. After swallowing, she said: "I was hungry. I was so worried last night that I didn't eat."

"There's more if you want it."

She shook her head. "We have to save it. I don't know how long we'll be traveling and we may have trouble getting more." Miriamele looked up. "Can you shoot? I brought a bow and a quiver of arrows." She pointed to the unstrung bow hanging beside her saddle.

Simon shrugged. "I've shot one, but I'm no Mundwode. I could probably hit a cow from a dozen paces or so."

Miriamele giggled. "I was thinking of rabbits or squirrels or birds, Simon. I don't think there will be many cows standing around."

He nodded sagely. "Then we'd better do as you say and save our food."

Miriamele sat back and placed her hands on her stomach. "As long as the fire's going . . ." She stood and went to her saddlebags. She brought out a pair of bowls and a small drawstring sack and returned to the fire, then placed two small stones in the embers to heat. "I brought some calamint tea."

"You don't put salt and butter in it, do you?" Simon asked, remembering the Qanuc and their odd additions.

"Elysia's mercy, no!" she said, laughing. "But I wish we had some honey."

While they drank the tea—Simon thought it a great improvement on

Mintahoq *aka*—Miriamele talked about what they would do that day. She did not want to resume riding until sundown, but there were other things to be accomplished.

"You can teach me something about swordplay, for one thing."

"What?" Simon stared at her as though she had asked him to show her how to fly.

Miriamele gave him a scornful glance, then got up and walked to her saddlebag. From the bottom she drew out a short sword in a tooled scabbard. "I had Freosel make it for me before we left. He cut it down from a man's sword." Her disdainful look gave way to a wry, strangely self-mocking grin. "I said I wanted it to protect my virtue when we marched on Nabban." She looked hard at Simon. "So teach me."

"You want me to show you how to use a sword," he said slowly.

"Of course. And in turn, I will show you how to use a bow." She raised her chin slightly. "I can hit a cow at a great deal more than a few paces—not that I have," she said hurriedly. "But old Sir Fluiren taught me how to shoot a bow when I was a little girl. He thought it was amusing."

Simon was nonplussed. "So you are going to shoot squirrels for the dinner pot?"

Her expression turned cool again. "I didn't bring the bow for hunting, Simon—the sword, either. We are going somewhere dangerous. A young woman traveling these days would be a fool to go unarmed."

Her calm explanation made him suddenly cold. "But you won't tell me where."

"Tomorrow morning. Now come—we're wasting time." She picked up the sword and drew it from the scabbard, letting the leather slide to the wet ground. Her eyes were bright, challenging.

Simon stared. "First, you don't treat your scabbard that way." He picked it up and handed it to her. "Put the blade away, then buckle on the sword belt."

Miriamele scowled. "I already know how to buckle a belt."

"First things first," Simon said calmly. "Do you want to learn or not?"

The morning passed, and Simon's irritation at having to teach swordsmanship to a girl passed with it. Miriamele was fiercely eager to learn. She asked question after question, many of which Simon had no answer to, no matter how much he wracked his memory for all the things Haestan, Sludig, and Camaris had tried to teach him. It was hard to admit to her that he, a knight, did not know something, but after a few short but unpleasant exchanges he swallowed his pride and said frankly that he did not know why a sword's hilt only stuck out on two sides and not all around, it just did. Miriamele seemed happier with that answer than she had been with his previous attempts at mystification, and the rest of the lesson passed more swiftly and pleasantly.

Miriamele was surprisingly strong for her size, although when Simon thought about what she had been through his surprise was less. She was quick as well, with good balance, although she tended to lean too far forward, a habit that could quickly prove fatal in an actual fight, since almost any opponent would be larger than she was and have a longer reach. All in all, he was impressed. He sensed that he would quickly run out of new things to tell her, and then it would just be practice and more practice. He was more than a little glad they were sparring with long sticks instead of blades; she had managed during the course of the morning to give him a few nasty swipes.

After they took a long pause for water and a rest, they changed places: Miriamele instructed Simon in the care of the bow, paying special attention to keeping the bowstring warm and dry. He smiled at his own impatience. As Miriamele had been unwilling to sit through his explanations of swordsmanship—much of it taken in whole cloth from Camaris' teachings to him—he himself was itching to show her what he could do with a bow in his hand. But she was having none of it, and so the remainder of the afternoon was spent learning the proper draw. By the time shadows grew long, Simon's fingers were red and raw. He would have to think of some way to acquire finger-leathers like Miriamele's if he was going to be shooting in earnest.

They made a meal for themselves with bread and an onion and a little jerked meat, then saddled the horses.

"Your horse needs a name," Simon told her as he fastened Homefinder's belly strap. "Camaris says your horse is part of you, but it's also one of God's creatures."

"I'll think about it," she said.

They looked one last time around the camp to make sure they had left no trace of their presence—they had buried the fire ashes and raked the bent grass with a long branch—then rode out into the disappearing day.

"There's the old forest," Simon said, pleased. He squinted against the first dawn light. "That dark line, there."

"I see it." She headed her horse off the road, aiming due north. "We will go as far toward it as we can today instead of stopping—I am going to break my own rule and ride in daylight. I'll feel safer when we're there."

"We aren't going back to Sesuad'ra?" Simon asked.

"No. We're going to Aldheorte—for a while."

"We're going to the forest? Why?"

Miriamele was looking straight ahead. She had thrown her hood back, and the sun was in her hair. "Because my uncle may send people after me. They won't be able to find us if we're in the woods."

Simon remembered all too well his experiences in the great forest. Very few of them had been pleasant. "But it takes forever to travel through there."

"We won't be in the woods long. Just enough to be sure that no one finds us."

Simon shrugged. He had no idea where exactly she wanted to go, or why, but she had obviously been planning.

They rode on toward the distant line of the forest.

★   ★   ★

They reached the outskirts of the Aldheorte late in the afternoon. The sun had sunk toward the horizon; the grassy hills were painted with slanting light.

Simon supposed they would stop and make camp in the thin vegetation of the forest's outer edge—after all, they had now been riding steadily since the evening before, almost a day straight, with only a few short naps stolen along the way—but Miriamele was determined to get well in, safe from accidental discovery. They rode through the increasingly close-leaning trees until riding was no longer practical, then led the horses another quarter of a league. When the princess at last found a site that was to her liking, the forest was in the last glow of twilight; beneath the thick tree canopy the world was all muted shades of blue.

Simon dismounted and hurriedly started a fire. When that was crackling healthily, they made camp. Miriamele had picked the site in part because of a small streamlet that trickled nearby. As she searched for the makings of a meal, he walked the horses over to the water to drink.

Simon, after a full day spent almost entirely in the saddle, found himself strangely wakeful, as though he had forgotten what sleep was. After he and Miriamele had fed themselves, they sat beside the fire and talked about everyday matters, although more by Miriamele's choice than Simon's. He had other things on his mind, and thought it strange that she should so earnestly discuss Josua and Vorzheva's coming child and ask for more stories about the battle with Fengbald when there were so many questions still unanswered about their present journey. At last, frustrated, he held up his hand.

"Enough of this. You said you would tell me where we are going, Miriamele."

She looked into the flames for a while before speaking. "That's true, Simon. I have not been fair, I suppose, to bring you so far on trust alone. But I didn't ask you to come with me."

He was hurt, but tried not to show it. "I'm here, though. So tell me—where are we going?"

She took a deep breath, then let it out. "To Erkynland."

He nodded. "I guessed that. It wasn't hard, listening to you at the Raed. But where in Erkynland? And what are we going to do there?"

"We're going to the Hayholt." She looked at him intently, as if daring him to disagree.

Aedon have mercy on us, Simon thought. Out loud, he said: "To get Bright-Nail?" Although it was madness even to consider it, there was a certain excitement to the thought. He—with help, admittedly—had found and secured Thorn, hadn't he? Perhaps if he brought back Bright-Nail as well, he would be . . . He didn't even dare to think the words, but a sudden picture came to him—he, Simon, a sort of knight-of-knights, one who could even court princesses. . . .

He pushed the picture back into the depths. There was no such thing, not really. And he and Miriamele would never come back from such a foolhardy venture in any case. "To try to save Bright-Nail?" he asked again.

Miriamele was still looking at him intently. "Perhaps."

"Perhaps?" He scowled. "What does that mean?"

"I said I would tell you where we were going," she responded. "I didn't say I would tell you everything in my head."

Simon irritatedly picked up a stick and broke it in half, then dumped the pieces into the firepit. " 'S Bloody Tree, Miriamele," he growled, "why are you doing this? You said I was your friend, but then you treat me like a child."

"I am not treating you like a child," she said hotly. "You insisted on coming with me. Good. But my errand is my own, whether I am going to get the sword or heading back to the castle to get a pair of shoes that I left behind by mistake."

Simon was still angry, but he couldn't suppress a bark of laughter. "You probably *are* going back for shoes or a dress or something. That would be just my luck—to get killed by the Erkynguard in the middle of a war for trying to steal shoes."

A little of Miriamele's annoyance had dissipated. "You probably stole enough things and got away with it when you were living at the Hayholt. It will only be fair."

"Stole? Me?"

"From the kitchens, constantly. You told me yourself, although I knew it already. And who was it who stole the sexton's shovel and put it in the gauntlet of that armor in the Lesser Hall, so that it looked like Sir Whoever was going out to dig a privy pit?"

Surprised she had remembered, Simon let out a quiet, pleased chortle. "Jeremias did that with me."

"You dragged him into it, you mean. Jeremias would never have done something like that without you."

"How did you know about that?"

Miriamele gave him a disgusted look. "I told you, you idiot, I followed you around for weeks."

"You did, didn't you." Simon was impressed. "What else did you see me do?"

"Mostly sneak off and sit around mooning when you were supposed to be working," she snapped. "No wonder Rachel had to pinch your ears blue."

Offended, Simon straightened his back. "I only sneaked off to have some time to myself. You don't know what it's like living in the servants' quarters."

Miriamele looked at him. Her expression was suddenly serious, even sad. "You're right. But you don't know what it was like being me, either. There certainly wasn't much chance to be off by myself."

"Maybe," Simon said stubbornly. "But I'll bet the food was better in your part of the Hayholt."

"It was the same food," she shot back. "We just ate it with clean hands." She looked pointedly at his ash-blackened fingers.

Simon laughed aloud. "Ah! So the difference between a scullion and a princess is clean hands. I hate to disappoint you, Miriamele, but after spending a day up to my elbows in the washing tub, my hands were *very* clean."

She looked at him mockingly. "So then I suppose there is no difference between the two at all."

"I don't know." Simon grew suddenly uncomfortable with the discussion; it was moving into painful territory. "I don't know, Miriamele."

Sensing that something had changed, she fell silent.

Insects were creaking musically all around, and the shadowy trees loomed like eavesdroppers. It was strange to be in the forest again, Simon thought. He had grown used to the vast distances to be seen from atop Sesuad'ra and the unending openness of the High Thrithing. After that, Aldheorte seemed confining. Still, a castle was confining, too, but it was the best defense against enemies. Perhaps Miriamele was right: for a while, anyway, the forest might be the best place for them.

"I'm going to sleep," she said suddenly. She stood up and walked to the spot where she had unrolled her bed. Simon noted that she had placed his bedroll on the far side of the campfire from her own.

"If you wish." He couldn't tell if she was mad at him again. Perhaps she'd just run short of things to say. He felt like that around her sometimes, once all the talk of small things was finished. The big things were too hard to speak of, too embarrassing . . . and too frightening. "I think I'll sit here for a while."

Miriamele rolled herself in her cloak and lay back. Simon watched her through the shimmer of the fire. One of the horses made a soft, contented-sounding noise.

"Miriamele?"

"Yes?"

"I meant what I said the night we left. I will be your protector, even if you don't tell me exactly what I'm protecting you *from.*"

"I know, Simon. Thank you."

There was another gap of silence. After a while, Simon heard a thin sound, quietly melodious. He had a moment of apprehension before he realized it was Miriamele humming softly to herself.

"What song is that?"

She stirred and turned toward him. "What?"

"What song is that you were humming?"

She smiled. "I didn't know I was humming. It's been running through my head all this evening. It's one my mother used to sing to me when I was little. I think it's a Hernystiri song that came from my grandmother, but the words are Westerling."

Simon stood and walked to his bedroll. "Would you sing it?"

Miriamele hesitated. "I don't know. I'm tired, and I'm not sure I can remember the words. Anyway, it's a sad song."

He lay down and pulled his cloak over him, abruptly shivering. The night was growing cold. The wind lightly rattled the leaves. "I don't care if you get the words right. It would just be nice to have a song."

"Very well. I'll try." She thought for a moment, then began to sing. Her voice was husky but sweet.

"In Cathyn Dair there lived a maid,"

she began. Although she sang quietly, the slow melody ran all through the darkened forest clearing.

"In Cathyn Dair, by Silversea,
The fairest girl was ever born
And I loved her and she loved me.

"By Silversea the wind is cold
The grass is long, the stones are old
And hearts are bought, and love is sold
And time and time the same tale told
In cruel Cathyn Dair.

"We met when autumn moon was high
In Cathyn Dair, by Silversea,
In silver dress and golden shoon
She danced and gave her smile to me.

"When winter's ice was on the roof
In Cathyn Dair, by Silversea,
We sang beside the fiery hearth
She smiled and gave her lips to me.

"By Silversea the wind is cold
The grass is long, the stones are old
And hearts are bought, and love is sold
And time and time the same tale told
In cruel Cathyn Dair.

"When spring was dreaming in the fields
In Cathyn Dair, by Silversea,
In Mircha's shrine where candles burned
She stood and pledged her troth to me.

"When summer burned upon the hills
In Cathyn Dair, by Silversea,
The banns were posted in the town
But she came not to marry me.

"By Silversea the wind is cold
The grass is long, the stones are old
And hearts are bought, and love is sold
And time and time the same tale told
In cruel Cathyn Dair.

"When Autumn's moon had come again
In Cathyn Dair, by Silversea,
I saw her dance in silver dress
The man she danced for was not me.

"When winter showed its cruel claws
In Cathyn Dair, by Silversea,
I walked out from the city walls
No more will that place torment me.

"By Silversea the wind is cold
The grass is long, the stones are old
And hearts are bought, and love is sold
And time and time the same tale told
In cruel Cathyn Dair . . ."

"That's a pretty song," Simon said when she had finished. "A sad song." The haunting tune still floated through his head; he understood why Miriamele had been humming it all unawares.

"My mother used to sing it to me in the garden at Meremund. She always sang. Everyone said she had the prettiest voice they'd ever heard."

There was silence for a while. Both Simon and Miriamele lay wrapped in their cloaks, nursing their secret thoughts.

"I never knew my mother," Simon said at last. "She died when I was born. I never knew either of my parents."

"Neither did I."

By the time the oddness of this remark sifted down through Simon's own distracted thoughts, Miriamele had rolled over, placing her back toward the fire—and toward Simon. He wanted to ask her what she meant, but sensed that she did not want to talk anymore.

Instead, he watched the fire burning low and the last few sparks fluttering upward into the darkness.

29

Windows Like Eyes

⁂

The rams stood so close together that there was scarcely room to move between them. Binabik sang a quiet sheep-soothing song as he threaded his way in and out among the woolly obstacles.

"Sisqi," he called. "I need to speak to you."

She was sitting cross-legged, retying the knots of her ram's harness. Around her several of the other troll men and women were seeing to final tasks before the prince's company resumed its march into Nabban. "I am here," she said.

Binabik looked around. "Would you come with me somewhere more quiet?"

She nodded and set the harness down on the ground. "I will."

They snaked their way back out through the herd of jostling rams and climbed up the knoll. When they sat down in the grass the milling camp lay spread below them. The tents had been dismantled early that morning, and all that remained of what had been a small city for three days was a formless, moving mass of people and animals.

"You are fretful," Sisqi said abruptly. "Tell me what is wrong, beloved—although we have certainly seen enough bad fortune in the last few days to make anyone sad for a long time."

Binabik sighed and nodded. "That is true. The loss of Geloë is a hard one, and not only because of her wisdom. I miss *her*, too, Sisqi. We will not see anyone like her again."

"But there is more," Sisqi prompted him gently. "I know you well, Binbiniqegabenik. Is it Simon and the princess?"

"That is the root of it. Look—I will show you something." He pulled apart the sections of his walking stick. A long white shaft tipped with blue-gray stone slid out.

"That is Simon's arrow." Sisqi's eyes were wide. "The gift of the Sithi. Did he leave it behind?"

"Not on purpose, I think. I found it tangled in one of the shirts Gutrun made for him. He took with him little but the clothes he wore on his back, but he did take the sack that held his most treasured possessions—Jiriki's mirror, a piece of stone he brought from Haestan's cairn, other things. I believe the

White Arrow must have been left by mistake. Perhaps he had taken it out for some other purpose and forgot to return it to the sack." Binabik lifted the arrow until it caught the morning sun and gleamed. "It reminds me of things," he said slowly. "It is the mark of Jiriki's debt to Simon. A debt which is no less than the one *I* owe, on my master Ookequk's behalf, to Doctor Morgenes."

A sudden look of fear came to Sisqi's face, although she did her best to hide it. "What do you mean, Binabik?"

He stared at the arrow miserably. "Ookequk promised help to Morgenes. I took on that oath. I swore to help protect young Simon, Sisqi."

She took his hand in hers. "You have done that and more, Binabik. Surely you are not to guard him day and night for the rest of your life."

"This is different." He carefully slid the arrow back into his walking stick. "And there is more than my debt, Sisqi. Both Simon and Miriamele are already in danger traveling alone in the wilderness, even more so if they go where I fear they do. But they are also a risk to the rest of us."

"What do you mean?" She was having trouble keeping the pain from her words.

"If they are caught, they will eventually be taken to Pryrates, King Elias' advisor. You do not know him, Sisqi, but I do, at least from tales. He is powerful, and reckless in his use of that power. And he is cruel. He will learn from them whatever they know about us, and Simon and Miriamele both know a great deal—about our plans, about the swords, everything. And Pryrates will kill them, or at least Simon, in the getting of that knowledge."

"So you are going to find them?" she asked slowly.

He hung his head. "I feel I must."

"But why you? Josua has an entire army!"

"There are reasons, my beloved. Come with me when I speak to Josua and you will hear the reasons. You should be there, in any case."

She looked at him defiantly. "If you go after them, then I will go with you."

"And who will keep our people safe in a strange land?" He gestured at the trolls moving below. "You at least speak some of the Westerling speech now. We cannot both go and leave our fellow Qanuc altogether deaf and mute."

Tears were forming in Sisqi's eyes. "Is there no other way?"

"I cannot think of one," he said slowly. "I wish I could." His own eyes were damp as well.

"Chukku's Stones!" she swore. "Are we to suffer everything we have suffered to be together, only to be separated again?" She squeezed his fingers tightly. "Why are you so straight-backed and honorable, Binabik of Mintahoq? I have cursed you for it before, but never so bitterly."

"I will come back to you. I swear, Sisqinanamook. No matter what befalls, I will come back to you."

She leaned forward, pushing her forehead against his chest, and wept. Binabik wrapped his arms around her and held tightly; tears rolled down his cheeks as well.

"If you do not come back," she moaned, "may you never have a moment's peace until Time is gone."

"I will come back," he repeated, then fell silent. They stayed that way for a long time, locked in a miserable embrace.

"I cannot say I like this idea, Binabik," said Prince Josua. "We can ill-afford to lose your wisdom—especially now, after Geloë's death." The prince looked morose. "Aedon knows what a blow that has been to us. I feel sick inside. And we have not even a body to weep over."

"And that is as she was wishing it," Binabik said gently. "But, speaking about your first worry, it is my thinking that we can even less be suffering the loss of your niece and Simon. I have made you know my fears about that."

"Perhaps. But what about discovering the use of the swords? We still have much to learn."

"I have little help left for giving to Strangyeard and Tiamak," said the little man. "Nearly all of Ookequk's scrolls I have already made into Westerling. Those few of them that are remaining still, Sisqi can be helping with them." He indicated his betrothed, who sat silently beside him, her eyes red. "And then, I must also be saying with regret, when that task is being finished she will take the remaining Qanuc and return to our people."

Josua looked at Sisqi. "This is another great loss."

She bowed her head.

"But you are many now," Binabik pointed out. "Our people suffer, too, and these herdsmen and huntresses will be needed at Blue Mud Lake."

"Of course," said the prince. "We will always be grateful that your people came to our aid. We will never forget, Binabik." He frowned. "So you are determined to go?"

The troll nodded. "There are many reasons it is seeming the best course to me. It is also my fear that Miriamele hopes to get the sword Bright-Nail—perhaps with thinking she can hurry the end of this struggle. That is frightening to me, since if Count Eolair's story was true, the dwarrows have already confessed to the minions of the Storm King that Minneyar is the sword that is resting now in your father's grave."

"Which is likely the end of our hopes, in any case," Josua said gloomily. "For if he knows that, why would Elias leave it there?"

"The Storm King's knowing and the knowing of your brother may not be the same thing," Binabik observed. "It is not an unheard-of strangeness for allies to be hiding things from each other. The Storm King may not be knowing that *we* also have this knowledge." He smiled a yellow smile. "It is a thing of great complication, is it not? Also, from the story that the old man Towser was so often telling—the story of how your brother acted when Towser was giving him the blade—it is possible that those who have the taint of Stormspike cannot bear its nearness."

"It is a great deal to hope for," Josua said. "Isgrimnur? What do you make of all this?"

The duke shifted on the low stool. "About which? The swords, or the troll's going off after Miri and the boy?"

"Either. Both." Josua waved his hand wearily.

"I can't say much about the swords, but what Binabik has to say makes a kind of sense. As to the other . . ." Isgrimnur shrugged. "Someone should go, that's clear. I brought her back once, so I'll go again if you want, Josua."

"No." The prince shook his head firmly. "I need you here. And I would not separate you from Gutrun yet again for the sake of my headstrong niece." He turned to the troll. "How many men would you take, Binabik?"

"None, Prince Josua."

"None?" The prince was astonished. "But what do you mean? Surely it would be safer to take at least a few good men, as you did on the journey to Urmsheim?"

Binabik shook his head. "I am thinking that Miriamele and Simon will not hide from me, but they would be hiding with certainness from mounted soldiers pursuing them. Also, there are places Qantaqa and I can go that even riders of great skill, like Hotvig's Thrithings-men, cannot. I can be more silent, too. No, it is a better thing if I go by myself."

"I do not like it," Josua said, "and I can see that your Sisqi does not like it either. But I will consider it, at least. Perhaps it *would* be best—there is more of me than just an uncle's love that fears what might happen if Miriamele and Simon fall into my brother's hands. Certainly something must be done." He lifted his hand and rubbed at his temples. "Let me think on it a while."

"With certainty, Prince Josua." Binabik stood. "But remember that even Qantaqa's wonderful nose cannot be tracking a scent that has been too long on the ground." He bowed, as did Sisqi, then they turned and went out.

"He is small—they both are," Josua said reflectively. "But not only do I wish the trolls were not leaving, I wish I had a thousand more like them."

"He's a brave one, that Binabik, right enough," said Isgrimnur. "Seems sometimes as if that's all we have left."

Eolair watched the fly buzzing near his horse's head for some time. The horse, but for an occasional ear-flick, seemed little bothered, but Eolair continued to stare. There was not much else to look at while riding through this westernmost part of Hernystir on the fringes of the Frostmarch, and the fly also reminded him of something he could not quite summon to mind, but which was nevertheless bidding for his attention. The Count of Nad Mullach watched the tiny black speck for some time before he finally realized why it seemed significant.

This is the first fly I've seen in a while—the first since the winter came down, I think. It must be getting warmer.

This rather ordinary thought gave rise to a host of other, less usual speculations.

Could it be that somehow the tide has turned? he wondered. *Could Josua and his people have accomplished something that has diminished the Storm King's power and pushed back his magical winter?* He looked around at the small, tattered troop of Hernystiri that rode behind him, and at the great company of Sithi who led them, their banners and armor ablaze with color. *Could the fact that Jiriki's folk have entered the battle somehow have tipped the scale in our favor? Or am I making too much out of the tiniest of signs?*

He laughed to himself, but grimly. This last year and its attendant horrors seemed to have made him as omen-drunk as his ancestors of Hern's day.

His ancestors had been on Eolair's mind more than a little in the last few days. The army of Sithi and men riding toward Naglimund had recently stopped at Eolair's castle at Nad Mullach on the River Baraillean. In the two days the army was quartered there, the count had found another three score men from the surrounding area who were willing to join the war party—most of them more for the wonder of riding with the fabled Peaceful Ones, Eolair suspected, than out of any sense of duty or thirst for revenge. The young men who agreed to join the company were mostly those whose families had been lost or scattered during the recent conflict. Those who still had land or loved ones to protect had no desire to ride off to another war, no matter how noble or all-encompassing the cause—nor could Eolair have commanded them to do so: the landholders of Hernystir had not possessed that right since King Tethtain's day.

Nad Mullach had been less harshly treated than Hernysadharc, but it had still suffered during Skali's conquest. In the short time he had, Eolair rounded up those few of his retainers who remained and did his best to set things on the right course again. If he did manage somehow to return from this mad war that was growing madder by the day, he wanted nothing more than to put down the reins of responsibility as soon as possible and live once more in his beloved Nad Mullach.

His liege-folk had held out long against the small portion of Skali's army that had been left to besiege them, but when those prisoned within the castle's walls began to starve, Eolair's cousin and castellain Gwynna, a stern, capable woman, opened the gates to the Rimmersmen. Many of the fine things that had been in Eolair's line since not long after Sinnach's alliance with the Erl-king were destroyed or stolen, and so were many objects that Eolair himself had brought back from his travels throughout Osten Ard. Still, he had consoled himself, the walls still stood, the fields—under a blanket of snow—were still fertile, and the wide Baraillean, unhindered by war or winter, still rushed past Nad Mullach on its way to Abaingeat and the sea.

The count had commended Gwynna for her decision, telling her that had he been in residence he would have done the same. She, to whom the sight of

Skali's outlanders in her great house had been the most galling thing imaginable, was a little comforted, but not much.

Those outlanders, perhaps because their master was far away in Hernysadharc, or perhaps because they were not themselves of Skali's savage Kaldskryke clan, had been less hateful in their occupation than the invaders in other parts of Hernystir. They had treated their conquered prisoners poorly, and had plundered and smashed to their hearts' content, but had not indulged in the kind of rape, torture, and senseless killing that had marked Skali's main army as it drove on Hernysadharc.

Still, despite the comparative lightness of the damage to his ancestral home, as he rode out of Nad Mullach Eolair was nevertheless filled with a sense of violation and shame. His forebears had built the castle to watch over their bit of the river valley. Now it had been attacked and defeated, and the current count had not even been at home. His servants and kin had been forced to make their way alone.

I served my king, he told himself. *What else could I do?*

There was no answer, but that did not make it any easier to live with the memories of shattered stone, scorched tapestries, and frightened, hollow-eyed people. Even should both war and spirit-winter end tomorrow, that harm had already been done.

"Would you like something more to eat, my lady?" Eolair asked.

He could not help wondering what Maegwin in her madness made of the rather poor fare that had been their lot so far on the trip toward Naglimund. Nothing much could be expected of a war-ravaged countryside, of course, but the count was curious how hard bread and leathery onions could be considered food fit for gods.

"No, Eolair, thank you." Maegwin shook her head and smiled gently. "Even in a land of unending pleasure, we must rest from pleasure occasionally."

Unending pleasure! The count smiled back despite himself. It might not be bad to be as touched as Maegwin, at least during meals.

A moment later he chided himself for the uncharitable thought. *Look at her. She's like a child. It's not her fault—perhaps it was the blow Skali struck her. It may not have killed her, as she thinks, but it might have disordered her brains.*

He stared at her. Maegwin was watching the sunset with evident pleasure. Her face seemed almost to glow.

What is that term they use in Nabban? "Holy fools." That's what she looks like— someone who is no longer of the earth.

"The sky of heaven is more beautiful than I would have imagined," she said dreamily. "I wonder if perhaps it is our own sky, but we see it now from the other side."

And even were there some cure, Eolair wondered suddenly, *what right have I to take this away from her?* The thought was shocking, like cold water dashed in his face. *She is happy—happy for the first time since her father went off to war and his*

death. She eats, she sleeps, she talks to me and others . . . even if most of it is arrant
nonsense. How would she be better off if she came back to her senses in this dreadful time?

There was no answer to that, of course. Eolair took a deep breath, fighting
off the weariness that assailed him when he was with Maegwin. He stood and
walked to a patch of melting snow nearby, washed his bowl, then returned to
the tree where Maegwin sat, staring out across the rolling fields of grass and
gray snow toward the ruddy western sky.

"I am going to talk to Jiriki," he told her. "Will you be well here?"

She nodded, a half-smile tilting her lips. "Certainly, Count Eolair."

He bowed his head and left her.

The Sithi were seated upon the ground around Likimeya's fire. Eolair
stopped some distance away, marveling at the strangeness of the sight. Although
close to a dozen of them sat in a wide circle, no one spoke: they merely looked
at each other as though they carried on some wordless conversation. Not for
the first time, the Count of Nad Mullach felt the hairs on the back of his neck
rise in superstitious wonder. What strange allies!

Likimeya still wore her mask of ashes. Heavy rains had swept down on the
traveling army the day before, but her strange face-painting seemed just as it
had been, which made the count suspect that she renewed it each day. Seated
across from her was a tall, narrow-featured Sitha-woman, thin as a priest's staff,
with pale sky-blue hair drawn up atop her head in a birdlike crest. It was only
because Jiriki had told him that Eolair knew that this stern woman, Zinjadu,
was even older than Likimeya.

Also seated at the fire was Jiriki's red-haired, green-garbed uncle Khendraja'aro, and Chekai'so Amber-Locks, whose shaggy hair and surprisingly open
face—Eolair had even seen this Sitha smile and laugh—made him seem almost
human. On either side of Jiriki sat Yizashi, whose long gray witchwood spear
was twined about with sun-golden ribbons, and Kuroyi, who was taller than
anyone else in the entire company, Sithi or Hernystiri, and so pale and cold-
featured that but for his tar-black hair he might have been a Norn. There were
others, too, three females and a pair of males that Eolair had seen before, but
whose names he did not know.

He stood uncomfortably for some time, uncertain of whether to stay or go.
At last, Jiriki looked up. "Count Eolair," he said. "We are just thinking about
Naglimund."

Eolair nodded, then bowed toward Likimeya, who lowered her chin briefly
in acknowledgment. None of the other Sithi gave him much more attention
than a flick of feline eyes. "We will be there soon," he said.

"A few days," agreed Jiriki. "We Zida'ya are not used to fighting against a
castle held by enemies—I do not think we have done it since the last evil days
back in Venyha Do'sae. Are there any among your folk who know Josua's stronghold well, or about such fighting? We have many questions."

"Siege warfare . . . ?" said Eolair uncertainly. He had thought that the frighteningly competent Sithi would have prepared for this long before. "There are a few of my men who have fought as mercenaries in the Southern Islands and the Lakeland wars, but not many. Hernystir itself has been peaceful during most of our lifetimes. As to Naglimund . . . I suppose that *I* know it best of any Hernystirman still living. I have spent much time there."

"Come and sit with us." Jiriki gestured to an open place near Chekai'so.

Black-haired Kuroyi said something in the liquid Sithi tongue as Eolair seated himself on the ground. Jiriki showed a hint of a smile. "Kuroyi says that surely the Norns will come out and fight us before the walls. He believes that the Hikeda'ya would never hide behind stone laid by mortals when the Zida'ya have come to resolve things at last."

"I know nothing of the . . . of those we call Norns," Eolair said carefully. "But I cannot imagine that if their purpose is as deadly earnest as it seems, they will give up the advantage of a stronghold like Naglimund."

"I believe you are correct," said Jiriki. "But it is hard to convince many of my people that. It is hard enough for most of us to believe that we go to war with the Hikeda'ya, let alone that they might hide within a fortress and drop stones on us as mortal armies do." He said something in the Sithi speech to Kuroyi, who replied briefly, then fell silent, his eyes cold as bronze plates. Jiriki next turned to the others.

"It is impolite for us to speak in a language Count Eolair does not know. If anyone does not feel comfortable speaking Hernystiri or Westerling, I will be happy to render your words for the count's understanding."

"Mortal tongues and mortal strategies. We will all have to learn," Likimeya said abruptly. "It is a different age. If the rules of mortals now make the world spin, then we must learn those rules."

"Or decide whether it is possible to live in such a world." Zinjadu's voice was deep yet strangely uninflected, as though she had learned Westerling without ever having heard it spoken. "Perhaps we should let the Hikeda'ya have this world of mortals that they seem to desire."

"The Hikeda'ya would destroy the mortals even more readily than they would destroy us," Jiriki said calmly.

"It is one thing," spoke up Yizashi Grayspear, "to fulfill an ancient debt, as we have just done at M'yin Azoshai. Besides, those were mortals we routed, and the descendants of bloody Fingil's ship-men besides. It is another thing to go to war with other Gardenborn to aid mortals to whom we owe no such debt— including those who hunted us long after we lost Asu'a. This Josua's father was our enemy!"

"Then does the hatred never end?" Jiriki replied with surprising heat. "Mortals have short lives. These are not the ones who warred on our scattered folk."

"Yes, the lives of mortals are short," said Yizashi dispassionately. "But their hatreds run deep, and are passed from parents to children."

Eolair was beginning to feel distinctly uncomfortable but did not think the time was right for him to speak up.

"It is possible that you forget, noble Yizashi," said Jiriki, "that it was the Hikeda'ya themselves who brought this war to us. It was they who invaded the sanctity of the Yásira. It was truly Utuk'ku's hand—not that of the mortal catspaw who wielded the dagger—which slew First Grandmother."

Yizashi did not reply.

"There is little point in this," Likimeya said. Eolair could not help noticing how the depths of Likimeya's eyes cast the light back, glowing orange as the stare of a torchlit wolf. "Yizashi, I asked you and these others, the House of Contemplation, the House of Gathering, all the houses, to honor your debts to the Grove. You agreed. And we are set upon our course because we need to thwart Utuk'ku Seyt-Hamakha's plans, not just repay an old debt or avenge Amerasu's murder."

Black-browed Kuroyi spoke up. "The mortals have a saying, I am told." His voice was measured and eerily musical, his Hernystiri somehow over-precise. " *'The enemy of my enemy is my friend . . . for a little while.'* Silvermask and her kin have chosen one set of mortals to be their allies, so we will choose those mortals' enemies to be *our* allies. Utuk'ku and her minions have also broken the Pact of Sesuad'ra. I find no shame in fighting beside Sudhoda'ya until the issue is settled." He raised his hand as though to ward off questions, but the circle was completely still. "No one has said I must love these mortal allies: I do not, and feel sure that I will not, whatever happens. And if I live until these days end, I will return to my high house in hidden Anvi'janya, for I have long been surfeited with the company of others, whether mortal or Gardenborn. But until then, I will do as I have promised to Likimeya."

There was a long pause after Kuroyi had finished. The Sithi again sat in silence, but Eolair had the feeling that some issue was in the air, some tension that sought resolution. When the quiet had gone on so long that he was beginning to wonder again whether he should leave, Likimeya lifted her hands and spread them flat in the air before her.

"So," she said. "Now we must think about this Naglimund. We must consider what we will do if the Hikeda'ya do not come out to fight."

The Sithi began to discuss the upcoming siege as though there had been no dispute over the honorability of fighting beside mortals. Eolair was puzzled but impressed by their civility. Each person was allowed to speak as long as he wished and no one interrupted. Whatever dissension there had been—and although Eolair found the immortals difficult to fathom, he had no doubt there had been true disagreement—now seemed vanished: the debate over Naglimund, although spirited, was calm and apparently free of resentment.

Perhaps when you live so long, Eolair thought, *you learn to exist by such rules—learn you must exist by such rules. Forever is a long time to carry grudges, after all.*

More at ease now, he entered the discussion—hesitantly at first, but when he saw that his opinion was to be given due weight he spoke openly and confidently about Naglimund, a place he knew almost as well as he knew the Taig in Hernysadharc. He had been there many times: Eolair had often found that

Josua's was a useful ear for introducing things into the court of his father, King John Presbyter. The prince was one of the few people the Count of Nad Mullach knew who would listen to an idea on its own merits, then support it if he found it good, regardless of whether it benefited him.

They talked long; eventually the fire burned down to glowing coals. Likimeya produced one of the crystal globes from her cloak and set it on the ground before her where it gradually grew bright; soon it cast its cool lunar glow all around the circle.

Eolair met Isorn on his way back from the council of the Sithi.

"Ho, Count," the young Rimmersman said. "Out for a stroll? I have a skin of wine here—from your own Nad Mullach cellars, I think. Let's find Ule and share it."

"Gladly. I have had a strange evening. Our allies . . . Isorn, they are like nothing and no one I have ever seen."

"They are the Old Ones, and heathen on top of it," Isorn said blithely, then laughed. "Apologies, Count. I sometimes forget that you Hernystiri are . . ."

"Also heathens?" Eolair smiled faintly. "No offense was taken. I have grown used to being the outsider, the odd one, during my years in Aedonite courts. But I have never felt so much the odd man as I did tonight."

"The Sithi may be different from us, Eolair, but they are bold as thunder."

"Yes, and clever. I did not understand all that was spoken of tonight, but I think that we have neither of us ever seen a battle like the one that will take place at Naglimund."

Isorn lifted an eyebrow, intrigued. "That is something to save and tell over that wine, but I am glad to hear it. If we live, we will have stories to amaze our grandchildren."

"If we live," Eolair said.

"Come, let us walk a little faster." Isorn's voice was light. "I am getting thirsty."

They rode across the Inniscrich the next day. The battlefield where Skali had triumphed and King Lluth had received his death-wound was still partially blanketed in snow, but that snow was full of irregular hummocks, and here and there a bit of rusted metal or a weathered spearhaft stuck up through the shrouding white. Although many prayers and curses were quietly spoken, none of the Hernystiri had any great interest in lingering at the site where they had been so soundly defeated and so many of their people had died, and for the Sithi it had no significance at all, so the great company passed by swiftly as they rode north along the river.

The Baraillean marked the boundary between Hernystir and Erkynland: the people of Utanyeat on the river's eastern side called it the Greenwade. These days, there were few living near either bank, although there were still fish to catch. The weather might have grown warmer, but Eolair could see that the land was almost lifeless. Those few survivors of the various struggles who still scratched out their lives here on the southern edge of the Frostmarch now fled before the approaching army of Sithi and men, unable to imagine any good that yet one more troop of armored invaders might bring.

At last, a week's journeying north of Nad Mullach—even when they were not in full charge the Sithi moved swiftly—the host crossed the river and moved into Utanyeat, the westernmost tip of Erkynland. Here the land seemed to grow more gray. The thick morning mists that had blanketed the ground during the ride across Hernystir no longer dispersed with the sun's ascension, so that the army rode from dawn to dusk in a cold, damp haze, like souls in some cloudy afterlife. In fact, a deathly pall seemed to hang over all the plains. The air was cold and seemed to reach directly into the bones of Eolair and his fellows. But for the wind and the muffled hoofbeats of their own horses, the wide countryside was silent, devoid even of birdsong. At night, as the count huddled with Maegwin and Isorn before the fire, a heavy stillness lay over everything. It felt, Isorn remarked one night, as though they were passing through a vast graveyard.

As each day brought them deeper into this colorless, cheerless country, Isorn's Rimmersmen prayed and made the Tree-sign frequently, and argued almost to bloodletting over insignificant things. Eolair's Hernystiri were no less affected. Even the Sithi seemed more reserved than usual. The ever-present mists and forbidding silence made all endeavor seem shallow and pointless.

Eolair found himself hoping that there would be some sign of their foes soon. The sense of foreboding that hung over these empty lands was a more insidious enemy, the count felt sure, than anything composed of flesh and blood could ever be. Even the frighteningly alien Norns were preferable to this journey through the netherworld.

"I feel something," said Isorn. "Something pricks at my neck."

Eolair nodded, then realized the duke's son probably could not see him through the mist, although he rode only a short distance away. "I feel it, too."

They were nine days out of Nad Mullach. Either the weather had again gone bad, or in this small part of the world the winter had never abated. The ground was carpeted in snow, and great uneven drifts lay humped on either side as they rode up the low hill. The failing sun was somewhere out of sight, the afternoon so gray there might never have been such a thing as a sun at all.

There was a clatter of armor and a flurry of words in the liquid Sithi speech from up ahead. Eolair squinted through the murk. "We are stopping." He spurred his horse forward. Isorn followed him, with Maegwin, who had ridden silently all day, close behind.

The Sithi had indeed reined up, and now sat silently on their horses as if waiting for something, their bright-colored armor and proud banners dimmed by the mist. Eolair rode through their ranks until he found Jiriki and Likimeya. They were staring ahead, but he saw nothing in the shifting fog that seemed worth their attention.

"We have halted," said the count.

Likimeya turned to him. "We have found what we sought." Her features seemed stony, as though her whole face had now become a mask.

"But I see nothing." Eolair turned to Isorn, who shrugged to show that he was no different.

"You will," said Likimeya. "Wait."

Puzzled, Eolair patted his horse's neck and wondered. There was a stirring as the wind rose again, fluttering his cloak. The mists swirled, and suddenly something dark appeared as the murk before them thinned.

The great curtain wall of Naglimund was ragged, many of its stones tumbled out like the scales of a rotting fish. In the midst of its great, gray length was a rubble-filled gap where the gate had stood, a sagging, toothless mouth. Beyond, showing even more faintly through the tendrils of mist, Naglimund's square stone towers loomed up beyond the walls, the dark windows glaring like the empty, bone-socket eyes of a skull.

"Brynioch," Eolair gasped.

"By the Ransomer," said Isorn, just as chilled.

"You see?" Likimeya asked. Eolair thought he detected a dreadful sort of humor in her voice. "We have arrived."

"It is Scadach." Maegwin sounded terrified. "The Hole in Heaven. Now I have seen it."

"But where is Naglimund-town?" Eolair asked. "There was a whole city at the castle's foot!"

"We have passed it, or at least its ruins," Jiriki said. "What little remains of it is now beneath the snows."

"Brynioch!" Eolair felt quite stupefied as he stared first at the insignificant-seeming lumps of earth and snow behind them, then turned back to the huge pile of crumbling stone just ahead. It seemed dead, yet as he gazed at it his nerves felt tight as lute strings and his heart was pounding. "Do we just ride in?" he asked no one in particular. Just thinking about it was like contemplating a headfirst crawl into a dark tunnel full of spiders.

"I will not go in that place," Maegwin said harshly. She was pale. For the first time since her madness had descended, she looked truly and completely fearful. "If you enter Scadach, you leave Heaven and its protection. It is a place from which nothing returns."

Eolair did not even have the heart to say anything soothing, but he reached out and took her gloved hand. Their horses stood quietly side by side, vaporous breath mingling.

"We will not ride into that place, no," Jiriki said solemnly. "Not yet."

Even as he spoke, flickering yellow lights bloomed in the depths of the black tower windows, as though whatever owned those empty eyes had just awakened.

Rachel the Dragon slept uneasily in her tiny room deep in the Hayholt's underground warrens.

She dreamed that she was again in her old room, the chambermaids' room that she knew so well. She was alone, and in her dream she was angry: her foolish girls were always so hard to find.

Something was scratching at the door; Rachel had a sudden certainty that it was Simon. Even in the midst of the dream, though, she remembered that she had been fooled once before by such a noise. She went carefully and quietly to the doorway and stood beside it for a moment, listening to the furtive noises outside.

"Simon?" she said. "Is that you?"

The voice that came back was indeed that of her long-lost ward, but it seemed stretched and thin, as though it traveled a long distance to reach her ear.

"Rachel, I want to come back. Please help me. I want to come back." The scratching resumed, insistent, strangely loud. . . .

The onetime Mistress of Chambermaids jerked awake, shivering with cold and fear. Her heart was beating very fast.

There. There was that noise again, just as she had heard it in the dream—but now she was awake. It was a strange sound, not so much a scratching as a hollow scraping, distant but regular. Rachel sat up.

This was no dream, she knew. She thought she had heard something like it as she was falling off to sleep, but had dismissed it. Could it be rats in the walls? Or something worse? Rachel sat up on her straw pallet. The small brazier with its few coals did no more than give the room a faint red sheen.

Rats in stone walls as thick as these? It was possible, but it didn't seem likely. *What else would it be, you old fool? Something is making that noise.*

Rachel sat up and moved stealthily toward the brazier. She took a handful of rushes from her carefully collected pile and dipped one end into the coals. After they had caught, she lifted the makeshift torch high.

The room, so familiar after all these weeks, was empty but for her stores. She bent low to look into the shadowy corners, but saw nothing moving. The scraping noise was a little fainter now but still unmistakable. It seemed to be coming from the far wall. Rachel took a step toward it and smacked her bare foot against her wooden keepsake chest, which she had neglected to push back against the wall after examining its sparse contents the night before. She let out a muffled shriek of pain and dropped a few of the flaming rushes, then quickly hobbled to her jug for a handful of water to put them out. When this was done, she stood on one foot while she rubbed her smarting toes.

When the pain subsided, she realized that the noise had also stopped. Either her surprised cry had frightened the noise maker away—likely if it were a rat or mouse—or merely warned the thing that someone was listening. The thought of something sitting quietly within the walls, aware now that someone was on the other side of the stone, was not one that Rachel wished to pursue.

Rats, she told herself. *Of course it's rats. They smell the food I've got in here, little demon imps.*

Whatever the cause had been, the noise was gone now. Rachel sat down on her stool and began to pull on her shoes. There was no point trying to sleep now.

What a strange dream about Simon, she thought. *Could it be his spirit is restless? I know that monster murdered him. There are tales that the dead can't rest till their murderers are punished. But I already did my best to punish Pryrates, and look where it got me. No good to anyone.*

Thinking of Simon condemned to some lonely darkness was both sad and frightening.

Get up, woman. Do something useful.

She decided that she would set out more food for poor blind Guthwulf.

A brief sojourn to the room with a slit of window upstairs confirmed that it was almost dawn. Rachel stared at the dark blue of the sky and the faded stars and felt a little reassured.

I'm still waking up regular, even if I live in the dark most days like a mole. That's something.

She descended to her hidden room, pausing in the doorway to listen for the scraping noises. The room was silent. After she had found suitable fare for both the earl and his feline familiar, she donned her heavy cloak and made her way down the stairwell to the secret passageway behind the tapestry on the landing.

When she arrived at the spot where she customarily left Guthwulf's meal, she found to her distress that the previous morning's food had not been touched: neither man nor cat had come.

He's never missed two days running since we started, she thought worriedly. *Blessed Rhiap, has the poor man fallen down somewhere?*

Rachel collected the untouched food and put out more, as though somehow a slightly different arrangement of what was really the same dried fruit and dried meat could tempt back her wandering earl.

If he doesn't come today, she decided, *I'll have to go and look for him. He has no one else to see to him, after all. It's the Aedonite thing to do.*

Full of worry, Rachel made her way back to her room.

❧

The sight of Binabik seated on a gray wolf as though it were a war-horse, his walking-stick couched like a lance, might have been comical in other circumstances, but Isgrimnur felt no urge even to smile.

"Still I am not sure this is the best thing," Josua said. "I fear we will miss your wisdom, Binabik of Yiqanuc."

"Then that is being all the larger reason for me to begin my journey now, since it will be ended so much more soon." The troll scratched behind Qantaqa's ears.

"Where is your lady?" Isgrimnur asked, looking around. Dawn was creeping into the sky overhead, but the hillside was deserted except for the three men and the wolf. "I would think she'd want to come and say farewell."

Binabik did not meet his eye, but rather stared at Qantaqa's shaggy neck. "We were saying our farewells in the earliness of the morning, Sisqi and I," he said quietly. "It is a hard thing for her to see me riding away."

Isgrimnur felt a great wash of regret for all the unwise, unthinking remarks he had ever made about trolls. They were small and strange, but they were certainly as bold-hearted as bigger men. He extended his hand for Binabik to clasp.

"Ride safely," the duke said. "Come back to us."

Josua did the same. "I hope you find Miriamele and Simon. But if you do not, there is no shame in it. As Isgrimnur said, come back to us as soon as you can, Binabik."

"And I am hoping that things will be going well for you in Nabban."

"But how will you find us?" Josua asked suddenly, his long face worried.

Binabik stared at him for a moment, then, surprisingly, let out a loud laugh. "How can I be finding an army of grasslanders and stone-dwellers mixed together, led by a dead hero of great famousness and a one-handed prince? I am thinking that it will not be difficult obtaining word of you."

Josua's face relaxed into a smile. "I suppose you are right. Farewell, Binabik." He raised his hand, exposing for a moment the dulled manacle he wore as a reminder of his imprisonment and the debt he owed his brother for it.

"Farewell, Josua and Isgrimnur," said the troll. "Please be saying that for me to the others as well. I could not bear to be making good-byes to all at once." He leaned forward to whisper something to the patiently waiting wolf, then turned back toward them. "In the mountains, we are saying this: *'Inij koku na siqqasa min taq'*—'When we meet again, that will be a good day.'" He sunk both his hands into the wolf's hackles. "*Hinik,* Qantaqa. Find Simon. *Hinik ummu!*"

The wolf leaped forward up the wet hillside. Binabik swayed on her broad back but kept his seat. Isgrimnur and Josua watched until the strange rider and his stranger mount topped the hill's crest and vanished from sight.

"I fear I will never see them again," said Josua. "I am cold, Isgrimnur."

The duke put his hand on the prince's shoulder. He was not himself feeling either very warm or very happy. "Let's go back. We have near a thousand people we need to get moving by the time the sun is above the hilltops."

Josua nodded. "So we do. Come, then."

They turned and retraced their own footsteps in the sodden grass.

30

A Thousand Leaves, A Thousand Shadows

✦

Miriamele and Simon spent the first week of their
flight in the forest. The traveling was slow and painfully laborious, but Miriamele had decided long before her escape that it would be far better to lose time
than to be captured. The daylight hours were spent struggling through the
dense trees and matted, tangling undergrowth, all to the tune of Simon's grumbling. They led their horses more often than they rode them.

"Be happy," she told him once as they rested in a clearing, leaning against
the trunk of an old oak. "At least we are getting to see the sun for a few days.
When we leave the forest again, we'll be riding by night."

"At least if we ride at night I won't have to look at the things that are tearing
all the skin off my body," Simon said crossly, rubbing at his tattered breeches
and the bruised flesh underneath.

It was heartening, Miriamele discovered, to have something to do. The
feeling of helpless dread that had gripped her for weeks faded away, leaving her
able to think clearly, to see everything around her as if with new eyes . . . and
even to enjoy being with Simon.

She did enjoy his company. Sometimes she wished she didn't enjoy it quite
so much. It was hard not to feel as though she were tricking him somehow. It
was more than just not telling him all her reasons for leaving Uncle Josua and
setting out for the Hayholt. She also felt as though she were not wholly clean,
not wholly fit to be with someone else.

It is Aspitis, she thought. *He did this to me. Before him, I was as pure as anyone
could want to be.*

But was that really true? He had not forced himself upon her. She had let
him do what he wished—in some ways she had welcomed it. In the end, Aspitis had proved to be a monster, but the way in which he came to her bed was
no different than that in which most men came to their sweethearts. He had
not savaged her. If what they had done was wrong and sinful, she bore equal
blame.

And what, then, of Simon? She had very mixed feelings. He was not a boy any more but a man, and a part of her feared the man he had become, as it would fear any man. But, she thought, there was also something about him that had remained strangely innocent. In his earnest attempts to do right, in the poorly-hidden hurt that he showed when she was short with him, he was still almost childlike. This made her feel even worse, that in his transparent regard for her he had no clue as to what she was truly like. It was precisely when he was kindest to her, when he most admired and complimented her, that she felt most angry with him. It seemed he was being willfully blind.

It was a dreadful way to feel. Luckily, Simon seemed to understand that his sincere affection was somehow painful to her, so he fell back on the jesting, mocking friendship with which she was more comfortable. When she could be around him without thinking about herself, she found him good company.

Despite growing up in the courts of her grandfather and father, Miriamele had found little opportunity to be with boys. King John's knights were mostly dead or long since retired to their estates scattered about Erkynland and elsewhere, and in her grandfather's later years the king's court had become empty of almost any but those who had to live near the king for the sake of their day-to-day livelihoods. Later, when her mother had died, her father had frowned on her spending time even with the few boys and girls of her age. He had not filled the void with his own presence, but had instead mewed her up with unpleasant old men and women who lectured her about the rituals and responsibilities of her position and found fault with everything she did. By the time her father had become king, Miriamele's solitary childhood was over.

Leleth, her handmaiden, had been almost her only young companion. The little girl had idolized Miriamele, hanging on the princess' every word. In turn, Leleth had told long stories about growing up with brothers and sisters—she was the youngest of a large baronial family—while her mistress listened in fascination, trying not to be jealous of the family she had never had.

That was why it had been so difficult to see Leleth again upon reaching Sesuad'ra. The lively little girl she remembered had vanished. Before they had fled the castle together, Leleth had been quiet sometimes, and many things frightened her, but it was as though some completely different creature now lived behind the little girl's eyes. Miriamele had tried to remember if there had ever been any sign of the sort of things that Geloë had discovered in the child, but could think of little, except that Leleth had been prone to vivid, intricate, and sometimes frightening dreams. Some of them had seemed so detailed and unusual in Leleth's retelling that Miriamele had been more than half certain the little girl had invented them.

When Miriamele's father had ascended to his own father's throne, she found herself both surrounded by people and yet terribly lonely. Everyone at the Hayholt had seemed obsessed with the empty ritual of power, something Miriamele had lived with for so long that it held no interest for her. It was like watching a confusing game played by bad-tempered children. Even the few young men

who paid court to her—or rather to her father, for most of them had been interested in little more than the riches and power that would fall to the one who
received her marriage-pledge—had seemed to her like some other type of
animal than she, boring old men in the bodies of youths, sullen boys masquer-
ading as adults.

The only ones in all of Meremund or the Hayholt who seemed to enjoy life
for what it was rather than what gain could be coaxed from it were the servants.
In the Hayholt especially, with its army of maids and grooms and scullions, it
was as though an entirely different race of people lived side by side with her
own bleak peers. Once, in a moment of terrible sadness, she had suddenly seen
the great castle as a kind of inverted lich-yard, with the creaking dead walking
around on top while the living sang and laughed below.

Thus Simon and a few others had first come to her attention—boys who
seemed to want nothing much more than to be boys. Unlike the children of
her father's nobles, they were in no hurry to take on the clacking, droning,
mannered speech of their elders. She watched them dawdling through their
chores, laughing behind their hands at each other's foolish pranks, or playing
hoodman blind on the commons grass, and she ached to be like them. Their
lives seemed so simple. Even when a more mature wisdom taught her that the
lives of the serving-folk were hard and wearisome, she still dreamed sometimes
that she could put off her royalty as easily as a cloak and become one of their
number. Hard work had never frightened her, but she was terrified of solitude.

"No," Simon said firmly. "You should never let me get this close to you."

He moved his foot slightly and twisted the hilt of his sword so that its cloth-
wrapped blade pushed hers away. Suddenly, he was pressing against her. His
smell, compounded of sweat and leather jerkin and the sodden fragments of a
thousand leaves, was very strong. He was so tall! She forgot that sometimes.
The sudden impact of his presence made it hard for Miriamele to think clearly.

"You've left yourself open now," he said. "If I used my dagger, you wouldn't
have a chance. Remember, you'll almost always be fighting someone with more
reach."

Instead of trying to bring her sword back where it would do some good, she
let it drop, then put both hands against Simon's chest and pushed. He fell back,
stumbling, before he regained his balance.

"Leave me alone." Miriamele turned and walked a few steps away, then
stooped to pick up a few branches for the fire so her shaking hands would have
something to do.

"What's wrong?" Simon asked, taken aback. "Did I hurt you?"

"No, you didn't hurt me." She took her armful of wood and dumped it into
the circle they had cleared on the forest floor. "I'm just done with that game for
a while."

Simon shook his head, then sat to undo the rags wound about his sword.

They had made camp early today, the sun still high above the treetops.

Miriamele had decided that tomorrow they would follow the little streamlet that had long been their companion down to the River Road; the course of the stream had been bending in that direction for most of this day's journey. The River Road wound beside the Ymstrecca, past Stanshire and on to Hasu Vale. It would be best, she had reasoned, for them to take to the road at midnight and still have some walking time before dawn, rather than spend all of this night in the forest and then wait through daylight again so they could travel the road in darkness.

This had been her first opportunity to use her sword in several days, except for the inglorious purpose of clearing brush. It had even been she who had suggested an hour of practice before they ate their evening meal—which was one of the reasons her abrupt change of heart obviously puzzled Simon. Miriamele felt torn between a desire to tell him it wasn't his fault, and an obscure feeling that somehow it *was* his fault—his fault for being male, his fault for liking her, his fault for coming with her when she would have been happier being miserably alone.

"Don't mind me, Simon," she said at last, and felt weak for doing so. "I'm just tired."

Mollified, he finished his careful rewinding of the cloth, then dropped the ball of dusty fabric into his saddlebag before coming to join her beside the unlit fire. "I just wanted you to be careful. I told you that you lean too far."

"I know, Simon. You did tell me."

"You can't let someone bigger than you get that close."

Miriamele found herself wishing silently that he would stop talking about it. "I know, Simon. I'm just tired."

He seemed to sense that he had annoyed her again. "But you're good, Miriamele. You're strong."

She nodded, absorbed now with the flint. A spark fell into the curls of tinder, but failed to produce a flame. Miriamele wrinkled her nose and tried again.

"Do you want me to try?"

"No, I don't want you to try." She struck again without result. Her arms were getting weary.

Simon looked at the wood shavings, then up at Miriamele's face, then quickly back down again. "Remember Binabik's yellow powder? He could start a fire in a rainstorm with that. I saw him make one catch when we were on Sikkihoq, and there was snow, and the wind was blowing. . . ."

"Here." Miriamele stood, letting the flint and the steel bar tumble to the dirt beside the tinder. "You do it." She walked to her horse and began hunting through the saddlebags.

Simon seemed about to say something, but instead applied himself to the task of fire-lighting. He had no better luck than Miriamele for a long time. At last, when she had returned with a kerchief full of the things she had found, he finally caught a small spark and provoked it into flame. As she stood over him she saw that his hair was getting quite long, hanging down onto his shoulders in reddish curls.

He looked up at her shyly. His eyes were full of concern for her. "What's wrong?"

She ignored his question. "Your hair wants cutting. I'll do it after we eat." She undid the kerchief. "These are our last two apples. They're getting a little old, in any case—I don't know where Fengbald found them." She had been told about the source of much of Josua's confiscated foodstuffs. There was an obscure pleasure in eating what had once been destined for that strutting braggart. "There's still some dried mutton, too, but we're almost through with it. We may have to try out the bow sometime soon."

Simon opened his mouth, then shut it. He took a breath. "We'll wrap the apples in leaves and bury them in the coals. Shem Horsegroom used to do that all the time. Then it doesn't matter if they're a little old."

"If you say so," Miriamele replied.

Miriamele leaned back and licked her fingers. They still smarted a little from the hot apple skin, but it had been worth it. "Shem Horsegroom," she said, "is a man of astonishing wisdom."

Simon smiled. His beard was sticky with juice. "It was good. But now we don't have any more."

"I couldn't eat any more tonight, anyway. And tomorrow we'll be on the road to Stanshire. I'm sure we can find something almost as good along the way."

Simon shrugged. "I wonder where old Shem is," he asked after a few moments had passed. The fire popped and spat as the leaves in which the apples had cooked began to blacken. "And Ruben. And Rachel. Do you think they're all still living at the Hayholt?"

"Why shouldn't they be? The king still needs grooms and blacksmiths. And there must *always* be a Mistress of Chambermaids." She offered a faint smile.

Simon chortled. "That's true. I can't imagine anyone getting Rachel to leave unless she wanted to. You might as well try to drag a porcupine out of a hollow stump. Even the king—your father, I mean—couldn't make her leave until she was ready."

"Sit up." Miriamele felt the sudden need to do something. "I said I was going to cut your hair."

Simon felt at the back of his head. "Do you think it needs it?"

Miriamele's look was stern. "Even sheep get sheared once a season."

She got out her whetstone and sharpened her knife. The noise of the blade on the stone was like a louder echo of the crickets that chirped beyond the light of the small fire.

Simon peered over his shoulder. "I feel like I'm about to be carved for the Aedonmansa feast."

"You never know what may happen when the dried meat runs out. Now look straight ahead and be quiet." She stood behind him, but there was not enough light to see. When she sat, his head was too far above her. "Stay there," she said.

She dragged over a large stone, digging a rut in the moist earth; when she sat on it, she was just the right height. Miriamele lifted Simon's hair in her hands and stared at it judiciously. Just a little off the bottom . . . No. Quite a bit off the bottom.

His hair was finer than it looked. Although it was thick, it was quite soft. Nevertheless, it was grimed with the days of travel. She thought of how her own must look and frowned. "When is the last time you bathed yourself?" she asked.

"What?" He was surprised. "What do you mean?"

"What do you think I mean? Your hair is full of bits of sticks and dirt."

Simon made a noise of disgust. "And what do you expect when I've been crawling through this stupid forest for days and days?"

"Well, I can't cut it like this." She thought for a moment. "I'm going to wash it."

"Are you mad? What do I want it washed for?" He drew up his shoulders protectively, as though she had threatened to stick the knife into him.

"I told you. So I can cut it." She stood and went to fetch the water skin.

"That's drinking water," Simon protested.

"I'll fill it again before we set out," she said calmly. "Now lean your head back."

She had thought momentarily of trying to warm the water, but she was just cross enough at his complaining to enjoy the spluttering noises he made as she disgorged the chilly contents of the water skin on his head. She then took her sturdy bone comb, which Vorzheva had given her back at Naglimund, and combed out the snarls as best she could, ignoring Simon's indignant protests. Some of the twigs were so entangled she had to unbind them with her fingernails, difficult work which made her lean close. The scent of wet hair added to his pungent Simon-smell was somehow quite pleasant, and Miriamele found herself humming quietly.

When she had done the best she could with the knots, she took up her knife again and began to trim his hair. As she had suspected, merely taking off the ragged ends was not entirely satisfying. Moving quickly in case Simon should begin to complain again, she began to cut in earnest. Soon the back of his neck came into view, pale from the long months hidden from the sun.

As she stared at Simon's neck, at the way it broadened at its base, at the line of red-gold hairs gradually thickening toward the hairline, she was suddenly moved.

There is something magical about everyone, she thought dreamily. *Everyone.*

She ran her fingers lightly up his neck and Simon jumped.

"Hoy! What are you doing? That tickles."

"Oh, shut your mouth." She smiled behind his back where he could not see.

She trimmed the hair up over his ears as well, leaving just a little bit to hang down in front where the beard began. She lifted the front and shortened that as well, then stepped to the side to make sure it would not fall down into his eyes. The snowy streak was as vivid as lightning.

"This is where the dragon's blood splashed you." The white hair felt no different than the red as it trailed across her fingertips. "Tell me again what it was like."

Simon seemed about to make some flippant remark, but paused instead, then spoke softly. "It was . . . it was not like anything, Miriamele. It just happened. I was frightened, and it was like someone was blowing a horn inside my head. It burned when it touched me. I don't remember much more until I woke up in the cave with Jiriki and Haestan." He shook his head. "There was more to it than that. Some things are hard to explain."

"I know." She let the strands of damp hair fall, then took a breath. "I'm finished."

Simon raised his hands to pat at the back and sides. "It feels short," he said. "I wish I could see it."

"Wait until morning, then have a look in the stream." She felt herself smiling again, stupidly, for no reason. "If I had known you were so vain, I would have brought one of my mirrors."

He turned a look of mock contempt upon her, then sat up straight. "I *do* have a mirror," he crowed. "Jiriki's! It's in my sack."

"But I thought that it was dangerous!"

"Not just to look at." Simon rose and headed for his saddlebags, in which he began to rummage energetically, like a bear seeking honey in a hollow tree. "Found it," he said. A frown crossed his face. He withdrew the hand that held the mirror, then reached back into the saddlebags with the other and continued to search.

"What is it?"

Simon withdrew his drawstring bag and brought it over to the fire. He handed her the Sithi mirror, which she held carefully, almost fearfully, while he scrabbled with increasing desperation in the large sack. At last he stopped and looked up at her, his eyes wide, his face a picture of loss. "It's gone."

"What's gone?"

"The White Arrow. It's not in here." He took his hands out of the sack. "Aedon's Blood! I must have left it in the tent. I must have forgotten to put it back that time." His face then registered a deeper shock. "I hope I didn't leave it up on Sesuad'ra!"

"You took it back to your tent, didn't you? That day you wanted to give it to me?"

He nodded slowly. "That's right. It must have been in there somewhere. At least that means it's probably not lost." He looked down at his empty hands. "But I don't have it." He laughed. "I tried to give it away. It didn't like that, I guess. Sithi gifts, Binabik told me, don't take them lightly. Remember on the river, when we were first traveling together? I was showing off with it and I fell out of the boat."

Miriamele smiled sadly. "I remember."

"I've done it this time, though, haven't I?" he said morosely, and sighed. "Still, it can't be helped. If Binabik finds it, he'll take care of it. And it's not like I need to have it to prove something to Jiriki. If I ever see him again." He shrugged and tried to smile. "May I have the mirror back?"

He held it up and carefully examined his hair. "It's good," he said. "It's short in the back. Like Josua's or someone like that." He looked up at her. "Like Camaris."

"Like a knight."

Simon looked down at his hand for a moment, then reached out and took Miriamele's, enfolding her fingers in his warm grasp. He did not quite meet her eyes. "Thank you. You did it very handsomely."

She nodded, desperately wanting to pull her hand free, to be not so close, but at the same time happy to feel his touch. "You are welcome, Simon."

At last, almost reluctantly, he let her go. "I suppose we should try to sleep if we're going to get up at midnight," he said.

"We should," she agreed.

They packed away their few goods and unfurled their bedrolls in friendly, if slightly uneasy, silence.

Miriamele was awakened in the middle of the night by a hand over her mouth. She tried to scream, but the hand clamped even more tightly.

"No! It's me!" The hand lifted.

"Simon?" she hissed. "You idiot! What are you doing?"

"Quiet. There's someone out there."

"What?" Miriamele sat up, staring uselessly into the darkness. "Are you sure?"

"I was just falling asleep when I heard it," he said into her ear, "but it wasn't a dream. I listened after I was wide awake and I heard it again."

"It's an animal—a deer."

Simon bared his teeth to the moonlight. "I don't know any animals that talk to themselves, do you?"

"What?"

"Quiet!" he whispered. "Just listen."

They sat in silence. It was hard for Miriamele to hear anything over the pounding of her own heart. She sneaked a glance at the fire. A few embers still glowed: if there was a person out there, they had demonstrated their presence quite thoroughly. She wondered if it would do any good now to throw dirt on the coals.

Then she heard it, a crackling noise that seemed a good hundred paces away. Her skin tingled. Simon looked at her significantly. The sound came again, a little more distant this time.

"Whatever it is," she said quietly, "it sounds like it's leaving."

"We were going to try to make our way down to the road in a few hours. I don't think we should risk it."

Miriamele wanted to argue—this was her journey, after all, her plan—but found that she could not. The idea of trying to make their way along the tangled riverbank by moonlight, while something followed along after them . . . "I agree," she said. "We'll wait until light."

"I'll stay up for a while and keep watch. Then I'll wake you and you can let me sleep for a while." Simon sat himself cross-legged with his back against a stump. His sword was across his knees. "Go on, sleep." He seemed tense, almost angry.

Miriamele felt her heart slowing a little. "You said it was talking to itself?"

"Well, it could be more than one person," he said, "but it didn't seem to make enough noise for two. And I only heard one voice."

"What was it saying?"

She could dimly see Simon shake his head. "I couldn't tell. It was too quiet. Just . . . words."

Miriamele settled back onto her bedroll. "It might just be some cotsman. People do live in the forest."

"Might be." Simon's voice was flat. Miriamele suddenly realized that he sounded that way because he was frightened. "There are all kinds of things in these woods," he added.

She let her head fall back until she could see a few stars peeping through holes in the forest roof. "If you start to feel sleepy, don't be a hero, Simon. Wake me up."

"I will. But I don't think I'll be sleepy for a while."

Neither will I, she thought.

The idea of being stalked was a dreadful one. But if someone was following them, someone her uncle had sent, why would the stalker go away again without doing anything? Perhaps it had been forest outlaws who would have slaughtered them in their sleep if Simon had not awakened. Or perhaps it had only been an animal after all, and Simon had imagined the words.

Miriamele at last drifted into an uneasy sleep, a sleep haunted by dreams of antler-headed, two-legged figures moving through the forest shadows.

It took them a good part of the morning to make their way out of the forest. The reaching branches and foot-snagging undergrowth almost seemed to be trying to hold them back; the mist rising from the forest floor was so treacherously dense that if they had not had the sound of the stream to keep them on track, Miriamele felt sure they might just as easily have gone in the wrong direction. At last, sore and sweaty and even more tattered than they had been at dawn, they emerged onto the sodden downs.

After a short ride across the uneven meadowland they reached the River Road late in the morning. There was no snow here, but the sky was dark and threatening, and the thick forest mist seemed to have followed them—the land was shrouded in fog as far as they could see.

The River Road itself was almost empty: as they rode along they met only one wagon, which bore an entire family and its belongings. The driver, a care-worn man who looked older than he probably was, seemed almost overwhelmed by the effort of nodding to Simon and Miriamele as they passed. She turned to watch the wagon wheeling slowly eastward behind a thin-shanked ox, and wondered if they were going to Sesuad'ra to cast their fortunes with Josua. The man, his scrawny wife, and their silent children had looked so sad, so tired, that it was painful to think that they might be traveling toward a place she knew to be deserted. Miriamele was tempted to warn them that the prince was already marching south, but she hardened her heart and turned around. Such a favor would be dangerous foolishness: appearing in Erkynland with knowledge of Josua would attract far more attention than was healthy.

The few small settlements they passed as morning wore into afternoon seemed almost deserted; only a few plumes of gray wafting from the smoke holes of houses, a gray just a little darker than the surrounding mist, suggested that people still went about their lives in this depressing place. If these had been farming communities, there was little sign of it now: the fields were full of dark weeds and there were no animals to be seen. Miriamele guessed that if the times were as bad here as she had heard reported of other parts of Erkynland, the few cows and sheep and pigs not yet eaten were being jealously guarded.

"I'm not sure we should stay on this road too much longer." Miriamele squinted up from the broad, muddy causeway into the reddening western sky.

"We've barely seen a dozen people all day," Simon replied. "And if we're being followed, we're best out in the open, where we can see anyone behind us."

"But we'll be coming to the outskirts of Stanshire soon." Miriamele had traveled in this area a few times with her father, and had a fairly good idea of where they were. "That's a much bigger town than any of these little places we've passed. There'll be people on the road there, that's certain. Maybe guardsmen, too."

Simon shrugged. "I suppose. What are we going to do, ride through the fields?"

"I don't think anyone will notice or care. Haven't you seen how all the houses are shuttered? It's too cold for people to be looking out the windows."

In answer, Simon exhaled a puff of foggy breath and smiled. "As you say. Just be careful we don't run the horses into a bog or something. It'll be dark soon."

They turned their mounts off the road and through a hedge of loose brush. The sun was almost gone now, a thin slice of crimson on the horizon all that remained. The wind increased, whipping through the long grass.

Evening had settled in across the hilly landscape by the time they saw the first signs of Stanshire. The village lay on both sides of the river, joined by a central bridge, and on the northern bank the clutter of houses extended almost to the eaves of the forest. Simon and Miriamele stopped on a hilltop and looked down on the twinkling lights.

"It's smaller," Miriamele said. "It used to fill this entire valley."

Simon squinted. "I think it still does—see, there are houses all the way across. It's just that only half of them have fires, or lamps burning, or whatever." He pulled off his gloves to blow on his fingers. "So. Where shall we stay tonight? Did you bring any money for an inn?"

"We are not going to sleep indoors."

Simon raised an eyebrow. "No? Well, at least we can find a hot meal somewhere."

Miriamele turned to look at him. "You don't understand, do you? This is my father's country. I have been here before myself. And there are so few travelers on the road that even if we weren't recognized by anyone, people would want to ask us questions." She shook her head. "I can't take the chance. We can probably send you in somewhere to buy some food—I did bring some money—but stay in a hostel? We might as well hire a trumpeter to walk before us."

It was hard to tell in the dim light, but Simon seemed to be flushing. There was certainly an angry edge to his voice. "If you say so."

She calmed her own temper. "Please, Simon. Don't you think that I would love a chance to wash my face and sit down on a bench and eat a real supper? I'm trying to do what's best."

Simon looked at her for a moment, then nodded. "I'm sorry. That's good sense. I was just disappointed."

Miriamele felt a sudden gust of affection for him. "I know. You're a good friend."

He looked up sharply, but said nothing. They rode down the hillside into the Stanshire valley.

There was something wrong with Stanshire. Miriamele remembered it from her visit some half-dozen years before as a bustling, thriving town populated mostly by miners and their families, a place where even at night the narrow streets were full of lamplight—but now the few passersby seemed in a hurry to be inside once more, and even the town's inns were quiet as monasteries and nearly empty.

Miriamele waited in the shadows outside *The Wedge and Beetle* while Simon spent some of their cintis-pieces on bread and milk and onions.

"I asked the owner about some mutton and he just stared at me," Simon said. "I think it's been a very bad year."

"Did he ask you any questions?"

"He wanted to know where I came from." Simon was already nibbling on his bread. "I told him I was a chandler from Hasu Vale, looking for some work. He looked at me funny again, then said, 'Well, you've found there's no work to be had here, haven't you?' It's just as well *he* didn't need some work because I've forgotten everything Jeremias ever told me about how to make candles. But he asked me how long since I'd left Hasu Vale, and was it true what everyone said, that there's hauntings in the hills there."

"Hauntings?" Miriamele felt a thin line of ice along her spine. "I don't like the sound of that. What did you tell him?"

"That I'd been gone a long time, of course. That I'd been traveling in the south looking for work. Then, before he could start asking me about *that,* I told him my wife was waiting in the wagon up on the River Road and that I had to go."

"Your *wife?*"

Simon grinned. "Well, I had to tell him something, didn't I? Why else would a man take his food and hurry back out into the cold?"

Miriamele made a disgusted noise, then clambered up into the saddle. "We should find a place to sleep, at least for a while. I'm exhausted."

Simon looked around. "I don't know where we could go here—it's hard to tell which houses are empty, even if there's no smoke and no light. The people may have left, or they just might not have any firewood."

As he spoke, a light rain began to fall.

"We should move farther out," she said. "On the western edge of town we can probably find an empty barn or a shed. Also there's a quarry out there, a big one."

"Sounds splendid." Simon took a bite from one of the rather shriveled-looking onions. "You lead."

"Just don't eat my supper by mistake," she said darkly. "And don't spill any of that milk."

"No, my lady," he replied.

As they rode west on Soakwood Road, one of Stanshire's main thorough-fares, Miriamele found herself oddly disturbed by Simon's words. It was indeed impossible to tell if any of the darkened houses and shops were occupied, but she had a distinct sense of being watched, as though hidden eyes peered out through the cracks in the window shutters.

Soon enough they reached the farmland outside town. The rain had eased, and was now little more than a drizzle. Miriamele pointed out the quarry, which from their vantage point on Soakwood Road was a great black nothing-ness. When the road had climbed a little higher up the hill, they could see a flickering of reddish light on the lower walls of the quarry.

"Someone's got a fire there," said Simon. "A big one."

"Perhaps they're digging stone," Miriamele replied. "Whatever they're doing, though, we don't need to know about it. The fewer people who see us, the bet-ter." She turned them off the wide road and down one of the small lanes, away from the quarry and back toward the River Road. The path was muddy, and finally Miriamele decided that it would be better to light a torch than risk a broken leg for one of the horses. They dismounted, and Simon did his best to hold off the misting rain with his cloak while Miriamele struggled with the flint. At last she managed to strike a spark that set the oily rag burning.

After riding a little farther they found a likely shelter, a large shed standing in a field that had gone mostly to weeds and bramble. The house to which it apparently belonged, several hundred paces away down the glen, looked deserted. Neither Miriamele nor Simon were certain that the house was truly empty, but the shed at least seemed relatively safe, and they would certainly be drier and happier than beneath open sky. They tethered their horses to a gnarled—and sadly barren—apple tree behind the shed, out of sight of the house below.

Inside, the torchlight revealed a heap of damp straw in the middle of the dirt floor, as well as a few rusting tools with splintered or missing handles leaned against the wall in anticipation of repair. A corroded scythe was depressing to Miriamele in its forgotten uselessness, but also heartening in that it suggested no one had used this shed for some time. Reassured, she and Simon went back out and fetched their saddlebags.

Miriamele kicked the straw into two even piles, then laid out her bedroll on one of them. She looked around critically. "I wish we could risk a real fire," she said, "but I do not even like the torch."

Simon had stuck the burning brand into the dirt of the floor, away from the straw. "I need to be able to see to eat," he said. "We'll put it out soon."

They devoured what remained of their meal hungrily, washing the dry bread down with draughts of cool milk. As they wiped fingers and lips clean on their sleeves, Simon looked up.

"So what do we do tomorrow?" he asked.

"Ride. If the weather stays like this, we might as well ride by day. In any case, we'll see no towns of any size until we reach the walls of Falshire, so there shouldn't be many people on the road."

"If the rest of the countryside around here is anything like Stanshire," Simon said, "we won't see half a dozen people all day."

"Perhaps. But if we hear anything greater than a few riders coming toward us, we should get off the road, just to be safe."

There was a silence as Miriamele took a last drink from the water skin, then crawled onto her bedroll and pulled her cloak over her.

"Are you going to tell me any more about where we're going?" Simon asked at last. She could hear from his voice that he was trying to be careful, that he didn't want to make her angry. She was touched by his cautiousness, but also felt more than a little cross at being treated like a child susceptible to tantrums.

"I don't want to talk about it now, Simon." She turned away, not liking herself, but unwilling to spill out her secret heart. She could hear him clamber onto his own bedroll, then a quiet curse as he realized he had not snuffed the torch. He crawled back across the shed.

"Don't soak it," she said. "It will make it easier to light the next time we need it."

"Indeed, my lady." Simon's voice was sour. There was a sizzle and the light was gone. After a few moments, she heard him return to his sleeping spot.

"Good night, Simon."

"Good night." He sounded angry.

Miriamele lay in darkness and thought about what Simon had asked. Could she even explain to him? It would sound so foolish to someone else, wouldn't it? Her father was the one who had started this war—or rather, she felt sure, he had started it at Pryrates' urging—so how could she explain to Simon that she needed to see him, to talk to him? It wouldn't just sound foolish, she decided, it would sound like the worst and most reckless sort of madness.

And maybe that's true, she thought gloomily. *What if I am just fooling myself? I could be captured by Pryrates and never see my father at all. Then what would happen? That red-robed monster would have every secret of Josua's that I know.*

She shuddered. Why didn't she tell Simon what she planned? And more importantly, why hadn't she told Uncle Josua instead of just running away? Just the little bit she *had* told him had made him angry and suspicious . . . but maybe he was right. Who was she, one young woman, to decide what was right and wrong for her uncle and all his followers? And wasn't that what she was doing, taking their lives into her hands to satisfy a whim?

But it's not a whim. She felt herself divided into warring factions, like her father and uncle, two halves in conflict. She was coming apart. *It's important. No one can stop this but my father, and only I know what started it. But I'm so frightened. . . .*

The magnitude of what she had done and what she planned to do came rising up, until she suddenly felt she might choke. And no one knew but her—no one!

Something inside her seemed about to break beyond mending. She took in a great gulp of breath.

"Miriamele? Miriamele, what's wrong?"

Fighting to control herself, she did not reply. She could hear Simon moving nearby, the straw rustling.

"Are you hurt? Are you having a bad dream?" His voice was closer, almost beside her ear.

"No," she gasped, then sobbing took her voice away.

Simon's hand touched her shoulder, then tentatively moved up to her face. "You're crying!" he said, surprised.

"Oh . . ." She struggled to speak. "I'm so . . . I'm so . . . *lonely!* I want t-to go h-h-home!" She sat up and bent forward, pressing her face into the damp cloak over her knees. Another great storm of weeping overtook her. At the same time, a part of her stood as though separate, watching her own performance with disgust.

Weak, it told her spitefully. *No wonder you won't get what you want. You're weak.*

". . . Home?" Simon said, wondering. "Do you want to go back to Josua and the others?"

"No, you idiot!" Anger at her own stupidity momentarily cut through the sobs so that she could speak, "I want to go home! I want things to be the way they used to be!"

In the dark, Simon reached for her and pulled her close. Miriamele struggled for a moment, then let her head fall against his chest. Everything hurt. "I'll protect you," he said softly. There was a curious note in his voice, a sort of quiet exultation. "I'll take care of you, Miriamele."

She pushed herself away from him. In the sliver of moonlight that leaked through the shed's doorway, she could see his tousle-haired silhouette. "I don't want to be protected! I'm not a child. I just want things to be right again."

Simon sat unmoving for a long moment, then she felt his arm again around her shoulder. His voice was gentle when she expected to have her own anger returned.

"I'm sorry," he said. "I'm scared, too. I'm sorry."

And as he spoke, she realized suddenly that this was Simon beside her, that he was not her enemy. She let herself sag back against his chest, craving for a moment the warmth and solidity of him. A fresh torrent of tears came rushing up and spilled out of her.

"Please, Miri," he said helplessly. "Don't cry." He put his other arm around her and held her tightly.

After a while the storm of weeping subsided. Miriamele could only lean against Simon, without strength. She felt his fingers run along her jaw, tracing the path of her tears. She pushed in closer, burrowing like a frightened animal, until she felt her face rub against his neck, his hidden blood pulsing against her cheek.

"Oh, Simon," she said, her voice ragged. "I'm so sorry."

"Miriamele," he began, then fell silent. She felt his hand on her chin, cupping it gently. He turned her face up to his, to his warm breath. He seemed about to say something. She could feel the words suspended between them, trembling, unspoken. Then she felt his lips upon hers, the gentle scratch of his beard around her mouth.

For a moment, Miriamele felt herself floating in some unfixed place, in some unrecorded time. She sought a huddling place, somewhere to flee from the pain that seemed all around her like a storm. His mouth was soft, careful, but the hand that touched her face was shaking. She was shaking, too. She wanted to fall into him, to dive into him like a quiet pool.

Unbidden, a picture came to her like a shred of dream: Earl Aspitis, his fine golden hair gleaming in lamplight, bending above her. The arm around her was suddenly a confining claw.

"No," she said, pulling away. "No, Simon, I can't."

He let go of her quickly, like someone caught pilfering. "I didn't . . ."

"Just leave me alone." She heard her own voice, flat and cold. It did not match the swirl of violent feelings inside her. "I'm . . . I just . . ." She, too, was at a loss for words.

In the silence, there was a sudden noise. A long moment passed before Miriamele realized that it came from outside the shed. It was the horses, whinnying nervously. An instant later, a twig crackled just beyond the door.

"There's someone out there!" she hissed. The confusion of the moment before fell away, replaced by the ice of fear.

Simon fumbled for his sword; finding it, he stood and moved to the door. Miriamele followed.

"Should I open it?" he asked.

"We don't want to be caught in here," she whispered sharply. "We don't want to be trapped."

Simon hesitated, then pushed the door outward. There was a flurry of movement outside. Someone was hurrying away, a shadow lurching toward the road through the misted moonlight.

Simon kicked free of the cloak tangled about his legs, then sprang out the door after the fleeing shape.

31

Flamedance

Simon was filled with anger, a high, wild fury that pushed him on like a wind at his back. The figure running before him faltered and he drew closer. He felt as he thought Qantaqa must feel when she ran some small fleeing thing to ground.

Spy on me! Spy on me, will you?!

The shadowy form stumbled again. Simon lifted his sword, ready to hew the sneaking creature down in its tracks. Another few paces . . .

"Simon!" Something caught at his shirt, tugging him off stride. "Don't!"

He lowered his hand to regain his balance and his sword caught in the weedy grass and sprang from his fingers. He pawed at the ground, but could not find it in the deep brush, in the dark. He hesitated for a moment, but the dark shape before him had regained its stride and was pulling away. With a curse, Simon abandoned the sword and ran on. A dozen strong paces and he had caught up again. He wrapped his arms around his quarry's midsection and tumbled them both to the ground.

"Oh, sweet Usires!" the thing beneath him shrieked. *"Don't burn me! Don't burn me!"* Simon grabbed the thrashing arms and held on.

"What are you doing?!" Simon hissed. "Why have you been following us?"

"Don't burn me!" the man quavered, struggling to keep his face turned away. He flailed his spindly limbs in seeming terror. "Weren't following no one!"

Miriamele arrived, Simon's sword clutched in both hands. "Who is it?"

Still angry, although even he was not quite sure why, Simon took the man's ear in his hand—as Rachel the Dragon had oftentimes done with a certain recalcitrant scullion—and twisted it until the face swung toward him.

His prisoner was an old man; Simon did not know him. The man's eyes were wide and blinking rapidly. "Didn't mean no harm, old Heanwig didn't!" he said. "Don't burn me!"

"Burn you? What are you babbling about? Why were you following us?"

Miriamele looked up suddenly. "Simon, we can't stay here shouting. Let's take him back."

"Don't burn Heanwig!"

"Nobody's burning anybody," Simon grunted. He dragged the old man onto his feet less gently than he might have, then marched him toward the shed. The intruder sniffled and pleaded for his life.

Simon retained his hold on the old man while Miriamele tried to relight the torch. She eventually gave up and took another from her saddlebag. When it was burning, Simon let go of the prisoner and then sat with his back against the door so that the old man could not make another bolt for freedom.

"He doesn't have any weapons," Simon said. "I felt his pockets."

"No, masters, got no nothing." Heanwig seemed a little less frightened, but still pathetically eager not to offend. "Please, just let me go and I'll tell no one."

Simon looked him over. The old man had the reddened cheeks and nose of a veteran tosspot, and his eyes were bleary. He was staring worriedly at the torch, as though it were now the greatest danger in the room. He certainly didn't seem much of a threat, but Simon had learned long ago from Doctor Morgenes' small-outside, large-inside chambers that things could be other than they appeared. "Why were you following us?" he demanded. "And why do you think we'd burn you?"

"Don't need to burn no one," the old man said, "Old Heanwig means no harm. He won't tell nobody."

"Answer my question. What are you doing here?"

"Was just looking for place to sleep, masters." The old man chanced a quick survey of the shed. "Slept here before once or twice. Didn't want to be outside tonight, no, not tonight."

"Were you following us in the forest? Did you come to our camp last night?"

The old man looked at him with what seemed genuine surprise. "Forest? In Oldheart? Heanwig won't go there. Things and beasties and such—that's a bad place, masters. Don't you go to that Oldheart."

"I think he's telling the truth," said Miriamele. "I think he was just coming here to sleep." She fished the water skin out of her saddlebag and gave it to the old man. He looked at it for a moment with suspicion. Understanding, Miriamele lifted it to her own mouth and drank, then passed it to him. Reassured, the old man swallowed hungrily, then looked at her as accusingly as if his fear of poison had been confirmed.

"Water," he murmured sullenly.

Miriamele stared at him, but Simon slowly smiled. He leaned across and fished out the other skin bag, the one Miriamele had told him she was saving for cold nights or painful injuries. Simon squirted a little bit of the red Perdruin into a bowl and held it out where the old man could see. Heanwig's trembling fingers reached for it, but Simon pulled the bowl back.

"Answer our questions first. You swear you were not searching for us?"

Heanwig shook his head emphatically. "Never seen you before. Won't remember you when you're gone. That's a promise." His thin hands snaked out again.

"Not yet. Why did you think we'd burn you?"

The old man looked at him, then at the wine, plainly torn. "Thought you were those Fire Dancers," he said at last, with obvious reluctance. "Thought you meant to burn me like they burned old Wiclaf who used to be First Hammerman up to quarry."

Simon shook his head, puzzled, but Miriamele leaned closer, fear and distaste in her expression. "Fire Dancers? Are there Fire Dancers here?"

The old man looked at her as though she had asked whether fish could swim. "Town be full of them. They chased me, chased Heanwig. But I hid from them." He smiled a weak smile, but his eyes remained wary and calculating. "They be in quarry tonight, dancing and praying to their Storm Lord."

"The quarry!" Miriamele breathed. "That's what the lights were!"

Simon was still not sure he trusted the old man. Something was bothering him, like a fly buzzing beside his ear, but he could not decide what it was. *"If he's telling the truth."*

"I tell the truth," Heanwig said with sudden force. He tried to draw himself up straight, fixing Simon with his rheumy eyes. "I was coming here for a bit of sleep, then I heard you. Thought the Fire Dancers were here—they roam all through town at night. People with houses bar their doors, do you see, but Heanwig's got no house no more. So I ran."

"Give the wine to him, Simon," Miriamele said. "It's cruel. He's just a frightened old man."

Simon made a face and handed Heanwig the bowl. The old man sniffed it and a look of rapture crossed his age-spotted features. He tilted the bowl and drank thirstily.

"The Fire Dancers!" Miriamele hugged herself. "Mother of Mercy, Simon, we don't want to get caught by them. They're all mad. Tiamak was attacked by some in Kwanitupul, and I saw others light themselves on fire and burn to death."

Simon looked from Miriamele to the old man, who was licking his wrinkled lips with a tongue that looked like something which made its home in a seashell. He felt an unlikely urge to reach out and cuff the old tosspot, although the man had done little enough, really. Simon suddenly remembered how he had raised the sword, that moment of fury when he might have slain this poor wretch, and was horribly ashamed.

What sort of knight would cut down a feeble drunkard?

But what dreadful fate had sent the old man to frighten the horses and break twigs in the very moment when he was finally holding Miriamele in his arms? They had been kissing! She, the princess, the beautiful Miriamele, had been kissing Simon!

He turned his gaze from the old man to Miriamele once more. She, too, had been watching Heanwig drain his bowl, but now her eyes flicked up to Simon's for a moment. Even in the torchlight, he could see her blush. Fate was cruel . . . but a little earlier, it had been kind as well. Oh, sweet Fate, sweet Luck!

Simon abruptly laughed. The greater part of his anger dissipated like chaff before the wind. The loveliest girl in all of Aedondom, clever and quick—and she had kissed him. Called him by his name! He could still feel the shape of her face on his fingertips. What right had he to complain?

"So what do we do?" he asked.

Miriamele avoided his eye. "We will stay the night. Then in the morning we will get as far away from the Fire Dancers as we can."

Simon darted a glance at Heanwig, who was looking hopefully toward the saddlebags. "And him?"

"We will let him stay here for the night, too."

"And what if he drinks all the wine and takes it into his head to strangle us in our sleep?" Simon protested. Even he found it rather silly to say such things about the bony, shivering old man, but he desperately wanted to be alone with Miriamele once more.

As if she understood this and was equally determined *not* to see it happen, Miriamele said: "He'll do nothing of the sort. And we will take turns sleeping. Will that make you feel better, Simon? You can guard the wine."

The old man looked from one to the other, evidently trying to decide where the battle lines were drawn. "Old Heanwig won't be no bother. You don't need to stay up, young masters. You be tired. Old fellow like me doesn't need sleep. I'll stay up and watch for them Fire Dancers."

Simon snorted. "I'm certain you would. Let's toss him out, Miriamele. If he isn't the one who followed us, there's no reason to keep him."

"There's a perfectly good reason. He's an old man and he's frightened. You forget, Simon, I've seen the Fire Dancers and you haven't. Don't be cruel just because you're in a bad mood." She gave him a stern look, but Simon thought he saw a tiny flash of knowing amusement in it.

"No, don't send me out to those Fire Dancers," Heanwig begged. "They burned Wiclaf, they did. I saw it. And him not harming nobody. They lit him on fire down Pulley Road, screaming *'Here's what's coming! Here's what's coming!'* " Heanwig trailed off, shuddering. What had started out as a self-serving justification had become real as the memory played out before his mind's eye. "Don't send me away, masters. I'll never speak no word." His abrupt sincerity was apparent.

Simon looked from Miriamele to the old man, then back to the princess. He had been neatly outflanked. "Oh, very well," he growled. "But I'm staying up on first watch, old man, and if you do anything the least bit suspicious, you'll be out that door and into the cold so fast your head will spin."

He gave Miriamele a last look compounded of annoyance and longing, then settled back against the shed door.

Simon awoke in the early morning to discover Miriamele and the old man both up and chatting amiably. Simon thought that Heanwig looked even worse in daylight, his seamed features smudged with dirt, his clothes so tattered and soiled that even poverty could not excuse it.

"You should come with us," Miriamele was saying. "You'll be safer than by yourself. At least join us until you're far away from the Fire Dancers."

The old man shook his head doubtfully. "Those mad folk be most everywhere, these days."

Simon sat up. His mouth was dry and his head hurt, as though *he* were the drunkard of the company. "What are you saying? You can't bring him with us."

"I certainly can," said Miriamele. "You may accompany me, Simon, but you may not tell me where I can go or who I can bring along."

Simon stared at her for a moment, sensing an argument that he had no hope of winning, no matter what he did. He was still weighing his next words when he was saved from the useless engagement by Heanwig.

"Are you bound for Nabban?" the old man asked. "I never have seen those parts."

"We're going to Falshire," Miriamele said. "Then on to Hasu Vale."

Simon was just about to upbraid her for telling this complete stranger their travel plans—what had happened to the need for caution she had lectured *him* about?—when the old man made a gasping noise. Simon turned, angry already at the thought that the old tosspot was now going to be sick right in front of them, but was startled by the look of horror on Heanwig's mottled face.

"Going to Hasu Vale!?" His voice rose. "What, be ye mad? That whole valley runs haunted." He scrambled a cubit toward the door, grasping fruitlessly for a handhold in the moldering straw beneath him, as though the two travelers had threatened to drag him to the hated place by force. "Sooner I'd crawl down into quarry with those Fire Dancers."

"What do you mean, haunted?" Miriamele demanded. "We've heard that before. What does it mean?"

The old man stared at her, eyes rolling to show the whites. "Haunted! Bad 'uns, bogies from out the lich-yard. Witches and suchlike!"

Miriamele stared at him hard. After a year like the last one, she was not inclined to dismiss such talk as superstition. "We're going there," she said at last. "We have to. But you don't have to travel any farther than you want to."

Heanwig got shakily to his feet. "Don't want to go west'ard. Heanwig'll stay here'bouts. There's folk in Stanshire as still have a morsel to spare, or a drop, even in bad times." He shook his head. "Don't go there, young mistress. *You* been kind." He looked pointedly at Simon to make it clear who had not been.

The old sot, Simon thought grumpily. *Who gave him the wine, anyway? Who didn't break his head when he could have?*

"Go south—you'll be happy there," Heanwig continued, almost pleading. "Stay out the Vale."

"We must go," said Miriamele. "But we won't make you come."

Heanwig had been sidling toward the door. Now he stopped with his hand already on the wood and ducked his head. "I thank you, young mistress. Aedon's Light be on you." He paused, at a loss for words. "Hope you come back again safe."

"Thank you, too, Heanwig," Miriamele replied solemnly.

Simon suppressed a groan of irritation, reminding himself that a knight did not make faces and noises like a scullion did—especially a knight who wished to stay on the good side of his lady. And at least the old man apparently would not be traveling with them. That was an acceptable reward for a little forbearance.

As they rode out of Stanshire into the countryside, the rain began to fall once more. At first it was little more than a flurry of drops, but by the time mid-morning came, it was falling in great sheets. The wind rose, carrying the rain toward them in cold, cascading slaps of water.

"This is as bad as being on a ship in storm," Miriamele shouted.

"At least on a ship you have oars," Simon called back. "We're going to need some soon."

Miriamele laughed, pulling her hood down low over her eyes.

Simon felt warmer just knowing he had amused her. He had been feeling a little ashamed of the way he had treated the old man; almost as soon as Heanwig had gone shuffling away down the lane, heading back toward the center of Stanshire, Simon had felt his bad temper evaporate. It was hard to say now what it was about the old man that had so perturbed him—he hadn't really done anything.

They headed back toward the River Road along a succession of wagon-rutted lanes that now were little more than sluices of mud. The countryside began to look more wild. The farmlands around Stanshire, although mostly given over to weeds, still bore the mark of past human care in the fences and stone walls and an occasional cottage, but as the town and its outlying settlements fell away behind them, the wilderness reasserted itself.

It was a peculiarly bleak place. The nearly endless winter had stripped all of the trees but the evergreens, and even the pines and firs seemed to have suffered unkind handling. Simon thought the strange, twisted shape of the trunks and branches resembled the writhing human bodies in the mural of The Day of Weighing-Out which stretched across the wall of the Hayholt's chapel. He had spent many a boring hour in church staring in fascination at the scenes of torment, marveling at the invention of the anonymous artist. But here in the real, cold, wet world, the gnarled shapes were mostly disheartening. Leafless oaks and elms and ash trees loomed against the sky, skeletal hands that clenched and unclenched as the wind bent them. With the sky bruised almost black by clouds and the rain flung slantwise across the muddied hillsides, it made a much drearier picture than even the decorations in the chapel.

Simon and Miriamele rode on through the storm, mostly unspeaking. Simon was chagrined that the princess had not once mentioned, or even hinted at, their kiss of the night before. It was not a day conducive to flirtatious conversation, he knew, but she seemed to be pretending it had never even happened. Simon did not know what to do about this: several times he was on the verge of asking her, but he could not think of anything to say about it that would not sound stupid in the light of day. That kiss had been a bit like his arrival in Jao é-Tinukai'i, a moment in which he had stepped out of time. Perhaps, like a trip to a fairy-hill, what they had shared the night before had been something magical, something destined to fade as quickly from memory as an icicle melting in the sun.

No. I won't let it fade. I'll remember it always . . . even if she doesn't.

He stole a glance at Miriamele. Most of her face was hidden by the hood, but he could see her nose and part of her cheek and her sharp chin. She looked almost Sitha-like, he thought, graceful and beautiful, yet not quite knowable. What was going on in her head? How could she cling to him as she had, then say nothing about it afterward, until he wondered if he had dreamed the whole thing or was going mad? Surely she had returned that kiss as eagerly as he had given it? Little as he knew of women and kissing, he could not believe that the way she had responded meant nothing.

Why don't I just ask her? I'll go mad if I don't find out. But what if she laughs at me, or gets angry—or doesn't remember?

The idea that Miriamele might have no strong emotions corresponding to the feelings that churned within him was chilling. His resolve to make her talk abruptly vanished. He would think about it more.

But I want to kiss her again.

He sighed. The sound was lost in the hissing tumult of the rain.

The River Road was muddy and almost entirely empty; as Simon had predicted, they passed fewer than a dozen other travelers all day. Only one man bothered to do more than nod, a short, bandy-legged fellow whose knob-kneed horse pulled a tented wagon full of tinker's goods. Hoping for information about what might lie ahead, Simon took courage at his pleasant greeting and asked the man to stop. The tinker stood in the downpour, apparently glad for someone to talk to, and told them that there was a way station ahead that they should reach not long after sundown. He said he was on his way out from Falshire, and described that city as quiet and the business he had done there as poor. After quietly making sure that Miriamele approved, Simon invited the man to come join them beneath a stand of pines that kept out most of the rain. They handed him the wineskin, and while their new acquaintance took a few healthy swallows, Simon repeated his story of being an itinerant chandler.

"Thank you kindly." The tinker handed back the wineskin. "Cuts the chill a bit, that does." He nodded. "You'll be hoping to do some trade for Saint Tunath's and Aedonmansa, then. Good luck to you. But if you'll pardon advice not asked for, I think you'd best go no farther west than Falshire."

Simon and Miriamele locked eyes briefly before turning back to the traveler.

"Why is that?" asked Simon.

"People just say it's bad there." The man's grin seemed forced. "You know the sort of tales. Bandits, the like. Some talk of odd happenings in the hills." He shrugged.

Simon pressed him for details, but the man did not seem inclined to elaborate. Simon had never heard of a traveling tinker who would not happily finish a proffered wineskin while regaling his listeners with tales of his journeying; whether this man was an exception to the rule, or whether there was something that had disturbed him enough to keep him quiet, Simon could not tell. He seemed a reasonable sort.

"We're looking for nothing but a roof over our heads and a few fithings worth of work here and there," said Simon.

The tinker cocked an eyebrow at the sword on Simon's belt and the metal hauberk protruding beyond his sleeves. "You're tolerable well-armed for candle-making, sirrah," he said gently. "But I suppose that shows what the roads are like these days." He nodded with a sort of careful approval, as if to suggest that whatever he thought of a chandler wearing the gear of a knight—albeit a tattered knight who had seen better times—he saw no reason to ask further questions.

Simon, catching the implicit message that he was expected to adopt the same courteous disinterest, offered the tinker a handclasp as they all walked back to the road.

"Anything you need?" the man asked as he once more took the bridle of his horse, which had been standing patiently in the rain. "I get a few things in trade from them as has not a cintis-piece to pay—some vegetables, little bits of metal clutter . . . shoeing-nails, the like."

Simon said that they had everything they needed until they reached Falshire: he was quite sure that the things they most needed would not be in the back of a rain-soaked wagon. But Miriamele asked to see the vegetables, and picked out a few spindly carrots and four brown onions, giving the tinker a coin in return. Afterward they waved him farewell as he took his horse and went squelching away east along the muddy road.

As the gray afternoon wore away, the rain continued to spatter down. Simon was growing tired of it pounding on his head.

Wish I'd remembered to bring my battle-helm, he thought. *But that'd probably be like sitting under a bucket and having someone throw stones at you—rattle, rattle, rattle till you go mad.*

To entertain Miriamele, he tried to sing a song called "Badulf and the Straying Heifer" that Shem Horsegroom had taught him, which had a rainstorm in it and seemed appropriate, but most of the words had slipped his memory, and when he sang the parts he remembered, the wind flung rain down his gullet until he thought he would strangle. He abandoned the experiment at last and they continued in silence.

The sun which had been invisible all day at last sank beneath the rim of the world, leaving behind a deeper darkness. They rode on as the rain turned even colder, until their teeth were chattering and their hands grew numb on the reins. Simon had begun to doubt that the tinker had spoken truly when at last they found the way station.

It was only a shed, four walls and a roof, with a smoke hole and a circle of stones dug into the floor for a fireplace. There was a covered spot outside at the back to tie the horses, but Simon, after unsaddling them, tethered them in a copse nearby where they would be almost as dry, and would be able to crop at the thin grass.

The last inhabitant of the station—Simon guessed it was the tinker himself, who had seemed a decent and conscientious fellow—had brought in fresh wood before leaving. It had to be new-gathered, because it was still wet and proved difficult to light: Simon had to restart it three times after the smoldering tinder fizzled out against the damp branches. He and the princess made themselves a stew with some carrots and one of the onions and a bit of flour and dried beef from Miriamele's stores.

"Hot food," proclaimed Simon, sucking his fingers, "is a wonderful thing." He held the bowl up and licked the last drops of gravy from the bottom.

"You're getting stew on your beard," Miriamele said sternly.

Simon pushed open the door of the way station, then leaned out and let his cupped palms fill with rainwater. He drank some and used the rest to rub the grease from his whiskers. "Better?"

"I suppose." Miriamele began arranging her bedroll.

Simon got up, patting his stomach contentedly. He went and dragged his own bedroll loose from the saddle, then came back and laid it out close to Miriamele's. She stared at it silently for a moment; then, without looking up, pulled hers around the fire, putting several cubits of straw-matted floor between them.

Simon pursed his lips. "Should we keep watch?" he said at last. "There's no bar on the door."

"That would be wise. Who first?"

"Me. I have a lot to think about."

His tone finally made Miriamele look up. She eyed him warily, as though he might do something sudden and frightening. "Very well. Wake me when you get tired."

"I'm tired now. But so are you. Sleep. I'll get you up after you've had a little time to rest."

Miriamele settled back without protest, wrapping her cloak tightly about her before she closed her eyes. The way station was silent but for the patter of rain on the roof. Simon sat motionless for a long time, watching the flickering firelight play across her pale, composed features.

Sometime in the earliest hours after midnight, Simon caught himself nodding. He sat up, shaking his head, and listened. The rain had stopped, but water was still dripping from the way station roof and drizzling on the ground outside.

He crawled over to wake Miriamele, but paused by the bedroll to look at her in the red light of the dying embers. She had twisted in her sleep, dislodging the cloak she used as a blanket, and her shirt had pulled loose from the top of the men's breeches she wore, exposing a measure of white skin along her side and the shadowed curve of her lowest ribs. Simon felt his heart turn over in his chest. He longed to touch her.

His hand, seemingly of its own volition, stole out; his fingers, gentle as butterflies, lit upon her skin. It was cool and smooth. He could feel goosebumps rise beneath his touch.

Miriamele made a groggy noise of irritation and brushed at him, flicking as though the butterflies had become less pleasant insects a-crawling. Simon quickly withdrew his hand.

He sat for a moment trying to catch his breath, feeling like a thief who had been nearly surprised in his crime. At last he reached out again, but this time only clasped her shoulder and gave a careful shake.

"Miriamele. Wake up, Miriamele."

She grunted and rolled over, turning her back to him. Simon shook her again, a little more strongly this time. She made a sound of protest and her fingers groped for her cloak without success, as though she sought protection from whatever cruel spirit plagued her.

"Come, Miriamele, it's your turn to keep watch."

The princess was sleeping soundly indeed. Simon leaned closer and spoke into her ear. "Wake up. It's time." Her hair was against his cheek.

Miriamele only half-smiled, as though someone had made a small joke. Her eyes remained shut. Simon slid down until he was lying next to her and stared for a few long moments at the curve of her cheek glowing in the emberlight. He slid his hand down from her shoulder and let it fall across her waist, then moved forward until his chest touched her back. Now her hair was all along his cheek and his body wrapped hers. She made a noise that might have been contentment and pushed back against him ever so slightly, then fell silent once more. Simon held his breath, fearing she would wake, fearing that he himself would cough or sneeze and somehow spoil this achingly splendid moment. He felt her warmth all down the length of his body. She was smaller than he, much smaller: he could wrap around her and protect her like a suit of armor. He thought he would like to lie this way forever.

As the two lay like nestling kittens, Simon drifted into sleep. The need to keep a watch was forgotten, eased from his mind like a leaf carried away by a river current.

Simon woke up alone. Miriamele was outside the way station, using a leafless branch to groom her horse. When she came in, they broke their fast on bread and water. She said nothing of the night before, but Simon thought he detected a little less brittleness in her manner, as though some of her chill had melted away while they lay huddled in sleep.

They traveled six more days on the River Road, slowed by the monotonous rains that had turned the broad track into sloppy mud. The weather was so miserable and the road generally so empty that Miriamele's fear of discovery seemed to lessen, although she still kept her face covered when they passed through smallish towns like Bregshame and Garwynswold. Nights they slept in way stations or beneath the leaky roofs of roadside shrines. As they sat together each night in the hour between eating and sleeping, Miriamele told Simon stories of her childhood in Meremund. In return, he recounted his days among the scullions and chambermaids; but as the nights passed, he spoke more and more about his time with Doctor Morgenes, of the old man's good humor and occasionally fierce temper, of his contempt for those who did not ask questions and his delight in life's unexpected complexity.

The night after they passed through Garwynswold, Simon abruptly found himself in tears as he related something Morgenes had once told him about the wonders of beehives. Miriamele stared, surprised, as he struggled to control himself; afterward she looked at him in a strange way he had not seen before, but although his first impulse was shame, he could not truthfully see anything contemptuous in her expression.

"I wish he had been my father or my grandfather," he said later. They had retired to their respective bedrolls. Although Miriamele was, as usual, an arm's length away, he felt that she was in some way nearer to him than she had been any night since they had kissed. He had held her since then, of course, but she had been asleep. Now she lay nearby in the darkness, and he almost thought he felt some unspoken agreement growing between them. "He was that kind to me. I wish he was still alive."

"He was a good man."

"He was more than that. He was . . . He was someone who did things when they needed to be done." Simon felt a tightening in his chest. "He died so that Josua and I could escape. He treated me like . . . like I was his own. It's all wrong. He shouldn't have had to die."

"Nobody should die," Miriamele said slowly. "Especially while they're still alive."

Simon lay in silence for a moment, confused. Before he could ask her what she meant, he felt her cool fingers touch his hand, then nestle into his palm.

"Sleep well," she murmured.

When his heart had slowed, her hand was still there. He fell asleep at last, still cupping it as gently as if it were a baby bird.

More than the rains and gray mist plagued them. The land itself, under the pall of bad weather, was almost completely lifeless, dreary as a landscape of stones and bones and spiderwebs. In the towns, the citizens appeared tired and frightened, unwilling even to regard Simon and Miriamele with the curiosity and suspicion that were usually a stranger's due. At night the windows were shuttered, the mucky streets empty. Simon felt as though they passed through ghost villages, as though the actual inhabitants had long departed, leaving only the insubstantial shades of previous generations, all doomed to a weary, pointless haunting of their ancestral homes.

In dim afternoon on their seventh day out of Stanshire, Simon and

Miriamele rounded a bend in the river road and saw the squat bulk of Falshire Castle looming on the western horizon before them. Green grazing land had once covered the castled hill like a king's train, but now, despite the heavy rains, the hillside fields were barren; near the hillcrest some were even patched with snow. At the base of the hill lay the walled city, bestriding the river that was its lifeblood. From docks along the shore Falshire's hides and wool were loaded on boats to travel to the Kynslagh and beyond, returning with the gold and other goods that had long made Falshire one of the richest cities in Osten Ard, second in importance in Erkynland only to Erchester.

"That castle used to be Fengbald's," said Miriamele. "And to think my father would have had me marry him! I wonder which of his family lords it there now." Her mouth tightened. "If the new master is anything like the old one, I hope the whole thing falls down on him."

Simon peered into the diffuse western light that made the castle seem only an oddly-shaped black crag, then pointed to the city below to distract her attention. "We can be in Falshire-town before nightfall. We can have a true meal tonight."

"Men always think of their stomachs."

Simon thought the assertion unfair, but was pleased enough to be called a man that he smiled. "How about a dry night in a warm inn, then?"

Miriamele shook her head. "We have been lucky, Simon, but we are getting closer to the Hayholt every day. I have been in Falshire many times. There is too good a chance someone might recognize me."

Simon sighed. "Very well. But you don't mind if I go in somewhere and get us something to eat like I did in Stanshire, do you?"

"As long as you don't leave me waiting all night. It's bad enough being a poor traveling chandler's wife without having to stand in the rain while the husband's inside slurruping down ale by a hot fire."

Simon's smile became a grin. "Poor chandler's wife."

Miriamele looked at him dourly. "Poor chandler if he makes her angry."

The inn called *The Tarbox* was brightly torchlit, as if for some festive holiday, but as Simon peered in through the doorway he thought the mood inside seemed far from merry. It was crowded enough, with perhaps two or three dozen people scattered around the wide common room, but the talk among them was so quiet that Simon could hear the rainwater dripping off the cloaks that hung beside the door.

Simon made his way between the crowded benches to the far side of the common room. He was aware of many heads turning to watch him pass, and a slight increase in the buzz of conversation, but he kept his eyes to himself. The landlord, a thin, tuft-haired fellow whose face sparkled with the sweat of the roasting oven, looked up as he approached.

"Yes? D'you need a room?" He looked at Simon's tattered clothes. "Two quinis the night."

"Just a few slices of that mutton and some bread. And perhaps some ale as well. My wife's waiting outside. We've far to go."

The landlord shouted at someone across the room to have patience, then glared at Simon suspiciously. "You'll need your own jug, for none of mine's walking out the door." Simon lifted his jug and the man nodded. "Six cintis for all. Pay now."

A little nettled, Simon dropped the coins on the table. The landlord picked them up and examined them, then pocketed the lot and scurried off.

Simon turned to survey the room. Most of the denizens seemed to be Falshire-folk, humble in garb and settled in their residence: there were very few who looked as though they might be travelers, despite the fact that this was one of the closest inns to the city gates and the River Road. A few returned his gaze, but he saw little malice or even curiosity. The people of Falshire, if this room was any indication, seemed to have much in common with the sheep they raised and sheared.

Simon had just turned back to look for the landlord when he sensed a sudden stirring in the room. He wondered if the Falshire-folk had indeed had more of a reaction to him than he'd realized. Then a chill breeze touched the back of his neck.

The door of the inn was open again. Standing before a curtain of water sluicing down from the roof outside, a trio of white-robed figures calmly surveyed the room. It was not Simon's imagination that all the other folk in the common room shrank back a little into themselves. Furtive glances were darted, conversations grew quieter or louder, and some of the patrons nearest the door sidled slowly away.

Simon felt a similar urge. *Those must be Fire Dancers,* he thought. His heartbeat had grown swifter. Had they seen Miriamele? But what would she have meant to them in any case?

Slowly Simon leaned back against the long table, putting on an air of mild interest as he watched the newcomers. Two of the three were large, as muscled as the dockers who worked the Hayholt's sea gate, and carried blunt-ended walking staves that looked more useful for skull-cracking than hiking. The third, the leader by his position in front, was small, thick, and bull-necked, and also carried one of the long cudgels. As he lowered his rain-soaked hood, his squarish, balding head glinted in the lamplight. He was older than the other two and had clever, piggy eyes.

The hum of conversation had now reached something like its normal level once more, but as the three Fire Dancers moved slowly into the common room they still received many covert stares. The robed men seemed to be openly searching the room for something or somebody; Simon had a moment of helpless fear as the leader's dark eyes lighted on him for a moment, but the man only lifted an amused eyebrow at Simon's sword, then shifted his attention to someone else.

Relief swept over Simon. Whatever they wanted, it was apparently not him.

Sensing a presence at his shoulder, he turned quickly and found the inn's pro-
prietor standing behind him with a pitted wooden platter. The man gave Simon
the mutton and bread, which Simon wrapped in his kerchief, then poured an
appropriate measure of ale into the jug. Despite the attention these tasks required, the landlord's eyes scarcely left the three newcomers, and his reply to
Simon's courteous thanks was distracted and incomplete. Simon was glad to be
going.

As he opened the door, he caught a quick glimpse of Miriamele's pale, worried face in the shadows across the street. A loud, mocking voice cut through
the room behind him.

"You didn't *really* think that you could leave without our noticing, did you?"

Simon went rigid in the doorway, then slowly turned. He had a parcel in one
hand and a jug in the other, his sword hand. Should he drop the ale and draw
the blade, or make the jug useful somehow—perhaps he could throw it? Haestan had taught him a little about tavern brawls, although the guardsman's main
recommendation had been to avoid them.

He completed his pivot, expecting to confront a sea of faces and the threatening Fire Dancers, but found to his astonishment that no one was even looking in his direction. Instead, the three robed men stood before a bench in the
corner farthest from the fire. The two seated there, a man and woman of middle years, looked up at them helplessly, faces slack with terror.

The leader of the Fire Dancers leaned forward, bringing his catapult-stone
of a head almost to the level of the tabletop, but though his position suggested
discretion, his voice was pitched to carry through the room. "Come, now. You
didn't really think that you could just walk away, did you?"

"M-Maefwaru," the man stuttered, "we, we could not . . . we thought
that . . ."

The Fire Dancer laid a thick hand on the table, silencing him. "That is not
the loyalty that the Storm King expects." He seemed to speak quietly, but
Simon could hear every word from the doorway. The rest of the room watched
in sickly fascinated silence. "We owe Him our lives, because He has graced us
with a vision of how things will be and a chance to be part of it. You cannot
turn your back on Him."

The man's mouth moved, but no words came out. His wife was equally silent, but tears ran down her face and her shoulders twitched. This was obviously a meeting much feared.

"*Simon!*"

He turned to look back out the inn's door. Miriamele was only a few paces
away in the middle of the muddy road. "What are you doing?" she demanded
in a loud whisper.

"Wait."

"Simon, there are Fire Dancers in there! Didn't you see them?!"

He raised his hand to stay her, then wheeled to face the interior. The two
large Fire Dancers were forcing the man and woman up from their bench,

dragging the woman across the rough wood when her legs would not support her. She was crying in earnest now; her companion, pinioned, could only stare at the ground and murmur miserably.

Simon felt anger flame within him. Why didn't anyone in this place help them? There must be two dozen seated here and only three Fire Dancers.

Miriamele tugged at his sleeve. "Is there trouble? Come, Simon, let's go!"

"I can't," he said, quietly but urgently. "They're taking those two people somewhere."

"We can't afford to be caught, Simon. This is not a time for heroes."

"I can't just let them take those people, Miriamele." He prayed that someone else in the crowded room would stand up, that some general movement of resistance would begin. Miriamele was right: they couldn't afford to do anything foolish. But no one did more than whisper and watch.

Cursing himself for his stupidity, and God or Fate for putting him in this position, Simon pulled his sleeve from Miriamele's grasp and took a step back into the common room. He carefully set the supper parcel and jug down beside the wall, then curled his hand around the hilt of the sword Josua had given him.

"Stop!" he said loudly.

"Simon!"

Now all heads *did* turn toward him. The last to swivel around was that of the leader. Although he was only a little shorter than an average man, there was something curiously dwarflike in his large, cleft-chinned head. His tiny eyes flicked Simon up and down. This time there was no amusement.

"What? Stop, you say? Stop what?"

"I don't think those people want to go with you." Simon addressed the male captive, who was struggling weakly in the grip of one of the large Fire Dancers. "Do you?"

The man's eyes flicked back and forth between Simon and his chief captor. At last, miserably, he shook his head. Simon knew then that what the man feared must be truly terrible, that he would risk making this situation worse in the desperate—and unlikely—hope that Simon could save him from it.

"You see?" Simon tried, with mixed results, to keep his voice firm and calm. "They do not wish to accompany you. Set them free." His heart was pounding. His own words sounded curiously formal, even deliberately high-flown, as if this were a Tallistro story or some other chronicle of imaginary heroism.

The bald man looked around the room as if to judge how many might be prepared to join Simon in resistance. No one else was moving; the entire room seemed to share a single held breath. The Fire Dancer turned back to Simon, a grin curling his thick lips. "These folk betrayed their oath to the Master. This is no concern of yours."

Simon felt an immense fury wash over him. He had seen all the bullying he had the stomach for, from the countrywide misdeeds of the king to the precisely pointed cruelties of Pryrates. He tightened his grip on the hilt. "I am making it my concern. Take your hands from them and get out."

Without further argument, the leader spat out a word and the follower who held the woman let her go—she slumped against the table, knocking a bowl onto the floor—and leaped toward Simon, his blunt-headed staff swinging in a wide arc. A few people shouted in fear or excitement. Simon was frozen for an instant, his sword only halfway out of his scabbard.

Idiot! Mooncalf!

He dropped to the floor and the staff whistled over his head, knocking several cloaks from the wall and becoming entangled in one of them. Simon seized the moment and threw himself forward into the man's legs. They both fell, tumbling, and Simon's sword came free of the scabbard and thumped into the floor rushes. He had hurt his shoulder—his attacker was heavy and solidly built—and as he disentangled himself and pulled free, the Fire Dancer managed to catch him with a cudgel blow to his leg which stung cold as a knife wound. Simon rolled toward his lost sword and was hugely grateful when he felt it beneath his fingers. His attacker was up and moving toward him, his cudgel darting out like a striking snake. From the corner of his eye, Simon could see that the second big man was coming toward him as well.

First things first, was the inane thought that ran through his head, the same thing Rachel had always told him about doing his chores when he wanted to go climb or play a game. He rose to a standing crouch, his sword held before him, and deflected a blow from his first attacker. It was impossible to remember all the things he had been taught in the muddle of noise and movement and panic, but he was relieved to find that as long as he could keep his sword between himself and the Fire Dancer, he could keep the man at bay. But what would he do when the second arrived?

He received an answer of sorts a moment later, when a blur of movement at the edge of his vision warned him to duck. The second man's staff whickered past and clacked against the first man's. Simon took a step backward without turning and then whirled and swung his blade around as hard as he could. He caught the man behind him across the arm, drawing an angry shriek. The Fire Dancer dropped his staff and stumbled back toward the doorway, clutching his forearm. Simon returned his attention to the man in front of him, hoping that the second man was, if not defeated, at least out of the battle for a few desperately-needed moments. The first attacker had learned the lesson of not getting too close, and was now using the length of his club to keep Simon on the defensive.

There was a crash from behind; Simon, startled, almost lost sight of the foe before him. Seeing this, the man aimed another whirling blow at his head. Simon managed to get his blade up in time to deflect it; then, as the Fire Dancer raised the staff once more, Simon brought his sword up, sweeping the cudgel even farther upward so that it struck the low timbers of the roof and caught in the netting below the thatch. The Fire Dancer stared up for a moment in surprise; in that instant, Simon took a step forward, lodged the sword against the man's midsection and pushed it home. He struggled to pull the blade free, conscious that at any moment the other attacker, or even the leader, might be upon him.

Something struck him from the side, flinging him against a table. For a moment, he was staring into the alarmed face of one of the common-room drinkers. He whirled to see that the person who had shoved him, the bald man Maefwaru, was pushing his way between the tables, headed toward the door; he did not pause to look down at either of his minions, the one Simon had slain or the other, who lay in a curious position near the doorway.

"It will not be so easy," Maefwaru shouted as he vanished through the door and into the rainy night.

A moment later Miriamele stepped back into the room. She looked down at the Fire Dancer laying there, the one Simon had wounded on the arm. "I've broken our jug on his head," she said, excited and breathless. "But I think the one who just ran out is going to come back with more of his friends. Curse my luck! I couldn't find anything to hit him with. We'll have to run."

"The horses," Simon panted. "Are they . . . ?"

"A few steps away," replied Miriamele. "Come."

Simon bent and snatched up the supper sack he had left on the floor. The kerchief was wet, soaked by the ale that had splashed from the jug which lay in pieces around the limp Fire Dancer. He looked around the room. The man and woman that Maefwaru and his henchmen had threatened were cringing against the far wall, staring as bewilderedly as any of the inn's other customers.

"You had better get out of here, too," he called to them. "That bald one will bring back more. Go on—run!"

Everyone was looking at him. Simon wanted to say something clever or brave—heroes usually did—but he couldn't think of anything. Also, there was real blood on his sword and his stomach seemed to have crawled up into his throat. He followed Miriamele out the door, leaving behind two bodies and a room full of wide eyes and open, speechless mouths.

32

The Circle Narrows

※

The swirl of snow had lessened, but the wind still moved angrily across the hillside beneath Naglimund, fluting in the teeth of the broken wall. Count Eolair nudged his horse toward Maegwin's mount, wishing he could shield her somehow, not just from the cold but also from the horror of the naked stone towers, the windows now flickering with light.

Yizashi Grayspear rode forward from the ranks of the Sithi, his lance couched beneath one arm. He lifted the other and waved something that looked like a silver baton. His hand flashed in a wide arc, making a loud musical noise which had something of the metallic in it; the silver thing in his hand opened like a lady's fan, spreading into a glittering, semicircular shield.

"A y'ei g'eisu!" he shouted up at the blankly staring keep. *"Yas'a pripurna joshoi!"*

The lights in Naglimund's windows seemed to waver like wind-fluttered candles as shadows moved in their depths. Eolair felt himself almost overwhelmed with the urge to turn and ride away. This was no longer a human place, and the poisonous terror he was feeling was nothing like the anticipatory fear before any human battle. He turned to Maegwin. Her eyes were closed and her mouth moved in silent speech. Isorn seemed similarly unnerved, and when Eolair turned in his saddle and looked back, the pale faces of his fellow Hernystiri were as gape-mouthed and hollow-eyed as a row of corpses.

Brynioch preserve us, the count thought desperately, *we do not belong in this. They will bolt in a moment if I do the wrong thing.*

Deliberately, he tugged his sword from its scabbard and showed it to his men, then held it high over his head for a moment before dropping it to his side. It was only a small show of bravery, but it was something.

Now Jiriki and his mother Likimeya rode forward, halting on either side of Yizashi. After a moment's whispered conversation, Likimeya spurred her horse a few paces ahead. Then, startlingly, she began to sing.

Her voice, thin at first against the rude piping of the wind, grew slowly stronger. The impenetrable Sithi tongue flowed out, slurring and clicking yet somehow as smooth as warm oil poured from a jar. The song rose and fell, pulsed, then rose again, each time growing more powerful. Although Eolair understood nothing of the words, there was something clearly denunciatory to the roll and swoop of it, something challenging in the cadence. Likimeya's voice chimed like a herald's brazen horn, and as with the call of a horn, there was a ring of cold metal beneath the music.

"What goes on here?" whispered Isorn.

Eolair gestured for silence.

The mist floating before the walls of Naglimund seemed to thicken, as though one dream was ending and another beginning. Something changed in Likimeya's voice. It took a moment before Eolair recognized that the mistress of the Sithi had not altered her song, but rather that another voice had joined it. At first the new thread of melody clung close to the challenge-song. The tone was as strong as Likimeya's, but where hers was metal, this new voice was stone and ice. After some long moments the second voice began to sing around the original melody, weaving a strange pattern like a glass filigree over Likimeya's belling tones. The sound of it made the Count of Nad Mullach's skin stretch and tingle and his body hair lift, even beneath the layers of clothing.

Eolair raised his eyes. His heart began to beat even more swiftly.

Through the dimming fog, a thin black shadow appeared atop the castle wall, rising into view as smoothly as though lifted by an unseen hand. It was man-sized, Eolair decided, but the mist subtly distorted its shape, so that one moment it seemed larger, the next smaller and thinner than any living thing. It looked down on them, black-cloaked, face invisible beneath a large hood—but Eolair did not need to see its face to know that it was the source of the high, stone-edged voice. For long moments it only stood in the swirling mist atop the wall, embroidering upon Likimeya's song. Finally, as if by some prior agreement, they both fell still at the same moment.

Likimeya broke the silence, calling out something in the Sithi tongue. The black apparition answered, its words ringing like shards of jagged flint, and yet Eolair could hear that the words they spoke were much the same, the differences mainly in rhythm and the greater harshness of the robed creature's speech. The conversation seemed interminable.

There was a movement behind him. Eolair flinched; his horse startled, kicking snow. Sky-haired Zinjadu, the lore-mistress, had brought her own mount to where the mortals stood.

"They speak of the Pact of Sesuad'ra." Her eyes were fixed on Likimeya and her opposite. "They speak of old heartbreaks and the mourning songs yet to be sung."

"Why so much talk?" asked Isorn raggedly. "The waiting is dreadful."

"It is our way." Zinjadu's lips tightened; her thin face seemed carved in pale golden stone. "Although it was not respected when Amerasu was slain."

She offered nothing more. Eolair could only wait in uneasy fear and, ultimately, a kind of horrible boredom as challenge and response were offered.

Finally the thing on the wall turned its attention away from Likimeya for a moment; its eyes lit on the count and his few scores of Hernystirmen. With a movement almost as broad as a traveling player's, the black-robed one flung back its hood, revealing a sleet-white face and thin hair just as colorless which rose in the wind, floating like the strands of some sea-plant.

"*Shu'do-tkzayha!*" the Norn said in a tone almost of exultation. "Mortals! They will yet be the death of your family, Likimeya Moon-Eyes!" He, if it was a he, spoke the Westerling tongue with the harsh precision of a game-keeper imitating a rabbit's death squeal. "Are you so weak that you summoned this rabble to aid you? It is hardly Sinnach's great army!"

"You have usurped a mortal's castle," said Likimeya coldly. Beside her Jiriki still sat his horse stiffly, his sharp-boned face empty of any recognizable emotion; Eolair wondered again how anyone could ever feel they knew the Sithi. "And your master and mistress have entered into the disputes of mortals. You have little to crow about."

The Norn laughed, a noise like fingernails on slate. "We use them, yes. They are the rats that have dug into the walls of our house—we might skin them for gloves, but we do not invite them in to sup at our table! That is your weakness, as it was Amerasu Ship-Born's."

"Do not speak of her!" Jiriki cried. "Your mouth is too foul to hold her name, Akhenabi!"

The thing on the wall smiled, a folding of white. "Ah, little Jiriki. I have heard tales of you and *your* adventuring—or should I say meddling. You should have come to live in the north, in our cold land. Then you would have grown strong. This tolerance for mortals is a terrible weakness. It is one reason why your family has grown dissolute while mine has grown ever sterner, ever more capable of doing what needs to be done." The Norn turned and lifted his head, directing his words now to Eolair and the nervously whispering Hernystiri. "Mortal men! You risk more than your lives fighting beside these immortals. You risk your souls as well!"

Eolair could hear the rustle of frightened speech behind him. He spurred his horse forward a few paces and raised his sword. "Your threats are empty!" he shouted. "Do your worst! Our souls are our own!"

"Count Eolair!" Maegwin called. "No! It is Scadach, the Hole in Heaven! Go no closer!"

Akhenabi leaned down, fixing the count with black-bead eyes. "The captain of the mortals, are you? So, little man, if you do not fear for your sake, or for your troop, what of the mortals still prisoned within these walls?"

"What are you saying?!" Eolair shouted.

The creature in the black robe turned and lifted both arms. A moment later two more figures clambered up into view beside him. Although they also wore heavy cloaks, their clumsy movements marked them as something other than the spider-graceful Norns.

"Here are some of your brethren!" trumpeted Akhenabi. "They are our guests. Would you see *them* die for the sake of your immortal allies as well?"

The two figures stood silently, slumped and hopeless. The faces in the wind-lashed hoods were clearly those of men, not Gardenborn.

Eolair felt himself fill with helpless rage. "Let them go!"

The Norn laughed again, pleased. "Oh, no, little mortal. Our guests are enjoying themselves too much. Would you like to see them show their joy? Perhaps they will dance." He lifted his hand and made a florid gesture. The two figures began slowly to revolve. Horribly, they lifted their arms in a parody of a courtly dance, swaying from side to side, stumbling together in front of the grinning Norn. They locked arms for a moment, teetering precariously along the edge of the high wall, then pulled apart and resumed their solitary postur-ing.

Through the tears of fury that misted his eyes, Eolair saw Jiriki spur his horse a few ells nearer the wall. The Sitha lifted a bow; then, in a movement so swift as to be almost invisible, he withdrew an arrow from the quiver on his saddle, nocked it, and drew the bow until it trembled in a wide arc. Atop the wall, the Norn Akhenabi's grin widened. He made a wriggling movement, almost a shiver; a moment later he had disappeared, leaving only the two sham-bling shapes in hideous lockstep.

Jiriki let his arrow fly. It struck one of the two dancers in the foot, jerking back the leg and overbalancing both the one struck and the one to whom he clung. They flailed briefly at the air, then toppled off the wall, dropping twenty ells to hit with a terrible smacking noise on the snow-covered rocks beneath. Several of the Hernystiri shouted and groaned.

"Blood of Rhynn!" Eolair screamed. "What have you done?!"

Jiriki rode forward, scanning the now empty wall cautiously. When he reached the huddled bodies, he dismounted and kneeled, then waved Eolair forward.

"Why did you do that, Jiriki?" the count demanded. His throat felt as tight as if someone's fingers were curled around it. "The Norn was gone." He stared down at the twisted, dark-robed figures. The hands and fingers protruding from their robes were splayed as though they still grabbed at a safety they would never find. "Did you think to spare them torture? What if we drove out the Norns—is there no chance we could rescue them?"

Jiriki said nothing, but reached down with surprising gentleness and turned over the nearest of the bodies, tugging a little to pull it free of the partner with which it was entwined. He folded back the hood.

"Brynioch!" Eolair choked. "Brynioch of the Skies preserve us!"

The face had no eyes, only black holes. The skin was waxy, and in places had burst from the force of the fall, but it was clear that this corpse was not fresh.

"Whoever he was, he has been dead since Naglimund's defeat," Jiriki said softly. "I do not think there are any living prisoners within the walls."

Count Eolair felt his gorge rising and turned away. "But they . . . moved . . . !"

"One of the Red Hand is lord here," Jiriki said. "That is now confirmed, for no others have the strength to do this. Their power is a part of their master's."

"But why?" Eolair said. He looked at the humped corpses, then turned his gaze outward, toward the massing of men and Sithi in the snow. "Why would they do this?"

Jiriki shook his head, his own hair as white and fluttering as that of the creature that had mocked them from the wall. "I cannot say. But Naglimund will not fall without a full tithing of horrors, that is certain."

Eolair looked at Maegwin and Isorn waiting fearfully for him to return. "And there is no turning back."

"No. I fear the final days have begun," said Jiriki. "For good or ill."

Duke Isgrimnur knew that he should be paying close attention to everything that was going on around him, to the people of Metessa, to the arrangements and manpower in the baronial hall. Metessa was the easternmost of Nabban's major outer states, and might be the place where Josua's challenge stood or fell. Success here could hinge on the smallest detail, so Isgrimnur had plenty to occupy him—but it was difficult to attend to his duties while the little boy followed him around like a shadow.

"Here," the duke said after he had almost trod upon the child for the dozenth time, "what are you up to? Don't you have somewhere to be? Where's your mother?"

The pale-haired, thin-faced little boy looked up at him, showing no fear of the large, bearded stranger. "My mother told me to stay away from the prince and you other knights. I did not agree."

The child was unnervingly well-spoken for his years, the duke reflected, and his Westerling was almost as good as Isgrimnur's own. It was odd to see how Prester John's Warinsten language had spread so thoroughly in only a couple of generations. But if things fell apart, as they seemed to be doing, would not the common tongue, like everything else, soon slip away? Empires were like sea-walls, he thought sadly, even those which embodied the best of hopes. The tide of chaos beat at them and beat at them, and as soon as no one was shoring up the stones any more . . .

Isgrimnur shook his head, then growled at the youngling a little more sternly than he intended. "Well, if your mother told you to stay away from the knights, what are you doing here? This is men's business tonight."

The boy deliberately raised himself until the top of his head reached the duke's bottom rib. "I will be a man some day. I am tired of living with the women. My mother is afraid I will run away to fight in war, but that is just what I will do."

There was something so unintentionally comic in his fierce determination that Isgrimnur smiled despite himself. "What's your name, lad?"

"Pasevalles, Sir Foreign Knight. My father is Brindalles, Baron Seriddan's brother."

"A knight is not the only thing in the world to be. And war is not a game. It is a terrible thing, little Pasevalles."

"I know that," said the boy readily. "But sometimes there is no choice, my father says, and there must be men who will fight."

The duke thought of Princess Miriamele in the ghant nest, and of his own beloved wife standing with an ax before Elvritshalla, ready to defend it to her death before Isorn persuaded her at last to let it go and flee with the rest of the family. "Women also fight."

"But women cannot be knights. And I am going to be a knight."

"Well, I suppose since I am not your father, I cannot send you back to your chambers. And I certainly can't seem to be rid of you. You might as well come with me and tell me a little about the place."

Pleased, Pasevalles bounced up and down a few times like a puppy. Then, just as suddenly, he stopped and fixed Isgrimnur with a suspicious glance. "Are you an enemy?" he asked sharply. "Because if you are, Sir Foreign Knight, I cannot show you things that might hurt my uncle."

Isgrimnur's grin was sour. "In these days, young fellow, it's hard to say who is enemy to who. But I can promise you that my liege-lord Prince Josua intends no harm to any who live in Metessa."

Pasevalles considered this for a moment. "I will trust you," he said at last. "I think you tell the truth. But if you do not, then you are no knight, who would lie to a young child."

Isgrimnur's grin widened. *Young child! This mannikin could give Count Eolair lessons in politicking.* "Tell me nothing that would help your uncle's enemies, and I will try not to ask anything that would put your honor in danger."

"That is fair," said the boy gravely. "That is knightly."

Metessa was more than just another Nabbanai hedge-barony. Situated beside the outermost edges of the Thrithings, it was a wide and prosperous piece of country, hilly and wide-meadowed. Even after the unseasonal snows, the rolling terrain gleamed greenly. One of the Stefflod's branches wound through the grasslands, a ribbon of silver foil bright even beneath the dull gray skies. Sheep and a few cows dotted the hillsides.

Chasu Metessa, the baronial keep, had stood atop one of the highest hills since the days of the later Imperators, looking down on these valleys full of small farms and freeholdings just as Isgrimnur did now.

He turned from the window to find Pasevalles pacing impatiently. The boy said: "Come and see the armor."

"That sounds like the kind of thing I shouldn't see."

"No, it's *old* armor." He was disgusted by Isgrimnur's obtuseness. "Very old."

The Rimmersman allowed himself to be tugged along. The child's energy seemed without bound.

If Isorn had been this demanding, he thought wryly, *I would likely have taken him out to the Frostmarch and left him, like they did in the old days when they had one mouth too many to feed.*

Pasevalles led him through a warren of hallways, past more than a few of the keep's inhabitants, who looked at Isgrimnur with alarm, to a corner tower that seemed a fairly late addition to the ancient hill fortress. After they had climbed far more stairs than were good for Isgrimnur's aching back, they reached a cluttered room near the top. The ceiling had not been recently swept—a canopy of cobwebs hung down almost to head height—and a heavy patina of dust covered the floor and all the crude furnishings, but Isgrimnur was nevertheless impressed with what he saw.

A series of wooden armor-stands ranged the room like silent guardsmen. Unlike the rest of the objects in the circular chamber, they were comparatively clean. On every stand hung a set of armor—but not modern armor, as Pasevalles had so crossly pointed out: the helmets and breastplates and curious metal-strip skirts were of a type that Isgrimnur had seen before only in very old paintings in the Sancellan Mahistrevis.

"This is armor from the Imperium!" he said, impressed. "Or damn clever copies."

Pasevalles drew himself up to his full height. "They are *not* copies! They are real. My father has been keeping them for years. My grandfather bought them in the great city."

"In Nabban," Isgrimnur mused. He walked along the rows, examining the various costumes, his warrior's eye seeing which were flawed in design, which simply missing pieces from the original arrangement. The metal the old Imperatorial craftsmen had used was heavier than that now used, but the armor was splendidly made. He leaned close to examine a helm with a twining sea-dragon crest. To get a better look, he puffed away a fine layer of dust.

"These have not been polished in some time," he said absently.

"My father has been ill." Little Pasevalles' voice was suddenly querulous. "I try to keep them clean, but they are too tall for me to reach and too heavy for me to lift down."

Isgrimnur looked around the room, thinking. The uninhabited armor suits seemed like watchers at a Raed, waiting for some decision. There were still many things for him to do. Surely he had spent enough time with this boy? He walked to the tower window and peered out into the gray western sky.

"We will not eat for some hour or so yet," he said at last, "and your uncle and Prince Josua will not be speaking of the other important things that must be discussed until afterward. Go and get your father's cleaning things—at least a whisking broom to get the dust off. You and I can make short work of this."

The boy looked up, eyes wide. "Truly?"

"Truly. I am in no hurry to go back down all those stairs, in any case." The boy was still staring. "Bless me, child, go on. And bring a lamp or two. It'll be dark soon."

The boy sped out of the room and down the narrow stairwell like a hare. Isgrimnur shook his head.

The banqueting hall of Chasu Metessa had a fireplace along each wall, and was warm and bright despite the chilliness of the season. The courtiers, landed folk from all over the valley, seemed to be dressed in their finest: many of the women wore long shimmery dresses and hats almost as weirdly inventive as those to be seen at the Sancellan Mahistrevis itself. Still, Isgrimnur noted the air of worry that hung like a fog in the huge, high-raftered chamber. The ladies talked swiftly and brightly and laughed at tiny things. The men were mostly quiet; what little they did say was spoken behind their hands.

A cask of Teligure wine had been breached at the start of things and its contents shared out around the room. Isgrimnur noticed that Josua, who was seated at the right of their host Baron Seriddan, had raised his goblet to his lips many times, but had not yet allowed the page beside him to refill it. The duke approved of Josua's forbearance. The prince was not much of a drinker at the best of times, but since the chance of dislodging Benigaris from the ducal throne might rest on the knife-edge of tonight's doings, it was doubly important that Josua's wits be sharp and his tongue cautious.

As he surveyed the room, the duke was stopped short by a pale glimmer in the doorway, far across the room. Squinting, Isgrimnur suddenly smiled deep in his beard. It was the boy Pasevalles, who had doubtless once more escaped from his mother and her ladies. He had come, Isgrimnur had no doubt, to watch Real Knights at table.

He may just get an eyeful.

Baron Seriddan Metessis rose from his seat at the head of the table and lifted his goblet. Behind him a blue crane, symbol of the Metessan House, spread its long wings across a wall banner.

"Let us salute our visitors," the baron said. He smiled ironically, his sun-browned, bearded face wrinkling. "I am doubtless a traitor already, just for letting you inside the gates, Prince Josua—so it does no further harm to drink your health."

Isgrimnur found himself liking Seriddan, and respecting him more than a bit. He little resembled the duke's fondly-held image of an effete Nabbanai baron: his thick neck and seamed peasant face made Seriddan look more a genial rogue than the hereditary master of a great fiefdom, but his eyes were shrewd and his manner deceptively self-mocking. His command of Westerling was so good that little Pasevalles' fluency no longer seemed surprising.

After the glasses were drained, Josua rose and lifted his own cup to thank the folk of Chasu Metessa for their hospitality. This was greeted by polite smiles and murmurs of approval that seemed more than a little forced. When the prince sat down, the whisper of table talk began to grow once more, but Seriddan gestured for quiet.

"So," he said to Josua, loud enough for everyone at the table to hear. "We have fulfilled the obligations that good Aedonites owe to their fellows—and some would say we have done far more than that, considering you appeared in our lands unasked for, and with an army at your back." Above the smiling mouth, Seriddan's stare was cool. "Will we see your heels in the morning, Josua of Erkynland?"

Isgrimnur suppressed a noise of surprise. He had assumed that the baron would send the lesser folk of his household away so that he could talk to the prince in privacy, but apparently Seriddan had other ideas.

Josua, too, was taken aback, but quickly said: "If you hear me out and are unmoved, Baron, you will indeed see our heels soon after sunrise. My people are not camped outside your walls as a threat to you. You have done me no wrong, and I will do you none either."

The baron stared at him for a long moment, then turned to his brother. "Brindalles, what do you think? Does it not seem odd that an Erkynlandish prince would wish to pass through our lands? Where might he be going?"

The brother's thin face bore many similarities to the baron's, but the features that looked roguishly dangerous on Seriddan seemed merely tired and a trifle unsettled on Brindalles.

"If he is not going to Nabban," came the mild reply, "he must be planning to walk straight to the sea." Brindalles' smile was wan. It was hard to think that such a diffident man could be the father of bright-burning Pasevalles.

"We *are* going on to Nabban," said Josua. "That is no secret."

"And what purpose could you have that is not dangerous to me and dangerous to my liege-lord, Duke Benigaris?" Seriddan demanded. "Why should I not make you a prisoner?"

Josua looked around the now-silent room. Chasu Metessa's most important residents all sat at the long table, watching with rapt attention. "Are you certain you wish me to speak so openly?"

Seriddan gestured impatiently. "I will not have it said that I misunderstood you, whether I let you pass through my lands or hold you here for Benigaris. Speak, and my people here will be my witnesses."

"Very well." Josua turned to Sludig, who despite having drained his wine cup several times was watching the proceedings with a wary eye. "May I have the scroll?"

As the yellow-bearded Rimmersman fumbled in the pocket of his cloak, Josua told Seriddan: "As I said, Baron: we go to Nabban. And we go in hopes of removing Benigaris from the Sancellan Mahistrevis. In part, that is because he is an ally of my brother, and his fall would weaken the High King's position. The fact that Elias and I are at war with each other is no secret, but the reasons why are less well-known."

"If you think they are important," Seriddan said equably, "tell them. We have plenty of wine, and we are at home. It is your little army that may or may not be leaving with the dawn."

"I will tell you, because I would not ask allies to fight unknowing," said Josua.

"*Héa!* Allies? Fight!?" The baron scowled and sat straighter. "You are walking a dangerous road, Josua Lackhand. Benigaris is my liege-lord. It is mad even to contemplate letting your people pass, knowing what I know, but I show respect for your father by letting you speak. But to hear you talk of me fighting beside you—madness!" He waved his hand. Some two dozen armed men, who had been standing back against the shadowed walls all during the meal, came rustlingly to attention.

Josua did not flinch, but calmly held Seriddan's eye. "As I said," he resumed, "I will give you the reasons that Elias must be driven from the Dragonbone Chair. But not now. There are other things to tell you first." He reached and took the scroll from Sludig's hand. "My finest knight, Sir Deornoth of Hewenshire, was at the battle of Bullback Hill when Duke Leobardis, Benigaris' father, came to relieve my castle at Naglimund."

"Leobardis chose your side," Seriddan said shortly. "Benigaris has chosen your brother's. What the old duke decided does not affect my loyalty to his son." Despite his words, there was a certain veiled look in the baron's eyes; watching him, Isgrimnur suspected Seriddan might just wish that the old duke were still alive and that his loyalty could be more comfortable. "And what does this Sir What-may-be-his-name have to do with Metessa?"

"Perhaps more than you can know." For the first time there was an edge of impatience in Josua's tone.

Careful, man. Isgrimnur tugged anxiously at his beard. *Don't let your sorrow over Deornoth betray you. We're farther along than I had thought we'd be. Seriddan's listening, anyway.*

As if he heard his old friend's silent thought, Josua paused and took a breath. "Forgive me, Baron Seriddan. I understand your loyalty to the Kingfisher House. I only wish to tell you things you deserve to know, not tell you where your duties lie. I want to read you Deornoth's words about what happened near Bullback Hill. They were written down by Father Strangyeard . . ." the prince pointed to the archivist, who was trying to make himself unobtrusive down near the long table's far end, "and sworn to before that priest and God Himself."

"Why are you reading some piece of parchment?" Seriddan asked impatiently. "If this man has a story to tell, why does he not come here before us?"

"Because Sir Deornoth is dead," said Josua. "He died at the hands of Thrithings mercenaries King Elias sent against me."

At this there was a small stir in the room. The Thrithings-folk were objects of both contempt and fear to the outland baronies of Nabban—contempt because the Nabbanai thought them little more than savages, fear because when the Thrithings-men went into one of their periodic raiding frenzies, outland fiefdoms such as Metessa bore the greatest part of the suffering.

"Read." Seriddan was clearly angry. Isgrimnur thought that the canny baron might already sense the snare into which his own cleverness had delivered him. He had hoped to deal with the odd and difficult situation of the prince by forcing Josua to speak his treason in front of many witnesses. Now the baron must sense that Josua's words might not be so easily dismissed. It was an awkward spot. But even now, Metessa's master did not disperse the other folk sitting at table: he had made his gambit and he would live with it. The Duke of Elvritshalla found himself appreciating the man anew.

"I had Deornoth tell his story to our priest before the battle for New Gadrinsett," Josua said. "What he saw was important enough that I did not wish to chance it might die with him, as there seemed little likelihood we would survive that fight." He held up the scroll, unrolling it with the stump of his right wrist. "I will read only the part that I think you need to hear, but I will gladly give the whole thing to you, Baron, so that you may read it at your ease."

He paused for a moment, then began. The listeners along the table leaned forward, greedy for more strangeness on what was already a night that would be discussed in Metessa for a long time.

"... When we came upon the field, the Nabbanai had ridden after Earl Guthwulf of Utanyeat and his men of the Boar and Spears, who were falling back with great swiftness to the slope of Bullback Hill. Duke Leobardis and three hundred knights came at them in such a wise as to pass between Utanyeat and the High King's army, which was still some way distant, as we thought.

"Prince Josua, fearing that Leobardis would be delayed too long and that thus the king could come against him in the unprotected open lands south of Naglimund, brought many knights out of the castle to save Nabban from the king, and also perhaps to capture Utanyeat, who was the greatest of King Elias' generals. Josua himself led us, and Isorn Isgrimnurson and a score of Rimmersmen were with us too.

"When we struck against the side of the Boar and Spears, we at first did bring them great woe, for they were outnumbered manyfold. But Guthwulf and the king had prepared a trap, and soon it was sprung. Earl Fengbald of Falshire and several hundred knights came down a-horse from the woods at the top of Bullback Hill.

"I saw Duke Leobardis and his son Benigaris at the outermost edge of the fighting, behind their men-at-arms. As Fengbald's falcon-crest came down the hill, I saw Benigaris draw his sword and stab his father in the neck, slaying him in the saddle so that Leobardis fell across his horse's withers, bleeding most piteously ..."

At this last sentence, the silence abruptly dissolved into shocked cries and rebukes. Several of Baron Seriddan's liege-men stood, shaking their fists in fury as though they would strike Josua down. The prince only looked at them, still holding the parchment before him, then turned to Seriddan. The baron had retained his seat, but his brown face had paled except for bright spots of color high on each cheek.

"Silence!" he shouted, and glared at his followers until they sank back onto

their benches, full of angry muttering. Several of the women had to be helped
from the room; they stumbled out as though they themselves had been stabbed,
their intricate hats and veils suddenly as sad as the bright flags of a defeated
army. "This is an old story," the baron said at last. His voice was tight, but Isgrimnur thought there was more than rage there.

He feels the snare drawing closed.

Seriddan drained his goblet, then banged it down on the tabletop, making
more than a few people jump. "It is an old tale," he said again. "Often repeated,
never proved. Why should I believe it now?"

"Because Sir Deornoth saw it happen," said Josua simply.

"He is not here. And I do not know that I would believe him if he were."

"Deornoth did not lie. He was a true knight."

Seriddan laughed harshly. "I have only *your* word on that, Prince. Men will
do strange things for king and country." He turned to his brother. "Brindalles?
Have you heard any reason here tonight that I should not throw the prince and
his followers into one of the locked cells beneath Chasu Metessa to wait for
Benigaris' mercy?"

The baron's brother sighed. He held his two hands close together, touching
at the fingertips. "I do not like this story, Seriddan. It has an unpleasantly truth-
ful ring, since those who prepared Leobardis for burial spoke wonderingly of
the evenness of the wound. But the word of any one man, even Prince Josua's
knight, is not enough to condemn the Lord of Nabban."

Wit is not lacking in the family blood! the Duke of Elvritshalla noted. *But on such
hard-headed men must our luck ride. Or fail.*

"There are others who saw Benigaris' terrible deed," Josua said. "A few of
them are still alive, although many died when Naglimund was conquered."

"A thousand men would not be enough," Seriddan spat. "*Héa!* What, should
the flower of Nabbanai nobility follow you—an Erkynlander and enemy of the
High King—against the rightful heir to the Kingfisher House, on the strength
of the writings of a dead man?" A murmur of agreement rose from Chasu
Metessa's other inhabitants. The situation was growing ugly.

"Very well," said Josua. "I understand, Baron. Now I will show you something that will convince you of the seriousness of my undertaking. And it may
also answer your fears about following an Erkynlander anywhere." He turned
and gestured. A hooded man seated near Strangyeard at the shadowy end of the
table abruptly rose. He was very tall. Several of the men-at-arms drew their
swords; the hiss of emerging blades seemed to make the room grow cold.

Do not fail us, Isgrimnur prayed.

"You said one thing that was not true, Baron," Josua said gently.

"Do you call me a liar?"

"No. But these are strange days, and even a man as learned and clever as you
cannot know everything. Even were Benigaris not a patricide, he is *not* first
claimant on his father's dukedom. Baron, people of Metessa, here is the true
master of the Kingfisher House . . . Camaris Benidrivis."

The tall figure at the end of the table pushed back his hood, revealing a snowfall of white hair and a face full of sadness and grace.

"What . . . ?" The baron was utterly confused.

"Heresy!" shouted a confused landowner, stumbling to his feet. "Camaris, he is dead!"

One of the remaining women screamed. The man beside her slumped forward onto the table in a drunken faint.

Camaris touched his hand to his breast. "I am not dead." He turned to Seriddan. "Grant me forgiveness, Baron, for abusing your hospitality in this manner."

Seriddan stared at the apparition, then rounded on Josua. "What madness is this?! Do you mock me, Erkynlander?"

The prince shook his head. "It is no mockery, Seriddan. This is indeed Camaris. I thought to reveal him to you in private, but the chance did not come."

"No." Seriddan slapped his hand on the table. "I cannot believe it. Camaris-sá-Vinitta is dead—lost years ago, drowned in the Bay of Firannos."

"I lost only my wits, not my life," the old knight said gravely. "I lived for years with no memory of my name or my past." He drew a hand across his brow. His voice shook. "I sometimes wish I had never been given either back again. But I have. I am Camaris of Vinitta, son of Benidrivis. And if it is my last act, I will avenge my brother's death and see my murdering nephew removed from the throne in Nabban."

The baron was shaken, but still seemed unconvinced. His brother Brindalles said: "Send for Eneppa."

Seriddan looked up, his eyes bright, as though he had been reprieved from some awful sentence. "Yes." He turned to one of his men-at-arms. "Fetch Eneppa from the kitchen. And tell her *nothing,* on pain of your life."

The man went out. Watching his departure, Isgrimnur saw that little Pasevalles had disappeared from the doorway.

The folk remaining at table whispered excitedly, but Seriddan no longer seemed to care. While he waited for his man to return, he downed another goblet of wine. Even Josua, as if he had given something a starting push and could no longer control it, allowed himself to finish his own cup. Camaris remained standing at the foot of the table, a figure of imposing stolidity. No one in the room could keep their eyes off him for long.

The messenger returned with an old woman in tow. She was short and plump, her hair cut short, her simple dark dress stained with flour and other things. She stood anxiously before Seriddan, obviously fearing some punishment.

"Stand still, Eneppa," the baron said. "You have done nothing wrong. Do you see that old man?" He pointed. "Go and look at him and tell me if you know him."

The old woman sidled toward Camaris. She peered up at him, starting a little when he looked down and met her eyes. "No, my lord Baron," she said at last. Her Westerling was awkward.

"So." Seriddan crossed his arms before his chest and leaned back, an angry little smile on his face.

"Just a moment," Josua said. "Eneppa, if that is your name, this is no one you have seen in recent days. If you did know him, it was long ago."

She turned her frightened-rabbit face from the prince back to Camaris. She appeared ready to turn from him just as quickly the second time, then something caught at her. She stared. Her eyes widened. Abruptly, her knees bent and she sagged. Swift as thought, Camaris caught her and kept her from falling.

"Ulimor Camaris?" she asked in Nabbanai, weeping. *"Veveis?"* There followed a torrent in the same language. Seriddan's angry smile vanished, replaced by an expression that was almost comically astonished.

"She says that they told her I had drowned," Camaris said. "Can you speak Westerling, good woman?" he asked her quietly. "There are some here who do not understand you."

Eneppa looked at him as he steadied her, then let her go. She was dazed, crumpling the skirt of her dress in her gnarled fingers. "He . . . he is Camaris. *Duos preterate!* Have . . . have the dead come back to us again?"

"Not the dead, Eneppa," said Josua. "Camaris lived, but lost his wits for many years."

"But although I know your face, my good woman," the old knight said wonderingly, "I do not recognize your name. Forgive me. It has been a long, long time."

Eneppa began to cry again in earnest, but she was laughing, too. "Because that is not my name in that time. When I work in your father's great house, they call me *Fuiri*—'flower.' "

"Fuiri." Camaris nodded. "Of course. I remember you. You were a lovely girl, with smiles in full measure for everyone." He lifted her wizened hand, then bent and kissed it. She stared open-mouthed as though God Himself had appeared in the room and offered her a chariot ride through the heavens. "Thank you, Fuiri. You have given me back a little of my past. Before I leave this place, you and I will sit by the fire and talk."

The sniffling cook was helped from the room.

Seriddan and Brindalles both looked stunned. The rest of the baron's followers were equally amazed, and for some time no one said anything. Josua, perhaps sensing the battering that the baron had taken this night, merely sat and waited. Camaris, his identity now confirmed, allowed himself to sit down once more; he, too, fell into silence. His half-lidded gaze seemed fixed on the leaping flames in the fireplace at the table's far side, but it was clear to Isgrimnur that he was looking at a time, not a place.

The stillness was interrupted by a sudden burst of whispering. Heads turned. Isgrimnur looked up to see Pasevalles walking straddle-legged into the room; something large and shiny was cradled against his small body. He stopped just inside the doorway, hesitated as he looked at Camaris, then moved awkwardly to stand before his uncle.

"I brought this for Sir Camaris," the boy said. His bold words were belied by his shaky voice. Seriddan stared at him for a moment, then his eyes widened.

"That is one of the helmets from your father's room!"

He nodded solemnly. "I want to give it to Sir Camaris."

Seriddan turned helplessly to his brother. Brindalles looked at his son, then briefly at Camaris, who still was lost in thought. At last, Brindalles shrugged. "He is who he says he is. There is no honor he has not earned, Seriddan." The thin-faced man told his son: "You were right to ask first." His smile was almost ghostly. "I suppose sometimes things must be taken down and dusted off and put to use. Go ahead, boy. Give it to him."

Isgrimnur watched in fascination as Pasevalles walked past clutching the heavy sea-dragon helm, his eyes as fearfully fixed as though he walked into an ogre's den. He stopped before the old knight and stood silently, although he looked as though any moment he might collapse beneath the weight of the helmet.

At last, Camaris looked up. "Yes?"

"My father and my uncle said I may give you this." Pasevalles struggled to lift the helm closer to Camaris, who even sitting down still towered above him. "It is very old."

A smile stretched across Camaris' face. "Like me, eh?" He reached out his large hands. "Let me see it, young sir." He turned the golden thing to the light. "This is a helm of the Imperium," he said wonderingly. "It *is* old."

"It belonged to Imperator Anitulles, or so I believe," said Brindalles from across the room. "It is yours if you wish it, my lord Camaris."

The old man examined it a moment more, then carefully put it on. His eyes disappeared into the shadows of the helm's depths, and the cheek-guards jutted past his jaw like blades. "It fits tolerably well," he said.

Pasevalles stared up at the old man, at the coiling, high-finned sea-worm molded along the helmet's crest. His mouth was open.

"Thank you, lad." Camaris lifted the helmet off and placed it on the table beside him. "What is your name?"

"P-Pasevalles."

"I will wear the helm, Pasevalles. It is an honor. My own armor has gone to rust years ago."

The boy seemed transported to another realm, his eyes bright as candle-flame. Watching him, Isgrimnur felt a twinge of sorrow. After this moment, after this experience with knighthood, how could life hold much but disappointment for this eager child?

Bless you, Pasevalles, the duke thought. *I hope your life is a happy one, but for some reason I fear it won't be so.*

Prince Josua had been watching. Now, he spoke.

"There are other things you must know, Baron Seriddan. Some of them are frightening, others infuriating. Some of the things I must tell you are even

more amazing than Camaris alive. Would you like to wait until the morning?
Or do you still wish us locked up?"

Seriddan frowned. "Enough. Do not mock me, Josua. You will tell me what
I need to know. I do not care if we are awake until cockcrow." He clapped his
hands for more wine, then sent all but a few of his benumbed and astonished
followers home.

Ah, Baron, Isgrimnur thought, *soon you'll find yourself down in the pit with the
rest of us. I could have wished you better.*

The Duke of Elvritshalla pulled his chair closer as Josua began to speak.

33

White Tree, Black Fruit

⚜

At first it seemed a tower or a mountain—surely nothing so tall, so slender, so bleakly, flatly white could be anything alive. But as she approached it, she saw that what had seemed a vast cloud surrounding the central shaft, a diffuse milky paleness, was instead an incredible net of branches.

It was a tree that stood before her, a great, white tree that stretched so high that she could not see the top of it; it seemed tall enough to pierce the sky. She stared, overwhelmed by its fearsome majesty. Even though a part of her knew that she was dreaming, Miriamele also knew that this great stripe of white was a very important thing.

As she drew closer—she had no body: was she walking? Flying? It was impossible to tell—Miriamele saw that the tree thrust up from the featureless ground in one smooth shaft like a column of irregular but faultlessly polished marble. If this ivory giant had roots, they were set deep, deep underground, anchored in the very heart of the earth. The branches that surrounded the tree like a cloak of worn gossamer were already slender where they sprouted from the trunk, but grew even more attenuated as they reached outward. The tangled ends were so fine that at their tips they vanished into invisibility.

Miriamele was close to the great tree now. She began to rise, passing effortlessly upward. The trunk slipped past her like a stream of milk.

She floated up through the great cloud of branches. Out beyond the twining filaments of white, the sky was a flat gray-blue. There was no horizon; there seemed nothing else in the world but the tree.

The web of branches thickened. Scattered here and there among the stems hung little kernels of darkness, clots of black like reversed stars. Rising as slowly as swansdown caught in a puff of wind, Miriamele reached out—suddenly she had hands, although the rest of her body still seemed curiously absent—and touched one of the black things. It was shaped like a pear, but was smooth and turgid as a ripe plum. She touched another and found it much the same. The next one that passed beneath her fingers felt slightly different. Miriamele's fingers tightened involuntarily and the thing came loose and fell into her grasp.

She looked down at the thing she had captured. It was as taut-skinned as the others, but for some reason it felt different. It might have been a little warmer. She knew, somehow, that it was ready—that it was ripe.

Even as she stared, and as the tendrils of the white tree fell endlessly past her on either side, the black fruit in her hands shuddered and split. Nestled in the heart of it, where a *peach would have hidden its stone, lay an infant scarcely bigger than a finger. Eyelids tiny as snowflakes were closed in sleep. It kicked and yawned, but the eyes did not open.*

So every one of these fruits is a soul, *she thought. Or are they just . . . possi-bilities? She didn't quite know what these dream-thoughts meant, but a moment later she felt a wash of fear.* But I've pulled it loose! I've plucked it too soon! I have to put it back!

Something was still drawing her upward, but now she was terrified. She had done something very wrong. She had to go back, to find that one branch in the net of manyfold thousands. Maybe it was not too late to return what she had unwittingly stolen.

Miriamele grabbed at the tangle of branches, trying to slow her ascent. Some of them, narrow and brittle as icicles, snapped in her hands; a few of the black fruits worked loose and went tumbling down into the gray-white distances below her.

No! She was frantic. She hadn't meant to cause this damage. She reached out her hand to catch one of the falling fruits and lost her grip on the tiny infant. She made a desperate grab, but it was out of her reach.

Miriamele let out a wail of despair and horror. . . .

It was dark. Someone was holding her, clutching her tightly.

"No!" she gasped. "I've dropped it!"

"You haven't dropped anything," the voice said. "You're having a bad dream."

She stared, but could not make out the face. The voice . . . she knew the voice. "Simon . . . ?"

"I'm here." He moved his mouth very close to her ear. "You're safe. But you probably shouldn't shout any more."

"Sorry. I'm sorry." She shivered, then began to disengage herself from his arms. There was a strong damp smell to the air and something scratchy beneath her fingers. "Where are we?"

"In a barn. About two hours' ride outside the walls of Falshire. Don't you remember?"

"A little. I don't feel very well." In fact, she felt dreadful. She was still shiv-ering, yet at the same time she felt hot and even more bleary than she usually did when she woke up in the middle of the night. "How did we get here?"

"We had a fight with the Fire Dancers."

"I remember that. And I remember riding."

Simon made a sound in the darkness that might have been a laugh. "Well, after a while we stopped riding. You were the one who decided to stop here."

She shook her head. "I don't remember."

Simon let go of her—a little reluctantly, it was clear even to her dulled sen-sibilities. Now he crawled away over the thin layer of straw. A moment later something creaked and thumped and a little light leaked in. Simon's dark form was silhouetted in the square of a window. He was trying to find something to prop the shutter.

"It's stopped raining," he said.

"I'm cold." She tried to dig her way down into the straw.

"You kicked off your cloak." Simon crawled back across the loft to her side. He found her cloak and tucked it up beneath her chin. "You can have mine, too, if you want."

"I think I'll be happy with this," Miriamele said, although her teeth were still chattering.

"Do you want something to eat? I left your half of the supper—but you broke the ale jug on that big fellow's head."

"Just some water." The idea of putting food in her stomach was not a pleasant one.

Simon fussed with the saddlebags while Miriamele sat hugging her knees and staring out the open window at the night sky. The stars were invisible behind a veil of clouds. After Simon brought her the water skin and she drank, she felt weariness sweep over her again.

"I feel . . . bad," she said. "I think I need to sleep some more."

The disappointment was plain in Simon's voice. "Certainly, Miri."

"I'm sorry. I just feel so ill. . . ." She lay back and pulled the cloak tight beneath her chin. The darkness seemed to spin slowly around her. She saw Simon's shadowed silhouette against the window once more, then shadows came and took her back down.

By early morning Miriamele's fever was quite high. Simon could do little for her but put a damp cloth on her forehead and give her water to drink.

The dark day passed in a blur of images: gray clouds sweeping past the window, the lonely sound of a solitary dove, Simon's worried face rising above her as periodically as the moon. Miriamele discovered that she did not much care what happened to her. All the fear and concern that had driven her was leached away by the illness. If she could have chosen to fall asleep for a year, she would have; instead, she bobbed in and out of consciousness like a shipwrecked sailor clinging to a spar. Her dreams were full of white trees and drowned cities with seaweed waving in their streets.

In the hour before dawn of their second day in the barn, Miriamele awakened to find herself clear-headed again, but terribly, terribly weak. She had a sudden fear that she was alone, that her companion had left her behind.

"Simon?" she asked. There was no answer. *"Simon!?"*

"Humf?"

"Is that you?"

"What? Miriamele? Of course it's me." She could hear him roll over and crawl toward her. "Are you worse?"

"Better, I think." She stretched out a shaking hand until she found his arm, then finger-walked down it until she could clasp his hand. "But still not very well. Stay with me for a little while."

"Of course. Are you cold?"

"A bit."

Simon caught up his cloak and laid it atop her own. She felt so strengthless that the very gesture made her want to cry—indeed, a cold tear formed and trickled down her cheek.

"Thank you." She sat in silence for a while. Even this short conversation had tired her. The night, which had seemed so large and empty when she woke, now seemed a little less daunting.

"I think I'm ready to go back to sleep now." Her voice sounded fuzzy even in her own ears.

"Good night, then."

Miriamele felt herself slipping away. She wondered if Simon had ever had a dream as strange as the one about the white tree and the odd fruits it bore. It seemed unlikely. . . .

When she awoke to the uncertain light of a slate-gray dawn, Simon's cloak was still covering her. He was sleeping nearby, a few wisps of damp hay his only covering.

Miriamele slept a great deal during their second day in the barn, but when she was not sunk in slumber, she felt much healthier, almost her old self. By midday she was able to take some bread and a morsel of cheese. Simon had been out exploring the local countryside; while she ate he told her of his adventures.

"There are so few people! I saw a couple on the road out of Falshire—I didn't let them see me, I promise you—but almost no one else. There's a house down below that's almost falling apart. I think it belongs to the people who own this barn. There are holes in the roof in a few places, but most of the thatching is good. I don't think anyone's living there now. If we need to stay longer, that might be a drier place than this."

"We'll see," said Miriamele. "I may be able to ride tomorrow."

"Perhaps, but you'll have to be able to move around a bit first. This is the first time you've sat up since the night we left Falshire." He turned toward her suddenly. "And I almost got killed!"

"What?" Miriamele had to grab for the waterskin to keep herself from choking on the dry bread. "What do you mean?" she demanded when she had recovered. "Was it Fire Dancers?"

"No," Simon said, his eyes wide, his expression solemn. A moment later he grinned. "But it was a near thing, even so. I was coming back uphill from the field next to the house. I had been picking some . . . some flowers there."

Miriamele looked at him quizzically. "Flowers? What did you want with flowers?"

Simon went on as though the question had not been asked. "Something made a noise and I looked up. Standing there at the top of the rise behind me was a bull."

"Simon!"

"He didn't look very friendly, either. He was all bony, and his eyes were red, and he had bloody scratches along his sides." Simon dragged his fingers down his ribs, illustrating. "We stood there staring at each other for a moment, then he began to lower his head and make huffing noises. I started walking backward toward where I'd been. He came down the hill after me, making these little dancing steps, but going faster and faster."

"But Simon! What did you do?"

"Well, running downhill in front of a bull seemed fairly stupid, so I dropped the flowers and climbed the first good-sized tree that I reached. He stopped at the bottom—I got my feet up out of the way just as he got there—then all of a sudden he lowered his head, and . . . *thump!*" Simon brought his fist into his open palm, "he smacked up against the trunk. The whole tree shook and it almost knocked me off the branch I was hanging on, until I got my legs wrapped around good and tight. I pulled myself up until I was sitting on the branch, which was a good thing, because this idiot bull began butting his head against the tree, over and over until the skin began to peel off his head and there was blood running down his face."

"That's terrible. He must have been mad, poor animal."

"Poor animal! I like that!" Simon's voice rose in mock-despair. "He tries to kill your special protector and all you can say about him is 'poor animal.'"

Miriamele smiled. "I'm glad he didn't kill you. What happened?"

"Oh, he got tired at last and went away," Simon said airily. "Walked on down the dell, so that he wasn't between me and the fence anymore. Still, as I was running up the slope, I kept thinking I heard him coming up behind me."

"Well, you had a close call." Unable to help herself, Miriamele yawned; Simon made a face. "But I'm glad you didn't slay the monster," she continued, "even if you are a knight. He can't help being mad."

"Slay the monster? What, with my bare hands?" Simon laughed, but sounded pleased. "But maybe killing him would have been the kindest thing to do. He certainly seemed past saving. That's probably why whoever lived there left him behind."

"Or he may have gone mad *because* they left him behind," Miriamele said slowly. She looked at Simon and saw that he had heard something odd in her voice. "I'm tired, now. Thank you for the bread."

"There's one thing more." He reached into his cloak and produced a small green apple. "The only one within walking distance."

Miriamele stared at it suspiciously for a moment, then sniffed it before taking a tentative bite. It was not sweet, but its tartness was very pleasant. She ate half, then handed the rest to Simon.

"It was good," she said. "Very good. But I still can't eat much."

Simon happily crunched up the rest. Miriamele found the hollow she had made for herself in the straw and stretched out. "I'm going to sleep a little more, Simon."

He nodded. He was looking at her so carefully, so thoroughly, that Miriamele had to turn away and pull her cloak up over her face. She was not strong enough to support such attention, not just now.

She awakened late in the afternoon. Something was making a strange noise—thump and swish, thump and swish. A little frightened and still very weak, Miriamele lay unmoving and tried to decide whether it might be someone looking for them, or Simon's bull, or something entirely different and possibly worse. At last she nerved herself and crawled silently across the loft, trying not to make any noise as she moved over the thin carpet of straw. When she reached the edge, she peered over.

Simon was on the ground floor of the barn practicing his sword strokes. Despite the coolness of the day, he had taken off his shirt; sweat gleamed on his pale skin. She watched him as he measured a distance before him, then lifted his sword with both hands, holding it perpendicular to the floor before gradually lowering its point. His freckled shoulders tensed. *Thump*—he took a step forward. *Thump, thump*—he pivoted to the side, moving around the almost stationary sword, as though he held someone else's blade trapped against it. His face was earnest as a child's, and the tip of his tongue protruded pinkly from his mouth as he gripped it between his teeth in solemn concentration. Miriamele suppressed a giggle, but she could not help noticing how his skin slid over his lean muscles, how the fanlike shapes of his shoulder blades and the knobs of his backbone pushed against the milky skin. He stopped, the sword again held motionless before him. A drop of sweat slid from his nose and disappeared into his reddish beard. She suddenly wanted very much for him to hold her again, but despite her desire, the thought of it made her stomach clench in pain. There was so much that he did not know.

She pushed herself back from the edge of the loft as quietly as she could, retreating to her hollow in the straw. She tried to fall into sleep once more, but could not. For a long time she lay on her back, staring up at the shadows between the rafters as she listened to the tread of his feet, the hiss of the blade sliding through the air, and the muffled percussion of his breath.

Just before sunset Simon went down to look at the house again. He came back and reported that it was indeed empty, although he had seen what looked like fresh bootprints in the mud. But there was no other sign of anyone about, and Simon decided that the tracks most likely belonged to another harmless wanderer like the old drunkard Heanwig, so they gathered up their belongings and moved down. At first Miriamele was so light-headed that she had to lean on Simon to keep from falling, but after a few dozen steps she felt strong enough to walk unaided, although she was careful to keep a good grip on his arm. He went very slowly, showing her where the track was slippery with mud.

The cottage appeared to have been deserted for some time, and there were, as Simon had pointed out, some holes in the thatching, but the barn had been even draftier, and the cottage at least had a fireplace. As Simon carried in some split timbers he had found stacked against the wall outside and struggled to get a fire started, Miriamele huddled in her cloak and looked around at their home for the night.

Whoever had lived here had left few reminders of their residence, so she guessed that the circumstances which had driven the owners away had not come on suddenly. The only piece of furniture that remained was a stool with a splintered leg squatting off-kilter beside the hearth. A single bowl lay shattered on the stone beside it, every piece still in the spot where it had tumbled to a halt, as if the bowl had fallen only moments before. The hard clay of the floor was covered with rushes which had gone damp and brown. The only signs of recent life in the room were the innumerable cobwebs hanging in the thatches or stretching in the corners, but even these looked threadbare and forlorn, as if it had not been a good season even for spiders.

"There." Simon stood up. "That's got it. I'm going to fetch down the horses."

While he was gone, Miriamele sat before the fire and hunted through the saddlebags for food. For the first time in two days, she was hungry. She wished the house's owners had left their stew pot—the hook hung naked over the growing fire—but since it was gone she would make do with what she had. She pushed a couple of stones into the fire to heat, then rooted out the few remaining carrots and an onion. When the stones were hot enough, she would make some soup.

Miriamele scanned the ceiling critically, then unrolled her bedroll in a spot that looked like it was far enough from the nearest hole to stay dry in case the rains returned. After a moment's thought she unrolled Simon's nearby. She left what she considered to be a safe distance between them, but his bedroll was still closer than she would have preferred had there not been a leaky roof to deal with. When all was arranged, she found her knife in the saddlebag and got to work on the vegetables.

"It's blowing hard now," Simon said as he came back in. His hair was disarranged, standing out in strange tufts, but his cheeks were red and his smile was wide. "It will be a good night to be near a fire."

"I'm glad we moved down here," she said. "I feel much better tonight. I think I'll be able to ride tomorrow."

"If you're ready." As he walked past her to the fireplace, he put his hand on her shoulder for a moment, then trailed it gently across her hair. Miriamele said nothing, but went on chopping the carrots into a clay bowl.

The meal had not been anything either of them would remember fondly, but Miriamele felt better for having something hot in her stomach. When she had rinsed the bowls and scoured them with a dry twig, she put them away, then crawled onto her bedroll. Simon fussed with the fire for a bit, then laid himself down as well. They spent a silent interval staring at the flames.

"There was a fireplace in my bedroom at Meremund," Miriamele said quietly. "I used to watch the flames dancing at night when I couldn't sleep. I saw pictures in them. When I was very little, I thought I saw the face of Usires smiling at me once."

"Mmmm," Simon said. Then: "You had your *own* room to sleep in?"

"I was the only child of the prince and heir," she said a little crisply. "It is not unheard of."

Simon snorted. "It's unheard of by me. I slept with a dozen other scullions. One of them, Fat Zebediah, used to snore like a cooper cutting slats with a handsaw."

Miriamele giggled. "Later on, in the last twelvemonth when I lived in the Hayholt, Leleth used to sleep in my room. That was nice. But when I was in Meremund, I slept by myself, with a maid just on the other side of the door."

"That sounds . . . lonely."

"I don't know. I suppose it was." She sighed and laughed at the same time, a funny noise that made Simon lift his head beside her. "Once I was having trouble sleeping, so I went in to my father's room. I told him that there was a cockindrill under my bed, so that he would let me sleep with him. But that was after my mother died, so he only gave me one of his dogs to take back with me. 'He's a cockindrill-hound, Miri,' he said to me. 'By my faith, he is. He'll keep you safe.' He was always a bad liar. The dog just lay by the door and whimpered until I finally let him out again."

Simon waited for a while before speaking. The flames made jigging shadows in the thatching overhead. "How did your mother die?" he asked at last. "No one ever told me."

"She was shot by an arrow." Miriamele still hurt when she thought of it, but not as badly as she once had. "Uncle Josua was taking her to my father, who was fighting for Grandfather John along the edge of the Meadow Thrithing during the uprising there. Josua's troop was surprised in broad daylight by a much larger force of Thrithings-men. He lost his hand defending her, and did succeed in winning free, but she was struck down by a stray arrow. She was dead before sunset."

"I'm sorry, Miriamele."

She shrugged, even though he could not see her. "It was long ago. But losing her gave my father even more misery than it gave me. He loved her so much! Oh, Simon, you only know what my father has become, but he was a good man once. He loved my mother more than he loved anything else in the world."

And thinking of her father's gray, grief-stricken face, of the pall of anger that had descended on him and never lifted, she began to cry.

"And that's why I have to see him," she said finally, her voice unsteady. "That's why."

Simon rustled atop his bedroll. "What? What do you mean? See who?"

Miriamele took a deep breath. "My father, of course. That's why we're going to the Hayholt. Because I have to speak to my father."

"What nonsense are you talking?" Simon sat up. "We're going to the Hayholt to get your grandfather's sword, Bright-Nail."

"I never said that. You did." Despite the tears, she felt herself grow angry.

"I don't understand you, Miriamele. We are at war with your father. Are you going to go see him and tell him there's a cockindrill under your bed again? What are you saying?"

"Don't be cruel, Simon. Don't you dare." She could feel the tears threatening to become a torrent, but a small ember of fury was burning inside her as well.

"I'm sorry," he said, "but I just don't understand."

Miriamele pressed her hands together as tightly as she could, and concentrated on that until she felt herself in control again. "And I have not explained to you, Simon. I'm sorry, too."

"Tell me. I'll listen."

Miriamele listened to the flames crackle and hiss for a while. "Cadrach showed me the truth, although I don't think he realized it. It was when we were traveling together, and he told me of Nisses' book. He had once owned it, or a copy of it."

"The magical book that Morgenes talked about?"

"Yes. And it is a powerful thing. Powerful enough that Pryrates learned that Cadrach had owned it and so Pryrates . . . sent for him." She fell silent momentarily, remembering Cadrach's description of the blood-red windows and the iron devices with the skin and hair of the tortured still on them. "He threatened him until Cadrach told him all the things he remembered. Cadrach said that Pryrates was particularly interested in talking with the dead—'Speaking through the Veil,' he called it."

"From what I know of Pryrates, that doesn't surprise me." Simon's voice was shaky, too. Obviously he had his own memories of the red priest.

"But that was what showed me what I needed to know," Miriamele said, unwilling to lose the thread of her idea now that she was finally talking about it out loud. "Oh, Simon, I had wondered so long why my father changed the way he did, why Pryrates was able to turn him to such evil tasks." She swallowed. There were still tears standing wet on her cheeks, but for the moment she had found a new strength. "My father loved my mother. He was never the same after she died. He did not marry, did not even consider it, despite all the wishes of my grandfather. They used to have terrible arguments about it. 'You need a son to be your heir,' Grandfather used to say, but my father always told him he would never marry again, that he had been given a wife and then God had taken her back." She paused, remembering.

"I still don't understand," said Simon quietly.

"Don't you see? Pryrates must have told my father that he could talk to the dead—that he could let my father speak with my mother again, perhaps even see her. You don't know him, Simon. He was heartsick with losing her. He would have done anything, I think, to have her back, even for a little while."

Simon drew in a long breath. "But that's . . . blasphemy. That's against God."

Miriamele laughed, a little shrilly. "As if that would have stopped him. I told you, he would have done *anything* to have her back. Pryrates must have lied to him and told him that they could reach her . . . beyond the Veil, or whatever that horrible book called it. Maybe the priest even thought that he could. And he used that promise to make my father first his patron, then his partner . . . then his slave."

Simon pondered this. "Perhaps Pryrates *did* try," he said finally. "Perhaps that is how they reached through to . . . to the other side. To the Storm King."

The sound of this name, even as quietly it had been spoken, was greeted with a skirl of wind in the thatches above, a rush of sound so abrupt that Miriamele flinched.

"Perhaps." The thought made her cold. To think of her father waiting eagerly to speak with his beloved wife and finding that *thing* instead. It was a little like the terrifying old story of what the fisherman Bulychlinn brought up in his nets. . . .

"But I still don't understand, Miriamele." Simon was gentle but stubborn. "Even if all that is true, what good will it do to speak to your father?"

"I'm not sure it will do any good." And that was true: it was hard to picture any happy result from their meeting after so much time and so much anger and sorrow. "But if there's even a small chance that I can show him sense, that I can remind him that this began out of love, and so convince him to stop . . . then I have to take that chance." She lifted a hand and wiped at her eyes: she was crying again. "He just wanted to see her. . . ." After a moment she steadied herself. "But you do not have to go, Simon. This is my burden."

He was silent. She could sense his discomfort.

"It is too great a risk," he said at last. "You might never get to see your father, even if that would do any good. Pryrates might catch you first, and then no one would ever hear from you again." He said it with terrible conviction.

"I know, Simon. I just don't know what else to do. I have to speak to my father. I have to show him what's happened, and only I can do it."

"You're determined, then?"

"I am."

Simon sighed. "Aedon on the Tree, Miriamele, it's madness. I hope you change your mind by the time we get there."

Miriamele knew there would be no change. "I have been thinking about it for a long time."

Simon slumped back onto his bedroll. "If Josua knew, he'd tie you up and carry you a thousand leagues away."

"You're right. He would never allow it."

In the darkness, Simon sighed again. "I have to think, Miriamele. I don't know what to do."

"You can do anything but stop me," she said evenly. "Don't try to stop me, Simon."

But he did not reply. After a while, despite all the fear and furor, Miriamele felt the heaviness of sleep pulling her down.

She was startled awake by a loud roar. As she lay with her heart pounding, something flashed up in the ceiling, brighter than a torch. It took a moment for her to realize that the source had been a sky-spanning sheet of lightning glaring through the holes in the roof. There was another crash of thunder.

The room smelled even damper and closer than it had before. When the next lightning flash came, Miriamele saw in its momentary brilliance a torrent of raindrops pouring through the ragged thatching. She sat up and felt along the floor. The rain was falling well short of her, but it was splashing on Simon's boots and the bottoms of his breeches. He was still asleep, snoring quietly.

"Simon!" She shook him. "Get up!"

He grunted, but showed no other signs of wakefulness.

"Simon, you have to move. You're being rained on."

After a few more shakes, he rolled over. Complaining muzzily, he helped Miriamele pull his bedroll closer to hers, then flopped onto it with every sign of going immediately back to sleep.

As she lay listening to the rain patter on the straw, she felt Simon move closer. His face was very close to hers in the dark; she could feel his warm breath on her cheek. It was oddly peaceful, despite all the danger they had seen and still faced, to lie here and listen to the storm with this young man close beside her.

Simon stirred. "Miriamele? Are you cold?"

"A little."

He moved closer still, then reached out his arm and put it under her neck, tipping her in toward his chest so that she could feel him the whole length of her. She felt trapped but not frightened. His mouth was now pressed against her cheek.

"Miriamele . . ." he said softly.

"Sssshhh." She stayed huddled against him. "Don't say a word."

They remained that way for some time. Rain rattled in the thatch. From time to time thunder sounded in the distance like giants' drums.

Simon kissed her cheek. Miriamele felt his beard tickling along her jaw, but it seemed so strangely right that she did not squirm. He turned her head slightly, then his lips met hers. The thunder rumbled again from farther away, something happening in another place, another time.

Why does there have to be more than this? Miriamele wondered sadly. *Why should there be all the complications?* Simon had put his other arm around her, gentle but insistent, and now they were pressed together, body against body. She could feel his lean, muscled arms and his hard chest against her stomach, against her breasts. If only time could stop!

Simon's kisses were stronger now. He lifted his face and buried it in her hair.

"Miriamele," he whispered, hoarse-throated.

"Oh. Oh, Simon," she murmured back. She was not quite sure what she wanted, but she knew she would be happy just kissing him, just holding him.

His face was against her neck now, sending chills all through her. It felt wonderful, but also frightening. He was a boy, but he was a man as well. She stiffened, but he brought his face back to hers. Again he kissed her, clumsy but ardent, pushing a little too hard. She lifted her hand to his bearded face and gentled him, so that their lips could meet and touch—oh, so softly!

Even as they shared breath, his hand was moving across her face, across her neck. He touched her everywhere he could without losing the warmth pressed between them, running his fingers across the swell of her hip, letting his hand rest in the hollow beneath her arm. She tingled, yearning to rub hard against him, but she felt a strange softness, too, as though they were slowly drowning together, sinking down into dark ocean depths. She could hear her own heartbeat above the rustle of rain in the straw.

Simon rolled farther, until he was half above her, then drew back a little. He was only a shadow, which she found somehow frightening. She reached up until she could feel his cheek, the delicate rasp of his beard. His mouth moved.

"I love you, Miriamele."

Her breath caught. Suddenly there was a knot of coldness in her stomach. "No, Simon," she whispered. "Don't say that."

"But it's true! I think I've loved you since I first saw you, up in the tower with the sun in your hair."

"You can't love me." She wanted to push him off, but she had no strength. "You don't understand."

"What do you mean?"

"You . . . you *can't* love me. It's wrong."

"Wrong?" he said angrily. His body was now quivering against her, but it was the trembling of suppressed fury. "Because I'm a commoner. I'm not good enough for a princess, is that it?" He twisted away, kneeling in the straw beside her. "Damn your pride, Miriamele. I fought a dragon! A dragon, a real dragon! Isn't that enough for you!? Do you prefer somebody like Fengbald—a m-m-murderer, but a m-murderer with a t—title?" He fought against tears.

The rawness in his voice tore at her heart. "No, Simon, that's not it! You don't understand!"

"Tell me, then!" he snapped. "Tell me what I don't understand!"

"It's not you. It's me."

There was a long silence. "What do you mean?"

"Nothing's wrong with you, Simon. I think you're brave, and kind, and everything you should be. It's me, Simon. I'm the one who doesn't deserve to be loved."

"What are you talking about?"

She gasped and shook her head violently. "I don't want to talk any more. Leave me alone, Simon. Find someone else to love. There will be plenty who would be happy to have you." She rolled over, turning her back to him. Now, when she most wanted the relief of tears, tears would not come. She felt high and cold and strange.

His hand clutched her shoulder. "By the bloody Tree, Miriamele, would you talk to me!? What are you saying?"

"I'm not pure, Simon. I'm not a maiden." There. It was out.

It took him several moments to respond. "What?"

"I have been with a man." Now that she was talking, it was easier than she had thought it would be. It was like listening to someone else speak. "The nobleman from Nabban I told you about, the one who took Cadrach and me aboard his ship. Aspitis Preves."

"He raped you . . . ?" He sounded stunned, but anger was growing. "That . . . that . . ."

Miriamele's laugh was short and bitter. "No, Simon, he did not rape me. He held me prisoner, yes, but that was later. He was a monster—but I let him come to my bed and I did not resist." Then, to bolt the door for good, so that Simon would leave her alone, so that she would bring him no further suffering after this night: "I wanted him to. I thought he was beautiful. I wanted him to."

Simon made an inarticulate noise, then stood up. His breath sawed in and out, in and out. For all she could see of him in the darkness, he could have been shape-changing: he seemed wordless and bedeviled as a trapped animal. He growled, then ran for the door of the cottage. It crashed open as he fled out into the dying storm.

After a few moments Miriamele went and pulled the door closed again. He would be back, she felt sure. Then he would leave her, or they would go on together, but things would be different. That was what she wanted. That was what she needed.

Her head felt empty. Those few thoughts almost seemed to echo, like stones rattled down a well.

She waited a long time for sleep. Just as she was beginning to slip away, she heard Simon come back in. He dragged his bedroll to the far corner and lay down. Neither of them spoke.

Outside, the storm had passed, but water still dripped from the ceiling. Miriamele counted the drops.

By midday the next day, Miriamele felt herself recovered enough to ride. They set out under dark clouds of more than one kind.

After all the pain and emotion of the night before they were both flat with each other, bruised and sullen like two swordfighters waiting for their final bout. They spoke no more than was necessary, but Miriamele saw signs of Simon's anger all day, from the over-brisk way he saddled and readied his horse to the way he rode ahead of her, just close enough to stay in sight.

For her part, Miriamele felt a sort of relief. The worst was out now and there was no turning back. Now Simon would know her for what she was, which could only be for the good, ultimately. It hurt to have him despise her, as he so obviously did at present, but it was better than leading him on falsely. Nevertheless, she could not shake the feeling of loss. It had been so warm, so nice, to kiss him and hold him without thinking. If only he had not talked of love. If only he had not forced her to consider her responsibilities. Deep down, she had known that anything more than friendship between them would mean living in a lie, but there had been moments, sweet moments, when she had allowed herself to pretend it could be different.

Making the best time they could on the terrible, muddy roads, they rode well beyond the reach of Falshire by evening time, out into the wildlands west of the city. When darkness came down—little more than a thickening of the already murky day—they found a wayside shrine to Elysia and made their beds on its floor. After a sparse meal and even sparser conversation, they retired to their bedrolls. This time it did not seem to bother Simon when Miriamele unfurled her pallet on the opposite side of the fire from his.

After her first day in the saddle following several days of illness, Miriamele felt ready to sink into sleep immediately, but sleep would not come. She moved several times, trying to find a comfortable position, but nothing seemed to help. She lay in darkness, staring up at nothing, listening as a light rain pattered the roof of the shrine.

Would Simon leave her, she wondered? It was an unexpectedly frightening thought. She had said several times that she was willing to make this journey by herself, as she had originally planned, but she realized now that she did not want to travel alone. Perhaps she had been wrong to tell him. Perhaps it would have been better to give him some more face-saving lie: if she had disgusted him too completely, he might simply go back to Josua.

And she did not want him to go, she realized. It was more than the idea of traveling these gloomy lands by herself that disturbed her. She would miss him.

It was odd to think about, now that she had probably thrown up an un-breachable wall between them, but she did not want to lose him. Simon had worked his way into her heart in a way no other friend ever had. His boyish silliness had always charmed her when it didn't irritate her, but now it was counterbalanced by a serious air that was very handsome. Several times she had caught herself watching him in surprise, amazed he had become a man in such a short time.

And there were other qualities that had become dear to her as well, his kind-ness, his loyalty, his open-mindedness. She doubted that the most traveled of her father's courtiers faced life with the same unprejudiced interest as Simon did.

It was frightening even to contemplate losing all those things if he left her.

But she *had* lost him now—or at least, there would always be a shadow over their friendship. He had seen the stain that was at the core of her; she had made it as visible and unpleasant as she could. She was not willing to suffer for lies any more, and seeing the way he felt about her was more suffering than she could stand. He was in love with her.

And she had been falling in love with him.

The thought hit her with unexpected force. Was that true? Wasn't love sup-posed to come like a bolt of sky-fire, to blind and stun? Or at the least, like a sweet perfume that rose and filled the air until one could think of nothing else? Surely her feelings for Simon had been different. She thought of him, of the laughable way his hair looked in the morning, of his earnest glances when he was worried for her.

Elysia, Mother of God, she prayed, *take this pain away. Did I love him? Do I love him?*

It didn't matter now, in any case. She had taken steps of her own to remove the hurt. Letting Simon continue to think of her as a chaste maiden worthy of his youthful ideals would be worse than anything—worse even than losing him completely, if that was the result.

So why, then, was the pain still so very strong?

"Simon . . . ?" she whispered. "Are you awake?"

If he was, he did not answer. She was alone with her thoughts.

The next day seemed even darker. The wind was sharp and biting. They rode swiftly, unspeaking, with Simon again keeping Homefinder a short distance ahead of Miriamele and her still-nameless steed.

By late morning they came to the fork where the River Road joined the Old Forest Road. Two corpses hung in iron cages at the crossing, and had clearly done so for some time: It was impossible to tell from the wind-tossed rags of clothing or the grinning bones who these unfortunates had been. Miriamele and Simon both made the sign of the Tree as they crossed, passing as far from the clanking cages as they could. They took the Old Forest Road turning, and soon the River Road vanished from sight behind the low hills to the south.

The road began to dip downward. On the north side they could now see the edge of Aldheorte Forest, which flowed onto and over the foothills there. As they passed down through the outskirts of Hasu Vale and into the shelter of the hills the wind became less, but Miriamele did not feel comforted. Even at midday the valley was dark and almost silent except for the slow drip of the morning's rains from the leafless branches of oak and ash. Even the evergreens seemed full of shadow.

"I don't like this valley, Simon." She spurred forward. He slowed to allow her to catch up. "It was always a quiet, secretive place—but it feels different now."

He shrugged, looking away across the deep-shaded hillside. It was only when he stared so long at the unchanging landscape that she understood he did not want to meet her eyes. "I have not liked most of the places we've been." His voice was cold. "But we are not traveling for pleasure."

She felt a flare of anger. "That's not what I meant and you know it, Simon. I mean that this valley feels . . . I don't know, dangerous."

Now he did turn. His smile was a smirk that hurt her to see. "Haunted, you mean? Like that old drunkard said?"

"I don't *know* exactly what I mean," she said furiously. "But I can see it was a waste of time talking about it with you."

"No doubt." He gently but deliberately touched his spurs to Homefinder's side and sent her trotting forward. Watching his straight back, Miriamele fought down the urge to shout at him. What had she expected? No, more to the point, what had she wanted, after all? Wasn't it best he had been told the truth? Perhaps things would be easier when some time had passed, when he realized they could still be friends.

The road descended deeper into the valley, so that the thick-mantled hills seemed to be growing even higher on either side. The road was deserted, and the few rough cottages they saw perched on the hillsides seemed equally uninhabited, but at least it seemed they would be able to find shelter somewhere tonight—which was a reassuring thought, since Miriamele did not in the least wish to spend a night here out of doors. She had conceived a serious dislike of Hasu Vale, although nothing had actually happened to make her feel that way. Still, the smothering quality of the stillness and the thick, overgrown hillsides—and perhaps, just a little bit, her own sorrow—conspired to make her look forward to the moment they rode out of this valley again and saw the headlands of Swertclif, even though that would mean that Asu'a and her father were very, very close.

It was also disheartening to think of spending another strained, silent night with Simon. Before their last unpleasant exchange, he had spoken to her only a few times today, and then only about practical things. He had discovered what he claimed were new footprints near the shrine where they had spent the night and had told her about them soon after they set out, but he had seemed quite offhand and uncaring about it. Miriamele secretly thought it likely that the muddy footmarks were their own, since they had tramped about a great deal while searching for firewood. Other than that, Simon had conversed with her only about whether it was time to stop and eat and rest the horses, and to issue curt thanks when she had given him food or shared the water skin. It would not be a pleasant night, she felt sure.

They were in the deeps of the valley when Simon abruptly stopped, pulling back on Homefinder's reins so that the mare paced nervously from side to side for a long moment after she halted.

"There's somebody on the road ahead," he said quietly. "There. Just through the trees." He pointed to a spot where the path hooked to one side and passed out of sight. "Do you see them?"

Miriamele squinted. The early twilight had turned the road before them into a dim streak of gray. If something was moving beyond the trees, she could not see it from her angle. "We're getting near the town."

"Come, then," he said. "It's probably just someone on their way home, but we haven't seen anyone else all day." He eased Homefinder ahead.

As they rounded the bend they came upon two figures hunching along in the middle of the road, both of them carrying buckets. When the noise of Simon and Miriamele's horses reached the pair, they flinched and looked over their shoulders as guiltily as thieves surprised. Miriamele felt sure that they were just as startled as Simon to find other travelers on the road.

The pair moved to the verge of the road as the riders approached. From what Miriamele could see of their dark, hooded cloaks, they were probably local people, hill-folk. Simon lifted his hand to his brow in salute.

"God give you good day," he said.

The nearest of the pair looked up at him and cautiously raised his own hand to return the greeting, but stopped abruptly, staring.

"By the Tree!" Simon reined up. "You're the ones from the tavern in Falshire."

What is he doing? Miriamele wondered fearfully. *Are they Fire Dancers? Ride on, Simon, you idiot!*

He turned toward her. "Miriamele. Look here."

Unexpectedly, the two hooded folk dropped to their knees. "You saved our lives," a woman's voice said.

Miriamele pulled up and stared. It was the woman and man that the Fire Dancers had threatened.

"That's true," the man said. His voice was unsteady. "May Usires bless you, good knight."

"Please, get up." Simon was clearly pleased yet embarrassed. "I'm sure someone else would have helped you if we hadn't."

The woman stood, unmindful of the mud on the knees of her long skirt. "None seemed in a hurry to help," she said. "That's the way. Those who are good are given the pain."

The man darted a glance at her. "That's enough, wife. These folk don't need your tellin' what's wrong with the world."

She looked back at him with poorly hidden defiance. "It's a shame, that's all. A shame the world works thus."

The man turned his attention back to Simon and Miriamele. He was middle-aged, with a face reddened and wrinkled by years of harsh sun. "My wife has her ideas, mind, but the bottom of it's true enough. You saved our lives, that you did." He forced a smile. He seemed nervous; having his life saved must have been almost as frightening as not having it saved. "Have you a place to stay for tonight? My wife's Gullaighn and I am Roelstan, and we would be pleased to offer you what shelter we have."

"We cannot stop yet," Miriamele said, unsettled by the thought of staying with strangers.

Simon looked at her. "You have been ill," he said.

"I can ride farther."

"Yes, you probably can, but why turn down a roof over our heads, even for one night?" He turned to look at the man and woman, then moved his horse closer to Miriamele. "It may be the last chance to get out of the wind and rain," he murmured, "the last until . . ." He broke off, unwilling even to whisper any hint of their destination.

Miriamele was certainly weary. She hesitated a moment longer, then nodded her head.

"Good," said Simon, then turned to the man and woman. "We would be glad of shelter." He did not offer their own names to these strangers; Miriamele silently approved of that at least.

"But we have nothing worthy of such good folk, husband." Gullaighn had a face that might have been kindly, but fear and hard times had made the skin slack, the eyes sorrowful. "It is no favor to bring them to our rude place."

"Be quiet, woman," her husband said. "We will do what we can."

She appeared to have more to say, but instead closed her mouth in a grim line.

"It's settled, then," he said. "Come. It is not much farther."

After a moment's consideration, Simon and Miriamele dismounted so that they could walk beside their hosts. "Do you live here in Hasu Vale?" asked Simon.

Roelstan laughed shortly. "For a short time only. We lived once in Falshire."

Miriamele hesitated before speaking. "And . . . and were you Fire Dancers?"

"To our sorrow."

"They are a powerful evil." Gullaighn's voice was thick with emotion. "You should have nothing to do with them, my lady, nor anything they've touched."

"Why were those men after you?" Simon reflexively fingered the hilt of his sword.

"Because we left," Roelstan said. "We could stand it no longer. They are mad, but like dogs, even in their madness they can do harm."

"But it is not so easy to escape them," said Gullaighn. "They are fierce and they do not let go. And they are everywhere." She lowered her voice. "Everywhere!"

"By the Ransomer, woman," Roelstan growled, "what are you trying to do? You have seen this knight wield a sword. He has naught to fear from them."

Simon walked a little straighter. Miriamele smiled, but a look at Gullaighn's anxious face made the smile fade. Could she be right? Might there be more Fire Dancers about? Perhaps by tomorrow it would be time to leave the main road again and travel more secretively.

As if echoing her thoughts, Roelstan stopped and waved at a track climbing up from the Old Forest Road, winding away into the wooded hillside. "We have made our place up there," he said. "It is no good to be too close to the road, where the smoke of a fire might bring visitors less welcome than you two."

They followed Roelstan and Gullaighn up the narrow path. After the first few turnings the road had disappeared behind them, hidden beneath a blanket of treetops. It was a long and steep climb through the close-leaning trees, and the dark cloaks of their guides became harder and harder to follow as twilight came on. Just as Miriamele began to think that they would see the moon before they saw a place to stop, Roelstan halted and pulled back the thick branch of a pine tree that had hung across their path.

"Here it is," he said.

Miriamele led her horse through after Simon, and found herself in a wide clearing on the hillside. In the center was a house made of split timbers, plain but surprisingly large. Smoke twined from a hole in the roof.

Miriamele was taken aback. She turned to Gullaighn, suddenly full of misgivings. "Who else lives here?"

The woman gave no answer.

Miriamele saw movement in the doorway of the house. A moment later, a man emerged onto the dark hard-packed earth before the door. He was short and thick-necked, clothed in a white robe.

"We meet again," said Maefwaru. "Our visit in the tavern was too short."

Miriamele heard Simon curse, then the scrape of his sword leaving the scabbard. He pulled at her bridle to turn her horse around.

"Don't," Maefwaru said. He whistled. A half-dozen more white-robed figures stepped from the shadows around the edge of the clearing. In the twilight, they seemed ghosts born from the secretive trees. Several of them had drawn their bows.

"Roelstan, you and your woman move away." The bald man sounded almost pleasant. "You have done what you were sent to do."

"Curse you, Maefwaru!" Gullaighn cried. "On the Day of Weighing-Out, you will eat your own guts for sausages!"

Maefwaru laughed, a deep rumble. "Is that so? Move, woman, before I have someone put an arrow in you."

As her husband dragged her away, Gullaighn turned to Miriamele with eyes full of tears. "Forgive us, my lady. They caught us again. They made us!"

Miriamele's heart was cold as a stone.

"What do you want with us, you coward?" Simon demanded.

Maefwaru laughed again, wheezing a little. "It is not what *we* want of you, young master. It is what the Storm King wants of you. And we will find out tonight, when we give you to Him." He waved to the other white-robed figures. "Bind them. There is much to do before midnight."

As the first of the Fire Dancers seized his arms, Simon turned to Miriamele, his face full of anger and desperation. She knew that he wished to fight, to make them kill him instead of simply surrendering, but was afraid to for her sake.

Miriamele could give him nothing. She had nothing left inside of her but stifling dread.

34

A Confession

✹

"Unto her side he came, he came,"

sang Maegwin,

"A youth dressed all in sable black
With golden curls about his head
And silken cape upon his back.

'And what would you my lady fair?'
That golden youth did smile and say.
'What rare gift may I give to you,
So you will be my bride this day?

The maiden turned her face aside.
'There is no gift so rich, so fine,
That I would give you in return
That rare thing that is only mine.'

The youth he shook his golden head
And laughed and said, 'Oh, maiden sweet
You may turn me away today,
But soon find that you can't say no.
My name is Death, and all you have
Will come to me anyway . . .'"

It was no use. Over the sound of her own melody, she could still hear the odd wailing that seemed to portend so much unhappiness.

Maegwin's song trailed off and she stared into the flames of the campfire. Her cold-cracked lips made it painful to sing. Her ears stung and her head hurt. Nothing was as it should be—nothing was as she had expected.

It had *seemed* at first that things were going the way they should. She had been a dutiful daughter to the gods: it was no surprise that after her death she should be raised up to live among them—not as an equal, of course, but as a trusted subordinate, a beloved servant. And in their strange way the gods had proved every bit as wondrous as she had imagined they would, with their in-human, flashing eyes and their rainbow-hued armor and clothing. Even the land of the gods had been much as she had expected, like her own beloved Hernystir, but better, cleaner, brighter. The sky in the godlands seemed higher and more blue than a sky could be, the snow whiter, the grass so green that its verdancy was almost painful. Even Count Eolair, who had also died and come to this beautiful eternity, seemed more open, more approachable; she had been able to tell him without fear or shyness that she had always loved him. Eolair, relieved like her of the burden of mortality, had listened with kind concern—almost like a god himself!

But then things had begun to go wrong.

Maegwin had thought that when she and the other living Hernystiri had faced their enemies, and by doing so brought the gods out into the world, they had somehow tipped a balance. The gods themselves were at war, just as the Hernystiri—but the gods' war had not been won. The worst, it seemed, was yet to come.

And so the gods had ridden across the broad white fields of Heaven, search-ing for Scadach, the hole into outer darkness. And they had found it. Cold and black it was, bounded in stone quarried from eternity's darkest recesses, just as the lore-masters had taught her—and full of the gods' direst enemies.

She had never believed that such things could exist, creatures of pure evil, shining vessels of emptiness and despair. But she had seen one stand on the ageless wall of Scadach, heard its lifeless voice prophesy the destruction of gods and mortals alike. All that was wrong lay behind that wall . . . and now the gods were trying to bring the wall tumbling down.

Maegwin would have guessed that the ways of gods were mysterious. What she would not have guessed was just how mysterious they could be.

She raised her voice in song again, still hoping that she could blot out the disturbing noise, but gave it up after a few moments. The gods themselves were singing, and their voices were much stronger than hers.

Why don't they stop? she thought desperately. *Why don't they leave it alone?!*

But it was useless to wonder. The gods had their reasons. They always did.

Eolair had long since given up trying to understand the Sithi. He knew they were not gods, whatever Maegwin's poor, fevered mind might see, but neither were they a great deal more comprehensible than the Lords of Heaven.

The count turned away from the fire, turned his back on Maegwin. She had been singing to herself, but had fallen silent. She had a sweet voice, but set against the chanting of the Peaceful Ones it sounded thin and discordant. It was not her fault. No mortal voice would sound like much when set against . . . this.

The Count of Nad Mullach shivered. The chorus of Sithi voices rose again. Their music was as impossible to ignore as were their catlike eyes when they stared you in the face. The rhythmic song gained in volume, pulsing like the oar-master's call to his rowers.

The Sithi had been singing for three days, clustered before the bleak walls of Naglimund in the flurrying snow. Whatever they were doing, the Norns within the castle did not ignore them: several times the white-faced defenders had mounted to the tops of the walls and let fly a volley of arrows. A few of the Sithi had been killed in these attacks, but they had their own archers. Each time, the Norns were driven from the walls and the Sithi voices would rise once more.

"I don't know that I can stand this much longer, Eolair." Isorn appeared qut of the whirl of mist, his beard jeweled with frost. "I had to go hunting just to get away, but the noise followed me as far as I went." He dropped a hare onto the ground near the fire. Red dribbled from the arrow-wound in its side, staining the snow. "Good day, Lady," the duke's son said to Maegwin. She had stopped singing, but did not look up at him. She seemed incapable of seeing anything but the wavering fire.

Eolair received Isorn's curious look and shrugged. "It is not really such a terrible sound."

The Rimmersman raised his eyebrows. "No, Eolair, it is beautiful in its way. But it is too beautiful for me, too strong, too strange. It is making me ill."

The count frowned. "I know. The rest of the men are unsettled, too. More than unsettled—frightened."

"But why are the Sithi doing this? They are risking their lives—two more were killed yesterday! If this is some fairy ceremony they must perform, can they not sing out of bowshot?"

Eolair shook his head helplessly. "I do not know. Bagba bite me, I do not know anything, Isorn."

As continual as the noise of the ocean, the voices of the Sithi washed across the camp.

Jiriki came in the dark before dawn. The slumbering coals picked out his sharp features in scarlet light.

"This morning," he said, then squatted, staring at the embers. "Before noon."

Eolair rubbed his eyes, trying to bring himself fully awake. He had been sleeping fitfully, but sleeping nonetheless. "This . . . this morning? What do you mean?"

"The battle will begin." Jiriki turned and gave Eolair a look that on a more familiar face might have betokened pity. "It will be dreadful."

"How do you know that the battle will start then?"

"Because that is what we have been working toward. We cannot fight a siege—we are too few. Those you call Norns are fewer than we are, but they sit inside a great shell of stone, and we do not have the engines mortals make for such battles nor the time to build them. So we will do it our way."

"Does it have something to do with the singing?"

Jiriki nodded in his oddly avian way. "Yes. Make your men ready. And tell them this: whatever they may think or see, they are fighting against living creatures. The Hikeda'ya are like you and like us—they bleed. They die." He fixed Eolair with an even, golden stare. "You will tell them that?"

"I will." Eolair shivered and leaned closer to the fire, warming his hands before the dreaming coals. "Tomorrow?"

Jiriki nodded again, then stood. "We will have our best chance while the sun is high. If we are lucky, it will be over before the darkness comes."

Eolair couldn't imagine rugged Naglimund being brought down in so short a time. "And if it's *not* over? What, then?"

"Things will be . . . difficult." Jiriki took a step backward and vanished into the mist.

Eolair sat before the coals for a little while, clenching his teeth to keep them from chattering. When he was sure he would not embarrass himself, he went to waken Isorn.

Buffeted by brisk winds, the gray and red tent rode the peak of the hill like a sailing ship breasting a high wave. A few other tents shared the hilltop; many more were scattered down the slope and clustered in the valley. Beyond them lay Lake Clodu, a vast blue-green mirror, still as a contented beast.

Tiamak stood outside the tent, lingering despite the chill breeze. So many people, so much movement, so much life! It was disturbing to look down on that great sea of people, frightening to know that he was so close to the grinding stones of History, but still it was somehow hard to turn away. His own little story had been quite swallowed up by the great tales that stalked through Osten Ard in these days. It sometimes seemed that a sack full of the mightiest dreams and nightmares had been emptied out. That Tiamak's own small accomplishments, fears, and desires seemed likely to be ignored was the best he could hope for. An equally strong possibility was that they might be trampled entirely.

Shivering a little, he finally lifted the tent flap and stepped through.

It was not, as he had feared when Jeremias brought him the prince's summons, a council of war. Such things made him feel completely useless. Only a few waited—Josua, Sir Camaris, Duke Isgrimnur, all seated on stools, Vorzheva propped up in her bed, and the Sitha-woman Aditu, cross-legged on the floor at Vorzheva's side. The only other person in the tent was young Jeremias, who had apparently been very busy this afternoon. Just now, he was standing before the prince, trying to look attentive while gasping slightly for air.

"Thank you for your haste, Jeremias," said Josua. "I understand completely.

Please just go back and tell Strangyeard to come when he can. After that, you are released."

"Yes, your Highness." Jeremias bowed, then headed for the door.

Tiamak, who was still standing in the doorway, smiled at the approaching youth. "I did not have a chance to ask you before, Jeremias: how is Leleth? Is there any change?"

The youth shook his head. He tried to keep his voice even, but the pain was obvious. "Just the same. She never wakes up. She drinks a little water, but takes no food." He rubbed fiercely at his eye. "No one can do anything."

"I am sorry," said Tiamak gently.

"It's not your fault." Jeremias moved uncomfortably from one foot to the other. "I have to go take Josua's message back to Father Strangyeard."

"Of course." Tiamak stepped out of the way. Jeremias slipped past him and was gone.

"Tiamak," the prince called, "please come and join us." He pointed to an empty stool.

When the Wrannaman was seated, Josua looked around. "This is very difficult," he said at last. "I am going to do a terrible thing and I apologize for it now. Nothing can excuse it but the strength of our need." He turned to Camaris. "My friend, please forgive me. If I could do this some other way, I would. Aditu feels that we should know whether you went to the Sithi home of Jao é-Tinukai'i, and if you did, why."

Camaris raised his tired eyes to Josua's. "Is a man permitted no secrets?" he asked heavily. "I promise you, Prince Josua, that it is nothing to do with this struggle against the Storm King. On the honor of my knighthood."

"But someone who does not know all the history of our people—and Ineluki was one of us, once—may not know all the ties of blood and fable." Aditu spoke without Josua's reluctance, clearly and forcefully. "Everyone here knows you are an honorable man, Camaris, but you may not realize whether what you have seen or learned is useful."

"Will you not tell just me, Camaris?" Josua asked. "You know I hold your honor as high as my own. You certainly need not spill all your secrets to a room full of people, if that is what you fear, even though they are your friends and allies."

Camaris looked at him for a moment. His gaze seemed to soften; he struggled visibly with some impulse, but after a moment he shook his head violently. "No. A thousand pardons, Prince Josua, but to my shame I cannot. There are some things that even the Canon of Knighthood cannot drive me to."

Isgrimnur was wringing his large hands together, clearly pained by Camaris' discomfort. Tiamak had not seen the Rimmersman so unhappy since they had left Kwanitupul. "And me, Camaris?" the duke asked. "I have known you longer by far than anyone here. We both served the old king. If it is something to do with Prester John, you can share it with me."

Camaris sat straighter, but it seemed to be weak opposition to something that was bending him down inside. "I cannot, Isgrimnur. It would put too great a burden on our friendship. Please, ask me not."

Tiamak felt the tension in the room. The old knight seemed to be backed into a corner no one else could see.

"Can you not leave him alone?" Vorzheva's voice was raw. She draped her hands over her round belly as though to protect the child from so much unpleasantness and sorrow.

Why am I here? Tiamak wondered. *Because I traveled with him when he was witless? Because I am a Scrollbearer? With Geloë dead and Binabik gone, the League is a sorry collection just now. And where is Strangyeard?*

A thought suddenly came to him. "Prince Josua?"

The prince looked up. "Yes, Tiamak?"

"Forgive me. This is not my place, and I do not know all the customs . . ." he hesitated, "but you Aedonites have a tradition of confession, do you not?"

Josua nodded. "Yes."

He Who Always Steps on Sand, Tiamak prayed silently, *let me walk the right path now!*

The Wrannaman turned to Camaris. The old knight, for all his dignified bearing, looked back at him with the eyes of a hunted animal. "Could you not tell your story to a priest," Tiamak asked him, "—perhaps Father Strangyeard, if he is the proper kind of holy man? That way, if I understand things rightly, your story would be between you and God. But also, Strangyeard knows as much about the Great Swords and our struggle as any man living. He could at least tell the rest of us whether we should truly look elsewhere for answers."

Josua slapped his hand on his knee. "You are indeed a Scrollbearer, Tiamak. You have a subtle mind."

Tiamak stored Josua's compliment away to be appreciated later and kept his gaze on the old knight.

Camaris stared. "I do not know," he said slowly. His chest rose and fell as he took a long breath. "I have not told this story, even in the confessional. That is part of my shame—but not the greatest part."

"Everyone has shame, everyone has done wrong." Isgrimnur was obviously growing a little impatient. "We do not want to drag this out of you, Camaris. We only wish to know whether any dealings you might have had with the Sithi can answer some of our questions. Damn it!" he added as an afterthought.

A wintry smile moved across Camaris' face. "You were always admirably forward, Isgrimnur." The smile fell away, revealing a terrible, trapped emptiness. "Very well. Send for the priest."

"Thank you, Camaris." Josua stood up. "Thank you. He is praying at young Leleth's bedside. I will fetch him myself."

Camaris and Strangyeard had walked far down the hill together. Tiamak stood in the doorway of Josua's tent and watched them, wondering despite the praise of his cleverness if he had done the right thing. Perhaps something he had heard Miriamele say was correct: they might have done Camaris no favor by waking him from his witless state. And forcing him to dredge up such obviously painful memories seemed no kinder.

The pair, the tall knight and the priest, stood for a long time on the windy hillside—long enough for a long bank of clouds to roll past and finally reveal the pale afternoon sun. At last Strangyeard turned and started back up the hill; Camaris remained, staring out across the valley to the gray mirror of Lake Clodu. The knight seemed carved in stone, something that might wear away to a featureless post but would still be standing in that spot a century from now.

Tiamak leaned into the tent. "Father Strangyeard is coming."

The priest struggled up the hill hunched over, whether against the cold or because he now bore the burden of Camaris' secrets, Tiamak could not guess. Certainly the look on his face as he made his way up the last few ells bespoke a man who had heard things he would have been happier not knowing.

"Everyone is waiting for you, Father Strangyeard," Tiamak told him.

The archivist nodded his head distractedly. His eye was cast down, as though he could not walk without watching where he set his feet. Tiamak let him pass, then followed him into the comparative warmth of the tent.

"Welcome back, Strangyeard," said Josua. "Before you begin, tell me: how is Camaris? Should we send someone to him?"

The priest looked up in startlement, as though it was a surprise to hear a human voice. The look he gave Josua was curiously fearful, even for the timid archivist. "I . . . I do not know, Prince Josua. I do not know much . . . much of anything at this moment."

"I'll go see to him," Isgrimnur grumbled, levering himself up off the stool.

Father Strangyeard raised his hand. "He . . . wishes to be alone, I think." He fidgeted with his eye-patch for a moment, then ran his fingers through his sparse hair. "Oh, merciful Usires. Poor souls."

"Poor *souls?*" said Josua. "What are you saying, Strangyeard? Can you tell us anything?"

The archivist wrung his hands. "Camaris *was* in Jao é-Tinukai'i. That much . . . oh, my . . . that much he told me before he asked for the seal of confession, knowing that I would tell you. But the reason, and what happened there, are locked behind the Door of the Ransomer." His stare wandered around the room as if it hurt him to look at anything too long. Then his eye fell on Vorzheva, and for some reason lingered there as he talked. "But this much I can say, I believe: I do not think that his experiences have aught to do with the present situation, nor is there anything to be learned from them about the Storm King, or the Three Great Swords, or any of the other things you need to know to fight this war. Oh, merciful Usires. Oh, dear." He patted at his thin red hair again. "Forgive me. Sometimes it is hard to remember that I am merely the doorkeeper of the Ransomer, and that the burden is not mine to bear, but God's. Ah, but it is hard right now."

Tiamak stared. His fellow Scrollbearer looked as though he had been visited by vengeful spirits. The Wrannaman moved closer to Strangyeard.

"Is that all?" Josua seemed disappointed. "Are you certain that the things he knows cannot help us?"

"I am not certain of anything but pain, Prince Josua," the archivist said quietly but with surprising firmness. "But I truly think it unlikely, and I know for certain that to force anything more from that man would be cruel beyond belief, and not just to him."

"Not just to him?" Isgrimnur said. "What does that mean?"

"Enough, please." Strangyeard seemed almost angry—something Tiamak had not imagined possible. "I have told you what you needed to know. Now I would like to leave."

Josua was taken aback. "Of course, Father Strangyeard."

The priest nodded. "May God watch over us all."

Tiamak followed Strangyeard out through the tent door. "Is there something I can do?" he asked. "Perhaps just walk with you?"

The archivist hesitated, then nodded. "Yes. That would be kind."

Camaris was gone from the spot where he had stood; Tiamak looked for him, but saw no sign.

When they had traveled some way down the hill, Strangyeard spoke in a musing voice. "I understand now . . . why a man would wish to drink himself into oblivion. I find it tempting myself at this moment."

Tiamak raised an eyebrow but said nothing.

"Perhaps drunkenness and sleep are the only ways God has given us to forget," Strangyeard continued. "And sometimes forgetting is the only cure for pain."

Tiamak considered. "In a way, Camaris was as one asleep for two score years."

"And we awakened him." Strangyeard smiled sadly. "Or, I should say, God allowed us to awaken him. Perhaps there is a reason for all this. Perhaps there will be some result beside sorrow after all."

He did not, the Wrannaman thought, sound as though he believed it.

♔

Guthwulf paused and let the air wash over him, trying to decide which of the passageways led upward—for it was upward that the sword-song was leading him. His nostrils twitched, sniffing for the faintest indication from the damp tunnel air as to which way he should go. His fingers traveled back and forth along the stone walls on either side, questing like eyeless crabs.

Disembodied, alien speech washed over him once more, words that he did not hear so much as feel. He shook his head, trying to drive them from his brain. They were ghosts, he knew, but he had learned that they could not harm him, could not touch him. The chittering voices only interfered with what he truly wanted to hear. They were not real. The sword was real, and it was calling.

*   *   *

He had first felt the pull return several days before.

As he awakened into the confusion of blind solitude, as he had so many times, a thread of compelling melody had followed him up out of sleep into his waking blackness. It was more than just another of his pitiful dreams: this was a powerful feeling, frightful and yet comfortably familiar, a song without words or melody that rang in his head and wrapped him with tendrils of longing. It tugged at him so strongly that he scrambled clumsily to his feet, eager as a young swain called by his beloved. The sword! It was back, it was near!

Only as the last clinging remnants of his slumbers left him did he remember that the sword was not alone.

It was never alone. It belonged to Elias, his once-friend, now bitter enemy. Much as Guthwulf ached to be near it, to bask in its song as he would the warmth of a fire, he knew he would have to approach cautiously. Miserable as his current life was, he preferred it to what Elias would do to him if he was captured—or worse, what Elias would let that serpent Pryrates do to him.

It never occurred to him that it would be even better simply to leave the sword alone. The song of it was like the splash of a stream to a traveler dying of thirst. It drew him, and he had no choice but to follow its call.

Still, some animal cunning remained. As he felt his way through the well-learned tunnels, he knew he needed not only to find Elias and the sword, but also to approach them in such a way so as to avoid discovery and capture, as he had managed once before to spy on the king from a shelf of rock above the foundry floor. To this end, he followed the sword's compelling summons but remained at as great a distance as he could, like a hawk circling its master on a long trace. But trying to resist the complete pull was maddening. The first day he followed the sword, Guthwulf forgot completely to go to the spot where the woman regularly left food for him. By the second day—which, to the blind Earl of Utanyeat, was whatever came between one sleep and the next—the sword's call beating within him like a second heartbeat had almost dissolved the memory that such a spot even existed. He ate what crawling things his groping hands encountered, and drank from any moving trickle of water he could find. He had learned in his first weeks in the tunnels what happened when he drank from standing pools.

Now, after three sleeps full of sword-dreams, he had wandered far beyond any of the passageways familiar to him. The stones he felt beneath his hands had never met his touch before; the tunnels themselves, but for the always-present phantom voices and the equally constant pull of the Great Sword, seemed completely alien.

He had some small idea of how long he had been searching for the sword this time, and, in a rare moment of clear thinking, he wondered what the king was doing down in the hidden places beneath the castle for such a long time.

A moment later, a wild, glorious thought came to him.

He's lost the sword. He's lost it down here somewhere, and it's just sitting, waiting for whoever finds it! Waiting for me! Me!

He did not even realize that he was slavering in his dusty beard. The thought of having the sword all to himself—to touch, to listen to, to love and to worship—was so horrifyingly pleasurable that he took a few steps and then fell to the floor, where he lay quivering until darkness took his remaining senses.

After he had regained his wits, Guthwulf rose and wandered, then slept once more. Now he was awake again, and standing before the branching of two tunnels, trying to decide which one was most likely to lead him upward. He knew, somehow, that the sword was above him, just as a mole beneath the ground knows which way to dig to reach the surface. In other lucid moments he had worried that perhaps he was grown so sensitive to the sword's song that it was leading him upward to the king's very throne room, where he would be caught and slaughtered just as a mole would be if it dug its way up into the kennels.

But even though he had been moving steadily upward, he had started very deep. He felt sure the rise had not been anything so great as he feared. He was also certain that in his roundabout way he was moving ever outward, away from the core of the castle. No, the beautiful, terrifying thing that drew him, the living, singing blade, must be somewhere here beneath the earth, coffined in rock just as he was. And when he found it, he would not be lonely any more. He only had to decide which of these tunnels to follow. . . .

Guthwulf raised his hands and reflexively rubbed at his blind eyes. He felt very weak. When was the last time he had eaten? What if the woman gave up on him and stopped putting out food? It had been so nice to eat real food. . . .

But if I find the sword, if I have it all to myself, he gloated, *I won't care about any of that.*

He cocked his head. There was a scratching noise just beyond him somewhere, as though something were trapped inside the stone. He had heard that noise before—in fact, he heard it ever more frequently of late—but it was nothing to do with what he sought.

The scratching ended, and still he stood in painful indecision before the forking tunnels. Even when he put down stones for markers, it was so easy to become lost, but he was certain that one of these passages led upward to the heart of the song—the crooning, sucking, soul-drowning melody of the Great Sword. He did not want to go the wrong way and spend another endless time trying to find his way back. He was weak with hunger, numb with weariness.

He might have stood for an hour or a day. At last, beginning as gently as a dust devil, a wind came tugging at his hair, a puff of breeze from the right-hand turning. Then, a moment later, a flurry of *somethings* welled up out of the tunnel and floated past him—the spirits that haunted the dark nether-roads. Their voices echoed in his skull, dim and somehow hopeless.

. . . The Pool. We must seek him at the Pool. He will know what to do . . .

Sorrow. They have called down the final sorrow . . .

As the twittering things blew past, blind Guthwulf slowly smiled. Whatever they were, spirits of the dead or bleak products of his own madness, they always came to him out of the depths, from the deepest, oldest parts of the labyrinth. They came from below . . . and he wished to climb.

He turned and shuffled into the left-hand tunnel.

The remains of Naglimund's massive gate had been plugged with rubble, but since it was lower than the surrounding wall and the piles of broken stone offered purchase for climbing feet, it seemed to Count Eolair the logical place for an assault to begin. He had been surprised when the Sithi had concentrated themselves before a blank and undamaged stretch of wall.

He left Maegwin and the contingent of anxious mortal warriors under Isorn's command, then crept up the snowy hillside to join Jiriki and Likimeya in the shell of a broken building a few hundred ells from Naglimund's outwall. Likimeya gave him a cursory glance, but Jiriki nodded.

"It is almost time," the Sitha said. "We have called for the *m'yon rashí*—the strikers."

Eolair stared at the contingent of Sithi before the wall. They had stopped singing, but had not moved away. He wondered why they should risk the arrows of the Norns when whatever their singing was intended for seemed finished. "Strikers? Do you mean battering rams?"

Jiriki shook his head, smiling faintly. "We have no history of such things, Count Eolair. I imagine we could devise such an engine, but we decided to fall back on what we know instead." His look darkened. "Or rather, what we learned from the Tinukeda'ya." He gestured. "Look, the m'yon rashí come."

A quartet of Sithi were approaching the wall. Although he did not recognize them, Eolair thought they looked no different than the hundreds of other Peaceful Ones camped in Naglimund's shadow. All were slender and golden-skinned. Like most of their fellows, no two seemed quite alike in the color of either their armor or the hair that streamed from beneath their helms; the m'yon rashí gleamed against the snow like misplaced tropical birds. The only difference the count could see between these and any other of Jiriki's people was that each bore a dark staff long as a walking-stick. These staffs were of the same odd gray-black stuff as Jiriki's sword Indreju; each was knobbed with a globe of some blue crystalline stone.

Jiriki turned from the Hernystirman and called out an order. His mother rose from her crouch and added words of her own. A contingent of Sithi archers moved up until they surrounded the group near the walls. The bowmen nocked arrows and drew, then froze in place, eyes scanning the empty walls.

The leader of the m'yon rashí, a female Sitha with grass-green hair and armor of a slightly deeper green, lifted her stick and slowly swung it toward the wall as if she forced it against the flowing current of a river. When the blue gem struck, all the m'yon rashí chanted a single loud syllable. Eolair felt a tremor in his bones, as though a tremendous weight had struck the ground nearby. For a moment the earth seemed to shift beneath him.

"What . . . ?" he gasped, struggling to find his balance. Before him, Jiriki raised a hand for silence.

The other three Sithi stepped forward to join the woman in green. As they all chanted, each in turn brought his staff forward to strike in a rough triangle around the first; each syrup-slow impact reverberated through the earth and up through the feet of Eolair and the other observers.

The Count of Nad Mullach stared. For a dozen ells up and down the wall from where the m'yon rashí stood, the snow slid off the stones. Around the jeweled heads of the four staffs, Eolair saw that the stone had turned a lighter shade of gray, as though it had sickened somehow—or as though it were covered with a web of fine cracks.

Now the Sithi lifted their striking-rods away from the wall. Their chanting grew louder. The leader struck again, a little more swiftly this time. The silent thunder of her blow rolled through the icy ground. The rest followed suit, each strike emphasized by a loudly chanted word. As they struck for the third time, bits of stone began to shiver loose from the top of the high wall, falling down to vanish into the high snow.

The count could not contain his astonishment. "I have never seen the like!"

Jiriki turned, his high-boned face serene. "You should go back to your folk. It will be only a moment more and they should be ready."

Eolair could not take his eyes from the strange spectacle. He walked backward down the hill, steadying himself with his arms outstretched whenever the shifting ground threatened to topple him from his feet.

At the fourth impact, a great section of the wall crumbled and fell inward, leaving a hole at the top that looked as though some huge creature had taken a bite from it. Eolair at last realized the imminence of what Jiriki had told him and hurried the rest of the way down to Isorn and the waiting Hernystiri.

"Ready!" he cried. "Be ready!"

There was a fifth shuddering, the strongest yet. Eolair lost his balance and fell forward, tumbling down the hill until he rolled to a stop, his nose and mouth stinging and cold from the snow. He half-expected his troop to laugh, but they were staring wide-eyed up the hill past him.

Eolair looked back. Naglimund's great wall, as thick as the height of two men, was dissolving like a wave-struck sand castle. There was a loud rasping of stone on stone, but that was all. The wall fell down into the banks of white with an eerily muffled sound. Great gouts of snow were thrown up everywhere, so that a fog of white flakes filled the air, obscuring all.

When it cleared, the m'yon rashí had retreated. A hole a dozen ells across was opened into Naglimund and its shadows. Slowly, a sea of dark figures was filling that hole. Eyes gleamed. Spear-points glimmered.

Eolair struggled to his feet. "Men of Hernystir!" he cried. "To me! The hour has come!"

But the count's troops did not budge, and instead it was the horde within Naglimund that came surging out through the breach, swift and uncountable as termites swarming from a shattered nest.

There was a great clang of blade on shield from the Sithi ranks, then a flight of arrows hissed out, felling many of the first Norns rushing down the hillside. Some of the Norns carried bows as well, and clambered up onto the castle wall to shoot, but for the most part neither side seemed content to wait. With the eagerness of lovers, the ancient kindred rushed forward to meet each other.

The battle before Naglimund quickly became a scene of horrible confusion. Through the swirling snow, Eolair saw that more than the slender Norns had issued from the crack in the wall. There were giants, too, creatures tall as two men and covered with gray-white fur, yet armored like humans, each bearing a great club which crushed bones like dry sticks.

Before the count could even retreat toward his men, one of the Norns was upon him. Incredibly, though a helm hid most of his pale face and armor covered his torso, the black-eyed creature wore no shoes, his long feet carrying him across the powdery snow as though it were solid stone. He was swift as a lynx. As Eolair stared in amazement, he almost lost his head to the Norn's first sweeping blow.

Who could fathom such madness? Eolair pushed all thoughts but survival from his mind.

The Norn bore only a small arm shield, and with his light sword was far faster than the Count of Nad Mullach. Eolair found himself instantly plunged into a defensive struggle, wading backward down the hill, encumbered by his heavy armor and shield, almost betrayed several times by treacherous footing. He fended off several blows, but the Norn's exultant grimace told Eolair that it was only a matter of time before his sinewy opponent found a fatal opening.

Abruptly, the Norn stood straight, his jet eyes puzzled. A moment later he sagged forward and fell. A blue fletched arrow quivered in the back of his neck.

"Keep your men together, Count Eolair!" Jiriki waved his bow as he shouted from up the slope. "If they are separated from each other, they will lose heart. And remember—these foes can bleed and die!" The Sitha turned his horse and spurred back into the thick of battle; in a moment he was obscured by snow and the twisting shapes of battle.

Eolair hurried downhill toward the Hernystiri. The hillside echoed with the shrieks of horses and men and even stranger creatures.

The confusion was almost complete. Eolair and Isorn had only just managed to rally their men for a charge up the hill when two of the white giants appeared at the top of the rise, carrying between them the trunk of a tree. With a choking roar, the giants came rushing down on Eolair's men, using the tree like a scythe to crush all who were caught between them. Bones shattered and red-soaked forms vanished beneath the churned snow. A terrified Hernystirman managed to put an arrow into one giant's eye, then a few more feathered the second until it was reeling. Still, two more men were smashed to death by the flailing tree trunk before the remaining Hernystiri dragged the giant down and killed him.

Eolair looked up to see that most of the Norns were engaged with the Sithi. Horrible as was the chaos of battle, the count was still compelled to stop and stare. Never since the dawn of time had such a thing been seen, the immortals at war. Those that were visible through the snow seemed to move with a ghastly, serpentine swiftness, feinting, leaping, swinging their dark swords like they were willow wands. Many contests seemed settled before the first blow was struck; indeed, in many of the single combats, after much dancelike movement, only one blow *was* struck—the blow that ended the fight.

There was a sour skirling of pipes from atop the hillside. Eolair looked up to see what seemed to be a line of trumpeters atop the stone, their long, tubelike instruments lifted to the gray sky. But the piping noise came from some musicians in the shadows of Naglimund below, for when the Norns atop the wall puffed their cheeks and blew, what came from their tubes was not sound but a cloud of dust as orange as sunset.

Eolair watched in sickened fascination. What could it be? Poison? Or just some other incomprehensible ritual of the immortals?

As the plume of orange floated down across the hillside, the tide of battle seemed to surge and writhe beneath it—but no one fell. If poison, the count thought, it was of a more subtle sort than he had heard of. Then Eolair felt a burning in his own throat and nostrils. He gasped for breath, and for a moment thought he would surely choke and die. A moment later he could breathe again. Then the sky dropped down upon him, the shadows began to stretch, and the snow seemed to catch fire.

Eolair was filled with a fear that blossomed like a great, black, ice-cold flower. Men were screaming all around him. He was screaming, too. And the Norns that now came surging forward out of the ruined shell of Naglimund were demons that even the priests had never dreamed. The count and his men turned to run, but the Sithi behind them, merciless and golden-eyed, were just as terrifying as their corpse-white cousins.

Trapped! Eolair thought, all else subsumed in panic. *Trapped! Trapped! Trapped!*

Something grabbed him and he lashed out, scratching with his nails to pull free of the horrible thing, a monster with a great yellow-tendriled face and shrieking mouth. He raised his sword to kill it, but something else struck him from behind and he fell sideways into the cold whiteness with the monstrous thing still clutching at him, still clawing at his arms and face. He was pushed face forward into the freezing snow, and though he struggled, he could not get free.

What is happening? he suddenly thought. There were monsters, yes, giants and Norns—but nothing so near. *And the Sithi*—he remembered how ghastly they had looked, how he had been certain that they intended to trap Eolair and the other Hernystiri between themselves and the Norns, then crush the mortals—*the Sithi are not our foes . . . !*

The weight on his back had lessened. He slipped free and sat up. There was no monster. Isorn crouched in the snow beside him, hanging his head like a sick calf. Although the madness of battle still raged around him, and his own men were snapping at each other and struggling brother against brother like crazed dogs, Eolair felt the terrible fear ebbing away. He reached up and pawed at his chilled face, then held out his gloved hand and stared at the orange-tinted snow.

"The snow washed it away," he said. "Isorn! It is some poison they have blown at us! The snow washes it away!"

Isorn retched and nodded weakly. "Mine has come off, too." He gasped and spat. "I tried . . . to kill you."

"Quickly," Eolair said, struggling to his feet. "We must try and get it off the others. Come!" He scooped up an armful of snow, scraping off the thin sprinkling of orange dust, and staggered to a small knot of squealing, struggling men nearby. They were all bleeding, but most only shallowly from wounds made by nails and teeth: although the poison had maddened them, it had made them clumsy and ineffectual as well. Eolair smashed clean snow into each face he could reach.

After he and Isorn had managed to bring some semblance of sanity back to the nearest men, they hurriedly explained and sent those they had rescued off to help others. One man did not get up. He had lost both eyes and was bleeding to death, staining all the ground around him. Eolair pulled the man's cloak over his ruined face and then stooped to gather more snow.

The Sithi did not seem to be anywhere near as badly stricken by the dusty poison as Eolair and his men. Some of the immortals closest to the walls seemed dazed and slowed, but none showed symptoms of the unrestrained madness that had swept the Hernystiri. Still, the hillside was full of dreadful sights.

Likimeya and a few Sithi were surrounded by a company of Norn foot soldiers, and though Jiriki's mother and her companions were mounted and able to deal deadly blows from above, one by one they were being pulled down into a mass of white hands that waved and swayed like some terrible plant.

Yizashi Grayspear faced a howling giant who already held a crushed Sithi body in each hand. The Sitha horseman, his face as sternly impassive as a hawk's, spurred forward.

Jiriki and two others had knocked another of the giants to his knees, and now hacked at the still-living monster as though they butchered an ox. Great jets of blood fountained up, covering Jiriki and his companions in a sticky mist.

The limp body of Zinjadu, her pale-blue hair clotted with red, had been hoisted on the spears of a group of Norns as they ran back toward Naglimund's walls in triumph. Chekai'so and dark Kuroyi rode them down before they could bear their prize to safety, and each killed three of their white-skinned brethren, although both took many wounds. When they had slaughtered the Norns, Chekai'so Amber-Locks draped Zinjadu's corpse across his saddle. His own streaming blood mixed with hers as he and Kuroyi bore her back toward the Sithi camp.

★   ★   ★

The day wore on, full of madness and misery. Behind the mist and snow, the sun rose past noon and began to fall. The broken west wall of Naglimund began to glow with the light of a murky afternoon, and the snows grew even more red.

Maegwin walked along the edge of the battle like a ghost—as indeed she was. At first she had hidden behind the trees, afraid to witness such horrible things, but eventually her better sense had led her out again.

If I am dead, then what do I fear?

But it was hard to look at the bloody forms that lay scattered about the snowy hillside and not fear death.

Gods do not die, and mortals die but once, she reassured herself. *When this is settled, they will all rise again.*

But if they should all rise again, then what was the point of this battle? And if the gods could not die, then what did they fear from the demon hordes out of Scadach? It was puzzling.

Pondering, Maegwin walked slowly beside slayers and slain. Her cloak fluttered behind her, and her feet left small, even prints in the froth of white and scarlet.

35

The Third House

Simon was furious. They had walked into a trap, as sweetly and stupidly as spring lambs led to the killing block.

"Can you move your hands at all?" he whispered to Miriamele. His own wrists were bound very securely: the two Fire Dancers who had done the job had some experience with knots.

She shook her head. He could barely see her in the deepening night.

They were kneeling side by side at the center of the forest clearing. Their arms had been tied behind their backs and their ankles roped. Seeing Miriamele trussed and helpless, the idea of brute animals readied for slaughter returned and black anger rose inside Simon once more.

I'm a knight! Doesn't that mean anything? How could I let this happen?

He should have known. But he had been busy strutting like a mooncalf over the man Roelstan's compliments. "You have seen this knight wield a sword," the traitor had said. "He has naught to fear from Fire Dancers."

And I believed him. I am not fit to be a knight. I am a disgrace to Josua and Morgenes and Binabik and everyone who's ever tried to teach me anything.

Simon engaged in another futile struggle with his bonds, but the ropes held him in an unbreakable grip.

"You know something of these Fire Dancers, don't you?" he whispered to Miriamele. "What are they going to do with us? What do they mean when they say they're going to give us to the Storm King? Burn us?"

He felt Miriamele shudder against him. "I don't know." Her voice was flat, dead. "I suppose so."

Simon's terror and anger were for a moment overcome by a stab of regret. "I let you down, didn't I?" he said quietly. "Some protector."

"It's not your fault. We were tricked."

"I wish I could get my hands on that Roelstan's throat. His wife was trying to tell us something was wrong, but I was too stupid to listen. But he—*he . . . !*"

"He was frightened, too." Miriamele spoke as from a great and lofty height, as though the things of which she spoke were of little import. "I don't know if I could give my own life up to save the lives of strangers. Why should I hate those two for not being able to?"

" 'S Bloody Tree." Simon didn't have the strength to waste pity on treacherous Roelstan and Gullaighn. He had to save Miriamele somehow, had to burst these bonds and fight his way free. But he didn't have the slightest idea how to begin.

The business of the Fire Dancer camp went on around them. Several white-robed folk were tending the fire and preparing a meal; others were feeding the goats and chickens, while still others sat and talked quietly. There were even a few women and children among them. But for the two bound prisoners and the omnipresent gleam of white robes, it might have been the onset of evening in any rural steading.

Maefwaru, the Fire Dancers' leader, had taken a trio of his lieutenants into the large cottage. Simon did not much wish to think about what they might be discussing.

The evening grew deeper. The white-clad figures ate a frugal meal, none of which they offered to share with the prisoners. The fire danced and fluttered in the wind.

"Get them up." Maefwaru's eyes flicked across Simon and Miriamele, then rolled up to the blue-black sky. "It is nearing the time."

Two of his helpers dragged the prisoners to their feet. Simon's feet were numb, and it was difficult to balance with his ankles tied together; he swayed and would have fallen if the Fire Dancer behind him had not grabbed his arms and jerked him upright once more. Beside him, Miriamele also teetered. Her captor wrapped an arm around her, handling her as casually as if she had been a log.

"Don't you touch her," Simon snarled.

Miriamele gave him a tired look. "It does no good, Simon. Let it go."

The Fire Dancer at her side grinned and pawed at her breasts for a moment, but a sharp sound from Maefwaru sobered him fast. As the robed man turned to face his chief, Miriamele hung in his grasp, her face devoid of feeling.

"Idiot," Maefwaru said harshly. "These are not children's toys. They are for Him—for the Master. Do you understand?"

Miriamele's captor swallowed and nodded rapidly.

"It is time to go." Maefwaru turned and headed for the edge of the clearing.

The Fire Dancer behind Simon gave him a rough shove. Simon toppled like a felled tree. His breath flew out in a great huff and the night swam with points of light.

"Their legs are tied," the Fire Dancer said slowly.

Maefwaru whirled. "I know that! Take the ropes off their legs."

"But . . . but what if they run?"

"Tie a rope to their arms," said the leader. "Tie the other end around your waist." He shook his bald head in thinly concealed disgust.

Simon felt a flash of hope as the robed man produced a knife and bent to saw through the knots at his ankles. If Maefwaru was the only clever one, as seemed to be the case, perhaps there was some hope after all.

When he and Miriamele were both able to walk, the Fire Dancers tied ropes around both of them, then pushed them ahead as though they were balky oxen, prodding them with spear-points if they stumbled or lagged. The spears were oddly formed, short and yet slim-hafted and very sharp, not quite like anything Simon had seen before.

Maefwaru stepped through the vegetation at the edge of the clearing and disappeared, evidently leading them somewhere out of the clearing. Simon was a little relieved. He had been watching the fire for a long time and having very bad thoughts about it. At least they would be taken to some other place; it might be that their chance of escape would improve. Perhaps there would even be an opportunity as they traveled. He looked back and was dismayed to see that what seemed like the entire enclave of Fire Dancers was following them, a line of white trailing off into the gloom.

What had appeared to be solid forest was instead a well-packed trail that switched back and forth as it wound uphill. It was hard to see its progress more than a few ells ahead: the ground was thick with mist, a grayish murk that seemed to absorb sound as thoroughly as it masked sight. But for the muffled tread of two-score feet, the woods were silent. Not a nightbird sang. Even the wind had quieted.

Simon's mind was racing, but as quickly as he thought of plans for escape, he had to abandon each in turn as impossible. He and Miriamele were vastly outnumbered and in an unfamiliar place. Even if they managed to jerk themselves free from the Fire Dancers who held their ropes, they would be unable to use their arms for balance or clearing a path, and would be caught within moments.

He looked back at the princess plodding along behind him. She looked cold and miserable and drearily resigned to whatever might come. At least they had let her keep her cloak. In her only moment of spirit, she had convinced one of their captors to allow her to wear it against the night breeze. Simon had not been so lucky. His cloak had gone, along with his sword and Qanuc knife. The horses and saddlebags had been taken somewhere, too. The only things left to him now were the clothes he wore and his life and soul.

And Miriamele's life, too, he thought. *I have sworn to protect it. That is still my responsibility.*

There was some comfort in that. While he had breath in him, he had a purpose.

He was slapped in the face by a hanging branch. He spat out wet fir needles. Maefwaru was a small ghostly shape in the murk before him, leading them ever higher.

Where are we going? Perhaps it would be better if we never found out.

They stumbled on through the gray mist like damned souls trying to walk out of Hell.

★   ★   ★

It seemed they had been walking for hours. The mists had thinned a little, but the silence was still heavy, the air thick and damp. Then, as swiftly as the passing of winter twilight, they emerged from a tangle of trees and found themselves on the hilltop.

While they had passed through the shadows of the wooded hill a great wash of clouds had covered the sky overhead, extinguishing the moon and stars, so that now the only light came from a few torches and the leaping flames of a huge bonfire. The summit's sloping ground bulged with strange vast shapes, forms limned with flickering red light so that they seemed to move fitfully, like sleeping giants. Once these might have been pieces of some great wall or other large structure; now they lay scattered and broken, smothered beneath a matted carpet of vines and grass.

In the middle of the wide hilltop one piece of stone had been cut free from vegetation—a huge pale rock, angular as an ax head, that jutted to twice the height of a man. Between the high bonfire and this naked stone stood three motionless dark-robed shapes. They looked as though they had been waiting for a long time—perhaps as long as the rocks themselves had waited. As the Fire Dancers pushed the prisoners toward the center of the hill, the dark trio turned, almost in unison.

"Hail, Cloud Children!" Maefwaru shouted. "Hail to the Master's first Chosen. We have come as He wished."

The black-robed things regarded him silently.

"And we have brought more even than we promised," Maefwaru continued. "Praise to the Master!" He turned and waved to his underlings, who hurried Simon and Miriamele forward; but as they approached the bonfire and the silent watchers, the Fire Dancers slowed, then stopped and looked helplessly back to their leader.

"Tie them to that tree, there." Maefwaru gestured impatiently at the wind-gnarled corpse of a pine standing some twenty paces from the fire. "Hurry—it is almost midnight."

Simon grunted in pain as one of their captors pulled his arms behind his back to secure them to the tree. As soon as the Fire Dancers had finished and withdrawn, he edged toward Miriamele until their shoulders touched, in part because he was frightened, and hungry for a little of her warmth, but also so that they might more easily whisper without attracting attention.

"Who are those three dark ones?" he asked under his breath.

Miriamele shook her head.

The nearest of the black-robed figures slowly turned toward Maefwaru. "And these are for the Master?" it said. The words were as cold and sharp as the edge of a knife. Simon felt his legs weaken. There was an unmistakable sound to the voice, a sour yet melodic accent he had heard only in moments of terror . . . the hiss of Stormspike.

"They are," said Maefwaru, nodding his blunt head eagerly. "I dreamed of the red-haired one some moons ago. I know that the Master gave me that dream. He wants this one."

The robed thing seemed to regard Simon for a moment. "Perhaps," it said slowly. "But did you bring another as well, in case the Master has other plans for these? Did you bring blood for the Binding?"

"I did, oh, yes!" In the presence of these strange beings the cruel Fire Dancer chieftain had become as humble and ingratiating as an old courtier. "Two who tried to flee the Master's great promise!" He turned and gestured to the knot of other Fire Dancers still waiting nervously at the edge of the hilltop. There was shouting and a convulsion of activity, then a handful of the white-robed figures dragged two others forward. One of the captured pair had lost his hood in the struggle.

"God curse you!" shouted Roelstan, sobbing. "You promised that if we brought you those two we'd be forgiven!"

"You *have* been forgiven," Maefwaru said cheerfully. "I forgive you your foolishness. But you cannot escape punishment. No one flees the Master."

Roelstan collapsed, sagging to his knees while the men around him tried to tug him back onto his feet. His wife Gullaighn might have fainted; she hung limply in the arms of her captors.

Simon's heart seemed to rise into his throat; for a moment, he could not breathe. They were powerless, and there was no help to be expected this time. They would die here on this windswept hill—or the Storm King would take them, as Maefwaru had said, which would surely be unimaginably worse. He turned to look at Miriamele.

The princess seemed half-asleep, her eyes lidded, her lips moving. Was she praying?

"Miriamele! Those are Norns! The Storm King's servants!"

She ignored him, absorbed in her own thoughts.

"Damn you, Miriamele, don't do this! We have to think—we have to get free!"

"Shut your mouth, Simon!" she hissed.

He was thunderstruck. "What!?"

"I'm trying to get something." Miriamele pushed against the dead tree, her shoulders moving up and down as she fidgeted behind her back. "It's at the bottom of the pocket of my cloak."

"What is it?" Simon strained closer, until his hands could feel her fingers beneath the cloth. "A knife?"

"No, they took my knife. It's your mirror—the one Jiriki gave you. I've had it since I cut your hair." Even as she spoke, he felt the wooden frame slide free from the pocket and touch his fingers. "Can you take it?"

"What good will it do?" He gripped it as firmly as he could. "Don't let go yet, not until I've got it. There." He tugged it loose, holding it tightly in his bound hands.

"You can call Jiriki!" she said triumphantly. "You said that it was to be used in direst need."

Simon's momentary elation ebbed. "But it doesn't work that way. He doesn't just appear. It's not that kind of magic."

Miriamele was silent for a moment. When she spoke, she, too, was more subdued. "But you said it brought Aditu when you were lost in the forest."

"It took her days to find me. We don't have days, Miri."

"Try it anyway," she said stubbornly. "It can't hurt. Maybe Jiriki is somewhere close by. It can't hurt!"

"But I can't even see it," Simon protested. "How can I make it work without being able to look into it?"

"Just try!"

Simon bit back further argument. He took a deep breath, then forced himself to think of his own face as it had looked the last time he had seen it in the Sithi glass. He could remember things generally, but suddenly could not remember details—what color were his eyes, exactly? And the scar on his cheek, the burning mark of dragon's blood—how long was it? Past the bottom of his nose?

For a brief moment, as the memory of the searing pain from Igjarjuk's black blood washed through him, he thought he felt the frame of the looking glass warm beneath his fingers. A moment later, it was cold again. He tried to summon the feeling back, but was unsuccessful. He kept on fruitlessly for long moments.

"It's no use," he said wearily. "I can't do it."

"You're not trying hard enough," Miriamele snapped.

Simon looked up. The Fire Dancers were paying no attention to Miriamele or him, their interest fixed instead on the weird scene beside the bonfire. The two renegades, Roelstan and Gullaighn, had been carried to the top of the large stone and forced onto their backs. Their four captors stood atop the rock holding their ankles, so that the prisoners' heads hung down, arms dangling helplessly. "Usires Aedon!" Simon swore. "Look at that!"

"Don't look," said Miriamele. "Just use the mirror."

"I told you, I can't. And it wouldn't do any good anyway." He paused for a moment, watching the contorted, upside-down mouth of Roelstan, who was shouting incoherently. The three Norns stood before him, looking up as if at some interesting bird sitting on a branch.

"Bloody Tree," Simon swore again, then dropped the mirror to the ground.

"Simon!" Miriamele said, horrified. "Have you gone mad? Pick it up!"

He lifted his foot and ground his heel into the looking glass. It was very strong, but he hooked it over so that it was tilted against the tree, then stepped down hard. The frame did not give, but the crystalline surface broke with a faint percussive sound; for a moment, the scent of violets rose around them. Simon kicked it again, scattering transparent shards.

"You *have* gone mad!" The princess was in despair.

Simon closed his eyes. *Forgive me, Jiriki,* he thought. *But Morgenes told me any gift that cannot be thrown away is not a gift but a trap.* He crouched as deeply as he could, but the rope that held him to the trunk would not allow his fingers to reach the shattered mirror.

"Can you get to that?" he asked Miriamele.

She stared at him for a moment, then slid herself as low as she could. She, too, was several handlengths short of the goal. "No. Why did you do it?"

"It was no good to us," Simon said impatiently. "Not in one piece, anyway." He caught at one of the larger shards with his foot and dragged it closer. "Help me."

Arduously, Simon got his toe beneath the piece of crystal and tried to lift it high enough for Miriamele's abbreviated reach, but the contortion was too difficult and it slid away, tumbling to the ground once more. Simon bit his lip and tried again.

Three times the shard fell free, forcing them to begin over. Fortunately, the Fire Dancers and the black-robed Norns seemed caught up in the preparations for their ritual, whatever it might be. When Simon sneaked a glance toward the center of the clearing, Maefwaru and his minions were on their knees before the stone. Roelstan had stopped shouting; he made weak sounds and thrashed, striking his head against the stone. Gullaighn hung motionless.

This time, as the jagged thing began to slide off his boot again, Simon lurched to the side and managed to trap it against the leg of Miriamele's breeches. He pushed his own leg against it to keep it from falling, then lowered his foot to the ground before he toppled.

"Now what?" he asked himself.

Miriamele pushed against him, then slowly moved up onto her toes, lifting the shard higher along Simon's leg. It sliced through the rough cloth with surprising ease, drawing blood, but Simon remained as still as he could, unwilling to let a little pain deter them. He was impressed by Miriamele's cleverness.

When she had lifted herself as high as she could, they moved again so that the crystal fragment rested primarily on Simon, then Miriamele eased herself back down. Next it was Simon's turn. The process was excruciatingly slow, and the crystal itself seemed sharper than any normal mirror-glass. By the time the shard was almost close enough for Simon to grasp in his hand, both prisoners had legs ribboned with blood.

As he strained his fingers toward it, and found it still just beyond reach, Simon felt the hackles on his neck rise. Across the hilltop, the Norns had begun to sing.

The melody rose like a serpent rearing above its coils. Simon found himself starting to slide away into a sort of dream. The voices were cold and fearsome, but also strangely beautiful. He thought he heard the hollow echo of measureless caverns, the musical drip of slow-melting ice. He could not understand the words, but the ageless magic of the song was unmistakable. It drew him along like a subterranean stream, down, down into darkness. . . .

Simon shook his head, trying to drive the grogginess away. Neither of the captives dangling across the top of the rock was struggling now. Beneath them, the Norns had spread out until they formed a rough triangle around the jut of stone.

Simon strained against the rope as hard as he could, wincing as the hemp bit into his wrists; it tormented his flesh as though he were bound in smoldering metal. Miriamele saw the tears form in his eyes and leaned against him, pushing her head against his shoulder as though she could somehow force the pain away. Simon strained, gasping for air. At last, his fingers touched the cold edge. Just the light contact sliced his skin, but the thin bright line of pain signaled victory. Simon sighed in relief.

The Norns' song ended. Maefwaru rose from his kneeling position and made his way forward to the stone. "Now is the time," he cried. "Now the Master shall see our loyalty! It is time to call forth His Third House!"

He turned and said something to the Norns in a voice too low for Simon to hear, but Simon was paying little attention in any case. He grasped the shard of crystal in his fingers, unmindful of shedding a little more of his own blood as long as it did not make his hold too slippery, then turned and began feeling blindly for Miriamele's bound wrists.

"Don't move," he said.

Maefwaru had been given a long knife that glinted in the wavering firelight like something from a nightmare. He stepped to the rock, then reached up and grabbed Roelstan's hair, pulling it so hard that the captive's ankles were almost tugged loose from the grip of the Fire Dancers atop the rock. Roelstan raised his hands as if to fight, but his movements were horribly slow: he might have been drowning in great depths. Maefwaru pulled the blade across Roelstan's neck and stepped back, but could not avoid all the blood that spurted free; darkness spattered his face and white robe.

Roelstan thrashed. Simon stared, sickened but fascinated, as streams of blood ran down the face of the pale rock. Gullaighn, hanging upside down beside her dying husband, began to shriek. Where the red liquid pooled at the base of the stone, the ground-hugging mist turned crimson, as though the blood itself had been rendered into fog.

"Simon!" Miriamele bumped against him. "Hurry!"

He reached out to find her fingers, then followed them up to the knots around her wrists. He placed the slick fragment of crystal against the bristling rope and began to saw.

They still faced the bonfire and the bloody stone. Miriamele's eyes were wide in her pale face. "Please hurry!"

Simon grunted. It was difficult enough just keeping the crystal in his lacerated, blood-dripping hand. And what was happening in the center of the hilltop was making him even more frightened than he had been.

The red mist had spread until it surrounded and partially obscured the great stone. The Fire Dancers were chanting now, cracked voices unpleasantly echoing the poison-sweet song of the Norns.

There was a movement in the mist, a pale bulky something that Simon at first thought was the stone itself given magical life. Then it strode forward out of the reddened darkness on four huge legs and the earth seemed to shudder beneath its tread. It was a great white bull, bigger than any Simon had ever seen, taller than a man at its shoulders. Despite its solidity, it seemed oddly translucent, as though it had been sculpted from fog. Its eyes burned like coals, and its bone-hued horns seemed to cradle the sky. On its back, riding like a knight on a horse, sat a massive black-robed figure. Terror beat out from this apparition like the heat of a summer sun. Simon felt first his fingers, then his hands go nerveless, so that he could not tell if he was still holding the precious shard. All he could think of was escaping from that terrible, empty black hood. He wanted only to throw himself against the weight of his ropes until they burst, or gnaw them until he was free to run and run and run. . . .

The chanting of the Fire Dancers grew ragged, shouts of awe and terror intermixed with the ritualistic words. Maefwaru stood before his congregation, waving his thick arms in horrified glee.

"Veng'a Sutekh!" he shouted. "Duke of the Black Wind! He is come to make the Master's Third House!"

The great figure atop the bull stared down at him, then the hood turned slowly, surveying the hilltop. Its invisible eyes passed across Simon like a freezing wind.

"Oh, Usires on the T-T-Tree!" Miriamele moaned. "W-What is it?"

Strangely, for a moment Simon's madness lessened, as though the fear had become too great to sustain any longer. He had never heard Miriamele so frightened, and her horrified voice pulled him back from the brink. He realized that he still held the bit of crystal clutched between his stiffened fingers.

"It is a bad . . . a bad thing," he panted. "One of the Storm King's . . ." He caught at her wrist and began sawing away once more. "Oh, Miri, hold still."

She was gulping air. "I'll . . . try. . . ."

The Norns had turned and were speaking to Maefwaru, who alone of his congregation seemed able to stand the sight of the bull and its rider: the rest of the Fire Dancers groveled in the tangled undergrowth, their chanting now entirely given way to sobs of almost ecstatic fear. Maefwaru turned and gesticulated toward the tree where Simon and Miriamele were tied.

"They're c-coming for us," Simon stuttered. As he spoke, the shard sliced through the last strands of Miriamele's ropes. "Cut mine, quick."

Miriamele half-turned, trying to use her fluttering cloak to hide what they were doing from their captors. He could feel her vigorous movements as she dragged the edge of the crystal fragment back and forth across the thick hemp. The Norns were making their way slowly across the hilltop toward them.

"Oh, Aedon, they're coming!" Simon said.

"I'm almost through!" she whispered. He felt something gouge into his wrist, then Miriamele cursed. "I dropped it!"

Simon hung his head. So it was hopeless, then. Beside him, he felt Miriamele hastily winding her own severed rope around her wrists once more so that it would appear she was still bound.

The Norns came on, their graceful walk and billowing robes making them almost seem to float over the rough ground. Their faces were expressionless, their eyes black as the holes between stars. They converged around the tree and Simon felt his arm caught in a cold, unbreakable grip. One of the Norns severed the rope that had leashed the prisoners, then Simon and Miriamele were drawn stumbling across the hilltop toward the looming stone and the terrifying shape that had appeared from the red mist.

He felt his heart speeding as he neared the bull and its rider, racing faster with each step until he thought it would burst through the walls of his chest. The Norns who held him were frighteningly alien, implacably hostile, but the fear they inspired was as nothing before the all-crushing terror of the Storm King's Red Hand.

The Norns flung him to the ground. The bull's hooves, each wide as a barrel, were only a few cubits away. He did not want to look, wanted only to keep his face pressed against the shielding vegetation, but something drew his head inexorably upward until he was staring at what seemed a shimmer of flame in the depths of the black hood.

"We have come to raise the Third House," the thing said. Its stony voice rumbled both without and within Simon, shaking the ground and his bones as well. *"What is . . . this?"*

Maefwaru was so frightened and excited that his voice was a squeal. "I had a dream! The Master wanted this one, great Veng'a Sutekh—I know that he did!"

An invisible something abruptly grasped Simon's mind as a falcon's claws might seize a rabbit. He felt his thoughts shaken and flung about with brutal abandon, so that he fell down onto his face, shrieking with pain and horror. He only dimly heard the thing speak again.

"We remember this little fly—but it is no longer wanted. The Red Hand has other business now . . . and we need more blood before we are ready. Add this one's life to that of the others upon the Wailing Stone."

Simon rolled over onto his back and stared up at the clouded, starless sky as the world reeled about him.

No longer wanted . . . The words spun crazily in his head. Someone somewhere was calling his name. *No longer wanted . . .*

"Simon! *Get up!*"

He dimly recognized Miriamele's voice, heard its shrill terror. His head lolled. There was a form approaching him, a pale smear in his blurry sight. For an appalling moment he thought it might be the great bull, but his vision cleared. Maefwaru was stalking toward him, the long knife held up so that it glinted in the bonfire's wavering light.

"The Red Hand wants your blood," the Fire Dancer chieftain said. His eyes were completely mad. "You will help to build the Third House."

Simon struggled to free himself from the tangling grasses and clamber up onto his knees. Miriamele had thrown off her false bonds, and now flung herself toward Maefwaru. One of the Norns caught at her arm and tugged her to his black-cloaked breast, pulling her as close as a lover would—but to Simon's surprise, the immortal did no more than hold her helpless; the Norn's black eyes were intent on Maefwaru, who had continued toward Simon without sparing an instant's attention to the girl.

Everything seemed to pause; even the fire seemed to slow in its fluttering. The Red Hand, the Norns, Maefwaru's cowering followers, all stood or lay still, as if waiting. The blocky Fire Dancer chieftain raised his knife higher.

Simon tugged furiously at his restraints, straining until he thought he could feel his muscles pulling free from his bones. Miriamele had cut through part of the rope.

If only . . . if only . . .

The rope snapped. Simon's arms flew outward, and the coil slithered down his arm and dropped to the ground. Blood dribbled down his wrists and hands where the shard had cut him, the ropes had scored him.

"Come, then," he gasped, and lifted his hands before him. "Come and get me."

Maefwaru laughed. Beads of sweat stood out on his brow and bald scalp. The thick muscles of his neck jumped as he pulled another knife from inside his robe. For a moment Simon thought the Fire Dancer was going to throw it to him, to make it a fair fight, but Maefwaru had no such intentions. A blade in each hand, he took another step toward Simon. He stumbled, caught himself, then strode forward another pace.

A moment later Maefwaru straightened up, bringing his hands to his neck so suddenly that he gashed himself with his own knife. His furious joy turned to puzzlement, then his legs folded beneath him and he toppled forward into the undergrowth.

Before Simon could make sense of what was happening, a shadowy form flew past him and struck the Norn who prisoned Miriamele, knocking the white-skinned thing to the ground. The princess tumbled free.

"*Simon!*" someone shouted. "*Take the knife!*"

Dazed, Simon saw the long blade that still gleamed in Maefwaru's fist. He dropped to a knee—the night air was suddenly full of strange noises, growls and shouts and a strange rumbling hum—and tugged it loose from the Fire Dancer's death-grip, then stood up.

Even as his two fellows hurried to his aid, the Norn who had held Miriamele was rolling on the ground with a gray, snarling something. The princess had crawled away; now, as she saw Simon, she scrambled to her feet and ran toward him, tripping on clinging vines and leaf-hidden stones.

"*Here, come here!*" someone shouted from the edge of the hilltop. "*This is the way!*"

As Miriamele reached him, Simon grabbed her hand and ran toward the voice. A pair of Fire Dancers leaped up to stop them, but Simon slashed one with Maefwaru's knife, opening a red wound through the white robe; Miriamele escaped the other, scratching at the man's panicky face as she pulled free of his grasp. The rumbling roar of the thing atop the bull—it was speaking, Simon realized, but now he could no longer understand it—grew until Simon's head hammered.

"Over here!" A small figure had emerged from the trees at the edge of the hilltop. The roiling bonfire painted the little man in flame-colored light.

"Binabik!"

"Run to me," the troll cried. "With swiftness, now!"

Simon could not help taking a look back. By the sacrificial stone, the great bull snorted and pawed at the ground, tearing great furrows in the damp earth. Ineluki's servitor was glowing, red light leaking through the black robes, but it made no move to pursue Simon and Miriamele, as though reluctant to leave the circle of blood-drenched ground. One of the Norns lay with its neck ragged and red; another was sprawled nearby, a victim of one of the troll's darts. The third black-robed figure was struggling with whatever had torn out its fellow's throat. But the Fire Dancers were finally gathering their wits, and as Simon watched, half a dozen of Maefwaru's followers turned to follow the escaping prisoners. An arrow flew past Simon's ear and vanished into the trees.

"Down here," Binabik said, hopping nimbly ahead of them down the hill. He gestured for Simon and Miriamele to move past him, then stopped and raised his hands to his mouth. *"Qantaqa!"* he shouted. *"Qantaqa sosa!"*

As they plunged down the hillside into the trees, the confusing roar grew slightly less behind them. Before they had taken a score of steps, two shapes loomed before them in the mist—two horses.

"They are tied with looseness," the troll called down to them. "Climb and ride!"

"Here, Binabik, ride with me," Simon panted.

"There is no need," he replied. Simon looked up to see a large gray shape appear on the foggy rise just above Binabik. "Brave Qantaqa!" Binabik grabbed the wolf's hackles and pulled himself up onto her back.

The noise of pursuit was rising again. Simon fumbled with the reins, pulling them free at last. Beside him, Miriamele dragged herself up by her saddle horn. Simon struggled onto his horse's back—it was Homefinder! After all the other mad things that had happened, Simon was so astonished to be reunited with his horse that he simply stopped thinking. Qantaqa leaped past with Binabik on her back, loping rapidly down the hillside. Simon clutched Homefinder's neck and dug in his heels, following the wolf's bobbing tail through the clutching branches, down into darker shadows.

The night had become a sort of waking dream, a blur of twisted trees and damp murk; when Binabik finally stopped, Simon was not sure how long they had been traveling. They were still on the hill slope, but in deep trees, cut off from even a sight of the cloudy sky. The darkness had become so thick that they had been moving at a walk for some time, Simon and Miriamele straining to see Qantaqa's gray form though the wolf was only cubits ahead of them.

"Here," Binabik said quietly. "Here is shelter."

Simon dismounted and followed the sound of his voice, leading Homefinder by the reins.

"Be keeping your head low," the troll said. There was an echo behind his words.

The damp, spongy ground gave way to something drier and more firmly packed. The air was musty.

"Now, stop where you are standing." Binabik fell silent but for some rustling noises. Long moments passed. Simon stood and listened to his own heavy breathing. His heart was still pounding, his skin still damp with cold sweat. Could they really be safe? And Binabik! Where had he come from? How had he arrived, so improbably, so fortunately?

There was a hiss and a flicker, then a blossom of flame rose at the end of a torch clutched in the troll's small hand. The light revealed a long, low cavern, its farthest end out of sight around a bend in the rock.

"Deeper in we are going," he said. "But it would not be safe for traveling in here with no light."

"What is this place?" Miriamele asked. The sight of her bloodied legs and pale, frightened face made Simon's heart cinch in pain.

"A cave, only." Binabik smiled, a welcome and familiar baring of yellow teeth. "Trust it for a troll to be finding a cave." He turned and gestured for them to follow. "Soon you can rest."

The horses balked at first, but after a few moments' soothing they allowed themselves to be led on. The cave was strewn with dry branches and leaves. Here and there the bones of small animals winked up from the litter on the floor. Within a few hundred paces they had reached the innermost end, a grotto that was a little loftier and a great deal wider than the outer tunnel. At one end a sheet of water ran down a flat stone and drizzled into a small pool; Simon tethered Miriamele's steed and Homefinder to a stone beside it.

"Here we will make our home for the evening," said Binabik. "The wood I have left here is dry, and the smoke it is making will not be great." He pointed up to a dark crevice in the roof. "I was making a fire here last night. The smoke is carried up there, so breathing is possible."

Simon sank down onto the floor. The dry brush crackled beneath him. "What about the Norns and the others?" At this moment he didn't really much care. If they wanted him, they could come and get him. Every inch of his body seemed to throb painfully.

"I am doubting they will find this place, but I am doubting even more they will be searching long." The troll began piling wood atop the ashes in the circle of stones he had made the night before. "The Norns were at some great task, and seemed to need you only for your blood. I am thinking that there will be blood enough among those remaining mortals for the task to be completed."

"What did they want, Binabik?" Miriamele's eyes were fever-bright. "What were they saying about the Third House? And what was that . . . that thing?"

"That fearsome thing was one of the Red Hand," Binabik said, his matter-of-fact tone betrayed by the worried look on his face. "I have never seen with my eyes anything like it, although Simon was telling me stories." He shook his head, then took his flint to put a spark to the wood. "I do not know what its purpose was, although it seems clear to me that it was doing the Storm King's bidding. I will think on that more." As the fire caught, he lifted his pack and began to search in it. "Now, let me be cleaning those cut places you both have."

Simon sat quietly as the troll dabbed at Miriamele's various wounds with a damp rag and rubbed something from a small pot on each. By the time it was his turn, Simon felt his eyes drooping. He yawned.

"But how did *you* get here, Binabik?" He winced as the little man probed a painful spot. "What . . . what . . . ?"

The troll laughed. "There will be time enough for all telling soon. First, though, food and sleeping are needed." He eyed them both. "Perhaps first sleeping, then food?" He rose to his feet and dusted his hands off on his wide breeches. "There is something you will be pleased to see." He pointed to something lying in the darkness near where Homefinder and Miriamele's mount stood drinking from the pool.

"What?" Simon stared. "Our saddlebags!"

"Yes, and with your sleeping-beds still upon them. A luckiness it was for me that the Fire Dancers had not removed them. I left them here when I followed you up the hill. It was a risk, but I did not know what might be in them that would be bad for losing." He laughed. "Neither did I wish to make you ride laden horses in the dark."

Simon was already dragging loose his bedroll and examining the saddlebags. "My sword!" he said, delighted. Then his face fell. "I had to break Jiriki's mirror, Binabik."

The little man nodded. "That I was seeing. But I doubt I could have helped your escaping if you had not freed your hands. A sad but clever sacrifice, friend Simon."

"And my White Arrow," he mused. "I left that back at Sesuad'ra." He tossed Miriamele her bedroll, then found a relatively smooth place to unroll his own. "I have not taken very good care of my gifts. . . ."

Binabik smiled a tiny smile. "You are having too much worry. Sleep for a while now. I will wake you later with something warm to eat." He returned to the task of building the fire. The torchlight played on his round face.

Simon looked at Miriamele, who had already curled up and closed her eyes.

She did not seem too badly hurt, although she was clearly as exhausted as he. So they had survived, somehow, after all. He had not failed his pledge.

He sat up suddenly. "The horses! I have to unsaddle them!"

"I will be doing all," Binabik assured him. "It is time for your resting."

Simon lay back on the bedroll and watched the shadows playing along the cavern roof. Within moments he was asleep.

36

A Wound in the World

✲

Simon awakened to the delicate patter of falling water.
He had been dreaming about being caught in a ring of fire, flames that
seemed to grow closer and closer. Somewhere outside the fiery circle, Rachel
the Dragon had been calling him to come and do his chores. He had tried to
tell her that he was trapped, but smoke and ashes had filled his mouth.

The water sounded as lovely as morningsong in the Hayholt chapel. Simon
crawled across the rustling cavern floor and dipped his hands in the pool, then
stared at his palms for a moment, unable to tell by the light of the low fire
whether the water looked safe. He smelled it and touched it briefly with his
tongue, then drank. It was sweet and cold. If it was poisonous, then he was
willing to die that way.

Mooncalf. The horses drank from it, and Binabik used it to wash our cuts.

Besides, even poisoning would be preferable to the doom that had almost
been theirs . . . last night?

The cold water made the wounds on his wrists and hands sting. All his muscles ached, and his joints were stiff and sore. Still, he did not feel quite as dreadful as he might have expected to. Perhaps he had been asleep longer than a few
hours—it was impossible to tell what time of day it might be. Simon looked
around the cavern, searching for clues. How long had he slept? The horses still
stood quietly nearby. On the far side of the campfire he could see Miriamele's
golden hair peeping out from beneath her cloak.

"Ah, Simon-friend!"

He turned. Binabik was trotting up the tunnel toward the central chamber,
his hands cupped before him. "Greetings," said Simon. "And good morning—
if it *is* morning."

The troll smiled. "It is indeed that time, although the middle-day will be soon
arriving. I have just been out in the cold and misted woods, stalking a most elusive
game." He held up his hands. "Mushrooms." He walked to the fire and spilled his
treasures out on a flat stone, then began sorting through them. "Gray-cap, here.
And this is being a rabbit-nose—and tasting far better than any true rabbit's nose,
I am thinking, as well as having much less messiness to prepare." He chortled. "I
will cook these and we will break our fast with great enjoyment."

Simon grinned. "It's good to see you, Binabik. Even if you hadn't rescued us, it would be very good to see you."

The troll cocked an eyebrow. "You both did much to make your own rescuing, Simon—and that is a fortunate thing, since you seem to be flinging yourself constantly into odd troubles. You said once that your parents were being common folk. It is my thought that at least one of them was not a person at all, but a moth." He smiled wryly and gestured toward the fire. "You are always heading toward the nearest burning flame."

"It does seem that way." Simon found himself a seat on an outcropping of stone, shifting gingerly to find the least painful position. "So now what do we do? How did you find us?"

"As to what thing we should be doing," Binabik wrinkled his brow in concentration as he cut up mushrooms with his knife, " 'eat' is being my suggestion. I decided that it would be more kindness to let you sleep than to wake you. You must now be feeling great hungriness."

"Great hungriness," Simon affirmed.

"As to the other question, I think I will be waiting until Miriamele is also awake. Much as I enjoy talking, I do not want to be telling all my stories twice."

"If you wanted me awake," Miriamele said crossly from her bedroll, "then talking so loud is just the way to go about it."

Binabik was unperturbed. "We have made a favor for you, then, for I will soon have food for you both. There is clean water here for washing, and if you wish to go outside, I have looked around with care and there does not seem anyone about."

"Oh," Miriamele groaned. "I hurt." She dragged herself off her bedroll, wrapped her cloak about her, then staggered out of the cavern.

"She isn't very cheerful in the mornings," Simon offered with some satisfaction. "Not used to getting up early, I suppose." He had never liked getting out of bed much either, but a scullion was given little say over how early he would rise or when he would work, and Rachel had always made it quite clear that sloth was the greatest of all sins.

"Who would be having much cheer after what you went through last night?" said Binabik, frowning. He tossed the mushroom bits into a pot of water, added some powdery substance from a pouch, then set the pot on the outermost edge of the coals. "I am surprised that the things you have been seeing in this year gone past have not made you mad, Simon, or at least trembling and fearful always."

Simon thought about this for a moment. "I do get frightened sometimes. Sometimes it all seems so *big*—the Storm King, and the war with Elias. But all I can do is what is in front of me." He shrugged. "I'll never understand it all. And I can only die once."

Binabik looked at him shrewdly. "You have been talking to Camaris, my knightly friend. That sounds with great similarity to his Canon of Knighthood— although the words have true Simon-like humbleness." He peered into his pot and agitated the contents with a stick. "Just a few things to add, then I will be leaving it to itself for a time." He tossed in a few strips of dried meat, chopped a small and rather lopsided onion into pieces and added those as well, then gave the mixture another stir.

When he had finished this chore, the troll turned and pulled his hide bag close to him, rummaging through it with an air of great concentration. "There is something in here I thought might give you interest . . ." he said absently. After a few moments, he pulled a long parcel wrapped in leaves out of the sack. "Ah. Here."

Simon took it, knowing it by the feel even before it was unwrapped. "The White Arrow!" he breathed. "Oh, Binabik, thank you! I was sure I had lost it."

"You did lose it," said the troll dryly. "But since I was coming for visiting you in any case, it seemed that I might as well be carrying it along."

Miriamele reentered. Simon held up his prize. "Look, Miri, my White Arrow! Binabik brought it!"

She gave it barely a glance. "That was kind, Simon. I'm glad for you."

He stared at her as she made her way to her saddlebags and began searching for something. What had he done to make her mad now? The girl was more changeable than weather! And wasn't *he* supposed to be upset with *her*?

Simon snorted quietly and turned back to Binabik. "Are you going to tell us how you found us?"

"Patience!" Binabik waved a stubby paw. "Let us have our food and a little peace, first. Princess Miriamele has not even come for joining us yet. And there is other news as well, some of it not happy." He bent over his sack and rooted some more. "Ah. Here they are." The troll produced yet another parcel, a small drawstring bag. He upended it and his knucklebones tumbled out onto a flat rock. "While we are waiting, I will find what the bones may be telling me." The bones made a soft clicking noise as he gentled them in his hands then tipped them out onto the stone. He squinted.

"The Shadowed Path." The troll grinned sourly. "That is not the first time I have been seeing that." He rolled them out again. "The Black Crevice." Binabik shook his head. "Still we are having that, as well." He shook the bones for a final time and spilled them before him. *"Chukku's Stones!"* His voice was unsteady.

"Is Chukku's Stones a bad throw?" Simon asked.

"It is a cursing word," Binabik informed him. "I was using it because I have never been seeing this pattern of bones." He leaned closer to the pile of yellowed objects. "A little like Wingless Bird," he said. "But not." He lifted one of the bones, which was delicately perched on two of its fellows, then took a deep breath. "Could this be Mountains Dancing?" He looked up at Simon, eyes bright, but not in a way Simon liked. "I have never been seeing it, and have not known anyone who was seeing it. But I think I was hearing of it once, when Ookequk my master talked to a wise old woman from Chugik Mountain."

Simon shrugged helplessly. "What does it mean?"

"Changing. Things changing. Large things." Binabik sighed. "If it is indeed

Mountains Dancing. If I had my scrolls, I could perhaps be discovering with sureness." He swept up the bones and dropped them back into their pouch; he seemed more than a little frightened. "It is a throw that has only been appearing a few times ever since the Singing Men of Yiqanuc have written their lives and learning on hides."

"And what happened?"

Binabik put the pouch away. "Let me wait before more talking, Simon. I must be thinking on this."

Simon had never taken the troll's bone oracles too seriously—they had always seemed as general and unhelpful as a fortune-reader from a traveling fair—but he was shaken now by Binabik's obvious uneasiness.

Before he could press the troll for more information, Miriamele returned to the fire and sat down. "I'm not going back," she said without preamble. Binabik, like Simon, was taken by surprise.

"I am not understanding your meaning, Princess Miriamele."

"Yes, you do. My uncle sent you to bring me back. I'm not going." Her face was as hard and determined as Simon had ever seen it. Now he understood her preoccupation. He also felt more than a little anger. Why was she always so stubborn, so cross? It almost seemed she enjoyed pushing people away from her with words.

Binabik spread his palms in the air. "I could not make you do anything that was not your wanting, Miriamele—and I would not try such doing." His brown eyes were full of concern. "But, yes, your uncle and many others worry for you. They worry about your safeness, and they worry about what you plan. I will *ask* you to be coming back . . . but making I cannot do."

Miriamele looked slightly relieved, but her jaw was still set. "I'm sorry, Binabik, if you have traveled so far for nothing, but I am not returning. I have something to do."

"She wants to tell her father that this whole war is a mistake," Simon muttered sullenly.

Miriamele gave him a look of disgust. "That's not why I'm going, Simon. I told you the reason." She haltingly explained to Binabik her ideas about what might have led Elias to the clutches of the Storm King.

"I am thinking you may indeed have discovered his mistake," Binabik said when she had finished. "It is close to some of my own supposing—but that does not mean that there is any likeliness you will be succeeding." He frowned. "If your father has been brought close to the Storm King's power, whether by the trickiness of Pryrates or something else, he may be like a man who drinks too much *kangkang*—telling him that his family is starving and his sheep are wandering away may not be heard." He laid a hand on Miriamele's arm. She flinched, but did not pull away. "Also—and this is a hard thing for my heart to be saying—it is perhaps true that your father the king *cannot* anymore survive without the Storm King. The sword Sorrow is a thing of great power, a strong, strong thing. Perhaps if it is taken from him, he will go sliding into madness."

Miriamele's eyes welled with tears, but her expression remained grim. "I am not trying to take the sword from him, Binabik. Only to tell him that things have gone too far. My father—my *real* father—would not have wanted so much harm to come from his love for my mother. Everything that has happened since must be the work of others."

Binabik raised his hands again, this time in resignation. "*If* you have guessed the reasons for his madness, for this war, for his pact with the Storm King. And if he can be hearing you. But as I told you, I cannot stop your journey. I can only accompany you to help keep you from harm."

"You're going to come with us?" Simon asked. He was very pleased and strangely relieved to think that someone else would share what felt like a heavy burden.

The troll nodded, but his smile was long gone. "Unless you are to be returning with me to Josua, Simon? That might be reason for not going on."

"I have to stay with Miriamele," he pronounced firmly. "I gave my oath as a knight."

"Even though I didn't ask for it," said Miriamele.

Simon felt a moment's angry pain, but remembered the Canon of Knighthood and mastered himself. "Even though you didn't ask for it," he repeated, glowering at her. Despite the terrible times they had shared, she seemed determined to hurt him. "I still have my duty. And," he said to Binabik, "if Miriamele is going to the Hayholt, *I'm* going to Swertclif. Bright-Nail is there, and Josua needs it. But I can't think of any way to get into the castle to get Sorrow," he added reflectively.

Binabik sat back and let loose a weary sigh. "So Miriamele is going to the Hayholt to plead with her father for stopping the war, and you are going there to be rescuing one of the Great Swords, just your single knightly self?" He leaned forward suddenly and dragged the stirring stick through the mixture simmering in the pot. "Are you hearing how like younglings you sound? I was thinking you were both wiser after your many dangers and almost-dyings than to take such things on yourselves."

"I'm a knight," said Simon. "I'm not a child any more, Binabik."

"That is just meaning that the damage you can be doing is greater," the troll said, but his tone was almost conciliatory, as though he knew he could not win the argument. "Come, let us be eating. This is still a happy meeting, even if the times are those of unhappiness."

Simon was relieved to have the argument end. "Yes, let's eat. And you still haven't told us how you found us."

Binabik gave the stew another stir. "That and other news when you have been eating your food," was all he said.

When the sound of contented chewing had slowed a little, Binabik licked his fingers and took a deep breath. "Now that your stomachs at least are full, and we are safe, there is grim news that needs telling."

As Simon and Miriamele sat in growing horror, the troll described the Norns' attack on the camp and its aftermath.

"Geloë dead?" Simon felt as though the earth was eroding beneath him; soon there would be nowhere safe left to stand. "Curse them! They are demons! I should have been there! A knight of the prince . . . !"

"It is perhaps true you should both have been there," Binabik said gently, "or at least that you two should not have left. But you could have done nothing, Simon. Everything was happening with great suddenness and silence, and only one target there was."

Simon shook his head, furious with himself.

"And Leleth." Miriamele rubbed away tears. "That poor child—she has had nothing but pain."

After they had sat in mournful silence for a while, Binabik spoke again. "Let me now be speaking of a less sad thing—how I was finding you. In truth, there is not a great deal for telling. Qantaqa it was who did the most of the tracking. She has a cunning nose. My only fear would be that we would fall too far behind—horses are traveling faster than wolves over long distances—and that the smells would grow too old. But our luck held.

"I was following you into the edge of Aldheorte Forest, and there things grew muddled for some time. I had the most worry that we would lose you in that place, since it was slow going, and then it was raining, too. But clever Qantaqa managed to keep your trail."

"Was it you, then?" Simon asked suddenly. "Were you the one who was skulking around our camp in the forest?"

The troll looked puzzled. "I am not thinking it was. When did this thing happen?"

Simon described the mysterious lurker who had approached the camp and then retreated into darkness.

Binabik shook his head. "It was not me. I would not have been talking to myself, although perhaps I might have been saying words to Qantaqa. But I am promising you," he drew himself up proudly, "Qanuc do not make so much noise. Especially in the forest at night. Very concerned with not becoming a meal for something large, we Qanuc are." He paused. "And the time is wrong, also. We would have been a day or two days at least behind you then. No, it was doubtless one of the things you were guessing, a bandit or a forest cotsman." Still, he considered for a few moments before continuing with his tale.

"In any manner, Qantaqa and I followed you. We were forced to make our hunting secret—I had no wish for riding Qantaqa into a large town like Stanshire—so I could only have hope that you were coming out of these places again. We wandered about on the outskirts of the large settlements trying to find your track. Several times I thought that I had made it too difficult for Qantaqa's scenting, but always she found you again." He scratched his head, contemplating. "I suppose that if you had not emerged, I would have then been forced to go searching for you. I am glad I did not need to do that thing—I would have had to leave Qantaqa out in the wildlands, and I would have myself been an easy target for Fire Dancers or frightened villagers who had never been seeing a troll." He smiled slyly. "The people of Stanshire and Falshire have *still* not seen a troll."

"When did you find us?"

"If you think on it, Simon, you will be guessing very easily. I had no reason to hide from you, so I would have been greeting you as soon as I came upon you—unless some reason there was not to."

Simon considered. "Because we were with someone you didn't know?"

The troll nodded, satisfied. "Exactly. A young man and woman may be traveling in Erkynland and speaking to strangers without too much attention. A troll may not."

"So it must have been when we were with that man and woman—the Fire Dancers. We met other people, but we were alone each time afterward."

"Yes. I came upon you here in Hasu Vale—I had been making camp in this very cave the night before—and followed you and that pair up into the hills. Qantaqa and I were watching all from the trees. We saw the Fire Dancers." He frowned. "They have become numerous and unafraid—by spying on other travelers along the road and listening to their gossip I was learning that. So I saw what these Fire Dancers did, and when they were taking you to the hilltop, I freed your horses and followed." He grinned, pleased with his own cleverness.

"Thank you, Binabik," Miriamele said. Some of her earlier frosty manner had disappeared. "I haven't said that yet."

He smiled and shrugged. "We all are doing what we can when we are able. As I was once before telling Simon, we three have saved each other's lives enough times that the tallying is no longer important." As he picked up a hank of moss and began to scrub his bowl, Qantaqa strode silently into the cavern. Her fur was wet; she shook herself, sending a fine spray of droplets everywhere.

"Ah." Binabik placed the bowl on the floor before the wolf. "*You* may be performing this task, then." As Qantaqa's pink tongue scoured out the last bits of stew, the troll stood up. "So, that is the telling. Now, if we are going carefully, I think we can leave this place today. We will stay away from the road until Hasu Vale is being safely behind."

"And the Fire Dancers won't find us?" Miriamele asked.

"After the last night's doings, I am doubting that there are many left, or that they are wishing to do much of anything but hide. I am thinking that the Storm King's servant gave them as much fright as it gave to you." He bent to begin picking up. "And now their chieftain is dead."

"That was one of your black-tipped darts," Simon said, remembering Maefwaru's puzzled expression as he clutched at his throat.

"It was."

"I'm not sorry." Simon went to tie up his bedroll. "Not sorry at all. So you're really going to come with us."

Binabik thumped his chest with the heel of his hand. "I am not believing what you do is wise or good. But I cannot be letting you go off when I might be able to help you survive." He frowned, pondering. "I wish there was some way for sending a message back to the others."

Simon remembered the trolls in Josua's camp, and especially Sisqi, the loved one Binabik must have left behind to come here. The magnitude of the little man's sacrifice struck him and he was suddenly ashamed. Binabik was right: Simon and Miriamele were behaving like wayward children. But one look at the princess convinced him that she could no more be talked out of this than the waves could be argued out of crashing onto the beach—and he could not imagine himself leaving her to face her fate alone. Like Binabik, he was trapped. He sighed and picked up the bedroll.

Either Binabik was a good guide or the Fire Dancers had, in fact, given up looking for them. They saw nothing living during their afternoon's journey through the damp, thick-forested hills of Hasu Vale except for a few jays and a single black squirrel. The woods were densely crowded with trees and ground plants, and every trunk was blanketed in spongy moss, but the land still seemed strangely inactive, as though everything that lived there slept or waited silently for the intruders to pass.

An hour after sunset they made camp beneath a rocky overhang, but the accommodations were far less pleasant than the dry and secret cave. When the rains came and water ran streaming down the hillside, Simon and the others were forced to huddle as far back under the overhang as they could. The horses, appearing none too pleased, were tethered at the front where they were inter- mittently lashed by rain. Simon hoped that since horses often stood in fields during bad weather, they would not suffer too badly, but he felt obscurely guilty. Surely Homefinder, a knight's companion, deserved better treatment?

After she hunted, Qantaqa came and curled herself against all three of them as they huddled in a row, making up with the warmth she provided for the strong smell of damp wolf that filled the shelter. They fell asleep at last, then awakened at dawn, stiff and sore. Binabik did not want to light a fire in such an exposed place, so they ate a little dried meat and some berries the troll gathered, then set out again.

It was a difficult day's traveling, the hillsides and dales slippery with mud and wet moss, the rain blowing up in sudden squalls that lashed them with water and slapped branches into their faces; when the rain ceased, the mist crept back in, hiding treacherous pitfalls. Their progress was achingly slow. Still, Simon was impressed that his trollish friend could find a way at all with no sun visible and the road far away and out of sight.

Sometime after noon Binabik led them along the hillside past the outskirts of the town of Hasu Vale itself. It was difficult to make out much more through the close-knit trees than the shapes of some rough houses, and—when the mist was momentarily cleared by a stiff wind—the snaking course of the road, a dark streak some furlongs away. But the town seemed just as muted and lifeless as the forest: nothing but gray mists rose around the smoke holes of the cottages, and there was no sign of people or animals.

"Where has everyone gone?" Miriamele asked. "I have been here. It was a lively place."

"Those Fire Dancers," Simon said grimly. "They've scared everyone away."

"Or perhaps it is the things with which the Fire Dancers have been making celebration on the hilltops at night," Binabik pointed out. "It is not necessary, I am thinking, to *see* those things, as you two were seeing, to know that something is wrong. It is a feeling in the air."

Simon nodded. Binabik was right. This entire area felt much like Thisterborg, the haunted hill between the forest and Erchester, the place where the Anger Stones stood . . . the place where the Norns had given Sorrow to King Elias. . . .

He did not like thinking about that horrible night, but for some reason the memory suddenly seemed important. Something was pulling at him, scattered thoughts that wanted to be fit together. The Norns. The Red Hand. Thisterborg. . . .

"What's that?" Miriamele cried in alarm. Simon jumped. Homefinder startled beneath him and slipped a little in the mud before finding her footing.

A dark shape had appeared in the mist before them, gesticulating wildly. Binabik leaned forward against Qantaqa's neck and squinted. After a long, tense moment, he smiled. "It is nothing. A rag caught by the wind. Someone's lost shirt, I am thinking."

Simon squinted, too. The troll was correct. It was a tattered bit of clothing wrapped around a tree, the sleeves fluttering in the wind like pennants.

Miriamele made the sign of the Tree, relieved.

They rode on. The town vanished into the thick greenery behind them as quickly and completely as if the wet, silent woods had swallowed it.

They camped that evening in a sheltered gully at the base of the valley's western slope. Binabik seemed preoccupied; Simon and Miriamele were both quiet. They ate an unsatisfying meal and made some small talk, then everyone took refuge in the darkness and the need to sleep.

Simon again felt the awkward distance that existed now between himself and Miriamele. He still did not quite know what to feel about the things she had told him. She was no maiden, and it was by her own choice. That was painful enough, but the way she had told him, the manner in which she had lashed out at him as though to punish, was even more infuriatingly confusing. Why was she so kind to him sometimes, so hateful at others? He would have liked to believe that she was playing the come-hither, go-away games that young court women were taught to play with men, but he knew her too well: Miriamele was not one for that kind of frippery. The only solution that he could find to this puzzle was that she truly wanted him for a friend, but was afraid that Simon wanted more.

I do *want more,* he thought miserably. *Even if I won't ever have it.*

He did not fall asleep for a long time, but instead lay listening to the water pattering through the leaves to the forest floor. Huddled beneath his cloak, he probed at his unhappiness as he might at a wound, trying to find out how much pain came with it.

By the middle of the next afternoon they climbed out of the valley, leaving Hasu Vale behind. The forest still stretched out at their right hands like a great green blanket, vanishing only at the horizon. Before them was the hilly grass country that lay between the Old Forest Road and the headlands at Swertclif.

Simon could not help wishing that this journey with Binabik and Miriamele could be more like the first heady days they had traveled together after leaving Geloë's lake house, so many months ago. The troll had been full of songs and silliness during that journey; even the princess—pretending then to be the servant girl Marya—had seemed excited and happy to be alive. Now the three of them went forward like soldiers marching toward a battle they did not expect to win, each immersed in private thoughts and fears.

The empty, rolling country north of the Kynslagh did not inspire much cheer in any case. It was fully as dreary and lifeless as Hasu Vale, equally as wet, but did not afford the hiding places, and security to be found in the densely forested valley. Simon felt that they were terribly exposed, and could not help marveling at the astonishing courage—or stupidity, or both—of walking virtually unarmed into the High King's gateyard. If there were left any scrap of the companions or their tale when these dark times had someday passed, surely it would make a wonderful, unbelievable song! Some future Shem Horsegroom, perhaps, might tell some wide-eyed scullion: *"Do ye listen, lad, whilst I tell ye of Brave Simon and his friends, them who rode open-eyed and empty-handed into the very Jaws of Darkness. . . ."*

Jaws of Darkness. Simon liked that. He had heard that in a song of Sangfugol's.

He suddenly thought of what that darkness really meant—the things he had seen and felt, the dreadful, clutching shadows waiting beyond the light and warmth of life—and his skin went shudderingly cold from head to foot.

It took them two days to ride across the hilly meadowlands, two days of mist and frequent cold rains. No matter which direction they traveled, the winds seemed always to be blowing into their faces. Simon sneezed the entirety of the first night and felt warm and unstable as melting candle wax. He was a bit recovered by morning.

In mid-afternoon of the second day, the headlands of Swertclif appeared before them, the raw edge of the high, rocky hill on whose summit the Hayholt perched. As he stared into the twilight, Simon thought he could see an impossibly slim white line looming beyond Swertclif's naked face.

It was Green Angel Tower, visible even though it stood the better part of a league beyond the nearest side of the hill.

Simon felt something tingle up his back, lifting the hairs on the nape of his neck. The tower, the great shining spike that the Sithi had built when the castle was theirs, the tower where Ineluki had lost his earthly life—it was waiting, still waiting. But it was also the site of Simon's own boyhood wanderings and imaginings. He had seen it, or something like it, in so many dreams since he had left his home that now it almost seemed like just another dream. And below it, out of sight beyond the cliff, lay the Hayholt itself. Tears welled up in Simon, but only dampened his eyes. How many times had he yearned for those mazy halls, the gardens and scullion hiding-holes, the warm corners and secret pleasures?

He turned to look at Miriamele. She, too, was staring fixedly into the west, but if she thought of the pleasures of home, her face did not show it. She looked like a hunter who had finally run a dangerous but long-sought quarry to ground. He blinked, ashamed that she might see him tearful.

"I wondered if I'd ever see it again," he said quietly. A flurry of rain struck his face and he wiped his eyes, grateful for the excuse. "It looks like a dream, doesn't it? A strange dream."

Miriamele nodded but said nothing.

Binabik did not hurry them away. He seemed content to wait and let Qantaqa nose the ground while Simon and Miriamele sat and silently gazed.

"Let us make camp," he said finally. "If we are riding another short time, we can find shelter at the base of the hills." He gestured toward Swertclif's massive face. "Then in the morning we will have better light for . . . whatever we may be doing."

"We're going to John's barrow," Simon said, more firmly than he felt. "At least that's what I'm doing."

Binabik shrugged. "Let us be riding. When we have a fire and food will be time for making of plans."

The sun vanished behind Swertclif's broad hump long before evening. They rode forward in cold shadow. Even the horses seemed uneasy: Simon could feel Homefinder's unwillingness, and thought that if he allowed her she would turn and race in the opposite direction.

Swertclif waited like an infinitely patient ogre. As they drew closer, the great dark hill seemed to blot out the sky as well as the sun, spreading and swelling until it seemed they could not turn away from it even if they tried. From the slope of its outermost foothills, they saw a flash of gray-green to the south, just beyond the cliffs—the Kynslagh, visible for the first time. Simon felt a pang of joy and regret, as he remembered the familiar, soothing song of the gulls and thought of the fisherman-father he had never known.

At last, when the hill's almost perpendicular face stood above them like a vast wall, they made camp in a ravine. The winds were less here, and Swertclif itself blocked much of the rain. Simon smiled grimly at the thought that the ogre's waiting was over: he and his companions were going to sleep in its lap tonight.

No one wanted to be first to speak of what they would do tomorrow. The making of the fire and the preparation of a modest supper were undertaken with a minimum of conversation and little of the fellowship that usually enlivened the evenings. Tonight Miriamele did not seem angry but preoccupied, and even Binabik was hesitant in his actions, as though his thoughts were elsewhere.

Simon felt surprisingly calm, almost cheerful, and was disappointed that his companions did not share his mood. This was a dangerous place, of course, and the next day's doings would be fearful—he was not letting himself think too much about where the sword was and what needed to be done to find it—but at least he was doing something. At least he was performing the kind of task for which he had been knighted. And if it worked—oh, glory! If it worked, surely Miriamele would see that taking the sword to Josua would be more important than trying to convince her mad father to halt a war that was doubtless already beyond his power to stop. Yes, surely when they had Bright-Nail—think of it, Bright-Nail! Prester John's famous sword!—in hand, Miriamele would realize that they had obtained the greatest prize they could hope for, and he and Binabik could coax her back to the comparative safety of her uncle's camp.

Simon was considering these ideas and letting his meal settle when Binabik finally began to speak.

"Once we are climbing this hill," the troll said slowly, "we will be having great difficulty to turn back. We are having no knowledge whether there are soldiers above—perhaps Elias has placed guards for protecting his father's sword and tomb. If we are going any farther westward, we will be coming to where people in that great castle can be seeing us. Do you have certainness—real, real true certainness!—that you both want this? Please think before you are speaking."

Simon did as his friend asked. After a while, he knew what he wished to say. "We are here. The next time we are so close to Bright-Nail, there may be men fighting everywhere. We may never be able to get near it. So I think it would be foolish not to try to take it now. I'm going."

Binabik looked at Simon, then slowly nodded. "So we will go to take the sword." He turned to the princess. "Miriamele?"

"I have little to say about it. If we need to use the Three Swords, then that will mean I have failed." She smiled, but it was a smile Simon did not like at all. "And if I fail to convince my father, I doubt that whatever happens afterward will mean much to me."

The troll made a close-handed gesture. "There is never sure knowledge. I will help you as I can, and Simon will also, I am not doubting that—but you must not give up any chance of coming out again. Thinking of this sort will make you careless."

"I would be very happy to come out again," said Miriamele. "I want to help my father understand so that he will cease the killing, then I want to say farewell to him. I could never live with him after what he has done."

"I am hoping that you get the thing you are wishing for," Binabik replied.

"So—first we are to go sword-searching, then we will decide what can be done for helping Miriamele. For such weighty efforts, I have need of sleep."

He lay down, curling against Qantaqa, and pulled his hood over his face. Miriamele continued to stare into the campfire. Simon watched her awkwardly for a short while, then pulled his own cloak tight around him and lay back. "Good night, Miriamele," he said. "I hope . . . I hope. . . ."

"So do I."

Simon threw his arm over his eyes and waited for sleep.

He dreamed that he sat atop Green Angel Tower, perched like a gargoyle. Someone was moving beside him.

It was the angel herself, who had apparently left her spire and now seated herself beside him, laying a cool hand on his wrist. She looked strangely like the little girl Leleth, but made of rough bronze and green with verdigris.

"It is a long way down." The angel's voice was beautiful, soft but strong.

Simon stared at the tiny rooftops of the Hayholt below him. "It is."

"That is not what I mean." The angel's tone was gently chiding. "I mean down to where the Truth is. Down to the bottom, where things begin."

"I don't understand." He felt curiously light, as though the next puff of wind might send him sailing off the tower roof, whirling like a leaf. It seemed that the angel's grip on his arm was the only thing that held him where he sat.

"From up here, the matters of Earth look small," she said. "That is one way to see, and a good one. But it is not the only one. The farther down you go, the harder things are to understand—but the more important they are. You must go very deep."

"I don't know how to do that." He stared at her face, but despite its familiarity it was still lifeless, just a casting of rough metal. There was no hint of friendship or kindness in the stiff features. "Where should I go? Who will help me?"

"Deep. You." The angel suddenly stood; as her hand released him, Simon felt himself beginning to float free of the tower. He clutched a curving bit of the roof and clung. "It is hard for me to talk to you, Simon," she said. "I may not be able to again."

"Why can't you just tell me?" he cried. His feet were floating off the edge; his body fluttered like a sail, trying to follow. "Just tell me!"

"It is not so easy." The angel turned and slowly rose back to her plinth atop the tower roof. "If I can come again, I will. But it is only possible to talk clearly about less important things. The greatest truths lie within, always within. They cannot be given. They must be found."

Simon felt himself tugged free of his handhold. Slowly, like a cartwheel spun loose from its axle, he began to revolve as he floated out. Sky and earth moved alternately past him, as though the world were a child's ball in which he had been imprisoned, a ball now sent rolling by a vengeful kick. . . .

Simon awakened in faint moonlight, sweating despite the chill night air. The dark bulk of Swertclif hung above him like a warning.

*   *   *

The next day found Simon considerably less certain about things than he had been the night before. As they readied for the climb, he found himself worrying over the dream. If Amerasu had been right, if Simon had truly become more open to the Road of Dreams, could there be a meaning to what he had been told by the dream angel? How could he go deeper? He was about to climb a tall hill. And what answer was within? Some secret that even *he* didn't know? It just didn't make sense.

The company set out as the sun began to warm in the sky. For the first part of the morning they rode up through the foothills, mounting Swertclif's lower reaches. As the lower, gentler slopes fell away behind them, they were forced to dismount and lead the horses.

They stopped for a mid-morning meal—a little of the dried fruit and bread that Binabik had brought with him from Josua's camp stores.

"I am thinking it is time to leave the horses behind us," said the troll. "If Qantaqa is still wishing to come, she will climb on her own instead of carrying me upon her back."

Simon had not thought about having to leave Homefinder. He had hoped there would be a way to ride to the summit, but the only level path was the one on the far side of Swertclif, the funeral road that led across the top of the headland from Erchester and the Hayholt.

Binabik had brought a good quantity of rope in his saddlebag; he sacrificed enough of it for Simon and Miriamele to leave their mounts tied on long tethers to a low, wind-curled tree within reach of a natural rocky pool full of rainwater. The two horses had ample room to graze during the half a day or more they would be required to wait. Simon laid his face against Homefinder's neck and quietly promised her he would be back as soon as he could.

"Any other things there are that need doing?" asked Binabik; Simon stared up at the pinnacle of Swertclif and wished he could think of something that would forestall the climb a little longer. "Then let us be going," the troll said.

Swertclif's eastern face was not as sheerly vertical as it seemed from a distance. By traversing diagonally, the company, with Qantaqa trailing behind, were even able occasionally to walk upright, although more often than not they went crouching from handhold to cautious handhold. In only one spot, a narrow chink between the cliff face and a standing stone, did Simon feel any worry, but he and his two companions inched through while Qantaqa, who had found some private wolfish path, stood on the far side with her tongue dangling pinkly, watching their struggles with apparent amusement.

A few hours after noon the skies darkened and the air grew heavy. A light rain swept across the cliff face, wetting the climbers and worrying Simon. It was not so bad where they were, but it looked to get more difficult very soon, and there was nothing pleasant about the idea of trying to cross some of the steeply angled stones if they were slick with rain. But the small shower passed, and although the clouds remained threatening, no larger storm seemed imminent.

The climb did grow steeper, but it was better than Simon had feared. Binabik was leading, and the little man was as surefooted as one of his Qanuc sheep. They only used the rope once, tying themselves for safety as they leapt from one grassy shelf to another over a long, slanting scree of naked stones. Everyone made the jump safely, although Miriamele scratched her hands and Simon banged his knee hard when he landed. Qantaqa seemed to find this part laughably easy as well.

As they paused for breath on the far side of this crossing, Simon found that he was standing just a few cubits below a small patch of white flowers—starblooms—whose petals gleamed like snowflakes in the dark green grass that surrounded them. He was heartened by the discovery: he'd seen very few flowers since he and Miriamele had first left Josua's camp. Even the Wintercap or Frayja's Fire that one might expect to see at this cold time of the year had been scarce.

The climb up Swertclif's face took longer than they had anticipated: as they toiled up the last long rise, the sun had sunk low in the sky, gleaming a hand-breadth above the horizon behind the pall of clouds. They were all bent nearly double now and working hard for breath; they had been using their hands for balance and leverage so frequently in this last stage that Simon wondered what Qantaqa must think to see all her companions turned as four-footed as she. When they stepped up and could at last stand upright on the grassy verge of Swertclif's summit, a sliver of sun broke through, washing the rounded hill with pale light.

The mounds of the Hayholt's kings lay before them, some hundred ells from where they stood struggling to regain breath. All except one of the barrows were nothing more than grassy humps, so rounded by time as to seem part of the hill: that one, which was surely John's, was still only a pile of naked stones. At the hill's distant western edge lay the dim bulk of the Hayholt; the needle-thin spire of Green Angel Tower was brighter than anything else in sight.

Binabik cocked an eye up at the weak sun. "We are being later than my hope. We will not be able to go down again before we are in darkness." He shrugged. "There is nothing that will help that. The horses will be able to feed themselves until the morning when we can return to them."

"But what about . . ." Simon looked at Qantaqa, embarrassed; he had been about to say "wolves,""'. . . what about wild animals? Are you sure they'll be all right?"

"Horses can be defending themselves very well. And I have seen few animals of any kind or name in these lands." Binabik patted Simon's arm. "And also there is nothing we can be doing otherwise except risking a broken neck or other unfortunate crunching or snapping of bones."

Simon took a breath and started off toward the barrows. "Come on, then."

The seven mounds were laid out in a partial circle. Space had been left for others to share this place. Simon felt a twinge of superstitious fear as he thought about that. Who else would lie here someday? Elias? Josua? Or neither? Perhaps the events that had been set in motion meant that nothing expected would ever happen again.

They walked into the center of the incomplete circle and stopped. The wind stirred and bent the grasses. The hilltop was silent. Simon walked to the first barrow, which had sunk into the waiting earth until it was scarcely a man's height, though it stretched several times that in length and was nearly equally wide. A verse floated into Simon's head, a verse and a memory of black statues in a dark, silent throne room.

>*"Fingil first, named the Bloody King."*

he said quietly,

>*"Flying out of the North on war's red wing."*

Now that he had spoken the initial verse, it seemed unlucky to stop. He moved to the next barrow, which was as old and weatherworn as the first. A few stones glinted in the grass, like teeth.

>*"Hjeldin his son, the Mad King dire*
>*Leaped to his death from the haunted spire."*

The third was set close to the second, as if the one buried there still sought protection from his predecessors.

>*"Ikferdig next, the Burned King hight*
>*He met the fire-drake by dark of night."*

Simon paused. There was a gap between this trio of mounds and the next, and there was also another verse prodding his memory. After a moment, it came.

>*"Three northern kings, all dead and cold*
>*The north rules no more in lofty Hayholt."*

He moved to the second group of three, the song swiftly coming back to him now, so that he did not have to search for words. Miriamele and Binabik stood in silence, watching and listening.

>*"The Heron King Sulis, called Apostate*
>*Fled Nabban, but in Hayholt he met his fate*

>*"The Hernystir Holly King, old Tethtain*
>*Came in at the gate, but not out again*

>*"Last, Eahlstan Fisher King, in lore most high*
>*The dragon he woke, and in Hayholt he died."*

Simon took a deep breath. It almost seemed that he was saying a magical spell, that a few more words might bring the barrows' inhabitants up from their centuried sleep, grave ornaments clinking as they broke through the earth.

> *"Six kings have ruled in Hayholt's broad halls*
> *Six masters have stridden her mighty stone walls*
> *Six mounds on the cliff over deep Kynslagh-bay*
> *Six kings will sleep there until Doom's final day . . ."*

When he finished, the wind grew stronger for a moment, flattening the grass and moaning as it whirled across the hilltop . . . but nothing else happened. The mounds remained silent and secretive. Their long shadows lay on the sward, stretching toward the east.

"Of course, there are seven kings here now," he said, breaking the silence. Now that the moment had come, he was tremendously unsettled. His heart was rattling in his ribs and he suddenly found it hard to speak without the words catching in his throat. He turned to face the last barrow. It was higher than the rest, and the grass had only partly covered the pile of stones. It looked like the shell of an immense sea-creature stranded by the waves of some ancient flood.

"King John Presbyter," said Simon.

"My *grandfather.*"

Struck by the sound of Miriamele's voice, Simon turned. She appeared positively haunted, her face colorless, her eyes hollow and frightened.

"I can't watch this," she said. "I'm going to wait over there." She turned and made her way around Fingil's barrow, sinking down out of sight at last as she sat, presumably to look out to the east and the hilly land they had just crossed.

"Let us be working, then," said Binabik. "I will not be enjoying this task, but you spoke rightly, Simon: we are here, and it would be foolishness not to take the sword."

"Prester John would want us to," he said with more confidence than he felt. "He would want us to do what we can to save his kingdom, his people."

"Who knows what the dead are wishing?" Binabik said darkly. "Come, let us work. Still we must be making at least some shelter for ourselves before night comes, for hiding the light of a fire if nothing else. Miriamele," he called, "can you look to see if some of those shrubs there along the hill could provide some wood for burning?"

She raised her hand in acknowledgment.

Simon bent to John's cairn and began tugging at one of the stones. It clung to the grassy earth so tenaciously that Simon had to put his boot on the stone beside it to help him pull it free. He stood up and wiped sweat from his face. His chain mail was too bulky and uncomfortable for this sort of work. He unlaced it and removed it, then took off the padded jerkin, too, and laid them both in the grass beside the mound. The wind clawed at him through his thin shirt.

"Halfway across Osten Ard we have been traveling," Binabik said as he dug his fingers into the earth, "and no one was thinking to find a shovel."

"I have my sword," said Simon.

"Save it until there is real need." A little of the troll's usual dryness had returned. "Gouging at stones has a dulling effect on blades, I am told. And we may be needing a sword with some sharpness. Especially if anyone notices us at our work digging up the High King's father."

Simon shut his eyes for a moment and said a brief prayer asking Aedon's forgiveness—and Prester John's, too, for good measure—for what they were about to do.

The sun was gone. The gray sky was beginning to turn pink at its western edge, a color that Simon usually found pleasant, but which now looked like something beginning to spoil. The last stone had been pulled out of the hole in the side of Prester John's grass-fringed cairn. The black nothingness that lay beyond looked like a wound in the flesh of the world.

Binabik fumbled with his flints. When at last he struck a spark, he lit the end of the torch and shielded it from the brisk wind until it caught. Unwilling to stare at the waiting blackness, Simon looked out instead across the dark green of the hilltop. Miriamele was a small figure in the distance, bending and rising as she scavenged for the makings of a campfire. Simon wished he could stop now, just turn and go. He wished he had never thought of such a foolish thing to do.

Binabik waved the flame inside the hole, pulled it out, then pushed the torch back inside again. He got down on his knees and took a cautious sniff. "The air, it is seeming, is at least good." He pushed more clods of earth from the edge of the hole before poking his head through. "I can see the wooden sides of something. A boat?"

"*Sea-Arrow.*" The gravity of what they were doing had begun to settle on Simon like a great weight. "Yes, Prester John's boat. He was buried in it."

Binabik edged in a little farther. "There is plenty of room for me to stand in here," he said. His voice was muffled. "And the timbers above are seeming to me quite sturdy."

"Binabik," said Simon. "Come out."

The little man backed up until he could turn to look. "What is wrong, Simon?"

"It was my idea. I should be the one to go in."

Binabik raised an eyebrow. "No one is wishing to take from you the glory of finding the sword. It is only that I am being smallest and best suited for cave-wandering."

"It's not the glory—it's in case anything happens. I don't want you hurt because of my stupid idea."

"Your idea? Simon, there is no blame here. I am doing what I think is being best. And I am thinking there is nothing inside here to hurt anyone." He paused. "But if you wish . . ." He stepped aside.

Simon lowered himself to his hands and knees, then took the torch from the troll's small hand and pushed it into the hole before him. In the flickering light he could see the great muddy sweep of *Sea-Arrow*'s hull; the boat was curved like a huge dead leaf, like a cocoon . . . as though something within it was waiting to be reborn.

Simon sat up and shook his head. His heart was hammering.

Mooncalf! What are you afraid of? Prester John was a good man.

Yes, but what if his ghost was angry about what had happened to his kingdom? And surely no spirit liked its grave being robbed.

Simon took in a gulp of air, then slowly eased himself through the hole in the side of the mound.

He slid down the crumbling slope of the pit until he touched the boat's hull. The dome of spars and mud and white root tendrils stretching overhead seemed a sky created by a feeble, half-blind god. When he finally took another breath, his nostrils filled with the smells of soil and pine sap and mildew, as well as stranger scents he could not identify, some of them as exotic as the contents of Judith the Kitchen Mistress' spice jars. The sweet strength took him by surprise and set him choking. Binabik popped his head through the hole.

"Are you well? Is there badness to the air?"

Simon regained his breath. "I'm well. I just . . ." He swallowed. "Don't worry."

Binabik hesitated, then withdrew.

Simon looked at the side of the hull for what seemed a very long time. Because of the way it was wedged in the pit, the wales rose higher than his head. Simon could not see a way to climb with one hand, and the torch was too thick to be carried comfortably in his mouth. After a moment in which he was strongly tempted to turn and clamber back out again and let Binabik solve the problem, he wedged the butt of the torch in beside one of the mound timbers, then threw his hands over the wale and pulled himself up, kicking his feet in search of a toehold. The wood of *Sea-Arrow*'s hull felt slimy beneath his fingers but held his weight.

Simon pulled the top half of his body over the wale and hung there for a moment, balanced, the edge of the boat pushing up against his stomach like a fist. The sweet, musty odor was very strong. Looking down, he almost cursed—biting back words that might be unlucky and were certainly disrespectful—when he realized that he had placed the torch too low for its light to reach into the boat's hull. All he could see beneath him were ill-defined lumps of shadow. Of course, he thought, it should be simple enough to find a single body and the sword it held, even in darkness: he could do it by touch alone. But there was not a chance in the world that Simon was going to try that.

"Binabik!" he shouted. "Can you come help me?" He was proud of how steady his voice sounded.

The troll clambered over the lip of the hole and slid down the incline. "Are you trapped somehow?"

"No, but I can't see anything without the torch. Can you get it for me?"

As Simon hung over the dark hull, the wooden wale trembled. Simon had a moment's fear that it might collapse beneath him, a fear that was not made less by a quiet creaking that drifted through the underground chamber. Simon was almost certain that the noise came from the tormented wood—the king's boat had been two years in the wet ground, after all—but it was hard not to imagine a hand . . . an ancient, withered hand . . . reaching up from the shadowed hull. . . .

"Binabik!?"

"I am bringing it, Simon. It was higher than I could be reaching."

"Sorry. Just hurry, please."

The light on the roof of the barrow changed as the flame was moved. Simon felt a tapping on his foot. Balancing as carefully as he could, he swung his legs around, pivoting until he was lying with his stomach along the length of the wale and could reach down and take the torch from Binabik's upstretched hand. With another silent prayer—and his eyes half-shut for fear of what he might see—Simon turned and leaned over the void of the inner hull.

At first it was hard to see anything. He opened his eyes wider. Small stones and dirt had worked loose from the barrow ceiling and covered much of *Sea-Arrow*'s contents—but the detritus of the grave had not covered everything.

"Binabik!" Simon cried. "Look!"

"What!?" The troll, alarmed, rushed along the hull to a spot where the boat touched the wall of the barrow, then clambered up, nimble as on a high Mintahoq trail. Balancing lightly atop the wale, he worked his way over until he was near Simon.

"Look." Simon gestured with the shaking torch.

King John Presbyter lay in the bosom of *Sea-Arrow*, surrounded by his funeral gifts, clad still in the magnificent raiment in which he had been buried. On the High King's brow was a golden circlet; his hands were folded on his chest, resting on his long snowy beard. John's skin, but for a certain waxy translucency, looked as firm as the flesh of a living man. After several seasons in the corrupting earth, he seemed to be only sleeping.

But, terrifyingly strange as it was to see the king whole and uncorrupted, that was not all that had made Simon cry out.

"*Kikkasut!*" Binabik swore, no less surprised than Simon. A moment later he had clambered down into the hull of the boat.

A search of the grave and its effects confirmed it: Prester John still lay in his resting place on Swertclif—but Bright-Nail was gone.

37

Heartbeats

✦

"Just because Varellan is my brother does *not* mean I will suffer stupidity," Duke Benigaris snarled at the knight who kneeled before him. He smacked his open palm on the arm of his throne. "Tell him to hold firm until I arrive with the Kingfishers. If he does not, I will hang his head from the Sancellan's gate-wall!"

"Please, my lord," said his armorer, who was hovering just to one side, "I beg you, do not thrash about so. I am trying to measure."

"Yes, do sit still," added his mother. She occupied the same low but ornate chair she had when her husband ruled in Nabban. "If you had not been making such a pig of yourself, your old armor would still fit."

Benigaris stared at her, mustache twitching with fury. "Thank you, Mother."

"And do not be so cruel to Varellan. He is hardly more than a child."

"He is a dawdling, simpering halfwit—and it is you who spoiled him. Who talked me into letting him lead the troops at the Onestrine Pass, in any case?"

Dowager Duchess Nessalanta waved her hand in airy dismissal. "Anyone could hold that pass against a ragtag mob like Josua's. *I* could. And the experience will do him good."

The duke jerked his arm free of the armorer's grasp and slammed it on the chair arm once more. "By the Tree, Mother! He has given up two leagues in less than a fortnight, despite having several thousand foot soldiers and half a thousand knights. He is falling back so fast that by the time I ride out the front door, I will probably trip over him."

"Xannasavin says there is nothing to fret about," she replied, amused. "He has examined the skies carefully. Benigaris, please calm yourself. Be a man."

The duke's stare was icy. His jaw worked for a moment before he spoke. "One of these days, Mother, you will push me too far."

"And what will you do—throw me into the cells? Cut off my head?" Her look become fierce. "You need me. Not to mention the respect you owe the one who bore you."

Benigaris scowled, took a deep breath, then turned his attention back to the knight who had delivered young Varellan's message. "What do you wait for?" he demanded. "You heard what I had to say. Now go and tell him."

The knight rose and made an elaborate bow, then turned and walked from the throne room. The ladies in colorful dresses who were talking quietly near the door watched him go, then huddled and began discussing something that caused them to giggle loudly.

Benigaris again tugged his wrist free of the armorer's clutch, this time so he could snap his fingers at one of the pages, who trotted over with a cup of wine.

The duke took a draught and wiped his mouth. "There is more to Josua's army than we first thought. People say that the High King's brother has found a mighty knight who fights at the head of his army. They are claiming it is Camaris. Seriddan of Metessa believes it, or at least he has joined them." He grimaced. "Traitorous dog."

Nessalanta laughed sourly. "I didn't give Josua as much credit as he deserved, I admit. It is a clever ploy. Nothing arouses the common folk like the mention of your uncle's name. But Seriddan? You ask me to worry about him and a few other puny barons from the wilderness? The Metessan Crane hasn't flown from the palace towers in five hundred years. They are nobodies."

"So you are quite sure that this talk of Sir Camaris is just a ploy?" Benigaris' words, intended to be mocking, came out a little hollow.

"Of course it is! How could it be him? Camaris is forty years dead."

"But his body was never found. Father always agonized because he couldn't give his brother an Aedonite burial."

The duchess made a noise of dismissal but kept her eyes on her needlework. "I knew Camaris, my brave son. You did not. Even if he had joined a monastery or gone into hiding, word would have leaked out: he was so madly honest he could never have lied to anyone who asked him who he was. And he was so self-satisfied, such a meddler, that it is not possible he would have stood by while Prester John fought the second Thrithings War without leaping in to be Camaris the Magnificent, Camaris the Holy, Camaris the Great." Nessalanta pricked her finger and cursed under her breath. "No, this is no living Camaris that Josua has found—and it is certainly no ghost. It is some tall imposter, some oversized grassland mercenary with his hair whitened with powder. A trick. But it makes no difference in any case." She examined her stitchery for a moment, then put the hoop down with an air of satisfaction. "Even the real Camaris could not unseat us. We are too strong . . . and his age is gone, gone, gone."

Benigaris looked at her appraisingly. "Unseat *us* . . . ?" he began, but was interrupted by a movement at the room's far end. A herald with the golden kingfisher sigil on his tabard had appeared in the throne room doorway.

"Your Highness," the man said in loud ceremonial tones. "Count Streáwe of Ansis Pelippé arrives at your summons."

The duke settled back, a smile tightening his lips. "Ah, yes. Send the count in."

Streáwe's litter was carried through the doors and set near the great high-arched windows that overlooked the sea, windows covered today in heavy draperies to keep out the cold air. The count's minions lifted out his chair and put it down before the dais that bore the ducal throne.

The count coughed, then caught his breath. "Greetings, Duke," he wheezed. "And Duchess Nessalanta, what a pleasure to see you! As usual, please forgive my sitting without your leave."

"Of course, of course," Benigaris said cheerfully. "And how is your catarrh, Streáwe? I cannot think that it is helped by our cold sea air. I know how warm you keep your house on Sta Mirore."

"As a matter of fact, Benigaris, I had wished to speak to you of just that . . ." the old man began, but the duke cut him short.

"First things first, I regret to say. Forgive me my impatience, but we are at war as you know. I am a blunt man."

Streáwe nodded. "Your straightforwardness is well-known, my friend."

"Yes. So, to the point, then. Where are my riverboats? Where are my Perdruinese troops?"

The count raised a white eyebrow ever so slightly, but his voice and manner remained unperturbed. "Oh, all are coming, Highness. Never fear. When has Perdruin not honored a debt to her elder sister Nabban?"

"But it has been two months," Benigaris said with mock sternness. "Streáwe, Streáwe, my old friend . . . I might almost think that you were putting me off— that for some reason you were trying to stall me."

This time the count's eyebrows betrayed no surprise, but nevertheless a subtle, indefinable change ran across his face. His eyes glittered in their net of wrinkled flesh. "I am disappointed that Nabban could think such a thing of Perdruin after our long and honorable partnership." Streáwe dipped his head. "But it is true that the boats you wish for river transport have been slow in coming—and for that I apologize most abjectly. You see, even with the many messages I have sent back home to Ansis Pelippé, detailing your needs with great care, there is no one who can get things accomplished in the way that I can when I take them in hand personally. I do not wish to malign my servitors, but, as we Perdruinese say, 'when the captain is below decks, there are many places to stretch a hammock.'" The count brought his long, gnarled fingers up to brush something from his upper lip. "I should go back to Ansis Pelippé, Benigaris. As sad as I should be to lose the company of you and your beloved mother—" he smiled at Nessalanta, "—I feel confident that I could send your riverboats and the troop of soldiers we agree on within a week after returning." He coughed again, a wracking spasm that went on for some moments before he regained his wind. "And for all the beauty of your palace, it is, as you said, a trifle airier than my own house. My health has worsened here, I fear."

"Just so," said Benigaris. "Just so. We all fear for your health, Count. It has been much on my mind of late. And the men and boats, too." He paused, regarding Streáwe with a smile that seemed increasingly smug. "That is why I could not allow you to leave just now. A sea voyage at this moment—why, your catarrh would certainly worsen. And let me be brutally honest, dear Count . . . but only because Nabban loves you so. If you were to grow more ill, not only would I hold myself responsible, but certainly it would also slow the arrival of boats and men even more. For if they are haphazard now, with your careful instructions, imagine how laggard they would become with you ill and unable to oversee them at all. There would be many hammocks stretched then, I'm sure!"

Streáwe's eyes narrowed. "Ah. So you are saying that you think it best I do not leave just now?"

"Oh, dear Count, I am *insisting* you remain." Benigaris, tiring at last of the ministrations of his armorer, waved the man away. "I could not forgive myself if I did anything less. Surely after the boats and your troop of soldiers arrive to help us defend against this madman Josua, the weather will have turned warm enough that you can safely travel again."

The count considered this for a moment, giving every impression of weighing Benigaris' arguments. "By Pelippa and her bowl," he said at last, "I can see the sense of what you are saying, Benigaris." His tight grin displayed surprisingly good teeth. "And I am touched at the concern you show for an old friend of your father's."

"I honor you just as I honored him."

"Indeed." Streáwe's smile now became almost gentle. "How lovely that is. Honor is in such short supply in these grim days." He waved a knobby hand, summoning his bearers. "I suspect that I should send another letter to Ansis Pelippé, urging my castellain and boatwrights to hasten their efforts even more."

"That sounds like a very good idea, Count. A very good idea." Benigaris sat back against the throne and finger-brushed his mustache. "Will we see you at table tonight?"

"Oh, I think you will. Where else would I find such kind and considerate friends?" He leaned forward on his chair, sketching a bow. "Duchess Nessalanta— a pleasure as always, gracious lady."

Nessalanta smiled and nodded. "Count Streáwe."

The old man was lifted back into his litter. After the curtain was drawn, his four servitors carried him from the throne room.

"I do not think you needed to be so ham-fisted," said Nessalanta when the count had gone. "He is no danger to us. Since when have sticky-fingered Perdruinese ever wanted more than to earn a little gold?"

"They have been known to accept coins from more than one pocket." Benigaris lifted his cup. "This way, Streáwe will have a much stronger wish to see *us* victorious. He is not a stupid man."

"No, he certainly is not. That is why I don't understand the need to use such a heavy hand."

"Everything I know, Mother," said Benigaris heartily, "I learned from you."

Isgrimnur was growing annoyed.

Josua could not seem to keep his attention on the matters at hand; instead, every few moments he went to the door of the tent and stared back up the valley at the monastery standing on the hillside, a humble collection of stone buildings that glowed golden-brown in the slanting sunlight.

"She is not dying, Josua," the duke finally growled. "She is only expecting a child."

The prince looked up guiltily. "What?"

"You have been staring at that place all afternoon." He levered his bulk off the stool and walked to Josua's side, then placed a hand on the prince's shoulder. "If you are so consumed, Josua, then go to her. But I assure you she is in good hands. What my wife doesn't know about babies isn't worth knowing."

"I know, I know." The prince returned to the map spread out on the table-top. "I cannot stop my mind churning, old friend. Tell me what we were talking about."

Isgrimnur sighed. "Very well." He bent to the map. "Camaris says there is a shepherd's trail that runs above the valley. . . ."

Someone made a discreet noise in the doorway of the tent. Josua looked up. "Ah, Baron. Welcome back. Please come in."

Seriddan was accompanied by Sludig and Freosel. All exchanged greetings as Josua brought out a jug of Teligure wine. The baron and Josua's lieutenants bore the marks of a day's muddy riding.

"Young Varellan has dug in his heels just before Chasu Yarinna," the baron said, grinning. "He has more grit than I thought. I had expected him to fall back all the way to the Onestrine Pass."

"And why hasn't he?" Isgrimnur asked.

Seriddan shook his head. "Perhaps because he feels that once the battle for the pass begins, there is no turning back."

"That might mean that he is not so sure of our weakness as his brother Benigaris is," Josua mused. "Perhaps he may prove willing to talk."

"What is just as likely," said Sludig, "is that he is trying to keep us out of the pass until Duke Benigaris comes up with reinforcements. Whatever they might have thought of our strength to start with, Sir Camaris has changed their minds, I promise you."

"Where is Camaris?" Josua asked.

"With Hotvig and the rest up at the front." Sludig shook his head in wonder-ment. "Merciful Aedon, I heard all the stories, but I thought they were just cradle songs. Prince Josua, I have never seen anything like him! When he and Hotvig's horsemen were caught between two wings of Varellan's knights two days ago, we were all sure that he was as good as dead or captured. But he broke the Nabbanai knights like they were kindling wood! One he cut nearly in half with a single stroke. Sheared right through him, armor and all! Surely that sword is magical!"

"Thorn is a powerful weapon," said Josua. "But with it or without it, there has never been a knight like Camaris."

"His horn Cellian has become a terror to the Nabbanmen," Sludig contin-ued. "When it echoes down the valley, some of them turn and ride away. And out of every troop Camaris defeats, he takes one of the prisoners and sends him back to say: 'Prince Josua and the others wish to talk with your lord.' He has beaten down so many that he must have sent two dozen Nabbanai prisoners back by now, each one carrying the same message."

Seriddan raised his wine cup. "Here's to him. If he is a terror now, what must he have been like in the height of his powers? I was a boy when Camaris . . ." he laughed shortly, "—I almost said 'died.' When he disappeared. I never saw him."

"He was little different," Isgrimnur said thoughtfully. "That is what surprises me. His body has aged, but his skills and fighting heart have not. As though his powers have been preserved."

"As though for one final test," Josua said, measuring out the words. "God grant that it is so—and that he succeeds, for all our sakes."

"But I am puzzled." Seriddan took another sip. "You have told me that Camaris hates war, that he would rather do anything than fight. Yet I have never seen such a killing engine."

Josua's smile was sad, his look troubled. "Camaris at war is like a lady's maid swatting spiders."

"What?" Seriddan lowered his eyebrows and squinted, wondering if he was being mocked.

"If you tell a maid to go and kill the spiders in her lady's chamber," the prince explained, "she will think of a hundred excuses not to do anything. But when she is finally convinced that it must be done, no matter the horror she feels, she will dispatch every single spider with great thoroughness, just to make sure she does not have to take up the task again." His faint smile disappeared. "And that is Camaris. The only thing he hates worse than warfare is *unnecessary* warfare—especially killings which could have been avoided by making a clean ending the first time. So once he is committed, Camaris makes sure that he does not have to do the same thing twice." He raised his glass in salute to the absent knight. "Imagine how it must feel to do best in all the world what you least wish to do."

After that, they drank their wine in silence for a time.

Tiamak limped out across the terrace. He found a place on the low wall and hoisted himself up, then sat with his legs dangling and basked in the late afternoon light. The Frasilis Valley stretched before him, two rippling banks of dark soil and gray-green treetops with the Anitullean Road snaking between them. If he narrowed his eyes, Tiamak could make out the shapes of Josua's tents nestled in the purple shadows of the hillside to the southwest.

My companions may think we Wrannamen live like savages, he thought to himself, *but I am as happy as anyone to be in one place for a few days and to have a solid roof over my head.*

One of the monks walked by, hands folded in his sleeve. He gave Tiamak a look that lasted the length of several steps, but only nodded his head in formal greeting.

The monks do not seem happy to have us here. He felt himself smiling. *Unwilling as they are to be caught up in a war, how much more dubious must they be about having women and marsh men within the cloisters, too?*

Still, Tiamak was glad that Josua had chosen this spot as a temporary refuge, and that he had allowed his wife and many others to remain here as the army moved farther down the gorge. The Wrannaman sighed as he felt the cool, dry breeze, the sunshine on his face. It was good to have shelter, even for just a little while. It was good that the rains had let up, that the sun had returned.

But as Josua said, he reminded himself, *it means nothing. A respite is all—the Storm King has not been slowed by anything we have done so far. If we cannot solve the riddles before us, if we cannot gain the swords and learn how to use them, this moment of peace will mean nothing. The deadly winter will return—and there will be no sunshine then. He Who Always Steps on Sand, let me not fail! Let Strangyeard and me find the answers we seek!*

But answers were becoming fewer and farther between. The search was a responsibility that had begun to feel more and more burdensome. Binabik was gone, Geloë was dead, and now only Tiamak and the diffident priest remained of all the Scrollbearers and other wise ones. Together they had pored over Morgenes' manuscript, searching it minutely from one end to the other in hope of finding some clues they had missed, some help with the riddle of the Great Swords. They had also scrutinized the translated scrolls of Binabik's master Ookequk, but so far these had provided nothing but a great deal of trollish wisdom, most of which seemed to concern predicting avalanches and singing away the spirits of frostbite.

But if Strangyeard and I do not find more success soon, Tiamak thought grimly, *we may have more need of Ookequk's wisdom than we will like.*

In the past few days, Tiamak had set Strangyeard to relate every bit of information that the archivist possessed about the Great Swords and their undead enemy—his own book-learning, the things old Jarnauga had taught him, the experiences of the youth Simon and his companions, everything that had happened in the last year that might contain some clue to their dilemma. Tiamak prayed that a pattern might show somewhere, as the ripples in a river demonstrated the presence of a rock beneath the surface. In all the lore of these wise men and women, these adventurers and accidental witnesses, *someone* must know something of how to use the Great Swords.

Tiamak sighed again and wiggled his toes. He longed to be just a little man with little problems again. How important those problems had seemed! And how he longed to have only those problems now. He held up his hand and looked at the play of light across his knuckles, a gnat that crept across the thin dark hairs on his wrist. The day was deceptively pleasant, just like the surface of a stream. But there was no question that rocks or worse lay hidden beneath.

✦

"Please lie back, Vorzheva," said Aditu.

The Thrithings-woman made a face. "Now you talk like Josua. It is only a little pain."

"You see what she's like." Gutrun wore an air of grim satisfaction. "If I could tie her to that bed, I would."

"I do not think that she needs to be tied to anything," the Sitha woman replied. "But Vorzheva, neither is there any dishonor in lying down when you are in pain."

The prince's wife reluctantly slumped back against the cushions and allowed Gutrun to pull the blanket up. "I was not raised to be weak." In the light filtering down from the high small window she was very pale.

"You are not weak. But both your life and the child's life are precious," Aditu said gently. "When you feel well and strong, move around as you like. When you are hurting or weak, lie down and let Duchess Gutrun or me help you." She stood and took a few steps toward the door.

"You are not going to leave?" Vorzheva asked in dismay. "Stay and talk to me. Tell me what is happening outside. Gutrun and I have been in this room all day. Even the monks do not speak to us. I think they hate women."

Aditu smiled. "Very well. My other tasks can wait in such a good cause." The Sitha seated herself upon the bed once more, folding her legs beneath her. "Duchess Gutrun, if you wish to stretch your legs, I will be here to sit with Vorzheva for a little while longer."

Gutrun sniffed dismissively. "I'm just where I should be." She turned back to her sewing.

Vorzheva reached out her hand and clasped Aditu's fingers. "Tell me what you have seen today. Did you go to Leleth?"

The Sitha nodded, her silver-white hair swinging. "Yes. She is just a few rooms away—but there is no change. And she is growing very thin. I mix nurturing herbs with the small draughts of water she will swallow, but even that is not enough, I fear. Something still tethers her to her body—to look at her she seems only to be sleeping—but I wonder how much longer that tie will hold." A troubled look seemed to pass over Aditu's alien face. "This is another way that Geloë's passing has lessened us. Surely the forest woman would know some root, some leafy thing that might draw Leleth's spirit back."

"I'm not sure," Gutrun said without looking up. "That child was never more than half here—I know, and I cared for her and held her as much as anyone. Whatever happened to her in the forest when she traveled with Miriamele, those dogs and merciful Usires only knows what else, it took a part of her away." She paused. "It's not your fault, Aditu. You've done all that anyone could, I'm sure."

Aditu turned to look at Gutrun, but betrayed no change of expression at the duchess' conciliatory tone. "But it is sad," was all she said.

"Sad, yes," Gutrun replied. "God's wishes often make His children sad. We just don't understand, I suppose, what He plans. Surely after all she suffered, He has something better in mind for little Leleth."

Aditu spoke carefully. "I hope that is so."

"And what else do you have to tell me?" Vorzheva asked. "I guessed about Leleth. You would have told me first if there was any new thing."

"There is not much else to relate. The Duke of Nabban's forces have fallen back a little farther, but soon they will stop and fight again. Josua and the others are trying to arrange a truce so that they can stop the fighting and talk."

"Will these Nabbanai talk to us?"

Aditu shrugged sinuously. "I sometimes wonder if I understand even the mortals I know best. As to those who are completely strange to me . . . I certainly cannot offer any firm idea as to what these men may do. But the Nabbanai general is a brother of the ruling duke, I am told, so I doubt that he will be very sympathetic to anything your husband has to say."

Vorzheva's face contorted. She gasped, but then waved the solicitous Aditu back. "No, I am well. It was just a squeezing." After a moment she took a deep breath. "And Josua? How is he?"

The Sitha looked to Gutrun, who raised her eyebrows in a gesture of amused helplessness. "He was just here this morning, Vorzheva," the duchess said. "He is not in the fighting."

"He is well," Aditu added. "He asked me to send his regards."

"Regards?" Vorzheva sat up. "What sort of word is that from a man, from a husband? Regards?"

"Oh, Elysia, Mother of Mercy," Gutrun said in disgust. "You know that he cares for you, Vorzheva. Let it go."

The Thrithings-woman sank back, her hair spreading against the pillow like a shining dark cloth. "It is only because I cannot *do* anything. Tomorrow I will be stronger. Tomorrow I will walk to where I can see the battle."

"Only if you can drag *me* that far," said the duchess. "You should have seen her, Aditu—she couldn't stand this morning, the pains were so dreadful. If I had not caught her, she would have fallen down right on the stone floor."

"If she is strong enough," Aditu said, "then for her to walk is certainly good—but carefully, and not too great a distance." She paused, looking at the Thrithings-woman carefully. "I think perhaps you are too excitable to look at the battle, Vorzheva."

"Hah." Vorzheva's disgust was plain. "You said your people hardly ever have children. Why are you now so wise about what I should do?"

"Since our birthings are so infrequent, we take them all the more seriously." Aditu smiled regretfully. "I would greatly love to bear a child one day. It has been a privilege to be with you while you carry yours." She leaned forward and pulled back the coverlet. "Let me listen."

"You will only say that the baby is too unhappy to go walking tomorrow," Vorzheva complained, but she did not prevent Aditu from laying a golden cheek against her tautly rounded stomach.

Aditu shut her upturned eyes as though she were falling asleep. For a long moment, her thin face seemed set in almost perfect repose. Then her eyes opened wide, a flashing of brilliant amber. *"Venyha s'ahn!"* she hissed in surprise. She lifted her head for a moment, then placed her ear back against Vorzheva's belly.

"What?" Gutrun was out of her chair in a heartbeat, stitchery tumbling to the floor. "The child! Is the child . . . is something wrong?"

"Tell me, Aditu." Vorzheva was lying perfectly still, but her voice cracked at the edges. "Do not spare me."

The Sitha began to laugh.

"Are you mad?" Gutrun demanded. "What is it?"

Aditu sat up. "I am sorry. I was marveling at the continuing astonishment I feel around you mortals. And when I think that my own people count themselves lucky if we birth a handful of children in a hundred years!"

"What are you talking about?" Gutrun snapped. Vorzheva looked too frightened to ask any more questions.

"I am talking about mortals, about the gifts you have that you do not know." She laughed again, but more quietly. "There are two heartbeats."

The duchess stared. "What . . . ?"

"Two heartbeats," Aditu said evenly. "Two children are growing inside of Vorzheva."

38

Sleepless in Darkness

✥

Simon's disappointment was an emptiness deep and hollow as the barrow in which they stood. "It's gone," he whispered. "Bright-Nail isn't here."

"Of that there is being little doubt." In the torchlight, Binabik's face was grim. "Qinkipa of the Snows! I almost am wishing we did not find out until we had come here with Prince Josua's army. I do not wish to take him such news."

"But what could have happened to it?" Simon stared down at the waxen face of Prester John as though the king might wake from his deathly sleep to give an answer.

"It seems plain to me that Elias knew its value and took it away. I am not doubting it is sitting in the Hayholt now." The troll shrugged; his voice was heavy. "Well, we knew always that we must be taking Sorrow from him. Two swords or one seems to me a small difference only."

"But Elias couldn't have taken it! There was no hole until we dug one!"

"Perhaps he was taking it out shortly after John was buried. The marks would be gone after such a time passing."

"That doesn't make any sense," Simon stubbornly insisted. "He could have kept it in the first place if he wanted it. Towser *said* that Elias hated it—that he couldn't wait to get rid of it."

"I have no certain answers, Simon. It is being possible that King Elias did not know its value then, but heard of it later. Perhaps Pryrates was discovering its power and so had it removed. There are many things possible." The troll passed his torch to Simon, then crawled off the wale of Prester John's boat and began to clamber back up toward the hole they had made. The twilit sky shone through, blue-gray and muddy with clouds.

"I don't believe it." Simon's hands, weary with digging, painfully sore still from the ordeal in Hasu Vale, hung limply in his lap. "I don't *want* to believe it."

"The second, I am afraid, is the truer thing," Binabik said kindly. "Come, friend Simon, we will see if Miriamele has made a fire. Some hot soup will be making the situation a little easier for thinking about." He climbed to the lip of the hole and wriggled out, then turned. "Hand the torches to me, then I will be helping you out."

Simon barely heard the troll's words. His attention abruptly caught by something, he held both torches higher, leaning out over the boat once more to stare at the base of the barrow's far wall.

"Simon, what are you seeking still?" Binabik called. "We have already nearly turned the poor king's body overside-up in searching."

"There's something on the other side of the mound. Something dark."

"Oh?" A trace of alarm crept into Binabik's tone. "What dark something are you seeing?" He leaned farther in through the entrance they had dug, blocking the view of the sky.

Simon took both torches in one hand, then slid along the wale of *Sea-Arrow* until he could get close enough to confirm his suspicions. "It's a hole!"

"That does not seem to me surprising," the troll said.

"But it's a big one—right into the side of the mound. Maybe it's the one they used to get in."

Binabik stared at the spot where he pointed, then suddenly vanished from the opening. Simon inched closer. The ragged hole in the side of the barrow was as wide as an ale cask.

The troll reappeared. "I see nothing on the outer side that matches," he called. "If they were making their hole there they covered it with great care, or they were doing it long ago; the grass is untouched."

Simon made his way carefully around to the narrow stern. He let himself down from the wale into *Sea-Arrow* and moved as carefully as he could to the other railing, then clambered up. There was a space little more than a cubit wide between the outside of the hull and the barrow's wall of mud and timber. He slid down to the floor so that he could examine the hole more closely, bringing the torch close to the shadowed gap. Surprise set his neck tingling. "Aedon," he said quietly. "It goes *down*."

"What?" Binabik's voice reflected some impatience. "Simon, there are things to do before the darkness is becoming full."

"It goes down, Binabik! The tunnel beyond this hole goes down!" He thrust his torches into the opening and leaned as close as he dared. There was nothing to see but a few gleaming, hair-thin roots; beyond them the torchlight faded as the tunnel wound down and away into blackness.

After a moment, the troll said: "Then we will be examining it more tomorrow, after we have had a chance for thinking and sleeping. Come up, Simon."

"I will," said Simon. "Go ahead." He moved closer. He knew he should be more frightened than he was—anything that made a hole this large, animal or human, was nothing to sneer at—but he felt an unmistakable certainty that this gaping rent in the earth had something to do with Bright-Nail's disappearance. He stared into the empty hole, then lifted the torch out of the way and squinted.

There was a gleam down in the darkness—some object that reflected the torchlight.

"Something's in there," he called.

"Something of what sort?" Binabik said worriedly. "Some animal?"

"No, something like metal." He leaned into the hole. He smelled no animal spoor, only a faint acridity like sweat. The gleaming thing seemed to lie a short way down the tunnel, just where it bent out of sight. "I can't reach it without going in."

"We will be looking for it in the morning, then," Binabik said firmly. "Come now."

Simon edged a little way into the hole. Maybe it was closer than it looked—it was hard to tell by torchlight. He held the burning brands before him and moved forward on his elbows and knees until he was entirely into the tunnel. If he could just extend himself to full length, it should be almost within his grasp. . . .

The soil beneath him abruptly gave way and Simon was flailing in loose dirt. He grabbed at the tunnel wall, which crumbled but held for a moment as he braced himself with arms outstretched. His legs continued to slip downward through the oddly soft earth until he was buried waist-deep in the tunnel floor. One of the torches had fallen from his grip and lay sizzling against the damp soil just a few handbreadths from his ribs. The other was pinioned by his palm, rammed against the tunnel wall; he could not have dropped it even if he wished. He felt strangely empty, unafraid.

"Binabik!" he shouted. "I've fallen through!"

Even as he struggled to work himself free, he felt the soil shifting beneath him in a very strange way, unstable as sand beneath a retreating wave.

The troll stared, eyes so wide the whites gleamed. *"Kikkasut!"* he swore, then shouted: *"Miriamele! Come here quickly!"* Binabik scrambled down the incline into the barrow, working his way around the broad hull of the boat.

"Don't come too close," Simon cautioned him. "The dirt feels strange. You might fall through, too."

"Then do not be moving." The little man gripped the protruding edge of the boat's buried keel and stretched his arm toward Simon, but his reach was short by more than a cubit. "Miriamele will bring our rope." The troll's voice was quiet and calm, but Simon knew that Binabik was frightened.

"And there's something . . . something *moving* down there," Simon said anxiously. It was a dreadful sensation, a compression and relaxation of the soil that held him, as though some great serpent twisted its coils in the depths. Simon's dreamlike sense of calm evaporated, replaced by mounting horror. "B-Bin . . . *Binabik!*" He could not get his breath.

"Do not be moving!" his friend said urgently. "If you can but . . ."

Simon never heard the rest of what the troll meant to say. There was a sharp stinging around his ankles as though they had been suddenly wrapped in nettles, then the earth twitched again beneath him and he was swallowed. He barely had time to close his mouth before the clotted soil rose up and closed over his head like an angry sea.

Miriamele saw Binabik emerge from the hole. As she stacked the brambles and twigs she had gathered, she watched him hover beside the entrance they had dug into the mound, talking to Simon, who was still inside the barrow. She wondered dully what they had found. It seemed so pointless, somehow. How could all the swords in the world, magical or not, put a stop to the runaway wagon that her father's maddened grief had set in motion? Only Elias himself could cry halt, and no threat of magical weapons would make him do that. Miriamele knew her father only too well, knew the stubbornness that ran through him just as his blood did. And the Storm King, the shuddersome demon glimpsed in dreams, the master of the Norns? Well, her father had invited the undead thing into the land of mortals. Miriamele knew enough old stories to feel sure that only Elias could send Ineluki away again and bar the door behind him.

But she knew that her friends were set on their plan, just as she was on hers, and she would not stand in their way. Still, she had not for a moment wished to descend with them into the grave. These were strange days, yes, but not strange enough that she wished to discover what two years in the disrespectful earth had done to her grandfather John.

It had been difficult enough to go to the burial and watch his body lowered into the ground. She had never been close to him, but in his distant way, he had loved her and been kind to her. She had never been able to imagine him young, since he had already been ancient when she was a small girl, but she had once or twice seen a glint in his eye or a hint in his stooped posture that suggested the bold, world-conquering man he must have been. She did not want even those few memories to be sullied by . . .

"Miriamele! Come here quickly!"

She looked up, startled by the fearful urgency in Binabik's tone. Despite his call the little man did not look back to her, but slid into the gouge in the barrow's side and vanished, quick as a mole. Miriamele leaped to her feet, knocking over her pile of gathered brush, and hurried across the hilltop. The sun had died in the west; the sky was turning plum-red.

Simon. Something has happened to Simon.

It seemed to take forever to cross the intervening distance. She was out of breath when she reached the grave, and as she dropped to her knees dizziness swept over her. When she leaned into the hole, she could see nothing.

"Simon has . . ." Binabik shouted, "Simon has . . . *No!*"

"What is it? I can't see you!"

"Qantaqa!" the troll shrieked. *"Qantaqa sosa!"*

"What's wrong!?" Miriamele was frantic. "What is it!"

Binabik's words came in ragged bursts. "Get . . . torch! Rope! *Sosa, Qantaqa!*" The troll suddenly let out a cry of pain. Miriamele kneeled in the opening, terrified and confused. Something dreadful was happening—Binabik clearly needed her. But he had told her to get the torch and the rope, and every instant she delayed might help doom the troll and Simon both.

Something huge pushed her aside, bowling her over as though she were an infant. Qantaqa's gray hindquarters disappeared down the incline and into the shadows; a moment later the wolf's furious snarl rumbled up from the depths. Miriamele turned and ran back toward the place where she had begun her fire, then stopped, remembering that the rest of their belongings were somewhere closer to Prester John's mound. She looked around in desperation until she saw them lying on the far side of the half-circle of graves.

Panting, her hands shaking so badly that it was difficult even to hold the flint and steel in her hands, Miriamele worked frantically until the torch caught. She grabbed a second brand; as she searched in desperation for rope, she set this torch alight with the first.

The rope was not among their belongings. She let out a string of Meremund river-rider curses as she hurried back to the mound.

The coil of rope lay half-buried in the dirt Simon and the troll had excavated. Miriamele wrapped it loosely about her so she could keep her hands free, then scrambled down into the barrow.

The inside of the grave was as strange as a dream. Qantaqa's low growling filled the space like the hum of an angry beehive, but there was another sound, too—a strange, insistent piping. At first, as her eyes became used to the darkness, the flickering torchlight showed her only the long, broad curve of *Sea-Arrow* and the sagging timbers jutting through the barrow's earthen roof like ribs. Then she saw movement—Qantaqa's agitated tail and back legs, all that was visible of her past the stern of the boat. The earth around the wolf was aboil with small dark shapes—rats?

"Binabik!" she screamed. "Simon!"

The troll's voice, when it came, was hoarse and tattered with fright. "No, run away! This place is being . . . full of *boghanik*! Run!"

Terrified for her companions, Miriamele scrambled around the side of the boat. Something small and chittering leaped down from the wale above her head, raking her face with its claws. She shrieked and knocked it away, then pinned it to the ground with the torch. For a horrifying instant she saw a wizened little manlike thing writhing beneath the burning brand, matted hair sizzling, sharp-toothed mouth stretched in a shrill of agony. Miriamele screamed again, pulling the torch away as she kicked the dying thing into the shadows.

Her pulse beating in her temples until she felt her head would burst, she forced her way forward. Several more of the spidery things swarmed toward her, but she swiped at them with the twin torches and they danced back. She was close enough now to touch Qantaqa, but felt no urge to do so: the wolf was hard at work, moving swiftly in the confined space, breaking necks and tearing small bodies.

"Binabik!" she cried. "Simon! I'm here! Come toward the light!"

Her call brought another cluster of the chittering terrors toward her. She hit two with her torch, but the second almost pulled the brand from her grasp before it fell to the earth, squealing. A moment later she saw a shadow above her and jumped back, raising the torch again.

"It is me, Princess," Binabik gasped. He had climbed up onto *Sea-Arrow*'s railing. He stooped for a moment and vanished, then reemerged, only his eyes clearly visible in the blood and earth that smeared his face. He thrust the butt of a long spear down for her to grasp. "Take this. Do not let them become close!"

She grasped the spear, then was forced to turn and sweep a half dozen of the things against the barrow wall. She dropped one of the torches. As she bent, another of the shriveled creatures pranced toward her; she speared it as a fisherman might. It wriggled on the spearhead, slow to die.

"Simon!" she shouted. "Where is he?" She picked up the second torch and held it toward Binabik, who had ducked down into the boat once more, and now stood with an ax clutched in his hands, a weapon nearly as long as the troll was tall.

"I cannot be holding the torch," Binabik said breathlessly. "Push it into the wall." He raised the ax over his head and then jumped down beside her.

Miriamele did as he said, jamming the butt of the torch into the crumbling earth.

"*Hinik Aia!*" Binabik shouted. Qantaqa backed up, but the wolf seemed reluctant to disengage; she made several snarling rushes back toward the chirping creatures. While she was engaged on one such sortie, another swarm of the things scurried around her. Binabik swept several into bloody ruin with the ax and Miriamele fended off others with jabs of the spear. Qantaqa finished her engagement and swept in to finish off the raiding party. The rest of the crowding creatures sputtered angrily, their white eyes gleaming like a hundred tiny moons, but they did not seem anxious to follow Miriamele and her companions as they backed toward the hole.

"Where is Simon?" she asked again. Even as she spoke, she knew she did not want to hear the answer. There was a kind of cold nothingness inside her. Binabik would not leave Simon behind if he still lived.

"I am not knowing," Binabik said harshly. "But he is beyond our power for helping. Lead us into the air."

Miriamele pulled herself up and through the hole in the mound. She emerged from the darkness into the violet of evening and a chilly wind. When she turned to extend the spear's haft down into the barrow for Binabik to clasp, she saw the creatures capering in impotent anger around the base of *Sea-Arrow*, their shadows made long and even more grotesque by torchlight. Just before Binabik's shoulders rose to block the hole, she caught a momentary glimpse of her grandfather's pale, serene face.

The troll huddled before the paltry fire, his face a soiled mask of loss. Miriamele tried to find her own pain and could not. She felt empty, scoured of feeling. Qantaqa, reclining nearby, cocked her head to one side as if puzzled by the silence. Her chops were sticky with gore.

"He was falling through," Binabik said slowly. "One moment he was before me, then he was gone. I was digging and digging, but there was only dirt." He shook his head. "Digging and digging. Then the *boghanik* came." He coughed and spat a glob of mud onto the fire. "So many they were, up from the dirt like worms. And more were coming always. More and more."

"You said it was a tunnel. Maybe there were other tunnels." Miriamele heard the unreal calmness of her voice with wonder. "Maybe he just fell through into another tunnel. When those things, those . . . diggers . . . go away, we can search."

"Yes, with certainty." Binabik's voice was flat.

"We'll find him. You'll see."

The troll ran his hand across his face and brought it away smeared with dirt and blood. He stared at it absently.

"There's water in the skin bag," she said. "Let me clean those cuts."

"You are also bleeding." Binabik pointed a stubby black finger at her face.

"I'll get the water." She stood on shaky legs. "We'll find Simon. You'll see."

Binabik did not reply. As Miriamele walked unsteadily toward their packs, she reached up to dab at her jaw, at the spot where the digger's claws had raked her. The blood was almost dry, but when she touched her cheeks, they were wet with tears—tears that she had not even known she was crying.

He's gone, she thought. *Gone.*

Her eyes blurred so that she almost stumbled.

ꙮ

Elias, High King of Osten Ard, stood at the window and stared up at the pale, looming finger of Green Angel Tower, silvered by moonlight. Wrapped in silence and secrecy, it seemed a specter sent from another world, a bearer of strange tidings. Elias watched it as a man who knows he will live and die a sailor watches the sea.

The king's chamber was as disorderly as an animal nest. The bed in the middle of the room was naked but for the sweat-stained pallet; the few blankets that remained lay tangled on the floor, unused, home now to whatever small creatures could bear the chilly air that Elias found more a necessity than a comfort.

The window at which the king stood, like all the other windows of the long chamber, was flung wide. Rainwater was puddled on the stone tiles beneath the casements; on some particularly cold nights it froze, making streaks of white across the floor. The wind had also carried in leaves and stems and even the stiffened corpse of a sparrow.

Elias watched the tower until the moon haloed the angel's silhouette atop the spire. At last he turned, pulling his tattered robe about him, his white skin showing through the gaps where the threads had rotted in their seams.

"Hengfisk," he whispered. "My cup."

What had seemed another clump of bedding wadded in the corner of the room now unfurled itself and stood. The silent monk scurried to a table just inside the chamber door and uncapped a stone ewer. He filled a goblet with dark, steaming liquid, then brought it to the king. The monk's ever-present smile, perhaps a little less wide than usual, glimmered faintly in the dark room.

"I shall not sleep again tonight," the king said. "It is the dreams, you know." Hengfisk stood silently, but his bulging eyes offered complete attention.

"And there is something else. Something I can feel but cannot understand." He took his goblet and returned to the window. The hilt of the gray sword Sorrow scraped against the stone sill. Elias had not taken it off in a long time, even to sleep; the blade had pressed its own shape into the pallet beside the indentation of the king's form.

Elias raised his cup to his lips, swallowed, then sighed. "There is a change in the music," he said quietly. "The great music of the dark. Pryrates has said nothing, but I know. I do not need that eunuch to tell me everything. I can *see* things now, hear things . . . smell things." He wiped his mouth with the sleeve of his robe, leaving a new smear of black among the countless others already dried on the cloth. "Somebody has changed things." He paused for a long moment. "But perhaps Pryrates isn't merely hiding it from me." The king turned to regard his cupbearer with an expression that was almost sane. "Perhaps Pryrates himself doesn't know. It wouldn't be the only thing he doesn't know. I still have a few secrets of my own." Elias brooded. "But if Pryrates doesn't realize how . . . how things have changed . . . now what might *that* mean, I wonder?" He turned back to the window, watching the tower. "What might that mean?"

Hengfisk waited patiently. Finally, Elias finished his draught and held out the cup. The monk took it from the king's hand and returned it to the table beside the door, then moved back to his corner. He curled himself against the wall, but his head stayed up, as though he waited further instruction.

"The tower is waiting," Elias said quietly. "It has been waiting a long time."

As he leaned against the sill a wind arose and set his dark hair fluttering, then lifted some of the leaves from the floor and sent them whispering and rattling around the chamber.

"Oh, Father . . ." the king said softly. "God of Mercy, I wish I could sleep."

⚜

For a horrifying time, Simon felt himself drowning in cold, damp earth. Every nightmare he had ever had of death and burial flooded through him as dirt filled his eyes, his nose, pinioned his arms and legs. He clawed until he could not feel his hands at the ends of his arms, but still the choking earth surrounded him.

Then, just as abruptly as the earth had swallowed him, it seemed to vomit him out once more. His legs, kicking like a drowning man's, were suddenly thrashing without resistance; an instant later he felt himself tumbling downward in a great avalanche of loose soil. He landed heavily, the breath he had held so long pushed out of him in a painful hiss. He gasped and swallowed dirt.

He was on his knees for long moments, choking and retching. When the flashes of light swarming before his eyes began to disperse, he lifted his head. There was light somewhere—not much, but enough to show him the vague outlines of a rounded space only a little wider than he was. Another tunnel? Or just a pit down in the depths, a grave of his very own where the air would soon give out?

A small flame seemed to have sprouted from the loose mound of soil upon which he crouched. That was the source of light. When he could force his trembling limbs to move, he crawled toward it and discovered that it was the tip of one of his torches, the only part of the burning brand that had not been buried in the great fall of earth. As carefully as he could, he worked his hand into the loamy earth and freed the torch, then flicked off the clinging dirt, cursing distractedly when he scorched his fingers. When it was as clean as he could get it, he turned it upside down so that the small flame could spread; soon the glow widened.

The first thing Simon saw was that he was indeed in another tunnel. In one direction it led downward, just like the one he had entered from the barrow, but *this* tunnel had no opening to the world above: the end was just beside him, a featureless spill of dirt, a great blunt nothingness of damp clods and loose soil. He could see no light or anything else beyond it; whatever gap he had fallen through was now choked with earth.

The second thing he saw was a dull glint of metal in the pile of dirt before him. He reached to pick it up, and was distractedly disappointed at how easily it came loose, how small an object it was. It was not Bright-Nail. It was a silver belt buckle.

Simon lifted the mud-smeared buckle up to catch the torchlight. When he wiped the dirt away with his fingers, he laughed, a harshly painful sound that died quickly in the narrow confines. So this was what he had risked his life for—*this* was the lure that had dropped him into the prisoning depths. The buckle was so scratched and worn that the markings were only faintly recognizable. Some kind of animal head was at the center of it, something square-snouted like a bear or pig; around it were a few slender things that might be sticks or arrows. It was old and meaningless. It was worthless.

Simon plunged his torch handle into the ground, then abruptly scrambled up the mound of soil. The sky *must* be somewhere above. His terror was growing strong. Surely Binabik was digging for him! But how would the troll find him if Simon did not help!? He slid back a cubit for every cubit he scrambled at first, until he found a way to move without dislodging so much soil. At last he climbed far enough that he could lay his hands against the loose earth at the tunnel's end. He dug there frantically, freeing a shower of dirt, but more dirt kept appearing to take its place. As long moments passed his movements became even more uncontrolled. He tore at the unresisting earth, gouged it away in great handfuls, bringing down avalanches of soil from above, but all to no effect. Tears streamed down his face, mixing with the beads of sweat until his eyes stung. There was no end to it, no matter how he dug.

He stopped at last, shuddering, covered in settling dirt almost to his waist. His heart was racing so swiftly that it took him a moment to realize that the tunnel had grown darker. He turned to see that his heedless digging had almost buried the torch once more. Simon stared, suddenly afraid that if he crawled back down the slope, down the pile of loose earth, sliding soil would cover the flame completely. Once extinguished, there would be no relighting it. He would be in complete and utter blackness.

He carefully freed himself from the small landslide that prisoned his legs, moving as delicately as he once had while stalking frogs across the Hayholt's moat.

Gently, gently, he told himself. *Not the dark, no. Need the light. There won't be anything left for them to find if I lose the light.*

A tiny avalanche was stirred. Clods of dirt went tumbling down the pile and a small slide stopped just short of the flame, which wavered. Simon's heart nearly stopped.

Gently. Gently. Very gently.

When his hands pushed into the crumbly soil beneath the torch, he held his breath; when he had lifted it free, he let the breath out again. There was such a narrow line—really only a fraying edge of shadow—between the darkness and the light.

Simon went through the process of cleaning the torch all over again, singeing the same fingers, cursing the same curses, until he discovered that his sheathed Qanuc knife was still strapped to his leg. After saying a prayer in gratitude for this, what seemed his first piece of luck in some time, he used the bone blade to finish the task. He wondered briefly how long the torch would continue to burn, but pushed the thought away. There was no chance of clawing his way out, that seemed clear. So he would move a little farther down the tunnel and wait for Binabik and Miriamele to dig down from above. Surely they would be doing so soon. And there was plenty of air, when he stopped to think of it. . . .

As he tipped the torch over so that the whole head caught fire once more, another patter of dirt came tumbling down the slope. Simon was so intent on what he was doing that he did not look up until a second fall of earth caught his attention. He held up the torch and squinted at the plugged end of the tunnel. The dirt was . . . *moving.*

Something like a tiny black tree pushed up from the soil, flexing flat, slender branches. An instant later another sprouted next to it, then a small lump forced its way up between them. It was a head. Blind white eyes turned toward him and nostrils twitched. A mouth opened in a terrible semblance of a human grin.

More hands and heads were pushing up through the dirt. Simon, who had been staring in shocked terror, lurched up onto his knees, holding his torch and knife before him.

Bukken! Diggers! His throat clenched.

There were perhaps half a dozen in all. As they freed themselves from the loose earth they bunched together, twittering quietly among themselves, their spindly, hairy limbs so intertwined and their movements so twitchingly sudden that he could not count them accurately. He waved the torch at them and they shrank back, but not far. They were being cautious, but they were certainly not frightened.

Usires Aedon, he prayed silently. *I am in the earth with the diggers. Save me now. Somebody please save me.*

They advanced in a clump, but then suddenly separated, skittering toward the walls. Simon shouted in fear and smacked the nearest with his torch. It shrilled in agony but leaped and wrapped its legs and arms about his wrist; sharp teeth sank into his hand so that he almost dropped the torch. His shout turning to a wordless rasp of pain, he smashed his arm against the wall of the tunnel, trying to dislodge the thing. Several more, heartened by the removal of the flame, pranced forward, piping eagerly.

Simon slashed at one and caught it with his knife, tearing at the moldy bits of rags the diggers wore like garments, cutting deeply into the meat beneath. He drove his other hand against the wall again, as hard as he could, and felt small bones break. The thing that had clutched his wrist dropped free, but Simon's hand was throbbing as though bitten by a venomous serpent.

He moved back, sliding awkwardly down the slope on his knees, struggling to keep his balance on the loosely-packed earth as the diggers ran at him. He swung his torch back and forth in a wide arc; the three creatures still standing stared back at him, shriveled little faces drawn tight, mouths open in hatred and fear. Three. And two small crumpled forms lying in the dirt where he had kneeled a moment before. So had there been only five . . . ?

Something dropped from the tunnel roof onto the top of his head. Ragged claws scraped at his face and a hand grabbed his upper lip. Simon shrieked and reached up, grabbed the squirming body as hard as he could, then pulled. After a moment's struggle it came free with several tufts of his hair clutched in its fists. Still screaming in disgust and terror, he smashed it down against the ground, then flung the broken body toward the others. He saw the remaining three tumble back into the shadows before he turned and crawled away down the tunnel as fast as he could, cursing and spluttering, spitting to rid his mouth of the vile taste of the digger's oily skin.

Simon expected any moment to feel something clutch at his legs; when he had crawled for some time he turned and raised the torch. He thought he saw a faint, pale gleam of eyes, but couldn't be sure. He turned and continued scrambling downward. Twice he dropped the torch, snatching it up as swiftly and fearfully as if it were his own heart tumbled from his breast.

The diggers did not seem to have pursued him. Simon felt some of the fear dropping away, but his heart still pounded. Beneath his hands and knees, the soil of the tunnel had become firmer.

After a while he stopped and sat back. The torchlight showed nothing following in the featureless tunnel behind him, but something was different. He looked up. The roof was much farther away—too far to touch while sitting down.

Simon took a deep breath, then another. He stayed where he was until he felt as though the air in his lungs was beginning to do him some good once more, then held up the torch and repeated his inspection. The tunnel had indeed grown wider, higher. He reached out to touch the wall and found that it was almost as solid as mud brick.

With a last look behind him, Simon struggled up onto his feet. The roof of the tunnel was a handsbreadth above his head.

Weary beyond belief, he raised the torch before him and began to walk. He knew now why Binabik and Miriamele had not been able to dig down to him. He hoped the diggers had not caught Binabik in the barrow. It was something he could not think about for more than a moment—his poor friend! The brave little man! But Simon had his own very immediate problems.

The tunnel was featureless as a rabbit warren, and led downward, ever deeper into the earth's black places. Simon desperately wanted to return to the light, to feel the wind—the last thing he wanted was to be in this place, this long, slender tomb. But there was nowhere else to go. He was alone again. He was utterly, utterly alone.

Aching in every joint, struggling to push away each dreadful thought before it could find a resting place in a mind which felt no less pained than his body, Simon plodded down into shadow.

39

The Fallen Sun

✵

Eolair stared at the remnants of his Hernystiri troop. Of the hundred or so who had left their western land to accompany him, only a little more than two score remained. These survivors sat huddled around their fires at the base of the hillside below Naglimund, their faces gaunt, their eyes empty as dry wells.

Look at these poor, brave men, Eolair thought. *Who would ever know that we were winning?* The count felt as drained of blood and courage as any of them; he felt insubstantial as a ghost.

As Eolair walked from one fire to the next, a whisper of strange music came wafting down the hill. The count saw the men stiffen, then whisper unhappily among themselves. It was only the singing of the Sithi, who were walking sentry outside Naglimund's broken walls . . . but even the Hernystirmen's Sithi allies were alien enough to make mortals anxious. And the Norns, the Sithi's immortal cousins, sang, too.

A fortnight of siege had razed Naglimund's walls, but the white-skinned defenders had only retreated to the inner castle, which had proved surprisingly resistant to defeat. There were forces at play that Eolair could not understand, things that even the mind of the shrewdest mortal general could not grasp— and Count Eolair, as he often reminded himself, was no general. He was a landowner, a somewhat unwilling courtier, and a skilled diplomat. Small surprise that he, like his men, felt that he was swimming in currents too powerful for his weak skills.

The Norns had established their defenses by the means of what sounded, when Jiriki described it to him, like pure magic. They had "sung a Hesitancy," Jiriki explained. There was "Shadow-mastery" at work. Until the music was understood and the shadows untangled, the castle would not fall. In the interim, clouds gathered overhead, stormed briefly, then retreated. At other times, when the skies were clear, lightning flashed and thunder boomed. The mists around Naglimund's keep sometimes seemed to become diamond hard, sparkling like glass; at other moments they turned blood red or ink black, and sent tendrils swirling high above the walls to claw at the sky. Eolair begged for explanation, but to Jiriki, what the Norns were doing—and what his own people were trying to do in retaliation—was no stranger than wooden hoardings or siege engines or any of the other machinery of humankind's wars: the Sitha terms meant little or nothing to Eolair, who could only shake his head in fearful wonder. He and his men were caught up in a battle of monsters and wizards out of bardic songs. This was no place for mortals—and the mortals knew it.

Pondering, walking in circles, the count had returned to his own fire.

"Eolair," Isorn greeted him, "I have saved the last swallows for you." He motioned the count toward the fire and held up a wineskin.

Eolair took a swallow, more out of comradeship than anything else. He had never been much of a drinker, especially when there was work to do: it was too hard to keep a cool head at a foreign court when one washed large dinners down with commensurate amounts of spirits. "Thank you." He brushed a thin skin of snow from the log and sat down, pushing his bootsoles near to the fire. "I am tired," he said quietly. "Where is Maegwin?"

"She was out walking earlier. But I am certain she has gone to sleep by now." He gestured to a tent a short distance away.

"She should not walk by herself," Eolair said.

"One of the men went with her. And she stays close by. You know I would not let her go far away, even under guard."

"I know." Eolair shook his head. "But she is so sick-spirited—it seems a criminal thing to bring her to a battlefield. *Especially* a battlefield like this." His hand swept out and gestured to the hillside and the snow, but Isorn certainly knew that it was not the terrain or weather that he meant.

The young Rimmersman shrugged. "She is mad, yes, but she seems to be more at ease than the men."

"Don't say that!" Eolair snapped. "She is not mad!" He took a shaky breath.

Isorn looked at him kindly. "If this is not madness, Eolair, what is? She speaks as though she is in the land of your gods."

"I sometimes wonder if she is not right."

Isorn lifted his arm, letting the firelight play across the jagged weal that ran from wrist to elbow. "If this is Heaven, then the priests at Elvritshalla misled me." He grinned. "But if we are dead already, then I suppose we have nothing left to fear."

Eolair shuddered. "That is just what worries me. She *does* think that she is dead, Isorn! At any moment she may walk out into the middle of the fighting again, as she did the first time she slipped away. . . ."

Isorn put a wide hand on his shoulder. "Her madness seems more clever to me than that. And she may not be as terrified as the men, but she is not un-afraid. She doesn't like that damned windy castle or those damned, filthy white things any more than we do. She has been safe so far and we will keep her that way. Surely you do not need more things to worry about?"

The count smiled wearily. "So, Isorn Isgrimnurson, you are going to take up your father's job, I see."

"What do you mean?"

"I have seen what your father does for Josua. Picks the prince up when he wants to lie down, pokes his ribs and sings him songs when the prince wants to weep. So you will be my Isgrimnur?"

The Rimmersman's grin was wide. "My father and I are simple men. We do not have the brains to worry like you and Josua."

Eolair snorted and reached out for the wineskin.

For the third night running, the count dreamed of the most recent skirmish inside Naglimund's walls, a nightmare more vivid and terrifying than anything mere imagination could contrive.

It had been a particularly dreadful battle. The Hernystirmen, now wearing masks of cloth rubbed with fat or tree sap to keep off the Norn's madness-dust, had become as frightening to look at as the rest of the combatants; those mortals who had survived the first days of the siege now fought with terrified determination, knowing that nothing else would give them a chance of leaving this haunted place alive. The greatest part of the struggle had taken place in the narrow spaces between scorched, crumbling buildings and through winter-blasted gardens—places where Eolair had once walked on warm evenings with ladies of Josua's court.

The dwindling army of Norns defended the stolen citadel with a kind of heedless madness: Count Eolair had seen one of them shove forward against a sword rammed through his chest, working his way up the blade to kill the mortal that clutched the hilt before dying in a coughing spray of red.

Most of the giants had also died, but each one exacted a horrible toll of men and Sithi before it fell. Dreaming, remembering, Eolair was again forced to watch one of the huge brutes grab Ule Frekkeson, one of the few Rimmersmen who had accompanied the war party out of Hernysadharc, then swing him around and dash his brains out against a wall as easily as a man might kill a cat. As a trio of Sithi surrounded him, the Hunë contemptuously shook the almost headless corpse at them, showering them with gore. The hairy giant then used Ule's body as a club, killing one of the Sithi with it before the spears of the other two punched into the monster's heart.

Squirming in the dream's unshakable grasp, Eolair helplessly watched dead Ule used as a weapon, smashed left and right until his body began to come apart. . . .

He woke quivering, head throbbing as though it might burst. He pressed his hands against his temples and squeezed, trying to relieve the pressure. How could a man see such things and keep his reason?

A hand touched his wrist.

Terrified, Eolair gasped and flung himself to one side, scrabbling for his sword. A tall shadow loomed in the doorway of his tent.

"Peace, Count Eolair," said Jiriki. "I am sorry I startled you. I called from outside the door, but I thought you must be asleep since you did not reply. Please forgive my intrusion."

Eolair was relieved, but angry and embarrassed. "What do you want?"

"Forgive me, please. I came because it is important and time is short."

The count shook his head and took a slow breath. "What is it? Is something wrong?"

"Likimeya asks that you come. All will be explained." He lifted the tent flap and stepped back outside. "Will you come? I will wait for you to dress."

"Yes . . . yes, certainly I will."

The count felt a sort of muted pride. Likimeya had sent her son for him, and since these days Jiriki seemed involved only in things of the first and most crucial order, the Sithi must indeed think it important that Eolair come. A moment later his pride turned to a gnawing of disquiet: could circumstances be so bad that they were searching for ideas or leadership from the master of two score terrified mortal warriors? He had been sure they were winning the siege.

It took only a few moments to secure his sword belt and pull on his boots and fur-lined cloak. He followed Jiriki across the foggy hillside, marveling that the footfalls of the Sitha, who was as tall as Eolair and almost as broad, should only dimple the snow while his own boots dug deep gouges in the white crust.

Eolair looked up to where Naglimund crouched on the hilltop like a huddled, wounded beast. It was almost impossible to believe that it had once been a place where people danced and talked and loved. Prince Josua's court had been thought by some rather grim—but, oh, how those who had mocked the prince would feel their mouths dry and their hearts flutter if they saw what grim *truly* meant.

Jiriki led the count among the gossamer-thin tents of the Sithi, tents that gleamed against the snow as though they were half-soaked in moonlight. Despite the hour, halfway between midnight and dawn, many of the Fair Folk were out; they stood in solemn clusters and stared at the sky or sat on the ground singing quietly. None of them seemed at all bothered by the freezing wind that had Eolair clutching his hood close beneath his chin. He hoped that Likimeya had a fire burning, if only out of consideration for the frailties of a mortal visitor.

"We have questions to ask you about this place you call Naglimund, Count Eolair." There was more than a hint of command in Likimeya's voice.

Eolair turned from the blaze to face Jiriki, his mother, and tall, black-haired Kuroyi. "What can I tell you that I have not told you already?" The count felt a mild anger at the Sithi's confusing habits, but found it hard to hold that emotion in the presence of Likimeya's powerful, even gaze. "And is it not a little late to be asking, since the siege began a fortnight ago?"

"It is not such things as the height of walls and the depth of wells that we need to know." Jiriki sat down beside the count, the cloth of his thin shirt glinting. "You have already told us much that has helped us."

"You spent time in Naglimund when the mortal prince Josua ruled here." Likimeya spoke briskly, as though impatient with her son's attempts at diplomacy. "Does it have secrets?"

"Secrets?" Eolair shook his head. "Now I am completely confounded. What do you mean?"

"This is not fair to the mortal." Kuroyi spoke with an emotionless reserve that was extreme even for the Sithi. "He deserves to know more. If Zinjadu had lived, she could tell him. Since I failed my old friend and she is now voyaging with the Ancestors, I will take her place as the lore-giver." He turned to Likimeya. "If Year-Dancing House approves, of course."

Likimeya made a wordless musical noise, then flicked her hand in permission.

"Jiriki i-Sa'onserei has told you something of the Road of Dreams, Count Eolair?" Kuroyi asked.

"Yes, he has told me a little. Also, we Hernystiri still have many stories of the past and of your people. There are those living among us who claim they can walk the Dream Road, just as you taught our ancestors to do." He thought sourly of Maegwin's would-be mentor, the scryer Diawen: if some Hernystiri did still have that power, it had little to do with good sense or responsibility.

"Then I am sure he has spoken of the Witnesses, too—those objects that we use to make the journeying easier." Kuroyi hesitated, then reached into his milk-white shirt and produced a round, translucent yellow object that caught the firelight like a globule of amber or a ball of melted glass. "This is one such—my own." He let Eolair look for a moment, then tucked the thing away again. "Like most others, it is of no use in these strange times—the Dream Road is as impassable as a road of this world might be in a terrible blizzard.

"But there are other Witnesses, too: larger, more powerful objects that are not moveable, and are linked to the place where they are found. Master Witnesses, they are called, for they can look upon many things and places. You have seen one such."

"The Shard?"

Kuroyi nodded his head once. "In Mezutu'a, yes. There were others, although most are now lost to time and earth-changes. One lies beneath the castle of your enemy King Elias."

"Beneath the Hayholt?"

"Yes. The Pool of Three Depths is its name. But it has been dry and voiceless for centuries."

"And this has something to do with Naglimund? Is there something of that sort here?"

Kuroyi smiled, a narrow, wintery smile. "We are not sure."

"I don't understand," the count said. "How can you not be sure?"

The Sitha lifted his long-fingered hand. "Peace, Eolair of Nad Mullach. Let me finish my tale. By the standards of the Gardenborn it is quite short."

Eolair shifted slightly; he was glad for the firelight, which disguised his flush of embarrassment. How was it that among these folk he was as easily cowed as a child—as if all his years of statecraft had been forgotten? "My apologies."

"There have always been in Osten Ard certain places," Kuroyi resumed, "which act much like Master Witnesses . . . but in which no Master Witness seems to be present. That is, many of the effects are there—in fact, sometimes these places exhibit more powerful results than *any* Witness—but no object can be found which is responsible. Since we first came to this land long ago, we have studied such places, thinking that they might answer questions we have about the Witnesses and why they do what they do, about Death itself, even about the Unbeing that made us flee our native land and come here."

"Forgive me for interrupting again," said Eolair, "but how many of these places exist? And where are they?"

"We know of only a handful between far Nascadu and the wastelands of the white north. *A-Genay'asu'e*, we call them—'Houses of Traveling Beyond' would be a crude rendering in your tongue. And we Gardenborn are not the only ones to sense the power of these places: they often draw mortals as well, some merely seekers-after-knowledge, some god-maddened and dangerous. What mortals call Thisterborg, the hill near Asu'a, is one such spot."

"I know it." Remembering a black sled and a team of misshapen white goats, Eolair felt his flesh tighten. "Your cousins the Norns also know about Thister-borg. I saw them there."

Kuroyi did not seem surprised. "We Gardenborn have been interested in these sites since long before the families parted. The Hikeda'ya, like us, have made many attempts to harness the might of such places. But their power is as wild and unpredictable as the wind."

Eolair pondered. "So there is not a Master Witness here at Naglimund, but rather one of these things, a . . . Beyonding House? I cannot remember the words in your tongue."

Jiriki looked toward his mother, smiling and nodding with what almost looked like pride. Eolair felt a flash of annoyance; was a mortal who could listen and reason such a surprise to them?

"An *A-Genay'asu*. Yes, that is what we believe," said Kuroyi. "But it came to our attention late, and there was never a chance to find out before the mortals came."

"Before the mortals came with their iron spikes." Likimeya's soft voice was like the hiss that preceded a whip-crack. Surprised by her vehemence, Eolair looked up, then just as quickly turned his gaze back to Kuroyi's more placid face.

"Both Zida'ya and Hikeda'ya continued to come to this place after men built their castle here at Naglimund," the black-haired Sitha explained. "Our presence frightened the mortals, though they saw us only by moonlight, and even then only rarely. The man the Imperators had given to rule over the locality filled the fields all around with the iron that gave the place its name: Nail Fort."

"I knew that the nails were there to keep out the Peaceful Ones—what we Hernystiri call your folk," said Eolair, "but since it was built in the era when your people and ours were at peace, I could not understand why the place should have needed such defenses."

"The mortal named Aeswides who had it done may have felt a certain shame that he had trespassed on our lands in building this keep so close to our city Da'ai Chikiza, on the far side of those hills." Kuroyi gestured toward the east. "He may have feared that we would some day come and take the place back; he may also have thought that those of our folk who still made pilgrimage to this place were spies. Who knows? In fact, he traveled less and less out of the gates, and died at last a recluse—afraid, it was said, even to leave his own well-guarded chamber for terror of what the dreaded immortals might do." Kuroyi's cool smile returned. "Strangely, although the world is already full of fearful things, mortals seem always to hunt for new worries."

"Nor do we relinquish the old ones." Eolair returned the tall Sitha's smile. "For, like the cut of a man's cloak, we know that the tried and true is best in the long run. But I doubt you have brought me here only to tell about what some long-dead mortal did."

"No, we have not," Kuroyi agreed. "Since we were driven from the land at a time when we considered it better policy not to interfere, and to let the mortals build where they wished, we have unanswered questions still about this place."

"And we need those questions answered now, Count Eolair," Likimeya broke in. "So tell us: this place you call Naglimund—is it known among mortals for strangeness of any kind? Apparitions? Odd happenings? Is it reputed a haunt of spirits of the dead?"

The count frowned as he considered. "I must say that I have never heard anything like that. There are other places, many others, some within a league of my birthplace, of which I could tell you a whole night's worth of tales. But not Naglimund. And Prince Josua was always a lover of odd lore—I feel sure that if there were such stories, it would have been his pleasure to relate them." He shook his head. "I am sorry to force you to tell such a long tale yourself for so little result."

"We still think it likely that this place *is* an A-Genay'asu," Jiriki said. "We have thought so since long before Asu'a fell. Here, Count Eolair, you look thirsty. Let me pour for you."

The Hernystirman gratefully accepted another cup of mulled . . . something; whatever it was, it tasted of flowers and warmed him very nicely. "In any case," he said after he had taken a few sips, "what does it mean if Naglimund *is* such a place?"

"We are not certain. That is one of the things that worries us." Jiriki sat down across from Eolair and raised a slim hand. "We had hoped that the Hikeda'ya came here only to pay their part of the bargain with Elias, and that they had remained here because it was a way station between Stormspike and the castle that stands on Asu'a's bones."

"But you do not think that any longer." It was a statement, not a question.

"No. Our cousins have fought too hard, long past the time when they could have gained anything from resisting. This is not the final confrontation. However much Utuk'ku has reason to hate us, it is not a blind anger: she would not throw away the lives of so many Cloud Children to hold a useless ruin."

Eolair had not heard much about the Norn Queen, Utuk'ku, but what he had was shuddersome. "So what does she want? What do *they* want?"

Jiriki shook his head. "They want to remain in Naglimund. That is all we know for certain. And it will be dreadful work to drive them out. I fear for you and your remaining soldiers, Count Eolair. I fear for all of us."

A horrible thought occurred to the Hernystirman. "Forgive me, since I know little of these things—although perhaps more now than I would have wished—but you said that these Beyonding places had something to do with the secrets of . . . of death?"

"All mysteries are one mystery until they are solved," said Kuroyi. "We have tried to learn more about Death and Unbeing from the A-Genay'asu'e, yes."

"These Norns we are fighting are living creatures—but their master is not. Could they be trying to bring the Storm King . . . back to life?"

Eolair's question brought neither derisive laughter nor shocked silence.

"We have thought on this." Likimeya was blunt. "It cannot happen."

"Ineluki is dead." Kuroyi spoke more softly, but with equal firmness. "There are some things we know about only little, but death we know very well." His lips twitched in a tiny, dry smile. "Very well, indeed. Ineluki is dead. He cannot return to this world."

"But you told me he was in Stormspike," Eolair said to Jiriki. "You said that the Norns do as he bids. Are we at war against something imaginary?"

"It is indeed confusing, Count Eolair," Jiriki replied. "Ineluki—although he is not truly Ineluki any more—has no more existence than a sort of dream. He is an evil and vengeful dream, one that possesses all the craftiness that the Storm King had in life, as well as knowledge of the ultimate darknesses no living thing has ever had . . . but he is only a dream, for all of that. Trust that I speak truly. As we can travel on the Road of Dreams, and see and feel things there, so Ineluki can speak to his followers in Nakkiga through the Breathing Harp, which is one of the greatest of the Master Witnesses—although I would guess that Utuk'ku alone has the skill even to understand him. So he is not a thing, Eolair, with an existence in this world." He gestured to the walls of the tent. "He is not real, like this cloth is real, like the ground is real beneath our feet. But that does not mean he cannot do great evil . . . and Utuk'ku and her servitors are more than real enough."

"Forgive me if I seem stubborn," Eolair said, "but I have heard much tonight that is still confused in my head. If Ineluki cannot return, then why are the Norns so eager to hold Naglimund?"

"That is the question we must answer," said Jiriki. "Perhaps they hope to use the A-Genay'asu to make their master's voice clearer. Perhaps they intend to tap its force in some other way. But it is clear that they want this place very much. One of the Red Hand is here."

"The Red Hand? The Storm King's servants?"

"His greatest servants, since like him they have passed through death and into the outer realms. But they cannot exist in this world without an immense expenditure of power by him every moment they are embodied, for they are almost as much of a deadly contradiction as he is. That is why when one of them attacked us in our fastness at Jao é-Tinukai'i, we knew that the time had come to take up arms. Ineluki and Utuk'ku must have been desperate to expend so much force to silence Amerasu." He paused. Eolair stared, bewildered by the unfamiliar names. "I will explain this to you at a later time, Count Eolair." Jiriki stood. "I am sure you are weary, and we have talked much of your sleeping time away."

"But this Red Hand creature is here? Have you seen it?"

Jiriki pointed at the campfire. "Do you have to touch the flames to know that the fire is hot? He is here, and that is why we have not been able to overcome their most important defenses, why we must instead knock down stone walls and struggle with sword and spear. A large portion of Ineluki's power is burning down in the heart of Naglimund's keep. But for all his might, the Storm King has limits. He is spread thin . . . so there must be some reason he wishes this place to remain in the hands of the Hikeda'ya."

Eolair stood, too. The blur of strange ideas and names had begun to tell on him: he was indeed feeling the need for sleep. "Perhaps the Norns' task is something to do with the Red Hand, then," the count said. "Perhaps . . ."

Jiriki's smile was sad. "We have cursed you with our own plague of 'perhaps,' Count Eolair. We had hoped you would give us answers, but instead we have weighed you down with questions."

"I have not been free of them since old King John died." He stifled a yawn. "So this is nothing strange." He laughed. "What a thing to say! It is *maddeningly* strange. But not unusual. Not in these times."

"Not in these times," agreed Jiriki.

Eolair bowed to Likimeya, then nodded a farewell to stone-faced Kuroyi before walking out into the cold wind. Thoughts were buzzing in his head like flies, but he knew that nothing useful could be done about any of them. Sleep was what he needed. Perhaps, if he was lucky, he would sleep right through the remainder of this gods-cursed siege.

Maegwin had quietly left her tent while the weary guard—he seemed a sad and ragged sort to have received Heaven's favor, but who was she to question the gods?—gossiped by the fire with one of his fellows. Now she stood in the deep shadows of a copse of trees, not a hundred cubits downslope from the tumbled walls of Naglimund. Above her loomed the silhouette of the blocky stone keep. As she stared at it, wind sifted snow across her boots.

Scadach, she thought. *It is the Hole in Heaven. But what lies beyond?*

She had seen the demons that had come swarming through from the Outer Darkness—horrible corpse-white things and shaggy, monstrous ogres—and had watched the gods and a few dead mortal heroes fight with them. It was clear that the gods wished this wound in heaven's flesh healed so that no more evil could creep in. For a while it had seemed that the gods would win easily. Now she was not so sure.

There was . . . *something* inside Scadach. Something dark and hideously strong, something that was empty as a flame is empty, but that nevertheless had a kind of brooding life. She could feel it, could almost hear its dreadful ruminations; even the faint part of its brooding that licked against her mind cast her into despair. But at the same time, there was something oddly familiar about the thoughts of whatever lurked in Scadach, whatever godsbane burned so angrily in the deeps. She felt strangely drawn, as to a darkly fascinating sibling: that horrid something . . . was much like her.

But what could that mean? What a mad thought! What could there be in that gnawing, spiteful heat that was *anything* like her, a mortal woman, king's daughter, slain beloved of the gods now privileged to ride with them across the fields of heaven?

Maegwin stood in the snow, silent, motionless, and let the incomprehensible thoughts of the thing within Scadach wash over her. She felt its turmoil. Hatred, that was what it felt . . . and something more. A hatred of the living coupled with an agonized longing for quietude and death.

She shivered. How could heaven be so cold, even in this black outer fringe? *But I don't long for death! Perhaps I did when I was alive, for a time. But now that is behind me. Because I died—I died—and the gods lifted me up to their country. Why should I still feel that so strongly? I am dead. I am no longer afraid, as I once was. I did my duty and brought the gods to save my people—no one can say I did not. I no longer mourn for my brother and father. I am dead, and nothing can harm me. I have nothing in common with that . . . thing out there in the darkness, beyond those walls of heaven-stone.*

A sudden thought came to her. *But where is my father? And where is Gwythinn? Didn't they both die heroes? Surely the gods have lifted them up and carried them away after their deaths, just as they did me. And surely they would have demanded to be allowed to fight here, at the side of the Masters of Heaven. Where are they?*

Maegwin stood, dumbfounded. She shivered again. It was wretchedly cold here. Were the gods playing some trick on her? Was there still some test she had yet to pass before she could be reunited with her father and brother, with her long-dead mother Penemhwye? How could that be?

Troubled, Maegwin turned and hurried back down the slope toward the lights of the other homeless souls.

More than five hundred pikemen of Metessa stood shoulder to shoulder in the neck of the Onestrine Pass, shields lifted above their heads so that it seemed some great centipede had lodged in the narrows between the cliffs. The baron's men wore boiled leather cuirasses and iron helms, armor that was nicked and abraded from long use. The Crane banner of their House waved above the serried pikes.

Nabbanai bowmen along the canyon walls filled the sky with a swarm of arrows. Most bounced harmlessly from the shield roof, but some found their way through the locked shields. Wherever a Metessan fell, though, his fellows drew together.

"The bowmen cannot move them!" Sludig enthused. "Varellan must charge! By the Aedon, the baron's men are proud bastards!" He turned to Isgrimnur with a look of glee on his face. "Josua has chosen his allies well!"

The duke nodded, but could not match Sludig's excitement. As he stood with the elite of Josua's forces, what was now being called the prince's household guard—a curious phrase Isgrimnur thought, considering the prince had no house—the duke only wanted the fighting to end. He was tired of war.

As he stared out across the narrowing valley, he was struck by how the ridged hills on both sides resembled a cage of ribs, the Anitullean Road its breastbone. When Prester John had fought his way through to victory in this same Frasilis Valley more than fifty years before, it was said that so many had died that the bodies were not all buried for months. The pass and the open land to the north of the valley had been littered with bones, the sky black with carrion birds for days.

And to what purpose? Isgrimnur wondered. *Less than a man's lifetime has passed and here we are again, making more feasts for the vultures. Over and over and over. I am sick with it.*

He sat uncomfortably in the saddle, looking down the length of the pass. Below him stood the waiting ranks of the prince's newest allies, their house banners bright in the noon sun, an aviary of Goose, Pheasant, Tern, and Grouse. Seriddan's neighboring barons had not been slow to follow his lead: none seemed happy with Duke Benigaris, and the resurrected Camaris was difficult to ignore.

Isgrimnur was struck by the circularity of the situation. Josua's forces were led by a man thought long-dead, and they were fighting a crucial battle in the very place where Prester John, Josua's father and Camaris' closest friend, had won his greatest triumph. It should have been a good omen, Isgrimnur thought . . . but instead he felt the past reaching up to squeeze the life out of the present, as though History was some great and jealous monster that wished to force all that followed after into unhappy mimicry.

This is no life for an old man. The duke sighed. Sludig, watching raptly as the battle developed, was oblivious. *To fight a war, you must believe it can accomplish something. We fight this one to save John's kingdom, or perhaps even to save all of mankind . . . but isn't that what we always think? That all wars are useless—except the one we're fighting now?*

He fingered his reins. His back was stiff, sore already, and he had not even put it to any hard work. Kvalnir hung sheathed at his side, untouched since he had sharpened it and polished it in the sleepless hours last night.

I'm just tired, he thought. *I want Elvritshalla back. I want to see my grandchildren. I want to walk with my wife by the Gratuvask when the ice is breaking up. But I can have none of those things until this damnable fighting is over.*

And that is why we do it, he decided. *Because we hope it will bring us peace. But it never, never does. . . .*

Sludig cried out. Isgrimnur looked up, startled, but his carl's shout had been one of glee.

"Look! Camaris and the horsemen are coming down on them!"

When it had become clear that bowshot would not dislodge Seriddan's Metessan shield wall from the center of the pass, Varellan of Nabban had ordered another charge by his knights. Now that Varellan's forces had committed themselves to pushing the prince's troops back down the valley, Camaris and Hotvig's Thrithings-men had come down from the hillroads and thrown themselves into the side of Varellan's larger force.

"Where is Camaris?" Sludig said. "Ah! There! I see his helm!"

Isgrimnur could see it, too. The sea-dragon was little more than a flaming smear of gold from this distance, but its wearer stood tall in his stirrups, a visible circle of dismay spreading around him as the Nabbanai knights struggled to stay out of Thorn's black reach.

Prince Josua, who had been watching the battle from a point about a hundred cubits downslope from Isgrimnur and Sludig, now turned Vinyafod toward them. "Sludig!" he called. "Tell Freosel I want his troop to wait until he counts his fingers ten times after I give the sign for the rest of us to charge."

"Yes, Highness." Sludig wheeled his steed around and jogged toward where Freosel and the rest of Josua's household troop stood in fretting anticipation.

The prince continued upslope until he was at Isgrimnur's side. "Varellan's youth is finally beginning to show. He has proved himself overeager."

"There are worse faults in a commander," Isgrimnur replied, "but you're right. He should have been content to hold the mouth of the pass."

"But he thought he saw a weakness when he threw us back yesterday." Josua squinted up at the sky. "Now he is committed to pushing us back. We are lucky. Benigaris, for all his rashness in other matters, would never have taken such a risk."

"Then why did he take the chance of sending little brother in the first place?"

Josua shrugged. "Who knows? Perhaps he underestimated us. Remember also that Benigaris does not rule alone in Nabban."

Isgrimnur grunted. "Poor Leobardis. What did he do to deserve such a wife and son?"

"Again, who knows? But perhaps there is some end that we cannot see to all this."

The duke shrugged.

The prince was watching the flow of the battle critically, eyes shadowed in the depths of his helm. He had drawn Naidel, which lay across his saddle and knee. "Almost time," he said. "Almost time."

"They are still many more than us, Josua." Isgrimnur pulled Kvalnir from its sheath. There remained a momentary pleasure in this: the blade had stood him well in many a contest, witnessed by the fact that he was still here, still alive, with aching back and chafing armor and doubts and all.

"But we have Camaris—and you, old friend." Josua grinned tightly. "We can ask for no better odds." His gaze had not left the neck of the pass. "May Usires the Ransomer preserve us." The prince solemnly made the sign of the Tree on his breast, then lifted his hand. Naidel caught the sunlight, and for a moment Isgrimnur found it hard to breathe. "To me, men!" Josua cried.

A horn sounded on the slopes above him. From the narrows of the pass, Cellian blared back an answer.

As the prince's troops and the rebel barons and their men charged up the road, Isgrimnur could not help marveling. They had become a real army at last, several thousand strong. When he remembered how it had begun, Josua and a dozen other bedraggled survivors slipping out of Naglimund through a back door, he felt heartened. Surely God the Merciful could not bring them so far only to dash their hopes!

The Metessans had held firm. Josua and his army swirled around and past them; the pikemen, freed from their deadly chore, dragged their wounded back down the road. The prince's forces flung themselves on Varellan's knights, whose superior numbers and heavy armor had been overwhelming even the ferocity of Camaris and the Thrithings-men.

Isgrimnur held back at first, lending aid where he could, but unwilling to throw himself into the thick, where lives seemed to be measured in instants. He spotted one of Hotvig's men unhorsed, standing over his dying steed and warding off the pike of a mounted knight. Isgrimnur rode forward, bellowing a challenge; when the Nabbanai knight heard him and turned, the Thrithings-man leapt forward and shoved his sword in beneath the man's arm where there was no shielding metal on his leather coat. As the knight toppled, bleeding, Isgrimnur felt a twitch of fury at his ally's dishonorable tactic, but when the rescued man shouted his thanks and legged down the slope, back into the heart of the struggle, the duke did not know any longer what to think. Should the Thrithings-man have died to preserve the lie that war could be honorable? But did another man deserve death because he believed that lie?

Slowly, as the afternoon turned, Isgrimnur found himself drawn deeper into the bloody conflict, slaying one man and driving several others back, bloodily wounded. He sustained only minor hurts himself, but only because luck was with him. He had stumbled once, and his opponent's swinging two-handed sword blow had glanced off the top of his helm; had he not fallen, it would likely have separated head from neck. Isgrimnur fought with none of his old battle rage, but fear brought out a strength he had forgotten he had. It was like the ghant nest all over again: everywhere he turned there were hard-shelled things that wanted to kill him.

Upslope, Josua and his knights had pushed Varellan's force back almost to the outer lip of the pass. Surely, thought Isgrimnur, some of those who fought in the front line must be able to see the broad valley below, green in the sunlight—except that to look at anything except the man in front of you and his weapon was to court swift death.

The knights of Nabban bent, but did not give. If they had made a mistake in trying to push their earlier advantage, they would make no mistake now. Whatever Prince Josua wanted, it was clear that he and his army would have to take it with their own hands.

As the sun began to dip down toward the horizon, Isgrimnur momentarily found himself in a backwater of the fighting, a spot in which the struggle had ended for a time; all around the bodies of murdered men lay sprawled like the leavings of a receding tide.

Just down the hill Isgrimnur saw a gleam of gold: it was Camaris. The duke watched him in amazement. Hours since the battle had begun, and although his movements seemed a little slower, still the old knight fought on with undiminished purpose. Camaris sat upright in his saddle, his movements as regular and unexcited as those of a farmer at work in his field. The battle horn swung at his side. Thorn whistled through the air like a black scythe, and where it touched, headless bodies fell like harvested wheat.

He's not as fierce as he ever was, Isgrimnur marveled, *he's fiercer. He fights like a damned soul. What is in that man's head? What gnaws at his heart?*

Isgrimnur suddenly felt shame that he stood watching as Camaris, twenty years his senior, fought and bled. The most important battle, perhaps, that had ever been fought, and it still hung in the balance, unclaimed. He was needed. Old and tired of war he might be, but he was still an experienced blade.

He lightly dug his spurs into his mount's side, heading toward the place where Sir Camaris now kept three foot soldiers at bay. It was a spot blocked from view by a web of low trees. Even though he had little doubt that Camaris could hold out until others reached him, it might be some while before they spotted him . . . and in any case, Camaris in the saddle was an inspiration to the rest of Josua's troops that would be a shame to waste behind concealing shrubbery.

Before he had gone more than a dozen cubits, Isgrimnur saw an arrow suddenly sprout from his horse's chest, just before his leg; the horse reared, shrilling with agony. Isgrimnur felt a burning pain in his own side, then a moment later he was tumbling free of his saddle. The ground rose up and hit him like a club. His horse, struggling for balance on the rocky slope, wavered above him with front legs flailing, then its shadow descended.

The last thing Isgrimnur saw and felt was a tremendous concussion of light, as though the sun had dropped from the sky to land on top of him.

40

Empires of Dust

✦

It was maddening. Simon was parched, his mouth dry as bone dust, and all around him echoed the sound of dripping water . . . but there was no water to be found. It was as though some demon had looked into his thoughts, then plucked out his fondest desire and turned it into a cruel trick.

He stopped, peering into the darkness. The tunnel had widened, but still led downward, and there had been no place to turn, no crossing corridors. Whatever made that dripping was now behind him, as though he had passed it somehow in the featureless shadows.

But that can't be! The sound was before me, and now it's behind me—but it was never beside me. Simon fought to keep down his fear, which felt like a living thing inside him, all tiny clicking scales and scrabbling claws.

He might be lost beneath the ground, he told himself, but he was not dead. He had been trapped in tunnels like these before and had come out into the sun again. And now he was older; he had seen things that few others had seen. Somehow, he would survive. And if he didn't? Then he would face the end without shame.

Brave words, mooncalf, an inner voice mocked him. *Brave words now. But when a sunless day and a moonless night pass with no water? When the torch burns out?*

Be quiet, he told the inner voice.

✦

"King John went down the darksome hole,"

Simon sang quietly. His throat hurt, but he was growing tired of the monotony of his bootheels clumping against the stone. Not to mention the miserable, lonely way the sound made him feel.

"To seek the fiery beast below,
Through caveish haunt of toad and troll,
Where none but he had dared to go . . ."

Simon frowned. If only this *were* the haunt of trolls. He would have given anything for Binabik's companionship—not to mention a skin full of water followed by a healthy swallow of *kangkang*. And if Prester John had brought nothing but a sword down into the earth—which he hadn't, come to think of it: wasn't that what the Hernystirman Eolair had come to Sesuad'ra to tell them? That John had found Minneyar somewhere down in the ground?—then what had he done for light? Simon had one torch, and its flame was beginning to look a little thin around the edges. It was all very well to go thumping and bumping about looking for dragons, but the songs never said much about food and water and trying to make fires.

Old cradle songs and missing swords and tunnels in the dark, fetid earth. How had his life ever come to revolve around such things? When Simon had prayed for knightly adventures, he had hoped for more noble things—battlefields and gleamingly polished armor, deeds of bravery, the love of the multitudes. He had found those, more or less, but they had not been what he had expected. And time and time again he was drawn back into this madness of swords and tunnels, as though he were being forced to play some childhood game long past the point where he had tired of it. . . .

His shoulder bumped against the wall and he almost fell. The torch dropped from his grasp and lay on the tunnel floor. Simon stared at it stupidly for a moment before suddenly regaining his senses. He snatched it up and held it tightly, as though the torch itself had tried to escape.

Mooncalf.

He sat down heavily. He was tired of walking, tired of empty nothingness and solitude. The tunnel had become a winding hole through irregular slabs of rock, which likely meant he was now deep among the bones of Swertclif; he seemed to be bound for the center of the earth.

Something in his pocket chafed against his leg, catching his attention. What was he carrying? He had been stumbling down these passageways for what seemed like hours, and he had not even bothered to see what oddments he had brought with him when he fell through the crumbling earth.

Emptying out the pockets stitched on his breeches, wincing and making soft sounds at the stinging of his abraded fingers, he discovered that he had not missed much by postponing his inventory. There was a stone, a round smooth one that he had picked up because he liked the heft of it, and the almost featureless belt buckle, which he had thought he discarded. He decided to keep it, thinking vaguely that it could be used for scratching or digging.

The only significant find was a bit of dried meat from yesterday's midafternoon meal. He looked longingly at the wrinkled strip, which was about the length and width of his finger, then put it aside. He had a feeling that he would want it more later than he did even now.

That accounted for his pockets. The gold ring Morgenes had sent to him was still on his finger, almost invisible under a layer of dirt, but whatever use or significance it might have in the world of sunlight was meaningless here: he could not eat it, and it would not frighten an enemy. His Qanuc knife was still in the sheath tied to his leg. Other than that and the torch, he was truly defenseless. His sword was somewhere above the ground—with Binabik and Miriamele, if they had escaped the diggers—along with his White Arrow, his cloak, his armor, and the rest of his meager possessions. He was nearly as empty-handed as when he had fled the castle almost a year before. And he was back in the black earth again. In the smothering earth . . .

Stop it, he ordered himself. *What was it Morgenes said? "Not what's in your hands, but what's in your head." That's something, anyway. I have a lot more in my head than I did then.*

But what good will it do me if I die of thirst?

He struggled to his feet and began walking again. He had no idea where the tunnel might lead, but it must lead somewhere. It must. The possibility that this direction might finish as the other end had, in an impenetrable wall of fallen dirt or stone, was not something he could afford to consider.

> *"Down pitch-black pit went young King John."*

Simon sang again, quieter than before,

> *"Where Fire-Drake lurked on hoard of gold,*
> *And no one knew that he had gone.*
> *For not a person had he told . . ."*

It was strange. Simon did not *feel* mad, but he was hearing things that were not truly there. The sound of splashing water had returned, louder and more forceful than before, but now it seemed to come from all sides, as though he walked through the curtain of a waterfall. Mixed with it, just barely separable from the hiss and spatter, was the murmur of speech.

Voices! Perhaps there are cross-tunnels somewhere nearby. Perhaps they lead to people. To real, living people . . .

The voices and the water-sounds stayed with him for a time without revealing their source, then faded away, leaving him again with the noise of his footsteps as his only company.

Confused and weary, frightened by what the phantom sounds might mean, he almost stepped into a hole in the tunnel floor. He tripped and then caught himself, braced his hand against the wall, and stared down. The light of another torch seemed to gleam in the depths below, and for a moment he thought his heart would stop.

"Who . . . Who's th . . ." As he leaned down, the light below him seemed to rise.

A reflection. Water.

Simon dropped to his knees and pushed his face toward the tiny pool, then stopped as its smell came up to him, oily and unpleasant. He dipped his fingers in and brought them out. The water seemed oddly slippery on his skin. He brought the torch forward for a better look. A sheet of flame leapt up and slapped hotly against his face; he shouted in pain and surprise as he tumbled backward. For a moment it seemed the whole world had caught fire.

Sitting splay-legged on the ground, he lifted his hand to his cheek and felt gingerly across his features. The skin was as tender as if he had been too long in the sun, and he could feel the hairs of his beard turned crisp and curled, but everything seemed to be in its proper place. He looked down to see a flame dancing in the hole in the tunnel floor.

Usires Aedon! he cursed silently. *Mooncalf's luck. I find water and it's the kind that burns—whatever that is.*

A tear coursed down his hot cheek.

Whatever was in the pool was burning merrily. Simon stared at it, so disappointed to find his drinking water undrinkable that he could not for a long time make sense of what he was seeing. At last, something Morgenes had once said came back to him.

Perdruinese Fire—that's what it is. The doctor said it's found in caves. The Perdruin-folk used to make catapult balls of it and throw it at their enemies and burn them to cracklings. That was the kind of history lesson that Simon had paid close attention to—the sort where interesting things happened. *If I had more sticks and more rags, I could use it to make torches.*

Shaking his head, he clambered to his feet and started down the tunnel once more. After a few paces he stopped and shook his head again.

Mooncalf. Stupid mooncalf.

He returned to the burning pool and sat down, then took off his shirt and began to tear strips of cloth from the hem. The Perdruinese Fire was pleasantly warm.

Rachel would skin me if she saw me ruining a perfectly good shirt. He giggled too loudly. The echoes rolled down the corridor into empty darkness. *It would be good to see Rachel again,* he realized. The idea seemed strange but indisputable.

When he had a dozen strips—his shirt now ended not far beneath his armpits—he sat and stared at the flames for a moment, trying to decide how to dip the cloth without burning the skin off his hands. He considered using the torch but decided against it. He had no idea how deep this hole in the tunnel ran and he was afraid he might drop the brand. Then the only light he possessed would be one he could not move.

At last, after long moments of thought, he set the torch to one side, then began shoveling loose dirt from the cracks between slabs of stone into the hole. After he had poured in a score of handfuls, the flame flickered and died. He waited a little longer, having no idea of how long it might take to cool, then shoveled the sticky dirt away until there was an open space into which he could dip the rags. When he had soaked all the strips of cloth, he put one aside and then rolled each of the others tightly and set them all side by side on the last and largest piece he had torn from his shirt. He bundled up this makeshift sack and hung it on his belt. The remaining strip he carefully wrapped around the torch just below the flame, then turned the brand until the cloth soaked in Perdruinese Fire caught. It burned brightly, and Simon nodded. He still needed food and water, but if he managed carefully, he would not have to worry about losing his light for some while yet. Lost and alone he might be, but he was not just Simon Mooncalf—he was the fabled Seoman Snowlock as well.

But he would much rather have been just Simon, and free to walk upon the green world with his friends.

Choices, he thought unhappily, could be both a blessing and a curse.

Simon had already slept once, curled in a ball on the hard tunnel floor with a fresh rag of Perdruinese Fire wrapped around his torch. When he awakened from a panicky dream in which all light was gone and he crawled through muddy blackness, the torch's flame was still burning steadily.

Since then, he had walked for what seemed like several more hours. His thirst had grown greater and greater until every step seemed to leach moisture from his body, until he could think of almost nothing but finding water. The strip of meat was still in his pocket—just the thought of eating the dry, salty thing made his head ache, despite a hunger almost as great as his thirst.

Now, suddenly, the monotonous stone and earth walls of the tunnel had been breached. A cross tunnel, a ragged but substantial hole that was clearly not natural, opened out on either side. After a near-infinity of choiceless plodding, he had a decision to make: should he go forward, right, or left?

What he wanted, of course, was a path leading upward, but neither of the two branches seemed anything but level. He walked a little way down each in turn, sniffing the air, looking and listening for anything that might be a sign of open air or water, but to no avail: the cross tunnel seemed as devoid of interest as the one through which he had been trudging since Aedon only knew when.

He moved back to the main tunnel and stood for a moment, trying to decide where he might be. Surely he was somewhere far beneath Swertclif itself—he could not have walked downward at such a steady angle for so long without having descended to beneath the hill itself. But his way had wound so many times he could not possibly guess where he might stand in relation to the world above. He would just have to make a choice and see what happened.

If I only ever turn one direction, I can at least find my way back to where I've been.

Based on nothing definite, he resolved to take the left-hand tunnel, and to always take the left-hand turning from here on. Then, if he decided he had made a bad decision, he would just turn around and take all the turns back to the right.

He turned to the left and stumbled on.

At first the tunnel seemed no different than the one he had left, a tube of uneven stone and earth without any sign of use or purpose. Who had made these grim holes? It must have been men, or manlike beings, for in places he felt sure he could see spots where rock been chipped or broken away to open the meandering course.

His thirst and dreary loneliness were such that he did not notice the soft voices again until they were all about him once more. This time, though, there was a sensation of movement as well—a plucking at his clothes like the touch of the wind, a hurrying of shadows that made the light in the tunnel seem to flicker. The voices were wailing softly in a language he could not understand. As they passed around him or through him he felt a sad coldness. These were memories . . . of a sort. These were lost things, shapes and feelings that had come unstuck from their own time. He was nothing to them, and they, disturbing as they might be, were really nothing to him.

Unless I become one of these myself. He felt bubbles of fear rising within him. *Unless someday some other wandering mooncalf feels a Simon-shadow brushing past him saying "Lost, lost, lost . . ."*

It was a horrible thought. Long after the flurry of almost-shapes was gone and the voices were silent, it stayed with him.

He had turned three more times, on each occasion choosing the left-hand direction, when at last things began to change.

Simon was considering going back—his last turning had led him into a tunnel that now sloped sharply downward—when his eye was caught by a blotchiness along the walls. He brought his torch close and saw that the cracks of the stone were full of moss. Moss, he felt sure, meant water somewhere nearby. He was so parched that he pulled loose a matted handful and put it in his mouth. After a few tentative chews he managed to swallow it. Bile rose in his throat, and for a moment he thought he might be ill. It was dreadfully bitter, but there *was* moisture in it. If he had to, he could eat it and probably stay alive for a while—but he prayed he could find some other alternative.

He was staring at the tiny fronds, trying to decide whether he could stomach a second helping, when he noticed pale marks in the gap where he had pulled loose the first handful. He squinted and held the torch closer. It was the remains of some kind of design, that was clear—great curving parallels and eroded shapes that might have been leaves or petals. Time had worn them away almost completely, but they seemed to have some of the looping grace of carvings he had seen in Da'ai Chikiza and Sesuad'ra. Sithi work? Had he gone so deep so quickly?

Simon looked around at the tunnel itself, at the crude, jagged-faced stones. He couldn't imagine the Sithi making such a place, even for the most basic of purposes. But if they had not dug these tunnels, why would there be Sithi carving on the walls?

He shook his head. Too many questions when the only ones that mattered were, where could he find some water—and which way was out?

Although he began to examine the walls carefully as he walked, his discovery of the moss was not immediately followed by anything more useful. The tunnel now began to widen, and the next two passageways he chose seemed more artfully constructed, the walls symmetrical, the floor even. Then, as he explored yet another branching, he put his foot down on nothing.

With a shout of horrified surprise, Simon caught at the entrance of the tunnel. His torch flew from his hand and tumbled down into the darkness where he had nearly gone himself. As he watched in fearful anticipation, it struck and then rolled; it stopped at last, flickering . . . but did not go out.

Stairs. His torch was lying on a flight of rough stairs leading downward. The first half-dozen steps had crumbled or been broken away, leaving nothing behind but a few rough edges.

He did not want to go down. He wanted to go up.

But stairs! Maybe there's something real down there—some place that makes sense. What could be worse than what's already happening?

Nothing. Everything.

It was a left-hand turning, so he would not be completely lost if it proved a bad choice. But it would be much easier to drop down the gap comprised by the missing steps—a distance almost twice his height—than to climb back up again if he changed his mind. Perhaps he should take one of the other paths. . . .

What nonsense are you thinking? he berated himself. He would have to go down just to retrieve his torch.

Simon sat, dangling his legs over the stairless gap, and pulled the strip of dried meat from his pocket. He broke off a small piece and sucked on it meditatively as he looked down. The torchlight showed the steps had been chiseled square, but left unfinished: they were made to be useful, nothing else. Looking at them, there was no way to tell whether they led anywhere.

He chewed and stared. His mouth filled with saliva as he savored the salty, smoky taste. It was wonderful to have something solid between his teeth again!

Simon rose, then turned and went back up the corridor, feeling with his hand when the light grew dim, until he found more moss clinging to the wall. He pulled loose several handfuls, then shoved the sticky mass into his pocket. He returned to the stairwell and peered down until he felt he had located the best spot to land. He slid his legs over, then rolled onto his front and let himself down as carefully as he could, gritting his teeth as the stone scraped against his stomach and chest. When he was almost hanging full length, he let go.

A piece of loose stone, perhaps a fragment of the missing steps, was lying in wait for him like a viper. He felt one foot touch before the other, then the first foot rolled over at the ankle. A flash of pain shot through his leg.

Tears in his eyes, Simon lay on the topmost step for a moment, cursing his luck. He sat up, slid forward until he could reach the fallen torch, then set it down beside him and took off his boot to examine his injured ankle.

He could bend it reasonably well, although each change of position was painful. He decided that it was not broken—but what could he have done about it if it were? He pulled off his shirt and tore loose yet another strip, then pulled

the ever-shrinking garment back on. When he had bound the cloth around his
ankle and foot as snugly as he could, he pulled the boot back on and tested
himself. He could walk, he decided, but it would hurt.

Walk, then. What else can you do?

He began his limping descent.

Simon had hoped that the stairs would lead him down to some place more
real than the endless, pointless tunnels. But the more real his surroundings
became, the more they also became unreal.

After several score small but painful descents, the stairs ended and Simon
hobbled out through a jagged hole into another corridor, a passage quite unlike
the tunnels through which he had been traveling. Moss-festooned and almost
black with the dirt of ages, it was nevertheless made of carefully-cut dressed
stone; its walls were thick with carvings. But when he stared at these carvings
for more than an instant, those that were just at the corners of his vision seemed
to shimmer and move, as though they were not marks in stone at all, but rather
some kind of parchment-thin creatures, slender as thread. The walls and floor
seemed somehow unstable, too: when Simon looked away for a moment in his
plodding progress, lured by yet another smear of movement at the edge of his
eye, or was distracted by the flickering of the torch flame, they appeared to
change. The long straight corridor suddenly had an upward slant, or seemed
abruptly narrower. If he turned away and then looked back, everything was as
it had been before.

Nor were these the only tricks this place played on him. The noises that he
had heard before returned, voices and rushing water now joined by a strange,
abstract music, all sourceless and ghostly. Unexpected scents washed over him,
too, rushes of sweet flowery air one moment that quickly gave way to dank
emptiness once more, only to be supplanted a moment later by the harsh smell
of something burning.

It was too much. Simon wanted to lie down, to go to sleep and wake up with
everything stable and unchanging. Even the monotony of the tunnels above
was preferable to this. He might have been trudging at the bottom of the sea,
where the currents and uneven light made everything sway and dance and
shimmer.

*How long did you think you could walk in the empty earth before you went mad,
Mooncalf?*

I'm not going mad, he told himself. *I'm just tired. Tired and thirsty. If only there
weren't all these water-noises. They just make things worse.*

He pulled some of the moss from his pocket and chewed as he walked, forcing himself to swallow the hateful stuff.

There was no question that he was walking in a place in which people . . .
in which *someone* . . . had once lived. The ceiling rose higher above him, the
floor was level beneath the rubble and dust, and the crossing passages, almost

all of them choked with stone and soil, were faced with carved arches, soiled
and worn to pebble-smoothness but clearly the work of careful craft.

Simon paused for a moment before one of these entranceways. As he stood
resting his throbbing ankle, staring at the jumble of rocks and dirt that plugged
it, the mound of dirt seemed to darken, then turn black. A small light bloomed
in that blackness, and Simon suddenly felt he was looking *through* the doorway.
He took a step closer. In the darkness beyond he saw a single spot of luminance,
an orb of light dimly glowing. Near it, bathed in faint radiance, was . . . a face.

Simon gasped. The face lifted, as though the person sitting in near-darkness
had heard him, but the high-slanted eyes did not meet his, staring instead out
past him. It was a Sitha face, or seemed so in the moment he could observe it,
a world of pain and concern in the shining eyes. He saw the lips move in
speech, the eyebrows rise in sad inquiry. Then the darkness blurred, the light
vanished, and Simon was standing with his nose a finger's breadth away from a
doorway choked with rubble.

Dry. Dry. Dead. Dead.

A sob hitched in his throat. He turned back to the long corridor.

Simon didn't know how long he had been staring at the flame of his torch.
It wavered before him, a universe of yellow light. It was a terrible effort to
wrench his gaze away.

The walls on both sides had turned to water.

He stopped, staring in awe. Somehow the tunnel floor had become a narrow
walkway over a great darkness and the walls had retreated: they no longer
touched the floor on which he stood, and their stone facing was completely
covered by flowing sheets of water. He could hear it rushing down into the
emptiness below, see the uneven reflection of the torch as it played across the
liquid expanse.

Simon moved to the edge of the walkway and stretched out his hand, but his
fingers did not reach. He could feel a faint dew of mist on his fingertips, and
when he drew the hand back and touched it to his mouth, there was a faint taste
of wet sweetness. He leaned out again, swaying perilously over the darkness,
but still could not touch even a fingertip to the sheeting water. He cursed in
fury. If he only had a bowl, a cup, a spoon!

Think, Mooncalf! Use your head!

After a moment's consideration, he put his torch down on the walkway and
shucked his tattered shirt over his head. He got down on his knees; then,
clutching one sleeve, he flung the rest of it out as far as he could. It touched
lightly against the cascade and was pulled downward. He yanked it back, his
heart beating faster as he felt the shirt's new heaviness. He threw back his head,
then pushed the sodden cloth against his mouth. The first drops were like
honey on his tongue. . . .

The light flickered. Everything in the long chamber seemed to lurch to one
side. The rush of the water grew louder, then hissed away into silence.

Simon's mouth was full of dust.

He gagged and spat, spat again, then fell to the floor in a panicked fury, growling and thrashing like a beast with a thorn in its side. When he looked up, he could still see the walls and the gap that stretched between them and the walkway on which he crouched—that much was real—but there was no sheeting water, only a lighter-colored smear on the stone wall where his shirt had flicked loose a few centuries' worth of grime.

Simon shook with tearless sobbing as he wiped the dirt from his face and rubbed the last of crumbs of soil from his swollen tongue. He tried to eat a little of the moss to take the taste of the dust away, but it was so foul he was almost sick again. He spat the leafy wad down into the abyss.

What kind of cursed, haunted place is this? Where am I?

I'm alone, alone.

Still shaking, he dragged himself to his feet, looking for a safer place to lie down for a while and sleep. He needed to get away. There was no water. There was no water anywhere. And no safety either.

Faint voices up in the shadows of the high ceiling sang words he could not understand. A wind he could not feel fluttered the torch flame.

Am I alive?

Yes, I am. I am Simon, and I am alive, and I will not give up. I am not a ghost.

He had slept twice more, and had chewed enough of the bitter moss to keep himself moving in between rests. He had used more than half of his treated rags to keep the torch burning. It was difficult to remember a time when he had not seen the world by wavering torchlight, or when the world itself had not consisted of unpeopled stone corridors and whispering, bodiless voices. He felt as though his own essence had begun to melt away, as though he were becoming a chittering shade.

I am Simon, he reminded himself. *I met the dragon and I won the White Arrow. I am real.*

As in a dream, he moved through the halls and corridors of a great castle. For illuminated moments swift as the whiteflash of lightning, he could see it in full life, the halls full of faint golden faces, the walls pale, shining stone that reflected the colors of the sky. It was a place unlike anything he had ever seen, with streams prisoned in stone banks that ran from room to room, and waterfalls that frothed down the walls of chambers. But for all the splashing, it was still dream-water. Each time he reached, the promise turned to grit in his hands; the walls darkened and slouched, the light dimmed, the beautiful fretwork withered away, and Simon found himself walking in ruined stone halls again, a homeless spirit in a vast tomb.

The Sithi lived here, he told himself. *This was Asu'a, shining Asu'a. And somehow they are still here . . . as though the stones themselves are dreaming of the old days.*

A poisonously seductive idea began to make itself felt. Amerasu Ship-Born had said that somehow Simon lived closer to the Dream Road than others—he had seen the Parting of the Families during his vigil atop Sesuad'ra, hadn't he? Perhaps, then, if he could discover some way to do it, he could . . . step across. He would go *into* the dream, he would live in beautiful Asu'a and plunge his face into the living streams that meandered through the palace—and this time they would not turn to dust. He would live in Asu'a, and never come back again to this dark, haunted world of crumbling shadows. . . .

Never come back to your friends? Never come back to your duty?

But the dream-Asu'a was so beautiful. In the instants of its flickering existence, he could see roses and other startlingly bright flowers climbing up the walls to bask in the sun from the high windows. He could see the Sithi, the dream-people who lived here, graceful and strange as bright-plumed birds. The dream showed a time before Simon's kind had destroyed the Sithi's greatest house. Surely the immortals would welcome a lost traveler . . . Oh, Mother of Mercy, might they welcome him in from the darkness . . . ?

Weak and weary, Simon stumbled on a loose paving stone and fell to his hands and knees. His heart felt like an anvil in his chest. He could not move, could not go another step. Anything was better than this mad loneliness!

The wide room before him pulsed, but did not disappear. Out of the nebulous cloud of moving forms, one of the figures became clearer. It was a Sitha woman, skin golden as sunlight, hair a cloud of nightblack. She stood between two twining trees laden with silvery fruit, and her eyes slowly turned to Simon. She paused. A strange look came over her face, as though she had heard a voice calling her name in a lonely place.

"Can . . . can you see me?" Simon gasped. He scrabbled toward her across the floor. She continued to stare at the spot where he had been.

Terror rushed through him. He had lost her! His limbs turned boneless and he slumped forward onto his belly. Behind the black-haired woman a fountain of water sparkled, the drops that flew through the slanting light of the windows glowing like gems. She closed her eyes, and Simon felt a questing touch at the farthest edge of his mind. She seemed only a few short steps away, but at the same moment as distant as a star in the sky. "Can't you see me!?" he howled. "I want to come inside! Let me in!"

She stood as immobile as a statue, her hands folded before her. The high-windowed chamber grew dark, until she alone stood in a column of radiance. Something brushed against Simon's thoughts, light as a spider's step, soft as a butterfly's breath.

Go back, little one. Go back and live.

Then she opened her eyes and looked at him again. Her eyes were full of a wisdom so vast and kind that Simon felt himself lifted and held and known. But her words were bitter for him.

This is not for you.

She began to fade. For a moment, she was only another shadowy figure in the ancient parade of shapes. Then the beautiful airy room itself flickered and vanished. Simon was sprawled in the dirt. His torch burned fitfully on the ground, half a pace from his outstretched fingers.

Gone. Left me behind.

Simon cried until he could not cry any more, until he was hoarse with weeping and his face hurt. He dragged himself to his feet and went on.

He had almost forgotten his name—he had certainly forgotten how many times he had slept, and how many times he had sucked at the diminishing wad of moss crammed in his pocket—when he found the great stairs.

There were only a few rags left to replace the one that burned on his torch. Simon was thinking about what that meant, and realizing that he had gone too far to find his way back to the pool of Perdruinese Fire before he was plunged into darkness, when he walked through one of the sweeping portals of the labyrinthine castle and found himself on a vast landing. Above and below this open place stretched a flight of wide stairs circling around emptiness, an uncountable sweep of steps that curled up into shadow and down into darkness.

The stairs! A memory, dim as a fish in a muddy pond, came floating up. *The . . . Tan'ja Stairs? Doctor Morgenes said . . . said . . .*

Long ago, in another life, another Simon had been told to look for stairs like these—and they had led him upward to night air and moonlight and damp green grass.

Then that means . . . if I go up . . .

A shockingly ragged laugh burst out and echoed in the stairwell. Something, bats or sad little memories, fluttered away into the darkness above, rustling like a handful of parchments. Simon began climbing the stairs, his throbbing ankle, his terrible thirst, his utter, utter loneliness almost forgotten.

I'll breathe the air. I'll see the sky. I'm . . . I'm . . . I'm Simon. I won't be a ghost.

Before he had gone half a hundred steps upward, he found that a section of the wall had tumbled down, smashing the outermost edge of the steps so that a ragged gap faced out into the empty darkness. The rest of the staircase was blocked by fallen stone.

"Bloody *Tree!*" he screamed in rage. "Bloody, Bloody *Tree!*"

". . . *ree . . .*" the echo repeated. ". . . *ee . . .*"

He waved the torch over his head in a furious challenge to the empty air; the flame billowed and streaked across the black. At last, defeated, he hobbled back down the wide stairs.

He remembered little of his first journey up the Tan'ja Stairs almost a year before, a journey that had taken place through both outer and inner darknesses . . . but surely there had not been so many of these damnable steps! It was almost impossible to believe that he could descend so far without finding himself in the pits of Hell.

His plodding descent seemed to take at least a day. There was no way off: the arches that led from the landings were blocked by rubble, and the only other escape would be over the baluster and a plummet down into . . . who knew what? By the time he stopped at last to sleep on one of the dusty landings, he wished he had never stepped onto the stairs at all, but the thought of dragging himself all the way back up that near-infinitude of steps to the spot where he had entered was horrifying. No, down was the only direction left to him. Surely even these monstrous stairs must come to an end somewhere! Simon curled up and fell into a thick slumber.

His dreams were powerful but confusing. Three almost painfully vivid images haunted him—a young fair-haired man bearing a torch and a spear down a steeply-sloping tunnel; an older man, robed and crowned, with a sword lying across his knees and a heavy book opened on top of it; a tall figure, hidden in shadow, who stood straight-backed in the middle of a strangely mobile floor. Again and again the same three visions appeared, changing slightly, showing more while revealing nothing. The spearman cocked his head as though he heard voices. The gray-haired man looked up from his reading as though disturbed by a sudden noise, and a bloom of red light filled the darkness, painting the man's strong features scarlet. The shadow-shape turned; a sword was in his hand, and something like antlers lifted from his brow. . . .

Simon awakened with a gasp, sweat cooling on his forehead, limbs a-tremble. This had not been the stuff of ordinary sleep: he had fallen into some rushing river of dream and been carried along like a piece of bark, helplessly careening. He sat up and rubbed his eyes, but he was still on the broad landing, still adrift on the ocean of stairs.

Dreams and voices, he thought desperately. *I need to get away from them. If they don't leave me alone, I'll die.*

His second-to-last rag was now on the torch. Time was running out. If he did not find his way soon, if he did not find the air and the sun and moon once more, he would be alone in darkness with the shadows of dead time.

Simon hurried down the steps.

The Tan'ja Stairs became a blur, and Simon himself was a cracked millwheel, his legs going up, down, up, down, every other step bringing a sharp pain as he forced his wounded ankle to bear the weight of his hurried descent. Shallow breaths fluted in and out of his dry mouth. If he had not been mad before, madness finally took him now. The stairs were the teeth of a mouth that wanted to swallow him, but as fast as he bounded downward, falling and not feeling the pain, clambering to his feet and plunging down to the next step, he could not escape. There were always more teeth. Always more white, even teeth. . . .

The voices that had been silent so long rose up around him like the choir of monks in the Hayholt's chapel. Simon paid them no heed. All he could do was fling himself down step after step after step. Something in the air was different, but he could not let himself pause to decide what it was: the voices were haunting him, the teeth taunting, waiting to snap closed.

Where there should have been a step, there was instead a flat white expanse of . . . something. Simon, in mid-leap downward, was brought up short and sent tumbling forward. His elbows cracked painfully against stone. He lay for a moment, whimpering, clutching his torch so hard his knuckles throbbed. Slowly he lifted his head. The air was . . . the air smelled . . . damp.

The wide landing stretched before him, then ended in blackness. There were no more stairs, or at least none he could see.

Still making pained noises, Simon crawled forward until the blackness was just before him. As he leaned out, his arm swept a small scree of dust and gravel over the edge.

Plink. Plink, plink. The sound of small stones falling into water. And not falling very far.

Panting, he leaned out, holding his torch as far over the darkness as he could. He could see a reflection just a few ells below, a wavering smudge of fiery light. Hope welled up in him, and that was somehow worse than any of his pain.

It's a trick, he mourned. *It's another trick. It's dust . . . dust . . . dust . . .*

Still, he crawled around the edge of the landing, looking for a way down. When he discovered a small and elegantly carved staircase, he crab-climbed down the steps on his hands and knees. The stairwell ended in a circular landing and a small spit of pale stone that stretched out over the blackness. The torch light did not reveal how far it extended, but he could see the sweep of the pool's sides as they vanished away into the shadows in either direction. It was huge— almost a small lake.

Simon dropped onto his stomach and extended his hand, then stopped, sniffing. If this great pond were full of Perdruinese Fire and he brought his torch close, there would be nothing of Simon left but a scrap of cinder. But there was no oily smell. He dipped his hand in and felt the water close over it, cold and just as wet as wet should be. He sucked his fingers. There was a faint metallic tang—but it *was* water.

Water!

He scooped it up in a double handful and lifted it to his mouth, more dribbling on his chin and neck than went down his throat. It seemed to tingle and sparkle on his tongue and fill his veins with warmth. It was glorious—better than any liquor, more wonderful than any drink he had ever tasted. It was water. He was alive.

Simon was light-headed with joy. He drank until he was uncomfortably full, until his stomach pressed against the waistband of his breeches; the cool, slightly tangy water felt so splendidly wet that it was difficult to stop. He poured it over his head and face, splashing so vigorously that he almost doused the torch, which made him laugh until the echoes crisscrossed. When he had moved his light up the stairwell to safety, he went back and drank more, then took off his ragged shirt and breeches and scrubbed himself all over, letting the water run off him in wonderfully wasteful excess. At last his fatigue overcame him. He lay singing happily until he fell asleep on the wet stone.

★   ★   ★

Simon awakened slowly, as if swimming upward from a great depth. For long moments he did not know where he was or what had happened. The powerful rush of dream-pictures had come to him again, whirling through his sleeping head like leaves in a great windstorm. The sword-bearing men were part of it, but there had also been a flash of shields as an armored host rode out through a tall silver gate, a splintery array of towers in rainbow hues, a glint of yellow as a raven cocked its head to reveal a bright eye, a circle that flashed gold, a tree with bark pale as snow, a dark wheel turning. . . .

Simon rubbed his temples, trying to clear away the clinging images. His head, which had felt hollow and airy when he was bathing himself, now throbbed and pounded. He groaned and sat up. He would be plagued by dreams, it seemed, no matter what happened. But there were other things to think about, things about which he could *do* something—or at least try. Food. Escape.

He looked up to where his torch lay on one of the steps of the narrow staircase. He had been foolish, risking his light with all that splashing. And it would not burn much longer. He had found water, but his predicament was still deathly grim.

The light of the torch suddenly seemed to grow. Simon squinted, then realized it was not the torch, but that rather the whole great chamber was filling with smoky light. And there was . . . *something* . . . very near. Something strong. He could feel it like hot breath on his neck.

Simon rolled over, conscious of his nakedness, his helplessness. He could see the great pool more clearly, could make out the fantastically elaborate carvings that covered the near walls and ceiling far overhead, but even with the spreading light he still could not see the pool's far side: a sort of mist seemed to hang over the water, obscuring his view.

As he gaped, a shadowy figure appeared in the mist at the pool's center, a shape exaggerated by the gray fog and directionless light. It was tall and billow-cloaked, with horns . . . antlers . . . growing from its head.

The figure bowed—not in reverence, it seemed, but in despair.

Jingizu.

The voice rolled through Simon's mind, mournful yet angry, powerful and cold as ice that cracked and split stone. The mist swirled and eddied. Simon felt his own thoughts swept away before it.

Jingizu. So much sorrow.

For a moment, Simon's spirit flickered like a candle in a storm wind. He was being extinguished by the force of the thing that hovered in the mists. He tried to scream, but could not; he was being eaten by its terrible emptiness. He felt himself dwindling, fading, vanishing. . . .

The light shifted again, then abruptly died. The pool became a wide black oval once more, and the only light was the dim yellow glow of his guttering torch.

For some moments, Simon lay gasping for air like a fish dragged into a boat. He was afraid to move, to make a sound, terrified the shadowy thing would return.

Merciful Aedon, give me rest. The words of the old prayer came up unbidden. *In Your Arms will I sleep, upon Your bosom* . . .

He no longer had the slightest urge to cross over to the dream-side, to join the ghosts of this place. Of all the things he had seen and felt since tumbling down into the ground, this place seemed the strangest, the most terrifyingly powerful. Water or no water, he could not stay. And soon his light would be gone, and the darkness would swallow him.

Quivering, he kneeled at the bottom of the stairwell and drank his fill once more. Cursing the lack of a water skin, he dragged on his breeches and boots, then dunked his shirt into the pool. It would stay wet for a while and he could squeeze out water when he needed it. He picked up the torch and began searching for a way out. His ankle had stiffened, but for the moment the pain was unimportant. He had to leave this place.

The pool, which a moment before had been a fount of terrifying visions, was now only a silent circle of black.

41

A Meandering of Ink

✾

Miriamele was as gentle with the bandages as she could be, and Binabik said not a word, but she could tell that the pain of his blistered hands was fierce.

"There." She tied a careful knot. "Now just let them alone for a while. I'll get us something to eat."

"All that digging, and with nothing for result," the troll said mournfully. He examined his cloth-wrapped paws. "Dirt and more dirt and more dirt."

"At least those . . . things didn't come back." The sun had dropped behind the western horizon; Miriamele was finding it difficult to see into the depths of the pack. She sat down and smoothed her cloak across her lap, then dumped out the contents. "Those diggers."

"I am almost wishing that they had, Miriamele. I would have been getting some pleasure in killing more of them. Like Qantaqa, I would be growling as their blood came out."

Miriamele shook her head, disturbed by Binabik's uncharacteristic savagery, but also worried by her own hollowness. She felt no such anger—there was almost nothing inside her at all. "If he . . . survived, then he will find a way to come back to us again." The ghost of a smile crept across her face. "He's stronger than I ever thought he might be, Binabik."

"I remember when I was first meeting him in the forest," the little man said. "Like a hatchling, like the young of a bird, he looked to me, his hair pointing up and every other way. I was thinking then, 'Here is one who would be quickly dying if I had not found him.' He seemed to me as helpless as the most wobbling-legged of lambs gone stray from the herd. But he has surprised me many times since then, many times." The troll fluted a sigh. "If there was something beneath his falling beside more dirt and *boghanik,* then I am thinking he will find a way out."

"Of course he will." Miriamele stared at the array of wrapped bundles in her lap. Her eyes were misty, and she had forgotten what she was looking for. "Of course he will."

"So we will go on, and trust in the luck that has kept him well for so long a time in all the moments of terrible peril." Binabik spoke as though afraid he would be contradicted.

"Yes. Certainly." Miriamele brought her hands to her face, kneading her temples as though that might make her scattered thoughts more manageable. "And I will say a prayer for Elysia the Mother of God to look after him."

But many prayers are said every day, she thought. *And only a few are answered. Curse you, Simon, why did you go away?*

Simon was almost a stronger presence lost than he had been while still with them. Miriamele, despite the deep affection she felt for Binabik, found it difficult to sit with him over the thin stew she had made for their supper: that they should be alive and eating seemed an insult to their absent friend. Still, they were both grateful for the bit of meat—a squirrel that Qantaqa had brought back. Miriamele wondered whether the wolf had done her own hunting first or felt she should bring a prize to her master before pursuing her own needs, but Binabik professed not to know.

"She only brings me such things on occasion, and usually when I am sad or hurt." He showed a tiny flash of teeth. "This time I am both things, I suppose."

"Bless her for it anyway," Miriamele said, and meant it. "Our larder is nearly bare."

"I am hoping . . ." the troll began, then abruptly fell silent. Miriamele was quite sure that he was thinking about Simon, who even if he survived would be somewhere beneath the ground without food. Neither of them spoke more until the meal was finished.

"So now what is the thing to be doing?" Binabik asked gently. "I do not wish to seem . . ."

"I am still going to find my father. Nothing has changed that."

Binabik looked at her but did not speak.

"But you do not have to come with me." Disliking the sound of her voice, she added: "It might be better if you don't. Maybe if Simon finds his way out he will come to this place. Someone should wait for him. And anyway, this is not your duty, Binabik. He's my father, but he's your enemy."

The troll shook his head. "When we come to the place at which no back-turning can happen, then I will decide. This is not seeming a safe spot to me for waiting." He looked briefly over to the distant Hayholt; in the evening light the castle was only a blackness that contained no stars. "But perhaps I could stay hidden somewhere with Qantaqa and come at certain times to look." He made an open-handed gesture. "Still, it is too soon for such thinking. I do not even know what plan you have made for your castle entrance." He turned and waved toward the invisible keep. "You may have some way for persuading your father the king, but you would not be taken to him if you present yourself at the gate, I am thinking. And if Pryrates is receiving you, he may decide it is of more convenience for you to be dead and not interfere with his plans for your father. You would become vanished."

Miriamele twitched involuntarily. "I am not stupid, Binabik, no matter what my uncle and others may think. I have some ideas of my own."

Binabik spread his palms. "I do not think you are anything like being stupid, Miriamele. I am not knowing anyone who thinks that."

"Perhaps." She got to her feet and walked across the damp grass toward her pack. Rain was coming down in a light mist. After rummaging in the bag, she found the bundle she had sought and carried it back to the small fire. "I spent a long time on Sesuad'ra making these."

Binabik unrolled the bundle, then slowly smiled. "Ah."

"And I copied them onto hides as well," she said with more than a little pride, "because I knew they would last that way. I saw those scrolls you and Sis . . . Sis . . ."

"Sisqinanamook," Binabik said, frowning over the skins. "Or 'Sisqi' is easier for lowlander tongues." His face went blank for a moment, then his features resumed life and he looked up at Miriamele. "So you copied the maps that Count Eolair was bringing."

"I did. He said that they were of the old dwarrow tunnels. Simon came out of the castle through them, so I thought that might be a way to get back in without being caught."

"It is not all being tunnels." Binabik stared at the meandering lines drawn on the skins. "The old Sithi castle is beneath the Hayholt, and it was of great largeness." He squinted. "These are not easy for reading, these maps."

"I wasn't sure what any of it meant, so I copied it all, even the little drawings and marks on the side," Miriamele said humbly. "I only know that these are the right maps because I asked Father Strangyeard." She felt a sudden bite of fear. "They *are* the right maps, aren't they?"

Binabik nodded slowly, black hair bouncing against his forehead. "They are looking like maps of this place, indeed—see, there is what you call the Kynslagh." He pointed to a large curving crescent at the edge of the topmost map. "And this must be Swertclif which lies beneath us even now."

Miriamele leaned forward to look, following Binabik's small finger with eager attention. A moment later, she felt a wash of intense sadness. "If that's where we are, the spot where Simon fell through has no tunnels."

"Perhaps." Binabik sounded genuinely unsure. "But maps and charts are being made at particular times, Miriamele. Just as likely it is that other tunnels have been made since the drawing of this thing."

"Elysia, Mother of Mercy, I hope that's true."

"So where was Simon emerging from his tunnels?" Binabik asked. "I seem to have a memory that it was . . ."

"In the lich-yard, just on the other side of the wall from Erchester," Miriamele finished for him. "I saw him there, but he ran away when I called to him. He thought I was a ghost."

"There are many tunnelings that seem to emerge around that place. But these were made long before Erchester and the rest were being built. I am doubting these landmarks still remain." He looked up as Qantaqa returned from her hunting, her shaggy pelt pearled with rain.

"I think I know more or less where he must have come up," Miriamele said. "We can look, anyway."

"That we will do." Binabik stretched. "Now, one more night we will be sleeping in this place. Then down to the horses."

"I hope they've had enough to eat. We didn't expect to leave them this long."

"I can be promising you that if they were finishing the grass, the next thing they chewed through would be the leather traces that held them. The horses will not suffer for want of finding food, but we may not be finding the horses."

Miriamele shrugged. "As you are always saying, there's nothing we can do about it until we get there."

"I say it because it has a great truthfulness," Binabik replied gravely.

Rachel the Dragon knew what she would find, but her resignation did not make it less of a blow. For the eighth day in a row, the food and water she had put out were untouched.

Offering a sad prayer for patience to Saint Rhiappa, Rachel gathered up those things that would not keep and put them in her sack. She would eat the small apple and the bit of hardening bread tonight. She replaced the neglected offerings with fresh ones, then lifted the lid on the bowl of water to make sure it was still clean and drinkable.

She frowned. Where was that poor man Guthwulf? She hated to think of him wandering blind in the darkness, unable to find his way back to the regular meals that she had been providing him. She was half-tempted to go and look for him—had in fact roamed a little wider than normal in the last few days—but knew that it would be inviting trouble. The farther down into these tunnels she went, the greater the chance that she would fall and hit her head, or tumble into a hole. Then she would be helpless. She might worry about blind Guthwulf, but no one at all was worrying about old Rachel.

These thoughts made her frown deepen. Just as such things might happen to her, so might they have happened to Guthwulf. He might be only a few furlongs away, lying injured. The thought of someone needing her care when she could not give it was like an itch inside of her, a hot frustration. Once she had been the mistress of all the castle servants, a queen of sorts; now she could not even do what was necessary for one poor sightless madman.

Rachel shouldered her bag and stumped back up the stairs, heading toward her hidden sanctuary.

When she had pulled aside the tapestry and pushed the door inward on its well-oiled hinges, she lit one of her lanterns and looked around. In a way, it was almost restful living in such a solitary fashion: the place was so small it was easy to keep clean, and since only she came here, she knew that everything was done in just the right way.

Rachel set the lamp on the stool she used as a table and pulled her chair next to it, wincing. The damp was in her bones tonight, and her extremities ached. She did not feel much like sewing, but there was little else to do, and it was still at least an hour before the time she would go to bed. Rachel was determined not to lose her routine. She had always been one to wake up just moments before the horn blare of the night sentries giving over duty to the morning watch, but these days only her morning trip upstairs to get water from the room with an outside window helped her retain a connection with the world beyond. She did not want anything to strain the tenuous contact with her old life, so she would sew for at least an hour before she allowed herself to lie down, no matter how her fingers cramped.

She took out her knife and cut the apple into small sections. She ate it carefully, but when she was finished her teeth and gums hurt, so she dipped the heel of bread into her water cup to soften before she ate it. Rachel grimaced. Everything hurt tonight. There was a storm coming, that seemed sure—her bones told her. It didn't seem fair. There had only been a few days in the past week when she had actually been able to see sunlight out of the window upstairs, and now even that was to be snatched away.

Rachel found her needlework hard going. Her mind kept flittering away, something that normally would not have affected her stitchery at all, but which tonight was causing her to stop for long moments between every few movements of the needle.

What would things have been like if Pryrates hadn't come? she wondered.

Elias might not have been a wonderful king like his sainted father, but he was strong and shrewd and capable. Perhaps he would have outgrown his churlishness and his bad companions; the castle would have remained in her control, the long tables snowy with their spotless cloths, the flagstones swept and mopped to a high gleam. The chambermaids would be working industriously— under Rachel's stern gaze, *everyone* worked industriously. Well, almost everyone . . .

Yes, Simon. If the red priest hadn't come to blight their lives, Simon would still be here. Perhaps he would have found some work to suit him by now. He would be bigger—oh, they grew so quickly at that age—maybe even with a man's beard, although it was hard to imagine anything manly about young Simon. He would come by sometimes to visit her at the end of the day, maybe even share a cup of cider and a little talk. She would keep a careful eye that he wasn't getting too big for his breeches, that he wasn't making a fool of himself over the wrong sort of girls—it wouldn't do to let that boy get too far out of hand. . . .

Something wet fell onto her hand. Rachel started.

Crying? Crying, you old fool? After that mooncalf boy? She shook herself angrily. *Well, he's in better hands than yours now, and tears won't bring him back.*

Still, it would have been nice to see him grown, a man, but still grinning that same impudent grin. . . .

Rachel put down her needlework in disgust. If she was not going to get any sewing done, it was a waste of time to pretend. She would find something else to do, instead of just sitting in her chair moping and dreaming like some ancient crone beside the fireplace. She wasn't dead yet. There was still work for her to do.

Someone *did* need her. Pacing slowly back and forth in the tiny chamber, ignoring the dull throb of her joints, Rachel decided that she would indeed go and look for Earl Guthwulf. She would be careful, and she would keep as safe as she could, but it was her Aedonite duty to find out whether the poor man was hurt somewhere, or sick.

Rachel the Dragon began making plans.

A great curtain of rain swept across the lich-yard, bending the knee-high grass and splattering on the old tumbled stones.

"Did you find anything?" Miriamele called.

"Nothing that is pleasant." She could barely hear the troll for the hissing of the rain. She bent closer to the crypt door. "I am finding no tunnel," he elaborated.

"Then come out. I'm soaking wet." She pulled her cloak tight and looked up.

Beyond the lich-yard, the Hayholt loomed, its spires dark and secretive against the muddy gray sky. She saw light glimmering in the red windows of Hjeldin's Tower and crouched lower in the grass, like a rabbit covered by the shadow of a hawk. The castle seemed to be waiting, quiet and almost lifeless. There were no soldiers on the battlements, no pennants fluttering atop the roofs. Only Green Angel Tower with its sweep of pure white stone seemed somehow alive. She thought of the days she had hidden there, spying on Simon as he day-dreamed through idle afternoons in the bell chamber. As constricting and smothering as the Hayholt had seemed to her then, it had been a comparatively cheerful place. The castle that stood before her now waited like some ancient hard-shelled creature, like an old spider brooding at the center of its web.

Can I actually go there? she wondered. *Maybe Binabik is right. Maybe I am being stubborn and headstrong to think I can do anything at all.*

But the troll might be wrong. Could she afford to gamble? And more importantly, could she walk away from her father, knowing that the two of them might never again meet on this earth?

"You were speaking the truth." Binabik slipped out through the crypt door, shielding his eyes with his hand. "The rain is falling down very strongly."

"Let's go back to where we left the horses," Miriamele said. "We can shelter there. So you found nothing?"

"Another place with no tunnels." The troll wiped mud from his hands onto his skin breeches. "But there were quite a few dead people, none of them good to be spending time with."

Miriamele made a face. "But I'm sure that Simon came up here. It has to be one of these."

Binabik shrugged and set out toward the clutch of wind-rattled elms along the lich-yard's south wall. As he walked, he pulled up his hood. "Either you are remembering it with some slight wrongness, or the tunnel is hidden in a way I cannot discover. But I have scrabbled in all the walls, and been lifting all the stones . . ."

"I'm certain it's not you," she said. A flare of lightning lit the sky; the thunder followed a few moments later. Suddenly an image of Simon struggling in the dark earth appeared before her mind's eyes. He was gone, lost forever, despite all the brave things she and the troll had said. She gasped and stumbled. Tears coursed down her rain-wet cheeks. She stopped, sobbing so hard she could not see.

Binabik's small hand closed about hers. "I am here with you." His own voice trembled.

They stood together in the rain for a long time. At last Miriamele grew calmer. "I'm sorry, Binabik. I don't know what to do. We have spent the whole day searching and it hasn't done us any good." She swallowed and wiped water from her face. She could not speak of Simon. "Perhaps we should give up. You were right: I could never walk up to that gate."

"Let us make ourselves dry, first." The little man tugged her forward, hurrying them toward shelter. "Then we will talk over what are the things we should do."

"We have looked, Miriamele," said Binabik. The horses made anxious noises as the thunder caromed across the sky once more. Qantaqa stared up at the clouds as though the great sound were something she would like to chase and catch. "But if you wish it, I will wait and look again when the rain is gone— perhaps the searching would be safer by night."

Miriamele shuddered at the thought of exploring the graves after dark. Besides, the diggers had proved that there was far more to fear in these crypts than just the restless spirits of the dead. "I don't want you to do that."

He shrugged. "Then what is your wishing?"

She looked at the map. The wandering lines of ink were nearly invisible in the dark, storm-curtained afternoon. "There are other lines that must be other tunnels going in. Here's one."

Binabik screwed up his eyes as he studied the map. "That one is seeming to me to come out in the rock wall over the Kynslagh. Very difficult it would be to find, I think, and it would be even more beneath the nose of your father and his soldiers."

Miriamele nodded sadly. "I think you're right. What about this one?"

The troll considered. "It is seeming to be in the place the town now stands."

"Erchester?" Miriamele looked back, but could not see over the tall lich-yard wall. "Somewhere in Erchester?"

"Yes, are you seeing?" He traced the line with his short finger. "If this is the little forest called Kynswood, and this is where we are now standing . . ."

"Yes. It must be almost in the middle of the town." She paused to consider. "If I could disguise my face, somehow . . ."

"And I would be disguising my height and my troll-ness?" Binabik asked wryly.

She shook her head, feeling the idea solidify. "No. You wouldn't need to. If we took one horse, and you rode with me, people would think you were a child."

"I am honored."

Miriamele laughed a little wildly. "No, it would work! No one would look at you twice if you kept your hood pulled low."

"And what would we do with Simon's horse, and with Qantaqa?"

"Perhaps we could bring them with us." She didn't want to give up. "Maybe they would think Qantaqa was a dog."

Now Binabik laughed, too, a sudden huff of mirth. "It is one thing to make people be thinking a small man like me is a child, but unless you could find a cloak for her as well, no one will ever have belief that my companion is anything but a deadly wolf from the White Waste."

Miriamele looked at Qantaqa's shaggy gray bulk and nodded sadly. "I know. It was just a thought."

The troll smiled. "But the rest of your idea is good. There are just a few things we must do, I am thinking. . . ."

They finished their work in a grove of linden trees on the edge of a fallow field just west of the main road, a few furlongs from Erchester's northernmost city gate.

"What did you put in this beeswax, Binabik?" Miriamele scowled, probing with her tongue. "It tastes terrible!"

"That is not for touching or tasting," he said. "It will come loose. And the answer is being, just a little dark mud for color."

"Does it really look like teeth are missing?"

Binabik cocked his head, eyeing the effect. "Yes. You are appearing very scruffy and not-princess-like."

Miriamele ran her hand through her dirt-matted hair and carefully stroked her muddy face. *I must be a sight.* She could not help being pleased for some reason. *It is like a game, like a Usires Play. I can be anyone I want to.*

But it was not a game, of course. Simon's face loomed before her; she abruptly and painfully remembered what she was doing, what dangers it would bring—and what had already been lost so that she could get to this place.

It is to end the pain, the killing, she dutifully reminded herself. *And to bring my father back to his senses.*

She looked up. "I'm ready, I suppose."

The troll nodded. He turned and patted Qantaqa's broad head, then led the wolf a short distance away and crouched beside her, burying his face in her neck fur to whisper in her ear. It was a long message, of which Miriamele could hear only the throaty clicking of trollish consonants. Qantaqa twisted her head to the side and whined softly but did not move. When Binabik had finished; he patted her again and touched his forehead to hers.

"She will not let Simon's horse stray far away," he said. "Now it is time for us to be going forward."

Miriamele swung up into the saddle, then leaned down to extend a hand to the little man; he scrambled up and seated himself before her. She tapped her heels against the horse's side.

When she looked back, Simon's horse Homefinder was cropping grass at the base of a rain-dripping tree. Qantaqa sat erect, ears high, yellow eyes intent on her master's small back.

The Erchester Road was a sea of mud. The horse seemed to spend almost as much time unsticking itself as it did walking.

The city gate proved to be unbolted. The delicately-weighted portal swung open with only a light push from Miriamele, creaking gently. She waded back across the muddy wagon ruts and remounted, then they rode in between the tall gate towers, rain drizzling down on them from the clotted gray skies.

"There are no guards," she whispered.

"There is no one at all that I am seeing."

Just inside the gate lay Battle Square, a vast expanse of cobblestones with a green in the center, the site of countless parades and festivals. Now the square was empty but for a few stark-ribbed dogs rooting in debris at the mouth of one of the alleys. The square looked as though it had been unused for some time, forgotten by all except the scavengers. Wide puddles rippled beneath the rain. The green had become a desolate patch of pockmarked mud.

The echo of the horse's hooves caught the dogs' attention. They stared, tongues lolling, dark eyes wary; a moment later the pack turned and fled splashing down the alleyway.

"What has happened here?" Miriamele wondered.

"I think we can be guessing," said Binabik. "You saw other nearby towns and villages, and I saw such emptiness all through the snowy lands of the north. And this place, do you see, is closest of all to what has happened at the Hayholt."

"But where have all the people gone? From Stanshire, from Hasu Vale, from . . . from here? They didn't just disappear."

"No. Some may have been dying when the harvests were not coming in, but others have just gone to the south, I am thinking. This year has been a fearful enough thing for those of us who are having some knowledge of what is happening. For those who were living here, it must have seemed that they were suddenly finding themselves under a curse."

"Oh, Merciful Elysia." Her unhappiness was strangely mixed with anger and pity. "What has my father done?"

Binabik shook his head.

As they entered broad Main Row, there at last appeared some signs of human life: from the cracks of a few shuttered windows firelight flickered, and somewhere farther up the thoroughfare a door banged shut. Miriamele even thought she could hear a faint voice raised in prayer, but somehow she could not imagine a person from whom such a ragged sound would come; rather, it seemed that some wandering spirit had left behind its mournful cry.

As they turned the bend in Main Row, a figure in a ragged cloak appeared from one of the narrow cross streets in front of them and went shambling slowly away up the road. Miriamele was so surprised to see an actual person that she reined up and sat staring for long moments. As if sensing the presence of strangers, the figure turned; for an instant a look of fear showed on the wrinkled face beneath the hood—it was difficult to tell if it was a man or a woman—then the cloaked shape scuttled rapidly forward and vanished down an alleyway. When Miriamele and Binabik drew even with the place, there was no sign of anyone. All the doors that faced the narrow byway looked as though they had been boarded up for some time.

"Whoever that was, *they* were scared of *us.*" Miriamele could not keep the pained surprise out of her voice.

"Can you feel blame for them about that?" The little man waved his hand at the haunted streets. "But it is no matter. I am not doubting that many ghastly things have been happening here—but it is not our task to be worrying about such happenings. We are looking for something."

"Of course," Miriamele replied quickly, but her mind did not fix easily on what the little man was saying. It was hard to tear her eyes from the mud-spattered walls, the gloomy, empty streets. It looked as though a great flood had rushed through and swept all the people away. "Of course," she said again. "But how will we find it?"

"On the map, the tunnel end looked as though it was being in the center of the town. Are we going in that direction?"

"Yes. Main Row goes through town all the way up to the Nearulagh Gate."

"Then what is that thing being?" Binabik pointed. "It seems to block any going forward." A few furlongs ahead, a huge dark mass straddled the road.

"That?" Miriamele was still so disoriented that it took her a long moment to recognize it. "Oh. That's the back of Saint Sutrin's—the cathedral."

Binabik was silent for some moments. "And it is at the center of the town?"

"More or less." Something in the tone of the troll's voice finally dragged her attention back from the dreamlike emptiness of Main Row. "Binabik? What is it? Is something wrong?"

"Let us just wait until we are seeing it from more closely. Why is there no golden wall? I thought from the traveler's tales told to me that such a wall was being a famous thing about this Saint Sutrin's."

"It's on the other side—the side that faces the castle."

They continued up Main Row. Miriamele wondered whether there might be people here after all—if instead of almost deserted, the city might actually be full-tenanted. Perhaps if all the inhabitants were as fearful as the one she had seen, they were even now watching quietly from behind shuttered windows and through cracks in the walls. Somehow that was just as bad as imagining the people of Erchester all gone.

Or perhaps it was something stranger still. On either side of the road, the stalls which had once housed the various small merchants were empty, but now she thought she could feel a sort of anticipation, as though these hollow holes waited to be filled with some new kind of life—something as unlike the farmers, peasants, and townsfolk who had once bustled through their lives here as mud was unlike dry, sunlit soil.

The golden facade of Saint Sutrin's had been peeled away by scavengers; even the famous stone reliefs were gouged almost into unrecognizability, as though the gold that had covered them had been smashed loose with hammers in the course of a single hasty hour.

"It was beautiful." Miriamele had not much room left for sadness or surprise. "When the sun was on it, it looked like the church was covered in holy flames."

"In times of badness, gold is being worth more than beauty," Binabik mused, squinting up at the crushed faces of the saints. "Let us go and try the door."

"Do you think it's here? The tunnel?"

"You saw from the map that it was coming up in the center of this town of Erchester. I am guessing that this place goes deeper than any other in the town."

The great wooden doors did not open easily, but Miriamele and Binabik both lowered their shoulders; the hinges groaned and the doors grated open almost a cubit, allowing them to slip inside.

The forechamber had also lost much of its decoration. The pedestals on either side of the door were empty, and the huge tapestries that had once made the chamber walls into windows that looked out on the days of Usires Aedon now lay crumpled on the flagstones, crisscrossed with muddy footprints. The room stank of damp and decay, as though it had been long deserted, but light glowed from the great chapel beyond the forechamber doors.

"Someone is here," Miriamele said quietly.

"Or at least they are still coming for lighting the candles."

They had only taken a few steps when a figure appeared in the inner doorway.

"Who are you? What do you seek in God's house?"

Miriamele was so surprised to hear another human voice that for a moment she did not reply. Binabik took a step forward, but she put her hand on his shoulder. "We are travelers," she said. "We wanted to see Saint Sutrin's. The doors were never closed in the past."

"Are you Aedonites?"

Miriamele thought there was something familiar about the voice. "I am. My companion is from a foreign land, but he has been of service to Mother Church."

There was a moment's hesitation before the man spoke again. "Enter, then, if you swear you are not enemies."

Miriamele doubted from the tremulousness of his tone that the man speaking could have stopped them if they *were* enemies, but she said: "We are not. Thank you."

The shadowy figure vanished from the doorway and Miriamele led Binabik through. She was still wary. In this haunted city, anyone could live in a cathedral. Why not then use it as a trap spider used its burrow, as a lure to the incautious?

It was not much warmer inside than out, and the great chapel was thick with shadows. Only a dozen candles burned in the huge room, and their light was scarcely enough to illuminate the vaulting high overhead. Something was strange about the dome as well. After a few moments' scrutiny, Miriamele realized that all of the glass was gone but for a few splinters clinging to the lead frame. A solitary star glimmered in the naked sky.

"Smashed by the storm," a voice said beside her. She flinched, startled. "All our lovely windows, the work of ages, shattered. It is a judgment on Mankind."

Standing beside her in the dim light was an old man in a dirty gray robe, his face sagging into a thousand wrinkles, his white-wisped, balding head covered with a lopsided hat of strange shape. "You look so sad," he murmured; his accent marked him as an Erkynlander. "Did you ever see our Saint Sutrin's before . . ." he hesitated, as he tried to find a word, but could not. "Did you ever see it . . . before?"

"Yes." Miriamele knew it was better policy to profess ignorance, but the old man seemed so pathetically proud that she did not have the heart. "I saw it. It was very beautiful."

"Only the great chapel in the Sancellan Aedonitis could compare," he said wistfully. "I wonder if it still stands? We hear little from the South these days."

"I am sure it does."

"Ah, yes? Well, that is very good." Despite his words, he sounded faintly disappointed that his cathedral's rival had not suffered a similarly ignoble fate. "But, may our Ransomer forgive us, we are poor hosts," he said suddenly, catching Miriamele's arm with a gently trembling claw. "Come in and shelter from the storm. You and your son—" he gestured to Binabik, who looked up in surprise; the old man had already forgotten what Miriamele had told him, "—will be safe here. They have taken our beautiful things, but they have not taken us from the watchful-ness of God's eye."

He led them up the long aisle toward the altar, a block of stone with a rag stretched over it, mumbling as he went about the wonderful things that had once stood here or there and the horrible things that had happened to them. Miriamele was not listening to him closely: she was preoccupied by the scatter of shadowy human shapes which leaned against the walls or lay in corners. One or two were draped lengthwise across the benches as though in sleep. All to-gether, there seemed to be several dozen people in the huge chapel, all silent and apparently unmoving. Miriamele had a sudden, horrid thought. "Who are all these folk?" she asked. "Are they . . . dead?"

The old man looked up, surprised, then smiled and shook his head. "No, no, they are pilgrims like yourself, travelers who sought a safe haven. God led them here, and so they shelter in His church."

As the old man recommenced his description of the splendors of Saint Sutrin's as it once had been, Miriamele felt a tug at her sleeve.

"Ask him whether there is anything beneath this place like that thing we are searching," the troll whispered.

When the man paused for a moment, Miriamele seized her chance. "Are there tunnels beneath the cathedral?"

"Tunnels?" The question set an odd light burning in the old man's rheumy eye. "What do you mean? There are the catacombs, where all the bishops of this place lie resting until the Day of Weighing-Out, but no one goes there. It is . . . holy ground." He seemed disturbed, staring past the altar at nothing Miriamele could see. "That is not a place for any traveler. Why do you ask?"

Miriamele did not wish to upset him any further. "I was told once that there was a . . . a holy place here." She bowed her head. "Someone dear to me is in danger. I had thought that maybe there was a special shrine. . . ." What had seemed a lie had come to her quickly, but as she thought about it, she realized it was only truth: someone dear to her *was* in peril. She should light a candle for Simon before they left this place.

"Ah." The old man seemed mollified. "No, it is not that sort of place, not at all. Now come, it is almost time for the evening *mansa.*"

Miriamele was surprised. So the rites were still celebrated here, even though the church seemed little more than a shell. She wondered what had happened to fat, blustering Bishop Domitis and all his priestly underlings.

The man led them to the first row of benches facing the altar, then gestured for them to sit down. The irony did not escape Miriamele: she had often sat there before at her father's side, and at her grandfather's before that. The old man walked to a place behind the stone and its ragged covering, then lifted his arms in the air. "Come, my friends," he said loudly. "You may return now."

Binabik looked at Miriamele. She shrugged, unsure of what the man wanted them to do.

But they were not the ones who had been addressed. A moment later, whir-ring and flapping, a host of black shapes descended from the shadowy wreckage of the dome. Miriamele gave out a little squeak of surprise as the ravens settled upon the altar. Within moments almost a score of them stood wing to wing on the altar cloth, oily feathers gleaming in the candlelight.

The old man began to speak the *Mansa Nictalis,* and as he did, the ravens preened and ruffled.

"What is this thing?" Binabik asked. "It is not a part of your worship that I have heard of."

Miriamele shook her head. The old man was clearly mad. He was addressing the Nabbanai words to the ravens, who strutted back and forth along the altar giving voice to harsh, grating cries. But there was something else about the scene that was almost as strange as the eerie ceremony, some elusive thing. . . .

Abruptly, as the old man lifted his arms and made the ritual sign of the Great Tree, she recognized him. This was Bishop Domitis himself at the altar—or his wasted remains, since he seemed shriveled to half his previous weight. Even his voice was different: deprived of the great bellows of flesh, it had become reedy and thin. But as he rolled into the sonorous cadences of the *mansa,* much of the old Domitis seemed to return; in her weary mind she could see him again as he once had been, swelled bullfrog-great with self-importance.

"Binabik," she whispered. "I know him! He is the bishop of this place. But he looks so different!"

The troll was eyeing the capering ravens with a mixture of amusement and uneasiness. "Can you then be persuading him to help us?"

Miriamele considered. "I don't think so. He seems very protective of his church, and he certainly didn't seem to want us wandering around down in the catacombs."

"Then I am thinking that is just the place we must go," Binabik said quietly. "We must be looking for the chance to come to us." He looked up at Domitis, who stood with head thrown back and eyes closed, his arms widespread as if in imitation of his avian congregation. "I have something that I must be doing now. Wait for me here. It will take me only a little time." He got up quietly from the bench, then turned and moved quickly back down the aisle toward the front of the cathedral.

"Binabik!" Miriamele called softly, but the troll only raised his hand before disappearing into the forechamber. Unsettled, she turned reluctantly to watch the rest of the odd performance.

Domitis seemed to have completely forgotten the presence of anyone but himself and the ravens. A pair of these had flown up from the altar to settle on his shoulders. They clung there as he swayed; as he windmilled his arms in the fervor of his speech, they flapped their great black wings to maintain balance on their perches.

Finally, as the bishop began the last stages of the *mansa,* the whole flock of birds rose up and began circling his head like a croaking thundercloud. Whatever humor the ritual had held was gone: Miriamele suddenly found the whole thing frightening. Was there no corner of the world left that had not succumbed to madness? Had *everything* been corrupted?

Domitis intoned the last Nabbanai phrases and fell silent. The ravens circled a few moments more, then went whirling up toward the ruptured dome like a whirlwind, vanishing into the shadows with only the echoes of their rasping cries left hanging in the air behind them. When even those had died and the cathedral had fallen quiet, Bishop Domitis, now almost gray with expended effort, bent down behind the altar.

When some time had passed and he had not stood up again, Miriamele began to wonder whether the old man had fallen into some sort of fit, or had perhaps even dropped dead. She got to her feet and moved cautiously toward the altar, keeping an eye cocked toward the ceiling as she went, half-fearing that at any moments the ravens might descend again, talons and beaks flailing. . . .

Domitis was curled on a ragged blanket behind the altar, snoring softly. In repose, the loose skin of his face seemed even more formless, sagging into long folds so that he seemed to wear a mask of melted candlewax. Miriamele shuddered and hurried back to her chair, but after a few moments even that began to feel too exposed. The room was still full of silent figures, but it was not difficult to imagine that they were only feigning sleep, waiting to be sure her companion was not returning before they rose and came toward her. . . .

Miriamele waited for what seemed a long time. The forechamber was colder even than the broken-domed chapel, but escape was within reach at a moment's notice. A little of the night wind slipped through the partially open door, which made her feel closer to freedom and hence a great deal safer, but she still jumped when the door hinges screeched.

"Ah," said Binabik, slipping inside, "it is still raining with great forcefulness." He shook water onto the stone floor.

"Bishop Domitis has gone to sleep behind the altar. Binabik, where did you go?"

"To take your horse back to where Homefinder and Qantaqa wait. Even if we are not finding what we seek here, we can easily travel through the town by walking. But if we find a tunnel-entering-place, I am fearing that we would come back at a later time to find your horse as part of some hungry person's soup."

Miriamele had not thought of that, but she did not doubt that he was right. "I'm glad you did it. Now what should we do?"

"Go hunting for our tunnel," said Binabik.

"When Bishop Domitis was talking about the catacombs, he kept looking over to the back of the cathedral, that wall behind the altar."

"Hmmm." The troll nodded. "You are wise for noticing and remembering. That is, I am thinking, the first place we should search."

"We have to be quiet—we don't want to wake him up."

"Like snow-mice we will be, our pads whispering on the white crust." Binabik squeezed her hand.

Her worries about the slumbering Domitis were unfounded. The old man was snoring thinly but emphatically, and did not even twitch as they padded by. The great wall behind the altar, which had once been covered in a tiled representation of Saint Sutrin's martyrdom, was now only crumbling mortar with a few remaining spots of ceramic color. At one end of the wall, tucked behind a rotting velvet drapery, stood a low door. Binabik gave it a tug and it opened easily, as though it had been used with some frequency. The troll peered inside, then turned. "Let us be taking some candles," he murmured. "That way we can be saving the torches in our packs for a later time."

Miriamele went back and plucked two of the candles from the sconces. She felt a little shame, since Domitis had been kind to them in his own strange way, but she reasoned that their greater goal outweighed the sin of theft, and would benefit the bishop as well—maybe one day he would even see his beloved cathedral rebuilt. She could not help wondering if the ravens would be welcome then. She hoped not.

Each holding a candle, Miriamele and Binabik went carefully down the narrow staircase. Centuries of human traffic had worn a groove like a dry river bed in the center of the stone steps. They stepped off the stairs into the low-ceilinged catacombs and stopped to look around. The walls on either side were honeycombed with niches, each containing a silent stone effigy of a figure in repose, most wearing the robes and other symbols of church office. But for these, the narrow halls seemed entirely empty.

Binabik pointed at one turning that seemed less traveled. "This way, I am thinking."

Miriamele peered down the shadowy tunnel. The pale plaster walls were unmarked; no would-be saints lay here, it seemed. She took a deep breath. "Let's go."

In the cathedral above, a pair of ravens dropped down from the ceiling and, after circling briefly, settled on the altar. They stood side by side, bright eyes glaring at the door to the catacombs. Nor were they the only observers. A figure detached itself from the shadows along the wall and crept silently across the cathedral. It moved past the altar, stepping just as carefully as had Miriamele and the troll, then paused for a while outside the vault door as though listening. When a short time had passed, the dark shape slipped through the doorway and went pattering quietly down the stairs.

After that, nothing was heard in the dark cathedral but the bishop's even snoring and the faint rustle of wings.

42

Roots of the White Tree

❧

Simon stared at the amazing thing for a long time. He took a step closer, then danced back nervously. How could it be? It must be a dream-picture, like so many other illusions in these endless tunnels.

He rubbed his eyes and then opened them again: the plate still stood in the niche by the stair landing, chest-high. On it, arranged as prettily as at a royal banquet, was a small green apple, an onion, and a heel of bread. An unadorned bowl with a cover stood beside it.

Simon shrank back, looking wildly from side to side. Who would do such a thing? What would make someone leave a perfectly good supper in the middle of an empty stairwell in the depths of the earth? He raised his guttering torch to inspect the magical offering once more.

It was hard to believe—no, it was impossible. He had been wandering for hours since leaving the great pool, trying to stay on an upward course but not at all sure that the curving bridges, downsloping corridors, and oddly constructed stairways were not taking him even further into the earth, no matter how many steps he climbed. All that time the flame of his torch had been growing fainter, until it was little more than a wisp of blue and yellow which might be blown out by any errant breeze. He had all but convinced himself that he would be lost forever, that he would starve and die in darkness—and then he had found this . . . this *miracle*.

It was not just the food itself, although the sight of it filled his mouth with saliva and made his fingers twitch. No, it meant there must be people somewhere nearby, and likely light and fresh air as well. Even the walls, which were rough-cobbled human work, spoke of the surface, of escape. He was as good as saved!

Hold a moment. He caught himself with hand outstretched, almost touching the skin of the apple. *What if it's a trap? What if they know someone is down here, and they're trying to lure him out?*

But who would "they" be? No one could know he was down here but his friends and the bestial diggers and the shadowy ghosts of the Sithi in their dream-castle. No, someone had brought supper down here, then for some reason had walked away, forgetting it.

If it was even real.

Simon reached, ready for the food to vanish, to turn to dust . . . but it did not. His hand closed on the apple. It was hard beneath his fingers. He snatched it up, sniffed it briefly—what did poison smell like, anyway?—and then took a bite.

Thank you, merciful Usires. Thank you.

It was . . . wonderful. The fruit was far from ripe, the juice tart, even sour, but it felt like he held the living green earth in his hand again, that the life of the sun and wind and rain was crisping between his teeth and tongue, running down his throat. For a moment he forgot all else, savoring the glory of it.

He lifted the cover from the bowl, sniffed to make sure it was water, then drank it down in thirsty gulps. When the bowl was empty, he grabbed the plate of food and darted back down the corridor, searching for a place to hide and eat in safety.

Simon fought with himself to make the apple last, even though each bite seemed like a year of his life given back to him. When he had finished it, and had licked every bit of juice from his fingers, he stared longingly at the bread and onion. With masterful self-control, he tucked them both into the pockets of his breeches. Even if he found his way back to the surface, even if he was near some place where people were, there was no guarantee he would be fed. If he came up within Erchester or one of the small villages along the Kynslagh, he might find a place to hide and even some allies; if he came up in the Hayholt, all hands might be turned against him. And if he was wrong about what the plate signified—well, he would be grateful to have the rest of the meal when the thrilling effect of an entire apple wore off.

He picked up the torch—it was even dimmer now, the flames a transparent azure—and stepped back out into the corridor, then paced forward until he reached the branching place. A chill passed through him. Which way had he turned? He had been in such a hurry to put distance between himself and anyone who might return for the food that he had acted without his normal care. Had he turned left, as he should have? Somehow that did not seem correct.

Still, he could do nothing but trust to the way he had done it so far. He took the rightward branching. Within moments, he became convinced that he had chosen wrongly: this way led down. He retraced his steps and took another of the corridors, but this one also sloped away downward. A few moments' examination proved that *all* the branches went down. He walked back toward where he had eaten the apple and found the stem he had dropped, but when he held the guttering torch close to the ground he saw that the only footprints on the dusty floor led back the way he had come.

Curse this place! Curse this mad maze of a place!

Simon trudged back to the branching. Something had happened, it was clear—the tunnels had shifted again in some strange way. Resigned, he chose the downward path that seemed least steep and started on his way again.

The corridor twisted and turned, leading him back into the depths. Soon the walls again showed signs of Sithi work, hints of twining carvings beneath the centuries of grime. The passageway widened, then widened again. He stepped out into a vast open area and knew it only from the far-ranging echoes of his bootheels: his torch was little more now than a smoldering glow.

This cavernous place seemed as high-ceilinged as that which had held the great pool. As Simon moved forward and his eyes adjusted to the greater dimensions, his heart lifted. It was like the chamber of the pool in another way as well: a great staircase ran upward into the darkness, following the curve of the walls. Something else gleamed faintly in the middle of the chamber. He moved closer, and the dying light of his torch revealed a great circle of stone that might have been the base of a fountain; at its center, set in black earth but stretching up to many times Simon's height, was a tree. Or at least it *seemed* to be a tree—there was a suggestion of humped and knotted roots at the bottom, and amazingly tangled branches above—but no matter how close he held the torch, he could see no detail of it, as though it were draped in clinging shadow.

As he leaned nearer, the shadow-tree rattled in an unfelt wind, a sound like a thousand dry hands rubbing against each other. Simon leaped back. He had been about to touch it, certain it was carved stone. Instead he turned and hurried past it to the base of the winding stairway.

As he circled around the perimeter of the chamber, picking his way up the steps by fading torchlight, he was still intensely aware of the tree standing at the room's center. He could hear the breathing sound of its leaves as they moved, but he could *feel* its existence even more strongly; it was as palpable in the darkness as someone lying beside him in a bed. It was not like anything he had felt before—less starkly powerful than the pool, perhaps, but somehow more subtle, an intelligence vast, old, and unhurried. The pool's magic was like a roaring bonfire—something that could burn or illuminate, but would do neither unless someone was present to use its power. Simon could not imagine anyone or anything *using* the tree. It stood and dreamed and waited for no one. It was not good or evil, it simply was.

Long after he had left the base of the stairway behind him, he could feel its living presence.

The light from his torch grew less and less. At last, after he had climbed some hundreds of steps, it finally died. Having anticipated its passing for so long did not make the moment any less dreadful: Simon slumped down and sat in complete darkness, too tired even to weep. He ate a mouthful of bread and some onion, then squeezed some of the last of the water from his drying shirt. When he had finished, he took a deep breath and began to crawl up the stairs on his hands and knees, feeling before him in the blackness.

It was hard to tell whether the voices that followed him were phantoms of the underground realm or the chattering of his own drifting thoughts.

Climb up. All will be ready soon.

On your knees again, mooncalf?

Step after stone step passed beneath his hands. His fingers were numb, his knees and shins aching dully.

The Conqueror is coming! Soon all will be ready.

But one is missing!

It does not matter. The trees are burning. All is dead, gone. It does not matter.

Simon's mind wandered as he clambered up the winding track. It was not hard to imagine that he had been swallowed whole, that he was in the belly of some great beast. Perhaps it was the dragon—the dragon that was spoken of in the inscription on his ring. He stopped and felt his finger, reassured by the feel of the metal. What had Binabik said the inscription meant? *Dragon* and *Death?*

Killed by a dragon, maybe. I've been swallowed by one, and I'm dead. I'll climb around and around inside it forever, here in the dark. I wonder if anyone else has been swallowed? It's so lonely. . . .

The dragon is dead, the voices told him. *No, the dragon is death,* others assured him.

He stopped and ate a little more of his food. His mouth was dry, but he did not take more than a few drops of water before resuming his four-legged climb.

Simon stopped to catch his breath and rest his aching leg for perhaps the dozenth time since entering the stairwell. As he crouched, panting, light suddenly flickered around him. He thought wildly that his torch had blazed again, until he remembered that the dead brand was stuck beneath his belt. For a startlingly beautiful moment the whole stairwell seemed full of pale golden light, and he looked up the shaft into infinite distance, up past a shrinking spiral of stairs to a hole that led straight to heaven. Then, with a silent concussion, a ball of angry flame bloomed in the heights above him, turning the very air red, and for a moment the stairwell became hot as forge fire. Simon shouted in fear.

No! the voices screamed. *No! Speak not the word! You will summon Unbeing!*

There was a crack louder than any thunder, then a blue-white flash that dissolved everything in pure light. An instant later everything was black once more.

Simon lay on the stairs, panting. Was it truly dark again, or had the flare blinded him? How could he know?

What does it matter? asked a mocking voice.

He pressed his fingers against his closed eyelids until faint sparkles of blue and red moved in the darkness, but it proved nothing.

I will not know unless I find something that I know I should be able to see.

He had a hideous thought. What if, blinded, he crawled past a way out, a lighted doorway, a portal open to the sky?

Can't think. I'll climb. Can't think.

He struggled upward. After a while he seemed to lose himself entirely, drifting away to other places, other times. He saw Erchester and the countryside beyond as they had looked from the bellchamber atop Green Angel Tower—the rolling hills and fenced farms, the tiny houses and people and animals laid out below him like wooden toys on a green blanket. He wanted to warn them all, tell them to run away, that a terrible winter was coming.

He saw Morgenes again. The lenses that the old man wore glinted in a beam of afternoon light, making his eyes flash as though some greater-than-ordinary fire burned within him. Morgenes was trying to tell him something, but Simon, young, stupid Simon, was watching a fly buzzing near the window. If only he had listened! If only he had known!

And he saw the castle itself, a fantastic hodgepodge of towers and roofs, its banners rippling in a spring wind. The Hayholt—his home. His home as it had been, and would never be again. But, oh, what he would give to turn Time in its track and send it rolling backward! If he could have bargained his soul for it . . . what was a soul worth, anyway, against the happiness of home restored?

The sky behind the Hayholt lightened as if the sun had emerged from behind a cloud. Simon squinted. Perhaps it was not spring after all—perhaps it was high summer . . . ?

The Hayholt's towers faded, but the light remained.

Light!

It was a faint, directionless sheen, no brighter than moonglow through fog—but Simon could see the dim form of the step before him, his dirt-crusted, scabby hand flattened upon it. He could see!

He looked around, trying to determine the source of the light. As far as he could see ahead of him, the steps wound upward. The light, faint as swamp-fire, came from somewhere above.

He got to his feet, swayed woozily for a moment, then began to walk upright once more. At first the angle seemed strange and he had to clutch the wall for support, but soon he felt almost human. Each step, laborious as it seemed, was taking him closer to the light. Each twinge of his wounded ankle was taking him nearer to . . . what? Freedom, he hoped.

What had seemed an unlimited vista during the blinding flash of light now abruptly closed off above him. The stairs opened out onto a broad landing, but did not continue upward. Instead, the stairwell had been sealed off with a low ceiling of crude brick, as though someone had tried to cork the stair-tower like the neck of a bottle—but light leaked through at one side. Simon shuffled toward the glow, crouching so that he would not bump his head, and found a place where the bricks had fallen down, leaving a crevice that seemed just wide enough for a single person to climb. He jumped, but his hands could only touch the rough brick lining the hole; if there was an upper side, it was out of his reach. He jumped again, but it was useless.

Simon stared up at the opening. A heavy, defeated weariness descended on him. He slumped down to the landing and sat for a moment with his head in his hands. To have climbed so far!

He finished off the heel of bread and weighed the onion in his hand, wondering if he should just eat it; at last, he put it away again. It wasn't time to give up yet. After a few moments of thought, he crawled over to the scatter of bricks that had crumbled loose from the ceiling and began piling them one atop the other, trying to find an arrangement that was stable. When he had made the sturdiest pile he could, he clambered atop it. Now, as he reached up, his hands stretched far into the crevice, but he still could not feel any upper surface. He tensed his muscles, then leaped. For a moment, he felt a lip at the upper part of the hole; an instant later his hands failed their grip and he slid back down, tumbling from the pile of bricks and twisting his sore ankle. Biting his lip to keep from shouting at the pain, he laboriously stacked the bricks again, climbed atop them, crouched, and jumped.

This time he was prepared. He caught the top of the hole and hung, wincing. After taking a few strong breaths, he pulled upward, his whole body trembling with the strain.

Farther, farther, just a little farther . . .

The broken edges of brick passed before him. As he pulled himself higher, his elbows pushed against the brick, and for a moment it seemed that he would be trapped, wedged and left hanging in the hole like a game bird. He sucked in another breath, clenched his teeth against the pain of his arms, and pulled. Quivering, he inched higher; he braced himself for a short moment against the back of the hole, then pulled again. His eyes rose past the top of his hole, then his nose, then his chin. When he could, he threw his arm out onto the surface and clutched, pressing his back against the brick, then brought the other arm out as well. Using his elbows as levers, he worked his way up out of the crevice, ignoring the scrape of stone along his back and sides, then slid forward onto his chest and kicked like a swimmer until the whole of his length was lying on dank stone, safe.

Simon lay for a long time, sucking air, trying not to think about how much his arms and shoulders hurt. He rolled over on his back and stared up at another ceiling of stone, this one only a little higher above him than the last had been. Tears trickled down his cheeks. Was this to be the next variation in his torments? Would he be forced to pull himself up by sheer strength through hole after hole, forever? Was he damned?

Simon pulled the wet shirt from his breeches and squeezed it to get a few drops into his mouth, then sat up and looked at what was around him.

His eyes widened; his heart seemed to expand inside his chest. This was something different.

He was sitting on the floor of what was obviously a storeroom. It was human-made, and full of human implements, although none seemed to have been touched for some time. In one corner was a wagon wheel with two of its spokes missing. Several casks stood against another wall, and beside them were piled cloth sacks bulging with mysterious contents. For a moment, all Simon could think about was the possibility that they might contain food. Then he saw the ladder beside the far wall, and realized where the light was coming from.

The upper part of the ladder vanished through an open hatch door in the ceiling, a square full of light. Simon stared, gape-mouthed. Surely someone had heard his anguished prayers and had set it there to wait for him.

He roused himself and moved slowly across the room, then clutched the rungs of the ladder and looked upward. There was light above, and it seemed like the clean light of day. After all this time, could such a thing be?

The room above was another storeroom. It had a hatch door and ladder as well, but in the upper part of the wall there was a small, narrow window—through which Simon could see gray sky.

Sky!

He had thought that he had no more tears to cry, but as he stared at the rectangle of clouds, he began to weep, sobs of relief like a lost child reunited with a parent. He sank to his knees and offered a prayer of thanks. The world had been given back to him. No, that was not true: *he* had found the world once more.

After resting a few moments, he mounted the ladder. On the upper side of the hatchway he found a small chamber full of masonry tools and jars of paint and whitewash. This room had an ordinary door and ordinary rough plaster walls. Simon was delighted. Everything was so blessedly ordinary! He opened the door carefully, suddenly aware that he was in a place where people lived, that much as he wished to see another face and hear a voice that did not issue from empty shadows, he had to be cautious.

Outside the door lay a huge chamber with a floor of polished stone, lit only by small high windows. The walls were covered with heavy tapestries. On his right, a wide staircase swept upward and out of sight; across the chamber a smaller set of steps rose to a landing and a closed door. Simon looked from side to side and listened, but there seemed no one about but him. He stepped out.

Despite all the cleaning implements in the various storerooms, the large chamber did not seem to have benefited from their use: pale freckles of mold grew on the tapestries and the air was thick with the damp, close smell of a place long-untended.

The astonishment of being in daylight again, the glory of escape from the depths, was so strong that Simon did not realize for some time that he stood in a place he knew well. Something in the shape and arrangement of the windows or some dimly perceptible detail in one of the fading tapestries finally pricked his memory.

Green Angel Tower. The awareness came over him like a dream, the familiar turned strange, the strange become familiar. *I'm in the entry hall. Green Angel Tower!*

That surprising recognition was followed by one much less pleasant.

I'm in the Hayholt. In the High King's castle. With Elias and his soldiers. And Pryrates.

He stepped back into the shadows along the wall as though any moment the

Erkynguard would crash through the tower's main door to take him prisoner. What should he do?

It was tempting to consider climbing up the wide staircase to the bellchamber, the place that had been his childhood refuge. He could look down and see every corner of the Hayholt; he could rest and try to decide what to do next. But his swollen ankle was throbbing horridly, and the thought of all those steps made him feel weak.

First he would eat the onion he had saved, he decided. He deserved a small celebration. He would think later.

Simon slipped back into the closet, then considered that even that place might be a little too frequented. Perhaps the tower's entry chamber only *seemed* unvisited. He clambered down the ladder into the storeroom beneath, grunting softly at the ache in his arms and ankle, then pulled the onion from his pocket and devoured it in a series of greedy bites. He squeezed the last of his water down his throat—whatever else might happen, rain was sluicing through all the castle gutters and drizzling down past the windows, so soon he would have all the water he wanted—and then lay back with his head resting against one of the sacks and began organizing his thoughts.

Within moments he fell asleep.

"We tell lies when we are afraid," said Morgenes.

The old man took a stone from his pocket and tossed it into the moat. There was a flirt of sunlight on the ripples as the stone disappeared. "Afraid of what we don't know, afraid of what others will think, afraid of what will be found out about us. But every time we tell a lie, the thing that we fear grows stronger."

Simon looked around. The sun was vanishing behind the castle's western wall; Green Angel Tower was a black spike, boldly silhouetted. He knew this was a dream. Morgenes had said this to him long ago, but they had been in the doctor's chambers standing over a dusty book at the time, not outside in the fading afternoon. And in any case, Morgenes was dead. This was a dream, nothing more.

"It is, in fact, a kind of magic—perhaps the strongest of all," Morgenes continued. "Study that, if you wish to understand power, young Simon. Don't fill your head with nattering about spells and incantations. Understand how lies shape us, shape kingdoms."

"But that's not magic," Simon protested, lured into the discussion despite himself. "That doesn't do anything. Real magic lets you . . . I don't know. Fly. Make bags of gold out of a pile of turnips. Like in the stories."

"But the stories themselves are often lies, Simon. The bad ones are." The doctor cleaned his spectacles on the wide sleeve of his robe. "Good stories will tell you that facing the lie is the worst terror of all. And there is no talisman or magic sword that is half so potent a weapon as truth."

Simon turned to watch the ripples slowly dissipating. It was wonderful to stand and *talk with Morgenes again, even if it was only a dream. "Do you mean that if I said to a great dragon like the one that King John killed: 'You're an ugly dragon,' that would be better than cutting its head off with a sword?"*

Morgenes' voice was fainter. "If you had been pretending it wasn't a dragon, then yes, that would be the best thing to do. But there is more, Simon. You have to go deeper still."

"Deeper?" Simon turned back, angry now. "I've been down in the earth, Doctor. I lived and I came up again. What do you mean?"

Morgenes was . . . changing. His skin had turned papery and his pale hair was full of leaves. Even as Simon watched, the old man's fingers began to lengthen, changing into slender twigs, branching, branching. "Yes, you have learned," the doctor said. As he spoke, his features began to disappear into the whorls on the white bark of the tree. "But you must go deeper still. There is much to understand. Watch for the angel—she will show you things, both in the ground and far above it."

"Morgenes!" Simon's anger was all gone. His friend was changing so swiftly that there was almost nothing manlike left of him, only a faint suggestion in the shape of the trunk, an unnatural trembling in the tree's limbs. "Don't leave me!"

"But I have left you already," the doctor's voice murmured. "What you have of me is only what is in your head—I am part of you. The rest of me has become part of the earth again." The tree swayed slightly. "Remember, though—the sun and stars shine on the leaves, but the roots are deep in the earth, hidden . . . hidden. . . ."

Simon clutched at the tree's pale trunk, his fingers scrabbling uselessly against the stiff bark. The doctor's voice was silent.

Simon sat up, nightmare-sweat stinging his eyes, and was horrified to discover himself in darkness.

It was all a dream! I'm still lost in the tunnels, I'm lost. . . .

A moment later he saw starlight through the storeroom's high window.

Mooncalf. Fell asleep and it got dark outside.

He sat up, rubbing his sore limbs. What was he to do now? He was hungry and thirsty, and there seemed little chance that he would find anything to eat here in Green Angel Tower. Still, he was more than a little reluctant to leave this relatively safe place.

Have I climbed out of the dark ground only to starve to death in a closet? he chided himself. *What kind of knight would do that?*

He got to his feet and stretched, noting the dull ache in his ankle. Perhaps just a foray out to get some water and see the lay of the land. Certainly it would be best to do such things while it was still dark.

Simon stood uncertainly in the shadows outside Green Angel Tower. The Inner Bailey's haphazard roofs made a familiar jumble against the night sky, but Simon did not feel at all comfortable. It was not just that he was an outlaw in his childhood home, although that was disconcerting enough: there was also something strange in the air that he could not name, but which he nevertheless could sense quite clearly. The maddening slipperiness of the world below-ground had somehow seeped up into the everyday stones of the castle itself. When he tilted his head to one side, he could almost see the buildings ripple and change at the edge of his sight. Faint blurs of light, like phantom flames, seemed to flicker along the edges of walls, then quickly vanish.

The Hayholt, too? Had all the world broken loose from its moorings? What was happening?

With some difficulty, he nerved himself to go exploring.

Although it seemed the great castle was deserted, Simon soon discovered it was not. The Inner Bailey was dark and quiet, but voices whispered down corridors and behind closed doors, and there were lights in many of the higher windows. He also heard snatches of music, odd tunes and odder voices that made him want to arch like a cat and hiss. As he stood in the deep concealing shadows of the Hedge Garden, he decided that the Hayholt had somehow become spoiled, a fruit left to sit for too long now grown soft and rotten beneath the outer shell. He could not quite say what was wrong, but the whole of the Inner Bailey, the place that had been the center of Simon's childhood world, seemed to have sickened.

He went stealthily to the kitchen, the lesser pantry, the chapel—even, in a moment of high daring, to the antechamber of the throne room, which opened onto the gardens. All the outer doors were barred. He could find no entrance anywhere. Simon could not remember any time before when that had been so. Was the king frightened of spies, of a siege? Or were the barriers not to keep out intruders, but to make sure that those who were inside remained there? He breathed quietly and thought. There were windows that could not be closed, he knew, and other secret ways—but did he want to risk such difficult entrances? There might be fewer people about at night, but judging by the barred doors, those who were up, especially if they were sentries, would be even more alert to unexpected noises.

Simon returned to the kitchen and pulled himself up into the branches of a small, barren apple tree, then climbed from there onto the ledge of the high window. The thick glass was gone, but the window slot had been wedged full of stones; there would be no way to remove them without making a terrible clatter. He cursed silently and descended.

He was sore and still terribly hungry, despite the luxury of a whole onion. He decided that he had wasted his time on the doors of the Inner Bailey. On the far side of the moat, though, the Middle Bailey might prove less well-protected.

There were several distressingly naked patches of ground between the two baileys. Despite not having seen a single guard or, in fact, a single other person, Simon had to force himself to cross these open stretches; each time he dashed for the safety of shadows as soon as he was clear. The bridge across the moat was the most unnerving part. He began to cross it and then changed his mind twice. It was at least thirty ells long, and if someone appeared while he was in the middle, he would be as obvious as a fly walking on a white wall.

At last he blew out a shaky breath, drew in a deep gasp of air, and sprinted across. His steps sounded as loud to him as thunder. He forced himself to slow down and cross at a silent walk, despite the thumping of his heart. When he reached the far side he ducked into a shed where he sat until he felt steady again.

You're doing well, he told himself. *No one's around. Nothing to fear.*

He knew that was a lie.

Plenty to fear, he amended. *But no one's caught you yet. Not in a while, anyway.*

As he got to his feet, he could not help wondering why the bridge over the moat had been down in the first place if all the doors were barred and windows blocked against some feared attack.

And why wasn't Green Angel Tower locked up? He could think of no answer.

Before he had taken a hundred paces across the muddy thoroughfare in the center of Middle Bailey, he saw something that made him shrink back into the darkness again, his terrors suddenly returned—this time with reason.

An army was camped in the bailey.

It had taken him some long moments to realize it, since so few fires burned, and since the tents were made of dark cloth that was almost invisible in the night, but the entire bailey seemed to be full of armed men. He could see perhaps a half dozen on the nearer outskirts, sentries by the look of them, cloaked and helmeted and carrying long pikes. In the dim light he could not see much of their faces. Even as he stood hidden in a crack between two of the bailey's buildings, wondering what to do next, another pair of cloaked and hooded figures passed him. They also carried long spears, but he could see immediately that they were different. Something in the way they carried themselves, something in their graceful, deceptively swift strides, told him beyond doubt that these were Norns.

Simon sank farther back into the concealing darkness, trembling. Would they know he was here? Could they . . . smell him?

Even as he wondered, the black-robed creatures paused only a short way from his hiding place, alert as hunting dogs. Simon held his breath and willed himself to total stillness. After a long wait, the Norns abruptly turned in unison, as though some wordless communication had passed between them, and continued on their way. Simon waited a few shaky moments, then cautiously poked his head around the wall. He could not see them against the darkness, but he could see the human soldiers move out of their way, quick as men avoiding a snake. For an instant the Norns were silhouetted against one of the watchfires, twin hooded shapes that seemed oblivious to the humans around them. They slipped from the light of the fire and vanished once more.

This was something unexpected. Norns! The White Foxes, here in the Hayholt itself! Things were worse even than he had imagined. But hadn't Geloë and the others said that the immortals couldn't come back here? Perhaps they had meant that Ineluki and his undead servitors couldn't return. But even if that last was true, it seemed little solace just now.

So the Middle Bailey was full of soldiers, and there were Norns moving freely around the keep, silent as hunting owls. Simon's skin prickled. He had no doubt that the Outer Bailey was also full of Black Rimmersmen, or Thrithings mercenaries, or whatever cutthroats Elias had bought with Erkynland's gold and the Storm King's magic. It was hard to believe that many of the king's own Erkynguard, even the most ruthless, would remain in this haunted place with the corpse-faced Norns: the immortals were too frighteningly different. It had been easy to see in just a brief instant that the soldiers in the Middle Bailey were frightened of them.

Now I have a reason to escape besides just my own skin. Josua and the others need to know what is going on in here. He felt a momentary surge of hope. *Maybe knowing the Norns are here with Elias will bring Jiriki and the rest of the Sithi. Jiriki's kin would have to help the mortals then, wouldn't they?* Simon tried to think carefully. *In fact, I should try to escape now—if I can. What good will I do Josua or anyone else if I don't get out?*

But he had barely learned anything. He was exactly what any war leader most valued—an experienced eye in the middle of the enemy camp. Simon knew the Hayholt like a farmer knew his fields, like a blacksmith knew his tools. He owed it to his good fortune in surviving this far—good fortune, yes, he reminded himself, but his wits and resourcefulness had helped him, too—to take all he could from the situation.

So. Back to the Inner Bailey. He could last a day or two without food if necessary, since water seemed to be abundantly available. Plenty of time to spy out what useful things he could, then find a way out past the soldiers to freedom. If he had to, he could even make his way back under the castle and through the dark tunnels again. That would be the surest way to escape undetected.

No. Not the tunnels.

It was no use pretending. Even for Josua and the others, that was something he could not do.

He was approaching the bridge to the Inner Bailey when a loud clatter made Simon pull back into the shadows once more. When he saw the group of mounted shapes riding out onto the span, he silently thanked Usires for not bringing him to the bridge a few moments earlier.

The company seemed made up of armored Erkynguardsmen, strangely dispirited-looking for all their martial finery. Simon had only a moment to wonder what their errand might be when he saw a chillingly familiar bald head in their midst.

Pryrates! Simon pushed back against the wall, staring. A choking hatred rose up inside of him. There the monster was, not three score paces away, his hairless features limned by faint moonlight.

I could be on him in a moment, he thought wildly. *If I walked up slowly, the soldiers wouldn't worry—they'd just think I was one of the mercenaries who'd drunk too much wine. I could crush his skull with a rock. . . .*

But what if he failed? Then he would easily be captured, any use he might be to Josua finished before it had begun. And worse, he would be the red priest's prisoner. It was just as Binabik had said: how long would it be until he told Pryrates every secret about Josua, about the Sithi and the swords—until he begged to tell the alchemist anything he wanted to hear?

Simon could not help shuddering like a taunted dog at the end of a rope. The monster was so close . . . !

The company of horsemen stopped. The priest was berating one of the Erkynguards, his raspy voice faint but unmistakable. Simon leaned as far forward as he could without losing the shadow of the wall, cupping his hand behind his ear so that he could hear better.

". . . or I will ride *you!*" the priest spat.

The soldier said something in a muffled voice. Despite his height and the sword he wore sheathed on his hip, the man cowered like a terrified child. No one dared speak sharply to Pryrates. That had been true even before Simon had fled the castle.

"Are you mad or just stupid?" Pryrates' voice rose. "I cannot ride a lame horse for days, all the way to Wentmouth. Give me yours."

The soldier got down, then handed the reins of his mount to the alchemist. He said something else. Pryrates laughed.

"Then you will lead mine. It will not hurt you to walk, I think, since it was your idiocy that . . ." The rest of his mocking remark was too soft to hear, but Simon thought he heard another reference to Wentmouth, the rocky height in the south where the Gleniwent River met the sea. Pryrates pulled himself up into the guardsman's saddle, his scarlet robe appearing for a moment from beneath his dark cloak like a bloody wound. The priest spurred down off the bridge and onto the mud of the Middle Bailey. The rest of the company followed after him, trailed on foot by the soldier leading Pryrates' horse.

As they passed by his hiding spot, Simon found that he was clutching a stone in his hand; he could not remember picking it up. He stared at the alchemist's head, round and bare as an eggshell, and thought about what pleasure he would feel to see it cracked open. That evil creature had killed Morgenes, and God Himself alone knew how many others. His fear mysteriously fled, Simon struggled against the almost overwhelming urge to shout his fury and attack. How could the good ones like the doctor and Geloë and Deornoth die when such a beast was allowed to live? Killing Pryrates would be worth the loss of his own life. An unimaginable vileness would be gone from the world. *Doing the necessary*, Rachel would have called it. *A dirty job, but one as needs doing.* But it seemed his life was not his to give.

He watched the company troop past. They circled around the tents and vanished, moving toward the Lesser Gate that led to the outermost bailey. Simon dropped the rock he had been clutching into the mud and stood, trembling.

A thought came to him suddenly, an idea so wild and mad that he frightened himself. He looked up at the sky, trying to guess how much time remained until dawn. By the chill, empty feel of the air, he felt sure the sun was at least a few hours away.

Who was most likely to have taken Bright-Nail from the mound? Pryrates, of course. He might not even have told King Elias, if that suited his purposes. And where would it be if that was true? Hidden in the priest's stronghold—in Hjeldin's Tower.

Simon turned. The alchemist's tower, unpleasantly squat beside the pure sweep of Green Angel, loomed over the Inner Bailey wall. If there were lights inside, they were hidden: the scarlet windows were dark. It looked deserted— but so did everything else at the center of the great keep. The whole of the Hayholt's interior might have been a mausoleum, a city of the dead.

Did he dare to go inside—or at least try? He would have to have light. Perhaps there were extra torches or a hooded lantern he could use somewhere in Green Angel Tower. It would be a fearful, terrible risk. . . .

If he had not seen Pryrates leaving with his own eyes, if he had not heard the red priest talk of riding to Wentmouth, Simon would not even have thought of it: just the idea of making his way into the ill-omened tower when hairless, black-eyed Pryrates might be sitting inside, waiting like a spider at the center of his web, made his stomach heave. But the priest was gone, that was undeniable, and Simon knew he might never have such a chance again. What if he found Bright-Nail?! He could take it and be gone from the Hayholt before Pryrates even returned. *That* would be a satisfying trick to play on the redrobed murderer. And wouldn't it be fine to ride into Prince Josua's camp and show them Bright-Nail flashing in the sun? Then he would *truly* be Simon, Master of the Great Swords, wouldn't he?

As he moved quickly and quietly across the bridge, he found himself staring at the bailey wall before him. Something about it had changed. It had grown . . . lighter.

The sun was coming up, or at least as much of the sun as would appear on this gray day. Simon hurried a little. He had been wrong.

A few more hours, eh? You've been lucky. What if you'd been rattling around outside the door of Hjeldin's Tower, when the sun came up? Mooncalf, still a mooncalf.

Still, he was not entirely unrepentant. Knights and heroes had to be bold, and what he was considering now was a bold plan indeed. He would simply have to wait until tomorrow night's darkness to accomplish it. It would be a marvelous, brave thing to do.

But even as he hurried back toward his hiding hole in Green Angel Tower, he wished his friends were around to talk him out of it.

The sun had set a few hours before. A fine drizzle was descending from the night sky. Simon stood in Green Angel Tower's doorway and prepared himself to step out.

It was not easy. He was still feeling weak and hungry, although after sleeping the day away he had found the remains of someone's supper, a crust of bread and a scanty rind of cheese, on a plate in an alcove off the tower's antechamber. Both bread and cheese were dry, but still seemed only hours old, not days or weeks; even as he gobbled them down he had wondered whose meal it had been. Did Barnabas the sexton still care for the tower and its great bells? If so, he was doing a poor job.

Thinking of Barnabas had made Simon realize that not once in the time he had returned had he heard Green Angel's bells. Now, as he stood in the doorway of the tower, waiting for darkness, the thought came to him again. The great echoing cry of the bronze bells had been the heartbeat of the Hayholt as he had known it, an hourly reminder that things went on, that time passed, that life continued. But now they were silent.

Simon shrugged and stepped out. He paused to cup his hands beneath a stream of rainwater running down from the roof, then drank thirstily. He wiped his hands on his breeches and stared at the shadow of Hjeldin's Tower against the violet sky. There was nothing left to do. There was no reason to wait any longer.

Simon made his way along the outer perimeter of the bailey, using the cover of the buildings to keep himself hidden from any eyes that might be watching. He had almost walked into the arms of Pryrates and the soldiers the night before; despite the seeming emptiness of the keep, he would take nothing for granted. Once or twice he heard wisps of conversation drift past, but he saw no living people who might have been responsible. A long, sobbing laugh floated by. Simon shivered.

As he moved out around the edge of one of the outbuildings, he thought he saw a flicker of light in the tower's upper windows, a momentary gleam of red like a coal that still hid smoldering life. He stopped, cursing quietly to himself. Why should he be so sure that just because Pryrates was gone, the tower would be empty? Perhaps the Norns lived there.

But perhaps not. Surely even the priest needed servants to look after him, to sweep the floors and light the lamps, just as Simon had once done for Doctor Morgenes. If anyone moved inside the tower, it was likely some terrified castle-dweller forced to labor in the red priest's stronghold. Perhaps it was Rachel the Dragon. If so, Simon would rescue her as well as Bright-Nail. Wouldn't she be astonished—he would have to be careful not to frighten her too badly. She must have wondered where in the world her wayward scullion had gone.

Simon turned before he reached the tower doors and clambered into a patch of ivy growing along the bailey wall. Hero or not, he was no fool. He would wait to see if there was any sign the tower was occupied.

He huddled, holding his knees. The bulk of the tower overhead, its blunt dark stones, made him uncomfortable. It was hard not to feel it waited for him like a giant feigning sleep, anticipating the moment when Simon would come within reach. . . .

Time seemed to pass very slowly. When he could stand the waiting no longer, he dragged himself out of the ivy, which seemed to cling more strongly than it should. No one had come near the doorway; no one was moving anywhere about the Inner Bailey. He had seen no more lights in the windows, nor had he heard anything but the moaning of the wind in the towertops. It was time.

But how to get in? There was scarcely any chance he would be able to unlock the huge black doors—someone as secretive as Pryrates must have bolts on his fortress gateway that could keep out an army. No, it would undoubtedly take climbing. The gatehouse that stood around and over the front door was probably his best chance. From the top of it he could perhaps find a way up to one of the upper windows. The stones of the walls were heavy and crudely set: climbing holds should not be too difficult to find.

He ducked into the shelter of the gatehouse and paused for a moment to look at the black timbers of the front doors. They were indeed massive—Simon guessed that even men with axes would not penetrate them in anything less than half a day. Testing, he grasped one of the massive door handles and pulled. The right side door swung out silently, startling Simon so that he stumbled backward, out into the thin rain.

The doors were open—unlocked! For a moment he wanted only to run, certain it was a trap set just for him; but as he stopped, hands raised as though to ward off a blow, he realized that was unlikely. Or perhaps there were more certain protections inside . . . ?

Simon hesitated a moment longer, his heart rattling.

Don't be a fool. Either go in or stay out. Don't stand around in the middle of everything waiting to be noticed by someone.

He clenched his fists and stepped through, then pulled the door shut behind him.

There was no need yet for the torch in his belt, which he had refurbished with oil from one of Green Angel Tower's storage rooms: one already burned in a bracket on the wall of the high antechamber, making shadows shiver in the corners. Simon could not help wondering who had lit it, but quickly dismissed the useless thought: he could only begin looking, try to move quietly, and listen for anyone else who might be in Hjeldin's Tower with him.

He walked across the antechamber, dismayed by the loud hiss his boot soles made rubbing on the stone. Stairs led upward along one wall to the highest, darkest parts of the tower. They would have to wait.

So many doors! Simon chose one and opened it gently. The torchlight bleeding in from the antechamber revealed a room filled entirely with furnishings made from bones that had been tied and glued together, including one large chair which had, as if in mockery of the High King's throne, an awning made entirely from skulls—human skulls. Many of the bones still had bits of dark dry flesh stuck to them. From somewhere in the room came the fizzing chirp of what sounded like a cricket. Simon felt his stomach rising into his throat and hurriedly shut the door.

When he had recovered a little he took his own brand and lit it from the wall torch. If he was really going to look for the sword, he would have to be able to see even into the dark corners, no matter what he might find there.

He went back to the bone room, but further inspection turned up nothing but the dreadful furnishings, an incredible array of bones. Simon hoped some of them were animal bones, but doubted it. The insistent buzz of the cricket drove him out once more.

The next chamber was filled wall to wall with tubs covered by stretched nets. Things Simon could not quite make out slithered and splashed in dark fluid; from time to time a slippery back or an oddly-terminated appendage pushed against the netting until it bulged upward. In another room Simon found thousands of tiny silvery figures of men and women, each carved with amazing accuracy and realism: each little statue was a perfect representation of a person frozen in a position of fear or despair. When Simon lifted one of them, the shiny metal felt slippery and strangely warm against his skin. A moment later, he dropped it and backed quickly out of the room. He was sure he had felt it squirm in his grip.

Simon made his way from one room to the next, continuously disturbed by what he found, sometimes by the sheer unpleasantness of the priest's possessions, sometimes by their incomprehensibility. The last room on the ground floor contained a few bones as well, but they were far too large to belong to anything human. They were boiling in a great vat that hung above an oil flame, filling the damp room with a powerful but unrecognizable stink. Viscous black fluid ran in oozing drops from a spigot on the vat's side into a wide stone bowl. The fetid steam swirling up made Simon's head reel and the scar on his cheek sting. A quick search discovered no trace of the sword, and he retreated gratefully to the relatively clean air outside.

After hesitating a moment, he climbed the stairs to the next level. There was undoubtedly more to be discovered beneath the tower, down in its catacombs— but Simon was in no hurry to do that. He would put such a search off for last, and pray that he found the sword before then.

A room full of glass beakers and retorts much like things Morgenes had possessed, a chamber whose walls and ceiling were draped with inordinately thick spiderwebs—his search of that one was brief and perfunctory—another which seemed an indoor jungle full of trailing vines and fat, rotting blossoms, Simon passed through them all, feeling more and more like some peasant boy from a story who had entered a witch's magical castle. Some of the chambers had contents so dreadful he could do no more than peer for a moment into the shadowed interior before shoving the door closed again. There were some things he simply could not force himself to do: if the sword was in one of these rooms, it would have to remain unrescued.

One room that did not at first seem so dreadful held only a single small cot, oddly woven from a mesh of leather straps. At first he thought this might be the place Pryrates slept . . . until he saw the hole in the stone floor and the stains beneath the cot. He left quickly, shuddering. He didn't think he could spend much longer in this place and keep his sanity.

On the fifth floor of the priest's storehouse of nightmares, Simon hesitated.

This was the level at which the great red windows were set: if he moved from room to room with his torch, it was quite possible someone elsewhere in the keep might notice the moving flicker of light in what should be an empty tower. After some consideration, he set his torch in one of the high brackets on the wall. He would have to search in near-darkness, Simon realized, but he had spent enough time below ground that he thought he might be better suited for that than almost anyone except a Sitha . . . or a Norn.

Only three chambers opened off the landing. The first was another feature-less room with a cot, although this one had no drain in the floor. Simon had no problem believing that this was indeed Pryrates' sleeping place: something in the stark emptiness of the room seemed appropriate. Simon could picture the black-eyed priest lying on his back staring up into nothing, plotting. There was also a privy, a strangely natural possession for someone so unnatural.

The second chamber was some sort of reliquary. The entire room was lined with shelves, and every inch of shelf space was taken up by statues. These were not all of a type, like the silver figurines on the first floor, but all shapes and sizes, some that looked like saint's icons, others lopsided wooden fetishes that might have been carved by children or lunatics. It was fascinating, in a way. Had Simon not felt the terror of this strange tower all around him, the incred-ible risk he was taking just being here, he might have liked to take some time to look at the bizarre collection. Some were made from wax and had candle wicks protruding from the heads, others were little more than conglomerations of bones and mud and feathers, but each was recognizably a figure of some sort, although many seemed more animal than human. But nowhere was there any-thing like a sword. The eyes of some of the images seemed to follow Simon as he backed out again.

The last and largest room was perhaps the red priest's study. Here the great scarlet windows were most visible, since they covered a large part of the curved wall, although with night sky outside they were dark. The room itself was lit-tered with scrolls and books and a collection of other objects as haphazardly odd and dispiriting as anything he had seen in any of the other chambers. If he could not find the sword here, his only hope was the catacombs beneath the tower. The roof above was full of star-gazing equipment and other strange machinery— he had seen that late in the afternoon from one of Green Angel Tower's narrow windows; Simon doubted there would be anything so valuable hidden out there, but he would look anyway. No sense avoiding anything that might save him a trip down below Hjeldin's monument. . . .

The study was thick with shadows and extremely cluttered, almost the entire floor covered with objects, although the walls were curiously empty of furnish-ings or anything else. At the room's center a high-backed chair faced away from the door toward the high windows. It was surrounded by free-standing cabi-nets, each one overflowing with parchments and heavy bound books. The wall beneath the windows, Simon saw by the faint torchlight, was covered in pale, painted runes.

He took a few steps toward the wall, then stumbled slightly. Something was wrong: he felt an odd tingling, a faintly nauseating unsteadiness in his bones and his guts. A moment later, a hand shot out from the darkness of the chair and fastened onto his wrist. Simon screamed and fell down, but the hand did not let go. The powerful grip was cold as frost.

"What have we here?" a voice said. "A trespasser?"

Simon could not yank himself free. His heart sped so swiftly that he thought he would die of fear. He was pulled slowly back onto his feet, then tugged around the chair until he could look into the pale face that gazed at him from its shadows. The eyes that met his were almost invisible, faint smears of reflected light that nevertheless seemed to hold him just as strongly as the bony hand on his wrist.

"What have we here?" his captor repeated, and leaned forward to stare at him.

It was King Elias.

43

An Ember in the Night Sky

Despite the urgency of his errand and the dull ache of his tailbone, Tiamak could not help pausing in wonder to watch the proceedings on the broad hillside.

It occurred to him that he had spent so much of his life reading scrolls and books that he had found very little chance to experience the sort of things about which they were written. Except for his brief stay in Ansis Pelippé and his monthly forays to the Kwanitupul market, the hurly-burly of life had not intruded much on his hut in the banyan tree. Now, in this last year, Tiamak had been caught up in the great movements of mortals and immortals. He had fought monsters beside a princess and a duke. He had met and spoken with one of the legendary Sithi. He had seen the return of the greatest knight of the Johannine Age. Now, as though the pages of one of Doctor Morgenes' dusty volumes had taken on magical life, he stood beneath cloudy skies watching the surrender of an army after a life or death struggle in the famous Onestrine Pass. Surely any scholar worth his quill pen would give everything he had to be here.

Then why, Tiamak wondered, did he feel such intense longing to see his banyan tree again?

I am as They Who Watch and Shape have made me, he decided. *I am not a hero, like Camaris or Josua or even poor Isgrimnur. No, I belong with Father Strangyeard and the others like us—the small, the quiet. We do not want the eyes of people on us all the time, waiting to see what we do next.*

Still, when he considered some of the things he had seen and even done, he was not quite sure that he would have passed them up, even if given a choice.

As long as I can keep dodging She Who Waits to Take All Back a while longer, that is. I would not mind having a family some day. I would not mind a wife and children who would fill the house with some laughter when I am old.

But that would mean finding a Wran-bride, of course. Even had he any taste for the tall, fish-skinned women of the drylander cities, he doubted any of them would be eager to live on crab soup in a tree house in the marsh.

Tiamak's thoughts were interrupted by Josua's voice. He started to move toward the prince to deliver his message, but found his way blocked by several large soldiers who, caught up as they were with the spectacle before them, seemed in no hurry to make room for the small man.

"I see you are here already," the prince said to someone. The Wrannaman stood on his tiptoes, straining to see.

"Where else would I go, Prince Josua?" Varellan rose to greet the victor. Benigaris' younger brother, even with cuts and bruises on his face and his arm in a sling, looked strangely unsuited to his role as war-leader. He was tall, and handsome enough in a thin, pale way, but his eyes were watery and his posture apologetic. He looked, Tiamak thought, like a sapling that had not received enough sun.

Josua faced him. The prince wore still a torn surcoat and battered boots, as though the battle had ended only moments ago instead of two full days before. He had not left camp in that time, engaged in so many duties that Tiamak doubted he had slept more than an hour here or there. "There is no need for shame, Varellan," Josua said firmly. "Your men fought well, and you did your duty."

Varellan shook his head furiously, looking for a moment like an unhappy child. "I failed. Benigaris will not care that I did my duty."

"You failed in one thing," Josua told him, "but your failure may bring more good than you know—although not much of it will come to your brother."

Camaris stepped up silently to stand beside the prince. Varellan's eyes opened wider, as though his uncle were some larger-than-life monster—as, Tiamak thought, in a way he was. "I cannot be happy about what has happened, Prince Josua," said Varellan tightly.

"When we are finished with this, you will find out things that may change your mind."

Varellan grimaced. "Have I not heard enough of such things already? Very well, then let us be finished. You already took my war banner. I would have preferred to give this to you on the battlefield as well."

"You were wounded." Josua spoke as though to a son. "There is no shame in being carried off the field. I knew your father well: he would have been proud of you."

"I wish I could believe that." Varellan, made awkward by the arm sling, pulled a slender golden rod from his belt; a carving of a high-crested bird's head sat atop it. He winced as he kneeled. "Prince Josua, here is my commission, the warmaster's baton of the Benidrivine House. For those men who are in my command, I give you our surrender. We are your prisoners."

"No." A stirring of surprise went through the watchers at Josua's words. "You do not surrender to me."

Varellan looked up, puzzled and sullen. "My lord?"

"You have not surrendered your Nabbanai soldiers to a foreign army. You have been defeated by the rightful heir of your household. Despite your brother's patricide—I know you do not believe me yet, Varellan—the Benidrivine

House still will rule, even when Benigaris is in shackles." Josua stepped back. "It is to Camaris-sá-Vinitta you surrender, not to me."

Camaris seemed more surprised than Varellan. The old knight turned questioningly to Josua; then, after a moment's hesitation, he extended a long arm and gently took the baton from the young man's hand.

"Rise, nephew," he said. "You have brought only honor on our House."

Varellan's face was a confusion of emotions. "How can that be?" he demanded. "Either you and Josua are lying and I have lost our most important pass to a usurper, or I have sent hundreds of brave soldiers to die in the cause of the man who murdered my father!"

Camaris shook his head. "If your error was innocent, then there is no blame." He spoke with a curious heaviness, and his gaze seemed fixed on something other than the suffering young man before him. "It is when evil is done by choice, however small or foolish the undertaking may seem, that God mourns." He looked to Josua, who nodded. The old knight then turned to face the watching soldiers and prisoners. "I declare that all who will fight with us to free Nabban shall themselves be free men," Camaris cried, loud enough that even the most distant parts of the gathering could hear him. He raised the baton, and for a moment the battle-light seemed to be on him again. "The Kingfisher House will restore its honor."

There was a loud shout from the men. Even Varellan's defeated army seemed surprised and heartened by what they had seen.

Tiamak took the onset of more general celebration to elbow his way through the crowd of soldiers and sidle up to Josua; the prince was having a few quiet words with Varellan, who was still angry and bewildered.

"Your Majesty?" The Wrannaman stood by the prince's elbow, uncomfortably conscious of his small stature in the midst of all these armored giants. How could little Binabik and his troll-kin—none of them much more than two-thirds Tiamak's size—stand it?

Josua turned to see who had spoken. "A moment, please, Tiamak. Varellan, this goes far deeper than even what your brother did at Bullback Hill. There are things that you must hear that will seem strange beyond belief—but I am here to tell you that in these days, the impossible has become the actual."

Tiamak did not want to stand waiting for Josua to tell the whole story of the Storm King's war. "Please, your Majesty. I have been sent to tell you that your wife, Lady Vorzheva, is giving birth."

"What?!" Josua's attention was now complete. "Is she well? Is anything amiss?"

"I cannot say. Duchess Gutrun sent me as soon as the time came. I rode all the way from the monastery. I am not used to riding." Tiamak resisted the temptation to rub his aching rump, deciding that as casual as his relations with nobility had become, there were perhaps some boundaries still. But he did ache. There was something foolishly dangerous about riding around on an animal so much bigger than he was. It was a drylander custom he did not see himself adopting.

The prince looked helplessly at Varellan, then at Camaris. The old knight's lips creased in a ghostly smile, but even this seemed to have pain in it. "Go, Josua," he said. "There is much I can tell Varellan without you." For a moment he paused and his face seemed to crumple; tears welled in his eyes. "May God give your wife a safe birthing."

"Thank you, Camaris." Josua seemed too distracted to take much note of the old man's reaction. He turned. "Tiamak. I apologize for my bad manners. Will you ride back with me?"

The Wrannaman shook his head. "No, thank you, Prince Josua. I have other things I need to do."

And one of them is recover from the ride here, he added silently.

The prince nodded and hurried away.

"Come," Camaris was saying as he laid his long arm across Varellan's shoulder. "We need to talk."

"I'm not sure that I wish to hear what you will tell me," the young man replied. He seemed only half-joking.

"I am not the only one who should speak, nephew," the old knight said. He wiped his eyes with his sleeve. "There is much I would hear from you of my home and of my family. Come."

He led Varellan off toward the row of tents pitched along the ridge-line. Tiamak watched them go with a faint sense of disappointment.

There it is. I may be in the thick of things, but I am still an outsider. At least if this were written in a book, I would know what they will say to each other. There is indeed something to be said for a lonely banyan tree.

After a few moments watching the retreating figures, Tiamak shivered and wrapped his cloak closer about himself. The weather had turned cold again; the wind seemed to have knives in it. He decided it was time to go in search of a little wine to relieve the aching of his back and fundament.

★

The mist that surrounded Naglimund was poisonously chill. Eolair would have given much to be in front of the fire in his great hall at Nad Mullach, with war a distant memory. But war was here, waiting just a short distance up the slope.

"Stand fast," he told the Hernystiri who huddled behind him. "We will move soon. Remember—they all bleed. They all die."

"But we die faster," one of the men said quietly.

Eolair did not have the heart to rebuke him. "It is the waiting," he murmured to Isorn. The duke's son turned a pale face toward him. "These are brave men. It is the waiting and the not-knowing that undoes them."

"It is not just that." Isorn gestured with his chin toward the fortress, a craggy shadow in the mists. "It is this place. It is the things we fight."

Eolair ground his teeth together. "What is keeping the Sithi? It might be different if we could understand what our allies are doing. I swear, it seems they are waiting for the wind to change or some particular birds to fly overhead. It is like fighting beside an army of scryers."

Isorn, despite his own tension, turned a look of pity on the count. Eolair felt it almost as a rebuke. "They know best how to battle their kinfolk."

"I know, I know." Eolair slapped at his sword-hilt. "But I would give much . . ."

A high-pitched note sang along the hillside. Two more horns joined in.

"Finally!" the Count of Nad Mullach breathed. He turned in the saddle. "We follow the Sithi," he called to his men. "Stay together. Protect each other's backs, and do not lose yourselves in this gods-cursed murk."

If Eolair expected to hear an answering shout from the men, he was disappointed. Still, they followed him as he spurred up the slope. He looked back and saw them wading through the snow, grim and silent as prisoners, and he wished again he had brought them to some better fate.

What should I expect? We are fighting an unnatural enemy, our allies are no less strange, and now the battle is not even on our own soil. It is hard for the men to see this is for the good of Hernystir, let alone for the good of their villages and families. It is hard for me to see that, though I believe it.

The mists swirled about them as they drove toward Naglimund's shadowy wall. Beyond the gap he could see only the faintest signs of moving shapes, although a trick of hearing made the shrill cries of the Norns and the birdlike war-songs of the Sithi seem to echo all around. Suddenly the great hole in the wall was before them, a mouth opening to swallow the mortals whole.

As Eolair rode through, the air was torn by a flash of light and a booming crash. For a moment all seemed to go inside out; the mist turned black, the shadowy forms before him white. His horse reared, screaming, and fought the reins. A moment later another great smear of light rubbed against his eyes, blinding him. When Eolair could see again, his terrified horse was heading back toward the breach in the wall, right into the reeling mass of the count's own troop. Eolair yanked furiously at the reins, to no effect. With a strangled curse, he pulled himself free of the stirrups and rolled out of the saddle, then crashed to the snowy ground as his mount ran wildly, scattering the reeling soldiers before him and trampling several.

As he lay struggling to catch his breath, Eolair felt rough hands close on him and drag him to his feet. Two of his Hernystirmen were staring at him, eyes wide with fear.

"That . . . that light . . ." one of them stammered.

"My horse ran mad," the count shouted above the din. He smacked snow loose from his leggings and surcoat and strode forward. The men fell in behind him. Isorn's horse had not bolted; still mounted, the young Rimmersman had vanished somewhere in the mists ahead.

Naglimund's inner court looked like some kind of nightmarish foundry. Mist hung everywhere like smoke, and flames leaped periodically from the high windows and traveled along the stone walls in great blazing curtains. The Sithi were already at close quarters with the Norn defenders; their shadows, magnified by flames and fog, stretched out across the castle like warring gods. For a moment Eolair thought he knew what Maegwin saw. He wanted to fall down on his face until it all went away.

A horseman appeared out of the fog. "They are hard pressed before the inner keep," Isorn called. He had a bloody streak down his jaw. "That is where the giants are."

"Oh, gods," Eolair said miserably. He waved his men to follow, then set out at a lope after Isorn. His boots sank into the snow at each step, so that he felt as though he labored up a steep hill. Eolair knew his mail-coat was too heavy to let him run for very long. He was breathing hard already, and not one blow struck.

The battle before the inner keep was a chaos of blades and mist and near-invisible foes into which Eolair's men quickly vanished. Isorn stopped to pick up a fallen pike and ride against a bloodied giant who held half a dozen Sithi at bay with his club. Eolair sensed movement nearby and turned find a dark-eyed Norn rushing toward him waving a gray ax. The count traded strokes with his attacker for a moment, then his foot slipped and he dropped to a knee. Before his foe could take advantage, he scooped a handful of snow and flung it up in a white shower toward the Norn's face. Without waiting to see if it had distracted his opponent, Eolair lunged forward, sweeping his sword around at ankle-height. There was a resounding crunch of steel against bone and his enemy fell atop him.

The next moments passed in what seemed a profound stillness. The sounds of battle dropped away, as though he had passed through into some other realm—a silent world only a cubit wide and a few inches deep where nothing existed but his own panicked struggle, his failing wind, and the bony fingers clawing at his throat. The white face hovered before him, grinning mirthlessly like some Southern devil mask. The thing's eyes were flat dark pebbles; its breath smelled like a cold hole in the ground.

Eolair had a dagger at his belt, but he did not want to let go even an instant to reach for it. Still, despite his advantage in size, he could feel his hands and arms losing their strength. The Norn was gradually crushing the muscles of Eolair's neck, closing his windpipe. He had no choice.

He released his grip on the Norn's wrists and snatched at his sheath. The fingers on his throat tightened and the silence began to hiss; blackness spread across the cubit-wide world. Eolair hammered with the knife at the thing's side until the pressure slackened, then he clutched his dying enemy like a lover, trying to prevent the Norn from reaching any weapon of its own. At last the body atop him ceased struggling. He pushed and the Norn rolled off, flopping into the snow.

As Eolair lay gasping for breath, the dark-haired head of Kuroyi appeared at the edge of his cloudy vision. The Sitha seemed to be deciding whether the count would live or not; then, without saying a word, he vanished from Eolair's view.

Eolair forced himself to sit up. His surcoat was sodden with the Norn's fast-cooling blood. He glanced at the sprawled corpse, then turned to stare, arrested even in the midst of chaos. Something about the shape of his enemy's face and slender torso was . . . wrong.

It was a woman. He had been fighting a Norn woman.

Coughing, each breath still burning in his throat, Eolair struggled to his feet. He should not feel ashamed—she had almost killed him—but he did. *What kind of world . . . ?*

As the silence in his head receded, the singing of Sithi and Cloud Children pressed in on him anew, combining with the more mundane screams of anger and shrieks of pain to fill the air with a complicated, frightening music.

Eolair was bleeding in a dozen places and his limbs felt heavy as stone. The sun, which had been shrouded all day, seemed to have gone down into the west, but it was hard for him to tell whether it was sunset or the leaping flames that stained the mists red. Most of the defenders of Naglimund's inner keep had fallen: only a final knot of Norns and the last and largest of the giants remained, all backed into a covered passageway before the keep's tall doors. They seemed determined to hold this ground. The muddy earth before them was piled with bodies and drenched with blood.

As the battle slackened, the count ordered his Hernystirmen back. The dozen who still stood were dull-eyed and sagging with weariness, but they demanded to see the battle through to the end; Eolair felt a fierce love for them even as he cursed their idiocy out loud. This was the Sithi's fight now, he told them: long weapons and swift reflexes were needed, and the staggering mortals had nothing left to offer but their failing bodies and brave hearts. Eolair held to his call for retreat, sending his men toward the relative safety of Naglimund's outwall. He was desperate to bring some of them out of this nightmare alive.

Eolair remained to hunt for Isorn, who had not answered the war horn's summons. He stumbled along the outskirts of the struggle, ignored by the Sithi warriors trying to force the giant out of the shelter of the arched doorway, where he was inflicting terrible injuries even in his dying moments. The Sithi seemed in a desperate hurry, but Eolair could not understand why. All but a few of the defenders were dead; those who remained were protecting the doors to the inner keep, but whoever was still inside seemed content to let them die doing so rather than try to bring them inside. Eventually, the Sithi would pick them off—Jiriki's folk had few arrows left, but several of the Norns had lost their shields, and the giant, half-concealed behind one of the arch pillars, already had a half-score of feathered shafts lodged in his shaggy hide.

Where Eolair walked, the bodies of mortals and immortals alike lay scattered as if the gods had flung them down from heaven. The count passed by many faces he recognized, some of them young Hernystirmen with whom he had sat at the campfire only the night before, some Sithi whose golden eyes stared up into nothing.

He found Isorn at last, on the far side of the keep. The young Rimmersman was lying on the ground, limbs awkwardly splayed, his helmet tumbled beside him. His horse was gone.

Brynioch of the Skies! Eolair had spent hours in the freezing wind, but when he saw his friend's body, he went colder still. The back of Isorn's head was soaked with blood. *Oh, gods, how will I tell his father?*

He hurried forward and grasped Isorn's shoulder to turn him over. The young Rimmersman's face was a mask of mud and fast-melting snow. As Eolair gently wiped some of it away, Isorn choked.

"You live!"

He opened his eyes. "Eolair?"

"Yes, it's me. What happened, man? Are you badly wounded?"

Isorn took in a great rasping wheeze of breath. "Ransomer preserve me, I don't know—it feels like my head is split open." He lifted a shaking hand to his head, then stared at his reddened fingers. "One of the Hunën struck me. A great hairy thing." He sagged back and closed his eyes, giving Eolair another fright before he opened them again. He looked more alert, but what he said belied it. "Where's Maegwin?"

"Maegwin?" Eolair took the young man's hand. "She is in the camp. You are inside Naglimund, and you've been hurt. I'll go find some folk to help me with you . . ."

"No," Isorn said, impatient despite his weakness. "She was here. I was chasing her when . . . when the giant clubbed me. He did not strike me full."

"Maegwin . . . here?" For a moment it was as though the northerner had begun speaking another tongue. "What do you mean?"

"Just as I said. I saw her walk past the outskirts of the fighting, right through the courtyard, heading around the keep. I thought I was seeing things in the mist, but I know she's been strange. I followed, and saw her just . . . there . . ." he winced at the pain as he pointed toward the far corner of the blocky keep, "and followed. Then that thing caught me from behind. Before I knew it, I was lying here. I don't know why it didn't kill me." Despite the chill, sweat beaded on his pale forehead. "Perhaps some of the Sithi came up."

Eolair stood. "I'll get help for you. Don't move any more than you have to."

Isorn tried to smile. "But I wanted to take a walk in the castle gardens tonight."

The count draped his cloak over his friend and sprinted back toward the front of the keep, skirting the siege of the keep's great doors. He found his Hernystirmen huddled beside a gap in the outwall like sheep terrified of thunder, and took four of the healthiest back to carry Isorn to the camp. As soon as he saw they had him safe, he returned to his search for Maegwin; it had taken all the restraint he possessed to see his friend out of harm's way first.

It did not take him long to find her. She was curled on the ground at the

back of the keep. Although he could see no marks of violence on her anywhere, her skin felt deathly cold to his touch. If she breathed, he could find no
sign of it.

When his wits returned sometime later, he was carrying Maegwin's limp
body in his arms, staggering across the camp at the base of the hill below Naglimund. He could not remember how he had gotten there. Men's faces looked
up as he approached, but at that moment their expressions had no more meaning for him than the bright eyes of animals.

"Kira'athu says that she is alive, but very close to death," said Jiriki. "I bring
you my sorrow, Eolair of Nad Mullach."

As the count looked up from Maegwin's pale, slack face, the Sitha healer rose
from the far side of the pallet and went quietly past Jiriki and out of the tent.
Eolair almost called her back, but he knew that there were others who needed
her help, his own men among them. It was clear that there was little more she
could do here, although Eolair could not have said what exactly the silver-
haired Sitha woman had done; he had been too busy willing Maegwin to live
to pay attention, clutching the young woman's cold hand as though to lend her
some of his own feverish warmth.

Jiriki had blood on his face. "You've been hurt," Eolair pointed out.

"A cut, no more." Jiriki made a flicking movement with his hand. "Your
men fought bravely."

Eolair turned so he could speak without craning his neck, but he retained
his grip on Maegwin's fingers. "And the siege is over?"

Jiriki paused for a moment before replying. Eolair, even in the depth of his
mourning, felt a sudden fear.

"We do not know," the Sitha finally said.

"What does that mean?"

Jiriki and his kin had a quality of stillness in them at all times that marked
them off from Eolair and his mortal fellows, but even so it was clear that the
Sitha was disturbed. "They have sealed the keep with the Red Hand still inside.
They have sung a great Word of Changing and there is no longer a way in."

"No way in? How can that be?" Eolair pictured huge stones pushed against
the inside of the entrance. "Is there no way to force the doors?"

The Sitha moved his head in a birdlike gesture of negation. "The doors are
there, but the keep is not behind them." He frowned. "No, that is misleading.
You would think us mad if I told you that, since the building clearly still
stands." The Sitha smiled crookedly. "I do not know if I can explain to you,
Count. There are not words in any mortal tongue that are quite right." He
paused. Eolair was astonished to see one of the Sithi looking so distraught,
so . . . human. "They cannot come out, but we cannot enter in. That is enough
to know."

"But you brought down the walls. Could you not knock down the stones of
the keep as well?"

"We brought down the walls, yes, but if the Hikeda'ya had been given time earlier to do what they have now accomplished, those walls would still be standing. Only some all-important task could have kept them from doing that before we laid siege. However, even if we now took down every stone of the keep and carried it a thousand leagues away, we still could not reach them—but they would still be there."

Eolair shook his head in weary confusion. "I do not understand, Jiriki. If they cannot come out and the rest of Naglimund is ours, then there is no worry, is there?" He had reached his limit with the vague explanations of the Peaceful Ones. He wanted only to be left in peace with Lluth's dying daughter.

"I wish it were so. But whatever purpose brought them here is still not understood—and it is likely that as long as they can stay in this place, close to the A-Genay'asu, they can still do what they came to do."

"So this whole struggle has been for nothing?" Eolair let go of Maegwin's hand and rose to his feet. Rage flared within him. "For nothing? Three score or more brave Hernystirmen slaughtered—not to mention your own people— and Maegwin . . ." he waved helplessly, ". . . like *this*! For *nothing*?!" He lurched forward a few steps, arm raised as though to strike at the silent immortal. Jiriki reacted so swiftly that Eolair felt his wrists caught and held in a gentle yet un-breakable grip before he saw the Sitha move. Even in his fury, he marveled at Jiriki's hidden strength.

"Your sorrow is real. So is mine, Eolair. And we should not assume that all has been for naught: we may have hindered the Hikeda'ya in ways we do not yet realize. Certainly we are alerted now, and will be on our guard for whatever the Cloud Children may do. We will leave some of our wisest and oldest sing-ers here."

Eolair felt his anger subside into hopelessness. He slumped, and Jiriki re-leased his arms. "Leave them here?" he asked dully. "Where are you going? Back to your home?" A part of him hoped that it was true. Let the Sithi and their strange magics return to the secret places of the world. Once Eolair had wondered if the immortals still existed. Now he had lived and fought with them, and doing so had experienced more horror and more pain than he had ever thought possible.

"Not to our home. Here, do you see?" Jiriki lifted the tent flap. The night sky had cleared; beyond the campfires hung a canopy of stars. "There. Beyond what we call the Night Heart, which is the bright star above the corner of Na-glimund's outwall."

Puzzled and irritated, Eolair squinted. Above the star, high in the sable sky, was another point of light, red as a dying ember.

"That one?" he asked.

Jiriki stared at it. "Yes. It is an omen of terrible power and significance. Among mortal peoples, it is called the Conqueror Star."

The name had a disturbingly familiar sound, but in his grief and emptiness Eolair could summon no memories. "I see it. What does it mean?"

Jiriki turned. His eyes were cold and distant. "It means the Zida'ya must return to Asu'a."

For a moment the count did not understand what he was being told. "You are going to the Hayholt?" he said finally. "To fight Elias?"

"It is time."

The count turned back to Maegwin. Her lips were bloodless. A thin line of white showed between her eyelids. "Then you will go without me and my men. I have had enough of killing. I will take Maegwin back so she may die in Hernystir. I will take her home."

Jiriki lifted a long-fingered hand as though he would reach out to his mortal ally. Instead, he turned and pulled the tent flap open once more. Eolair expected some dramatic gesture, but the Sitha only said: "You must do what you think best, Eolair. You have given much already." He slid out, a dark shadow against the starlit sky, then the flap fell back into place.

Eolair slid down beside Maegwin's pallet, his mind full of despair and confusion. He could not think any more. He laid his cheek against her unmoving arm and let sleep take him.

"How are you, old friend?"

Isgrimnur groaned and opened his eyes. His head pounded and ached, but that was as nothing to the pain below his neck. "Dead. Why don't you bury me?"

"You will outlive us all."

"If it feels like this, that is no gift." Isgrimnur sat a little straighter. "What are you doing here? Strangyeard told me that Varellan was to surrender today."

"He did. I had business here at the monastery."

The duke stared at Josua suspiciously. "Why are you smiling? It doesn't look a thing like you."

The prince chuckled. "I am a father, Isgrimnur."

"Vorzheva has given birth?" The Rimmersman shot out his furry paw and clasped Josua's hand. "Wonderful, man, wonderful! Boy or girl?"

The prince sat down on the bed so that Isgrimnur would not have to stretch so far. "Both."

"Both?" Isgrimnur's look turned to suspicion again. "What nonsense is that?" Realization came, if slowly. "Twins?"

"Twins." Josua seemed on the verge of laughing aloud with pleasure. "They are fine, Isgrimnur—they are fat and healthy. Vorzheva was right, Thrithings-women are strong. She hardly made a noise, though it took forever for them both to come."

"Praise Aedon," the Rimmersman said; he made the sign of the Tree. "Both babies and their mother, all safe. Praise be." Moisture appeared in the corner of his eye. He wiped it away brusquely. "And you, Josua, look at you. You are practically dancing. Who would have thought fatherhood would suit you so?"

The prince still smiled, but something more serious was beneath. "I have something to live for, now, Isgrimnur. I did not understand it would be like this. They must come to no harm. You should see them—perfect, perfect."

"I will see them." Isgrimnur began struggling with his covers.

"You will not!" Josua was shocked. "You will not get out of that bed. Your ribs . . ."

"Are still where they're supposed to be. They've just been dented by a tipped-over horse. I've felt worse. Most of the punishment was taken by my head, and that is all bone, anyway."

Josua had grasped Isgrimnur's broad shoulders, and for a moment it seemed that he would actually try to wrestle the duke back into bed. Reluctantly, he let go. "You're being foolish," he said. "They are not going anywhere."

"Nor will I be either if I never move around." Grunting with pain, Isgrimnur put his bare feet down on the cold stone floor. "I saw what happened to my father Isbeorn. When he was thrown from his horse, he stayed in bed the whole winter. After that he could never walk again."

"Oh, goodness. What is he . . . what is he doing?" Father Strangyeard had appeared in the doorway, and was staring at the duke with profound unhappiness.

"He is getting up to see the children," said Josua in a tone of resignation.

"But . . . but . . ."

"Blast you, Strangyeard, you sound like a chicken," Isgrimnur growled. "Make yourself useful. Get me something to sit on. I am not such a fool that I am going to stand up in there while I make faces at Josua's heirs."

The priest, alarmed, hurried back out again.

"Now come and help me, Josua. It's too bad we don't have one of those Nabbanai harnesses for lifting an armored man onto a horse."

The prince braced himself against the edge of the bed. Isgrimnur grabbed Josua's belt and pulled himself upright. By the time he was standing, the duke was breathing heavily.

"Are you well?" Josua asked worriedly.

"No. I hurt damnably. But I'm on my feet, and that's something." He seemed reluctant to move further. "How far is it?"

"Just down the hall a short way." Josua slid his shoulder under the older man's arm. "We will go slowly."

They moved carefully out into the long, cool hallway. After a couple of dozen paces, Isgrimnur stopped to rest. "I will not be able to sit a horse for a few days, Josua," he said apologetically.

"A few days!" Josua laughed. "You brave old fool. I will not let you on a horse for a month at least."

"I won't be left behind, damn you!"

"No one is going to leave you behind, Isgrimnur. I am going to need you more than ever in the days ahead, whether you can fight or not. My wife is not going to ride, either. We will find a way to get you to Nabban, and to wherever we go from there."

"Traveling with the women and children." The disgust in his voice did not mask the fear.

"Only until you are healed," Josua soothed him. "But don't lie to me, Isgrimnur. Don't tell me that you are ready when you are not. I mean it when I say that I need you, and I will not have you making yourself so weak that your wounds don't heal." He shook his head. "I should be hanged for letting you get out of bed."

The duke was a little cheerier. "A new father cannot refuse a request. Didn't you know that? An old Rimmersgard custom."

"I'm sure," said Josua sourly.

"And besides, even with smashed ribs, I could beat you the best day of your life."

"Come on, then, old war-horse," the prince sighed. "You can tell me about it when we get you to a bench."

Duchess Gutrun left the protective circle around Vorzheva's bed to give Isgrimnur a furious scolding for leaving his bed. She had been running back and forth between the two rooms for days, and was plainly exhausted. The duke did not argue, but sank onto the bench Strangyeard had dragged in with the air of an recalcitrant child.

Vorzheva was propped against a mound of blankets with an infant in each arm. Like Gutrun, she was pale and obviously tired, but this did not diminish the proud serenity that shone from her like a lantern's hooded glow. Both babies were swaddled so that only their black-haired heads peeped out. Aditu squatted near Vorzheva's right shoulder, staring at the nearest child with rapt interest.

When he had caught his breath, Isgrimnur leaned forward, stealing a glance at the Sitha woman. There seemed a strange hunger in her eyes, and for a moment the duke was reminded of old stories about the Sithi stealing mortal children. He pushed away the disconcerting thought.

"They look fine," he said. "Which is which?"

"The boy is in my right arm. And this is the girl."

"And what will they be called?"

Josua took a step closer, staring down at his wife and children with unalloyed pride. "We will name the boy Deornoth, in memory of my friend. If he grows up half so noble a man, I will be proud." He shifted his gaze to the other small, sleeping face. "The girl is Derra."

"It is the Thrithings word for star." Vorzheva smiled. "She will burn bright. She will not be like my mother and sisters, a prisoner of the wagons."

"Those are good names," Isgrimnur said, nodding. "When is the First Blessing to be?"

"We leave here in three days' time," Josua replied, still staring at his family.

"We will have the ceremony before we ride." He turned. "If Strangyeard can do it then, that is."

"Me?" The archivist looked around as though there might be someone else of that name in the room. "But we are in Nabban, now, Josua. There is a church on every hillside. And I have never performed a First Blessing."

"You married Vorzheva and me, so of course we would have no one else," Josua said firmly. "Unless you do not want to."

"Want to? I shall be honored, of course. Of course! Thank you, Prince Josua, Lady Vorzheva." He began to edge toward the door. "I had better find a copy of the ceremony and learn it."

"We're in a monastery, man," Isgrimnur said. "You shouldn't have to look far."

But Strangyeard had already slipped out. The duke felt sure that the attention had been too much for him.

Gutrun made a brisk throat-clearing noise. "Yes. Well, if all of you are quite finished with your talking, I think it's time for Vorzheva and the little ones to get some rest." She turned on her husband. "And *you* are going back to bed, you stubborn old bear. It nearly stopped my heart when I saw you carried back here on a sling, and it was just as bad when I saw you staggering in today. Have you no sense, Isgrimnur?"

"I'm going, Gutrun," he mumbled, embarrassed. "Don't bully me."

Aditu's voice was quiet, but her melodious tones carried surprisingly well. "Vorzheva, may I hold them for a moment?"

"She needs to rest." Gutrun was sharp; Isgrimnur thought he saw something beyond her usual firmness in her eyes—a touch of fear, perhaps. Had she had the same thought he had? "The babies, too."

"Just for a moment."

"Of course," said Vorzheva, although she, too, looked a little startled. "You had only to ask."

Aditu leaned down and carefully took the children, first the girl, then the boy, and balanced them in her arms with great care. For a long moment she looked at both of them in turn, then she closed her eyes. Isgrimnur felt an inexplicable touch of panic, as though something fearful had been set into motion.

"They will be as close as brother and sister can be," Aditu intoned, her voice suddenly solemn and powerful, *"although they will live many years apart. She will travel in lands that have never known a mortal woman's step, and will lose what she loves best, but find happiness with what she once despised. He will be given another name. He will never have a throne, but kingdoms will rise and fall by his hand."* The Sitha's eyes opened wide, but seemed to gaze far beyond the confines of the room. *"Their steps will carry them into mystery."* After a moment her eyes closed; when they opened once more, she seemed as natural as it was possible for a Sitha to seem to mortals.

"Is this some curse?" Gutrun was frightened but angry. "What right have you to put Sithi magics on these Aedonite children?"

"Peace, wife," Isgrimnur said, although he, too, was shaken by what he had seen.

Aditu handed the children back to Vorzheva, who stared at the Sitha in superstitious bafflement.

Josua also seemed unhappy, but he was clearly trying to keep his voice even. "Perhaps it was meant as a gift. Still, Aditu, our customs are not yours. . . ."

"This is *not* something we Sithi do." Aditu seemed a little surprised herself. "Oh, sometimes there are prophesies that go with certain of our births, but it is not a regular custom. No, something . . . came to me. I heard a voice in my ear, as one sometimes does on the Road of Dreams. For some reason I thought it was . . . young Leleth."

"But she is down the hall, next to my room," said Isgrimnur. "She has been asleep for weeks—and she never talked when she was awake. What nonsense is this?"

"I do not know." Aditu's golden eyes were bright. Her own surprise gone, she seemed to be enjoying the discomfiture she had caused. "And I am sorry if I made anyone frightened."

"That is enough," Gutrun said. "This is upsetting Vorzheva."

"I am not upset," said the new mother mildly. She, too, had recovered some of her good humor. Isgrimnur wondered if things like this happened among her wagon-folk. "But I am now tired."

"Let us get you back to bed, Isgrimnur." Josua darted a last worried glance at his wife. "We will think on this later. I suppose Aditu's . . . words . . . should be written down—although if they are true, I do not know that I wish to know the future. Perhaps they are better forgotten."

"Please forgive me," Aditu said to him. "Someone wanted those words spoken. And I do not think they portend ill. Your children seem fated for great things."

"I am not sure that any such portent could be good," Josua replied. "I, for one, have had quite enough of great things." He moved to Isgrimnur's side and helped the duke to rise.

When they were in the corridor again, Isgrimnur asked: "Do you think that was a true prophesy?"

Josua shook his head. "I have been living with dreams and omens too long to say it could not be, but as with all such things, it no doubt has its tricks and twists." He sighed. "Mother of Mercy, old friend, it seems that even my children will not be free of the mysteries that plague us."

Isgrimnur could think of nothing to say to comfort the prince. Instead, he changed the subject. "So Varellan has surrendered. I wish I had been there to see the end of the battle. And is Camaris well? And Hotvig and the rest?"

"Both wounded, but not seriously. We are in surprisingly good strength, thanks to Seriddan and the other Nabbanai barons."

"So we march on to the city itself. Where do you think Benigaris will try to draw his line?"

Bent beneath Isgrimnur's broad arm, the prince shrugged. "I do not know. But he will draw it, never fear—and we may not come out of that battle so luckily. I do not like to think about fighting house to house down the peninsula."

"We will get the lay of the land, Josua, then decide." As they reached his bedside, Isgrimnur found himself looking forward to getting into bed as eagerly as a young man might anticipate a day free from chores.

You're turning soft, he told himself. But at this moment, he did not care. It would be good to lay his aching bones down.

"The children are splendid, Josua." He adjusted himself on the pallet. "Do not fret on Aditu's words."

"I always fret," the prince said, smiling weakly. "Just as you always bluster."

"Are we really so set in our habits?" Isgrimnur yawned to cover a grimace at the fierce aching of his ribs and back. "Then maybe it is time for the young ones to push us aside."

"We must leave them a better world than this one if we can. We have made a terrible muck of the one we were given." He took Isgrimnur's hand for a moment. "Sleep now, old friend."

Isgrimnur watched the prince walk out, happy to see that some of the bounce still remained in his step.

I hope you get the chance to see those two children grow. And that they get to do it in that better world you spoke of.

He leaned back and closed his eyes, waiting for the welcome embrace of sleep.

44

The Shadow King

Simon's entire life had shrunk to the length of two arms, his and the king's. The room was dark. Elias held him in a cold-fingered grip as unbreakable as any manacle.

"Speak." The voice was accompanied by a puff of vapor like dragon-spume, although Simon's own breath was invisible. "Who are you?"

Simon struggled for words, but could make no sound. This was a nightmare, a terrible dream from which he could not awaken.

"Speak, damn you. Who are you?" The faint gleam of the king's eyes narrowed, almost vanishing into the shadows that hid his face.

"N-n-nobody," Simon stammered. "I . . . I'm n-nobody. . . ."

"Are you?" There was a note of sour amusement. "And what brings you here?"

Simon's head was empty of thoughts or excuses. "Nothing."

"You are nobody . . . and your business is nothing." Elias laughed quietly, a sound like parchment being torn. "Then you certainly belong in this place, with all the other nameless ones." He tugged Simon a step closer. "Let me look at you."

Simon was forced in turn to look directly at the king. It was hard to see him clearly in the faint light, but Simon thought he did not look quite human. There was a sheen to his pale arm, faint as the glow of swamp water, and although the chamber was dank and very cold, all of Elias' skin that Simon could see was beaded with moisture. Still, for all his fevered look, the king's arm was knotted with muscle and his grip was like stone.

A shadowy something lay against the king's leg, long and black. A sheath. Simon could feel the thing that was in it, the sensation as faint yet unmistakable as a voice calling from far away. Its song reached deep into the secret part of his thoughts . . . but he knew he could not let it fascinate him. His real danger was far more immediate.

"Young, I see," Elias said slowly. "And fair-skinned. What are you, one of Pryrates' Black Rimmersmen? Or Thrithings-folk?"

Simon shook his head but said nothing.

"It is all the same to me," Elias murmured. "Whatever tools Pryrates chooses for his work, it is all the same to me." He squinted at Simon's face. "Ah, I see you flinch. Of course I know why you are here." He laughed harshly. "That damned priest has his spies everywhere—why would he not have one in his own tower, where he keeps secrets that he will not show even to his master, the king?"

Elias' clutch loosened for a moment. Simon's heart sped again in anticipation that he might be able to make a try for freedom, but the king was only settling himself in a different position; before Simon could do more than think about escape, the claw tightened again.

But it's something to watch for, Simon told himself, struggling to keep hope from dying. *Oh, if he does, I pray I can get the door downstairs open again!*

A sudden tug on his arm dragged Simon to his knees.

"Down, boy, where I can see you without stretching my neck. Your king is tired and his bones ache." There was a moment of silence. "Strange. You do not have the face of a Rimmersman or Thrithings-rider. You look more like one of my Erkynlandish peasants. That red hair! But they say that the grasslanders were of Erkynland once, long ago. . . ."

The sense of being in a dream returned. How could the king see the color of his hair in this darkness? Simon struggled to make his breathing even, to keep his fear down. He had faced a dragon—a real dragon, not a human one like this—and he had also survived in the black dreadfulness of the tunnels. He must keep his wits about him and watch for any opportunity.

"Once all of Erkynland—all of the lands of Osten Ard—were like the grasslands," Elias hissed. "Nothing but petty tribes squabbling over pastureland, horse-stealing savages." He took a deep breath and let it out slowly; the odor was strangely like metal. "It took a strong hand to change that. It takes a strong hand to build a kingdom. Do you not think that the hill-folk of Nabban cried and wailed when the Imperator's guardsmen first came? But their children were thankful, and their children's children would have had it no other way. . . ."

Simon could make no sense of the king's rambling, but felt a fluttering of hope as the deep voice trailed off and silence fell. After waiting for a score of rapid heartbeats, Simon pulled as gently as he could, but his arm was still held. The king's eyes were hooded and his chin appeared to have sunk onto his chest. But he was not sleeping.

"And look what my father built," Elias said abruptly. His eyes opened wide, as though he could see beyond the shadowed room and its disturbing furniture. "An empire such as the old Nabbanai masters only dreamed about. He carved it out with his sword, then protected it from jealous men and vengeful immortals. Aedon be praised, but he was a man—a *man!*" The king's fingers tightened on Simon's wrist until it felt as though the bones were grinding together. Simon let out a gasp of pain. "And he gave it to me to tend, just the way one of your peasant ancestors passed his son a small patch of land and a raddled cow. My father gave me the world! But that was not enough—no, it was not enough that I hold his kingdom, that I keep its borders strong, that I protect it from those who would take it away again. No, that is only part of ruling. Only part. And it is not enough."

Elias seemed completely lost now, droning away as if to an old friend. Simon wondered if he was drunk, but there was no liquor on his breath, only that strange leaden smell. Simon's sense of being trapped rose again, choking him. Would he be kept here by the mad king until Pryrates returned? Or would Elias tire of talking and administer king's justice himself to the captured spy?

"This is what your master Pryrates will never understand," Elias continued. "Loyalty. Loyalty to a person, or loyalty to a cause. Do you think he cares what happens to you? Of course you don't—even a peasant lad like you is not so thick. It would be hard to spend a moment in the alchemist's company without knowing his only loyalty is to himself. And that is where he does not understand me. He only serves me because I have power: if he could wield the power himself, he would happily slit my throat." Elias laughed. "Or he would try, in any case. I wish he *would* try. But I have a greater loyalty, to my father and to the kingdom he built, and I would suffer any pain for it." His voice broke suddenly; for a moment, Simon felt sure the king would weep. "I *have* suffered. God Himself knows that I have. Suffered like the damned souls roasting in Hell. I have not slept . . . have not slept . . ."

Again the king fell silent. Made wary by the last such pause, Simon did not move, despite the dull throbbing of his knees pressed against the hard stone floor.

When he spoke again, Elias' voice had lost some of its harshness; he sounded almost like an ordinary man. "Look you, boy, how many years do you have? Fifteen? Twenty? If Hylissa had lived, she might have borne me a son like you. She was beautiful . . . shy as a young colt, but beautiful. We never had a son. That was the problem, you know. He might have been your age now. Then none of this would have happened." He pulled Simon closer; then, horribly, he rested a cold hand atop Simon's head as though performing some ritual blessing. Sorrow's double-guarded hilt was only a few inches away from Simon's arm. There was something dreadful about the sword, and the idea that it might touch his flesh made Simon want to pull away screaming, but he was even more terrified by what might happen if he woke the king from this strange speaking dream. He held his arm rigid, and did not move even as Elias began slowly to stroke his hair, though it sent chills down his neck.

"A son. That is what I needed. One that I could have raised as my father raised me, a son that could understand what was needed. Daughters . . ." He paused and took several rasping breaths. "I had a daughter. Once. But a daughter is not the same. You must hope that the man she marries will understand, will have the right blood, for he will be the one who rules. And what man who is not his own flesh and blood can a father trust to inherit the world? Still, I would have tried. I would have tried . . . but she would not have it. Damned, insolent child!" His voice rose. "I gave her everything—I gave her life, curse her! But she ran away! And everything fell to ashes. Where was my son? Where was he?"

The king's hand tightened in Simon's hair until it seemed he must tear it loose from the scalp. Simon bit his lip to keep silent, frightened again by the turn Elias' madness had taken. The voice from the shadows of the chair was growing louder. "Where have you been? I waited until I could not wait any longer. Then I had to make my own arrangements. A king cannot wait, you see. Where were you? A king cannot wait. Otherwise things begin to fall apart. Things fall apart, and everything my father gave me would be lost." His voice rose to a shout. *"Lost!"* Elias leaned forward until his face was only a hand-breadth from Simon's. "Lost!" he hissed, staring. His face was glossy with sweat. "Because you did not come!"

A rabbit in the fox's jaw, Simon waited, heart hammering. When the king's hand loosened in his hair he ducked his head, waiting for the blow to fall.

"But Pryrates came to me," Elias whispered. "He had failed me in his first task, but he came to me with words, words like smoke. There was a way to make things right." He snorted. "I knew that he only wanted power. Don't you see, that is what a king does, my son. He uses those who seek to use *him*. That is the way of it. That is what my father taught me, so listen well. I have used him as he has used me. But now his little plan is unraveling and he thinks to hide it from me. But I have my own ways of knowing, do you see? And I need no spies, no peasant boys skulking about. Even did I not hear the voices that howl through the sleepless nights, still the king is no fool. What is this trip to Wentmouth, that Pryrates should go there yet again even as the red star is rising? What is at Wentmouth but a hill and a harbor flame? What is to be done there that has not been done already? He says it is part of the great design, but I do not believe him. I do not believe him."

Elias was panting now, hunched over with his shoulders moving as though he tried to swallow and could not. Simon leaned away, but his arm was still firmly prisoned. He thought that if he flung himself backward as hard as he could he might break free, but the idea of what would happen if he failed—if he only brought the king's attention back to where he was and what he was doing—was enough to make him stay shivering on his knees beside the chair. Then the king's next words pushed thought of escape from his mind.

"I should have known that there was something wrong when he told me about the swords," the king grated. "I am no fool, to be frightened with such kitchen tales, but that sword of my father's—it burned me! Like it was cursed. And then I was given . . . the other one." Although it hung at his hip only a few scant inches away, the king did not look at Sorrow, but instead turned his haunted stare up toward the ceiling. "It has . . . changed me. Pryrates says it is for the best. Said that I will not gain what he promised me unless the bargain is kept. But it is inside me like my own blood now, this sorcerous thing. It sings to me all through the night hours. Even in the daytime it is like a demon crouched beside me. Cursed blade!"

Simon waited for the king to say more, but Elias had fallen into another rough-breathing silence, his head still tilted back. At last, when it seemed that the king had truly fallen asleep, or had forgotten entirely what he had been saying, Simon nerved himself to speak.

"A-and your f-f-father's sword? Where is it?"

Elias lowered his gaze. "It is in his grave." His eyes held Simon's for a moment, then the muscles of his jaw tightened and his teeth appeared in a mirthless grin. "And what is it to you, spy? Why does Pryrates wish to know about that sword? I have heard it spoken of in the night. I have heard much." His hand reached up and the fingers wrapped around Simon's face like bands of steel. Elias coughed harshly and wheezed for breath, but his clutch did not loosen. "Your master would have been proud of you if you had escaped to tell him. The sword, is it? The sword? Is that part of his plan, to use my father's sword against me?" The king's face was streaming sweat. His eyes seemed entirely black, holes into a skull full of twittering darkness. "What does your master plan?" He heaved in another difficult breath. "T-t-tell me!"

"I don't know anything!" cried Simon. "I swear!"

Elias was shaken by a wracking cough. He slid back in the chair, letting go of his prisoner's face; Simon could feel the icy burn where the fingers had been. The hand on his wrist tightened as the king coughed again and gasped for breath.

"God curse it," Elias panted. "Go find my cupbearer."

Simon froze like a startled mouse.

"Do you hear me?" The king let go of Simon's wrist and waved at him angrily. "Get the monk. Tell him to bring my cup." He sucked in another draught of air. "Find my cupbearer."

Simon pushed himself back along the stone until he was out of the king's reach. Elias was sunken in shadow once more, but his cold presence was still strong. Simon's arm throbbed where the king had squeezed it, but the pain was as nothing next to the heartbreaking possibility of escape. He struggled to his feet, and doing so, knocked over a stack of books; when they thumped to the floor Simon cringed, but Elias did not move.

"Get him," the king growled.

Simon moved slowly toward the door, certain that at any moment he would hear the king lurch to his feet behind him. He reached the landing, out of sight of the chair; then, within a moment, he was on the stairway. He did not even grab for his torch, though it was within arm's reach, but hurried down the stairs in darkness, his feet as surefooted as if he walked a meadow in sunlight. He was free! Beyond all hope, he was free! Free!

On the stairs just above the first landing a small, dark-haired woman stood. He had a momentary glimpse of her yellowish eyes as she stepped out of his way. Silent, she watched him pass.

He hit the tower's outside doors at a rush and burst through into the foggy, moonlit Inner Bailey, feeling as though he could suddenly sprout wings and mount up into the clouded sky. He had only taken two steps before the cat-silent, black-cloaked figures were upon him. They caught him as firmly as the king had, holding both his arms pinioned. The white faces stared at him dispassionately. The Norns did not seem at all surprised to have captured an unfamiliar mortal on the steps of Hjeldin's Tower.

♛

As Rachel shrank back in alarm, the bundle in her hand fell to the rough stone floor. She flinched at the noise it made.

The crunch of footsteps grew louder and a glow like dawn crept up the tunnel: they would be upon her in a moment. Backed into a crevice in the stone wall, Rachel looked around for somewhere to hide her lamp. At last, in desperation, she put the treacherously bright thing between her feet and bent over it, draping her cloak around her like a curtain so that its hem spread out onto the ground. She could only hope that the torches they carried blinded them to the light that must leak from beneath. Rachel clenched her teeth and silently prayed. The oily smell of the lamp was already making her feel ill.

The men who were approaching moved at a leisurely pace—far too leisurely to miss an old woman hiding behind her cloak, she was fearfully certain. Rachel thought she would die if they stopped.

". . . they like those white-skinned things so much, they should put *them* to work," a voice said, becoming audible above the noise of footfalls. "All the priest has us doing is carrying away stones and dirt and running errands. That's no job for guardsmen."

"And who are you to say?" another man asked.

"Just because the king gives Red-robe a free hand doesn't mean that we . . ." the first began, but was interrupted.

"And I suppose *you* would tell him otherwise?" a third cackled. "He would eat you for supper and toss the bones away!"

"Shut your mouth," the first snapped, but there was not much confidence in his tone. He resumed more quietly. "All the same, there's something dead wrong down here, dead wrong. I saw one of those corpse-faces waiting in the shadows to talk to him. . . ."

The scrape of boots on stone diminished. Within a few moments, the corridor was silent again.

Gasping for air, Rachel flapped her cloak out of the way and staggered from the alcove. The fumes of the lamp seemed to have seeped right into her head; for a moment the walls tilted. She put a hand out to steady herself.

Blessed Saint Rhiap, she breathed voicelessly, *thank you for protecting your humble servant from the unrighteous. Thank you for making their eyes blind.*

More soldiers! They were all over the tunnels beneath the castle, filling the passageways like ants. This group was the third that she had seen—or, in this instance, heard—and Rachel did not doubt there were many more that she had not. What could they want down here? This part of the castle had lain unexplored for years, she knew—that was what had given her the courage to search here in the first place. But now something had caught the attention of the king's soldiers. Pryrates had put them to work digging, it seemed—but digging after what? Could it be Guthwulf?

Rachel was full of frightened anger. That poor old man! Hadn't he suffered enough, losing his sight, driven out of the castle? What could they want with him? Of course, he had been the High King's trusted counselor before he had fled: perhaps he knew some secrets that the king was desperate to have. It must be terribly important to set so many soldiers tracking around in this dreary underworld.

It *must* be Guthwulf. Who else would there be to search for down here? Certainly not Rachel herself: she knew she counted for little in the games of powerful men. But Guthwulf—well, he had fallen out with Pryrates, hadn't he? Poor Guthwulf. She had been right to look for him—he was in terrible danger! But how could she continue her search with the passageways crawling with the king's men—and worse things, if what the guardsmen seemed to be saying was true? She would be lucky if she made her own way back to sanctuary undiscovered.

That's so, she told herself. *They nearly had you that time, old woman. It a presumption to expect the saint to save you again if you persist in foolishness. Remember what Father Dreosan used to say: 'God can do anything, but He does not protect the prideful from the doom they summon.'*

Rachel stood in the corridor while she waited for her breathing to slow. She could hear nothing in the corridor but her own swift-drumming heartbeat.

"Right," she said to herself. "Home. To think." She turned back up the corridor, clutching her sack.

The stairs were hard going. Rachel had to stop frequently to rest, leaning against the wall and thinking angry thoughts about her increasing infirmity. In a better world, she knew, a world not so smirched with sin, those who walked the path of righteousness would not suffer such twinges and spites. But in this world all souls were suspect, and adversity, as Rachel the Dragon had learned at her mother's knee, was the test by which God weighed them. Surely the burdens she carried now would lighten her in the Great Scales on that fated day.

Aedon Ransomer, I hope so, she thought sourly. *If my earthly burdens get any heavier, on the Day of Weighing-Out I will float away like a dandelion seed.* She grinned wryly at her own impiety. *Rachel, you old fool, listen to you. It's not too late to endanger your soul!*

There was something oddly reassuring in that thought. Strengthened, she renewed her assault on the stairs.

She had passed the alcove and climbed a flight past it before she remembered about the plate. Surely nothing would be different than when she had looked on her way down that morning . . . but even so, it would be wrong to shirk. Rachel, Mistress of Chambermaids, did not shirk. Although her feet ached and her knees protested, although she wanted nothing but to stagger to her little room and lie down, she forced herself to turn and go back down the stairs.

The plate was empty.

Rachel stared at it for long moments. The meaning of its emptiness crept over her only gradually.

Guthwulf had come back.

She was astonished to find herself clutching the plate and weeping. *Doddering old woman*, she berated herself. *What on God's earth are you crying for? Because a man who has never spoken to you or known your name—who likely doesn't even know his own name any more—came and took some bread and an onion from a plate?*

But even as she scolded herself she felt the dandelion-seed lightness that she had only imagined earlier. He was not dead! If the soldiers were looking for him, they had not yet found him—and he had come back. It was almost as though Earl Guthwulf had known how worried she was. That was an absurd thought, she knew, but she could not help feeling that something very important had happened.

When she had recovered, she wiped her tears briskly with her sleeve, then took cheese and dried fruit from her sack and filled the plate again. She checked the covered bowl; the water was gone too. She emptied her own water skin into the bowl. The tunnels were a dry and dusty place, and the poor man would certainly be thirsty again soon.

The happy chore finished, Rachel resumed her ascent but this time the stairs seemed gentler. She had not found him, but he was alive. He knew where to come, and would come again. Perhaps next time he would stay and let her speak to him.

But what would she say?

Anything, anything. It will be someone to talk to. Someone to talk to.

Singing a hymn beneath her breath, Rachel made her way back to her hidden room.

Simon's strength seemed to drain out. As the Norns took him across the Inner Bailey courtyard his knees gave way. The two immortals did not falter, but lifted him by the arms until only his toes dragged along the ground.

By their silence and their frozen faces, they might have been statues of white marble magicked into movement; only their black eyes, which flicked back and forth across the shadowy courtyard, seemed to belong to living creatures. When one of them spoke quietly in the hissing, clicking tongue of Stormspike, it was as surprising as if the castle walls had laughed.

Whatever the thing had said, its fellow seemed to agree. They turned slightly and bore their prisoner toward the great keep that contained the Hayholt's chief buildings.

Simon wondered dully where they were taking him. It didn't seem to matter much. He had been small use as a spy—first walking into the king's clutches, then practically throwing himself into the arms of these creatures—and now he would be punished for his carelessness.

But what will they do? Exhaustion battled with fear. *I won't tell them anything. I won't betray my friends. I won't!*

Even in his numb state, Simon knew that there was little chance that he would keep his silence when Pryrates returned. Binabik was right. He had been a wretched, damnable fool.

I will find a way to kill myself if I have to.

But could he? The Book of Aedon said it was a sin . . . and he was afraid to die, afraid to set out on that dark journey by his own choice. In any case, it seemed unlikely that he would be given any chance for such an escape. The Norns had taken his Qanuc bone knife, and they seemed capable of effortlessly countering anything he might try.

The walls of the inner keep, covered in carvings of mythical beasts and only slightly better-known saints, appeared through the gloom. The door was half-open; deep shadow lay beyond. Simon struggled briefly, but he was held far too firmly by unyielding white fingers. He stretched his neck in desperation, trying to get a last view of the sky.

Hanging in the murky northern night between Pryrates' stronghold and Green Angel Tower was a spot of shimmering red light—an angry scarlet star.

The poorly lit corridors went on and on. The Hayholt had always been called the greatest house of all, but Simon was dully surprised at how large it truly was. It almost seemed that new passageways were being created just on the far side of every door. Although the night outside had been calm, the corridors were full of chilly breezes; Simon saw only a few, flitting shapes at the far ends of passageways, but the shadows were lively with voices and strange sounds.

Still clutching him firmly, the Norns dragged Simon through a doorway that opened onto a steep, narrow stairwell. After a long climb down, during which he was wedged so close between the two silent immortals that he thought he could feel their cold skin drawing the heat from his body, they reached another empty corridor, then quickly turned down into another stairwell.

They're taking me down to the tunnels, Simon thought in despair. *Down into the tunnels again. Oh, God, down into the dark!*

They stopped at last before a large door of iron-bound oak. One of the Norns produced a great crude key from its robe and pushed it into the lock, then tugged the door open with a flick of its white wrist. A billow of hot, smoky air pushed out, stinging Simon's nose and eyes.

He wavered stupidly for a long moment, waiting for whatever would happen next. At last he looked up. The Norns' flat, expressionless black eyes stared back at him. Was this the prison chamber, he wondered? Or was this the place where they threw the bodies of their victims?

He found the strength to speak. "If you want me to go in there, then you might as well make me go in." He stiffened his muscles to resist.

One of the Norns gave him a push. Simon caught at the door and teetered for a moment on the threshold, then overbalanced and toppled through into emptiness.

There was no floor.

A moment later he discovered that there *was* a floor, but that it was several cubits lower than the doorway. He hit on broken stone and tumbled forward with a shout of startlement and pain. He lay for a moment, panting, and stared up at the play of firelight across the surprisingly high ceiling. The air was full of strange hissing noises. The lock clanked overhead as the key was turned.

Simon rolled over and found that he was not alone in this place. A half-dozen strangely clad men—if they were men: their faces were almost entirely covered by dirty rags—stood a short distance away, staring at him. They made no move toward him. If they were torturers, Simon thought, they must be tired of their work.

Beyond them lay a large cavern that seemed to have been fitted for animals rather than men. A few ragged blankets were piled against the walls like empty nests; a trough of water, reflecting the scarlet glow, seemed full of molten metal. Instead of a solid stone wall, which Simon would have expected to see at the back of a prison chamber, the far side of the cavern was an opening into some bigger place beyond, a great space full of flickering, fiery light. Somewhere a pained voice cried out.

He stared, amazed. Had he been carried all the way down to the flame pits of Hell? Or had the Norns built their own version to torment their Aedonite prisoners?

The figures before him, which had been standing stolidly as grazing animals, suddenly dispersed and moved quickly to the sides of the cavern. Simon saw a terrifyingly familiar silhouette appear in the open space between the two caverns. Without thinking, he scuttled to one side and pushed himself back into a shadowed recess, then pulled a stinking blanket up to his eyes.

Pryrates still had his back to the smaller cavern and to Simon, shouting to someone out of sight; the alchemist's head reflected an arc of fire. After a few last words, he turned and came forward, bootheels crunching in shattered stone. He crossed the cavern and climbed stone stairs to the narrow ledge, then pushed the flat of his hand against the door. It swung outward, then thumped shut again behind him.

Simon had thought himself beyond any further fear or surprise, but now he was slack-mouthed with astonishment. What was Pryrates doing here when he had said he was going to Wentmouth? Even the king thought he had gone to Wentmouth. Why should the alchemist deceive his master?

And where is "here" anyway?

Simon looked up quickly at a sound nearby. One of the rag-masked figures was approaching him, moving with the aching slowness of a very old man. The man, for his eyes above the cloth were clearly human, stopped before Simon and stared at him for a moment. He said something, but it was too muffled for Simon to understand.

"What?"

The man reached up and slowly peeled the stiff cloth away from his face. He was almost impossibly gaunt, and his seamed face was covered with gray whiskers, but there was something about him that suggested he might be younger than he looked.

"Lucky this time, eh?" said the stranger.

"Lucky?" Simon was puzzled. Had the Norns put him in with madmen?

"The priest. Lucky that'un had other business this time. Lucky there be no more . . . tasks he needs prisoners for."

"I don't know what you're talking about." Simon stood up out of his crouch, feeling the bruises from his most recent fall.

"You . . . you be no forge man," said the stranger, squinting. "Dirty you be, but there's no smoke on you."

"The Norns captured me," Simon said after a moment's hesitation. He had no reason to trust this man—but he had no reason not to. "The White Foxes," he amended when he saw no recognition on the other's gaunt face.

"Ah, those devils." The man furtively made the sign of the Tree. "We see 'em sometimes, but only at a ways off. Godless, unnatural things they be." He looked Simon up and down, then moved a little closer. "Don't tell no one else that you be not a forge man," he whispered. "Here, come here."

He led Simon a little to one side. The other masked men looked up, but seemed little interested in the newcomer. Their eyes were empty as the stares of landed fish.

The man reached down into a snarl of blankets and at last clawed up a smoke-mask and a dirty, tattered shirt. "Here, take this—was Old Bent Leg's, but won't miss it where he be gone. Look like everyone else, you will."

"Is that good?" Simon was finding it hard to keep his overstuffed head working. He was in the forge, it seemed. But why? Was this his only punishment for spying, to work in the castle's foundry? It seemed surprisingly mild.

"If you don't want to get worked to death," the man said, then began coughing, long dry rasps that sounded as though they came all the way up from his feet. It was some time before he could talk again. "If Doctor sees you be a new 'un," he wheezed, "he'll get his work out of you, never fear. And more. A right bad 'un, he be." The man said it very convincingly. "Don't want him noticing you."

Simon looked down at the soiled scraps of cloth. "Thank you. What's your name?"

"Stanhelm." The man coughed again. "And don't tell others you be new either, or they'll run to Doctor so fast your eyes'll pop out. Tell 'em you worked with ore buckets. Those'uns sleep in 'nother hole on t'other side, but White

Foxes and soldiers dump all runaways back through this door, 'matter which side 'uns ran from." He reflected sadly. "Few of us left and work to do. That's why 'uns brought you back and didn't kill you. What be your name, lad?"

"Seoman." He looked around. The other forge men had fallen back into unheeding silence. Most had curled themselves up on their thin blankets and closed their eyes. "Who is this Doctor?" For a split instant the sound of the name had filled him with wild hope, but Morgenes, even if he had lived through the dreadful blaze, would never be someone to occasion fear in men like these.

"You'll meet 'un soon enough," Stanhelm said. "Don't be in no hurry."

Simon wrapped the strip of cloth about his face. It smelled of smoke and dirt and other things, and did not seem very easy to breathe through. He told Stanhelm so.

"You keep it wet. Thank Ransomer Himself you've got it, you will. Otherwise, fire goes right down your throat and burns innards." Stanhelm prodded the shirt with a blackened finger. "Put that on, too." He looked nervously over his shoulder at his fellow forge workers.

Simon understood. As soon as he pulled on the shirt, he would no longer be different—he would not draw attention. These were bent, almost broken men, that was clear. They did not want to be noticed if they could avoid it.

When his head poked free of the neck hole and he could see again, a looming shape was lurching toward him. For an instant, Simon thought one of the snow-giants had somehow found its way south to the Hayholt.

The great head turned slowly from side to side. The mask of ruined flesh wrinkled in anger.

"Too much sleeping, little rat-men," the thing rumbled. "Work to do. The priest wants everything finished now."

Simon thanked Usires for the tattered fabric that made him another faceless captive. He knew this one-eyed monster.

Oh, Mother of Mercy. They've given me to Inch.

45

Cunning as Time

✦

"Do you think Simon could be down here somewhere?"

Binabik looked up from his dried mutton, which he had been tearing into small pieces. It was the morning meal, if morning could be said to exist in a sunless, skyless place. "If he is," the little man said, "I am thinking there is only a small chance we will find him. I am sorry, Miriamele, but here there are many leagues of tunnels."

Simon wandering alone and in darkness. The thought hurt too much—she had been so cruel to him!

Desperate to think of something else, she asked: "Did the Sithi really build all this?" The walls stretched high above, so that the torchlight failed before it found the upper reaches. They were roofed over by purest black; but for the absence of stars and weather, she and the troll might be sitting beneath the open night sky.

"With help they built it. The Sithi were having the assisting of their cousins, I have read—in fact, they were the people who were making the maps you copied. Other immortals, masters of stone and earth. Eolair said some still are living beneath Hernystir."

"But who could live down here?" she wondered. "Never seeing the day . . ."

"Ah, you are not understanding." The troll smiled. "Asu'a was full of light. The castle you were living in had its building on the top of the Sithi's great house. Asu'a was buried so that the Hayholt could be born."

"But it won't *stay* buried," Miriamele said grimly.

Binabik nodded. "We Qanuc have a believing that the spirit of a murdered man cannot rest, and stays on in the body of an animal. Sometimes it is following the one who killed him, sometimes it is staying in the place he was loving most. Either way, there is no rest for it until the truth has been discovered and the crime has been given its punishment."

Miriamele thought of the spirits of all the murdered Sithi and shivered. She had heard more than a few strange echoes since they had entered the tunnels beneath Saint Sutrin's. "They can't rest."

Binabik cocked an eyebrow. "There is more here than just restless spirits, Miriamele."

"Yes, but that's what the . . ." she lowered her voice, ". . . that's what the Storm King is, isn't he? A murdered soul looking for vengeance."

The troll looked troubled. "I am not happy to be talking of such things here. And he brought his own death upon him, I am remembering."

"Because the Rimmersmen had surrounded this place and were going to kill him anyway."

"There is truth in what you say," Binabik admitted. "But please, Miriamele, no more. I do not know what things are in this place, or what ears might be listening, but I am thinking that the less we speak of such matters, the happier we will be. In many ways."

Miriamele inclined her head, agreeing. In fact, she wished now she had never mentioned it. After more than a day wandering in these disturbing shadows, the thought of the undead enemy was already close enough.

They had not penetrated far into the tunnels the first night. The catacomb passages beneath Saint Sutrin's had gradually become wider and wider, and soon had begun to slant steadily downward into the earth; after the first hour, Miriamele thought that they must have descended beneath even the bed of the many-fathomed Kynslagh. They had soon found a relatively comfortable spot to stop and eat a meal. After sitting down for a short while, both of them had realized just how weary they truly were, so they had spread their cloaks and slept. Upon awaking, Binabik had relit their torches from his firepot—a tiny earthenware jug in which a spark was somehow kept smoldering—and after a few bites of bread and some dried fruit washed down with warm water, they had set out again.

The day's traveling had brought them down many twisting paths. Miriamele and Binabik had done their best to stay close to the general directions on the dwarrow map, but the tunnels were snaky and confusing; it was hard to feel very confident that they were following the correct course. Wherever they were, though, it was clear that they had left the realms of humankind. They had descended into Asu'a—in a way, they had circled back into the past. Trying to fall asleep, Miriamele had found her thoughts reeling. Who could know the world had so many secrets in it?

She was no less overwhelmed this morning. A well-traveled child, even for a king's daughter, she had seen many of the greatest monuments of Osten Ard, from the Sancellan Aedonitis to the Floating Castle at Warinsten—but the minds that had conceived this strange hidden castle made even the most innovative human builders seem timid.

Time and falling debris had crushed much of Asu'a into dust, but enough of it remained to show how matchless it had been. Spectacular as the ruins of Da'ai Chikiza had seemed, Miriamele quickly decided, these far surpassed them. Stairways, seemingly unsupported, rose and twisted into darkness like cloth streamers bending in the wind. Walls curved upward, then spread out overhead into spectacular fan-shaped arrays of multicolored, attenuated rock, or bent back on themselves in rippling folds; every surface was alive with carvings of animals and plants. The makers of this place seemed able to stretch stone like hot sugar-candy and etch it like wax.

What had clearly been streambeds, although they now held only sifting dust, ran in and out from one room to the other along the broken floors, stitched by tiny, ornate bridges. Overhead, great sconces shaped like fantastically unlikely flowers grew downward from the carved vines and leaves that festooned the ceilings. Miriamele could not help wishing she could have seen them when they had bloomed full of light. Judging by the traces of color that still remained in the grooves of the stone, the palace had been a garden of colors and radiance almost beyond imagining.

But although chamber after ruined chamber dazzled her eyes, there was also something about these endless halls that set her teeth on edge. For all their beauty, they had clearly been made for inhabitants who saw things differently than a mortal could: the angles were strange, the arrangements unsettling. Some high-arched chambers seemed far too vast for their furnishings and decorations, but other rooms were almost frightening in their closeness, so cramped and tangled with ornament that it was hard to imagine more than one person occupying them at any given time. Stranger still, the remnants of the Sithi castle did not seem entirely dead. In addition to the faint sounds which might be voices and the odd shifts of the air in what should be a windless place, Miriamele saw an elusive shimmer everywhere, a hint of unseen movement at the corner of her eye, as though nothing was quite real. She imagined she could blink and find Asu'a restored—or, equally likely, find bare cavern walls and dirt.

"God is not here."

"What is that you are saying?" asked Binabik.

Their meal finished, they were walking again, carrying their packs down a long, high-walled gallery, across a narrow bridge that stretched through emptiness like the flight of an arrow. The torchlight did not reach past the darkness below them.

She looked up, embarrassed. "I'm not sure. I said, 'God is not here.'"

"You are not liking this place?" Binabik showed a small yellow smile. "I have fear of these shadows, too."

"No—I mean, yes, I'm afraid. But that's not what I meant." She held her torch higher, staring at a string of carvings on the wall beyond the gap. "The people who lived here weren't anything like us. They didn't think about us. It's hard to believe it's the same world as the one I know. I was taught to believe that God is everywhere, watching over everything." She shook her head. "It's hard to explain. It seems like this place is out of God's sight. Like the place itself doesn't see Him, so He doesn't see it."

"Is that making you more afraid?"

"I suppose so. It just seems as though the things happening here don't have much to do with the things I was taught."

Binabik nodded solemnly. In the yellow torchlight, he looked less like a child than he sometimes did. Outlined by shadow, his round face had an air of gravity. "But some would be saying that the things happening are exactly what your church is telling of—a battle between the armies of goodness and badness."

"Yes, but it can't be that simple," she said emphatically. "Ineluki—was he good? Bad? He tried to do what was right for his people. I just don't know any more."

Binabik paused, then reached out a small hand to take hers. "Your questions are sensible ones, and I am not thinking that we should hate . . . our enemy. But do not be naming him, please!" He squeezed her fingers for emphasis. "And make yourself assured of one thing: whatever he was being once, he has now become a dangerous thing, more dangerous than anything you know or can be thinking about. Do not be forgetting that! He will kill us and all of the people we love if his wishes are done. Of that I have certainty."

And my father? she wondered. *Is he only an enemy now, too? What if somehow I find my way to him, but there is nothing left of what I loved? That will be like dying. I won't care what happens to me then.*

And then it came to her. It was not that God was not watching, it was that no one was going to tell her right from wrong; she had not even the solace of doing something just because someone else had ordered her not to. Whatever decisions she made, she would have to make herself, then live by them.

She held Binabik's hand for a moment longer before they resumed walking. At least she had the company of a friend. What would it be like to be alone in such a place?

By the time they had slept three times in the ruins of Asu'a, even its crumbling magnificence could no longer hold Miriamele's attention. The dark halls seemed to breed memories—unimportant pictures of her childhood in Meremund, her days as a captive princess in the Hayholt. She felt herself suspended between the Sithi's past and her own.

They found a wide staircase leading upward, an expanse of dusty steps with balusters carved into the form of rose hedges. When Binabik's inspection of the map suggested that this was part of their path, she felt a rush of happiness. They would be going upward, after so long in the depths!

But something more than an hour plodding up the apparently endless stairs soon cooled even that excitement; Miriamele's mind went wandering again.

Simon is gone, and I never had a chance to . . . to really talk to him. Did I love him? It would never have come to anything—how could he care for me after I told him about Aspitis? But perhaps we could have been friends. But did I love him?

She looked down at her booted feet, climbing, climbing, the stairs passing beneath her like a slow waterfall.

It's useless to wonder . . . but I suppose I did. Thinking this, she felt something vast and unformed struggling inside her, a grief that threatened to turn into madness. She fought it down, afraid of its strength. *Oh, God, is this all there is to life? To have something precious and to realize it only after it's too late?*

She almost stumbled over Binabik, who had stopped abruptly on the step above her, his head nearly even with hers. The troll lifted a hand to his mouth, warning her to be silent.

They had just mounted past a landing where several archways led outward from the staircase, and at first Miriamele thought the quiet noise must come from one of them, but Binabik pointed up the stairwell. His meaning was clear: someone else was on the stairs.

Miriamele's contemplative mood evaporated. Who could be walking these dead halls? Simon? That seemed too much to hope. But who else would be roaming the shadow-world? The restless dead?

Even as they backed down toward the landing, Binabik fumbled his walking-stick into two pieces, pulling free the section that held a knife blade. Miriamele felt for her own knife as the sound of footfalls grew louder. Binabik shrugged off his pack and dropped it quietly to the stone floor near Miriamele's feet.

A shape came down the darkened stairwell, moving slowly and confidently into the torchlight. Miriamele felt her heart pressing against her ribs. It was a man, one she had not seen before. In the depths of his hood, his eyes bulged as though with surprise or fright, but his teeth were bared in a bizarre grin.

A moment passed before Binabik gasped in recognition. "Hangfish!"

"You know him?" Her voice sounded shrill to her, the quaver of a frightened little girl.

The troll held the knife before him as a priest might a holy Tree. "What do you want, Rimmersman?" he demanded. "Are you lost?"

The smiling man did not reply, but stretched his arms wide and took another step downward. There was something terribly but indefinably wrong about him.

"Get away, you!" she cried. Involuntarily, she took another step backward toward one of the arched doorways. "Binabik, who is he?"

"I know who he was," the troll said, still brandishing the knife. "But I am thinking he has become something else. . . ."

Before Binabik had finished speaking, the pop-eyed man moved, scuttling down the stairs with shocking speed. In an eye-blink he had closed with the troll, grabbing the wrist of Binabik's knife hand and wrapping his other arm around the little man. After a moment's struggle, the two tumbled to the floor and rolled off the landing to the steps below. Binabik's torch flew free and bounced down the stairs ahead of them. The troll gasped and grunted with pain, but the other was silent.

Miriamele had scarcely an instant to stare open-mouthed before several large hands snaked out of the shadowy archway and folded around her, seizing her wrists and clutching at her waist, the fingers rough but somehow tentative where they touched her skin. Her own torch was knocked to the ground. Before she had finished drawing breath to shout her alarm, something was pulled down over her head, shutting out the light. A sweet odor filled her nose and she felt herself slipping away, half-formed questions dissolving, everything fading.

"Why will you not come and sit beside me?" said Nessalanta, like a spoiled child denied a treat. "I have not spoken to you for days."

Benigaris turned from the railing of the rooftop garden. Below him, the first fires of evening had been lit. Great Nabban twinkled in the lavender twilight. "I have been occupied, Mother. Perhaps it has escaped your attention that we are at war."

"We have been at war before," she said airily. "Merciful God, such things never change, Benigaris. You wanted to rule. You must grow up and accept the burdens that come with it."

"Grow up, is it?" Benigaris turned from the railing with his fists clenched tight. "It is you who are the child, Mother. Do you not see what is happening? A week ago we lost the Onestrine Pass. Today I have been told that Aspitis Preves has taken to his heels and Eadne Province has fallen! We are losing, this war, damn you! If I had gone myself instead of sending that idiot brother of mine . . ."

"You are not to say a word against Varellan," Nessalanta snapped. "Is it his fault that your legion was full of superstitious peasants who believe in ghosts?"

Benigaris stared at her for a long moment; there was no love in his gaze. "It *is* Camaris," he said quietly.

"What?"

"It is Camaris out there, Mother. You can say anything you wish, but I have heard the reports from the men who have been on the battlefield. If it is not him, then it is one of our ancestors' old war gods returned to earth."

"Camaris is dead," she sniffed.

"Did he elude some trap you set for him?" Benigaris moved a few steps closer. "Is that how my father became duke of Nabban in the first place— because you arranged to have Camaris killed? If so, it appears you failed. Perhaps for once you chose the wrong tool."

Nessalanta's face contorted in fury. "There are no tools in this country strong enough for my will. Don't I know that!" She stared at her son. "They are all weak, all dull-edged. Blessed Ransomer, if only I had been born a man—then none of this would have happened! We would not be bowing to any northern king on a chair of bones."

"Spare me your dreams of glory, Mother. What did you arrange for Camaris? Whatever it was, he seems to have survived it."

"I did nothing to Camaris." The dowager duchess rearranged her skirts, recovering a little of her calm. "I admit that I was not unhappy when he fell into the ocean—for a strong man, he was the weakest of all. Quite unsuitable to rule. But I had nothing to do with it."

"I almost believe you, Mother. Almost." Benigaris smiled thinly. He turned to find one of his courtiers standing in the doorway, looking out with poorly-hidden apprehension. "Yes? What do you want?"

"There . . . there are many folk asking for you, my lord. You said you wished to be told . . ."

"Yes, yes. Who is waiting?"

"The Niskie, for one, my lord. He is still outside the audience chamber."

"Have I not enough to occupy me? Why won't he take the hint and go? What does the damned sea-watcher want, anyway?"

The courtier shook his head. The long feather in his cap swayed before his face, fluttered by the evening breeze. "He will not speak to any but you, Duke Benigaris."

"Then he will sit there until he dries out and lies gasping on the floor. I have no time to listen to Niskie chatter." He turned to look out over the lights of the city. "And who else?"

"Another messenger from Count Streáwe, Lord."

"Ah." Benigaris pulled at his mustache. "As expected. I think we will let that wine sit in the cask a little longer. Who else?"

"The astrologer Xannasavin, Lord."

"So he has arrived at last. Very grieved, I'm sure, to keep his duke waiting." Benigaris nodded slowly. "Send him up."

"Xannasavin is here?" Nessalanta smiled. "I'm sure he has wonderful things to tell us. You'll see, Benigaris. He'll bring us good news."

"No doubt."

Xannasavin appeared within moments. As though to take attention away from his own lean height, the astrologer carefully lowered himself to his knees.

"My lord, Duke Benigaris, and my lady, Duchess Nessalanta. A thousand, thousand pardons. I came as soon as I received your summons."

"Come and sit beside me, Xannasavin," said the duchess. "We have seen too little of you lately."

Benigaris leaned against the railing. "My mother is right—you have been much absent from the palace."

The astrologer rose and went to sit near Nessalanta. "My apologies. I have found that sometimes it is best to get away from the splendor of court life. Seclusion makes it easier to hear what the stars tell me."

"Ah." The duke nodded as though some great riddle had been solved. "That is why you were seen in the marketplace dickering with a horse merchant."

Xannasavin flinched minutely. "Yes, my lord. In fact, I thought it might help me to ride beneath the night sky. Your court is so full of pleasurable distractions, and these are important times. I felt my mind should be clear so I might better serve you."

"Come here," Benigaris said.

The astrologer rose from his seat, smoothing the folds from his dark robe, then went to stand beside the duke at the garden railing.

"What do you see in the sky?"

Xannasavin squinted. "Oh, many things, my lord. But if you wish me to read the stars aright, I should go back to my chamber and get my charts. . . ."

"But the last time you were here, the sky was so full of good fortune! You needed no charts then!"

"I had studied them for long hours before coming up, my . . ."

Benigaris put his arm around the astrologer's shoulder. "And what of the great victories for the House of the Kingfisher?"

Xannasavin squirmed. "They are coming, my lord. See, look there in the sky." He pointed toward the north. "Is that not as I foretold to you? Look, the Conqueror Star!"

Benigaris turned to follow Xannasavin's finger. "That little red spot?"

"Soon it will fill the sky with flame, Duke Benigaris."

"He did predict that it would rise, Benigaris," Nessalanta called from her chair. She seemed disgruntled at being left out. "I'm sure everything else he said will come true as well."

"I'm certain it will." Benigaris stared at the crimson pinhole in the evening sky. "The death of empires. Great deeds for the Benidrivine House."

"You remember, my lord!" Xannasavin smiled. "These things that worry you are only temporary. Beneath the great wheel of heaven, they are only a moment of wind across the grass."

"Perhaps." The duke's arm was still draped companionably across the astrologer's shoulders. "But I worry for you, Xannasavin."

"My lord is too kind, to spare a thought for me in his time of trial. What is your worry, Duke Benigaris?"

"I think you have spent too much time looking up at the sky. You need to widen your view, look down at the earth as well." The duke pointed to the lanterns burning in the streets below. "When you stare at something too long, you lose sight of other things that are just as important. For instance, Xannasavin, the stars told you that glory would come to the Benidrivine House—but you did not listen closely enough to the marketplace gossip that Lord Camaris himself, my father's brother, leads the armies against Nabban. Or perhaps you *did* listen to the gossip, and it helped you make your sudden decision to take up riding, hmm?"

"M–my lord wrongs me."

"Because, of course, Camaris is the oldest heir of the Benidrivine House. So the glory for the house that you spoke of might very well be *his* victory, might it not?"

"Oh, my lord, I do not think so . . . !"

"Stop it, Benigaris," Nessalanta said sharply. "Stop bullying poor Xannasavin. Come sit by me and we will have some wine."

"I am trying to help him, Mother." Benigaris turned back to the astrologer.

The duke was smiling, but his face was flushed, his cheeks mottled. "As I said, I think you have spent too much time staring at the sky, and not enough paying attention to more lowly things."

"My lord . . ."

"I will remedy that." Benigaris abruptly stooped, dropping his arm down to Xannasavin's hip and wrapping his other arm around it. He straightened, grunting with the effort; the astrologer swayed, his feet a cubit off the ground.

"No, Duke Benigaris, no . . . !"

"Stop that!" shrieked Nessalanta.

"Go to hell." Benigaris heaved. Xannasavin toppled over the railing, his arms grabbing at nothing, and plummeted out of sight. A long moment later a wet smack echoed up from the courtyard.

"How . . . how *dare* you . . . ?!" Nessalanta stammered, her eyes wide with shock. Benigaris rounded on her, face contorted with rage. A thin stream of blood trickled down his forehead: the astrologer had pulled loose some of his hair.

"Shut your mouth," he snarled. "I ought to throw you over, too, you old she-wolf. We are losing this war—losing! You may not care now, but you are not so safe as you think. I doubt that whey-faced Josua will let his army rape women and kill prisoners, but the people who whisper in the market about what happened to Father know you are just as guilty as I am." He wiped blood from his face. "No, I don't need to do you in myself. Likely there are more than a few peasants sharpening their knives right now, just waiting for Camaris and the rest to show up at the gates before they start the festival." Benigaris laughed angrily. "Do you think the palace guard is going to throw their lives away protecting you when it's plain that everything is lost? They're just like the peasants, Mother. They have lives to lead, and they don't care who sits on the throne here. You old fool." He stared at her, his mouth working, fists trembling.

The dowager duchess shrank back in her chair. "What are you going to do?" she moaned.

Benigaris threw out his arms. "I am going to fight, damn you. I may be a murderer, but what I have I will keep—until they take it from my dead hands." He stalked to the doorway, then turned. "And I do not want to see you again, Mother. I don't care where you go or what you do . . . but I do not want to see you."

He pushed through the door and disappeared.

"Benigaris!" Nessalanta's voice rose to a scream. "Benigaris! Come back!"

♔

The silent monk had wrapped the fingers of one hand around Binabik's throat; even as he pressed down, his other hand brought the troll's own knife-hand up, forcing the blade closer and closer to Binabik's sweating face.

"Why . . . are . . . you . . . ?" The fingers cinched tighter, cutting off the little man's air and his words. The monk's pale, sweating face hung close; it gave off a feverish heat.

Binabik arched his back and heaved. For a moment he partially broke the monk's hold, and he used that sliver of freedom to kick himself off the edge of the stair, tumbling them both over so that when they rolled to a halt, Binabik was on top. The troll leaned forward, putting all his weight behind his knife, but Hengfisk held it away with one hand. Although he was thin, the monk was nearly twice the troll's size; only the odd jerkiness of his movements seemed to be keeping him from a swift victory.

Hengfisk's fingers slithered around the troll's neck once more. Frantic, Binabik tried to push the hand away with his jaw, but the monk's grip was too strong.

"Miriamele!" Binabik gasped. "Miriamele!" There was no answering cry. The troll was choking now, fighting for breath. He could not force his blade closer to Hengfisk's relentlessly smiling face or dislodge the hand around his throat. The monk's knees rose and squeezed Binabik's ribs so that the little man' could not wriggle free.

Binabik turned his head and bit Hengfisk's wrist. For a moment the fingers at his neck clamped even more tightly, then skin and muscle parted beneath the troll's teeth; hot blood welled in his mouth and spilled down his chin.

Hengfisk did not cry out—his grin did not even slacken—but he abruptly twisted, using his legs to throw Binabik to one side. The troll's knife slipped from his hand and skittered free, but he was too occupied trying not to skid off the edge of the step and down into darkness to do anything about it. He came to a halt, palms flat on the stone, feet dangling beneath the baluster and past the brink, then pulled himself forward with hands and knees, desperate to recover his knife. It was lying only inches from Hengfisk, who crouched against the wall, protuberant eyes glaring at the troll, hand drizzling red onto the stair.

But his grin had vanished.

"*Vad . . . ?*" Hengfisk's voice was a hollow croak. He looked from side to side and up and down, as though he suddenly found himself somewhere unexpected. The expression he turned at last on Binabik was full of confused horror.

"Why are you attacking me?" Binabik rasped. Blood was smeared on his chin and cheeks. He could barely speak. "We were not having friendship . . . but . . ." He broke off in a fit of coughing.

"Troll . . . ?" Hengfisk's face, which moments before had been stretched in glee, had gone slack. "What . . . ? Ah, horrible, so horrible!"

Astonished by the change, Binabik stared.

"I cannot . . ." The monk seemed overwhelmed with misery and bafflement. His fingers twitched. "I cannot . . . oh, merciful God, troll, it is so *cold . . . !*"

"What has happened to you?" Binabik pulled himself a little nearer, keeping a watchful eye on the dagger, but though it lay only a short distance from Hengfisk's hand, the monk seemed oblivious.

"I cannot tell. I cannot speak it." The monk began to weep. "They have filled me . . . with . . . pushed me aside . . . how could my God be so cruel . . . ?"

"Tell me. Is there some helping thing I can do?"

The monk stared at him, and for a brief moment something like hope flickered in his bulging, red-rimmed eyes. Then his back stiffened and his head jerked. He screamed with pain.

"Hengfisk!" Binabik threw his hands up as though to ward off whatever had stabbed at the monk.

Hengfisk jerked, arms extended straight out, limbs shaking. "Do not . . . !" he shouted. *"No!"* For an instant he seemed to master himself, but his gaunt face, when he turned it back to Binabik, began to ripple and change as though serpents roiled beneath the flesh. "They are false, troll." There was a terrible, deathly weight to his words. "False beyond believing. But as cunning as Time itself." He turned awkwardly and took a few staggering steps down the stairway, passing so close that Binabik could have reached out to touch him. "Go," the monk breathed.

Unnerved even more than he had been by the attack, Binabik crawled forward and picked up his knife. A sound behind him made him whirl. Hengfisk, his lips skinned back in a grin once more, was lurching up the steps. Binabik had time only to lift his arms before the monk fell upon him. Hengfisk's stinking robe wrapped around them both like a shroud. There was a brief struggle, then stillness.

Binabik crawled out from beneath the body of the monk. After regaining his breath, he rolled Hengfisk over onto his back. The hilt of his bone knife protruded from the monk's left eye. Shuddering, the troll pulled the blade free and wiped it on the dark robe. Hengfisk's last smile was frozen on his face.

Binabik picked up his fallen torch and stumbled back up the steps to the landing. Miriamele had vanished, and the packs that had contained their food and water and other important articles were gone, too. Binabik had nothing but his torch and his walking stick.

"Princess!" he called. The echoes caromed into the emptiness beyond the stairs. "Miriamele!"

Except for the body of the monk, he was alone.

"He must have gone mad. Are you certain that is what he wants?"

"Yes, Prince Josua, I am certain. I spoke to him myself." Baron Seriddan lowered himself onto a stool, waving away his squire when the young man tried to take his cloak. "You know, if this is not a trick, we could hardly wish for a better offer. Many men will die before we take the city walls, otherwise. But it *is* strange."

"It is not at all what I expected of Benigaris," Josua admitted. "He demanded that it be Camaris? Is he so tired of life?"

Baron Seriddan shrugged, then reached out to take the cup his squire brought him.

Isgrimnur, who had been watching silently, grunted. He understood why the baron and Josua were puzzled. Certainly Benigaris was losing—in the last month, the coalition assembled by Josua and the Nabbanai barons had pushed the duke's forces back until all that remained in Benigaris' control was the city itself. But Nabban was the greatest city in Osten Ard, and its seaport made a true siege difficult. Some of Josua's allies had provided their own house navies, but these were not enough to blockade the city and starve it into submission. So why should the reigning Duke of Nabban offer such an odd bargain? Still, Josua was taking the news as though it were *he* who would have to fight Camaris.

Isgrimnur shifted his aching body into a more comfortable position. "It sounds mad, Josua—but what have we to lose? It is Benigaris who is trusting our good faith, not the other way around."

"But it's madness!" Josua said unhappily. "And all he wants if he wins is safe passage for himself and his family and servants? Those are surrender terms—so why should he wish to fight for them? It makes no sense. It must be a trick." The prince seemed to be hoping someone would agree with him. "This sort of thing has not been done in a hundred years!"

Isgrimnur smiled. "Except by you, just a few short months ago in the grasslands. Everyone knows *that* story, Josua. They'll be telling it around the campfires for a long time."

The prince did not return his smile. "But I used a trick to force Fikolmij into that! And he never dreamed that his champion might lose. Even if Benigaris does not believe that this is truly his uncle, he must have heard what sort of warrior he is! None of it makes sense!" He turned to the old knight, who had been sitting in the corner, still as a statue. "What do you think, Sir Camaris?"

Camaris spread his broad hands palms upward before him. "It must end. If this is how the ending will come, then I will play my part. And Baron Seriddan speaks truly: we would be fools to throw away this chance out of suspicion. We may save many lives. For that alone, I would do whatever is needed."

Josua nodded. "I suppose so. I still do not understand the why of it, but I suppose I must agree. The people of Nabban do not deserve to suffer because their lord is a patricide. And if we accomplish this, we have a greater task before us—one for which we will need our army whole and strong."

Of course, Josua's down-mouthed, Isgrimnur realized. *He knows that we have horrors before us that may overshadow the slaughter in the Onestrine Pass so gravely that we think back on that battle as a day of sport. Only Josua, of all of us in this room, survived the siege of Naglimund. He's fought the White Foxes. Of course he's grim.*

Out loud, he said: "Then it's settled. I just hope somebody will help me find a stool for my fat old backside so I can watch it happen."

Josua looked at him a little sourly. "It is not a tourney, Isgrimnur. But you will be there—we all will. That seems to be what Benigaris wants."

Rituals, Tiamak thought. *My people's must seem as odd to the drylanders as these to me.*

He stood on the windy hillside, watching as Nabban's great city gates swung wide. A small procession of horsemen emerged, the leader dressed in plate armor that gleamed even beneath the cloudy afternoon skies. One of the other riders carried the huge blue and gold banner of the Kingfisher House. But no horns blew.

Tiamak watched Benigaris and his party ride toward the place where the Wrannaman stood with Josua's company. As they waited, the wind grew stronger. Tiamak felt it through his robe and shivered.

It is bitterly cold. Too cold for this time of year, even near the ocean.

The riders stopped a few paces short of the prince and his followers. Josua's soldiers lounged in scattered ranks about the bottom of the hillside, caught up in the moment and watching attentively. Faces also peered from the windows and rooftops of outer Nabban and from the city walls. A war had been abruptly halted so that this moment could take place. Now all the participants stood waiting, like toys set up and then forgotten.

Josua stepped forward. "You have come, Benigaris."

The leading rider pushed up the visor of his helm. "I have, Josua. In my way, I am an honorable man. Just like you."

"And you intend to abide by the terms you gave Baron Seriddan? Single combat? And all you ask if you win is safe conduct for your family and retainers?"

Benigaris flexed his shoulders impatiently. "You have my word. I have yours. Let us get on with this. Where is . . . the great man?"

Josua looked at him with some distrust. "He is here."

As the prince spoke, the circle of people behind him parted and Camaris stepped forward. The old knight wore chain mail. His surcoat was without insignia, and he held the antique sea-dragon helmet under his arm. Tiamak thought that Camaris looked even more unhappy than usual.

As he stared at the old man's face, Benigaris' sour smile curled the ends of his mustaches. "Ah. I was right. I told her." He nodded toward the knight. "Greetings, Uncle."

Camaris said nothing.

Josua lifted his hand. He seemed to be finding the scene increasingly distasteful. "So, then. Let us get on with it." He turned to the Duke of Nabban. "Varellan is here, and he has not been mistreated. I promise that whatever happens, we will treat your sister and mother with kindness and honor."

Benigaris stared at him for a long moment, his eyes cold as a lizard's. "My mother is dead." He snapped his visor down, then turned his horse and rode a short way back up the hillside.

Josua wearily beckoned Camaris. "Try not to kill him."

"You know I can promise nothing," the old knight said. "But I will grant him quarter if he asks."

The wind grew sterner. Tiamak wished he had taken up drylander clothing more completely: breeches and boots would be a decided improvement over the bare legs and sandals that his robe barely protected from the cold. He shivered as he watched the two riders turn toward each other.

He Who Bends the Trees must have woken up angry, he thought, echoing something his father had often said. The idea sent a deeper chill through him than had the wind. *But I do not think that it is the weatherlord of the Wran who sends this cold. We have another enemy, one who has lain quiet for a long time—and there is no question that he can command wind and storms.*

Tiamak stared up at the hillside where Camaris and Benigaris faced each other across a distance that a man could walk in a few short moments. They were only separated by a short span, and were bound close by ties of blood, but it was clear that an impassable gulf stretched between them.

And meanwhile the Storm King's wind blows, Tiamak thought. *As these two, uncle and nephew, dance some mad drylander ritual . . . just like Josua and Elias. . . .*

The two riders abruptly spurred toward each other, but they were nothing but a blur to Tiamak. A sickening notion had crept over him, black and frightening as any storm cloud.

We have been thinking all along that King Elias was the tool of Ineluki's vengeance. And the two brothers have gone brawling from Naglimund to Sesuad'ra, biting and scratching at each other so that Prince Josua and the rest of us have had no chance to do anything but survive. But what if Elias is as benighted about what the Storm King plans as we are? What if his purpose in some vast plan is only to keep us occupied while that dark, undead thing pursues some completely different end?

Despite the cold air on the hill, Tiamak felt beads of sweat cooling on his forehead. If this was true, what could Ineluki be planning? Aditu swore that he could never come back from the void into which his death spell had cast him—but perhaps there was some other revenge he schemed for that was far more terrible than simply ruling humankind through Elias and the Norns. But what could it be?

Tiamak looked around for Strangyeard, anxious to share this worry with his fellow Scrollbearer, but the priest was hidden by the milling crowd. The people around the Wrannaman were shouting excitedly at something. It took the distracted Tiamak a moment to realize that one of the mounted men had unhorsed the other. A brief stab of fear was allayed when he saw that it was gleaming-armored Benigaris who had fallen.

A murmur ran through the crowd when Camaris dismounted. Two boys ran forward to lead the horses away.

Tiamak put aside his suspicions for the moment and squeezed between Hotvig and Sludig, who were standing just behind the prince. The Rimmersman looked down in annoyance, but when he saw Tiamak he grinned. "Knocked him rump over plume! The old man is giving Benigaris a stern lesson!"

Tiamak winced. He could never understand his companions' pleasure at such things. This "lesson" might end in death for one of the two men who were now circling each other, shields up and longswords at the ready. Black Thorn looked like a stripe of emptiest night.

At first it seemed the combat would not last long. Benigaris was an able fighter, shorter than Camaris but stocky and broad-shouldered; he swung the heavy blade as easily as a smaller man might have brandished Josua's Naidel, and was well-trained in the use of his shield. But to Tiamak, Camaris seemed another kind of creature entirely, graceful as a river otter, swift as a striking serpent. In his hands, Thorn was a complicated black blur, a web of glinting darkness. Although he knew nothing good of Benigaris, Tiamak could not help feeling sorry for him. Surely this whole ridiculous battle would be over in a few moments.

The sooner Benigaris gives up, Tiamak thought, *the sooner we can get out of this wind.*

But Benigaris, it rapidly became clear, had other plans. After looking almost helpless through the first score of strokes, Nabban's duke suddenly took the battle to Camaris, crashing blow after blow on the old knight's shield and deflecting those that his opponent returned. Camaris was forced back, and Tiamak could feel the worry that ran through Josua's party like a whisper.

He is an old man, after all. Older than my father's father was when he died. And perhaps he has even less heart for this battle than for others.

Benigaris rained strokes against Camaris' shield, trying to push home his advantage as the old knight gave ground; the duke was grunting so loudly that everyone on the hillside could hear him above the clang of iron. Even Tiamak, with almost no knowledge of drylander swordplay, wondered how long he could keep up such an attack.

But he doesn't necessarily have to last a long time, Tiamak realized. *Just until he beats down Camaris' guard and finds an opening. He is gambling.*

For a moment Benigaris' gamble appeared to have paid. One of his hammering blows caught Camaris with his shield too low, skimmed off its upper edge and struck the old knight on the side of the helmet, staggering him. The crowd made a hungry sound. Camaris regained his footing and lifted his shield as though it had become almost impossibly heavy. Benigaris waded in.

Tiamak was not quite sure what happened next. One moment the old knight was in a crouch, shield raised in what looked like helplessness against Benigaris' battering sword; the next, he had somehow caught Benigaris' shield with his own and knocked it upward, so that for a moment it hung in the air like a blue and gold coin. When it fell to the earth, Thorn's black point was at the duke's gorget.

"Do you yield, Benigaris?" The voice of Camaris was clear, but there was a hint of a weary tremor.

In answer, Benigaris knocked Thorn aside with a mailed fist, then thrust his own blade at Camaris' unprotected belly. The old man seemed to contort as the sword touched his mail-clad midsection. For an instant Tiamak thought he might have been skewered, but instead Camaris whirled all the way around.

Benigaris' sword slid past him, and as Camaris finished his circular turn Thorn came with him in a flat, deadly arc. The black blade crunched into Benigaris' armor just below his ribs. The duke was driven to one knee; he wobbled for an instant, then collapsed. Camaris pulled Thorn free of the rent in the breast plate and a freshet of blood followed it.

Beside Tiamak, Sludig and Hotvig were cheering hoarsely. Josua did not seem so happy.

"Merciful Aedon." He turned to look at his two captains with more than a little anger, but his eye lit on the Wrannaman. "At least we can thank God Camaris was not killed. Let us go to him, and see what we can do for Benigaris. Did you bring your herbs, Tiamak?"

The marsh man nodded. He and the prince began to push their way forward through the knot of people that was quickly forming around the two combatants.

When they reached the center of the crowd, Josua put a hand on Camaris' shoulder. "Are you well?"

The old man nodded. He appeared exhausted. His hair hung down his forehead in sweaty twists.

Josua turned to the fallen Benigaris. Someone had removed the duke's helmet. He was pale as a Norn, and there was a froth of blood on his lips. "Lie still, Benigaris. Let this man look at your wound."

The duke turned his bleary eyes on Tiamak. "A marsh man!" he wheezed. "You are a strange one, Josua." The Wrannaman kneeled down beside him and began looking for the catch-buckles on the breastplate, but Benigaris struck his hands away. "Leave me alone, damn you. Let me die without having some savage paw at me."

Josua's mouth tightened, but he motioned Tiamak to step back. "As you wish. But perhaps there is something that can be done for you. . . ."

Benigaris barked a laugh. A bubble of bloody spittle caught in his mustache. "Let me die, Josua. That is what is left for me. You can have . . ." he coughed more red froth, ". . . you can have everything else."

"Why did you do it?" Josua asked. "You must have known you could not win."

Benigaris mustered a grin. "But I frightened you all, didn't I?" His face contorted, but he regained control. "In any case, I took what was left to me . . . just as my mother did."

"What do you mean?" Josua stared at the dying duke as though he had never seen anything quite like him.

"My mother realized . . . with help from me . . . that her game was over. There was nothing left but shame. So she took poison. I had my own way."

"But you could have escaped, surely. You still control the seas."

"Escape to where?" Benigaris spat another scarlet gobbet. "To the loving arms of your brother and his pet wizard? And in any case, the damnable docks belong to Streáwe now—I thought I was holding him prisoner, but he was gnawing away at my power from within. The count is playing us all off each other for his own profit." The duke's breath sawed in and out. "No, the end had come—I saw it as soon as the Onestrine Pass fell. So I chose my own death. I was duke less than a year, Josua. No one would ever have remembered me as anything but a father-murderer. Now, if anyone survives, I will be the man who fought Camaris for the throne of Nabban . . . and damned near won."

Josua was looking at Benigaris with an expression that was not quite recognizable. Tiamak could not let the question go unasked.

"What do you mean, 'if anyone survives'?"

Benigaris looked at the Wrannaman with contempt. "It talks." He slowly turned back to the prince. "Oh, yes," he said, his labored breathing not disguising his relish, "I forgot to tell you. You have won your prize—but you may not get much joy from it, Josua."

"I almost felt sorry for you, Benigaris," the prince said. "But the feeling has passed." He stood up.

"Wait!" Benigaris raised a bloody hand. "You really should know this, Josua. Stay just a moment. I won't embarrass you long."

"Speak."

"The ghants are crawling up out of the swamps. The riders have begun coming in from the Lakelands and the coast towns along Firannos Bay bearing the tale. They are swarming. Oh, there are more of them than you can imagine, Josua." He laughed, bringing up a fresh welter of blood. "And that's not all," he said gleefully. "There was another reason I had no desire to flee Nabban by boat. The kilpa, too, seem to have gone mad. The Niskies are terrified. So you see, not only did I buy myself a clean and honorable death . . . but it is a death you and yours might find yourself envying very soon."

"And your own people?" Josua asked angrily. "Do you care nothing for them? If what you say is true, they are already suffering."

"My people?" Benigaris wheezed. "No more. I am dead, and the dead have no loyalty. And in any case, they are your people now—yours and my uncle's."

Josua stared at him for a long moment, then turned and strode away. Camaris tried to follow him, but he was quickly surrounded by a curious mob of soldiers and Nabbanai citizens and could not break away.

Tiamak was left to kneel beside the fallen duke and watch him die. The sun was almost touching the horizon, and cold shadows were stretching across the hillside, when Benigaris finally stopped breathing.

46

Prisoned on the Wheel

♔

Simon had at first thought the great underground forge was someone's attempt to recreate Hell. After he had been captive there for nearly a fortnight, he was certain of it.

He and the other men seemed barely to have fallen into their ragged nests at the end of one backbreaking day before one of Inch's assistants—a handful of men less terrifying but no more humane than their master—was braying at them to get up and start the next. Almost *dizzy* with weariness before the work had even begun, Simon and his fellow prisoners would gulp down a cupful of thin porridge that tasted of rust, then stumble out to the foundry floor.

If the cavern where the workers slept was unpleasantly hot, the vast forge cavern was an inferno. The stifling heat pressed against Simon's face until his eyeballs felt dry as walnut shells and his skin seemed about to crisp and peel away. Each day brought a long, dreary round of backbreaking, finger-burning labor, made bearable only by the man who brought the water dipper. It seemed eons between drinks.

Simon's one piece of luck was that he had fallen in with Stanhelm, who alone among the wretches working in the forge seemed to have retained most of his humanity. Stanhelm showed the new prisoner the spots to go and catch a breath where the air was a little cooler, which of Inch's minions to avoid most scrupulously, and, most importantly, how to look like he belonged in the forge. The older man did not know that Simon had a particular reason to stay nameless and unnoticed, but sensibly believed that no one should invite Inch's attention, so he also taught the new prisoner what was expected of all the workers, the greatest part of which was cringing subservience; Simon learned to keep his eyes lowered and work fast and hard whenever Inch was near. He also tied a strip of rag around his finger to cover his golden ring. He was unwilling to let such a precious thing out of his grasp, but he knew it would be a terrible mistake to let others see it.

Stanhelm's work was to sort bits of waste metal for the crucibles. He had Simon join him at it, then taught his new apprentice how to tell copper from bronze and tin from lead by tapping the metal against stone or scratching its surface with a jagged iron bar.

A strange jumble of things passed through their hands on the way to the smelter, chains and pots and crushed bits of plating whose original purpose was unguessable, wagon rims and barrel bands, sacks full of bent nails, fire irons, and door hinges. Once Simon lifted a delicately wrought bottle rack and recognized it as something that had hung on the wall of Doctor Morgenes' chamber, but as he stared, caught for a moment in an eddying memory of a happier past, Stanhelm nudged him in warning that Inch was approaching. Simon hurriedly tossed it into the pile.

The scrap metal was carried to the row of crucibles that hung in the forge fire, a blaze as large as a house, fed with a seemingly unending supply of charcoal and heated by bellows that were themselves pumped by the action of the foundry's massive water wheel, which was three times as high as a man and revolved ceaselessly, day and night. Fanned by the bellows, the forge fire burned with such incredible ferocity that it seemed a miracle to Simon the very stone of the cavern did not melt. The crucibles, each containing a different metal, were moved by a collection of blackened chains and pulleys which were also connected to the wheel. Yet another set of chains, so much larger than the links that moved the crucibles that they seemed made to shackle giants, extended upward from the wheel's hub and vanished into a darkened crevice in the forge chamber's roof. Not even Stanhelm wanted to talk about where those went, but Simon gathered it had something to do with Pryrates.

In stolen moments, Stanhelm showed Simon the whole process, how the scrap was melted down to a glowing red liquid, then decanted from the crucibles and formed into sows, long cylindrical chunks of raw metal which, when cool, were carried away by sweating men to another part of the vast chamber where they would be shaped into whatever it was that Inch supplied to his king. Armor and weapons, Simon guessed, since in all the great quantities of scrap, he had seen almost no articles of war that were not damaged beyond use. It made sense that Elias wished to convert every unnecessary bit of metal into arrow heads and sword blades.

As the days passed, it became more and more clear to Simon that there was little chance he would escape from this place. Stanhelm told him that only a few prisoners had escaped during the past year and all but one had quickly been dragged back. None of the recaptured had lived long after returning.

And the one who escaped was Jeremias, Simon thought. *He only managed it because Inch was foolish enough to let him go upstairs on an errand. I doubt I will get such a chance.*

The feeling of being trapped was so powerful, the impulse to flee so intense, that at times Simon could hardly stand it. He thought obsessively about being carried upward by the great water wheel chains to whatever dark place they went. He dreamed of finding a tunnel leading out of the great chamber, as he had during his first escape from the Hayholt, but they were all filled in now, or led only to other parts of the forge. Supplies from the outside came with Thrithings mercenary guards armed with spears and axes, and the arrival of anything was always supervised by Inch or one of his chieftains. The only keys hung rattling on Inch's broad belt.

Time was growing short for his friends, for Josua's cause, and Simon was helpless.

And Pryrates has not left the castle, either. So it is likely only a matter of time until he comes back here. What if he is not in such a hurry next time? What if he recognizes me?

Whenever he seemed to be alone and unwatched, Simon hunted for anything that might help him to escape, but he found little that gave him any hope. He pocketed a piece of scrap iron and took to sharpening it against the stone when he was supposed to be sleeping. If Pryrates discovered him at last, he would do what damage he could.

Simon and Stanhelm were standing near the scrap pile, panting for breath. The older man had cut himself on a jagged edge and his hand was bleeding badly.

"Hold still." Simon tore a piece from his ragged breeches for a bandage and began to wrap it around Stanhelm's wounded hand. Exhausted, the older man wobbled from side to side like a ship in high winds. "Aedon!" Simon swore unhappily. "That's deep."

"Can't go no more," Stanhelm muttered. Above the face mask, his eyes had finally taken on the lifeless glaze that marked the rest of the forge's laborers. "Can't go no more."

"Just stand there," Simon said, pulling the knot tight. "Rest."

Stanhelm shook his head hopelessly. "Can't."

"Then don't. Sit down. I'll go find the dipper man, get you some water."

Something large and dark passed before the flames, blocking the light like a mountain obscuring a sunset.

"Rest?" Inch lowered his head, peering first at Stanhelm, then at Simon. "You are not working."

"He h—hurt his hand." Avoiding the overseer's eyes, Simon stared instead at Inch's broad shoes, noting with numbed bemusement that one flat, blunt toe poked through on each. "He's bleeding."

"Little men are always bleeding," Inch said matter-of-factly. "Time to rest later. Now there is work to do."

Stanhelm swayed a little, then abruptly sagged and sat down. Inch stared at him, then stepped closer.

"Get up. Time to work."

Stanhelm only moaned softly, cradling his injured hand.

"Get up." Inch's voice was a deep rumble. "Now."

The seated man did not look at him. Inch leaned down and smacked Stanhelm on the side of the head so hard that the forge worker's head snapped to one side and his body rocked. Stanhelm began to cry.

"Get up."

When this did not produce any better results, Inch lifted his thick fist high and struck Stanhelm again, this time knocking him into a splay-limbed sprawl.

Several of the other forge workers had stopped to stare, watching Stanhelm's punishment with the crushed calm of a flock of sheep who have seen one of their number taken by a wolf, and know that for a while at least they are safe.

Stanhelm lay silent, only barely moving. Inch lifted his boot above the man's head. "Get up, you."

Simon's heart was racing. The whole thing seemed to be happening too fast. He knew he would be a fool to say anything—Stanhelm had clearly reached his breaking point and was as good as dead. Why should Simon risk everything?

It's a mistake to care about people, he thought angrily.

"Stop." He knew it was his own voice, but it sounded unreal. "Let him be."

Inch's wide, scarred face swung around slowly, his one good eye blinking in the scorched flesh. "You don't talk," he growled, then gave Stanhelm an off-hand kick.

"I said . . . let him be."

Inch turned away from his victim and Simon took a step backward, looking for someplace to run. There was no turning back now, no escape from this confrontation. Terror and long-suppressed rage battled inside him. He yearned for his Qanuc knife, confiscated by the Norns.

"Come here."

Simon took another step backward. "Come and get me, you great sack of guts."

Inch's ruined face screwed up in a snarl and he lunged forward. Simon darted out of his reach and turned to run across the chamber. The other workers gaped as the master of the forge lumbered after him.

Simon had hoped to tire the huge man, but had reckoned without his own weariness, the weeks of injury and deprivation. Within a hundred strides he felt his strength ebbing, although Inch still plodded some distance behind him. There was nowhere to hide, and there was no escape from the forge; better to turn and fight in the open, where he could best use whatever advantage of speed still remained to him.

He bent to pick up a large chunk of stone. Inch, certain that he had Simon captured, but wary of the stone, moved steadily but slowly closer.

"Doctor Inch is master here," he rumbled. "There is work to do. You . . . you have . . ." He growled, unable to find words to describe the magnitude of Simon's crimes. He took another step forward.

Simon flung the stone at his head. Inch dodged and it thumped heavily against his shoulder instead. Simon found himself filling with a dark exhilaration, a rising fury that surged through him almost like joy. This was the creature who had brought Pyrates to Morgenes' chamber! This monstrosity had helped kill Simon's master!

"Doctor Inch!" Simon shouted, laughing wildly as he bent for another stone. *"Doctor?!* You are not fit to call yourself anything but Slug, but Filth, but

Half-Wit! Doctor! Ha!" Simon flung the second stone, but Inch side-stepped and it clattered across the cavern floor. The big man leaped forward with startling speed and hit Simon a glancing blow that knocked him off his feet. Before he could regain his balance, a wide hand closed on his arm. He was jerked upright, then flung headfirst across the stone floor. Tumbling, he hit his head, then lay for a moment, dazed. Inch's meaty hands closed on him again. He was lifted up, then something struck his face so hard that he heard thunder and saw lightning. He felt his cloth mask pull away. Another blow rocked him, then he was free and toppling to the ground. Simon lay where he had fallen, struggling to understand where he was and what had happened.

"You make me angry . . ." said a deep voice. Simon waited helplessly for another blow, hoping it would be strong enough to take away the pain in his head and the sickness in his guts forever. But for long moments nothing happened.

"The little kitchen boy," Inch said at last. "I know you. You are the kitchen boy. But you have hair on your face!" There was a sound like two stones being rubbed together. It took some time for Simon to realize that Inch was laughing. "You came back!" He sounded as pleased as if Simon were an old friend. "Back to Inch—but I am Doctor Inch now. You laughed at me. But you won't laugh any more."

Thick fingers squeezed him and he was jerked up from the floor. The sudden movement filled his head with blackness.

Simon struggled to move but could not. Something held him with his arms and legs extended, stretched to their utmost.

He opened his eyes to the tattered moon face of Inch.

"Little kitchen boy. You came back." The huge man leaned closer. He used one hand to pinion Simon's right arm against whatever stood behind, then raised the other, which clutched a heavy mallet. Simon saw the spike being held against his wrist and could not hold back his shout of terror.

"Are you afraid, kitchen boy? You took my place, the place that should have been mine. Turned the old man against me. I didn't forget." Inch raised the mallet and brought it down hard against the head of the spike. Simon gasped and twitched helplessly, but there was no pain, only a tightening of the pressure on his wrist. Inch hammered the spike in deeper, then leaned back to examine his work. For the first time Simon realized that they were high above the cavern floor. Inch was standing on a ladder that leaned against the wall just below Simon's arm.

But it *wasn't* the wall, Simon saw a moment later. The rope around his wrist was now spiked to the forge's immense water wheel. His other wrist and both ankles had already been secured. He was spread-eagled a few cubits beneath the wheel's edge, ten cubits above the ground. The wheel was not moving, and the sluice of dark water seemed farther away than it should.

"Do whatever you want." Simon clenched his teeth against the scream that wanted to erupt. "I don't care. Do anything."

Inch tugged at Simon's wrists again, testing. Simon could begin to feel the downward pull of his weight against the bonds and the slow warmth in the joints of his arms, precursor of real pain.

"Do? I do nothing." Inch placed his huge hand on Simon's chest and gave a push, forcing Simon's breath out in a surprised hiss. "I waited. You took my place. I waited and waited to be Doctor Inch. Now *you* wait."

"W-wait for what?"

Inch smiled, a slow spread of lips that revealed broken teeth. "Wait to die. No food. Maybe I will give you water—it will take longer that way. Maybe I will think of . . . something else to do. Doesn't matter. You will wait." Inch nodded his head. "Wait." He pushed the mallet's handle into his belt and climbed down the ladder.

Simon craned his neck, watching Inch's progress with stupefied fascination. The overseer reached the bottom and waved for a pair of his henchmen to take the ladder away. Simon sadly watched it go. Even if he somehow escaped his bonds, he would surely fall to his death.

But Inch was not finished. He moved forward until he was almost hidden from Simon's view by the great wheel, then pulled down on a thick wooden lever. Simon heard a grinding noise, then felt the wheel jerk, its sudden motion rattling his bones. It slipped downward, shuddering as it went, then splashed into the sluice, sending another jolt through Simon.

Slowly . . . ever so slowly . . . the wheel began to turn.

At first it was almost a relief to be rotated down toward the ground. The weight shifted from both his arms to his wrist and ankle, then gradually the strain moved to his legs as the chamber turned upside down. Then, as he rolled even further downward, blood rushed to his head until it felt as though it would burst out through his ears. At the bottom of his revolution, water splashed just beyond him, almost wetting his fingertips.

Above the wheel, the immense chains were again reeling up into darkness.

"Couldn't stop it for long," rumbled a downside-up Inch. "Bellows don't work, buckets don't work—and the Red Rat Wizard's tower don't turn." He stood staring for a moment as Simon slowly began to rise toward the cavern ceiling. "It does lots of things, this wheel." His remaining eye glittered in the light from the forge. "Kills little kitchen boys."

He turned and lumbered off across the chamber.

It didn't hurt that much at first. Simon's wrists were so securely bound, and he was stretched so tightly against the wheel's wide rim, that there was very little movement. He was hungry, which kept him clearheaded enough to think; his mind revolved far more swiftly than the prisoning wheel, circling through the events that had brought him to this place and through dozens of unlikely possibilities for escape.

Perhaps Stanhelm would come when it was sleeping time and cut him loose, he told himself. Inch had his own chamber somewhere in another part of the forge: with luck, Simon could be freed without the hulking overseer even knowing. But where would he go? And what made him think that Stanhelm was still alive, or if he was, that he would risk death again to save a person he barely knew?

Someone else? But who? None of the other foundrymen cared if Simon lived or died—nor could he much blame them. How could you worry about another person when every moment was a struggle to breathe the air, to survive the heat, to perform backbreaking work at the whim of a brutish master?

And this time there were no friends to rescue Simon. Binabik and Miriamele, even should they somehow make their way into the castle, would surely never come here. They sought the king—and had no reason to believe Simon still lived, anyway. Those who had rescued him from danger in the past—Jiriki, Josua, Aditu—were far away, on the grasslands or marching toward Nabban. Any friends who had once lived in the castle were gone. And even if he somehow managed to free himself from this wheel, where would he go? What could he do? Inch would only catch him again, and next time the forge-master might not devise such a gradual torment.

He strained again at his bonds, but they were heavy ropes woven to resist the strains of forge work and they gave not at all. He could work at them for days and only tear the skin from his wrists. Even the spikes that held the knotted ropes against the wheel's timbers were no help: Inch had carefully driven them between the strands so that the rope would not split.

The burning in his arms and legs was worsening. Simon felt a drumbeat of real dread begin inside him. He could not move. No matter what happened, no matter how bad it got, no matter how much he screamed and struggled for release, there was nothing he could do.

It would almost be a relief, he thought, if Pryrates came and found that Inch held him prisoner. The red priest would do terrible things to him, but at least they would be different terrible things—sharp pains, long pains, little ones and great ones. This, Simon could tell, was only going to become steadily worse. Soon his hunger would become a torment as well. Most of a day had passed since he had last eaten, and he was already thinking on his last bowl of scum-flecked soup with a regret bordering on madness.

As he turned upside-down once more, his stomach lurched, momentarily freeing him from hunger. It was little enough to be grateful for, but Simon's expectations were becoming very slight.

The pain that burned his body was matched by a fury that grew within him as he suffered, a helpless rage that could find no outlet and so began to gnaw at the very foundations of his sanity instead. Like an angry man he had once seen in Erchester, who threw everything in his house out of the window, piece by piece, Simon had nothing to fling at his enemies but what was his own—his beliefs, his loves, his most cherished memories.

Morgenes and Josua and Binabik and the others had used him, he decided.

They had taken a boy who could not even write his own name and had made him a tool. Under their manipulation and for their benefit he had been driven from his home, had been made an exile, had seen the death of many he held dear and the destruction of much that was innocent and beautiful. With no say in his own destiny he had been led this way and that, and told just enough half-truths to keep him soldiering on. For the sake of Josua he had faced a dragon and won—then the Great Sword had been taken from him and given to someone else. For Binabik's sake he had stayed on in Yiqanuc—who could say that Haestan would have been killed if the company had left earlier? He had come with Miriamele to protect her on her journey, and had suffered because of it, both in the tunnels and now on this wheel where he would likely die. They had all taken from him, taken everything he had. They had used him.

And Miriamele had other crimes to answer for. She had led him on, treated him like an equal even though she was a king's daughter. She had been his friend, or had said she was, but she had not waited for him to come back from the quest to the northern mountains. No, instead she had gone off on her own without even a word left for him, as though their friendship had never existed. And she had given herself to another man—delivered her maidenhood to someone she did not even like! She had kissed Simon and let him think that his hopeless love had some meaning . . . but then she had thrown her own deeds in his face in the cruelest manner possible.

Even his mother and father had abandoned him, dying before he could ever know them, leaving him with no life and no history but what the chamber-maids had given him. How could they!? And how could God let such a thing be?! Even God had betrayed him, for God had not been there. He was said to watch all creatures of His world, but He obviously cared little for Simon, the least of His children. How could God love someone and leave them to suffer as Simon had suffered, for no fault other than trying to do right?

Yet with all his fury at these so-called friends who had abused his trust, he had greater hatred still for his enemies: Inch, the brute animal—no, worse than any animal, for an animal did not torture; King Elias who had thrown the world into war and blighted the earth with terror and famine and death; silver-masked Utuk'ku, who had set her huntsman after Simon and his friends and had killed wise Amerasu; and the priest Pryrates, Morgenes' murderer, who had nothing in his black soul but self-serving malice.

But the greatest author of all Simon's suffering, it seemed, was he whose ravening hatred was so great that even the grave could not contain it. If anyone deserved to be repaid in torment, it was the Storm King. Ineluki had brought ruin to a world full of innocents. He had destroyed Simon's life and happiness.

Sometimes Simon felt that hate was keeping him alive. When the agony became too strong, when he felt life slipping away, or at least passing out of his control, the need to survive and revenge himself was something to which he could cling. He would stay alive as long as he could, if only to return some measure of his own suffering to all who had abused him. Every miserable lonely night would be recompensed, every wound, every terror, every tear.

Revolving through darkness, in and out of madness, Simon made a thousand oaths to repay pain for pain.

At first it seemed a firefly, flitting on the edge of his vision—something small that glowed without light, a point of not-black in a world of blackness. Simon, his thoughts floundering in a wash of ache and hunger, could make no sense of it.

"Come," a voice murmured to him. Simon had been hearing voices through this entire second day—or was it the third?—upon the wheel. What was another voice? What was another speck of dancing light?

"Come."

Abruptly he was pulled free, free of the wheel, free of the ropes that burned his wrists. He was tugged onward by the spark, and could not understand how escape could be accomplished so easily . . . until he looked back.

A body hung on the slowly circling rim, a naked white-skinned form sagging in the ropes. Flame-hued hair was sweat-plastered on its brow. Chin sagged on chest.

Who is that? Simon wondered briefly . . . but he knew the answer. He viewed his own form with dispassion. *So that's what I looked like? But there's nothing left in it—it's like an empty jar.*

The thought came to him suddenly. *I'm dead.*

But if that was so, why could he still dimly feel the ropes, still feel his arms yanked to the straining length of their sockets? Why did he seem to be both in and out of his body?

The light moved before him again, summoning, beckoning. Without will, Simon followed. Like wind in a long dark chimney, they moved together through chaotic shadows; almost-things brushed at him and passed through him. His connection to the body hanging upon the wheel grew more tenuous. He felt the candle of his being flickering.

"I don't want to lose me! Let me go back!"

But the spark that led him flew on.

Swirling darkness blossomed into light and color, then gradually took on the shapes of real things. Simon was at the mouth of the great sluice that turned the water wheel, watching the dark water tumble down into the depths below the castle, headed for the foundry. Next he saw the silent pool in the deserted halls of Asu'a. Water trickled down into the pool through the cracks in the ceiling. The mists that floated above the wide tarn pulsed with life, as though this water was somehow revivifying something that had long been almost lifeless. Could that be what the flickering light was trying to show him? That water from the forge had filled the Sithi pool? That it was coming to life again?

Other images flowed past. He saw the dark shape that grew at the base of the massive stairwell in Asu'a, the tree-thing he had almost touched, whose alien thoughts he had felt. The stairway itself was a spiraling pipe that led from the roots of the breathing tree up to Green Angel Tower itself.

As he thought of the tower, he abruptly found himself staring at its pinnacle, which reared like a vast white tooth. Snow was falling and the sky was thick with clouds, but somehow Simon could see through them to the night sky beyond. Hovering low in the northern darkness was a fiery ember with a tiny smear of tail—the Conqueror Star.

"Why have you brought me here, to all these places?" Simon asked. The spot of light hovered before him as though listening. *"What does this mean?"*

There was no answer. Instead, something cold splashed against his face.

Simon opened his eyes, suddenly very much an inhabitant of his painful flesh once more. A distorted shape hung upside down from the ceiling, piping like a bat.

No. It was one of Inch's henchmen, and Simon himself was hanging head-down at the lowest point of the wheel's revolution, listening to the axle squeak. The henchman turned another dipper full of water over Simon's face, pouring only a little of it into his mouth. He gasped and choked, trying to swallow, then licked his chin and lips. As Simon began his upward turn, the man walked away without a word. Little drops ran down from Simon's head and hair, and for a while he was too busy trying to catch and swallow them before they dripped away to wonder at his strange vision. It was only when the wheel brought him down the other side again that he could think.

What did that mean? It was hard to hold a coherent thought against the fire in his joints. *What was that glowing thing, what was it trying to show me? Or was it just more madness?*

Simon had experienced many strange dreams since Inch had left him—visions of despair and exaltation, scenes of impossible victory over his enemies and of his friends suffering dreadful fates, but he had also dreamed of far less meaningful things. The voices he had heard in the tunnels had returned, sometimes as a faint babble barely audible above the splashing and groaning of the wheel, other times clear as someone whispering in his ear, snatches of speech that always seemed just tantalizingly beyond his comprehension. He was beset by fantasies, dizzy as a storm-battered bird. So why should this vision be any more real?

But it felt different. Like the difference between wind on your skin and someone touching you.

Simon clung to the memory. After all, it was something to think about, something beside the horrible gnawing in his stomach and fire in his limbs.

What did I see? That the pool down below the castle is alive again, filled up by the water that's splashing right under this wheel? The pool! Why didn't I think of it before? Jiriki—no, Aditu—said that there was something in Asu'a called the Pool of Three Depths, a Master Witness. That must be what I saw down there. Saw? I drank from it! But what does that matter, even if it's true? He struggled with his thoughts. Green Angel Tower, that tree, the pool—are they all linked somehow?

He remembered his dreams of the White Tree, dreams that had plagued him for a long time. At first he had thought it was the Uduntree on frozen Yijarjuk, the great ice waterfall that had stunned him with its magnificence and improbability, but he had come to think it had another meaning as well.

A white tree with no leaves. Green Angel Tower. Is something going to happen there? But what? He laughed harshly, surprising himself by the rasping noise—he had been silent for many, many hours. *And what can I do about it anyway? Tell Inch?*

Still, something *was* happening. The Pool was alive, and Green Angel Tower was waiting for something . . . and the water wheel kept turning, turning, turning.

I used to dream about a wheel, too—a great wheel that spun through Time, that pulled the past up into the light and pushed everything alive down into the ground . . . not a huge piece of wood paddling dirty water, like this.

Now the wheel was carrying him down once more, tipping him so that the blood again rushed to his head and made his temples pound.

What did the angel tell me in that other dream? He grimaced and choked back a cry. The pain as it moved to his legs felt like someone jabbing him with long needles. *"Go deeper,"* she said. *"Go deeper."*

Time's walls began to crumble around Simon, as though the wheel that carried him, like the wheel that had haunted his dreams, plunged directly through the fabric of the living moment, pushing it down into the past and dredging up old history to spill across the present: The castle below him, Asu'a the Great, dead for five centuries, had become as real as the Hayholt above. The deeds of those who were gone—or those like Ineluki who had died but still would not go—were as vital as those of living men and women. And Simon himself was spun between them, a bit of tattered skin and bone caught on the wheel-rim of Eternity, dragged without his consent through the haunted present and the undying past.

Something was touching his face. Simon surfaced from delirium to feel fingers trailing across his cheek; they caught in his hair for a moment, then slid free as the wheel pulled him away. He opened his eyes, but either he could not see or the torches in the chamber had all been extinguished.

"What are you?" asked a quavering voice. It was just to one side, but he was moving away from it. "I hear you cry out. Your voice is not like the others. And I can feel you. What are you?"

The inside of Simon's mouth was swollen so that he could barely breathe. He tried to speak, but nothing came out except a soft gargle of noise.

"What are you?"

Simon struggled to answer, wondering even as he did so if this was another dream. But none of those, for all their rustlingly intrusive presence, had touched him with solid flesh.

An eternity of time seemed to pass as he made his way to the top of the wheel where the great chains sawed noisily upward, then began his downward turn again. By the time he reached the bottom he had worked up enough spit for something close to speech, although the effort tore at his aching throat.

"Help . . . me . . ."

But if someone was there, they did not speak or touch him again. His circle continued, uninterrupted. In darkness, alone, he wept without tears.

The wheel turned. Simon turned with it. Occasionally water splashed on his face and trickled into his mouth. Like the Pool of Three Depths, he thirstily absorbed it to keep the spark inside him alive. Shadows flitted through his mind. Voices hissed in the porch of his ear. His thoughts seemed to know no boundary, but at the same time he was trapped in the shell of his tormented, dying body. He began to yearn for release.

The wheel turned. Simon turned with it.

He stared into a grayness without form, an infinite distance that seemed somehow near enough to touch. A figure hovered there, faintly glimmering, gray-green as dying leaves—the angel from the tower-top.

"Simon," the angel said. "I have things to show you."

Even in his thoughts, Simon could not form the words to question her.

"Come. There is not much time."

Together they passed through things, moving crossways to another place. Like a fog evaporated by strong sun, the grayness wavered and melted away, and Simon found himself watching something he had seen before, although he could not say where. A young man with golden hair moved carefully down a tunnel. In one hand was a torch, in the other a spear.

Simon looked for the angel, but there was only the man with the spear and his stance of fearfully poised expectation. Who was he? Why was Simon being shown this vision? Was it the past? The present? Was it someone coming to rescue him?

The stealthy figure moved forward. The tunnel widened, and the torchlight picked out the carvings of vines and flowers that twined on the walls. Whenever this might be, the past, future, or present, Simon now felt sure that he knew *where* it was happening—in Asu'a, in the depths below the Hayholt.

The man stopped abruptly, then took a step backward, raising his spear. His light fell upon a shape that bulked huge in the chamber before him, the torch-glare glittering on a thousand red scales. An immense clawed foot lay only a few paces from the archway in which the spearman stood, the talons knives of yellow bone.

"Now look. Here is a part of your own story. . . ."

But even as the angel spoke, the scene faded abruptly.

*　　*　　*

Simon awoke to feel a hand on his face and water running between his lips. He choked and spluttered, but at the same time did his best to swallow every life-preserving drop.

"You are a man," a voice said. "You are real."

Another draught of water was poured over his face and into his mouth. It was hard to swallow while dangling downside-up, but Simon had learned in his hours on the wheel.

"*Who . . . ?*" he whispered, forcing the word out through cracked lips. The hand traced across his features, delicate as an inquisitive spider.

"Who am I?" the voice asked. "I am the one who is here. In this place, I mean."

Simon's eyes widened. Somewhere in another chamber a torch still burned, and he could see the silhouette before him—the silhouette of a real person, a man, not a murmuring shadow. But even as he stared, the wheel drew him up again. He felt sure that when he came back around this living creature would be gone, leaving him alone once more.

"Who am I?" the man pondered. "I had a name, once—but that was in another place. When I was alive."

Simon could not stand such talk. All he wanted was a person, a real person to speak with. He let out a strangled sob.

"I had a name," the man said, his voice becoming quieter as Simon rotated away. "In that other place, before everything happened. They called me Guthwulf."

PART FOUR

✹

The Blazing Tower

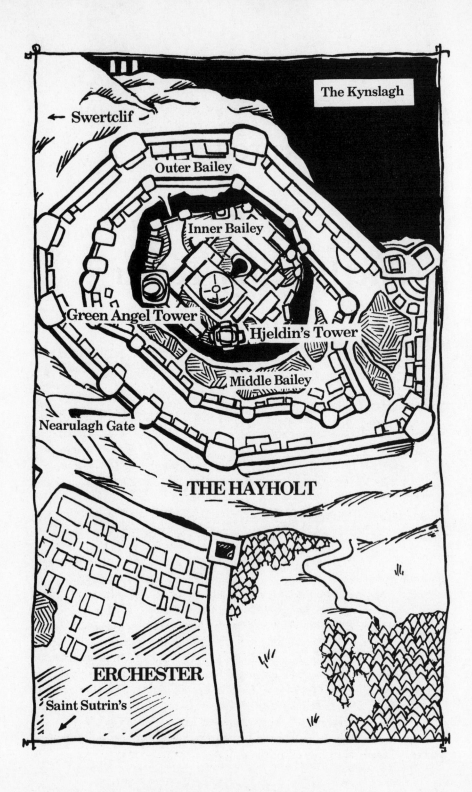

The Kynslagh

← Swertclif

Outer Bailey

Inner Bailey

Green Angel Tower

Hjeldin's Tower

Middle Bailey

Nearulagh Gate

THE HAYHOLT

ERCHESTER

Saint Sutrin's

47

The Frightened Ones

✦

Miriamele awakened slowly into darkness. She was moving, but not of her own power, carried by somebody or something as though she were a bundle of clothing. The cloying sweetness was still in her nose. Her thoughts were muddy and slow.

What happened? Binabik was fighting that terrible grinning man. . . .

She dimly remembered being grasped and pulled back into darkness. She was a prisoner . . . but of whom? Her father? Or worse . . . far worse . . . Pryrates?

Miriamele kicked experimentally, but her legs were firmly held, restrained by something less painful than ropes or chains, but no more yielding; her arms were also pinioned. She was helpless as a child.

"Let me go!" she cried, knowing it was useless, but unable to restrain her frustration. Her voice was muffled: the sack, or whatever it was, still covered her face.

Whoever held her did not reply; the bumpy progress did not slow. Miriamele struggled a bit longer, then gave up.

She had been drifting in a half-sleep when whoever carried her stopped. She was set down with surprising gentleness, then the sack was carefully lifted from her head.

At first the light, though dim, hurt her eyes. Dark figures stood before her, one leaning so close that at first she did not recognize the silhouetted shape as a head. As her eyes adjusted, she gasped and scrambled backward until hard stone halted her. She was surrounded by monsters.

The nearest creature flinched, startled by her sudden movement. Like its fellows, it was more or less manlike, but it had huge dark eyes with no whites, and its gaunt, lantern-jawed head bobbed on the end of a slender neck. It reached out a long-fingered hand toward her, then drew it back as though it feared she would bite. It said a few words in a tongue that sounded something like Hernystiri. Miriamele stared back in horrified incomprehension. The creature tried again, this time in halting, oddly-accented Westerling.

"Have we brought harm to you?" The spidery creature seemed genuinely worried. "Please, are you well? Is there aught we can give to you?"

Miriamele gaped and tried to slide out of the thing's reach. It did not seem inclined to hurt her—at least not yet. "Some water," she said at last. "Who are you?"

"Yis-fidri am I," the creature replied. "These others are my fellows, and that is my mate Yis-hadra."

"But *what* are you?" Miriamele wondered if the seeming kindness of these creatures could be a trick of some sort. She tried to look unobtrusively for her knife, which was no longer sheathed at her waist; as she did so, she took in her surroundings for the first time. She was in a cavern, featureless but for the rough surface of the rock. It was dimly illuminated, all glowing pink, but she could see no source for the light. A few paces away, the packs she and Binabik had carried lay beside the cavern wall. There were things inside them she could use as a weapon if she had to. . . .

"What are we?" The one called Yis-fidri nodded solemnly. "We are the last of our people, or at least the last who have chosen this way, the Way of Stone and Earth." The other creatures made a musical sound of regret, as though this meaningless remark had great significance. "Your people have known us as dwarrows."

"Dwarrows!" Miriamele could not have been more surprised had Yis-fidri announced they were angels. Dwarrows were creatures of folktale, goblins who lived in the earth. Still, as unbelievable as it seemed, they stood here before her. And more, there was something almost familiar in Yis-fidri's manner, as though she had known him or someone like him before. "Dwarrows," she repeated. She felt a terrified laugh bubbling inside her. "Yet another story springs to life." She sat up straighter, trying to hide her fright. "If you mean me no harm, then take me back to my friend. He is in danger."

The saucer-eyed creature looked mournful. He made a melodious sound and one of the other dwarrows stepped forward with a stone bowl. "Take of this and drink. It is water, as you asked."

Miriamele sniffed at it suspiciously for a moment, then realized that if they could bring her here so easily the dwarrows had little need to poison her. She drank, savoring the feel of the chill, clean water on her dry throat. "Will you take me back to him?" she asked again when she had finished.

The dwarrows looked nervously at each other, heads wavering like poppies in a windy field. "Please, mortal woman, ask not for that," Yis-fidri said at last. "You were in a perilous place—more perilous than you can know—and you carried something there which you should not have. The balance is exceeding delicate." The words sounded stilted and almost comical, but his reluctance was very clear.

"Perilous!?" A spark of indignation kindled. "What right do you have to snatch me away from my friend? I will decide what is perilous for me!"

He shook his head. "Not for you—or not for you only. Dreadful things are in the balance, and that place . . . it is not good." He seemed very uncomfortable, and the other dwarrows swayed a little behind him, humming nervously to themselves. Despite her unhappiness, Miriamele almost laughed at the odd spectacle. "We cannot let you go there. We are deeply sorry. Some of our number will return and look for your friend."

"Why didn't you help him? Why couldn't you bring him with us if it was so important that we not be there?"

"We were sorely afraid. He did fight with an Unliving One, or so it seemed. And the balance is very delicate there."

"What does that mean?!" Miriamele stood up, for a moment more angry than fearful. "You cannot do this!" She began to edge toward a shadowy place on the cavern wall that she thought might be a tunnel mouth. Yis-fidri reached out and caught at her wrist. His thin fingers were callused and hard as stone. There was deceptive strength, great strength, in this slender dwarrow.

"Please, mortal woman. We will tell you all that we are able. Content yourself for now to stay with us. We will seek for your friend."

She struggled, but it was hopeless. She might have been pulling against the weight of the earth.

"So," she said at last. Fright was turning to hopelessness. "I have no choice. Tell me what you know, then. But if Binabik is hurt because of what you've done, I'll . . . I'll find a way to punish you, whoever you are. I will."

Yis-fidri hung his great head like a dog being scolded. "It is not our wont to force others against their will. We have ourselves suffered too much at the hands of bad masters."

"If I must be your prisoner, at least call me by my name. I'm Miriamele."

"Miriamele, then." Yis-fidri let go of her arm. "Forgive us, Miriamele, or at least judge us not until all we have to say is heard."

She lifted the bowl and took another drink. "Tell me, then."

The dwarrow looked around at his fellows, at the circle of huge dark eyes, then began to talk.

"And how is Maegwin?" Isorn asked. His bandage gave him a strange, swollen-headed appearance. Icy air crept past the tent flap to ripple the flames of the small fire.

"I had thought she might be coming back to us," Eolair sighed. "Last night she began to move a little and take deeper breaths. She even spoke a few words, but they were whispered. I could make no sense of them."

"But that is good news! Why are you so long-faced?"

"The Sitha woman came to see her. She said it was like a fever—that sometimes the sufferer comes near to the surface, like a drowning man coming up for air one last time, but that does not mean . . ." Eolair's voice shook. He made an effort to control himself. "The healer said that she was still just as close to death, if not closer."

"And you believe the Sitha?"

"It is not an illness of the flesh, Isorn," the count said quietly. "It is a wound to her soul, which was already damaged. You saw her in the last weeks." He twined his fingers, then untwined them. "And the Sithi know more of these things than we do. Whatever happened to Maegwin left no marks, no broken bones or bleeding cuts. Give thanks that your own injury is something that can be mended."

"I do, by my faith." The young Rimmersman frowned. "Ah, Merciful Usires, Eolair, that is more grim news, then. And is there nothing anyone can do?"

The count shrugged. "The healer says it is beyond her powers. She can work only to make Maegwin comfortable."

"A cursed fate for such a good woman. Lluth's family is haunted somehow."

"No one would have said so before this year." Eolair bit his lip before continuing. His own sorrow grew until it seemed it must escape or kill him. "But, Murhagh's Shield, Isorn, no wonder that Maegwin sought the gods! How could she not think they had deserted us? Her father killed, her brother tortured and hacked to pieces, her people driven into exile?" He fought for a breath. *"My* people! And now poor Maegwin, maddened and then left dying in the snows of Naglimund. It is more than the absence of the gods—it is as though the gods were determined to punish us."

Isorn made the sign of the Tree. "We can never know what Heaven plans, Eolair. Perhaps there are greater designs for Maegwin than we can understand."

"Perhaps." Eolair pushed down his anger. It was not Isorn's fault that Maegwin was slipping away, and everything he said was kind and sensible. But the Count of Nad Mullach did not want kindness and sense. He wanted to howl like a Frostmarch wolf. "Ah, Cuamh bite me, Isorn, you should see her! When she is not lying still as death, her face stretches in terror, and her hands clutch," he raised his own hands, fingers curled, "like this, as if she sought something to save her." Eolair slapped his palms against his knees in frustration. "She needs something, and I cannot give it to her. She is lost, and I cannot find her to bring her back!" He gasped raggedly.

Isorn stared at his friend. The light of understanding kindled in his eyes. "Oh, Eolair. Do you love her?"

"I don't know!" The count put his hands to his face for a moment before continuing. "I thought once I might be coming to it, but then she turned harsh and cold to me, pushing me away whenever she could. But when the madness came over her, she told me that she had loved me since she was a child. She was certain I would scorn her, and did not like to be pitied, so she kept me ever at bay so I would not discover the truth."

"Mother of Mercy," Isorn breathed. He reached out his freckled hand and grasped Eolair's. The count felt the broad strength of the contact and held on for a long moment.

"Life is already a confounding maze without wars between immortals and such. Ah, gods, Isorn, will we never have peace?"

"Someday," said the Rimmersman. "Someday we must."

Eolair gave his friend's hand a parting squeeze before he let it go. "Jiriki said the Sithi plan to leave within two days. Will you go with them, or back to Hernystir with me?"

"I am not sure. The way my head feels, I cannot ride at anything like speed."

"Then go with me," the count said as he rose. "We are in no hurry, now."

"Be well, Eolair."

"And you. If you like, I'll come back later with some of that Sithi wine. It would do you miles of good, and take the sting of that wound away."

"It will take more than that away," Isorn laughed. "My wits will go, too. But I do not care. I am going nowhere, and am expected to do nothing. Bring the wine when you can."

Eolair patted the younger man's shoulder, then pushed out through the door flap into the biting wind.

As he reached the place where Maegwin lay, he was struck again by the power of Sithi craft. Isorn's small tent was well-made and sturdy, but cold air crept in on all sides and melting snow seeped through at the base. Maegwin's tent was of Sithi make, since Jiriki had wished her to rest in as much comfort as she could, and though its glistening cloth was so thin as to be translucent, stepping across the threshold was like walking into a well-built house. The storm that gripped Naglimund could have been leagues away.

But why should that be so, Eolair wondered, when the Sithi themselves seemed almost unaware of cold or damp?

Kira'athu looked up as Eolair entered. Maegwin, stretched out on the pallet beneath a thin blanket, was moving restlessly, but her eyes were still closed and the deathlike pallor had not left her face.

"Any change?" Eolair asked, knowing the answer already.

The Sitha gave a small, sinuous shrug. "She is fighting, but I do not think she has the strength to break the grip of whatever has her." The Sitha seemed emotionless, her golden eyes unrevealing as a cat's, but the count knew how much time she spent at Maegwin's side. They were just different, these immortals; it was senseless trying to judge them by their faces and even voices. "Has she spoken any words to you?" Kira'athu asked suddenly.

Eolair watched as Maegwin's fingers clawed at the blanket, scrabbling for something that was not there. "She has spoken, yes, but I could not hear her well. And what I did hear was only babble. There were no words in it I recognized."

The Sitha raised a silvery eyebrow. "I thought I heard . . ." She turned to look at her ward, whose mouth now moved soundlessly.

"Thought you heard what?"

"The speech of the Garden." Kira'athu spread her hands, curving the fingers to meet the thumbs. "What you would call Sithi speech."

"It is possible that she learned some in the time we have all traveled and fought together." Eolair moved closer. It tugged at his heart to see Maegwin's hands searching restlessly.

"It is possible," the healer agreed. "But it seemed spoken as the Zida'ya would speak it . . . almost."

"What do you mean?" Eolair was confused and more than a little irritated.

Kira'athu rose. "Forgive me. I should speak to Jiriki and Likimeya about it rather than trouble you. And it matters little, in any case, I think. I am sorry, Count Eolair. I wish I could give you happier news."

He sat down on the ground at Maegwin's side. "It is not your fault. You have been very kind." He reached out his hand so Maegwin could grip it, but her cold fingers moved skittishly away. "Bagba bite me, what does she want?"

"Is there something she usually carries with her or wears about her neck?" Kira'athu asked. "Some amulet or other thing that gives her comfort?"

"I can think of nothing like that. Perhaps she needs water."

The Sitha shook her head. "I have given her to drink."

Eolair leaned down and began fumbling absently in the saddlebags that contained the strew of Maegwin's belongings. He took out a scarf of warm wool and pressed it into her hands, but Maegwin only held it a moment before pushing it away. Her hands began to search again as she murmured wordlessly in her throat.

Desperate to give Maegwin some kind of comfort, he began to pull other things out of the bags, placing them one at a time beneath her fingers—a bowl, a wooden bird that had apparently come from the Taig's Hall of Carvings, even the hilt of a sheathed knife. Eolair was not very happy to find this last. Afraid that with her mind clouded she might do herself an injury, he had forbidden her to bring it from Hernysadharc. Maegwin had apparently flouted his orders. But none of these things, nor the other small objects he gave to her, seemed to soothe her. She pushed them away, the movements of her hands angry and abrupt as a small child's, although her face was still empty.

His fingers closed on something heavy. He lifted it out and stared at the chunk of cloudy stone.

"What is that?" Kira'athu was surprisingly sharp.

"It was a gift from the dwarrows." He lifted it so she could see its face. "See, Yis-fidri carved Maegwin's name upon it—or so he told me."

Kira'athu took the stone from him and turned it in her slender fingers. "That is indeed her name. Those are the craft-runes of the Tinukeda'ya. Dwarrows, do you say?"

Eolair nodded. "I led Jiriki to their place in the earth, Mezutu'a." He took the stone back and held it, weighing it, watching the firelight become confused in its depths. "I did not know she had this with her."

Maegwin suddenly moaned, a deep sound that made the count flinch. He turned hurriedly to the bed. She made another sound which seemed to have words in it.

"*Lost,*" Kira'athu murmured, moving closer.

Eolair's heart clenched. "What do you mean?"

"That is what she said. She is speaking in the Garden-tongue."

The count stared at Maegwin's furrowed brow. Her mouth moved again, but no sound came but a wordless hiss; her head whipped from side to side upon the pillow. Suddenly, her hands reached out and scrabbled at Eolair's. When he released the stone to take them, she snatched it from him and pulled it against her breasts. Her feverish writhing subsided and she fell silent. Her eyes were still closed, but she seemed to have fallen back into a more peaceful sleep.

Eolair watched, dumbfounded. Kira'athu bent over her and touched her brow, then smelled her breath.

"Is she well?" the count asked finally.

"She is no closer to us. But she has found a little rest for a while. I think that stone was what she sought."

"But why?"

"I do not know. I will speak to Likimeya and her son, and anyone else who might have some knowledge. But it changes nothing, Eolair. She is the same. Still, perhaps where she walks, on the Dream Road or elsewhere, she is less afraid. That is something."

She pulled the blanket up over Maegwin's hands, which now clasped the dwarrow-stone as though it were a part of her.

"You should rest yourself, Count Eolair." The Sitha moved to the doorway. "You will be no good to her if you fall ill as well."

A breath of cold air moved through the tent as the flap opened and closed.

Isgrimnur watched Lector Velligis leave the throne room. The huge man's litter was carried by eight grimacing guards, and was led out, as it had been led in, by a procession of priests bearing sacred objects and smoking censers. Isgrimnur thought they resembled a traveling fair on its way to a new village. Spared kneeling by his injuries, he had watched the new lector's performance from a chair against the wall.

Camaris, for all his noble look, appeared uncomfortable on the high ducal throne. Josua, who had kneeled beside the chair while Lector Velligis offered his blessing, now rose.

"So." The prince dusted his knees with his hand. "Mother Church recognizes our victory."

"What choice did Mother Church have?" Isgrimnur growled. "We won. Velligis is one of those who always puts his money on the favorite—any favorite."

"He is the lector, Duke Isgrimnur," said Camaris sternly. "He is God's minister on earth."

"Camaris is right. Whatever he was before, he has been elevated to the Seat of the Highest. He deserves our respect."

Isgrimnur made a noise of disgust. "I'm old and I hurt and I know what I know. I can respect the Seat without loving the man. Did taking the Dragon-bone Chair make your brother a good king?"

"No one ever claimed a kingship made its possessor infallible."

"Try telling that to most kings," snorted Isgrimnur.

"Please." Camaris raised his hand. "No more. This is a wearisome day, and there is more yet to be done."

Isgrimnur looked at the old knight. He *did* look tired, in a way that the duke had never seen. It would have seemed that freeing Nabban from his brother's killer should have brought Camaris joy, but instead it seemed to have sapped the life from him.

It's as if he knows he's done one of the things he's meant to do—but only one. He wants to rest, but he can't yet. The duke thought he finally understood. *I've wondered why he was so strange, so distant. He does not wish to live. He is only here because he believes God wishes him to finish the tasks before him.* Clearly any questioning of God's will, even the infallibility of the lector, was difficult for Camaris. *He thinks of himself as a dead man.* Isgrimnur suppressed a shudder. It was one thing to yearn for rest, for release, but another to feel that one was already dead. The duke wondered momentarily whether Camaris might, more than any of them, understand the Storm King.

"Very well," Josua was saying. "There is one person left we must see. I will speak to him, Camaris, if you do not mind. I have been thinking about this for some time."

The old knight waved his hand, uncaring. His eyes were like ice chips beneath his thick brows.

Josua signaled a page and the doors were thrown open. As Count Streáwe's litter was carried in, Isgrimnur sat back and picked up the mug of beer he had hidden behind his chair. He took a long sip. Outside it was afternoon, but the chamber's ceiling-high windows were barred against the storm that lashed the seas beneath the palace, and torches burned in the wall sconces. Isgrimnur knew that the room was painted in delicate colors of sea and sand and sky, but in the torchlight all was muddy and indistinct.

Streáwe was lifted from his litter and his chair was set down at the base of the throne. The count smiled and bowed his head. "Duke Camaris. Welcome back to your rightful home. You have been missed, my lord." He swiveled his white head. "And Prince Josua and Duke Isgrimnur. I am honored that you have summoned me. This is noble company."

"I am not a duke, Count Streáwe," said Camaris. "I have taken no title, but only revenged my brother's death."

Josua stepped forward. "Do not mistake his modesty, Count. Camaris does rule here."

Streáwe's smile broadened, deepening the wrinkles around his eyes. Isgrimnur thought he looked like the most grandfatherly grandfather that God ever made. He wondered if the count practiced before a looking glass. "I am glad you took my advice, Prince Josua. As you see, there were indeed many folk unhappy with Benigaris' rule. Now there is joy in Nabban. As I came up from the docks, people were dancing in the public square."

Josua shrugged. "That is more to do with the fact that Baron Seriddan and the others have sent their troops into the town with money to spend. This city did not suffer much because of Benigaris, difficult as times are. Patricide or no, he seems to have ruled fairly well."

The count eyed him for a moment, then appeared to decide a different approach was warranted. Isgrimnur found himself enjoying the show. "No," Streáwe said slowly, "you are correct there. But people *know*, don't you think? There was a sense that things were not right, and many rumors that Benigaris had slain his father—your dear brother, Sir Camaris—to achieve the throne. There were problems that were certainly not all Benigaris' fault, but there was also much unrest."

"Unrest which you and Pryrates both helped to kindle, then fanned the flames."

Perdruin's ruler looked genuinely shocked. "You link me with Pryrates!?" For a moment his courtly mask fell away, showing the angry, iron-willed man beneath. "With that red-cloaked scum? If I could walk, Josua, we would cross swords for that."

The prince stared at him coldly for a moment, then his face softened. "I do not say you and Pryrates worked in concert, Streáwe, but that you each exploited the situation for your own ends. Very different ends, I'm sure."

"If that is what you meant, then I name myself guilty and throw myself on the mercy of the throne." The count seemed mollified. "Yes, I work in the ways I can to protect my island's interests. I have no armies to speak of, Josua, and I am always prey to the whims of my neighbors. 'When Nabban rolls over in its sleep,' it is said in Ansis Pelippé, 'Perdruin falls out of bed.'"

"Well argued, Count," Josua laughed. "And quite true, as far as it goes. But it is also said that you are perhaps the wealthiest man in Osten Ard. *All* the result of your vigilance on Perdruin's behalf?"

Streáwe drew himself up straighter. "What I have is none of your business. I understood you sought me as an ally, not to insult me."

"Spare me your false dignity, my good Count. I find it hard to believe that calling you wealthy is an insult. But you are right about one thing: we wish to speak with you about certain matters of mutual interest."

The count bobbed his head solemnly. "That is better to hear, Prince Josua. You know that I support you—remember the note I sent with my man Lenti!— and I am anxious to speak about ways that I can help you."

"That we can help each other, you mean." Josua raised his hand to still Streáwe's protest. "Please, Count, let us avoid the usual dancing. I am in a fierce hurry. There, I have given up a bargaining token already by telling you so. Now please do not waste our time with false protestations of this or that."

The old man's lips pursed and his eyes narrowed. "Very well, Josua. I find myself oddly interested. What do you want?"

"Ships. And sailors to man them. Enough to ferry our armies to Erkynland."

Surprised, Streáwe waited a moment before replying. "You intend to set sail for Erkynland now? After fighting fiercely for weeks to take Nabban, and with the worst storm in years sweeping down on us out of the north even as we speak?" He gestured toward the shuttered windows; outside, the wind wailed across the Sancelline Hill. "It was so cold last night that the water froze in the Hall of Fountains. The Clavean Bell barely rang over God's house, it was so icy. And you wish to go to sea?"

Isgrimnur felt a clutch of shock at the count's mention of the bell. Josua turned for a moment and caught the Rimmersman's eye, warning him not to speak. Obviously he, too, remembered Nisses' prophetic poem.

"Yes, Streáwe," said the prince. "There are storms and storms. We must brave some to survive others. I will take ship as soon as I can."

The count lifted his hands, showing open, empty palms. "Very well, you know your own business. But what would you have me do? Perdruin's ships are not warships, and they are all at sea. Surely Nabban's great fleet is what you need, not my trading vessels." He gestured to the throne. "Camaris is master of the Kingfisher House now."

"But you are master of the docks," Josua replied. "As Benigaris said, he thought you were his prisoner, but all the time you were gnawing him away from within. Did you use some of that gold they say fills the catacombs below your house on Sta Mirore? Or something more subtle—rumors, stories . . . ?" He shook his head. "It matters not. The thing is, Streáwe, you can help us or hinder us. I wish to discuss with you your price, whether in power or gold. There is provisioning to do as well. I want those ships loaded and on their way in seven days or less."

"Seven days?" The count showed surprise for the second time. "That will not be easy. And you have heard about the kilpa, have you not? They are running like quinis-fish—but quinis-fish do not pull sailors over the rails and eat them. Men are reluctant to go to sea in these dark days."

"So we have started the bargaining?" Josua asked. "Granted and granted. Times are difficult. What do you want, power or gold?"

Abruptly, Streáwe laughed. "Yes, we have started bargaining. But you underestimate me, Josua, or you undervalue your own coffers. You have something that might be more use to me than either gold or power—something that in fact brings both in its train."

"And what is that?"

The count leaned forward. "Knowledge." He sat up, a slow smile spreading across his face. "So now I have given *you* a bargaining token in return for your earlier gift." The count rubbed his hands in barely restrained enjoyment. "Let us speak in earnest, then."

Isgrimnur groaned softly as Josua sat down beside Perdruin's master. Despite the prince's stated hurry, it was indeed going to be a complicated dance. This was clearly something Streáwe enjoyed too much to do quickly, and something Josua took too seriously to be rushed through. Isgrimnur turned to look at Camaris, who had been silent during the whole discussion. The old knight was staring at the shuttered windows as if they were an intricately absorbing picture, his chin resting on his hand. Isgrimnur made another noise of pain and reached for his beer. He sensed a long evening ahead.

Miriamele's fear of the dwarrows was dwindling. She was beginning to remember what Simon and others had told her of Count Eolair's journey to Sesuad'ra. The count had met dwarrows—he called them *domhaini*—in the mines below Hernystir's mountains. He had called them friendly and peaceful, and that seemed to be true: except for snatching her from the stairs, they had not harmed her. But they still would not let her go.

"Here." She gestured to the saddlebags. "If you are so certain that something I am carrying is harmful, or dangerous, or . . . or whatever, search for yourselves."

As the dwarrows conferred in anxious, chiming voices, Miriamele considered escape. She wondered if dwarrows ever slept. But where had they brought her? How could she find her way out, and where would she go then? At least she still had the maps, although she doubted she could read them as efficiently as Binabik had.

Where *was* Binabik? Was he alive? She felt almost ill as she remembered the grinning thing that had attacked the troll. Another friend was lost somewhere in the shadows. The little man had been right—this had been a foolish journey. Her own stubbornness had perhaps brought death to her two closest friends. How could she live with that knowledge?

By the time the dwarrows had finished their discussion, Miriamele did not much care what they had decided. Gloom had settled on her, sapping her strength.

"We will search among your possessions, by your leave," Yis-fidri said. "In respect of your customs, my wife Yis-hadra only will touch them."

Miriamele was bemused by the dwarrow's circumspection. What did they think she had brought down into the earth, the dainty small-clothes of a castle-dwelling princess? Tiny, fragile keepsakes? Scented notes from admirers?

Yis-hadra approached timidly and began to examine the contents of the saddlebags. Her husband came and kneeled beside Miriamele. "We are sorely grieved that things should be thus. It is truly not our way—never have we pressed our will by force on another. Never." He seemed desperate to convince her.

"I still do not understand the danger you fear."

"It was the place you and your two companions walked. It is . . . it is—there are no words that I know in mortal tongues to explain." He flexed his long fingers. "There are . . . powers, things which have been sleeping. Now they awaken. The tower stairwell in which you climbed is a place where these forces are strong. Every day they become stronger. We do not yet understand what is happening, but until we do, nothing must happen which might upset the balance. . . ."

Miriamele waved for him to stop. "Slowly, Yis-fidri. I am trying to understand. First of all, that . . . thing that attacked us on the stairs was not a companion of ours. Binabik seemed to recognize him, but I have never seen him before."

Yis-fidri shook his head, agitated. "No, no, Miriamele. Be not insulted. We know that what your friend fought was no companion—it was a walking hollowness full of Unbeing. Perhaps it was a mortal man once. No, I meant that companion who followed a little behind you."

"*Behind* us? There were only two of us. Unless . . ." Her heart skipped. Could it have been Simon, searching for his friends? Had he only been a short distance away when she had been taken? No, that would be too cruel!

"Then you were followed," Yis-fidri said firmly. "For good or ill, we cannot say. We just know that three mortals were upon the stairs."

Miriamele shook her head, unable to think about it. Too much confusion was piled atop too much sorrow.

Yis-hadra made a birdlike sound. Her husband turned. The she-dwarrow held up Simon's White Arrow.

"Of course," Yis-fidri breathed. The other dwarrows leaned closer, watching raptly. "We felt it, but knew it not." He turned to Miriamele. "It is not our work or we would know it as verily as you know your own hand at the end of your arm. But it was made by Vindaomeyo, one of the Zida'ya to whom we taught our skills and craft. And see," he reached to take it from his wife, "here is a piece of one of the Master Witnesses." He pointed to the cloudy blue-gray arrowhead. "No surprise that we felt it."

"And carrying it on the stairwell was a danger somehow?" Miriamele wanted to understand, but terror had battered her for a long time, and weariness was now pulling at her like an undertow. "How could that be?"

"We will explain if we can. Things are changing. Balances are delicate. The red stone in the sky speaks to the stones of the earth, and we Tinukeda'ya hear the voices of those stones."

"And these stones tell you to snatch people off the staircase?" She was exhausted. It was hard not to be rude.

"We did not wish to come here," Yis-fidri said gravely. "Things that happened in our home and elsewhere drove us ever southward, but when we reached this place through the old tunnels, we realized that the menace here is even greater. We cannot go forward, we cannot go back. But we must understand what is happening so that we can decide how best to escape it."

"You're going to run away?" Miriamele asked. "That's why you're doing all these things? To give yourself a chance to run away?"

"We are not warriors. We are not our once-masters, the Zida'ya. The way of the Ocean Children has always been to make do, to survive."

Miriamele shook her head in frustration. They had trapped her and torn her away from her friend, but only so they could escape something she did not understand. "Let me go."

"We cannot, Miriamele. We are sorry."

"Then let me go to sleep." She crawled away toward the wall of the cavern and curled herself in her cloak. The dwarrows did not hinder her, but began talking among themselves again. The sound of their voices, melodious and incomprehensible as cricket calls, followed her down into sleep.

48

A Sleeping Dragon

✦

Oh, please, God, *don't let him be gone!*
The wheel carried Simon upward. If Guthwulf still spoke in the darkness below, Simon could not hear him above the creak of the wheel and the clanking of the heavy chains.

Guthwulf! Could it be the same man Simon had so often glimpsed, the High King's Hand with his fierce face? But he had led the siege against Naglimund, had been one of King Elias' most powerful friends. What would he be doing here? It must be someone else. Still, whoever he was, at least he had a human voice.

"Can you hear me?" Simon croaked as the wheel brought him down again. Blood, regular as the tide at evening, was rushing into his head once more.

"Yes," Guthwulf hissed. "Don't speak so loudly. I have heard others here, and I think they would hurt me. They would take away all I have left."

Simon could see him, a dim, bent figure—but large, as the King's Hand had been, broad shoulders evident despite his stoop. He held his head in an odd way, as though it hurt him.

"Can I have . . . more water?"

Guthwulf dipped his hands into the sluice beneath the wheel; as Simon swung low enough to reach, he poured the water over the prisoner's face. Simon gasped and begged for more. Guthwulf filled his palms three more times before Simon rose out of reach. "You are on . . . on a wheel?" the man said, as though he could not quite believe it.

His thirst quenched for the first time in days, Simon wondered at the question. Was he simple-minded? How could anyone who wasn't blind doubt it was a wheel?

Suddenly Guthwulf's odd way of holding his head made sense. Blind. Of course. No wonder he had felt at Simon's face.

"Are you . . . Earl Guthwulf?" Simon asked as the wheel headed downward again. "The Earl of Utanyeat?" Remembering what his benefactor had said, he kept his voice low. He had to repeat the question when he was nearer.

"I . . . think I was." The earl's hands hung limply, dripping. "In another life. Before my eyes were gone. Before the sword took me. . . ."

The sword? Had he been blinded in battle? In a duel? Simon dismissed the thought: there were more important things to think about. His belly was full of water, but nothing else. "Can you bring me food? No, can you free me? Please!? They are tormenting me, torturing me!" So many words rasped his tender throat and he broke into a fit of coughing.

"Free you . . . ?" Guthwulf sounded distinctly shaken. "But . . . you do not wish to be here? I'm sorry, things are . . . so different. I have trouble remembering."

He's a madman. The only person who might help me, and he's mad!

Aloud, he said: "Please. I am suffering. If you don't help me, I'll die here." A sob choked him. Talking about it suddenly made it real. "I don't want to die!"

The wheel began to carry him up again.

"I . . . could not. The voices will not let me do anything," Guthwulf whispered. "They tell me that I must go and hide, or someone will take everything I have from me." His voice took on a horribly wistful tone. "But I could hear you there, making noises, breathing. I knew you were a real thing, and I wanted to hear your voice. I have not spoken to anyone for so long." His words grew faint as the wheel took Simon away. "Are you the one who left me food?"

Simon had no idea what the blind man was talking about, but heard him hesitating, troubled by Simon's pain. "I did!" He tried to be heard above the wheel without shouting. Was the man out of hearing? "I did! I brought you food!"

Please let him be there when I get back, Simon prayed. *Please let him be there. Please.*

As Simon neared the bottom again, Guthwulf reached out his hand once more and let it trail across Simon's features. "You fed me. I do not know. I am afraid. They will take everything from me. The voices are so loud!" He shook his shaggy head. "I cannot think now. The voices are very loud." Abruptly, he turned and lurched away across the cavern and vanished into the shadows.

"Guthwulf!" Simon cried. "Don't leave me!"

But the blind man was gone.

The touch of a human hand, the sound of a voice, had awakened Simon to his terrible pain once more. The passing hours or days or weeks—he had long since given up trying to mark time—had begun to smear into a gradually increasing nothingness; he had been floating in fog, drifting slowly away from the lights of home. Now he was back again, and suffering.

The wheel turned. Sometimes, when all the forge chamber's torches were lit, he saw masked, soot-blackened men hustling past him, but none ever spoke to him. Inch's helpers brought him water with excruciating infrequency, and did not waste words on him when they did. On a few occasions he even saw the huge overseer standing silently, watching as the wheel bore Simon around. Strangely, Inch did not seem interested in gloating: he came only to inspect Simon's misery, as a householder might pause to mark the progress of his vegetable garden while on the way to some other duty.

The pain in Simon's limbs and belly was so constant that he could not remember what it was like to feel any other way. It rolled through him as though his body were only a sack to contain it—a sack being tossed from hand to hand by careless laborers. With each rotation of the wheel, the pain rushed to Simon's head until it seemed his skull would burst, then pushed through his empty, aching guts to lodge in his feet once more, so that it seemed he stood on blazing coals.

Neither did the hunger go away. It was a gentler companion than the agony of his limbs, but still a dull and unceasing hurt. He could feel himself becoming less with every revolution—less human, less alive, less interested into holding onto whatever made him Simon. Only a dim flame of vengefulness, and an even dimmer spark of hope that someday he might come home to his friends, kept him clinging to the remains of his life.

I am Simon, he told himself until it was hard to remember what that meant. *I won't let them take that. I am Simon.*

The wheel turned. He turned with it.

Guthwulf did not return to speak to him. Once, as he floated in a haze of misery, Simon felt the person who gave him water touch his face, but he could not move his lips to make a sound of inquiry. If it was the blind man, he did not stay.

Even as Simon felt himself shrinking away to nothingness, the forge chamber seemed to grow larger. Like the vision the glowing speck had shown him, it seemed opened to the entire world—or rather, it seemed that the world had collapsed in upon the foundry, so that often Simon felt himself to be in many different places at the same moment.

He felt himself trapped upon the empty, snow-chilled heights, burning with the dragon's blood. The scar upon his face was a searing agony. Something had touched him there, and changed him. He would never be the same.

Below the forge, but also inside Simon, Asu'a stirred. The crumbled stone shivered and bloomed anew, gleaming like the walls of Heaven. Whispering shadows became golden-eyed, laughing ghosts. Ghosts become Sithi, hot with life. Music as delicately beautiful as dew-spotted spiderwebs stretched through the resurrected halls.

A great red streak climbed into the sky above Green Angel Tower. The heavens surrounded it, but the other stars seemed only timid witnesses.

And a great storm rolled down out of the north, a whirling blackness that vomited wind and lightning and turned everything beneath it to ice, leaving only dead, silent whiteness in its wake.

Like a man floundering in a whirlpool, Simon felt himself at the center of powerful currents with no strength to alter them. He was a prisoner of the wheel. The world was turning toward some mighty, calamitous change, but Simon could not even lift his hand to his burning face.

"*Simon.*"

The fog was so thick he could not see. Gray blankness surrounded him. Who called him? Couldn't they see he needed to sleep? If he waited, the voice would go away. Everyone went away if he waited long enough.

"*Simon.*" The voice was insistent.

He did not want voices any more. He wanted nothing except to go back to sleep, a dreamless, endless sleep. . . .

"*Simon. Look at me.*"

Something was moving in the grayness. He did not care. Why couldn't the voice leave him be? "*Go away.*"

"*Look at me, Simon. See me, Simon. You must reach out.*"

He tried to shut out the troubling presence, but something inside him had been awakened by its voice. He looked into the emptiness.

"*Can you see me?*"

"*No. I want to sleep.*"

"*Not yet, Simon. There are things you must do. You will have your rest someday—but not today. Please, Simon, look!*"

The moving something took on a more definite form. A face, sad and beautiful, yet lifeless, hovered before him. Something like wings or flowing garments moved around it, barely distinct from the gray.

"*Do you see me?*"

"*Yes.*"

"*Who am I?*"

"*You're the angel. From the tower.*"

"*No. But that doesn't matter.*" The angel moved closer. Simon could see the discolorations on her weathered bronze skin. "*I suppose it is good you can see me at all. I have been waiting for you to come close enough. I hope you can still get back.*"

"*I don't understand.*" The words were too difficult. He wanted only to let go, to float back into uncaring, to sleep. . . .

"*You must understand, Simon. You must. There are many things I must show you, and I have only a little time left.*"

"*Show me?*"

"*Things are different here. I cannot simply tell you. This place is not like the world.*"

"*This place?*" He labored to make sense. "*What place is this?*"

"*It is . . . beyond. There is no other word.*"

A faint memory came to him. "*The Dream Road?*"

"*Not exactly: that road travels along the edge of these fields, and even to the borders of the place where I will soon go. But enough of this. We have little time.*" The angel seemed to float away from him. "*Follow me.*"

"*I . . . I can't.*"

"*You did before. Follow me.*"

The angel receded. Simon did not want her to go. He was so lonely. Suddenly, he was with her.

"You see," she said. *"Ah, Simon, I waited so long for this place—to be here all the time! It is wonderful! I am free!"*

He wondered what the angel meant, but he had no strength for more riddles. *"Where are we going?"*

"Not where, but when. You know that." The angel seemed to give off a sort of joy; if she had been a flower, Simon thought, she would have been standing in a patch of sunlight, surrounded by bees. *"It was so terrible those other times when I had to go back. I was only happy here. I tried to tell you that once, but you could not hear me."*

"I don't understand."

"Of course. You have never heard my voice until now. Never my own voice, that is. You heard hers."

There were no words, Simon realized suddenly. He and the angel were not speaking as people spoke; rather, she seemed to give him her ideas and they found a home in his head. When she talked of "her," of the other whose voice he had heard, he did not perceive it as a word, but as a feeling of a protecting, holding, loving, but still somehow dangerous, female.

"Who is 'her'?"

"She has gone on ahead," the angel said, as though he had asked a completely different question. *"Soon I will join her. But I had to wait for you. Simon. It doesn't bother me, though. I am happy here. I'm just glad I didn't have to go back."* Simon felt "back" as a trapped, hurting place. *"Even before, when I first came here, I never wanted to go back . . . but she always made me."*

Before he could question further—before he could even decide whether, in this strange dream, he *wanted* to question further—Simon found himself in the tunnels of Asu'a. A familiar scene spread before him—the fair-haired man, the torch, the spear, the great glittering *something* that lay just beyond the archway.

"What is this?"

"Watch. It is your story—or part of it."

The spearman took a step forward, every inch of him aquiver with fearful expectation. The great beast did not move. Its red claw lay curled on the ground just a few paces before his feet.

Simon wondered if the beast slept. His own scar, or the memory of it, stung him.

Run away, man, he thought. *A dragon is more than you can know. Run away!*

The spearman took another cautious step, then stopped. Simon was suddenly closer, looking into the wide chamber as though he saw through the eyes of the golden-haired man. What he saw was at first hard to take in.

The room was huge, with a ceiling that stretched up beyond the limits of the torchflame. The walls had been blasted and melted by great fires.

It's the forge, Simon realized. *Or that's what it is now. This must be the past.*

The dragon lay sprawled across the cavern floor, red-gold, as though the countless scales mirrored the torchlight. It was larger than a house, its tail a seemingly endless coil of looping flesh. Great wings stretched from its haunches to the elongated spurs behind its front claws. It was magnificent and terrifying in a way that even the ice-dragon Igjarjuk had not been. And it was completely and utterly dead.

The spearman stared. Simon, floating in a dream, stared.

"Do you see?" the angel whispered. *"The dragon was dead."*

The spearman took a step forward to prod the inert claw with his spear. Reassured, he moved into the great chamber of melted stone.

Something pale lay beneath the dragon's breast.

"It's a skeleton, Simon whispered. *"A person's skeleton."*

"Hush," the angel said in his ear. *"Watch. This is your story."*

"What do you mean?"

The spearman moved toward the pile of white bones, his fingers tracing the sign of the Tree in the air. The shadow of his hand leaped across the wall. He leaned close, still moving slowly and stealthily, as though any moment the dragon might suddenly roar back to life—but the man, like Simon, could see the ragged holes where the dragon's eyes had been, the withered, blackened tongue that lolled from the gaping mouth.

The man reached down and reverently touched the human skull that lay beside the dragon's breastbone like a pearl from a broken necklace. The rest of the bones were scattered close by. They were blackened and warped. Looking at them, Simon suddenly remembered Igjarjuk's scalding blood, and felt a pang of sadness for the poor wretch who had slain this creature and received his own death. For slain it he had, it seemed; the only bones which still hung together were a forearm and hand, and they were wrapped around the hilt of a sword driven nearly to the hilt in the dragon's belly.

The spearman stared at this odd sight for a long time, then at last lifted his head, looking wildly around the cavern as though in fear someone might be watching. His face was somber, but his eyes gleamed feverishly. In that instant Simon almost recognized him, but the grayness of his thoughts was not entirely dispersed; when the fair-haired man turned back to the skeleton, the recognition faded.

The man dropped his spear and detached the skeletal hand from the sword's hilt with trembling care. One of the fingers broke loose. The man held it for a moment, his expression unreadable, then kissed the bone and tucked it into his shirt. When the hilt was freed, the man put his torch down on the stone, then took the sword in a firm grip. He placed his boot against the dragon's arching breastbone and pulled. Muscles rippled on his arms and cords stood out in his neck, but the sword did not come free. He rested for a moment, then spat on his palms and gripped the sword again. At last it slid out, leaving a puckered hole between the gleaming red scales.

The man lifted the sword before him, his eyes wide. At first Simon thought the blade a simple, almost crude piece of work, but its lines were clean and

graceful beneath the char of dragon's blood. The man regarded it with an admiration so frank that it was almost greedy, then lowered it abruptly and looked
around again, as though still afraid someone might be watching. He picked up
the torch and began to move back toward the chamber's arched doorway, but
stopped to stare at the dragon's leg and clawed front foot. After a long moment's
consideration, he kneeled and began sawing away with the blackened sword at
the leg's narrowest point, just in front of the wing-spur.

It was hard labor, but the man was young and powerfully built. As he
worked, he looked up anxiously, staring into the shadows of the vast room as
though a thousand scornful eyes were watching him. Sweat was trickling down
his face and limbs. He seemed possessed, as though some wild spirit had taken
hold of him; when he had sawed almost halfway through the thing he suddenly
stood and began hacking with the sword, smashing at the arm with blow after
blow until bits of tissue spun away on all sides. Simon, still a helpless but fascinated observer, saw that the man's eyes were full of tears, that his youthful face
was contorted in a grimace of pain and horror.

Finally the last of the flesh parted and the claw rolled free. Shivering like a
terrified child, the man shoved the sword through his belt, then hefted the huge
claw up onto his shoulder as though it were a side of beef. His face still full of
misery, he staggered out of the chamber and disappeared up the tunnel.

"He felt the Sithi ghosts," the angel whispered to him. Simon had been so
caught up in the man's private torment that he was startled by her voice. *"He
felt them shame him for his lie."*

"I don't understand." Something was tickling his memory, but he had been in
the gray for so long. . . . *"What was that? And who was the other one—the skeleton,
the one who killed the dragon?"*

"That is part of your story, Simon." And suddenly the cavern was gone and they
were in nothingness once more. *"There is much still to show you . . . and there is
very little time."*

"But I don't understand!"

"Then we must go deeper still."

The gray wavered, then dissolved into another of the visions that had come
to him in sleep upon the Tan'ja Stairs.

A large room opened before him. A few candles made all the light, and
shadows hung in the corners. The room's sole occupant sat in a high-backed
chair at the room's center, surrounded by a scatter of books and scrolls.

Simon had glimpsed this person during his stairwell dream. As in that earlier
vision, the man sat in the chair with a book spread open in his lap. He was past
middle age, but in his calm, thoughtful features there still remained a trace of
the child he had once been, an innocent sweetness only slightly diminished by
a long hard life. His hair had mostly gone to gray, although it still held darker
streaks and much of his short beard remained light brown. He wore a circlet on
his brow. His clothes, though simple in form, were well-made and of good
cloth.

As with the man in the dragon's lair, Simon felt a twinge of recognition. Before the dream, he had never seen this person—yet, in some way, he knew him.

The man looked up from his reading as two other figures entered the room. One, an old woman with her white hair caught up in a ragged scarf, came forward and kneeled at the man's feet. He put his book aside, then stood and gave the woman his hand to help her up. After saying a few words that Simon could not hear—as with the dragon-dream, all these shapes seemed voiceless and remote—the man walked across the chamber and squatted beside the old woman's companion, a little girl of seven or eight years. She had been crying: her eyes were puffy and her lip trembled with anger or fright. She avoided the man's gaze, pulling fitfully at her reddish hair. She, too, wore simple clothing, an unadorned dark dress, but despite her disarray she looked well cared for. Her feet were bare.

At last the man reached out his arms for her. She hesitated, then flung herself at him and buried her face against his chest, crying. Tears came to the man as well, and he held her for a long time, stroking her back. At last, with clear reluctance, he let her go and stood. The girl ran from the room. The man watched her go, then turned to the old woman. Without saying another word, he slipped a thin golden ring from his finger and gave it to her; she nodded and wrapped her fingers around it as he leaned down and kissed her forehead. She bowed to him; then, as if her own composure was fast slipping, she turned and hurried away.

After a long moment the man walked to a book-covered chest that lay beside the wall, opened it, and withdrew a sheathed sword. Simon recognized it immediately: he had seen that sparsely decorated hilt only moments before, standing in a dragon's breast. The man held the sword carefully, but did not look at it for more than a moment; instead, he cocked his head as though he heard something. He made the Tree sign with slow deliberation, lips moving in what might have been prayer, then returned to his seat. He set the sword across his lap, then picked up his book and opened it, spreading it atop the sword. But for the set of his jaw and the faintest tremor in his fingers as he turned the pages, he might have been thinking only of a good night's sleep—but Simon knew that he was waiting for something far different.

The scene wavered and dissipated like smoke.

"*Do you see? Do you understand now?*" the angel asked, impatient as a child.

Simon felt as though he groped at a large sack. Something was inside it, and he could feel strange corners and significant bumps, but just when he thought he knew what it contained, his imagination failed. He had been in the gray fog a long time. Thinking was difficult—and it was hard to care.

"*I don't know. Why can't you just tell me, angel?*"

"*It is not the way. These truths are too strong, the myths and lies around them too great. They are surrounded on all sides by walls I cannot explain, Simon. You must see them and you must understand for yourself. But this has been your story.*"

His story? Simon thought again about what he had seen, but meaning seemed to slither away from him. If he could only remember what things had been like before, the names and stories he had known before the grayness surrounded him . . . !

"Hold to them," the angel said. *"If you can get back, these truths will be of use to you. And now there is one more thing I must show you."*

"I'm tired. I don't want to see any more." The urge for restful oblivion had returned, pulling at him like a powerful current. All he had gained from this visitor was confusion. Go back? To the world of pain? Why should he bother? Sleep was easier, the drowsy emptiness of not caring. He could just let go, and all would be so easy. . . .

"Simon!" There was fear in the angel's voice. *"Don't! You must not give up."*

Slowly the angel's verdigrised features appeared once more. Simon wanted to ignore her, but although her face was a mask of lifeless bronze, there was something in her voice, some note of true need, that would not let him.

"Why can't I rest?"

"I have only a little while left with you, Simon. You were never near enough before. Then I must give you a push to send you back or you will wander here forever."

"Why do you care?"

"Because I love you." The angel spoke with sweet simplicity that held neither obligation or reproach. *"You saved me—or you tried. And there are others I love who need you. There is only a small chance that the storm can be turned away—but it is the only chance that remains."*

Saved her? Saved the angel who stood on the tower top? Simon felt exhausting confusion tug at him again. He could not afford to wonder.

"Then show me, if you must."

This time the translation from gray nothing to living vision seemed more difficult, as though this place was somehow harder to Teach, or as though her powers were flagging. The first thing Simon saw was a great circular shadow, and for a long time he saw nothing else. The shadow grew ragged at one edge. Tracings of light appeared there, then became a figure.

Even in the dislocated netherworld of the vision, Simon felt a stab of fear. The figure that sat at the edge of the shadowy circle wore a crown of antlers. Before it, point down, double-guarded hilt clutched in its hands, was a long gray sword.

The enemy! His mind was empty of names, but the thought was clear and cold. The black-hearted one, the frozen yet burning thing that caused the world's misery. Simon felt fear and hatred burning inside him so strongly that for a moment the vision flickered and threatened to vanish.

"See!" The angel's voice was very faint. *"You must see!"*

Simon did not want to see. His entire life had been destroyed by this monstrosity, this demon of ultimate evil. Why should he look?

To learn the way to destroy it, he told himself, struggling. *To keep my anger strong. To find a reason to go back to the pain.*

"Show me. I will watch."

The image strengthened. It took Simon a moment to realize that the darkness which surrounded the enemy was the Pool of Three Depths. It gleamed beneath the cloak of shadows, the stone carvings uncorrupted, the pool itself alight and scintillant, shifting as though the very water were alive. Washed by the liquidly shifting glow, the figure sat on a pedestal on a peninsula of stone with the Pool all around.

Simon dared to look closer. Whatever else it might be, this version of the enemy was a living creature, skin and bone and blood. His long-fingered hands moved fretfully on the pommel of the gray sword. His face was covered by shadow, but his bowed neck and shoulders were those of one horribly burdened.

His attention captured, Simon saw with surprise that the antlers upon the enemy's head were not horns at all, but slender branches: his crown was carved from a single circlet of some silvery-dark wood. The branches still bore a few leaves.

The enemy lifted his head. His face was strange, as were the faces of all the immortals Simon had seen—high-cheeked and narrow-chinned, pale in the shifting light, and surrounded by straight black hair, much of which hung in twisted plaits. His eyes were wide open, and he stared across the water as though in desperate search. If something was there, Simon could not see it. But it was the expression upon the enemy's face that Simon found most disconcerting. There was anger, which did not surprise him, and an implacable determination in the set of the long jaw, but the eyes were haunted. Simon had never seen such unhappiness. Behind the stern mask lurked devastation, an inner landscape that had been scoured to bare rock, a misery that had hardened into something like the stuff of the earth itself. If this being ever wept again, it would be tears of fire and dust.

Sorrow. Simon remembered the name of the gray sword. *Jingizu. So much sorrow.* He felt a kind of convulsion of despair and anger. He had never seen anything as terrible, as frightening, as the enemy's suffering face.

The vision wavered.

". . . *Simon* . . ." The angel's voice was as quiet as a leaf tumbling across the grass. ". . . *must send you back.* . . ."

He was alone in misty gray nothingness. *"Why did you show me that? What is it supposed to mean?"*

". . . *Go back, Simon. I am losing you, and you are far away from where you should be.* . . ."

"But I need to know! I have so many questions!"

". . . *I waited for you so long. I am called to go on, Simon.* . . ."

And now he did feel her slipping away. A very different kind of fear caught at him. *"Angel! Where are you?!"*

". . . *I am free now* . . ." Faint as feather brushing feather. *"I have waited so long.* . . ."

And suddenly, as the last touch of her voice slid away, he knew her.

"Leleth!" he cried. *"Leleth! Don't leave me!"*

A sense of her smiling, of Leleth free and flying at last, brushed him, then was gone. Nothing came in its place.

Simon was suspended in emptiness, without direction or understanding. He tried to move as he and Leleth had moved, but nothing happened. He was lost in the void, more lost than he had ever been. He was a rag blowing through the darkness. He was utterly alone.

"Help me!" he screamed.

Nothing changed.

"Help me," he murmured. *"Someone."*

Nothing changed. Nothing would ever change.

49

The Rose Unmade

The ship plunged again. As the cabin timbers creaked, Isgrimnur's empty cup bounced from his hand and clanked to the floor.

"Aedon preserve us! This is horrible!"

Josua's smile was thin. "True. Only madmen are at sea in this storm."

"Don't joke," Isgrimnur growled, alarmed. "Don't joke about boats. Or storms."

"I was not jesting." The prince gripped his chair with his hand as the cabin lurched again. "Are we not mad to let the fear of a star in the sky hurry us into this attack?"

The duke glowered. "We are here. Heaven knows, I don't want to be, but we are here."

"We are here," Josua agreed. "Let us only give thanks that for now Vorzheva and the children and your Gutrun are safe in Nabban."

"Safe until the ghants get there." Isgrimnur winced, thinking of the horrid nest. "Safe until the kilpa decide to try dry land."

"Now who is the worrier?" Josua asked gently. "Varellan, as we saw, has become an able young man, and a good portion of Nabban's army stayed there with him. Our ladies are much safer than we are."

The ship shuddered and pitched. Isgrimnur felt the need to talk, to do anything besides listen to what sounded like the timbers of the hull being wrenched apart. "I have been wondering something. If the Niskies are cousins to the immortals, as Miriamele told us, then how are we to trust them? Why should they favor our fairy-folk over the Norns?" As if summoned by his words, a Niskie's song, alien and powerful, rose once more above the shouting winds.

"But they do." Josua spoke loudly. "One of the sea-watchers gave her life so Miriamele could escape. What stronger answer do you need?"

"They haven't kept the kilpa as far away as *I'd* like." He made the sign of the Tree. "Josua, we have been attacked three times already!"

"And would have been attacked more often were it not for Nin Reisu and her brother and sister Niskies, I have no doubt," said Josua. "You have been on deck. You've seen the cursed things swimming all around. The seas are choked with them."

Isgrimnur nodded somberly. He had indeed seen the kilpa—far too many of them—swarming about the fleet, active as eels in a barrel. They had boarded the flagship several times, once in daylight. Despite the agony of his ribs, the duke had killed two of the hooting things himself, then spent hours trying to wash the oily, foul-smelling blood from his hands and face. "I know," he said at last. "It is as if they have been sent by our enemy to hold us back."

"Perhaps they have." Josua poured a bit of wine into his cup. "I find it strange that the kilpa should rise and the ghants should come pouring out of the swamps at just the same moment. Our enemy's reach is long, Isgrimnur."

"Little Tiamak believes that was happening in the ghant nest when we found him—that somehow Stormspike was using him and the other Wrannamen to talk to those bugs." The thought of Tiamak's countrymen used by the ghants, burned up like candles and then discarded, and of the hundreds of Nabbanai mariners dragged away to a hideous death by the kilpa, made Isgrimnur curl his fist and wish for something to hit. "What kind of a demon could do such things, Josua? What kind of an enemy is this, that we cannot see and cannot strike?"

"The greatest enemy we have." The prince sipped his wine, swaying as the ship pitched again. "An enemy we must defeat, no matter the cost."

The cabin door swung open. Camaris steadied himself, then entered, his scabbard scraping the doorframe. The old knight's cloak drizzled water on the floor.

"What did Nin Reisu say?" Josua asked as he poured wine for Camaris. "Will *Emettin's Jewel* hold together for one more night?"

The old man drained his cup and stared at the lees.

"Camaris?" Josua moved toward him. "What did Nin Reisu say?"

After a moment, the knight looked up. "I cannot sleep."

The prince shared a worried look with Isgrimnur. "I do not understand."

"I have been up on deck."

Isgrimnur thought that was obvious from the water puddling on the floor. The old knight seemed even more fearfully distracted than was usual. "What's wrong, Camaris?"

"I cannot sleep. This sword is in my dreams." He pawed fitfully at Thorn's hilt. "I hear it . . . singing to me." Camaris tugged it a short way out of the scabbard, a length of pure darkness. "I carried this sword for years." He struggled for words. "I . . . felt it sometimes, especially in battle. But never this way. I think . . . I think it is alive."

Josua looked at the blade with more than a little distrust. "Perhaps you should not carry it, Camaris. You will be forced to take it up soon enough. Put it somewhere safe."

"No." The old man shook his head. His voice was heavy. "No, I dare not. There are things to learn. We do not know how to use these Great Swords against our enemy. As you said, the time is fast coming. Perhaps I can understand the song it sings. Perhaps . . ."

The prince lifted his hand as if to dispute him, then let it fall. "You must do as you think best. You are Thorn's master."

Camaris looked up solemnly. "Am I? I thought so, once."

"Come, have some more wine," Isgrimnur urged him. He tried to rise from his stool but decided against it. The battles with the kilpa had set back his recovery. Wincing, he signaled to Josua to refill the old man's cup. "It is hard not to feel haunted when the wind howls and the sea flings us about like dice in a cup."

"Isgrimnur is right." Josua smiled. "Here, drink up." The room lurched once more, and wine splashed onto his wrist. "Come, while there is more in the cup than on the floor."

Camaris was silent for long moments. "I must speak to you, Josua," he said abruptly. "Something weighs upon my soul."

Puzzled, the prince waited.

The knight's face seemed almost gray as he turned to the duke. "Please, Isgrimnur, I must talk with Josua alone."

"I am your friend, Camaris," said the duke. "If anyone is to blame for bringing you here, it's me. If something is plaguing you, I want to help."

"This is a shame that burns. I would not tell Josua, but that he needs to hear it. Even as I lie sleepless for fear of what the sword will do, God punishes me for my secret sin. I pray that if I make this right, He will give me the strength to understand Thorn and its brother swords. But please do not force me to bare this shame to you as well." Camaris looked truly old, his features slack, his eyes wandering. "Please. I beg you."

Confused and more than a little frightened, Isgrimnur nodded. "As you wish, Camaris. Of course."

Isgrimnur was debating whether he should wait in the narrow passageway any longer when the cabin door opened and Camaris emerged. The old knight brushed past, hunched beneath the low ceiling. Before Isgrimnur could get more than half his question out, Camaris was gone down the passageway, thumping from wall to wall as *Emettin's Jewel* heaved in the storm's grip.

Isgrimnur knocked at the cabin door. When the prince did not answer, he carefully pushed it open. The prince was staring at the lamp, his blasted expression that of a man who has seen his own death.

"Josua?"

The prince's hand rose as though tugged by a string. He seemed entirely leeched of spirit. His voice was flat, terrible. "Go away, Isgrimnur. Let me be alone."

The duke hesitated, but Josua's face decided him. Whatever had happened in the cabin, there was nothing he could give the prince at this moment but solitude.

"Send for me when you want me." Isgrimnur backed out of the room. Josua did not look up or speak, but continued to watch the lamp as though it were the only thing that might lead him out of ultimate darkness.

✷

"I am trying to understand." Miriamele's head ached. "Tell me again about the swords."

She had been with the dwarrows for several days, as far as she could tell: it was hard to know for certain here in the rocky fastness below the Hayholt. The shy earth-dwellers had continued to treat her well, but still refused to free her. Miriamele had argued, pleaded—even raged for a long hour, demanding to be released, threatening, cursing. As her anger spent itself, the dwarrows had murmured among themselves worriedly. They seemed so shocked and unsettled by her fury that she had almost felt ashamed of herself, but the embarrassment passed as quickly as the anger.

After all, she had decided, *I did not ask to be brought here. They say their reasons are good—then let their reasons make them feel better. I shouldn't have to.*

She was convinced of, if not reconciled to, the reasons for her captivity. The dwarrows seemed to sleep very little if at all, and only a few of them at a time ever left the wide cavern. Whether they were telling her the entire truth or not, she did not doubt that there was something out there that frightened the slender, wide-eyed creatures very badly.

"The swords," said Yis-fidri. "Very well, I will try better to explain. You saw that we knew the arrow, even though we did not make it?"

"Yes." They had certainly seemed to know *something* significant was in the saddlebags, although it was possible they could have made up the story on the spot after finding it.

"We did not make the arrow, but it was crafted by one who learned from us. The three Great Swords *are* of our making, and we are bound to them."

"You made the three swords?" This was what had confused her. It did not match what she had been told. "I knew that your people made Minneyar for King Elvrit of Rimmersgard—but not that they forged the other two as well. Jarnauga said that the sword Sorrow was made by Ineluki himself."

"Speak not his name!" Several of the other dwarrows looked up and chimed a few unsettled words which Yis-fidri answered before turning back to Miriamele. "Speak not his name. He is closer than he has been in centuries. Do not call his attention!"

It's like being in a whole cave full of Strangyeards, thought Miriamele. *They seem afraid of everything.* Still, Binabik had said much the same thing. "Very well. I won't say . . . his name. But that story is not what I was told. A learned man said that . . . he . . . made it himself in the forges of Asu'a."

The dwarrow sighed. "Indeed. We were the smiths of Asu'a—or at least some of our people were . . . some who had not fled our Zida'ya masters, but who were still Navigator's Children for all that, still as like to us as two chunks of ore from the same vein. They all died when the castle fell." Yis-fidri chanted a brief lament in the dwarrow tongue; his wife Yis-hadra echoed him. "He used the Hammer that Shapes to forge it—*our* Hammer—and the Words of Making that we taught to him. It might as well have been our own High Smith's hand that crafted it. In that terrible instant, wheresoever we were, scattered across the world's face . . . we felt Sorrow's making. The pain of it is with us still." He fell silent for a long time. "That the Zida'ya allowed such a thing," he said at last, "is one of the reasons we have turned away from them. We were so sorely diminished by that one act that we have ever since been crippled."

"And Thorn?"

Yis-fidri nodded his heavy head. "The mortal smiths of Nabban tried to work the star-stone. They could not. Certain of our people were sought out and brought secretly to the Imperator's palace. These kin of ours were thought by most mortals to be only strange folk who watched the oceans and kept the ships safe from harm, but a small number knew that the old lore of Making and Shaping ran deep in all the Tinukeda'ya, even those who had chosen to remain with the sea."

"Tinukeda'ya?" It took a moment to sink in. "But that's what Gan Itai . . . those are Niskies!"

"We are all Ocean Children," said the dwarrow gravely. "Some decided to stay near the sea which forever separates us from the Garden of our birth. Others chose more hidden and secretive ways, like the earth's dark places and the task of shaping-stone. You see, unlike our cousins the Zida'ya and Hikeda'ya, we Children of the Navigator can shape ourselves just as we shape other things."

Miriamele was dumbfounded. "You're . . . you and the Niskies are the same?" Now she understood the phantom of recognition that had troubled her upon first seeing Yis-fidri. There *was* something in his bones, in his way of moving, that reminded her of Gan Itai. But they looked so different!

"We are not the same any more. The act of shaping ourselves takes generations, and it changes more than just our outward seeming. But much does not change. The Dawn Children and Cloud Children are our cousins—but the sea-watchers are our sisters and brothers."

Miriamele sat back, trying to grasp what she had been told. "So you and the Niskies are the same. And Niskies forged Thorn." She shook her head. "You are saying, then, that you can feel all the Great Swords—even more strongly than you felt the White Arrow?" A sudden thought came to her. "Then you must know where Bright-Nail is—the sword that was called Minneyar!"

Yis-fidri smiled sadly. "Yes, although your King John hung it with many prayers and relics and other mortal magicks, perhaps in the hope of concealing its true nature. But you know your own arms and hands, Princess Miriamele, do you not? Would you know them any the less if they were still joined to you, but were clothed in some other mortal's jacket and gloves?"

It was strange to think of her magnificent grandfather working so hard to hide Bright-Nail's heritage. Was he ashamed of owning such a weapon? Why? "If you know these swords so well, can you tell me where Bright-Nail is now?"

"I cannot say, 'it is such and such a place,' no. But it is somewhere near. Somewhere within a few thousand paces."

So it was either in the castle or the under-castle, Miriamele decided. That didn't help much, but at least her father had not had it thrown in the ocean or carried off to Nascadu. "Did you come here because you knew the swords were here?"

"No. We were fleeing other things, routed from our city in the north. We knew already that two of the swords were here, but that meant little to us at that time: we fled away through our tunnels and they led us here. It was only as we drew close to Asu'a that we came to understand that other forces were also at work."

"And so now you're caught between the two and don't know which way to run." She said it with more than a little disapproval, but knew even so that what the dwarrows faced was much like her own situation. She, too, was driven by things bigger than herself. She had fled her father, trying to put the entire world between the two of them. Now she had risked her life and the lives of her friends to come back and find him, but feared what might happen if she succeeded. Miriamele pushed the useless thoughts away. "Forgive me, Yis-fidri. I'm tired of sitting for so long, that's all."

It had been good to rest the first day, despite her anger over her imprisonment, but now she was aching to be on her way, to move, to *do* something, whatever that might be. Otherwise, she was trapped with her thoughts. They made painful company.

"We are truly sorry, Miriamele. You may walk as much as you wish here. We have tried to give you all that you need."

It was fortunate for them that she had the packs that held the remaining provisions, she reflected. If she had been forced to subsist on the dwarrows' food—fungi and small, unpleasant burrowing creatures—she would be a much less congenial prisoner. "You cannot give me what I need as long as I am held captive," she said. "Nothing can change that, no matter what you say."

"It is too perilous."

Miriamele bit back an angry reply. She had already tried that approach. She needed to think.

Yis-hadra scraped at a bit of the cavern wall with a curved, flat-ended tool. Miriamele could not quite tell what Yis-fidri's wife was doing, but she seemed to be enjoying it: the dwarrow was singing quietly beneath her breath. The more Miriamele listened, the more the song fascinated her. It was scarcely louder than a whisper, but it had something in it of the power and complexity of Gan Itai's kilpa-singing. Yis-hadra sang in rhythm with the movement of her long, graceful hands. Music and movement together made one singular thing. Miriamele sat beside her for some time, transfixed.

"Are you building something?" she asked during a lull in the song.

The dwarrow looked up. A smile stretched her odd face. "This *s'h'rosa* here—this piece of stone that runs through the other stone . . ." she indicated a darker streak, barely visible in the glow of the rose crystal. "It wishes to . . . come out. To be seen."

Miriamele shook her head. "It wishes to be seen?"

Yis-hadra pursed her wide mouth thoughtfully. "I do not have your tongue well. It . . . needs? Needs to come out?"

Like gardeners, Miriamele thought bemusedly. *Tending the stone.*

Aloud, she said: "Do you carve things? All the ruins of Asu'a I've seen are covered with beautiful carvings. Did the dwarrows do that?"

Yis-hadra made an indecipherable gesture with curled fingers. "We prepared some of the walls, then the Zida'ya created pictures there. But in other places, we gave care to the stone ourselves, helping it . . . become. When Asu'a was built, Zida'ya and Tinukeda'ya still worked side by side." Her tone was mournful. "Together we made wonderful things."

"Yes. I saw some of them." She looked around. "Where is Yis-fidri? I need to talk to him."

Yis-hadra appeared embarrassed. "Is it I have said something bad? I cannot speak your tongue as I can the tongue of the mortals of Hernystir. Yis-fidri speaks more well than I."

"No." Miriamele smiled. "Nothing bad at all. But he and I were talking about something, and I want to talk to him more."

"Ah. He will come back in a little time. He has left this place."

"Then I'll just watch you work, if you don't mind."

Yis-hadra returned the smile. "No. I will tell you something about the stone, if you like. Stones have stories. We know the stories. Sometimes I think we know their stories better than our own."

Miriamele sat down with her back against the wall. Yis-hadra continued with her task, and as she did so, she talked. Miriamele had never thought much about rocks and stone, but as she listened to the dwarrow's low, musical voice, she saw for the first time that they were in a way living things, like plants and animals—or at least they were to Yis-hadra's kind. The stones moved, but that movement took eons. They changed, but no living thing, not even the Sithi, walked alive beneath the sky long enough to see that change. The dwarrow-folk studied and cultivated, and even in a way loved, the bones of the earth. They admired the beauty of glittering gems and shining metals, but they also valued the layered patience of sandstone and the boldness of volcanic glass. Every one of them had its own tale, but it took a certain kind of vision and wisdom to understand the slow stories that stones told. Yis-fidri's wife, with her huge eyes and careful fingers, knew them well.

Miriamele found herself oddly touched by this strange creature, and for a while, listening to Yis-hadra's slow, joyful speech, she forgot even her own unhappiness.

Tiamak felt a hand close around his arm.

"Is that you?" Father Strangyeard's voice sounded querulous.

"It is me."

"We shouldn't either of us be out on deck," the archivist said. "Sludig will be angry."

"Sludig would be right," Tiamak said. "The kilpa are all around us." But still he did not move. The closed quarters of the ship's cabin had been making it hard to think, and the ideas that were moving at the edge of his mind seemed too important to lose just because of a fear of the sea-creatures—however worthy of fear they might be.

"My sight is not good," Strangyeard said, peering worriedly into the darkness. He held his hand beside his good eye to shield against the strong winds. "I should probably not be walking the deck at night. But I was . . . worried for you, you were gone so long."

"I know." Tiamak patted the older man's hand where it lay on the weathered rail. "I am thinking about the things I told you earlier—the idea had when Camaris fought Benigaris." He stopped, noticing for the first time the ship's odd movement. "Are we anchored?" he asked at last.

"We are. The Hayefur is not lit at Wentmouth, and Josua feared to come too close to the rocks in darkness. He sent word with the signal-lamp." The archivist shivered. "It makes it worse, though, having to sit still. Those nasty gray things . . ."

"Then let us go down. I think the rains are returning, in any case." Tiamak turned from the rail. "We will warm some of your wine—a drylander custom I have come to appreciate—and think more about the swords." He took the priest's elbow and led him toward the cabin door.

"Surely this is better," Strangyeard said. He braced himself against the wall as the ship dipped into a trough between the waves, then handed the sloshing cup to the Wrannaman. "I had better cover the coals. It would be terrible if the brazier tipped over. Goodness! I hope everyone else is being careful, too."

"I think Sludig is allowing few others to have braziers, or even lanterns, except on deck." Tiamak took a sip of the wine and smacked his lips. "Ah. Good. No, we are the privileged ones because we have things to read and time is short."

The archivist lowered himself to the pallet on the floor, pitching gently with the motion of the ship. "So I suppose we should be back at our work again." He drank from his own cup. "Forgive me, Tiamak, but does it not seem futile to you sometimes? Hanging all our hopes on three swords, two of which are not even ours?" He stared into his wine.

"I came late to these matters, in a way." Tiamak made himself comfortable. The rocking of the ship, however pronounced, was not that different from the way the wind rattled his house in the banyan tree. "If you had asked me a year ago what chance there was that I would be aboard a boat sailing for Erkynland to conquer the High King—that I would be a Scrollbearer, that I would have seen Camaris reborn, been captured by the ghants, saved by the Duke of Elvrit-shalla and the High King's daughter . . ." He waved his hand. "You see what I am saying. Everything that has happened to us is madness, but when we look back, it all seems to have followed logically from one moment to the next. Perhaps someday capturing and using the swords will seem just as clear in its sense."

"That is a nice thought." Strangyeard sighed and pushed his eyepatch, which had shifted slightly, back into place. "I like things better when they have already happened. Books may differ, one from the other, but at least most every book claims to know the truth and set it out clearly."

"Someday we will perhaps be in someone else's book," Tiamak offered, smiling, "and whoever writes it will be very certain about how everything came to pass. But we do not have that luxury now." He leaned forward. "Now where is the part of the doctor's manuscript that tells of the forging of Sorrow?"

"Here, I think." Strangyeard shuffled through one of the many piles of parchment scattered about the room. "Yes, here." He lifted it to the light, squinting. "Shall I read something to you?"

Tiamak held out his hand. He had an immense fondness for the Archive Master, a closeness he had not felt to anyone since old Doctor Morgenes. "No," he said gently, "let me read. Let us not put your poor eyes to any more work tonight."

Strangyeard mumbled something and gave him the sheaf of parchment.

"It is this bit about the Words of Making that sticks in my head," Tiamak said. "Is it possible that all these swords were made with these same powerful Words?"

"But why would you think so?" Strangyeard asked. His face became intent. "Nisses' book, at least as Morgenes quotes it, does not seem to say that. All the swords came from different places, and one was forged by mortals."

"There must be *something* that links them all together," Tiamak replied, "and I can think of nothing else. Why else should possessing them all give us such power?" He shuffled through the parchments. "Great magic went into their forging. It must be this magic that will bring us power over the Storm King!"

As he spoke, the song of a Niskie rose outside, piercing the mournful sound of the winds. The melody throbbed with wild power, an alien sound even more disturbing than the distant rumble of thunder.

"If only there were someone who knew of the swords' forging," Tiamak murmured in frustration; his eyes stared at Morgenes' precise, ornate characters, but did not really see them. The Niskie song rose higher, then vibrated and fell away on a note of keening loss. "If only we could speak to the dwarrows who made Minneyar—but Eolair says they were far to the north, many leagues beyond the Hayholt. And the Nabbanai smiths who forged Thorn are centuries dead." He frowned. "So many questions we have, and still so few answers. This is tiring, Strangyeard. It seems that every step forward takes us two paces back into confusion."

The archivist was silent while Tiamak looked for the well-thumbed pages that described Ineluki creating Sorrow in the forges below Asu'a. "Here it is," he said at last. "I will read."

"Just a moment," said Strangyeard. "Perhaps the answer to one is the answer to both."

Tiamak looked up. "What do you mean?" He dragged his thoughts away from the page before him.

"Your other idea was that somehow we have been purposely kept in confusion—that the Storm King has played Elias and Josua off against each other while he pursued some goal of his own."

"Yes?"

"Perhaps it is not just some secret goal he has that he wishes to conceal. Perhaps he also tries to hide the secret of the Three Swords."

Tiamak felt a glimmer of understanding. "But if all the contention between Josua and the High King has been arranged just to keep us from understanding how to use the swords, it might mean that the answer is quite simple— something we would quickly see if we were not distracted."

"Exactly!" Strangyeard, in pursuit of an idea, had lost his usual reticence. "Exactly. Either there is something so simple that we could not fail to see it if we were not caught up in the day-to-day struggle, or there is someone or someplace vital to us that we cannot reach as long as this war between brothers continues."

They Who Watch and Shape, marveled Tiamak, *it is good to have someone to share my thoughts with—someone who understands, who questions, who searches for meaning!* For a moment he did not even miss his home in the swamp. Aloud, he said: "Wonderful, Strangyeard. It is something well worth considering."

The archivist colored, but spoke confidently. "I remember when we were first fleeing Naglimund, Deornoth said that the Norns seemed to wish to keep us from going certain directions—at that time it was deeper into Aldheorte. Instead of trying to kill us, or capture us, they seemed to try to . . . drive us." The priest wiped absently at his chill-reddened nostrils, not yet recovered from the sojourn on deck. "I think perhaps they were keeping us from the Sithi."

Tiamak put the pages he was holding down: there would be time enough for them later. "So perhaps there is something the Sithi know—perhaps even they do not realize it! He Who Always Steps on Sand, how I wish we had questioned young Simon more closely about his time with the immortals." Tiamak stood up and moved toward the cabin door. "I will go tell Sludig that we wish to talk to Aditu." He stopped. "But I do not know how she could cross from one ship to another. The seas are so dangerous now."

Strangyeard shrugged. "It will do no harm to ask."

Tiamak paused, tilting back and forth with the ship's movement, then abruptly sat down again. "It can wait until the morning, when it would be a safe crossing. There is much we can do first." He picked up the parchments again. "It could be anything, Strangyeard—anything! We must think back on all the places we have been, the people we have met. We have been reacting to only what was in front of us. Now it is up to you and me to think on what we did *not* see while we were busy watching the spectacle of pursuit and war."

"We should talk to others, too. Sludig himself has seen much, and certainly Isgrimnur and Josua should be questioned. But we do not even know what questions to ask." The priest sighed and shook his head mournfully. "Merciful Aedon, but it is a pity that Geloë is not here with us. *She* would know where to begin."

"But she is not, as you said, and neither is Binabik. So we must do it on our own. This is our fearful duty, just as it is Camaris' task to swing a sword, and Josua's to bear the burdens of leadership." Tiamak looked at the untidy mess of writings in his lap. "But you are right: it is hard to know where to begin. If only someone could tell us more about the forging of these swords. If only that knowledge had not been lost."

As the two sat, lost for a moment in glum silence, the Niskie's voice rose again, cutting through the clamor of the storm like a sharp blade.

At first the very size of the thing prevented Miriamele from understanding what it was. Its dawn-colored brilliance and massive velvety petals, the dew drops sparkling like glass globes, even the thorns, each one a great spike of dark curving wood, all seemed things that must be absorbed and considered individually. It was only after a long while—or what seemed a long while—that she could comprehend that the vast thing spinning slowly before her eyes was . . . a rose. It revolved as though its stem were being twirled by gigantic yet invisible fingers; its scent was so powerful that she felt the whole universe choked in perfume, and yet even as it smothered her, it filled her with life.

The wide, unbroken plain of grass above which the rose turned began to shudder. The sod buckled upward beneath the mighty bloom; gray stones appeared, tall and angular, pushing up through the earth like moles nosing toward sunlight. As they burst free, and as she saw for the first time that the long stones were joined at the bottom, she realized that what she saw was a huge hand pushing up from below the world's surface. It lifted, grass and clotted dirt tumbling away; the stony fingers spread wide, encircling the rose. A moment later the hand closed and squeezed. The huge rose ceased turning, then slowly vanished in the crushing grip. A single wide petal scudded slowly from side to side as it floated to the ground. The rose was dead. . . .

★   ★   ★

Miriamele struggled up, blinking, her heart rattling inside her chest. The cavern was dark but for the faint pink glow of a few of the dwarrow's crystals, as it had been when she had drifted off to sleep. Nevertheless, she could tell something was different.

"Yis-fidri?" she called. A shape detached itself from the wall nearby and moved toward her, head bobbing.

"He still has not returned," said Yis-hadra.

"What happened?" Miriamele's head was throbbing as though she had been struck a blow. "Something just happened."

"It was very strong, this one." Yis-hadra was clearly upset: her immense eyes were wider than usual and her long fingers twitched spasmodically. "Some . . . change is happening here—a change in the bones of the earth and in the heart of Asu'a." She sought for words. "It has been happening for some time. Now it grows stronger."

"What kind of change? What are we going to do?"

"We do not know. But we will do nothing until Yis-fidri and the others are come back."

"The whole place is falling down around our ears . . . and you're not going to do anything?! Not even run away?"

"It is not . . . falling down. The changing is different." Yis-hadra laid a trembling hand on Miriamele's arm. "Please. My people are frightened. You make it worse."

Before Miriamele could say anything else, a strange silent rumble moved through her, a sound too low to hear. The entire chamber seemed to shift— for a moment, even Yis-hadra's odd, homely face became something unliving, and the roseate light from the dwarrow's batons deepened and chilled to glaring white, then azure. Everything seemed to be skewed. Miriamele felt herself slipping away sideways, as though she had lost her grip on the spinning world.

A moment later, the crystal lights warmed again and the cavern was once more as it had been.

Miriamele took several shaky breaths before she could speak. "Something . . . *very* bad . . . is happening."

Yis-hadra rose from her crouch, swaying unsteadily. "I must see to the others. Yis-fidri and I try to keep them from becoming too fearful. Without the Shard, without the Pattern Hall, there is little left to hold us together."

Shivering, Miriamele watched the dwarrow go. The mass of stone all around her felt like the confining walls of a tomb. Whatever Josua and old Jarnauga and the others had feared was now happening. Some wild power was coursing through the stones beneath the Hayholt just as blood ran through her own body. Surely there was only a little time left.

Is this where it will end for me? she wondered. *Down here in the dark, and never knowing why?*

*   *   *

Miriamele did not remember falling asleep again, but she awakened—more gently this time—sitting upright along the cavern wall, pillowed against the hood of her cloak. Her neck was sore, and she rubbed it for a moment until she saw someone squatting by her pack, a dim outline in the faint rose light of the dwarrow-crystals.

"You there! What are you doing?"

The figure turned, eyes wide. "You are awake," the troll said.

"Binabik?" Miriamele stared for a moment, dumbfounded, then sprang to her feet and ran to him. She caught him up in a hug that squeezed out a breathless laugh. "Mother of Mercy! Binabik! What are you doing? How did you get here?"

"The dwarrows found me wandering on the stairs," he said as she set him down. "I have been here a little time. I did not want to wake you, but I am full of hunger, so I have been searching in the packs. . . ."

"There's a little trail-bread left, I think, and maybe some dried fruit." She rummaged through her belongings. "I am so happy to see you—I didn't know what had become of you! That thing, that monk! What happened?"

"I killed him—or perhaps I was releasing him." Binabik shook his head. "I cannot say. He was himself for a moment, and warned that the Norns were . . . what did he say? . . . 'false beyond believing'." He took the piece of hard bread Miriamele offered. "I knew him as a man once. Simon and I met him in St. Hoderund's ruins. We were not being friends, Hengfisk and I—but to look into his eyes. . . ! Such a terrible thing should not be done to anyone. Our enemies have much to be answering for."

"What do you think of the dwarrows? Did they tell you why they took me?" A thought occurred to her. "Are *you* a prisoner now, too?"

"I do not know if prisoner is being the correct word," Binabik said thoughtfully. "Yes, Yis-fidri was telling me much when they found me, as we were making our way back to this place. At least for a while he was."

"What do you mean?"

"There are soldiers in the tunnels," the troll replied. "And others, too— Norns, I think, although we did not see them as we did the soldiers. But the dwarrows were certainly feeling them, and I do not think they were pretending for the benefit of me. They were full of terror."

"Norns? Here? But I thought they couldn't come to the castle!"

Binabik shrugged. "Who can say? It is their deathless master who is barred from this place, but I did not think it likely the living Norns would wish to enter here. Still, if everything I have been thinking was truth was now proved false, it would no longer be a surprising thing to me."

Yis-fidri approached, then stooped and crouched beside them, the padded leather of his garments creaking. Despite his kind, sad face, Miriamele thought that his long limbs gave him something of the appearance of a spider picking its way across a web.

"Here is your companion safe, Miriamele."

"I'm glad you found him."

"And not a moment too soon did we come upon him." Yis-fidri was clearly worried. "There are mortal men and Hikeda'ya swarming through the tunnels. Only our skill in hiding the doorway to this chamber keeps us safe."

"Do you plan to stay here forever? That won't help anything." The joy of Binabik's return had worn off a little, and now she felt desperation returning. They were all trapped in an isolated cavern while the world around them seemed to be moving toward some terrible cataclysm. "Don't you feel what is happening? All the rest of your folk felt it."

"Of course we feel it." For a moment Yis-fidri almost sounded angry. "We feel more than you. We know these changes of old—we know what the Words of Making can do. And the stones speak to us as well. But we have no strength to stop what is happening, and if we call attention to ourselves, that will be the end. Our freedom is of no use to anyone."

"Words of Making . . . ?" Binabik asked, but before he could finish his question, Yis-hadra appeared and spoke softly to her husband in the dwarrow tongue. Miriamele looked past her to where the rest of the tribe huddled against the cavern's far wall. They were clearly disturbed, eyes wide in the dim light, chattering quietly among themselves with much nodding and shaking of their large heads.

Yis-fidri's thin face wore a look of alarm. "Someone is outside," he said.

"Outside?" Miriamele pulled the pack closed. "What do you mean? Who?"

"We know not. But someone is outside the hidden door to this chamber, trying to get in." He flapped his hands anxiously. "It is not mortal soldiers, for whoever it is, they have some power over things—we shielded that door to the limits of the Tinukeda'ya's art."

"The Norns?" Miriamele breathed.

"We know not!" Yis-fidri stood and put his thin arm around Yis-hadra. "But we must hope that even though they have found the door, they cannot force it. There is nothing more we can do."

"There must be another way out, isn't there?"

Yis-fidri hung his head. "We took a risk. Hiding two doors makes both of them more vulnerable, and we feared to expend too much Art when things are so unbalanced. . . ."

"Mother of Mercy!" Miriamele cried. Anger fought with hopeless terror inside her. "So we're trapped." She turned to Binabik. "God help us, what choice do we have?"

The troll looked tired. "Are you asking if we will fight? Of course. The Qanuc are not giving their lives away. *Mindunob inik yat,* we say—'my home will be your tomb.'" His laugh was grim. "But with certainty, even the fiercest troll would rather find a way to keep his cave without himself dying."

"I found my knife," said Miriamele, drumming her fingers nervously on her leg. She struggled to keep her voice steady. Trapped! They were trapped with no way out, and the Norns were at the door! "Merciful Elysia, I wish I'd brought a bow. I only have Simon's White Arrow, but I'm sure he would approve if I feathered a Norn with it. I suppose I can use it to stab someone."

Yis-fidri looked at them in disbelief. "You could not save yourself from the Hikeda'ya with a bow and a whole quiver full of Vindaomeyo's most perfect arrows, let alone with only a knife."

"I don't think we *will* save ourselves," Miriamele snapped. "But we have come too far to let them take us as though we were frightened children." She took a breath to calm herself. "You are strong, Yis-fidri—I felt it when you carried me off. Surely you won't just let them kill you?"

"It is not our way, fighting," Yis-hadra spoke up. "We have never been the strong ones—not strong that way."

"Then stay back." Inwardly, Miriamele thought she sounded like the worst kind of boastful tavern brawler, but it was already hard enough to think about what might be coming. Just looking at the trembling, terrified dwarrows sapped her resolve, and the fear that lay beneath felt like a hole into which she might tumble and fall forever. "Take us to the door. Binabik, let's at least pick up some stones. The good Lord knows this place is full of them."

The huddled dwarrows watched them with distrust, as though the very act of preparing a resistance made them almost as dangerous as the enemy outside. Miriamele and Binabik quickly gathered a pile of stones, then Binabik broke down his walking-stick and placed the knife section in his belt, then readied the blowpipe.

"Better to use this first." He pushed a dart into the tube. "Perhaps a death they cannot see will make them a little more slow for coming in."

The doorway appeared to be only another section of the striated cavern wall, but as Miriamele and the troll stood before it, a faint silvery line began to creep up the stone.

"Ruyan guide us!" Yis-fidri said miserably. "They have breached the wards!" There was a chorus of fearful noises from his fellow.

The silver gleam crept up the rock face, then coursed across the length of a man's reach and started down again. When a whole section was bounded by a thread of light, the stone inside the glow slowly began to swivel inward, scraping as it moved against the cavern floor. Miriamele watched its ponderous movement with terrified fascination, trembling in every limb.

"Do not step to the front of me," whispered Binabik. "I will tell you when it is safe for moving."

The door ground to a halt. As a figure appeared in the narrow opening, Binabik raised his blowpipe to his mouth. The dark shape tottered and fell forward. The dwarrows moaned in fear.

"You hit him!" Miriamele exulted. She hefted a rock, ready to try for the next one through while Binabik loaded another dart . . . but no one else moved into the doorway.

"They're waiting," Miriamele whispered to the troll. "They saw what happened to the first one."

"But I was doing nothing!" said Binabik. "My dart is still unflown."

The figure raised its head. *"Close . . . the . . . door."* Each word was an agonized effort. *"They are . . . behind me. . . ."*

Miriamele gaped in astonishment. "It's Cadrach!"

Binabik stared first at her, then at the monk, who had collapsed again. He put down his walking-stick and ran forward.

"Cadrach?" Miriamele slowly shook her head. "Here?"

The dwarrows rushed past her, hurrying to shut the door.

50

The Graylands

✦

The colorless fog went on forever, without floor or ceiling or any visible limit at all. Simon floated in the middle of nothingness. There was no movement, no sound.

"Help me!" he shouted, or tried to, but his voice never seemed to leave his own head. Leleth was gone, her last touch upon his thoughts now grown cool and distant. "Help! Someone!"

If any shared the empty gray spaces with him, they did not answer.

And what if there is someone or something here? Simon thought suddenly, remembering all he had been told about the Road of Dreams. *It might be something I don't want to meet.* This might not be the Dream Road, but Leleth had said it was close. Binabik's master Ookequk had met some dreadful thing while *he* walked the road—and it had killed him.

But would that be worse than just floating here forever, like a ghost? Soon there will be nothing left of me worth saving.

Hours went by with nothing changing. Or it might have been days. Or weeks. There was no time here. The nothingness was perfect.

After a long empty space, his weak and scattered thoughts again coalesced.

Leleth was supposed to push me back, back to my body, to my life. Maybe I can do it myself.

He tried to remember what it felt like to be inside his living body, but for a long while could form only disjointed and disturbing images of the most recent days—burrowing diggers grinning into the torchlight, the Norns gathered whispering on the hilltop above Hasu Vale. Gradually he summoned a vision of the great wheel, and a naked body prisoned upon it.

Me! he exulted. *Me, Simon! I'm still alive!*

The figure hanging on the wheel's rim was shadowy and without much form, like a crudely carved image of Usires on His Tree, but Simon could feel the intangible connection between it and him. He tried to give the shape a face, but could not remember his own features.

I've lost myself. The realization crawled over him like a blanket of killing frost. *I don't remember what I look like—I don't have a face!*

The figure on the wheel, even the wheel itself, wavered and became indistinct.

No! He clung to the wheel, willing its circular shadow to stay before his mind's eye. *No! I'm real. I'm alive. My name is Simon!*

He struggled to remember how he had looked in Jiriki's mirror—but first had to draw up the memory of the mirror itself, its cool feel beneath his fingers, the delicate smoothness of its carvings. It had warmed at his touch until it felt like a living thing.

Suddenly he could recall his own face prisoned in the Sithi glass. His red hair was thick and unkempt, slashed by a white streak; down his cheek from eye to jaw ran the mark of the dragon's blood. The eyes did not reveal all that went on behind them. It was not a boy who looked back from Jiriki's mirror, but a rawboned young man. It was his own face, Simon realized, his own face returned to him.

He narrowed his will, straining to force his own features onto the shadowy form hanging on the wheel. As the mask of his face grew upon the dim figure, everything else became clearer, too. The forge chamber grew out of the indistinct gray nothing, faint and ghostly, but unquestionably a real place from which Simon was separated only by some short, indefinable distance. Hope flooded back into his heart.

But no matter how he tried, he could not push any farther. He wanted desperately to return—even to the wheel—yet it remained tantalizingly out of reach: the more he struggled, the greater the distance seemed between the Simon that floated in the dreamworld and his empty, slumbering body.

I can't reach it! Defeat pulled at him. *I can't.*

With that realization, his vision of the wheel dimmed, then vanished. The phantom forge evaporated as well, leaving him adrift once more in the colorless void.

He summoned up the strength to try again, but this time could bring into existence only the faintest glimmering of the world he had left behind. It faded swiftly. Furious, despairing, he tried again and again, but was unable to break through. At last, his will flagged. He was defeated. He belonged to the void.

I'm lost. . . .

For a while Simon knew nothing but hollowness and hopeless pain.

He did not know if he had slept or passed over into some other realm, but when he could feel himself think again, something else had finally come to share the emptiness. A single mote of light glowed faintly before him, like a candle flame seen through a thick fog.

"Leleth!? Leleth, is that you?"

The spark did not move. Simon willed himself toward the gleam of light.

At first he could not say if it grew nearer, or whether, like a star on the horizon, it remained remote and beyond reach no matter how he traveled. But even though Simon could not be sure that the spark was any closer, things began to change around him. Where once there had been only airy nothingness, he now began to see faint lines and shapes which gradually became sharper and more distinct until at last he could make out the forms of trees and stones—but all were transparent as water. He was passing along a hillside, but the very earth below him and the vegetation that shrouded it seemed only scarcely more real than the void that stretched overhead in place of the sky. He seemed to be moving through a landscape of clear glass, but when he lost his way for a moment and stepped into a rock in his path, he passed through it.

Am I the ghost? Or is it this place?

The light *was* nearer. Simon could see its warm glow reflected faintly in the fog of tree-shapes that ringed it round. He moved closer.

The radiance hovered on the edge of a ghostly valley, perched at the end of a jut of translucent stone. It was cradled in the arms of a dim, smoky figure. As he drew closer, the phantom turned. Ghost or angel or demon, it had the face of a woman. The eyes widened, although they did not quite seem to see him.

"Who is there?" The shadowy woman's face did not move, but there was no question in his mind that it was she who spoke. Her voice was reassuringly human.

"I am. I'm lost." Simon thought of how he would feel, approached in this deathly emptiness by a stranger. "I mean no harm."

A ripple passed through the woman's form, and for a moment the gleam of light she cradled against her breast glowed more brightly. Simon felt it as a spreading warmth inside him and was strangely comforted. "I know you," she said slowly. "You came to me once before."

He could make no sense of that. "I am Simon. Who are you? What is this place?"

"My name is Maegwin." She sounded uneasy. "And this is the land of the gods. But surely you know both those things. You were the gods' messenger."

Simon had no idea what she meant, but he was desperately hungry for the company of another creature, even this ghost-woman. "I am lost," he repeated. "May I stay here and talk to you?" It seemed somehow important that he have her permission.

"Of course," she said, but the uncertainty had not left her voice. "Please, be welcome."

For a moment he could see her more clearly; her sorrowful face was framed by thick hair and the hood of a long cloak. "You are very beautiful," he said.

Maegwin laughed, something Simon felt more than heard. "In case I had forgotten, you have reminded me that I am far from the life I knew." There was a pause. The glowing light pulsed. "You say you are lost?"

"I am. It's hard to explain, but I am not here—at least, the rest of me is not." He considered telling her more, but was hesitant to open himself completely even to this melancholy, harmless-seeming spirit. "Why are *you* here?"

"I wait." Maegwin's voice was regretful. "I do not know who or what I am waiting for. But I know that is what I do."

For a time the two of them did not speak. The valley shimmered below, pellucid as mist.

"It all seems so far away," Simon said at last. "All the things that seemed so important."

"If you listen," Maegwin replied, "you can hear the music."

Simon listened, but heard absolutely nothing. That in itself was astonishing, and for a moment he was overwhelmed. There was nothing at all—no wind, no birdsong, no soft babble of voices, not even the muffled bumping of his own heart. He had never imagined a quiet so absolute, a peace so deep. After all the madness and uproar of his life, he seemed to have come to the still center of things.

"I fear this place a little," he said. "I'm afraid that if I stay here too long, I won't even want to go back to my life."

He could feel Maegwin's surprise. "Your life? Are you not already long dead? When you came to me before, I thought you must be an ancient hero." She made an unhappy sound. "What have I done? Could it be that you did not know you were dead?"

"Dead?" Shock and fury and more than a little terror surged through him. "I'm not dead! I'm still alive, I just can't get back. I'm alive!"

"Then what are you doing here with me?" There was something very strange in her voice.

"I don't know. But I'm alive!" And although he said it in part to combat his own sudden apprehension, he felt it, too—ties that had grown weak but were nevertheless quite real still bound him to the waking world and his lost body.

"But surely only the dead come here? Only the dead, like me?"

"No. The dead go on." Simon thought of Leleth flying free and knew he spoke truly. "This is a waiting place—a between-place. The dead go on."

"But how can that be, when I . . ." Maegwin suddenly fell silent.

Simon's frightened anger did not dissipate, but he felt the flame of his life still inside him, a flame that had dimmed but had not yet blown out, and he was comforted. He knew he was alive. That was all he had to cling to, but it was everything.

He felt something strange beside him. Maegwin was crying, not in sounds, but in great shuddering movements that caused her entire being to waver and almost dissipate, like breeze-stirred smoke.

"What's wrong?" As odd and unsettling as all this was, he did not want to lose her, but she had become alarmingly insubstantial. Even the light she bore seemed to have grown fainter. "Maegwin? Why are you crying?"

"I have been such a fool," she keened. "Such a fool!"

"What do you mean?" He tried to reach out to her, to take her hand, but the two of them could not touch. Simon looked down and saw nothing where his body should be. It was odd, but in this dreamlike place it did not seem as terrifying as it might have elsewhere. He wondered how he looked to Maegwin. "Why have you been a fool?"

"Because I thought I knew all. Because I thought even the gods waited to see what I would do."

"I don't understand."

For a long time she did not reply. He felt her sorrow flow through him in great gusts, angry and mournful in turn. "I will explain—but first tell me who you are, how you came to be in this place. Oh, the gods, the gods!" Her sorrow threatened to sweep her away again. "I have made too many assumptions. Far, far too many."

Simon did as she asked, starting slowly and hesitantly at first, then gaining confidence as bit by bit his past returned to him. He was surprised to find that he could remember names which only a little while before had been misty holes in his memory.

Maegwin did not interrupt, but as his recitation went on she became slightly more substantial. He could see her clearly again, her bright, wounded eyes, her lips pressed together tightly as though to keep them from trembling. He wondered who had loved her, for certainly she was a woman someone could love. Who mourned for her?

When he spoke of Sesuad'ra, and of Count Eolair's mission from Hernysadharc, she broke her silence for the first time, asking him to tell more of the count and what he had said.

As Simon described Aditu, and what the Sitha-woman had said about the Dawn Children riding to Hernystir, Maegwin again began to weep.

"Mircha clothed in rain! It is as I feared. I have almost destroyed my people with my madness. I did not die!"

"I don't understand." Simon leaned a little closer, basking in the warmth of her glow. It made the strange ghostly landscape a little less empty. "You didn't die?"

The shadow-woman began to speak of her own life. Simon realized with dawning amazement that he did indeed know of her, although they had never met: she was Lluth's daughter, sister of Gwythinn the Hernystirman Simon had seen at Josua's councils in Naglimund.

The story she told, and then the further tale of dreams and misunderstandings and accidents that she and Simon pieced together from fragments and guesses, was terrible indeed. Simon, who had spent much of his time on the wheel in a fury of self-pity, found himself sickened by Maegwin's losses—her father, her brother, her very home and country taken from her in a way that even he, for all his sorrows, had not experienced. And the cruel tricks that fate, with Simon's unwitting help, had played on her! No wonder she had lost her wits and imagined herself dead. He ached for her.

When Maegwin had finished, the phantom valley again fell into total silence.

"But why are you here?" Simon finally asked.

"I do not know. I was not led here, like you. But after I touched the mind of the thing in what I thought was Scadach—in Naglimund, if that is where it was—I was nowhere at all for a time. Then I awoke to this place, this land, and knew I was waiting." She paused. "Perhaps it was you I was meant to wait for."

"But why?"

"I do not know. But it seems we fight the same fight—or rather we did fight it, since I see no way that either of us will leave this place."

Simon waited and thought. "That thing . . . that thing at Naglimund. What was it like? What did . . . what did you *feel* when you touched its thoughts?"

Maegwin struggled to find a way to explain. "It . . . it burned. Being so near to it was like putting my face in the door of a kiln—I feared it would scorch away my very being. I did not sense words, as I do from you, but . . . ideas. Hatred, as I told you—a hatred of the living. And a longing for death, for release, which was almost as strong as the longing for revenge." She made a sad noise. For a moment her light dimmed. "That was when I was first troubled about my own thoughts, for *I* felt that longing for death, too—and if I was already dead, how could I desire to be released from life?" She laughed, a bittersweet sensation that pricked at Simon's being. "Mircha shelter me! Listen to us! Even after all that has passed, this is a madness beyond all understanding, dear stranger. That you and I should be in this place, this *moiheneg*," she used a Hernystiri word or thought that Simon did not understand, "talking of our lives, although we do not even know whether we still live."

"We have stepped out of the world," Simon told her, and suddenly everything seemed different. He felt a sort of calm descend upon him. "Perhaps we've been given a gift. For a time, we've been allowed to step outside the world. A time to rest." Indeed, he felt more like himself than he had since he had fallen through the earth of John's barrow. Meeting Maegwin had done much to make him feel like a living thing again.

"A time to rest? Perhaps for you, Simon—and if that is so, I am happy for you. But I can only look on the foolishness I made of my life and mourn."

"Was there anything else you learned from . . . from the burning thing?" He was anxious to distract her. Her sorrow over her mistakes seemed only barely contained, and he feared that if it overwhelmed her he would find himself alone again.

Maegwin shimmered slightly. An unfelt wind seemed to toss her cloudy hair. "There were thoughts for which I have no words. Pictures I cannot quite explain. Very strong, very bright, as though they were close to the center of the flames that give that spirit life."

"What were they?" If the burning presence Maegwin described was what he thought it was, any clue to its plans—and by extension to the designs of its undead master—might help avert an endless age of blackness.

If I can even get back, he reminded himself. *If I can escape this place.* He pushed the disturbing thought away. Binabik had taught him to do only what he could at any given time. '*You cannot catch three fish with two hands,*' the little man often said.

Maegwin hesitated, then the glow began to spread. "I will try to show you."

In the valley of glass and shadows before them, something moved. It was another light, but where the one that Maegwin held against her breast was soft and warm, this one blazed with a fierce intensity; as Simon watched, four more points of radiance sprang up around it. A moment later the central light grew into a licking flame, stretching upward—but even as the flame grew, it changed color, becoming paler and paler until it was white as frost; the licking tendrils of fire stiffened into immobility even as they reached up and outward. Simon gaped at what they had become. At the center of the four-cornered ring of flames now loomed a tall white tree, beautiful and unearthly. It was the thing that had haunted him so long. The white tree. The blazing tower.

"It's Green Angel Tower," he murmured.

"This is where all the thoughts of the spirit in Naglimund are bent." Maegwin's voice was suddenly weary, as though showing Simon the tree had taken nearly all her strength. "That idea burns inside it, just as those flames burn around the tree." The vision wavered and fell away, leaving only the shadowy, insubstantial landscape.

Green Angel Tower, Simon thought. *Something is going to happen there.*

"One other thing." Maegwin had grown markedly fainter. "Somehow it thought of Naglimund as . . . the Fourth House. Does that mean something?"

Simon had a dim recollection of hearing something similar from the Fire Dancers on the hilltop over Hasu Vale, but at this moment it meant little to him. He was consumed by the thought of Green Angel Tower. The tower, and its mirror-phantom the White Tree, had haunted his dreams for almost a year. It was the last Sithi building in the Hayholt, the place where Ineluki had spoken the dreadful words that had slain a thousand mortal soldiers and had barred him forever from the living world of Osten Ard. If the Storm King desired some ultimate revenge, perhaps by giving some dread power to his mortal ally Elias, what more likely place for it to happen than the tower?

Simon felt a frustrated rage sweep over him. To know this, to see at last the outlines of the Enemy's ultimate plan, but to be helpless to do anything—it was maddening! More than ever he needed to be able to act, yet instead he was condemned to wander as an unhomed spirit while his body hung useless and uninhabited.

"Maegwin, I have to find a way out of this . . . this place. I must go back, somehow. Everything we have both fought for is there. Green Angel Tower in the Hayholt—that is the White Tree. I must go back!"

The shadowy figure beside him took a long time to respond. "You wish to go back to that pain? To all your suffering?"

Simon thought of all that had happened and still might happen, of his tormented body on the wheel and the agony he had fled in coming here, but it did not change his resolve. "Aedon save me, I have to. Don't you want to go back, too?"

"No." Maegwin's dim form shuddered. "No. I have no strength left, Simon. If something was not keeping me here, I would already have let go of everything that held me." She took what seemed to be a deep breath; when she spoke again, her voice trembled on the edge of weeping. "There are some I have loved, and I know now that many of them are still among the living. One in particular." She steadied herself. "I loved him—loved him until I was sick with it. And perhaps he even cared for me a little and I was too stupidly prideful to see it . . . but that is not important now." Her voice grew ragged. "No, that is not true. There is nothing in the living world more important to me than that love—but it is not to be. I would not go back and start again, even if I could."

Her pain was so great that Simon was left without words. There were some things that could not be made better, he realized. Some sorrows were irreparable.

"But I believe that *you* must go back," she said. "It is different for you, Simon. And I am glad to know that, to find that there are still those who wish to live in the world. I would not wish the way I feel on anyone. Return, Simon. Save those you love if you can—and those I love, too."

"But I can't." And now his thwarted anger at last gave way to desolation. There was no way to return. He and Maegwin would be here discussing the minutiae of their lives for eternity. "I don't know why I even said it, because I can't. I've tried. I don't have the strength to find my body again."

"Try. Try once more."

"Don't you think I did? Don't you believe I tried as hard as I could? It's out of my reach!"

"If you are right, we have forever. It will do no harm to try once more."

Simon, who knew that he had already exerted his powers to the utmost and failed, choked down bitter words. She was right. If he were to be any help to his friends, if he were to have even a remote chance to gain revenge for all he and Maegwin and thousands of others had suffered, he must try again—however unlikely success might be.

He tried to empty his mind of all his fears and distractions. When he had achieved a small measure of calm, he called up the image of the waterwheel, willing it into existence so that it turned in a great smoky circle over the ghostly valley. Then he summoned the image of his own face, his particular and only face, paying special attention this time to what was *behind* the features as well, the dreams and thoughts and memories that made him Simon. He tried to make the shadowy figure bound to the wheel come alive with Simon-ness, but already felt himself at the limits of his strength.

"Can you help me, Maegwin?" As the wheel grew more substantial she had grown dimmer; she was now little more than a glow of hazy light. "I can't do it."

"Try."

He struggled to keep the wheel before him, tried to summon the pain and terror and unending loneliness that went with it. For a moment he almost felt the rough wood scraping his back, heard the splashing of the wheels and the grating clash of the great chains, but then it began to slip away once more. Fading, the wheel trembled like a reflection in a rippling pond. It had been so close, but now it was receding from his reach. . . .

"Here, Simon."

And suddenly Maegwin's presence was all around him—even, somehow, inside of him. The glow that she had cradled as long as they spoke she now passed to him; it felt warm as the sun. "I think this is why I was brought here to wait. It is time for me to go on—but it is time for you to return."

Her strength filled him. The wheel, the forge chamber, the gnawing pain of his living body, all the things that at this moment meant life to him were suddenly very close.

But Maegwin herself was far away. Her next words seemed to come from a great distance, faint and dwindling rapidly.

"I am going on, Simon. Take what I give you and use it: I do not need my life any more. Do what you must. I pray it will be enough. If you meet Eolair . . . no, I will tell him myself. Someday. In another place . . ."

Her brave words did not mask her fear. Simon felt every bit of her terror as she let go and allowed herself to slip away into the dark unknown.

"Maegwin! Don't!"

But she was gone. The glow she had held was part of Simon, now. She had given him the only thing she had left—the bravest, most terrible gift of all.

Simon fought as he had never fought before, determined not to waste Maegwin's sacrifice. Although the living world was so close he could feel it, still some inexplicable barrier separated him from the body he had left behind—but he could not let himself fail. Using the strength Maegwin had given him, he forced himself closer, embracing the agony, the fear, even the helplessness that would be his if he returned. There was nothing he could do unless he accepted what was real. He pushed and felt the barrier ripping. He pushed again.

Murky gray turned to black, then red. As he passed back from the nether realms into the waking world, Simon screamed. He hurt. Everything hurt. He was reborn into a world of pain.

The scream continued, rasping from his dried throat and cracked lips. His hand was on fire, full of scorching agony.

"Quiet!" The frightened voice was very close. "I am trying . . ."

He was back on the wheel. His head was pounding, and splintered wood rubbed against his skin. But what was wrong with his hand? It felt as though someone were trying to tear it from his wrist with hot pincers. . . .

It moved! He could move his arm!

Again there came a tremulous whisper. "The voices say I must hurry. They will be coming soon."

Simon's left arm was free. As he tried to flex it, a flaming bolt of pain leaped into his shoulder—but the arm moved. He opened his eyes and goggled dizzily.

A figure hung upside down before him; beyond, the forge cavern itself was inverted as well. The dark shape was sawing at his right arm with something that caught the gleam of one of the torches at the far side of the cavern. Who was it? What was it doing? Simon could not make his crippled thoughts follow each other.

A throbbing, burning pain now crept into his right hand. What was happening?

"You brought me food. I . . . I could not leave you. But the voices say I must hurry!"

It was hard to think with both of his arms on fire, but slowly Simon began to understand. He was hanging head-downward on the wheel. Someone was cutting him free. Someone . . .

". . . Guthwulf . . . ?"

"Soon the others will notice. They will come. Do not move—I cannot see and I fear I will cut you." The blind earl was working furiously.

Simon ground his teeth as the blood rushed back into his arms, trying to choke back another scream. He had not believed such misery was possible.

Free. It will be worth it. I'll be free. . . . He shut his eyes again, his jaws clamped together. His other arm was loose, and now both dangled beside his head. The change of position was excruciating.

He dimly heard Guthwulf wade a few steps, then felt the rhythmic sawing begin on his ankle.

Only a few moments, Simon promised himself, trying desperately to stay silent. He remembered what the chambermaids had told him when, as a child, he had wept over a small hurt. *"It won't mean anything tomorrow. You'll be happy then."*

One ankle came free, and the misery of its release was equaled by the strain now put on the other. Simon turned his head and sank his teeth into his own shoulder. Anything to keep from making noise that might bring Inch or his minions.

"Almost . . ." said Guthwulf hoarsely. There was an instant of slow movement, a sense of slippage, then Simon abruptly fell. Stunned, he found himself drowning in cold water. He thrashed helplessly, but could not feel his limbs. He did not know which direction was up.

Something grasped his hair and yanked. A moment later, another hand curled chokingly around his neck beneath his chin. Simon's mouth came up out of the water, and he gasped in a long breath. For a moment his face was pressed against Guthwulf's lean stomach while his rescuer struggled to get a better grip. Then Simon was dragged forward and dumped onto the rim of the sluice. His hands still did not work properly; he clung in place with his elbows, almost oblivious to the shrieking pain of his joints. He did not want to go back into that water again.

"We must . . ." he heard Guthwulf begin, then the blind man gasped and something smashed against Simon, who slid backward and only barely retained his hold on the edge of the sluice.

"What happens here?!" Inch's voice was a dreadful rumbling growl. "You do not touch my kitchen boy!"

Simon felt hope fade, replaced with sick terror. How could this happen? It was wrong! That he should have come back from death, from nothingness, only to have Inch show up a few moments too soon—how could Fate play such a monstrous trick?

Guthwulf gave a choking cry, then Simon could hear nothing but frenzied splashing. He slowly let himself back down until his feet touched the slippery bottom of the sluice. Putting weight on his wounded legs sent a blinding cloud of black fire through his head and back, but he stood. After his torments he knew he should not even be able to move, but he still retained some of the strength given to him by Maegwin's sacrifice; he felt it smoldering in him like a low-banked fire. He forced himself to remain upright in the slow-moving water until he could see again.

Inch had waded into the sluice, and now stood waist-deep in the center like some beast of the swamps. In the dim torchlight, Simon saw Guthwulf burst up from beneath the water, struggling wildly to escape the overseer's clutches. Inch grabbed the blind man's head and pushed him back under.

"No!" Simon's crippled voice was barely louder than a whisper. If it carried across the short distance, Inch gave him no heed. Still, the silence nagged at Simon in some obscure way. Was he deaf? No, he had heard both Guthwulf and Inch. So why did the chamber seem so quiet?

Guthwulf's arms jerked above the surface, but the rest of him remained submerged in the dark waters.

Simon stumbled toward them, thrashing against the slow current. The great wheel hung unmoving above the waterway. As he saw it, Simon realized why the cavern was strangely quiet: Guthwulf had somehow managed to lift the wheel so he could cut Simon free.

As he neared Inch, the cavern began to grow lighter, as though dawn had somehow found its way down through the rock. Shadowy figures were approaching, a few of them bearing torches. Simon thought they must be soldiers or Inch's henchmen, but when they came a little closer he saw their wide, frightened eyes. The forge workers had been roused, and now came hesitantly forward to see what was causing the uproar.

"Help!" Simon rasped. "Help us! He cannot stop you all!"

The tattered men stopped, as though Simon's words alone might make them traitors, liable to Inch's punishment. They stared, too cowed even to whisper among themselves.

Inch was paying neither Simon nor his slave labor any attention. He had allowed Guthwulf to surface briefly, gasping and spitting, and now was shoving him back into the water again. Simon lifted his hands, still numb with their long binding, and struck at Inch as hard as he could. He might as well have kicked a mountain. Inch turned to look at him. The overseer's scarred face was curiously expressionless, as though the act of violence in which he was engaged took all his attention.

"Kitchen boy," Inch boomed. "You do not run away. You are next." He reached out a huge hand and jerked Simon forward. He released his grip on drowning Guthwulf long enough to pick Simon up with both hands and throw him out of the sluiceway onto the hard stone. All Simon's breath blew out, and another rush of pain coursed through him, fiercer even than the simmering agony of his limbs. For a moment he could not make his battered body respond.

Simon sensed somebody stooping over him. Certain it was Inch come to finish the job, he curled into a ball.

"Here, lad," someone whispered, and tried to help him into a sitting position. Stanhelm, the forge worker who had befriended him, was crouching at his side. The older man seemed barely able to move: one arm curled uselessly in front of his chest, and his neck was bent at an odd angle.

"Help us." Simon struggled to rise. His chest felt dagger-stabbed with each breath.

"Nothing left of me." Even Stanhelm's speech was slurred. "But look to yon wheel, lad."

While Simon fought to make sense of this, one of Inch's helpers strode over.

"Don't touch him," he snarled. "He's Doctor's."

"Shut your mouth," said Stanhelm. The henchman lifted his hand as if to strike, but suddenly several other forge men moved in on either side of him. Some of them held bits of iron scrap, heavy and sharp-edged.

"You heard," one of them growled quietly at Inch's man. "Shut your mouth."

The man looked around, judging his chances. "You'll pay pretty when Doctor hears. He'll be done with that'un in a moment."

"Then go watch," spat another of the forge workers. The men seemed frightened, but somehow they had drawn a line: if they were not yet willing to fight back against the hulking overseer, neither would they stand by and see Inch's crony harm Simon or Stanhelm. The henchman cursed and backed off, then hurried to the safety of his master's vicinity.

"Now, lad," Stanhelm whispered. "Look to yon wheel."

Dizzied by all that was happening, Simon stared at the forge man as he tried to make sense out of his words. Then he turned slowly and saw.

The great wooden paddlewheel had been lifted up so that it hung almost twice a man's height above the watercourse. Inch, who had pursued floundering Guthwulf a short way down the sluice, now stood beneath the wheel.

Stanhelm extended a bent and shaking arm. "There. Them are the works."

Simon struggled to his feet and took a few shaky steps toward the vast framework. The lever which he had seen Inch use was cocked, secured by a rope. Simon slowly tugged the rope free, straining his burning muscles and cramped hands, then grasped the lever itself in slippery, numbed fingers. Inch had pushed Guthwulf under again; he watched his victim's suffering with calm interest. The blind man was floundering away from his tormentor, toward Simon, and now appeared to be beyond the wheel's rim.

Simon said the few words of the Elysia prayer that he could remember, then heaved on the wooden lever. It moved only slightly, but the frame that held the wheel groaned. Inch looked up and around, then gradually turned his monocular gaze toward Simon.

"Kitchen boy! You . . ."

Simon heaved again, this time lifting his feet from the ground so that all his weight hung on the lever. He screamed with the pain of holding on. The frame groaned again, then, with a grating squeal, the lever banged down and the wheel shuddered and dropped into the sluice with a thunderous splash. Inch tried to dive forward out of the way, but disappeared beneath the huge paddles.

For a moment nothing moved in the whole cavern but the wheel, which began, slowly, to revolve. Then, as if the frothing channel gave birth to a monster, Inch burst to the surface howling in anger, water running from his wide-stretched mouth.

"Doctor!" he spluttered, waving his fist. "Can't kill me! Not Doctor Inch!" Simon slumped to the ground. He had done all he could.

Inch took a sloshing step forward, then began to fly. Simon stared, overwhelmed. The world had run entirely mad.

Inch's body lifted out of the water. Only when all of him was in view could Simon see that the foundry-master's broad belt had somehow caught on the fittings of one of the vast paddle blades.

The waterwheel bore Inch upward. The giant was in a frenzy now, bellowing as he was manhandled by something even larger than he was. He twisted at the end of the blade, struggling to free himself, reaching back to smash at the wooden paddle with his fist. As the wheel swung him up toward the top of its rotation, he reached out for the great chains which twined around its axle and climbed up out of sight into the shadows of the cavern ceiling. Inch's huge hands grasped the slippery links. He clung tightly. As they pulled upward past the wheel, he was stretched to his utmost for an instant. Then the buckle of his belt snapped loose and he fell free of the paddle. He clung to the massive chain with both his arms and legs.

Inch was still not coherent, but his echoing roar changed to a note of triumph as the chains carried him slowly upward. He swung away from the wheel so he could drop into the water below, but when he let go, he fell only a little way and then tipped over. He slammed against the chain and dangled, head downward. His foot had slid through the center of one of the wide, oily links and was wedged there.

The overseer thrashed, trying to pull himself up to free his foot. Howling and sputtering, he tore his own leg bloody, but he could not drag his weight high enough. The chain carried him up toward the unseen heights.

His cries grew fainter as he vanished into the shadows overhead, then a horrendous agonized cry echoed down, a rasping gargle with nothing human in it. The wheel lurched in its rotation for a moment and stopped, bouncing a little from side to side as the current pushed at the immobilized paddle blades. Then the wheel began to turn again, forcing the obstruction through the monumental grinding gears that turned Pryrates' tower-top. A drizzle of dark fluids rained down. Bits of something more solid spattered across the waterway.

Moments later, what remained of Inch slowly descended into the light, wrapped around the huge chain like meat on a cooking skewer.

Simon stared idiotically for a moment, then bent, retching, but there was nothing in his stomach to bring up.

Someone was patting his head. "Run, lad, if you got place to go. Red priest'll come quick. His tower stopped turning for a good long time when wheel was up."

Simon squinted against the black flecks that danced before his eyes, fighting to make sense of things. "Stanhelm," he gasped. "Come with us."

"Can't. Nothing left of me." Stanhelm gestured with his chin at his twisted, badly-healed legs. "Me and others'll keep the rest shut up. Say Inch had a bit of accident. King's soldiers won't do us badly—they need us. You run. Didn't belong here."

"Nobody belongs here," Simon gasped. "I'll come back for you."

"Won't be here." Stanhelm turned away. "Go on now."

Simon clambered to his feet and stumbled toward the watercourse, pain arrowing through him with every step. A pair of forge workers had lifted Guthwulf out of the water; the blind man lay on the cavern floor, struggling for air. The men who had saved him stared, but did nothing further to help. They seemed curiously numbed and slow, like fish in a winter pond.

Simon bent and tugged at Guthwulf. The last of the strength Maegwin's sacrifice had lent him was eddying away.

"Guthwulf! Can you get up?"

The earl flailed his hands. "Where is it? God help me, where is it?"

"Where is what? Inch is dead. Get up! Hurry! Where do we go?"

The blind man choked and spat water. "Can't go! Not without . . ." He rolled over and forced himself up onto hands and knees, then began scrabbling along the ground beside the watercourse, pawing as though to dig himself a hole.

"What are you doing?"

"Can't leave it. I'll die. Can't leave it." Suddenly, Guthwulf gave an animal cry of joy. "Here!"

"Aedon's mercy, Guthwulf, Pryrates will be here any moment!"

Guthwulf took a few staggering steps. He lifted something that reflected a yellow strip of torchlight. "I should never have brought it," he babbled. "But I needed something to cut the rope." He gasped in more air. "They all want to take it."

Simon stared at the long blade. Even in the shadowy forge chamber, he knew it. Against all sense, against all likelihood . . . here was the sword they had sought.

"Bright-Nail," he murmured.

The blind man suddenly lifted his free hand. "Where are you?"

Simon took a few painful steps closer. "I'm here. We have to go. How did you get here? How did you come to this place?"

"Help me." Guthwulf put out his arm.

Simon took it. "Where can we go?"

"Toward the water. Where the water goes down." He began to limp along the edge of the channel. The forge workers drifted back to let them pass, watching with nervous interest.

"You're free!" Simon croaked at them. "Free!" They stared at him as though he spoke a foreign tongue.

But how are they free, unless they follow us? The forges are still locked, the doors still barred. We should help them. We should lead them out.

Simon had no strength left. Beside him, Guthwulf was mumbling, shuffling his feet like a lame old man. How could they save anyone? The forge workers would have to make their own way.

The water ran foaming down through a fissure in the cavern wall. As Guthwulf felt his way along the stone, Simon was momentarily certain that the blind earl had lost what few wits he had left—that they had escaped drowning once, but would now be washed down into blackness. But there was a narrow track along the edge of the watercourse, one that Simon could never have found in the shadows. Guthwulf, to whom light was useless, made his way downward, tracking the wall with his fingers as Simon struggled to help him and still remain balanced. They passed out of the last gleams of torchlight and into blackness. The water churned noisily beside them.

The darkness was so complete that Simon had to struggle to remember who he was and what he was doing. Fragments of the things Leleth had showed him floated up from his memory, colors and pictures as swirlingly confused as an oil film on a puddle. A dragon, a king with a book, a frightened man looking for faces in the shadows—what did all these things mean? Simon did not want to think any more. He wanted to sleep. To sleep . . .

The roar of the water was very loud. Simon emerged suddenly from a haze of pain and confusion to find himself leaning sideways at a precarious angle. He grabbed at the cracked wall of the fissure, pulling himself upright. "Guthwulf!"

"They speak so many tongues," the blind man murmured. "Sometimes I think I understand them, but then I am lost again." He sounded very weak. Simon could feel him trembling.

"I can't . . . go much longer." Simon clung to the rough stone. "I have to stop."

"Almost." Guthwulf took another stumbling step along the slender track. Simon forced himself away from the wall, struggling to retain his clutch on the blind man.

They trudged on. Simon felt several openings in the stone wall pass beneath his fingers, but Guthwulf did not turn. When the tunnel began to resonate with loud voices, Simon wondered if he were sliding into Guthwulf's madness, but after a short while he saw a gleam of amber torchglow on the cavern wall and realized that someone was coming down the sluiceway behind them.

"They're after us! I think it's Pryrates." He slipped and released his hold on the blind man to steady himself. When he reached out again, Guthwulf was gone.

A moment of complete panic ended when Simon found the opening to a spur tunnel. Guthwulf was just inside. "Almost," the earl panted. "Almost. The voices—Aedon, they're screaming!—but! I have the sword. Why are they screaming?"

He headed down the tunnel, lurching against the walls. Simon kept his hand against the earl's back as Guthwulf turned several more times. Soon Simon could no longer remember all the turnings. That was hopeful—whoever followed them should find it no easier.

The trudge through blackness seemed to go on and on. Simon felt bits of himself drifting away, until he thought himself a spirit again, an unhomed ghost like the one that had roamed the gray spaces alone.

Alone except for Leleth. And Maegwin.

Thinking of those who had helped him there, he reached down for a last increment of resolve and struggled on.

Walking in a daze, he did not notice that they had stopped until he felt Guthwulf abruptly drop forward; when Simon's hand found him again, the blind man was crawling. When Guthwulf stopped, Simon reached down and felt crumpled cloth strewn across the stone. A nest. Letting his hand travel farther across the floor, Simon touched the earl's quivering leg, then the cold metal of the sword.

"Mine," Guthwulf said reflexively. His voice was muddy with fatigue. "This, too. Safe."

At that moment, Simon no longer cared about the sword, about Pryrates or any soldiers who might be following, or even whether the Storm King and Elias might bring the whole world tumbling down around his ears. Every breath burned, and his arms and legs were a-twitch with agonizing cramps. His head hammered like the bells in Green Angel Tower.

Simon found a place of his own amid the scattered rags, then surrendered to the dark pull.

51

Living in Exile

✷

Jiriki took his hands off the dwarrow-stone.

Eolair did not need to be told. "She is gone." The count stared at Maegwin's pale face, relaxed now as though in sleep. "Gone." He had been preparing himself for this moment, but still felt as though a huge emptiness had opened inside him, a void that would never be filled. He reached out and grasped her hands, which were still warm.

"I am sorry," said Jiriki.

"Are you?" Eolair did not look at him. "What can the short life of a mortal mean to your kind?"

The Sitha did not speak for a moment. "The Zida'ya die, just as mortals do. And when those we held in our hearts have passed from us, we, too, are unhappy."

"Then if you understand," Eolair said, struggling for control, "please leave me alone."

"As you wish." Jiriki stood, a catlike unfolding from his seat on the pallet. He seemed about to say something more, but instead went silently out of the tent.

Eolair stared at Maegwin for a long time. Her hair, damp with sweat, lay in tight curls across her forehead. Her mouth seemed to hint at a smile. It was almost impossible to believe that life had left her.

"Oh, the gods have been cruel masters," he groaned. "Maegwin, what did we do to be so ill-treated?" Tears started in his eyes. He buried his face in her hair, then kissed her cooling cheek. "It has all been a cruel, cruel trick. It has all been for nothing, if you are dead." His body was shaken by sobs. For a while he could only rock back and forth, clutching her hand. The dwarrow-stone was still in her other palm, held against her breast as though to keep it from theft.

"I never knew. I never knew. You foolish woman, why did you tell me nothing? Why did you pretend? Now all is gone. All is lost. . . ."

Jiriki, white hair streaming in the wind, was waiting for him when he emerged. Eolair thought he looked like a storm-spirit—like a harbinger of death.

"What do you want?"

"As I said, Count Eolair, I am very sorry. But there are things I think you should know—things that I discovered in the last moments of the Lady Maegwin's life."

Oh, Brynioch preserve me, he thought wearily. The world was too much for Eolair, and he did not think he could bear any more Sithi riddles.

"I am tired. And we must leave tomorrow for Hernystir."

"That is why I wish to tell you now," Jiriki said patiently.

Eolair stared at him for a moment, then shrugged. "Very well. Speak."

"Are you cold?" Jiriki asked this with the careful solicitousness of one who had learned that although he never suffered from the elements, others did. "We can walk to one of the fires."

"I will survive."

Jiriki nodded slowly. "That piece of stone was given to Maegwin by the Tinukeda'ya, was it not? By those you call *domhaini?*"

"It was a gift from the dwarrows, yes."

"It was much like the great stone you and I visited in Mezutu'a beneath the mountain—the Shard, the Master Witness. When I touched this small stone, I felt much of Maegwin's thought."

Eolair was disturbed by the idea of the immortal being with Maegwin in her last moments, being with her in a way he could not. "And can you not leave those thoughts in peace—let them go with her to her barrow?"

The Sitha hesitated. "It is difficult for me. I do not wish to force things upon you. But there are things I think you should know." Jiriki laid his long fingers against Eolair's arm. "I am not your enemy, Eolair. We are all hostages to the whims of a mad power." He let his hand fall. "I cannot claim to know for certain all that she felt or thought. The ways of the Dream Road—the path that Witnesses such as the dwarrow-stone open—are very confusing these days, very dangerous. You remember what happened when I touched the Shard. I was reluctant even to risk the Other Pathways, but felt that if there was a chance I could help, I should."

From a mortal Eolair would have found this self-serving, but there was something about the Sitha that suggested an almost frightening sincerity. Eolair felt a little of his anger slip away.

"In that muddle of thoughts and feelings," Jiriki continued, "I did understand two things, or at least I am fairly sure that I did. I believe that at the end her madness lifted. I did not know the Maegwin that you knew, so I cannot be certain, but her thoughts seemed clear and unmuddied. She thought of you. I felt that very strongly."

Eolair took a step backward. "She did? You do not say that to soothe me, as a parent might to a child?"

The Sitha's smooth face momentarily showed surprise. "Do you mean tell you something that is not true, deliberately? No, Eolair. That is not our way."

"She thought of me? Poor woman! And I could do nothing for her." The count felt tears returning, but made no attempt to hide them. "This is no favor, Jiriki."

"It was not meant to be. These are things you deserve to know. Now I must ask you a question. There is a young mortal named Seoman who is linked to Josua. Do you know him? More importantly, did Maegwin know him?"

"Seoman?" Eolair was bewildered by the sudden shift of the conversation. He thought for a moment. "There was a young knight named Simon, tall, red-haired—is that who you mean? I think I heard some call him Sir Seoman."

"That is him."

"I doubt very much that Maegwin knew him. She never traveled to Erkynland, and I believe that was where the young man lived before running away to serve Josua. Why?" Eolair shook his head. "I do not understand this."

"Nor do I. And I fear what it might mean. But in those last moments, it seemed Maegwin thought also of young Seoman, almost as though she had seen him or spoken with him." Jiriki frowned. "It is our ill luck that the Dream Road is so murky now, so unrewarding. It was all I could do to glean that much. But something is happening in Asu'a—the Hayholt—and Seoman will be there. I fear for him, Count Eolair. He is . . . important to me."

"But that is where you are going anyway. That is fortunate, I suppose." Eolair did not want to think any more. "I wish you luck finding him."

"And you? Even if Seoman had some significance for Maegwin? Even if she had some message from him, or for him?"

"I am done with that—and so is she. I will take her back to Hernystir to be buried on the mountain beside her father and brother. There is much to do to rebuild our country, and I have been absent too long."

"What help can I give you?" Jiriki asked.

"I want no more help." Eolair spoke more sharply than he had intended. "We mortals are very good at burying our dead."

He turned and walked away, pulling his cloak tight against the flurrying snows.

Isgrimnur limped out onto the deck, cursing his aching body and his halting progress. He did not notice the shadowy figure until he had nearly stumbled into it.

"Greetings, Duke Isgrimnur." Aditu turned and regarded him for a moment. "Is it not chill weather for one of your folk to be out in the wind?"

Isgrimnur hid his startlement by an elaborate readjustment of his gloves. "Perhaps for the southern folk like Tiamak. But my people are Rimmersmen, my lady. We are hardened to the cold."

"Am I your lady?" she said with amusement. "I certainly hold no mortal title. And I cannot believe that Duchess Gutrun would approve of any other meaning."

He grimaced, and was suddenly grateful for the chill wind on his cheeks. "It is just politeness, my la . . ." He tried again. "I find it difficult to call by their first name someone who . . . who . . ."

"Who is older than you are?" She laughed, a not unpleasant sound. "Another problem for which I am to blame! I truly did not come to you mortals to discomfort you."

"Are you really? Older than me?" Isgrimnur was not sure if it was a polite question—but after all, she had brought it up.

"Oh, I should think so . . . although my brother Jiriki and I are both accounted quite young by our folk. We are both children of the Exile, born since Asu'a fell. To some, like my uncle Khendraja'aro, we are barely even real people, and certainly not to be trusted with any responsibility." She laughed again. "Oh, poor Uncle. He has seen so many outrageous things happen in these last days—a mortal brought to Jao é-Tinukai'i, the breaking of the Pact, Zida'ya and humans fighting side by side again. I fear that he will finish his present duty to my mother and Year-Dancing House and then simply let himself die. Sometimes it is the strongest who are the most brittle. Do you not think so?"

Isgrimnur nodded. For once, he understood what the Sitha-woman meant. "I have seen that, yes. Sometimes those who act the strongest are really the most frightened."

Aditu smiled. "You are a very wise mortal, Duke Isgrimnur."

The duke coughed, embarrassed. "I am a very old, very sore mortal." He stared out across the choppy bay. "And tomorrow we make landfall. I am glad we have been able to shelter here in the Kynslagh—I don't think most of us could have taken much more of the storms and the kilpa on the open sea, and God knows I hate boats—but I still don't understand why Elias has not lifted a hand in his own defense."

"He has not yet," Aditu agreed. "Perhaps he feels that his Hayholt walls are defense enough."

"Could be." Isgrimnur voiced the fear that others in the prince's fleet shared. "Or perhaps he is expecting allies—the kind of allies he had at Naglimund."

"That could also be true. Your people and my people have both wondered much about what is intended." She shrugged, a sinuous gesture that might have been part of a ritual dance. "Soon it will not matter. Soon we will learn first hand, as I think you say."

They both fell silent. The wind was not strong, but its breath was bitterly cold. Despite his rugged heritage, Isgrimnur found himself pulling his scarf higher on his neck.

"What happens to your fairy-folk when they get old?" Isgrimnur asked suddenly. "Do they just get wiser? Or do they turn silly and mawkish, as some of ours do?"

"'Old' means something different to us, as you know," Aditu replied. "But the answer is: there are as many different answers as there are Zida'ya, as is no doubt true with mortals. Some grow increasingly remote; they do not speak to anyone, but live entirely in their own thoughts. Others develop fondnesses for things others find unimportant. And some begin to brood on the past, on wrongs and hurts and missed chances.

"The oldest one of all, the one you call the Norn Queen, has grown old in that way. She was known once for her wisdom and beauty, for grace beyond measurement. But something in her was balked and grew bent, and so she curled inward into malice. As the years almost beyond counting rolled past, all that was once admirable became twisted." Aditu had suddenly become serious in a way that Isgrimnur had not seen before. "That is perhaps the greatest sorrow of our folk, that the ruin of the world should be brought about by two who were among the greatest of the Gardenborn."

"Two?" Isgrimnur was trying to reconcile the stories he had heard of the silver-masked queen of ice and darkness with Aditu's description.

"Ineluki . . . the Storm King." She turned back to look across the Kynslagh, as though she could see the old Asu'a looming beyond the darkness. "He was the brightest-burning flame ever kindled in this land. Had the mortals not come—had your own ancestors not come, Duke Isgrimnur—and attacked our great house with iron and fire, he might have led us out of the shadows of exile and back into the light of the living world again. That was his dream. But any great dream can flower into madness." She was silent for a while. "Perhaps we must all learn to live with exile, Isgrimnur. Perhaps we must all learn to live with smaller dreams."

Isgrimnur said nothing. They stood for a while in the wind, silent but not uncomfortably so, before the duke turned and sought the warmth of the cabins.

✲

Duchess Gutrun looked up in alarm when she felt the cold air. "Vorzheva! Are you mad? Bring those children away from the windows."

The Thrithings-woman, one child cradled in each arm, did not move. Beyond the open window stretched Nabban, vast but strangely intimate; the city's famous hills made the houses and streets and buildings seem built almost on top of each other. "There is no harm in air. On the grasslands, we live all our lives out in the open."

"Nonsense," Gutrun said crossly. "I've been there, Vorzheva, don't forget. Those wagons are almost like houses."

"But we only sleep in them. Everything else—eating, singing, loving—we do beneath the sky."

"And your men cut their cheeks with knives, too. Does that mean you're going to do that to poor little Deornoth?" She bristled at the mere thought.

The Thrithings-woman turned and gave her companion an amused look. "You do not think the little one should wear scars?" She gazed at the male infant's sleeping face, then laid a finger along his cheek, pretending to consider it. "Oh, but they are so handsome to see. . . ." She darted a sideward glance, then burst out laughing at the Rimmerswoman's horror. "Gutrun! You think I mean it for true!"

"Don't even say such things. And bring those poor babies away from the window."

"I am showing them the ocean where their father is. But you, Gutrun, you are very angry and unhappy today. Are you not well?"

"What is there to be happy about?" The duchess sank down again onto her chair and picked up her sewing, but only turned the cloth in her hands. "We are at war. People are dying. It is not even a week since we buried little Leleth!"

"Oh, I am sorry," Vorzheva said. "I did not mean to be cruel. You were very close to her."

"She was just a child. She suffered terrible things, may God grant her peace."

"She did not seem to have any pain at the end. That is something. Did you think she would come awake, after all that time?"

"No." The duchess frowned. "But that does not make the sadness less. I hope I am not the one who must tell young Jeremias when he comes back." Her voice dropped. "If he comes back."

Vorzheva looked at the older woman intently. "Poor Gutrun. It is not just Leleth, is it? You are frightened for Isgrimnur also."

"My old fellow will come back well," Gutrun muttered. "He always does." She peered up at Vorzheva, who still stood before the open window, a sweep of ash-gray sky behind her. "But what of you, who feared so much for Josua? Where is *your* worry?" She shook her head. "Saint Skendi protect us, I should not speak of such things. Who knows what ill luck it could bring?"

Vorzheva smiled. "Josua will come back to me. I had a dream."

"What do you mean? Has all that nonsense of Aditu's turned your head?"

"No." The Thrithings-woman looked down at her girl-child; Vorzheva's thick hair fell like a curtain, so that for a moment the faces of both mother and daughter were hidden. "But it was a true dream. I know. Josua came to me and said, 'I have what I always have wanted.' And he was at peace. So I know that he will win, and he will come back to me."

Gutrun opened her mouth to say something, then shut it again. Her face was fearful. Quickly, while Vorzheva still gazed at little Derra, the duchess made the sign of the Tree.

Vorzheva shivered and looked up. "Perhaps you are right, Gutrun. It *is* getting cold. I will shut the windows."

The duchess levered herself up from her chair. "Nonsense. I'll do it. You take those little ones right back and get under the blankets." She paused in front of the window. "Merciful Elysia," she said. "Look."

Vorzheva turned. "What?"

"It's snowing."

"You would think we were stopping for a visit to a local shrine," Sangfugol observed. "That these were boat-loads of pilgrims."

Tiamak was huddled with the harper and Strangyeard on a windy, snow-clad slope east of Swertclif. Below them, landing boats bounced Josua's army across the choppy Kynslagh toward the shore; the prince and the martial arm of his household were at the landing site, overseeing the complex enterprise.

"Where is Elias?" Sangfugol demanded. "Aedon's Bones, his brother is landing an army on his doorstep. Where is the king?"

Strangyeard winced ever so slightly at the oath. "You sound as though you want him to come! We know where the High King is, Sangfugol." He gestured toward the Hayholt, a cluster of spiky shadows almost hidden by whirling snow. "Waiting. But we do not know why."

Tiamak sank deeper into his cloak. His bones felt frozen. He could understand that the prince might not want them underfoot, but surely they could have found a place to stay out of the way that was less exposed to the wind and snow?

At least I have drylander breeches now. But I still do not want to end my days here, in this cold place. Please let me see my Wran again. Let me go to the Wind Festival one more time. Let me drink too much fern beer and play snatch-the-feather. I don't want to die here and be unburned and unremembered.

He shivered and tried to slough off such glum thoughts. "Has the prince sent scouts toward the castle?"

Sangfugol shook his head, pleased to be knowledgeable. "Not in close. I heard him tell Isgrimnur that stealth was useless, since the king must have seen us coming days ago, and heard of it long before that. Now that he has made sure Elias has no soldiers hidden in Erchester—soldiers! No one is there but dogs and rats!—Josua will send outriders ahead when the company moves up to set the siege."

As the harper went on to explain how, in his estimation, the prince should go about deploying his forces, Tiamak saw someone slogging up the hill through the snow.

"Look!" Father Strangyeard pointed. "Who is that?"

"It's young Jeremias." Sangfugol was a little nettled to be interrupted. "Been driven out like the rest of us, I suppose."

"Tiamak!" Jeremias called. "Come with me! Hurry!"

"Goodness!" Strangyeard fluttered his hands. "Perhaps they've found something important!"

Tiamak was already standing. "What is it?"

"Josua says come quickly. The Sitha-woman is sick."

"Shall we come, Tiamak?" Strangyeard asked. "No, I am sure you would rather not be crowded. And what help or comfort could *I* give to one of the Sithi?"

The Wrannaman started down the hill, leaning into the wind. As the snow crunched beneath his feet, he was again grateful for Sangfugol's loan of boots and breeches, although both were too large.

I am in a strange place, he marveled. *A strange time. A marsh man wading through the snows of Erkynland to help one of the Sithi. It must be They Who Watch and Shape who have drunk too much fern beer.*

Aditu had been taken to a makeshift shelter, a cloth cargo cover that had been stretched across the bottom branches of a tree on a rise above the shoreline. Josua and Sludig and a few of the soldiers stood by awkwardly, hunched beneath the low roof. "Sludig found her," the prince said. "I feared she had surprised some of my brother's spies, but there are no marks of violence upon her and Sludig said he saw no signs of struggle. No one heard anything, either, although she was only a hundred paces up from the shore." He frowned worriedly. "It is like Leleth after Geloë died. She is sleeping, but will not wake."

Tiamak stared at the Sitha's face. With her eyes closed she appeared nearly human. "I did little for Leleth," he said, "and I have no idea what effect my herbs would have on one of the immortals. I do not know what I can do for Aditu."

Josua made a gesture of helplessness. "At least see that she is comfortable."

"Did you see anything that might have caused it?" Tiamak asked Sludig.

The Rimmersman shook his head vigorously. "Nothing. I found her as you see her, lying on the ground with no one else nearby."

"I must get back to watch over the unloading. Unless there is something . . ." Josua seemed distracted, as though even this upsetting event was not quite enough to hold his full attention. The prince had always been a bit remote, but in the day since they had made landfall, the Wrannaman had found him to be unusually preoccupied. Still, Tiamak decided, with what lay ahead of them all, the prince had a right to be a little distracted.

"I will stay with her, Prince Josua." He bent and touched the Sitha's cheek. Her skin was cool, but he had no idea whether that was unusual.

"Good. My thanks, Tiamak." Josua hesitated for a moment, then ducked out from beneath the lean-to. Sludig and the other soldiers followed.

Tiamak squatted beside Aditu. She was dressed in mortal clothes, pale breeches and a jacket made of hide, neither of them heavy enough for the weather—but Sithi cared little about weather, Tiamak reminded himself. She was breathing shallowly, and one hand was curled into a fist. Something about the way her long fingers were bent caught Tiamak's interest; he opened her hand. Her grip was surprisingly strong.

Nestled in Aditu's palm was a small round mirror, scarcely larger than an aspen leaf. Its frame was a narrow ring of what appeared to be shiny bone, minutely carved. Tiamak lifted it up and balanced it gently in his own hand. It was heavy for its size and oddly warm.

A tingling, prickling sensation crept through his fingers. He tilted the mirror so that he could see his face reflected; as he moved the angle, he could find no trace of his own features, but only roiling darkness. He brought it closer to his face and felt the tingling grow more pronounced.

Something struck his wrist. The mirror tumbled from his hand onto the damp ground.

"Leave it." Aditu withdrew her hand and let herself fall back, covering her eyes with her long fingers. Her voice was thin and strained. "Do not touch it, Tiamak."

"You are awake!" He looked at the mirror where it lay in the grass, but felt no particular urge to flout Aditu's warning.

"Yes, I am now. Were you sent to take care of me? To heal me?"

"To watch over you, anyway." He moved a little closer to her. "Are you well? Is there anything I can get you?"

"Water. Some snowmelt would be a good thing."

Tiamak scrambled out from under the heavy cloth and scooped up a double handful of snow, then brought it back. "I have no cup or bowl."

"It does not matter." She sat up, not without effort, and received it in her cupped palms. She pushed some of it into her mouth and rubbed the rest on her face. "Where is the mirror?"

Tiamak pointed. Aditu bent and plucked it from the grass; a moment later, her hand was empty again. Tiamak had not seen where she put it. "What happened to you?" he asked. "Do you know?"

"Yes and no." She pressed her hands against her face. "You have learned something of the Witnesses?"

"A little."

"The Dream Road, the place we Zida'ya go when we use such Witnesses as the mirror you held for a moment, has been almost completely barred to us since Amerasu Ship-Born was slain in the Yásira. Because of this, I have not been able to confer with Jiriki or Likimeya my mother or any of my people since I left them. But I have been thinking about the things you and Strangyeard asked me—even though, as I told you, I have no answers myself. I agree that your questions may be very important. I hoped that since we are now closer to my kin, perhaps I could somehow let them know I needed to speak with them."

"And you failed?"

"Worse than that, I may have done something foolish. I underestimated how things have changed on the Dream Road."

Tiamak the Scrollbearer, glutton for knowledge, was starting to settle in for the tale before he remembered his nominal duty. "Is there anything else I can bring to you, Lady Aditu?"

She smiled at something, but did not explain. "No. I am well."

"Then please tell me what you meant about the Dream Road."

"I will tell you what I can—but there is a reason I said 'yes and no' when you asked whether I knew what had happened. I am not quite sure what *did* happen. The Road of Dreams was far more chaotic than I have ever found it, but that I expected. What I did not expect was some terrible *thing* to be waiting for me there."

Tiamak was uneasy. "What do you mean, a 'thing'? A demon? One of our . . . enemies?"

"It was not like that." Aditu's amber eyes narrowed in concentration. "It was . . . a structure, I suppose. Something very powerful and very strange that had been . . . built there. There is no other word. It was something as huge and menacing in its own way as the castle that Josua plans to attack here in the waking world."

"A castle?" Tiamak was mystified.

"Nothing so simple, nothing so much like anything you know. It was a construction of the Art, I believe—an intelligent construction, not like the shadow-things that spontaneously spring into being along the Other Ways. It was a maelstrom of smoke and sparks and black energies—a thing of great power, something that must have been long in the building. I have never seen or heard of anything like it. It caught me up as a whirlwind draws in a leaf, and I only barely won free again." She pressed her temples again. "I was lucky, I think."

"Is it a danger to us? And if it is, is there anything you can think of that might help solve this riddle?" The Wrannaman was reminded of his earlier thought about unfamiliar ground: this was territory about which he knew nothing.

"I find it hard to believe that such an unusual thing would *not* have something to do with Ineluki and the other events of these days." She paused, considering. "One thought I had might mean something, although it means nothing to me. When I first perceived it, I heard or felt the word *'Sumy'asu.'* In the speech of the Gardenborn, that means 'The Fifth House.'"

"The Fifth House?" repeated Tiamak, mystified.

"Yes." Aditu lay back. "It means nothing to me, either. But that was the name I heard when I first encountered this powerful thing."

"I will ask Strangyeard," said Tiamak. "And I suppose we should tell Josua, too. In any case, he will be relieved to hear you are well."

"I am tired. I think I will lie here quietly a while and think," Aditu made a gesture unfamiliar to the Wrannaman. "My thanks to you, Tiamak."

"I did nothing."

"You did what you could." She closed her eyes and leaned back. "The Ancestors may understand all this—but I do not. I am frightened. I would give much to speak to my kin."

Tiamak rose and made his way back out onto the Kynslagh's snowy shores.

The cart rolled to a stop and the wooden wheels fell silent. The Count of Nad Mullach was certain that he would be very tired of the painful sound of their creaking by the time his journey was finished.

"Here we say farewell," he called to Isorn. He left his horse in the care of one of the soldiers and walked through the snow to the young Rimmersman, who dismounted and embraced him.

"Farewell, indeed." Isorn looked to the cart and Maegwin's shrouded body. "I cannot tell you my sorrow. She deserved better. So do you, Eolair."

The count gave him a last handclasp. "In my experience," he said with more than a touch of bitterness, "the gods do not seem to care much what their servants deserve—or at least the rewards they give are too subtle for my understanding." He closed his eyes for a moment. "But enough. She is dead, and all the lamenting in the world, all the railing against Heaven, cannot bring her back. I will bury her with her loved ones and then I will help Inahwen and the rest of my folk do what they can to rebuild."

"And after that?"

Eolair shook his head. "I think that depends on whether the Sithi are able to stop Elias and his ally. I hope you do not think I wish you ill luck if I say that we may keep the caves of the Grianspog prepared in case we need them again."

Isorn smiled thinly. "You would be a fool not to."

"And you will go with them? Your own people will be looking for help, now that Skali is gone."

"I know. But I must find my family, and Josua. My wounds have healed well enough that I can ride, so I will go with the Sithi. The only mortal, I will be. It will get lonely on the way to Erchester."

Eolair smiled. "The way that Jiriki's folk ride, I do not think it will be a long journey." He looked to his ragged troop of men. He knew that they preferred crossing the blizzard-ridden Frostmarch to any more travels with the immortals. "But if things go in such a way that the men of Hernystir are needed, send word to Hernysadharc. I will find a way to come."

"I know."

"Fare you well, Isorn."

Eolair turned and walked back toward his horse. As he mounted, Likimeya and Jiriki, who had been hanging back, rode toward them.

"Men of Hernystir." Likimeya's eyes were bright beneath her black helm. "Know that we honor you. Not since the days of Prince Sinnach have your folk and ours fought side by side. Your fallen lie with our own dead, both here and in your home country. We thank you."

Eolair wanted to ask the stern-faced Sitha what value there had been in the deaths of four score Hernystiri, but this was not the time to recommence such an argument. His men stood, nervous but silent, wanting only to be on their way.

"You freed Hernystir from a great scourge," he replied dutifully. There were observances that had to be made. "We thank you and honor you, as well."

"May you find some peace at the end of your journey, Count Eolair," said Jiriki. His dark blade Indreju hung at his hip. He, too, was armored and looked every bit as much a strange warrior god as his mother. "And when you find it, may it last."

"May Heaven preserve you." Eolair swung up into his saddle, then waved his arm, signaling the carter. The wheels slowly began to turn. Maegwin's shroud rippled in the stiff, sharp wind.

And as for me, he thought, *may the gods from this moment leave me alone. They have broken my people and my life. Let them now turn their attention elsewhere so we can begin to build anew.*

When he looked back, the Rimmersman and the Sithi still stood motionless, outlined by the rising sun. He raised his arm; Isorn returned the gesture of leavetaking.

Eolair looked west across the snows. "Come, my countrymen," he called to his tattered band. "We are going home."

52

Song of the Red Star

✴

"Here, drink." The troll held out a water skin. "I am Binabik of Mintahoq. Ookequk was my master. And you are Padreic. He was speaking of you many times."

"Padreic is dead," the monk gasped. He took a sip of water, letting some run down his chin. He was clearly exhausted. "I am a different man now." He put up a trembling hand to push the bowl away. "By all the gods, old and new, that was a powerful ward on the door. I have not tried to defeat such a thing in two decades. I think it almost killed me." He shook his head. "Better if it had, perhaps."

"Listen to you!" Miriamele cried. "You appear from nowhere, but you are still spouting the same nonsense. What are you doing here?"

Cadrach would not meet her eye. "I followed you."

"Followed me? From where?"

"All the way to Sesuad'ra—then followed after you when you fled." He looked at the dwarrows, who had closed the stone door and now stood in huddled colloquy at the far end of the cavern, peering at the newcomer as though he might be a Norn in disguise. "And there they are—the *domhaini*." He grimaced. "I thought I felt their clever hand in that door-ward, but I couldn't be sure. I had never encountered one of theirs so new-minted."

Miriamele would not be distracted. "What are you doing here, Cadrach? And who is following you?"

The monk turned his gaze down to his own hands, which were clenched in the folds of his tattered robe. "I fear I have brought the Norns down on you and your allies. The white monsters have been following me almost since I descended through the catacombs. I have been hard-pressed to stay ahead of them."

"So you led them to us?" Miriamele still did not know what she felt about seeing Cadrach again. Since he had deserted her and the rest of the company in the Lake Thrithing, she had done her best to put him out of her mind. She still felt shame about the argument over Tiamak's parchment.

"They will never take me again," the monk said fervently. "If I had not been able to force the door, I would have thrown myself down the Tan'ja Stairs before falling into their hands."

"But now the Norns are outside, you say, and the cavern has only one door for leaving," Binabik pointed out. "This is not much good you have done for yourself, Cadrach or Padreic or whichever name you now wear." Binabik had heard many stories about the monk from her and from Simon. Miriamele could see his respect for what the Hernystirman had once been warring with distrust of anyone who could betray one of the troll's friends. He shrugged. "Chukku's Stones! Enough of talking. Let us be seeing to important things now." He rose and padded across the cavern toward the dwarrows.

"Why did you run away, Cadrach? I told you I was sorry about Tiamak's parchment . . . about all that."

The monk finally turned his eyes to hers. His gaze was curiously flat. "Ah, but you were right. Miriamele. I am a thief and a liar and a drunkard, and that is the truth of many years. That I did a few honest deeds does not change that."

"Why do you always say such things?" she demanded. "Why are you so determined to see the worst in yourself?"

The look on his face became something almost accusatory. "And why are you determined to see the best in me, Miriamele? You imagine that you know all about the world, but you are only a young girl, after all is said and done. There are limits to your imagination, to your understanding of how black a place the world truly is."

Stung, Miriamele turned away and busied herself looking in the saddlebag. He had only been back a few moments, and already she wanted to strangle him—yet she was searching diligently for something to feed him.

I suppose I might as well keep him healthy until I decide to kill him.

Cadrach was leaning against the cavern wall, head thrown back and eyes closed, overcome with exhaustion. She took the opportunity to look him over. He had grown even thinner since he had abandoned her on the grasslands; his face sagged, the skin deprived of its padding of flesh. Even in the pink light of the dwarrows' stones, the monk looked gray.

Binabik returned. "Our safeness may not last long. Yis-fidri is telling me the door-wards will never be as strong now that they have once been forced. Not all the Norns are being masters like your monkish friend, but some of them might be. And even if none of them can open it, it is likely that Pryrates will not be prevented."

"Masters? What do you mean?"

"Lore-masters. Learned in the Art—what folk who are not Scrollbearers sometimes are calling magic."

"Cadrach said he couldn't do magic any more."

Binabik shook his head in bemusement. "Miriamele, once Padreic of Crann-hyr was perhaps the most adept user of the Art in all of Osten Ard—although that was in part being so because other Scrollbearers, even the greatest, Mor-genes, chose not to risk its deepest currents. It is seeming that Cadrach has not lost his skills, either—how else did he force the dwarrows' door?"

"It all happened so fast. I suppose I hadn't thought about it." She felt a brief upsurge of hope. Perhaps fate had brought the monk here for a reason.

"I did what I had to," Cadrach said abruptly. Miriamele, who had thought he was asleep, jumped. "The White Foxes would have caught me in a few more moments. But I am not what I was, troll. Working the Art takes discipline and hard work . . . and peace. I have been a stranger to those things for many years." He let his head fall back against the cavern wall. "Now the well is dry. I have no more to give. Nothing."

Miriamele was determined to have answers. "You still have not explained why you followed me, Cadrach."

The monk opened his eyes. "Because there is nothing else. The world holds nothing else for me." He hesitated, then looked at Binabik angrily, as though the little man was eavesdropping on something he had no right to hear. The words came slowly. "Because . . . because you were kind to me, Miriamele. I had forgotten what it feels like. I could not go with you to face the questions, the looks, the disgust of all those others—Duke Isgrimnur and the rest—but neither could I let go of that small touch of life . . . life as it once was. *I could not let go.*" He reached up with both hands and rubbed at the skin of his face, then laughed wretchedly. "I suppose I am not so much a dead man as I thought."

"Was it you who followed Simon and me in the forest?"

"Yes, and through Stanshire and Falshire as well. It was only when this one joined you," he indicated Binabik, "that I had to fall farther behind. That wolf has a keen nose."

"You were not much help when the Fire Dancers caught us."

Cadrach only shuddered.

"So you followed us all the way here?"

"I lost your track after Hasu Vale. It was pure luck I found you again. If you had not come to Saint Sutrin's, where I had found a sheltering roof courtesy of that madman Domitis, I think we would never have met again." He laughed again, harshly. "Think on that, my lady. *Your* luck went bad when you entered God's house."

"Enough of this." Miriamele was losing patience with Cadrach's self-loathing. "You are here. What do we do now?"

Before the monk could offer any suggestion, Yis-fidri came shambling up. The dwarrow looked mournfully at Cadrach, then turned to Miriamele and Binabik. "This man is right in one thing. Someone else is now outside this cavern. The Hikeda'ya have come."

There was a silence as the words sank in.

"Are you certain?" Miriamele held little hope they were wrong, but the thought of being hemmed in the cavern with the corpse-faced Norns outside was dreadful. The White Foxes had been fearsome enough as characters in her uncle's tales of the fall of Naglimund, but on the hillside above Hasu Vale she had seen them for herself. She never wished to see them again—but she doubted she would be so lucky. Her panic, which had abated with the surprise of

Cadrach's entrance, now returned. She was suddenly short of breath. "You're certain it's the Norns, not just some of my father's soldiers?"

"This man we did not expect," said Yis-fidri, "but we know what things move through our tunnels. The door does for now hold them out, but soon that may change."

"If these are your tunnels, you must know a way we can escape!"

The dwarrow said nothing.

"Perhaps we will after all be using those stones we gathered," Binabik said. "We should give thought to trying an escape before more of our enemies arrive." He turned to Yis-fidri. "Can you tell how many are being outside?"

The dwarrow fluted what sounded like a question to his wife. After listening to her reply, he turned. "The number of one hand's fingers, perhaps. But that will not be true for long."

"That few?" Miriamele sat up. "We should fight! If your folk will help us, surely we can defeat so few of them and escape!"

Yis-fidri shrank back, plainly uneasy. "I have told you. We are not strong. We do not fight."

"Listen to what the Tinukeda'ya say." Cadrach's voice was cold. "Not that it will make much difference soon, but I for one prefer to await the end here rather than be spitted on one of the White Foxes' spears."

"But the end is certain if we wait. At least if we try to escape, there is a chance."

"There is no chance either way," the monk replied. "At least here, we can make our peace and die by our own choice when it suits us."

"I cannot believe what a coward you are!" cried Miriamele. "You heard Yis-fidri! A half-dozen Norns at the most! That is not the end of the world. We have a chance!"

Cadrach turned to her. Sorrow and disgust and barely-concealed fury warred in his expression. "It is not the Norns that I fear," he said finally. "But it *is* the end of the world."

Miriamele caught something unusual in his tone, something beyond even his ordinary pessimism. "What are you talking about, Cadrach?"

"The end of the world," he repeated. He took a deep breath. "Lady, if you and I and this troll could somehow slaughter every Norn in the Hayholt—every Norn in Stormspike, too—still it would make no difference. It is too late to do anything. It was *always* too late. The world, the green fields of Osten Ard, the people of its lands . . . they are doomed. And I have known it since before I met you." He looked up imploringly. "Of course I am bitter, Miriamele. Of course I am almost mad. Because I know beyond doubt that there is no hope."

Simon woke from cloudy, chaotic dreams into utter darkness. Someone was moaning nearby. Every part of his body throbbed, and he could barely move his wrists and ankles. For long moments he was certain he had been captured and was bound in some black cell, but at last he remembered where he was.

"Guthwulf?" he croaked. The moans continued, unchanging.

Simon rolled over onto his stomach and crawled toward the sounds. When his swollen fingers encountered something, he stopped and explored clumsily until he found the earl's shaggy-bearded face. The blind man was blazing with fever.

"Earl Guthwulf. It's Simon. You saved me from the wheel."

"Their home is burning!" Guthwulf sounded terrified. "They cannot run—there are strangers with black iron at the gates!"

"Do you have water here? Is there food?"

He felt the blind man struggle to sit up. "Who's there? You can't take it! It sings for me. For me!" Guthwulf grabbed at something, and Simon felt a cold metal edge drag painfully along his forearm. He swore and lifted the arm to his mouth, tasting blood.

Bright-Nail. It seemed impossibly strange. *This fever-ridden blind man has Bright-Nail.*

For a moment he considered simply pulling it from Guthwulf's weakened grasp. After all, how could this madman's need outweigh that of entire nations? But even more troubling than the idea of stealing the sword from a sick man who had saved his life was the fact that Simon was lost without light somewhere in the tunnels beneath the Hayholt. Unless for some incomprehensible reason the blind earl kept a torch or lantern, without Guthwulf's knowledge of this maze he might wander forever in the shadows. What good would Bright-Nail be then?

"Guthwulf, do you have a torch? Flint and steel?"

The earl was murmuring again. Nothing Simon could understand seemed useful. He turned away and began to search the cavern by touch, wincing and groaning at the pain each movement caused.

Guthwulf's nesting place was small, scarcely a dozen paces wide—if Simon had been on his feet and pacing—in either direction. He felt what seemed to be moss growing in the cracks of the stone beneath him. He broke some off and smelled it: it did not seem to be the same plant that had sustained him in Asu'a's ruined halls. He put a little on his tongue, then spat it out again. It tasted even more foul than the other. Still, his stomach hurt so much that he knew he would be trying it again soon.

Except for the various rags strewn about the uneven stone floor, Guthwulf seemed to have few possessions. Simon found a knife with half its blade snapped off. When he reached to tuck it into his belt, he suddenly realized he did not have one, nor any other clothes.

Naked and lost in dark. Nothing left of Simon but Simon.

He had been splashed by the dragon's blood, but afterward, he had still been Simon. He had seen Jao é-Tinukai'i, had fought in a great battle, had been kissed by a princess—but he was still the same kitchen boy, more or less.

Now everything had been taken from him, but he still had what he had begun with.

Simon laughed, a dry, hoarse sound. There was a sort of freedom in having so little. If he lived to the next hour, it would be a triumph. He had escaped the wheel. What more could anyone do to him?

He put the broken knife against the wall so he could find it again, then continued his search. He encountered several objects he could see no purpose for, oddly shaped stones that felt too intricate to be natural, bits of broken pottery and splintered wood, even the skeletons of some small animals, but it was only as he reached the far side of the cavern that he found something truly useful.

His numb, stiffened fingers touched something wet. He snatched his hand away, then slowly reached out again. It was a stone bowl half full of water. On the ground beside it, as wonderful as any miracle from the Book of Aedon, was what felt like a lump of stale bread.

Simon had the bread to his mouth before he remembered Guthwulf. He hesitated, his stomach raging, then tore a piece loose and dipped it in the water and put it in his mouth. He ate two more small pieces the same way, then held the bowl carefully in his aching, trembling hand and crawled to where Guthwulf lay. Simon dipped his fingers in the water and let some dribble into the earl's mouth; he heard the blind man swallow thirstily. Next he took a morsel of bread and moistened it, then fed it to his ward. Guthwulf did not close his mouth, and seemed unable to chew or swallow it. After a moment, Simon retrieved it and ate it himself. He felt exhaustion creeping over him.

"Later," he told Guthwulf. "Later you will eat. You will be well again, and so will I. Then we will leave here."

Then I will take Bright-Nail to the tower. That is what I took back my life to do.

"The witchwood is in flames, the garden is burning. . . ." The earl squirmed and twisted. Simon moved the bowl away, terrified it might be spilled. Guthwulf groaned. *"Ruakha, ruakha Asu'a!"*

Even from a short distance away, Simon could feel his raging heat.

The man lay on the ground, his face pressed against the stone. His clothes and skin were so dirty it was hard to see him. "That's everything, master. I swear it!"

"Get up." Pryrates kicked him in the ribs, but not hard enough to break anything. "I can scarcely understand you."

He rose to his haunches, whiskered mouth quivering in fear. "That's all, master. They run away. Down watercourse."

"I know that, fool."

The alchemist had given his soldiers no directions since they had returned from their fruitless search, and now they stood uneasily. Inch's remains had been removed from the chains that turned Pryrates' tower top; they lay in an

untidy heap beside the sluice. It was obvious that most of the guardsmen wished
they had been allowed to cover such of the overseer as had been recovered, but
since they had received no order from Pryrates, they were studiously looking
anywhere else.

"And you do not know who these people were?"

"'Twas the blind man, master. Some have seen him, but none ever catched
him. He takes things sometime."

A blind man living in the caverns. Pryrates smiled. He had a reasonably
good idea who that might be. "And the other? One of the foundrymen being
punished, I take it?"

"That it was, master. But Inch called him something else."

"Something else? What?"

The man paused, his face a mask of terror. "Can't remember," he whispered.

Pryrates leaned down until his hairless face was only a handbreadth from the
man's nose. "I can *make* you remember."

The forge man froze like a serpent-tranced frog. A small whimper escaped
his throat. "I be trying, master," he squeaked, then: "'Kitchen Boy'! Doctor
Inch called him 'Kitchen Boy'!"

Pryrates straightened up. The man slumped, his chest heaving.

"A kitchen boy," the priest mused. "Could it be?" Suddenly he laughed, a
rasping scrape of sound. "Perfect. Of course it would be." He turned to the
soldiers. "There is nothing else for us to do here. And the king has need of us."

Inch's henchman stared at the alchemist's back. His lips moved as he worked
up the nerve to speak. "Master?"

Pryrates turned slowly. "What?"

"Now . . . now that Doctor Inch be dead . . . well, who do you wish to . . .
to take charge here? Here in king's forge?"

The priest looked sourly at the grizzled, ash-blackened man. "Sort that out
yourselves." He gestured at the waiting soldiers, marking out half of the score
of men. "You lot will stay here. Do not bother protecting Inch's cronies—I
should not have left him in charge of this place so long. I want you only to make
sure that wheel stays in the water. Too many important things are driven by it
to risk a second occurrence of a folly like this. Remember: if that wheel stops
turning again, I will make you very, very sorry."

The designated guards took up positions along the edge of the watercourse;
the rest of the soldiers filed out of the forge. Pryrates' stopped in the doorway
to look back. Under the impassive gaze of the guardsmen, Inch's chief henchman was quickly being surrounded by a tightening ring of grim forge workers.
Pryrates laughed quietly and let the door crunch shut.

Josua sat up, startled. The wind was howling fiercely, and the shape in the
tent's door loomed giant-size.

"Who is there?"

Isgrimnur, who had been nodding during the long silence, snorted in surprise and fumbled for Kvalnir's hilt.

"I cannot stand it any longer." Sir Camaris swayed in the doorway like a tree in a strong wind. "God save me, God save me . . . I hear it even in my waking hours now. In the darkness it is all there is."

"What are you talking about?" Josua rose and went to the tent flap. "You are not well, Camaris. Come, sit down here beside the fire. This is no weather to be out wandering."

Camaris shook off his hand. "I must go. It is time. I can hear the song so clearly. It is time."

"Time for what? Go where? Isgrimnur, come help me."

The duke struggled to his feet, wheezing at the pain of stiff muscles and still-tender ribs. He took Camaris by the arm and found the muscles tight as wet knots.

He is terrified! By the Ransomer, what has done this to him?

"Come, sit." Josua urged him toward a stool. "Tell us what ails you."

The old knight abruptly pulled away and took a few staggering steps backward out into the snow. Thorn's long scabbard bumped against his leg. "They are calling, each to each. They *need*. The blade will go where it will go. It is time."

Josua followed him out onto the hillside. Isgrimnur, puzzled and worried, limped after, pulling his cloak tight against the wind. The Kynslagh lay below, a dark expanse beyond the blanketing white. "I cannot understand you, Camaris," the prince called over the wind. "What is it the time for?"

"Look!" The old man threw up an arm, pointing into the murk of storm clouds. "Do you not see?"

Isgrimnur, like Josua, looked upward to the sky. A dull spot of ember-red burned there. "The Conqueror Star?" he asked.

"They feel it. It is time." Camaris took another retreating step, wobbling as though he might at any moment tumble backward down the hill. "God grant me strength, I can resist it no longer."

Josua caught the duke's eye, silently asking his help. Isgrimnur walked forward and he and the prince again grasped Camaris' arms. "Come in from the cold," Josua begged.

Sir Camaris yanked himself free—his strength never ceased to astonish Isgrimnur—and for a moment his hand strayed to Thorn's silver-wrapped hilt.

"Camaris!" Isgrimnur was shocked. "You would draw blade against us!? Your friends!?"

The old man stared at him for a moment, his eyes curiously unfocused. Then, slowly, the duke saw his tension ease. "God help me, it is the sword. It sings to me. It knows where it wants to go. Inside." He gestured limply toward the dark bulk of the Hayholt.

"And we will take you there—and the sword, too." Josua was calm. "But there is the simple matter of breaching the walls that we must deal with first."

"There are other ways," said Camaris, but his wild energy had faded. He allowed himself to be led into Josua's tent.

Camaris downed the cup that Josua had filled for him in a single gulp, then drained a second serving. This worried Isgrimnur almost as much as the strange things the old knight had said: Camaris was renowned as a moderate man. Still, by his haunted look, the old knight now seemed to welcome anything that might bring him relief from the agony Thorn caused him.

Camaris would say nothing more, although Josua pressed him for information in what Isgrimnur thought was an exceedingly solicitous yet awkward manner. Ever since the night on the ship, Isgrimnur had seen Josua's attitude to the old knight change, as though even the old man's presence made him dreadfully uncomfortable. Isgrimnur wondered, not for the first time, what terrible thing Camaris had told him.

After a while, the prince gave up and returned to the discussion interrupted by the knight's appearance.

"We know now that there are indeed forces still within the castle walls, Isgrimnur—considerable forces of men, mercenaries as well as the Erkynguard." Josua frowned. "My brother shows more patience than I would have suspected. Not even a sally while we were landing."

"Patience . . . or perhaps Elias has some worse fate planned for us." The duke tugged at his beard. "For that matter, Josua, we do not even know that your brother is still alive. Erchester is all but deserted, and the few people we have managed to find there wouldn't know if Fingil himself had come back from the grave and was sitting on the Dragonbone Chair."

"Perhaps." The prince sounded doubtful. "But I cannot rid myself of the feeling that I would know if Elias were dead. In any case, even if Pryrates rules him, or has even taken the throne himself, we are still faced with the Storm King and the Scroll League's angry star."

Isgrimnur nodded. "Someone is in there, right enough. Someone knows our plans. And they took your father's sword."

Josua's mood darkened. "That was a blow. Still, when I saw that Swertclif was unguarded, I had little hope left we would find it there."

"We always knew we would have to go inside the Hayholt to get that fairysword, Sorrow." Isgrimnur pulled at his beard again and made a noise of disgust. War was difficult enough without these magical complexities. "I suppose we can go in for two as easily as one."

"If it is even inside the walls," Josua pointed out. "That hole in the side of my father's cairn looked a hurried thing to me—not what I would have expected from Pryrates or my brother, who need hide their works from no one."

"But who else would do it?"

"We still do not know what happened to my niece and Simon and the troll."

Isgrimnur grunted. "I doubt that Miriamele or young Simon would have taken the blade and just disappeared. Where are they? They both know what Bright-Nail is worth to us."

Camaris' sudden outcry made the duke flinch.

"*All* the swords! God's Nails, I can feel them, all three! They sing to each other—and to me." He sighed. "Oh, Josua, how I wish I could silence them!"

The prince turned. "Can you truly feel Bright-Nail?"

The old knight nodded. "It is a voice. I cannot explain, but I hear it—and so does Thorn."

"But do you know where it is?"

Camaris shook his head. "No. It—the part that calls to me—is not in a place. But they wish to come together inside the walls. There is need. The time is growing short."

Josua grimaced. "It sounds as though Binabik and the others were right. Hours are marching by: if the swords are any use to us, we must find them and discover that use soon."

Madness, thought Isgrimnur. *Our lives, our land, ruled by madness out of old tales. What would Prester John have thought, who worked so hard to drive the fairy-folk out of his kingdom and to push the shadows away?*

"We cannot fly over those walls, Josua," he pointed out. "We've won a victory in Nabban and sailed north in such a short time that folk will talk of it for years. But we cannot fly an army into the Hayholt like a flock of starlings."

"There are other ways . . ." Camaris whispered. Josua looked at him sharply, but before he could discover whether this was more singing-sword maundering or something useful, another shape appeared in the tent doorway, accompanied by a blast of chill air and a few snowflakes.

"Your pardon, Prince Josua." It was Sludig, in mail and helm. He nodded to Isgrimnur. "My lord."

"What is it?"

"We were riding the far side of Swertclif, as you asked. Searching."

"And you found something?" Josua stood, his face carefully expressionless.

"Not found something. Heard something." Sludig was obviously exhausted, as though he had ridden far and fast. "Horns in the far distance. From the north."

"From the north? How far away?"

"It is hard to say, Prince Josua." Sludig spread his hands, as though he could find the words by touch. "They were not like any horns I have heard. But they were very faint."

"Thank you, Sludig. Are there sentries on Swertclif?"

"On the near side, Highness, out of sight of the castle."

"I do not care if anyone sees them," the prince said. "I am more concerned about who might be coming down on us from the north. If you and your men are tired, ask Hotvig to take some of his grasslanders and ride down the far side toward the skirts of Aldheorte. Tell them to return immediately if they see something coming."

"I will, Prince Josua." Sludig went out.

Josua turned to Isgrimnur. "What do you think? Is the Storm King going to play the same hand he produced at Naglimund?"

"Perhaps. But you had castle walls, there. Here we have nothing before us but open land, and nothing behind us but the Kynslagh."

"Yes, but we have several thousand men here, too. And no innocents to worry over. If my brother's chief ally thinks he will find us as easy a nut to crack as before, he will be disappointed."

Isgrimnur stared at the fierce-eyed prince, then at Camaris, who held his head in his hands and stared at the tabletop.

Is Josua right? Or are we the last raveled end of John's empire, waiting for a final pull before it falls into threads?

"I suppose we'd better go and talk to a few of the captains." The duke got up and held his hands close to the brazier, trying to dispel some of the chill. "Better we tell them something's coming than they hear it by rumor." He made a noise of disgust. "Looks like we don't get much sleep."

Miriamele stared at Cadrach. She, who had heard him lie so many times, could not free herself of the horrifying certainty that this time he was telling the truth.

Or the truth as he sees it, anyway, she tried to comfort herself.

She looked at Binabik, who had narrowed his eyes in concentration, then returned to Cadrach's bleak face. "Doomed? Do you mean some danger beside that we already face?"

He met her stare. "Doomed beyond hope. And I have played no little part in it."

"What is it you are saying?" demanded Binabik.

The dwarrow Yis-fidri seemed to want little to do with this volatile and frightening conversation; he hesitated, fingers flexing.

"What I am saying, troll, is that all the scurrying about in caverns that we do here matters little. Whether we escape the White Foxes outside, whether your Prince Josua knocks down the walls, whether God Himself sends lightning down from Heaven to blast Elias to ash . . . none of it matters."

Miriamele felt her guts twist at the certainty in his voice. "Tell us what you mean."

The monk's hard face crumpled. "Aedon's mercy! Everything you have thought about me is true, Miriamele. Everything." A tear ran down his cheek. "God help me—although He has no reason to—I have done such foul things. . . ."

"Curse you, Cadrach, will you explain!"

As if this outburst had somehow pushed Yis-fidri past what he could bear, the dwarrow got up and moved away rapidly, going to join his whispering fellows on the other side of the cavern.

Cadrach wiped at his eyes and nose with his dirty sleeve. "I told you of my capture by Pryrates," he said to Miriamele.

"You did." And she in turn had told Binabik and others on Sesuad'ra, so she felt no need to retell the tale now.

"I told you that after I had betrayed the booksellers, Pryrates threw me out, thinking I was dead."

She nodded.

"That was not true—or at least it did not happen then." He took a breath. "He set me to spy on Morgenes and others I had known from my days as a Scrollbearer."

"And you did it?"

"If you think I hesitated, my lady, you do not know how fiercely a drunkard and coward can cling to his life—or how terrified of Pryrates' anger I was. You see, I *knew* him. I knew that the injuries he had done to my flesh in his tower were nothing set against what he could do if he truly wished to make me suffer."

"So you spied for him?! Spied on Morgenes?"

Cadrach shook his head. "I tried—by the Tree, how I tried! But Morgenes was no fool. He knew that I had fallen into dreadful straits, and that the red priest knew both of us from elder days. He gave me food and a night's lodging, but he was suspicious. He made sure there was nothing for me to find in either his chambers or his discourse that would be useful to someone like Pryrates." Cadrach shook his head. "If anything, my efforts only taught Morgenes that he had less time than he had hoped."

"So you failed?" Miriamele could not see where this was leading, but a deep dread was spreading through her.

"Yes. And I was terrified. When I went back to Hjeldin's Tower, Pryrates was angry. But he did not kill me, or do something worse, as I feared. Instead he asked me more questions about *Du Svardenvyrd*. I think by then he had already been touched by the Storm King and was beginning to bargain with him." Cadrach's look turned contemptuous. "As if any mortal could successfully bargain with one such as that! I doubt Pryrates has even yet realized what has come through the door he opened."

"We will talk of what things Pryrates has done later," said Binabik. "You are telling us now of things *you* have been doing."

The monk stared at him. "They are less separate than you think," he said at last. "Pryrates asked me many questions, but for one who had read *Du Svardenvyrd*—indeed, for one who knew Nisses' book so well that the memory of its words still haunts my thoughts daily—it was easy enough to see the direction behind his questions. Somehow he had been reached by the Storm King, and now Pryrates was eager to know about the three Great Swords."

"So Pryrates *does* know about the swords." Miriamele took a shaky breath. "I suppose he was the one who took Bright-Nail from the mound, then."

Cadrach held up his hand. "Pryrates dealt with me harshly for failing with Morgenes. Then he had me send a message to old Jarnauga in the north, asking for information about the Storm King. I suspect that the alchemist was looking for ways to defend himself against his new and very dangerous friend. He made me write it as he watched, then sent it himself with a sparrow he had filched from Morgenes. He let me go free again. He was sure I would not run away when he could so easily locate me."

"But you did run away," Miriamele said. "You told me so."

Cadrach nodded. "Eventually. But not then. My fear was too great. But at the same time I knew that Jarnauga would not respond. The Rimmersman and Morgenes were closer than Pryrates realized, and I had no doubt the doctor would have already written to tell Jarnauga about my unexpected visit. In any case, Jarnauga had been living in Stormspike's shadow for years and would not have opened his mind to anyone he did not know for certain to be untouched by Ineluki's long hand. So I knew that the imposture Pryrates had forced me to commit was useless, and that when the red priest discovered it, he would have no use left for me. My only worth was as one who had read Nisses' book and as a former Scrollbearer. But I had answered all of his questions about the book, and now he would discover that the other Scrollbearers had stopped trusting me years before. . . ." He broke off, struggling again with powerful emotions.

"Go on." Miriamele spoke a little more gently than before. Whatever he had done, he seemed to be genuinely suffering.

"I was in terror—stark terror. I knew that I had only a short time before Jarnauga's inevitably unhelpful reply. I wanted desperately to flee, but Pryrates would know the moment I left Erchester, and by his use of the Art would also know where I had gone. He had marked me in that high chamber of his tower. He would find me *anywhere*." Cadrach paused, struggling for self-control. "So I thought, and thought, and thought—but not, to my shame, of a way to escape Pryrates or thwart his plans. No, in my besottedness and my fear, I thought only of ways that I could please this horrid master, that I could convince him to grant me my pathetic life." He quivered, unable for a moment to continue.

"I had thought much about his questions," the monk finally resumed. "Especially about the three Great Swords. It was clear that they had some marvelous power, and equally clear that they meant something to the Storm King. What was not clear to anyone but me, I thought, was that the sword Minneyar, one of the three, was in fact Bright-Nail, the sword that had been buried with King John."

Miriamele gaped. "You knew?"

"Anyone who read the books of history that I had would have suspected it," Cadrach replied. "I am convinced Morgenes knew, but hid it in his own book about your grandfather so that only those who knew what to look for would find it, thus keeping it from common knowledge." He had regained a little composure. "In any case, I read the same sources Doctor Morgenes did, and had long held that opinion, although I had never shared it with anyone. And the more I thought about the marketplace gossip that claimed Elias would not handle his father's sword, that he had, against custom, buried it with his father, the more I felt sure that my guess was not just likely, but true.

"So I decided that if what *Du Svardenvyrd* seemed to suggest was *also* true—that the only weapons the Storm King feared were the Three Great Swords—what more pleasing gift could I bring to Pryrates than one of the swords? All three were thought to be lost. Surely if I produced one, I reasoned, Pryrates would find me useful."

Miriamele gaped at the monk in disgust and astonishment. "You . . . you traitor! Was it you who took the sword from my grandfather's barrow? And gave it to Pryrates!? God curse you if it was, Cadrach!"

"You may call curses on me all you like—and you will, with ample reason. But wait until you hear the whole tale."

I was right to try and drown him in Emettin Bay. I wish he had never been fished out. She waved angrily for him to continue.

"I went to Swertclif, of course," he said. "But the burial ground was closely guarded by the king's soldiers. It seemed that Elias meant to keep his father's grave safe. I waited two nights for a moment when I might get at the barrow, but no such moment came. And then Pryrates sent for me." He winced, remembering. "He had learned well from his studies. His voice was in my head—you cannot imagine how that feels! He forced me to come to him, come slinking like a disobedient child. . . ."

"Cadrach, there are Norns who are waiting outside this cavern," Binabik interrupted. "So far your story is telling us little that will help us."

The monk stared at him coldly. "Nothing will help us. That is what I am trying to explain—but I will not force you to listen."

"You will tell us everything," Miriamele declared, her rage fighting free. "We are fighting for our lives. Speak!"

"Pryrates called me to him again. As I knew he would, he told me that Jarnauga had sent only information of no worth, that it was clear the old Rimmersman did not trust me. 'You are useless to me, Padreic ec-Crannhyr,' the alchemist said.

"'What if I can tell you something that is *very* useful?' I asked. No, that is not the right word. I begged. 'If you will leave me my life, I will serve you faithfully. There are still things I know that might help you!' He laughed when I said that—laughed!—and told me that if I could give him even a single piece of information that was truly valuable, he would indeed spare me. So I told him that I knew the Great Swords were important to him, that all were lost, but that I knew where one of them was.

"'Do you think to tell me Sorrow is with the Norns of Stormspike?' he said scornfully. 'I know that already,' I shook my head—in fact, I had not known that myself, but I could guess how he had discovered it. 'That Thorn did not sink into the ocean with Camaris?' he continued.

"I hurriedly told him what I had discovered—that Minneyar and Bright-Nail were one and the same, that one of the Great Swords was even now buried less than a league from where we sat. In my eagerness to gain his favor, I even told him that I had tried to get it myself to bring it to him."

Miriamele scowled. "To think that I saw you as a friend, Cadrach—if you had even an idea of what this could mean to us all . . . !"

The monk ignored her, grimly following her order to finish the tale. "And when I was done . . . he laughed again. 'Oh, this is very sad, Padreic,' he hooted. 'Is this your great work of spycraft? Is this what you think will save you? I have known what Bright-Nail truly is since before you first entered this tower. And if you *had* moved it from its resting place, I would have plucked out your eyes and tongue with my own fingers. It will lie there on old John's rotting breast until the proper time. When the hour is right, the sword will come. All the swords will come.'"

Miriamele's thoughts suddenly went staggering. "The sword will come? He . . . he has known all along? Pryrates . . . wanted it left there?" She turned helplessly to Binabik, but the little man seemed just as amazed as she. "I don't understand. Elysia, Mother of Mercy, what are you telling us, Cadrach?"

"Pryrates knows all." A certain black satisfaction crept into the monk's voice. "He knew what Bright-Nail was, where it lay—and he saw no need to disturb it. I feel sure that everything your uncle and these . . ." he gestured toward Binabik, "latter-day Scrollbearers plan is already known to him. He is content to see it happen."

"But how can that be? How can Pryrates not fear the one power that can undo his master?" Miriamele was still astonished. "Binabik, what does this mean?"

The troll had lost his composure. He held up his trembling fingers, begging a moment to think. "It is much for considering. Perhaps Pryrates has a plan of some treachery against the Storm King. Perhaps he thinks to keep Ineluki's power restrained with the threatening of the swords' power." He turned to Cadrach. "He was saying 'the swords will come'? Those words?"

The monk nodded. "He knows. He *wants* Bright-Nail and the others brought here."

"But no sense in this am I seeing," said Binabik anxiously. "Why not then bring Prester John's blade in and hide it away until the time he waits is arrived?"

Cadrach shrugged. "Who can know? Pryrates has walked strange paths and learned hidden things."

As her shock lessened a little, Miriamele felt her rage at the monk return, battening on her fear. "How can you sit there so smugly? If you did *not* betray me and all I care about, it was not for lack of trying. I suppose he set you free then to spy some more? Is that why you arranged to accompany me from Naglimund? I thought you were just using me to further your own greed . . ." as she thought about it, despair seized her, "but . . . but you were working for Pryrates!" She turned away, unable to look at Cadrach any longer.

"No, my lady!" Amazingly, he sounded hurt and upset. "No, he did not release me—and I did not serve him again."

"If you expect me to believe that," she said with cold hatred, "you are truly mad."

"Is there more to your tale?" The tentative respect Binabik had earlier shown the monk had curdled into sour practicality. "Because we are still trapped here, still in danger that is most dreadful—although there is little else we can do, I am thinking, until the Norns prove they can force the dwarrows' door."

"There is a little more. No, Miriamele, Pryrates did not release me. As I told you, he had proved that I was worthless to him. I told you this much of the truth when we were in the landing boat—I was not even worth more tortures. Someone clubbed me, then I was tossed away like offal dumped behind a rich man's house. Except I was not left for dead out in the Kynswood as I told you before. Rather, I was dumped into a pit in the catacombs that run beneath Hjeldin's Tower . . . and that is where I awoke. In darkness."

He paused, as though this memory was even more painful than the ghastly things he had already told. Miriamele said nothing. She was furious and yet empty. If Cadrach's tale was true, then perhaps there really was no hope. If Pryrates was as powerful as this—if he had a stratagem to constrain even the Storm King to his will—then should Miriamele somehow find her father and convince him to end the war, the red priest would still find some method to have things his own way.

No hope. It was strange to think about. As unlikely as their chances had seemed, Josua and his allies had always had the slim hope of the swords to cling to. If that was gone . . . Miriamele felt dizzy. It seemed she had walked through a familiar door only to find a chasm yawning just beyond the threshold.

"I was alive, but wounded and dazed. I was in a terrible place—no living man should have to visit the black, black places beneath Pryrates' tower. And to go upward would mean escaping *through* the tower, past Pryrates himself. I could not imagine succeeding at that. The only tiny scrap of luck I had was that he likely thought me dead. So I went . . . another way. Down."

Cadrach had to pause for a long moment and wipe the sweat from his pale face. It was not particularly warm in the cavern.

"When we were in the Wran," he suddenly said to Miriamele, "I could not force myself to go down into the ghants' nest. That was because it was too much like . . . like going into the tunnels below Hjeldin's Tower."

"You were here before?" She stared at him, her attention unwillingly held. "Here beneath the castle?"

"Yes, but not in the places you have been, the places I have followed you." He wiped at his forehead again. "Ransomer preserve me, I wish my escape had been through the parts of this vast maze you saw! The way I came was far worse." He tried to find words but gave up. "Far, far worse."

"Worse? Why?"

"No." Cadrach shook his head. "I will not tell you. There are many ways in and out of here, and not all of them are . . . normal. I will speak no further on it, and if you could glimpse even a piece of what I saw, you would thank me for not telling you." He shivered. "But it felt like years that I was below the ground, and I saw and heard and felt things . . . things that . . ." He stopped, shaking his head again.

"Don't tell us, then. I don't believe you, in any case. How could you escape unnoticed? You said that Pryrates could find you, could summon you."

"I had—I still have—some little smatterings of the Art left to me. I was able to draw a . . . a sort of fog over me. I have kept it since. That is why you were not summoned to Sesuad'ra as Tiamak and the others were. They could not find us."

"But why didn't that shield you from Pryrates before, when he summoned you—when you couldn't run away and had to spy and sneak for him like the worst sort of traitor in the world?" She was disgusted with herself for being drawn back into a discussion. She was even angrier that she had ever wasted her trust and concern on someone who could do what the monk had done. She had defended him to the world, but it was she who had been the fool. He was a traitor through and through.

"Because he thinks I am dead!" Cadrach almost shouted. "If he knew I lived, he would find me soon enough. He would blow my poor shielding fog away like a strong wind and I would be naked and helpless. By all the gods old and new, Miriamele, why do you think I was so determined to get off Aspitis' ship? As I slowly came to realize that he was one of Pryrates' servitors I could think of nothing but that he might tell his master I still lived. Aedon save us, why do you think when we met him again on the Lakelands I begged you to kill him?" He mopped more sweat from his face. "I can only guess that Pryrates did not recognize the name 'Cadrach,' although I had used it before. But I have used many names—even that red-robed demon could not know them all."

"So you were making your way to freedom through the tunnels," Binabik prompted. "*Kikkasut!* This place is indeed like our Mintahoq cave-city—most that is important happens beneath the rock."

"Freedom?" Cadrach almost sneered. "How could anyone be free who lived with the knowledge I did? Yes, I finally made my way up from the very deepest depths; I think I was quite mad by then. I headed north, away from Pryrates and the Hayholt, although at the time I had no idea of where I would go. I wound up finally in Naglimund, thinking that I would be safest in a place sworn to oppose Elias and his chief counselor. But it was soon apparent that Naglimund, too, would be attacked and thrown down, so I took up the Lady Vorzheva's offer to accompany Miriamele south."

"You said you were not free because of the knowledge you had," said Miriamele slowly. "But you did not share that knowledge with anyone. That is perhaps the most wretched deed of all you have done, Cadrach. Fear of Pryrates might make you do terrible things, but to be free of him and still say nothing—while the rest of us have pondered and struggled and suffered and died . . ." She shook her head, trying to make her words reflect the chilly contempt she felt. "That I cannot forgive."

He looked at her without flinching. "Now you truly know me, Princess Miriamele."

A long silence fell, broken only by the faint singsong of the dwarrows muttering among themselves. Binabik was the one who ended it. "We have talked enough of these things. And I need time for pondering on what Cadrach has said. But something there is that is clear: Josua and the others search for Bright-Nail, and they have Thorn already. They plan to bring them here if they can, but they are knowing nothing of what this one says of Pryrates. If we were having no other reason for surviving and escaping, we now have one that is large." He made a close-fisted gesture. "But what is outside our door is the first thing that will prevent us. How will we be making an escape?"

"Or have we already lost the chance listening to Brother Cadrach's tale of treachery?" Miriamele took a breath. "There were a handful of Norns before—how long before there is an army?"

Binabik looked at Cadrach, but the monk had lowered his face into his hands.

"We must make an attempt at escaping. If only one of us can survive to bear the tale, then still it will be a victory."

"And even if all is lost," Miriamele said, "there will be some Norns who will not be around to see it. I would settle for even a victory like that." She meant it, she realized—and with that realization, a part of her seemed to turn cold and lifeless.

53

Hammer of Pain

"Prince Jiriki. At last we meet." Josua bowed, then extended his left hand; the manacle he wore as a remembrance of imprisonment was a shadow on his wrist. The Sitha made a strangely-jointed bow of his own, then reached out his hand to clasp Josua's. Isgrimnur could not help marveling at such a strange scene.

"Prince Josua." The new-risen sun turned both Jiriki's white hair and the snow faintly golden. "Young Seoman told me much about you. Is he here?"

Josua frowned. "He is not, to my regret. There is much to say—much to tell you, and much we hope you can tell us." He looked up at the looming walls of the Hayholt, falsely welcoming in the dawn light. "I am not sure which of us should say to the other: 'Welcome home.'"

The Sitha smiled coldly. "This is not our home any more, Prince Josua."

"And I am not sure it is mine, either. But come, it is foolish to stand in the snow. Will you come and break your fast with us?"

Jiriki shook his head. "Thanks to you for your courtesy, but I think not yet." He looked back at the milling Sithi, who had fanned out across the hillside and were rapidly setting up camp, the first colorful tents blooming like snowflowers. "My mother Likimeya, I think, speaks with my sister; I, too, would like to spend a short time with Aditu. If you would be kind enough to come to my mother's tent by the time the sun is above the treeline, bringing those of your household you deem necessary, we will begin to talk. There is, as you said, much to tell."

The Sitha gave a sort of graceful salute, bowed again, then turned and moved away across the snow.

"That's cheek," Isgrimnur muttered. "Making you come to them."

"It *was* their castle first." Josua laughed quietly. "Even if they do not wish to reclaim it."

Isgrimnur grunted. "As long as they help us put the bastards out, I suppose we can go to their house for a visit." He squinted. "Now who's that?"

A solitary rider had crested the hilltop behind the Sithi encampment. He was taller and more solidly-built than the immortals, but he slumped wearily in the saddle.

"God be praised!" Isgrimnur breathed, then shouted for joy. "Isorn! *Hah,* Isorn!" He waved his arms. The rider looked up, then spurred his horse down the hill.

"Ah, Father," he said after he had dismounted and received a backbreaking embrace from the duke, "I cannot tell you how good it is to see you. This brave Hernystiri mount," he patted his gray horse, "kept up with the Sithi almost all the way from Naglimund. They ride so fast! But we fell behind at the end."

"No matter, no matter," Isgrimnur chortled. "I only wish your mother was not behind in Nabban. Bless you, son, it makes my heart glad to see you."

"Indeed," said Josua. "You are a happy sight. What of Eolair? What of Hernystir? Jiriki said but little."

Isorn made a weary bow. "Everything I can tell you I will, Josua. Is there something to eat here? And somewhat to drink, too?"

"Come." Isgrimnur put his arm about his tall son. "Let your old father lean on you for just a few minutes—I was smashed beneath my horse in Nabban, did you know? But I am not finished yet! We will all break fast together. Aedon has blessed us this morning."

The afternoon had turned dark and the wind had risen, clawing at the walls of the tent. Silent Sithi had put out shining globes of light which were now warming into full brightness like small suns.

Duke Isgrimnur was beginning to feel restless. His back was giving him no peace, and he had been sitting propped on cushions—and how *did* a war party of Sithi manage to carry cushions, he could not help wondering—so long that he did not think he could rise to his feet without help. Even the presence of Isorn sitting nearby was not enough to keep his thoughts from turning sour.

The Sithi had destroyed Skali and his men—that was the first news Isorn had given him. The immortals had brought the Thane of Kaldskryke's head back to Hernysadharc in a sack. Isgrimnur knew he should rejoice that the man who had stolen his dukedom and brought so much unhappiness to Rimmersgard and Hernystir was dead, but he felt mostly his own age and infirmity, as well as a certain angry shame. The revenge he had sworn so loudly at Naglimund had been taken by someone else. If he regained Elvritshalla, it would be because the Sithi had earned it for him. That did not sit well. The unhappy duke was having trouble paying attention to the things that seemed to fascinate Josua and the immortals.

"All this talk of Houses and Stars is very well," he said crossly, "but what exactly are we going to *do?*" He folded his arms across his broad chest. *Someone* had to hasten things along. These Sithi were like an army of golden-eyed Josuas, seemingly content to talk and ponder until The Day of Weighing-Out—but the reality of the Hayholt would not go away. "We have siege engines, if you know what those are. We can knock the gates down eventually, or maybe even burrow under the walls. But the Hayholt was built stronger than anything in Osten Ard, and it won't happen fast. In the meantime, your Conqueror Star is right overhead."

Likimeya, who Isgrimnur supposed was the queen of the Sithi, though no one seemed to call her by that title, turned her faintly serpentine gaze on him. It was all the Rimmersman could do to meet her stare.

This one chills my blood. And I thought Aditu was strange.

"You are correct, mortal. If our understanding, and the lore of your Scroll-bearers is true, we have very little time." She turned to Josua. "We brought down Naglimund's walls in days—but that did not stop the Hikeda'ya from doing what they wished, or at least we do not think it did. We cannot afford to make that mistake here."

Prince Josua lowered his head, thinking. "But what else can we do? As Isgrimnur pointed out to me last night, we cannot fly over the walls."

"There are other ways into the castle you call the Hayholt," said Likimeya. The tall, black-haired Sitha beside her nodded. "We could not send an army in through those passages, nor would we wish to, but we can, and should, send a sufficient force. Ineluki has a hand in all this; he or your mortal enemies have doubtless made sure that these ways are guarded. But if we keep our foes' attention on what happens out here before the walls, we might succeed in getting a small troop inside."

"What 'other ways' do you mean?" Josua asked, frowning.

"Tunnels," said Camaris suddenly. "Ways in and out. John knew them. There is one on the cliffside below the Sea Gate." The old man had a slightly wild look, as though any moment he might begin raving again.

Likimeya nodded. The strings of polished stones braided into her hair clinked. "Just so—although I think we can choose a better entrance than the caves along the cliff. Do not forget, Prince Josua: Asu'a was ours once, and many of us were alive when it was still the great house of the Zida'ya. We know its hidden paths."

"The sword." Camaris rubbed his hand back and forth across Thorn's pommel. "It wants to go inside. It has been . . ." He broke off and fell silent. He had been strangely subdued through the entire day, but Isgrimnur could not help noticing that he seemed less daunted by the Sithi than any of the other mortals assembled in Likimeya's tent. Even Tiamak and Strangyeard, students of old lore, sat wide-eyed and silent except when forced into stammering speech.

Outside, the wind grew louder.

"That is another, and perhaps the most important, mystery," said Jiriki. "Your brother has one Great Sword, Prince Josua. This mortal knight, Sir Camaris, has another. Where is the third?"

Josua shook his head. "As I told you, it is gone from my father's barrow."

"And how will they serve us if we bring them all together?" Jiriki finished. "Still, it seems that Camaris must be one of those we send beneath the walls. We cannot afford the chance that we would gain the other two swords and have this black blade left outside." He steepled his long fingers. "I regret more than ever the fact that Eolair and I could not find the Tinukeda'ya of Mezutu'a—those you call dwarrows. They know more of sword-lore and forging than anyone, and they certainly made Minneyar. There is doubtless much they could have told us."

"Send in Camaris? Through some underground caverns?" Josua seemed more than dubious—there was an edge almost of despair to his words. "We face perhaps the greatest battle that Osten Ard has seen—certainly, it seems, one of the most important—and you say that we should send away our greatest warrior?" As Josua looked over to the old knight, Isgrimnur saw again the discomfort he had sensed earlier. What had Camaris told him?

"But surely you can see the sense of what my brother says, Prince Josua." Aditu had been almost deferentially silent through the afternoon. "If all the signs, if all the dreams and rumors and whispered lore are true, then it is the Great Swords that will thwart Ineluki's plan, not men—or even immortals—battling before the gates of the castle. That has been the wisdom by which you have planned everything."

"So because Thorn belongs to Camaris, he and he alone can take it inside? And not through the gate or over the walls with the army behind him, but like a sneak thief?"

"Thorn does not belong to me." Camaris seemed to be struggling just to speak slowly and rationally. "Methinks it is the other way around. Merciful Aedon, let me go, Josua. I doubt I can wait much longer before this thing drives me mad."

Josua looked at the old knight for a long time; something unspoken passed between them. "Perhaps there is sense in what you all say," the prince admitted at last. "But it will be a hard thing to lose Camaris. . . ." He paused. "To lose him for the coming battle. It will be hard on the men. They feel invincible when they follow him."

"Perhaps they should not know that he is gone," Aditu said.

Josua turned, startled. "What? How would we hide such a thing?"

"I think my sister has spoken wisely," said Jiriki. "If we hope to have a chance to send Sir Camaris into your brother's castle—and he will not be alone, Josua; there will be Zida'ya with him who know those places—but we do not wish to blow a trumpet and announce that we have done that, we must make it seem that Camaris is still here, even once the full siege has begun."

"The siege? But if our only hope is the swords and our true stroke is this company that we send in through your secret ways, what point is there in throwing away the lives of others?" the prince demanded angrily. "Are you saying we should sacrifice men in a bloody siege that we already know is starting too late to achieve success?"

Likimeya leaned forward. "We must sacrifice men and Zida'ya both." Isgrimnur caught a flicker in her amber stare that seemed almost like regret, or pain, but he dismissed it. He could not believe one so stern, so alien, felt anything but cool necessity. "Otherwise, we announce to our enemies that we have other hopes. We shout to them that we are waiting for some other stratagem to take effect."

"Why?" Isgrimnur could see that Josua was truly agonized. "Any sensible war-leader knows it is better practice to starve out a foe than to waste men's lives on thick stone walls."

"You are camped beside the Zida'ya. Those who are even now watching from behind those stone walls have made compact with Ineluki. Some may even be our kin, the Hikeda'ya. They will know that the Dawn Children see the red star in the sky overhead. The Conqueror Star, as you call it, tells us that we have only a few days at most, that whatever your mortal sorcerer plans to do on Ineluki's behalf must happen soon. If we appear to ignore that fact, we will fool no one. We must launch the siege immediately, and your people and ours must fight as though we have no other hope. And who knows? Perhaps we do not. Not all tales end happily, Prince Josua. We Gardenborn know that all too well."

Josua turned to Isgrimnur as if for support. "So we send our finest warrior, who is also our greatest inspiration, down into the earth. And we throw away the lives of our fighting men on a siege that we know cannot succeed. Duke Isgrimnur, have I gone mad? Is this all that is left to us?"

The Rimmersman shrugged helplessly. It was dreadful to watch Josua's honest torment. "What the Sithi-folk say makes sense. I'm sorry, Josua. It galls me, too."

The prince lifted his hand in a gesture of resignation. "Then I will do as you all say. Since my brother took the throne, I have been faced with horror after horror. It seems, as one of my teachers once told me, that God shapes us with a hammer of pain on an anvil of duty. I cannot imagine what shape we will be when He is finished." He sat back, waving to the others to continue. "Make certain only that Camaris is well-defended. He carries the one thing we have that we did not already possess when my brother and the Storm King broke Naglimund—and we have lost much else since then."

Isgrimnur looked at the old knight. Camaris was lost in thought, his eyes fixed on nothing visible, his lips moving.

The king was lurking in the passageway above the entrance to the forge. The soldiers, already nervous, startled when they saw the cloaked shape lurch forward out of the shadows. One of them even went so far as to draw his sword before Pryrates barked at him to put up; Elias, though, seemed oblivious to what would normally be a fatal error for a young guardsman.

"Pryrates," the king rasped. "I have been searching and searching. Where is my cupbearer? My throat is so dry. . . ."

"I will help you, Majesty." The priest turned his coal-black stare on the gawking soldiers, who quickly shifted their eyes sideways or down to their own chests. "The captain will take these men back to the walls. We are finished here." He waved them away with a flapping red sleeve.

When the noise of their footfalls grew faint in the corridor, Pryrates gently took the king's arm so that Elias could lean on him. The king's staring face was parchment-white, and he licked at his lips constantly.

"Did you say you had seen my cupbearer?"

"I will take care of you, Majesty. I think we will not see Hengfisk again."

"Has he . . . has he run away to . . . them?" Elias cocked his head as though treachery might have a sound. "They are all around the walls. You must know. I can feel them. My brother, and those bright-eyed creatures . . ." He pawed at his mouth. "You said they would be destroyed, Pryrates. You said all that resisted me would be destroyed."

"And so they will be, my king." The priest induced Elias to walk down the hallway, heading him through the maze of corridors toward the residences. They passed an open window where snow blew in and melted into puddles on the floor: outside, Green Angel Tower loomed against the swirling storm clouds. "You yourself will destroy them and usher in the Golden Age."

"And then the pain will go away," Elias wheezed. "I would not hate Josua so if he had not brought me such pain. If he had not stolen my daughter, too. He *is* my brother, after all . . ." the king clenched his teeth as though something had stabbed him, ". . . because family is blood. . . ."

"And blood is powerful magic," Pryrates said, half to himself. "I know, my king. But they turned against you. That is why I found you new friends— powerful friends."

"But you cannot replace a family," said Elias, a little sadly. He winced. "Ah, God, Pryrates, I am burning up. Where is that cupbearer?"

"A little farther, Majesty. Just a little farther."

"I can feel it, you know," Elias panted. He lay back on his mattress, which had rotted through in so many places that the horsehair stuck up all around him. A stained goblet, now empty, was clutched in his hand.

Pryrates paused in the doorway. "Feel what, Majesty?"

"The star, the red star." Elias pointed at the cobwebbed ceiling. "It is hanging overhead, staring at me like an eye. I hear the singing all the time."

"Singing?"

"The song it sings—or that the sword sings to the star. I cannot tell which." His hand fell and crawled like a white spider onto the long sheath. "It sings in my head. 'It is time, it is time,' the voices say, over and over." He laughed, a cracked, jagged sound. "Sometimes I awaken to find myself walking through the castle and I cannot remember how I came there. But I hear the song, and I feel the star burning into me whether it is day or night. It has a fiery tail, like a dragon. . . ." He paused. "I will go out to them."

"What!?" Pryrates returned to the king's bedside.

"I will go out to them—Josua and the others. Perhaps that is the time the sword means. Time to show them that I am different than they know. That their resistance is foolish." He brought his hands to his face. "They are . . . they are my blood, Pryrates."

"Your Highness, I . . ." The priest seemed momentarily unsure. "They are your enemies, Elias. They wish you only harm."

The king's laugh was almost a sob. "And you mean me only well, is that right? That is why every night since you took me to that hill I have suffered dreams that God would not visit upon sinners in Hell? That is why my body aches and burns until I can barely keep from screaming out loud?"

Pryrates frowned. "You have suffered, my king, but you know the reason. The hour is coming fast. Do not let your torments be for nothing."

Elias waved his hand. "Go away. I do not wish to talk any more. I will do what I think best. I am the master of this castle—of this land." He gestured violently. "Go away, damn you. I am in pain."

The alchemist bowed. "I pray you can rest, Majesty. I will go."

Pryrates left the king staring up into the shadows of the ceiling.

After standing silently in the corridor for long moments, the priest returned to the closed door and passed his hand over hinges and frame and door latch several times, mouth working soundlessly. When he had finished he nodded, then went briskly up the corridor, bootheels clicking.

Tiamak and Strangyeard walked close together as they made their way down the hillside. Snow was no longer falling, but it was piled high on the ground; they made slow progress despite the comparatively short distance between the Sithi camp and the fires of the prince's army.

"I am going to turn to ice in a moment," Tiamak said through clicking teeth. "How do your people live like this?"

Strangyeard was shivering, too. "This is a terrible cold by any measurement. And we have thick walls to hide behind, and fires—the lucky ones do, that is." He stumbled and went down on his knees in a thick drift. Tiamak helped him back up. The bottom half of the priest's robe was covered in clinging snow. "I am tempted to curse," Strangyeard said, and laughed unmerrily; his breath hovered as a cloud.

"Come, lean on me," urged Tiamak. The priest's disarranged hair and sad face tugged at his heart. "One day you must come see the Wran. It is not all pleasant, but it is never cold."

"Just n-now that sounds very n-n-nice."

The storm clouds had been borne away by the wind, and a salting of dim stars glimmered. Tiamak stared upward. "It looks so close."

Strangyeard followed his gaze, stumbled for a moment, then righted himself. The Conqueror Star seemed to hang almost directly over the Hayholt, a burning hole in the darkness with a tail like a smear of blood. "It is close," the priest said. "I can feel it. Plesinnen wrote that such stars spout bad air over the world. Until n-now, I was never sure whether I believed him—but if there was ever a star that dripped p-pestilence, that is it." He hugged himself. "I sometimes wonder if these are the final days, Tiamak."

The marsh man did not want to think about that. "All the stars here are a little strange. I keep thinking that I recognize the Otter or the Sand Beetle, but they seem stretched and changed."

Strangyeard squinted his single eye. "The stars look odd to me, too." He shivered and lowered his gaze to the knee-high snow. "I am frightened, Tiamak."

They staggered on toward the camp, side by side.

"The worst of it," said Tiamak, holding his hands close to the fire, "is that we have no better answer to our questions than we did when Morgenes sent the first sparrow to Jarnauga. The Storm King's plan is a complete puzzle, and so is the one scheme we have to stop him." The small tent was filling with smoke despite the opening near the top, but at this moment Tiamak did not care; as a matter of fact, it felt somewhat homelike.

"That is not completely true." Strangyeard coughed and waved away some of the smoke. "We know a few things—that Minneyar is Bright-Nail, for one."

"But that Hernystirman had to come tell us that," Tiamak said crossly. "You need not feel bad, Strangyeard. From what I heard, you did much to help them locate Thorn. But I have done little to warrant being a member of the League of the Scroll."

"You are too hard on yourself," the archivist said. "You brought the page of Nisses' book that helped bring back Camaris."

"Have you looked into his eyes, Strangyeard? Was that anything other than a curse to him? And now it seems he is losing those wits all over again. We should have left him alone."

The priest stood. "Forgive me, but this smoke . . ." He pulled the tent flap open and fanned vigorously. A blast of cold air pushed much of the smoke back inside and set them both to shivering anew. "I'm sorry," he said miserably.

Tiamak gestured for him to sit down. "It is a little better. My eyes are not stinging so." He sighed. "And this talk of a Fifth House—did you see how worried the Sithi looked? They may have said they did not know what it meant, but I believe they knew something. They did not like it." The Wrannaman shrugged his thin shoulders; he had already learned from Aditu that what the Sithi did not want to discuss remained a secret. They were polite, but could be stubbornly vague when they wished. "It matters little, I suppose. The siege begins tomorrow morning, and Camaris and the others will try to make their way inside, and whatever They Who Watch and Shape decide will happen . . . it will happen."

Strangyeard stared at him, his unpatched eye red-rimmed and watery. "You do not seem to get much solace from your Wran gods, Tiamak."

"They are mine," the marsh man said. "I doubt yours would bring me any greater peace." He looked up, and was startled by the archivist's pained expression. "Oh! I am sorry, Strangyeard. I did not mean to be insulting. I am just angry . . . and frightened, like you."

Please, let me not lose my friends. Then I would have nothing at all!

"Of course," the archivist said, then sighed. "And I am no different than you.

I cannot escape the feeling that something important is just before me—some simple thing, as you mentioned. I can feel its presence, but I cannot grasp it." He stared at his knit hands. "It is infuriating. There is some obvious mistake we have made, or will make, I am certain. It is as though I looked back and forth through a well-known book, looking for a page I have often read, but now I cannot find it." He sighed again. "It is no wonder we are neither of us very happy, my friend."

Tiamak warmed briefly at the word 'friend,' but then felt his sorrow return. "Something else is worrying me, too," he told the archivist.

"What is that?" Strangyeard leaned over and tugged the door flap open for a moment, then let it fall shut.

"I have realized that I must go down into the deeps with Camaris and the others."

"What? Blessed Elysia, Tiamak, what do you mean? You are no warrior."

"Exactly. And neither Camaris nor any of the Sithi have read Morgenes' book, or studied the archives at Naglimund, as you did, nor shared the wisdom of Jarnauga and Dinivan and Valada Geloë. But someone who has must go— otherwise, what if the people of this raiding party secure the swords and cannot guess how to use them? We will not get a second chance."

"Oh! Well, then . . . mercy! I suppose I should go, since I have had the most time to study these things of anyone remaining."

"Yes, Strangyeard, my good drylander friend, of all of us, you know the most about the swords. But you have only one eye, and the sight in that one is not good. And you are many years older than I am, and not so used to climbing and getting in and out of tight places. If Binabik of Yiqanuc were here, I would let him go and wish him well, since he is more learned in these things than I, and at least as capable in other ways—not to mention the least likely to get stuck in a narrow tunnel of any of us." Tiamak wagged his head sadly. "But Binabik is gone, and the wisewoman Geloë is gone, and all the old Scrollbearers are dead. So it falls to me, I think. You have taught me much in a short time, Strangyeard." He let out another heartfelt sigh. "I have evil dreams still about being in the ghant nest, of the pictures I saw in my head, of hearing my own voice clacking away in the dark. But I fear this may be worse."

After a long silence, the priest went and pawed through his belongings, coming back at last with a skin bag. "Here. This is a strong drink made from berries. Jarnauga brought it with him to Naglimund: he said it was a shield against the cold." He laughed nervously. "Cold we certainly have, don't we? Try a little." He passed Tiamak the sack.

The liquor was sweet and fiery. Tiamak swallowed, then took another swig. He passed the bag back to Strangyeard. "It is good, but strange-tasting. I am used to sour fern beer. Try some."

"Oh, I think it too potent for me," the priest stammered. "I wanted you . . . ."

"A little will help to keep out the chill—perhaps it will even help set free that elusive thought you spoke of."

Strangyeard hesitated, then lifted the sack to his lips. He took a tiny sip and worked it around his mouth, then took a little more. Tiamak was pleased to see he did not choke. "It's . . . hot," the priest said, wonderingly.

"It feels that way, does it not?" The Wrannaman sank back against one of the priest's saddlebags. "Have another, then pass it to me again. I will need more than a few swallows before I work up the nerve to tell Josua what I have decided."

The sack was mostly empty. Tiamak had heard the sentries change outside, and knew it must be near midnight. "I should go," he said. He listened to the words as he formed them, and was proud of how well-articulated they were. "I should go because I need to tell Prince Josua what I will do."

"What you will do, yes." Strangyeard was holding the wineskin by its cord strap and watching it swing back and forth. "That is good."

"So in a moment I will get up," Tiamak pointed out.

"I wish Geloë were here."

"Geloë? Here?" Tiamak frowned. "Drinking this Rimmersgard liquor?"

"No. Well, I suppose." Strangyeard reached up his free hand and set the skin swinging again. "Here to talk to us. She was a wise one. Frightening, a little— didn't she frighten you? Those eyes . . ." His forehead creased as he remembered Geloë's alarming stare. "But solid. Reassuring."

"Of course. We miss her." He got unsteadily to his feet. "Terrible thing."

"Why did those . . . things do it?" the priest wondered.

"Kill Geloë?"

"No, Camaris." Strangyeard carefully placed the skin on top of a blanket. "Why did they kill Camaris? No." He smiled, abashed. "I mean . . . why did they *try* to kill Camaris? Just him. Doesn't make sense."

"They wanted to take the sword. Thorn."

"Ah," Strangyeard replied. "Ah. P'raps so."

Tiamak struggled out through the tent flap. The chilly air was like a blow. He looked over at the priest, who had followed him out. "Where are you going?"

"With you," Strangyeard said matter-of-factly. "Tell Josua I'm going, too. Down in the tunnels."

"No, you're not." Tiamak was firm. "That would be a bad idea. I told you before."

"I'll come with you anyway. To talk with him." The priest's teeth were already chattering. "Can't let you walk in the cold by yourself." He staggered a few steps, then stopped, peering upward, and frowned broadly. "Look at that red star. Mad thing. Causing all this trouble. The stars should leave us alone." He raised his fist. "We're not afraid!" he called to the distant spot of light. "Not afraid!"

"You drank too much," Tiamak said as he took the archivist's elbow.

Strangyeard bobbed his head. "I might have done."

Josua watched the archivist and the Wrannaman lurch out of his tent and into the night, then turned to Isgrimnur. "I would never have believed it."

"A drunken priest?" The duke yawned despite the tension that roiled his stomach. "That's nothing strange." There was a dull pressure behind his eyes. It was past the middle of the night, and the next day promised to be something dreadful. He needed sleep.

"Perhaps, but a drunken Strangyeard?" Josua shook his head slowly. "I think that Tiamak is right about going, though—and he is, from what you've told me, a useful fellow."

"Wiry as a hound," Isgrimnur said. "Brave, too, and so well-spoken I'm still not used to it. I'll confess, I didn't think marsh men were that learned. Camaris could do far worse than to take Tiamak, even with his limp. That was a cockindrill bit him there, did you know?"

Josua's mind was on other things. "So that is two of our mortal contingent." He rubbed his temple. "I cannot think any more—it feels like three days have passed since this morning's sun rose. We will begin the siege tomorrow, and tomorrow evening will be time enough to make the final decision on who shall go." He rose and looked almost with tenderness at Camaris, who was stretched full-length on a pallet at the far side of the tent, moving fitfully in his sleep. The squire Jeremias, who seemed to attach himself to troubled folk, was curled up on a pile of blankets near the old knight's feet.

"Can you find your way back?" Josua asked the duke. "Take the lantern."

"I'll find my way right enough. Isorn will be up telling tales with Sludig and the rest, I have no doubt." He yawned again. "Wasn't there a time when we could stay up all night drinking, then fight in the morning, then start drinking all over again?"

"Maybe for you, Uncle Isgrimnur," Josua said with a tiny smile. "Never for me. God grant you good rest tonight."

Isgrimnur grunted, then picked up the lamp and made his way out of the tent, leaving Josua standing in its center, staring at the sleeping Camaris.

Outside the storm clouds had dispersed. The stars spread a faint light over the Hayholt's silent walls. The Conqueror Star seemed to hang just above Green Angel Tower like a flame above a candle.

Go away, you cursed, ill-omened thing, he demanded, but he knew that it would not comply.

Shivering in the chill, he stumped slowly through the snow toward his tent.

"Jeremias! Boy! *Wake up!*"

The young squire sat up, fighting his way out of sleep. "What?"

Josua stood over him, half-dressed. "He's gone. He's been gone far too long."

The prince snatched up his sword belt and leaned to pluck his cloak from the floor. "Put on your boots and come help me."

"What? Who's gone, Prince Josua?"

"Camaris, curse it, Camaris! Come and help me. No, rouse Isgrimnur and find some men to help. Have them bring torches."

The prince took a brand from the fire, then turned and pushed out through the door flap. He looked down at the snow, trying to make some sense out of the muddle of footprints. At last he chose a set of tracks that led downhill toward the Kynslagh. Within moments he was beyond the light of the few campfires still burning. The moon had vanished from the sky, but the Conqueror Star still burned like a signal beacon.

The trail twisted erratically, but within half a furlong it was clear that the footprints had turned toward the cliffs east of the Hayholt's seawall. Josua looked up to see a pale figure moving along the edge of the shoreline, silhouetted against the wall of empty blackness that was the Kynslagh.

"*Camaris!*" Josua called. The figure did not stop, but moved along unsteadily toward the edge, lurching like a puppet with knotted strings. The prince began to run, floundering in the deep snow, then slowed as he reached the cliffs. "Camaris," he said, his voice deceptively calm. "Where are you going?"

The old man turned to look at him. He wore no cloak, and his loose shirt flapped in the wind. Even seen by starlight there was something odd in his posture.

"It is Josua." The prince lifted his arms as though to embrace the old man. "Come back with me. We will sit by the fire and talk."

Camaris stared as though the words were animal noises, then began to make his way down the rocks. Josua hastened forward.

"Stop! Camaris, where are you going?" He scrambled over the edge, struggling to keep his balance on the muddy slope. "Come back with me."

The old knight whirled and pulled Thorn from its scabbard. Although he seemed fearfully confused, he handled the sword with unthinking mastery. His horn Cellian dangled on its baldric, drawing Josua's eye as it swung back and forth. "It is time," Camaris whispered. He was barely audible above the waves that slapped on the shore below.

"You cannot do this." Josua reached out his hand. "We are not ready. You must wait until the others can go with you." He advanced a few slithering steps down the slope. "Come back."

Camaris abruptly swung the sword in a wide, flat arc; it was nearly invisible in the darkness, but it hissed as it passed the prince's chest.

"Aedon's Blood, Camaris, do you not recognize me?" Josua took a step back. The old man raised the sword for another stroke.

"It is *time!*" he said, and swung, this time with deadly aim.

Josua threw himself backward. His feet skidded from beneath him and he whirled his arms for a moment, struggling for balance, then fell and tumbled down the slope, through long grasses and over mud and stones, landing at last in a drift of dirty snow where he lay for long moments, wheezing in pain.

"Prince Josua?!" A head appeared at the top of the rise. "Are you down there?"

Josua dragged himself onto his feet. Camaris had made his way down to the bottom of the hill and onto the beach. Now he was a ghostly shape moving along the cliff face. "I'm here," he called to Jeremias. "Damn it, where is the duke!?"

"He's coming, but I don't see him yet," the youth said excitedly. "I ran back after I told him. Shall I come down and help you? Are you hurt?"

Josua turned and saw Camaris hesitating before one of the black openings in the cliff wall. A moment later he vanished into the hole. "No!" Josua shouted, then called up to Jeremias: "Get Isgrimnur, make him hurry! Tell him Camaris has gone into one of the caves down here—I will mark which one! We will lose him if we wait any longer. I am going to bring him out."

"You . . . you . . ." The squire was confused. "You're going to follow him?"

"Damn me, I can't let him go down there himself—he is mad. Aedon knows what—he might fall, be lost . . . I will bring him back somehow, even if I have to outfight him myself and carry him back on my shoulder. But for God's sake, tell Isgrimnur to hurry with the torches and men. Go on, boy, run!"

Jeremias hesitated a moment longer, then vanished from the prince's sight. Josua crawled the short distance to where his torch lay sputtering on a muddy outcropping, then clambered down the slope to the beach. He quickly made his way to the place where Camaris had disappeared and found a cave mouth little different than any of the others along the cliff. Josua grabbed several stones and piled them next to the opening, then stepped in, holding the torch before him.

Isgrimnur stared at the soldiers. "What do you mean, gone?"

The man looked back at him, half-apologetic and half-defensive. "Just that, Duke Isgrimnur. The hole splits off, goes different ways. We thought we saw some marks, like from a torch-end, up on the walls, but we didn't find anybody that way. We searched the other passages, too. It's like wormholes in there, tunnels everywhere."

"And you shouted?"

"Called the prince's name loud as we could. Nobody called back."

Isgrimnur stared at the gap in the cliff wall, then looked at Sludig. "Ransomer preserve us," he groaned. "Both gone. We'll have to get the Sithi after them now." He turned to the soldier. "I'll be back before sunrise. Until then, keep looking and calling."

The man nodded. "Yes, sire."

Isgrimnur pulled at his beard for a moment, then began making his way back along the beach. "Oh, Josua," he said quietly. "You fool. And me, too. We've all been fools."

54

Abandoned Ways

⚜

Binabik touched her arm. "Miriamele, what are you thinking?"

"I'm trying to think of what we can do." Her head was pounding. The shadowed cavern seemed to be closing in. "We have to get out, somehow. We have to. I don't want to be trapped in here." She caught her breath and looked at Cadrach huddled against the wall on the far side of the cavern. "How could he do such things, Binabik? How could he betray us all that way?"

"He was not knowing you then," the troll pointed out. "So he could not be thinking that it was you he was betraying."

"But he didn't tell us afterward! He didn't tell us anything! All that time we were together."

Binabik lowered his head. "It is done. Now we must be thinking on other things." He gestured to the dwarrows, who were seated in a circle, singing quietly. "They are thinking the Norns come soon, they have said to me. Already the ward is crumbling. The door will not hold for a much lengthier time."

"And they're just going to sit and wait," said Miriamele bitterly. "I can't understand them any more than I can understand Cadrach." She stood and walked past the troll. "Yis-fidri! Why are you mooning around like this when the Norns are outside? Don't you understand what will happen to us?" She heard her voice rising shrilly, but she did not care.

The dwarrows stared up apprehensively, mouths agape. Miriamele thought they looked like a nestful of baby birds. "We are waiting . . ." he began.

"Waiting! That's just it, you're waiting." She quivered with anger. They were all waiting for those fishbelly-white things to come in and take them—take her and the troll, too. "Then let's open the door now. Why put it off any longer? Binabik and I will fight to win free and probably be killed—killed because you brought us here to this trap against our will—and you will sit and be slaughtered. So there is no sense waiting any longer."

Yis-fidri goggled. "But . . . perhaps they will go. . . ."

"You don't believe that! Come, open the door!" Her fear beat higher, rising like storm-tossed waves. She leaned down and grabbed the dwarrow's long wrist in her hand and tugged. He was as unmovable as stone. "Get up, damn you!" she shouted, and yanked as hard as she could. Alarmed, the dwarrows burbled at each other. Yis-fidri's eyes widened in consternation; with a flick of his powerful arm he dislodged Miriamele's grip. She fell back on the cavern floor, breathless.

"Miriamele!" Binabik hurried to her side. "Are you hurt?"

She shook off the troll's helping hand and sat up. "There!" she said triumphantly. "Yis-fidri, you didn't tell the truth."

The dwarrow stared at her as though she had begun to foam at the mouth. He curled his flat fingers protectively against his chest.

"You didn't," she said, and stood. "You will push *me* away to keep me from forcing you against your will, so why not the Norns? Do you want to die, then? Because the Norns will certainly kill you, kill me, kill us all. Or perhaps they will make you slaves again—is that what you are hoping for? Why do you resist me and not resist them?"

Yis-fidri turned briefly to his wife; she stared back at him, silent and solemn-eyed. "But there is naught we can do." The dwarrow seemed to be pleading for Miriamele's understanding.

"There is *always* something you can do," she snapped. "It may not change anything, but you will have tried. You are strong, Yis-fidri—you dwarrow-folk are very strong, and you can do many things: I watched your wife shaping stone. Maybe you have always run away before, but now there is nowhere left to hide. Stand with us, damn you!"

Yis-hadra said something in the dwarrow tongue, which brought a murmuring but swift reply from others in the group. Yis-fidri entered in, then for a long time the dwarrows argued among themselves, voices rushing and burbling like water chiming on stone.

At last Yis-hadra rose. "I will stand with you," she said. "You speak rightly. There is nowhere left to run, and we are almost the last of our kind. If we die, no one then will be left to tend and harvest the stone, no one to find the beautiful things in the earth. That would be a shame." She turned to her husband and again spoke rapidly to him. After a moment, Yis-fidri lidded his huge eyes.

"I will do as my wife does," he said with obvious reluctance. "But we do not speak for our fellow Tinukeda'ya."

"Then speak *to* them," Miriamele urged. "There is so little time!"

Yis-fidri hesitated, then nodded. The other dwarrows looked on, their strange faces fearful.

Miriamele crouched in blackness, her heart thudding. She could see nothing at all, but apparently enough light was still bleeding from the crystal batons to allow the dwarrows to see: Miriamele could hear them padding back and forth across the cavern as unhesitatingly as she herself would walk through a lamplit room.

She reached out to touch the small but reassuring shape of Binabik crouched beside her. "I'm frightened," she whispered.

"As who is not?" She felt him pat her hand.

Miriamele had opened her mouth to say something else when a slight sensation of movement passed through the stone behind her. At first she thought it was the strange shifting she had felt earlier, the thing that had so frightened Yis-hadra and the other dwarrows, but then a faint blue glow sprang up in the empty black where the door stood. It was not like any light she had seen, for it illuminated nothing else; it was only a pulsing sky-blue streak hanging in the darkness.

"They're coming," she gurgled. Her heart raced even more swiftly. All her brave words now seemed foolish. On the far side of Binabik, she heard Cadrach's harsh breathing grow louder. She half-expected him to cry out, to try to shout a warning to the Norns. She did not believe his claim that he had no Art that would help them against the Norns, nor even the strength left now to use those few skills he retained.

The blue line lengthened. A warm wind pushed through the chamber, tangible as a slap to her heightened senses. For the dozenth time since the dwarrows had darkened the cavern she tugged at the straps of her pack and wiped sweat from the handle of her dagger. She also clutched Simon's White Arrow; if the Norns grabbed her, she would stab at them with both hands. A shudder ran through her. The Norns. The White Foxes. They were only moments away. . . .

Yis-fidri said something quiet but emphatic in the dwarrow tongue. Yis-hadra replied in the same tone from somewhere across the cavern. The sound of moving dwarrows ceased. The chamber was silent as a grave.

The blue gleam grew in a rough oval until one end of the line met the other. For a moment the heat became greater, then the glow faded. Something scraped and then fell heavily. A rush of cold air swept into the chamber, but if the door had opened, no light came through.

Curse them! Despair swept over her. *They are too clever to come in with torches.* She clutched her knife tighter: she was shaking so violently she feared she might drop it.

Suddenly there was a booming rumble like thunder and a high-pitched shout that came from no human throat. Miriamele's heart leaped. The great stones the dwarrows had loosened above the cavern door were tumbling down—she could hear the Norns' high-pitched, angry wailing. Another crash was followed by a scraping, grinding noise, then many voices were shouting, none of them in human languages. After a moment Miriamele felt her eyes begin to sting. She took a breath and felt it burn all the way down.

"Up!" Binabik cried. "It is poison-smoke!"

Miriamele struggled to her feet, lost in the dark and feeling as though her insides were on fire. A powerful hand gripped her and led her stumbling through the blackness. The cavern was raucous with strange cries and shrieks and the sound of smashing stone.

The next moments were blind madness. She felt herself pulled through into chilly air; within moments she could breathe again, although she still could not see. The hand that held her let go, and a moment later she caught her foot on something and crashed to the ground.

"*Binabik!*" she shouted. She tried to rise, but something had entangled her. "Where are you!?"

Miriamele was seized again, but this time was lifted bodily and carried swiftly through the noisy darkness. Something struck her a glancing blow. For a moment whoever was carrying her stopped and put her down; there was a succession of strange noises, some of them grunts or gasps of pain, then a moment later she was snatched up again.

At last she touched down again on the hard stone. The darkness was absolute. "Binabik?" she called.

There was a spark nearby, then a flash. For a moment she saw the troll standing beside a cavern wall in the midst of darkness with his hand full of flame. Then he flung whatever he held outward, and it scattered in a shower of sputtering sparks. Tiny flames burned everywhere. Frozen as if painted on a tapestry were Binabik, several dwarrows, and almost a dozen other shadowy figures, all scattered about a long, high-ceilinged cavern. The stone door that had protected them lay in pieces behind her at the far end of this outer cavern.

She had scarcely an instant to marvel at the effect of the troll's fire-starting powder before a pale-faced shape raced toward her, long knife held high. Miriamele lifted her own blade, but her ankles seemed bound somehow and she could not get her feet beneath her. The knife lashed toward Miriamele's face, but the blade stopped abruptly a hand's length from her eyes.

The dwarrow that had caught the creature's arm jerked upward. There was a sound of something snapping; a moment later the Norn was pitched headfirst across the chamber.

"Go that way," Yis-fidri gasped, pointing toward a dark hole at the near end of the cavern. In the faint, flickering light he looked even more grotesque than the enemy he had dispatched: one of his arms hung limply, and the broken shaft of an arrow wagged in his shoulder. The dwarrow flinched as another arrow shattered against the cavern wall beside him.

Miriamele reached down and disentangled her feet from what had held them—a Norn bow. Its owner lay a few paces away, just inside the entrance to the dwarrow's hiding place; a thick shard of rock jutted from his crushed chest.

"Move quickly, quickly," said Yis-fidri. "We have surprised them, but there may be more coming." His brisk tones could not hide his terror; his saucer eyes seemed to bulge. One of the other dwarrows threw a stone at the Norn archer. The motion was awkward, but the missile flew so swiftly that the white-faced immortal staggered backward before the dwarrow's arm had finished moving, then crumpled to the cavern floor.

"Run!" Binabik called. "Before more archers are coming!"

Miriamele rushed after him into the tunnel mouth, still clutching the bow. She stooped on the run to pick up a few scattered Norn arrows. She put Simon's arrow through her belt for safekeeping, and nocked one of the black arrows; as she did so, she looked back. Yis-fidri and the other dwarrows were backing after her, keeping their frightened eyes fixed on the Norns. These inched along behind them, staying out of the dwarrows' long reach, but obviously not intending to let them escape so easily. Despite the carnage, the half-dozen bodies lying scattered in the outer chamber and the breached doorway, the Norns seemed as calm and unhurried as hunting insects.

Miriamele turned and hastened her pace. Binabik had lit a torch, and she followed its light down the uneven tunnel.

"They're still following!" she panted.

"Run, then, until we find a better place for fighting," the troll called back. "Where is the monk Cadrach?"

"Don't know," Miriamele said.

And maybe it would be better for everyone if he died back there. The thought felt cruel but just. *Better for everyone.*

She raced along after the bobbing torch.

"Josua is gone?" Isorn was stunned. "But how could he risk himself, even for Camaris?"

Isgrimnur did not know how to answer his son's question. He tugged fiercely at his beard, trying to think clearly. "Still, there it is," he said. He stared around the tent at the rest of the unhappy faces. "I have had soldiers hunting all through the caves for hours with no luck. The Sithi are preparing to go after the two of them, and Tiamak will accompany them. There is nothing more we can do about it." He blew out, fluttering his mustache. "Yes, damn me, Josua has hamstrung us, but now more than ever we must make sure we distract Elias. We can't waste tears."

Sludig peered out through the door flap. "It is nearly dawn, Duke Isgrimnur. And snowing again. The men know something strange has happened—they are growing restless. We should decide what to do, my lord."

The duke nodded. Inwardly he cursed the fate that had dropped Josua's command into his lap. "We will do what we planned. All that has changed from yesterday's council is that Josua is gone. So we will need not one mimic, but two."

"I am ready," Isorn said. "I have Camaris' surcoat, and see," he pulled his sword from its scabbard: blade and hilt were shiny black, "a little paint and it becomes Thorn." He caught Isgrimnur's discomfited look. "Father, you agreed to this and nothing has changed. Of all who can be trusted with the secret, only I am nearly tall enough to pass as Camaris."

The duke frowned. "It is so. But because you pretend to be Camaris, don't believe you *are* Camaris: you need to stay alive and on your horse so you can be seen. Take no foolish chances."

Isorn flashed him an unhappy glance, angry after all his experiences to be treated like a child. Isgrimnur almost regretted his fatherly worry—almost, but not quite. "So then. Who shall mime Josua?"

"Are there any that can fight with their left hands?" Sludig asked.

"S'right," said Freosel. "None'll believe Josua with a right hand."

Isgrimnur felt his frustration growing. This was madness—like choosing courtiers to act in the Tunath's Day pageant. "He need only be seen, not fight," Isgrimnur growled.

"But he must be somewhere in the fighting," Sludig insisted, "or no one will see him."

"I will do it," said Hotvig. The scarred Thrithings-man lifted his arm and his bracelets jangled. "I can fight with either hand."

"But . . . but he does not look like Josua," said Strangyeard apologetically, ". . . does he?" He had sobered since the duke had seen him earlier, but still seemed distracted. "Hotvig, you are . . . you are very broad in the chest. And your hair is too light."

"He will be wearing a helm," Sludig pointed out.

"The harper Sangfugol looks much like the prince," Strangyeard offered. "At least he is slender and dark-haired."

"Ha." Isgrimnur barked a laugh. "I would not send a singer into the middle of such a bloodletting. Even if he need not fight, he must sit his horse in the clamor of fierce fighting." He shook his head. "But I cannot spare you, either, Hotvig. We need your Thrithings-men—you are our fastest horsemen, and we must be ready in case the king's knights make a sally from the gate. Who else?" He turned to Seriddan. The Nabbanai captains had been silent, stunned by Josua's disappearance. "Have you any ideas, Baron?"

Before Seriddan could reply, his brother Brindalles stood. "I am close to the prince's size. And I can ride."

"No, that is foolish," Seriddan began, but Brindalles halted him with a raised hand.

"I am not a fighter like you, my brother, but this is something I can do. Prince Josua and these folk have risked much for us. They faced imprisonment or even death at our hands to bring us the truth, and then helped us to drive Benigaris from the throne." He looked around the tent somberly. "But what good is that to us if we do not survive to enjoy it, if our children are unhomed by Elias and his allies? I am still somewhat baffled by all this talk of swords and strange magics, but if this stratagem is truly necessary, then it is the least I can do."

Isgrimnur saw his calm resolve and nodded. "It is done, then. Thank you, Brindalles, and may Aedon give you good luck. Isorn, get him into things of Josua's as will fit, then you can take whatever else of Camaris' that you need. From what Jeremias said, I doubt he took his helm with him. Freosel?"

"Yes, Duke Isgrimnur?"

"Tell the engineers to make ready. Everyone else, go to your men and make ready. God's grace on us all."

"Yes," Strangyeard said suddenly. "Yes, of course—God's grace on us all."

He Who Always Steps on Sand, Tiamak prayed silently, *I am going into a dark place. I am far from our swamps, farther than I have ever been. Please do not lose sight of this marsh man!*

The sun was invisible beyond the storm, but the deep blue of night was beginning to pale. Tiamak looked up from the Kynslagh beach at the faint shadows that must be the turrets of the Hayholt. They seemed impossibly far away, distant and forbidding as mountains.

Bring me out alive and I will . . . and . . . He could not think of any promise that might tempt the protector-god. *I will honor you. I will do what is right. Bring me out alive again, please!*

The snow swirled and the wind moaned, whipping the black Kynslagh to a froth of waves.

"We go, Tiamak," Aditu said from behind him. She was near enough that he jumped in surprise at the sound of her voice.

Her brother disappeared into the black mouth of the cave. Tiamak followed; the noise of the wind began to diminish behind him.

Tiamak had been surprised to find the Sithi such a small group, and even more surprised to find Likimeya a part of it.

"But isn't your mother too important to leave your people and come down here?" he whispered to Aditu. As he scrambled down a boulder, clinging to the shining globe that Jiriki had given him, he saw Likimeya turn to look back at him with what he felt sure was disgust. He was embarrassed and angry with himself for underestimating the Sithi's keen ears.

Aditu slithered down beside him, nimble as a deer. "If someone must speak for Year-Dancing House, Uncle Khendraja'aro will be there. But the others will make their decisions as things happen, and all will do what needs to be done." She stopped to pick something off the floor and stared at it intently; it was too small for Tiamak to see. "In any case, there are things at least as important to be done down here, and so those most able to do them have come."

He and Aditu were at the back of the small company, trailing Jiriki and Li-kimeya, as well as Kira'athu, a small, quiet Sitha-woman, another woman named Chiya, who seemed to Tiamak inexplicably more foreign than even the rest of the alien group, and a tall, black-haired Sitha-man named Kuroyi. All moved with the odd grace Tiamak had long noted in Aditu, and except for Aditu and her brother, none seemed to take any more notice of the Wrannaman than of a dog following in the road.

"I found sand," Aditu called to the rest of the party. She had been careful to speak Westerling all morning, even with her kin, for which Tiamak was duly grateful.

"Sand?" Tiamak squinted at the invisible something she held prisoned between finger and thumb. "Yes?"

"We are now far in from the water's edge," she said. "But this is rounded, formed by the motion of stone in water. I would say we are still on Josua's track."

Tiamak had thought the Sithi were following the prince by some kind of immortals' magic. He did not know quite what to make of this revelation. "Can't you . . . don't you just . . . *know* where the prince and Camaris are?"

Her amused smile was very human. "No. There are things we can sometimes do to make finding someone or something easier—but not here."

"Not here? Why?"

The smile went away. "Because things are changing here. Can you not feel it? It is as powerful to me as the wind was loud outside."

Tiamak shook his head. "If anything dangerous comes toward us, I hope you will tell me. This is not my marsh, and I do not know where the dangerous sands lie."

"Where we go was our place once," Aditu said seriously. "But no more."

"Do you know your way?" Tiamak looked around at the sloping tunnel, the countless crevices and nearly identical cross-passages, black beyond the range of the lighted globes. The thought of being lost here was terrifying.

"My mother does, or at least she soon will. Chiya also lived here."

"Your mother lived in this place?"

"In Asu'a. She lived there for a thousand years."

Tiamak shivered.

The company followed no logical path that Tiamak could see, but he had long resigned himself to trusting the Sithi, although there was much about them that frightened him. Meeting Aditu on Sesuad'ra had been strange enough, but she had been singular, a freak, as Tiamak himself must have seemed to the drylanders. Seeing them together, either in their great numbers on the hillside east of the Hayholt, or here in a group that, despite making many decisions without discussion, seemed always in accord, he felt for the first time the true force of their strangeness. They had ruled all of Osten Ard once. History said they had been kind masters, but Tiamak could not help wondering if they had been truly kind, or had just given no attention at all, tyrannical or otherwise, to their mortal inferiors. If that was true, they had been cruelly repaid for their heedlessness.

Kuroyi halted and the others stopped with him. He said something in the liquid Sithi speech.

"Someone is there," Aditu quietly told Tiamak.

"Josua? Camaris?" He did not want to think it could be something worse.

"We will find out."

Kuroyi turned into a passageway and took a few steps downward. A moment later he danced back out, hissing. Aditu pushed past Tiamak and ran to Kuroyi's side. "Do not run!" she called into the dark space. "I am Aditu!"

After a few moments a figure appeared, sword leveled.

"Prince Josua!" Relief flowed through Tiamak. "You are safe."

The prince stared at them for a long moment, blinking in the light of the crystal globes. "Aedon's Mercy, it is truly you." He sank down heavily onto the floor of the tunnel. "My . . . my torch burned out. I have been in darkness some time. I thought I heard footsteps, but you walk so quietly I could not be sure. . . ."

"Have you found Camaris?" Tiamak asked.

The prince shook his head miserably. His eyes were haunted. "No. I lost sight of him soon after I followed him in. He would not stop, no matter how I called. He has gone! Gone!" He struggled to control himself. "I have left my men without a leader—deserted my people! Can you take me back?" He looked imploringly around the circle of Sithi.

"The mortal Duke Isgrimnur is performing ably in your place," said Likimeya. "We cannot afford the time to return you, nor any of our number, and you could not find your way back alone."

Josua lowered his head, bowed by shame. "I have done a foolish thing, and failed those who trusted me. It was all to find Camaris . . . but he has gone. And he has taken Thorn with him."

"Do not worry yourself over what is done, Prince Josua." Aditu spoke with surprising gentleness. "As for Camaris, do not fear. We will find him."

"How?"

Likimeya stared at Josua for a moment, then turned her glance up the passageway. "If the sword is being drawn toward Sorrow and the other blade, as seems true from what you have told us, then we know where he is bound." She looked at Chiya, who nodded. "We will go there by the straightest route, or close to it. Either we will find him, or we will reach the upper levels before him and can wait."

"But he could wander down here forever!" Josua said unhappily, and Tiamak remembered his own earlier thought.

"I do not think so," said Likimeya. "If some convergence of power is drawing the swords together—which may be our greatest hope, for it will bring Bright-Nail, too—then he will find his way, even with his wits as troubled as you say they were. He will be like a blind man searching for the fire in a cold room. He will find his way."

Jiriki extended his hand to the prince. "Come, Prince Josua. I have some food and water. Take some nourishment, then we will find him."

As the prince looked at him some of the hard edge of worry softened. "Thank you. I am grateful you found me." He took Jiriki's hand and stood, then laughed, mocking himself. "I thought . . . I thought I heard voices."

"I have no doubt you did," said Jiriki. "And you will hear more."

Tiamak could not help noticing that even the impassive Sithi did not look entirely comfortable with Jiriki's remark.

Slowly, almost imperceptibly, Tiamak's surroundings began to change. As he and Josua followed the immortals through the twisting passages, he first noticed that the floors seemed more level, the tunnels a little more regular. Soon he began to see the undeniable marks of intelligent shapers, hard angles, arches of stone that braced the wider crossings, even a few patches in the rock walls that seemed to have been carved, although the decorations were little more than repetitive patterns like waves or twining grass stems.

"These outermost reaches were never finished," Aditu told him. "Either they were built too late in Asu'a's life, or were abandoned in favor of more useful paths."

"Abandoned?" Tiamak could not imagine such a thing. "Who would do all the work of gouging through this stone and then abandon it?"

"Some of these passages were built by my people, with the help of the Ti-nukeda'ya—the dwarrows as mortals call them," she explained. "And that stone-loving folk carved some just for themselves, unconcerned with finishing or keeping, as a child might make a basket of grass stems and then toss it away when it is time to run home."

The marsh man shook his head.

Mindful of their mortal companions, the Sithi stopped at last for a rest in a wide grotto whose roof was covered with a tracery of slender stalactites. In the mellow light of the globes, Tiamak thought it looked entirely magical; for a moment, he was glad he had come. The world below, it seemed, was full of wonders as well as terrors.

As he sat eating a piece of bread and a savory but unfamiliar fruit the Sithi had brought, Tiamak wondered how far they had come. It seemed they had walked most of a day, but the full distance on the surface between where they had begun and the walls of the Hayholt would not have taken a fourth of that time. Even with the circuitous track of the tunnels, it seemed they should have reached something, but they were still wandering through largely featureless caverns.

It is like the spirit-hut of Buayeg in the old story, he decided, only half in jest. *Small outside, big inside.*

He turned to ask Josua if he had noticed the same oddity; the prince was staring at his own piece of bread as though he was too tired or distraught to eat. Abruptly the cavern shuddered—or seemed to: Tiamak felt a sensation of movement, of sudden slippage, but neither Josua nor the Sithi seemed to move in response to it. Rather, it was as though everything in the grotto had slid to one side, but the people inside had slid effortlessly with it. It was a frightening wrench, and for a long moment after it had passed Tiamak felt as though he occupied two places at the same time. A thrill of terror ran up his spine.

"What is happening!?" he gasped.

The obvious uneasiness of the Sithi did nothing to make him feel better. "It is that which I spoke of before," said Aditu. "As we draw closer to Asu'a's heart, it is getting stronger."

Likimeya stood and slowly looked around, but Tiamak felt sure that she was using more than her eyes. "Up," she said. "Time is short, I think."

Tiamak scrambled to his feet. The look on Likimeya's stern face frightened him badly. He suddenly wished he had kept his mouth closed, that he had stayed above ground with the rest of his mortal companions. But it was far too late to turn back.

"Where are we going?" Miriamele gasped.

Yis-hadra, who had replaced her wounded husband as leader, turned to stare. "Going?" said the dwarrow. "We are fleeing. We run to escape."

Miriamele stopped, bending over to catch her breath. The Norns had attacked them twice more as they fled through the tunnels, but without archers they had been unable to overcome the terrified dwarrows. Still, two more of the stone-tenders had fallen in the fighting, and the white-skinned immortals had by no means given up. Since the last struggle, Miriamele had already spotted the pursuers once when she had entered a passageway long and straight enough to permit a backward look; in that glimpse they had truly seemed creatures of the lightless depths—pale, silent, and remorseless. The Norns seemed in no hurry, as if they were merely trailing Miriamele and her companions until more of their kind came bearing bows and long spears. It had been as much as she could do not to sink to the ground in surrender.

She knew that they had been lucky to escape the dwarrows' cavern at all. If the White Foxes had anticipated any resistance, they had doubtless expected it to be close combat in a narrow corner. Instead, the dwarrows' desperate attack in the dark and the avalanches of falling stone they had engineered had caught the immortals by surprise, permitting Miriamele and her companions to flee. But she had no illusions they could trick the cunning Norns twice.

"We could be forced to run this way forever," she told Yis-hadra. "Perhaps you can outlast them, but we can't. In any case, our people are in danger up above."

Binabik nodded. "She speaks truth to you. Escaping is not enough for us. We have need of finding our way out from this place."

The dwarrow did not reply, but looked to her husband who was limping up the passageway toward them, trailed by the last of the dwarrows and Cadrach. The monk's face was ashen, as though he had been wounded, but Miriamele saw no injuries. She turned away, unwilling to waste sympathy on him.

"They are a distance behind us, now," said Yis-fidri wearily. "They seem full content to let us run ahead." He leaned back against the wall, letting his head rest against the stone. Yis-hadra went to him and probed gently with her wide fingers at the arrow wound in his shoulder. "Sho-vennae is dead, and three others," he groaned, then fluted a few words to his wife, who gave a cry of grief. "Smashed like delicate crystals. Gone."

"If we had not run, they would all be dead anyway—and you and the rest of us would be, too." Miriamele paused to fight back her anger and her horror of the pursuing Norns. "Forgive me, Yis-fidri. I am sorry about your people. I am truly sorry."

Sweat beaded on the dwarrow's brow, glimmering in the light of the batons. "Few mourn for the Tinukeda'ya," he replied softly. "They make us their servants, they steal from us the Words of Making, they even beg our help when they are in need—but they seldom mourn us."

Miriamele was ashamed. Surely he meant that she was as guilty of using the dwarrows—and Niskies, too, she thought, remembering Gan Itai's sacrifice— as even their one-time masters, the Sithi.

"Take us to where we can reach the world above," she said. "That is all I ask. Then go with our blessing, Yis-fidri."

Before the dwarrow could reply, Binabik suddenly spoke up. "The Words of Making. Were *all* the Great Swords being forged with these Making-Words?"

Yis-fidri looked at him with more than a little suspicion, then winced at something his wife was doing to his shoulder. "Yes. It was needful to bind their substance—to bring their being within the Laws."

"What laws are these?"

"Those Laws that cannot be changed. The Laws that make stone be stone, make water be water. They can be . . ." he searched for a word, "stretched or altered for a short time, but that brings consequences. *Never* can they be undone."

One of the dwarrows at the rear of the tunnel spoke anxiously.

"Imai-an says he can feel them coming," Yis-hadra cried. "We must run."

Yis-fidri pushed himself away from the tunnel wall and the group began its uneven progress once more. Miriamele's weary heart was racing. Would there never be an end to this? "Help us reach the surface, Yis-fidri," she begged. "Please."

"Yes! It is more than ever important!"

Miriamele turned at the distraught tone of Binabik's voice. The little man looked terrified. "What is it?" she asked him.

Sweat was running on his dark forehead. "I must think on this, Miriamele, but I have never had such fear as I do now. For the first time I believe I see behind the shadow that has been all our consideration, and I am thinking— Kikkasut! To be saying such words!—that the monk may have spoken rightly. There may be nothing left for our doing at all."

With those words hanging in the air, he turned from her and hastened after the dwarrows. As though his sudden despair had passed to her like a fever, she felt hopelessness enwrap her.

55

The Hand of the North

※

The winds shrieked around Stormspike's summit, but beneath the mountain all was silent. The Lightless Ones had fallen into a deep slumber. The corridors of Under-Nakkiga were nearly empty.

Utuk'ku's gloved fingers, slender and brittle as cricket legs, flexed upon the arm of her throne. She settled her ancient bones against the rock and let her thoughts move through the Breathing Harp, following its twistings and turnings until Stormspike fell away and she became pure mind moving through the black between-spaces.

The angry Dark One was gone from the Harp. He had moved himself to the place—if it could be called a place—where he could act in concert with her to enact the final step of their centuried scheme, but she could still feel the weight of his hatred and envy, personified in the net of storms that spread across the land above.

In Nabban, where the upstart Imperators had once ruled, snow piled high in the streets; in the great harbor high waves flung the anchored ships against each other, or drove them into the shore where their splintered timbers lay like the bones of giants. The kilpa, frenzied, struck at everything that moved across the water, and even began to make sluggish forays into the coastal towns. And deep within the heart of the Sancellan Aedonitis, the Clavean Bell hung silent, immobilized by ice just as the mortals' Mother Church was frozen by fear.

The Wran, although its interior was sheltered from the worst of the storm, nevertheless turned chillingly cold. The ghants, undeterred as a group, though countless individuals died in the harsh weather, continued to boil out of the swamps and harry the coastal villages. Those few mortals of Kwanitupul who braved the icy winds to walk outside went only in groups, armed with iron weapons and wind-whipped torches against the ghants who now seemed to be crawling in every shadowy place. Children were kept inside, and doors and windows were shuttered even during those few hours when the storm abated.

Even Aldheorte Forest slept beneath a blanket of white, but if its ageless trees suffered beneath the freezing hand of the North, they did so in silence. In the heart of the woods Jao é-Tinukai'i lay empty, misty with cold.

All the mortal lands lay trembling beneath Stormspike's hand. The storms kept Rimmersgard and the Frostmarch an icy wasteland, and Hernystir suffered only a little less. Before the Hernystiri could truly reclaim the homes from which they had been driven by Skali of Kaldskryke, they had been forced back into the caves of the Grianspog. The spirit of the people the Sithi had loved, a spirit which had flamed high for a short time, sank back to a guttering flicker.

The storm hung low over Erkynland. Black winds bent and broke the trees and piled snow high on the houses; thunder growled like an angry beast up and down the length of the land. The storm's malevolent heart, as it seemed, full of whirling sleet and jagged lightning, pulsed above Erchester and the Hayholt.

Utuk'ku noted all this with calm satisfaction, but did not pause to savor the terror and hopelessness of the hated mortals. She had something to do, a task she had awaited since her son Drukhi's pale, cold body had been set before her. Utuk'ku was old and subtle. The irony that it was her own great-great-grandchild who had led her to her revenge at last, that he was also a scion of the very family that had destroyed her happiness, was not lost on her. She almost smiled.

Her thoughts raced on, out along the whispery threads of being until they passed into the farther regions, the places only she of all the living could go. When she felt the presence of the thing she sought, she reached out for it, praying to forces that had been old in Venyha Do'sae that it would give her what she needed to accomplish her final, long-awaited goal.

A flare of joy passed through her. The power was there, more than enough for her purposes; now all that remained was to master it and make it hers. The hour was approaching, and Utuk'ku had no need to be patient any longer.

"My eyes are not good at the best of times," Strangyeard complained. "And with this sunless day and the blowing snow, I cannot see anything! Sangfugol, tell me what is happening, please!"

"There's nothing to see, yet." They were perched on the side of one of Swertclif's foothills, looking down on Erchester and the Hayholt. The tree beneath which the pair huddled and the low wall of stones they had made provided scant protection against the wind. Despite his hooded cloak and the two blankets he had wrapped around himself, the harper was shivering. "Our army is before the walls and the heralds have blown the trumpets. Isgrimnur or someone must be reading the Writ of Demand. I still don't see any of the king's soldiers . . . no, there are some shapes moving on the battlements. I had begun to wonder if anyone was inside at all. . . ."

"Who? Who is on the battlements?"

"Aedon's mercy, Strangyeard, I can't tell. They are shapes, that's all."

"We should be closer," the priest said fretfully. "This hillside is too distant in weather like this."

The harper darted a glance at him. "You must be mad. I am a musician, you are a librarian. We are too close as it is—we should have stayed in Nabban. But here we are, and here we will stay. Closer, indeed!" He blew into his cupped palms.

A faint clamor of horns drifted over the wind. "What is it?" Strangyeard asked. "What is happening?"

"They have finished the Writ and I suppose they've gotten no answer. That is just like Josua, to give Elias a chance to surrender honorably when we know already he will do nothing of the sort."

"The prince is . . . determined to do the right thing," Strangyeard replied. "Goodness, I hope he is well. It makes me sick to think of him and Camaris wandering lost in those caverns."

"There is that Nabbanman," Sangfugol said excitedly. "He does look rather like Josua—from here, anyway." He turned suddenly toward the priest. "Did you really suggest *I* should mimic the prince?"

"You look much like him."

Sangfugol stared at him with disgust and bitter amusement. "Mother of God, Strangyeard, do me no favors." He huddled deeper into his blankets. "Imagine me riding around waving a sword. Ransomer save us all."

"But we all must do what we can."

"Yes—and what I can do is play my harp, or my lute, and sing. And if we win, I will most assuredly do that. And if we don't—well, I may do that anyway if I live, but it won't be here. But what I *cannot* do is ride and fight and convince people that I am Josua."

They were silent for a time, listening to the wind.

"If we lose, I fear there will be nowhere else to run to, Sangfugol."

"Perhaps." The harper sat unspeaking a while longer, then said: "Finally!"

"What? Is something happening?"

"They are bringing forward the battering ram—save me, but it is a frightening thing. It has a great iron head on it that looks like a real ram, with curling horns and all. But it's so big! Even with all those men, it is a miracle they can push it along." He took a sharp breath. "The king's men are firing arrows from the walls! There, someone is down. More than one. But the ram is still going forward."

"May God keep them safe," Strangyeard said quietly. "It is so cold up here, Sangfugol."

"How can anyone shoot an arrow in this wind, let alone hit anything? Ah! Someone has fallen from the wall. That's one of theirs gone, in any case." The harper's voice rose in excitement. "It is hard to see what is happening, but our men are close to the walls now. There, someone has put up a ladder. There are soldiers swarming up it." A moment later he made a noise of surprise and horror.

"What do you see?" Strangyeard squinted his eye, trying to see through the swirling snows.

"Something was dropped on them." The harper was shaken. "A big stone, I think. I am sure they are all dead."

"May the Ransomer protect us," Strangyeard said miserably. "It has begun in earnest. Now we can only wait for the ending, whatever that may be."

Isgrimnur held his hands close to his face, trying to shield himself from the wind-flung snow. He was having great difficulty keeping track of what was happening, although the Hayholt's walls were less than five hundred cubits up the hillside from where he watched. Hundreds of armored men floundered in the drifts before the wall, busy as insects. Hundreds more, even dimmer shapes from Isgrimnur's vantage point, scurried about atop the Hayholt's walls. The duke cursed quietly. Everything seemed so damnably distant!

Freosel climbed onto the wooden platform the engineers had built between the bottom of the hill and the empty, storm-raddled husk of Erchester. The Falshireman was visibly struggling against the wind. "Ram's almost to the gates. The wind, it'll be our friend today—hard on their bowmen, it be."

"But we're not able to shoot any better," the duke snarled. "They've got free run of the walls and they're pushing our scaling ladders off easy as you please." He smacked his fist into his gloved hand. "The sun's been up for hours and all we've done is wear a few trenches in the snow."

The Falshireman looked at him quizzically. "Pardon, Sir Duke, but seems you think we should knock these walls down 'fore sunset."

"No, no. God knows the Hayholt is built strong. But I don't know how much time we have." He looked up into the murky sky. "That cursed star they all talk about is right overhead. I can almost feel it glaring. The prince and Camaris are gone. Miriamele's gone." He turned his gaze to the Hayholt, peering through the snow flurries. "And our men are going to freeze solid if we keep them out there too long. I wish we *could* knock the walls down by sunset—but I don't hold much hope."

Isorn pointed upward. The soldiers gathered around him looked up.

"There. On the walls."

Beside the helmeted heads peering through the crenellations were more than a few whose heads were bare; their faces were ghostly, and their white hair blew in the strong wind.

"White Foxes?" asked Sludig. He made the sign of the Tree.

"Indeed. And inside the Hayholt. Cursed things!" Isorn lifted his black-painted sword and waved it back and forth in challenge, but the distant figures on the walls did not seem to notice. "And curse Elias for whatever foul bargain he made."

Sludig was staring. "I have not seen them before," he cried above the tumult. "Merciful Aedon, they look like demons!"

"They *are* demons. And now the Hayholt is their nest."

"But they are doing nothing that I can see."

"Just as well," Isorn replied. "Perhaps they are too few. But they are fearsome archers. I wonder why none of them seem to have bows."

Sludig shook his head, mystified. He was unable to look away from the pale faces. "Preserve us," he said hoarsely.

♔

Baron Seriddan climbed heavily up the steps onto the platform, weighted by his armor. "What news?" Isgrimnur asked.

Seriddan took off his gloves and held his hands close to the brazier of coals. "Things go well, I suppose. Elias' men are firing on the ram and it is slow going to keep it moving uphill, but it will be against the gate soon. Some of the siege towers are also being moved into place, and they seem to be concentrating their arrows on them. We are lucky there is such wind today, and that it is so hard for the king's archers to see."

"That's what everyone keeps saying," the duke grumbled. "But I am going quietly mad here anyway. Curse Josua for leaving me this way." He scowled, then made the sign of the Tree. "Forgive me. I did not mean that."

Seriddan nodded. "I know. It is terrible not to know where he is."

"That's not all that's bothering me. There are still too many unanswered questions."

"What do you mean?"

"If all they need to do is stall us—if this flaming star truly signifies something will happen that helps Elias—then why didn't they even try to parley? And you'd think that the king would want to see his brother at the very least, if only to shout at him and call him a traitor."

"Perhaps Elias knows that Josua is not here."

Isgrimnur flinched. "How could he know that? Josua only disappeared last night!"

"You know more of these matters than I do, Duke Isgrimnur. You have been fighting the king and his magical allies a long time."

Isgrimnur walked to the front of the platform, staring at the Hayholt's shadowy walls. "Maybe they *do* know. Maybe they lured Camaris in somehow— but, damn me, that wouldn't mean Josua would come, too. They couldn't have planned on that."

"I cannot even guess," said the baron. "I only came to tell you that I'd like to take some of my men around to the western wall. I think it is time we gave them another spot to worry about."

"Go ahead. But that is another thing that troubles me: Elias doesn't seem very worried at all. With the battering ram so close, I would have expected at least one sortie to prevent us from dragging it into place."

"I cannot answer you." Seriddan clapped him on the arm. "But if this is all that the High King has left to offer, we will have the gate down in a matter of days at the most."

"We may not have days," Isgrimnur replied, frowning.

"But we do what we can." Seriddan clambered down and moved toward his horse. "Take heart, Duke Isgrimnur," he called. "Things are going well."

Isgrimnur looked around. "Jeremias!"

The boy pushed through a small knot of armored men at the back of the platform. "Yes, sire."

"See if you can find me some wine, boy. My guts are colder than my toes."

The squire hurried off toward the tents. Isgrimnur turned back to the windy, snow-smothered battlefield, glowering.

"God preserve us!" Sludig gaped in astonishment. "What are they doing?"

"Singing," said Isorn. "I saw it before the walls of Naglimund. It went on a long time." He stared at the two dozen Sithi, who had ridden forward and now stood calmly within bowshot of the walls, knee-deep in the drifting snows.

"What do you mean, *singing?*"

"It is how they fight—at least it is how they fight with their cousins, the Norns. If I understood better, I would explain it to you."

"And these are the allies we've been waiting for?" Sludig's voice rose in anger. "We battle for our lives—and they *sing*? Look! Our men are dying out there!"

"The Sithi can fight in other ways too, Sludig. You will see that, I think. And it worked for them at Naglimund, although I don't know how. They brought the walls down."

His companion snorted derisively. "I will put my faith in the ram and the siege-towers—and in men with strong arms." He looked up at the sky. "It's getting darker. But it cannot be much past midday."

"The storm is growing thicker, perhaps." Isorn restrained his horse, which was stepping nervously. "I do not like the looks of it, though. Do you see that cloud over the towers?"

Sludig stared, following Isorn's pointing finger. He blinked. "Lightning! Is this the Sithi's doing?" Indeed, almost the only thing that could be heard over the moaning wind was the strange, rhythmic rise and fall of the immortals' voices.

"I do not know, but it might be. I watched them at it before Naglimund for days, and still I could not tell you what they do. But Jiriki told me that his people work to counter certain magicks of the Norns." Isorn winced as thunder crashed, echoing across the hillside and down through the deserted streets of Erchester behind the prince's army. The lightning flashed again, seeming for a moment to freeze everything on and before the walls of the Hayholt—men, engines of war, flurrying snowflakes, even arrows in their flight—before the storm darkness returned. Another roar of thunder sounded. The wind howled even louder. "Perhaps that is why the Norns are not among the archers," Isorn continued loudly. "Because they are preparing some trick, some spell—something we will not like much. Oh, I saw horrors at Naglimund, Sludig. I pray Jiriki's people are strong enough to hold them back."

"This is madness!" Sludig shouted. "I can see almost nothing!"

Another crash came, this one a little softer. It was not thunder. "Praise Usires! They have brought the ram against the gates," Isorn called, excited. "See, Sludig, they have struck the first blow!" The black sword raised before him, he spurred his horse forward a few steps. With the sea-dragon helm on his head and his cloak whipping in the high wind, even Sludig could almost believe this was Camaris and not his liege-lord's son. "We must find Hotvig's riders and be ready to go in if they can breach the gate."

Sludig looked in vain for a messenger among the milling foot soldiers. "We should tell your father," he shouted.

"Go, then. I will wait. But hurry, man. Who would have thought we would be so close so soon?"

Sludig tried to say something, but it was lost in the noise of the storm. He turned his horse away and rode back down the hill toward Duke Isgrimnur's watching place.

"The ram is against the gate," Sangfugol said exultantly. "Look at it! It is big as three houses!"

"The gate is bigger." Strangyeard was shivering. "Still, I am astonished that there should be so little resistance."

"You saw Erchester. Everyone has fled. Elias and his pet wizard have made this place a wasteland."

"But there seem to be men enough inside the walls to defend the castle. Why did they dig no trenches to slow the siege engines? Why did they lay up so few stones to push down on the scaling ladders?"

"The stones they had did their work," Sangfugol replied, angry that Strangyeard did not share his excitement. "The men who wound up beneath them are as dead as you could wish."

"Elysia, Mother of our Ransomer!" The priest was shocked. "Sangfugol, do not speak so of our fallen soldiers! I only meant it is strange the defenders seem so ill-prepared for a siege Elias must have known was coming for weeks, even months."

"The king has gone mad," the harper replied. "You've heard what those who fled Erkynland say. And there are few left to fight with him. This will be no different than prodding a bear out of its cave. The bear is fierce, but it is an animal for all that, and must lose out to the cleverness of men."

"Cleverness?" The archivist did his best to shake the snow off his blanket. The wind slashed bitterly even through the low barrier of stones they had erected. "What have we done that is so clever? We have been led by the nose like oxen all along."

Sangfugol waved his hand airily, although he too was trembling with cold. "Having Isorn and that Nabban fellow pose as Camaris and Josua—that was a clever idea, you must admit . . . except for your little suggestion that *I* be the one to play the prince. And going beneath the Hayholt's walls by caverns and tunnels—that is something clever indeed! The king would not think of that in a thousand years."

Strangyeard, who was rubbing his hands together furiously in an effort to keep them warm, suddenly stopped. "The king might not—but his allies must know of those tunnels." His voice shook. "Surely the Norns must know."

"That is why *our* fairy-folk have gone down after the prince and Camaris. I've seen them, Aditu's brother and mother and the rest. They can take care of themselves, I have no doubt . . . even if the Norns know about the tunnels and are waiting for them, as you seem to think."

"That is *not* what I am thinking." Strangyeard stood. Snow fell from him and was promptly snatched away by the wind. "Not what I am thinking at all. The Norns know all about the tunnels." He stepped over the low wall of stones, knocking several loose.

"Hi! What are you doing?"

"I have to find Duke Isgrimnur. We are in more danger than we suspected." He turned and waded downhill through the drifts, leaning into the wind, frail but determined.

"Strangyeard!" cried Sangfugol. "Blast it, I am not staying here by myself. I'll come with you, whatever madness you're onto." He followed the archivist over the barrier. "You are heading right toward the fighting!" he shouted. "You'll be shot with an arrow!"

"I have to find Isgrimnur," Strangyeard called back.

Cursing richly, the harper hurried after him.

"Isorn's right, sire," said Sludig. "If we pass through the gate, we must make a great charge. The men have already seen the Norns and they are frightened. If we hesitate, the advantage will be the king's again. Who knows what will happen if he makes a sortie, and us fighting uphill?"

Isgrimnur stared at the Hayholt's high walls. It was only when seen against a storm like this that the works of man, even such a mighty construction as the Hayholt, seemed truly small. Perhaps they actually *could* knock down the gate. Perhaps Sludig and the others were right—Elias' kingdom was a rotting fruit waiting to fall from the vine.

There was another strange, sputtering flash of lightning over the tower tops. Thunder rolled, but following close behind it came a loud crash as the great ram was swung forward into the gate.

"Go, then," Isgrimnur told Sludig. His carl had not dismounted, but had brought his steam-puffing horse to the edge of the wooden structure where the duke stood. "Hotvig and his riders are still waiting at the edge of the Kynswood. No, better yet, you stay here." Isgrimnur summoned one of the newly returned outriders and gave him a message for the Thrithings-men, then sent him on his way. "You go back to Isorn, Sludig. Tell him to hold fast and let the first of the men-at-arms go through on foot. There will be no storied charges here, at least not until I see what Elias has waiting."

As the duke spoke, the ram smashed against the Nearulagh Gate. The timbers seemed to sag inward a little way, as though the huge bolts had been loosened.

"Yes, sire." Sludig turned his charger toward the walls.

The ram's engineers swung it forward once more. The iron-plated head crunched against the barrier. A length of wood splintered away down the length of the gate, and even through the storm noises Isgrimnur could hear the excited shouts of men all across the field. The ram was pulled back and then set in motion again. The Nearulagh Gate shattered and fell inward in an explosion of broken timbers and tumbling statuary. Snow swirled in the empty space. Isgrimnur goggled, almost unable to believe the gate was down. When the snow cleared, a few score of the castle's pikemen moved into the opening, braced against attack. No great hidden army charged outward.

A long moment passed as the two forces eyed each other through the snow-flurries. It seemed no one could move, that both sides were astonished by what had happened. Then a small, golden-helmeted figure lifted a sword and spurred forward. A score of mounted knights and several hundred foot soldiers surged toward the breach in the Hayholt's walls.

"Damn me, Isorn!" Duke Isgrimnur shouted. He leaned so far forward that he nearly lost his balance and toppled from the observation platform. "Come back! Where is Sludig!? Sludig! Stop him!" Someone was tugging at his sleeve, pulling him back from the edge of the platform, but Isgrimnur paid the intruder no mind. "Can't he see that it's too easy? *Isorn!*" He knew his voice could not possibly carry above the tumult. "Seriddan! Where are you!? Ride after him—by Dror's red mallet, where are my messengers!?"

"Duke Isgrimnur!" It was Strangyeard the archivist, still pulling at his sleeve.

"Get away, damn you!" Isgrimnur roared. "I do not need a priest, I need mounted knights. Jeremias, run to Seriddan," he called. "Isorn has forced our hand. Tell the baron to ride in."

Strangyeard was undaunted. "Please, Duke Isgrimnur, you must listen to me!"

"I have no time for you now, man! My son has just charged in like a fool. He must think he *is* Camaris—after all I told him!" He stalked across the platform, satisfying himself that everyone was in as much of a furious state of excitement as he was. The priest pursued him like a dog nipping at the heels of a bull. Finally Strangyeard grasped Isgrimnur's surcoat and yanked hard, pulling the duke off-balance and almost toppling him over.

"By all that's holy, Isgrimnur!" he shouted. "You must listen to me!"

The duke stared at the priest's reddened face. Strangyeard's eyepatch had slid almost onto his nose. "What are you on about?" Isgrimnur demanded. "We have knocked down the gates! We are at war, man!"

"The Norns must know about the tunnels," Strangyeard said urgently. Isgrimnur saw Sangfugol the harper skulking beside the platform, and wondered what both a priest *and* a harper were doing in the middle of things that did not concern them.

"What do you mean?"

"They must know. And if we can think to send somebody under the castle walls . . ."

The clamor of men as they charged up the hillside toward the shattered gate, even the grumbling of thunder and the moan of the wind, were suddenly overtopped by a hideous grinding noise, a rasp like fingernails on slate. Horses reared, and several of the soldiers on the platform lifted their hands to their ears.

"Oh, merciful Aedon," said Isgrimnur, staring up at the Hayholt. "No!"

The last of Isorn's company had fought their way through the opening in the wall. At their backs, thrusting up from the snowy ground and the wreckage left by the battering ram, a second gate was rising. It climbed upward swiftly, rasping like an ogre's teeth grinding on bone. Within a few moments the wall was sealed again. The new gate, beneath a layer of snow and mud, was covered with dull iron plates.

"Oh, God help me, I was right," Isgrimnur groaned. "They have trapped Isorn and the others. Sweet Usires." He stared in sick horror as the engineers rolled the ram forward and began hammering at the second gate. The metal-clad wood did not seem to give even an inch.

"They think they have trapped Camaris," Strangyeard said. "That is what they planned to do all along."

Isgrimnur turned and grabbed at the priest's robe, thrusting his face close to the smaller man's. "You knew? You *knew?!*"

"Goodness, Isgrimnur, no, I didn't. But I see it now."

The duke let him go and began shouting frantic orders, sending his remaining archers forward to help protect the engineers, who were receiving redoubled interest from the soldiers on the Hayholt's walls. "And find me that damn Sithi general!" he bawled. "The one in green! The fairy-folk must help us knock this new wall down!"

"But you still must listen to me, Isgrimnur," said the priest. "If the Sithi know of those tunnels, the Norns must, too. The Storm King, when he lived, was master of Asu'a!"

"What does that mean? Speak plainly, damn you!" Isgrimnur was furiously agitated. "My son is trapped in there with only a few men. We must break down this new gate and go in after him."

"I think you must look . . ." Strangyeard began, when another round of excited shouts interrupted him. This time, though, they came from behind Isgrimnur.

"Coming up through Erchester!" one of the mounted men screamed. "Look! It is the White Foxes!"

"I think you must look behind you, I was going to say." Strangyeard shook his head. "If we could go beneath the walls, so could they."

Even in near-darkness it was possible to see that the host moving up Main Row was not human. White faces gleamed in the shadows. White hands held long sharp spears. Now that they had been sighted and the need for stealth was gone, they began to sing, a triumphant chant that fell painfully on Isgrimnur's ears.

The duke allowed himself one moment of utter despair. "Ransomer preserve us, we have been snared like rabbits." He patted the priest's shoulder in silent thanks, then strode to the middle of the platform. "To me, Josua's men! To me!" He waved to Jeremias, calling for his horse.

The Norns came up Main Row, singing.

56

Beside the Pool

"**Up to the tree . . .**" Guthwulf mumbled. His face beneath Simon's hand was oven-hot and slippery with sweat. "To the flaming tree. Wants to go . . ."

The earl was getting worse, and Simon did not know what to do. He was still badly hobbled by his own wounds, knew almost nothing of the healing arts, and in any case was in a lightless place with nothing that might be of use in easing Guthwulf's fever. Because of a dim recollection that fevers had to burn themselves out, he had covered the suffering earl with some of the rags strewn about the floor, but he felt like a traitor putting warm things on someone who seemed to be burning up.

Helpless, he sat down beside Guthwulf once more, listening to him rave and praying that the earl would survive. The blackness pressed in on him like the crushing depths of the ocean, making it hard to breathe, to think. He tried to distract himself by remembering the things he had seen, the places he had been. More than anything he wanted to *do* something, but at this moment there seemed to be nothing to do but wait. He did not want to be left alone and lost in the empty places again.

Something touched his leg and Simon reached out, thinking that Guthwulf in his misery was looking for a hand to hold. Instead, Simon's fingers trailed across something warm and covered with fur. He let out a shout of surprise and scrabbled back, expecting momentarily to feel rats or something worse swarming over him. When there was no further contact he crouched, huddled into himself, for a long time. Then his feelings of responsibility for Guthwulf won out and he edged back toward the earl. A squeamish exploration found the furry thing again. It shrank back as he had, but did not go far. It was a cat.

Simon laughed breathlessly, then reached out and stroked the creature. It arched beneath his hand, but would not come to him. Instead it settled against the blind man and Guthwulf's movements became less agitated, his breathing quieter. The cat's presence seemed to soothe him. Simon, too, felt a little less alone, and resolved to be careful not to frighten the animal away. He fetched some of the remaining heel of bread and offered a pinch to the cat, who sniffed it but did not take any. Simon ate a few small pieces himself, then tried to find a comfortable position to sleep in.

Simon awakened, abruptly conscious that something had happened. In the darkness it was impossible to discern any changes, but he had the inescapable feeling that things had shifted somehow, that he was suddenly in an unfamiliar place with no knowledge of how he had come there. But the rags around him were the same, and Guthwulf's labored breathing, though quieter, still rasped away nearby. Simon crawled over to the earl, gently pushed aside the warm and purring cat, and was heartened to feel much of the cramping tension gone from the blind man's limbs. Perhaps he was recovering from the fever. Perhaps the cat had been his companion and its presence had restored a little of his sanity. In any case, Guthwulf had stopped raving. Simon let the cat clamber back into the crook of the earl's arm. It felt strange not to hear Guthwulf's voice.

During the earliest hours of his fever, the earl had been almost lucid for short stretches, although he was so plagued by his voices and former solitude that it was difficult to separate truth from terrifying dream. He talked about crawling through darkness, desperate to find Bright-Nail—although, strangely, he did not seem to think of it as a sword at all, but as something alive that summoned him. Simon remembered Thorn's disturbing vitality and thought he understood a little of what the earl meant.

It was hard to make sense out of the impressions of a half-mad blind man, but as Guthwulf spoke, Simon pictured the earl walking through the tunnels, lured by something that called to him in a voice he could not ignore. Guthwulf had gone far beyond his usual range, it seemed, and had heard and felt many terrible things. At last he had crawled, and when even those narrow ways were blocked, he had dug, fighting his way through the last cubits of earth that had separated him from the object of his obsession.

He dug into John's barrow, Simon realized, shuddering. *Like a blind mole after a carrot, scraping, scraping . . .*

Guthwulf had taken his prize and had somehow found his way back to his nest, but apparently even the joy of possessing the thing he had sought had not been enough to keep him in hiding. For some reason he had ventured out, perhaps to steal food from the forge—where else had the bread and water come from?—but perhaps for some deeper, more complicated reason.

Why did he come to me? Simon wondered. *Why would he risk being caught by Inch?* He thought again of Thorn, of how it had seemed almost to choose where it wished to go. *Maybe Bright-Nail wanted to find . . . me.*

The thought was a frighteningly seductive one. If Bright-Nail was being drawn to the great conflict that was coming, then maybe it somehow knew that Guthwulf would never willingly go up into the light again. As Thorn had chosen Simon and his fellows to bring it down from Urmsheim and back to Camaris, maybe Bright-Nail had chosen Simon to carry it up to Green Angel Tower to fight the Storm King.

Another dim recollection surfaced. *In my dream, Leleth said that the sword was part of my story. Is that what she meant?* The details were strangely misty, but he remembered the sad-faced man who had held the blade across his lap as he waited for something. *The dragon?*

Simon let his fingers trail away from the cat's back and down Guthwulf's arm until they reached Bright-Nail. The earl moaned, but did not resist as Simon gently pried his fingers away. His finger reverently traced the rough shape of the Nail, bound just below the guard. A nail from the Execution Tree of holy Usires! And some sacred relic of Saint Eahlstan was sealed inside the hollow hilt, he remembered. Prester John's sword. It was astonishing that a onetime scullion should ever touch such a thing!

Simon curled his hand around the hilt. It seemed to . . . fit. It lay in his hand as comfortably as though it had been made for him. All other thoughts about the blade, about Guthwulf, slid away. He sat in the dark and felt the sword to be an extension of his own arm, of himself. He stood, ignoring his aching muscles, and slashed at the lightless void before him. A moment later, horrified at the thought that he might accidentally strike Bright-Nail against the rock wall of the cavern and blunt its edge, he sat down again, then crawled away to his corner of the cavern and stretched out on the stone, clutching the sword to him as though it were a child. The metal was cold where it touched his skin, and the blade was sharp, but he did not want to let it go. Across the chamber, Guthwulf murmured uncomfortably.

Some time had passed, although Simon did not know whether he had slept or not, when he suddenly became aware that something was missing: he could no longer hear the earl breathing. For a moment, as he scrambled across the uneven floor, he clung to the wild hope that Guthwulf had grown well enough to leave the cavern, but the presence of Bright-Nail still gripped in his own fingers made that seem very unlikely: the blind man would not for a moment allow someone else to have his blade.

When Simon reached Guthwulf, the earl's skin was cool as river clay.

He did not weep, but his feeling of loss was great. His sorrow was not for Guthwulf the man, who except for these last dreamlike hours or days he had only known as a fearsome figure, but for himself, left alone once more.

Almost alone. Something bumped against his shin. The cat seemed to be trying to get his attention. It missed its companion, Simon felt sure. Perhaps it thought that somehow he could wake Guthwulf where it had failed.

"Sorry," he whispered, running his fingers down its back and gently tugging its tail. "He's gone somewhere else. I'm lonely, too."

Feeling empty, he sat for a moment and took stock of things. Now he had no choice but to brave the mazy, lightless tunnels, even though he doubted he would find his way out again without a guide. Two times he had stumbled through this haunted labyrinth, each time followed so closely by death that he heard its patient footsteps behind him; it was too much to hope that he would be lucky again. Still, there was little else he could do. Green Angel Tower stood somewhere above, and Bright-Nail must be carried there. If Josua and the others had not brought Thorn, he would do what he could, although it would doubtless end in failure. He owed that much to all those who had sold their dear lives for his freedom.

It was difficult to put Bright-Nail down—he already felt a little of Guthwulf's possessiveness, although there was nothing in the small cavern that might endanger the sword—but he could accomplish little with it clutched in his hand. He leaned it against one of the walls, then proceeded to the unpleasant task of undressing the dead earl. When he had removed Guthwulf's tattered clothing he took some of the rags scattered about the cavern and, in poor imitation of the priestly labors in the House of Preparing, wrapped the body. A part of him felt ridiculous for going to such lengths for a man who had, by all repute, been little-loved in his life, and who would lie here alone and undiscovered regardless, but Simon felt a stubborn urge to pay the blind man back. Morgenes and Maegwin had given their lives for him, and they had been given no memorial, no rites, except those in Simon's own heart. Guthwulf should not go to the Fields Beyond unheralded.

When he had finished, he stood.

"Our Lord protect you,"

he began, struggling to remember the words to the Prayer for the Dead,

"And Usires His only Son lift you up.
May you be carried to the green valleys
Of His domains,
Where the souls of the good and righteous sing from the hilltops,
And angels are in the trees,
Speaking joy with God's own voice. . . ."

"Thank you, Guthwulf," he said when the prayer was done. "I'm sorry to take the sword away from you, but I'll try to do what should be done."

He made the sign of the Tree—hoping that, despite the darkness, God would see and so take note of Guthwulf when at last the earl came before Him—then he pulled on Guthwulf's clothing and boots. A year before, he might have thought twice before donning a dead man's garb, but Simon had walked so close to death himself that he was now all practicality. It was warm and safe in the cavern, but who knew what cold winds, what sharp stones, awaited him?

As he drank off the last drops in the water bowl, the cat nudged his leg once more. "You can come with me or stay here," he told it. "Your choice." He took up Bright-Nail, then wrapped a rag around the blade just below the hilt and tied the earl's buckleless belt around the sword and his waist so his hands would be free. It was more than a slight relief to feel it against him once more.

As he felt his way toward the mouth of the cavern the cat was at his feet, twining in and out between his ankles. "You'll trip me," he said. "Stop that."

He edged a little distance along the passageway, but the creature was between his legs again and made him stumble. He reached down for it, then laughed hollowly at the stupidity of trying to catch a cat in blind darkness. The cat moved under his hand and then slipped away in the opposite direction. Simon paused.

"That way, not this way?" he said aloud. After a moment, he shrugged, then laughed again. Despite all the horror behind him and before him, he felt curiously free. "Very well, then, I'll follow you for a while. Which means I'll probably wind up sitting next to the largest rat hole in Osten Ard."

The cat bumped him, then slipped away up the corridor. Feeling along the walls, entirely surrounded by darkness, Simon trailed after it.

Yis-hadra stopped at the base of the stairs and chimed anxiously to her husband. Yis-fidri replied. They bent to examine the cracked stone baluster.

"This place," Yis-fidri said. "If you follow these steps upward, you will come at last to the mortal castle built atop this one."

"Where?" asked Miriamele. She dropped her bow and pack to the tunnel floor and slumped against the stone. "Where in the castle?"

"We know not," Yis-hadra said. "All has been built since our day. No Tinukeda'ya touched those stones."

"And you? Where will you go?" She looked up the stairwell. It spiraled up far beyond the weak light of the dwarrow's batons, twisting into darkness.

"We will find another place." Yis-fidri looked at his wife. "There are few of us left, but there are still places that will welcome our hands and eyes."

"It is time for *our* going," Binabik said urgently. "Who is knowing how far away the Norns are?"

Miriamele asked the dwarrows: "Why don't you come with us? You are strong, and we can use your strength. You should know by now that our fight is yours, too."

Yis-fidri shuddered and raised his long hands as though to fend her off. "Do you not understand? We do not belong in the light, in the world of Sudhoda'ya. We have already been changed by you, done things that Tinukeda'ya do not do. We have . . . we have killed some of those who were once our masters." He murmured something in the dwarrow-tongue and Yis-hadra and his other remaining folk chorused unhappily. "It will take us long to learn to live with that. We do not belong in the world above. Let us go to find the darkness and deep places we crave."

Binabik, who had spoken much to Yis-fidri during the last part of their flight, stepped forward and extended his small hand. "May you find safety."

The dwarrow looked at him for a moment as if he did not understand, then slowly put out his own spidery fingers and wrapped them around the troll's. "And you. I will not tell you my thoughts, for they are fearful and unhappy."

Miriamele bit back words of argument. The dwarrows wished to go. They had fulfilled the promise that she had forced out of them. They were already frightened and miserable; aboveground they might be less than useless, more a responsibility than an asset. "Farewell, Yis-fidri," she said, then turned to his wife. "Yis-hadra, thank you for showing me how you tend the stone."

The dwarrow bobbed her head. "May you also fare well."

Even as she spoke, the lights of the batons flickered and the underground chamber seemed to shift, another convulsion without movement; a moment later, when things were again as they had been, the remaining dwarrows began to whisper.

"We must go now," Yis-hadra said, her dark eyes wide with fear. She and her husband turned and led their troop of shuffling, spindle-legged kin away into the shadows. Within moments the corridor was as empty as if they had never existed. Miriamele blinked.

"We must go also." Binabik started up the stairs, then turned. "Where is the monk?"

Miriamele looked back. Cadrach, who had been at the rear of the assembled dwarrows, was sitting on the ground, his eyes half-closed. The flicker of Binabik's torch made him seem to sway.

"He's useless." She bent to pick up her belongings. "We should leave him here. Let him follow if he wants to."

Binabik frowned at her. "Help him, Miriamele. Otherwise, he is left for the Norns' finding."

She was not sure the monk didn't deserve just that, but she shrugged and went to him anyway. A tug on his arm brought him slowly to his feet.

"We're going."

Cadrach looked at her for a moment. "Ah," he said, then followed her up the ancient stairway.

As the company of Sithi led them farther into the deeps below the Hayholt, Tiamak and Josua found themselves staring around in astonishment, like Lakeland farmers on their first visit to Nabban.

"What a treasure trove this is!" Josua breathed. "And to think it was below me all those years I lived here. I would gladly spend a lifetime down here, exploring, studying. . . ."

Tiamak, too, was overwhelmed. The rough corridors of the outer tunnels had given way to a decayed splendor he could never have imagined, and even now could scarcely believe. Vast chambers which seemed to have been pains-takingly carved out of living rock, every surface a minutely detailed tapestry; seemingly endless stairways, thin and beautiful as spiderwebs, that curled up into shadow or stretched across black emptiness; entire rooms carved in the likeness of forest clearings or mountainsides with waterfalls, though everything in the chamber was solid stone—even as crumbling ruins, Asu'a the Great was astonishing.

They Who Watch and Shape, Tiamak thought, *seeing this place has made every bit of my suffering worthwhile. My lame leg, my hours in the ghant nest—I would not trade them if I must also lose the memories of this hour.*

As they wound through the dusty byways, Tiamak tore his eyes away from the wonders that surrounded him long enough to observe the strange behavior of his Sithi companions. When Likimeya and the others stopped to let the mortals rest, in a high-roofed chamber whose arching windows were clogged with dirt and rubble, Tiamak sat beside Aditu.

"Forgive me if my question is rude," he asked softly, "but do your people mourn their old home? You seem . . . distracted."

Aditu inclined her head, bending her graceful neck. "In part, yes. It is sad to see the beautiful things our people built in such a state—and for those who lived here . . ." she made an intricate gesture, "it is even more painful. Do you remember the chamber carved with great flowered steps—the Hall of Five Staircases, as we call it?"

"We stopped there a long time," Tiamak said, remembering.

"That was the place where my mother's mother, Briseyu Dawnfeather, died."

The marsh man thought of how Likimeya had stood expressionlessly in the center of that wide room. Who could know these immortals?

Aditu shook her head. "But such are not the greatest reasons we are, as you put it, distracted. There are . . . presences here. Things that should not be."

Tiamak had himself felt more than a touch of what he thought Aditu meant—a riffle of wind on the back of his neck that seemed insistent as probing fingers, echoes that almost sounded like faint voices. "What does it mean?"

"Something is awake here in Asu'a that should not be awake. It is hard to explain. Whatever it may be, it has given a semblance of life to what should not have one."

Tiamak frowned, unsure. "Do you mean . . . ghosts?"

Aditu's smile was fleeting. "If I understood First Grandmother when she taught me what the mortal word means, no. Not as such. But it is hard to show the difference. Your tongue is not suited for it, and you do not see or feel what we do."

"How can you tell?" He looked across to Josua, but the prince was staring fixedly at the ornately carved walls.

"Because if you did," Aditu replied, "I suspect you would not be sitting there so calmly." She rose and crossed the rubble-strewn floor to where her mother and Jiriki stood in quiet conversation.

In the middle of emptiness, Tiamak suddenly felt surrounded by danger. He slid closer to Josua.

"Do you feel it, Prince Josua?" Tiamak asked. "The Sithi do. They are frightened."

The prince looked grim. "We are all of us frightened. I would have liked a full night to prepare for this, but Camaris took that away from me. I try not to remember where it is we are going."

"And all with no idea of what to do when we get there," Tiamak mourned. "Was there ever a battle fought so confusedly?" He hesitated. "I have no right to question you, Prince Josua, but why *did* you follow Camaris? Surely others less crucial to our success than you could have tried to track him."

The prince stared ahead. "I was the only one there. I sought to bring him back before he was lost to us." He sighed. "I feared others would not come in time. But even more . . ."

The strange perturbation of air and stone came again, sudden and disorienting, cutting Josua off in mid-speech. The Sithi's lights jittered, although the immortals themselves seemed not to move. For a moment, Tiamak thought he sensed the presence of a host of others, a shadowy horde disposed all through the ruined halls. Then the feeling was gone and everything was as it had been but for an odd, lingering smell of smoke.

"Aedon's mercy!" Josua looked down at his feet as though surprised to discover them still on the ground. "What is this place?"

The Sithi had paused. Jiriki turned to the mortals.

"We must go faster," he said. "Can you keep up?"

"I have a lame leg," Tiamak replied. "But I will do my best."

Josua laid his hand on the Wrannaman's shoulder. "I will not leave you behind. I can carry you if need be."

Tiamak smiled, touched. "I do not think it will come to that, Prince Josua."

"Come, then. The Sithi need haste. We will try to give it to them."

They moved at a fast trot through the winding passageways. Watching the backs of the Sithi, Tiamak had little doubt that if they chose they could leave their mortal companions far behind. But they did not, and that said much: the Sithi thought that Tiamak and Josua could do something important. He ignored the pain in his leg and hurried on.

They seemed to run for hours, although Tiamak had no way of knowing if that was true: just as the substance of Asu'a itself seemed strangely unstable, so too did time move in a manner that Tiamak no longer trusted himself to interpret. The lag between steps sometimes seemed to stretch for long moments, then an instant later he would be in another part of the ruined sub-castle, still running, with no memory of the intervening journey.

He Who Always Steps on Sand, keep me sane until I have done whatever I can do, he prayed. Beside him, the prince too seemed in silent communication with something or someone.

For a while the Sithi were so far ahead that their lights were little more than a glow in the tunnel before them. Tiamak's own globe, jiggling in his clutch, provided inconstant light; he and Josua found themselves stumbling through wreckage they could barely see, suffering more than a few cuts and bruises, until they caught up to the immortals once more.

The Sithi had halted beneath a high archway where they stood silhouetted by a diffuse glow from the chamber beyond. As Tiamak hobbled to a stop beside them, gasping for breath, he wondered if they had finally reached the light of the upper world. As he sucked air into his lungs, he stared at the dragonlike serpent carved on the arch. Its tail stretched down one side and was carved across the dusty floor of the archway as well, then rose up the other side and back to the lintel, where the tip was clasped in its owner's mouth. There were still flecks of paint on its thousands of minute scales.

The smoky light behind the Sithi made them seem distorted, freakishly lean and without firm edges. The nearest, Jiriki, turned and looked back at the panting mortals. There was compassion on his face, but it battled with more pressing emotions. "Beyond is the Pool of Three Depths," he said. "If I tell you it is a Master Witness, you may have some idea of what kind of forces are at work here. This is one of the mightiest of the places of power; the great worms of Osten Ard once came to drink its waters and share their wordless wisdom, long before my people set foot in this land."

"Why have we stopped here?" Josua asked. "Is Camaris . . . ?"

"He may be, or he may have already been here and passed on. It is a place of potency as I said, and it is one of the sources of the change we have felt all around us. He may very well have been drawn here." Jiriki lifted his hand in warning; for the first time, Tiamak could see the weariness on the immortal's face. "Please do nothing without asking. Touch nothing except the floor where we walk. If something speaks to you, do not reply."

Tiamak was chilled. He nodded his understanding. There were a thousand questions he longed to ask, but the tension he saw in the Sithi was a strong argument for silence.

"Lead on," said Josua.

Appearing a little hesitant themselves, the Sithi stepped through the archway into a wide chamber full of indirect light. Where Tiamak could see the walls through the strange mistiness of the air, they seemed almost new-built, undamaged and ribbed with great sculpted pillars that stretched up toward the hidden ceiling. The pool, a circular expanse of scintillant water, lay in the center of the chamber. A circular staircase whose landing touched on the pool's far side spiraled up, massive yet graceful, and vanished in the mists above.

Something in the room was . . . alive. Tiamak could think of no other way to describe the sensation. Whether it was the pool itself, with its shifting blue and green glows flickering up from the depths, he could not say, but there was far more to this place than water and stone. The air was thunderstorm-taut, and he found he was holding his breath as they moved forward. The Sithi, moving as cautiously as hunters stalking a wounded boar, fanned out along the edge of the pool, growing unaccountably more distant from him with each single step. The smoky light glimmered.

"Camaris!" shouted Josua. Tiamak looked up, startled. The prince was staring at a shape beyond the farthest of the Sithi, a tall figure with a long shadow in one hand. The prince hastened around the tarn's rim; the Sithi, their attention pulled away from the pool, moved with him toward the solitary figure. Tiamak hurried after, the pain of his leg momentarily forgotten.

For an instant Tiamak thought the prince was mistaken, that whatever this shape was, it was not Camaris: for a blink of time he saw someone completely different, jet-haired and dressed in strange robes, with a branching crown upon his head. Then the chamber seemed to shudder and tip, and the Wrannaman stumbled; when he had regained his balance, he saw that it was indeed the old knight. Camaris looked up at the approaching figures and stepped back, his eyes wild with alarm, then leveled the black sword before him. Josua and the Sithi stopped beyond its reach.

"Camaris," said the prince. "It is Josua. Look, it is only me. I have been searching for you."

The old man stared at him, but the sword did not waver from its defensive position. "It is a sinful world," he replied hoarsely.

"I will go with you," said Josua. "Wherever you wish to go. Do not be afraid. I will not stop you."

Likimeya's voice was surprisingly gentle. "We can help you, *Hikka Ti-tuno*. We will not stay you, but we can make your pain less." She took a step forward, her hands held with palms upward. "Do you remember Amerasu Ship-Born?"

The old man's lips drew back in a grimace of pain or fear and he drew Thorn back as if to strike. Dark Kuroyi's sword hissed from its sheath as he stepped in front of Likimeya.

"There is no need," she said coldly. "Put up."

The tall Sitha hesitated for a moment, then slipped his witchwood sword back into place. Camaris lowered his black blade once more.

"Pity." Kuroyi sounded genuinely regretful. "I have always wondered what it would be to cross swords with the greatest of mortal warriors. . . ."

Before anyone else spoke again the light flared wildly, then the room was plunged into blackness. A moment later light returned, but this time the misty air was blue as the center of a flame. Tiamak felt a freezing wind that seemed to blow through him, and the tension of the air increased until his ears hammered.

"How you do love mortals." The dreadful voice sounded in his thoughts and all through his body; the words felt like insects skittering on the Wrannaman's skin. *"You cannot leave them alone."*

Tiamak and the others turned. In the roiling mists behind them a shape was forming, pale robed and silver masked, enthroned in midair above the pool. The sickly blue light did not reach much beyond the water, and the chamber was now walled with shadow. The Wrannaman felt terror seize him by the spine. He could not move, could only pray that he would be unnoticed. Storm-spike's queen—for who else could it be?—was as dreadful as any nightmare vision of She Who Waits to Take All Back.

Likimeya nodded her head. She held herself stiffly, as though even speaking took much effort. "So, Eldest. You have found a way to reach the Pool of Three Depths. That does not mean that you can use it."

The masked figure did not move, but Tiamak felt something almost like triumph emanate from it. *"I silenced Amerasu—I broke her before my huntsman dispatched her. Do you think you are her equal, child?"*

"By myself, no. But I have others here with me."

"Other children." A pale gloved hand lifted, wavering as the mist swirled.

Tiamak was dimly aware of movement on the edge of the circle of figures around him, but could not tear his eyes away from the shimmering silver mask.

"Camaris!" Josua cried. "He is leaving."

"Go," said Jiriki. "And you, too, Tiamak. Follow him."

"But what of you?" The prince's voice cracked. "And how will we find our way?"

"He is going where he is drawn." Jiriki moved closer to his mother, who already seemed locked in some silent struggle with the Norn Queen. The muscles of Likimeya's face were rippling. "And that is where you must go, too. This is our struggle here." Jiriki turned to face the pool.

"Go!" said Aditu urgently. She tugged at Tiamak's sleeve, pulling him off-balance and sending him stumbling toward Josua. "We will call on the power of the Oldest Tree and hold her at bay as long as we can, but we cannot defeat their plan here. Utuk'ku is already drawing on the Master Witness. I can feel it."

"But what is she doing? What is happening?" Tiamak heard his voice rising in terror.

"We cannot see that," Aditu moaned. Her teeth were clenched. "We have all we can do to hold her back. You and the others must accomplish whatever remains. This is *our* battle. Now go!" She turned away from him.

The pulsing radiance of the pool grew stronger, and lavender flames kindled along the walls, leaping as though in a fierce wind. The entire chamber felt tight as a drumhead. Tiamak thought he could feel himself shrinking, twisting, being slowly crushed by the forces now unleashed. Something powerful, yet without form or substance, was beating out at him from the misty shape that hovered over the water.

Fumbling as though they were battered by gale winds, the Sithi formed into a line before the pool and linked their hands, then began to sing.

As the immortals' strange music rose, the lights of the pool flickered wildly. Tiamak stared helplessly at the glowing mists, unable to remember how to move. The walls around the pool seemed to bend inward and then push out again, bend in and push out, as though the chamber breathed. On the rim of the pool Aditu staggered and slumped forward, but her brother, who stood beside her, pulled her upright; the song of the Sithi faltered for a moment, then resumed.

In response to their wailing music, something else began to form in the mists of the pool, something that rapidly became entangled with the pale shadow of the Norn Queen. Tiamak saw it as a dim, dark shape with a wide trunk, swaying branches, and phantom leaves that fluttered as though a wind caressed them. Aditu had said "the Oldest Tree"; Tiamak could sense this huge thing's antiquity, its deep roots and spreading, nurturing strength. For a moment he felt something like hope.

As if in response, the blue lights in the water began to burn even more fiercely, until the glare filled the chamber with blinding radiance. The tree shape grew less substantial. The Wrannaman felt himself sinking down to the ground as Utuk'ku's choking, freezing might surged out from the Pool of Three Depths.

"Tiamak!"

The voice was distant and far behind him; it meant little. Nothing could push through the fog that was filling his ears, his heart, his thoughts. . . .

High above the center of the pool, the Norn Queen seemed a creature made entirely of ice, but something black pulsed at the heart of her, and jagged flares of purple and blue played about her head and glinted from her shining mask. She spread her arms, then clenched her gloved fists. Kuroyi abruptly shrieked and fell away from the rest of the Sithi to writhe on the ground. The dark-haired Sitha began to deform into impossibly swift-changing shapes, as though invisible hands kneaded him like dough. The other Sithi slumped and fell back; the ghost-tree vanished completely. After a few moments Aditu and her kin recovered themselves and began fighting to close the gap where Kuroyi had been. They struggled as though immersed in deep water, striving to join hands once more. The fallen Sitha had stopped struggling and lay still. There was no longer anything manlike in his form.

Something jerked at Tiamak's arm, then jerked again. He turned slowly. Josua was screaming at him, but he could not hear the words. The prince pulled him up onto his feet and dragged him, stumbling, away from the pool. Tiamak's heart was rattling as though it might burst. His legs did not want to support him, but Josua kept tugging until Tiamak could move on his own, then the prince turned and lurched away in pursuit of Camaris. The old knight was several score paces ahead, walking stiff-legged toward the dark passages at the far side of the wide chamber. Tiamak limped slowly after them both.

The song of the Dawn Children rose again behind him, more raggedly this time. Tiamak did not dare look back. Blue light throbbed all across the cavern ceiling, and the shadows bloomed and vanished and then bloomed again.

Despite the strange shifting that seemed to be going on around him, despite the bodiless voices that sometimes shrieked or gibbered in the blackness, Simon did not surrender to fear. He had survived the wheel and then had passed over into the void and returned. He had won back his life, but he did not hold it as tightly as he once had, and so, in a way, his grip on it was more sure. What were little things like hunger or momentary blindness? He had been hungry before. He had wandered without light.

The cat padded silently ahead, turning at intervals to rub against him before moving on, leading him slowly through the twisting tunnels. He had long since given his safety over into the animal's care. There was nothing else to do, and no use worrying about it.

Something was happening around him, although he could not tell exactly what that something was. The ghostly presences and strange distortions were even stronger than before, and seemed to come now as regularly as waves dashing themselves upon a beach, sweeping all before them, then ebbing away again. He hardened himself to the sensations as he had hardened himself to his own aches.

Simon felt his way along the black corridors, Bright-Nail scraping the walls like a beetle's feeler, his fingers trailing through dust and dank moss and cobwebs and other things less pleasant. He could do nothing but what he was doing. He had faced the ice-dragon and shouted his name at it, had wandered the emptiness beyond dreams and clung to himself. He could not turn back from the task that was before him, and he would not.

Bright-Nail seemed to change along with his lightless surroundings. One moment it was a simple blade slapping against his hip, then a moment later it seemed to throb in time with the convulsions of the castle depths, becoming for a moment a living thing; at those times, it was hard to tell whether one of them was master, or whether Simon and the sword were, as he and the cat were, two creatures traveling the darkness together in strange partnership.

At such times, he could begin to hear its call in his thoughts; it was a faint presence, only a hint of the song that Guthwulf had seemed to hear, but it was growing steadily stronger. For brief moments he could almost understand it, as though it spoke to him in a language he had forgotten long ago, but which was slowly surfacing from the place in his memory where it had been buried. But Simon did not think he wanted to understand what the blade sang. Perhaps if he wandered long enough, he thought, he would indeed become like Guthwulf, and hear almost nothing but the sword's compelling music.

He hoped he would not be in darkness that long.

There came a time when the cat stopped and did not go on. It wreathed itself around his shins as though it wished to be stroked; when he bent to touch it, it pushed at his fingers with its muzzle, but did not continue on its way. He waited, finally wondering if he had not put far too much trust in a mere beast.

"Where next?" he said. His voice scarcely echoed: they were still in one of the narrower passages. "Go on, now. I'm waiting."

The cat rubbed against him, purring. After a few moments, Simon put his hands out and began searching carefully along the walls, looking for something—perhaps a doorway of some kind that did not reach the floor—which might have stopped their progress. Instead, on a shelf of rock set into the wall, nearly head high, he found a plate and a covered bowl.

I've been here before! he realized. *Unless some madman is leaving food all across the tunnels. But if so, bless him, bless him anyway.*

Simon said a prayer of thanks as he took the bread and dried meat and small wedge of cheese from the plate, then sat down and ate enough of each to feel happier and more prosperous than he had in a long while. He drank half the bowl of water, then after a moment's consideration, finished it off. He regretted the lack of a water skin, but if he had to carry the water without one, it might as well be inside him.

The cat was at him again, butting and purring. Simon broke off a sizable piece of the jerked meat to share with his guide—the cat took it so quickly its sharp teeth scraped his fingers—then put the remainder in the pocket of his shirt. He stood.

P'raps he won't want to lead me anymore, he thought. *This may have been all the little creature wanted.*

But the cat, as though some ritual had been successfully observed, slithered in and out between his ankles for a few moments, then started off again. Simon bent and felt first its head, then its back, then its tail pass beneath his fingers. He smiled an invisible smile and followed it.

It was so faint at first as to be almost unnoticeable, but gradually Simon realized that the walls around him were slowly becoming visible. The light was so dim that for hundreds of paces he thought it was only his eyes playing tricks on him, but eventually he realized that he was seeing the rough surfaces across which he dragged his hands. The cat, too, had become a real thing instead of just an idea, a hint of movement on the tunnel floor before him.

He followed the shadow-cat up through the coiling tunnels. These were rougher hewn than those which traversed the ruins of Asu'a, and he felt a growing certainty that he was back in the mortal castle once more. As he turned another bend, the dim netherlight became a torch in a wall bracket at the far end of a long passageway.

Light! Back again! He fell to his knees, unmindful for a moment of his aching limbs, and pressed his forehead against the stone floor. He stayed there, trembling. Light! He was in the world again.

Thank you, Maegwin. Bless you. Thank you, Guthwulf.

The cat was a gray shape against the gray stone. Something else tugged at his memory.

I've seen that cat before—or have I? The Hayholt was full of cats.

The air abruptly contracted and the walls shivered and then bowed inward as though to trap him. An image passed before his mind's eye, a great tree shivering in storm winds, its branches torn loose and spinning away. For a moment Simon felt as though he had been turned inside-out. Even when the vision had gone and all was as it had been, he remained on his knees for long moments, panting.

His four-footed guide stopped and looked around to see if he was still following, then continued on, as though the strange slippage was beneath a cat's notice. Simon clambered to his feet.

The creature paused in an archway. Simon saw a narrow staircase climbing up into darkness. The cat bumped his shin but did not move on.

"Should I go up here?" he whispered. He poked his head into the entranceway. High above, hidden by the twisting stairwell, another source of light glowed faintly.

He stared at the cat for a moment. The cat stared back, yellow eyes wide.

"Very well, then." He touched Bright-Nail, making sure the hilt was not tangled in the rags of his belt, then began to climb. After a few steps he turned and looked back. The cat still sat in the middle of the tunnel floor, watching. "Aren't you coming?"

The gray cat stood and slowly sauntered away down the corridor. Even if it had possessed the gift of speech, it could not more clearly have told him that from this point he was on his own.

Simon smiled grimly.

I suppose there's no cat in the world stupid enough to go where I'm going.

He turned and made his way up the shadowed stairs.

The stairwell opened at last into a broad windowless room imperfectly lit by an open hatch door in the ceiling. As he stepped out from behind the wooden screen that hid the stairway, he realized that he was in one of the storage rooms below the refectory. He had been in this place before as well, on the momentous, horrible day when he had discovered Prince Josua in Pryrates' prison cell . . . but that time the storeroom had been packed to the ceilings with all manner of food and other goods. Now the barrels that remained lay empty, many in splinters. Dusty mantles of spiderweb covered the remains, and the few spatters of flour left on the floor were crisscrossed with the tracks of mice. It looked as though no one had entered the room for some time.

Up above him, he knew, stood the refectory, and the hundreds of other close-huddled buildings of the Inner Bailey. Looming over them all was the ivory spike of Green Angel Tower.

As he thought of it, he felt Bright-Nail's song grow a little more insistent.

. . . *go there* . . . It was a whisper at the farthest edge of his thoughts.

Simon found and replaced the hatchway ladder, which had toppled to the floor, then began to climb. It creaked ominously, but held. Beneath its complaining he could hear a faint murmur, as though the hissing voices of the tunnels were following him up from the dark.

The only illumination in the refectory hall was the weak and unevenly pulsing gray light that leaked in through the high windows. The remaining tables and benches were scattered, some smashed to flinders, but most were gone entirely, perhaps taken to be burned as firewood. A bleak layer of dust lay everywhere, even on those things which had suffered a violent end, as though the destruction had happened a century before. A pair of rats scurried across one of the broken tables, paying Simon no heed.

The murmuring noise he had heard was louder here. The greatest part of it was the wind moaning outside the windows, but there were still hints of voices crying out in pain or anger or fear. Simon looked up and saw tiny flecks of snow whirling in past the broken shutters. He thought he could feel Bright-Nail stir, like a hunting beast catching the scent of blood.

He looked once more around the refectory—taking note, however distractedly, of the damage visited upon his home—then moved as quietly as he could toward the eastern portico. As he approached the door, he saw that it sagged on broken hinges and he despaired of opening it without noise, but as he came closer and heard the tumult outside he realized no one would hear him even if he were to kick it loose. The menacing song of the wind had grown, but the shouting voices and other noises had become louder still, until it sounded as if a great battle were being fought just outside the refectory door.

He crouched and placed his eye against the wedge of light where the door had edged free from its frame. It was hard at first to make sense of what he saw.

There *was* a battle just outside, or at least great knots of armored men were surging back and forth across the bailey. The chaos was abetted by the snows which covered the muddy ground and blew through the air like smoke, making everything murky; what sky he could see was full of streaming black clouds.

Lightning flashed, turning all to brilliant noon one instant, then, on its disappearance, making it seem for a moment as though all light had fled. It looked like a battle at the gates of Hell, a madness of shrieking faces and terrified horses, and it raged like an angry sea all across the snow-smothered bailey. Trying to make his way through such madness would be choosing to die.

On the far side, hopelessly out of Simon's reach, Green Angel Tower stood with its ivory spire wreathed in thunderheads. Lightning burst across the sky once more, a jagged, flaring chain that seemed to encircle the tower. Thunder shook his bones. Staring upward in that instant of savage illumination, Simon saw a pale face gazing from the great bellchamber windows.

57

The False Messenger

Miriamele was staggeringly exhausted. She could not imagine how Binabik, with his shorter legs, could still be moving. She was certain
they had been climbing for more than an hour. How could there be so many
steps? Surely by this time they could have reached the Hayholt if they had
started from the center of the earth.

Panting, she stopped to wipe sweat from her face and look back. Cadrach
was two flights down, barely visible in the torchlight. The monk would not
give up; Miriamele had to credit him for that.

"Binabik, wait," she called. "If I . . . if I go another step . . . my legs will fall off."

The troll paused, then turned and came back down. He handed her his water
skin, and as she drank, he said: "We have almost reached to the castle. I can feel
the changing of air."

Miriamele slumped down onto the wide smooth step, discarding the bow
and pack she had been tempted to toss away so many times in the past hour.
"What air? I haven't had any in my lungs since I don't remember when."

Binabik looked at her solicitously. "Mountain-clambering is what we Qanuc
learn before we can talk. You have been doing well to stay with me."

Miriamele did not bother with a reply. A few moments later Cadrach staggered up and toppled against the wall, then slid down onto the step an arm's
length from her. His pale face was moist, his eyes remote. She watched him
fight for breath, and after a moment's hesitation offered him the water skin. He
took it without looking up.

"Rest, both of you," said Binabik. "Then after will be time for the last
climbing. We are near, very near."

"Near to what?" Miriamele took the water skin from Cadrach's unresponsive fingers and had another drink, then passed it back to the troll. "Binabik, I
have been trying to find the breath to ask you—what is happening? Something
the dwarrows said, something you thought of . . ." She held his eye, although
she could see he wished to look away. "What is it?"

The troll fell silent, but he cocked his head as though listening. There was
nothing to be heard in the stairwell except the rough noise of their breathing.
He sat down beside her.

"It was indeed something the dwarrows were saying—although that alone would not have been making my thoughts leap so." Binabik stared at his feet. "There are other thoughts I have, too. Something I have been long pondering—the 'false messenger' of Simon's dream."

"In Geloë's house," Miriamele whispered, remembering.

"And he was not the only one. A message we were receiving in the White Waste, sparrow-carried—which now it is my thinking was sent by Dinivan of Nabban, since Isgrimnur later heard him speak it as well—also held a warning against false messengers."

Miriamele felt a pang at the memory of Dinivan. He had been so kind, so clever—yet he had been broken like a kindling-stick by Pryrates. Isgrimnur's tale of the horrors he had seen in the Sancellan Aedonitis still colored her nightmares.

A sudden thought came to her: she had fought Cadrach when he tried to take her out of the Sancellan, resisted him and called him a liar until he was forced to strike her senseless and carry her out—but he had, in fact, told her the truth. Why hadn't he simply run and saved himself, leaving her to make her own way?

She turned to look at him. The monk had still not caught his breath; he lay curled against the wall, his face blank as a wax doll's.

"So long have I wondered who could be such a messenger," Binabik continued. "Many are the messengers who have come to Josua, and also to Simon and Dinivan, the two who somehow had these warnings. Which messenger was meant?"

"And now you think you know?"

Binabik started to answer, then took a breath. "Let me tell you what I am thinking. Perhaps you will be finding some flaw—you too, Cadrach. I have hope only that I am wrong." He knitted the fingers of his small hands together and frowned. "The dwarrow-folk say the Great Swords were all having their forging with the help of Words of Making—words that the dwarrows say are used for pushing back the rules of the world."

"I didn't understand that."

"I will try for explaining," Binabik said unhappily. "But truly we are having little time to talk."

"When I've caught my breath, you can talk while we're climbing."

The troll nodded. "Then here is my explaining about the world's rules. One is that things want to fall downward." He put the stopper on the water skin and then dropped it, illustrating his point. "If some *other* kind of falling is wanted—to make this fall *upward,* that might be—that is one thing that the Art is being used for. To make something that is going against the world's rules."

Miriamele nodded. Beside her, Cadrach had raised his head as though listening, but he still stared out at the opposite wall.

"But if some rule must be broken for a long time, then the Art used must have great powerfulness, just as lifting a heavy thing once and then dropping it is easier than the holding of it in the air for hours. For such tasks, the dwarrows and others who were practicing the Art used . . ."

". . . The Words of Making," Miriamele finished for him. "And they used them when the Great Swords were forged."

Binabik bobbed his head. "They did that because all the Great Swords were forged of things that had no place in Osten Ard, things which were resisting the Arts used for creating a magical weapon. This needed overcoming, but not just for a moment. *Forever* was the time that these resisting forces must be subdued, so the most powerful Words of Making were being used." He spoke slowly now. "So those blades, it is my thinking, are like the pulled-back arm of the giant sling-stones your people use to attack walled cities—balanced so that one touch sends a vast rock flying like a tiny, tiny bird. Such great power is being restrained in each one of those swords—who knows what the power of three brought together may be doing?"

"But that's good," said Miriamele, confused. "Isn't that what we need—the strength to overcome the Storm King?" She looked at Binabik's sorrowful face and her heart grew heavy. "Is there some reason we can't use it?"

Cadrach shifted against the wall, turning his gaze at last on the troll. A gleam of interest had kindled in his eyes. "But who *will* use it?" the monk asked. "That is the question, is it not?"

Binabik nodded unhappily. "That is indeed what I am fearing." He turned to the princess. "Miriamele, why is Thorn being brought here? Why are Josua and others searching for Bright-Nail?"

"To use against the Storm King," Miriamele replied. She still did not see where the troll's questions were leading, but Cadrach evidently did. A grim half-smile, as of reluctant admiration, curled the monk's lips. She wondered who the admiration was for.

"But why?" asked the troll. "What was telling us to use them against our enemy? This is not something for tricking you, Miriamele—it is what I myself have been worrying until my head feels full of sharp stones."

"Because . . ." For a moment, she could not remember. "Because of the rhyme. The rhyme that told how to drive the Storm King away."

"When frost doth grow on Claves' bell . . ."

Binabik recited, his voice ringing strangely in the stairwell. His face twisted in what looked like pain.

"And Shadows walk upon the road
When water blackens in the Well
Three Swords must come again

"When Bukken from the Earth do creep
And Hunën from the heights descend

When Nightmare throttles peaceful Sleep
Three Swords must come again

"To turn the stride of treading Fate
To clear the fogging Mists of Time
If Early shall resist Too Late
Three Swords must come again . . ."

"I've heard it a hundred times!" she snapped. Anger only thinly covered her fear at the little man's strange expression. "What are you saying?"

Binabik lifted his hands. "Listen, listen to what it is telling, Miriamele. All the first parts are true things—diggers, giants, the great bell in Nabban—but at the end it only speaks of turning Fate, of clearing Time . . . and of Early fighting against Late."

"So?"

"What, then, is to say that it speaks to us!?" hissed Binabik.

She was so astonished by the troll's agitation that it took several moments before his words sank in. "Do you mean to say. . . ?"

"That it could just as easily be speaking of what will be helping *the Storm King himself!* For what are we mortals being to him if not the Lateness to his Earliness? Who is turning this Fate? And whose fate is it being?"

"But . . . but . . ."

Binabik spoke on in a fury, as though the words had been unbottled after a long fermentation and now foamed free. "Where did the idea to look for this rhyming come to us? From the dreams of Simon and Jarnauga and others! The Dream Road has been long compromised—Jiriki and the other Sithi have told that to us—but we were frightened enough to believe those dreams, desperate to have some way for fighting the returning Storm King!" He paused a moment, panting. "I am sorry, but I have so much angriness at my own stupidity . . . ! We took a twig of great slenderness and hung a bridge upon it without thinking more. Now we are over the middle of the chasm." He slapped his palms against his thighs. "Scrollbearers, we are now called. *Kikkasut!*"

"So . . ." She struggled to understand the ins and outs of what the troll had said; a throb of despair had begun beating inside her. "So the dreams about Nisses' book—*those* were the false messengers? The ones that led us to this rhyme?"

"That is what I am now thinking."

"But that doesn't make sense! Why would the Storm King play such a strange trick? If we cannot defeat him, why lead us to believe we could?"

Binabik took a breath. "Perhaps he has need of the swords, but cannot bring them himself. Pryrates was telling Cadrach that he knew where Bright-Nail was and did not wish it touched. Perhaps the red priest was having no plans of his own, and was doing only the Storm King's bidding. I am thinking the dark one in the north needs the great power that is in those blades." His voice broke.

"It . . . it is my great fear that all this has been a complicated game, like the Sithi's *shent,* created for making us bring the remaining swords."

Miriamele sat back against the wall, stunned. "Then Josua, Simon . . . all of us . . ."

"Have been doing the enemy's bidding all along," said Cadrach abruptly. Miriamele expected to hear satisfaction in his words, but there was none, only hollowness. "We have been his servants. The enemy has already won."

"Shut your mouth," she spat. "Damn you! If you had told us what you knew, we would likely have discovered this already." She turned to Binabik, struggling to keep her wits. "If you're right, is there anything we can do?"

The troll shrugged. "Try to be escaping, then find our way back to Josua and the others for warning them."

Miriamele stood. A few moments earlier she had been rested and ready to climb again. Now she felt as though an ox-yoke had been laid across her shoulders, a ponderous, painful weight that could not be shrugged off. There seemed little doubt that all was indeed lost. "And even if we find them, now we will have no weapons to use against the Storm King."

Binabik did not reply. The diminutive troll seemed to have shrunk even smaller. He rose and began clambering up the stairs again. Miriamele turned her back on Cadrach and followed him.

Order had been overthrown; screaming, grinding chaos raged before the Hayholt's walls. Pale Norns and shaggy, barking giants were everywhere, fighting with no discernible regard for their own lives, as though their only purpose was to strike horror into the hearts of their enemies. One of the giants had lost most of an arm to a warrior's ax-blow, but as it pushed through panicked human soldiers the huge beast swung the fountaining stub as vigorously as it did the club in its remaining hand, both combining to fill the surrounding air with a mist of red. Other giants were yet unwounded, and they quickly piled terrible carnage around themselves. The Norns, almost as fierce but far more canny, gathered themselves into small rings and stood shoulder to shoulder, their needle-sharp pikes facing outward. The swiftness and battle mastery of the white-skinned immortals was such that they seemed to fell two or three humans for each one of their own number that fell . . . and as they fought, they sang. Their eerie, strident voices echoed even above the clamor of combat.

And over all hung the Conqueror Star, glowing a sickly red.

Duke Isgrimnur raised Kvalnir in the air and shouted for Sludig, for Hotvig, but his voice was swallowed by the din. He turned his horse in circles, trying to find some area where the forces were concentrated, but already his army was scattered in a thousand separate pieces. Although he had been fighting vigorously for some time, Isgrimnur still could not quite believe what was

happening. They were under attack by creatures out of old stories. The battlefield, grim but familiar less than an hour before, had now become a nightmare
of otherworldly punishment.

Josua's standard had been thrown down; Isgrimnur searched in vain for
something he could use to give his forces a rallying point. A giant fell to the
snow, thrashing as it died with a dozen arrows crackling beneath it, and the
duke's horse bolted away despite his attempts to control it, pulling up at last in
an eddy of calm on the part of the northeastern hillside nearest the Kynswood.

When he had steadied his mount, Isgrimnur sheathed Kvalnir and removed his
helmet, then tugged his surcoat up, grunting at the pain in his back and ribs. For
a moment his bulky mail prevented him from pulling the garment over his head;
Isgrimnur struggled, cursing and sweating, horrified at the thought of being taken
by surprise and struck down in such a ridiculous position. The surcoat ripped at
the armholes and he yanked it free at last, then looked around for something to
which he could tie it. One of the Norns' pikes lay on the snow. Isgrimnur unsheathed his sword, then leaned over, grunting, and hooked it up so he could grab
the long shaft. As he tied the shirt sleeves to the smooth grayish wood, he stared
at the bladed tip that seemed to blossom like a knife-petaled flower. When he had
finished, he lifted the makeshift banner above his head and rode back into the
thick of the battle, roaring a Rimmersgard war song that even he could not hear.

He had already dodged one swinging blow from an ax-wielding Norn before he realized his helm was still swinging on his saddle horn. Kvalnir bounced
ineffectively from the creature's strange painted armor. Isgrimnur managed to
catch the returning blow on his arm, suffering only torn mail and a shallow
gouge in his flesh, but the Norn was very nimble on the slippery snow, and was
circling rapidly for another attack. The wind abruptly blew the banner across
the duke's face.

Killed by my own shirt, was his brief thought, then the cloth flapped away
again. A dark something heaved into his field of sight and the Norn staggered
sideways, blood erupting from a split helmet. The new arrival wheeled about
in a splash of snow and returned to ride down Isgrimnur's reeling enemy.

"You are alive," Sludig gasped, swiping his dripping ax against his cloak.

Isgrimnur took a breath, then shouted over the growing rumble of thunder.
"This is a damnable mess—where's Freosel?"

Sludig indicated a knot of struggling shapes a hundred cubits away. "Come.
And put your damned helmet on."

"They're coming down the walls!" someone shouted.

Isgrimnur looked over to see rope ladders unrolling at the far end of the
Hayholt's sloping outwall. The darkening sky and the dizzying flashes of inter-
mittent lightning made it hard to see anything clearly, but to Isgrimnur the
men making their way down the ladders looked like mortals.

"God damn their mercenary souls!" the duke growled. "And now we're
pinched from both sides. We're being forced back against the walls and we

won't have the advantage of numbers much longer." He turned and looked past his small, besieged company. Across the battlefield he could see determined clumps of men, Seriddan's Nabbanai legions and Hotvig's horsemen, trying to fight their way toward his surcoat-banner, which now waved on the strut of a scaling ladder socketed in the muddy ground. The question was whether Hotvig and the rest could cut their way through before Isgrimnur's small party was crushed between the Norns and the mercenaries.

Perhaps we should fall back toward the base of the castle walls, he thought, *even try to fetch up in front of that new gate.* There was little else he and Sludig and the rest could do: they were going to be forced back in any case, so they might as well pick their spot. The duke had noticed that none of Elias' soldiers were atop the gate: he guessed it might not be wide enough. If that was true, he and his small company could use it as a rearguard without having to worry about missiles from above. With their backs protected, they could hold off even the fearsome Norns until the rest of the soldiers fought through . . . or so he hoped.

And maybe if we make ourselves a little room we can force that cursed gate, or use those ladders, and go in after Isorn. No reason Elias shouldn't have some mortal foxes in his henyard for a change.

He turned back to the horde of pale, black-eyed creatures and their witchwood blades. Lightning split the sky again, eclipsing for a moment the scarlet smolder of the Conqueror Star. Dimly, Isgrimnur heard a bell tolling, and felt it in his gut and bones as well. For a moment he saw what looked like flames crawling at the edge of his vision, but then the storm-darkness fell again.

God help us, he thought distractedly. *That's the noon bell in the tower. And here it is black as night. Aedon, it's so dark. . . .*

"Oh! Mother of Mercy!" Miriamele looked down from the balcony, horrified. Below her perch on the king's residence, the Inner Bailey was a sea of men and horses that moved in strange rippling patterns of conflict. Snow whipped and circled in the wind, making everything indistinct. The sky was knotted with stormclouds, but the red star burned visibly behind them, its long tail casting a faint bloody glow over all. "Uncle Josua has begun the siege!" she cried. Their hurry to find him and warn him seemed to have been for nothing.

The climb up the stairs had led them at last to a door hidden in the lower recesses of the storerooms beneath the king's residence. Miriamele, who prided herself on her knowledge of the Hayholt's ins and outs, many of them discovered while in her Malachias disguise, had been shocked to discover that a passageway to old Asu'a had been beneath her nose all the time she had lived here—but there were more surprises waiting.

The second came when they emerged cautiously into the ground-level portions of the residence. Despite the howling of wind and the roar of wild voices outside, the many chambers of the residence were deserted and showed little evidence of any recent habitation. As they passed through the cold rooms and grimy hallways, Miriamele's fear of discovery had lessened, but her sense of things being wrong had grown steadily. Braced for any number of unhappy discoveries, she had entered her father's sleeping chamber only to find it not just empty, but in such a fetid and bestial state that she could not imagine who might have been living there.

Now they had emerged onto a small sheltered balcony off one of the third floor rooms, where they crouched behind its stone railing, peering through the ornamental slits at the madness below. The air smelled strongly of lightning-tang and blood.

"I fear that is true." Binabik spoke in a loud voice: between the uproar of combat and the howling winds, there was no fear of drawing attention. "People are fighting down below, and there are men and animals lying dead. But still something there is that is strange. I wish we could be seeing beyond the castle walls."

"What do we do?" Miriamele looked about frantically. "Josua and Camaris and the rest must still be outside. We have to get out to them somehow!"

The daylight, darkened by stormclouds until the whole of the castle seemed sunk in deep water, shifted and flickered strangely, then for a moment the world suddenly shouted and went white. A coil of lightning had snapped down like a fiery whip; thunder rattled the air and even seemed to shake the balcony beneath them. The lightning curled around Green Angel Tower, hung for a moment as the thunder echoes faded, then sputtered out of existence.

"How?" Binabik shouted. "I do not know this castle. What places might there be for escaping?"

Miriamele was having trouble thinking. The noises of wind and combat made her want to scream and cover her ears; the whirling clouds overhead dizzied her. She abruptly remembered Cadrach, who had been trailing along behind them, silent and unresponsive as a sleepwalker. Miriamele turned, certain that he had taken advantage of their confusion to sneak away, but the monk was crouched in the doorway, gazing up at the tempestuous, red-shot sky with a look of resignation.

"Perhaps we could get out through the seagate," she said to the troll. "If Josua's army is at the walls above Erchester, perhaps there will be only a few . . ."

Binabik's eyes widened. "Look there!" He thrust his hand through the slitted railing to point. "Is that not . . . ? Oh, Daughter of the Mountains!"

Miriamele squinted, trying to make sense out of the madness below her, and saw that there was more to the antheap-swirl of activity than just defenders running to and from the moat-bridge that led to the Middle Bailey. In fact, there seemed to be a fight of some kind taking place on the bridge itself. A large knot of armed men in the Middle Bailey was forcing a smaller troop of riders and footmen back across the moat. As she stared, one of the horses reared and tumbled from the span, taking its rider with it into the dark water. Were Josua's forces inside the wall already, and pushing toward the Inner Bailey? Could those few on the bridge be the last of her father's defenders? But then what of all the armored men just below her who were doing nothing to support the retreating horsemen? Who were they?

And then, as the small troop on the bridge was forced back even farther, she saw what Binabik had seen. One of the riders, standing almost impossibly tall in his saddle, swung his blade high overhead. Even in the false twilight she could see that the sword was black as coal.

"Oh, God, save us." Something cold clutched at her innards. "It's Camaris!"

Binabik was leaning forward, his face pressed against the stone rails. "I am thinking I see Prince Josua, too—there, in the gray cloak, riding near to Camaris." He turned to her, his face fearful. Another jagged lightning flash silvered the sky. "And there are so few with them—they could not have been fighting their way inside the walls, I am guessing. Somehow they have been tricked into bringing the sword into the castle."

Miriamele hammered her palms against the balcony floor. "What can we do?!"

The troll peered out through the rails again. "I am not knowing," he half-shouted. "I have no thoughts at all! *Kikkasut!* We will be cut in pieces if we go down to them—and they have already been bringing the sword! *Kikkasut!*"

"There are flames in the tower window," Cadrach said in a loud, flat tone.

Miriamele glanced briefly at both Green Angel Tower and Hjeldin's Tower, but except for the clot of writhing clouds above the tall spire of the first, she could see nothing unusual.

"See!" Binabik called. "Something is happening!" He sounded angry and puzzled. "What are they doing?"

Josua and Camaris and their small company of allies had been driven across the bridge and onto the soil of the Inner Bailey. But the rest of the mercenary troops milling haphazardly inside the bailey did not step up to cut them off; rather, a ragged gap formed in their ranks, a split which gradually opened into a path that led from the base of the moat-bridge to the front steps of Green Angel Tower. As the rest of the king's soldiers pushed their way across the bridge, Josua and his followers were forced toward the tower. Astoundingly, the mercenaries on either side did not menace them at all until Camaris, on his pale horse, tried to turn the troop sideways to cut his way through the wall of enemies. The king's forces resisted fiercely and the small company was thrown back, then driven again across the open space toward Green Angel's waiting steps.

"The tower!" said Miriamele. "They're forcing them to the tower! What . . . ?"

"The Sithi-place!" Binabik sprang up suddenly, all thought of hiding now gone. "The place where the Storm King was making his last battle. Your father and Pryrates are wanting the swords there!"

Miriamele stood. Her knees were weak. What monstrous thing was happening before them, as relentless and inescapable as the clutch of a nightmare? "We have to go to them! Somehow! Maybe . . . maybe there's still something we can do!"

Binabik grabbed his pack from the floor inside the balcony window. "Where and how are we going to them?" he asked her.

Miriamele stared at him, then at silent Cadrach. For a moment, her mind was empty of everything except the howling of the wind outside. At last, a memory fluttered up from the depths.

"Follow me." She shouldered her pack and Norn bow and ran across the damp stone toward the doorway and the residence stairs. Binabik hurried after her. She did not look back to see what Cadrach did.

�™

Tiamak and Josua scrambled up the stairwell, silent except for their labored breath, struggling to stay close behind Camaris. A flight above them the knight climbed steadily, unheeding as a sleepwalker, his powerful legs carrying him upward two steps at a time.

"How could any stairs stretch so high?" Tiamak gasped. His lame leg was throbbing.

"There are mysteries in this place I never dreamed." Josua held his torch high, and the shadows leaped from crevice to crevice along the richly-textured walls. "Who knew a whole world still remained down here?"

Tiamak shuddered. The silver-masked Norn Queen hovering over the Sithi's sacred pool was a mystery that the Wrannaman wished he had never discovered. Her words, her chill invincibility, and especially the dreadful power that had filled the cavern of the Pool of Three Depths, had haunted him all the way up the great staircase. "Our ignorance is thrown back at us," he panted. "We are fighting things we only guessed at, or glimpsed in nightmares. Now the Sithi are locked in struggle with that . . . she-thing, fighting, dying . . . and we do not even know why."

Josua turned his gaze from the old man's back to peer briefly at Tiamak. "I thought that was the task of the Scroll League. To know such things."

"Those who went before us knew more than we do," Tiamak replied. "And there is much that even Morgenes and the others never learned, much hidden even to Eahlstan Fiskerne, who they say was a true if secret friend to the Sithi. The immortals have always been tight-fisted with their lore."

"And who can blame them, after the harm mortals have done with nothing more than stone and iron and fire." Josua glanced at the marsh man again. "Ah, merciful God, we are wasting breath on talk. I see pain on your face, Tiamak. Let me carry you a while."

Tiamak, climbing doggedly, shook his head. "Camaris has not slowed. We would fall farther behind, and if we leave the stairs we might lose him again, with no Sithi this time to help us find our way. He would be alone, and we might wander here forever." He mounted several more steps before he had the breath to speak again. "If need be, let me trail behind. It is more important you stay with Camaris than with me."

Josua did not say anything, but at last nodded unhappily.

*   *   *

The terrible sensation of shifting eddied away, and with it the dancing lights that, for a moment, had made Tiamak think the great staircase was burning. He shook his head, trying to clear his rattled thoughts. What could be happening? The air seemed strangely hot, and he felt the hairs on his arm and neck prickling.

"Something dreadful is happening," Tiamak cried. He staggered in Josua's shadow, wondering if the increasing force of the strange slippages meant that the Norn Queen was defeating the Sithi. The thought fastened on him as though it had claws. Perhaps she had escaped the pool. Would she follow him and the prince up the darkened stairs, silver mask expressionless, white robes fluttering . . . ?

"He's gone!" Josua's voice was full of horror. "But how can that be?"

"What? Gone where?" Tiamak looked up.

The torchlight revealed a place where the stairwell abruptly stopped, capped by a low ceiling of stone. Camaris was nowhere in sight.

"There is no place he could have hidden!" the prince said.

"No, look!" Tiamak pointed toward a fissure in the ceiling wide enough to allow a man to crawl through.

Josua quickly lifted Tiamak up into the hole, then held him steady while the Wrannaman probed for something to grasp. Tiamak found he could almost push his head above the surface on the far side. He pulled himself up and through, fighting against his treacherous, weary muscles, and when he lay quivering on the stone floor he called down through the fissure: "Come! It's a storeroom!"

Josua tossed up the torch. With a helping hand from Tiamak, he struggled upward through the crack. Together they raced across the room, dodging the bits of wreckage strewn about, and climbed a rickety ladder through a hatchway. Beyond this was another storeroom, this one with a small window high in the wall. Threatening black clouds roiled in the box of sky visible there, and cold wind bled through. Another hatchway led to yet one more level.

As Tiamak put his aching leg to the bottommost rung, a crash resounded back through the hatch door, a sudden and violent sound. Josua, who climbed above him, sped up the ladder and disappeared.

When Tiamak made his way to the top, he found himself in a small, shadowy room, staring at the flinders of a door strewn outward into the chamber beyond. He could see torchlight in the chamber, and figures moving. Josua's voice rang out.

"You! May God send your black soul to hell!"

Tiamak hurried to the doorway, then stopped, blinking as he tried to make sense of the wide circular room that opened before him. On his left, the windows above the tall main doors streamed with scarlet-tinted light that vied with the dull glow of torches in the wall sconces. Just a few cubits before the Wrannaman, Camaris stood in the ruins of the smaller door which had blocked his own way out into the chamber; the old knight now stood motionless, as though

stunned. Josua was only an arm's length away from Camaris, Naidel unsheathed
and dangling in his hand. Two dozen paces beyond them, on the far side of the
stone floor, a small door in the wall mirrored the one Camaris had just burst
into flinders. On Tiamak's right, beyond a high arch, a great sweep of stairs
coiled upward out of sight.

But it was the figures on the bottom steps of this staircase that caught and
held Tiamak's eye, as they had Josua's—especially the bald man in the flapping
red robe, who stood tall in the midst of a strew of human bodies, like a fisherman in a shallow stream. One armored man he still held by the shoulders,
though the way the soldier's gold-helmeted head wagged suggested he had long
since stopped fighting.

"Damn you, Pryrates, let him go!" cried Josua.

The priest laughed. With a shrug, he effortlessly threw aside . . . Camaris,
who clattered on the stone flags and lay still, black blade clutched in his fist.

Tiamak stared in numb astonishment. The Camaris he and Josua had followed still stood nearby, wavering slightly like a tree in a stiff breeze. How
could there be two? Who sprawled there?

"Isorn!" Josua shouted, his voice ragged with grief. Tiamak suddenly remembered, and the terror that clutched him clamped tighter. The deception
they had conceived with the Sithi had come to this—this clutter of motionless
men? Nearly a dozen soldiers, including powerful young Isorn, and the priest
had defeated them with his bare hands? What could possibly stop Pryrates and
his immortal ally now? Josua and his companions had but one of the Great
Swords, and its wielder, Camaris, seemed lost in a dreaming daze. . . .

"I'll have your heart for this," Prince Josua snarled, leaping toward the stairway. Pryrates lifted his hands and a nimbus of oily yellow light flickered around
the alchemist's fingers. As Naidel came flashing toward him in a wide, deadly
arc, Pryrates' hand snaked out and caught the blade. The point of contact hissed
like a hot stone dropped into water, then the priest grabbed Josua's sword arm
and pulled him forward. The prince struggled, flailing at Pryrates with his
other, handless arm, but the priest caught that too and drew Josua toward him
until their faces were so close it seemed that the alchemist might kiss the prince.

"It is almost too easy," Pryrates said, laughing.

Tiamak, weak with fear, slid back into the shadows of the doorway. *I must
do something—but who am I?* The Wrannaman could barely stand upright. *A
little man, a nobody! I am no fighter! He would catch me and kill me like a tiny fish.*

"There is no hell deep enough for you," Josua grated. Sweat streamed down
his face, and his sword arm trembled, but he seemed as helpless as a child in the
priest's prisoning grip.

"And I will visit them all." Pryrates extended his arms again. The yellow
light wavered around him. "You are one of the few who have balked me, Lackhand. Now you will see that your interference comes to—*nothing*." He flung
Josua against the nearby arch. The prince struck hard and slid down to lie motionless beside a man dressed in his own gray surcoat and armor—the Nabbanai

baron's brother, Brindalles. The man's right arm, like Josua's, ended in a black leather cap, but Brindalles' arm was bent at an angle that made Tiamak's stomach lurch. There was no sign of life on the impostor's pale, blood-flecked face.

Tiamak shrank farther back into the shadows, but Pyrates did not even look at him. Instead, the priest moved up the stairwell, then stopped and turned to Camaris.

"Come, old one," he said, and smiled. Tiamak thought his grin as empty and mirthless as a crocodile's. "I can feel the ward solidifying, which means the time has come. You need carry your burden only a little farther."

Camaris took a step toward him, then stopped, shaking his head slowly. "No," he said hoarsely. "No. I will not let it . . ." Something of his real self had returned; Tiamak felt a faint swelling of hope.

Pyrates only crossed his arms on his scarlet breast. "It will be interesting to watch you resist. You will fail, of course. The pull of the sword is too strong for any mortal, even a tattered legend like yourself."

"Damn you," Camaris gasped. His body twitched and he shifted his balance back and forth, as though he fought some invisible thing that sought to tug him toward the stairs. The old knight sucked in a breath with a painful gasp. "What manner of creature are you?"

"Creature?" Pyrates' hairless face was amused. "I am what a man who accepts no limits can become. . . ."

While his last words still hung in the air, there was a sudden booming concussion. Where the door on the opposite side of the chamber had been, a murky cloud billowed. Several shadowy figures stumbled through, indistinguishable in the smoke.

"How exciting." Pyrates' tone was sardonic, but Tiamak saw a certain animation creep into the alchemist's face that had not been there before. The priest took a step downward and peered into the haze. A moment later he reeled back, gurgling, with a black arrow all the way through his neck, its head standing out a handspan beyond the skin. Pyrates stumbled in place for a moment, then fell and rolled down the stairs to lie beside his victims. Blood pooled beneath his head, as though his bright robes melted and ran.

Miriamele stared up and down the narrow hallways, struggling to regain her bearings. The Chancelry had been a daunting maze when she had lived in the castle, but it was even more confusing now. Familiar doors and hallways were not quite where they should be, and all the passages seemed the wrong lengths, as though the Chancelry's dimensions had somehow become shiftingly fluid. Miriamele struggled to keep her head. She was certain she could eventually find a way through, but she feared the loss of precious time.

As she waited for her companions, the freezing wind which whistled through the unshuttered windows rolled a few crumpled parchments past her feet.

Binabik trotted around the corner. "I did not mean that you should be waiting for me," he said. "I was stopping only because I saw these. They have come
through the window, I am thinking." He handed her three arrows of plainer
workmanship than the Norn shafts she had scavenged earlier. "There were others, too, but they had been broken by striking on the stone walls." Miriamele
had no quiver to put them in. She slipped them into the open corner of her pack
beside Simon's prize and the shafts she had saved from the tunnels. Even with
Binabik's additions she still had far fewer arrows than she would have liked, but
it was a relief to know that if it came to it, she need not sell her life cheaply.

Look at me, she marveled. *The world is ending, the Day of Weighing-Out has come
at last . . . and I'm playing at soldier.*

Still, it was better than letting the terror push through. She felt it coiling
inside her, and knew that if she let go of composure for even a moment she
would be overwhelmed.

"I wasn't waiting." She pushed away from the wall. "Just making sure I
know the way. This place was always difficult, but now it's almost impossible.
And it's not just this. . . ." She gestured at the smashed furniture and the ghostly
rags of parchment, the doors splintered off their hinges that lay across the passage. "There are other changes too, things I don't understand. But I think I'm
right, now. We must go quietly from here, wind or no wind—we're almost to
the chapel, and that's right beside the tower."

"Cadrach is coming." The troll said it as though he thought she might care.

Miriamele curled her lip. "I'm not waiting. If he can keep up, then let him."
She hesitated for a moment, then pulled one of the arrows from her pack and
nocked it, letting it sit loosely on the bowstring. Armed, she set off down the
narrow hallway. Binabik looked back, then scurried after her.

"He has been having as much hurt as us, Miriamele," said the troll. "Maybe
more. Who can say what things he or she would be doing under Pryrates' torturing?"

"The monk has lied to me more times than I can count." The thought of his
betrayals burned so fiercely inside her that for a moment she was not even
afraid. "One word of truth about the swords, about Pryrates, might have saved
us all."

Binabik's face was unhappy. "We are not losing everything yet."

"Not yet."

Cadrach caught up to them in the chaplain's walking hall. The monk said
nothing—perhaps in part because he was fighting for breath—but fell in behind
the troll. Miriamele allowed herself one icy stare.

As they reached the door, everything seemed to shift again. For a moment
Miriamele thought she saw pale flames running up the walls; she struggled not
to cry out as, for a dreadful instant, she felt herself torn apart. When the sensation passed, she did not feel as though she had been completely restored.

Long moments passed before she felt able to speak.

"The . . . chapel is on . . . the other side." Despite the incessant keening of the wind beyond the walls, Miriamele whispered. The terror inside her was struggling to break free and it took all her strength to keep it in place. Binabik was wide-eyed and unusually pale; Cadrach looked ill, his forehead moist, his gaze fever-bright. "On the far side there is a short hallway that leads directly into the tower. Look to your feet. With all these broken things about, you might trip and hurt yourself—" she pointedly addressed her concern only to Binabik, "—or make enough noise that whoever is inside will hear us coming."

The troll smiled wanly. "Like hare's feet are the steps of the Qanuc," he whispered. "Light on snows or rock."

"Good." Miriamele turned to stare at the monk, trying to divine what further treachery might lurk behind his watery gray eyes, then decided it did not matter. There was little Cadrach could do to worsen their situation: the time for stealth would be over in moments, and what had been their greatest hope seemed now to have been turned against them.

"Follow me, then," she told Binabik.

As she opened the door into the transept of the chapel, the cold reached out and grasped at her; a cloud of her steaming breath hung in the air. She paused for a moment and listened before leading her companions out onto the wide chapel floor. Snow had drifted into the corners and against the walls, and pools of water lay everywhere on the stone. Most of the benches were gone; the few tapestries that remained flapped in ragged, moldy strips. It was hard to believe it had once been a place of comfort and refuge.

The storm and the clamor of the struggle outside were also louder here. When she looked up, she learned the reason.

The great dome overhead had been ruptured, the glass saints and angels all tumbled and shattered into colored dust. Miriamele trembled, awed even after all she had experienced to see a familiar thing so changed. Snowflakes swirled lazily downward, and the storm-darkened sky, touched with the bloodlight of the flaming star, twisted in the broken frame like an angry face.

As they made their way across the front of the apse, past the altar, Miriamele saw that other forces beside impersonal nature had worked desecration here: crude hands had smashed the faces of the holy martyrs' statues, and had smeared others with blood and worse things.

Despite the dangerous footing, they made their way silently across to the far transept. She led them down a slender passageway to a door set deeply into the rock. She stooped and listened at the keyhole, but could hear nothing through the echoing din that leaked from above. A strange, painful, prickling sensation came over her, as though lightning were in the air—but lightning was in the air, she reminded herself.

"Miriamele. . . ." Cadrach sounded frightened.

She ignored him, trying the latch. "Locked," she said quietly, then shrugged against the crawling itch, which was worsening. "And too heavy for us to knock down."

"Miriamele!" Cadrach pulled at her sleeve. "Some kind of barrier is being formed. We will be trapped."

"What do you mean?"

"Can you not sense it pushing in on us? Feel your skin creep? A barrier is being formed and drawn inward to surround the tower. Pryrates' work—I feel his heedless power."

She stared at the monk, but there was no sign of anything but unfeigned concern on his face. "Binabik?" she asked.

"I am thinking he speaks rightly." He, too, was beginning to twitch. "We will be squeezed in a most comfortless way."

"Cadrach, you opened the dwarrows' door. Open this one."

"This is a simple lock, Lady, not a door-warding spell."

"But you have been a thief, too!"

He shivered. Wisps of hair were beginning to stand upright on his head, and Miriamele could feel a stirring on her own arms and scalp. "I have no lockpicks, no tools—it is useless. Perhaps it is just as well. I wager it will be a quick death."

Binabik hissed in exasperation. "I am not wanting any death, of quickness *or* slowness, if it can be escaped." He stared at the door for a moment, then threw down his pack and began to rummage in it.

Miriamele watched helplessly. The oppressive feeling was growing by the moment. Praying they could find some other way into the tower, she hurried back up the passageway, but within a dozen strides the air seemed to become grossly thicker, harder to breathe. A strange humming was in her ears and her skin burned. Unwilling to give up so easily, she took a few more steps; each was more difficult than the last, as though she waded in deepening mud.

"Come back!" Cadrach cried. "That will do you no good!"

She turned with difficulty and made her way back to the door. "You were right, there is no going back. But this thing, this barrier, moves so slowly!"

The monk was scratching frenziedly at his arms. "Such things take a certain time to appear, and the priest has expended much power summoning it. He obviously intends nothing should go in or come out."

Binabik had found a small leather sack and was rooting in it. "How do you know it's Pryrates?" Miriamele asked. "Perhaps it's . . . the other."

Cadrach shook his head mournfully, but there was a hard core of rage beneath. "I know the red priest's work. Gods! I shall never forget the feeling of his filthy presence in my head, in my thoughts. . . ."

"Miriamele, Cadrach," the troll said. "Lift me up."

They bent and raised him from the floor, then moved at his direction to the side of the door. The air seemed to be tightening around them: the effort to lift tiny Binabik seemed tremendous. The troll climbed until he stood with his feet on their quivering shoulders.

"It's . . . hard to . . . breathe," Miriamele panted. Something was buzzing in her ears. Cadrach's mouth hung open and his chest heaved.

"No speaking." Binabik reached up and poured a handful of something into the door's upper hinge.

Miriamele's ears were hammering now; she felt squeezed, as though held in a huge, crushing fist. A constellation of sparks spun in the shadows before her.

"Turn away your faces," Binabik gasped, then took something from his hand and smacked it sharply against the hinge.

A sheet of light filled Miriamele's eyes. The throttling fist became a giant open hand that slapped her away from the door. Despite the force, she fell backward only a little way and retained her feet, buoyed by the unseen but encroaching barrier. Binabik toppled from her shoulders and fell onto the ground between her and Cadrach.

When she could see again, the door lay a-tilt in its frame, half-obscured by drifting smoke.

"Through!" she said, and tugged the troll's arm. He snatched up his pack, then they pushed into the dark space, stumbling on the tipped door. For a moment Miriamele stuck in the doorway, her pack wedged, her bow snagged on the broken hinge, but she fought free at last. When they had passed over into Green Angel Tower's broad antechamber, the pressure was suddenly gone.

"Lucky we are the hinges were outside," Binabik gasped, fanning the air.

Miriamele stopped and stared. Through the murk she could see a flash of bright red on the tower's staircase. A moment later the smoke had cleared enough that she could clearly see Pryrates' gleaming pink skull. Bodies lay scattered at his feet, and Camaris stood before him in the room's center. The old man was staring at the priest with such hopeless misery that Miriamele felt her heart tear in her breast.

Grinning, Pryrates turned from the old knight and took a step down, swiveling his bottomless black eyes toward the doorway where she stood. The door's destruction seemed to have startled him no more than the fall of a tumbling leaf. Without thinking, Miriamele lifted her bow, straightened the arrow, drew, and fired. She aimed for the widest part of the priest's body, but the shaft flew high. It seemed a miracle when she saw Pryrates stumble backward. When she saw that the arrow stood from his throat, she was too dumbfounded at her own shot even to feel joy. The priest fell and rolled bonelessly down the few remaining steps to the antechamber floor.

"Chukku's Stones!" the troll gasped. "You have ended him."

"Uncle Josua!" she shouted. "Where are you? Camaris! It's a trick! They *wanted* us to bring the swords!"

I've killed him! The thought was a quiet bloom of exultation deep inside her. *I've killed the monster!*

"The sword must not be going any farther," cried Binabik.

The old knight took a few lurching steps toward them, but even with Pryrates face down on the floor, dead or dying, Camaris still seemed in the grip of some terrible power. Of Josua there was no sign; but for the old man, all in the chamber lay motionless.

Before anyone could speak again a bell rang in the tower high above, monstrously loud, lower and deeper than any bell Miriamele had ever heard. The very stones of the wide room shuddered, and she felt its tolling strike into her bones. For an instant the antechamber seemed to melt away, the waterstained tapestries replaced by walls of gleaming white. Lights glittered everywhere, like fireflies. As the cry of the bell faded, the illusion flickered and disappeared.

As Miriamele struggled to regain her wits, a figure rose slowly near the foot of the stairs, grasping at the stone arch for support. It was Josua, his cloak hanging raggedly, his thin shirt torn at the neck.

"Uncle Josua!" Miriamele hastened toward him.

He stared at her, eyes wide and, for a brief moment, uncomprehending. "You live," he said at last. "Thank God."

"It's a trick," she said even as she threw her arms around him. The small return of hope, when the greatest perils still remained, was painful as a knife-wound. "The false messenger—that was the rhyme about the swords! It was a trick. They *wanted* the swords here, wanted us to bring them!"

He gently disengaged himself. A trickle of blood showed along his high hairline. "Who wanted the swords? I do not understand."

"We were fooled, Prince Josua." Binabik came forward. "It has been the planning of Pryrates and the Storm King all along that the swords should be brought here. I am thinking the blades will be used in some great magic."

"We didn't find Bright-Nail," Miriamele said urgently. "Do you have it?"

The prince shook his head. "The barrow was empty."

"Then there's hope! It's not here!"

Josua opened his mouth to reply, but a loud moan of pain from Camaris stopped him.

"Ah, God, why do You torment me?" the old man cried. He lifted his free hand to his head as though he had been struck by a stone. "It is wrong—that answer is wrong!"

The prince's face was full of startled concern. "We must take him out of this place. Something in the sword drew him here. While he still has his wits about him, we must get him outside again."

"But Pryrates was making some barrier around the tower," said Binabik anxiously. "Our only hope is that now . . ."

"This is my punishment!" cried Camaris. "Oh, my God, there is too much blackness, too much sin. I am sorry . . . so sorry!"

Josua took a step toward him, then leaped away again as Thorn flickered through the air. The prince backed toward the stairwell, trying to keep himself between Camaris and whatever called him so powerfully.

"The thing Pryrates has begun is not yet being finished," Binabik shouted. "The sword must not be going further!"

Josua danced back from another awkward blow. He held Naidel before him, but seemed reluctant even to use it for defense, as though fearing he might hurt the old man. Miriamele, full of fluttering panic, knew that the prince would be killed if he did not resist with all his power.

"Uncle Josua! Fight back! Stop him!"

As Josua backed up the wide stairway and Camaris reached the bottom step, Binabik bolted from her side. He leaped across the motionless bodies lying before the stairs and threw himself at the back of the old knight's legs, knocking Camaris down. As Miriamele hurried forward to help the troll, another figure came up beside her. She was amazed to see that it was the Wrannaman, Tiamak.

"Take one of his arms, Lady Miriamele." The marsh man's eyes were wide with fear and his voice shook, but he was already reaching down. "I will take the other."

Although Binabik had wrapped both his arms and legs around the old knight's knees, Camaris was already beginning to rise. Miriamele grasped at the hand that sought to pull Binabik loose, but it slipped from her sweating grip. She clutched again at his upper arm and this time hung on as Camaris' long muscles bunched beneath her. A moment later all four of them tumbled to the floor again, landing among the scatter of bodies. Miriamele found herself staring down into the half-open eyes of Isorn, whose slack face was as white as one of the Norns. A scream tried to force its way out of her, but she was clinging so fiercely to Camaris' flailing arm that she could not think much about Isgrimnur's son. There was only the scent of fear-sweat and rolling bodies.

She caught a glimpse of Josua, who stood a short distance away on the stairs. Camaris again began to climb to his feet, dragging his attackers up with him.

"Josua," she panted. "He'll . . . get away from us! Kill him . . . if you have to . . . but stop him!"

The prince only stared. Miriamele could feel the old knight's tremendous strength. He would shake them off in a few moments.

"Kill him, Josua!" she screamed. Camaris was half-standing now, but Tiamak was draped around his sword arm; the knight's chest and stomach were unprotected.

"Something!" Binabik grunted in pain, struggling to hold Camaris' legs together. "Be doing something!"

But Josua only took a hesitant step forward, Naidel hanging slack in his hand.

Miriamele let go with one arm and hurriedly groped for Camaris' sword belt. When she had it, she slid off his arm and grasped the belt with both hands, then braced her legs against the bottom step and pulled backward as hard as she could. The old man swayed for a moment, but the tangling weight of Tiamak and Binabik were making his movements clumsy and he could not keep his balance. He tottered, then fell backward as heavily as an axed tree.

Miriamele's legs were caught beneath the knight. His collapse knocked the breath from her. When Camaris stirred after a long moment, she knew she did not have the strength to pull him down again.

"Ah, God," the knight murmured to the ceiling. "Free me from this song! I do not wish to go—but it is too strong for me. I have paid and paid. . . ."

Josua seemed almost as wracked with torment as Camaris. He took another step downward, then paused before backing up again. "Merciful God," said the prince. "Merciful God." He straightened, blinking. "Keep Camaris there as long as you can. I think I know who is waiting at the top of the stairs." He turned away.

"Come back, Josua!" cried Miriamele. "Don't go!"

"There is no time left," he called over his shoulder as he mounted upward. "I must get to him while I can. He is waiting for me."

She suddenly realized who he meant. "No," she whispered.

Camaris was still lying on the floor, but Binabik had not let go of the knight's legs. Tiamak had been flung to one side; he crouched at the foot of the stairs, rubbing a bruised arm and staring at Camaris with fearful anticipation.

"Tiamak, follow him," pleaded Miriamele. "Follow my uncle. Hurry! Don't let them kill each other."

The Wrannaman's eyes widened. He looked at her, then back to Camaris, his face solemn as a frightened child's. At last he clambered to his feet and hobbled up the stairs after Josua, who had already disappeared into the shadows.

Camaris drew himself into a sitting position. "Let me up. I do not wish to hurt you, whoever you are." His eyes were fixed on some distant point beyond the antechamber. "It is calling me."

Miriamele pulled herself free and, trembling, took his hand. "Sir Camaris, please. It is an evil spell that is calling you. Don't go. If you take the sword there, everything you have fought for may be destroyed."

The old knight lowered his pale eyes to meet hers. His face was bleak, drawn with terrible strain. "Tell the wind not to blow," he said hoarsely. "Tell the thunder not to roar. Tell this cursed sword not to sing and pull at me." But he seemed to sag, as though for a moment the summoning grew less powerful.

A wordless cry like a howl of animal fear rang through the antechamber. Miriamele suddenly remembered Cadrach. She whirled to look at him where he crouched by the doorway, but the monk yowled again and pointed.

Pryrates was climbing slowly to his feet, loose-limbed as a drunkard. The arrow still protruded from either side of his neck. A faint, putrescent glow played about the torn flesh.

But he's dead! Horror gusted through her. *He's dead! Sweet Elysia, Mother of God, I killed him!*

The priest staggered a step, groaning, then turned his sharklike gaze toward Miriamele. His voice was even harsher than before, ripped raw. "You . . . *hurt* me. For that, I will . . . I will keep you alive a long time, womanchild."

"Daughter of the Mountains," Binabik said hopelessly. He still clung to the old knight's legs. Camaris lay staring at the ceiling, oblivious to all but the call from above.

Swaying, the priest reached up and grasped the black shaft just behind the arrowhead and snapped it off, bringing a fresh dribble of blood from the wound. He took a couple of whistling breaths, then grasped the feathers and drew the rest of the arrow back out through his throat, his face stretched in a rictus of agony. He stared at the blood-smeared thing for a moment before tossing it disdainfully onto the floor.

"A Nakkiga shaft," he rasped. "I should have known. The Norns make strong weapons—but not strong enough." The bleeding had stopped, and now a tiny wisp of smoke wafted from one of the holes in his neck.

Miriamele had nocked another arrow, and now tremblingly drew her bow and leveled the black point at his face. "May . . . may God send you to Hell, Pryrates!" She struggled to form the words without falling into panicked shrieking. "What have you done with my father?!"

"He is upstairs." The priest laughed suddenly. He stood now without wavering, and seemed almost gleefully drunk on his own display of power. "Your father is waiting. The time we have both waited for is come. I wonder who shall enjoy it more?" Pryrates lifted his fingers and curled them. The air grew momentarily hotter around Miriamele's hand, then the arrow snapped. The suddenly empty bow almost flew from her grasp.

"It is not so pleasant tugging out arrows that I will stand and let you feather me all day, girl." Pryrates turned to look back across the antechamber at Cadrach. The broken doorway behind the monk, barred by the alchemist's ward, was full of shifting, crimson-streaked shadows. The priest beckoned. "Padreic, come here."

Cadrach gave a low moan, then stood and took a lurching step.

"Don't do it!" Miriamele called to him.

"Do not be so cruel," said Pryrates. "He wishes to attend his master."

"Fight him, Cadrach!"

The priest cocked his head. "Enough. Soon I shall have to go and attend to *my* duties." He lifted his hand again. "Come here, Padreic."

The monk staggered forward, sweating and mumbling. As Miriamele watched helplessly, he sank into a heap at Pryrates' feet, face pressed against the stone. He edged forward, quivering, and laid his cheek against one of the priest's black boots.

"That is better," Pryrates crooned. "I am glad you are not so foolish as to challenge me—glad that you *remember.* I feared you had forgotten me during your travels. And where *have* you been, little Padreic? You left me and went to keep company with traitors, I see."

"It is you who are being the traitor," Binabik shouted at him. He grimaced as Camaris shifted, trying at last to break the troll's grip on his legs. "To Morgenes, to my master Ookequk, to all who were taking you in and teaching you their secrets."

The priest looked up at him, amused. "Ookequk? So you are the fat troll's errand boy? This is splendid, indeed. All of my old friends gathered here to share this day with me."

Camaris was clambering to his feet. Binabik struggled to retain his hold, but the old man reached down and effortlessly dislodged him, then straightened, black Thorn dangling in his hand. He took a few hesitant steps toward the stairs.

"Soon, now," said Pryrates. "The call is very strong." He turned his attention to Miriamele. "I fear the rest of our conversation will have to wait. The ritual will soon reach a delicate moment. It would be good for me to be there."

Miriamele was desperate to distract him, to keep him away from her uncle and father. "Why do you do this, Pryrates? What can you gain?"

"Gain? Why, everything. Wisdom such as you cannot even imagine, child. The entire cosmos laid naked before me, unable to hide even its smallest secret." He extended his arms, and for a moment seemed almost to grow. His robe billowed, and eddies of dust whirled away across the chamber. "I will know things at which even the immortals can only guess."

Camaris suddenly cried out as though he had been stabbed, then stumbled toward the wide staircase. As he did, the great bell tolled again from somewhere above, making everything shiver and rock. The room wavered before Miriamele's eyes; flames licked up the walls, then vanished as the echoes faded away.

Miriamele's head was reeling, but Pryrates seemed unaffected. "That means the moment is very near," he said. "You hope to detain me while Josua confronts his brother." The priest shook his hairless head. "Your uncle can no more halt what is to come than he could carry this castle away on his shoulders. And neither can you. I hope I can find you when everything is finished, little Miriamele—I am not quite sure what will remain, but it would be a shame to lose you." His cold eyes flicked over her. "There is so much we will do. And we will have as long as we want—forever, if need be."

Miriamele felt her heart smothered in an icy fist.

"But you've failed!" she shouted at him. "The other sword isn't here! You've failed, Pryrates!"

He smiled mockingly. "Have I?"

She turned as something moved just at the edge of her vision. Camaris' resistance had faded at last, and he was shambling up the first flight of stairs; within moments he had vanished around the spiraling stairwell. She watched the old man go with dull resignation. They had done everything they could, but it had not been enough.

Pryrates stepped past Binabik and Miriamele to follow the old knight, then stopped at the base of the steps and slapped at his neck. He turned slowly to stare at the troll, who had just taken his blowpipe from his lips. Pryrates plucked something from behind his ear and examined it. "Poison?" he asked. "You are a fitting apprentice for Ookequk. He was always slow to learn."

He dropped the dart on the floor and ground it beneath his black boot, then mounted the stairs.

"He is fearing nothing," Binabik whispered, awed. "I do not . . ." He shook his head.

Miriamele stared at the priest's red garment until it had disappeared into the shadows. Her gaze moved down to the sad, broken bodies of Isorn and the other soldiers. The flame of her anger, which had nearly been extinguished by fear, suddenly sprang up again.

"My father is up there."

On the floor beside them, Cadrach lay weeping with his face buried in his sleeve.

Tiamak hurried up the stairs.

All our calculations, all our clever plans, our hopes, he mourned. *All for nothing. The swords were a trick, they said. We have been foolish, foolish. . . .*

He scrambled upward, ignoring the flare of pain each step brought as he fought to keep close to Josua, who was a slender gray shadow moving through the near-darkness above him. Tiamak's mouth was dry. *Something* waited at the top of these stairs.

Death, he thought. *Death, crouching like a ghant in the treetops.*

From somewhere above the bell thundered again, a shuddersome impact that shook him as an angry parent shakes a child. Flames flickered again before his eyes, and the very substance of things seemed to shred apart. It seemed an agonizingly long time before he could see the steps before him once more, and could make his clumsy, nerveless legs do what he bade them. The tower . . . was it coming to life? When everything else was about to die?

Why did she send me? What can I do? He Who Always Steps on Sand, I am so frightened!

Prince Josua pulled farther ahead, then disappeared from view, but the lame Wrannaman climbed on. Quick glances through the tower windows showed him brawling chaos raging across the unfamiliar terrain below. The Conqueror Star glared like an angry eye overhead. Snow cluttered the reddened skies, but he could make out the faint shapes of men swarming over the walls, small skirmishes forming along the battlements, other combats spilling across the open ground around the tower. For a moment Tiamak felt hope, guessing that Duke Isgrimnur and the rest of Josua's army must be forcing their way in—until he remembered the ward with which Binabik said the tower was sealed. Isgrimnur and the others would be unable to prevent whatever was to happen here.

So much was confusing. What exactly had Miriamele and the troll meant about the swords? They were a trick, somehow—and, more importantly, Pryrates and Elias wanted them brought here. But why? What had they planned? Clearly, Utuk'ku's presence beneath the castle had something to do with it. The Sithi had said they could slow her but not stop her. There had been some vast power in the Pool of Three Depths, and Tiamak felt sure the Norn Queen intended to harness it. The Sithi had been struggling to slow her, but they had seemed to be failing at even that task.

Tiamak heard Josua's voice close by. He paused, quivering, afraid to go the final steps. Suddenly he did not want to see whatever the prince had found at the top of the stairs. He squeezed his eyes tightly shut and prayed with all his strength that he would wake up in his banyan-tree hut once more, everything that had happened just an evil dream. But the sound of the restless winds outside never faded, and when he opened his eyes the pale, polished walls of Green Angel Tower's stairwell still surrounded him. He knew he must go on, although every hammerblow of his heart urged him to flee back down the stairs. His legs too weak to hold him upright, he sank to the stone, then climbed the last few steps on his hands and knees, until his head rose past the top step into cold wind and he found himself inside the airy bellchamber.

The huge bronze bells hung beneath the vaulted ceiling like poisonous green marsh flowers, and indeed, despite the buffeting wind, the chamber was filled with the odor of decaying flesh that such flowers produced. Around the center of the chamber a cluster of dark pillars rose to the ceiling, and on all four sides great arched windows opened out onto swirling snow and angry crimson clouds. Josua stood a few steps before Tiamak, facing the north window. The prince's attitude was stiff, as though he did not know what to do, how to stand. Facing him, seated before the window on a simple wooden stool, was his brother Elias.

The king wore a dark iron crown on his pale brow, and held in his hands a long gray something that Tiamak could not quite see. It had something of the shape of a sword, but Tiamak's eyes could not fasten on it properly, as though it did not entirely reside within the natural world. The king himself was dressed in full royal pomp, but his clothes were stained, and his cloak where the wind caught and lifted it showed more holes than cloth.

"Throw it away?" Elias said slowly. His eyes were still downcast, and he replied to whatever Josua had said with the air of one who had been daydreaming. "Throw it away? But I could never do that. Not now."

"For God's love and mercy, Elias!" Josua said desperately, "it is killing you! And it is meant to do more—whatever Pryrates has told you, he plans only evil!"

The king lifted his head, and Tiamak, though he was behind Josua and hidden by the shadows in the stairwell, could not help recoiling in horror. The red light from the windows played across the king's colorless face; muscles writhed beneath the skin like worms. But it was his eyes that made Tiamak choke back a shout of fear. A dull gleam smoldered in them, an inhuman light like the pallid glare of marsh-candles.

"Aedon save us," Josua gasped.

"But this is *not* Pryrates' plan." Elias' lips pulled back in a stiff smile, as though he could no longer make his face work properly. "I am the High King, do not forget: everything moves at my will. It is *my* plan. The priest has only done my bidding, and soon I will have no further need of him. And *you . . .*" he rose, unfolding himself with odd jerking movements until he stood at full height, the uncertain gray thing still resting point-down on the floor, ". . . you were my brother. Once."

"Once!?" Josua shouted. "Elias, what has happened to you? You have become something foul—something demonic!" He took a step back and almost fell into the hole of the stairwell, then turned Naidel's hilt in his trembling hand and made the sign of the Tree over his own breast. Thunder growled outside and the light flickered, but the king only stared at him blankly.

"I am no demon," the king said. He seemed to be considering the matter carefully. "No. But soon I will be more—much more—than a man. I can feel it already, feel myself opening to the winds that cry between stars, feel myself as a night sky where comets flare. . . ."

"May Usires the Ransomer forgive me," Josua breathed. "You are correct, Elias. You are no longer my brother."

The king's calm expression twisted into rage. "And whose is the fault?! You have envied me since you were a child and have done your best to destroy me. You took my wife from me, my beloved Hylissa, stole her and gave her to Death! I have not had a moment's peace since!" The king lifted a twitching hand. "But that was not enough—no, cutting out my heart was not enough for you, but you would have my rightful kingship, too! So you covet my crown, do you?" he bellowed. "Here, take it!" He wrenched at the dark circlet as Josua stared. "Cursed iron—it has burned me until I thought I would go mad!" Elias grunted as he ripped it free and cast it to the floor. A seared shadow-crown of torn, blackened flesh remained on his brow.

Josua took a step back, eyes wide with horror and pity. Tears ran down his cheeks. "I pray . . . Aedon's mercy! I pray for your soul, Elias." The prince lifted his leather-capped arm as though to push away what he saw. "Ah, God, you poor man!" He stiffened, then raised Naidel and extended it until the point trembled before the king's breast. "But you *must* surrender that cursed sword. There are only moments before Pryrates comes. I cannot wait."

The king dropped his chin, peering out at Josua from beneath his eyebrows, head lolling as if his neck was broken. A thick droplet of blood oozed from the place where the crown had been. "Ah. Ah. Is it that time, then? I grow confused, since everything has already happened—or so it seems . . ." He swept up the gray thing, and for a moment it hardened into existence, a long mottle-bladed sword with a double guard, streaked with fiery gleams. Tiamak quailed, but stayed where he was, unable to look away. The blade seemed a piece of the storm-tortured sky. "Very well. . . ."

Josua leaped forward with a wordless cry, Naidel darting like lightning. The king flicked Sorrow and knocked the blow aside, but did not return the thrust. Josua danced back, shaking as though fevered; Tiamak wondered if merely having the gray sword touch his own made him quiver so. The prince waded in again, and for long moments he strove to break through his brother's guard. Elias seemed to fight in a sort of dream, moving in sudden spasms, but only enough to block Josua's attacks, waiting until the last moment each time as though he knew where the prince would strike.

Josua at last drew back, gasping for breath. The sweat on his brow gleamed as lightning flickered in the distance.

"You see," Elias said, "it is too late for such crude methods." He paused for a moment; a rumble of thunder gently shook the bells. "Too late." The smoky light in his eyes flared as he lifted Sorrow. "But it is not too late for me to enjoy a little repayment for all the evil you have done me—my wife dead, my throne made unsafe, my daughter's heart poisoned against me. Later I will have other concerns. But for this time I can think on *you,* once-brother." He stepped forward, the sword a shadowy blur.

Josua fought a desperate battle of resistance, but the king had a more than human strength. He quickly backed Josua against the southern window, then, despite the strange stiffness of his movements, kept the prince pinned there with heavy blows that Josua only barely managed to keep from his vital spots. Slender Naidel was not enough to hold the king away, and within instants Josua tottered against the window-ledge, unable to protect himself any longer. Elias abruptly reached out and grasped Naidel by the blade, then yanked it from Josua's grip. Tiamak, desperate beyond sense, clambered up out of the stairwell and flung himself at the king's back as Sorrow rose overhead. The Wrannaman dragged at Elias' sword arm.

It was not enough to save the prince. Josua flung up his arms to protect himself, but the gray blade hammered down at his neck. Tiamak did not see the sword bite, but he heard the awful smash of impact and felt it shiver up the king's arm. Josua's head jerked and he flew to one side, blood streaming from his neck. He collapsed like an empty sack, then lay still.

Thrown off his balance, the king staggered sideways, then reached up and grasped the back of Tiamak's neck with his free hand. For a moment the Wrannaman's hands closed on Sorrow; the sword was so cold that it burned him. A horrible lance of chill pierced Tiamak's chest and his arms lost their feeling. He had time only to let out a scream of anguish for his pain, for Josua, for all that had gone so terribly wrong, then the king tugged him free and threw him aside. Tiamak felt himself skid across the bellchamber's stone floor, helpless, then something smashed against his head and neck.

He lay on his side, crumpled against the wall.

Tiamak was unable to speak or move. His already fading vision blurred as his eyes filled with tears. A great noise suddenly boomed through the chamber, shaking even the floor beneath him. Red light bloomed even more brightly beyond the windows, as though flames surrounded the tower—for a moment they leaped high enough that he could see them, and see the king's fire-drawn silhouette in the window. Then they were gone.

The bell had rung a third time.

58

The Tower

✹

Simon paused at the throne room door. Despite the strange calm he had felt on his trip through the Hayholt's underbelly, despite Bright-Nail hanging on his hip, his heart was thudding in his chest. Would the king be waiting silently in the dark, as in Hjeldin's Tower?

He pushed through the doorway, one hand falling to his sword hilt.

The throne room was empty, at least of people. Six silent figures flanked the Dragonbone Chair, but Simon knew them of old. He stepped inside.

The heraldic banners that had hung along the ceiling had fallen, worried free by the teeth of the wind that streamed in through the high windows. Flattened beasts and birds lay in tangled piles, a few of them even draped limply across the bones of the great chair. Simon stepped over a waterstained pennant; the falcon stitched upon it stared, eye wide as though shocked by its tumble from the heavens. Nearby, partially covered by other damp banners, lay a black cloth with a stylized golden fish. As Simon looked at it, a memory came drifting up.

The tumult was growing outside. He knew he had little time to spare, but the wisp of memory teased him. He moved toward the black malachite statues. The pulsing storm light made their features seem to writhe, and for a moment Simon worried that the same magics that made the entire castle shift and change might be bringing the stone kings to life, but to his relief they remained frozen, dead.

Simon stared at the figure standing just to the right of the great chair's yellowed arm. Eahlstan Fiskerne's face was lifted as though he looked to a glory beyond the windows, beyond the castle and its towers. Simon had gazed many times at the martyr-king's face, but this time was different.

He's the one I saw, he realized suddenly. *In the dream Leleth showed me. He was reading his book and waiting for the dragon. She said: "This is a part of your story, Simon."* His eyes dropped to the thin circlet of gold around his own finger. The fish symbol scribed on the band looked back at him. What was it Binabik had told him the Sithi writing on the ring meant? Dragons and death?

"The dragon was dead." That was what Leleth had whispered in that not-place, the window onto the past.

And King Eahlstan is a part of my story? Simon wondered. *Is that what Morgenes entrusted to me when he sent this ring to me? The greatest secret of the League of the Scroll—that its founder killed the dragon, not John?*

Simon was Eahlstan's messenger, across five centuries. It was a weight of honor and responsibility he could scarcely think of now, a richness to savor if he survived, a delicate secret that could change the lives of almost everyone he knew.

But Leleth had shown him something else, too. She had given him a vision of Ineluki, with Sorrow in his hands. And all Ineluki's malice was bent upon . . .

The tower! The peril of the present hour suddenly rushed back. *I must take Bright-Nail there. I have been wasting time!*

Simon turned to look again at Eahlstan's stone face. He bowed to the League's founder as to a liege-lord, relishing the strangeness of it all, then turned his back on the statue-flanked throne and walked quickly across the stone tiles.

The tapestries in the standing room were gone, and the stairway to the privy was exposed. Simon scrambled up the stairs and out through the privy's window-slit, nervous excitement struggling with terror inside him. The bailey might be full of armed men, but they had forgotten about Simon the Ghost-Boy, who knew the Hayholt's every nook and cranny. No, not just Simon the Ghost-Boy—Sir Seoman, Bearer of Great Secrets!

The cold wind hit him like a battering ram, almost toppling him from the ledge. The wind threw snow almost sideways, stinging his eyes and face so that Simon could scarcely see. He held on to the window-slit, squinting. The wall outside the window was a pace wide. Ten cubits below, armored men were shouting and metal clashed against metal. Who was fighting? Were those giants that he heard roaring, or was that only the storm? Simon thought he could make out huge white shapes thrashing in the murk, but he dared not look too long or too closely at what waited for him if he tumbled from the wall.

He turned his eyes upward. Green Angel Tower loomed overhead, thrusting out from the muddle of the Hayholt's roofs like the trunk of a white tree, the lord of an ancient forest. Black clouds clung to its head; lightning split the sky.

Simon let himself down from the ledge, then inched forward along the wall on his hands and knees. His fingers rapidly grew numb, and he cursed the luck that had lost his gloves. He clung to the icy stone and tried to keep low so the incessant winds would not pluck him loose.

Usires on the Tree! This wall was never so long before!

He might have been on a bridge above the pits of Hell. Screams of pain and rage, as well as less definable sounds, drifted up from the murk, some of them loud enough to make him flinch and almost lose his grip. The cold was terrible, and the wind kept shoving, shoving. He kept his eyes on the wall's narrow top until it ended. An emptiness as long as he was tall yawned before the wall's edge and the turret that surrounded Green Angel Tower's fourth floor. Simon crouched beside this gap, braced against the buffeting wind as he tried to nerve himself to jump. A surge of air shoved him hard enough to make him lean forward until he was almost lying down atop the wall.

There it is, he told himself. *You've done it a hundred times.*

But not in a blizzard, another part of him pointed out. *Not with armed men down below who would chop you to pieces before you even knew whether you'd survived the fall.*

He grimaced against the sleet and tucked his hands underneath his arms to bring some blood back into his fingers.

You carry the secrets of the League, he told himself. *Morgenes trusted you.* It was a reminder, an incantation. He touched Bright-Nail to make sure it was still secure in his belt—its quiet song rose to his touch like the back of a stroked cat—then carefully lifted himself to stand hunched at the corner of the wall. After teetering precariously for long moments, waiting for the wind to slacken just a little, he said a brief prayer and leaped.

The wind caught him in midair and shoved him to the side. He fell short of his landing. For a moment he was slipping away into empty space, but his clawing hand caught in one of the crenellations and he jerked to a halt, dangling. As the wind tugged at him the tower and sky seemed to twist above his head, as though any moment all of creation would go topside-down. He felt the stone sliding from beneath his damp fingers and quickly pushed his other hand into the gap as well, but it was scant help. His legs and feet dangled over nothingness, and his grip was giving way.

Simon tried to ignore the fierce pain that raced through his already aching joints. He might have been tied to the wheel all over again, stretched to the breaking point—but this time there was a way out of the torment. If he let go, it would be over in a moment, and there would be peace.

But he had seen too much, suffered too much, to settle for oblivion.

Straining until agony shot through him, he pulled himself a little higher. When his arms had bent as far as he could make them, one hand scrabbled free, searching for a firmer handhold. His fingertips at last found a crevice between stones; he hauled himself upward again, an involuntary shout of pain forcing its way out through his clenched teeth. The stone was slippery, and for a moment he almost fell back, but with a last jerk he pulled his upper body into the crenellation and slithered ahead, his legs still protruding.

A raven, sheltering beneath the tower's overhang, stared at him, its yellow eyes blank. He pulled himself a little farther forward and the raven danced away, then stopped with its head tipped to one side, watching.

Simon dragged himself toward the tower window, thinking only of getting out of the icy wind. His arms and shoulders throbbed, his face felt seared by the bitter cold. As he caught at the sill, he suddenly felt something seize him from head to foot, a burning tingle that ran up and down his skin, maddening as biting ants. The raven leaped into the sky in a flapping blur of black feathers, caromed once against the powerful wind, then flew upward out of sight.

The stinging grew stronger and his limbs twitched helplessly. Something began squeezing the air from his chest. Simon knew that he had leaped directly into a trap, a trap set just to catch and kill overeager scullions.

Mooncalf, he thought. *Once a mooncalf . . .*

He half-crawled, half-fell through the tower window and onto the stairway. The agonizing pressure abruptly ceased. Simon lay on the cold stones, shivering violently, and struggled to catch his breath. His head throbbed, especially the dragon-scar on his cheek. His stomach seemed to be trying to crawl up his throat.

Something shook the tower then, a deep pealing like some monstrous bell, a sound that rattled in Simon's bones and aching skull, unlike anything he had ever heard. For a long moment the world turned inside-out.

Simon huddled on the stairs, trembling. *That wasn't the tower's bells!* he thought when the echoes had died and his shattered thoughts had coalesced. *They rang every day, all my life. What was it? What's happening to everything!?*

A little more of the chill wore away, and blood rushed back to the places it had fled. More than just his cheek was throbbing. Simon ran his fingers across his forehead. There was the beginning of a lump above his right eye; even touching it lightly made him suck in his breath. He decided he must have struck his head on something as he flung himself through the window and onto the stairs.

It could have been worse, he told himself. *I could have hit my head when I was jumping to the battlement. I'd be dead now. But instead I'm in the tower—the tower where Bright-Nail needs to . . . wants to . . .*

Bright-Nail!

He reached down in a panic, but he had not lost the sword: it was still caught against his hip, tangled in his belt. At some point it had rubbed against him and cut him—two small snakes of dried blood coiled on his left forearm—but not badly. And he still had it. That was the important thing.

And the sword was quietly singing to him. He felt rather than heard it, a seductive pull that fought past the pain in his head and battered body.

It wanted to go up.

Now? Should I just climb? Merciful Aedon, it's so hard to think!

He raised himself and crawled to the side of the stairwell, then propped his back against the smooth wall as he tried to rub the knots from his muscles. When all his limbs seemed to bend again in more or less the way they should, Simon grabbed at the wall and pulled himself to his feet. Immediately, the world began to tip and spin, but he braced himself, hands pressed flat against the tracery of reliefs that covered the stone, and after some moments he could stand unaided.

He paused, listening to the wind moaning outside the tower walls and the faint din of battle. One additional sound gradually became louder. Footsteps were echoing up the stairwell.

Simon looked around helplessly. There was nowhere to hide. He drew Bright-Nail and felt it throb in his hand, filling him with a heady warmth like a swallow of the trolls' Hunt-wine. For a brief moment, he considered standing bravely with the sword in his hand, waiting to meet whoever was mounting the stairs, but he knew that was terrible foolishness. It could be anyone—soldiers,

Norns, even the king or Pryrates. Simon had the lives of others to think about, a Great Sword that must be brought to the final battle; these were responsibilities that could not be ignored. He turned and went lightly up the steps, holding Bright-Nail leveled before him so the blade would not scrape against something and give him away. Someone had already been on these stairs today: torches burned in the wall-sconces, filling the places between windows with jittering yellow light.

The stairs wound upward, and within a score of steps he came upon a thick wooden door set into the inner wall. Relief swept through him: he could hide in the room behind it, and if he was careful, peer out through the slot set high in the door to see who climbed behind him. The discovery had come not a moment too soon. Despite his haste, the trailing footfalls had not grown any fainter, and as he paused to fumble with the doorlatch they seemed to become quite loud.

The door pivoted inward. Simon peered into the shadows beyond, then stepped through. The floor seemed to sag beneath his feet as he turned and eased the door closed. He stepped away so the edge of the door could swing past without hitting him, and his back foot came down on nothing.

Simon made a sound of startled terror and grabbed at the inside door handle. The door swung into the room, tipping him even farther backward as he stabbed with his foot for something to stand on. Panic-sweat made his grip on the door handle treacherous. The torchlight leaking in through the doorway showed a floor that extended only a cubit past the door jamb and then fell away in rotted splinters. He could see nothing below but darkness.

He had barely regained his balance, pulling himself back onto the fragment of flooring with one hand, when the great and terrible bell rang a second time. For an instant the world fell away around him and the room with the missing floor filled with light and leaping flames. The sword, which he had held tightly even while dangling over nothingness, tumbled from his grip and fell. A moment later the flames were gone and Simon was tottering on the edge of floor. Bright-Nail—precious, precious thing, the hope of all the world—had disappeared into the shadows below.

The footfalls, which had stopped for long moments, started again. Simon pushed the door closed and huddled with his back against it, on a narrow strip of wood over empty blackness. He heard the footsteps pass his hiding place and move away up the stairwell—but he no longer cared who shared the tower with him. Bright-Nail was lost.

They were so high. The walls of the stairwell seemed to lean inward, closing on her like a swallowing throat. Miriamele swayed. If that ear-shattering bell rang a fourth time, she would surely lose her balance and fall. The plummet down the battering stairs would be unending.

"We are almost there," whispered Binabik.

"I know." She could feel *something* waiting for them just a short distance above: the very air trembled. "I don't know if I can go there. . . ."

The troll took her hand. "I am also frightened." She could scarcely hear him over the shrilling of the wind. "But your uncle is being there, and Camaris has now carried the sword up to that place. Pryrates is there, too."

"And my father."

Binabik nodded.

Miriamele took a deep breath and looked up to where a thin gleam of scarlet leaked past the bend of the stairwell. Death and even worse was waiting there. She knew she must go, but she also knew with terrible clarity that the moment she took her next step the world she had known would begin to end.

She ran her hands across her sweaty face.

"I'm ready."

Smoky light throbbed where the stairs opened into the chamber above. Thunder growled outside. Miriamele squeezed Binabik's arm, then patted at her belt, touching the dagger she had taken from the cold, unmoving hand of one of Isorn's men. She took another arrow from her pack and fitted it loosely on the string of her bow. Pryrates had been hurt once—even if she could not kill him, perhaps she could provide a crucial distraction.

They stepped up into the bloody glow.

Tiamak's thin legs were the first thing she saw. The Wrannaman lay unmoving against the wall with his robe rucked up around his knees. She choked back a cry and swallowed hard, then mounted higher; her face lifted into the streaming wind.

Dark clouds knotted the sky beyond the high windows, ragged edges agleam with the Conqueror Star's feverish light. Flecks of snow swirled like ashes beneath the chamber ceiling where the great bells hung. The sense of waiting, of a world in suspension, was very strong. Miriamele struggled for breath.

She heard Binabik make a small noise beside her. Camaris knelt on the floor beneath the green-skinned bells, his shoulders shaking, black Thorn held upright before him like a holy Tree. A few paces away stood Pryrates, scarlet robes rippling in the powerful wind. But neither of these held her attention.

"Father?" It came out as little more than a whisper.

The king's head lifted, but the motion seemed to take a long time. His pale face was skeletally gaunt, his eyes deep-sunken, gleaming like shuttered lamps. He stared at her, and she felt herself falling into shards. She wanted to weep, to laugh, to rush to him and help to make him well again. Another part of her, trapped and screaming, wanted to see this twisted thing that pretended to be him—that *could not* be the man who had raised her—obliterated, sent down into darkness where it could not trouble her with either love or terror.

"Father?!" This time her voice carried.

Pryrates cocked his head toward her; a look of annoyance hurried across his shiny face. "See? They pay no heed, Highness," he told the king. "They will always go where they do not belong. No wonder your reign has burdened you so."

Elias shrugged his shoulders in anger or impatience. His face was slack. "Send her away."

"Father, wait!" she cried, and took a step forward. "God help us, don't do this! I have crossed the world to speak to you! Don't do this!"

Pryrates held up his hands and said something she could not hear. Abruptly she was seized all over by some invisible thing that clung and burned, then she and Binabik were thrown back against the chamber wall. Her pack fell from her shoulder and tumbled onto the floor, spilling its contents. The bow flew from her hand and spun away out of reach. She fought, but the clinging force gave only enough to allow her a few slow, twitching movements. She could not move forward. Binabik struggled beside her, but with no more success. They were helpless.

"Send her *away*," Elias repeated, more angrily this time, his eyes looking at anything but her.

"No, Majesty," the priest urged, "let her stay. Let her *watch*. Of all the people in the world, it is your brother," he gestured to something Miriamele could not see, "—who is unfortunately beyond appreciating it now—and your treacherous daughter who forced you onto this path." He chortled. "But they did not know that the solution you found would make you even greater than before."

"Is she in pain?" the king asked brusquely. "She is no longer my daughter—but I will not see you torture her."

"No pain, Highness," he said. "She and the troll will merely be . . . an audience."

"Very well." The king at last met her eyes, squinting as though she were a mile distant. "If you had only listened," he said coldly, "if you had only obeyed me . . ."

Pryrates put a hand on Elias' shoulder. "All was for the best."

Too late. The emptiness and desperation Miriamele had been fighting broke free and spread through her like black blood. Her father was lost to her, and she was dead to him. All the risks, the suffering, had been for nothing. Her misery grew until she thought it would stop her heart.

A fork of lightning split the sky beyond the window. Thunder made the bells hum.

"For . . . *love.*" She forced her jaws to work against the alchemist's prisoning spell. Each faint word echoed in her own ears, as though she stood at the bottom of a deep well. She told him, but it was too late, too late. "You . . . I . . . did these things . . . for love."

"Silence!" the king hissed. His face was a rawboned mask of fury. "Love! Does it remain after worms have gnawed the bones? I do not know that word."

Elias slowly turned back to Camaris. The old knight had not moved from his spot on the floor, but now, as though some power in the king's attention compelled him, he crawled a few steps closer, Thorn scraping across the stone tiles before him.

The king's voice became curiously gentle. "I am not surprised to see that the black sword chose you, Camaris. I was told that you had returned to the living. I knew that if those tales were true, Thorn would find you. Now we will act together to protect your beloved John's kingdom."

Miriamele's eyes widened in horror as a figure that had been blocked from her sight by Camaris now became visible. Josua lay crumpled just a little to one side of her father, arms and legs splayed. The prince's face was turned away, but his shirt and cloak were sodden crimson around his neck, and blood had pooled beneath him. Miriamele's eyes filled with blurring tears.

"It is time, Majesty," said Pryrates.

The king extended Sorrow like a gray tongue until it nearly touched the old knight. Although Camaris was visibly struggling with himself, he began to lift Thorn to meet the shadowy blade in the king's hand.

Fighting against the same force that bound Miriamele, Binabik gave a muffled shout of warning, but still Thorn rose in the old man's trembling hands.

"God, forgive me," Camaris cried wretchedly. "It is a sinful world . . . and I have failed You again."

The two swords met with a quiet click that cut through the room. The noise of the storm diminished, and for a moment the only thing audible was Camaris' moan of anguish.

A point of blackness began to pulse where the tips of the two blades crossed, as though the world had been ripped open and some fundamental emptiness was beginning to leak through. Even through the bonds of the alchemist's spell, Miriamele could feel the air in the high chamber suddenly grow hard and brittle. The chill deepened. Traceries of ice began to form in the arches of the windows and along the walls, spreading like wildfire. Within moments the chamber was furred with a thin surface of ice crystals that shimmered in a thousand strange colors. Icicles were growing on the great bells, translucent fangs that gleamed with the light of the red star.

Pryrates lifted his arms triumphantly. Glinting flakes clung to his robe. "It has begun."

The somber cluster of bells at the ceiling did not move, but the bone-shaking sound of a greater bell rang out once more. Powdery ice fluttered as the tower trembled like a slender tree caught in storm winds.

Simon tugged at the handle and cursed quietly. This lower door was wedged shut—there would be no easy entry into the room beneath the missing floor—and now he heard footsteps coming up the stairwell again.

His joints still hurt fiercely, but he scrambled back up the stairs to the other door as quickly as he could, then stepped inside, taking care this time to stand at the very edge of the flooring, which had held his weight before. He was forced to move far to the side of the door as it closed. As the footfalls passed outside, he carefully made his way along the strip of wood to look through the door slit, but by the time he could reach it he glimpsed only a small dark shape vanishing up the stairwell, lurching strangely. He waited a score of heartbeats, listening, then crept outside and took a torch from the nearest bracket.

To his vast relief, Simon saw by the torch's light that there was indeed a bottom to the chamber below, and though parts of that lower floor had rotted through as well, it was mostly intact. Bright-Nail lay gleaming in a pile of discarded furniture. Seeing it lying there like a piece of splendid jewelry thrown onto a midden heap, Simon felt a violent pang. He must get it back. Bright-Nail must go to the tower. Even from a distance, he could feel its yearning.

A faint thread of the blade's song coiled through his thoughts as he found what seemed the most stable spot on the floor below, gripped the butt of the torch between his teeth, then slid his legs over the edge of the strip inside the doorway. He let himself down to the full extension of his arms, then dropped, his heart fluttering as he landed. The wood creaked loudly and sagged a little, but held. Simon took a step toward Bright-Nail, but his foot sank as though into muddy ground. He hurriedly pulled it back to see that a section of the floor a little larger than his boot sole had crumpled and fallen in.

Simon got down onto his hands and knees. He made his way across the treacherous surface with slow caution, taking more than a few splinters as he probed before him. The cry of the wind outside was muffled. The torch burned hot beside his cheek; its quavering flame threw his shadow up on the wall, a hunched thing like a beast.

He stretched out his hand. Nearer . . . nearer . . . there! His fingers closed around Bright-Nail's hilt, and instantly he could feel its song intensify, vibrating through him, making him feel welcome . . . and more. Its need became his need.

Up, he thought suddenly. The word seemed a glowing thing before his mind's eye. *It's time to go up.*

But that was easier said than accomplished. He sat back on his haunches, wincing as the floor creaked, and removed the torch from his teeth. He lifted it and looked around. This room was wider than the one above; the half of the ceiling that had not been the wood floor of the upper chamber was a slab of pale stone, seemingly without support. The walls were bare except for a faint scrawl of carvings, overlaid with dust and soot. There was nothing to afford any holds for climbing, and even if he jumped, he could not reach the bit of flooring that edged the doorway above.

Simon pondered for a moment. The sword's pull was a shadow behind his thoughts, an urgency like a quiet but steady drumbeat. He slid Bright-Nail into his belt, reluctantly releasing the hilt, then resettled the torch handle in his jaws. He crawled back across the floor toward the door he had tried from the stairs, but it was just as impassable from the inside: either damp weather or shifting timbers kept it firmly closed no matter how he pulled. He sighed, then crept back to the middle of the room.

Moving with extreme care, he dragged bits of broken furniture across the floor, setting each piece carefully on or beside the last, until he had made a shoulder-high pile near the sealed doorway. As he was sliding the scarred surface of a discarded table into place at the top of the heap, he again heard someone mounting the steps.

It was hard to tell, but this time there seemed to be more than one set of feet. He crouched in silence, steadying the tabletop with his hand, and listened to the footfalls move past the door beside him, then, after a few dragging moments, echo softly past the door above. He held his breath, wondering which of his many enemies might be climbing the tower, knowing that he would discover the answer all too soon. Bright-Nail tugged at his thoughts. It was hard to sit still.

When the noises had faded, Simon prodded at the pile until he was certain it was steady. He had tried to point all the jagged edges and snapped legs downward in case he fell, but he knew that if he did, he and the spiky pieces of broken chairs, stools, and heavy tables would probably break through the floor together and tumble down into yet a lower room. He did not think much of his chances if that happened.

Simon climbed the pile as gently as he could, laying his body flat across the tabletop until he could draw his legs up behind him. The flame of the torch he held in his teeth sizzled the ends of his hair. He clambered to his feet and felt the unsteady mass rock gently beneath him. Balancing carefully, he removed the torch and held it up, looking for the sturdiest spot on the edge of flooring overhead.

He was moving toward the edge of the teetering pile when the bell rang for a third time.

Even as the thunderous peal grabbed the entire tower and shook it, and the pile of wood fell away beneath him, Simon let go of the torch and leaped. One piece of the flooring overhead broke loose in his hand, but the other held. Panting, he grasped another section with his free hand and struggled to pull himself up, even as gusts of purple fire chased themselves across the walls and everything shifted and blurred. His arms, already tired, trembled. He pulled himself higher, reaching out a hand to grab at the doorsill, then lifted his leg until it was on the strip of floor. The echo of the bell faded, although he felt it still in his teeth and the bones of his skull. The lights flickered and died, but for a faint glow beneath him. He could smell smoke rising from the torch that now lay among the shards of the piled furniture.

Grunting with the strain, Simon dragged himself the rest of the way onto the safety of the narrow band of wood. As he lay gasping for air, he saw flames beginning to lick up from the floor below.

He scrabbled to one side as cautiously as haste would permit, pulled the door open, then sprawled forth onto the stairs. He tugged the door shut, leaving a few orphaned tendrils of smoke to float and dissipate, and waited for his hands to stop shaking quite so violently.

He pulled the sword from his belt. Bright-Nail was his once more. He was still alive, still free. Hope remained.

As he began to climb he felt the blade's song rise inside him, a chant of joy, of approaching fulfillment. He felt his own heart speed as it sang. Things would be set right.

The sword was warm in his grip. It seemed a part of his arm, of his body, a new organ of sense as alert and attuned as the nose of a hunting hound or the ears of a bat.

Upward. It is time.

The pain in his head and limbs flowed away, to be filled with the ever-rising triumph of Bright-Nail, clutched firmly in his hand, safe from all harm.

It is time at last. Things will be set right. It is time.

The sword's urging grew stronger. He found it hard to think of anything but putting one foot before the next, carrying himself up toward the top of the tower, to the place where Bright-Nail longed to go. Knotted, red-shot clouds showed in the windows he passed, scarred by the occasional jagged flicker of lightning, but the noise of the storm seemed curiously muffled. Far louder now, at least in his thoughts, was the song of the sword.

It's finally going to end, he thought. He could feel that, Bright-Nail's promise. The sword would bring a halt to all the confusions and dissatisfactions that had plagued him for so long; when it joined its brothers, everything would change. All that unhappiness would end.

There was no one else on the steps now. No one moved but Simon, and he could feel that everyone, everything, waited for him. All the world hung on the fulcrum of Green Angel Tower, and he would be the one to shift that balance. It was a wild, heady feeling. The sword pulled him on, singing to him, filling him with imprecise but powerful intimations of glory and release at every upward step.

I am Simon, he thought, and could almost hear trumpets flare and echo. *I have done mighty deeds—slain a dragon! Won a battle! Now, I bring the Great Sword.*

As he mounted up, the stairs shimmered before and behind, a downward-flowing river of ivory. The pale stone of the stairway wall seemed to glow, as if it reflected the light that burned within him. The sky-blue carvings were as heartbreakingly lovely as flowers strewn before the feet of a conqueror. Completion was ahead. An end to pain awaited him.

The bell tolled a fourth time, even more powerfully than before.

Simon staggered, shaken like a rat in a dog's teeth as the echoes boomed and resounded down the stairwell. A blast of freezing air rolled past him, blurring the carvings on the wall with a milky skin of ice. He almost dropped the sword again as he lifted his hands to his head and cried out. Stumbling, he grabbed at the frame of one of the tower's windows for support.

As he stood, shivering and moaning, the sky outside changed. The broad smear of clouds vanished, and for a long moment the full blackness of the sky opened before him, dotted with tiny, cold stars, as though Green Angel Tower had torn free of its moorings and now floated above the storm. He stared, teeth clenched against the bell's fading echoes. After three heartbeats the black sky clotted with gray and red and the tower was surrounded by storm once more.

Something tugged at his thoughts, fighting against Bright-Nail's unslackening pull.

This . . . is . . . wrong. The joy that he had shared, the feeling that he would somehow make things right, ebbed away. *Something bad is happening—something very bad!*

But he was already moving again, mounting the stairs toward the dim glow. He was not the master of his own body.

He struggled. His limbs felt distant, numb. He slowed himself, then managed to stop, shuddering in the freezing wind that blew down the stairwell. Tiny whiskers of ice hung from the walls, and his breath clouded about his head, but he could feel an even greater coldness lurking somewhere above him—a coldness that somehow *thought.*

He fought for a long time on the stairs, struggling to regain control of his own arms and legs—a struggle against nothing visible that went unobserved except by the cold, inhuman presence. He could feel its hungry attention as the sweat beading on his skin froze and fell tinkling onto the steps. Steam rose from his overheated body, and where the warmth left, deadening chill crept in.

The cold took Simon at last, filling him. It moved him like a puppet on a stick. He jerked and began to stagger upward once more, screaming silently from the prison of his skull.

He stepped up out of the stairwell and into the vaporous bellchamber; the ice-blanketed walls glimmered and sparkled. Storm clouds surrounded the high windows, and light and shadow moved sluggishly, as though the cold gripped them, too.

Miriamele and Binabik stood beside the door, writhing slowly, caught somehow like flies struggling in amber. His eyes widened as he saw them, and his heart thudded painfully behind his ribs, but he could not call out or even stop his feet from carrying him forward. Miriamele opened her mouth and made a muffled noise. Tears filled his eyes, and for a moment her pale face held him like a lamp in a dark room—but the thing that gripped him would not be denied. It swept him past his friends like a river current, tugging him toward the cluster of pillars at the center of the chamber.

Beneath the frost-furred bells three figures waited, one kneeling. The part of Bright-Nail that had entangled itself with him danced and leaped . . . but the still-Simon part quailed as Elias turned toward him with a face like a dead man's. The mottled gray sword in his two fists lay against black Thorn, and where they touched there was nullity, an emptiness that hurt Simon's mind.

Shivering, Camaris turned to Simon, his hair and brows powdery with ice. The old man's eyes stared in abject misery.

"My fault . . ." he whispered through chattering teeth.

Pryrates had watched Simon's lurching entrance. Now the priest nodded, smiling tightly. "I knew you were in the tower somewhere, kitchen boy—you and the last of the swords."

Simon felt himself drawn closer to the place where Thorn and Sorrow met. Through Bright-Nail, whose song coursed inside him, he could feel the music of the other two swords as well: the dancing throb of life that was within all of them grew stronger as the moment of their joining approached. Simon felt it like the speeding current of a river's narrows, but he could also feel that there was a barrier that somehow kept the blades apart. Although two of them were touching, and only a few cubits stood between them and the third, they all remained as widely separated as they had ever been.

But what was different now, what Simon felt deeply and wordlessly in his mind's inmost, was that soon there would be a great change. Some mighty universal wheel lay loose on its axle, ready to turn, and when it did all the barriers would fall, all the walls would vanish. The swords sang, waiting.

Before he knew it, he was stepping forward. Bright-Nail clicked against the other two blades. The shock of contact traveled not just through Simon, but through the room as well. The black emptiness where the swords met deepened, a hole into which the entire world might fall and perish. The light changed all around: the star-glow seeping in through the windows deepened, turning the chamber bloody, and then the dreadful bell tolled a fifth time.

Simon trembled and cried out as the tower shook and the energies of the swords, still pent but fighting now for release, traveled through him. His heart stuttered, hesitated, and almost stopped. His vision blurred and darkened, then gradually came back. He was inextricably caught in something that burned like fire, that dragged like a lodestone. He tried desperately to pull away, but a supreme effort only made him sway gently, caught on Bright-Nail's hilt like a fish dying on a hook. The bell's echoes died out.

Even through the music of the swords, Simon could sense the chill presence he had felt on the stairs growing stronger, vast and weighty as a mountain, cold as the gaps between stars. It was closer now, but at the same time it hovered just beyond some incomprehensible wall.

Elias, who seemed almost unmoved by the exuberating power of the swords, raked Simon with mad green eyes. "I do not know this one, Pryrates," he murmured, "—although there is something familiar about him. But it does not matter. All the bargains have been kept."

"Indeed." The priest moved past, so close that his robe touched Simon's arm. A buried part of Simon shrieked with disgust and fury, but no sound passed his quivering lips: he was now little more than something that held Bright-Nail. The sword's vaulting spirit, connected now to its brothers, uncaring of human struggles and human hatreds, waited only for whatever would happen next, eager as a dog expecting to be fed.

"All bargains are kept," Pryrates rasped as he took a place beside the king's shoulder, "and all is now set in motion. Soon Utuk'ku the Eldest will have harnessed the Pool of Three Depths. Then we will have completed the Fifth House, and all will change." He looked at Simon and his eyes glittered. "This one you do not know is Morgenes' kitchen-whelp, Highness." Pryrates grinned. "This *is* satisfying. I saw what you did to Inch, boy. Very thorough work. You saved me some tiresome effort."

Simon felt a powerful rage bubbling up inside him. In the red light the priest's smug face seemed to hang bodilessly, and for a moment Simon could see nothing else. He struggled to move his limbs, to pull Bright-Nail away from its brothers so he could smash out the murderer's life, but he was helpless. The flame of anger blazed without release, so hot that Simon felt sure it would scorch him to ashes from within.

The tower rocked again to the thunderous voice of the bell. Simon stared, even as the floor shook before him and his ears popped, but the bronze bells at the center of the chamber did not move. Instead, a ghostly shape appeared, a bell of sorts, but long and cylindrical. For a moment, as the phantom bell vibrated, Simon saw flames sheeting again outside the windows, the sky gone endlessly black.

When the noise had died, Pryrates lifted his hands. "She has conquered. It is time."

The king lowered his head. "God help me, I have waited long."

"Your waiting is over." The priest crossed his arms before his face, then lowered them. "Utuk'ku has captured the Pool of Three Depths. The swords are here, waiting only for the Words of Unmaking to release that which binds them, then the force that was prisoned within them will sing free and bring you everything that you have desired."

"Immortality?" asked Elias, shy as a child.

"Immortality. A life that outlasts the stars. You sought your dead wife, Highness, but you found something far greater."

"Do not . . . do not speak of her."

"Rejoice, Elias, do not grieve!" Pryrates brought his palms together and lightning scratched across the sky outside the tall windows. "You feared you would have no heir when your disobedient daughter ran away—but you yourself will be your own inheritor. You will never die!"

Elias lifted his head, his eyes shut as though he basked in a warming sun. His mouth trembled.

"Never die," he said.

"You have gained powerful friends, and in this hour they will pay you back for all your suffering." Pryrates stepped away from the king and thrust his red-sleeved arm toward the ceiling. "I invoke the First House!"

The great invisible bell sounded again, crashing like a hammer in a god's smithy. Flames ran through the bellchamber, capering across the icy walls. "On Thisterborg, among the ancient stones," Pryrates intoned, "one of the Red Hand is waiting. For his master and you he uses the power of that place and opens a crack into the between-places. He unfolds the first of the A-Genay'asu'e and brings forth the First House."

Simon sensed the cold, dreadful something that waited growing stronger. It was all around Green Angel Tower, drawing nearer, like a hunting beast coming stealthily through the darkness toward a campfire.

"At Wentmouth," Pryrates cried, "on the cliffs above the endless ocean where the Hayefur once burned for travelers from the lost West, the Second House is now built. The Storm King's servant is there, and a far greater flame lifts to the skies."

"Do . . . not . . ." Binabik, held by Pryrates' magics, struggled to move forward from the walls. His voice seemed to come from a great distance. "Do . . . not . . . !"

The priest flicked a gesture toward him and the troll was silenced, squirming helplessly.

Again the bell rang, and the power of it seemed to pulse on and on, reverberating. For a moment Simon heard voices rising outside, screams of pain and terror in the language of the Sithi. Red lights flickered in the icicles hanging from the bell-chamber's vaulted ceiling.

"Above Hasu Vale, beside the ancient Wailing Stone, where the Eldest before the Eldest once danced beneath stars that have burned out—the Third House is built. The Storm King's servant lifts another flame to the skies."

Elias suddenly took a wobbly step. Sorrow's blade dipped as he bent, although it still touched the other two swords. "Pryrates," he gasped, "something . . . something is burning . . . inside me!"

"Father!" Miriamele's voice was faint, but her face was contorted with terror.

"Because it is time, Majesty," the alchemist said. "You are changing. Your mortality must be scorched away by clean flame." He pointed at the princess. "Look, Elias! Do you see what your weakness does to you? Do you see what the sham of love would bring you? She would make you into an old man, sobbing for your meals, pissing in your bed!"

The king straightened up and turned his back on Miriamele. "I will not be held down," he gritted. Every word seemed an effort. "I will . . . take . . . what was promised."

Simon saw that the priest was smiling, though sweat trickled down his egg-smooth brow. "You will have it." He lifted his arms once more. Simon strained until he thought veins would burst in his temples, but could not pull free from the crossed swords. "In your brother's stronghold, Elias," Pryrates said, "in what was the very heart of his treachery—at Naglimund we build the Fourth House!"

Simon again saw the unfamiliar black sky framed in the window. At the bottom of the sill, the Hayholt had become a forest of pale, graceful towers. Flames ran among them. The strange sight did not vanish. The Hayholt was gone, replaced by . . . Asu'a? Simon heard shrieking Sithi voices echoing, and the roar of flames.

"And now the Fifth House!" cried Pryrates.

The tolling of the phantom bell this time brought back Simon's view of storm clouds and whirling snow. The high-pitched anguish of the Sithi gave way to the dulled shouts of mortals.

"In the Pool of Three Depths, Utuk'ku gives way to the last of the Storm King's servitors, and beneath us the fifth and final House is created." Pryrates spread his arms, palms down, and the whole tower trembled. A kind of sucking pull reached down the length of Bright-Nail, through Simon's arm, tugging at his heart and even his thoughts as though it sought to draw them out whole. Across from him, Camaris bared his teeth in an agonized grimace, Thorn quivering in his fist.

A fountain of icy blue light sprang up through the floor of the bellchamber, roaring and crackling as it passed through the blackness where the swords touched. Diminished and distorted by that passage, it continued up past Simon's face and spattered the glinting ceiling with blue sparks. Simon felt his body convulsing as tremendous energies flowed around him and through him. Inside his battered thoughts the swords thrilled exultantly, their spirits released. He tried to open his mouth and scream, but his jaws were locked tight, teeth grinding. The coruscating blue light filled his eyes.

"And now the three Great Swords have found their way to this place, beneath the Conqueror Star. Sorrow, defender of Asu'a, scourge of the living; Thorn, star-blade, banner of the dying Imperium; Bright-Nail, last iron from the vanished West."

As Pryrates called each name, the great bell rang. The tower and all around it seemed to shift with each sounding, the delicate towers and flames giving way to the squat, snow-covered roofs of the Hayholt, then appearing once more with the next reverberating clang.

Caught in the grip of terrible forces, Simon felt himself burning from within. He hated. Smoldering clouds of rage rose up inside him, hatred at being tricked, at seeing his friends murdered, at the terrible devastation that Pryrates and Elias had caused. He wanted to swing the sword in a deadly arc, to smash everything in sight, to kill those who had made him so horribly unhappy. He could not shriek— he could not even move except to twitch helplessly. The rage, ordinary escape blocked, seemed to pour out through his sword arm instead. Bright-Nail became a blur, something not quite real, as though part of it had gone away. Thorn was a dark smear in Camaris' hands. The old man's eyes had rolled up in his head.

Simon felt his monstrous anger and despair break free. The blackness where the swords met widened, an unending emptiness, a gate into Unbeing, and Simon's hate poured into it. The void began to crawl up Sorrow's length toward Elias.

"We harness the great fear." Pryrates moved to a spot behind the king, who now seemed as trapped and helpless as the other two swordbearers. The priest spread his arms wide, so that for a moment Elias seemed to have another pair of hands. "In every land, the fear has spread. The kilpa make the seas boil. The ghants crawl through the streets of the southern cities. The beasts of legend stalk the snows of the north. The fear is *everywhere*.

"We harness the great fear. In every land, brother is turned against brother. Plague and famine and the scourge of war turn people into raging demons.

"All the strength of fright and fury is ours, funneled through the pattern of the Five Houses." Suddenly Pryrates laughed. "You are all such small minds! Even your terrors are small ones. You feared to see your armies defeated? You will see more than that. You will see Time itself roll backward in its rut."

King Elias jerked and twitched as the blackness crawled up the blade toward him, but he seemed unable to release Sorrow. "God help me, Pryrates!" A convulsive shudder ran through him, a tremor of such power that he should have fallen to the floor. The nightdark void touched his hands. "Aaaah! God help me, I am burning up! My soul is on fire!"

"Surely you did not think it would be easy?" Pryrates was grinning. Sweat sheeted down his forehead. "It will get worse, you fool."

"I do not wish immortality!" Elias screamed. "Ah, God, God, God! Release me! I am burning away!" His voice was distorted, as though some inconceivable thing had invaded his lungs and chest.

"What you wish is not important," Pryrates spat back. "You will have your immortality—but it may not be all you had hoped."

Elias writhed. His shrieks were wordless now.

Pryrates extended his hands until they hovered on either side of Sorrow's hilt, only inches from Elias' own fingers. "It is time for the Words of Unmaking," he said.

The bell thundered, and once more Green Angel Tower was surrounded by the tragic delicacy of burning Asu'a. The stars in that black sky were cold and tiny as snowflakes. The tower seemed to shake like an agonized living thing.

"I have prepared the way!" Pryrates called. "I have crafted the vessel. Now, in this place, *let Time turn backward!* Roll back the centuries to the moment before Ineluki was banished to the realms beyond death. As I speak the Words of Unmaking, let him return! *Let him return!*" He lapsed into a bellowing chant in a language harsh as shattering stone, as cracking ice. The blackness spread out over Elias and for a moment the king vanished utterly, as though he had been pushed through the wall of reality. Then he seemed to absorb the blackness, or it flowed into him; he reappeared, thrashing and shrieking incoherently.

Elysia, Mother of Mercy! They've won! They've won! Simon's head seemed full of storm winds and flame, but his heart was black ice.

Once more the bell caroled, and this time the very air of the chamber seemed to grow solid and glassy, bending Simon's gaze as though he looked through a mirrored tunnel. There seemed no up or down. Outside, the stars began to smear across the sky in long white threads, tangling like wormholes in sod. Even as his life bled from him and out of Bright-Nail in searing waves, he felt the world turning inside out.

The bellchamber grew dark. Distorted shadows loomed and shifted across the icy chamber, then the walls seemed to open and fall away. Blackness flowed through, bringing with it a deeper chill, a freezing, ultimate cold.

Elias' agonized screams had become a choking near-silence. He and Pryrates were now the only things visible. The priest's hands flickered with yellow light; his face gleamed. All the warmth of the world was leaking away.

The king began to change.

Elias' silhouette bent and shifted, growing monstrously, even though his own contorted form was somehow still visible in the center of the darkness.

The deadening chill was inside Simon, too, seeping in where the flames of his fury had burned away his hope. His life was being drawn out of him, sucked clean like marrow from a bone.

The cold, cold thing that had waited so long was coming.

"Yes, you will live forever, Elias," intoned Pryrates. "But it will be as a flitting shadow within your own body, a shadow dwarfed by Ineluki's bright flame. You see, even with the wheel of Time turned backward in its track and all the doors opened to Ineluki once more, his spirit must have an earthly home."

The sounds of the storm outside had ceased, or could no longer penetrate through the strange forces that clutched the bellchamber. The fountain of blue light flowing upward from the Pool had narrowed to a silent stream that vanished into the blackness of the swords' joining and did not reemerge. When Pryrates had finished, there was no sound in the dark room but the rapid chuffing of the king's breath. Scarlet flames kindled in the depths of Elias' eyes, then his head rocked back as though his neck had snapped. Vaporous red light leaked from his mouth.

Simon watched in horror; through the swords he could feel the way being opened, just as Pryrates had said. Something too horrible to exist was forcing its way through into the world. The king's body jerked like a child's doll dangling on a string. Smoldering light seemed to spring forth from him everywhere, as though the very fabric of his body was fraying apart, revealing some burning thing beneath.

Somewhere Miriamele was screaming; her small, lost voice seemed to come from the other end of the universe.

The bellchamber was gone. All around, angles as strange as if reflected in broken mirrors, stood Asu'a's needle towers. They burned as the king's body burned, crumbled as Time itself was crumbling. Five centuries were sliding away into the frozen black void. Nothing would be left but ashes and stone and Ineluki's utter triumph.

"Come to us, Storm King!" shouted Pryrates. "I have made the way. The Words of Unmaking release the power of the swords, and Time turns withershins. History is undone! We shall write it anew!"

Elias writhed, and writhing grew larger, as though whatever filled him was too large for any mortal form and stretched him almost to the point of bursting. A suggestion of antlers flickered on the king's brow, and his eyes were pits of shifting, molten scarlet. His outline wavered, a moving tide of shadow that made it impossible to discern his true shape. The king's arms parted. One hand still held the elusive blur of nothingness that had been Sorrow; the other hand extended and the fingers spread, black as charred sticks. Emberlight played in the creases.

The thing paused, flickering and shifting. It seemed saggingly weary, like a butterfly newly emerged from a cocoon.

Pryrates took a step back and averted his face. "I have . . . I have done what you asked, mighty one." His smug grin was gone: the priest had willingly opened the door, but what had entered shocked even him. He took a deep breath and appeared to find some core of strength. His face again became feral. "The hour is come—but it is not your hour, it is *mine*. How could I trust one who hated every living thing to keep its bargain? I knew that once you had no need of me, your promises would be wind in darkness." He spread his wide-sleeved arms. "Mortal I may be, but I am no fool. You gave me the Words of Changing, thinking them a toy that would keep me childishly amused as I did your bidding. But I have learned, too. Those Words will become your cage, and then you will be *my* servant. All creation will bend to you—but you will bow to me!"

The unstable thing at the room's center eddied like blown smoke, but its black, scarlet-streaming heart remained solid. Pryrates began to chant loudly in something only recognizable as language because of the empty spaces between noises. The alchemist seemed to change, reeling in the red-shot darkness that surrounded the king like a fog; his limbs curled and snapped in a ghastly, serpentine way, then he faded into a coiling shadow, a wide rope of blackness that drifted around the place where the king or whatever had devoured him now stood. The shadowy coils tightened around the smoldering heart. The world seemed to bend farther inward, distorting the two shapes until only flame and steam and darkness pulsed at the center of the bellchamber.

The whole of creation seemed to collapse in on this place, on this moment. Simon felt his own terror surge out, crackling through his arms, through Bright-Nail and into the midst of the clotted dark.

The blackness bulged. Tiny arcs of lightning flickered about the room. Somewhere outside, Simon knew, the Asu'a of five centuries before was burning, its inhabitants dying at the hands of Fingil's long-dead army. And what of everyone else? Was all Simon knew gone, borne away by Time's circling wheel?

The lightnings jittered about the chamber. Something pulsed at the center, a storm of fire and thunderheads that suddenly gaped, filling the room with blinding light. Pryrates, his real form restored, staggered backward out of the beating radiance, which promptly collapsed back into shadow. For a moment the priest raised his arms triumphantly over his head, then he teetered and dropped to his knees. A vaguely manlike form coalesced out of the darkness and stood over him, a scarlet suggestion of a face fluttering atop its misshapen head.

Pryrates shuddered and wept. "Forgive me! Forgive my arrogance, my foolishness! Oh, please, Master, forgive me!" He crawled toward the thing, banging his forehead against the almost invisible floor. "I can still do you great service! Remember what you promised me, Lord—that if I served you well I would be first among mortals."

The thing retained its grip on shifting Sorrow, but extended its other blackened hand until it touched the alchemist. The fingers cupped his smooth wet head. A voice more powerful than the bell, as ragged and deadly as the hiss of freezing wind, scraped through the darkness. Despite everything else that had happened, Simon's eyes filled with frightened tears at the sound of it.

"YES. YOU WILL BE FIRST."

Jets of steam lifted from beneath the king's fingers. Pryrates shrieked and threw up his arms, grabbing at the hand, but the king did not move and Pryrates could not free himself. Runnels of flame sped down the alchemist's robe. Above him, the king's face was an indistinct lump of darkness, but eyes and ragged mouth blazed scarlet. The priest's scream was a sound no human throat should have loosed. Vapors enveloped him, but Simon saw his threshing arms steaming, cracking, shriveling into waggling things like tree limbs. After a long moment, the priest, all bones and burning tatters, fell to the floor and twitched like a smashed cricket. The jerking movements slowed, then stopped.

The thing that had been Elias slumped, head down, so that nothing could be seen of it but shadow. Still, Simon could feel it drinking the energies that raced through Bright-Nail, Thorn, and Sorrow, regaining the strength to control its stolen body. Pryrates had hurt it, somehow, but Simon could sense that it would be only the work of moments before it recovered. He felt a tiny flutter of hope, and tried to let go of his sword hilt, but it was as much a part of him as his arm. There was no escape.

As though it sensed his attempt to break free, the black thing looked up at him, and even as his heart stumbled and almost failed, he could glean its implacable thought. It had smashed Time itself to return. Even the mortal priest, no matter what powers he had wielded, would not have been allowed to close the door again—what possible chance could Simon have?

In this moment of horror, Simon suddenly felt the shock of the dragon blood that had once scorched his flesh and changed him. He stared at the unsteady black shape that had been Elias, the ruined husk and its fiery occupant, and felt an answering stab of pain where the dragon's black essence had scarred him. Through the pulsing unlight that moved between Bright-Nail and Sorrow, Simon felt not only the all-consuming hatred that had been the blood of the Storm King's deathly exile, but also Ineluki's terrible, mad loneliness.

He loved his people, Simon thought. *He gave his life for them but did not die.*

Staring helplessly across the short distance between them, watching as the thing regathered its strength, Simon remembered the vision Leleth had shown him of Ineluki beside the great pool. Such shattering unhappiness had been in that face, but the determination had been a mirror of Eahlstan's as he had sat in his chair and waited for the terrible worm he knew he must meet, the dragon that he knew would slay him. They were somehow the same, Ineluki and

Eahlstan, doing what must be done, though life itself was the price. And Simon was no different.

Sorrow. His thoughts flittered and died like moths in a flame, but he clung to this one. *Ineluki named his sword Sorrow. Why did she show me that?*

Something was moving at the edge of his vision. Binabik and Miriamele, freed by Pryrates' death, reeled a few steps forward. Miriamele fell to her knees. Binabik staggered closer, head held low as though he walked into a powerful wind.

"You will destroy this world," the troll gasped. Although his mouth was stretched wide, his words seemed quiet as the whir of velvety wings. "You have lost your belonging, Ineluki. There will be nothing for your governing. *You do not belong here!*"

The clot of darkness turned to look at him, then raised a flickering hand. Simon, seeing Binabik quail before the destroying touch, felt his fear and hatred rise anew. He fought against that surge of loathing, although he did not know why.

Hatred kept him alive in the dark places. Five centuries, burning in emptiness. Hatred is all he has. And I have hated, too. I have felt like him. We are the same.

Simon struggled to keep the image of the living Ineluki's suffering face before him. That was the truth beneath this horrible, burning thing. No creature in all the cosmos deserved what had happened to the Storm King.

"I'm sorry," he whispered to the face in his memory. "You should not have suffered so."

The surge of energy from Bright-Nail suddenly grew less. The thing that held Sorrow turned back to him, and waves of terror broke over Simon again. His heart was being crushed.

"No," he gasped, and groped inside himself for a solid place to stand and live. "I will . . . fear you, but I . . . *will not hate you.*"

There came a still instant that seemed like years. Then Sir Camaris rose slowly from his knees and stood, swaying. In his hands, Thorn still throbbed with blackness, but Simon felt the drain of its forces weaken, as though what he himself felt had somehow run down through the point of connection into Camaris as well.

"Forgiven . . ." the old knight croaked. "*Yes.* Let all be . . ."

There was a wavering at the center of the darkness that was the Storm King. For a moment, the scarlet light grew less, then died. A glowing red haze leaked free, agitated as a swarm of bees. In the center of the shadows, wreathed in smoke, the pale visage of King Elias shimmered into existence, his face contorted in pain. Wisps of smoke curled from his hair. Flames darted on his cape and shirt.

"*Father!*" Miriamele's entire being seemed in her cry.

The king turned his eyes to her. "*Ah, God, Miriamele,*" he breathed. His voice was not entirely human. "*He has waited too long for this. He will not let me go. I was a fool, and now . . . I am . . . repaid. I am sorry . . . daughter.*" He convulsed, and for a moment his eyes blazed red, though his knotted features still remained. *"He is too strong . . . his hate is too strong. He will . . . not . . . let me . . . go. . . ."*

His head began to sag. Emberlight bloomed in the cavern of his mouth.

Miriamele shouted wordlessly and lifted her arms. Simon felt rather than saw some fleeting thing snap past him.

A feathered white shaft sprouted from Elias' breast.

For a heartbeat the king's eyes were his own once more, and his gaze locked with Miriamele's. Then his features twisted. A roar louder than thunder tore from the king's gaping mouth and Elias toppled backward into shadow. The roar became an echoing, impossibly loud shriek that seemed to have no ending.

For a fleeting instant Simon felt an impossibly cold *something* scrabbling at the place where the dragon's blood had entered his heart, seeking to find refuge in him if its other host was denied to it. The thing's hunger was all-swallowing and desperate.

No. You do not belong here. Simon's thought echoed Binabik's words.

The clawing thing fell away, shrieking soundlessly.

Flames climbed up and outward where the king had stood, mushrooming beneath the roof of the bellchamber. A terrible cold blackness was at the center of them, but as Simon watched in shattered awe, it began to fragment into darting shadows. The world tipped again, and the tower shuddered. Bright-Nail throbbed in his grip, then dissolved in a whirl of black; a moment later, he was holding only dust. He lifted his trembling hand near his face to stare at the sifting powder, then stopped, astonished.

He could move again!

A chunk of stone from the ceiling overhead crashed down beside him, spattering him with sharp fragments. Simon took a reeling step. The chamber was afire, as though the stones themselves were burning. One of the blackened bells tumbled from the cluster at the ceiling and crashed to the floor, smashing a crater in the stone tiles. Shadowy figures moved around him, their motions distorted by the walls of flame.

A voice was calling his name, but he stood at the center of fiery chaos and saw no direction in which to turn. The swirling sky appeared in a jagged opening above his head as more stone fell. Something struck him.

59

Hidden from the Stars

✷

Tiamak stood awkwardly, waiting. The duke listened patiently to the two Thrithings-men, then nodded and replied; they turned and walked through the melting snow toward their horses, leaving the duke and the Wrannaman alone beside the fire.

When Isgrimnur looked up and saw his visitor, he did his best to smile. "Tiamak, what are you doing standing there? Aedon's Mercy, man, sit down. Warm yourself." The duke tried to beckon, but his arm sling prevented it.

Tiamak limped over and sat down on the log. For a moment he held his hands before the flames without speaking, then said: "I am so sorry about Isorn."

Isgrimnur turned his red-rimmed eyes away and stared across the foggy headland toward the Kynslagh. It was a long time before he spoke. "I do not know how I will tell my Gutrun. She will be heartbroken."

The silence stretched. Tiamak waited, unsure whether he should say more. He knew Isgrimnur far better than he had known the duke's tall son, whom he had met only once, in Likimeya's tent.

"He was not the only one to die," Isgrimnur said at last. He rubbed at his nose. "And there are the living to be taken care of." He picked up a stick and tossed it into the fire, then blinked at it with an intent fury. Tears glinted on his eyelashes. The silence grew again, swelling to almost frightening proportions before Isgrimnur broke it. "Ah, Tiamak, why wasn't it me? His life was ahead. I am old. My life is over."

The Wrannaman shook his head. He knew there was no answer to that question. No one could plumb the reasoning of They Who Watch and Shape. No one.

The duke dragged his sleeve across his eyes, then cleared his throat. "Enough. Time for mourning will come." He turned back to Tiamak, and the Wrannaman for the first time saw the truth of Isgrimnur's words: the duke *was* old, a man long past his prime. Only his great vitality had masked it, and now, as though the struts had been kicked from beneath him, he sagged. Tiamak felt anger that such a good man should suffer.

But everyone has suffered, he told himself. *Now is the time to gather strength, to try to understand and to decide what comes next.*

"Tell me what happened, Tiamak." The duke forced himself to sit upright, restoring a semblance of self-discipline he clearly needed. "Tell me what you saw."

"Surely I have little to say that you . . ." the Wrannaman began.

"Just tell me." Isgrimnur shifted his broken arm to a more comfortable position. "We have a while before Strangyeard can come and join us, but I imagine you have spoken to him already."

Tiamak nodded. "When I was putting salve on his wounds. Everyone has stories to tell, and none of them pleasant to hear." He composed himself for a moment, then began. "I traveled with the Sithi for what seemed a long time before we found Josua. . . ."

"So you believe Josua was dead already?" The calmness of the duke's deep voice was belied by the unhappy nervousness of his free hand, which passed in and out of his beard, tugging and plucking. His beard looked thinner and shabbier, as though he had pulled at it too often in recent days.

Tiamak nodded sadly. "He was struck very hard on the neck by the king's sword. There was a terrible noise when it hit, a snapping, and then the blood. . . ." The small man shuddered. "He could not have survived it."

Isgrimnur brooded for a moment, then shook his head. "Ah, well. I thank Usires Aedon in His mercy that at least Josua did not suffer. An unhappy man, though I loved him. An unhappy ending." He looked up at a shout in the distance, then turned his gaze back to the Wrannaman. "And you were then knocked senseless yourself."

"I remember nothing after I heard the bell again . . . until I awakened. I was still in the place where the bells hung, but I did not know it at first. All I could see was that I was surrounded by a whirlpool of fire and smoke and strange shadows.

"I tried to climb to my feet, but my head was spinning and my legs would not work properly. Someone caught at my arm and dragged at me until I could rise. At first I thought I had gone mad, because no one was there. Then I looked down and saw that it was Binabik who had helped me.

"'Hurry,' he told me, 'this place is falling into pieces.' He pulled at me again—I was dazed and did not entirely understand him. Smoke was everywhere and the floor was pitching beneath my feet with loud grinding noises. As I stood wavering, another shape appeared. It was Miriamele, and she was dragging a body across the floor with great effort. It took me a moment to see through the dust and ashes that it was the young man Simon.

"'I killed him,' Miriamele was saying over and over. Tears were streaming down her face. I did not understand why she thought she had killed Simon when I could see his fingers moving, his chest rising and falling. Binabik hastened to help her and they pulled Simon across the floor toward the stairwell. I followed them. A moment later the tower shook again and a great chunk of stone fell down and shattered on the spot where I had stood." Tiamak reached down and pointed at the cloth wrapped around his leg. "A piece flew free and cut me, but not badly." He straightened up.

"Miriamele wanted to go back for Josua, but the floor was shaking powerfully now, and more pieces of the ceiling and walls were crumbling. Binabik was doubtful, and they began to argue. My wits were coming back. I told them that the king had broken Josua's neck, that I had seen it happen. Miriamele was hard to understand—she seemed to be half-asleep, despite the tears—but she had begun to say something about Camaris when one of the bells broke loose and smashed down through the floor. We could hear it clang as it struck on something below. Smoke was everywhere. I was coughing, and my eyes were as wet as Miriamele's. I did not much care at the moment, but I felt sure that we would be burned or smashed to death, that I would never know what had happened to cause all this.

"Binabik grabbed Miriamele's arm, pointing to the ceiling, shouting that there was no time. Simon would be difficult enough to carry. She fought him for a moment, but her heart was not in it. The three of us picked Simon up as best we could—he was limp; it made him very difficult to carry—and we scuttled into the stairwell.

"The smoke was not so thick down below the first turn. The fire seemed to burn only in the bellchamber, although I heard Binabik say something that made it sound as if the whole tower had been in flames just instants before. But even if it was easier to breathe, I was still certain we would not survive to reach the ground: the tower was pitching like a tree in a strong wind. I have heard that in days long past one or two of the southernmost islands of Firannos Bay disappeared because the earth shook so hard that the sea swallowed them. If that is true, their last moments must have felt like this. We could barely keep on our feet in the narrow stairwell. Several times I was thrown against one of the walls, and we were lucky we only dropped poor Simon twice. Stone was shivering down and dust was everywhere, choking me as thoroughly as the smoke had."

Tiamak paused and pressed his fingers against his temples. His head hurt. Remembering the desperate flight down the stairs made it ache almost as badly as it had then.

"We had gone down a little farther—it was fearfully difficult to make our way, and the very steps seemed to be breaking apart beneath our feet—when a figure appeared out of the dust below us. It was smeared with ash and grime and blood, and its eyes stared. At first I thought it some horrible demon that Pryrates had summoned, but Miriamele cried 'Cadrach!', and I recognized him. I was astonished, of course—I had no idea how he of all people had appeared in this place. I could hardly hear him above the groaning and rumbling of the tower, but he said: 'I waited for you,' to no one in particular, then turned and led us down the stairs. I was angry and frightened, and I could not help wondering why he did not offer to help carry Simon, who was a terrible load for a young woman, a troll, and a small man like me to bear. Simon was now beginning to move a little more, mumbling to himself and struggling weakly. It made him even more difficult to carry.

"Then there was a time I can hardly remember. We went as fast as we could, but there seemed little chance we would escape before the tower collapsed completely. We were still very high up, maybe ten times a man's height. As we passed one of the windows, I saw the tower's spire hanging crookedly, as if the whole tower bowed from the waist. You notice strange things at such times, I suppose, and I saw that the bronze angel at the spire's tip had its arms extended as though it was poised to fly away. Suddenly the whole spire shivered, broke loose, and fell down out of sight.

"There were cracks in the walls of the stairwell wide enough to put your arm into, Isgrimnur. Through some of them I could see gray sky.

"Then the tower shook again, so strongly that we fell down on the stairs. It kept shaking; it was almost impossible to regain our feet, but we did at last. When we had scrambled down a few more paces, the twisting of the staircase suddenly opened onto nothing. The side of the tower wall had gone, fallen away outward: I could see it lying in great shards, spread out on the snow beneath, white on white. A great chunk of the staircase had gone with it, so that there was a gap many paces across, and beneath lay a fall of twenty cubits onto darkness and broken stone."

Tiamak paused for a moment. "What happened next is strange. Had I stayed in my swamp, I would not believe this tale from someone else. But I have seen things that have changed what I believe is possible."

Isgrimnur nodded somberly. "As have I. Go on, man."

"We were stopped at the gap, staring hopelessly at the bits of rubble working loose from the ragged edge and tumbling down into shadows."

"'So here it ends,' Miriamele said. I must say that she did not sound particularly upset. She was fey, Isgrimnur. She had worked as hard as any of us to stay alive, but she seemed to do it only to help the rest of us.

"'It is not over . . .' Cadrach said. The monk sank to his knees beside the edge of the pit and spread his hands flat over the nothingness. The tower was quivering itself apart, and it seemed to me that the man was praying—although I admit I could think of nothing better to do at that point. As he did, he twisted his face like a man lifting a heavy load. At last he looked over his shoulder to Miriamele. 'Now cross,' he said. His voice was strained.

"'Cross?' She stared at him. There was anger on her face, strong anger. 'What final trick of yours is this?'

"'You once said . . . only trust me again . . . when stars shone at midday,' the monk said softly. Every word was an effort. I could barely hear him, and I could not understand what he intended or what he was talking about. 'You saw them,' he said. 'They were there.'

"She looked at him for what seemed like a dreadfully long time as the tower trembled. Then she gently set Simon's shoulders down and took a step toward the pit. I reached out to pull her back, but Binabik stopped me. He had a strange look on his face. So did she, for that matter. So did Cadrach.

"Miriamele closed her eyes, then stepped out from the edge. I was certain that she would fall down and be killed, and I may have shouted something, but she walked out onto the solid air as though the stone steps were still there. Isgrimnur, there was nothing beneath her feet!"

"I believe you," the duke grunted. "I have been told Cadrach was once a mighty man."

"She opened her eyes and did not look down, but turned to Binabik and me and beckoned us to bring Simon. For the first time, there was something lively in her face again, but it was not happiness. We wrestled Simon down—he was groaning by then, awakening—and she reached up and took his feet, then began to back away over the nothingness. I could not believe what she was doing—what *I* was about to do! I slitted my eyes so I could see only Miriamele moving carefully downward, and followed her. Binabik was beside me, holding Simon's other shoulder. He looked between his feet, but then looked up again very quickly. Even a mountain-troll has some limits, it seems.

"It took us a long time. There were still things like steps beneath us; we could not see them, and we had no idea how far to either side they extended, so we went very carefully. The tower was making deep moaning noises now, as though its roots were being plucked from the ground. If I live a thousand years, Isgrimnur, I will never forget walking across nothingness and trying to stay on my feet as everything pitched and tipped! He Who Always Steps on Sand was truly with us. Truly.

"At last we reached a place where there was real stone. As I stepped onto it and let out my breath, I looked back. Cadrach was on the far side still. His face was gray as ashes and his sides were heaving. He looked like a drowning man before he sinks the last time. What strength did it take him to do what he had done? Nearly all, it seemed.

"Miriamele turned and called to him to cross, but he only lifted his hand and sat back. He could barely speak. 'Go on,' he said. 'You are not safe yet. That was all I had.' He smiled—smiled, Isgrimnur!—and said: 'I am not the man I was.'

"The princess cursed him and cursed him, but more rock was tumbling free, and Binabik and I shouted that there was nothing to be done, that if Cadrach could not, he could not. Miriamele looked down at Simon, then back at the monk. At last she said something I could not hear, then reached down for Simon's feet. As we hurried down the stairwell, I looked back and saw Cadrach sitting beside the broken edge, and the light from the gray sky shone on him through the broken wall. His eyes were closed. He might have been praying, or just waiting.

"We went down another flight, and then Simon was fighting to be let free. We set him down, since we could not carry him against his will—he is quite strong!—but neither could we wait to see if his wits were about him. Binabik pulled at his wrist, talking to him all the while, and he stumbled along with us.

"Dust was so thick from crumbling stone that I could barely breathe, and now there was fire, too, a blaze which had burned away one of the inner doors and was filling the stairwell with smoke. Beyond the windows we could see other pieces of the tower's upper stories topple past. Simon pointed to one of the windows and shouted we must go there. We thought he was addled, but he grabbed Miriamele and dragged her toward it.

"He was not addled, or at least in this he was not, for outside the window was a porch of stone—perhaps it has some drylander name—and beyond it the edge of a wall. It was still a long drop to the ground, but the wall was not far away, only a little farther than I am tall. But the tower was shaking itself to pieces, and we almost fell from the porch. More pieces were dropping. Simon suddenly bent down and grabbed at Binabik, said something to him—then flung him through the air! I was astonished! The troll landed on the edge of the wall, slipped a little on the snow, but held his balance. Miriamele went next, jumping without help; Binabik kept her from sliding off when she landed. Then Simon urged me, and I held my breath and jumped. I *would* have fallen if the other two had not been waiting, because the stone porch had begun to tip downward as I went, and I almost did not leap far enough.

"Now Simon stood, trying to find his balance, and Miriamele was screaming at him to hurry, hurry, and Binabik was shouting, too. Simon leaped and landed, and as he did, most of the porch dropped away, crashing into the snow beneath. We all three caught at him and pulled him to safety before he toppled off the wall.

"A few moments later the entire tower collapsed in on itself with a noise like nothing I have ever heard, louder than any thunderstorm . . . but you heard it. You know. Pieces of stone bigger than this tent smashed past us, but none hit the wall. Most of the tower fell inward, and a cloud of dust and snow and streaming smoke rose up as high as the tower had reached, then spread out across the castle grounds."

Tiamak took a deep breath. "We stood for a long time staring. It was as though I watched a god die. I learned later what Miriamele and the others had seen in the towertop, and that must have been stranger still. When we could think of moving again, Simon led us down through the throne room, past that astounding chair of bones, and out to meet you and the rest. I thanked my Wran deities that the fighting was all but over—I could not have lifted a hand if a Norn had put a knife to my neck."

He sat for a while, shaking his head.

Isgrimnur cleared his throat. "So nothing could have survived, then. Even if Josua or Camaris lived until the end, they would have been crushed."

"We will never know from what remains in that rubble," Tiamak said. "I cannot think we could recognize . . ." He remembered Isorn. "Oh, Isgrimnur, please, please forgive me. I forgot."

Isgrimnur shook his head. "The doors to the antechamber came open a short while before the end—I suppose Pyrates' dying put an end to his deviltry, his magical wall or whatever it was. Some of the soldiers nearby pulled out those of the fallen they could before the tower began to collapse. I, at least, have my son's body." He looked down, struggling for composure, then sighed. "Thank you, Tiamak. I am sorry to make you remember."

Tiamak laughed shakily. "I have not been able to stop talking about it. We are all of us in this camp babbling away at each other like children, and have been since the tower fell, since . . . since everything happened."

The duke stood, slowly and painfully. "I see Strangyeard coming. The others will meet us. Will you come along, Tiamak? These are important matters, and I would like you to be with us when we talk. We need your wisdom."

The Wrannaman gently bowed his head. "Of course, Isgrimnur. Of course."

♔

Simon wandered through the rubble of the Inner Bailey. The melting snow had shrunk away to reveal patches of dead grass, and here and there a freshet of new plant life which the sorcerous winter had not destroyed. The different hues of green and brown were soothing to his eyes. He had seen enough of black, ice-white, and blood-red to last him several lifetimes.

He only wished that everything followed such ordinary patterns of renewal. It was a short two days since the tower had fallen and the Storm King had been vanquished, a time when he and his friends should have been rejoicing over their victory, yet here he was, wandering and brooding.

He had slept through the night and the first day after their escape, a thick, bone-weary slumber. Binabik had come to him the second night, telling him stories, explaining, commiserating, then finally sitting with him in silence until Simon fell asleep once more. Others had visited him throughout the morning of this second day, friends and acquaintances reaching out, proving to themselves that he lived, just as the sight of these visitors showed Simon that the world still made a kind of sense.

But Miriamele had not come.

When the unclouded sun had begun to slide down past noon, he had nerved himself to go and see her. Binabik had assured him the night before that she lived and was not badly hurt, so he did not fear for her health, but the troll's reassurances had only made his other unhappiness stronger. If she was well, why had she not come to him or sent a message?

He had found her at her tent, in conversation with Aditu, who earlier that morning had been one of his own visitors. Miriamele had greeted him in a friendly enough fashion, and had exclaimed sorrowfully over his various wounds, as he had over hers, but when he expressed his sadness over the deaths of her uncle and father, she had suddenly grown cold and remote.

Simon wanted to believe it was no more than the justifiable bitterness of someone who had lived through a terrible time and had lost her family—not to mention her own unhappy role in her father's death—but he could not fool himself that there was nothing more to her reaction than that. She had been reacting to him, too, as though something about Simon still made her dreadfully uncomfortable. It made him miserable to see that distance in her eyes after all they had been through together, but he had also felt fury, wondering why he should be treated as though it had been his cruelty to her that had marred their trip into Erkynland, instead of the other way around. Although he had struggled to hide this anger, things had only grown chillier between them, and at last he had excused himself and gone out into the wind.

Into the wind and up the hill he had gone, to wander now through the slushy grounds of the abandoned Hayholt.

Simon paused, staring at the great pile of spread rubble that had once been Green Angel Tower. Small figures moved in the ruins, Erchester-folk scavenging for anything worth saving, either to trade for food or as a keepsake of what was already a fabled event.

It was strange, Simon reflected. He had gone as deep into the earth as anyone could, and had climbed equally as high, but he had not changed very much. He was a little stronger, perhaps, but he guessed that was a strength mostly caused by the inflexibility of scarred places; other than that, he was much the same. A kitchen boy, Pryrates had called him. The priest had been right. Despite his knighthood, despite all else that had happened, there would always be the heart of a scullion inside him.

Something caught his eye and he bent forward. A green hand lay at the bottom of the gulley beside his feet, fingers protruding from the mud in a frozen gesture of release. Simon leaned forward and scraped away some of the soggy clay, exposing an arm, then finally a bronze face.

It was the angel of the towertop, fallen to the earth. He poured a handful of puddle water over the high-boned face, clearing the eyes. They were open, but no life was in them. It was a tumbled statue, nothing more.

Simon stood up and wiped his hands on his breeches. Let someone else drag it from the muck and take it home. Let it sit in the corner of someone's cottage and whisper to them beguiling stories of the depths and heights.

But as he trudged away across the commons yard, turning his back on the wreckage of the tower, the angel's voice—Leleth's voice—came back to him.

"These truths are too strong," she had said, *"the myths and lies around them too great. You must see them and you must understand for yourself. But this has been your story."*

And she had showed him important things indeed. The proof of that, at least in part, lay scattered over a thousand cubits of ground behind him. But there had been more, something that had teased at the edge of his understanding, but which time and circumstance had kept him from pondering. Now the curious thread of memory came back to him, and would not be denied. He had come closest to seeing it in the throne room. . . .

His footsteps echoed across the tiles. There was no other sound. This was a place no one had yet come to scavenge—the mute specter of the Dragonbone Chair was enough to raise fearful hackles in the best of times, and these had not been the best of times.

The afternoon light, warmer than the last time he had been here, spilled down from the windows and gave a little color to the strew of fading banners, although the malachite kings were still cloaked in their own black stone shadows. Simon remembered a void of spreading nothingness and hesitated, his heart pounding, but he swallowed his momentary fear and stepped forward. That blackness was gone. That king was dead.

In full daylight the great throne looked less daunting than he remembered it. The great toothy mouth still menaced, but some vitality it had once had seemed gone. There was nothing in the eye sockets but cobwebs. Even the massive cage of wired bones sagged in places, and it was clear that some were missing, although none lay around the chair. Simon had a dim recollection of seeing yellowed bones somewhere else, but pushed it away: something different had caught his attention.

Eahlstan Fiskerne. He stood before the stone statue and examined it, trying to find the thing that would scratch the itching spot in his memory. When he had seen the martyr-king's face in his Dream Road vision, there had been something familiar about it. In the throne room before, on his way to the tower, he had thought the resemblance was to the statue he had looked at so often. But now he knew there was something else familiar about the face. It was much like another, one he had also seen many times—in Jiriki's mirror, in reflecting ponds, in the shiny surface of a shield. Eahlstan looked much like Simon.

He lifted his hand and stared at the golden ring, remembering. The Fisher King's people had gone into exile, and Prester John had later come to claim the killing of the dragon and with it the throne of Erkynland. Morgenes had entrusted him with the ring that told that secret.

"This is your story," the angel had said. Who else to entrust with the knowledge and record of Eahlstan's house than . . . Eahlstan's heir?

As he stood before the statue, the sudden, certain knowledge splashed him like cold water, raising goosebumps of fear and wonder.

Much of the afternoon slid by as Simon paced back and forth across the empty throne room, lost in thought. He was staring at Eahlstan's statue again when he heard a noise in the doorway behind him. He turned to see Duke Isgrimnur and a few others filing into the chamber.

The duke looked him over carefully. "Ah. So you know, do you?"

The young man said nothing, but his face was full of conflicting emotions. Isgrimnur observed Simon carefully, wondering how this could be the same person as the stripling brought to him on the plains south of Naglimund a year before, draped like a sack across the saddle of a riderless horse.

He had been tall even then, although surely not this tall, and the thick reddish beard had been only soft boy-whiskers—but there was more to the change. Simon had developed an air of calm, a stillness that might have been either strength or unconcern. Isgrimnur worried more than a little about what the boy might have become: what had happened to Simon seemed to have changed that stripling of a year ago beyond reclaiming, almost beyond recognizing. His childhood had been burned away, and now only manhood remained.

"I think I have realized some things, yes," Simon said at last. He carefully smoothed all expression from his face. "But I do not think they matter very much—even to me."

Isgrimnur made a noncommittal sound. "Well. We have been looking for you."

"Here I am."

As the group moved forward, Simon nodded toward the duke, then greeted Tiamak, Strangyeard, Jiriki, and Aditu. As Simon said a few quiet words to the Sithi, Isgrimnur saw for the first time how like them the young man had become, at least at this moment—reserved, careful, slow to speak. The duke shook his head. Who would ever have imagined such a thing?

"Are you well, Simon?" asked Strangyeard.

The youth shrugged and offered a half-smile. "My wounds are healing." He turned to Isgrimnur. "Jeremias brought me your message. I would have come to your tent, you know, but Jeremias insisted you would come to me when you were ready." He looked around the small company, his face closed and careful. "It looks like you're ready now, but you've come a long way up from camp to find me. Do you have more questions to ask?"

"Among other things." The duke watched the others seat themselves on the stone floor and made a face. Simon smiled with good-natured mockery and motioned to the Dragonbone Chair. Isgrimnur shook his head, shuddering.

"Very well, then." Simon collected a stack of fallen banners and put them down on the step below the throne dais.

With only one good arm, Isgrimnur took a little time to lower himself to the makeshift seat, but he was determined to do it without leaning on anyone. "I am glad to see you up and around, Simon," he said when he could talk without breathing hard. "You did not look well this morning."

The young man nodded and eased down beside him. He moved slowly, too, nursing many hurts, but Isgrimnur knew he would heal soon. The duke could not help feeling a sharp twinge of envy. "Where are Binabik and Miriamele?" asked Simon.

"Binabik will be here soon," Strangyeard offered. "And . . . and Miriamele . . ."

The youth's calm evaporated. "She's still here, isn't she? She hasn't run off, or been hurt?"

Tiamak waved his hand. "No, Simon. She is in camp and healing, just as you. But she . . ." He turned to Isgrimnur, seeking help.

"But there are things to be discussed without Miriamele here," the duke said bluntly. "That is all."

Simon absorbed this. "Very well. *I* have questions."

Isgrimnur nodded. "Ask them." He had been expecting this since he saw Simon standing in mute absorption before the statue of Eahlstan.

"Binabik said yesterday that bringing the swords was a trick, a 'false messenger'—that Pryrates and the Storm King wanted them all the time." Simon pushed at one of the sodden banners with the heel of his boot. "They needed them so they could turn back time to before Ineluki's last spell, before all the wards and prayers and whatnot had been laid on the Hayholt."

"All of us outside saw the castle change," the duke said slowly, caught off balance by Simon's question. He had been certain the youth would want to ask about his newly-discovered history. "Even as we fought against the Norns, the Hayholt just . . . melted away. There were strange towers everywhere, and fires burning. I thought I saw . . . ghosts, I suppose they were—ghosts of Sithi and Rimmersmen in ancient costume. They were at war, right in the midst of our own battle. What else could it have been?" The clean afternoon light flooding in through the high windows suddenly made it all seem unreal to Isgrimnur. Just days ago, the world had been gripped by sorcerous madness and deadly winter storms. Now a bird twittered outside.

Simon shook his head. "I believe that. I was *there*. It was worse inside. But why did they need us to bring the swords? Bright-Nail was less than a league away from Pryrates for two years. And surely, if they had really tried, they could have taken Thorn, either when we were coming back from Yiqanuc or when it was lying on a stone slab in Leavetaking House up on Sesuad'ra. It doesn't make sense."

Jiriki spoke up. "Yes, this is perhaps the hardest matter of all to understand, Seoman. I can explain some of it. As we were struggling with Utuk'ku at the Pool of Three Depths, much of her thought was revealed to us. She did not shield herself, but rather used that strength in her fight to capture and use the Pool. She believed there was little at that point we could do even if we understood the truth." His slow hand-spread seemed a gesture of regret. "She was correct."

"You held her off a long while," Simon pointed out. "And at a great price, from what I heard. Who knows what might have happened if the Storm King hadn't been forced to wait?"

Jiriki smiled thinly. "Of all of who fought beside the Pool, Likimeya understood the most in the short time we touched Utuk'ku's thoughts. My mother is recovering very slowly from the battle with her ancestor, but she has confirmed much that the rest of us suspected.

"The swords were almost living things. That will come as no surprise to anyone who bore one of them. A large part of their might was, as Binabik of Mintahoq suspected, the unworldly forces bound by the Words of Making. But almost as much of their power was in the effect those Words had. Somehow, the swords had life. They were not creatures like us—they had nothing in them that humans or even Sithi can fully understand—yet they lived. This was what made them greater than any other weapons, but it was also what made them difficult for anyone to rule or control. They could be called—their hunger to be together and to release their energies would eventually draw them to the tower—but they could not be compelled. Part of the terrible magic the Storm King needed for his plan to succeed, perhaps the most important part, was that the swords must come to the summoning themselves at the proper time. They must choose their own bearers."

Isgrimnur watched Simon think carefully before speaking. "But Binabik also told me that the night Miriamele and I left Josua's camp, the Norns tried to kill Camaris. But the sword had already chosen him—chosen him a long time ago! So why would they want him dead?"

"I may have the beginning of the answer to that," Strangyeard spoke up. He was still nearly as diffident as when Isgrimnur had first met him years before, but a little boldness had begun to show through in recent days. "When we fled Naglimund, the Norns who pursued us behaved very strangely. Sir Deornoth was the first to realize that they were . . . oh!" The archivist looked up, startled.

A gray shape had rushed into the throne room. It bounded up onto the steps before the dais, knocking Simon onto his side. The young man laughed, tangling his fingers in the wolf's hackles, trying to keep the probing muzzle and long tongue from his face.

"She is full of gladness to see you, Simon!" Binabik called. He was just coming through the doorway, trotting in a futile effort to keep pace with Qantaqa. "She has been waiting long to bring you greeting. I was keeping her away before, while your wounds were new-bandaged." The troll hurried forward, distractedly greeting the rest of the company as he wrestled Qantaqa to the stone floor beside the dais. She yielded, then stretched out between Binabik and Simon, huge and content. "You will be pleased for knowing I have found Homefinder this afternoon," the troll told the young man. "She wandered away from the fighting and was roaming in the depths of the Kynswood."

"Homefinder." Simon said the name slowly. "Thank you, Binabik. Thank you."

"I will take you for seeing her later."

When all had settled in once more, Strangyeard continued. "Sir Deornoth was the first to see that they were not so much chasing us as . . . herding us. They drove us out in fright, but they did not kill us when they surely could have. And they only became desperate to stop us when we turned toward the innermost depths of Aldheorte."

"Toward Jao é-Tinukai'i," said Aditu softly.

". . . And they also killed Amerasu when she had begun to see Ineluki's plan." Simon pondered. "But I still do not see why they tried to kill Camaris."

Jiriki spoke. "They were content when you had the sword, Seoman, although I am sure it made Utuk'ku unhappy when Ingen Jegger brought her the news that Dawn Children accompanied you. Still, she and Ineluki must have thought it doubtful we would so quickly grasp what they planned—and as it turned out, they were correct. Only First Grandmother perceived the lineaments of their plot. They removed her and sowed much other confusion beside. For those who dwelled in Stormspike, the Zida'ya were then little threat. They must have felt sure that when the time came, the black sword would select you or the Rimmersman Sludig or someone else to be its bearer. Josua would come for Bright-Nail—his father's sword, after all—and the final rituals could take place."

"But Camaris came back," said Simon. "I suppose they didn't suspect that might happen. Still, he had carried Thorn for decades. It only makes sense the sword would choose him again. Why should they fear him?"

Strangyeard cleared his throat. "Sir Camaris, may God rest his troubled soul—" the priest quickly sketched the Tree, "—confessed to me what he could not tell others. That confession must go with me to my grave." Strangyeard shook his head. "Ransomer preserve him! But the reason he confessed to me at all was that Aditu and Geloë wished to know whether he had traveled to Jao . . . whether he had met Amerasu. He had."

"He told Prince Josua his secret, I am sure," muttered Isgrimnur. Remembering that night, and Josua's terrible expression, he wondered again at what mere words could have made the prince look as he had. "But Josua is dead, too, God rest him. We will never know."

"But even though Father Strangyeard swears that it had nothing to do with our battles here," Jiriki said, "it seems that Utuk'ku and her ally did not know that. Nakkiga's queen knew that Amerasu had met Camaris—perhaps she somehow gleaned the knowledge from First Grandmother herself during their tests of will. Having Camaris suddenly and unexpectedly appear on the scene, perhaps with some special wisdom Amerasu might have given him, and also with his long experience of one of the Great Swords . . ." Jiriki shook his head. "We cannot know, but it seems they decided it was too much of a risk. They must have thought that with Camaris dead, the sword would find a new bearer, one less likely to complicate their scheme. After all, Thorn was not a loyal creature like Binabik's wolf."

Simon leaned back and stared at nothing. "So all our hopes, our quest for the swords, were a trap. And we walked into it like children." He scowled. Isgrimnur knew that it was himself he berated.

"It was a damnably clever trap," the duke offered. "One that must have been a-building for a long time. And in the end they failed."

"Are we sure?" Simon turned to Jiriki. "Do we *know* they've failed?"

"Isgrimnur has told how the Hikeda'ya fled when the tower fell—those that still lived. I am not sorry that he did not pursue them, for they are few now, and our kind give birth infrequently. Many died at Naglimund, and many here. The fact that they fled instead of fighting to the death tells much: they are broken."

"Even after Utuk'ku wrested control of the Pool from us," Aditu said, "we fought her still. And when Ineluki began to cross over, we felt it." The long pause was eloquent. "It was *terrible*. But we also felt it when his mortal body— King Elias' body—died. Ineluki had abandoned the nowhere-place which had been his refuge, and risked final dissolution to enter back into the world. He risked, and he lost. There is surely nothing left of him."

Simon raised an eyebrow. "And Utuk'ku?"

"She lives, but her power is destroyed. She, too, gambled much, and it was through her magics that Ineluki's being could be fixed in the tower during the moment when Time was turned withershins. The failure blasted her." Aditu fixed him with her amber eyes. "I saw her, Seoman, saw her in my thoughts as clearly as if she stood before me. The fires of Stormspike have gone dark and the halls are empty. She is all but alone, her silver mask shattered."

"You mean you saw her? Saw her face?"

Aditu inclined her head. "Horror of her own antiquity made her hide her features long ago—but to you, Seoman Snowlock, she would seem nothing but an old woman. Her features are lined and sagging, her skin mottled. Utuk'ku Seyt-Hamakha is the Eldest, but her wisdom was corrupted by selfishness and vanity ages ago. She was ashamed that the years had caught up with her. And now even the terror and strength she wielded is gone."

"So the power of *Sturmrspeik* and the White Foxes is finished," Isgrimnur said. "We have suffered many losses, but we could have lost far more, Simon— lost everything. We have much to thank you and Binabik for."

"And Miriamele," Simon said quietly.

"And Miriamele, of course."

The young man looked at the gathering, then turned back to the duke. "There's more brings you here, I know. You answered my questions. What are yours?"

Isgrimnur couldn't help noticing how Simon's confidence had grown. He was still courteous, but his voice suggested that he deferred to no one. Which was as it should be. But there was an undercurrent of anger which made Isgrimnur hesitate before speaking. "Jiriki has been talking to me about you, about your . . . heritage. I was astonished, I must say, but I can only believe him, since it fits with everything else we've learned—about John, about the Sithi, everything. I thought we would be bringing you the news, but something in your face told me you had already discovered it."

Simon's lips quirked in an odd half-smile. "I did."

"So you know that you are of the blood of Eahlstan Fiskerne," Isgrimnur forged on, "last king of Erkynland in the centuries before Prester John."

"And the founder of the Scroll League," Binabik added.

"And the one who *truly* killed the dragon," Simon said dryly. "What of it?" Despite his calm, something intense and powerful moved beneath the surface. Isgrimnur was puzzled.

Before Isgrimnur could say anything more, Jiriki spoke. "I am sorry I could not tell you earlier what I knew, Seoman, my friend. I feared it could only burden and confuse you, or perhaps lead you to take dangerous risks."

"I understand," Simon said, but he did not sound pleased. "How did you know?"

"Eahlstan Fiskerne was the first mortal king after the fall of Asu'a to reach out to the Zida'ya." The sun was setting outside, and the sky beyond the windows was turning dark. A brisk wind coursed through the throne room and ruffled some of the banners on the floor. Jiriki's white hair fluttered. "He knew us, and some of our folk came at times to meet with him in the caverns below the Hayholt—in the ruins of our home. He feared that what we Zida'ya knew would be lost forever, and even that we might turn against humankind entirely after the destruction that Fingil had wrought. He was not far wrong. There has been little love for mortals among my folk. There was also little love for immortals among Eahlstan's own kind. But as the years of his reign passed, small steps were taken, small confidences exchanged, and a delicate trust began to build. We who were involved kept it a secret." Jiriki smiled. "I say 'we,' but I myself was only the message-bearer, running errands for First Grandmother, who could not let her continuing interest in mortals be widely known, even within her own family."

"I was always jealous of you, Willow-Switch," said Aditu, laughing. "So young, and yet with such important tasks!"

Jiriki smiled. "In any case, whatever might have been if Eahlstan had lived and his line had continued did not come to pass. The fire-worm Shurakai came, and in killing it, Eahlstan was himself killed. Whether his eventual successor John knew something of Eahlstan's secret dealings with us and feared we would expose John's lie that he was the dragon-slayer or there was some other reason for his enmity toward us, I do not know. But John set out to drive us from the last of our hiding places. He did not find them all, and never came near to discovering Jao é-Tinukai'i, but he did us great harm. Almost all our contact with mortals ended during John's life."

Simon folded his hands. "I am sorry for the things my people have done. And I am glad to know my ancestor was such a man."

"Eahlstan's folk scattered before the wrath of the dragon. Eventually they settled into their exile, I am told," Jiriki said. "And when John came and conquered, all hope of regaining the Hayholt was gone. So they nursed their secret and went on, a fishing folk living close to the waters as they had been in the days of Eahlstan Fiskerne's ancestors. But Eahlstan's ring they kept in the royal family, and passed it down from parent to child. One of Eahlstan's great-grandchildren, a scholar like his forebear, studied the old Sithi runes from one of Eahlstan's treasured scrolls, then had the motto that was the family's pride—and Prester John's secret shame—inscribed upon the ring. That was what Morgenes held in trust for you, Seoman: your past."

"And I'm certain he would have told me some day." Simon had listened to Jiriki's tale with poorly-hidden tension. Isgrimnur stared, looking for the cracks in Simon's nature that he half-expected, but feared, to see. "But what has it to do with anything now? All the royal blood in the world did not make me less of a dupe for Pryrates and the Storm King. It's a pretty tale, no more. Half the noble houses in Nabban must have Imperators in their history. What of it?" His jaw was set belligerently.

Several of the company turned to Isgrimnur. The duke moved uncomfortably on the step. "Erkynland needs a ruler," he said at last. "The Dragonbone Chair is empty."

Simon's mouth opened, then closed, then opened again. *"And . . . ?"* he said at last. He stared at Isgrimnur distrustfully. "Miriamele is in good health and has only a few wounds. In fact, she is just the same as she ever was,"—the bitterness in his voice was plain—"so surely she will soon be able to rule."

"It is not her health that concerns us," said the duke gruffly. Somewhere, this conversation had gone wrong. Simon was acting like one awakened from his rightful sleep by a group of misbehaving children. "It is—damn it, it's her father!"

"But Elias is dead. She killed him herself. With the White Arrow of the Sithi." Simon turned to Jiriki. "Come to think of it, since that arrow certainly saved my life, I suppose we have evened our debt."

The Sitha did not respond. The immortal's face was, as usual, unrevealing, but something in his posture suggested he was troubled.

"The people have suffered so under Elias that they may not trust Miriamele," Isgrimnur said. "It's foolish, I know, but there it is. If Josua had lived, they might have welcomed him with open arms. The barons know the prince resisted Elias ever since he began to go bad, that he suffered terribly and fought his way back from exile. But Josua is dead."

"Miriamele did all those things, too!" Simon cried angrily. "This is nonsense!"

"We know, Simon," said Tiamak. "I traveled with her a long way. Many of us know of her bravery."

"Yes, I know it, too," Isgrimnur growled, his own irritation flaring. "But what is true does not matter here. She fled Naglimund before the siege started and she did not reach Sesuad'ra until after Fengbald had been defeated. Then she vanished again, and wound up in the Hayholt with her father at the very ending." He grimaced. "And there are tales, doubtless spread by that whoreson Aspitis Preves, that she was his doxy while he served Pyrates. Rumors are flying."

"But some of those things are true of me, too. Am *I* a traitor?"

"Miriamele is not a traitor, God knows—and *I* know." Isgrimnur glared at him. "But after what her father has done, she may not be trusted. The people want someone on the throne they can trust."

"Madness!" Simon slapped his hands against his thighs, then turned to the Sithi. He seemed ready to burst. "What do you two think of this?" he demanded.

"We do not concern ourselves in these kind of mortal affairs," Jiriki said a little stiffly.

"You are our friend, Seoman," Aditu added. "Whatever we can do for you to help you in this time, we will. However, we also have only respect for Miriamele, though we know her but little."

Simon turned to the troll. "Binabik?"

The little man shrugged. "I cannot say. Isgrimnur and the rest of you must be making decisions to settle it yourselves. You and Miriamele are both my friends. If you are wishing advice later, Simon, we will take Qantaqa off for walking and we will speak."

"Speak about what? People telling lies about Miriamele?"

Isgrimnur cleared his throat. "He means he will talk to you about accepting the crown of Erkynland."

Simon turned back to stare at the duke. This time, for all his newfound maturity, the young man could not hide any of his feelings. "You are . . . you are offering *me* the throne?" he asked derisively, incredulously. "This is madness! Me? A kitchen boy!"

Isgrimnur could not help smiling. "You are much more than a kitchen boy. Your deeds are already filling up songs and stories everywhere between here and Nabban. Wait until the Battle in the Tower is added to the tally."

"Aedon preserve me," Simon said in disgust.

"But there are more important things." The duke grew serious. "You are well-liked and well-known. Not only did you battle a dragon, you fought bravely for Sesuad'ra and Josua, and people remember that. And now we can tell them that you have the blood of Saint Eahlstan Fiskerne, one of the most beloved men ever to hold a throne. In fact, if it weren't true, I would be tempted to make it up."

"But it doesn't mean *anything*!" Simon exploded. "Don't you think I've thought about it? I've been doing nothing *but* thinking since the moment I realized. I am a scullion who was taught by a very wise, very kind man. I have been lucky in my friends. I have been caught up in terrible things, I did what I had to, and I lived through it. None of that has anything to do with who my great-great-however-many-greats-grandfather was!"

Isgrimnur waited a few moments after Simon finished, letting some of the youth's anger pass. "But don't you see," the duke said gently, "it doesn't matter whether it changes anything or not. As I said, I don't think it really matters much if it's *true* or not. Dror's red mallet, Simon, Prester John's story was a myth—a lie! I've had to struggle with that discovery myself in the last few days. But does it make him any less a king? People need to believe something whether you want them to or not. If you don't give them things to believe, they will make things up.

"Right now they are frightened of the future. Most of the world we know is in a shambles, Simon. And the survivors are wary of Miriamele because of who she is and because of uncertainty about what she's done—and because she's a young woman, to speak bluntly. The barons want a man, someone strong but not too strong, and they want no civil wars over a reigning queen's choice of husbands." Isgrimnur reached out to touch Simon's arm, but decided against it and drew his hand back. "Listen to me. The people who followed Josua love you, Simon, almost as much as they loved the prince. More in some ways, perhaps. You know and I know that what blood flows in you makes no difference—it's all red. But your people need to believe in something, and they are cold and hurting and homeless."

Simon stared at him. Isgrimnur could not help feeling the force of the young man's rage. He had grown indeed. He would be a formidable man—no, he was so already.

"And for such tricks you would have me betray Miriamele?" Simon demanded.

"Not betray," Isgrimnur said. "I will give you a few days to think about it, then I will go and put it to her myself. We will bury our dead tomorrow, and the people will see us all together. That will be enough for now." The duke shook his head. "I'm not going to lie to her, Simon—that's not my way—but I wanted you to have a chance to hear me first." He suddenly felt immensely sorry for the young man.

He probably thought he would have a chance to lick his wounds in peace—and he's got plenty of them. We all do.

"Think about it, Simon. We need you—all of us. It will be hard enough for me to pull my own dukedom together, not to mention what will happen to young Varellan, orphaned in Nabban, and whoever still remains in Hernystir. We need at least the appearance of the High King's Ward again, and someone the people trust sitting on the throne at the Hayholt."

He rose from the low stair, trying not to show how much his back hurt, bowed stiffly to Simon—which in itself was an odd sensation—and stumped away across the throne room, leaving the rest of the circle in silence. He could feel Simon's eyes on his back.

God help me, Isgrimnur thought as he emerged into the twilight. *I need a rest. A long rest.*

He looked up from the fire at the sound of footsteps. "Binabik?"

She moved forward into the light. Despite the cool spring night and the patches of still unmelted snow, her feet were bare. Her cloak fluttered in the breeze that swept down the hillside from the Hayholt.

"I couldn't sleep," she said.

For a moment Simon hesitated. He had not expected anyone, least of all her. After the day-long memorial for Josua, Camaris, Isorn, and the other dead, Binabik had gone off to spend the evening with Strangyeard and Tiamak, leaving Simon alone to sit before his tent and think. Her arrival seemed a thing he might have dreamed while staring into the campfire.

"Miriamele." He clambered awkwardly to his feet. "Princess. Sit down, please." He gestured to a stone near the fire.

She sat, drawing her cloak close around her. "Are you well?" she asked at last.

"I'm . . ." He paused. "I don't know. Things are strange."

She nodded. "It's hard to believe it's finished. It's hard to believe they're all gone forever."

He moved uncomfortably, not certain if she spoke of friends or enemies. "There are still lots of things to be done. People are scattered, the world has been turned upside-down. . . ." Simon waved his hand vaguely. "There's lots to do."

Miriamele leaned forward, stretching her hands toward the fire. Simon watched the light play across her delicate features and felt his heart clutch hopelessly. All the royal blood in the world might run in his veins, rivers of it, but it did not matter if she did not care for him. During all of today's rites for the fallen, she had not once met his eyes. Even their friendship seemed to have faded.

It would serve her right if I let them force me to take the throne. He turned away to stare at the flames, feeling low and mean-spirited. *But it is hers by right.* She was Prester John's granddaughter. What difference did it make that some ancestor of Simon's had been king two centuries ago?

"I killed him, Simon," she said abruptly. "I traveled all that way to speak to him, to try to let him know I understood . . . but instead I killed him." There was devastation in her words. "Killed him!"

Simon searched frantically for something to say. "You saved us all, Miriamele."

"He was a good man, Simon. Loud and short-tempered, perhaps, but he was . . . before my mother . . ." She blinked her eyes rapidly. "My own father!"

"You had no other choice." Simon ached to see her in such pain. "There was nothing else you could have done, Miri. You saved us."

"He knew me at the end. May God help me, Simon, I think he wanted me to do it. I looked at him . . . and he was so unhappy. He was in so much pain!" She rubbed at her face with her cloak. "I will not cry," she said harshly. "I am so weary of crying!"

The wind grew stronger, sighing through the grass.

"And sweet Uncle Josua!" she said, more quietly now, but with a core of urgency. "Gone, like everyone else. Gone. All my family gone. And poor, tormented Camaris. Ah, God. What kind of a world is this?" Her shoulders were heaving. Simon reached out and awkwardly took her hand. She did not try to pull away, as he felt sure she would. Instead, they sat in silence except for the crackling of the fire. "And C-Cadrach, too," she murmured at last. "Oh, Merciful Elysia, in some ways he is the worst. He wanted only to die, but he waited for me . . . for us. He stayed, despite all that had happened, despite all the terrible things I said to him." She lowered her head, staring at the ground. Her voice was painfully raw. "In his way, he loved me. That was cruel of him, wasn't it?"

Simon shook his head. There was nothing to say.

She suddenly turned to him, eyes wide. "Let's go away! We can take the horses and be half a dozen leagues from here by morning. I don't want to be a queen!" She squeezed his hand. "Oh, please don't leave me!"

"Go away? Where? And why would I leave you?" Simon felt his heart speed. It was hard to think, hard to believe he had truly understood her. "Miriamele, what are you talking about?"

"Curse you, Simon! Are you really as foolish as people used to think you were?" She now grasped his hand in both of hers; tears gleamed on her cheeks. "I don't care if you were a kitchen boy. I don't care that your father was a fisherman. I only want you, Simon. Oh, do you think I'm an idiot? I *am* an idiot, I suppose." Her laugh had a touch of wildness to it. She let go of his hand for a moment to wipe at her eyes again. "I've been brooding about this ever since the tower fell. I can't stand it! Uncle Isgrimnur and the others, they're going to make me take the throne, I know they will. And I'll go back to being the old Miriamele again, except this time it will be a thousand, thousand times worse! It will be a prison. And then I'll have to marry some other Fengbald—just because he's dead doesn't mean there aren't a hundred more just like him—and I'll never have another adventure, or be free, or do what I want to . . . and you'll go away, Simon! I'll lose you! The only one I really care about."

He stood, then pulled her up from the stone so he could put his arms around her. They were both shaking, and for a little time all he could do was grapple her to him and hang on, as though the wind might sweep her away.

"I've loved you so long, Miriamele." He could not keep his voice steady.

"You frighten me. You don't know how you frighten me." Her voice was muffled against his chest. "I don't know what you see when you look at me. But please don't go away," she said urgently. "Whatever happens, don't go away."

"I won't." He leaned back so he could see her. Her eyes were bright, fresh tears trembling on the lower lashes. His own eyes were blurring as well. He laughed; his voice cracked. "I won't leave you. I promised I wouldn't, don't you remember?"

"Sir Seoman. My Simon. You are my love." She sucked in her breath. "How did it happen?"

He leaned forward, pressing his mouth against hers, and as they clung to each other the starry sky seemed to spin around the place where they stood. Simon's hands moved beneath her cloak and he ran his fingers down the long muscles of her back. Miriamele shuddered and pulled him closer, rubbing her damp face against his neck.

Feeling the length of her pressed against him filled Simon with a kind of drunken, joyous madness. With his arms still locked around her, he took a few staggering steps toward the tent. He tasted the salt of her tears and covered her eyes and cheeks and lips with kisses as her hair swirled around him and stuck to his damp face.

Inside the tent, hidden from the prying stars, they wrapped themselves tightly around each other, clutching, drowning together. The wind plucked at the tent cloth, the only sound beside the rustle of clothes and the urgent hiss of their breathing.

For a moment the wind tugged the tent door open. In the thin starlight, her skin was pale as ivory, so smooth and warm beneath his fingers that he could not imagine ever wanting to touch anything else. His hand slid across the curve of her breast and ran down her hip. He felt something catch inside him, something almost like terror, but sweet, so sweet. She held his face between her hands and drank his breath, murmuring wordlessly all the while, gasping quietly as his mouth moved down her neck and onto the delicate arch of her collarbone.

He pulled her closer, wanting to devour her, wanting to be devoured. His eyes overspilled with tears.

"I've loved you so long," he whispered.

Simon awakened slowly. He felt heavy, his body warm and boneless. Miriamele's head nestled in the hollow of his shoulder, her hair pressed softly against his cheek and neck. Her slender limbs were wrapped around him, one arm splayed across his chest, the fingers tickling beneath his chin.

He pulled her nearer. She murmured sleepily and rubbed her head against him.

The tent flap rustled. A silhouette, a slightly darker spot against the night sky, appeared in the gap.

"Simon?" someone whispered.

Heart pounding, suddenly ashamed for the princess, Simon tried to sit up. Miriamele made an unhappy sound as he slid her arm lower.

"Binabik?" he asked. "Is that you?"

The dark shape pushed in, letting the flap fall shut behind.

"Quiet. I am about to light a candle. Say nothing."

There was a muted clinking as flint met steel, then a tiny glow sprang up in the grass near the tent door. A moment later a flame bobbed at the end of a wick and soft candlelight filled the tent. Miriamele made a groggy noise of protest and buried her face deeper in Simon's neck. He gaped in astonishment.

Josua's thin face hovered above the candle.

"The grave cannot hold me," said the prince, smiling.

60

Leavetaking

Simon's heart thumped.

"Prince Josua . . . ?"

"Quietly, lad." Josua leaned forward. His eyes widened for a moment as he saw the head pillowed on Simon's chest, but then his smile returned. "Ah. Bless you both. Make her marry you, Simon—not that it will take much coaxing, I think. She will make a splendid queen with you to help her."

Simon shook his head in amazement. "But . . . but you . . . surely . . ." He stopped and took a breath. "You're dead—or everyone thinks you are!"

Josua seated himself, holding the candle low so that the gleam was mostly shielded by his body. "I should be."

"Tiamak saw your neck broken!" Simon whispered. "And no one could have gotten out of that place after we did."

"Tiamak saw me *struck,*" Josua corrected him. "My neck should indeed have been broken—as it is, it still hurts fiercely. But I had my hand up." He extended his left arm and the tattered sleeve pulled back. Elias' manacle still hung on the swollen wrist, the metal flattened and scarred. "My brother and Pryrates forgot the gift they had given me. There is some poetry in that—or perhaps God wished to send a message about the value of suffering." The prince's sleeve rustled back into place. "I could barely use the hand for two days after I awoke, but the feeling is coming back now."

Miriamele stirred and opened her eyes. For a moment they widened in dread, then she sat up, clutching the blanket to her breast. "Uncle Josua!"

Smiling crookedly, he lifted his finger to his lips. She pulled the top part of the blanket around her—leaving most of Simon exposed to the cold air—and threw her arms around him, weeping. Josua, too, seemed almost overcome. After a few moments Miriamele pulled away, then looked down at her bare shoulders and colored. She hurriedly lay back on the bedroll again and pulled the blanket up to her chin. Simon took back his half of it with gratitude.

"How can you be alive?" she said, laughing and dabbing at her eyes with the blanket's edge.

Josua explained again, showing her the dented manacle.

"But how did you escape?" Simon was anxious now for the story to continue. "The tower fell!"

The prince's head moved from side to side. Shadows flittered on the tent wall. "That is one thing I cannot know for certain, but my guess is that Camaris picked me up and carried me down in the first moments. I have come close to many campfires in the past nights, and heard many things. It sounds as though the confusion and smoke and flames were such that he could have gone down the stairwell ahead of you. We first came into the tower from beneath, through the tunnels; I believe he went out that way as well. All I know for certain is that I woke up beneath the stars, alone on the beach beside the Kynslagh. But who except Camaris would have had the strength to carry me so far?"

"If he went down before us, then Cadrach must have seen." Miriamele fell silent, pondering this.

"It's a miracle," Simon breathed. "But why have you told no one? And what did you mean when you said Miriamele would be queen? Won't you . . . ?"

"You do not understand," the prince said quietly. There was a strange edge of merriment in his voice. "I am dead. I wish to stay that way."

"What?"

"Just as I said. Simon, Miriamele, I was never meant to rule. It was agony for me, but I saw no other course but to try to push Elias from the throne. Now God has opened a door for me, a door that I believed forever shut. To die or to take the crown were my only choices. Now, I have been given another."

Simon was stunned. For a long while he said nothing. Miriamele was silent, too. Josua watched them, a smile playing across his mouth.

"It is shocking, I know." The prince turned to his niece. "But you will be a far better ruler than I ever would—as will Simon."

"But you are John's true heir," Simon protested, "even more than Miriamele! And I'm just a kitchen boy you knighted! They say I'm a descendant of Saint Eahlstan, but that means nothing to me. It doesn't make me fit to rule Erkynland or anything else."

"I heard that tale, Simon. Isgrimnur and the others keep secrets poorly, if they ever meant to keep your heritage secret." Josua laughed quietly. "And I was not at all surprised to hear that you are of Eahlstan Fiskerne's blood. But as to whether that makes you more or less fit than me, Simon—you do not know all, even so. I am no more John's heir than you are."

"What do you mean?" Simon moved slightly so that Miriamele's head found a more comfortable position on his breast. She was not looking at Josua now, but up at Simon, her brow furrowed with worry or deep thought.

"Just as I said," the prince replied. "I am not John's son. Camaris was my father."

Simon sucked in his breath. "Camaris . . . ?"

Now Miriamele did look at the prince, as startled as Simon. "What are you talking about?"

"John was old when he married my mother, Efiathe of Hernysadharc," Josua said. "A measure of the distance in their years is that he felt no qualms about giving her a new name, Ebekah, as though she were a child." He frowned. "What happened after that is not particularly surprising. It is one of the commonest and oldest stories in the world, although I do not doubt she loved the king and he loved her. But Camaris was her special protector, a young man, as great and fabled a hero as John. What began as a deep respect and admiration between them grew into something more.

"Elias was John's child, but I was not. When my mother died birthing me, Camaris went mad. What could he think but that his sin had sentenced his beloved, who was also the wife of his closest friend, to death?" The prince shook his head. "His agony was such that he gave away everything he had, as one who knows he will die—and he must have felt he was dying, since every breath, every moment, was so full of pain and terrible shame. At last he took the horn Ti-tuno and went in search of the Sithi, perhaps to expiate the sin of participating in John's persecution of them, or perhaps, like Elias, he hoped the wise immortals could help him reach his beloved beyond death. Whatever the aim of his pilgrimage, Amerasu brought him secretly to Jao é-Tinukai'i, for reasons of her own. I have not discovered all that happened: my father was so distraught when he told me it was hard to make sense of everything.

"In any case, Amerasu met with him and took the horn back, perhaps to keep it for him, perhaps because it had belonged to her lost sons. Exactly what passed between them is still a mystery to me, but apparently whatever she told him was no comfort. My father left the forest deeps, still grieving. Soon after, when his despair finally outweighed even his terror of the sin of self-slaughter, he cast himself over the side of a ship into the Bay of Firannos. He survived somehow—he is fearfully strong, you know; that trait his blood certainly did not pass on to me!—but his wits were shadowed. He wandered through the southland, begging, living in the wilderness, subsisting on the charities of others, until he found his way at last to that Kwanitupul inn. In a way, I suppose, he knew peace for that time, despite the harshness of his life and his own poor wits. Then, after two score years, Isgrimnur found him, and soon peace was taken from him again. He awakened with the old horror still fresh in his mind, and the knowledge he had tried to murder himself added to it."

"Mother of Mercy!" Miriamele said feelingly. "That unhappy man!"

It was hard for Simon to encompass the breadth of the old knight's suffering. "Where is he now?"

Josua shook his head. "I do not know. Wandering once more, perhaps. I pray he did not try to drown himself again. My poor father! I hope that the demons that plague him are weaker now, although I doubt it. I will find him, and I will try to help him toward some kind of peace."

"So that's what you're going to do?" Simon asked. "Look for Camaris?"

Miriamele looked at the prince sharply. "What about Vorzheva?"

Josua nodded and smiled. "I will search for my father, but only after my wife and children are safe. There is much to be done, and it will be almost impossible for me to do any of it here in Erkynland where I am known." He laughed quietly. "You see, I am imitating Duke Isgrimnur and letting my beard grow to better my disguise." The prince rubbed his chin. "So tonight I ride south. Soon old Count Streáwe will have a late-night visitor. He owes me a favor . . . of which I will remind him. If anyone can spirit Vorzheva and the two children out of the Nabbanai court, it will be Perdruin's devious master. And he will enjoy the sport of it more than any payment I could ever make him. He loves secrets."

"The dead prince's wife and heirs disappearing." Simon could not resist a smile of his own. "That will make for a few stories and songs!"

"So it will. And I'm sure I will hear them and laugh." He reached over and squeezed Simon's arm, then leaned farther to embrace Miriamele, who clung to him for a long moment. "Now it is time for me to go. Vinyafod is waiting. It will be dawn soon."

Dreamlike as the conversation was, as the whole night had been, Simon was suddenly unwilling to let Josua go. "But if you find Camaris, and if you have Vorzheva with you, what then?"

The prince paused. "The southland will need at least one more Scrollbearer besides Tiamak, I believe—if the League will have me. And I can think of nothing I would like better than to put all the cares of battle and judgment behind me to read and think. Perhaps Streáwe can help me purchase *Pelippa's Bowl,* and I will be the landlord of a quiet inn at Kwanitupul. An inn where friends will always be welcome."

"So you are truly going?" asked Miriamele.

"Truly. I have been given the gift of freedom—a gift I had never expected to receive. I would be ungrateful indeed to turn my back on it." He stood up. "It was very strange to hear my funeral rites spoken at the Hayholt today. Everyone should have such a chance while they still live—it gives one much to think about." He smiled. "Let me have a few hours' start at least, but then tell Isgrimnur, and whatever others can be trusted, that I live. They will be wondering about the disappearance of Vinyafod in any case. But do tell Isgrimnur soon. It pains me greatly to think of my old friend mourning for me: the loss of his son is burden enough. I hope he will understand what I do."

Josua moved toward the tent flap. "And you two, your adventures are only beginning, I think—although I hope those to come are happier." He blew out the candle and the tent was dark again. "Just as I would be a fool not to take what I have been given, Simon, you will be a fool indeed if you do not marry my niece—and Miriamele, you will be a fool if you do not take him. The two of you have much work to do, and many things to set right, but you are young and strong, and you have been given a schooling like none the world has ever seen. May God bless you both, and good luck. I will be watching you. You will both be in my prayers."

The tent flap lifted. Stars glimmered above Josua's shoulder, then all was dark again.

Simon settled back, his head whirling. Josua alive! Camaris the prince's father! And he, Simon, with a princess lying beside him. The world was unimaginably strange.

"So?" Miriamele asked suddenly.

"What?" He held his breath, worried by the tone of her voice.

"You heard my uncle," she said. "Are you going to marry me? And what's this about the blood of Eahlstan? Have you been hiding something from me all this time to pay me back for my serving-girl disguise?"

He exhaled. "I only found out myself yesterday."

After a long silence, she said: "You haven't answered my other question." She took his face and pulled it near hers, running her finger along the sensitive ridge of his scar. "You said you would never leave me, Simon. Now are you going to do what Josua told you to do?"

For answer, he laughed helplessly and kissed her. Her arms curled around his neck.

They had gathered on the grassy hillside beneath the Nearulagh Gate. The great portal lay in ruins; birds fluttered above the stones, quarreling shrilly. Beyond the rubble the setting sun glinted from the wet roofs of the Hayholt. The Conqueror Star made a faint red smear in the northernmost corner of the darkening heavens.

Simon and Miriamele stood arm in arm, surrounded by friends and allies. The Sithi had come to say farewell.

"Jiriki." Simon gently disengaged himself from Miriamele and stepped forward. "I meant what I said before, although I said it in childish bad temper. Your arrow is gone, burned away when the Storm King vanished. Any debt between us is gone, too. You have saved my life enough times."

The Sitha smiled. "We will start afresh, then."

"I wish you didn't have to go."

"My mother and the others will recover more quickly in their homes." Jiriki gazed at the banners of his people ranged along the hillside, their bright clothes. "Look on that. I hope you will remember. The Dawn Children may never be gathered again in one place."

Miriamele stared down at the waiting Sithi and their bold, impatient horses. "It is beautiful," she said. "Beautiful."

Jiriki smiled at her, then turned back to Simon. "So it is time for my folk to go back to Jao é-Tinukai'i, but you and I will see each other before long. Do you remember I told you once that it took no magical wisdom to say we would meet again? I will say it once more, Seoman Snowlock. The story is not ended."

"All the same, I will miss you—we will miss you."

"It may be that things will be better in days to come between my folk and yours, Seoman. But it will not happen swiftly. We are an old people, slow to change, and most mortals still fear us—not without reason after what the Hike-da'ya have done. Still, I cannot but hope that something has indeed changed forever. We Dawn Children, our day is past, but perhaps now we will not simply disappear. Perhaps when we are gone there will be something of us left behind beside our ruins and a few old stories." He clasped Simon's hand and then drew him forward until they embraced.

Aditu followed her brother, light-footed and smiling. "Of course you will come to see us, Seoman. And we will come to you, too. You and I have many a game of shent yet to play. I fear to see what clever new strategies you will have learned."

Simon laughed. "I'm sure you fear my shent-playing the way you fear deep snow and high walls—not at all."

She kissed him, then went to Miriamele and kissed her too. "Be kind and patient with each other," the Sitha said, eyes bright. "Your days will be long together. Remember these moments always, but do not ignore the sad times, either. Memory is the greatest of gifts."

Many others, some who would stay to help in the rebuilding of Erchester and the Hayholt and remain for the coronation, others soon to return to their own cities and people, clustered around. The Sithi gravely and sweetly ex-changed farewells with them all.

Duke Isgrimnur pulled himself away from the crowd surrounding the im-mortals. "I'll be here yet a while, Simon, Miriamele—even after Gutrun's ship comes from Nabban. But we'll have to leave for Elvritshalla before summer begins." He shook his head. "There will be an ungodly lot of work to do there. My people have suffered too much."

"We couldn't hope to begin here without you, Uncle Isgrimnur," said Mir-iamele. "Stay as long as you can, and we will send with you whatever may help you."

The duke lifted her in his broad arms and hugged her. "I am so happy for you, Miriamele, my dear one. I felt like such a damnable traitor."

She smacked at his arm until he put her down. "You were trying to do what was best for everyone—or what you thought was best. But you should have come to me in any case, you foolish man. I would happily have stepped aside for Simon, or you, or even Qantaqa." She laughed and spun in a circle, dress flaring. "But now I am happy, Uncle. Now I can *work*. We will put things to rights."

Isgrimnur nodded, a melancholy smile nestling in his beard. "I know you will, bless you," he whispered.

There was a piercing shout of trumpets and a rumble from the crowd. The Sithi were mounting. Simon turned and lifted his hand. Miriamele pushed in beneath his arm, pressing against him. Jiriki, at the head of the company, stood in his stirrups and raised his arm, then the trumpets called again and the Sithi rode. Light from the dying sun gleaming on their armor, they picked up speed; within moments they were only a bright cloud moving along the hillside toward the east. Snatches of their song hung in the wind behind them. Simon felt his heart leap in his chest, full of joy and sadness both, and knew the sight would live with him forever.

After a long and reverent quiet, the gathering at last began splitting apart. Simon and his companions started to wander down toward Erchester. A great bonfire had been lit in Battle Square, and already the streets, so long deserted, were full of people. Miriamele dropped behind to walk with Isgrimnur, slowing her pace to his. Simon felt a touch on his hand and looked down. Binabik was there, Qantaqa moving beside him like a gray shadow.

"I wondered where you were," said Simon.

"My farewells to the Sithi-folk were being said this morning, so Qantaqa and I were at walking along the Kynswood. Some squirrels that were living there have now come to a sad end, but Qantaqa is feeling very cheerful." The troll grinned. "Ah, Simon-friend, I was thinking of old Doctor Morgenes, and of the prideful feeling that he would have if he saw what is happening here."

"He saved us all, didn't he?"

"Certain it is that his planning gave us the only chance we had. We were being tricked by Pryrates and the Storm King, but had we not been alerted, Elias' ravagings would have been worse. Also, the swords would have been finding other bearers, and no fighting back would have happened in the tower. No, Morgenes could not be knowing all, but he did what no other could have done."

"He tried to tell me. He tried to warn us all about false messengers." Simon looked down Main Row at the hurrying figures and the flicker of firelight. "Do you remember the dream I had at Geloë's house? I know that was him. That he was . . . watching."

"I do not know what happens after we are dying," Binabik said. "But I am thinking you are right. Somehow, Morgenes was watching for you. You were being like a family for him, even more than his Scroll League."

"I will always miss him."

They walked along for a while without speaking. A trio of children ran past, one of them trailing a strip of colorful cloth which the others, laughing and shrieking, tried to catch.

"I must go soon myself," said Binabik. "My people in Yiqanuc are waiting, wondering no doubt what has happened here. And, being most important, Sisqinanamook is there, also waiting. Like you and your Miriamele, she and I have a tale that is long. It is time that we were married before the Herder and Huntress and all the folk of Mintahoq." He laughed. "Despite everything, I am thinking her parents will still have a small sadness when they see I have survived."

"Soon? You're going soon?"

The troll nodded. "I must. But as Jiriki said to you, we will have many more meetings, you and I."

Qantaqa looked at them for a moment, then trotted ahead, sniffing the ground. Simon kept his eyes forward, staring toward the bonfire as though he had never seen such a thing. "I don't want to lose you, Binabik. You're my best friend in the world."

The troll reached up and took his hand. "All the more reason that we should not be long parted. You will come to Yiqanuc when you can—surely there is being a need for the first *Utku* embassy ever to the trolls!—and Sisqi and I will come to see you." He nodded his head solemnly. "You are my dearest friend also, Simon. Always we will be in each other's hearts."

They walked on toward the bonfire, hand in hand.

Rachel the Dragon wandered through Erchester, her hair bedraggled, her clothes tattered and soiled. All around, people ran laughing through the streets, singing, cheering, playing frivolous games as though the city were not falling apart around them. Rachel could not understand it.

For days she had hidden in her underground sanctuary, even after the terrible tremblings and shiftings had stopped. She had been convinced that the world had ended over her head, and felt no urge to leave her well-stocked cell to see demons and sorcerous spirits celebrating in the ruins of her beloved Hayholt. But at last curiosity and a certain resolve had gotten the better of her. Rachel was not the kind of woman to take even the end of the world without fighting back. Let them put her to their fiendish tortures. Blessed Rhiap had suffered, hadn't she? Who was Rachel to hesitate before the example of the saints?

Her first blinking, molelike view of the castle seemed to confirm her worst fears. As she made her way through the hallways, through the ruins of what had been her home and her greatest pride, her heart withered in her breast. She cursed the people or creatures who had done this, cursed them in a way that would have made Father Dreosan turn pale and hurry away. Wrath moved through her like a tide of fire.

But when she had finally emerged into the almost-deserted Inner Bailey, it was to discover one puzzlement after another. Green Angel Tower lay in a shambles of stone, and the destruction and fire-scorchings of recent battle were everywhere, but the few folk she encountered wandering through the desolation claimed that Elias was dead and that everything was to be made right again.

On the tongues of these, and of many others she met as she went down into Erchester, were the names of Miriamele, the king's daughter, and someone called Snowlock. These two, it was said—he a great hero of battles in the east, a dragon-slayer and warrior—had thrown down the High King. Soon they would be married. All would soon be made right. That was the refrain on every tongue: all would be made right.

Rachel had snorted to herself—only those who had never had the responsibilities she had would think this a task that could take less than years—but she could not help feeling curiosity and a faint flickering of hope. Perhaps better days were coming. The folk she met said Pryrates had died, too, burned to death somehow in the great tower. So a measure of justice had been done at least. Rachel's losses had finally been avenged, however tardily.

And perhaps, she had thought, Guthwulf could be saved and brought up again from darkness. He deserved a happier fate than to wander forever while the world aboveground returned to something like order.

Kind folk in Erchester had fed her from their own meager stores and given her a place to sleep. And all evening she had heard the stories of Princess Miriamele and the hero Snowlock, the warrior princeling with the dragon-scar. Perhaps, she had considered, when things were calm again she would offer her services to the new rulers. Surely a young woman like Miriamele, if she had been brought up at all well, would understand the need for order. Rachel did not think that her heart would ever entirely be in her work again, but felt sure she had something to offer. She was old, but there might still be use for her.

Rachel the Dragon looked up. While her thoughts had been meandering, her feet had led her down to the fringes of Battle Square, where a bonfire had been lit. As much as possible had been made of scant provisions, and a feast of sorts had been laid in the middle of the square. The remnants of Erchester's citizenry milled about, shouting, singing, dancing around the fire. The clamor was almost deafening. Rachel accepted a piece of dried fruit from a young woman, then wandered over to a shadowy corner to eat it. She sat down against the wall of a shop and watched the carryings-on.

A young man passed her, and his eye caught hers for a moment. He was thin and his face was sad. Rachel squinted. Something about him was familiar.

He seemed to have the same thought, for he wheeled and walked back toward her. "Rachel?" he asked. "Aren't you Rachel, the Mistress of Chambermaids?"

She looked at him, but could summon no name. Her head was full of the noise of people on the roofs shouting down to friends in the square. "I am," she said. "I was."

He stepped forward suddenly, frightening her a little, and put his arms around her. "Don't you remember me?" he asked. "I'm Jeremias! The chandler's boy! You helped me escape from the castle."

"Jeremias," she said, patting his back softly. So he had lived. That was a good thing. She was happy. "Of course."

He stepped back and looked at her. "Have you been here all along? No one has seen you in Erchester."

She shook her head, a little surprised. Why should anyone have been looking for her? "I had a room . . . a place I found. Under the castle." She raised her hands, unable to explain everything that had happened. "I hid. Then I came out."

Grinning, Jeremias grabbed her hand. "Come with me. There are people who will want to see you."

Protesting, although she did not quite know why—surely there was nothing better an old woman like her had to do—Rachel allowed herself to be led through the swirling crowds, right across Battle Square. With Jeremias tugging at her until she wanted to ask him to let go, they passed so close to the bonfire that she could feel its heat down into her cold bones. Within moments they had pushed through another knot of people and approached a line of armored soldiers who held them back with crossed pikes until Jeremias whispered something in the captain's ear. The sentries then let them through. Rachel had just enough strength to wonder what Jeremias had said, but too little breath to ask.

They stopped abruptly and Jeremias stepped past her toward a young woman sitting in the nearest of two tall chairs. As he spoke to her, the woman turned her gaze toward Rachel and her lips curled in a slow smile. The Mistress of Chambermaids stared at her in fascination. Surely that was Miriamele, the king's daughter—but she looked so much older! And she was beautiful, her fair hair curving around her face, shimmering in the fireglow. She looked every inch a queen.

Rachel felt a kind of gratitude sweep over her. Perhaps there would be some kind of order to life after all, at least a little. But what concern could Miriamele, this radiant creature as exalted as an angel, have with an old servant?

Miriamele turned and said something to the man sitting back in the shadows of the chair beside hers. Rachel saw him start, then clamber to his feet.

Merciful Rhiap, she thought. *He's so tall! This must be that Snowlock, that one they all speak of. Someone said his other name, what was it?*

". . . Seoman . . ." she said aloud, staring at his face. The beard, the scar, the streak of white in his hair—for a moment he was just a young man. Then she knew.

"*Rachel!*" In a few long steps he was before her. He stared down at her for a moment, his lips trembling, then a wide grin broke across his face. "Rachel!" he said again.

"Simon . . . ?" she murmured. The world had ceased to make any kind of sense. "You're . . . *alive?*"

He bent down and grabbed her, squeezing hard. He lifted her high in the air so that her feet wiggled above the ground. "Yes!" he laughed. "I'm alive! God knows how, but I'm alive! Oh, Rachel, you could never imagine what has happened, never, never, never!"

He put her down but took both her hands in his. She wanted to pull them free because tears were streaming down her cheeks. Could this be? Or had she finally gone mad? But there he was, red hair, idiot grin, big as life—bigger than life!

"Are *you* . . . Snowlock?"

"I am, I suppose!" He laughed again. "I am." He let go for a moment, then draped an arm around her. "There is so much to tell you—but we have time now, nothing but time." He lifted his head, shouting: "Quick! This is Rachel! Bring her wine, bring her food, get her a chair!"

"But what has happened?" She craned her neck to look up at him, impossibly tall, impossibly alive, but Simon for all that. "How can this be?"

"Sit," he said. "I will tell you all. And then we can begin the grand task."

She shook her head, dazed. "Grand task?"

"You were Mistress of Chambermaids . . . but you were always more. You were like a mother to me, but I was too young and stupid to see it. Now you shall have the honor you deserve, Rachel. And if you want it, you shall be the mistress of the entire Hayholt. Heaven knows, we need you. An army of servants will attend you, troops of builders, companies of chambermaids, legions of gardeners." He laughed, a man's loud laugh. "We will fight a war against the ruin we have made, and we will build the castle again. We will make our home a beautiful place once more!" He gave her a squeeze and steered her toward where Miriamele and Jeremias waited, smiling. "You will be Rachel the Dragon, General of the Hayholt!"

Tears trickled down her cheeks. *"Mooncalf,"* she said.

Afterword

✦

Tiamak pushed with his toe at the lilypad. The part of the moat in the shadow of the wall was quiet but for the hum of insects and the splashing of Tiamak's own feet dangling in the water.

He was watching a water beetle when he heard footsteps behind him.

"Tiamak!" Father Strangyeard sat down awkwardly beside him, but kept his sandaled feet out of the moat. "I heard you had arrived. How good it is to see you."

The Wrannaman turned and clasped the archivist's hand. "And you, dear friend," he said. "It is astonishing to see the changes here."

"A great deal can happen in a year," Strangyeard laughed. "And people have been hard at work. But what is *your* news since your last message?"

Tiamak smiled. "Much. I found the remnants of my townsmen, scattered mainly through other villages across the Wran. Many of them will come back to Village Grove, I think, now that the ghants have retreated to the deep swamp." His smile dwindled. "And my sister still does not believe half of what I tell her."

"Can you blame her?" asked Strangyeard gently. "I can scarcely believe the things I saw myself."

"No, I do not blame her." Tiamak's smile returned. "And I have finally finished *Sovran Remedys of the Wranna Healers.*"

"Tiamak, my friend!" Strangyeard was honestly delighted. "But that is wonderful! I am hungry for it! Is there a chance I can read it soon?"

"Very soon. I brought it with me. Simon and Miriamele said they would have copies made here. Four writing-priests, just to work on my book!" He shook his head. "Who would ever have dreamed?"

"Wonderful," Strangyeard said again. His smile was mysterious. "Come, should we not head back? I think it is almost time."

Tiamak nodded and reluctantly pulled his feet from the water. The lilypad floated back into place.

"I have heard that this will be more than a memorial," the Wrannaman said as they gazed at the incomplete shell of stone, littered with the boards and covering cloths of absent workers, that rose where Green Angel Tower had stood. "That there will be archives as well." He turned suddenly to look at his friend. "Ah. I suspect you know more about those four writing-priests than you told me."

Strangyeard nodded and blushed. "That is *my* news," he said proudly. "I helped draw the plans. It will be magnificent, Tiamak. A place of learning where nothing will be lost or hidden. And I will have many assistants to help me." He smiled and stared across the grounds. Two slow-moving figures made their way through the building site and passed through the recently completed doorway into the shadowed interior. "Most likely my eye will be so bad by the time the thing is finished—if God has not yet called me, that is—that I won't be able to see it. But that does not worry me. I see it already." He tapped his head and his gentle smile grew wider. "Here. And it is wonderful, my friend, wonderful."

Tiamak took the priest's arm. They made their way across the grounds of the Inner Bailey.

"As I said, it is astonishing to see the changes." The marsh man looked up at the castle's hodgepodge of roofs, almost all patched now, gleaming in the late afternoon sun. Higher up, a scaffolding had been erected over the dome of the chapel. A few workmen moved across it, tying things down for the night. Tiamak's gaze roved to the far side of the Inner Bailey wall and he paused. "Hjeldin's Tower—it has no windows in it any more. They were red, were they not?"

"Pyrates' tower . . . and storehouse." Strangyeard sketched the Tree on his breast. "Yes. Fire will be put to it, I expect, then it will be leveled to the ground. It has been sealed a long time, but no one is in much of a hurry to go inside, and Simon—King Seoman, I suppose I should say, although that still sounds faintly strange to me—wants the entrance to the catacombs beneath sealed as well." The archivist shook his head. "You know I think knowledge is precious, Tiamak. But I have not objected to any part of that plan."

The Wrannaman nodded. "I understand. But let us talk of more pleasant things."

"Yes." Strangyeard smiled again. "Speaking of such, I have come by a fascinating object—part of the castellain's account book from the time of Sulis the Apostate. Someone found it when they were cleaning up the Chancelry. There are some astonishing things in it, Tiamak—just astonishing! I think we just have time to stop by my chamber and get it on our way to the dining hall."

"Let us go then, by all means," Tiamak said, grinning, but as he fell in beside the archivist, he turned for a last look at Hjeldin's Tower and its empty windows.

"You see," Isgrimnur said softly. "They have covered it with fine stone, just as Miriamele said."

Gutrun wiped at her face with the scarf. "Read it to me."

The duke squinted down at the slab set into the floor. The place was open to the sky, but the light was fading fast. *"Isorn, son of Isgrimnur and Gutrun, Duke and Duchess of Elvritshalla. Bravest of men, beloved of God and all who knew him."* He straightened up, determined not to cry. He would be strong for his lost child. "Bless you, son," he whispered.

"He must be so lonely," Gutrun said, her voice quavering. "So cold in the ground."

"Hush." Isgrimnur put his arm around her. "Isorn is not here, you know that. He is in a better place. He would laugh to see us fret so." He tried to make his words firm. It did no good to question, to worry. "God has rewarded him."

"Of course." Gutrun sniffed. "But, Isgrimnur, I still miss him so!"

He felt his eyes misting and cursed quietly, then hastily made the Tree sign. "I miss him, too, wife. Of course. But we have our others to think of, and Elvritshalla—not to mention two godchildren down in Kwanitupul."

"Godchildren I cannot even brag about!" she said indignantly, then laughed and shook her head.

They stood a while longer, until the light had vanished and the stone slab had fallen into shadow. Then they went out again into the evening.

♛

They sat in the dining hall, filling the chairs around John's Great Table. All the wall sconces held torches, and candles were set about the table as well, so that the long room was full of light.

Miriamele rose, her blue gown whispering in the sudden silence. The circlet on her brow caught the torchlight.

"Welcome, all." Her voice was soft but strong. "This house is yours and always will be. Come to us whenever you wish, stay as long as you like."

"But be sure and be here at least once a year," Simon said, and raised his cup.

Tiamak laughed. "It is a long journey for some of us, Simon," he said. "But we will always do our best."

Beside him, Isgrimnur thumped his goblet on the table. He had been making healthy inroads into the supply of beer and wine. "He's right, Simon. And speaking of long journeys, I don't see little Binabik."

Simon stood up and put his arm around Miriamele's shoulder, pausing for a moment to pull her close and brush the top of her head with a kiss. "Binabik and Sisqi have sent a bird with a message." He smiled. "They are performing the Rite of Quickening—Sludig knows what I'm talking about, since it almost got us all killed—and then traveling with their folk down-mountain to Blue Mud Lake. After that, they will come to visit us here." Simon's grin widened. "Then, next year, Sludig and I will be off to visit them in high Mintahoq!"

Sludig nodded his head vigorously as various jests were made. "The trolls invited me," he said proudly. "First what-do-they-call-it—'Croohok'—they have ever asked." He raised his cup. "To Binabik and Sisqi! Long life and many children!"

The toast was echoed.

"Do you really think you will slip off on such an adventure without me?" asked Miriamele, eyeing her husband. "Leave me home to do all the work?"

"Good luck trying to outrun Miri," Isgrimnur chortled. "There's a woman who's already traveled more of the world than you have!"

Gutrun elbowed him. "Let them speak."

Isgrimnur turned and kissed her cheek. "Of course."

"Then we will go together," Simon said grandly. "We will make it a royal progress."

Miriamele gave him a sour glance, then turned to Rachel the Dragon, who had paused in the hall's far doorway to quietly berate a serving lad. Rachel's eyebrows had shot up at Simon's offhand remark. Now she and Miriamele shared a look of disgusted amusement.

"Do you have any idea what sort of trouble that will be?" Miriamele demanded. "To take the whole court into the mountains to Yiqanuc?"

Simon looked around the hall at the amused faces of the guests. He ran his fingers through his red beard and grinned. "I am not quite civilized yet, but they are doing their best." Miriamele poked his ribs, then leaned against him again. He lifted his goblet high. "It is so good to see you all. Another toast! To the Prince's Company! Would that Josua were here to see it—but I know he will be honored, wherever he is!" The rest of the companions laughed, all now privy to the secret.

Tiamak stood. "As a matter of fact, I bring word from . . . an absent friend. He sends his great love, and wishes you to know that he, his wife, and their children are well." The announcement was greeted with shouts of approval.

Isgrimnur rose abruptly, teetering a little. "And let us not forget to drink to all the others who also fought and fell that we could be here," he cried. "All of them." His voice shook a little. "God preserve their souls. May we never forget them!"

"Amen!" cried many others. When the cheers fell away, there was a long moment of silence.

"Now drink up," Miriamele ordered. "But keep your wits. Sangfugol has promised to play us a new song."

"And Jeremias will sing it. He has been practicing." The harper looked around. "I don't know where he has gotten to. It is annoying to have the singer unprepared."

"You mean some singers are prepared?" Isgrimnur laughed, then made a face of mock fear as Sangfugol waved a heel of bread at him threateningly.

"When your ears are other than stone, Duke Isgrimnur," Sangfugol replied with a certain frostiness, "then you can make jokes."

The hall had fallen back into merriment and general conversation when Jeremias appeared at Simon's shoulder and whispered something in his ear.

"Good," said Simon. "I am glad he came. But you, Jeremias, what are you doing, scuttling around like a servant? They are expecting you to sing later. Sit down here. Miri will pour you some wine." He got up and forced a protesting Jeremias into his chair, then walked toward the door.

In the entrance hall, a somber man with a dark horse-tail of hair awaited him, still wearing traveling clothes and a cloak.

"Count Eolair." Simon went forward to clasp the Hernystirman's hand. "I hoped you would come. How was your journey?"

Eolair looked at him keenly, studying him as though they had never met before. He bent his knee. "Well enough, King Seoman. The roads are still not good, and it is a long trip, but there is little fear of bandits anymore. It does me good to get away from Hernysadharc. But you know of rebuilding."

"It is Simon, please. And Queen Inahwen? How is she?"

Eolair nodded, half-smiling. "She sends her greetings. But we will play those tunes later, I suppose, when Queen Miriamele and others can hear them—in the throne room, where these things must be done." He looked up suddenly. "Speaking of throne rooms, was that not the Dragonbone Chair I saw in the courtyard outside? With ivy growing upon it?"

Simon laughed. "Out for everyone to see. Fear not—a little wind and a little damp won't hurt those bones. They are stronger than rock. And neither Miri nor I could bear to sit in the thing."

"Some children were playing on it." Eolair shook his head in wonderment. "That was something I never thought to see."

"To the castle children, it's only something to climb on. Although they were a little worried at first." He extended a hand. "Come, let me take you in and give you something to drink and to eat."

Eolair hesitated. "Perhaps I would be better off finding a bed. It was a long ride today."

Now it was Simon's turn to look at Eolair carefully. "Forgive me if I am speaking out of turn," he said, "but I have known something for a long time that you should know too. I would have waited until we had spoken more, you and I, but perhaps it would be best to tell you now." He took a breath. "I met Maegwin before she died. Did you know? But the strange thing was that we were really leagues apart."

"I know something of it," said the Count of Nad Mullach. "Jiriki was with us. He tried to explain. It was difficult to understand what he meant."

"There will be much to talk about later, but here is the one thing you must know." Simon's voice dropped. "She was herself at the last, and the only thing she regretted leaving was you, Count Eolair. She loved you. But by giving up her life she saved me and freed me to go to the tower. We might none of us be here today—Erkynland, Hernystir, everything else, all might be under cold shadows—were it not for her."

Eolair was silent for a while, his face expressionless. "Thank you," he said at last. A little of his brittleness seemed to have gone.

Simon gently took his arm. "Now come, please. Come and join us. Up the corridor you have a room full of friends, Eolair—some of them you don't even know yet!"

He led the count toward the dining hall. Firelight and the sound of laughing voices reached out to welcome them.

TELL THE WORLD THIS BOOK WAS

GOOD | BAD | SO-SO

Appendix

PEOPLE

ERKYNLANDERS

Barnabas—Hayholt chapel sexton

Deornoth, Sir—of Hewenshire, Josua's knight

Eahlferend—Simon's fisherman father

Eahlstan Fiskerne—"Fisher King," founder of League of Scroll

Ebekah, also known as Efiathe of Hernysadharc—Queen of Erkynland, John's wife, mother of Elias and Josua

Elias—High King, John's oldest son, Josua's brother

Fengbald—Earl of Falshire, High King's Hand

Freobeorn—Freosel's father, a blacksmith of Falshire

Freosel—Falshireman, constable of New Gadrinsett

Guthwulf—Earl of Utanyeat

Heanwig—old drunkard in Stanshire

Helfgrim—Lord Mayor of Gadrinsett (former)

Inch—foundry master

Isaak—Fengbald's page

Jack Mundwode—mythical forest bandit

Jeremias—former chandler's apprentice, Simon's friend

John—King John Presbyter, High King, also known as "Prester John"

Josua—Prince, John's younger son, lord of Naglimund, called "Lackhand"

Judith—Hayholt Mistress of Kitchens

Leleth—Geloë's companion, once Miriamele's handmaiden

Maefwaru—a Fire Dancer

Miriamele—Princess, Elias' daughter

Morgenes, Doctor—Scrollbearer, Simon's friend and mentor

Old Bent Legs—forge worker in Hayholt

Osgal—one of Mundwode's mythical band

Rachel—Hayholt Mistress of Chambermaids, also known as "The Dragon"

Roelstan—escaped Fire Dancer

Sangfugol—Josua's harper

Sceldwine—captain of the prisoned Erkynguardsmen

Shem Horsegroom—Hayholt groom

Simon—castle scullion (named "Seoman" at birth)

Stanhelm—forge worker

Strangyeard, Father—Scrollbearer, priest, Josua's archivist

Towser—King John's jester (original name "Cruinh")

Ulca—girl on Sesuad'ra, called "Curly Hair"

Welma—girl on Sesuad'ra, called "Thin One"
Wiclaf—former First Hammerman killed by Fire Dancers
Zebediah—a Hayholt scullion, called "Fat Zebediah"

HERNYSTIRI

Airgad Oakheart—famous Hernystiri hero
Arnoran—minstrel
Bagba—cattle god
Brynioch of the Skies—sky god
Bulychlinn—fisherman in old story who caught a demon in his nets
Cadrach-ec-Crannhyr—monk of indeterminate Order, also known as "Padreic"
Caihwye—young mother
Craobhan—called "Old," adviser to Hernystiri royal house
Croich, House—a Hernystiri clan
Cuamh Earthdog—earth god
Deanagha of the Brown Eyes—Hernystiri goddess, daughter of Rhynn
Diawen—scryer
Earb, House—a Hernystiri clan
Eoin-ec-Cluias—legendary Hernystiri harper
Eolair—Count of Nad Mullach
Feurgha—Hernystiri woman, captive of Fengbald
Frethis of Cuihmne—Hernystiri scholar
Gullaighn—escaped Fire Dancer
Gwynna—Eolair's cousin and castellain
Gwythinn—Maegwin's brother, Lluth's son
Hern—founder of Hernystir
Inahwen—Lluth's third wife
Lach, House—a Hernystiri clan
Lluth—King, father of Maegwin and Gwythinn
Llythinn—King, Lluth's father, uncle of John's wife Ebekah
Maegwin—Princess, daughter of Lluth
Mathan—goddess of household, wife of Murhagh One-Arm
Mircha—rain goddess, wife of Brynioch
Murhagh One-Arm—war god, husband of Mathan
Penemhwye—Maegwin's mother, Lluth's first wife
Rhynn of the Cauldron—a god
Siadreth—Caihwye's infant son
Sinnach—prince of Hernystir, also known as "The Red Fox"
Tethtain—former master of the Hayholt, "Holly King"

RIMMERSMEN

Dror—storm god

Dypnir—one of Ule's band

Einskaldir—Isgrimnur's man, killed in forest

Elvrit—first Osten Ard king of Rimmersmen

Fingil Bloodfist—first human master of Hayholt, "Bloody King"

Frekke Grayhair—Isgrimnur's man, killed at Naglimund

Gutrun—Duchess, Isgrimnur's wife

Hengfisk—Hoderundian priest, Elias' cupbearer

Hjeldin—Fingil's son, "Mad King"

Ikferdig—third Hayholt ruler, "Burned King"

Isgrimnur—Duke of Elvritshalla, Gutrun's husband

Isorn—son of Isgrimnur and Gutrun

Jarnauga—Scrollbearer, killed at Naglimund

Nisse—(Nisses) author of *Du Svardenvyrd*

Skali—Thane of Kaldskryke, called "Sharp-nose"

Sludig—Isgrimnur's man

Trestolt—Jarnauga's father

Ule Frekkeson—leader of renegade band of Rimmersmen, son of Frekke

NABBANAI

Aspitis Preves—Earl of Drina and Eadne

Benigaris—Duke of Nabban, son of Leobardis and Nessalanta

Benidrivis—first duke under John, father of Camaris and Leobardis

Brindalles—Seriddan's brother

Camaris-sá-Vinitta, Sir—John's greatest knight, also known as "Camaris Benidrivis"

Dinivan—Scrollbearer, secretary to Lector Ranessin, killed in Sancellan Aedonitis

Domitis—bishop of Saint Sutrin's cathedral in Erchester

Eneppa—Metessan kitchen woman, once called "Fuiri"

Elysia—mother of Usires Aedon, called "Mother of God"

Fluiren, Sir—knight of Sulian House, member of John's Great Table

Gavenaxes—knight of Honsa Claves (Clavean House) for whom Camaris was squire

Hylissa—Miriamele's mother, Elias' wife, killed in Thrithings

Lavennin, Saint—patron saint of Spenit Island

Leobardis—Duke of Nabban, killed at Naglimund

Metessan House—Nabbanai noble house, blue crane emblem

Munshazou—Pryrates' Naraxi serving woman

Nessalanta—Dowager Duchess, mother of Benigaris

Nuanni (Nuannis)—ancient Nabbanai sea god
Pasevalles—Brindalles' young son
Pelippa, Saint—called "Pelippa of the Island"
Plesinnen Myrmenis—ancient scholar
Pryrates—priest, alchemist, wizard, Elias' counselor
Ranessin—Lector of Mother Church, killed at Sancellan Aedonitis
Rhiappa, Saint—called "Rhiap" in Erkynland
Seriddan, Baron—Lord of Metessa, also known as "Seriddan Metessis"
Sulis, Lord—Nabbanai nobleman, former master of Hayholt, "Heron King,"
    also known as "The Apostate"
Thures—Aspitis' young page
Usires Aedon—Aedonite religion's Son of God
Varellan—youngest son of Leobardis, and Nessalanta, Benigaris' brother
Velligis—Lector of Mother Church
Xannasavin—Nabbanai court astrologer
Yistrin, Saint—saint linked to Simon's birth-day

SITHI

Aditu (no-Sa'onserei)—daughter of Likimeya and Shima'onari; Jiriki's sister
Amerasu y-Senditu no'e-Sa'onserei—mother of Ineluki, killed at Jao é-Tinukai'i,
    called "First Grandmother," also known as "Amerasu Ship-Born"
Benayha (of Kementari)—famed Sithi poet and warrior
Briseyu Dawnfeather—Likimeya's mother, wife of Hakatri
Chekai'so—called "Amber-Locks," member of Sithi clan
Chiya—member of Sithi clan, once resident of Asu'a
Contemplation House—Sithi clan
Drukhi—son of Utuk'ku and Ekimeniso, husband of Nenais'u
Gathering House—Sithi clan
Hakatri—Amerasu's son, vanished into West
Ineluki—Amerasu's son, killed at Asu'a, now Storm King
Initri—husband of Jenjiyana
Jenjiyana—wife of Initri, mother of Nenais'u, called "the Nightingale"
Jiriki (i-Sa'onserei)—son of Likimeya and Shima'onari, brother of Aditu
Khendraja'aro—uncle of Jiriki and Aditu
Kira'athu—Sitha healer
Kuroyi—called "the tall horseman," master of High Anvi'janya, leader of Sithi clan
Likimeya (y-Briseyu no'e-Sa'onserei)—mother of Jiriki and Aditu, called "Li-
    kimeya Moon-Eyes"
Mezumiiru—mistress of moon in Sithi legend
Senditu—mother of Amerasu
Shi'iki—father of Amerasu
Shima'onari—father of Aditu and Jiriki, killed at Jao é-Tinukai'i

Vindaomeyo—famed arrow-maker of Tumet'ai, called "the Fletcher"
Year-Dancing House—Sithi clan
Yizashi Grayspear—leader of Sithi clan
Zinjadu—of Kementari, called "Lore-Mistress"

QANUC

Binabik (Binbiniqegabenik)—Scrollbearer, Singing Man of Qanuc, Simon's friend
Chukku—legendary troll hero
Kikkasut—legendary king of birds
Nimsuk—Qanuc herder, one of Sisqi's troop
Nunuuika—the Huntress
Ookequk—Scrollbearer, Binabik's master
Qinkipa (of the Snows)—snow and cold goddess
Sedda—moon goddess
Sisqi (Sisqinanamook)—daughter of Herder and Huntress, Binabik's betrothed
Snenneq—herd-chief of Lower Chugik
Uammannaq—the Herder

THRITHINGS-FOLK

Fikolmij—Vorzheva's father, March-thane of Clan Mehrdon
Hotvig—High Thrithings randwarder, Josua's man
Lezhdraka—Thrithings-man, mercenary chieftain
Ozhbern—High Thrithings-man
Ulgart—a mercenary captain from the Meadow Thrithing
Vorzheva—Josua's wife, daughter of Fikolmij

PERDRUINESE

Charystra—landlady of *Pelippa's Bowl*
Lenti—Streáwe's servant, called "Avi Stetto"
Streáwe, Count—master of Perdruin
Tallistro, Sir—famous knight of John's Great Table
Xorastra—Scrollbearer, first owner of *Pelippa's Bowl*

WRANNAMEN

Buayeg—owner of "the spirit-hut" (Wrannaman fable)
He Who Always Steps on Sand—god

He Who Bends the Trees—wind god
Inihe Red-Flower—woman in Tiamak's song
Nuobdig—Husband of the Fire Sister in Wrannaman legend
Rimihe—Tiamak's sister
She Who Birthed Mankind—goddess
She Who Waits to Take All Back—death goddess
Shoaneg Swift-Rowing—man in Tiamak's song
They Who Breathe Darkness—gods
They Who Watch and Shape—gods
Tiamak—Scrollbearer, herbalist
Tugumak—Tiamak's father
Twiyah—Tiamak's sister
Younger Mogahib—man of Tiamak's village

NORNS

Akhenabi—spokesman at Naglimund
"Born-Beneath-Tzaaihta's-Stone"—one of Utuk'ku's Talons
"Called-by-the-Voices"—one of Utuk'ku's Talons
Ekimeniso Blackstaff—husband of Utuk'ku, father of Drukhi
Mezhumeyru—Norn version of "Mezumiiru"
Utuk'ku Seyt-Hamakha—Norn Queen, Mistress of Nakkiga
"Vein-of-Silverfire"—one of Utuk'ku's Talons

OTHERS

Derra—a half-Thrithings child
Deornoth—a half-Thrithings child
Gan Itai—Niskie of *Eadne Cloud*
Geloë—a wise woman, called "Valada Geloë"
Imai-an—a dwarrow
Ingen Jegger—Black Rimmersman, huntsman of Utuk'ku, killed at Jao é-
    Tinukai'i
Injar—Niskie clan living on Risa Island
Nin Reisu—Niskie of *Emettin's Jewel*
Ruyan Vé—patriarch of Tinukeda'ya, called "The Navigator"
Sho-vennae—a dwarrow
Veng'a Sutekh—called "Duke of the Black Wind," one of the Red Hand
Yis-fidri—a dwarrow, Yis-hadra's husband, master of the Pattern Hall
Yis-hadra—a dwarrow, Yis-fidri's wife, mistress of the Pattern Hall

"Badulf and the Straying Heifer"—a song Simon tries to sing to Miriamele

Battle of Clodu Lake—battle John fought against Thrithings-men, also known as "Battle of the Lakelands"

"Bishop's Wagon, The"—a Jack Mundwode song

Boar and Spears—emblem of Guthwulf of Utanyeat

Breathing Harp, The—Master Witness in Stormspike

Bright-Nail—sword of Prester John, formerly called "Minneyar," containing nail from the Holy Tree and finger-bone of Saint Eahlstan

"By Greenwade's Shore"—song sung at Bonfire Night on Sesuad'ra

Cellian—Camaris' horn, made from dragon Hidohebhi's tooth. (Original name: "Ti-tuno")

Citril—root for chewing, grown in south

Cockindrill—Northern word for "crocodile"

Conqueror Star—a comet, ominous star

Day of Weighing-Out—Aedonite day of final judgment

Door of the Ransomer—seal of confession

Du Svardenvyrd—near-mythical prophetic book by Nisses

Falcon, The—Nabbanai constellation

Fifty Families—Nabbanai noble houses

Floating Castle, The—famous monument on Warinsten

Frayja's Fire—Erkynlandish winter flower

Gardenborn, The—all who came from Venyha Do'sae

Good Peasant—character from the proverbs of the Book of Aedon

Gray Coast—part of the shent board

Gray-cap—mushroom

Great Swords—Bright-Nail, Sorrow, and Thorn

Great Table—John's assembly of knights and heroes

Green Column, The—Master Witness in Jhiná T'seneí

Hare, The—Erkynlandish constellation name

Harrow's Eve—Octander 30, day before "Soul's Day"

Hesitancy, a—Norn spell

High King's Ward—protection of High King over countries of Osten Ard

Hunt-wine—Qanuc liquor

Indreju—Jiriki's witchwood sword

Juya'ha—Sithi art: pictures made of woven cords

Kei-vishaa—Substance used by Gardenborn to make enemies drowsy and weak

Kingfisher, The—Nabbanai constellation

Kvalnir—Isgrimnur's sword

Lobster, The—Nabbanai constellation

Mansa Nictalis—Night ceremony of Mother Church

Market Hall—a domed building in central Kwanitupul

Mist Lamp—a Witness, brought out of Tumet'ai by Amerasu

Mixis the Wolf—Nabbanai constellation

Mockfoil—a flowering herb

Muster of Anitulles—Imperatorial battle-muster from Golden Age of Nabban

Navigator's Trust—Niskie pledge to protect their ships at all cost

Night Heart—Sitha star-name

Ocean Indefinite and Eternal—Niskie term for ocean crossed by Gardenborn

Oldest Tree—Witchwood tree growing in Asu'a

One Who Fled, The—Aedonite euphemism for the Devil

Pact of Sesuad'ra—agreement of Sithi and Norn to part

Pool of Three Depths, The—Master Witness in Asu'a

Prise'a—"Ever-fresh," a favorite flower of Sithi

Quickweed—Wran herb

Rabbit-nose—mushroom

Red knifebill—Wran bird

Rhao iye-Sama'an—the Master Witness at Sesuad'ra, called the "Earth-Drake's Eye"

Rhynn's Cauldron—Hernystiri battle-summoner

Rite of Quickening—Qanuc Spring ceremony

Saint Granis' Day—a holy day

Saint Rhiappa's—a cathedral in Kwanitupul

Sand Beetle, The—Wran name for constellation

Serpent, The—Nabbanai constellation

Shadow-mastery—Norn magics

Shard, The—Master Witness in Mezutu'a

Shent—a Sithi game of socializing and strategy

Snatch-the-feather—Wran gambling game

Sorrow—Elias' sword, a gift from Ineluki the Storm King

Speakfire, The—Master Witness in Hikehikayo

Spinning Wheel—Erkynlandish name for constellation

Sugar-bulb—Wran tree

Tarbox, The—inn at Falshire

Tethtain's Axe—sunk in the heart of a beech tree in famous Hernystiri tale

Thorn—black star-sword of Camaris

Ti-tuno—Camaris' horn, made from dragon's tooth, also known as "Cellian"

Tree, The—(or "Holy Tree," or "Execution Tree") symbol of Usires Aedon's execution

Twistgrass—Wran plant

Uncharted, The—subject of Niskie oath

Wailing Stone—dolmen above Hasu Vale

Wedge and Beetle, The—Stanshire inn

Wind Festival—Wrannaman celebration

Winged Beetle, The—Nabbanai constellation

Winged dolphin—emblem of Streáwe of Perdruin

Wintercap—Erkynlandish winter flower

"Woman from Nabban"—one of Sangfugol's songs

"Wormglass"—Hernystiri name for certain old mirrors

Yellow Tinker—Wran plant
Yrmansol—tree of Erkynlandish Maia-day celebration
Yuvenis' Throne—Nabbanai constellation

Knucklebones—Binabik's auguring tools. Patterns include:
  Wingless Bird
  Fish-Spear
  The Shadowed Path
  Torch at the Cave-Mouth
  Balking Ram
  Clouds in the Pass
  The Black Crevice
  Unwrapped Dart
  Circle of Stones
  Mountains Dancing

WORDS AND PHRASES

QANUC

Henimaatuq! Ea kup!—"Beloved friend! You're here!"
Inij koku na siqqasa min taq—"When we meet again, that will be a good day."
Iq ta randayhet suk biqahuc—"Winter is not being the time for naked swimming."
Mindunob inik yat—"My home will be your tomb."
Nenit, henimaatuya—"Come on, friends."
Nihut—"Attack"
Shummuk—"Wait"
Ummu Bok—"Well done!" (roughly)

SITHI

A y'ei g'eisu! Yas'a pripurna jo-shoi!—"You cowardly ones! The waves would not carry you!"
A-Genay'asu'e—"Houses of Traveling Beyond"
Hikeda'ya—"Cloud Children": Norns
Hikka Staja—"Arrow Bearer"
Hikka Ti-tuno—"Bearer of Ti-tuno"

M'yon rashí—(Sithi) "Breakers of Things"

Sinya'a du-n'sha é-d'treyesa inro—"May you find the light that shines above the bow"

Sudhoda'ya—"Sunset Children": Mortals

Sumy'asu—"Fifth House"

Tinukeda'ya—"Ocean Children": Niskies and dwarrows

Venyha s'ahn!—"By the Garden!"

Zida'ya—"Dawn Children": Sithi

NABBANAI

Á prenteiz—"Take him!" or "At him!"

Duos preterate!—"God preserve"

Duos Simpetis—"Merciful God"

Em Wulstes Duos—"By God's will"

Matra sá Duos—"Mother of God"

Otillenaes—"Tools"

Soria—"Sister"

Ulimor Camaris? Veveis?—"Lord Camaris? You live?"

HERNYSTIRI

Goirach cilagh!—"Foolish (or mad) girl!"

Moiheneg—"between" or "empty place" (a neutral ground)

Smearech fleann—"dangerous book"

RIMMERSPAKK

Vad es . . . Uf nammen Hott, vad es . . . ?—"What? In the name of God, what?"

OTHER

"Azha she'she t'chakó, urun she'she bhabekró . . . Mudhul samat'ai. Jabbak s'era memekeza sanayha-z'á . . . Ninyek she'she, hamut 'tke agrazh'a s'era yé . . ."—(Norn song) means Something Very Unpleasant

Shu'do-tkzayha!—(Norn) "mortals" (var. of Sithi "Sudhoda'ya")

S'h'rosa—(Dwarrow) Vein of stone

A GUIDE TO PRONUNCIATION

ERKYNLANDISH

Erkynlandish names are divided into two types, Old Erkynlandish (O.E.) and Warinstenner. Those names which are based on types from Prester John's native island of Warinsten (mostly the names of castle servants or John's immediate family) have been represented as variants on Biblical names (Elias—Elijah, Ebekah—Rebecca, etc.) Old Erkynlandish names should be pronounced like modern English, except as follows:

a—always *ah,* as in "father"

ae—*ay* of "say"

c—*k* as in "keen"

e—*ai* as in "air," except at the end of names, when it is also sounded, but with an *eh* or *uh* sound, i.e., Hruse—"Rooz-uh"

ea—sounds as *a* in "mark," except at beginning of word or name, where it has the same value as *ae*

g—always hard *g,* as in "glad"

h—hard *h* of "help"

i—short *i* of "in"

j—hard *j* of "jaw"

o—long but soft *o,* as in "orb"

u—*oo* sound of "wood," never *yoo* as in "music"

HERNYSTIRI

The Hernystiri names and words can be pronounced in largely the same way as the O.E., with a few exceptions:

th—always the *th* in "other," never as in "thing"

ch—a guttural, as in Scottish "loch"

y—pronounce *yr* like "beer," *ye* like "spy"

h—unvoiced except at beginning of word or after *t* or *c*

e—*ay* as in "ray"

ll—same as single *l*: Lluth—Luth

RIMMERSPAKK

Names and words in Rimmerspakk differ from O.E. pronunciation in the following:

j—pronounced *y:* Jarnauga—Yarnauga; Hjeldin—Hyeldin (*H* nearly silent here)

ei—long *i* as in "crime"
e—*ee*, as in "sweet"
ö—*oo*, as in "coop"
au—*ow*, as in "cow"

NABBANAI

The Nabbanai language holds basically to the rules of a romance language, i.e., the vowels are pronounced "ah-eh-ih-oh-ooh," the consonants are all sounded, etc. There are some exceptions.

i—most names take emphasis on second to last syllable: Ben-i-GAR-is. When this syllable has an *i*, it is sounded long (Ardrivis: Ar-DRY-vis) unless it comes before a double consonant (Antippa: An-TIHP-pa)

es—at end of name, *es* is sounded long: Gelles—Gel-leez

y—is pronounced as a long *i*, as in "mild"

QANUC

Troll-language is considerably different than the other human languages. There are three hard "k" sounds, signified by: *c, q,* and *k.* The only difference intelligible to most non-Qanuc is a slight clucking sound on the *q,* but it is not to be encouraged in beginners. For our purposes, all three will sound with the *k* of "keep." Also, the Qanuc *u* is pronounced *uh,* as in "bug." Other interpretations are up to the reader, but he or she will not go far wrong pronouncing phonetically.

SITHI

Even more than the language of Yiqanuc, the language of the Zida'ya is virtually unpronounceable by untrained tongues, and so is easiest rendered phonetically, since the chance of any of us being judged by experts is slight (but not nonexistent, as Binabik learned). These rules may be applied, however.

i—when the first vowel, pronounced *ih,* as in "clip." When later in word, especially at end, pronounced *ee,* as in "fleet": Jiriki—Jih-REE-kee

ai—pronounced like long *i,* as in "time"

' (apostrophe)—represents a clicking sound, and should be not voiced by mortal readers.

EXCEPTIONAL NAMES

Geloë—Her origins are unknown, and so is the source of her name. It is pronounced "Juh-LO-ee" or "Juh-LOY." Both are correct.

Ingen Jegger—He is a Black Rimmersman, and the "J" in Jegger is sounded, just as in "jump."

Miriamele—Although born in the Erkynlandish court, hers is a Nabbanai name that developed a strange pronunciation—perhaps due to some family influence or confusion of her dual heritage—and sounds as "Mih-ree-uh-MEL."

Vorzheva—A Thrithings-woman, her name is pronounced "Vor-SHAY-va," with the *zh* sounding harshly, like the Hungarian *zs*.

Acknowledgment, May 2016

All thanks and love to the following. They are Scrollbearers not just by name but by performance, and their expertise helped greatly with the 2016 reissue of these books.

Jeremy Erman

Jonathan Erman

Ron Hyde

Mark Gambal

Olaf Keith

Ylva von Löhneysen

Eva Maderbacher

Linda van der Pal

Cindy Squires

Lisa Tveit

Angela Welchel

Cindy Yan